DEATHWATCH
THE OMNIBUS

More tales of the Deathwatch from Black Library

DEATHWATCH: IGNITION
Various authors
A Warhammer 40,000 anthology

MISSION: PURGE
Gav Thorpe
A Deathwatch audio drama

DEATHWATCH: THE LAST GUARDIAN
C Z Dunn
A Deathwatch audio drama

DEATHWATCH
Jim Alexander and Graham Stoddart
A Deathwatch graphic novel

Further tales of the Inquisition

VAULTS OF TERRA: THE CARRION THRONE
Chris Wraight
An Inquisition novel

THE HORUSIAN WARS: RESURRECTION
John French
An Inquisition novel

AGENT OF THE THRONE: BLOOD AND LIES
John French
An Inquisition audio drama

• The Eisenhorn trilogy by Dan Abnett •
XENOS
MALLEUS
HERETICUS

• The Ravenor trilogy by Dan Abnett •
RAVENOR
RAVENOR RETURNED
RAVENOR ROGUE

PARIAH
Dan Abnett
An Eisenhorn vs Ravenor novel

WARHAMMER 40,000

DEATHWATCH
THE OMNIBUS

STEVE PARKER
IAN ST. MARTIN
JUSTIN D HILL
ANDY CHAMBERS
CHRIS WRAIGHT
NICK KYME
BRADEN CAMPBELL
BEN COUNTER
DAVID ANNANDALE
ANDY CLARK
GAV THORPE
ANTHONY REYNOLDS

BLACK LIBRARY

A BLACK LIBRARY PUBLICATION

Headhunted first published in the
Heroes of the Space Marines anthology in 2009.
Exhumed first published in the
Victories of the Space Marines anthology in 2011.
Deathwatch first published in 2013.
*The Alien Hunters, Machine Spirit, Rackinruin, Weaponsmith,
The Vorago Fastness* and *The Infinite Tableau* first published in
Deathwatch Xenos Hunters in 2012.
Onyx first published in 2014.
Swordwind first published in 2016.
Deathwatch: Kryptman's War first published as *Legends of the Dark
Millennium: Deathwatch* in 2016.
Storm of Damocles first published in 2016.
Whiteout first published in 2015.
Mission: Annihilate first published in 2013.
This edition published in Great Britain in 2017 by
Black Library,
Games Workshop Ltd.,
Willow Road,
Nottingham, NG7 2WS, UK.

10 9 8 7 6 5 4 3 2

Produced by Games Workshop in Nottingham.
Cover illustration by Lie Setiawan.

Deathwatch: The Omnibus © Copyright Games Workshop Limited 2017. Deathwatch: The Omnibus, GW, Games Workshop, Black Library, The Horus Heresy, The Horus Heresy Eye logo, Space Marine, 40K, Warhammer, Warhammer 40,000, the 'Aquila' Double-headed Eagle logo, and all associated logos, illustrations, images, names, creatures, races, vehicles, locations, weapons, characters, and the distinctive likenesses thereof, are either ® or TM, and/or © Games Workshop Limited, variably registered around the world.
All Rights Reserved.

A CIP record for this book is available from the British Library.

ISBN 13: 978 1 78496 622 5

No part of this publication may be reproduced, stored in a retrieval system, or transmitted in any form or by any means, electronic, mechanical, photocopying, recording or otherwise, without the prior permission of the publishers.

This is a work of fiction. All the characters and events portrayed in this book are fictional, and any resemblance to real people or incidents is purely coincidental.

See Black Library on the internet at
blacklibrary.com

Find out more about Games Workshop
and the world of Warhammer 40,000 at
games-workshop.com

Printed and bound by CPI Group (UK) Ltd, Croydon, CR0 4YY

It is the 41st millennium. For more than a hundred centuries the Emperor has sat immobile on the Golden Throne of Earth. He is the Master of Mankind by the will of the gods, and master of a million worlds by the might of his inexhaustible armies. He is a rotting carcass writhing invisibly with power from the Dark Age of Technology. He is the Carrion Lord of the Imperium for whom a thousand souls are sacrificed every day, so that he may never truly die.

Yet even in his deathless state, the Emperor continues his eternal vigilance. Mighty battlefleets cross the daemon-infested miasma of the warp, the only route between distant stars, their way lit by the Astronomican, the psychic manifestation of the Emperor's will. Vast armies give battle in His name on uncounted worlds. Greatest amongst his soldiers are the Adeptus Astartes, the Space Marines, bioengineered super-warriors. Their comrades in arms are legion: the Astra Militarum and countless planetary defence forces, the ever-vigilant Inquisition and the tech-priests of the Adeptus Mechanicus to name only a few. But for all their multitudes, they are barely enough to hold off the ever-present threat from aliens, heretics, mutants – and worse.

To be a man in such times is to be one amongst untold billions. It is to live in the cruellest and most bloody regime imaginable. These are the tales of those times. Forget the power of technology and science, for so much has been forgotten, never to be re-learned. Forget the promise of progress and understanding, for in the grim dark future there is only war. There is no peace amongst the stars, only an eternity of carnage and slaughter, and the laughter of thirsting gods.

CONTENTS

Headhunted *Steve Parker*	9
Exhumed *Steve Parker*	49
Deathwatch *Steve Parker*	77
The Alien Hunters *Andy Chambers*	395
Onyx *Chris Wraight*	433
Machine Spirit *Nick Kyme*	459
Swordwind *Ian St. Martin*	491
Deathwatch: Kryptman's War *Ian St. Martin*	507
Rackinruin *Braden Campbell*	663
Weaponsmith *Ben Counter*	677
The Vorago Fastness *David Annandale*	701
Storm of Damocles *Justin D Hill*	731
Whiteout *Andy Clark*	907

Mission: Annihilate 931
Gav Thorpe

The Infinite Tableau 937
Anthony Reynolds

To be Unclean
That is the Mark of the Xenos
To be Impure
That is the Mark of the Xenos
To be Abhorred
That is the Mark of the Xenos
To be Reviled
That is the Mark of the Xenos
To be Hunted
That is the Mark of the Xenos
To be Purged
That is the Fate of the Xenos
To be Cleansed
That is the Fate of all Xenos

– Catechism of the Xeno,
extract from *The Third Book of Indoctrinations*

HEADHUNTED

STEVE PARKER

Something vast, dark and brutish moved across the pinpricked curtain of space, blotting out the diamond lights of the constellations behind it as if swallowing them whole. It was the size of a city block, and its bulbous eyes, like those of a great blind fish, glowed with a green and baleful light.

It was a terrible thing to behold, this leviathan – a harbinger of doom – and its passage had brought agony and destruction to countless victims in the centuries it had swum among the stars. It travelled, now, through the Charybdis Subsector on trails of angry red plasma, cutting across the inky darkness with a purpose.

That purpose was close at hand, and a change began to take place on its bestial features. New lights flickered to life on its muzzle, shining far brighter and sharper than its eyes, illuminating myriad shapes, large and small, that danced and spun in high orbit above the glowing orange sphere of Arronax II. With a slow, deliberate motion, the leviathan unhinged its massive lower jaw, and opened its mouth to feed.

At first, the glimmering pieces of debris it swallowed were mere fragments, nothing much larger than a man. But soon, heavier, bulkier pieces drifted into that gaping maw, passing between its bladelike teeth and down into its black throat.

For hours, the monster gorged itself on space-borne scrap, devouring everything it could fit into its mouth. The pickings were good. There had been heavy fighting here in ages past. Scoured worlds and lifeless wrecks were all that remained now, locked in a slow elliptical dance around the local star. But the wrecks, at least, had a future. Once salvaged, they would be forged anew, recast in forms that would bring death and suffering down upon countless others.

For, of course, this beast, this hungry monster of the void, was no beast at all.

It was an ork ship. And the massive glyphs daubed sloppily on its hull marked it as a vessel of the Deathskull clan.

Re-pressurisation began the moment the ship's vast metal jaws clanged shut. The process took around twenty minutes, pumps flooding the salvage bay with breathable, if foul-smelling, air. The orks crowding the corridor beyond the bay's airlock doors roared their impatience and hammered their fists against the thick metal bulkheads. They shoved and jostled for position. Then, just when it seemed murderous violence was sure to erupt, sirens sounded and the heavy doors split apart. The orks surged forward, pushing and scrambling, racing towards the mountains of scrap, each utterly focused on claiming the choicest pieces for himself.

Fights broke out between the biggest and darkest-skinned. They roared and wrestled with each other, and snapped at each other with tusk-filled jaws. They lashed out with the tools and weapons that bristled on their augmented limbs. They might have killed each other but for the massive suits of cybernetic armour they wore. These were no mere greenskin foot soldiers. They were orks of a unique genus, the engineers of their race, each born with an inherent understanding of machines. It was hard-coded into their marrow in the same way as violence and torture.

As was true of every caste, however, some among them were cleverer than others. While the mightiest bellowed and beat their metal-plated chests, one ork, marginally shorter and leaner than the rest, slid around them and into the shadows, intent on getting first pickings.

This ork was called Gorgrot in the rough speech of his race, and, despite the sheer density of salvage the ship had swallowed, it didn't take him long to find something truly valuable. At the very back of the junk-filled bay, closest to the ship's great metal teeth, he found the ruined, severed prow of a mid-sized human craft. As he studied it, he noticed weapon barrels protruding from the front end. His alien heart quickened. Functional or not, he could do great things with salvaged weapon systems. He would make himself more dangerous, an ork to be reckoned with.

After a furtive look over his shoulder to make sure none of the bigger orks had noticed him, he moved straight across to the wrecked prow, reached out a gnarled hand and touched the hull. Its armour-plating was in bad shape, pocked and cratered by plasma fire and torpedo impacts. To the rear, the metal was twisted and black where it had sheared away from the rest of the craft. It looked like an explosion had torn the ship apart. To Gorgrot, however, the nature of the ship's destruction mattered not at all. What mattered was its potential. Already, visions of murderous creativity were flashing through his tiny mind in rapid succession, so many at once, in fact, that he forgot to breathe until his lungs sent him a painful reminder. These visions were a gift from Gork and Mork, the bloodthirsty greenskin gods, and he had received their like many times before. All greenskin engineers received them, and nothing, save the rending of an enemy's flesh, felt so utterly right.

Even so, it was something small and insignificant that pulled him out of his rapture.

A light had begun to flash on the lower left side of the ruined prow, winking at him from beneath a tangle of beams and cables and dented armour plates, igniting his simple-minded curiosity, drawing him towards it. It was small and green, and it looked like it might be a button of some kind. Gorgrot began clearing debris from the area around it. Soon, he was grunting and growling with the effort, sweating despite the assistance of his armour's strength-boosting hydraulics.

Within minutes, he had removed all obstructions between himself and the blinking light, and discovered that it was indeed a kind of button.

Gorgrot was extending his finger out to press it when something suddenly wrenched him backwards with irresistible force. He was hurled to the ground and landed hard on his back with a snarl. Immediately, he tried to scramble up again, but a huge metal boot stamped down on him, denting his belly-armour and pushing him deep into the carpet of sharp scrap.

Gorgrot looked up into the blazing red eyes of the biggest, heaviest ork in the salvage bay.

This was Zazog, personal engineer to the mighty Warboss Balthazog Bludwrekk, and few orks on the ship were foolish enough to challenge any of his salvage claims. It was the reason he always arrived in the salvage bay last of all; his tardiness was the supreme symbol of his dominance among the scavengers.

Zazog staked his claim now, turning from Gorgrot and stomping over to the wrecked prow. There, he hunkered down to examine the winking button. He knew well enough what it meant. There had to be a working power source onboard, something far more valuable than most scrap. He flicked out a blowtorch attachment from the middle knuckle of his mechanised left claw and burned a rough likeness of his personal glyph into the side of the wrecked prow. Then he rose and bellowed a challenge to those around him.

Scores of gretchin, the puniest members of the orkoid race, skittered away in panic, disappearing into the protection of the shadows. The other orks stepped back, growling at Zazog, snarling in anger. But none dared challenge him.

Zazog glared at each in turn, forcing them, one by one, to drop their gazes or die by his hand. Then, satisfied at their deference, he turned and pressed a thick finger to the winking green button.

For a brief moment, nothing happened. Zazog growled and pressed it again. Still nothing. He was about to begin pounding it with his mighty fist when he heard a noise.

It was the sound of atmospheric seals unlocking.

The door shuddered, and began sliding up into the hull.

Zazog's craggy, scar-covered face twisted into a hideous grin. Yes, there *was* a power source on board. The door's motion proved it. He, like Gorgrot, began to experience flashes of divine inspiration, visions of weaponry so grand and deadly that his limited brain could hardly cope. No matter; the gods would work through him once he got started. His hands would automatically fashion what his brain could barely comprehend. It was always the way.

The sliding door retracted fully now, revealing an entrance just large enough for Zazog's armoured bulk to squeeze through. He shifted forward with that very intention, but the moment never came.

From the shadows inside the doorway, there was a soft coughing sound.

Zazog's skull disintegrated in a haze of blood and bone chips. His headless corpse crashed backwards onto the carpet of junk.

The other orks gaped in slack-jawed wonder. They looked down at Zazog's body, trying to make sense of the dim warnings that rolled through their minds. Ignoring the obvious threat, the biggest orks quickly began roaring fresh claims and shoving the others aside, little realising that their own deaths were imminent.

But imminent they were.

A great black shadow appeared, bursting from the door Zazog had opened. It was humanoid, not quite as large as the orks surrounding it, but bulky nonetheless, though it moved with a speed and confidence no ork could ever have matched. Its long adamantium talons sparked and crackled with deadly energy as it slashed and stabbed in all directions, a whirlwind of lethal motion. Great fountains of thick red blood arced through the air as it killed again and again. Greenskins fell like sacks of meat.

More shadows emerged from the wreck now. Four of them. Like the first, all were dressed in heavy black ceramite armour. All bore an intricate skull and 'I' design on their massive left pauldrons. The icons on their right pauldrons, however, were each unique.

'Clear the room,' barked one over his comm-link as he gunned down a greenskin in front of him, spitting death from the barrel of his silenced bolter. 'Quick and quiet. Kill the rest before they raise the alarm.' Switching comm channels, he said, 'Sigma, this is Talon Alpha. Phase one complete. Kill-team is aboard. Securing entry point now.'

'Understood, Alpha,' replied the toneless voice at the other end of the link. 'Proceed on mission. Extract within the hour, as instructed. Captain Redthorne has orders to pull out if you miss your pick-up, so keep your team on a tight leash. This is *not* a purge operation. Is that clear?'

'I'm well aware of that, Sigma,' the kill-team leader replied brusquely.

'You had better be,' replied the voice. 'Sigma, out.'

It took Talon squad less than sixty seconds to clear the salvage bay. Brother Rauth of the Exorcists Chapter gunned down the last of the fleeing gretchin as it dashed for the exit. The creature stumbled as a single silenced bolt punched into its back. Half a second later, a flesh-muffled detonation ripped it apart.

It was the last of twenty-six bodies to fall among the litter of salvaged scrap.

'Target down, Karras,' reported Rauth. 'Area clear.'

'Confirmed,' replied Karras. He turned to face a Space Marine with a heavy flamer. 'Omni, you know what to do. The rest of you, cover the entrance.'

With the exception of Omni, the team immediately moved to positions covering the mouth of the corridor through which the orks had come. Omni, otherwise known as Maximmion Voss of the Imperial Fists, moved to the side walls, first the left, then the right, working quickly at a number of thick hydraulic pistons and power cables there.

'That was messy, Karras,' said Brother Solarion, 'letting them see us as we came out. I told you we should have used smoke. If one had escaped and raised the alarm…'

Karras ignored the comment. It was just Solarion being Solarion.

'Give it a rest, Prophet,' said Brother Zeed, opting to use Solarion's nickname. Zeed had coined it himself, and knew precisely how much it irritated the proud Ultramarine. 'The room is clear. No runners. No alarms. Scholar knows what he's doing.'

Scholar. That was what they called Karras, or at least Brothers Voss and Zeed did. Rauth and Solarion insisted on calling him by his second name. Sigma always called him Alpha. And his battle-brothers back on Occludus, homeworld of the Death Spectres Chapter, simply called him by his first name, Lyandro, or sometimes simply Codicier – his rank in the Librarius.

Karras didn't much care what anyone called him so long as they all did their jobs. The honour of serving in the Deathwatch had been offered to him, and he had taken it, knowing the great glory it would bring both himself and his Chapter. But he wouldn't be sorry when his obligation to the Emperor's Holy Inquisition was over. Astartes life seemed far less complicated among one's own Chapter-brothers.

When would he return to the fold? He didn't know. There was no fixed term for Deathwatch service. The Inquisition made high demands of all it called upon. Karras might not see the darkly beautiful crypt-cities of his home world again for decades... if he lived that long.

'Done, Scholar,' reported Voss as he rejoined the rest of the team.

Karras nodded and pointed towards a shattered pict screen and rune-board that protruded from the wall, close to the bay's only exit. 'Think you can get anything from that?' he asked.

'Nothing from the screen,' said Voss, 'but I could try wiring the data-feed directly into my visor.'

'Do it,' said Karras, 'but be quick.' To the others, he said, 'Proceed with phase two. Solarion, take point.'

The Ultramarine nodded curtly, rose from his position among the scrap and stalked forward into the shadowy corridor, bolter raised and ready. He moved with smooth, near-silent steps despite the massive weight of his armour. Torias Telion, famed Ultramarine Scout Master and Solarion's former mentor, would have been proud of his prize student.

One by one, with the exception of Voss, the rest of the kill-team followed in his wake.

The filthy, rusting corridors of the ork ship were lit, but the electric lamps the greenskins had strung up along pipes and ducts were old and in poor repair. Barely half of them seemed to be working at all. Even these buzzed and flickered in a constant battle to throw out their weak illumination. Still, the little light they did give was enough to bother the kill-team leader. The inquisitor, known to the members of Talon only by his call-sign, Sigma, had estimated the ork population of the ship at somewhere over twenty thousand. Against odds like these, Karras knew only too well that darkness and stealth were among his best weapons.

'I want the lights taken out,' he growled. 'The longer we stay hidden, the better our chances of making it off this damned heap.'

'We could shoot them out as we go,' offered Solarion, 'but I'd rather not waste my ammunition on something that doesn't bleed.'

Just then, Karras heard Voss on the comm-link. 'I've finished with the terminal, Scholar. I managed to pull some old cargo manifests from the ship's memory core. Not much else, though. Apparently, this ship used to be a civilian heavy-transport, Magellann class, built on Stygies. It was called *The Pegasus*.'

'No schematics?'

'Most of the memory core is heavily corrupted. It's thousands of years old. We were lucky to get that much.'

'Sigma, this is Alpha,' said Karras. 'The ork ship is built around an Imperial transport called *The Pegasus*. Requesting schematics, priority one.'

'I heard,' said Sigma. 'You'll have them as soon as I do.'

'Voss, where are you now?' Karras asked.

'Close to your position,' said the Imperial Fist.

'Do you have any idea which cable provides power to the lights?'

'Look up,' said Voss. 'See those cables running along the ceiling? The thick one, third from the left. I'd wager my knife on it.'

Karras didn't have to issue the order. The moment Zeed heard Voss's words, his right arm flashed upwards. There was a crackle of blue energy as the Raven Guard's claws sliced through the cable, and the corridor went utterly dark.

To the Space Marines, however, everything remained clear as day. Their Mark VII helmets, like everything else in their arsenal, had been heavily modified by the Inquisition's finest artificers. They boasted a composite low-light/thermal vision mode that was superior to anything else Karras had ever used. In the three years he had been leading Talon, it had tipped the balance in his favour more times than he cared to count. He hoped it would do so many more times in the years to come, but that would all depend on their survival here, and he knew all too well that the odds were against them from the start. It wasn't just the numbers they were up against, or the tight deadline. There was something here the likes of which few Deathwatch kill-teams had ever faced before.

Karras could already feel its presence somewhere on the upper levels of the ship.

'Keep moving,' he told the others.

Three minutes after Zeed had killed the lights, Solarion hissed for them all to stop. 'Karras,' he rasped, 'I have multiple xenos up ahead. Suggest you move up and take a look.'

Karras ordered the others to hold and went forward, careful not to bang or scrape his broad pauldrons against the clutter of twisting pipes that lined both walls. Crouching beside Solarion, he realised he needn't have worried about a little noise. In front of him, over a hundred orks had crowded into a high-ceilinged, octagonal chamber. They were hooting and laughing and wrestling with each other to get nearer the centre of the room.

Neither Karras nor Solarion could see beyond the wall of broad green backs, but there was clearly something in the middle that was holding their attention.

'What are they doing?' whispered Solarion.

Karras decided there was only one way to find out. He centred his awareness down in the pit of his stomach, and began reciting the Litany of the Sight Beyond Sight that his former master, Chief Librarian Athio Cordatus, had taught him during his earliest years in the Librarius. Beneath his helmet, hidden from Solarion's view, Karras's eyes, normally deep red in colour, began to glow with an ethereal white flame. On his forehead, a wound appeared. A single drop of blood rolled over his brow and down to the bridge of his narrow, angular nose. Slowly, as he opened his soul fractionally more to the dangerous power within him, the wound widened, revealing the physical manifestation of his psychic inner eye.

Karras felt his awareness lift out of his body now. He willed it deeper into the chamber, rising above the backs of the orks, looking down on them from above.

He saw a great pit sunk into the centre of the metal floor. It was filled with hideous ovoid creatures of every possible colour, their tiny red eyes set above oversized mouths crammed with razor-edged teeth.

'It's a mess hall,' Karras told his team over the link. 'There's a squig pit in the centre.'

As his projected consciousness watched, the greenskins at the rim of the pit stabbed downwards with cruelly barbed poles, hooking their prey through soft flesh. Then they lifted the squigs, bleeding and screaming, into the air before reaching for them, tearing them from the hooks, and feasting on them.

'They're busy,' said Karras, 'but we'll need to find another way through.'

'Send me in, Scholar,' said Voss from the rear. 'I'll turn them all into cooked meat before they even realise they're under attack. Ghost can back me up.'

'On your order, Scholar,' said Zeed eagerly.

Ghost. That was Siefer Zeed. With his helmet off, it was easy to see how he'd come by the name. Like Karras, and like all brothers of their respective Chapters, Zeed was the victim of a failed melanochromic implant, a slight mutation in his ancient and otherwise worthy gene-seed. The skin of both he and the kill-team leader was as white as porcelain. But, whereas Karras bore the blood-red eyes and chalk-white hair of the true albino, Zeed's eyes were black as coals, and his hair no less dark.

'Negative,' said Karras. 'We'll find another way through.'

He pushed his astral-self further into the chamber, desperate to find a means that didn't involve alerting the foe, but there seemed little choice. Only when he turned his awareness upwards did he see what he was looking for.

'There's a walkway near the ceiling,' he reported. 'It looks frail, rusting badly, but if we cross it one at a time, it should hold.'

A sharp, icy voice on the comm-link interrupted him. 'Talon Alpha, get ready to receive those schematics. Transmitting now.'

Karras willed his consciousness back into his body, and his glowing third eye sealed itself, leaving only the barest trace of a scar. Using conventional sight, he consulted his helmet's heads-up display and watched the last few per cent of the schematics file being downloaded. When it was finished, he called it up with a thought, and the helmet projected it as a shimmering green image cast directly onto his left retina.

The others, he knew, were seeing the same thing.

'According to these plans,' he told them, 'there's an access ladder set into the wall near the second junction we passed. We'll backtrack to it. The corridor above this one will give us access to the walkway.'

'If it's still there,' said Solarion. 'The orks may have removed it.'

'And backtracking will cost us time,' grumbled Voss.

'Less time than a firefight would cost us,' countered Rauth. His hard, gravelly tones were made even harder by the slight distortion on the comm-link. 'There's a time and place for that kind of killing, but it isn't now.'

'Watcher's right,' said Zeed reluctantly. It was rare for he and Rauth to agree.

'I've told you before,' warned Rauth. 'Don't call me that.'

'Right or wrong,' said Karras, 'I'm not taking votes. I've made my call. Let's move.'

Karras was the last to cross the gantry above the ork feeding pit. The shadows up here were dense and, so far, the orks had noticed nothing, though there had been a few moments when it looked as if the aging iron were about to collapse, particularly beneath the tremendous weight of Voss with his heavy flamer, high explosives, and back-mounted promethium supply.

Such was the weight of the Imperial Fist and his kit that Karras had decided to send him over first. Voss had made it across, but it was nothing short of a miracle that the orks below hadn't noticed the rain of red flakes showering down on them.

Lucky we didn't bring old Chyron after all, thought Karras.

The sixth member of Talon wouldn't have made it out of the salvage bay. The corridors on this ship were too narrow for such a mighty Space Marine. Instead, Sigma had ordered the redoubtable Dreadnought, formerly of the Lamenters Chapter but now permanently attached to Talon, to remain behind on Redthorne's ship, the *Saint Nevarre*. That had caused a few tense moments. Chyron had a vile temper.

Karras made his way, centimetre by centimetre, along the creaking metal grille, his silenced bolter fixed securely to the magnetic couplings on his right thigh plate, his force sword sheathed on his left hip. Over one massive shoulder was slung the cryo-case that Sigma had insisted he carry. Karras cursed it, but there was no way he could leave it behind. It added twenty kilogrammes to his already significant weight, but the case was absolutely critical to the mission. He had no choice.

Up ahead, he could see Rauth watching him, as ever, from the end of the gangway. What was the Exorcist thinking? Karras had no clue. He had never been able to read the mysterious Astartes. Rauth seemed to have no warp signature whatsoever. He simply didn't register at all. Even his armour, even his bolter for Throne's sake, resonated more than he did. And it was an anomaly that Rauth was singularly unwilling to discuss.

There was no love lost between them, Karras knew, and, for his part, he regretted that. He had made gestures, occasional overtures, but for whatever reason, they had been rebuffed every time. The Exorcist was unreachable, distant, remote, and it seemed he planned to stay that way.

As Karras took his next step, the cryo-case suddenly swung forward on its strap, shifting his centre of gravity and threatening to unbalance him. He compensated swiftly, but the effort caused the gangway to creak and a piece of rusted metal snapped off, spinning away under him.

He froze, praying that the orks wouldn't notice.

But one did.

It was at the edge of the pit, poking a fat squig with its barbed pole, when the metal fragment struck its head. The ork immediately stopped what it was doing and scanned the shadows above it, squinting suspiciously up towards the unlit recesses of the high ceiling.

Karras stared back, willing it to turn away. Reading minds and controlling minds, however, were two very different things. The latter was a power beyond his gifts. Ultimately, it wasn't Karras's will that turned the ork from its scrutiny. It was the nature of the greenskin species.

The other orks around it, impatient to feed, began grabbing at the barbed pole. One managed to snatch it, and the gazing ork suddenly found himself robbed of his chance to feed. He launched himself into a violent frenzy, lashing out at the pole-thief and those nearby. That was when the orks behind him surged forward, and pushed him into the squig pit.

Karras saw the squigs swarm on the hapless ork, sinking their long teeth into its flesh and tearing away great, bloody mouthfuls. The food chain had been turned on its head. The orks around the pit laughed and capered and struck at their dying fellow with their poles.

Karras didn't stop to watch. He moved on carefully, cursing the black case that was now pressed tight to his side with one arm. He rejoined his team in the mouth of a tunnel on the far side of the gantry and they moved off, pressing deeper into the ship. Solarion moved up front with Zeed. Voss stayed in the middle. Rauth and Karras brought up the rear.

'They need to do some damned maintenance around here,' Karras told Rauth in a wry tone.

The Exorcist said nothing.

By comparing Sigma's schematics of *The Pegasus* with the features he saw as he moved through it, it soon became clear to Karras that the orks had done very little to alter the interior of the ship beyond covering its walls in badly rendered glyphs, defecating wherever they pleased, leaving dead bodies to rot where they fell, and generally making the place unfit for habitation by anything save their own wretched kind. Masses of quivering fungi had sprouted from broken water pipes. Frayed electrical cables sparked and hissed at anyone who walked by. And there were so many bones strewn about that some sections almost looked like mass graves.

The Deathwatch members made a number of kills, or rather Solarion did, as they proceeded deeper into the ship's belly. Most of these were gretchin sent out on some errand or other by their slavemasters. The Ultramarine silently executed them wherever he found them and stuffed the small corpses under pipes or in dark alcoves. Only twice did the kill-team encounter parties of ork warriors, and both times, the greenskins announced themselves well in advance with their loud grunting and jabbering. Karras could tell that Voss and Zeed were both itching to engage, but stealth was still paramount. Instead, he, Rauth and Solarion eliminated the foe, loading powerful hellfire rounds into their silenced bolters to ensure quick, quiet one-shot kills.

'I've reached Waypoint Adrius,' Solarion soon reported from up ahead. 'No xenos contacts.'

'Okay, move in and secure,' Karras ordered. 'Check your corners and exits.'

The kill-team hurried forward, emerging from the blackness of the corridor into a towering square shaft. It was hundreds of metres high, its metal walls stained with age and rust and all kinds of spillage. Thick pipes ran across the walls at all angles, many of them venting steam or dripping icy coolant. There were broken staircases and rusting gantries at regular intervals, each of which led to gaping doorways. And, in the middle of the left-side wall, an open elevator shaft ran almost to the top.

It was here that Talon would be forced to split up. From this chamber, they could access any level in the ship. Voss and Zeed would go down via a metal stairway, the others would go up.

'Good luck using that,' said Voss, nodding towards the elevator cage. It was clearly of ork construction, a mishmash of metal bits bolted together. It had a bloodstained steel floor, a folding lattice-work gate and a large lever which could be pushed forward for up, or pulled backwards for down.

There was no sign of what had happened to the original elevator.

Karras scowled under his helmet as he looked at it and cross-referenced what he saw against his schematics. 'We'll have to take it as high as it will go,' he told Rauth and Solarion. He pointed up towards the far ceiling. 'That landing at the top; that is where we are going. From there we can access the corridor to the bridge. Ghost, Omni, you have your own objectives.' He checked the mission chrono in the corner of his visor. 'Forty-three minutes,' he told them. 'Avoid confrontation if you can. And stay in contact.'

'Understood, Scholar,' said Voss.

Karras frowned. He could sense the Imperial Fist's hunger for battle. It had been there since the moment they'd set foot on this mechanical abomination. Like most Imperial Fists, once Voss was in a fight, he tended to stay there until the foe was dead. He could be stubborn to the point of idiocy, but there was no denying his versatility. Weapons, vehicles, demolitions... Voss could do it all.

'Ghost,' said Karras. 'Make sure he gets back here on schedule.'

'If I have to knock him out and drag him back myself,' said Zeed.

'You can try,' Voss snorted, grinning under his helmet. He and the Raven Guard had enjoyed a good rapport since the moment they had met. Karras occasionally envied them that.

'Go,' he told them, and they moved off, disappearing down a stairwell on the right, their footsteps vibrating the grille under Karras's feet.

'Then there were three,' said Solarion.

'With the Emperor's blessing,' said Karras, 'that's all we'll need.' He strode over to the elevator, pulled the latticework gate aside, and got in. As the others joined him, he added, 'If either of you know a Mechanicus prayer, now would be a good time. Rauth, take us up.'

The Exorcist pushed the control lever forward, and it gave a harsh, metallic screech. A winch high above them began turning. Slowly at first, then with increasing speed, the lower levels dropped away beneath them. Pipes and landings flashed by, then the counterweight whistled past. The floor of the cage creaked and groaned under their feet as it carried them higher and higher. Disconcerting sounds issued from the cable and the assembly at the top, but the ride was short, lasting barely a minute, for which Karras thanked the Emperor.

When they were almost at the top of the shaft, Rauth eased the control lever backwards and the elevator slowed, issuing the same high-pitched complaint with which it had started.

Karras heard Solarion cursing.

'Problem, brother?' he asked.

'We'll be lucky if the whole damned ship doesn't know we're here by now,' spat the Ultramarine. 'Accursed piece of ork junk.'

The elevator ground to a halt at the level of the topmost landing, and Solarion almost tore the latticework gate from its fixings as he wrenched it aside. Stepping out, he took point again automatically.

The rickety steel landing led off in two directions. To the left, it led to a trio of dimly lit corridor entrances. To the right, it led towards a steep metal staircase in a severe state of disrepair.

Karras consulted his schematics.

'Now for the bad news,' he said.

The others eyed the stair grimly.

'It won't hold us,' said Rauth. 'Not together.'

Some of the metal steps had rusted away completely leaving gaps of up to a metre. Others were bent and twisted, torn halfway free of their bolts as if something heavy had landed hard on them.

'So we spread out,' said Karras. 'Stay close to the wall. Put as little pressure on each step as we can. We don't have time to debate it.'

They moved off, Solarion in front, Karras in the middle, Rauth at the rear. Karras watched his point-man carefully, noting exactly where he placed each foot. The Ultramarine moved with a certainty and fluidity that few could match. Had he registered more of a warp signature than he did, Karras might even have suspected some kind of extrasensory perception, but, in fact, it was simply the superior training of the Master Scout, Telion.

Halfway up the stair, however, Solarion suddenly held up his hand and hissed, 'Hold!'

Rauth and Karras froze at once. The stairway creaked gently under them.

'Xenos, direct front. Twenty metres. Three big ones.'

Neither Karras nor Rauth could see them. The steep angle of the stair prevented it.

'Can you deal with them?' asked Karras.

'Not alone,' said Solarion. 'One is standing in a doorway. I don't have clear line of fire on him. It could go either way. If he charges, fine. But he may raise the alarm as soon as I drop the others. Better the three of us take them out at once, if you think you can move up quietly.'

The challenge in Solarion's words, not to mention his tone, could hardly be missed. Karras lifted a foot and placed it gently on the next step up. Slowly, he put his weight on it. There was a harsh grating sound.

'I said *quietly*,' hissed Solarion.

'I heard you, damn it,' Karras snapped back. Silently, he cursed the cryo-case strapped over his shoulder. Its extra weight and shifting centre of gravity was hampering him, as it had on the gantry above the squig pit, but what could he do?

'Rauth,' he said. 'Move past me. Don't touch this step. Place yourself on Solarion's left. Try to get an angle on the ork in the doorway. Solarion, open fire on Rauth's mark. You'll have to handle the other two yourself.'

'Confirmed,' rumbled Rauth. Slowly, carefully, the Exorcist moved out from behind Karras and continued climbing as quietly as he could. Flakes of rust fell from the underside of the stair like red snow.

Rauth was just ahead of Karras, barely a metre out in front, when, as he put the weight down on his right foot, the step under it gave way with a sharp snap. Rauth plunged into open space, nothing below him but two hundred metres of freefall and a lethally hard landing.

Karras moved on instinct with a speed that bordered on supernatural. His gauntleted fist shot out, catching Rauth just in time, closing around the Exorcist's left wrist with almost crushing force.

The orks turned their heads towards the sudden noise and stomped towards the top of the stairs, massive stubbers raised in front of them.

'By Guilliman's blood!' raged Solarion.

He opened fire.

The first of the orks collapsed with its brainpan blown out.

Karras was struggling to haul Rauth back onto the stairway, but the metal under his own feet, forced to support the weight of both Astartes, began to scrape clear of its fixings.

'Quickly, psyker,' gasped Rauth, 'or we'll both die.'

'Not a damned chance,' Karras growled. With a monumental effort of strength, he heaved Rauth high enough that the Exorcist could grab the staircase and scramble back onto it.

As Rauth got to his feet, he breathed, 'Thank you, Karras... but you may live to regret saving me.'

Karras was scowling furiously under his helmet. 'You may not think of me as your brother, but, at the very least, you are a member of my team. However, the next time you call me psyker with such disdain, you will be the one to regret it. Is that understood?'

Rauth glared at him for a second, then nodded once. 'Fair words.'

Karras moved past him, stepping over the broad gap then stopping at Solarion's side. On the landing ahead, he saw two ork bodies leaking copious amounts of fluid from severe head wounds.

As he looked at them, wailing alarms began to sound throughout the ship.

Solarion turned to face him. 'I told Sigma he should have put me in charge,' he hissed. 'Damn it, Karras.'

'Save it,' Karras barked. His eyes flicked to the countdown on his heads-up display. 'Thirty-three minutes left. They know we're here. The killing starts in earnest now, but we can't let them hold us up. Both of you follow me. Let's move!'

Without another word, the three Astartes pounded across the upper landing and into the mouth of the corridor down which the third ork had vanished, desperate to reach their primary objective before the whole damned horde descended on them.

'So much for keeping a low profile, eh, brother?' said Zeed as he guarded Voss's back.

A deafening, ululating wail had filled the air. Red lights began to rotate in their wall fixtures.

Voss grunted by way of response. He was concentrating hard on the task at hand. He crouched by the coolant valves of the ship's massive plasma reactor, power source for the vessel's gigantic main thrusters.

The noise in the reactor room was deafening even without the ork alarms, and none of the busy gretchin work crews had noticed the two Deathwatch members until it was too late. Zeed had hacked them limb from limb before they'd had a chance to scatter. Now that the alarm had been sounded, though, orks would be arming themselves and filling the corridors outside, each filthy alien desperate to claim a kill.

'We're done here,' said Voss, rising from his crouch. He hefted his heavy flamer from the floor and turned. 'The rest is up to Scholar and the others.'

Voss couldn't check in with them. Not from here. Such close proximity to a reactor, particularly one with so much leakage, filled the kill-team's primary comm-channels with nothing but static.

Zeed moved to the thick steel door of the reactor room, opened it a crack, and peered outside.

'It's getting busy out there,' he reported. 'Lots of mean-looking bastards, but they can hardly see with all the lights knocked out.

What do you say, brother? Are you ready to paint the walls with the blood of the foe?'

Under his helmet, Voss grinned. He thumbed his heavy flamer's igniter switch and a hot blue flame burst to life just in front of the weapon's promethium nozzle. 'Always,' he said, coming abreast of the Raven Guard.

Together, the two comrades charged into the corridor, howling the names of their primarchs as battle-cries.

'We're pinned,' hissed Rauth as ork stubber and pistol fire smacked into the metal wall beside him. Pipes shattered. Iron flakes showered the ground. Karras, Rauth and Solarion had pushed as far and as fast as they could once the alarms had been tripped. But now they found themselves penned-in at a junction, a confluence of three broad corridors, and mobs of howling, jabbering orks were pouring towards them from all sides.

With his knife, Solarion had already severed the cable that powered the lights, along with a score of others that did Throne knew what. A number of the orks, however, were equipped with goggles, not to mention weapons and armour far above typical greenskin standards. Karras had fought such fiends before. They were the greenskin equivalent of commando squads, far more cunning and deadly than the usual muscle-minded oafs. Their red night-vision lenses glowed like daemons' eyes as they pressed closer and closer, keeping to cover as much as possible.

Karras and his Deathwatch Marines were outnumbered at least twenty to one, and that ratio would quickly change for the worse if they didn't break through soon.

'Orders, Karras,' growled Solarion as his right pauldron absorbed a direct hit. The ork shell left an ugly scrape on the blue and white Chapter insignia there. 'We're taking too much fire. The cover here is pitiful.'

Karras thought fast. A smokescreen would be useless. If the ork goggles were operating on thermal signatures, they would see right through it. Incendiaries or frags would kill a good score of them and dissuade the others from closing, but that wouldn't solve the problem of being pinned.

'Novas,' he told them. 'On my signal, one down each corridor. Short throws. Remember to cover your visors. The moment they detonate, we make a push. I'm taking point. Clear?'

'On your mark, Karras,' said Solarion with a nod.

'Give the word,' said Rauth.

Karras tugged a nova grenade from the webbing around his armoured waist. The others did the same. He pulled the pin, swung his arm back and called out, 'Now!'

Three small black cylinders flew through the darkness to clatter against the metal floor. Swept up in the excitement of the firefight, the orks didn't notice them.

'Eyes!' shouted Karras and threw an arm up over his visor.

Three deafening bangs sounded in quick succession, louder even than the bark of the orks' guns. Howls of agony immediately followed, filling the close, damp air of the corridors. Karras looked up to see the orks reeling around in the dark with their great, thick-fingered hands pressed to their faces. They were crashing into the walls, weapons forgotten, thrown to the floor in their agony and confusion.

Nova grenades were typically employed for room clearance, but they worked well in any dark, enclosed space. They were far from standard-issue Astartes hardware, but the Deathwatch were the elite, the best of the best, and they had access to the kind of resources that few others could boast. The intense, phosphor-bright flash that the grenades produced overloaded optical receptors, both mechanical and biological. The blindness was temporary in most cases, but Karras was betting that the orks' goggles would magnify the glare.

Their retinas would be permanently burned out.

'With me,' he barked, and charged out from his corner. He moved in a blur, fixing his silenced bolter to the mag-locks on his thigh plate and drawing his faithful force sword, Arquemann, from its scabbard as he raced towards the foe.

Rauth and Solarion came behind, but not so close as to gamble with their lives. The bite of Arquemann was certain death whenever it glowed with otherworldly energy, and it had begun to glow now, throwing out a chill, unnatural light.

Karras threw himself in among the greenskin commandos, turning great powerful arcs with his blade, despatching more xenos filth with every limb-severing stroke. Steaming corpses soon littered the floor. The orks in the corridors behind continued to flail blindly, attacking each other now, in their sightless desperation.

'The way is clear,' Karras gasped. 'We run.' He sheathed Arquemann and led the way, feet pounding on the metal deck. The cryo-case swung wildly behind him as he moved, but he paid it no mind. Beneath his helmet, his third eye was closing again. The dangerous energies that gave him his powers were retreating at his command, suppressed by the mantras that kept him strong, kept him safe.

The inquisitor's voice intruded on the comm-link. 'Alpha, this is Sigma. Respond.'

'I hear you, Sigma,' said Karras as he ran.

'Where are you now?'

'Closing on Waypoint Barrius. We're about one minute out.'

'You're falling behind, Alpha. Perhaps I should begin preparing death certificates to your respective Chapters.'

'Damn you, inquisitor. We'll make it. Now if that's all you wanted...'

'Solarion is to leave you at Barrius. I have another task for him.'

'No,' said Karras flatly. 'We're already facing heavy resistance here. I need him with me.'

'I don't make requests, Deathwatch. According to naval intelligence reports, there is a large fighter bay on the ship's starboard side. Significant fuel dumps. Give Solarion your explosives. I want him to knock out that fighter bay while you and Rauth proceed to the bridge. If all goes well, the diversion may help clear your escape route. If not, you had better start praying for a miracle.'

'Rauth will blow the fuel dumps,' said Karras, opting to test a hunch.

'No,' said Sigma. 'Solarion is better acquainted with operating alone.'

Karras wondered about Sigma's insistence that Solarion go. Rauth hardly ever let Karras out of his sight. It had been that way ever since they'd met. Little wonder, then, that Zeed had settled on the nickname '*Watcher*'. Was Sigma behind it all? Karras couldn't be sure. The inquisitor had a point about Solarion's solo skills, and he knew it.

'Fine, I'll give Solarion the new orders.'

'No,' said Sigma. 'I'll do it directly. You and Rauth must hurry to the command bridge. Expect to lose comms once you get closer to the target. I'm sure you've sensed the creature's incredible power already. I want that thing eliminated, Alpha. Do not fail me.'

'When have I ever?' Karras retorted, but Sigma had already cut the link. Judging by Solarion's body language as he ran, the inquisitor was already giving him his new orders.

At the next junction, Waypoint Barrius, the trio encountered another ork mob. But the speed at which Karras and his men were moving caught the orks by surprise. Karras didn't even have time to charge his blade with psychic energy before he was in among them, hacking and thrusting. Arquemann was lethally sharp even without the power of the immaterium running through it, and orks fell in a great tide of blood. Silenced bolters coughed on either side of him, Solarion and Rauth giving fire support, and soon the junction was heaped with twitching green meat.

Karras turned to Rauth. 'Give Solarion your frags and incendiaries,' he said, pulling his own from his webbing. 'But keep two breaching charges. We'll need them.'

Solarion accepted the grenades, quickly fixing them to his belt, then he said, 'Good hunting, brothers.'

Karras nodded. 'We'll rendezvous back at the elevator shaft.

Whoever gets there first holds it until the others arrive. Keep the comm-link open. If it goes dead for more than ten minutes at our end, don't waste any time. Rendezvous with Voss and Zeed and get to the salvage bay.'

Solarion banged a fist on his breastplate in salute and turned.

Karras nodded to Rauth. 'Let's go,' he said, and together, they ran on towards the fore section of the ship while Solarion merged with the shadows in the other direction.

'Die!' spat Zeed as another massive greenskin slid to the floor, its body opened from gullet to groin. Then he was moving again. Instincts every bit as sharp as his lightning claws told him to sidestep just in time to avoid the stroke of a giant chainaxe that would have cleaved him in two. The ork wielding the axe roared in frustration as its whirring blade bit into the metal floor, sending up a shower of orange sparks. It made a grab for Zeed with its empty hand, but Zeed parried, slipped inside at the same instant, and thrust his right set of claws straight up under the creature's jutting jaw. The tips of the long slender blades punched through the top of its skull, and it stood there quivering, literally dead on its feet.

Zeed stepped back, wrenching his claws from the creature's throat, and watched its body drop beside the others.

He looked around hungrily, eager for another opponent to step forward, but there were none to be had. Voss and he stood surrounded by dead xenos. The Imperial Fist had already lowered his heavy flamer. He stood admiring his handiwork, a small hill of smoking black corpses. The two comrades had fought their way back to Waypoint Adrius. The air in the towering chamber was now thick with the stink of spilled blood and burnt flesh.

Zeed looked up at the landings overhead and said, 'No sign of the others.'

Voss moved up beside him. 'There's much less static on the comm-link here. Scholar, this is Omni. If you can hear me, respond.'

At first there was no answer. Voss was about to try again when the Death Spectre Librarian finally acknowledged. 'I hear you, Omni. This isn't the best time.'

Karras sounded strained, as if fighting for his life.

'We are finished with the reactor,' Voss reported. 'Back at Waypoint Adrius, now. Do you need assistance?'

As he asked this, Voss automatically checked the mission countdown. Not good.

Twenty-seven minutes left.

'Hold that position,' Karras grunted. 'We need to keep that area secure for our escape. Rauth and I are–'

His words were cut off in mid-sentence. For a brief instant, Voss and Zeed thought the kill-team leader had been hit, possibly even killed. But their fears were allayed when Karras heaved a sigh of relief and said, 'Damn, those bastards were strong. Ghost, you would have enjoyed that. Listen, brothers, Rauth and I are outside the ship's command bridge. Time is running out. If we don't make it back to Waypoint Adrius within the next twelve minutes, I want the rest of you to pull out. Do *not* miss the pick-up. Is that understood?'

Voss scowled. The words *pull out* made him want to smash something. As far as his Chapter was concerned, they were curse words. But he knew Karras was right. There was little to be gained by dying here. 'Emperor's speed, Scholar,' he said.

'For Terra and the Throne,' Karras replied then signed off.

Zeed was scraping his claws together restlessly, a bad habit that manifested itself when he had excess adrenaline and no further outlet for it. 'Damn,' he said. 'I'm not standing around here while the others are fighting for their lives.' He pointed to the metal landing high above him where Karras and the others had gotten off the elevator. 'There has to be a way to call that piece of junk back down to this level. We can ride it up there and–'

He was interrupted by the clatter of heavy, iron-shod boots closing from multiple directions. The sounds echoed into the chamber from a dozen corridor mouths.

'I think we're about to be too busy for that, brother,' said Voss darkly.

Rauth stepped over the body of the massive ork guard he had just slain, flicked the beast's blood from the groove on his shortsword, and sheathed it at his side. There was a shallow crater in the ceramite of his right pauldron. Part of his Chapter icon was missing, cleaved off in the fight. The daemon-skull design now boasted only a single horn. The other pauldron, intricately detailed with the skull, bones and inquisitorial 'I' of the Deathwatch, was chipped and scraped, but had suffered no serious damage.

'That's the biggest I've slain hand-to-hand,' the Exorcist muttered, mostly to himself.

The one Karras had just slain was no smaller, but the Death Spectre was focused on something else. He was standing with one hand pressed to a massive steel blast door covered in orkish glyphs. Tiny lambent arcs of unnatural energy flickered around him.

'There's a tremendous amount of psychic interference,' he said, 'but I sense at least thirty of them on this level. Our target is on the upper deck. And he knows we're here.'

Rauth nodded, but said nothing. *We?* No. Karras was wrong in that. Rauth knew well enough that the target couldn't have sensed him. Nothing psychic could. It was a side effect of the unspeakable horrors he had endured during his Chapter's selection and training programmes – programmes that had taught him to hate all psykers and the terrible daemons their powers sometimes loosed into the galaxy.

The frequency with which Lyandro Karras tapped the power of the immaterium disgusted Rauth. Did the Librarian not realise the great peril in which he placed his soul? Or was he simply a fool, spilling over with an arrogance that invited the ultimate calamity. Daemons of the warp rejoiced in the folly of such men.

Of course, that was why Rauth had been sequestered to Deathwatch in the first place. The inquisitor had never said so explicitly, but it simply had to be the case. As enigmatic as Sigma was, he was clearly no fool. Who better than an Exorcist to watch over one such as Karras? Even the mighty Grey Knights, from whose seed Rauth's Chapter had been born, could hardly have been more suited to the task.

'Smoke,' said Karras. 'The moment we breach, I want smoke grenades in there. Don't spare them for later. Use what we have. We go in with bolters blazing. Remove your suppressor. There's no need for it now. Let them hear the bark of our guns. The minute the lower floor is cleared, we each take a side stair to the command deck. You go left. I'll take the right. We'll find the target at the top.'

'Bodyguards?' asked Rauth. Like Karras, he began unscrewing the sound suppressor from the barrel of his bolter.

'I can't tell. If there are, the psychic resonance is blotting them out. It's... incredible.'

The two Astartes stored their suppressors in pouches on their webbing, then Rauth fixed a rectangular breaching charge to the seam between the double doors. The Exorcist was about to step back when Karras said, 'No, brother. We'll need two. These doors are stronger than you think.'

Rauth fixed another charge just below the first, then he and Karras moved to either side of the doorway and pressed their backs to the wall.

Simultaneously, they checked the magazines in their bolters. Rauth slid in a fresh clip. Karras tugged a smoke grenade from his webbing, and nodded.

'Now!'

Rauth pressed the tiny detonator switch in his hand, and the whole corridor shook with a deafening blast to rival the boom of any artillery piece. The heavy doors blew straight into the room, causing immediate casualties among the orks closest to the explosion.

'Smoke!' ordered Karras as he threw his first grenade. Rauth discarded the detonator and did the same. Two, three, four small canisters bounced onto the ship's bridge, spread just enough to avoid redundancy. Within two seconds, the whole deck was covered in a dense grey cloud. The ork crew went into an uproar, barely able to see their hands in front of their faces. But to the Astartes, all was perfectly clear. They entered the room with bolters firing, each shot a vicious bark, and the greenskins fell where they stood.

Not a single bolt was wasted. Every last one found its target, every shot a headshot, an instant kill. In the time it took to draw three breaths, the lower floor of the bridge was cleared of threats.

'Move!' said Karras, making for the stair that jutted from the right-hand wall.

The smoke had begun to billow upwards now, thinning as it did.

Rauth stormed the left-side stair.

Neither Space Marine, however, was entirely prepared for what he found at the top.

Solarion burst from the mouth of the corridor and sprinted along the metal landing in the direction of the elevator cage. He was breathing hard, and rivulets of red blood ran from grape-sized holes in the armour of his torso and left upper arm. If he could only stop, the wounds would quickly seal themselves, but there was no time for that. His normally dormant second heart was pumping in tandem with the first, flushing lactic acid from his muscles, helping him to keep going. Following barely a second behind him, a great mob of armoured orks with heavy pistols and blades surged out of the same corridor in hot pursuit. The platform trembled under their tremendous weight.

Solarion didn't stop to look behind. Just ahead of him, the upper section of the landing ended. Beyond it was the rusted stairway that had almost claimed Rauth's life. There was no time now to navigate those stairs.

He put on an extra burst of speed and leapt straight out over them.

It was an impressive jump. For a moment, he almost seemed to fly. Then he passed the apex of his jump and the ship's artificial gravity started to pull him downwards. He landed on the lower section of the landing with a loud clang. Sharp spears of pain shot up the nerves in his legs, but he ignored them and turned, bolter held ready at his shoulder.

The orks were following his example, leaping from the upper platform, hoping to land right beside him and cut him to pieces. Their lack of agility, however, betrayed them. The first row crashed down onto the rickety stairs about two thirds of the way down.

The old iron steps couldn't take that kind of punishment. They crumbled and snapped, dropping the luckless orks into lethal free-fall. The air filled with howls, but the others didn't catch on until it was too late. They, too, leapt from the platform's edge in their eagerness to make a kill. Step after step gave way with each heavy body that crashed down on it, and soon the stairway was reduced almost to nothing.

A broad chasm, some thirty metres across, now separated the metal platforms that had been joined by the stairs. The surviving orks saw that they couldn't follow the Space Marine across. Instead, they paced the edge of the upper platform, bellowing at Solarion in outrage and frustration and taking wild potshots at him with their clunky pistols.

'It's raining greenskins,' said a gruff voice on the link. 'What in Dorn's name is going on up there?'

With one eye still on the pacing orks, Solarion moved to the edge of the platform. As he reached the twisted railing, he looked out over the edge and down towards the steel floor two-hundred metres below. Gouts of bright promethium flame illuminated a conflict there. Voss and Zeed were standing back to back, about five metres apart, fighting off an ork assault from all sides. The floor around them was heaped with dead aliens.

'This is Solarion,' the Ultramarine told them. 'Do you need aid, brothers?'

'Prophet?' said Zeed between lethal sweeps of his claws. 'Where are Scholar and Watcher?'

'You've had no word?' asked Solarion.

'They've been out of contact since they entered the command bridge. Sigma warned of that. But time is running out. Can you go to them?'

'Impossible,' replied Solarion. 'The stairs are gone. I can't get back up there now.'

'Then pray for them,' said Voss.

Solarion checked his mission chrono. He remembered Karras's orders. Four more minutes. After that, he would have to assume they were dead. He would take the elevator down and, with the others, strike out for the salvage bay and their only hope of escape.

A shell from an ork pistol ricocheted from the platform and smacked against his breastplate. The shot wasn't powerful enough to penetrate ceramite, not like the heavy-stubber shells he had taken at close range, but it got his attention. He was about to return fire, to start clearing the upper platform in anticipation of Karras and Rauth's return, when a great boom shook the air and sent deep vibrations through the metal under his feet.

'That's not one of mine,' said Voss.

'It's mine,' said Solarion. 'I rigged the fuel dump in their fighter bay. If we're lucky, most of the greenskins will be drawn there, thinking that's where the conflict is. It might buy our brothers a little time.'

The mission chrono now read eighteen minutes and forty seconds. He watched it drop. Thirty-nine seconds. Thirty-eight. Thirty-seven.

Come on, Karras, he thought. What in Terra's name are you doing?

Karras barely had time to register the sheer size of Balthazog Bludwrekk's twin bodyguards before their blistering assault began. They were easily the largest orks he had ever seen, even larger than the door guards he and Rauth had slain, and they wielded their massive two-handed warhammers as if they weighed nothing at all. Under normal circumstances, orks of this size and strength would have become mighty warbosses, but these two were nothing of the kind. They were slaves to a far greater power than mere muscle or aggression. They were mindless puppets held in servitude by a much deadlier force, and the puppeteer himself sat some ten metres behind them, perched on a bizarre mechanical throne in the centre of the ship's command deck.

Bludwrekk!

Karras only needed an instant, a fraction of a second, to take in the details of the fiend's appearance.

Even for an ork, the psychic warboss was hideous. Portions of his head were vastly swollen, with great vein-marbled bumps extending out in all directions from his crown. His brow was ringed with large, blood-stained metal plugs sunk deep into the bone of his skull. The beast's leering, lopsided face was twisted, like something seen in a curved mirror, the features pathetically small on one side, grotesquely overlarge on the other, and saliva dripped from his slack jaw, great strands of it hanging from the spaces between his tusks.

He wore a patchwork robe of cured human skins stitched together with gut, and a trio of decaying heads hung between his knees, fixed to his belt by long, braided hair. Karras had the immediate impression that the heads had been taken from murdered women, perhaps the wives of some human lord or tribal leader that the beast had slain during a raid. Orks had a known fondness for such grisly trophies.

The beast's throne was just as strange; a mass of coils, cogs and moving pistons without any apparent purpose whatsoever. Thick bundles of wire linked it to an inexplicable clutter of vast, arcane machines that crackled and hummed with sickly green light. In the instant Karras took all this in, he felt his anger and hate break over him like a thunderstorm.

It was as if this creature, this blasted aberration, sat in sickening, blasphemous parody of the immortal Emperor Himself.

The two Space Marines opened fire at the same time, eager to drop the bodyguards and engage the real target quickly. Their bolters chattered, spitting their deadly hail, but somehow each round detonated harmlessly in the air.

'He's shielding them!' Karras called out. 'Draw your blade!'

He dropped the cryo-case from his shoulder, pulled Arquemann from its scabbard and let the power of the immaterium flow through him, focusing it into the ancient crystalline matrix that lay embedded in the blade.

'To me, xenos scum!' he roared at the hulking beast in front of him.

The bodyguard's massive hammer whistled up into the air, then changed direction with a speed that seemed impossible. Karras barely managed to step aside. Sparks flew as the weapon clipped his left pauldron, sending a painful shock along his arm. The thick steel floor fared worse. The hammer left a hole in it the size of a human head.

On his right, Karras heard Rauth loose a great battle-cry as he clashed with his own opponent, barely ducking a lateral blow that would have taken his head clean off. The Exorcist's short-sword looked awfully small compared to his enemy's hammer.

Bludwrekk was laughing, revelling in the life and death struggle that was playing out before him, as if it were some kind of grand entertainment laid on just for him. The more he cackled, the more the green light seemed to shimmer and churn around him. Karras felt the resonance of that power disorienting him. The air was supercharged with it. He felt his own power surging up inside him, rising to meet it. Only so much could be channelled into his force sword. Already, the blade sang with deadly energy as it slashed through the air.

This surge is dangerous, he warned himself. I mustn't let it get out of control.

Automatically, he began reciting the mantras Master Cordatus had taught him, but the effort of wrestling to maintain his equilibrium cost him an opening in which he could have killed his foe with a stroke. The ork bodyguard, on the other hand, did not miss its chance. It caught Karras squarely on the right pauldron with the head of its hammer, shattering the Deathwatch insignia there, and knocking him sideways, straight off his feet.

The impact hurled Karras directly into Rauth's opponent, and the two tumbled to the metal floor. Karras's helmet was torn from his head, and rolled away. In the sudden tangle of thrashing Space Marine and ork bodies, Rauth saw an opening. He stepped straight in, plunging his shortsword up under the beast's sternum, shoving it deep, cleaving the ork's heart in two. Without hesitation, he then turned to face the remaining bodyguard while Karras kicked himself clear of the dead behemoth and got to his feet.

The last bodyguard was fast, and Rauth did well to stay clear of the whistling hammerhead, but the stabbing and slashing strokes of his shortsword were having little effect. It was only when Karras joined him, and the ork was faced with attacks from two directions at once, that the tables truly turned. Balthazog Bludwrekk had stopped laughing now. He gave a deafening roar of anger as Rauth and Karras thrust from opposite angles and, between them, pierced the greenskin's heart and lungs.

Blood bubbled from its wounds as it sank to the floor, dropping its mighty hammer with a crash.

Bludwrekk surged upwards from his throne. Arcs of green lightning lanced outwards from his fingers. Karras felt Waaagh! energy lick his armour, looking for chinks through which it might burn his flesh and corrode his soul. Together, blades raised, he and Rauth rounded on their foe.

The moment they stepped forward to engage, however, a great torrent of kinetic energy burst from the ork's outstretched hands and launched Rauth into the air. Karras ducked and rolled sideways, narrowly avoiding death, but he heard Rauth land with a heavy crash on the lower floor of the bridge.

'Rauth!' he shouted over the link. 'Answer!'

No answer was forthcoming. The comm-link was useless here. And perhaps Rauth was already dead.

Karras felt the ork's magnified power pressing in on him from all sides, and now he saw its source. Behind Bludwrekk's mechanical throne, beyond a filthy, blood-spattered window of thick glass, there were hundreds – no, thousands – of orks strapped to vertical slabs that looked like operating tables. The tops of their skulls had been removed, and cables and tubes ran from their exposed brains to the core of a vast power-siphoning system.

'By the Golden Throne,' gasped Karras. 'No wonder Sigma wants your ugly head.'

How much time remained before the ship's reactors detonated? Without his helmet, he couldn't tell. Long enough to kill this monstrosity? Maybe. But, one on one, was he even a match for the thing?

Not without exploiting more of the dangerous power at his disposal. He had to trust in his master's teachings. The mantras would keep him safe. They had to. He opened himself up to the warp a little more, channelling it, focusing it with his mind.

Bludwrekk stepped forward to meet him, and the two powers clashed with apocalyptic fury.

Darrion Rauth was not dead. The searing impact of the ork warlord's psychic blast would have killed a lesser man on contact, ripping his soul from his body and leaving it a lifeless hunk of meat. But Rauth was no lesser man. The secret rites of his Chapter, and the suffering he had endured to earn his place in it, had proofed him against such a fate. Also, though a number of his bones were broken, his superhuman physiology was already about the business of reknitting them, making them whole and strong again. The internal bleeding would stop soon, too.

But there wasn't time to heal completely. Not if he wanted to make a difference.

With a grunt of pain, he rolled, pushed himself to one knee, and looked for his shortsword. He couldn't see it. His bolter, however, was still attached to his thigh plate. He tugged it free, slammed in a fresh magazine, cocked it, and struggled to his feet. He coughed wetly, tasting blood in his mouth. Looking up towards the place from which he had been thrown, he saw unnatural light blazing and strobing. There was a great deal of noise, too, almost like thunder, but not quite the same. It made the air tremble around him.

Karras must still be alive, he thought. He's still fighting.

Pushing aside the agony in his limbs, he ran to the stairs on his right and, with an ancient litany of strength on his lips, charged up them to rejoin the battle.

Karras was failing. He could feel it. Balthazog Bludwrekk was drawing on an incredible reserve of power. The psychic Waaagh! energy he was tapping seemed boundless, pouring into the warlord from the brains of the tormented orks wired into his insane contraption.

Karras cursed as he struggled to turn aside another wave of roiling green fire. It buckled the deck plates all around him. Only those beneath his feet, those that fell inside the shimmering bubble he fought to maintain, remained undamaged.

His shield was holding, but only just, and the effort required to maintain it precluded him from launching attacks of his own. Worse yet, as the ork warlord pressed his advantage, Karras was forced to let the power of the warp flow through him more and more. A cacophony of voices had risen in his head, chittering and whispering in tongues he knew were blasphemous. This was the moment all Librarians feared, when the power they wielded threatened to consume them, when user became used, master became slave. The voices started to drown out his own. Much more of this and his soul would be lost for eternity, ripped from him and thrown into the maelstrom. Daemons would wrestle for command of his mortal flesh.

Was it right to slay this ork at the cost of his immortal soul? Should he not simply drop his shield and die so that something far worse than Bludwrekk would be denied entry into the material universe?

Karras could barely hear these questions in his head. So many other voices crowded them out.

Balthazog Bludwrekk seemed to sense the moment was his. He stepped nearer, still trailing thick cables from the metal plugs in his distorted skull.

Karras sank to one knee under the onslaught to both body and mind. His protective bubble was dissipating. Only seconds remained. One way or another, he realised, he was doomed.

Bludwrekk was almost on him now, still throwing green lightning from one hand, drawing a long, curved blade with the other. Glistening strands of drool shone in the fierce green light. His eyes were ablaze.

Karras sagged, barely able to hold himself upright, leaning heavily on the sword his mentor had given him.

I am Lyandro Karras, he tried to think. Librarian. Death Spectre. Space Marine. The Emperor will not let me fall.

But his inner voice was faint. Bludwrekk was barely two metres away. His psychic assault pierced Karras's shield. The Codicer felt the skin on his arms blazing and crisping. His nerves began to scream.

In his mind, one voice began to dominate the others. Was this the voice of the daemon that would claim him? It was so loud and clear that it seemed to issue from the very air around him. 'Get up, Karras!' it snarled. 'Fight!'

He realised it was speaking in High Gothic. He hadn't expected that.

His vision was darkening, despite the green fire that blazed all around, but, distantly, he caught a flicker of movement to his right. A hulking black figure appeared as if from nowhere, weapon raised before it. There was something familiar about it, an icon on the left shoulder; a skull with a single gleaming red eye.

Rauth!

The Exorcist's bolter spat a torrent of shells, forcing Balthazog Bludwrekk to spin and defend himself, concentrating all his psychic power on stopping the stream of deadly bolts.

Karras acted without pause for conscious thought. He moved

on reflex, conditioned by decades of harsh daily training rituals. With Bludwrekk's merciless assault momentarily halted, he surged upwards, putting all his strength into a single horizontal swing of his force sword. The warp energy he had been trying to marshal crashed over him, flooding into the crystalline matrix of his blade as the razor-edged metal bit deep into the ork's thick green neck.

The monster didn't even have time to scream. Body and head fell in separate directions, the green light vanished, and the upper bridge was suddenly awash with steaming ork blood.

Karras fell to his knees, and screamed, dropping Arquemann at his side. His fight wasn't over. Not yet.

Now, he turned his attention to the battle for his soul.

Rauth saw all too clearly that his moment had come, as he had known it must, sooner or later, but he couldn't relish it. There was no joy to be had here. Psyker or not, Lyandro Karras was a Space Marine, a son of the Emperor just as he was himself, and he had saved Rauth's life.

But you must do it for him, Rauth told himself. You must do it to save his soul.

Out of respect, Rauth took off his helmet so that he might bear witness to the Death Spectre's final moments with his own naked eyes. Grimacing, he raised the barrel of his bolter to Karras's temple and began reciting the words of the *Mortis Morgatii Praetovo*. It was an ancient rite from long before the Great Crusade, forgotten by all save the Exorcists and the Grey Knights. If it worked, it would send Karras's spiritual essence beyond the reach of the warp's ravenous fiends, but it could not save his life.

It was not a long rite, and Rauth recited it perfectly.

As he came to the end of it, he prepared to squeeze the trigger.

War raged inside Lyandro Karras. Sickening entities filled with hate and hunger strove to overwhelm him. They were brutal and relentless, bombarding him with unholy visions that threatened to drown him in horror and disgust. He saw Imperial saints defiled and mutilated on altars of burning black rock. He saw the Golden Throne smashed and ruined, and the body of the Emperor trampled under the feet of vile capering beasts. He saw his Chapter house sundered, its walls covered in weeping sores as if the stones themselves had contracted a vile disease.

He cried out, railing against the visions, denying them. But still they came. He scrambled for something Cordatus had told him.

Cordatus!

The thought of that name alone gave him the strength to keep up the fight, if only for a moment. To avoid becoming lost in the empyrean, the old warrior had said, one must anchor oneself to the physical.

Karras reached for the physical now, for something real, a bastion against the visions.

He found it in a strange place, in a sensation he couldn't quite explain. Something hot and metallic was pressing hard against the skin of his temple.

The metal was scalding him, causing him physical pain. Other pains joined it, accumulating so that the song of agony his nerves were singing became louder and louder. He felt again the pain of his burned hands, even while his gene-boosted body worked fast to heal them. He clutched at the pain, letting the sensation pull his mind back to the moment, to the here and now. He grasped it like a rock in a storm-tossed sea.

The voices of the vile multitude began to weaken. He heard his own inner voice again, and immediately resumed his mantras. Soon enough, the energy of the immaterium slowed to a trickle, then ceased completely. He felt the physical manifestation of his third eye closing. He felt the skin knitting on his brow once again.

What was it, he wondered, this hot metal pressed to his head, this thing that had saved him?

He opened his eyes and saw the craggy, battle-scarred features of Darrion Rauth. The Exorcist was standing very close, helmet at his side, muttering something that sounded like a prayer.

His bolter was pressed to Karras's head, and he was about to blow his brains out.

'What are you doing?' Karras asked quietly.

Rauth looked surprised to hear his voice.

'I'm saving your soul, Death Spectre. Be at peace. Your honour will be spared. The daemons of the warp will not have you.'

'That is good to know,' said Karras. 'Now lower your weapon. My soul is exactly where it should be, and there it stays until my service to the Emperor is done.'

For a moment, neither Rauth nor Karras moved. The Exorcist did not seem convinced.

'Darrion Rauth,' said Karras. 'Are you so eager to spill my blood? Is this why you have shadowed my every movement for the last three years? Perhaps Solarion would thank you for killing me, but I don't think Sigma would.'

'That would depend,' Rauth replied. Hesitantly, however, he lowered his gun. 'You will submit to proper testing when we return to the *Saint Nevarre*. Sigma will insist on it, and so shall I.'

'As is your right, brother, but be assured that you will find no taint. Of course it won't matter either way unless we get off this ship alive. Quickly now, grab the monster's head. I will open the cryo-case.'

Rauth did as ordered, though he kept a wary eye on the kill-team leader. Lifting Bludwrekk's lifeless head, he offered it to Karras, saying, 'The machinery that boosted Bludwrekk's power should be analysed. If other ork psykers begin to employ such things…'

Karras took the ork's head from him, placed it inside the black case, and pressed a four-digit code into the keypad on the side. The lid fused itself shut with a hiss. Karras rose, slung it over his right shoulder, sheathed Arquemann, located his helmet, and fixed it back on his head. Rauth donned his own helmet, too.

'If Sigma wanted the machine,' said Karras as he led his comrade off the command bridge, 'he would have said so.'

Glancing at the mission chrono, he saw that barely seventeen minutes remained until the exfiltration deadline. He doubted it would be enough to escape the ship, but he wasn't about to give up without trying. Not after all they had been through here.

'Can you run?' he asked Rauth.

'Time is up,' said Solarion grimly. He stood in front of the open elevator cage. 'They're not going to make it. I'm coming down.'

'No,' said Voss. 'Give them another minute, Prophet.'

Voss and Zeed had finished slaughtering their attackers on the lower floor. It was just as well, too. Voss had used up the last of his promethium fuel in the fight. With great regret, he had slung the fuel pack off his back and relinquished the powerful weapon. He drew his support weapon, a bolt pistol, from a holster on his webbing.

It felt pathetically small and light in his hand.

'Would you have us all die here, brother?' asked the Ultra-marine. 'For no gain? Because that will be our lot if we don't get moving right now.'

'If only we had heard *something* on the link…' said Zeed. 'Omni, as much as I hate to say it, Prophet has a point.'

'Believe me,' said Solarion, 'I wish it were otherwise. As of this moment, however, it seems only prudent that I assume operational command. Sigma, if you are listening–'

A familiar voice cut him off.

'Wait until my boots have cooled before you step into them, Solarion!'

'Scholar!' exclaimed Zeed. 'And is Watcher with you?'

'How many times must I warn you, Raven Guard,' said the Exorcist. 'Don't call me that.'

'At least another hundred,' replied Zeed.

'Karras,' said Voss, 'where in Dorn's name are you?'

'Almost at the platform now,' said Karras. 'We've got company. Ork commandos closing the distance from the rear.'

'Keep your speed up,' said Solarion. 'The stairs are out. You'll have to jump. The gap is about thirty metres.'

'Understood,' said Karras. 'Coming out of the corridor now.'

Solarion could hear the thunder of heavy feet pounding the upper metal platform from which he had so recently leaped. He watched from beside the elevator, and saw two bulky black figures soar out into the air.

Karras landed first, coming down hard. The cryo-case came free of his shoulder and skidded across the metal floor towards the edge. Solarion saw it and moved automatically, stopping it with one booted foot before it slid over the side.

Rauth landed a second later, slamming onto the platform in a heap. He gave a grunt of pain, pushed himself up and limped past Solarion into the elevator cage.

'Are you wounded, brother?' asked the Ultramarine.

'It is nothing,' growled Rauth.

Karras and Solarion joined him in the cage. The kill-team leader pulled the lever, starting them on their downward journey.

The cage started slowly at first, but soon gathered speed. Halfway down, the heavy counterweight again whooshed past them.

'Ghost, Omni,' said Karras over the link. 'Start clearing the route towards the salvage bay. We'll catch up with you as soon as we're at the bottom.'

'Loud and clear, Scholar,' said Zeed. He and Voss disappeared off into the darkness of the corridor through which the kill-team had originally come.

Suddenly, Rauth pointed upwards. 'Trouble,' he said.

Karras and Solarion looked up.

Some of the ork commandos, those more resourceful than their kin, had used grapnels to cross the gap in the platforms. Now they were hacking at the elevator cables with their broad blades.

'Solarion,' said Karras.

He didn't need to say anything else. The Ultramarine raised his bolter, sighted along the barrel, and began firing up at the orks. Shots sparked from the metal around the greenskins' heads, but it was hard to fire accurately with the elevator shaking and shuddering throughout its descent.

Rauth stepped forward and ripped the latticework gate from its hinges. 'We should jump the last twenty metres,' he said.

Solarion stopped firing. 'Agreed.'

Karras looked down from the edge of the cage floor. 'Forty metres,' he said. 'Thirty-five. Thirty. Twenty-five. Go!'

Together, the three Astartes leapt clear of the elevator and landed on the metal floor below. Again, Rauth gave a pained grunt, but he was up just as fast as the others.

Behind them, the elevator cage slammed into the floor with a mighty clang. Karras turned just in time to see the heavy counterweight smash down on top of it. The orks had cut the cables after all. Had the three Space Marines stayed in the cage until it reached the bottom, they would have been crushed to a fleshy pulp.

'Ten minutes left,' said Karras, adjusting the cryo-case on his shoulder. 'In the Emperor's name, run!'

Karras, Rauth and Solarion soon caught up with Voss and Zeed. There wasn't time to move carefully now, but Karras dreaded getting caught up in another firefight. That would surely doom them. Perhaps the saints were smiling on him, though, because it seemed that most of the orks in the sections between the central shaft and the prow had responded to the earlier alarms and had already been slain by Zeed and Voss.

The corridors were comparatively empty, but the large mess room with its central squig pit was not.

The Space Marines charged straight in, this time on ground level, and opened fire with their bolters, cutting down the orks that were directly in their way. With his beloved blade, Karras hacked down all who stood before him, always maintaining his forward momentum, never stopping for a moment. In a matter of seconds, the kill-team crossed the mess hall and plunged into the shadowy corridor on the far side.

A great noise erupted behind them. Those orks that had not been killed or injured were taking up weapons and following close by. Their heavy, booted feet shook the grillework floors of the corridor as they swarmed along it.

'Omni,' said Karras, feet hammering the metal floor, 'the moment we reach the bay, I want you to ready the shuttle. Do not stop to engage, is that clear?'

If Karras had been expecting some argument from the Imperial Fist, he was surprised. Voss acknowledged the order without dispute. The whole team had made it this far by the skin of their teeth, but he knew it would count for absolutely nothing if their shuttle didn't get clear of the ork ship in time.

Up ahead, just over Solarion's shoulder, Karras saw the light of the salvage bay. Then, in another few seconds, they were out of the corridor and charging through the mountains of scrap towards the large piece of starship wreckage in which they had stolen aboard.

There was a crew of gretchin around it, working feverishly with wrenches and hammers that looked far too big for their sinewy little bodies. Some even had blowtorches and were cutting through sections of the outer plate.

Damn them, cursed Karras. If they've damaged any of our critical systems...

Bolters spat, and the gretchin dropped in a red mist.

'Omni, get those systems running,' Karras ordered. 'We'll hold them off.'

Voss tossed Karras his bolt pistol as he ran past, then disappeared into the doorway in the side of the ruined prow.

Karras saw Rauth and Solarion open fire as the first of the pursuing orks charged in. At first, they came in twos and threes. Then they came in a great flood. Empty magazines fell to the scrap-covered floor, to be replaced by others that were quickly spent.

Karras drew his own bolt pistol from its holster and joined the firefight, wielding one in each hand. Orks fell before him with gaping exit wounds in their heads.

'I'm out!' yelled Solarion, drawing his shortsword.

'Dry,' called Rauth seconds later and did the same.

Frenzied orks continued to pour in, firing their guns and waving their oversized blades, despite the steadily growing number of their dead that they had to trample over.

'Blast it!' cursed Karras. 'Talk to me, Omni.'

'Forty seconds,' answered the Imperial Fist. 'Coils at sixty per cent.'

Karras's bolt pistols clicked empty within two rounds of each other. He holstered his own, fixed Voss's to a loop on his webbing, drew Arquemann and called to the others, 'Into the shuttle, now. We'll have to take our chances.'

And hope they don't cut through to our fuel lines, he thought sourly.

One member of the kill-team, however, didn't seem to like those odds much.

'They're mine!' Zeed roared, and he threw himself in among the orks, cutting and stabbing in a battle-fury, dropping the giant alien savages like flies. Karras felt a flash of anger, but he marvelled at the way the Raven Guard moved, as if every single flex of muscle and claw was part of a dance that sent xenos filth howling to their deaths.

Zeed's armour was soon drenched in blood, and still he fought, swiping this way and that, always moving in perpetual slaughter, as if he were a tireless engine of death.

'Plasma coils at eighty per cent,' Voss announced. 'What are we waiting on, Scholar?'

Solarion and Rauth had already broken from the orks they were fighting and had raced inside, but Karras hovered by the door.

Zeed was still fighting.

'Ghost,' shouted Karras. 'Fall back, damn you.'

Zeed didn't seem to hear him, and the seconds kept ticking away. Any moment now, Karras knew, the ork ship's reactor would explode. Voss had seen to that. Death would take all of them if they didn't leave right now.

'Raven Guard!' Karras roared.

That did it.

Zeed plunged his lightning claws deep into the belly of one last ork, gutted him, then turned and raced towards Karras.

When they were through the door, Karras thumped the locking mechanism with the heel of his fist. 'You're worse than Omni,' he growled at the Raven Guard. Then, over the comm-link, he said, 'Blow the piston charges and get us out of here fast.'

He heard the sound of ork blades and hammers battering the hull as the orks tried to hack their way inside. The shuttle door would hold but, if Voss didn't get them out of the salvage bay soon, they would go up with the rest of the ship.

'Detonating charges now,' said the Imperial Fist.

In the salvage bay, the packages he had fixed to the big pistons and cables on either side of the bay at the start of the mission exploded, shearing straight through the metal.

There was a great metallic screeching sound and the whole floor of the salvage bay began to shudder. Slowly, the ork ship's gigantic mouth fell open, and the cold void of space rushed in, stealing away the breathable atmosphere. Everything inside the salvage bay, both animate and inanimate, was blown out of the gigantic mouth, as if snatched up by a mighty hurricane. Anything that hit the great triangular teeth on the way out went into a wild spin. Karras's team was lucky. Their craft missed clipping the upper front teeth by less than a metre.

'Shedding the shell,' said Voss, 'in three… two… one…'

He hit a button on the pilot's console that fired a series of explosive bolts, and the wrecked prow façade fragmented and fell away, the pieces drifting off into space like metal blossoms on a breeze. The shuttle beneath was now revealed – a sleek, black wedge-shaped craft bearing the icons of both the Ordo Xenos and the Inquisition proper. All around it, metal debris and rapidly freezing ork bodies spun in zero gravity.

Inside the craft, Karras, Rauth, Solarion and Zeed fixed their weapons on storage racks, sat in their respective places, and locked themselves into impact frames.

'Hold on to something,' said Voss from the cockpit as he fired the ship's plasma thrusters.

The shuttle leapt forward, accelerating violently just as the stern of the massive ork ship exploded. There was a blinding flash of yellow light that outshone even the local star. Then a series of secondary explosions erupted, blowing each section of the vast metal monstrosity apart, from aft to fore, in a great chain of utter destruction. Twenty thousand ork lives were snuffed out in a matter of seconds, reduced to their component atoms in the plasma-charged blasts.

Aboard the shuttle, Zeed removed his helmet and shook out his long black hair. With a broad grin, he said, 'Damn, but I fought well today.'

Karras might have grinned at the Raven Guard's exaggerated arrogance, but not this time. His mood was dark, despite their survival. Sigma had asked a lot this time. He looked down at the black surface of the cryo-case between his booted feet.

Zeed followed his gaze. 'We got what we came for, right, Scholar?' he asked.

Karras nodded.

'Going to let me see it?'

Zeed hated the ordo's need-to-know policies, hated not knowing exactly why Talon squad was put on the line, time after time. Karras could identify with that. Maybe they all could. But curiosity brought its own dangers.

In one sense, it didn't really matter *why* Sigma wanted Bludwrekk's head, or anything else, so long as each of the Space Marines honoured the obligations of their Chapters and lived to return to them.

One day, it would all be over.

One day, Karras would set foot on Occludus again, and return to the Librarius as a veteran of the Deathwatch.

He felt Rauth's eyes on him, watching as always, perhaps closer than ever now. There would be trouble later. Difficult questions. Tests. Karras didn't lie to himself. He knew how close he had come to losing his soul. He had never allowed so much of the power to flow through him before, and the results made him anxious never to do so again.

How readily would Rauth pull the trigger next time?

Focusing his attention back on Zeed, he shook his head and muttered, 'There's nothing to see, Ghost. Just an ugly green head with metal plugs in it.' He tapped the case. 'Besides, the moment I locked this thing, it fused itself shut. You could ask Sigma to let you see it, but we both know what he'll say.'

The mention of his name seemed to invoke the inquisitor. His voice sounded on the comm-link. 'That could have gone better, Alpha. I confess I'm disappointed.'

'Don't be,' Karras replied coldly. 'We have what you wanted. How fine we cut it is beside the point.'

Sigma said nothing for a moment, then, 'Fly the shuttle to the extraction coordinates and prepare for pick-up. Redthorne is on her way. And rest while you can. Something else has come up, and I want Talon on it.'

'What is it this time?' asked Karras.

'You'll know,' said the inquisitor, 'when you need to know. Sigma out.'

Magos Altando, former member of both biologis and technicus arms of the glorious Adeptus Mechanicus, stared through the wide plex window at his current project. Beyond the transparent barrier, a hundred captured orks lay strapped down to cold metal tables. Their skulls were trepanned, soft grey brains open to the air. Servo-arms dangling from the ceiling prodded each of them with short electrically-charged spikes, eliciting thunderous roars and howls of rage. The strange machine in the centre, wired directly to the greenskins' brains, siphoned off the psychic energy their collective anger and aggression was generating.

Altando's many eye-lenses watched his servitors scuttle among the tables, taking the measurements he had demanded.

I must comprehend the manner of its function, he told himself. Who could have projected that the orks were capable of fabricating such a thing?

Frustratingly, much of the data surrounding the recovery of the ork machine was classified above Altando's clearance level. He knew that a Deathwatch kill-team, designation *Scimitar*, had uncovered it during a purge of mining tunnels on Delta IV Genova. The inquisitor had brought it to him, knowing Altando followed a school of thought which other tech-magi considered disconcertingly radical.

Of course, the machine would tell Altando very little without the last missing part of the puzzle.

A door slid open behind him, and he turned from his observations to greet a cloaked and hooded figure accompanied by a large, shambling servitor who carried a black case.

'Progress?' said the figure.

'Limited,' said Altando, 'and so it will remain, inquisitor, without the resources we need. Ah, but it appears you have solved that problem. Correct?'

The inquisitor muttered something and the blank-eyed servitor trudged forward. It stopped just in front of Altando and wordlessly passed him the black metal case.

Altando accepted it without thanks, his own heavily augmented body having no trouble with the weight. 'Let us go next door, inquisitor,' he said, 'to the primary laboratory.'

The hooded figure followed the magos into a chamber on the left, leaving the servitor where it stood, staring lifelessly into empty space.

The laboratory was large, but so packed with devices of every conceivable scientific purpose that there was little room to move. Servo-skulls hovered in the air overhead, awaiting commands, their metallic components gleaming in the lamplight. Altando placed the black case on a table in the middle of the room, and unfurled a long mechanical arm from his back. It was tipped with a las-cutter.

'May I?' asked the magos.

'Proceed.'

The cutter sent bright red sparks out as it traced the circumference of the case. When it was done, the mechanical arm folded again behind the magos's back, and another unfurled over the opposite shoulder. This was tipped with a powerful metal manipulator, like an angular crab's claw but with three tapering digits instead of two. With it, the magos clutched the top of the case, lifted it, and set it aside. Then he dipped the manipulator into the box and lifted out the head of Balthazog Bludwrekk.

'Yes,' he grated through his vocaliser. 'This will be perfect.'

'It had better be,' said the inquisitor. 'These new orkoid machines represent a significant threat, and the Inquisition must have answers.'

The magos craned forward to examine the severed head. It was frozen solid, glittering with frost. The cut at its neck was incredibly clean, even at the highest magnification his eye-lenses would allow.

It must have been a fine weapon indeed that did this, Altando thought. No typical blade.

'Look at the distortion of the skull,' he said. 'Look at the features. Fascinating. A mutation, perhaps? Or a side effect of the channelling process? Give me time, inquisitor, and the august Ordo Xenos will have the answers it seeks.'

'Do not take *too* long, magos,' said the inquisitor as he turned to leave. 'And do not disappoint me. It took my best assets to acquire that abomination.'

The magos barely registered these words. Nor did he look up to watch the inquisitor and his servitor depart. He was already far too engrossed in his study of the monstrous head.

Now, at long last, he could begin to unravel the secrets of the strange ork machine.

EXHUMED
STEVE PARKER

The Thunderhawk gunship loomed out of the clouds like a monstrous bird of prey, wings spread, turbines growling, airbrakes flared to slow it for landing. It was black, its fuselage marked with three symbols: the Imperial aquila, noble and golden; the 'I' of the Emperor's Holy Inquisition, a symbol even the righteous knew better than to greet gladly; and another symbol, a skull cast in silver with a gleaming red, cybernetic eye. Derlon Saezar didn't know that one, had never seen it before, but it sent a chill up his spine all the same. Whichever august Imperial body the symbol represented was obviously linked to the Holy Inquisition. That couldn't be good news.

Eyes locked to his vid-monitor, Saezar watched tensely as the gunship banked hard towards the small landing facility he managed, its prow slicing through the veils of windblown dust like a knife through silk. There was a burst of static-riddled speech on his headset. In response, he tapped several codes into the console in front of him, keyed his microphone and said, 'Acknowledged, One-Seven-One. Clearance codes accepted. Proceed to Bay Four. This is an enclosed atmosphere facility. I'm uploading our safety and debarkation protocols to you now. Over.'

His fingers rippled over the console's runeboard, and the massive metal jaws of Bay Four began to grate open, ready to swallow the unwelcome black craft. Thick, toxic air rushed in. Breathable air rushed out. The entire facility shuddered and groaned in complaint, as it always did when a spacecraft came or went. The Adeptus Mechanicus had built this station, Orga Station, quickly and with the minimum systems and resources it would need to do its job. No more, no less.

It was a rusting, dust-scoured place, squat and ugly on the outside, dank and gloomy within. Craft arrived, craft departed. Those coming in brought slaves, servitors, heavy machinery and fuel. Saezar didn't know what those leaving carried. The magos who had hired him had left him in no doubt that curiosity would lead to the termination of more than his contract. Saezar was smart enough to believe it. He and his staff kept their heads down and did their jobs. In another few years, the tech-priests would be done here. They had told him as much. He would go back to Jacero then, maybe buy a farm with the money he'd have saved, enjoy air that didn't kill you on the first lungful.

That thought called up a memory Saezar would have given a lot to erase. Three weeks ago, a malfunction in one of the Bay Two extractors left an entire work crew breathing this planet's lethal air. The bay's vid-picters had caught it all in fine detail, the way the technicians and slaves staggered in agony towards the emergency airlocks, clawing at their throats while blood streamed from their mouths, noses and eyes. Twenty-three men dead. It had taken only seconds, but Saezar knew the sight would be with him for life. He shook himself, trying to cast the memory off.

The Thunderhawk had passed beyond the outer picters' field of view. Saezar switched to Bay Four's internal picters and saw the big black craft settle heavily on its landing stanchions. Thrusters cooled. Turbines whined down towards silence. The outer doors of the landing bay clanged shut. Saezar hit the winking red rune on the top right of his board and flooded the bay with the proper nitrogen and oxygen mix. When his screen showed everything was in the green, he addressed the pilot of the Thunderhawk again.

'Atmosphere restored, One-Seven-One. Bay Four secure. Free to debark.'

There was a brief grunt in answer. The Thunderhawk's front ramp lowered. Yellow light spilled out from inside, illuminating the black metal grille of the bay floor. Shadows appeared in that light – big shadows – and, after a moment, the figures that cast them began to descend the ramp. Saezar leaned forward, face close to his screen.

'By the Throne,' he whispered to himself.

With his right hand, he manipulated one of the bay vid-picters by remote, zooming in on the figure striding in front. It was massive, armoured in black ceramite, its face hidden beneath a cold, expressionless helm. On one great pauldron, the left, Saezar saw the same skull icon that graced the ship's prow. On the right, he saw another skull on a field of white, two black scythes crossed behind it. Here was yet another icon Saezar had never seen before, but he knew well enough the nature of the being that bore it. He had seen such beings rendered in paintings and stained glass, cut from marble or cast in precious metal. It was a figure of legend, and it was not alone.

Behind it, four others, similarly armour-clad but each bearing different iconography on their right pauldrons, marched in formation. Saezar's heart was in his throat. He tried to swallow, but his mouth was dry. He had never expected to see such beings with his own eyes. No one did. They were heroes from the stories his father had read to him, stories told to all children of the Imperium to give them hope, to help them sleep at night. Here they were in flesh and bone and metal.

Space Marines! Here! At Orga Station!

And there was a further incredible sight yet to come. Just as the five figures stepped onto the grillework floor, something huge blotted out all the light from inside the craft. The Thunderhawk's ramp shook with thunderous steps. Something emerged on two stocky, piston-like legs. It was vast and angular and impossibly powerful-looking, like a walking tank with fists instead of cannon.

It was a Dreadnought, and, even among such legends as these, it was in a class of its own.

Saezar felt a flood of conflicting emotion, equal parts joy and dread.

The Space Marines had come to Menatar, and where they went, death followed.

'Menatar,' said the tiny hunched figure, more to himself than to any of the black-armoured giants he shared the pressurised mag-rail carriage with. 'Second planet of the Ozyma-138 system, Hatha Subsector, Ultima Segmentum. Solar orbital period, one-point-one-three Terran standard. Gravity, zero-point-eight-three Terran standard.' He looked up, his tiny black eyes meeting those of Siefer Zeed, the Raven Guard. 'The atmosphere is a thick nitrogen-sulphide and carbon dioxide mix. Did you know that? Utterly deadly to the non-augmented. I doubt even you Adeptus Astartes could breathe it for long. Even our servitors wear air tanks here.'

Zeed stared back indifferently at the little tech-priest. When he spoke, it was not in answer. His words were directed to his right, to his squad leader, Lyandro Karras, Codicier Librarian of the Death Spectres Chapter, known officially in Deathwatch circles as Talon Alpha. That wasn't what Zeed called him, though. 'Tell me again, Scholar, why we get all the worthless jobs.'

Karras didn't look up from the boltgun he was muttering litanies over. Times like these, the quiet times, were for meditation and proper observances, something the Raven Guard seemed wholly unable to grasp. Karras had spent six years as leader of this kill-team. Siefer Zeed, nicknamed Ghost for his alabaster skin, was as irreverent today as he had been when they'd first met. Perhaps he was even worse.

Karras finished murmuring his Litany of Flawless Operation and sighed. 'You know why, Ghost. If you didn't go out of your way to anger Sigma all the time, maybe those Scimitar bastards would be here instead of us.'

Talon Squad's handler, an inquisitor lord known only as Sigma, had come all too close to dismissing Zeed from active duty on several occasions, a terrible dishonour not just for the Deathwatch member in question, but for his entire Chapter. Zeed frequently tested the limits of Sigma's need-to-know policy, not to mention the inquisitor's patience. But the Raven Guard was a peerless killing machine at close range, and his skill with a pair of lightning claws, his signature weapon, had won the day so often that Karras and the others had stopped counting.

Another voice spoke up, a deep rumbling bass, its tones warm and rich. 'They're not all bad,' said Maximmion Voss of the Imperial Fists. 'Scimitar Squad, I mean.'

'Right,' said Zeed with good-natured sarcasm. 'It's not like you're biased, Omni. I mean, every Black Templar or Crimson Fist in the galaxy is a veritable saint.'

Voss grinned.

There was a hiss from the rear of the carriage where Ignatio Solarion and Darrion Rauth, Ultramarine and Exorcist respectively, sat in relative silence. The hiss had come from Solarion.

'Something you want to say, Prophet?' said Zeed with a challenging thrust of his chin.

Solarion scowled at him, displaying the full extent of his contempt for the Raven Guard. 'We are with company,' he said, indicating the little tech-priest who had fallen silent while the Deathwatch Space Marines talked. 'You would do well to remember that.'

Zeed threw Solarion a sneer, then turned his eyes back to the tech-priest. The man had met them on the mag-rail platform at Orga Station, introducing himself as Magos Iapetus Borgovda, the most senior adept on the planet and a xeno-heirographologist specialising in the writings and history of the Exodites, offshoot cultures of the eldar race. They had lived here once, these Exodites, and had left many secrets buried deep in the drifting red sands.

That went no way to explaining why a Deathwatch kill-team was needed, however, especially now. Menatar was a dead world. Its sun had become a red giant, a K3-type star well on its way to final collapse. Before it died, however, it would burn off the last of Menatar's atmosphere, leaving little more than a ball of molten rock. Shortly after that, Menatar would cool and there would be no trace of anyone ever having set foot here at all. Such an end was many tens of thousands of years away, of course. Had the Exodites abandoned this world early, knowing its eventual fate? Or had something else driven them off? Maybe the xeno-heirographologist would find the answers eventually, but that still didn't tell Zeed anything about why Sigma had sent some of his key assets here.

Magos Borgovda turned to his left and looked out the viewspex bubble at the front of the mag-rail carriage. A vast dead volcano dominated the skyline. The mag-rail car sped towards it so fast the red dunes and rocky spires on either side of the tracks went by in a blur. 'We are coming up on Typhonis Mons,' the magos wheezed. 'The noble Priesthood of Mars cut a tunnel straight through the side of the crater, you know. The journey will take another hour. No more than that. Without the tunnel–'

'Good,' interrupted Zeed, running the fingers of one gauntleted hand through his long black hair. His eyes flicked to the blades of the lightning claws fixed to the magnetic couplings on his thigh-plates. Soon it would be time to don the weapons properly, fix his helmet to its seals, and step out onto solid ground. Omni was tuning the suspensors on his heavy bolter. Solarion was checking the bolt mechanism of his sniper rifle. Karras and Rauth had both finished their final checks already.

If there was nothing here to fight, why were they sent so heavily armed, Zeed asked himself?

He thought of the ill-tempered Dreadnought riding alone in the other carriage.

And why did they bring Chyron?

The mag-rail carriage slowed to a smooth halt beside a platform cluttered with crates bearing the cog-and-skull mark of the Adeptus Mechanicus. On either side of the platform, spreading out in well-ordered concentric rows, were scores of stocky pre-fabricated huts and storage units, their low roofs piled with ash and dust. Thick insulated cables snaked everywhere, linking heavy machinery to generators supplying light, heat and atmospheric stability to the sleeping quarters and mess blocks. Here and there, cranes stood tall against the wind. Looming over everything were the sides of the crater, penning it all in, lending the place a strange quality, almost like being outdoors and yet indoors at the same time.

Borgovda was clearly expected. Dozens of acolytes, robed in the red of the Martian Priesthood and fitted with breathing apparatus, bowed low when he emerged from the carriage. Around them, straight-backed skitarii troopers stood to attention with lasguns and hellguns clutched diagonally across their chests.

Quietly, Voss mumbled to Zeed, 'It seems our new acquaintance didn't lie about his status here. Perhaps you should have been more polite to him, paper-face.'

'I don't recall you offering any pleasantries, tree-trunk,' Zeed replied. He and Voss had been friends since the moment they met. It was a rapport that none of the other kill-team members shared, a fact that only served to deepen the bond. Had anyone else called Zeed *paper-face*, he might well have eviscerated them on the spot. Likewise, few would have dared to call the squat, powerful Voss *tree-trunk*. Even fewer would have survived to tell of it. But, between the two of them, such names were taken as a mark of trust and friendship that was truly rare among the Deathwatch.

Magos Borgovda broke from greeting the rows of fawning acolytes and turned to his black-armoured escorts. When he spoke, it was directly to Karras, who had identified himself as team leader during introductions.

'Shall we proceed to the dig-site, lord? Or do you wish to rest first?'

'Astartes need no rest,' answered Karras flatly.

It was a slight exaggeration, of course, and the twinkle in the xeno-heirographologist's eye suggested he knew as much, but he also knew that, by comparison to most humans, it was as good as true. Borgovda and his fellow servants of the Machine-God also required little rest.

'Very well,' said the magos. 'Let us go straight to the pit. My acolytes tell me we are ready to initiate the final stage of our operation. They await only my command.'

He dismissed all but a few of the acolytes, issuing commands to them in sharp bursts of machine code language, and turned east. Leaving the platform behind them, the Deathwatch followed. Karras walked beside the bent and robed figure, consciously slowing his steps to match the speed of the tech-priest. The others, including the massive, multi-tonne form of the Dreadnought, Chyron, fell into step behind them. Chyron's footfalls made the ground tremble as he brought up the rear.

Zeed cursed at having to walk so slowly. Why should one such as he, one who could move with inhuman speed, be forced to crawl at the little tech-priest's pace? He might reach the dig-site in a fraction of the time and never break sweat. How long would it take at the speed of this grinding, clicking, wheezing half-mechanical magos?

Eager for distraction, he turned his gaze to the inner slopes of the great crater in which the entire excavation site was located. This was

Typhonis Mons, the largest volcano in the Ozyma-138 system. No wonder the Adeptus Mechanicus had tunnelled all those kilometres through the crater wall. To go up and over the towering ridgeline would have taken significantly more time and effort. Any road built to do so would have required more switchbacks than was reasonable. The caldera was close to two and a half kilometres across, its jagged rim rising well over a kilometre on every side.

Looking more closely at the steep slopes all around him, Zeed saw that many bore signs of artifice. The signs were subtle, yes, perhaps eroded by time and wind, or by the changes in atmosphere that the expanding red giant had wrought, but they were there all the same. The Raven Guard's enhanced visor-optics, working in accord with his superior gene-boosted vision, showed him crumbled doorways and pillared galleries.

Had he not known this world for an Exodite world, he might have passed these off as natural structures, for there was little angular about them. Angularity was something one saw everywhere in human construction, but far less so in the works of the hated, inexplicable eldar. Their structures, their craft, their weapons – each seemed almost grown rather than built, their forms fluid, gracefully organic. Like all righteous warriors of the Imperium, Zeed hated them. They denied man's destiny as ruler of the stars. They stood in the way of expansion, of progress.

He had fought them many times. He had been there when forces had contested human territory in the Adiccan Reach, launching blisteringly fast raids on worlds they had no right to claim. They were good foes to fight. He enjoyed the challenge of their speed, and they were not afraid to engage with him at close quarters, though they often retreated in the face of his might rather than die honourably.

Cowards.

Such a shame they had left this world so long ago. He would have enjoyed fighting them here.

In fact, he thought, flexing his claws in irritation, just about any fight would do.

Six massive cranes struggled in unison to raise their load from the circular black pit in the centre of the crater. They had buried this thing deep – deep enough that no one should ever have disturbed it here. But Iapetus Borgovda had transcribed the records of that burial; records found on a damaged craft that had been lost in the warp only to emerge centuries later on the fringe of the Imperium. He had been on his way to present his findings to the Genetor Biologis himself when a senior magos by the name of Serjus Altando had intercepted him and asked him to present his findings to the Ordo Xenos of the Holy Inquisition first.

After that, Borgovda never got around to presenting his work to his superiors on Mars. The mysterious inquisitor lord that Magos Altando served had guaranteed Borgovda all the resources he would need to make the discovery entirely his own. The credit, Altando promised, need not be shared with anyone else. Borgovda would be revered for his work. Perhaps, one day, he would even be granted genetor rank himself.

And so it was that mankind had come to Menatar and had begun to dig where no one was supposed to.

The fruits of that labour were finally close at hand. Borgovda's black eyes glittered like coals beneath the clear bubble of his breathing apparatus as he watched each of the six cranes reel in their thick polysteel cables. With tantalising slowness, something huge and ancient began to peek above the lip of the pit. A hundred skitarii troopers and gun-servitors inched forward, weapons raised. They had no idea what was emerging. Few did.

Borgovda knew. Magos Altando knew. Sigma knew. Of these three, however, only Borgovda was present in person. The others, he believed, were light-years away. This was *his* prize alone, just as the inquisitor had promised. This was *his* operation. As more of the object cleared the lip of the pit, he stepped forward himself. Behind him, the Space Marines of Talon Squad gripped their weapons and watched.

The object was almost entirely revealed now, a vast sarcophagus, oval in shape, twenty-three metres long on its vertical axis, sixteen metres on the horizontal. Every centimetre of its surface, a surface like nothing so much as polished bone, was intricately carved with script. By force of habit, the xeno-heirographologist began translating the symbols with part of his mind while the rest of it continued to marvel at the beauty of what he saw. Just what secrets would this object reveal?

He, and other radicals like him, believed mankind's salvation, its very future, lay not with the technological stagnation in which the race of men was currently mired, but with the act of understanding and embracing the technology of its alien enemies. And yet, so many fools scorned this patently obvious truth. Borgovda had known good colleagues, fine inquisitive magi like himself, who had been executed for their beliefs. Why did the Fabricator General not see it? Why did the mighty Lords of Terra not understand? Well, he would make them see. Sigma had promised him all the resources he would need to make the most of this discovery. The Holy Inquisition was on his side. This time would be different.

The object, fully raised above the pit, hung there in all its ancient, inscrutable glory. Borgovda gave a muttered command into a vox-piece, and the cranes began a slow, synchronised turn.

Borgovda held his breath.

They moved the vast sarcophagus over solid ground and stopped.

'Yes,' said Borgovda over the link. 'That's it. Now lower it gently.'

The crane crews did as ordered. Millimetre by millimetre, the oval tomb descended.

Then it lurched.

One of the cranes gave a screech of metal. Its frame twisted sharply to the right, titanium struts crumpling like tin.

'What's going on?' demanded Borgovda.

From the corner of his vision, he noted the Deathwatch stepping forward, cocking their weapons, and the Dreadnought eagerly flexing its great metal fists.

A panicked voice came back to him from the crane operator in the damaged machine. 'There's something moving inside that thing,' gasped the man. 'Something really heavy. Its centre of gravity is shifting all over the place!'

Borgovda's eyes narrowed as he scrutinised the hanging oval object. It was swinging on five taut cables now, while the sixth, that of the ruined crane, had gone slack. The object lurched again. The movement was clearly visible this time, obviously generated by massive internal force.

'Get it onto the ground,' Borgovda barked over the link, 'but carefully. Do not damage it.'

The cranes began spooling out more cable at his command, but the sarcophagus gave one final big lurch and crumpled two more of the sturdy machines. The other three cables tore free, and it fell to the ground with an impact that shook the closest slaves and acolytes from their feet.

Borgovda started towards the fallen sarcophagus, and knew that the Deathwatch were right behind him. Had the inquisitor known this might happen? Was that why he had sent his angels of death and destruction along?

Even at this distance, some one hundred and twenty metres away, even through all the dust and grit the impact had kicked up, Borgovda could see sigils begin to glow red on the surface of the massive object. They blinked on and off like warning lights, and he realised that was exactly what they were. Despite all the irreconcilable differences between the humans and the aliens, this message, at least, meant the same.

Danger!

There was a sound like cracking wood, but so loud it was deafening. Suddenly, one of the Deathwatch Space Marines roared in agony and collapsed to his knees, gauntlets pressed tight to the side of his helmet. Another Adeptus Astartes, the Imperial Fist, raced forward to his fallen leader's side.

'What's the matter, Scholar? What's going on?'

The one called Karras spoke through his pain, but there was no mistaking the sound of it, the raw, nerve-searing agony in his words. 'A psychic beacon!' he growled through clenched teeth. 'A psychic beacon just went off. The magnitude–'

He howled as another wave of pain hit him, and the sound spoke of a suffering that Borgovda could hardly imagine.

Another of the kill-team members, this one with a pauldron boasting a daemon's skull design, stepped forward with boltgun raised and, incredibly, took aim at his leader's head.

The Raven Guard moved like lightning. Almost too fast to see, he was at this other's side, knocking the muzzle of the boltgun up and away with the back of his forearm. 'What the hell are you doing, Watcher?' Zeed snapped. 'Stand down!'

The Exorcist, Rauth, glared at Zeed through his helmet visor, but he turned his weapon away all the same. His finger, however, did not leave the trigger.

'Scholar,' said Voss. 'Can you fight it? Can you fight through it?'

The Death Spectre struggled to his feet, but his posture said he was hardly in any shape to fight if he had to. 'I've never felt anything like this!' he hissed. 'We have to knock it out. It's smothering my... gift.' He turned to Borgovda. 'What in the Emperor's name is going on here, magos?'

'Gift?' spat Rauth in an undertone.

Borgovda answered, turning his black eyes back to the object as he did. It was on its side about twenty metres from the edge of the pit, rocking violently as if something were alive inside it.

'The Exodites...' he said. 'They must have set up some kind of signal to alert them when someone... interfered. We've just set it off.'

'Interfered with what?' demanded Ignatio Solarion. The Ultramarine rounded on the tiny tech-priest. 'Answer me!'

There was another loud cracking sound. Borgovda looked beyond Solarion and saw the bone-like surface of the sarcophagus split violently. Pieces shattered and flew off. In the gaps they left, something huge and dark writhed and twisted, desperate to be free.

The magos was transfixed.

'I asked you a question!' Solarion barked, visibly fighting to restrain himself from striking the magos. 'What does the beacon alert them to?'

'To that,' said Borgovda, terrified and exhilarated all at once. 'To the release of... of whatever they buried here.'

'They left it alive?' said Voss, drawing abreast of Solarion and Borgovda, his heavy bolter raised and ready.

Suddenly, everything slotted into place. Borgovda had the full context of the writing he had deciphered on the sarcophagus's surface, and, with that context, came a new understanding.

'They buried it,' he told Talon Squad, 'because they couldn't kill it!'

There was a shower of bony pieces as the creature finally broke free of the last of its tomb and stretched its massive serpentine body for all to see. It was as tall as a Warhound Titan, and, from the look of it, almost as well armoured. Complex mouthparts split open like the bony, razor-lined petals of some strange, lethal flower. Its bizarre jaws dripped with corrosive fluids. This beast, this nightmare leviathan pulled from the belly of the earth, shivered and threw back its gargantuan head.

A piercing shriek filled the poisonous air, so loud that some of the skitarii troopers closest to it fell down, choking on the deadly atmosphere. The creature's screech had shattered their visors.

'Well maybe *they* couldn't kill it,' growled Lyandro Karras, marching stoically forwards through waves of psychic pain, 'But *we* will! To battle, brothers, in the Emperor's name!'

Searing lances of las-fire erupted from all directions at once, centring on the massive worm-like creature that was, after so many long millennia, finally free. Normal men would have quailed in the face of such an overwhelming foe. What could such tiny things as humans do against something like this? But the skitarii troopers of the Adeptus Mechanicus had been rendered all but fearless, their survival instincts overridden by neural programming, augmentation and brain surgery. They did not flee as other men would have. They surrounded the beast, working as one to put as much firepower on it as possible.

A brave effort, but ultimately a wasted one. The creature's thick plates of alien chitin shrugged off their assault. All that concentrated firepower really achieved was to turn the beast's attention on its attackers. Though sightless in the conventional sense, it sensed everything. Rows of tiny cyst-like nodules running the length of its body detected changes in heat, air pressure and vibration to the most minute degree. It knew exactly where each of its attackers stood. Not only could it hear their beating hearts, it could feel them vibrating through the ground and the air. Nothing escaped its notice.

With incredible speed for a creature so vast, it whipped its heavy black tail forward in an arc. The air around it whistled. Skitarii troopers were cut down like stalks of wheat, crushed by the dozen, their rib cages pulverised. Some were launched into the air, their bodies falling like mortar shells a second later, slamming down with fatal force onto the corrugated metal roofs of the nearby storage and accommodation huts.

Talon Squad was already racing forward to join the fight. Chyron's awkward run caused crates to fall from their stacks. Adrenaline flooded the wretched remains of his organic body, a tiny remnant of the Astartes he had once been, little more now than brain, organs and scraps of flesh held together, kept alive, by the systems of his massive armoured chassis.

'Death to all xenos!' he roared, following close behind the others.

At the head of the team, Karras ran with his bolter in hand. The creature was three hundred metres away, but he and his squadmates would close that gap all too quickly. What would they do then? How did one fight a monster like this?

There was a voice on the link. It was Voss.

'A trygon, Scholar? A mawloc?'

'No, Omni,' replied Karras. 'Same genus, I think, but something we haven't seen before.'

'Sigma knew,' said Zeed, breaking in on the link.

'Aye,' said Karras. 'Knew or suspected.'

'Karras,' said Solarion. 'I'm moving to high ground.'

'Go.'

Solarion's boltgun, a superbly-crafted weapon, its like unseen in the armouries of any Adeptus Astartes Chapter but the Deathwatch, was best employed from a distance. The Ultramarine broke away from the charge of the others. He sought out the tallest structure in the crater that he could reach quickly. His eyes found it almost immediately. It was behind him – the loading crane that served the mag-rail line. It was slightly shorter than the cranes that had been used to lift the entombed creature out of the pit, but each of those were far too close to the beast to be useful. This one would do well. He ran to the foot of the crane, to the stanchions that were steam-bolted to the ground, slung his rifle over his right pauldron, and began to climb.

The massive tyranid worm was scything its tail through more of the skitarii, and their numbers dropped by half. Bloody smears marked the open concrete. For all their fearlessness and tenacity, the Mechanicus troops hadn't even scratched the blasted thing. All they had managed was to put the beast in a killing frenzy at the cost of their own lives. Still they fought, still they poured blinding spears of fire on it, but to no avail. The beast flexed again, tail slashing forward, and another dozen died, their bodies smashed to a red pulp.

'I hope you've got a plan, Scholar,' said Zeed as he ran beside his leader. 'Other than *kill the bastard*, I mean.'

'I can't channel psychic energy into *Arquemann*,' said Karras, thinking for a moment that his ancient force sword might be the only thing able to crack the brute's armoured hide. 'Not with that infernal beacon drowning me out. But if we can stop the beacon... If I can get close enough–'

He was cut off by a calm, cold and all-too-familiar voice on the link.

'Specimen Six is not to be killed under any circumstances, Talon Alpha. I want the creature alive!'

'Sigma!' spat Karras. 'You can't seriously think... No! We're taking it down. We have to!'

Sigma broadcast his voice to the entire team.

'Listen to me, Talon Squad. That creature is to be taken alive at all costs. Restrain it and prepare it for transport. Brother Solarion has been equipped for the task already. Your job is to facilitate the success of his shot, then escort the tranquilised creature back to the *Saint Nevarre*. Remember your oaths. Do as you are bid.'

It was Chyron, breaking his characteristic brooding silence, who spoke up first.

'This is an outrage, Sigma. It is a tyranid abomination and Chyron will kill it. We are Deathwatch. Killing things is what we do.'

'You will do as ordered, Lamenter. All of you will. Remember your oaths. Honour the treaties, or return to your brothers in disgrace.'

'I have no brothers left,' Chyron snarled, as if this freed him from the need to obey.

'Then you will return to nothing. The Inquisition has no need of those who cannot follow mission parameters. The Deathwatch even less so.'

Karras, getting close to the skitarii and the foe, felt his lip curl in anger. This was madness.

'Solarion,' he barked. 'How much did you know?'

'Some,' said the Ultramarine, a trace of something unpleasant in his voice. 'Not much.'

'And you didn't warn us, brother?' Karras demanded.

'Orders, Karras. Unlike some, I follow mine to the letter.'

Solarion had never been happy operating under the Death Spectre Librarian's command. Karras was from a Chapter of the Thirteenth Founding. To Solarion, that made him inferior. Only the Chapters of the First Founding were worthy of unconditional respect, and even some of those...

'Magos Altando issued me with special rounds,' Solarion went on. 'Neuro-toxins. I need a clear shot on a soft, fleshy area. Get me that opening, Karras, and Sigma will have what he wants.'

Karras swore under his helm. He had known all along that something was up. His psychic gift did not extend to prescience, but he had sensed something dark and ominous hanging over them from the start.

The tyranid worm was barely fifty metres away now, and it turned its plated head straight towards the charging Deathwatch Space Marines. It could hardly have missed the thundering footfalls of Chyron, who was another thirty metres behind Karras, unable to match the swift pace of his smaller, lighter squadmates.

'The plan, Karras!' said Zeed, voice high and anxious.

Karras had to think fast. The beast lowered its fore-sections and began slithering towards them, sensing these newcomers were a far greater threat than the remaining skitarii.

Karras skidded to an abrupt halt next to a skitarii sergeant and shouted at him, 'You! Get your forces out. Fall back towards the mag-rail station.'

'We fight,' insisted the skitarii. 'Magos Borgovda has not issued the command to retreat.'

Karras grabbed the man by the upper right arm and almost lifted him off his feet. 'This isn't fighting. This is dying. You will do as I say. The Deathwatch will take care of this. Do not get in our way.'

The sergeant's eyes were blank, lifeless things, like those of a doll. Had the Adeptus Mechanicus surgically removed so much of the man's humanity? There was no fear there, certainly, but Karras sensed little else, either. Whether that was because of the surgeries or because the beacon was still drowning him in wave after invisible wave of pounding psychic pressure, he could not say.

After a second, the skitarii sergeant gave a reluctant nod and sent a message over his vox-link. The skitarii began falling back, but they kept their futile fire up as they moved.

The rasping of the worm's armour plates against the rockcrete grew louder as it neared, and Karras turned again to face it. 'Get ready!' he told the others.

'What is your decision, Death Spectre?' Chyron rumbled. 'It is a xenos abomination. It must be killed, regardless of the inquisitor's command.'

Damn it, thought Karras. I know he's right, but I must honour the treaties, for the sake of the Chapter. We must give Solarion his window.

'Keep the beast occupied. Do as Sigma commands. If Solarion's shot fails...'

'It won't,' said Solarion over the link.

It had better not, thought Karras. Because, if it does, I'm not sure we *can* kill this thing.

Solarion had reached the end of the crane's armature. The entire crater floor was spread out below him. He saw his fellow Talon members fan out to face the alien abomination. It reared up on its hind-sections again and screeched at them, thrashing the air with rows of tiny vestigial limbs. Voss opened up on it first, showering it with a hail of fire from his heavy bolter. Rauth and Karras followed suit while Zeed and Chyron tried to flank it and approach from the sides.

Solarion snorted.

It was obvious, to him at least, that the fiend didn't have any blind spots. It didn't have eyes!

So far as Solarion could tell from up here, the furious fusillade of bolter rounds rattling off the beast's hide was doing nothing at all, unable to penetrate the thick chitin plates.

I need exposed flesh, he told himself. I won't fire until I get it. One shot, one kill. Or, in this case, one paralysed xenos worm.

He locked himself into a stable position by pushing his boots into the corners created by the crane's metal frame. All around him, the winds of Menatar howled and tugged, trying to pull him into a deadly eighty metre drop. The dust on those winds cut visibility by twenty per cent, but Solarion had hit targets the size of an Imperial ducat at three kilometres. He knew he could pull off a perfect shot in far worse conditions than these.

Sniping from the top of the crane meant that he was forced to lie belly-down at a forty-five degree angle, his boltgun's stock braced against his shoulder, right visor-slit pressed close to the lens of his scope. After some adjustments, the writhing monstrosity came into sharp focus. Bursts of Astartes gunfire continued to ripple over its carapace. Its tail came down hard in a hammering vertical stroke that Rauth only managed to sidestep at the last possible second. The concrete where the Exorcist had been standing shattered and flew off in all directions.

Solarion pulled back the cocking lever of his weapon and slid one of Altando's neuro-toxin rounds into the chamber. Then he spoke over the comm-link.

'I'm in position, Karras. Ready to take the shot. Hurry up and get me that opening.'

'We're trying, Prophet!' Karras snapped back, using the nickname Zeed had coined for the Ultramarine.

Try harder, thought Solarion, but he didn't say it. There was a limit, he knew, to how far he could push Talon Alpha.

* * *

Three grenades detonated, one after another, with ground-splintering cracks. The wind pulled the dust and debris aside. The creature reared up again, towering over the Space Marines, and they saw that it remained utterly undamaged, not even a scratch on it.

'Nothing!' cursed Rauth.

Karras swore. This was getting desperate. The monster was tireless, its speed undiminished, and nothing they did seemed to have the least effect. By contrast, its own blows were all too potent. It had already struck Voss aside. Luck had been with the Imperial Fist, however. The blow had been lateral, sending him twenty metres along the ground before slamming him into the side of a fuel silo. The strength of his ceramite armour had saved his life. Had the blow been vertical, it would have killed him on the spot.

Talon Squad hadn't survived the last six years of special operations to die here on Menatar. Karras wouldn't allow it. But the only weapon they had which might do anything to the monster was his force blade, *Arquemann*, and, with that accursed beacon drowning out his gift, Karras couldn't charge it with the devastating psychic power it needed to do the job.

'Warp blast it!' he cursed over the link. 'Someone find the source of that psychic signal and knock it out!'

He couldn't pinpoint it himself. The psychic bursts were overwhelming, drowning out all but his own thoughts. He could no longer sense Zeed's spiritual essence, nor that of Voss, Chyron, or Solarion. As for Rauth, he had never been able to sense the Exorcist's soul. Even after serving together this long, he was no closer to discovering the reason for that. For all Karras knew, maybe the quiet, brooding Astartes had no soul.

Zeed was doing his best to keep the tyranid's attention on himself. He was the fastest of all of them. If Karras hadn't known better, he might even have said Zeed was enjoying the deadly game. Again and again, that barbed black tail flashed at the Raven Guard, and, every time, found only empty air. Zeed kept himself a split second ahead. Whenever he was close enough, he lashed out with his lightning claws and raked the creature's sides. But, despite the blue sparks that flashed with every contact, he couldn't penetrate that incredible armour.

Karras locked his bolter to his thigh plate and drew *Arquemann* from its scabbard.

This is it, he thought. We have to close with it. Maybe Chyron can do something if he can get inside its guard. He's the only one who might just be strong enough.

'Engage at close quarters,' he told the others. 'We can't do anything from back here.'

It was all the direction Chyron needed. The Dreadnought loosed a battle-cry and stormed forward to attack with his two great power fists, the ground juddering under him as he charged.

By the Emperor's grace, thought Karras, following in the Dreadnought's thunderous wake, don't let this be the day we lose someone.

Talon Squad was *his* squad. Despite the infighting, the secrets, the mistrust and everything else, that still meant something.

Solarion saw the rest of the kill-team race forward to engage the beast at close quarters and did not envy them, but he had to admit a grudging pride in their bravery and honour. Such a charge looked like sure suicide. For any other squad, it might well have been. But for Talon Squad…

Concentrate, he told himself. The moment is at hand. Breathe slowly.

He did.

His helmet filtered the air, removing the elements that might have killed him, elements that even the Adeptus Astartes implant known as the Imbiber, or the multi-lung, would not have been able to handle. Still, the air tasted foul and burned in his nostrils and throat. A gust of wind buffeted him, throwing his aim off a few millimetres, forcing him to adjust again.

A voice shouted triumphantly on the link.

'I've found it, Scholar. I have the beacon!'

'Voss?' said Karras.

There was a muffled crump, the sound of a krak grenade. Solarion's eyes flicked from his scope to a cloud of smoke about fifty metres to the creature's right. He saw Voss emerge from the smoke. Around him lay the rubble of the monster's smashed sarcophagus.

Karras gave a roar of triumph.

'It's… it's gone,' he said. 'It's lifted. I can feel it!'

So Karras would be able to wield his psychic abilities again. Would it make any difference, Solarion wondered.

It did, and that difference was immediate. Something began to glow down on the battlefield. Solarion turned his eyes towards it and saw Karras raise *Arquemann* in a two-handed grip. The monster must have sensed the sudden build-up of psychic charge, too. It thrashed its way towards the Librarian, eager to crush him under its powerful coils. Karras dashed in to meet the creature's huge body and plunged his blade into a crease where two sections of chitin plate met.

An ear-splitting alien scream tore through the air, echoing off the crater walls.

Karras twisted the blade hard and pulled it free, and its glowing length was followed by a thick gush of black ichor.

The creature writhed in pain, reared straight up and screeched again, its complex jaws open wide.

Just the opening Solarion was waiting for.

He squeezed the trigger of his rifle and felt it kick powerfully against his armoured shoulder.

A single white-hot round lanced out towards the tyranid worm.

There was a wet impact as the round struck home, embedding itself deep in the fleshy tissue of the beast's mouth.

'Direct hit!' Solarion reported.

'Good work,' said Karras on the link. 'Now what?'

It was Sigma's voice that answered. 'Fall back and wait. The toxin is fast acting. Ten to fifteen seconds. Specimen Six will be completely paralysed.'

'You heard him, Talon Squad,' said Karras. 'Fall back. Let's go!'

Solarion placed one hand on the top of his rifle, muttered a prayer of thanks to the weapon's machine-spirit, and prepared to descend. As he looked out over the crater floor, however, he saw that one member of the kill-team wasn't retreating.

Karras had seen it, too.

'Chyron,' barked the team leader. 'What in Terra's name are you doing?

The Dreadnought was standing right in front of the beast, fending off blows from its tail and its jaws with his oversized fists.

'Stand down, Lamenter,' Sigma commanded.

If Chyron heard, he deigned not to answer. While there was still a fight to be had here, he wasn't going anywhere. It was the tyranids that had obliterated his Chapter. Hive Fleet Kraken had decimated them, leaving him with no brothers, no home to return to. But if Sigma and the others thought the Deathwatch was all Chyron had left, they were wrong. He had his rage, his fury, his unquenchable lust for dire and bloody vengeance.

The others should have known that. Sigma should have known.

Karras started back towards the Dreadnought, intent on finding some way to reach him. He would use his psyker gifts if he had to. Chyron could not hope to beat the thing alone.

But, as the seconds ticked off and the Dreadnought continued to fight, it became clear that something was wrong.

From his high vantage point, it was Solarion who voiced it first.

'It's not stopping,' he said over the link. 'Sigma, the damned thing isn't even slowing down. The neuro-toxin didn't work.'

'Impossible,' replied the voice of the inquisitor. 'Magos Altando had the serum tested on–'

'Twenty-five... no, thirty seconds. I tell you, it's not working.'

Sigma was silent for a brief moment. Then he said, 'We need it alive.'

'Why?' demanded Zeed. The Raven Guard was crossing the concrete again, back towards the fight, following close behind Karras.

'You do not need to know,' said Sigma.

'The neuro-toxin doesn't work, Sigma,' Solarion repeated. 'If you have some other suggestion...'

Sigma clicked off.

I guess he doesn't, thought Solarion sourly.

'Solarion,' said Karras. 'Can you put another round in it?'

'Get it to open wide and you know I can. But it might not be a dosage issue.'

'I know,' said Karras, his anger and frustration telling in his voice. 'But it's all we've got. Be ready.'

Chyron's chassis was scraped and dented. His foe's strength seemed boundless. Every time the barbed tail whipped forward, Chyron swung his fists at it, but the beast was truly powerful and, when one blow connected squarely with the Dreadnought's thick glacis plate, he found himself staggering backwards despite his best efforts.

Karras was suddenly at his side.

'When I tell you to fall back, Dreadnought, you will do it,' growled the Librarian. 'I'm still Talon Alpha. Or does that mean nothing to you?'

Chyron steadied himself and started forward again, saying, 'I honour your station, Death Spectre, and your command. But vengeance for my Chapter supersedes all. Sigma be damned, I *will* kill this thing!'

Karras hefted *Arquemann* and prepared to join Chyron's charge. 'Would you dishonour all of us with you?'

The beast swivelled its head towards them and readied to strike again.

'For the vengeance of my Chapter, no price is too high. I am sorry, Alpha, but that is how it must be.'

'Then the rest of Talon Squad stands with you,' said Karras. 'Let us hope we all live to regret it.'

Solarion managed to put two further toxic rounds into the creature's mouth in rapid succession, but it was futile. This hopeless battle was telling badly on the others now. Each slash of that deadly tail was avoided by a rapidly narrowing margin. Against a smaller and more numerous foe, the strength of the Adeptus Astartes would have seemed almost infinite, but this towering tyranid leviathan was far too powerful to engage with the weapons they had. They were losing this fight, and yet Chyron would not abandon it, and the others would not abandon him, despite the good sense that might be served in doing so.

Voss tried his best to keep the creature occupied at range, firing great torrents from his heavy bolter, even knowing that he could do little, if any, real damage. His fire, however, gave the others just enough openings to keep fighting. Still, even the heavy ammunition store on the Imperial Fist's back had its limits. Soon, the weapon's thick belt feed began whining as it tried to cycle non-existent rounds into the chamber.

'I'm out,' Voss told them. He started disconnecting the heavy weapon so that he might draw his combat blade and join the close-quarters melee.

It was at that precise moment, however, that Zeed, who had again been taunting the creature with his lightning claws, had his feet struck out from under him. He went down hard on his back, and the tyranid monstrosity launched itself straight towards him, massive mandibles spread wide.

For an instant, Zeed saw that huge red maw descending towards him. It looked like a tunnel of dark, wet flesh. Then a black shape blocked his view and he heard a mechanical grunt of strain.

'I'm more of a meal, beast,' growled Chyron.

The Dreadnought had put himself directly in front of Zeed at the last minute, gripping the tyranid's sharp mandibles in his unbreakable titanium grip. But the creature was impossibly heavy, and it pressed down on the Lamenter with all its weight.

The force pressing down on Chyron was impossible to fight, but he put everything he had into the effort. His squat, powerful legs began to buckle. A piston in his right leg snapped. His engine began to sputter and cough with the strain.

'Get out from under me, Raven Guard,' he barked. 'I can't hold it much longer!'

Zeed scrabbled backwards about two metres, then stopped.

No, he told himself. Not today. Not to a mindless beast like this.

'Corax protect me,' he muttered, then sprang to his feet and raced forward, shouting, '*Victoris aut mortis!*'

Victory or death!

He slipped beneath the Dreadnought's right arm, bunched his legs beneath him and, with lightning claws extended out in front, dived directly into the beast's gaping throat.

'Ghost!' shouted Voss and Karras at the same time, but he was already gone from sight and there was no reply over the link.

Chyron wrestled on for another second. Then two. Then, suddenly, the monster began thrashing in great paroxysms of agony. It wrenched its mandibles from Chyron's grip and flew backwards, pounding its ringed segments against the concrete so hard that great fractures appeared in the ground.

The others moved quickly back to a safe distance and watched in stunned silence.

It took a long time to die.

When the beast was finally still, Voss sank to his knees.

'No,' he said, but he was so quiet that the others almost missed it.

Footsteps sounded on the stone behind them. It was Solarion. He stopped alongside Karras and Rauth.

'So much for taking it alive,' he said.

No one answered.

Karras couldn't believe it had finally happened. He had lost one. After all they had been through together, he had started to believe they might all return to their Chapters alive one day, to be welcomed as honoured heroes, with the sad exception of Chyron, of course.

Suddenly, however, that belief seemed embarrassingly naïve. If Zeed could die, all of them could. Even the very best of the best would meet his match in the end. Statistically, most Deathwatch members never made it back to the fortress-monasteries of their originating Chapters. Today, Zeed had joined those fallen ranks.

It was Sigma, breaking in on the command channel, who shattered the grim silence.

'You have failed me, Talon Squad. It seems I greatly overestimated you.'

Karras hissed in quiet anger. 'Siefer Zeed is dead, inquisitor.'

'Then you, Alpha, have failed on two counts. The Chapter Master of the Raven Guard will be notified of Zeed's failure. Those of you who live will at least have a future chance to redeem yourselves. The Imperium has lost a great opportunity here. I have no more to say to you. Stand by for Magos Altando.'

'Altando?' said Karras. 'Why would–'

Sigma signed off before Karras could finish, his voice soon replaced by the buzzing mechanical tones of the old magos who served on his retinue.

'I am told that Specimen Six is dead,' he grated over the link. 'Most regrettable, but your chances of success were extremely slim from the beginning. I predicted failure at close to ninety-six point eight five per cent probability.'

'But Sigma deployed us anyway,' Karras seethed. 'Why am I not surprised?'

'All is not lost,' Altando continued, ignoring the Death Spectre's ire. 'There is much still to be learned from the carcass. Escort it back to Orga Station. I will arrive there to collect it shortly.'

'Wait,' snapped Karras. 'You wish this piece of tyranid filth loaded up and shipped back for extraction? Are you aware of its size?'

'Of course, I am,' answered Altando. 'It is what the mag-rail line was built for. In fact, everything we did on Menatar from the very beginning – the construction, the excavation, the influx of Mechanicus personnel – all of it was to secure the specimen alive, still trapped inside its sarcophagus. Under the circumstances, we will make do with a dead one. You have given us no choice.'

The sound of approaching footsteps caught Karras's attention. He turned from the beast's slumped form and saw the xeno-heirographologist, Magos Borgovda, walking towards him with a phalanx of surviving skitarii troopers and robed Mechanicus acolytes.

Beneath the plex bubble of his helm, the little tech-priest's eyes were wide.

'You… you bested it. I would not have believed it possible. You have achieved what the Exodites could not.'

'Ghost bested it,' said Voss. 'This is his kill. His and Chyron's.'

If Chyron registered these words, he didn't show it. The ancient warrior stared fixedly at his fallen foe.

'Magos Borgovda,' said Karras heavily, 'are there men among your survivors who can work the cranes? This carcass is to be loaded onto a mag-rail car and taken to Orga Station.'

'Yes, indeed,' said Borgovda, his eyes taking in the sheer size of the creature. 'That part of our plans has not changed, at least.'

Karras turned in the direction of the mag-rail station and started walking. He knew he sounded tired and miserable when he said, 'Talon Squad, fall in.'

'Wait,' said Chyron. He limped forward with a clashing and grinding of the gears in his right leg. 'I swear it, Alpha. The creature just moved. Perhaps it is not dead, after all.'

He clenched his fists as if in anticipation of crushing the last vestiges of life from it. But, as he stepped closer to the creature's slack mouth, there was a sudden outpouring of thick black gore, a great torrent of it. It splashed over his feet and washed across the dry rocky ground.

In that flood of gore was a bulky form, a form with great rounded pauldrons, sharp claws, and a distinctive, back-mounted generator. It lay unmoving in the tide of ichor.

'Ghost,' said Karras quietly. He had hoped never to see this, one under his command lying dead.

Then the figure stirred and groaned.

'If we ever fight a giant alien worm again,' said the croaking figure over the comm-link, 'some other bastard can jump down its throat. I've had my turn.'

Solarion gave a sharp laugh. Voss's reaction was immediate. He strode forward and hauled his friend up, clapping him hard on the shoulders. 'Why would any of us bother when you're so good at it, paper-face?'

Karras could hear the relief in Voss's voice. He grinned under his helm. Maybe Talon Squad was blessed after all. Maybe they would live to return to their Chapters.

'I said fall in, Deathwatch,' he barked at them; then he turned and led them away.

Altando's lifter had already docked at Orga Station by the time the mag-rail cars brought Talon Squad, the dead beast and the Mechanicus survivors to the facility. Sigma himself was, as always, nowhere to be seen. That was standard practice for the inquisitor. Six years, and Karras had still never met his enigmatic handler. He doubted he ever would.

Derlon Saezar and the station staff had been warned to stay well away from the mag-rail platforms and loading bays and to turn off all internal vid-picters. Saezar was smarter than most people gave him credit for. He did exactly as he was told. No knowledge was worth the price of his life.

Magos Altando surveyed the tyranid's long body with an appraising lens before ordering it loaded onto the lifter, a task with which even his veritable army of servitor slaves had some trouble. Magos Borgovda was most eager to speak with him, but, for some reason, Altando acted as if the xeno-heirographologist barely existed. In the end, Borgovda became irate and insisted that the other magos answer his questions at once. Why was he being told nothing? This was *his* discovery. Great promises had been made. He demanded the respect he was due.

It was at this point, with everyone gathered in Bay One, the only bay in the station large enough to offer a berth to Altando's lifter, that Sigma addressed Talon Squad over the comm-link command channel once again.

'No witnesses,' he said simply.

Karras was hardly surprised. Again, this was standard operating procedure, but that didn't mean the Death Spectre had to like it. It went against every bone in his body. Wasn't the whole point of the Deathwatch to protect mankind? They were alien-hunters. His weapons hadn't been crafted to take the lives of loyal Imperial citizens, no matter who gave the command.

'Clarify,' said Karras, feigning momentary confusion.

There was a crack of thunder, a single bolter-shot. Magos Borgovda's head exploded in a red haze.

Darrion Rauth stood over the body, dark grey smoke rising from the muzzle of his bolter

'Clear enough for you, Karras?' said the Exorcist.

Karras felt anger surging up inside him. He might even have lashed out at Rauth, might have grabbed him by the gorget, but the reaction of the surviving skitarii troopers put a stop to that. Responding to the cold-blooded slaughter of their leader, they raised their weapons and aimed straight at the Exorcist.

What followed was a one-sided massacre that made Karras sick to his stomach.

When it was over, Sigma had his wish.

There were no witnesses left to testify that anything at all had been dug up from the crater on Menatar. All that remained was the little spaceport station and its staff, waiting to be told that the excavation was over and that their time on this inhospitable world was finally at an end.

Saezar watched the big lifter take off first, and marvelled at it. Even on his slightly fuzzy vid-monitor screen, the craft was an awe-inspiring sight. It emerged from the doors of Bay One with so much thrust that he thought it might rip the whole station apart, but the facility's integrity held. There were no pressure leaks, no accidents.

The way that great ship hauled its heavy form up into the sky and off beyond the clouds thrilled him. Such power! It was a joy and an honour to see it. He wondered what it must be like to pilot such a ship.

Soon, the black Thunderhawk was also ready to leave. He granted the smaller, sleeker craft clearance and opened the doors of Bay Four once again. Good air out, bad air in. The Thunderhawk's thrusters powered up. It soon emerged into the light of the Menatarian day, angled its nose upwards, and began to pull away.

Watching it go, Saezar felt a sense of relief that surprised him. The Adeptus Astartes were leaving. He had expected to feel some kind of sadness, perhaps even regret at not getting to meet them in person. But he felt neither of those things. There was something terrible about them. He knew that now. It was something none of the bedtime stories had ever conveyed.

As he watched the Thunderhawk climb, Saezar reflected on it, and discovered that he knew what it was. The Astartes, the Space Marines... they didn't radiate goodness or kindness like the stories pretended. They were not so much righteous and shining champions as they were dark avatars of destruction. Aye, he was glad to see the back of them. They were the living embodiment of death. He hoped he would never set eyes on such beings again. Was there any greater reminder that the galaxy was a terrible and deadly place?

'That's right,' he said quietly to the vid-image of the departing Thunderhawk. 'Fly away. We don't need angels of death here. Better you remain a legend only if the truth is so grim.'

And then he saw something that made him start forward, eyes wide.

It was as if the great black bird of prey had heard his words. It veered sharply left, turning back towards the station.

Saezar stared at it, wordless, confused.

There was a burst of bright light from the battle-cannon on the craft's back. A cluster of dark, slim shapes burst forward from the under-wing pylons, each trailing a bright ribbon of smoke.

Missiles!

'No!'

Saezar would have said more, would have cried out to the Emperor for salvation, but the roof of the operations centre was ripped apart in the blast. Even if the razor-sharp debris hadn't cut his body into a dozen wet red pieces, the rush of choking Menatarian air would have eaten him from the inside out.

'No witnesses,' Sigma had said.

Within minutes, Orga Station was obliterated, and there were none.

Days passed.

The only thing stirring within the crater was the skirts of dust kicked up by gusting winds. Ozyma-138 loomed vast and red in the sky above, continuing its work of slowly blasting away the planet's atmosphere. With the last of the humans gone, this truly was a dead place once again, and that was how the visitors, or rather returnees, found it.

There were three of them, and they had been called here by a powerful beacon that only psychically gifted individuals might detect. It was a beacon that had gone strangely silent just shortly after it had been activated. The visitors had come to find out why.

They were far taller than the men of the Imperium, and their limbs were long and straight. The human race might have thought them elegant once, but all the killings these slender beings had perpetrated against mankind had put a permanent end to that. To the modern Imperium, they were simply xenos, to be hated and feared and destroyed like any other.

They descended the rocky sides of the crater in graceful silence, their booted feet causing only the slightest of rockslides. When they reached the bottom, they stepped onto the crater floor and marched together towards the centre where the mouth of the great pit gaped.

There was nothing hurried about their movements, and yet they covered the distance at an impressive speed.

The one who walked at the front of the trio was taller than the others, and not just by virtue of the high, jewel-encrusted crest on his helmet. He wore a rich cloak of strange shimmering material and carried a golden staff that shone with its own light.

The others were dressed in dark armour sculpted to emphasise the sweep of their long, lean muscles. They were armed with projectile weapons as white as bone. When the tall, cloaked figure stopped by the edge of the great pit, they stopped, too, and turned to either side, watchful, alert to any danger that might remain here.

The cloaked leader looked down into the pit for a moment, then moved off through the ruins of the excavation site, glancing at the crumpled metal huts and the rusting cranes as he passed them.

He stopped by a body on the ground, one of many. It was a pathetic, filthy mess of a thing, little more than rotting meat and broken bone wrapped in dust-caked cloth. It looked like it had been crushed by something. Pulverised. On the cloth was an icon – a skull set within a cog, equal parts black and white. For a moment, the tall figure looked down at it in silence, then he turned to the others and spoke, his voice filled with a boundless contempt that made even the swollen red sun seem to draw away.

'Mon-keigh,' he said, and the word was like a bitter poison on his tongue.

Mon-keigh.

DEATHWATCH

STEVE PARKER

DRAMATIS PERSONAE

TALON SQUAD

Lyandro Karras — First Codicier of the Death Spectres, aka Talon Alpha, aka *Scholar*

Darrion Rauth — Battle-brother of the Exorcists (First Company), aka Talon Two, aka *Watcher*

Ignacio Solarion — Battle-brother of the Ultramarines (Fourth Company), aka Talon Three, aka *Prophet*

Maximmion Voss — Brother-sergeant of the Imperial Fists (Second Company), aka Talon Four, aka *Omni*

Siefer Zeed — Battle-brother of the Raven Guard (Third Company), aka Talon Five, aka *Ghost*

Chyron Amadeus Chyropheles — Dreadnought of the Lamenters (Second Company), aka Talon Six

THE INQUISITION

Sigma — Inquisitor lord, Ordo Xenos (real name unknown)

Shianna Varlan — Interrogator class 3, Ordo Xenos, aka Lady Fara Devanon

Ordimas Arujo — Intelligence agent, Ordo Xenos, aka Asset 16, aka the Puppeteer

PROLOGUE

The tunnels were alive with them. The ceilings, walls, the floor; everywhere a tide of tooth and claw, of alien organisms cloaked in shadow, slavering and chittering with lethal intent as they swept towards the trespassers.

Insatiable.

Unstoppable.

They surged forwards, unified in purpose, compelled by a single terrible will, a cold intelligence that drove them on from much deeper and lower in this inky maze of twists and turns. The command was given in no language of sounds; it was a single, all-powerful impulse untranslatable to the human mind. The closest approximation would have been *Kill!*

But *kill* was too simple a word for this, an act so fundamental to the aliens' life-cycle, to the cancerous spread of their merciless race across all known space. The impulse reflected a complete cycle of purpose, of experience, of need:

Kill. Consume. Utilise. Adapt. Grow. Spread. Kill.

So it would go, on and on, until the universe held nothing left to devour.

Unless, of course, that cancer was cut out, excised with precision and lethal violence.

Three stood facing the xenos horde; three warriors, unafraid, heavily armed and clad in ceramite armour. Space Marines. The living legacy of the Emperor Himself. But what could three hope to do? They were almost certain to be overwhelmed here in the claustrophobic darkness. The numbers they faced were beyond count... And yet, they did not fear.

Kill was the thought in their minds, too – as much a part of their life-cycle as that of the ravening foe they faced.

Muzzle flare from two bolters strobed the tunnel intersection. The air beat with a deep tattoo, bolt after bolt after bolt. Chitinous ribcages shattered. Blood sprayed in dark fonts from punctured heads and torsos. Bodies burst from within as large-calibre rounds detonated deep inside alien flesh.

To the three, nothing felt so right as this killing of foes. They had been conditioned to it, programmed to live for it. It was hard-coded into every neuron. More than mere duty, it was a reason to live, the crux of their entire existence, the expression of everything they were and ever would be. Every enemy slain lifted them higher. Every mangled corpse that hit the ground pushed them that bit closer to the ceiling of their performance levels. Not a single bolt missed its mark, every shot a kill-shot.

Even so, it would not be enough.

'A curse on you, Karras,' hissed Ignacio Solarion under his breath. Two menacing shapes, humanoid but far from human, sped towards him, trying to flank him from the shadows to his left. He downed them without hesitation, a bolter-round to each brain. Over the vox-link, he barked at the others, 'We can't hold here waiting for those two fools. Not now. Fall back to RP2[1]!'

His bolter chugged to a sudden stop. With reflexes honed over a century of warfare, he dumped the empty mag and hammered home another just in time. Something on the ceiling reached bony arms towards him. Solarion didn't need to look up. Prox-alerts on his retinal display told him it was there. He turned the fat muzzle of his bolter straight upwards, fired and stepped back a pace.

A scream. A spray of hot blood. Something long-limbed and heavy crashed to the tunnel floor where he had stood. Solarion raised an armoured boot and stamped down hard, smashing the grotesque head flat on the tunnel floor. The body quivered and twitched as its nerves fired off one last time. No chance to admire his handiwork. Other targets were closing at speed. He marked each by distance – so few metres! – and dropped them as they came.

Bolt after bolt after bolt.

'We fall back *now*, brothers, or we die here for naught!' he growled.

'Stand and fight, Ultramarine,' another rumbled back at him. The voice belonged to Maximmion Voss, battle-brother of the Imperial Fists. 'Scholar will be here. I know it. Watcher, too. Give them a damned chance.'

'It's *our* chances that concern me!' Solarion shot back.

Five metres to the Ultramarine's left, there was a sudden blinding

---

1. RP – Rendezvous Point.

wash of white light. Voss had fired again. The flamer he carried sent out a torrent of ignited promethium that washed over the ranks of the charging foe, filling the tunnel with blazing, screeching bodies that thrashed and danced as they burned. In the close confines of the tunnels, the weapon was supremely effective... At least while its ammo lasted.

Voss dumped another depleted canister from under the flamer's neck, tugged a replacement from his webbing, and pressed it into place till it clicked in its housing. *Two tanks left.* He knew it wouldn't be enough – not if the others failed to link up with them soon. Galling as it was, Voss knew the Ultramarine was right. They had to fall back while they still had firepower enough to cover their retreat.

Throne, how he hated that word!

He spat a curse in Low Gothic – so much better for swearing than the higher tongue.

'Fine,' he told Solarion. 'Lead us out. Paper-face and I will keep the bastards off our backs.'

'I'm almost out,' added Siefer Zeed, third member of the embattled trio. 'Prophet! Throw me a magazine.'

Prophet!

Solarion scowled under his helm. The Raven Guard was a disrespectful fool, irreverent beyond any other Space Marine he had ever encountered. Nevertheless, between shots, he tossed Zeed a full bolter-mag, then turned and broke from the fight. At an armour-heavy trot, he led them westwards up the long, winding tunnel towards RP2 and the supply cache they had left there. Ammunition... More of it at RP1. They'd need that too, no doubt. And farther still, awaiting them at the exfil point, the sixth member of Talon Squad. That thought almost brought a smile to Solarion's narrow lips. The foul xenos would soon regret giving chase. Chyron would bring a storm of slaughter down upon them. It would be a fine sight, if any of them lived to see it.

Twenty metres up the tunnel, he turned to make sure the others were following and to give a burst of covering fire. Neither of the others could be trusted to fall back in the face of a fight. They were reckless and arrogant. They lacked proper battlefield discipline. It was a miracle they'd survived this long. That was why Solarion should have been chosen. Ultramarines fought smart, not just hard. He should have been made Alpha. Sigma would rue the day he let the bloody Death Spectre run this fiasco.

Voss and Zeed *were* following, however, walking backwards towards him but unable to move at speed while they held the enemy off. There was another blinding gush of white flame from Voss's weapon. It bought twenty metres of respite – a few seconds of breathing space only. Fresh pursuers would pour unflinching over the burning bodies of their dead.

'Run, fools!' shouted Solarion, and he dropped into a half-crouch with his bolter braced between breastplate and pauldron. More alien shapes appeared, moving into the space Voss had just cleared, their ropey muscles and glistening organic armour detailed in the flames that guttered on the bodies of their dead broodmates.

Solarion was about to pull his trigger and down the first when the tunnel wall on his immediate right exploded outwards. He was hammered against the far wall by the force of the blast, his armour pummelled by the impacts of countless fist-sized rocks. Scraped and dented, he rose from his knees with a half-stumble, shaking white stars from his vision. Thick dust obscured everything around him. His helmet optics buzzed with intermittent static. Warning glyphs flashed red. The vox-link hissed in his ear. He thought he heard shouting and bolter-fire.

Something monstrous reared up out of the dust cloud in front of him, serpentine and segmented from what little he could see.

The walls trembled with its unearthly battle-scream, high and shrill, and yet deep and throaty too, as if it screamed with two voices.

Huge clashing jaws swung towards Solarion, scything through the air, questing for prey.

'I'll give you something to scream about,' snarled the Ultramarine.

He raised his bolter and opened fire.

ACT I: THE CALL

How arrogant we were before His coming, and how naïve. The structures we trusted to maintain our unity were so fragile. Too fragile by far. We lost ourselves out there. We became strangers. We set off down different evolutionary paths. No wonder we faltered. No wonder we turned against each other. Had He not come to us then, chasing the shadows from the dark and the haze from our memories, we would have perished en masse, waging war against kin, not recognising each other, any difference seized upon as fuel for the fires of hate.

'He reminded us all that we were human, and He showed us that together, only together, could we endure the endless onslaught of those that were not.'

– Inscription at Bilahl (anon.), circa. 800.M31

1

Darkness, sudden and absolute, swallowed everything, even the noise of a fully staffed bridge. The crew fell silent all at once as if plunged into a vacuum. And silent it might have stayed but for Captain Sythero, his voice cutting through the blackness like a cracked whip.

'Mister Brindle!' he barked.

'Aye, sir,' came the reply about ten metres off to the left in that utter dark.

'I'd very much like to know what the hell is going on with my bloody ship! Back-up systems. Where are they? I want some light in here, and I want it now!'

As if the ship itself were listening, the bridge was suddenly painted in the red of emergency lighting. Everything reappeared, but dull, murky, revealed in hues of blood. The banks of monitor screens, however – both the captain's huge personal screens and those in the bridge control pits – remained as black and lifeless as space.

Crewmen at ancient metal consoles began desperately tapping on their runeboards, trying to get any kind of response from the *Ventria*'s primary systems.

Nothing.

First Officer Gideon Brindle hunched forwards over the screen of a secondary systems monitor which had finally flickered to life. 'Looks like we have full bio-support, sir,' he told the captain. 'Secondary and tertiary power units have kicked in for the air-scrubbers, waste reclamation, emergency lighting, shipboard communications, system resource monitors and door controls on all levels. No primary systems whatsoever.'

Brindle let that sink in for a moment before adding, 'I don't know how or why, sir, but we're locked out.'

Sythero hammered a fist on the ornate armrest of his command throne. 'Saints' balls! Do we at least have local space comms? Can we contact the *Ultrix* or GDC[2]?'

In the gloomy red light, the captain saw his first officer cross to the comms pit and confer with the men and women there. His body language gave the answer away before he voiced it.

No comms! What in Terra's name is going on here? Are we being jammed? Are we under attack?

'Orders, sir?' asked the first officer.

Sythero was stumped. What could he do without engines and weapons? If there were enemies out there... Damn it, the auspex arrays were as dead as everything else.

'No motive power at all, are we absolutely sure of that, Mister Brindle?'

'None, sir. We've been frozen out of all engine systems and sub-systems. We're sitting dead in the water.'

'I want observers at every viewport on this ship. I want eyes on anything that moves out there. Jump to it!'

Brindle was about to do exactly that when there was a sudden, ear-splitting burst of static over the ship's vox-speaker system. The monitors stuttered and rolled back to life, displaying not their usual scrolling columns of glyphs and pict-feeds, but a lone icon in razor-sharp detail. It was a leering white skull overlaid on a pillar of deep red.

No, not a pillar. A letter from the Gothic alphabet.

Captain Sythero squinted at it, puzzled, angry and deeply unsettled.

An eerie voice accompanied the image: flat, cold, emotionless and inhumanly deep. To those listening, it seemed the voice of some great and terrible entity, a being to which they might seem little more than worms or ants.

And so it was.

'Bow down before the glory of the God-Emperor and his most trusted agents,' throbbed the voice. 'Your ship's primary systems have been disabled on the authority of His Majesty's Holy Inquisition. This is a Centaurus level override. Do not attempt to circumvent it. You cannot. Do nothing. Say nothing. All systems will be restored in due course. Until then, know that we are watching you. That is all.'

The crew gaped at the wall-mounted vox-speakers in stunned silence.

'Your ruddy arse that's all!' roared Captain Sythero, leaping up from his throne. 'Brindle, open me a channel with that bastard right now!'

---

2. GDC – Ground Defence Command.

Brindle crossed hurriedly to his captain's side, wringing his hands anxiously. He leaned close and spoke low so that the others would not hear. 'With respect, sir, we had better sit tight. Whatever business they're about, let them get on with it. We ought to just keep our heads down.'

Sythero glared at his first officer. Brindle was no coward, he knew. He'd never had cause for complaint till now. But the man was barely fighting tremors. Fear was written all over his face. What had gotten into him?

'Listen, Gideon,' said Sythero in more conversational tones, using Brindle's first name in the hope of re-instilling a little of the man's usual confidence. 'I've got a crew of four hundred listed men here, and we're floating in space at the absolute mercy of anyone or anything that shows up. I've been charged with protecting that bloody rock out there, all the Imperial resources on it, not to mention about three million people. So, I don't care if the Emperor Himself shows up and asks me to wait it out. I want some bloody answers.'

Brindle nodded sympathetically, but spoke again, his eyes pleading. 'I've heard a lot of stories in my time, sir. And I've shared more than a few with your good self at table, not so? But have you ever heard me talk of the Inquisition, sir? Can you remember even one occasion?'

Sythero simply scowled, wishing his first officer would get to the point.

'That's because there are none, sir. Every sailor talks when the booze is flowing. Talk of every horror known to man and then some. Traitors, witches, heretics, ghosts, xenos, you name it. But I tell you this, sir. You'll never hear a word spoken about the Inquisition. Not a whisper, sir.' Brindle paused to swallow in a throat gone dry. 'You know why that is, captain? The people with those stories... They don't live long enough to tell them.'

The captain raised a dubious eyebrow. He would have scorned anyone else for such talk – tall tales of shadowy conspiracy seemed to be a favourite pastime among the Navy's lower ranks – but this was Gideon Brindle. The man was his rock. He never drank on duty. He could quote core Naval texts back to you verbatim if you asked, even when bone-tired. And right now, he was scared.

Captain Sythero had heard of the Inquisition, of course. He was an officer of thirty years' experience, not some pup fresh from the academy. The name had cropped up now and then in war rooms and briefings. But he had always considered them just another arm of the Adeptus Terra, and a small one at that. Weren't they mostly responsible for dealing with obscure religious matters? Something like that. As far as he knew, he had never run into them before.

Well, now he had, and somehow they had shut down his ship.

He folded his arms and stared out over his command bridge. The eyes of every crewman in that great long room had turned his way. He blew out a deep, frustrated breath, drew in another, and called out, 'Stand down all of you. It's not like we have any choice. Permission granted to rest at your stations until further notice. Mister Korren and Mister Hayter, stations six and ten. I'll want to know the moment something changes.'

Two grudging *yessirs* came back at him. The captain had never liked Korren and Hayter much, and he was not above demonstrating it.

He dropped back into his chair and rested his chin on a clenched fist. Brindle still stood beside him. The captain waved him off, gesturing for him to go and rest at his station. The first officer moved away. Before he had gone five metres, however, Captain Sythero called out to him again.

'Inquisitors are just men, Gideon,' he said. 'Just men and women like you or I.'

Brindle turned, but his eyes did not meet his captain's. They rested on that macabre icon still glowing from the nearest screen.

'I don't think so, sir,' he said. 'I don't think they're like us at all. But if we're lucky, we'll never find out the truth of it.'

Those words hung in the red gloom long after Brindle had returned to his chair. Captain Sythero turned them over and over in his head. Commanding a system defence ship, even all the way out here on the fringe, had always given him a sense of power, of importance. Four hundred trained men and women under his command. Forward weapons batteries that could level a city in minutes or cut through a battleship three times the *Ventria*'s size. How easily this Inquisition had come along and stripped him of that, ripped it away from him like a gossamer veil.

How had they shut him down? A Centaurus level override, the voice had said. Did that mean override codes had been pre-written into the ship's systems? The *Ventria* was a vessel of His Holy Majesty's Imperial Navy; it didn't seem possible. But if the overrides had been broadcast from an external source, a ship somewhere in-system, why hadn't the long-range auspex arrays picked it up? They had full-scan capabilities right out to the system's edge and beyond.

If the override codes had been broadcast from another ship, the implications of them falling into enemy hands were, frankly, terrifying.

I can't abide this. Naval Command needs to be told. This undermines every capability we have. To hell with the warnings. As soon as the override lifts…

* * *

Four hours and twenty-seven minutes later, it did lift. The *Ventria*'s primary systems came back online. Colours other than red flooded the bridge as if erasing a murder scene, restoring life, noise and activity. Cogitator screens and vocaliser units started churning out status reports and statistical data. The control pits buzzed in a frenzy.

Sythero thrust forwards in his chair and called out, 'Brindle, open me a two-way with the *Ultrix*. I want to speak to Captain Mendel at once. And make sure it's bloody secure.'

'Aye, sir,' said Brindle, punching the relevant runes.

A pale-skinned old man in a crisp Naval uniform soon appeared on the main display above Sythero's chair. He was clean shaven, with craggy features, and his white hair was oiled back smartly. A dark scar, legacy of a past wound, traced a path from his forehead down to his left ear. This was Mendel, captain of the *Ventria*'s sister vessel, and Sythero read on his face that the old man had known this call was coming. Typically a forceful and vigorous man despite his years, Mendel looked unusually weary now. There was no formal greeting. The old man simply held up a hand and said, 'Please, captain. If you're about to ask what I think–'

Sythero cut him off. 'Tell me the *Ultrix* hasn't just spent the last four hours in some kind of blasted lockdown!'

Mendel sighed and nodded. 'We just got all our primaries back online, same as you.'

'And that's all you've got to say about it? For Throne's sake, Mendel. What's going on here? Someone out there has override codes that leave two Naval warships completely defenceless, and you don't seem ready to do a damned thing about it. We could have been cut to pieces already. What's gotten into you, man?'

Mendel looked off to the side, gave an order to someone on his own bridge, and returned his attention to the link. 'You saw the insignia, same as I did, captain, and we only saw *that* because they wanted us to know we were not under attack. It was a courtesy. I'm not about to start asking questions to which I honestly don't want the answers. And trust me, you don't either. Do us both a favour and forget anything happened.'

'Like red hell I will! I'm going straight to Sector Command with this. The implications–'

'The implications don't bear thinking about, son,' interrupted Mendel. 'I'll assume you like breathing as much as I do, so I'll say this and then I'm done. I hope you'll credit me with at least a little age-based wisdom. Drop this thing completely, captain. Don't mention it in any reports. Don't record it in your log. If anyone ever asks, it was a glitch in the monitoring scripts. Nothing more. That's your story, and you stick to it.'

Sythero knew his expression betrayed his distaste, but it was clear, too, that he was alone in wanting to take the matter further. As is so often true, the resolve of a man standing alone is that much easier to shake. He cursed under his breath, wanting to do something, but not quite adamant enough to act against such strong counsel. Mendel and Brindle were neither of them fools, after all.

'If it happens again?' he asked the older captain, his tone signalling his acceptance of defeat.

'We stay nice and quiet, and wait it out,' replied Mendel. 'I've worked system defence for a dozen other worlds, captain, and I've only ever... Look, I doubt it'll happen again, but if it does...' He shrugged.

Sythero nodded, hardly satisfied but subdued at last. 'Very well, captain. In that case, I'll not keep you any longer.'

Mendel gave a sympathetic half-smile and signed off.

Sythero remained staring silently at the comms monitor long after it had gone blank. In the days that followed, the numerous duties of a Naval captain helped to push the matter further and further towards the back of his mind. But he never quite forgot it. From time to time, his mind would throw up the image of the skull-and-I symbol that had appeared on all his screens, and he would wonder at it, at the power it represented and the questions no one else seemed willing to ask.

Of the men he had ordered to the ship's viewports, only one reported anything unusual. Two hours and thirty-three minutes into the primary systems lock-out, Ormond Greeves, a low-ranking weapons tech assigned to one of the aft plasma-batteries, reported a brief flicker of fire skirting the edge of the dark hemisphere of the planet below. It looked, he said, as if something – perhaps a small craft, perhaps just debris – had entered the atmosphere of Chiaro at speed. Greeves had good eyes – he was a religious man, too, whose words were seldom, if ever, false. But his report was never entered in the ship's records.

Of what really happened that day in the orbit of the mine-world Chiaro, only those responsible could properly tell. But they were of the Holy Inquisition and, with but a single exception, they were answerable to no one.

2

'*Blackseed* has been planted,' said one hooded figure to another in a clear, toneless voice.

They sat across from each other at a table of polished wood, rich and dark, the grain unnaturally symmetrical. No Imperial iconography here. It was a simple room, lit by simple oil lamps with simple iron fixings. There were no glasses or dishes on the table, no tapestries or portraits on the walls. No need for such. This place, after all, and everything in it, was mere psychic projection. The figures, too, were projections only, in truth seated many light years away from each other, brought together by the life-sapping toil of the psychic choirs under their command. Nothing here was real save the words they shared and the wills behind them. Here in this mutual mindscape, no other could intrude without detection. No other could hear their words, for they were spoken in secrecy. And that was well.

'Fruition?' asked the other.

'Four years for a ten per cent conversion, given the reported gestation times. Nineteen years absolute if the magos's projections prove accurate. Monitors are in place, naturally, but if there are timeline problems...'

'You'll have the new assets you need. The Watch Commander may grudge it, but he will not refuse. The new accord bears your personal seal as arranged. The Deathwatch knows what it gains. You have other assets in place, of course.'

'Some of my best, and I'm positioning others now.'

'Nothing to which you are too attached, I hope.'

'You taught me better than that.'

A nod, acknowledging the compliment. 'You do me credit as ever.

May it always be so. If *Project Blackseed* bears fruit, your most fervent hope may be that much closer to reality.'

'Or it may not. In either case, your continued support–'

'Mutually beneficial, my old friend, as I've assured you before.'

'Even so, I would affirm my commitment once more if you would hear it.'

A raised hand. 'Your loyalty is not in doubt. We both know the sacrifices that must be made. Let the opposition believe you work against me. Small wounds I gladly bear for the greater prize. You have done well in laying false tracks. They follow where we send them. They shall not discover their error until it is too late. By then we will have taken them apart from the inside, and our benefactor will rise to power unopposed.'

'You mentioned new players.'

'Middle-rankers. Nothing that need concern you yet. They play the long game, as we do, hoping to establish their own candidate. Others who share our *outlook* are already on hand to check them. Focus on your own immediate objectives. If there is anything you would ask before we part minds…'

'Is she well?'

Always the same question, worded exactly the same way. His one true weakness.

His sister.

'She sleeps peacefully as always, my friend. Envy her that. And may the Imperium to which you restore her be a better place for both of you.'

'*Blackseed* will bear fruit.'

'But only if White Phoenix is at the centre. Any other and we gain nothing. The psykers were adamant. Along that path alone lies the weapon we need.'

'White Phoenix will be ordered to the relevant location when the time is right. Everything else will depend on successful extraction. I am sure the Deathwatch will not disappoint.'

'Let us hope not. The visions were less clear on that count. In any case, I shall await your report. We'll not speak again until this is over. Vigilance, my friend. *In nomine Imperator.*'

'Vigilance. And may His Glorious Light guide us all.'

3

Around him, death. Familiar. Comfortable. Not the screaming, churning, blood-drenched death of thousands falling in battle. This was quiet death. This was the pensive, sombre death of the graveyard in winter. This was death carved artfully in stone. Death in repose.

A crow cawed in the chill air, noisily protesting the intrusion of the tall figure in grey fatigues who approached uninvited.

Lyandro Karras grinned at the bird and nodded in salutation, but as he drew nearer, the bird cawed once more, a last harsh reproach, and left its perch on the tallest of the headstones. Pinions clapping, it beat a path through the frigid air.

Karras watched the crow's grudging departure until it vanished beyond a steep hill to his right. Falling snow danced for a moment in the wake of its passage.

We are both icons of death, my noisy friend, he thought, psychically tracking the bird's life-force as it moved farther and farther off, something he did out of long habit.

I precipitate it. My arrival signals the coming end. You come after to gorge on the spoils. And neither of us is welcome in gentle company. How misunderstood we are!

The words were not his own but quotes from a 31st millennium play by Hertzen. *Sunset on Deneb*, it was called. Karras had never seen it performed, but he had read it once during warp transit to a combat zone in the Janos subsector. That had been over a century ago. Thinking back, he allowed himself a moment of silent amusement as he remembered the improbable series of events that had befallen the play's hero, Benizzi Caldori. Stumbling from conflict to conflict, the poor fool, unable even to tie his own boot-laces, had ended up a Lord Militant charged with winning a sector-wide campaign against the abhorrent orks.

Karras made a mental note to recall the play in its entirety sometime. There were several lessons in the second and third acts worth reviewing.

Turning his thoughts away from petulant crows and ancient plays, he continued his journey, snow crunching beneath his boots with every broad stride. He walked without destination, as he had done for the past three days, untroubled by sub-zero temperatures that would have killed a normal man, glad simply to have been called back here after so long fighting out in the dark reaches.

Occludus.

The grave world.

Chapter-planet of the Death Spectres Space Marines.

Home.

As he walked, Karras let his fingers run over the snow-covered tops of the headstones he passed. History could not recall the people who had made them, nor those who lay beneath, though they were certainly human. The writing on the stones was in a sharp, angular script that had lost all its meaning far back in the mists of time. Despite the Chapter's efforts, no record could be found that told of the first colonies here. No archive explained how or why the entire planet had been dedicated to the interring of the dead.

And this world's greatest secret...

That was a thing the Chapter kept well buried, for there were still things in the universe that mankind was far from ready to know.

Thinking of this and of the long-dead multitude beneath his feet caused Karras to recall his own deaths.

The first he had experienced at the age of four S.I.[3], and it had lasted only twenty-three minutes and seven seconds. The poison they gave him stopped his heart and lungs – he'd had only one heart back then, and his lungs had as yet been unaltered. He remembered struggling frantically, unable to scream, his young muscles almost tearing as he wrestled with the restraints. Then the struggle left him and so did his worldly senses. His awareness awoke to the realms beyond reality. He had seen the nexus, the Black River of which others had spoken, its surface an inexplicable cylinder enclosing his mind, funnelling him towards the Beyond. He had felt its powerful currents pulling at him, dragging him towards an irreversible transition he was not yet ready to make.

In the lore of the Chapter, as it was written in ancient times, only those who died in battle could be reborn to serve again. The

---

3. S.I. – Standard Imperial: a single year of one thousand days in the official Imperial calendar.

Afterworld waited to embrace him, to swallow him, to deny him that eventual rebirth, and he fought as his betters had instructed, using mantras, wielding his mental strength where the physical had no meaning. Other presences, hungry and malign, closed in on him as he resisted, but they could not breach the flowing walls of the tunnel. They belonged to other dimensions and lacked the power to tear their way into his. Nevertheless, he heard them screaming in rage and frustration. He felt it, too. Their combined anger manifested itself as a hurricane-like force, fearfully strong. He reeled as it buffeted his awareness. Still the Black River pulled at him, but he held on.

How long had he fought in those strange dimensions? Time flowed differently there. Hours? Days? Longer? Bright as his young life-force was, his reserves reached their end at last. He was sapped. He could fight the flow no longer. There would be no return to the world of flesh. Not ever. He had failed himself and the Chapter both, and the price was an eternity without honour or glory.

No! I cannot die. I must not die. Not like this, without weapon in hand.

Thoughts of disappointing his *khadit*[4] were too much. That, too, was worse than death, a shame he refused to carry into the ever-after. Renewed strength infused his essence then, born of loyalty and natural tenacity both. He fought harder, a last desperate push, turning his rage upon the flowing nexus as if it were a sentient foe.

In the culmination of holy rites symbolic of the Great Resurrection itself, his immortal soul wrestled its way back to the physical plane. He gasped, flexed cold, stiff fingers, opened his eyes, and drank deep lungfuls of incense-heavy air. Lyandro Karras lived again, no longer an aspirant but a neophyte that day, embraced by the warrior cult that had taken him from his birth-parents and changed his fate to one of consequence.

The Black River terrified me back then.

As he crunched through the snow between avenues of ancient graves, he remembered his second death.

He had been eight S.I. – almost twenty-two Terran years – and he had lain dead for one hour, eleven minutes and twenty-eight seconds. Dispassionate eyes had watched him as he lay on an altar of black marble inlaid with fine golden script. Those around him, robed and hooded in dark grey, murmured ancient litanies in low, hypnotic monotone. Again, Karras had fought against the currents of the Black River as it surged all around him. Experience gave him more fortitude this time around, but his strengthened life-force

---

4. *khadit* – literally 'giver of knowledge'; shares a root with *ditah*, meaning 'father' in Occludian Low Gothic.

and growing psychic power also attracted more attention from the dreadful denizens on the other side of the walls. He felt them clawing frantically at the fabric of reality, scrabbling to get at him. They had come so much closer that second time, driven into a famished frenzy by the new vigour they sensed in him. But, as before, he won out. Bolstered by mantras taught since the earliest days of the Chapter, and the Deep Training passed to him by his khadit, he bested death and its raging currents once more.

When life at last returned to his cooling corpse, Karras rose once again. And once again, he ascended in rank, a neophyte no longer, a full battle-brother of the Chapter at last. The litanies ended. Silent smiles replaced thin-lipped concern. He stood now among equals, ready at last to visit death on mankind's enemies in the Emperor's holy name.

Karras remembered the look in the eyes of his khadit that day. *There* was the respect he craved. And beneath it, just for a fleeting second, something like the glimmer of an almost parental pride.

The third and final time Karras had died during the sacred rites of the Chapter, he was one hundred and nine years-old by the Terran count, and he lay as a corpse for a full Occludian day[5]. It was the greatest test he had faced thus far – a test which, this time, he undertook at his own behest. Success would elevate him within the Librarius, unlocking a path to greater psychic mastery that was, by grim necessity, closed to those of Lexicanium rank. If he survived, he would return to life as a Codicier, proud to stand among the most powerful of his psychic brethren. Only the most darkly blessed ever attempted the Third Ascension. The chances of a successful resurrection were far slimmer than with his previous deaths. His closest battle-brothers, bonded to him through incessant training and live combat, stood wordless and tense, anxious for his success. Some had counselled him against undergoing those rites, but Karras had been determined, sensing a greater destiny might lie along that path, not to mention a significant leap in power. He knew he had the potential to survive it. Thus, he had crossed over once again and felt familiar dark waters flow around him.

The currents of the Black River bothered him not at all that final time. He had mastered them by mastering himself. But his advanced psychic power was so great a beacon that it drew the attention of something new – a different order of beast from the Other Realm. Something sickening broke through that day, as Karras had known it must. It was a vast, pulsing thing of constantly changing forms, of countless mouths and tendrils, of strange grasping appendages that defied comparison with anything he had

5. The Occludian day is 27.3 hours.

known. It was rage and hate and hunger, and it fell upon him with savage glee. The battle was one of wills, of two minds struggling for supremacy with everything they had, and it had seemed to last aeons. In the end, they proved well-matched, the abomination and he. Both spent themselves utterly in the fight. They became locked together in mental exhaustion, and the currents began to drag them both into the mouth of oblivion. But Karras rallied. The prayers and hopes of his battle-brothers penetrated to his consciousness from the distant realm of the living, energising him for one last, desperate push.

The surge of psychic strength blasted him free, and the beast was dragged away by the Black River, raging and thrashing against its fate until it was swallowed by distance and time and absolute darkness.

Karras's cold corpse began to breathe again. Twin hearts kicked back to life.

He returned from death that day triumphant, a Codicier of the Death Spectres Librarius at last, and the Chapter rejoiced, for such gifted brothers were few.

In the long years since, Karras had served in that role, rarely setting foot back on Occludus. War had kept him away. He did the Chapter's work, the Emperor's work. It was what he had been born to do.

But, at last, his khadit had called him back.

There had been a development; an opportunity to earn great honour for himself and the Chapter both.

It was a rare chance to serve as never before.

'The time is soon,' his khadit had told him. 'One must return before the other departs. Until then, go out alone. Be with your thoughts. Think on who and what you are. Sense of self is the pillar that supports us when all else falls. Go. I will send for you when the time comes.'

So Karras had started walking. Walking and thinking. Remembering.

He sensed a trio of souls, such strong shining souls, approaching from the east at speed. Fellow Death Spectres; their ethereal signature was unmistakable, as familiar and comforting as the land itself. He turned into the freezing wind to meet their approach just as something vast and dark and angular rolled in over the hills, almost clipping them. It pulled up great skirts of loose snow as it came skimming towards his location. Powerful turbofan engines drummed on the air. It slowed and began a fiery, vertical descent, turning the snow all around it to steam. The craft settled on thick landing stanchions with a sharp hiss of hydraulic pistons. There was a loud clang. Orange light flowed like liquid over the snow as a boarding ramp lowered.

It was a Thunderhawk gunship from the Chapter's crypt-city, Logopol, and its arrival was a bittersweet thing to Karras.

His time out here alone was over. This visit to the Chapter world had been all too brief. What lay ahead, he knew, would make the trials of his past seem a mere game by comparison. He didn't need witchsight to tell him that.

Only one in twenty ever returned alive from service in the Deathwatch.

4

Evening came, such as it was in Cholixe. The sky never changed over the canyon-city. The slice that was visible between the towering walls of rock was a constant twilight purple pierced by las-bright stars. But, at the tone of the evening bell, more lamps were lit and the streets and alleys became busier. A simulated evening. People seemed to need that cycle of night and day. A hangover from the days of Old Terra, it comforted them, even so poorly approximated as this.

The men who lived here, stocky Nightsiders for the most part, moved in work-parties, either returning from a long hard shift in the mines, or departing for the start of one. Weary mothers led young children home from Ecclesiarchy-run schola while older children weaved between the flows of human traffic, kicking trash and calling out to each other in voices too coarse for their scant years.

The air was thick with the smell of grox oil from the streetlamps. It was a salty, burned-meat smell, and it clung to clothes and hair and skin. No bath or shower ever seemed to remove it completely. One came to ignore it in time, but it still bothered Ordimas Arujo. He had only been on Chiaro a year.

It still struck him, too, the oppressive nature of the place. Hemmed in between the sheer cliffs, which rose four kilometres high on either side, the city blocks were pressed together like people in an overcrowded train. The tallest buildings, precariously top-heavy and shoddily built, loomed like dark, hungry giants over the inhabitants, as if readying to fall upon them and feed. Thick black utility cables hung between them like the strands of some chaotic spider's web, humming with electrical power and badly digitised voices. Alleyways were often so narrow here that the broad-shouldered men from the mines had to walk sideways down them just to get to their own tenement doors.

Such was the life of the average Chiarite, at least here in Cholixe. Those of loftier rank mostly lived and worked in structures cut straight into the canyon walls. Their broad diamonite windows, warm with steady golden light, looked out over the city below; not the best view perhaps, but Ordimas suspected the air was a lot cleaner up there. He could imagine how it felt to look down on this grimy, oily pit of a town while one drank fine liquor from a crystal goblet after a hot shower.

Not this time.

He had known both the high life and the lowest in his many travels, but man-of-station was not his role here on Chiaro. Here, he was a humble street performer. Here, he was the Puppeteer.

It was the younger children of Cholixe for whom Ordimas regularly performed. Day after day, at the southern edge of Great Market Square, he set up his benches and the little plastex stage on which his stories played out. The local vendors had no love for him, always scowling and cursing at him, warding themselves against black fate with the sign of the aquila while he and his assistant arranged the stage. But they had no authority to move him on, and he paid them no mind. They didn't interest him much. The children, however…

So many more than before. And so strange, this new generation.

As the modest crowd watched his marionettes dance on the tiny stage, Ordimas peered out from behind the gauzy screen that hid him. *Aye. So strange.* While half the audience laughed, clapped and gasped at all the proper moments, the others sat as cold and motionless as mantelpiece figurines. Nothing reached them. No words passed between them. No flicker of emotion or interaction at all. There were boys and girls both, and all seemed to share a queer aspect. Their hair was somewhat thinner than it ought to be. Their skin had an unhealthy tint to it. And their eyes, those unblinking eyes… He couldn't be certain, not absolutely, but they seemed to have a strange shining quality, like the eyes of wolves or cats, only to be seen when thick shadow passed over them.

Most unsettling of all, however, was a fact more related to their mothers than to the children themselves. Ordimas had seen these women before here in the market. He had a good eye for beauty, despite, or perhaps because of, his own wretched form. He often watched the young women pass by. That's why he was certain, without a shadow of a doubt, that some of their pregnancies had lasted less than three months.

Three months. It shouldn't be possible.

Yet here they were, standing over their tiny charges as his performance came to an end, living their lives as if nothing was amiss. It was absurd.

His marionettes took a bow signalling the end of the show. Ordimas manipulated one cross-frame so that the puppet of Saint Cirdan, having vanquished the warboss Borgblud in the final act, raised its sword aloft. 'For the glory of the Emperor!' Ordimas piped in the character's reedy voice.

'For the glory of the Emperor!' echoed half the children with delight.

Ordimas tapped a pedal with his foot and the curtain fell on the little stage. From the more normal-looking children there came rapturous applause and cries of joy. From the others, only lifeless stares. After a moment, these latter rose to their feet and, wordlessly as always, sought out their mothers at the back of the crowd.

'You're up,' said Ordimas, turning to his young assistant.

The boy, Nedra, nodded with a grin and, taking the cloth cap from his head, he went out among the audience to call for coin. Ordimas heard him thanking those mothers who spared a centim or two. He didn't need the money, of course. Ordimas was already rich beyond the dreams of most men, though he looked far from it. His Lordship was a generous employer, despite the two having never actually met. Still, what puppeteer performed for free in the Imperium? It was important not to raise undue suspicions while his intelligence was still incomplete. Just a few more days and the report would be ready. Besides, the boy Nedra was earning his keep. He was proud of his job as Ordimas's assistant. *So kind, that boy.* He had never once looked on Ordimas with disgust or loathing, though he himself was already showing signs that he would be a handsome young man in a few years if given half a chance.

Ordimas would be sorry to leave him, but he'd see the boy a'right. He always did. There was always some waif or stray that he picked up on long assignments, especially when sent among the downtrodden. When he left – and he always did – he hoped he left them with a better life than before; better than they would have had, at any rate.

He had trained Nedra well. There would still be a puppet show in Great Market Square after Ordimas left the planet.

Packing his marionettes into their case, Ordimas only wondered if, a year from now, there would be any *natural* children left here to enjoy it.

5

The Thunderhawk flight back to Logopol was brief, a little over an hour, and Karras was back in time to witness the arrival of the black drop-shuttle that would, all too soon, carry him up into orbit. The atmosphere in the fortress-monastery's massive east hangar was solemn, even more so than usual. Karras stood on his khadit's left, wordless and, despite mentally reciting a mantra against doubt, more than a little anxious. Each cut a tall, powerful figure, but Athio Cordatus, the Mesazar, Master of the Librarius, had a certain heavy solidity that Karras had yet to develop. It was a hard, powerful thickness common to Space Marines who survived the wars of five centuries or more. It made the old warrior seem like a living mountain, even now, out of armour, dressed in his hooded robe of blue and gold. Karras and Cordatus shared a brief look as the black shuttlecraft settled onto its stanchions and powered down its engines.

Across from the Librarians stood the entire Third Company of the Death Spectres Space Marines, here to witness in sorrow and respect the return to the Chapter of one of their own. Unlike the two psykers, the battle-brothers of Third Company stood in full plate, eschewing only their helms as per the occasion. Each held a polished bolter across his broad armoured chest.

The shuttle's ramp rang dully on the hangar floor. A slim figure in a tight black officer's uniform and stiffened cap descended. He marched three metres from the bottom of the ramp and dropped to one knee, head bowed, waiting.

Captain Elgrist stepped from his place at the head of Third Company and walked out to meet the officer from the shuttle. Karras watched him. It had been many years, many battles, but Elgrist looked well, resplendent in fact, with his white cloak flaring out behind him as he marched. Still, there was pain written on his face. It was he who had nominated Stephanus for Deathwatch service, and the Chapter had lost one of its finest as a result.

Though Elgrist and the black-clad officer spoke at normal volume in the vast and windy hangar, the gene-boosted hearing of the Space Marines in attendance picked up every word.

'Rise,' said Elgrist. 'I am Rohiam Elgrist, the Megron[6] and the Third Captain.'

The officer from the shuttle stood as commanded and, straightening to attention, looked up into all-red eyes. The Third Captain stood almost eighty centimetres taller than he. Swallowing in a dry throat, the officer steeled himself and said, 'I am honoured, lord. My name is Flight Lieutenant Carvael Qree of the *Adonai*. Address me as you please. I... I'm afraid my duty is not a happy one.'

'Nevertheless,' said Elgrist, 'you are welcome here on this hallowed ground, lieutenant. We are aware of the duty that has brought you to Logopol. Would that it were indeed happier.'

'Aye, lord. If it be any comfort to you, I am told he died well, saving the brothers of his kill-team and ending a threat that would have seen many thousands slaughtered by xenos tooth and claw. That, of course, is all I was told. There are protocols–'

'The Deathwatch operates in shadow. We know this. We accept this. Still, your words offer comfort. His brothers shall be glad to know he died well and for good gain.'

Qree opened a latched leather tube on his belt and withdrew a furled scroll which, in the palms of both hands, he offered up to the Third captain. 'Watch Commander Jaeger asked that I deliver this with the body. It is encrypted, of course, but I am told your Chapter already possesses the key. I fear that you will find few answers within, but perhaps the contents will further honour the fallen.'

Elgrist took the scroll in a large gauntleted hand and nodded.

'It shall be passed to the Megir.' Seeing the lieutenant's confusion, Elgrist added, 'To the Chapter Master.'

That much was a lie, of course. The Megir could not be troubled with such things. His burden was too great by far. But the Imperium at large must never know what lay below Logopol. It was to Athio Cordatus that the scroll would be given. It was the Mesazar who commanded the Chapter while the First Spectre sat suffering in a chamber deep below the city's catacombs.

Flight Lieutenant Qree inclined his head. 'I see. Well, I believe

---

6. *The Megron* – a position roughly equivalent to *Master of the Flag* in other Space Marine Chapters.

this concludes the first part of my duty, my lord. Shall I signal for the body to be…'

He almost said *unloaded* but the word struck him as disrespectful. Silence hung for a moment while Qree grasped for a more appropriate term. After the span of a few seconds, however, Captain Elgrist interceded.

'If you would, lieutenant. Please.'

'At once, m'lord.'

Qree reached up and pressed a brass stud in his starched black collar. Into this stud, he muttered, 'Begin the procession.' A moment later, six figures in black robes of mourning descended the shuttle ramp. They carried censers that trailed wisps of pungent incense as they swung to and fro with each slow, deliberate step. They sang softly and deeply as they descended, a low, humming lament that reached out to the aural senses of all present and held them fast. The quality of sorrow in that soft, hypnotic song was palpable. Normal men would weep to hear it, and Lieutenant Qree fought hard to keep tears from his eyes, not with complete success. The assembled Space Marines wept not, but their battle-worn faces, all ghostly white with blood-red eyes, betrayed the deep sadness that pulled on their hearts.

Karras felt it tug at his own hearts as his psychic awareness was pricked by their grief. Stephanus would have made captain one day, but that honour had been taken from him, swapped for another. He had died in battle, which was proper, but he had fallen surrounded not by his Occludian brothers but by strangers from other worlds, other Chapters. Such was the end of a Deathwatch operative. Was it worth it? Was Deathwatch service the greater of the two honours, or the lesser? Putting his prejudice aside, Karras searched himself for an honest answer, knowing full well that he, like Stephanus, might return here on a shuttle crewed by men in robes of mourning.

But he would reach no real conclusion, he decided, until service was upon him. Time would answer the questions that soul-searching could not.

Between the six hooded mourners, a long, thick, lidless sarcophagus of black onyx appeared, floating silently on the air, keeping pace perfectly with its escort, upheld and propelled by tiny anti-gravitic motors. The mourners reached the bottom of the ramp and guided the onyx block to Captain Elgrist. There, a few metres in front of him, they dropped to their right knees and bowed their heads. The song stopped.

Qree threw back his shoulders, chest out, chin raised, took a deep breath, and said in a sonorous voice, 'To his beloved brothers, to those that forged him, to those that knew him best, we commend the body of the fallen in the name of the Deathwatch. May his sacrifice be honoured until the ending of all things.'

'So shall it be,' boomed the Third Captain in response.

'So shall it be,' echoed the assembled brothers, Karras and his master included.

At a nod from Elgrist, four sergeants moved forwards from the ranks of Third Company and walked towards the floating sarcophagus. The six robed mourners rose from their knees, bowed low to the Third captain, turned, and silently drifted back up the shuttle ramp. The Space Marine sergeants took up position around the sarcophagus, each raising his right hand to his lips then touching his fingers to the cold forehead of their fallen comrade.

Captain Elgrist turned to face Qree once more.

'Your duty is done and done well, lieutenant. One has returned. Another shall leave with you.' Here, he indicated Karras with a nod. Qree looked over, caught Karras's eye, and bowed. Karras nodded back.

'Chapter-serfs will attend your crew while Brother Karras says his goodbyes,' Elgrist continued. 'Your shuttle will be refuelled.' He gestured to an archway in the hangar's north wall. 'You may take repast in the antechamber beyond that door and make ablutions as you will. Third Company thanks you for your service.'

'It was my honour, though not my pleasure, my lord.'

'Go in peace, then, and may you long serve the Golden Throne.'

Qree bowed, at which point Elgrist turned and strode to the head of the four sergeants. At a word, he led them to the great arched corridor that dominated the western wall and would take them towards the heart of the crypt-city. As the sergeants and the sarcophagus passed beneath the sculpted arch, the remaining battle-brothers of Third Company turned as one and marched in ordered lines, following their captain and the body of Brother Stephanus out of the massive hangar. Karras and Cordatus watched them go.

'A day of saddened hearts,' said Karras.

'And yet we are blessed,' said his khadit. 'Most that fall in Deathwatch service are never recovered. While the gene-seed was ruined before it could be extracted, he shall at least be mummified properly and interred in the holy catacombs of his Chapter world. Would that every brother could be honoured so, but it is the exception rather than the rule.'

These last words were said pointedly, their message clear:

Be one of the exceptions.

Serfs bearing the Chapter sigil emerged from one of the north passageways and moved towards the shuttle. They were masked with steel – each face a polished, grinning skull – and robed in black, all but one who wore the white robes and gold skull-mask of the upper ranks. This one went to Qree and, after a few words, led him away from the hangar. Moments later, the rest of the shuttle crew descended and followed the other serfs into the antechamber Elgrist had indicated.

'Do not keep them overlong, my *khajar*[7]' said Cordatus. 'May I assume all your affairs are in order?'

'I am ready in all but mind,' answered Karras.

Cordatus smiled. 'No one is ever truly ready for such a duty, and I can do little more to prepare you. The Deathwatch holds rigidly to its protocols of secrecy, and for reasons I'll not venture to question. But you will adapt. You are worthy at least to try. Before you leave, the Megir has asked that you attend him.'

The Megir.

First Spectre, Grandmaster of the Order, Lord of Occludus...

...The Eye that Pierces the Veil.

It was very rare for the Megir to see anyone but the First Captain, the High Chaplain, or Cordatus himself. Karras had not laid eyes on the First Spectre since his ascension to that position, but his power could be felt everywhere. Logopol pulsed with it. One could feel it resonating even in orbit. To Karras, it was part of being home.

'Go,' said Cordatus. 'Robed as you are. Enter the great dome barefoot and kneel before him to make your obeisance. When you exit, send me a thought and I shall meet you back here.'

'It will be as you say, my lord. I go with haste.'

One did not keep the Megir waiting.

Dismissed, Karras left the hangar, taking the great archway by which Third Company had departed. His mind was reeling. He had never imagined the Megir would call upon him before he entered service with the Deathwatch. In truth, he was unsettled and utterly unprepared. His khadit had spoken of the Shariax only occasionally, and all warmth seemed to bleed from him whenever he had.

It is the Throne of Glass from which no First Spectre ever rises alive. It is both the Chapter's greatest burden and its greatest gift. Without it, all hope of the Great Resurrection is lost. Ah, what a price we pay for faith.

On the very day of his ascension, the First Spectre had gone alone into the darkest depths of Logopol and had never come back. It was always so, a custom thousands of years old, beginning with Corcaedus the Founder who, driven by a vision from the Emperor Himself, had brought his Death Spectres to Occludus.

The vision had shown him exactly where to delve. He had found

---

7. *khajar* – literally *receiver of wisdom*; the term by which a khadit addresses his foremost student. The word shares an etymological root with *jari*, the Occludian Low Gothic for *son*.

the great dome – the Temple of Voices – sitting silent, patient, in its vast cavern many kilometres below ground. Within the dome, he found the ancient secret it had kept hidden since before the dawn of the Imperium.

On his command, Logopol had been built directly above it.

So much history. So much significance. The destiny of the Chapter. Its purpose.

Karras didn't feel ready. Not for this.

But he kept walking.

6

Athio Cordatus watched his khajar emerge into the hangar, dressed now in dark blue fatigues and black boots, flanked by serfs and servitors carrying his wargear and the limited belongings permitted by the Deathwatch.

Karras looked hollow, stunned even. It was clear he had been profoundly disturbed by his time with the Megir. Cordatus didn't need to ask why. The Megir as Karras would have remembered him was a vision of strength and power, of boundless vitality and an insatiable hunger for victory in battle. Not so the figure that now led the Chapter from his life-leeching throne. There in the depths sat a withered thing, muscles atrophied, bone structure starkly visible beneath skin that was gradually turning black. His beard and hair, white as Occludian snow, had grown long and thin. He no longer moved, no longer spoke with lips and breath. His body was undergoing slow petrifaction. In due course, he would turn completely to stone. The Shariax did this, but the power it offered in return, a power unknown anywhere else in all the worlds of man, made such suffering a dark necessity. The Chapter could not fulfil its destiny without it.

We waited so long for him, thought Cordatus. *So many others were lost along the way. But in Lyandro Karras, the calculations, the breeding, the manipulation; it has all come together at last. The sacrifice of the Chapter Masters will not be in vain.*

Whatever visions or words the First Spectre had shared with Karras were a matter for the two alone. Cordatus would not ask. He would, no doubt, be summoned below after his khajar left for space. The Megir would share anything he needed to know then.

Cordatus dared not explain the depths of the Chapter's hopes to Karras. At least, not directly or in any great detail. The sharing of that knowledge would alter the very future it suggested. But there were other methods to steer him along the critical path. Cordatus had seeded several prime futures with a series of psychic messages, each intended to corral Karras in the necessary direction. Only time would tell if those messages were ever received. The act of placing them had taken Cordatus beyond the previous limits of his capabilities. It had stretched him to a point perilously close to absolute psychic collapse, after which, warded or not by his tattoos and holy amulets, he would have been unable to resist possession. There was no thought more chilling to a Librarian: that a daemon of the warp might swallow his soul, claim his body, and turn his powers upon the Order he loved above all else... The word *nightmare* was hardly adequate.

As Cordatus had scored his messages in the surface of time to come, the Black River had surged and crashed around him, carrying him almost into the Afterworld. But he was not the Mesazar for nothing. Few among even the most powerful Librarians of the Adeptus Astartes would have survived, but among those few Athio Cordatus stood as one.

When you return, my khajar... if you return... it may be I who sits atop the Shariax. I would pray to Terra to be spared such a fate, but it is inevitable, and it is my duty. I shall embrace it for the sake of the Order, though I am a lesser man than the First Spectre, and I may not last as long.

Cordatus watched his khajar march to the middle of the hangar and stop, facing the sleek black shuttle that would take him up to the *Adonai*. Behind him, the serfs and servitors trundled to a halt. Arranged in ranks on either side of the hangar, every Space Marine in Logopol, with the exception of the members of Third Company and those others whose duties could not be postponed, stood in attendance, dressed in full plate to honour their brother on his leaving. The mood was grim. This was not like a standard departure. All those present knew the odds were against Karras ever returning, alive or dead.

Cordatus had used Karras's time below to have the tech-priests dress him in full power armour. The Chief Librarian stood now as a polished, gleaming vision of power and position, his shimmering ceramite replete with purity seals, the sculpted icon of the Crux Terminatus, and several formal pieces inscribed or embossed with details and renderings of his greatest personal glories. From his massive pauldrons, a thick cloak trailed all the way to the hangar floor.

In truth, Cordatus felt overdressed as he looked at his khajar.

Karras had donned simple combat fatigues of dark Librarius blue. He seemed almost naked in comparison to the armoured might of the others. But that was as it should be. Instructions from the Deathwatch were explicit: those sequestered into service were to arrive out of armour. They would not wear it again until the taking of Second Oath. To those who had never served, that meant little. But Cordatus remembered his own term of service, despite the intervening centuries. Those days of relentless training without his second skin had made him feel like a damned neophyte again. Karras would not relish it, as he himself had not, but there was purpose behind it. His khajar would come to see that quickly.

Flight Lieutenant Qree, who had since re-boarded the shuttle to make final preparations for take-off, descended the craft's ramp now and stopped in front of Karras. He bowed low and spoke a few words of greeting. Karras couldn't manage a smile. He nodded. The lieutenant bowed again, turned sharply and marched back to the shuttle, followed now by Karras's serfs and baggage servitors. The First Codicier stood alone, the eyes of his battle-brothers on him. It was time.

Cordatus was glad he was here for this. His combat duties in The Cape of Lost Hope – the stellar tip of the local spiral arm – had ended only weeks ago with the detestable dark eldar beaten back at last, though they would return in due course. Cordatus believed the timing to be no accident. Perhaps it was the hand of Fate intervening on his behalf, or perhaps the hand of the Emperor Himself or the countless spirits of humanity's dead. Whatever the cause, Cordatus had again been able to take a direct hand in steering this warrior on whom so much depended.

Time to bid him farewell.

He marched forwards, stopped before his khajar, met his gaze and offered formal salute. This he did in the ancient manner of the Chapter, left hand held flat at the abdomen, palm up, right hand clenched in a vertical fist resting on the palm of the left. It was the *masrahim*, the salute of skull and stone. Its meaning was simple, but it was not a salute made lightly: *I will honour you in death as I do now in life.*

Karras, though still shaken badly by what he had seen in the Temple of Voices, managed to return the salute, eyes locked with those of his teacher, red locked to red.

Cordatus could see the torment there. He knew it all too well himself. Today, for the first time, Karras had seen the Megir upon the Throne of Glass. He was bound to be profoundly disturbed. Cordatus's own hearts broke every time he went below at the psychic call of his old friend and master.

Better Corcaedus had never found the Shariax.

No. That wasn't true, and such thought bordered on Chapter heresy. If the vision of the Founder ever came to pass, all the sacrifice in the galaxy would be made worthwhile, even – and it burned Cordatus to concede it – the soul of Lyandro Karras.

'My khajar,' said Cordatus. 'You carry the honour of the Order on your shoulders. The reputation of the Chapter is in your hands. Do not stain it. Serve well. Earn the respect of those around you. Show by your example the strength and quality of the Death Spectres.'

'It shall be as you command, khadit. They shall know us by our strength and spirit. This I swear on my life.'

Preserve that life, my son, thought Cordatus. *Preserve it at any cost.*

He did not voice this.

Instead, he placed a hand on Karras's shoulder and sent a command-pulse to a servitor waiting silently in the shadows. The mind-wiped man-machine ambled forwards, cog-knees whirring and jinking. In its metal pincers it held a weapon, long and slender, of such history and power that it had a soul of its own – and not a mere machine-spirit to be coaxed into operation with oils and litanies, but a soul that burned as bright as any man's.

'*Arquemann?*' asked Karras in confusion as the servitor stopped on his right.

'Aye,' said Cordatus. 'I entrust it to you now, may you serve each other well in the trials to come.'

'I-I cannot,' stammered Karras. This was a thing too great. The weapon, he knew, had once been laid at the feet of the Golden Throne on Terra. The Founder, to whom it had once belonged, had placed it before the Emperor just seconds before receiving his vision. After the Shariax itself, and the bones and armour of Corcaedus, this ancient force sword was the holiest relic on Occludus.

He shook his head and took a staggering step back. 'Khadit,' he said. 'I dare not even touch it.'

'You can and will,' ordered Cordatus. 'The First Spectre commands. You cannot disobey. Please, khajar. Take it with honour and gladness. *Arquemann* is sensitive to the thoughts of those who wield it, and it will serve you better if you accept it with pride.'

Karras reached out hesitantly, reverently, and touched the flat of the blade. Witchlight coruscated along it as the sword sensed his psychic strength. Karras felt the sword's spirit probing his own, learning his signature, even… could it be… evaluating him? Was that possible? If so, what was the sword's assessment? Athio Cordatus had wielded it in battle since the ascension of the Megir. Great honour had been earned in the time since. Did the weapon now rage at this transfer to a lesser warrior?

Karras gripped the hilt and lifted the blade before him. He felt a sharp mental jolt as his power was joined with the blade's own. Was this acceptance? There was a psychic pulse, a flash of fractured images, of monstrous foes wounded or cut down. Were these the sword's memories, or glimpses of things yet to be? It was long seconds before he remembered to take a breath.

'Decline cryostasis on your journey to the Watch fortress,' Cordatus advised him. 'Spend those weeks training with the blade. There will be time for you and *Arquemann* to bond properly on the journey through the warp. Practise with it often and to extremes, and together you will become a force formidable beyond the limitations you thought you had. So it was with me.'

Farewell, proud weapon. No other can fill the gap you leave.

'You honour me more than I deserve, khadit,' said Karras, breaking eye contact, looking down in contrition. 'But then, you have always honoured me more than I deserve.'

Cordatus grinned. 'Let me be the judge of that.'

The grin was short-lived. He could draw this out no longer. 'Our time together is again at its end, khajar. We part once more. If destiny wills it, we shall stand together again and speak words of greeting rather than farewell. Such is my fervent hope. Now face your brothers proudly, lift your voice, and call out those words so sacred to our Order.'

Karras slung *Arquemann* over his head and one shoulder, hanging the sword diagonally across his back by its black harness. He turned to face the Space Marines in their ordered ranks by the south wall and let the sight of them lift his hearts. They were glorious, all of them.

Remember this, he told himself. *Hold to it. Remember who you honour.*

In a loud, clear voice he called out to those he faced, 'Fear not death, we who embody it in His name.'

The response erupted like thunder from the throats of all assembled.

'We fear not Death!' they bellowed. 'For we are Death incarnate!'

'Now go,' said Cordatus. 'Depart to honour and glory, scion of the Spectres of Death. And may your deeds be written in the blood of many foes!'

Cordatus stepped aside, armour plates scraping quietly as he moved. Karras fixed unblinking eyes on the ramp of the black shuttle and marched past him in heavy silence. There was yet much he wanted to say to his khadit, but the time for words was past. He doubted he could have found the appropriate ones to express all he felt.

Instead, as Karras reached the base of the ramp, he paused, then turned and saluted the Master of the Librarius once more, fist on palm, the masrahim.

In response, Cordatus raised a clenched fist into the air and boomed out, 'The First Codicier!'

Sixty-eight Space Marines raised their armoured right fists as one. 'The First Codicier!' they roared, and the words echoed back at Karras from the hangar's great stone walls.

He turned from them and stalked up the ramp, conscious of the weight of *Arquemann* and of his duty both. It did not do to dwell on partings. They were hard enough. Instead, he centred his mind on the immediate future. He faced the unknown. Unlike those whose gifts pierced the veils of time, Karras saw only fragments in dreams, misted generalities, blurred visions of possibility and chance almost impossible to distinguish from the typical conjurings of a dreaming mind. His gifts were given more to psychic combat that to scrying.

He knew this much, however:

The Deathwatch would either make him or destroy him.

Athio Cordatus watched the shuttle ramp slowly rise. It sealed with all the dark finality of a sarcophagus lid.

I should be rejoicing, he thought bitterly. *This is all as destiny dictates. And yet...*

The craft's engines rose in pitch to a deafening roar. Shakily at first, the shuttle lifted slowly into the air. With a twin burst of flame from the small vents in its nose, it backed out into the open air beyond the hangar mouth. There, a black shadow against a heavy, snow-filled sky, it turned and rose, lifting out of sight on a trail of fire and smoke.

Cordatus dismissed the others and strode to the hangar's edge. He looked out into the charcoal grey afternoon long after the glow of the shuttle's jets had gone from sight.

'Return to us alive, Lyandro,' he murmured to himself. 'The Watch will change you in the ways we need, but only if you survive it. You must return alive.

'For without the Cadash[8], mankind will falter and die.'

---

8. *Cadash* – translates approximately from Old Occludian as 'the living chalice'.

7

Nedra finished counting out the coins from the last performance, added the total to that of the morning show and proudly announced the sum to Ordimas, who lay on his shabby cot dozing lightly.

'Three ducats and seventeen centims! That's half a ducat more than yesterday, boss.'

Ordimas opened his left eye, looked over at the boy and threw him a grin. 'Take thirty of those centims and get us something hot to eat, my lad. We've earned it. Before that, though, take another twenty and ask old Skaiman in the next block to fix those shoes.' He pointed a finger at Nedra's feet. 'They're about to fall off. Shoes first. I don't want my dinner getting cold before you get back.'

Nedra practically jumped off his stool. 'Really, boss? It's okay?'

Ordimas closed his eyes again and gave a short nod. 'Just don't waste it on re-processed grox-burgers from the stand. I want real food tonight. Your choice, hear, but something decent.'

Joy suited Nedra. It suited those bright eyes and that face so void of malice. Ordimas thought back to the day he had found the boy, a little less than a year ago. Nedra had been hiding in a length of broken outflow pipe on the city's southern edge. His sobs had given him away. He had been brutally beaten by one of the miners after refusing to surrender the contents of his begging bowl. He still bore the scars, inside and out. Ordimas had never found the perpetrator. It was too late now to hope he ever would. A pity, that; dispensing a little righteous violence would have been very satisfying. Now, though...

Only a few more days. Damn it, I'll miss you, boy.

'On your way, now,' he told Nedra. 'I need a nap.'

The boy pocketed the coins, grabbed a cloth bag from a hook by the door, tugged his cap on, yanked the door open, and vanished off into the street.

The door swung shut. Ordimas listened as Nedra trotted past the rusting window shutters. When the sound had faded, he swung his short legs over the side of the cot and stood up. The twisted leg ached as he moved. It always did, but he'd learned to ignore it most of the time. Turning and leaning down, he pulled a black plasteel case from beneath the cot, carried it over to the table and sat. It bore no markings, but it was heavy and its construction was flawless, a thing far too valuable to belong to a mere street performer. There was a keypad on the surface. Ordimas tapped in a twenty-four digit access code, fingers moving in a blur. There was a soft hiss as the stasis seal disengaged. The lid slid backwards about two centimetres before rotating into a vertical position, revealing the powerful field cogitator and burst-comms unit within.

Ordimas leaned forwards and let a small laser lens in the unit's upper housing scan his left retina. There was a half-second delay before the glossy black screen flickered to life.

Select function, it said.

'Report 227a/Cholixe,' Ordimas told the machine in a hushed voice.

Review previous entry(s)? Begin new entry(s)? Other?, asked the machine.

'Begin new entry.'

Ready for connection.

Ordimas did something then that he could never let Nedra see. Raising thumb and forefinger to his right eye, he pressed inwards at the corners. After a second, a rubbery skin – the white of the eye, the brown iris, the black pupil – came away in his hand. Beneath this overlay, sitting deep in the eye socket, was an orb of gunmetal-grey. In the centre of the orb glowed a red lens about half the diameter of a one-centim coin.

He hunched forwards to bring his optical implant in line with the unit's scan-lens. The machine spent a moment acquiring him before a pencil-thin beam of red light formed a bridge between them. This was the data-stream, and Ordimas committed all the day's relevant observations to it. Smells, sights, sounds, even those elements that only his subconscious had noted; everything was transferred to the machine's crystal matrix memory drive.

It took less than a minute.

When it was done, Ordimas leaned back and fitted his false eye-cover into place.

'Save entry and transmit,' he told the machine.

Entry saved. Beginning transmission...
Several minutes passed.
Transmission sent. Select next function.
'Stand by,' said Ordimas.

If he judged right, and he usually did, Nedra wouldn't return for another forty minutes. Ordimas left the machine on the table. He was thirsty. He was always thirsty after a transfer. He walked to the tiny kitchen, turned on the noisy, flickering lume-strip in the ceiling and poured himself a cup of watered wine. He drank half on the spot, the cold liquid soothing his throat, then returned to the table. There he sat, thinking and sipping from the cup.

He wouldn't miss this filthy cesspit of a city. Part of him wasn't looking forward to leaving, but only because of the boy. He remembered the sorrow he'd felt at leaving the others. It always lessened in time, but he never forgot them, not any of them. Despite his hopes, the realist in him knew most of those children were probably dead by now. His Lordship didn't send Ordimas Arujo to safe, healthy places. His arrival anywhere meant a cancer had developed already, something deeply wrong, something that the Great and the Powerful needed him to observe on their behalf.

Chiaro was no different. The whole planet was like a giant workhouse. The Imperium's rapacious hunger for resources had forced two different peoples to settle this hellish world – the Hasmiri, or Daysiders, and the Garrahym, known here on Chiaro as the Nightsiders. And how they hated each other for all their religious and genetic differences. Both were Imperial loyalists, of course. They worshipped the Emperor as the Ecclesiarchy demanded of them. But the writings of their patron saints were, in places, at great odds. The Daysiders mined provium, darksilver and carzum – all of which were used in the Geller field projectors so important to warp transit. They toiled beneath the heat-blistered rock of the baking sunward hemisphere. The Nightsiders, on the other hand, worked far beneath the deep-frozen surface of the void-facing hemisphere where no sunlight ever reached the ground. They searched for veins of soledite and margonite, both of which were found only on a scattered two-dozen or so Imperial worlds. Ordimas didn't know what these materials were used for. Very few did.

For all their differences, both peoples endured the same daily reality. Life on Chiaro was only possible in the Twilight Band. That meant living in the canyon, the Nystarean Gorge, and one of the two cities built within it: Cholixe or Najra.

I can't take him with me. That hasn't changed. I can't stop working for His Lordship, either. Old Ordimas knows too much by half. There's no retirement for the likes of me, unless I count death a retirement, which I guess it is.

A winking glyph on the little screen caught his eye, and he wondered how long it had been flashing at him while he sat there thinking.

One message, it said. *Priority A-2.*

Ordimas's breath caught in his throat. It was the first A-2 communiqué he had ever received. His Lordship never initiated comms before an assignment was properly completed. At least, he had never done so before.

Ordimas licked his lips, suddenly dry.

'Display message,' he told the machine.

Recipient: Asset 16
Source: Priority A-2 DSC – Key 'Sigma'
Identicode: Classified 'Uridion: Eyes Only'
Most recent transmission received. Under review. New orders as follows:
Contrive entry to active mining sector as part of work-detail. Gather observational intelligence. Everything relevant. One shift sufficient. Two days hence, rendezvous with Ordo representative, field code White Phoenix. Transfer all data to representative and exfiltrate. Expect off-world transport options limited. White Phoenix will advise.
Protocols and data-files attached. Access by opticom only. Full auto-erase will begin immediately after transfer.
That is all.
Ave Imperator.

White Phoenix? That assignation wasn't familiar to Ordimas. He sensed an urgency in the message he couldn't put his finger on. The work-party placement meant a stealth kill first. He didn't look forward to using the drug. His genes were his curse, and he knew all too well that he would never be free. His unique chromosomal heritage had brought him to the attention of the Holy Inquisition in the first place.

And once you're in, you never get out.

Familiar footsteps sounded outside, echoing along the alleyway, announcing the return of young Nedra. But something was wrong. Ordimas read dismay in the sound. Almost panic.

Thrusting his face forwards, closer to the machine, he whispered, 'Session end.' The unit on the table closed and locked itself abruptly. With a hiss, the stasis-seal re-engaged. Ordimas hefted the case off the table and hastily slung it back under his cot. He was rising just as Nedra burst through the door.

Ordimas turned and saw at once that his young charge was shaking. Nedra's eyes were brimming with tears yet to spill. He stood fighting to hold them back.

'I-I saw him, boss,' he stammered.

Ordimas didn't need to ask who. He'd seen Nedra like this only once before.

'Where?'

'The meat market,' managed the boy.

Only a few blocks away! Ordimas felt raw hatred clench his stomach. A scowl twisted his lop-sided face. 'Did he see you?'

Nedra shook his head and the first tear spilled over, rolling and dropping from his cheek. Conscious of it as it splashed on the toe of one of his newly repaired shoes, the boy turned aside, not wanting his boss to see him break down. Other tears began to flow.

'I'm sorry, boss,' he sniffed. 'I didn't get any food. I...'

'Peace, lad,' said Ordimas, moving to the boy's side. He laid a hand on Nedra's shoulder. 'It's well that you found him. I've business with the bastard.' *And I may be able to kill two birds with one stone*, he thought. 'Come. Show him to me.'

Nedra shook his head. 'I can't. He's twice your size, boss. Big as a bull grox. Let's just stay here. I'll get some bread from Clavian's on the corner. We'll eat.'

'No! You'll take me to him. And don't underestimate me, boy. There's much about old Ordimas Arujo that none would guess, not even you.'

Nedra turned again, gaping, tears forgotten. Ordimas had never spoken to him so sharply before. It was like being slapped. A stony, unfamiliar hardness had entered the puppeteer's gaze. In those eyes, the boy glimpsed a cold confidence in the stunted, hunch-backed little man. There was no change in his physical stature, but Ordimas seemed strangely taller and stronger than he ever had before, unruffled and somehow suddenly dangerous.

'I... I'll take you there,' said Nedra, though his own words shocked him. He seemed to be speaking them against his will. 'I'll show you, but please...'

Ordimas allowed himself a predator's grin. It had been over a year since he'd last killed. This ill-minded oaf, this abuser of the weak, was a Nightside miner. Ordimas had his new orders: infiltrate one of the work-parties, get into the mines, and report anything of note. Fate had brought two separate threads together this day. Such moments were a gift. He flexed his fingers and rolled his misshapen shoulders. With a touch, he confirmed the presence of the short black knife in his waistband, its blade coated in a very rare and potent paralytic. With another touch, he confirmed the injector packs filled with their milky purple drug, nestled patiently in a side pouch he never removed save to make ablutions. The pouch sat on his left hip beneath the hem of his dirty, sack-cloth shirt, each tiny phial inside it worth more Imperial ducats than an entire Cholixe city block.

Readiness was ever his way. He had everything he needed. It was time for some real work.

As he herded Nedra out into the alleyway, he thought of his favourite line from a book – the only children's storybook he had ever owned. It was a line from which he had often drawn strength and confidence in the past, especially in the face of danger, and it was simply this:

The smaller the scorpion, the deadlier the sting.

8

'He is superb,' admitted Sergeant Saigan. 'You cannot deny it.'

'I've never said otherwise,' murmured Captain Shrike.

From a balcony high in the western towers of the Ravenspire, the two Raven Guard Space Marines looked down on a training ground within the fortress-monastery's inner wall. The subject of their conversation, a battle-brother named Siefer Zeed, was surrounded by twenty-three others, all of whom wielded blunted training weapons. They had asked Zeed for training outside the standard Chapter curriculum. Shrike knew he should have been pleased, but it rankled. In the eyes of most captains, Siefer Zeed was an unrepentant troublemaker. If only the Chapter Master agreed...

'You cannot keep passing him over, captain,' said Saigan. 'Not even sergeant rank? By rights, he should have been inducted into the Wing long ago. Every soul in the Chapter knows it. How long will you set him aside?'

Shrike felt a surge of fresh irritation and forced himself to suppress it. Saigan was right, and he knew it. That was what bothered him most; he knew he had waited too long to honour Zeed. The insult had been dealt. It could not be taken back now, even had he strolled out onto the training field this very morning and reversed his position.

He gazed off into the distance, angry that things had gone this far. Far away, the barrier of the force-dome shimmered, shielding the Ravenspire from the void of space, fractionally distorting the horizon. Beyond the barrier, across that dusty grey expanse where no breathable atmosphere existed, Shrike could see another heavy transport lifting off from the freight station at Leiros, hauling freshly processed metals from Deliverance to the planet Kiavahr.

That vast orange orb wasn't visible above the Ravenspire today. The atmospheric enclosure fields were high enough for clouds to form within, and today they had.

Fourteen hours ago, an adept from the Chapter's communicarum had brought word of a ship seeking approach clearance. Shrike had been expecting it. Soon enough, a shuttle from that ship would descend through those clouds.

I am committed now, but no matter. I was right to do it this way.

Lowering his eyes again, he watched as Zeed selected three battle-brothers from the group surrounding him and told them to attack him from each side. Then, slowly at first so the others could study his movements, he began a series of simultaneous parries and attacks that would have brutally disarmed and eviscerated his foes.

Zeed's balance and control were superb, beyond anything the Chapter had seen for long years. Shrike harboured momentary doubts that even he could stand against him. He knew he should have been proud to count Zeed among the men of his company. Yet he could not.

'I would have been glad to honour him, Saigan, if he would only follow doctrine. But he will not listen. He is rebellious, arrogant, even disrespectful at times.'

'And his brothers love him for it,' said Saigan with a half-grin on that scarred, leathery face of his. 'These below...' he said, gesturing at the crowd around Zeed. 'These are only the brothers for whom this hour is free from other duties. Many more wished they could attend, but for duty.'

'You do not help his case, sergeant. That he leads others astray is what counts against him most. He has become a problem. He should have become the Chapter's champion instead. Corax knows, he's an exceptional asset in the field. But I can't allow him to continue like this. The more his legend grows, the more he draws his battle-brothers away from the true teachings. You've seen the sensorium feeds. No sense of strategic avoidance. He throws himself headlong into any fight he can find like a damnable madman.'

A light rain began to fall now. The wind whipped at Shrike's cloth tabard. Down on the grassy training field, Zeed had finished teaching his three-foe execution pattern in slow-motion. Now he demonstrated it at full speed.

Shrike heard Saigan curse quietly under his breath.

Zeed was a dark blur. Up towards the high balcony, there came the clash of training claws on ceramite as he disabled the three brothers attacking him with zeal. The sound was all too brief. If the flow of deadly movement had taken more than a single second, it was not by much. The brothers being instructed clashed their right fists on their breastplates in awed applause. Zeed stepped out of the centre, selected one of the others to take his place, then carefully led him through the series of defensive counter-attacks.

'I've half a mind to take lessons with him myself,' grunted Saigan. He sensed Shrike tense in anger at the words, and added, 'Sorry, captain. I was just–'

Shrike raised a hand in placation. 'Forget it, old friend. If I am angry, it is with myself. I cannot help thinking I could have guided him better, that his flaws are the result of my own failings.'

'That cannot be so, captain. Truly, is it not always the way? The most exceptional are ever the most pig-headed and independent.' He laughed then. 'Without meaning offence, so it was with you. I remember Captain Thune despairing of your unruliness. In days long past, of course.'

'Perhaps I was lucky, Saigan. Perhaps Thune was a better mentor than I have been. I tried with Zeed. I still do. But the more I try, the more he seems to rebel. I can expend no more energy on him. There are others to whom I must turn my attention. They deserve the same opportunities I have given Zeed.'

'Then what is to be done with him?'

Even as Saigan said this, a black shape materialised, dropping into view beneath the rain-laden clouds to the far south-west. It was sleek and fast, and the roar of its engines echoed over the hills beneath the Ravenspire like peals of deep thunder.

Shrike nodded in the direction of the approaching craft.

'For a time, at least, the problem will be out of my hands. You see that ship? There is my solution, temporary though it may prove. The Deathwatch has come for him. In truth, it is a greater honour than I can offer him here. May it quell this talk of passing him over. I see that look, Saigan. I'll not deny it is a convenient and easy path to take. But Zeed is worthy of joining the Watch. None can argue that. May he find guidance and wisdom among brothers from other Chapters since he will not listen to those of his own. And may he return to us recast, better suited to serve among us.'

'If he returns at all,' said Sergeant Saigan darkly. The ease of the captain's solution did not sit well with him. Deathwatch service ought not to be used to rid one of an inconvenience. Moreover, Saigan himself had long dreamed of such an honour. Those who returned alive were often judged the best candidates for a captaincy whenever one arose.

'Quite,' said Shrike, and he turned from the balcony and went inside to descend the great stone stairs on his way to meet the black shuttle.

9

They found the man in question just as he was leaving the square, a large brown bottle in one hand, a bag of grox cuts in the other. Ordimas marked him well: a little shy of two metres tall, notably broad and deep-chested like so many of the Nightsiders. He was thickly bearded but with a shaved head. The crude tattoo on his neck identified him as either a member or former member of the local criminal organisation known as the Rockheads.

Meaning he can fight, thought Ordimas, *but I wasn't planning on going toe-to-toe.*

As the brute made his way out of the square, Ordimas ordered Nedra home.

'No,' said the boy, standing firm. 'I said I'd show you. Now, let's go back together.'

Ordimas frowned. 'Lad, have I ever done ill by you?'

Nedra looked at the ground and shook his head.

'Do you take me at my word?'

'You know I do,' muttered the boy.

'Then do as I ask. Have faith in me now. I have business that you can't be part of. Not this time. So go home and wait for me. Eat. Sleep. Practise with the puppets. When I return – and I will return, though it may be a day or two – I'll want to see that you can perform Harvald's *The Smiting of the Traitor* at least as well as I. Is that understood? If you can, you'll have your first official public appearance at our next showing.'

Nedra's eyes went wide. For a long time, he had waited to perform publicly. He wanted to make Ordimas proud. His fear for the little man's safety still hung over him, but he nodded obediently and turned to go.

At the last second, he turned back and, on a whim, reached out for Ordimas and drew him into a crushing hug.

No further words passed between them, but Ordimas felt his heart breaking in that embrace, knowing that, after this last reconnaissance was done, he would have to leave the boy forever.

I would have stayed, lad, he thought. *Even in this dingy slum, living this pitiful false life. I'd have stayed until you were a bit older at least. But His Lordship won't allow that. I live only while I'm useful; a man owned until death.*

I'll see you right, though, son. Mark my words. This little freak, this smallest of scorpions, will see you right.

Nedra released him and ran off towards home at a sprint. Ordimas didn't have time to watch him go, or to dwell further on their inevitable parting. He moved off into the crowds, slipping between them like a fish between river reeds. Someone spat on his hunched-back and hissed, 'Filthy twist!', but he paid them no heed. The miner had slipped down a side-street, and Ordimas had to keep moving at speed to keep him within sight.

Out of the market square, that proved a lot easier; the alleys were thick with shadow. Most people avoided them.

The miner never noticed his diminutive pursuer. He roughly shouldered his way past anyone on his path, walking with the swagger of one who was known and feared here on his own patch. The Rockheads controlled most criminal business in Cholixe – drugs, women, weapons, smuggling, and much else besides. They were known for being ruthless and brutal; the very qualities which had allowed them to crush their competition. Even the Civitas enforcers here on Chiaro, few as there were, tolerated the gang's activities rather than wage all-out war on them. An uneasy accord existed. With their local monopoly on illicit products and services, the Rockheads had their claws deep in the Garrahym labour force. They could tilt the miners into striking if they wanted to, even rioting. The administrators and law-enforcers knew the cost of denying labourers their few, limited pleasures. So, within tolerable limits, the Rockheads prospered.

Arrogant oaf, thought Ordimas. *Your tattoo won't protect you from me.*

But it would pose something of a problem later.

The miner had stopped at the door of a corner hab just up ahead and was delving into his pocket for his keys. He seemed to be having trouble finding them. Ordimas checked the street. No good. There were too many people around. Best not to act in haste. Patient observation was called for here.

The miner began hammering a big fist on the door. 'Mira!' he barked over the pounding. 'Open up! I forgot my gackin' keys.'

A moment later, the door opened. The miner shoved it wide, and charged inside, cursing the woman in his way, calling her every name he could think of.

Ordimas slipped into a shadowed doorway on the right with a good view of the corner hab. The alcove was strewn with garbage and the smell from the gutters was foul, but it provided good cover. He dragged tattered papers and plastic bags over himself until he was completely cloaked from notice. And there he waited for his time to strike.

He didn't have to wait long. After forty minutes or so, voices were raised in the hab. Ordimas picked up the miner's name. The woman, Mira, was screaming it.

'Please, Mykal! Don't!'

The muffled sounds of a struggle followed. Suddenly, the hab door flew open, and a short, petite woman came racing out holding her cheek. Her clothes were torn, and she bled from one corner of her mouth. The miner, Mykal, came to the doorway and shouted after her, 'Aye, run! You can come back when you remember your gackin' place!'

Mira didn't hang around to shout back. She was already gone from the street when Ordimas rose from the cover of the shadows and the garbage. Mykal, he noticed, had slammed the door so hard behind him that the auto-lock hadn't had time to click into place. The momentum of the metal door was so great when it struck the frame that it rebounded and swung half open again.

Mykal had already retreated back inside the hab, too hasty or angry to notice, or perhaps too sure of himself to care.

Ordimas bolted across the street and slid into the hab like a shadow, leaving the door open for now, knowing that the noise of closing it might alert his target.

Once inside, he slid the short knife from its sheath at his lower back and crept forwards, feline-stealthy, down a gloomy, smoky hallway. The air smelt of mould and lho-stick residue. The wallpaper was curled and patchy with fungal growth. These people lived even worse than he and Nedra did.

But not for long, Mykal, he thought as he stalked towards the kitchen at the far end of the hall. He could hear grunting and grumbling over the sound of fat sizzling in a hot pan. At the doorway, he paused long enough for a split-second scan of the place. There was Mykal, alone at the hob, back towards the door like an idiot.

Ordimas gripped his knife tighter and stepped silently into the room.

Time's up, you son-of-a-bitch. May daemons gorge on your soul.

Mykal made a short, gasping moan when the little knife punched into his lower back. It was the last breath that ever left his lungs. The neurotoxin on the blade raced through him in an instant, shutting down each of his organs, burning through his neurons, starving his brain of oxygen.

Ordimas stepped deftly aside just in time as the big man toppled backwards stiff as a board, eyes wide open and already glassy.

The little hunchback leaned over his mark, looking down into his face from only inches away. 'You've had that coming a while, gacker,' he murmured.

There was little time to take real satisfaction in the deed. Morphosis would take an hour or so. He had to work fast. It was this moment, more than any other, that Ordimas dreaded. He knew the price he would pay later for using the drug. Taking it was bad enough, but the crash was another type of torture entirely.

Quickly, he stripped both himself and the corpse, placing everything on the floor in two piles. Taking one of the drug-capsules from its pouch, he uncapped it, pressed the tiny needle into the flesh of his chest, and crushed the flexible plastic bubble that contained the purple liquid.

The drug shot into him. He gritted his teeth, muffling a scream that desperately wanted to get out. The pain was as intense as ever, a fire that coursed along every last nerve in his body. He saw stars. His skin itched all over. He felt his heart hammering so fast he thought it would burst. But none of this was new to him. He knew it would subside.

Within three minutes it had, and the drug, acting on Ordimas's unique genetics, started to take its intended effect. Ordimas felt his joints loosen. He lay down on the floor next to the body of Mykal. His bones became less rigid. Normal breathing became difficult. He forced himself to relax and take shorter, shallower breaths, establishing a rhythm he knew would work best from past experience.

The moment was at hand. Mustering all the strength his now flaccid muscles had left, he shifted his head over to the arm of the dead miner and took a tiny bite of his flesh. He didn't need much; just some tissue, some blood, a little hair.

He swallowed, no longer sickened by this, though in his early days of service to His Lordship, he had struggled with the notion, raging at himself because he dared not refuse. Not so now. One small bite was all he needed. That hardly made him a cannibal.

The changes in his body took a new direction almost at once, guided not just by the intake of genetic material but by his eidetic imprint of how the man had looked when alive. He closed his eyes, holding that image of Mykal in vivid detail, knowing the process couldn't be rushed. It was always better to lie back and let it happen.

Fifty-eight minutes later, two near-identical bodies lay on the kitchen floor of that dirty corner hab; two men of thick muscle and bearded face. Of the original Ordimas Arujo, there was no sign left save the pile of humble clothes, the knife and the drug pouch. Two bodies, but only one stretched and rose to its feet:

Ordimas as Mykal – puppeteer of another sort entirely.

'What shall we do about that tattoo?' wondered Ordimas aloud, testing the qualities of his newly configured vocal cords, attempting to mimic Mykal's voice from the memory of the words the miner had hurled after his battered woman. Ordimas was trained for this, too, of course, and his mimicry was near perfect despite only hearing the mark speak clearly twice. Unique vocal habits and idiosyncrasies were something he would have to guess at, but Ordimas had observed enough of the Rockheads in bars and on street corners to know he had a feel for their patterns of speech.

Still naked, he leaned close to the cold corpse to get a better look at the tattoo. Tattoos, scars, the holes of piercings; these were things his gift alone could not mimic. He had to think of a way–

There was a crash of breaking glass to his left and the sound of a scream suddenly muffled by two hands.

Ordimas whipped his head around to face the source.

There in the kitchen doorway stood Mira, pale as a ghost, eyes wide like a panicked animal, her hands pressed tight over her mouth.

Ashra's arse! thought Ordimas. *I should have locked the door after the kill.*

The woman probably had her own key, of course. Still, forcing her to unlock it would have bought him valuable extra seconds. In any case, it was too late for *should-haves*; here she was, frozen in fear, then suddenly frozen no more.

She turned and bolted into the hall.

Ordimas flew after her, fighting to coordinate his new limbs as he ran.

10

Bolter-fire stitched the earthworks behind which Second Company held fast.

'Get those lascannons ready!' barked Sergeant Voss. 'Those tanks will move up any second. I want them taken out. And someone move those bloody fuel drums. If a stray bolt hits them, we'll all be cooked meat!'

Paradaxis, third planet of the Arcaydes system, had drawn the interest of the foul traitors known as the Word Bearers. No one knew why. They had struck suddenly, ships slipping from the warp so close to Imperial planetary defences that, within hours, the Naval Defence Monitors were overwhelmed and obliterated. Chaos drop-ships fell by the dozen, concentrating on the eastern regions of the Frajian continent, particularly around the bustling trade city Diasport.

Imperial Guard regiments garrisoning the city had dug in to offer every bit of resistance they could muster. Via both astropathic and deep space relay communications, they had sent out a desperate call for aid.

It was by chance alone that the Imperial Fists Second Company were in the subsector. They were two days out. Those two days almost ended the fight. The Guard regiments were little more than tattered remnants when the Fists arrived. Had it not been for the support of a redoubtable civilian militia determined to protect their homes and families, the city of Diasport would have fallen before the Adeptus Astartes could have made any difference.

As it was, Maximmion Voss and the rest of his company, under the command of the renowned Second Captain Rudiel Straker, found themselves fighting against the clock. Whoever had designed the defences of Diasport ought to have been executed, at least in Voss's eyes. The city's guns were mostly on the coast, intended to prevent an attack by sea. The land to the west of the city had been given over to agriculture with little thought for effective fortification. So it was that Second Company fought from hastily constructed earthworks behind which they had dug and blasted out a complex trench network. Razor wire and tank traps added to the mix. It wasn't much, not against the vile forces of Traitor Marines, but, given the identity of the Chapter defending the city, it was proving enough.

Once ordered to hold ground, the Imperial Fists were unrivalled. They were the finest defensive fighters and counter-siege specialists in the modern Imperium. Voss intended to prove that.

He ran along the primary trench, heading south, his powerful legs pounding the muddy duckboards. He was unusually short for a Space Marine. In the militia, there were standard humans – *mundanes*, some of the brothers called them – who cast as long a shadow as he did. Few cast a shadow as wide, however, for what Voss lacked in height, he more than compensated for in hard, grainy muscle. There was nothing he could do about his height, and not a few of the Chapter's Apothecaries looked at him askance whenever he passed by. Perhaps it was a kind of unconscious compensation, but Voss had become prone to voluntary sessions of extreme physical training. His muscles swelled beyond their already significant gene-boosted mass. His armour had to be adjusted by the Chapter's tech-servitors. Then it had to be adjusted again, and again. Finally, he had been told – no, commanded! – to grow no thicker. His strength and power had outstripped those around him, but concerns had arisen about his mobility in the field. So far, these had not been borne out. But nevertheless, with some reluctance, Voss had acceded to the demands of his superiors. He grew no bigger and, from that moment, trained only to maintain what he had.

What he had remained formidable. As he ran to shore up a potential weakness in the southern defences, he carried not one but two portable Hellfire missile launchers, fully loaded, one in either armoured hand.

Bolter and autocannon-rounds whipped and whined over his head. To his right, the earthworks shuddered. Dirt leapt into the air to shower down on his bright yellow helmet and pauldrons. A tank round – high explosive – had missed him by a few metres only. Voss kept running. Up ahead, he could see the battle-brothers of Squad Richter pouring bolter and plasma-fire onto the kill-zone from the firing step. Suddenly, as one, they ducked. Another tank round whistled over them, smacking into the rear wall of the trench.

The brothers of Squad Richter closest to the impact threw themselves to safety barely half a second before the rear wall blasted outwards. Voss was shoved sideways by the force of another blast a second later, but he was sure-footed and steady. He did not fall, nor did he drop his armaments.

He reached Squad Richter a few seconds later. They were rising to their feet, shaking off clods of wet earth. Voss recognised a battle-brother called Varagrim, a heavy weapons specialist like himself. 'Var!' he shouted. 'Look sharp!'

He tossed one of the missile launchers and Varagrim caught it, knees bending momentarily with the weight of the weapon as it landed in his outstretched hands.

'With me,' ordered Voss as he leapt up onto the firing step and put the other missile launcher to his shoulder.

Varagrim didn't argue. Sergeant Richter had fallen to a heavy artillery barrage just two days prior. Sergeant Voss had assumed command of Squads Voss and Richter both.

Voss poked his visor up above the lip of the trench and cursed. It wasn't any kind of conventional armoured vehicle that had fired those shots into the trench. Before him, not three hundred metres away and scuttling forwards fast, was a multi-legged metal monstrosity. Hideous, daemonic faces cast in gold and bronze leered at the loyalists, mocking them, daring them to stand and fight. And die.

'Defiler,' spat Varagrim, joining him on the step.

Aye, thought Voss. *Curse the luck.*

Defilers were damned difficult to disable. Knock out the treads of a tank and it became a sitting target. Easy prey. But the thickly-armoured, spider-like limbs of the Defiler were harder to hit. More than that, should one of the legs be disabled, the others could compensate, keeping the Chaos abomination mobile. If one managed to stagger it, however, there was a short window of opportunity...

'We've only two missiles,' said Voss to Varagrim. 'I want you to target the front right leg.'

'Surely we should both fire on the hull, sergeant!'

'Not while it still has full mobility. Trust me, brother. The next step that monster takes, I want you to cripple that leg.'

Varagrim hesitated only a moment, then nodded.

'As you say, brother-sergeant.'

Behind the Defiler, a squad of Chaos Marines advanced, using the walking tank to shield themselves from the fury of the defenders. If the Defiler breached the earthworks, the Traitors would spill into the trenches and all advantage would be lost. Voss was confident of his company's strength in hand-to-hand combat, but it was a numbers game here, and the Chaos filth outnumbered his brothers by a factor of three to one.

What in Dorn's holy name brought these bastards here?

Perhaps he would never know. It was enough for now that they had to be stopped.

'Fire!' he barked to Varagrim.

There was a shriek of igniting fuel and a bright flash of back-blast. The first missile screamed towards the Defiler on a trail of white smoke.

It struck the leg squarely on the knee joint, staggering the unholy machine, biting off great chunks of thick armour and crippling the pistons beneath. The Defiler swayed and struggled to its articulated knees. That instant of immobility was the window Voss had been waiting for. He painted the Defiler's hull dead-centre with his weapon's targeting laser.

'Get clear,' he yelled, warning any behind him of the imminent back-blast.

He pressed the firing stud and let fly.

The launcher's tube coughed out its deadly payload, kicking hard in Voss's hands.

With a piercing scream, the missile spiralled towards its mark. There was a short, sharp boom before blinding fire erupted outwards, followed immediately by a great billowing cloud of thick black smoke. As the wind pulled the smoke aside like a great curtain, Voss saw the ruined machine collapse in the mud. A secondary explosion rocked it from inside, the walker's magazine detonating, blowing out the rest of its hull armour in a wave of deadly shrapnel that scythed into the Chaos Marines close by.

'Now,' Voss roared over the link. 'Take them!'

Along the trench, a blazing fusillade poured out towards the Traitor Marines, now wounded and exposed. Bolts punched deep into spiked armour, ruining the corrupt and twisted flesh within. Bright plasma fire arced into their ranks, burning and melting all it touched. It was slaughter. Righteous slaughter. The Imperial Fists revelled in it, feeling their blood rise.

'Sergeant Voss,' barked a stern voice on the vox-link. 'Do you read me, sergeant?'

'Captain?' answered Voss.

'You are relieved, sergeant. Fall back to Command HQ at once.'

'The battle is not over, my lord. I have much to do here. My squad await–'

'Your squad will be fused with Squad Richter for now. Brother Berren will assume command. I'm promoting him to sergeant as of this moment.'

'A good choice, my lord, but I cannot leave the field while the enemy yet lays siege.'

'You can and will, Maximmion. That is an order, and you shall not disobey. Your petition has been approved. A shuttle has arrived. You are to don the black of the Deathwatch, sergeant. The honour of the Chapter must be served.'

Voss was stunned to silence, but only for a heartbeat. He had hoped, of course, but he had not dared to assume.

'The honour of the Chapter *will* be served, captain.'

'For the primarch, sergeant.'

'For the primarch,' said Voss. 'For he and the Chapter both.'

11

One arm went around her waist and lifted her clear off the floor. The other snaked over her shoulder, a big hand clapping tight over her mouth before she could call out.

Ordimas caught her as she was reaching for the handle on the inside of the front door. He wrestled her back to a doorway on the left of the hall that led into a dark main room. Two stained and rickety chairs sat before a smudge-screened pict-viewer. Lho-stick butts and empty bottles littered a table on the left.

With his hand still on her mouth, Ordimas dropped Mira, the dead miner's woman, down into one of the chairs and, staying behind her, pressed his face close to her ear.

'I'm not here for you, girl,' he said softly. 'But I can't let you report what you've seen. Not until my business is done. We both know that man was cruel to you, Mira. It is Mira, right? We both know you'll be better off without him, Mira. So what I propose is this. I'm going to ask you some questions, and you're going to answer them. You're going to help me. And then I'll help you. I will have to tie you up when I leave, and gag you. But when my work is done, I'll contact an associate of mine. She'll come and free you. And if you do exactly as I say, and don't interfere with my plans in any way, I'll see to it you're compensated. She'll bring money, but only if you comply.'

When he told her the exact amount he would be paying her, she went rigid. Ordimas remained silent to let the significance of the amount sink in. The woman gradually relaxed.

'Good girl,' he told her. 'We both know what that money could do for you, so keep that in mind. Because you won't like the alternative. I'm good to my friends, Mira, but I'm a daemon to my enemies. I never forgive, and I never forget. Take my word on that.'

Mira nodded.

Slowly, Ordimas removed his hand from her mouth. She didn't scream.

All the same, he made sure to stay behind her for now. Seeing him naked in front of her, an almost perfect likeness of her freshly slain partner, would most probably unhinge her. Ordimas didn't need that. It was bad enough that he had to speak to her in Mykal's voice. And it was the voice that he asked her about now.

'Do I sound like him?'

Mira made to turn and face him.

'No,' said Ordimas. 'Face forwards. It'll be easier for you that way, at least for now.'

'H-he spoke a bit rougher than you,' she said. 'More rasping, sort of. Something he did by choice. He put it on to sound meaner.'

Ordimas nodded and added more gravel to his tone.

'Like this?'

Mira gave a shudder. 'Saints! What... what in the nine hells *are* you?'

'Just a man,' said Ordimas. 'A man with a job to do. If that improves your lot, so much the better, yes?'

Mira was silent. Seconds passed before she said, 'He cursed a lot, Mykal did. Gacking this. Gacking that.'

'Understood. Any physical habits? Anything other Rockheads would know him for?'

Mira nodded, still facing the wall. 'He cracked his knuckles a lot. He thought it intimidated people. He chewed that fungal stuff from the mines, too. Greywort. You'll find some in his pockets if you check. He was always spittin' it in the sink. Foul stuff.'

Ordimas didn't particularly want to mimic that habit – greywort was a mild psychotropic that induced euphoria in certain quantities – but he knew he could suppress the effect if he was careful with the dose. He wouldn't take any unless offered. He needed to be sharp for this.

'Right- or left-handed?' he asked.

'Right,' said Mira.

'Wait here,' he told her.

He went back into the kitchen and put on the dead man's clothes, conscious of how different that felt to the habitual, almost automatic act of putting on his own. Then he stuffed his discarded clothes into a stinking, half-filled garbage bag, tied it shut, and jammed it in a corner beneath five or six others already filled almost to bursting. Then he put his belt, with its dagger and injectibles, around his waist and cinched it. His new waist was three notches bigger than his true waist. 'Lucky the damned thing still fits,' he mumbled to himself and went back through to the main room.

'Okay, listen, Mira. I'm going to move in front of you now. I need you to keep it together, all right? I need to know everything you can tell me about his shifts, his friends, what he does in the mines, what business he's into with the Rockheads. I need everything you can give me, Mira. It's important. Just keep thinking about that money. I can't pay you if I don't pull this off.'

'I... I understand. I'll help you, but you better not be lying about that money.'

'I'm not,' said Ordimas. 'I'll make sure you get what you're due. Is there a quill and ink around here somewhere?'

She told him he'd find them on an old desk in the corner of the next room. Ordimas, having bound her tightly to the chair, fetched them and went to the kitchen where the miner's dead body lay cooling on the floor. With his knife, he cut the tattooed flesh from Mykal's neck, took the flesh, quill and ink to the couple's dingy bathroom, and copied the design onto his own skin. It took six minutes. Like any agent worth his salt, Ordimas had an eye for detail. The replica was near flawless.

For the next two hours, Mira coached him. He dressed in Mykal's overalls – a rough, orange one-piece thermasuit with I-8 printed on the back in big white letters. This was the man's work-party allocation, and Ordimas's primary concern was making sure the other men of I-8 sensed nothing out of the ordinary. By the end of his time with Mira, he had Mykal's identity and mannerisms down so well that the woman suddenly began to weep. Ordimas thought she might be doubting her sanity. The scene she had returned to in the kitchen would have shaken anybody's hold on reality. But it wasn't that.

'I won't miss him,' she sobbed, still tied to her chair. 'I'm glad he's dead, but I shouldn't be. It seems wrong. Especially now that...'

'Now that what?'

'Now that I'm carrying his child. He could never manage it before. Children, I mean. Then suddenly he comes home from his shift one day and it's the most important thing in the world. I never understood him.'

So there were two living beings tied to the chair – Mira and her unborn child. That was a complication, but only if Ordimas allowed it to be.

'It's not wrong to be glad, Mira,' he told her. 'No child should grow up with a man like that as a father. There're things you don't know about him. But it doesn't matter now. He's gone.'

There was a heavy knock at the front door and a gruff voice from outside, 'Time to go, Myk. Get your arse out here, brother.'

Mira started. 'That's Nordam. He and Mykal go to work together.'

'A Rockhead?' asked Ordimas.

'No. Just a co-worker.'

'Okay,' said Ordimas. 'Last chance, Mira. If I blow this, we're both gacked and you'll never see that money. Is there anything you've forgotten?'

Mira thought hard, brow creasing. Then she found something.

'The Rockheads have a hand-sign.'

'I know it,' said Ordimas. He'd seen gang-members greet each other with it. He clenched his right fist and rapped it against the side of his skull. 'Right?'

Mira shook her head. 'It used to be that,' she told him. 'For some of them, it still is, I think. But Mykal told me they changed it.' She made a gesture with her hand – fingers splayed in twos with the thumb extended so that the hand looked like it had three digits instead of five.

'Do this and put your hand over your heart,' she told him.

Ordimas tried it. She nodded. 'That's it.'

He was suspicious. Had she changed her mind? Was this new hand-sign intended to give him away? No. Looking at her hard, using all his abilities to read people, he convinced himself that this woman was telling the truth. Mykal had abused her for Throne-knew-how-long. She wouldn't miss him. The money she hoped to gain by aiding Ordimas would buy her a new life.

More thumping sounded at the door, angry and impatient.

'Time's up,' said Ordimas, and he withdrew behind Mira's chair.

She tensed. 'You'll remember the money?' she said, voice desperate with thin hope. 'You'll remember your promise, right?'

By way of answer, Ordimas moved close behind her. He looped a powerful arm round her neck, locked his grip on his opposite shoulder, and quickly, quietly choked her to death. She barely struggled. Ultimately, she had known deep down her death was at hand. Her last thought was one of self-contempt; how could she have even remotely believed in a happy ending? When had life ever granted her a boon?

After checking for a pulse that was no longer there, Ordimas went to the front door and stepped out, greeting the broad-shouldered man on the step with a grunt. He closed the door behind himself and heard it lock, then the two men set off down the street.

There was little conversation, which suited Ordimas fine.

It was time to go to work.

12

Two hours ago, Karras had felt it. The pressure had eased. The voices died to a whisper, then to nothing at all. The rage and hate that had pricked the air inside the *Adonai* since it had entered the warp had finally ebbed away. The thrumming psychic resonance of the ship's Geller fields no longer intruded on his enhanced awareness. He breathed easier. Warp transit was no smooth matter for a psyker, not even an experienced Codicier of the Librarius. For most of the journey, combat rituals and relentless training had helped to focus his mind. It was as Cordatus had said: *Arquemann* felt like a part of him now, an extension of his lethal will. He had never felt as deadly as he did wielding the rune-inscribed blade. Even so, as focused as he had been, he had nevertheless remained sharply aware of the attentions of the warp's ravenous entities. They had been fixed on him for weeks as the ship sailed the tides of the immaterium.

It was only the *Adonai*'s powerful Geller fields that kept those on board safe. With the exception of the ship's Navigator and astropaths – themselves powerful psykers – the rest of the crew were far less sensitive than Karras to the chilling daemonic howls and screams of frustration, if they were even aware of the warp entities at all. Crewmen got restless, of course. They had sleepless, torment filled nights. There were more instances of argument, even flashes of physical violence. But the Geller fields had held.

Now, in the austere, candlelit chamber that was his temporary quarters, Karras sat on the edge of his stone cot, glad that the worst part of the journey was over.

A junior crewman, barely out of boyhood it seemed, had brought provisions to him here in his quarters about half an hour ago: fruit and watered wine. He had been shaking so much when Karras bade him enter that he'd almost spilled the contents of the tray. Karras grinned, remembering the speed of the boy's terrified retreat. He lifted the clay goblet to his lips.

The wine was cool and refreshing as it slid down his throat.

They were like skittish birds sometimes, these little humans. Their fear over such simple things was beyond his comprehension. A miracle they had ever set forth into space at all!

He ate some of the fruit – a platter of bright, fleshy segments, pre-skinned or peeled, from half a dozen worlds. Not exactly the right stuff to maintain a hard-training Space Marine, but it would be back to nutrient-dense amino-porridge and triglyceride gel soon enough.

He was about to reach for another slice of black pear when, from the vox-speaker in the corner of his chamber, the voice of Captain Paninus Orlesi rang out, tinny and riddled with low static.

'My lord passenger,' said Orlesi. 'Our destination is now in visual range. If you'll meet me in the forward observation gallery, upper deck, I thought we might view it together. I think you'll find the sight more than worthy of your time, my lord. I shall be there in ten minutes, if you'd care to meet me.'

Twelve minutes later, Karras entered the viewing gallery. It was a broad, dimly lit space with deep, luxurious burgundy carpeting. In the centre of the carpet, a golden aquila, the two-headed eagle sigil of the Imperium of Man, had been woven into the fabric. Even at a cursory glance, Karras could see that it was beautiful and extremely expensive work. So too were the rich oil-paintings that lined the walls to left and right, each highlighted in the warm oval illumination of its own wall-mounted lamp. A chandelier of pale green crystal dominated the ceiling, so low, and Karras so tall, that its polished centre almost brushed his head as he strode beneath it.

Not realising he had company, the captain stood with hands clasped behind his back, gazing out through the wide armourglass window at the gallery's far end. Karras continued towards him, announcing himself by clearing his throat.

Orlesi turned to greet him, a smile on his florid features, teeth bright under a thick, well-oiled black moustache. He bowed. 'My lord, I'm heartened that you decided to come. We're on final approach. I'm sure you won't think your time wasted.'

'Naturally, I'm curious about our destination, captain. I would not have missed this opportunity.'

Orlesi gestured towards the window, inviting Karras to enjoy the view.

Whatever Karras had been expecting – some smaller variation of a Ramilies star fort, perhaps – it was not this.

'Watch Fortress Damaroth,' said Orlesi with theatrical emphasis.

Damaroth. Centre of Deathwatch operations in the Centaurus Arm of the Ultima Segmentum.

The actual coordinates of Damaroth were classified at the very highest level, known only to those pledged to a lifetime of service. The Space Marines seconded here only temporarily were never told exactly where *here* was. They were brought on Deathwatch ships and they departed on Deathwatch ships. They did not need to know.

Shrouded in secrecy until now, Damaroth was at last revealed to Karras's eyes. There it sat, hanging in space, rotating slowly in a wispy nebula of greenish blue. It was a striking sight.

A ring! A vast artificial ring around a glowing moon.

He was silent for long moments looking at that strange place. The ring structure was black on the nightward side, its shape a curving shadow against the backdrop of the gas cloud. Countless warning and docking lights blinked in waves of red and green respectively, still tiny at this distance. The sunward extent of the Watch fortress was lit in shades of silvery grey. The outer surface seemed smooth but for the telltale shadows of huge communications pylons and the kilometre-wide dishes of the advanced auspex arrays. Karras could see no edges where blocks joined other blocks. It was as if the ring was cast or carved from a single piece.

That's not possible. Not at this size. Cast by whom? And when?

The inner surface of the ring, permanently facing the small bright moon in the centre, was, by contrast a study in complexity. At this range, it was hard even for gene-boosted eyes to make sense of the apparent jumble of structures there. But as Karras continued to stare in silence, and the *Adonai* crept closer, things began to resolve themselves.

'About three-and-a-half thousand kilometres in diameter,' said Orlesi. 'With a circumference of some eleven thousand. Quite something, isn't she?'

Karras had seen many wonders in a lifetime of warfare among the stars, and yet he was stunned. 'We didn't build that,' he murmured. 'Not human hands.'

Orlesi shook his head. 'Not the basic structure, no. We don't know who or what built it. We know it's old. According to Mechanicus paleotechs, it's older than any other artificial structure in the Imperium. Apart from the others, that is.'

'The others?' said Karras.

'There are six ring-and-moon arrangements like this one – six that we know of so far – each sitting somewhere out on the dark, empty rimward edges of the galaxy. With the approval and cooperation of the High Lords of Terra and the Inquisition's Ordo Xenos, Deathwatch High Command commissioned Watch fortresses to be established on all of them once the proper research was completed. Not that the tech-priests found much. As I say, the basic structure is ancient beyond human history, and it was only the basic structure that remained – no trace of the beings that made them, nor of the technologies they used. The facilities you see down there on the inner surface are all Imperial in origin. Impressive in their own right, I'd say. Gravity is a solid one-gee throughout, with a fully breathable atmosphere. The magnetosphere and ozone layer are generated by Mechanicus facilities at the moon's poles, everything maintained at close to Terran standards. Ideal for human life. We may not have built the foundations, but I'd say we've done a damned fine job with the rest of it, what?'

Orlesi chuckled at his own understatement.

'What else can you tell me?' Karras asked, eyes fixed on the Watch fortress as it grew larger and larger in his vision.

'Not much, I'm afraid,' said Orlesi, humour giving way to thoughtfulness once more. 'I've shuttled warriors like your honoured self back and forth for almost a century in real terms, and I know little more now than I did back then.'

Xenos hunters, thought Karras, *living and training on a xenos structure. As will I.*

He felt a twinge of revulsion. Like all Space Marines, he had been psycho-conditioned to loathe all things alien. Yet none fought mankind's inhuman foes with more zeal than the Deathwatch. If they had deemed it right to utilise this structure in their interminable war, Karras could hardly argue.

'Given its size, large sections of the ring's inner surface remain unexploited. There are four massive docking facilities, each equidistant, all largely automated, equipped to rival any star port in Imperial space. Conveniently, each of the docks is named for a compass direction, giving the ring an artificial north, south, east and west. The *Adonai* has only ever dropped anchor, so to speak, in the South Dock. There are always ships coming and going, I know that much. I've seen everything from Cobra-class destroyers like this one to Overlord–class battlecruisers, all belonging to the Holy Inquisition, the Adeptus Mechanicus, or to the Watch itself. As far as the Watch's own fleet goes, I've no idea of its exact strength. At any given time, most of its ships are deployed to conflict zones or sent to serve at various Watch stations, as I expect you will be, sooner or later. And that's about all I'm privy to, I'm afraid. Or at least, all I can talk about.'

Karras could have probed further. With a flexing of his power, he could have ripped the man's entire knowledge, his every living memory, from his mind. Such a thing was within his abilities if the subject was otherwise unprepared and undefended. But the Deathwatch operated in secrecy for a reason. Karras was no hypocrite. His own Chapter held many things close to its chest. Besides, a mind-rip had other consequences; some subjects went mad, others dropped dead on the spot.

Minute by minute, the dark underside of the Ring of Damaroth swelled until it dominated the entire viewing window.

'I'll beg your leave now, my lord,' said Orlesi. 'We're on final approach and I must return to the bridge.'

'You have it,' said Karras.

'You're welcome to join me, my lord. Or you may stay here as long as you wish. Either way, you'll have a fine view of the docks as we come in.'

'I shall stay here, captain,' said Karras, 'where I can enjoy the view in silence. I would not wish to cause any distraction on the bridge.'

'Very good, my lord.'

Orlesi offered a last quick bow and marched from the room, leaving Karras alone at the window.

Soon after, the prow of the *Adonai* rose above the upper edge of the great ring, and the viewing gallery was bathed in the strange eldritch glow of the moon of Damaroth itself.

In that glow, Karras could see that the massive construct bristled with weapon batteries all along its length, everything from torpedo and missile tubes to las and plasma cannons of immense size, arranged so as to provide defensive fire in every conceivable direction. Karras was duly impressed. He had come here with few preconceptions, but he had never imagined that the Deathwatch might boast a facility of such incredible size and armament.

No. Not one, but six, he reminded himself.

The Watch, as Captain Orlesi called it, must surely have incredible wealth and resources behind it – more even than a First Founding Chapter. There were key-worlds throughout the Imperium which could hardly boast static defences of this magnitude. No doubt the facility had mobile defences too, though none were yet apparent.

The inner surface of the ring, visible to the left and right of the moon's cloud-covered sphere, became easier to make out now. Karras noted the sharp spires and windowed domes, the crenellated towers and great buttressed walls, all of which bore the elaborate gothic craftsmanship so typical of the Imperium's architecture. These details were not what drew his attention most, however. What grabbed him were the incredible shining pavilions that stretched for hundreds of kilometres on each of their sides. They were sprawling constructions of arched plasteel and shimmering diamonite. He had seen such structures before in the wealthier cities to which he had been deployed in the past. Usually, lush gardens lay beneath, filled with flora and fauna of a bewildering variety, often not even native to the world on which the pavilions were built. Such places were beloved of the aristocracy, an expensive indulgence which Karras actually found quite worthy since it appealed to his own inclinations towards knowledge and study. But what were such extravagant structures doing on a Watch fortress? He didn't imagine for a second that the Deathwatch indulged itself in the luxury of such botanical gardens.

The *Adonai* moved into its docking lane now, and the prow dropped once more, angling towards a gaping rectangular aperture in the ring's upper edge. Bright, flickering lights could be seen inside that space. At this distance, still many kilometres out, Karras could just make out the flanks of other, larger ships already docked there, gripped in position by a profusion of thick metal arms and magnetic clamps.

Minutes passed. The mouth of the docking bay gaped wider. It was elaborately crafted, a bas-relief of countless leering skulls worked into the metal of the aperture's broad border. In the centre of that relief was a skull far larger than the others and bearing a certain distinct difference. Karras was all too familiar with that icon. It was the skull motif of the Deathwatch, easily identifiable by the glowing red lens in its left eye socket, and the crossed bones behind it. If he was judged worthy, Karras would bear that very icon on his left pauldron.

I am worthy. I should not doubt it. I would not have been called otherwise.

He wished he felt as certain of that as he ought to.

To either side of the docking bay, a great statue stood guard. Each was a robed manifestation of death almost a kilometre in height, its grinning skull partly covered by a sculpted hood. Karras marvelled at the detail. Even the texture of the fabric had been worked into the dark stone. In bony fingers, the statue on the left held open a thick book. It stood posed with hollow eye sockets cast down, as if caught frozen in time, reading from stone pages. The statue on the left held the haft of a massive sword in a two-handed grip, blade pointed down, tip planted between skeletal feet. This figure's hollow gaze was turned outwards into space.

Each of these skeletal giants stood atop a plinth that jutted out from the edge of the hangar's mouth. On the plinth of the book-reading figure, the inscription read, *With strength of mind, you shall discern their weakness.* On the plinth of the sword-bearing one was inscribed, *With strength of body, you shall exploit that weakness.*

Body and mind both; ignore one and you undermined the other. Irrefutable. No warrior worth his steel could afford to forget it.

The *Adonai* shifted a fraction, imperceptibly but for Karras's heightened senses. Her starboard thrusters flared briefly, compensating further for the ring's clockwise rotation, after which her approach vector was perfectly matched to the movement of the dock. Karras could make out smaller ships now. The inner dimensions of the docking bay staggered him. He had seen none bigger save the unrivalled facilities at the segmentum's Naval headquarters, Kar Duniash. He counted over forty ships of varying size, none much smaller than the *Adonai*. Around each craft, maintenance drones weaved a slow, shifting dance as they moved silently to and fro on jets of hot plasma. Some would stop, clamp themselves to the hull of this or that ship, and swing articulated arms into play. The bright glare of oxy-acetylene torches was everywhere. Fountains of sparks rained bright and brief.

Slow, steady and smooth, the *Adonai* passed within the great mouth of the docking bay.

Flying servitor drones swarmed out to meet the craft and assist it in coming to rest.

Orlesi's voice sounded from small speakers worked cleverly into the room's chandelier. 'All personnel brace for docking.'

The ship swung to port, and the view shifted. A mass of metal gantries and loading cranes passed by on the left and right. Cables swung from beams and junction boxes, hanging everywhere like vines in a dense jungle. Clouds of greasy steam hissed from massive wall-vents. Karras could see red-robed tech-priests and servitor slaves scurrying or trundling back and forth along metal walkways and hazard-striped landings. Huge servo-arms reached out to grasp the hull of the *Adonai*. There was a mighty clang. The ship shuddered to a halt. The thrumming of its engines faded and stopped.

It was then that Karras's eyes were drawn to a figure hovering in the shadow of a dark doorway directly in front of the ship. The silhouette was bulky, its lines describing the unmistakable shape of Space Marine power armour.

Karras was suddenly sharply aware of a fresh presence in the gallery, powerful but not hostile. It was not a physical presence, but it was projected so strongly that he almost turned to greet it, half expecting to see someone behind him.

Now he knew the figure in the dark doorway for what it was.

Like always recognises like, he thought.

Welcome to Watch Station Damaroth, Death Spectre, pulsed the presence.
Welcome to the Watch.

ACT II: THE WATCH

'The scrying of prime futures carries with it a unique set of problems. One of the most fundamental is simply this: the mere act of attempting prophecy may alter the very futures one tries to perceive.'

– Athio Cordatus, 947.M31

1

The train that carried the miners of I-8 to work was a noisy, juddering locomotive: built of black iron, windowless, twelve cars long. The first and last were engine cars, and the second and eleventh were filled with grim, barrel-chested men setting out for their twenty-hour shift. All the other cars were empty – open-topped freight wagons returning to the active parts of the mine to be refilled with raw ore for the topside refineries.

So far, Ordimas seemed to be doing fine. It helped that Mykal wasn't known for good conversation. Those others who were not Rockheads had learned not to take liberties with him, and the other Rockheads in the group – five surly, cruel-faced men all bearing the neck tattoo of the gang – had given only nods of greeting. Clearly they didn't talk about gang business in the presence of others. Ordimas sensed the silence went beyond this somehow, but he couldn't put his finger on it. There was a strange air in the passenger car, almost meditative, as if each man sat straining to hear a faint voice only he could perceive. That didn't seem natural. Not for men like these. The carriage should have been filled with rough banter, tall tales, or at least some griping about the long work-shift ahead. There was none of it.

The journey to the assigned work-site was just over two hours long with a stop of ten minutes at halfway for the massive turntable at Maddox Point to rotate them onto the proper track. Eventually, the train pulled into its destination – a grimy steel platform lined with yellow-painted loading cranes – and the side doors were hauled open. Everyone rose and took work-helmets from the overhead storage bays. Ordimas did likewise, exited the train with the rest and followed as they marched off down a gloomy, lantern-lit side tunnel of jagged black rock.

There were none of the great mining machines of the Adeptus Mechanicus here. No massive titanium-jawed monsters, no gargantuan drill-faced juggernauts. These tunnels were small and narrow, a recent excavation searching for untapped veins. The men of I-8 worked at different spots along the tunnel wall, cutting to both left and right, and there was a significant bonus for anyone who found a good score. Still, even with the prospect of a reward, the work was punishing and dangerous, and little allowance was made for accident or injury. Nightsiders died so often in cave-ins and las-cutter accidents that the work-parties had a constant flow of rookies coming in. Ordimas would have been better off choosing a rookie to mimic instead of a *face* like Mykal, but vengeance for Nedra had driven his choice and that was something he couldn't bring himself to regret.

The shift supervisor – a big, red-faced man named Yunus, whom everyone called simply *chief* – led everyone to their positions at the tunnel wall, checked his chrono, and called out for the official start of the shift. There would be a short break in six hours.

Under cover of adjusting his safety helmet, Ordimas watched the man next to him for a few moments to see what he should be doing. This man was called Seulus and, when he caught Ordimas looking at him, he grinned, put down his las-cutter, and came over.

Ordimas forced himself to relax. So far, scowling and keeping to himself had been enough. He hadn't aroused any suspicions, but all it might take was one wrong word.

Seulus stopped beside him, leaned in close, and said, 'Soon, brother. Soon.'

He made the hand-sign the miner's woman had mentioned back in Cholixe.

Ordimas limited his response to a nod and mirrored the sign, fingers splayed in twos, hand over heart. The other miner seemed satisfied.

'The chief will be round in an hour for us,' said Seulus. 'The other work-party are about twenty minutes from here. Section C. Not far. Just be ready.'

'I'm always ready,' Ordimas grunted back. The voice was Mykal's. He just hoped the words were something Mykal would have said. Evidently they were, because Seulus snorted derisively like he'd heard them a thousand times. Then, he went back to his downed las-cutter, lowered his goggles, hefted it and got to work burning into the rock with its blinding beam.

Having seen enough to at least look like he knew what he was doing, Ordimas hefted his own cutter, lowered his goggles, and followed suit. The cutter soon got hot, and the constant vibration numbed his hands so that he had to take small breaks every five or six minutes to shake feeling back into them. This wasn't a problem unique to Ordimas. Seulus, he was glad to see, was forced to do the same.

Before long, the chief appeared, marching towards them from the far end of the tunnel with a promethium lantern in his right hand and something dark and indistinct gripped in his left.

He gestured for Ordimas, Seulus and two others from further up the tunnel to gather round. Eyeing each of them intently, he told them, 'Everything is ready, kindred. We'll go by autocart. Once we get to Section C, I want you two to block the far end of the tunnel.' He said this to Ordimas and Seulus. 'Zonnd and Brinte will block the near end. The others will attack with me. Be ready to take down anyone who tries to break away. Understood?'

Ordimas saw by the lamplight that the black object in the chief's hand was a stun-cudgel, enforcer issue. What was this man doing with a Civitas-grade weapon? One did not come by such things accidentally. Enforcers were nothing if not careful with their gear. The punishments for any losses were severe.

Each of the men around the chief nodded their understanding. Supervisor Yunus thumbed the activation rune on his cudgel and it hummed softly to life. Having checked the weapon's charge, he thumbed it off again. 'Time for the real work to start. Follow Brinte here to the autocarts. I'll gather the others.'

Brinte turned, and led the way while the chief went off to brief the rest of I-8. Ordimas kept a wary eye on those around him as he followed.

What in the Eye of Terror is going on here? he asked himself. *Why are we going to attack another work-party?*

Whatever the reason, it looked like His Lordship had thrown Ordimas Arujo into deep water once again.

As always, it was up to Ordimas to get himself out of it alive.

2

At the edge of the plasteel walkway by which the *Adonai* had settled, Captain Orlesi and Karras gripped wrists. The smaller man's eyes shone with a level of emotion that surprised the Death Spectre.

'Fight well and hard, my lord,' Orlesi said emphatically. 'Don't have the old girl and I ferry you back to Occludus in an onyx box, will you? I ask that with all my heart.'

Like Brother Stephanus, thought Karras. *I must not forget. I must not be complacent. Stephanus was mighty among us. And yet, he did not survive all the Deathwatch demanded of him.*

In his mind's eye, he saw Athio Cordatus glaring at him, demanding he serve with honour and survive to return home.

Watch over me, khadit. If even Stephanus was not equal to the tasks set him, how can I hope to be?

Karras offered the captain a wan smile. 'May the Emperor light your way, captain,' he said, 'and may the winds favour you.' It was an archaic phrase Karras had heard spoken before among parting Naval officers. He could see that it surprised Orlesi to hear it now, but the look of surprise was soon replaced by one of appreciative pleasure. Karras released the man's wrist and turned. Followed by a train of baggage servitors from the ship, he strode out to meet in body the Deathwatch Librarian who had already welcomed him in mind.

Marnus Lochaine of the Storm Wardens Chapter was not just any Librarian, as Karras soon learned. He was Chief Librarian of Watch Fortress Damaroth, a member of the Watch Council and the supreme authority governing the Librarians sent to train here. It was Lochaine who would oversee the special training each psychic

Space Marine would undertake above and beyond the standard xenos hunter programme. It was Lochaine's assessment that would alter the fate of each, at least in the short term. But these were details Karras discovered only later. At the moment of their meeting, Lochaine was one more unknown in a day filled with them.

Behind the Storm Warden, a row of twelve smartly attired male serfs appeared, standing to sharp attention. These were members of the Rothi – the order of menials that served the brothers of the Watch. Each wore a smooth mask of white porcelain, the Deathwatch icon emblazoned in silver at the outer corner of the left eyehole. As Lochaine briefly introduced himself to the new arrival, the Rothi stood in silence, shoulders back, eyes front, chests out. They were dressed in crisp, black two-piece uniforms and boots, military in appearance, with a broad grey belt. In this and in their austere military bearing, they were all identical, but their similarities to each other went beyond that. They were indistinguishable from each other in both height and build. Masked as they were, they could not be told apart. Karras let his mind reach out a psychic tendril and sent it flickering over their auras.

Clones, he thought. *Can it be? They're prohibited throughout the Imperium. Does the Watch have a special dispensation?*

It was hardly the time to ask. Lochaine was looking at him expectantly. Karras made his formal introduction and passed the other Librarian an official scroll of secondment bearing the seal of his Chapter. Lochaine nodded as he read it, then rolled it up and handed it to one of the Rothi with instructions to deliver it to the Watch Commander. With formal introductions over, Lochaine directed six of the Rothi to take Karras's effects to his new quarters. These quarters, Karras was told, were located far above the docking bay in a chapel-barracks on the inner surface of the great ring. The remaining six Rothi he instructed to attend Captain Orlesi, who stood waiting patiently at the ramp to his ship, quietly observing the proceedings from afar.

As Karras watched the Rothi silently obey, his eyes caught movement on the far right. Dark, power-armoured figures were boarding a sleek, black Sword-class frigate some distance away.

Lochaine followed the Death Spectre's gaze.

'Scorpion Squad,' he said simply. 'Still at full strength, by Terra's blessing.'

'Where are they going?' asked Karras.

'Deployment details are classified as standard. Only the Watch Council and the squad itself have access to that information.'

Karras cursed. What was he thinking? This wasn't Logopol.

'You'll get used to all the cloak-and-dagger soon enough,' said

Lochaine. 'I once stood in your place. Can't say I liked it much either – all the silence, the blank stares, the evasion and the half-truths. Reasons enough for it, as you'll come to see, but it takes a little faith at first. Come, brother. There are matters to settle before you can see your quarters.'

He turned and led Karras away from the South Dock. Behind them, the Sword-class Frigate carrying Scorpion Squad began its departure, engines roaring with a noise like unrelenting thunder. As Karras and Lochaine moved into a corridor, a thick bulkhead door rolled shut behind them and the noise of the departing craft died to a low rumble.

While they walked, Karras cast his mind back, searching for what he knew of the First Librarian's parent Chapter. It was not much. He had heard very little of the Storm Wardens. Prior to this moment he had never met one, nor could he recall mention of them in Imperial archives or oral legends. His thoughts lingered on that a moment. The glories of most Chapters quickly became tales of legend, often wildly embellished, that spread like wildfire among the Imperium's civilian populations. Who had not heard, for example, of the great Battle for Macragge, or the legendary First and Second Wars of Armageddon? Of the Gildar Rift and the Purge of Kadillus? What child did not grow up dreaming of life as a warrior of the Adeptus Astartes? Ironic, then, that the arrival of Space Marines heralded bloodshed and death on a scale of which few mortals could conceive even in nightmare. Not many civilian witnesses lived through that reality.

Space Marines went where needed, where the cancers that ailed the Imperium were most malignant. The trillions who eagerly devoured tales of the legendary warriors were the lucky ones, living safe lives, spared the truth, content to worship their heroes in blissful ignorance. Their simplistic view was something the lords of the Imperium gladly encouraged, for such tales – even the vast number of fictional ones – were a beacon of hope in these darkest of times. The absence of any such tales about a given Chapter usually spoke of deliberate suppression and secrecy. What, if anything, did the Storm Wardens hide?

Nothing like the Shariax, I'll wager.

Secretive or not, as they walked and talked, Karras found it easy to like the First Librarian. In the Storm Warden's eyes, he found little sign of judgement. If Lochaine bore any prejudices, he hid them well enough. It was not always so. Other Chapters, most especially those formed from the much-lauded Ultramarines gene-seed, tended to look askance at those bearing the mark of genetic mutation. The bone-white skin and hair and the all-red eyes of the Death

Spectres marked them at once as having a flawed melanchromic organ[9]. Less outwardly obvious was the absence of a functioning mucranoid[10] and Betcher's gland[11]. His own lack of these advantages bothered Karras not at all, for he had never known them. If it bothered anyone else, let them stand apart as they pleased.

Lochaine was pale-skinned himself, but he was no albino. He had a thick, heavy brow and dark, deep set eyes above tattooed cheeks and a jaw covered with short, dark stubble. He looked rough and unruly to Karras, far from the noble and austere image projected by Athio Cordatus. But Karras could sense his power, that fierce, bright aura betraying an immense force held in supremely well-exercised control. Lochaine's power was equal to his own at least. Perhaps even a degree greater.

Having taken a sequence of turns, the two Librarians now marched along a gloomy stone tunnel. It was broad and high-ceilinged, the walls cold and wet, and the stonework was unadorned by any decoration. It was a dank place, lit every five metres or so by lumes in the ceiling that cast pools of milky white light in the damp air. 'We're in the mid-levels,' Lochaine told him. 'There are coolant pipes in the walls. Moisture tends to gather.'

'How many levels are there?'

Having asked, he suddenly wondered how far questions would be tolerated. Was it anathema to seek knowledge here? Operating in shadow outside the walls of the Watch fortress was one thing, but how much curiosity would be tolerated within? Plausible deniability was critical to an organisation like the Inquisition's Ordo Xenos, with whom the Deathwatch worked so closely. The Ordo often sanctioned actions about which the greater part of humanity must never know. The most terrible and controversial of these was Exterminatus – the absolute eradication of all life on a given world. Open knowledge of this recourse, and of just how regularly it was deemed necessary, could split the Imperium like an axe. Fear would turn to panic, which might cause outright revolt. From there, it was a small step to galactic civil war and to bloodshed the likes of which had not been seen since the horrors of the mad Ecclesiarch Goge Vandire. No. The less that was known, the better. But it was more than simple deniability. The alien enemies of the Imperium were legion, and among them were cruel and ancient intellects to rival mankind's

---

9. Melanchromic organ – the phase 13 implant responsible for cutaneous protection from radiation.

10. Mucranoid – the phase 16 implant controlling sweat-gland secretions to protect against climatic extremes.

11. Betcher's gland – the phase 17 implant allowing internal production of a corrosive toxin projected by spitting.

best. Any information about the Deathwatch could conceivably be seized upon and utilised for strategic gain.

Karras well understood the necessity for *need to know*. He just had to find the boundaries.

Lochaine laid some of them out for him.

'There are three hundred and twelve levels in total, the uppermost being the first. It's the first that we Space Marines mostly keep to. Everything we need is there, save the hangars and docking bays. Do not be hesitant to ask questions, brother, so long as they are the right questions. The Deathwatch operates entirely unlike any other Chapter in the Imperium. Make it easier on yourself. Abandon your preconceptions. Empty your cup so that it might be filled anew.'

'The brothers who returned to Occludus alive would tell me nothing,' said Karras.

Lochaine nodded. 'I'm sure they wanted to, but everyone who *dons the black*, as we say, becomes honour-bound, sworn by oath to say nothing of their time among us. That's not to mention the hypno-induction, too, of course.'

'And not just for the Space Marines,' said Karras, thinking now of Captain Orlesi.

Lochaine picked up on the direction of his thoughts. 'The captain is a good man. He knows well the limits of his business. But you're right. We don't gamble on honour and loyalty. He has undergone hypno-induction, though it's a far more dangerous and unpleasant experience for a normal man.'

The dank tunnel through which they walked soon terminated in a wide archway. Beyond it, they entered a chamber with a ceiling twice as high as that of the corridor. Each of the walls to left and right boasted an entrance to a wide elevator, though neither were currently waiting at this level. In the far wall, the archways to two other corridors led deeper into the complex. Two large ventilator fans turned lazily behind their grilles in the ceiling, the lumes behind them throwing the shadows of the rotating blades down onto the stone floor below. Everything was stained dark by age and moisture. Lochaine strode forwards, stopping at a wall-embedded servo-skull by the elevator on the left. 'Summon,' he barked at the age-browned skull. In the skull's left socket, a light winked from red to green, acknowledging the command. In a small screen below the skull, numerical runes began counting upwards from six.

As they waited, Lochaine turned serious.

'You'll forgive the necessity, brother, but I must now give you the same warning I give all who are selected for the honour of serving. You see, Damaroth is not like any fortress-monastery you'd care to name. Tensions run high here. Rivalry is common and old grudges between Chapters often bear out. Unworthy infighting is all too common. Only the truly exceptional are seconded to the Deathwatch, and that makes for a lot of egos, a lot of pride. Don't mistake me. You seem well grounded. But there are plenty of others who insist on making things more difficult than they ought to be. I ask you not to rise to provocation. These others… Their minds will be tempered in time, but hunger for glory and honour is rife. To be certain, it has its time and its place, but that is not here at Damaroth. Focus only on what matters. Do your Chapter proud. Unlock your potential. There is so much for you to learn. Put your trust in us, do as ordered, and you shall see.'

'I came here to honour my Chapter,' Karras told him, rankled somewhat at the tone and nature of the warning, despite its worthy intention. 'To honour my Chapter and to serve the Imperium. I intend to do both to the limits of my ability. I did not come here for self-glorification or personal satisfaction. Let your mind rest easy on that.'

Lochaine noted the suppressed anger in Karras's voice. 'Do not be offended, brother. As I say, it is a speech I make to all who come, regardless of integrity and origin.'

There was a chime and a toneless voice emanated from the elevator servo-skull.

'Level sixty. Stand clear.'

'Forgive me for what happens next,' said Lochaine.

'What?'

Suddenly, Karras felt a tremendous force suppressing his psychic power and locking his muscles tight. At once, he fought back, but he had been caught off guard. Though he strained, grunting with effort, he could not move. He glared at Lochaine and saw the Chief Librarian's eyes burning with white flame. This was balefire, also known as witchfire, the ethereal flame that ignited whenever a Librarian exercised his true strength.

'Damn you,' Karras barely managed through clenched teeth. 'What–'

The elevator doors drew open and a single Space Marine stepped out, dressed in the black armour of the Deathwatch with the winged-helix icon of the Apothecarion on his right knee-guard.

He looked Karras up and down. 'So this is the Death Spectre,' he said; his voice was somewhat nasal. 'Fearsome looking, isn't he? Mark those red eyes.'

'Get it over with, Asphodal,' said Lochaine.

The Apothecary marched to Karras's side and raised a pistol-like device to his neck. Karras felt several needles pierce the skin below his left ear.

'Put your faith in us, brother,' said Asphodal. 'We mean no harm, no offence. All arrivals must endure this. A little undignified, perhaps, but you will understand the need for it soon enough.'

Karras was hardly listening. His blood roared in his ears. He was here to serve with honour. This was a grave insult, an outrage he would not forget nor soon forgive. Had he been able, he would have smashed his forehead into the face of the Apothecary and blasted Lochaine with balefire of his own.

He was a Death Spectre, damn it!

The Apothecary pulled a trigger. There was a sharp hiss and a strange sensation of simultaneous freezing and burning that spread from Karras's neck throughout his entire body. Darkness fell over him. How could this be? He was a Space Marine. His body had been engineered to overcome any known paralytic drug.

Dimly, he felt his centre of balance shift. Strong hands caught him.

Before darkness descended fully, he heard two voices speaking close to him one more time.

'Throne curse that we have to do this. He'll hate us for it.'

'What makes you so sure?'

'Because I did.'

3

No one should have been here. This was an old section of the Underworks known as the Arraphel mine. Rich in its day, it had been abandoned over three hundred years ago, its thick, branching veins of precious ore utterly stripped. Silent and dark it had lain since then, frost riming the long-unwalked tunnels, but it was not silent and dark now. Ordimas rode in the last of three autocarts that trundled noisily along the dusty tunnel floors. The unconscious forms of the H-6 miners lay before him on the deck of the cart, ringed by the men who had assaulted them. The victims lay heaped together, wrists and ankles bound, mouths gagged. Looking down at the slumped forms, Ordimas's thoughts returned unbidden to Mira. He searched his feelings for guilt, and was glad to find none. He knew the type well enough. She'd only have found herself another abuser... and she would have talked. Eventually, people always did. Granting her a quick, painless death, that had been a mercy. Or was he merely justifying his actions? How many had he killed in his lifetime? Close to a hundred now, he guessed, and each so that he might get the job done. His Lordship cared not about deaths in such trivial numbers. His game, after all, was played out on a much grander scale.

He turned his eyes from the victims on the autocart floor to the men seated across from him. He still couldn't work it out: the silent almost drone-like behavior of the rest of Mykal's crew, making it almost too easy to pass for Mykal among them; the stun-cudgel assault on the other mining party; this grim, silent convoy into a long-ignored part of the mine.

What in the blasted warp are we doing here? What's going on?

An entire work-crew, kidnapped, loaded up, and driven down here to these mined-out branches! Ordimas scrabbled to make sense of it. He knew he was in great danger. Raised adrenaline levels would have told him as much, even if the prickling of his neck hairs and the goose-bumps on his skin hadn't. The dour, uncommunicative behaviour of his fellows was a blessing, now as before. No probing questions, no awkward conversations that could have tripped him up. But the strange silence still made him feel deeply uneasy, and the men trussed up at his feet, like pigs bound for the cook-fire… that was more unsettling still.

He caught one of the I-8 crew, Nendes, looking at him. They locked gazes for a second. Ordimas nodded in silent acknowledgement. Nendes nodded back and raised his hand to his chest in the three-pronged salute. Ordimas copied it as before. What did it mean? Not so much as a flicker of human emotion showed on Nendes's face, but his gaze moved on, and Ordimas breathed a shallow sigh of relief.

Whatever happens, he told himself, whatever you see, *don't give yourself away. Be steady. Maintain the mask. Maintain the mask.*

Despite years in the service of His Lordship, who wielded almost holy authority in the Emperor's name, Ordimas didn't really believe in the Emperor of Mankind. Most people, he suspected, didn't really believe. Hope and belief were often mistaken for each other. In the cold light of day, all he could rely on were his wits and his skills. It was these that had gotten him through all those times he'd been sure he would die. It was these that he turned to now, knowing he had to be ready for whatever lay ahead.

At that moment, what lay ahead was a massive plasteel door some ten metres across. Supervisor Yunus, riding the first cart in the line, stood and raised his hand for the others to halt. The autocarts rolled to a growling stop in a line facing the plasteel door. Suddenly, as if from nowhere, two men in enforcer uniforms stepped into the cart headlights. They wore helmets and carapace armour, and in their gloved hands, each brandished a lethal wide-bore riot-gun. These they levelled at the men on the first cart.

'Unity,' the one on the left called out.

It was Yunus who spoke in reply.

'The gift of the Master.'

'Strength,' challenged the guard.

'And life everlasting,' said Yunus.

The guard lowered his riot-gun. 'In whatever form that be.' Saying this, he nodded to his companion, who also lowered his weapon.

'Your group is the last to arrive,' said the one on the right. 'You have new kindred?'

Yunus nodded and gestured to the bodies heaped on the carts behind him. The guard moved down the row of idling vehicles, inspecting the haul of victims that lay in the back of each. When he got to Ordimas's cart, he nodded approvingly. He looked up, directly at Ordimas, and said, 'They will soon awaken to the blessings of the Master.'

Ordimas thought it deathly unwise to speak at that moment, so he nodded once, face impassive, and returned his gaze to the slumbering victims.

The guard walked back to his companion at the metal door. 'All is well,' he said.

The other guard then walked to the wall and struck a number of runes on a dark panel there. Ordimas wondered how he could see them in such low light. The headlamps of the carts lit the area immediately in front of them, but nothing else. Then it occurred to him that these men had been standing here in utter darkness for… How long? Ordimas could see clearly in the dark thanks to the opticom aug sitting in his right eye socket. Watching the man at the panel, it suddenly became clear that these guards could see just as well. Someone had augged them, too? Who? That kind of upgrade was well beyond the reach of some backwater Civitas precinct. Who had supplied the augs? Who were these men? If they were enforcers, what in nine hells were they doing down here in the freezing darkness?

New kindred, the man had said. More than anything, it was those words that made Ordimas's skin truly crawl. These people sounded like cultists.

The tunnel began to shudder as the vast doors slowly split apart. More darkness lay beyond. After thirty seconds or so, the doors finally ground all the way back into their housing, and the way ahead lay open.

The guard on the right ushered the carts forwards now, and Ordimas swayed a little as his vehicle started into motion.

As his cart rumbled past the enforcers, he looked down and tried to read the name and number embossed on the golden badge worn by the one on the right.

Cartigan. 899-00-213.

Was this man really Enforcer Cartigan? Or was the uniform stolen?

It wouldn't be hard to find out, if he ever got out of here. He had hacked the local Civitas cogitator mainframe a number of times over the last year on the orders of His Lordship. He would look up this Cartigan. Maybe he was listed as missing.

If I get out.

As if in answer to that thought, the plasteel doors ground shut behind him with a deafening clang.

The carts rolled on. The tunnel was wide here. It curved slowly down to the left. It seemed to go quite a distance, half a kilometre at least, before another source of light could be seen up ahead. Another five minutes and the convoy emerged into a wide chamber dimly lit by grox-oil lamps that cast everything in pale, flickering orange.

In the centre of the chamber, two broad lift shafts plunged down into the abyssal black depths. The lift platform on the left was raised, already here in the chamber, waiting to take the new arrivals to Arraphel's lowest levels. The shaft on the right gaped open, its platform waiting at the bottom, and no light shone upwards from within it.

We're going deep, thought Ordimas with a lurch in his stomach. He struggled with an overwhelming urge to turn, leap from the cart, and run from here. He had come this far on experience, grit and cool nerves, but the very idea of descending these shafts with these people made him blanch.

I'm terrified, he admitted to himself. *Something is down there, waiting, and I'm not going to like it. Throne help me, if something goes wrong, if I'm discovered, if the mask slips...*

He was already well beyond the point of no return. He acknowledged that now. There was nothing he could do. He had to ride this out, see where it led, and hope to Holy Terra that he lived to breathe the open air again.

Yunus barked out more orders and, one by one, the carts all rumbled in an orderly fashion onto the open lift platform. Even with all three vehicles, there was plenty of room to spare. Then the chief jumped down from his vehicle, walked to the control console at the platform's edge, and tapped a code into its lambent green runeboard.

Ordimas heard gears grind to life in the shaft walls and, with a violent judder, the platform began its long descent.

There were work-lumes set in the shaft walls, as there were with most shafts in the Underworks, but they were not lit. Apart from the headlamps of the carts, the only light Ordimas could see now was the square of orange above him at the top of the shaft.

As the minutes of slow descent stretched out and the pressure in his ears gradually increased, he looked straight up, watching that square become smaller and smaller, and with it, his hopes of getting out alive.

4

Karras awoke to a hammering pain in the back of his head and neck. He opened his eyes to find himself in a lume-lit room, measuring, he estimated, about eight metres on each of its sides. His vision was blurry at first, but it soon sharpened. He was not alone. Across from him, seated in a high-backed chair of grey stone, was a large Space Marine in black fatigues.

Lochaine!

The Chief Librarian was less imposing out of armour, but not by much. That didn't stop Karras. He surged forwards without thinking, pinning Lochaine to the back of his chair with his left hand while his right hovered before the Storm Warden's throat, fingers rigid, poised to strike a blow that would crush the other's windpipe.

'What did you do?' raged Karras. 'What in damnation did you do to me?'

Lochaine sighed. 'Sit down, brother. You won't spill blood here.'

For a moment, they stayed like that, the Death Spectre frozen in his confusion and rage, the Storm Warden quietly waiting, face impassive.

It was then that realisation dawned. It hit Karras like a thunder hammer. Always before, when rage had overtaken him, his gift had risen, the flow of power boiling up to meet his violent needs.

Not so now.

It was this, as much as the truth in Lochaine's words, that forced Karras back into his own stone chair. His alabaster face retained its murderous snarl, but rage had already given way to grave concern. Why had his talent not manifested?

Lochaine knew.

'We had no choice,' he told Karras. 'It is always the way with the Librarians who come. Do not feel that you have been singled out. I endured the very same when I first arrived here, and I raged as you do, but I soon saw the need.'

'You... you have sealed my power?'

Karras's blood ran cold. For as long as he could remember, the gift had been with him, guiding him, protecting him, setting him apart from other men, even from other Space Marines.

Athio Cordatus had told him to cleave to self-image in times of doubt. But Karras's self-image was inextricably woven to the witching ways that made him such an asset to his noble order.

'You must understand the nature of this organisation,' Lochaine continued. 'Space Marines from hundreds of Chapters are pledged to serve the Watch with honour. Every last brother who dons the black is desperately needed. Promises must be made. And once made, kept. Every Chapter has its secrets, Death Spectre.' The emphasis on those last two words could not be missed. But Lochaine couldn't know anything. Like he said, every Chapter had its secrets. That didn't mean he knew what they were.

'The powers we yield could be used to pry them from a brother's mind. I won't insult you by spelling out what that would mean to the Deathwatch. It cannot be permitted. Long ago, compacts were made. The Deathwatch assures as much confidentiality as it asks. Until you have taken Second Oath, your psychic power must be suppressed.'

As Lochaine spoke, Karras focused inwards, desperately searching for the least remnant of his power that might remain to him. It was there, a muted flickering of eldritch energy deep within him, like a raindrop where once had blazed a lake of fire, so far removed from the glorious flow he had known that he almost cried out in despair.

'This... I...'

Lochaine leaned forwards, forearms resting on his knees. 'Be patient with us, brother. You will see in time that we do this not only to preserve the accords, but for your benefit also. We Librarians are ever too dependent on our gifts. You'll gain much from training without. You'll rediscover what it's like to fight with only physical strength. Before your deployment, the warp-field suppressor will be fully removed.'

Karras tried to isolate and locate the source of the pain in his head and neck. He stretched a thickly muscled arm over his head and reached back, feeling the base of his skull, the back of his neck, tracing his spine as far down as he could. That wasn't very far. The muscle mass of his shoulders and biceps meant he could not reach lower than the centre of his trapezius. It was, however, enough. His fingers brushed cold metal.

'We graft them to the spine. Easily removed with the proper rituals when the time comes, but don't try to pull it off yourself. Permanent paralysis won't help your fighting abilities.'

'It's not just a suppressor, is it?' Karras growled.

'Sharp, brother. Keep thinking like that and you might just make it to the end of your term alive. No, it's not just a suppressor.'

'So all those seconded here receive implants?'

Lochaine nodded. 'Standard procedure. A tracking device with a neural interrupt. It's how we keep order here, enforce the boundaries and such. There is much in the archives here at Damaroth that is classified at the highest levels, information of a nature that, if leaked, could destabilise the treaties and accords that hold the Imperium together. The Deathwatch is ancient, Karras, and the scrolls and datacores collected here record countless things best forgotten.'

To this, a more bullish Space Marine might simply have said, *Destroy them!*

Not so a Librarian. Not Lyandro Karras. To a Librarian, knowledge was its own justification, and as vital to victory as a keen blade and a loaded bolter.

Those who stick their heads in the sand find only the darkness of ignorance. Shy not from the horror and shame of the past. The hardest memories teach the strongest lessons.

When had his khadit told him that? Long ago. A century now. It was as true as it would always be. Karras could see the need to track battle-brothers while they remained at the Watch fortress. That did not make the method any less insulting.

'The implant will shut off muscle control should you try to breach a restricted area. You'll drop, as limp as an empty sack, until a Watch sergeant issues the override command. Likewise if a fight gets a little too intense. We can't have Space Wolves and Dark Angels killing each other.'

'You could have asked, Storm Warden,' hissed Karras. 'Had you explained, I would have complied.'

'And what if you had not? Do you think we could just ship you home? No. I told you, Karras. The Watch needs every last Space Marine it calls upon. Would that we could take more. Trust is a luxury few can afford in this Imperium. And we don't have time to build it. So we no longer ask. We do what we must. Do you imagine we could negotiate the use of such implants with a White Scar? A Black Templar? It was tried. That we resort to such extremes ought to tell you how well *that* played out.'

Karras cursed. To be tracked like an animal... To be robbed of his gifts and forced to train without the power he had always commanded...

Things were not as he had imagined them to be. Where was the honour in this?

Stephanus. How did you react? Were you as indignant as I?

Whether Stephanus had railed against his own implant or not, he had remained to serve for over thirty years with great pride. He had brought glory to his Chapter. Indignant or not, Karras could do no less.

'You believe the end justifies the means, Brother Lochaine. Very well. Your judgement is better informed than mine. But it is a bad start for us, as it must be with the others.'

Lochaine shrugged. 'As I said, I felt the same way. I got over it. You will, too. Your training will begin tomorrow at 0200 hours. From that moment forth, you will have precious little time to dwell on injured pride.'

Lochaine rose from his stone chair. Karras did likewise.

'Within the hour, that pounding in your head will dissipate. You will quickly cease to notice the physical presence of the implant. The absence of your gifts will bother you as much as you let it. Try to remember that it's only temporary.'

He turned to leave, but Karras stopped him.

'Tell me, brother,' he said. 'How is it done? Among my own, my power was considered great. I needed no psychic hood. On the battlefield, I burned my foes to ash with the white fire of the soul.'

'It will be great again,' said the Storm Warden, 'when the time is right. As to the method – like so much else here, that is not for you to know.'

He walked to the chamber door, big shoulders rolling. The doors slid apart before him, but, as he was about to step through, Lochaine stopped and spoke over his shoulder.

'I will call for you in one hour, Karras. Wear the robes we have prepared for you. They are lying on your cot. You will receive First Induction from the Watch Council today.'

Karras said nothing.

'After induction,' continued Lochaine, 'things will change. For the duration of your service, you must be Deathwatch first and a Death Spectre second. I know how that sounds. I remember how it sounded to me. But come to terms with it quickly, for your own sake. Only in this way shall you earn glory for your Chapter. So it is with all who honour the ancient accords.'

Karras stared at Lochaine coldly. It seemed impossible to think that way. A Death Spectre second? His mind rebelled, offended by the mere notion.

Yet his secondment could work no other way.

It will be hard. Throne, will it be hard.

'One more thing,' said Lochaine. 'You should know that the moment these doors close behind me, the soft gloves come off. Do not forget that I am Chief Librarian here. You are subordinate to me for a reason. From this moment forward, you will address me in the manner to which I am entitled. You will address me as *my lord*. Is that clear, Codicier?'

Karras stiffened. Lochaine's voice was sharp with command.

'Crystal clear,' he said, then added after the briefest pause, 'my lord.'

'One hour, Karras. Be ready.'

Lochaine strode out and the steel jaws of the chamber doors crunched shut behind him.

Karras turned and surveyed his new quarters. Small. Simple. Spartan in the extreme. *Good.*

There were recesses in each wall, waist high from the floor, each bearing a small bronze figure – icons of death like the ones at the entrance to the great docking bay. Apart from his simple stone cot, there was a black granitwood bookshelf stocked with approved texts, and a marble font filled with clear, ice-cold water. To the left and right, stone archways led into two antechambers. In one of these, Karras found the force sword *Arquemann* and the few personal effects he had been allowed to bring, one of which was the oldest known copy of Belvedere's *Tribulatus Terrarum* – a fine, if somewhat dramatised account of the political events that led to the Schism of Mars.

Arquemann had been mounted on the wall. Beneath it, on a black iron rack, one of the Rothi had lit votive candles. He had recognised the sword's relic status. Karras silently approved.

He reached out a hand to *Arquemann*'s hilt, whispering to the sword.

'Deathwatch first? They ask too much. My death in battle, this I offer freely for the honour of the Megir. An eternity of service, never again to see the domed mausoleums and polished crypts of Logopol? Even this I would endure. But the Chapter I will always put first.'

Even before the Imperium, he admitted to himself guiltily.

He half expected the spirit of the force sword to flare in response. In their time training on the *Adonai*, the blade had joined its power to Karras's just as his khadit had said it would, reacting to the strength and sense of honour within the warrior's soul. How would it react to this last, less-than-honourable thought?

Karras felt nothing from the haft. He moved his fingers to the keen shimmering edge of the blade itself. Still nothing.

Damn them.

In sealing his power, they had cut him off from the soul of the ancient weapon. He almost lashed out, almost struck his heavy fists against the wall. But he mastered himself. It took a moment, but he did it. With a growl, he turned from the antechamber and went to investigate the other.

In the second antechamber, he came upon a sight that doused the fires of his frustration.

It was a gloomy, candlelit room, but bright enough to his enhanced eyes. On every wall was hung polished, resin-coated alien skulls and strange helms fashioned by inhuman hands. Each item had a parchment scroll beneath it, some far older and more worn than others. Crossing to the grotesque skull of a massive ork, Karras read the parchment. His eyes widened in surprise. He crossed to a bladed helm of dark metal, easily recognisable as the mask of some eldar abomination. He read the scroll beneath that one, too. Each artefact in the room was the same – a trophy, placed here to honour the Space Marine who had taken it.

He knew those names. Every last one of those Space Marines had been a Death Spectre. A few of those represented here had even returned to Occludus alive.

It was a shrine to the long service of Karras's Chapter, and he immediately felt abashed, regretting his anger of only moments ago.

He looked down. The black marble flagstones beneath his feet were engraved with four words in High Gothic:

They served with honour.

He scowled at himself.

As I must. And I will add trophies of my own.

He bowed and said a silent prayer for the souls of those long passed, then strode back into the main chamber where a heavy robe lay spread on his cot. He sat on the cot's edge and gathered up the coarse black material in his hands.

Looking down at it, he blew a deep breath out between his teeth.

How can I do any less than follow their example? They died to honour the ancient accord. They earned the respect of the Deathwatch with blood and sweat. And I had thought to be granted it simply for qualifying. I see how naive that was. The respect of my kin was hard earned on Occludus. By Terra, I died three times to get it!

Let us hope I don't have to die this time, too.

As Marnus Lochaine strode along a corridor already some distance from Karras's quarters, a voice sounded in his ear, transmitted there by the tiniest of vox devices.

'He is angry, then?'

'Naturally,' replied Lochaine.

'Will he overcome it?'

'Did I?'

'Didn't you, brother? How disappointing. You think he will harbour a grudge, even once his power has been returned?'

'It will spur him on. I believe his performance will benefit.'

'You see a little of yourself in him.'

There was humour in the voice.

'Not so little,' replied Lochaine with a private grin.

'Any clue as to why the inquisitor is so interested in this one?'

'Beyond his exceptional record, no. Not yet. He does not seem particularly pliant. Nor is he an outright rebel, so far as I can judge. But inquisitors do not make demands lightly. There may be prophecy involved. The psykers of the Ordo Xenos may have seen something we have not. His futures are so turbulent, so murky. The Librarius cannot read them. We cannot explain it, but whatever has drawn the eye of the Inquisition to Lyandro Karras, it must be significant.'

'As must the reason these others were flagged. The Ordo did not broker the new accord for our benefit alone. What game are they playing, I wonder. Observe this Death Spectre closely, old friend. He will be trained under Watch Sergeant Kulle.'

'Kulle?' said Lochaine. 'Is that wise? I would have thought, given the pedestal his Chapter places–'

'There are worse things than a little respect. Of all the Watch sergeants, it is Kulle who has the most experience operating under an Inquisition handler. It is he who can best prepare this Karras for whatever awaits him beyond our walls.'

'I detest this,' said Lochaine. 'Could we not have refused the Ordo's request? This inquisitor already has two kill-teams at his disposal, and four of the teams assigned to him in the past have been wiped out completely. The Ordo goes too far this time. Handing us a list–'

'No, brother. We will not refuse them. I had thought the issue resolved between us, but clearly I was wrong, so I tell you again: the new accord takes priority. It will prove its value in time. We may lose another kill-team to those crows, but the Deathwatch as a whole – not just sector-wide, but throughout the Imperium – is gaining a vital source of new blood at a critical time. We both know the importance of that strength now.

'Let this be an end to it, Marnus. I have spoken with finality. I'll not retread the matter. Not with you and not with Watch Chaplain Kayphe. I will see you in the Hall of Induction within the hour. There are preparations to be made before these newcomers take First Oath.'

'My lord's will,' said Lochaine curtly.

He dropped the link.

5

The chamber was vast – a dank echoing space cut deep in the rocky heart of Chiaro. Ordimas gazed in grim wonder as he stood among the miners, not just the men of I-8 but dozens more crews, hundreds of hard-faced, grit-stained men, all unspeaking, expectant, rigid with anticipation.

The chamber had the air of a cathedral, though it was far from grand or elaborate. Its austerity lent it atmosphere, as did the echoes that bounced back from the walls. There was a broad stone platform on the south side, its surface raised about a metre from the floor. A wide doorway gaped open at the platform's rear, about four metres across and two metres high, thick with inky shadows. Smaller portals led to tunnels that snaked off northwards. It was through one of these that Ordimas and the men of I-8 had entered. Other doorways led to tunnels east and west. The walls and floor of the large chamber were flat and smooth, almost glassy – a telltale sign that they had been fashioned with energy tools. Perhaps the place had once been an assembly area or a mess for the labourers who had toiled here before Arraphel had been bled dry.

Ordimas looked up. The roof – what little could be seen of it in the lamp-lit gloom – was rough, indicating that this had once been a natural cavern. Evenly spaced along the hall's length, great pillars stretched to that distant ceiling, their sides cut square, the corners chamfered. Iron braziers hung from each side of the pillars, their fires spreading a milky yellow haze in the close air, but giving off little or no warmth that Ordimas could feel. His breath, he noted, was still misting in the air before him. He was glad of his, or rather Mykal's, thermasuit.

We're not deep enough for magma heat, he thought, *but still deep.*

When the men of I-8 had arrived, Yunus had ordered them to park their carts in a broad side tunnel and carry their unconscious prisoners on their shoulders. Ordimas had done a quick count of the autocarts already parked there. Fifty-six of them. Whatever dark business was afoot, it involved far more people than just Yunus's crew. He couldn't have imagined at that point just how many would be convening here. Close to a thousand people, surely! Covertly, he studied them.

Most were miners or auxiliary crews, dressed in the thermasuits necessary for working Nightside. Here and there, orange overalls could be seen peeking out from beneath thick padding cinched with tool harnesses.

This must be almost the entire labour force for the local zone.

More unsettling still was the presence of others, people who clearly didn't belong down here. Among the silent crowd, he saw armed enforcers, robed members of the Ecclesiarchy, Administratum functionaries, even a fair number of civilians. Among this latter group were several dozen women, glassy-eyed, clad in thick woollen robes without marking. They stood together in ordered rows on the left of the platform, as silent as the others. A number of enforcers stood by them, riot-guns and assault stubbers cradled in their arms.

Other enforcers stood guard at the corners of the raised platform. Ordimas thought of that platform now as a stage, and the connection sent his mind back to happier thoughts, thoughts of puppetry and of Nedra.

Let me live to see him again. If I die down here, he'll think I abandoned him.

He chided himself.

You will abandon him, you fool. As soon as the order comes in, there will be no choice.

Still, while there was time, he wanted a chance to prepare the boy. Any explanation he gave for leaving would be better than none.

Supervisor Yunus had ordered the men of I-8 to place the bodies of their H-6 victims onto the cold, hard surface of the stage-like platform. Still bound and gagged, they were lowered face-down onto the frosty stone. Dozens of other bodies had already been laid out in neat lines. These, too, were bound and gagged, the victims of other crews or, perhaps, the victims of the civs and enforcers who'd come. There were women and men both, but no children. Ordimas could at least be thankful for that.

Some of the victims stirred to consciousness. He watched, hands clenched into fists, helpless to do anything, as they struggled against their bonds, screaming in fear and panic from behind their thick gags. An enforcer on the stage would stride forwards every time this happened and strike the writhing victim hard at the base of his or her skull with the stock of his gun.

A dark pox on these people, cursed Ordimas, *and whatever bloody cult they follow.*

As to the nature of the cult, answers still eluded him. It was not one he had ever encountered before, he felt sure. The Imperium was riddled with strange cults. There were always people ready to follow some false idol or other, despite the consequences. Heretics seemed to spread and multiply like cockroaches, and the only course of action was to stamp them out.

Those around him remained silent, watching the dark doorway at the back of the stage, waiting passively, and Ordimas began to marvel at the patience of the strange congregation. His own was starting to fray. He couldn't hold Mykal's shape forever, though another dose of cyanomorphide[12] would extend it... If he could only self-administer more without drawing attention.

Something shifted. He felt it before he saw it. A ripple of something ran through the hall, a change on the air, the aura of someone or something approaching. The members of the gathering dropped to their knees. Ordimas, his senses supercharged by fear and tension, dropped with them, a mere fraction of a second behind, so little a delay that no one noticed. No eyes were on him anyway. Not now, for shapes began to appear, filtering from the broad space in the back wall and out onto the platform.

The men that appeared were impressively large, that much was obvious, but their hooded robes hid any sign of features beyond their size. Some walked tall and powerful, their strides easy with animal grace. Others seemed to hunch over and limp, and Ordimas was sharply reminded of his own true shape and of the fact that he was watching all this unfold with eyes set, not in his own face but in the borrowed face of dead, contemptible Mykal.

A dead man I'll be joining if I'm not careful.

Upright or hunched, the longer Ordimas studied them, the clearer it became that all these newcomers were misshapen. The lay of their robes on back and shoulder seemed to hint at twisted masses of bone and muscle. Surely they were cloaked thus because they were grotesquely deformed, as he was without the influence of his priceless drug.

Normally, on seeing other hunchbacks and malformed souls, Ordimas would feel a spasm of sympathy, of understanding and a

---

12. Cyanomorphide – a 'nucleocode' drug also known as Shift which, in combination with ingested samples of genetic material, allows certain mutants to mimic the physical form of others.

kind of unspoken camaraderie. Not so here. Something about these men turned his stomach, and he wondered at that. Something at the back of his mind was repulsed by them, though he could as yet see no exposed flesh.

The strange men took up evenly spaced positions against the wall at the back of the stage. There they stood, as silent and still as the congregation kneeling on the floor. Now the final figure appeared, and the sight of him sent fingers of ice running down Ordimas's back.

He was tall, this figure that strode smoothly out of the dark doorway, and his robes were of a bluish purple rendered almost black in the weak light from the wall sconces. In his hand he carried a long stave of gleaming metal, dark gold in colour, with a red gem set in a headpiece shaped like three curving claws.

Like the hand sign they use, thought Ordimas.

His face was striking: utterly hairless, the skin smooth and pale with a bluish tint and a waxy sheen. It was an ageless face with no wrinkles or scars, but with none of the softness of youth. Ordimas could not guess how old this man was. He seemed at once both ancient and yet just entering his prime. But it was his eyes that were most remarkable. In the dim yellow light, they seemed to glow by themselves, like those of a wolf or cat.

I've seen that before.

Those eyes swept the crowd from end to end, assessing all they saw. Had those eyes lingered a fraction of a second longer on Ordimas? Or was it just his imagination?

He felt his stomach clench with fresh fear.

Dimly, he became aware of something in his mind. Nothing overt. Nothing violent. It was a subtle thing, the brushing of a psychic veil so light that its touch might be mere fancy. Then it was gone.

The august figure on the stage – among these others, he could not be mistaken for anything less than a supreme aristocrat – raised his staff and called out in a clear, crisp, pleasing voice, 'Thou art the children of the Master. Gather, ye, to this sanctum and give Him praise.'

The men and women on the chamber floor crossed their arms over their chests, each hand making that now-familiar three-pronged sign, and intoned in one droning voice, 'As we love, so we come to serve.'

The tall man nodded and lowered his staff. 'All are one under the Master. All are loved. All are treasured. By His gift alone shall the time of peace and happiness come. We are His people, and His benediction has spared us from disease, madness, hunger and fear. He has raised us up, so that we might bring others into His light.' Here, he gestured to the bound figures that lay on the stage behind him. 'Thus, you have brought these men and women here today, that they might awaken to new hope and come to know the Master's boundless love. Like you, they shall be granted life everlasting that they might better contribute to the coming of the Master's divine kingdom.'

Ordimas consciously opened his senses to everything – the sights, the smells, the sounds. He took it all in, knowing that his opticom was recording it all. This was why His Lordship had sent him down here. This cult was the reason he had been assigned to Chiaro in the first place.

And the children in the marketplace... That's where I've seen such eyes. I was not mistaken. They're a part of this somehow.

He glanced sidelong at the group of robed women waiting by the stage.

By the saints, don't let it be that.

Three of the bound captives on the stage had come awake again during the tall man's speech. They thrashed and kicked helplessly, desperate to break their bonds, driven by raw, mortal dread. The enforcers at the corners stepped forwards to pacify them, but a wave of something rippled through the air of the chamber once again. Ordimas had the sudden inexplicable urge to move backwards, but the command was not meant for him. He stood where he was while the enforcers on stage reacted. They bowed low and retreated, leaving the bound figures to twist and vent their muffled screams in utter futility.

At another mental pulse, the cloaked men at the back of the stage moved forwards. They stooped over the kidnapped victims and reached down, then hefted them up, one victim over each broad shoulder, and turned to filter back through the dark doorway. The number of victims was odd, so the last of the robed figures carried only one body. Ordimas watched that hulking, misshapen man as he hauled his limp human cargo towards the dark portal. Just for a second, one of those long robe sleeves slid back, and Ordimas caught a brief flash – a glimpse, no more – of pale blue flesh, of fingers ending in curved black claws with a wicked gleam. Then the figure moved beyond sight, off down the tunnel and deeper into the maze beyond.

Mutants? thought Ordimas. Once again, he focused his gaze on the tall, strange man with the stave. *A psyker leading a mutant cult, harvesting people and converting them somehow? No. Something is missing. The miners and these others... They show no sign of mutation. What makes them obedient? If it was just a matter of psychic force, I'd be feeling it, warded or not. How is he controlling them?*

There was also the matter of the strange children to consider: the three-month gestation period, the eerie eyes, the cold, inhuman way they eschewed any normal childlike interaction. That didn't tie up all too cleanly with rogue psykers or mutant cults.

How are they linked to this?

Ordimas was to have his answer all too soon, and, in later moments of reflection, no matter how much he burned with the shame and horror of it, he could not forget what he did in that cold stone hall, deep in the rock of a cursed, doomed planet.

6

'Too slow. Too damned slow. I want another eight seconds shaved off this, or we keep running it till you drop.'

Watch Sergeant Andreas Kulle of the Silver Skulls Chapter stood behind a bank of flickering monitors with two other Deathwatch Space Marines and a trio of supporting tech-adepts clothed in the black and silver robes of Watch Support. High above, the moon of Damaroth filled two-thirds of the sky with its lambent blue bulk. Cloud patterns churned slowly, lazily on its surface.

Karras, his fatigues damp with sweat, sighed and looked up. He breathed deeply, taking a moment to mentally reset himself.

No shadows here. So much ambient light.

He glanced to his left, then to his right. Far off in the distance, the inner surface of the Watch fortress's great ring could be seen curving up towards the glowing moon. Even with his eyesight boosted far beyond that of a normal man, any detail of the structures on those far curves was lost to the vast expanse and the bluish haze.

The training was so different, so precise. Karras hadn't felt like this since his days as a Scout. There were similarities, of course: the endless hours of sensorium review and neuro-reactive simulation overseen by Lochaine and the rest of the Watch Librarius; the live-fire range practice and close combat drills designed with the physiology of alien opponents in mind. These things he had taken to with ease and familiarity. But this...

'You've got six minutes to prepare and board the Stormraven before we run it again,' Kulle boomed. 'Do better. Codicier Karras, a word please.'

Karras dropped his gaze from the heavens and walked over to

the group behind the monitors. Passing him, a small army of servitors walked and trundled into kill-block Ophidion to restore the building to its pre-assault state. It was the twentieth time they had done so since morning repast.

'Karras,' said Kulle with a nod. The Space Marines flanking him on either side, both being groomed for Watch sergeant status, also nodded, like mirror images on some kind of time delay.

'Sergeant,' said Karras.

'Analysis, please.'

'Much as before, sergeant. For the most part, it's the smoke-and-clear on that final room. Without enhanced vision modes or any kind of real-time tactical data-feed, our coordination is suffering. We're still adapting to this kind of rooftop insertion, and operating without power armour is causing the team to overcompensate. We're rushing things, so our timings are all over the place.'

Kulle looked at the brothers standing silently on either side.

'Comments,' he demanded.

The one on the left – hard-faced Brother Ghan of the Aurora Chapter – was eager to speak first. 'They should have the method of entry down by now, sergeant. This performance is unacceptable. Eight seconds is a lifetime in tactical asset recovery.'

Karras had to force himself not to scowl at the acerbic, red-bearded Space Marine. How fast had *he* adjusted to Deathwatch methodology? Fast-roping, rooftop insertions, window entries; in general, Space Marine warfare was waged without the need for such subtle things. Brutal and direct was standard. The Adeptus Astartes marched proudly out to sow death among man's foes. They didn't sneak in through windows with silenced weapons. Such work was for assassins.

Assassins and Deathwatch operatives, apparently.

A kill-team was a precision tool, called upon to handle anti-xenos operations that other forces simply could not – the exact words of the Watch Commander at the induction ceremony. Well, what better way to cripple an enemy force than eliminate its leadership? Fast, efficient, effective. A single bolter-round could change the face of an entire war.

Perhaps there *was* something to be said for this kind of approach.

'Brother Procion?' said Kulle.

The other observer, bearing the silver cross icon of the Iron Knights, smiled. 'Brother Karras mastered this MoE on the third run. He speaks as if the fault were shared when it is not. Of course, to some extent, an Alpha *should* see the team's flaws as his own. But it is the Fire Lord who is slowing them down. Brother Uphreidi should switch positions with the Invader, Mannix. Dropping from the rear hatch might suit him better.'

'Thoughts, Karras?' said Kulle.

'Uphreidi and Mannix shall switch as recommended,' replied Karras. 'I thank Brother Procion for the advice.'

Karras saw Ghan scowl and shake his head. Kulle and Procion missed it. The Aurora Space Marine rarely offered anything but criticism, and none of it particularly useful. He verbally compared everything he saw against his own past performance, seeing this training session only as a chance to expound his own virtues in front of Kulle.

Procion, on the other hand, had been constructive from the start. Still, Karras was frustrated, and the source of that frustration was Watch Sergeant Andreas Kulle.

Was Kulle really running this exercise for the benefit of the new Watch members? Or was his true goal the evaluation of the ne-sergeants[13] he had brought along?

Karras felt he and the other trainees deserved better than that.

'You asked for another eight seconds cut, sergeant,' he said brusquely. 'Might I ask how you yourself would achieve it?'

Kulle met Karras's gaze and found it hard and penetrating, like a spear-tip.

There it is, thought the Silver Skull. *He knows I've been distracted. Ghan and Procion have waited long enough for our decision, but I needed to be absolutely sure. Very well, Death Spectre. I have all the information I need, in any case.*

'Brother Procion. Brother Ghan. You are dismissed for now,' said Kulle without turning to them. 'Return to quarters and write up your conclusions. Have them ready by evening assembly. I'll read them after last litany.'

Both the Space Marines looked less than happy at being sent off, but saluted Kulle stiffly with right fist to chest. 'For the honour of the Watch,' they intoned together. Then they turned and stalked towards a cluster of block-shaped buildings a few hundred metres to the south. One of these blocks was the Mag-line node from where they would take an auto-carriage back to their chapel-barracks.

Karras did not imagine the journey would be one of friendly banter. He looked at Kulle, awaiting his attention.

The Watch sergeant's light grey eyes followed the two candidates as they departed. When they were gone, he said, 'Ghan won't make it. He served with distinction on Squad Cerberus for eighteen years, but he hasn't the mindset for a Watch sergeant. He'll be given another kill-team or he'll be released to return to his Chapter. Procion, though…'

---

13. ne-sergeants – candidates for advancement to the position of Watch sergeant. By Deathwatch conventions, the prefix ne– denotes a candidate under consideration for further honour.

The sergeant turned his gaze back to Karras. 'In a Deathwatch kill-team, the weakness of one is the weakness of all. The Alpha *must* know the identity and nature of the weakest link. It is his role to correct for that weakness or, if possible, to eliminate it entirely.'

'I did not realise it was Uphreidi who was slowing the insertion,' said Karras.

'You suspected another,' said Kulle, grinning. 'Good. I have the advantage of the monitors, and you are operating without helm or gift, so allowances must be made, but I'm glad you saw it. The insertion *is* an issue, as Procion pointed out, but storming the final room – the smoke-and-clear stage of the assault – is at least half of your problem. You realise that one of your team is deliberately hampering you?'

'Hampering, yes, but deliberately?'

Kulle dropped his grin. 'I told Procion and Ghan not to say anything. I'm glad you noticed. It is the Ultramarine, Solarion. He has been undermining the team's performance since the first run, clearing the west hallway at a stroll, breaching his assigned door a full second after everyone else goes in. If it were just incompetence, I would swap him out, but the Deathwatch sequesters no incompetents to its ranks. If he were such, he would not be here. I've seen his feeds. He is an exemplary operator. He is almost certainly throwing you off by choice. Have you clashed before? Is there some history we should know about?'

Karras was speechless. The Ultramarine? They had not even shared words before this day.

A flat, grille-distorted voice spoke from beside the bank of monitors on the left. It was one of the tech-priests. 'The kill-block is reset, Watch sergeant. The servitor crews have withdrawn. The Stormraven is ready.'

'What will you do about Solarion?' Kulle asked Karras.

As the Stormraven powered up its turbines on the far right, Karras wrestled with a fury that had lit inside him. Turning his will upon it like a torrent of icy water, he forced himself to extinguish it. Emotion would not serve. It was efficiency the Deathwatch demanded. He could see only one way to get it.

'I'll partner with him. Mannix will take the west hall. Solarion moves with me. We'll see how he likes that.'

Kulle's grin returned, predatory, like the blade-toothed smile of a Cestean crocophid. 'Just don't *accidentally* shoot him, brother. A friendly fire incident will look bad on my report.'

His gaze shifted over Karras's right shoulder to the area by the ammo tables where the others had finished resupplying and prepping their weapons. Dropping his grin, he shouted over at them:

'Back in the Stormraven, you cack-handed sloths. The twenty-first time is the charm!'

7

Higgan Dozois ran his eyes over the woman's form for the thousandth time, drinking it in with the same pleasure he always did. It was something he did on reflex now, something he seemed incapable of resisting. There she stood before the viewport, back towards him, utterly indifferent to him despite every card he had played over the last seven weeks. He rolled his gaze over the sweep of her hips, the long slender legs in their glossy black breeches, the shapely calves that fitted snugly into the tops of her spike-heeled boots. She shifted, and her black hair shimmered in the pale cream light of the viewing deck.

What a torment she is, thought Dozois. *I swear she delights in taunting me. Only an hour to groundside, and then it's over. All those weeks, all those hours together, and she's given me nothing. If she wasn't paying so well...*

It still rankled despite that princely sum. He had been a gentleman from the start, naturally. She had dined nightly at the captain's table. He had given her the very best quarters on his ship, save his own, of course. He had plied her with fine wines, rare dishes, high-minded conversation, games for two. He had even stated his desires plainly when all else had proven futile. But this woman, born of a Noble House with more financial troubles than his own if reports read true, rebuffed his every advance.

Dozois, who was not an unhandsome man and heir to a significant portion of his House's wealth, could not understand it. He had always enjoyed a fine measure of success with female passengers. But then, he had never wanted to bed a woman quite so much as he wanted Lady Fara Devanon. Once again, he allowed his eyes to trace those hips. *Exquisite*. Perhaps that was the problem. Perhaps she sensed his eagerness and was repulsed by it. *Far too late to affect indifference now,* thought Dozois. *Journey's end.* He and his crew had brought her, as contracted, to Chiaro. Her House sought to secure industrial supply contracts here, though why it should hope to do so on a planet so far from any major Imperial trading lanes was beyond him. She had made some vague reference to a distant familial tie here. Dozois had been too busy admiring the graceful line of her neck to pay much attention.

He had examined her cargo on loading, as was his right: mining lasers and heavy machinery for the most part, some consumables, very little of interest to him personally. They would sell, he guessed – perhaps even at a decent mark-up – but, according to his own sources, Chiaro's output had been in decline for decades. It rather looked as if House Devanon was locking the gates after the grox had bolted, so to speak.

All of which means what? Dozois asked himself bitterly. *What do you care? Get her off the* Macedon *and be done with it.*

He had other contracts waiting and, while none would pay quite as well as the Devanon contract, they ought at least to cause him less frustration.

Lady Fara spoke, bringing him back to the moment. Even her smooth voice, the voice of a woman trained and educated to the upper limits of her House's provision, stoked the fires of his lust.

'I had seen picts, of course,' she told him without turning from the window. 'But its strangeness only really becomes apparent to the naked eye, don't you think?'

Dozois walked across to stand by her side. Even a metre away, he imagined he could feel the heat of her body. Testily, he tried to focus on the planet below.

'I've seen no rock like it,' he conceded. 'Though I've seen countless eggs of that very shape.'

The lady didn't bother to laugh.

'You see the dark band there?' she said, pointing. 'The Nystarean Gorge. It runs the entire circumference of the planet. Four kilometres deep on average. Quite remarkable.'

Dozois followed the direction of the woman's long finger. 'I've read the dossier,' he told her, and was surprised at the churlish quality in his voice. Quickly, he reeled himself in and added in gentler tones, 'There's an ongoing debate, I believe, about the origin of the canyon. Solid arguments that it's artificial, you know. Crafted by some ancient xenos race, they say. Then again, they say many things, don't they?'

'I could believe it, captain. In fact, I'm sure I could believe anything about this world. Strangeness seems built into its very fabric.'

Dozois couldn't dispute that. Chiaro was unique in all his experience, and his travels had taken him to the rimward boundaries of two segmenta. Nothing he had seen looked quite like this.

Chiaro's axis of rotation pointed directly at the heart of its local star, Ienvo, meaning that, unlike other worlds, there was no day-night cycle. To the ground-dwellers who lived on the canyon floor, only the stars in the sky appeared to change as the planet rolled on its axis. The floor of the Nystarean Gorge was suitable for human habitation, but nowhere else was. Chiaro's northern hemisphere was constantly bathed in Ienvo's flesh-crisping glare, while the southern hemisphere was eternally dark and deathly cold.

Nightside and Dayside, thought Dozois, *and men eking out an existence in the narrow gap between. Poor sods. Give me a captain's life or none at all.*

The Nystarean Gorge might be habitable, but men didn't fill all that much of it. There were only two major cities on Chiaro: Najra and Cholixe. A mere six hundred and ninety kilometres stood between them.

Cholixe, the larger of the two, was populated mostly by the Garrahym people, a racial minority on their home world of Delta III Ragash. The Garrahym had been brought to Chiaro en masse to work the freezing mines of Nightside. According to the files Lady Fara had shared, the Garrahym were a hardy, stocky breed prone to quick violence and high alcohol consumption. These facts in themselves were of little interest to Dozois – his holds carried little alcohol and even less weaponry. But he knew from experience that elements of such a culture would also be prone to certain chemical addictions – a fact that did much to brighten his mood. As profitable as Lady Fara's patronage might be for the captain and crew of the *Macedon*, he could hardly have kept his ship in fuel if not for his trade in *yaga*. The shipping and selling of the illegal narcotic root was punishable by death, but it was so potent and so difficult to detect through traditional scanning methods, that modest quantities could easily be hidden, then suitably diluted and mixed with reagents once the target market was reached. There would be demand in Cholixe, Dozois was sure. Few ships other than Adeptus Mechanicus cargo freighters ever landed here, and the priests of the Omnissiah offered no competition in black-market goods. They cared little for anything save their mad obsession with technology.

Najra, the smaller of Chiaro's two cities despite being the official capital, was a different matter. Dozois did not plan to go there. For whatever reason, Lady Fara's appointments were in Cholixe only, and she had commissioned transport solely to that city. A pity in some respects, for Dozois preferred the bustle of planetary capitals when he went groundside, but he doubted he would be missing all that much this time around. Najra's populace were far less likely to indulge in the dangerously addictive joys of his wares. The people of that city were Hasmiri: devout, hard-working, and pledged to the ascetical teachings of their beloved Saint Sufra. They worked Dayside, excavating and mining the machine-cooled tunnels below the northern hemisphere's baking surface. Sufra had been one of those sour-faced saints who spent his whole life condemning pleasure in any and every form. No. There would be little business for Dozois among the Hasmiri.

Just Cholixe, then, Dozois told himself. *Just the Garrahym. Drop, sell and split. And good riddance to this devil-temptress!*

'Don't you think?'

Dozois started, suddenly aware the lady had been speaking to him while his thoughts had turned to business.

'Forgive me, m'lady,' he said with a forced smile. 'I was miles away. You were talking about the origin of the gorge? No conclusive explanations, even after millennia of human occupation. I think we may never know the answers to Chiaro's riddles. Then again, if the Martian priesthood ever did uncover its secrets, would we ever know? I doubt it.'

Lady Fara turned to face him and smiled back with red lips of the most exquisite shape. Dozois thought he heard blood rushing through his ears, red cells rasping on the inner surface of his veins. 'There are some mysteries we ought not to solve, don't you think?' the lady purred. 'What would life be without a little mystery?'

Now or never, thought the captain. *A last charge.*

'Mystery has its place,' he concurred, leaning slightly forwards, 'and yet, what satisfaction is there in a question unanswered? We have an hour, dear Fara,' he said, deliberately opting to drop her rightful prefix. 'Shall we not finally answer the question which has hung over us both since you came aboard?'

Lady Fara feigned confusion. 'And what question is that, my good captain?'

See how she plays the game.

Dozois inched a little closer and made bed-eyes. 'The question that always stands between a man and a woman, my dear. Simply, how good would it be?'

Lady Fara lapsed abruptly into delighted, almost musical laughter. She put a cool white hand to his cheek and, once her laughter had subsided, told him, 'I have enjoyed you so, captain. Truly, your company and your humour have made a long, dull journey that much more bearable, and for that I thank you.'

Dozois's smile was painted on. She... she was actually *laughing* at him. Did she think him some kind of joke?

'I must rouse my entourage,' she told him, dropping her hand from his face. 'We must make ready for the drop. Until then.'

With that, she turned and strode towards the doors at the far end of the room. The yellowing scan-skull above the doorway detected her. Red lights blinked green in its sockets. The door hissed open with twin bursts of greasy steam. Dozois stood numb, watching her go. Without turning, Fara Devanon slinked through the door and out into the corridor, hips rolling like the flanks of a sleek black panther.

The captain turned his eyes back to the viewport and to the bizarre planet below.

Seven weeks, he thought bitterly. *Seven bloody weeks. And nothing for me but mockery. To the blasted warp with you, whore. May your precious mysteries swallow your soul down there.*

Shianna Varlan, Interrogator Class 3 of the Ordo Xenos of His Imperial Majesty's Holy Orders of the Inquisition, stalked off down the corridor at a steady pace, heels clicking on the plasteel floor. She followed a route that would take her back to her quarters aboard the *Macedon* for the last time, and to the aides that awaited her there. So much to do in this last hour before boarding the drop-shuttle. This accursed journey was almost over, thank the Throne. It had been all too long and tortuous. The insufferable captain had barely given her a moment's peace: invitations every time he sat at table, requests for her personal company at regular readings given by the ship's chaplain, the constant battering innuendo while they played hand after hand of *Heretic!* together. His eyes were on her all the time. She detested it. The way his gaze played over her was almost a physical, tangible thing, like invisible hands groping. All men were the same, little better than beasts.

No. Not all, Shianna, she reminded herself. *His Lordship is different.*

Still, such unwelcome attention was hardly new to her. Fine genes were one of the primary assets for which she had been chosen, and she used them to the fullest, as she was expected to, even commanded to. But orders or not, it made her feel unclean, and that in turn made her wrathful. She had hated Dozois from the first, that simple, foolish man. But, as was always the case, greater need had forced her to put personal feelings aside. She had played her role to perfection: Lady Fara Devanon, aristocratic daughter of a minor House struggling to improve its lot; a woman firm in the knowledge of her feminine allure, but aware, too, that this was a coin to be spent only once. Give a man like Dozois exactly what he sought and you lost all power over him. The character Lady Fara, much like the woman who played her, valued her self-respect.

Pray we do not meet under other circumstances, you inbred fool! For I'll surely kill you if we do.

Thoughts only, an empty threat, but the mental image that accompanied them pleased her. In all likelihood, she would never see Dozois again after today. It was time to put the foolish man aside, time to focus on the next phase of the operation. Her transit to Chiaro was at its end. On arrival in Cholixe, her work would begin in earnest.

She knew little of what lay ahead, but that was hardly new either. According to His Lordship, there were other assets already in play. Something on Chiaro had demanded the special attention of the Ordo Xenos. She would discover its nature soon enough.

And then, if so commanded, she would destroy it.

8

The black bulk of the Stormraven assault transport hovered ten metres over the kill-block roof on tongues of blue fire. Cables dropped from side and rear hatches. There was a sharp shout from inside.

'Kill-team, go!'

Three slab-muscled figures in black fatigues dropped at speed, controlling their descent with gloved hands only. Slung across their backs were boltguns, slightly smaller and more compact than those they were used to. Cinched around waist and chest, they wore combat webbing stocked with grenades and other tactical equipment. Boots hit the rooftop with a subdued, tread-muffled thump. Immediately, the three spread out, securing east, west and north edges of the building, leaning out, visually sweeping the windows and balconies below for sign of enemy sentries.

Two others dropped a second later. Onboard winches whipped the droplines back up, and the Stormraven lifted away, tilting as it left the infil point.

The last two figures to drop darted to the north edge of the roof. As soon as they were in place, all five operatives pulled a small pistol-like device from a holster in their webbing, pressed the muzzle to the permacrete lip at the edge of the roof, and pulled the trigger. There was a crumping sound and five little coughs of dust. Each figure pulled on his pistol and a length of black polyfibre cable started to unspool from inside the grip. With a brief tug to check each line was secure, the five stepped onto the permacrete lip, turned, and dropped backwards from the edges of the roof.

Karras pushed off with his legs, flying out a little way from the surface of the wall, and released the trigger on the pistol. He dropped about three metres, then pulled the trigger again, arresting his descent. He swung back in and braced his legs on the wall, then bunched his muscles, ready for another push off. To his right, Ignacio Solarion, the Ultramarine, did the same. When Karras had paired them up, he'd said nothing, but the look on his face had hardly been one of joy.

Below, a broad semicircular balcony extended out from the wall. From that balcony, a wide set of plastek double-doors offered access to the kill-block's rooms and corridors.

Together, Karras and Solarion dropped to the balcony and abandoned their ziplines. They took position on either side of the double doors, backs pressed to the wall. Solarion looked over at Karras, his pale blue eyes cold and hard. Karras nodded for him to proceed. From his webbing, Solarion took a small canister with a long, tubular nozzle, then stuck his head out to check there were no hostiles on the other side of the panes of transparent plastek Seeing none, he stepped to the centre, lifted his canister, and began to spray a large, irregular outline – bigger than himself – directly onto the glassy surface. Corrosive black foam began to bubble as it ate away at the windows' molecular bonds.

With the outline finished, Solarion returned the canister to its pouch and gripped the doors' outer handles.

Karras was counting in his head. At sixteen, he gave the go.

Solarion tugged the handles and two large pieces of frame and glass came away in his hands – no shattering, only the slightest sound of breakage.

The Ultramarine turned and laid the pieces carefully down. Karras moved inside in a half-crouch, bolter raised, stock pressed to shoulder. He heard quiet footfalls behind him as Solarion followed.

SpACE, thought Karras, sweeping the room.

The Watch sergeants had drummed it into them since the beginning of day two.

Spacing, Angles, Corners, Exits.

This room was clear, but it might not have been. Kulle kept changing enemy dispersal every time he sent them in. He kept changing the sentry patrol patterns, too.

Beyond the door in the far side lay the north hallway from which he and Solarion would proceed to the objective room. Moving fast, Karras placed himself on the right of the door. Solarion took his place on the left. Each signalled readiness to the other. So far, so good.

Karras reached out a gloved hand and pressed the access rune. The door slid sideways into its housing. Before it had finished, Karras was already out in the corridor, muzzle covering the left.

'Contact!'

A ghostly eldar sentry spun and, on seeing Karras, raised the fluted muzzle of its alien pistol.

Karras's bolter coughed quietly and the tall, slender alien crumpled, then flickered with greenish static, blurred into lower resolution and disappeared altogether. In the wall behind where it had stood, a small black crater bled thin wisps of smoke. A hololithic projector in the ceiling above buzzed briefly, its indicator light changing from green to red. Karras turned.

Behind him, Solarion had taken out a similar target.

'Let's move,' said Karras, indicating southwards. Together, Karras hugging the left wall and Solarion the right, they stalked off down the now unguarded corridor. As they proceeded closer to the central chamber at the far end, they kept their muzzles level, covering the metal apertures on either side and the corridor junction ahead where the path split east and west. There was no time to clear each side chamber in this high-speed secure-for-extraction exercise.

The scenario was simple: three high-value Imperial Naval personnel had been taken alive by so-called dark eldar during a xenos assault on an Imperial outpost. The Navy personnel each held critical strategic information, none of which overlapped, meaning all three needed to be recovered alive before they could be broken by cruel xenos torture or mind-manipulation. They were designated Apollon-level assets; the loss of even one during the operation meant a mission failure.

Kill-block Ophidion didn't look like any space port Karras had ever seen, of course, but that hardly mattered. A little imagination was often called for during training.

A metal door on the right slid upwards and a spidery figure emerged: black hair pinned up with small white bones, pointed ears on either side of a long, narrow, olive-skinned face.

Solarion dropped the target before its shoulders had even cleared the doorway. The image of the dark eldar spun, flickered and rezzed out, giving its simulated cohorts in the room behind it ample warning that they were under attack. Bone-like muzzles suddenly bristled from the doorway. Enemy fire blazed into the hallway. The holo-projected shots whined and buzzed through the air above Karras's head, given worrying realism by the kill-block's advanced audio system.

'Blood and blazes!' he hissed.

Solarion dropped to a full crouch and fired back, bolts smacking into the doorframe behind which the hostiles hid. These rounds didn't detonate as bolter-rounds usually did. They were practice bolts, nicknamed *clippers* – low-velocity, non-explosive slugs of the type used in kill-block training as standard. Sparks leapt from each harmless impact.

Multiple roused targets in hard cover, thought Karras bitterly. *The run is practically scuppered already. That idiot knows better. Kulle was right about him trying to undermine me.*

Over the link, he heard the others report that they were in position around the target room. Karras couldn't let them storm that room without either he or Solarion coming in from the north side. He wouldn't send them in to be cut down knowing that Kulle always kept the hostages heavily guarded. There would be too many foes inside for three operatives to handle without a casualty or two, Space Marines or not.

Gritting his teeth, he made his decision. He marked the distance to the door from which all the fire was coming, then pulled a smoke grenade from his webbing. Arming it, he tossed it just in front of the enemy. With a hiss, thick grey smoke billowed out, quickly filling the confines of the corridor and much of the side chamber. Visibility dropped to nothing, but Karras had everything he needed in his head. He tugged a frag grenade free and burst into a low run. The aliens were blind-firing now. He did his best to cut a safe path through their simulated barrage. Behind him, Solarion was still firing at the shrouded door, though he could no more see it now than Karras could. At least his fire offered some suppression. Maybe Karras wouldn't be cut to pieces.

Or maybe I will, but he has left me no choice.

Between the smoke and the covering fire, it was enough. As Karras passed the door, he didn't slow, but he tossed the primed frag grenade inside, and kept running straight through the choking cloud and beyond it. Ahead of him, where the corridors formed a T-junction, the north entrance to the objective room loomed large. He put on a burst of speed. Over the link, he growled, 'Space Marines, breach in three...'

His feet pounded the floor. Six metres to go.

'Two...'

Closer.

'One...'

Closer.

'Go,' he barked. Behind him, his grenade detonated. Like the clipper rounds in his bolter, the grenade was a modified training version, packed with only enough explosive to generate a loud noise. Smoke still lingered to hide the results from view, but four projected dark eldar flickered into non-existence and a cluster of indicator lights turned from green to red.

Karras was already beyond thinking about any of that. All that mattered was the hostage room, the double-doors of which raced towards him. He was supposed to breach them with a small demo charge, but there was no time. Solarion had seen to that. With a grunt, he hurled himself forwards, slamming his left shoulder hard into the centre of the doors.

There was a great crack as locks and hinge mechanisms ripped from the frame. Like a living juggernaut, Karras exploded through it to the other side, just as his other three team members – Uphreidi, Mannix, and Ansul of the Sons of Sanguinius – stormed the room from south, east and west. Silenced bolters coughed. The dark eldar within had heard the grenade detonate just a fraction of a second before the kill-team burst in – all save Solarion, that is, who was now bringing up the rear. Eight of the cruel-faced xenos had spun towards the doors, raising their strange weapons a moment too late. Clipper rounds whipped through them and they vanished like ghosts. That had been in the first second. In the next, Karras's team cut down the four remaining foes, all of whom were moving to execute their hostages – three small, nervous-looking men in the starched uniforms and gold brocade of the Admiralty. One of the dark eldar almost succeeded, his black sword about to fall, but there came the sound of a single muffled shot from behind Karras, and the alien disappeared with his vile kin.

That last kill belonged to Solarion. He stepped into the room and looked around.

'Clear,' said Brother Mannix.

'Clear,' echoed each of the others.

'Secure the exits,' Karras told them. 'Overwatch on all approaches.'

The three Naval personnel disappeared now, just like the eldar, fizzling out as if they had never been there at all. Of course, they hadn't.

Adrenaline pumping, hearts still hammering in his ears, Karras opened a vox-channel to Watch Sergeant Kulle.

'Alpha here, sergeant. Objectives secured. No casualties. Ready for exfil.'

'What was that in the hallway, Alpha? That was a damned mess. If you hadn't rammed those doors, we'd be looking at total asset loss.'

'I know, sergeant,' Karras growled. He glared over at Solarion. The Ultramarine had his back to him, his eyes turned outwards to the corridor he was covering.

That fool. What's his issue? I'll have an explanation, by the Throne.

'What was our time?'

'Better,' said Kulle. 'You shaved off three seconds with that death-or-glory run of yours. Still, that's not how we like to see things done around here.'

'It shouldn't have happened.'

'No, it should not. But you thought fast. You'll be remembered for it.'

'I think... What?'

There was a pause on the other end of the link that Karras didn't much like, then Kulle said, 'You're a dead man, Karras. Right about now, you'd be doubled over on the floor vomiting up what's left of your dissolving organs. When you rushed the side doorway and dropped that grenade, an enemy round took you in the upper left thigh. The dark eldar use powerful toxins. Some of them are beyond even the *Purifier's*[14] abilities. You would have lived long enough to storm the room, but, if this were anything but an exercise, I'd be talking to your Two right now, not to you. Even your progenoids[15] would be lost.'

Karras stood stunned. His progenoids ruined? So, not only had the surly Ultramarine gotten him killed, he had robbed him of the honour of providing that final genetic legacy to his Chapter. No Space Marine could stomach thoughts of such a death.

He thundered over to where Solarion stood and spun him violently around. Placing a big hand on the Ultramarine's throat, Karras slammed him against the doorframe and drove him up into the air, his back pressed hard against it.

Solarion reacted at once, throwing a blistering left hook at Karras's temple. But Karras still had a free hand. He raised his elbow and redirected the blow.

'If you ever do anything like that again, you piece of–'

Solarion brought his knees up fast and used them to lever Karras back. Overextended, Karras had to let the Ultramarine drop. Solarion landed in stance, ready to defend himself.

'Ever do what, witchblood?' he spat.

'You know damned well,' said Karras, eyes blazing at the slur.

Solarion's snarl became a sneer. 'I told them you weren't equal to this. The Death Spectres? What great part have you played in history? A third-tier Chapter stuck out in the middle of nowhere. Your home world isn't even within the bounds of the Imperium. And they put *you* in charge of *me*?'

Eyes still on Karras, he bent and retrieved his fallen bolter.

'I was called to Damaroth because I'm the best,' insisted Solarion,

---

14. The Purifier – phase 14 implant known more properly as the oolitic kidney, which purges toxins from a Space Marine's body.

15. Progenoids – two extremely important glands – phase 18 implants – that grow inside a living Space Marine; they contain the genetic seeds of all other implant organs and are used to make more Space Marines. There is no other way.

his conviction absolute. 'The Ultramarine before me was a kill-team leader, and the one before him. I'll not be subordinate to the likes of you.'

'I didn't make that decision,' Karras threw back.

'But it suits you well enough.'

Karras felt something stir that he had thought locked away. His rage must have broken through somehow, momentarily pushing him beyond the limiting power of the warp field suppressor on his spine.

His gift flared like a struck match, not the blaze it should have been, not even close to the eldritch strength he had known before, but it was there, enough to feel, enough to lash out with before he could restrain himself.

Balefire licked upwards from his eyes. The space around him pulsed.

Solarion was lifted into the air by powerful invisible hands and hurled against the far wall. He crashed into it with a grunt, then dropped hard to the floor. He righted himself quickly and stood glaring across the room at Karras. A strange smile spread his lips. 'And now you've struck me,' he said with icy calm.

Karras felt an immediate rush of shame. This was not how things should be. He knew the glory of the Ultramarines. He would never, could never, have imagined attacking one like this.

What has gotten into me? Where is my self-control? Is my anger due to the insult, or to the sealing of my power? I had not thought my equilibrium so dependent on it. They were right to seal it away. I see now that my dependence is a weakness I must overcome.

There was blood on Solarion's lip. He wiped it off with the back of his hand. The other three Space Marines stood in tense silence, unsure whether to step in or not. They had all heard it; Karras's honour had been insulted beyond reasonable tolerance, even to the most lenient among them. But the Ultramarines were greatly respected. For the most part, at least, they were paragons of what it meant to be a Space Marine.

Karras heard Kulle lambasting them over the link.

'Stand down, both of you! Do not force me to use the neural interrupt. Codicier Karras, I want to see you down here now.' He paused before adding, 'You're not supposed to be able to do that.'

Karras briefly considered apologising to Solarion, but the fool had insulted his Chapter. The psychic assault had been wrong, but the Ultramarine's ignorant words were no less so. Instead, he said nothing and strode from the room. There was a staircase to the left, down the west corridor, that led to the front exit on the ground level. He took this and, as he walked down the steps, he heard Kulle addressing him again, this time on a closed channel. 'They told me the suppression field was set to maximum. What did you do?'

'He went too far,' said Karras, voice flat now.

'It happens. But overloading the implant... That does not.'

Karras couldn't find it in himself to care about the implant and the expectations the Watch Council placed on it. His power had overridden it only briefly, just long enough to make a bad situation worse. It had subsided now. He tried to call it up again, to create a ball of balefire in his hand, but the implant blocked him as before. It was fury that had overcome it, not will or need. Just rage, plain and simple.

'The Ultramarine crossed the line, sergeant,' he told Kulle, 'but my response crossed it further. I will endure whatever punishment I must.'

'We shall see,' said Kulle. 'For my part, I say he had it coming, but I shall have to consult with the council.'

'I understand.'

'Now,' said the Silver Skull, 'get your team down here and prep for the next run. You've got six minutes.' After a pause, he added, 'I'll have to work out how to report this.'

Karras halted on the stairs, unable to believe what he was hearing.

'Are you serious, sergeant?' he asked. 'We're to run the exercise again?'

'I don't joke about kill-block training, Librarian. Not ever. Get down here and prep for infil. We've still got five seconds to cut!'

9

Captain Dozois's farewell surprised Varlan with its brevity. She had gotten deeper under his skin than she had realised. He was bitter and angry, and he struggled visibly to keep it in check. During a descent that felt much longer than it was, he refused to look at her. When addressed, he clenched his jaw and offered only one-word answers or made short, mumbled comments mostly directed at himself. That suited Varlan fine. She was relieved when they finally hit groundside, knowing the moment she would be free of his company was close at hand. Even then, however, with the cargo shuttle settling on its thick metal feet, Dozois sat tense, barely looking at her across the craft's well-appointed passenger cabin. She half expected him to order her out.

There was the matter of his fee, of course, and for that, he finally had to engage her directly. Varlan, or rather Lady Fara as she was still known to him, presented a black case made of a hard, light ceramic. Dozois placed the case on his lap, entered the code exactly as the lady instructed, and opened it. The gems within sparkled in the light from the overhead lumes. He called a child-sized servitor out from an alcove in the wall and had it run a substance analysis. Emeralds from the vaults of House Devanon, just as agreed. Superb quality. Everything checked out. Paid in full, he closed the case and handed it to his first officer, Sarapho, whom he ordered to await him in his quarters.

When the doors hissed shut behind Sarapho's back, Dozois stood stiffly and offered his hand. 'Our business is concluded, Lady Fara,' he said coolly, meaning to dismiss her without further ado.

Varlan stood, much amused by the change in his demeanour since earlier in the day, and took the outstretched hand. She noted that he did not give hers a playful squeeze this time. He had abandoned all hope at last. Throne knew, it had taken long enough. *If only the captain of the* Macedon *had been a woman*, Varlan thought to herself.

'Will you be staying groundside for long, captain?' she asked.

'A week, perhaps,' Dozois replied, not quite meeting her gaze. 'Maybe two. We'll secure provisions, fuel and such – see what the locals have to offer by way of trade goods. I have other concerns awaiting my attention, however, so I can't dally overlong on this rock. I doubt our paths will cross again before I return to my ship.'

'Oh, how regrettable,' Varlan lied, and did not care that he knew it. 'Still, such is the busy life of a starship captain. I shan't keep you. I shall simply thank you again for your hospitality and wish you every success.'

If it was a polite smile Dozois attempted, he failed. It came out as a bizarre sort of anguished sneer.

'Emperor guide you and watch over you, lady,' he said without feeling, and promptly released her hand.

Varlan turned and strode to the cabin's forward exit. Before she passed beyond it, she stopped to nod her thanks one last time, half expecting the captain's eyes to be on her as usual. But Dozois was already making for the other exit in the far wall.

She didn't quite know if she felt perversely disappointed or satisfied, or both.

One week, she thought. *Maybe two. Will this operation be concluded by then? I'd not travel with him outwards unless so ordered. Better to wait for a Mechanicus ship, though the next won't be due for months.*

She'd know better after consulting with the Ordo's assets on the ground.

Minutes later, descending the shuttle's ramp to the black rockcrete of the landing field, Varlan was met by her aides, Oroga and Myrda. The twins fell in behind her, walking in step, lens-eyes scanning the tall stacks of cargo crates for any sign of threat. Their heavy arm-augmetics were concealed by coat sleeves and kratyd-skin gloves. Knives and stunners were likewise well concealed. To the untrained eye, they would have seemed mere aides. To the trained, they would have appeared bodyguards, for they moved with a predator's balance and grace. In truth, they filled both roles, allowing Varlan to maintain such a small retinue that she tended to draw far less attention than she otherwise might. Accountability was forever an issue in her work. She was under no illusions about that; drawing an excess of scrutiny by storming around cities with a large, intimidating group of oath-bonded warriors and agents would render her far less useful to His Lordship. While her false identity remained solid, she had undercover access to Imperial social strata beyond what could normally be reached. Lady Fara Devanon had as comprehensive and verifiable a history as any member of a minor House, even if it was entirely fabricated. Varlan would do nothing to jeopardise that. Which is why, when a gaggle of short men in blue tunics walked out to meet her from the space port's main arrivals building, she hid her irritation. She had suspected this might happen. From the moment Chiaro GDC had received the *Macedon*'s passenger list, her name would have been flagged. Nobility always drew note. Sure enough, the local governor had sent his agents to greet her, and here they were.

The men, of which there were four, stopped in Varlan's path and bowed low. She sensed Oroga and Myrda readying themselves for violence – a subtle repositioning apparent only to her. The twins were as adept at concealment as she was. Their readiness to kill was a thing sensed on the air rather than seen. It seemed that the men in blue tunics did not sense it. They paid no heed whatsoever.

Or perhaps they do, and are themselves adept at concealment.

An interrogator took nothing at face value.

As the men emerged from their bows, one spoke. 'Do I have the honour of addressing the notable and esteemed Lady Fara Devanon?' he said, his tone high, slightly wheezy, like wind in a hollow reed.

'To whom would I be responding, sir?' replied Varlan with a demure smile.

The man returned the smile broadly, though the gesture did not reach his eyes. Varlan thought it gave him the aspect of a frightened ape.

'My lady,' he said, 'we are aides to the Lord High Arbitrator Nenahem Sannra, Planetary Governor of Chiaro under His Holiness the Emperor of Mankind. My name is Suliman, though you may call me Sul if it pleases you. I am Aide Primaris to the Lord High Arbitrator.'

'Then I bid you well met, Sul, and I ask what business you have with me. I have only just arrived from a seven-week warp journey. You will understand if suitable lodgings and rest are my current priority.'

Sul dipped his bald, liver-spotted head. He was not a young man. 'Indeed, ma'am,' he said. 'But perhaps, on that very matter, I can speak to your benefit, for my lord has sent me to ask that you and your party take accommodation in his Cholixe apartments. So fine and noble a visitor is rare on Chiaro, and my lord wishes to extend to you his hospitality. He tells me that the Houses of Sannra and Devanon may actually be related through a distant link with House Nandol.'

Varlan allowed herself a smile at that, well aware that her own master had arranged for this false information to be inserted into the relevant archives during her voyage here. 'Indeed. My paternal grandfather mentioned such to me once, as I recall. We lament the passing of House Nandol. Much was lost when they fell into ruin.'

Sul's expression spoke of a sorrow unfelt, but well feigned, 'Much was lost,' he echoed, 'but perhaps not all if a distant connection would persuade you to accept my lord's courtesy.'

Varlan had already decided it suited her to accept. Whatever lay ahead for her, currying the favour of the supreme authority on the planet ought to prove valuable. If not, it would further cement her false identity at the very least.

'Then the offer is accepted with gratitude,' she told Sul. 'However, I have certain commercial interests to which I must first attend. They should not take up more than an hour or so.' Here, she gestured to the tall stacks of metal crates to the left of the drop-shuttle – her cargo, already unloaded by the space port's servitors and slaves. Each crate bore the interlocking three-moon design of the seal of her purported House. 'Confer with my aide,' she said, indicating Myrda. 'When my business here is concluded, we shall be glad to follow your directions to the Lord High Arbitrator's estate.'

'You need follow no directions, my lady,' said Sul. 'We have armoured transports awaiting your leisure. We shall take you to my lord's apartments ourselves if you've no objection. But, please, do not hurry yourself on our account. We are instructed to wait as long as need be.'

Armoured, thought Varlan. *He needn't have said that. Interesting that he chose to. It seems all is not well on Chiaro, and the planetary governor is aware of it. Let us hope he is as free with his tongue as he is with his accommodation.*

'Your master's kindness is much appreciated,' Varlan told the little man. 'As is your service. Myrda? If you would, my dear.'

Myrda stepped forwards, introduced herself to the men in blue, and herded them away from the interrogator. Varlan maintained a grateful smile until their backs were turned. Then she spoke in urgent undertones to Oroga, who remained by her side.

'The cargo?' she asked.

'It will be taken to a storage facility close to the city centre,' answered Oroga in his deep baritone. 'The port servitors will start loading it onto freight cars as soon as you give the word. The buyers' representatives will inspect it this evening.'

'Have the servitors start loading at once. As for the buyers, encourage a bidding war for the sake of our cover. The sale itself is in your hands. Allow it to drag on if you can. We've no idea how much time we'll need here. If matters on Chiaro require our attention long-term, we'll have to contrive a solid pretence. Have you contacted the asset?'

Oroga nodded. 'Yes, ma'am. He was waiting for us nearby. I received a coded burst transmission three minutes after we landed. He seems well informed. He has secured a meeting place and awaits you there now. Access is by a small equipment storage hut to the left of the main arrivals building. It's just over there. You should be able to slip inside without drawing attention. Use the building's shadow. I've remotely disabled the appropriate lumes.'

Varlan turned and looked over at a little concrete block with a metal door, hardly discernable at all but for the lamps around the landing port's perimeter and the lit windows of the arrival and departure buildings.

Cholixe is so dark, she thought. *Eternal twilight. No true day. No true night. That ought to serve us well. Always in shadow are the affairs of the Inquisition conducted.*

'Neither myself nor Myrda had time to green-light the structure, ma'am,' said Oroga. 'Give the word and I shall go in your stead.'

'We're sure Asset 16 sent the message?'

'Identicode verification was immediate. It was a Thanatos-level code. Those codes are still listed green. They have not been compromised.'

'Then I will go alone.' She tapped her throat three times and Oroga nodded. He reached up and tapped his own twice. In her ear, Varlan heard the clicks.

Good. We have line-of-sight comms at least.

The implanted vox-comms augmentation she shared with her two aides was working as intended for now. She'd test it from inside the rendezvous structure to verify non-LoS capability. She didn't hold out much hope, however. Chiaro's rare metals were known to cause problems with small-scale, non-shielded communications devices.

'We'll take advantage of the Lord High Arbitrator's offer for now,' she told Oroga. 'See where that leads us. I'll know more once I debrief Asset 16. Now, walk with me towards the arrivals building. When I break away for the rendezvous, keep walking to the main door, then wait for me in the shadows there. I'll vox if I need you.'

'I'll be ready,' said Oroga, falling into step.

'I know you will,' said Varlan, and she set off across the dark rockcrete.

Having dismissed his pilot, ordering the man to get some rest, Higgan Dozois used the cargo shuttle's forward vid-picters to watch Lady Fara discreetly from the cockpit. On the main monitor, he saw her strike out for the arrivals building, then peel away from her aide, the male one, as they entered thick shadow. For a moment, he lost sight of her there. Then he saw movement – a door quickly opened and quickly shut, a slender figure passing within. He would not have seen anything at all but for the very dimmest orange glow of a work-lume somewhere inside the small square structure.

That was a utility hut. What was she doing? Why hadn't she gone straight to passenger processing?

From that moment, he discovered a burning need within him, a fire fed by seven weeks of frustration. There was something strange about Lady Fara Devanon, he convinced himself. He should have seen it before. She was not *right* somehow.

He decided a foolish thing then.

He decided to make her business his own.

10

Hour after endless hour the Space Marines drilled; over and over again in every conceivable form of close combat and small-unit special operations. The programme was organised into ten-hour cycles. First, the trainees would assemble in the main chapel for fifteen minutes of litany led by a senior Watch Chaplain called Qesos, a tall Space Marine of the Revilers Chapter with an unusually narrow frame and gaunt features. Despite his somewhat spare physique, his words smote the dank air of the nave like hammer on anvil, firing the blood of the assembled Space Marines for the rigours of the exercises to come.

After prayers, in which they petitioned the Emperor and the primarchs for increases in their already formidable skills, the Space Marines would assemble in the East Auditorium – a large skylighted hall hung with banners and pennants recalling the most glorious endeavours of those who had been trained here in days past. It was here, in this auditorium, facing the newest oath-takers on the tiered stone benches, that the Watch captains would announce the cycle's squad allocations and outline the training ahead. After this, there would be stern reminders, if any were needed, of the codes and strictures under which all those accepted into the Watch were expected to operate. During these, there were no small amount of side glances cast between bitter rivals. Already, Brother Keanor of the Dark Angels had engaged in unsanctioned combat — too artful to be labelled brawling — with brothers from not one but three other Chapters. Likewise Brother Iddecai of the Minotaurs had been involved in his fair share of violent encounters, though in his particular case, it was clear to all that Iddecai had been the instigator each time.

The Watch Council punished these infractions through a combination of verbal denouncement – a stain on the honour of those involved – and something far, far worse. For as many cycles as was deemed necessary, the transgressor was incarcerated in a Penance Box – essentially a coffin, of height and width barely greater than his own. Locked in and fitted with a heavy psychostim helm, he was forced to endure sensorium feeds in which brothers from his own Chapter faced off against overwhelming enemy forces. These feeds had been recorded during real wars in days long past, and the penitent Space Marine sentenced to endure them now was helpless to do anything as he saw and felt those around him – his blood, his kin – cut to pieces by enemy fire or torn to red tatters by claw and fang. It was a terrible punishment, for it struck at the very heart of the those who received it.

Brotherhood: was there anything more important to a Space Marine? One fought for the Emperor, true. But one died for one's brothers.

Even Iddecai, forced to experience the three hundred years-past slaughter of over sixty fellow Minotaurs at the hands of a vast eldar host, found the burning anguish too much to bear. It quickly dampened his hunger for picking fights with other Deathwatch trainees.

Karras had wondered if he, too, would be punished after the incident with the Ultramarine. But, due in great measure to the phrasing of Kulle's report, it did not come to that. At the end of the exercise at kill-block Ophidion, Kulle had ordered him to the apothecarion so that his implant might be examined and, despite appearing to function as expected, be replaced.

Karras had accepted the new implant in cold silence tinged with a mixture of resentment and lingering shame.

With prayers and tencycle squad allocations over, the Space Marines would leave the East Auditorium, moving to pre-arranged assembly points in the groups to which they had been assigned. There, a Watch sergeant would brief them further and accompany them to the relevant training facility. Most of the Deathwatch training in those first hundred cycles centred around the kill-blocks. There were over thirty of them, each of varying size and complexity, each configurable to a given scenario. No Chapter in all Imperial space boasted such fine training facilities, but then no Chapter placed such singular emphasis on covert anti-xenos operations. Stormraven drops, special weapons and equipment training, fast-roping, stealth infiltration, asset recovery, assassination – all this and much more, the new arrivals studied and practised over and over until it came as natural to them as breathing. They learned fast, for even among Space Marines they were the chosen elite, and here were taught the skills that separated Deathwatch operatives from all others. This was a war fought not face to bloodied face on the battlefield, where superior force and top-down strategy won the day, but behind the lines, from the shadows, sudden and brief and scalpel-precise.

After physical training, usually lasting five to six hours per cycle, the trainees were given individual programmes of Librarius study. The Damaroth Archive had the distinction of being one of the top two repositories for xenos-related material in the entire segmentum, the other being located at the local Ordo Xenos headquarters on Talasa Prime. But this period of study contained far more than simple book-learning. The Deathwatch Librarius had at its disposal an incredible archive of sensorium recordings taken from human-xenos conflicts across the Imperium. Some of these dated back to the very earliest days of the Deathwatch, back to when the Imperium was still groggily pushing itself to its feet after the treachery of Horus and his faithless cohorts, and the enshrinement of the Emperor upon the Golden Throne.

The sensorium records – the very same resource used for punishment – provided a level of education that was unmatched. Seated in stone chairs with psychostim helms on their heads, Karras and the others would relive hellish battles through the senses of Space Marines long gone. As with the Penance Box, they could not influence these recordings. The battlefields they walked had gone quiet long ago. They were observers only, but the bloodshed that unfolded all around them was heart-stoppingly vivid – the sights, the smells, the sounds, everything.

They saw through the eyes of a stoic Black Templar as he and his brothers were finally gunned down by tau battlesuits on a desert salt pan beneath triple suns. Had they executed a fighting retreat they might just have survived. Pride made them stand their ground and the price was their lives. The lesson, though fatal to those who taught it, was not wasted.

In other recordings, they lived through the final moments of a tyranid assault on a missile defence base at a classified location somewhere in Ultramar. The forces of the Ultramarines Fourth Company held on as long as they could for air support that never came. Karras winced as a pair of huge, slavering jaws closed over the legs of the Space Marine through whose senses he was experiencing the dreadful rout. The Ultramarine had been bitten in half at the waist and swallowed in two twitching pieces. Throne alone knew how anyone had recovered his helmet and the data crystal it contained.

They witnessed, too, the lethally methodical advance of the deadly necrons. Those skeletal figures of black metal bone seemed to press forwards almost lazily. They never charged at speed – so utterly sure of victory, of the irresistible force they represented. Time and again, it seemed the Space Wolves that fought them were making progress, only for the thin black bodies on the ground to rise up and take arms again, corpses called endlessly back to life. Nothing would avail the Space Wolves. They fell back, dying as they gave ground.

All this and more, Karras and the others lived through, feeling the pain and loss of those whose experiences they distantly relived. These were some of the hardest sessions for Karras, for he could do nothing to help the brave Space Marines. He felt fresh pity for those brothers, such as Iddecai, forced to experience the loss of their Chapter brothers in a Penance Box. These were battles lost to time, and yet, through the sensorium feeds, they seemed as real and as tangible as the stone armrests beneath his straining, white-knuckled hands. Often after such a session, despite none of them originating with his own noble order, he would rise from the stone chair riddled with grief, blazing with anger, fists clenched, desperately seeking an enemy to kill in revenge for what he had seen. He was far from alone in this. These sessions were harrowing in the extreme. Though the Watch Council made sure to filter the experiences by Chapter, ensuring that only the perpetrators of misdemeanours witnessed the loss of their kin, still many cried out in raw anguish and struggled against the titanium bindings that kept them restrained. It mattered not that the dying wore different colours, different iconography, and spoke with accents unfamiliar. The effect was powerful all the same.

The Watch Librarians, Lochaine foremost among them, insisted it was necessary. No one was exempt; not by Chapter, not by rank. The sessions became hated, for they represented all that was worst about defeat: the loss of great heroes, the helplessness, the grief, anger and guilt.

Despite all this distress, Karras quickly came to see the value of these feeds. No one could deny the effects. Seeing how each xenos breed fought first-hand was absolutely invaluable. Karras vicariously looked straight into the alien eyes of several threat-species he had never even heard of. He learned how they moved, how they struck, the weapons they wielded. But it went beyond that. Something else happened that was, perhaps, more significant still.

Despite their differences, the Space Marines started to come together.

Like several others, Karras was, at one point, even compelled to approach Solarion. He did this after enduring the horrific feed from the Ultramarines Fourth Company.

'Do not speak,' he told Solarion, cornering him in the Refectorum. 'I need no response. I wish only to tell you this: your brothers fought like gods of war. The sacrifice of those that fell is a testament to the glory of your Chapter. My brothers and I would have been proud to fight beside them.'

That was it. He turned and left immediately, still moved by what he had seen, not wishing to give the Ultramarine a chance to sour the sentiment.

Typically, after two or three hours of archival and sensorium study, the Space Marines would once again return to the main chapel to give thanks for all they had learned. Many who had stood in that same gloomy echoing space only eight hours earlier returned bearing fresh injuries of varying severity. The training was extreme because Deathwatch operations, by their very nature, were extreme. Yet no deaths occurred. There had not been a Space Marine death on Damaroth for over a century, for the Watch could ill afford to lose even a single battle-brother seconded to its ranks. This did not mean, however, that it could not push them to the very edge. Often, the Rothi would filter silently into the chapel after the post-training litanies were complete to clean congealed blood from the smooth marble flagstones.

After these litanies, the Space Marines would move to the Refectorum where, once per ten-hour cycle, they would consume a bowl of nutrient-dense gruel or, if they wished to eat alone, could acquire a meal-replacement block and return with it to their cells. These meal-replacements were affectionately known as bricks, and the name was well earned. They were the length and width of a typical Space Marine's index finger, coloured like sandstone and grooved deeply so that they could be broken into three smaller chunks. They were textured like sandstone, too – rough, gritty and requiring significant pressure from the jaw muscles to break them down.

At first, Karras took his with iced water, eating back in the silence of his sparse quarters. After the first dozen cycles, however, he decided he was missing a unique opportunity and began to eat regularly in the Refectorum among his fellows. It did not serve anyone, he told himself, to hide away in solitude. A kill-team was a team. He would live and die by the honour and skill of the Space Marines who served beside him. With that in mind, he made efforts to get to know those around him, at the very least by sight. Mostly, he just observed them, for few seemed willing to approach. Librarians often found themselves segregated, even within their own Chapters, for the feelings their powers generated in their Chapter brothers were conflicting in nature.

Tolerate not the psyker, the witch, the shaman. Their power is the gateway to madness and corruption.

And yet, were Librarians not the supreme embodiment of anti-xenos war: soldiers whose physical talents were matched only by their psychic weaponry? Most alien species represented a threat on both counts. Only the psyker was capable of combating the latter aspect effectively.

Seated in the Refectorum cycle after cycle with the stone benches empty on either side of him, it was apparent to Karras that, in their discomfort at his presence, these elite battle-brothers were not so different from many others he had known, and he took to reading ancient texts from the Watch Librarius to distract himself from their prejudice as he ate.

But there were exceptions. During one such meal, with the Refectorum at only a third of its capacity, he met for the first time the most unusual and irreverent Space Marine he had ever encountered.

'The one that bloodied Prophet's lip,' said the figure that suddenly appeared in front of him.

Karras looked up from his gruel and across the stone table. Before him stood a striking battle-brother in a black tunic belted with silver. In his hands, he held a clay bowl and spoon like those on the table in front of Karras.

'Prophet?' Karras asked, confused.

'The Ultramarine you threw into a wall.'

'Ignacio Solarion,' said Karras. His brow creased. 'Do you seek to shame me with such a reminder? Very well. I admit I was wrong to lose my composure. What is that to you?'

The stranger, ignoring the warning tone, asked if he might sit. Despite his misgivings, Karras gestured to the bench on the other side of the table. The other Space Marine dropped onto it, smiling to himself. His skin was as white as sun-bleached bone, exactly the shade of Karras's own. The similarities stopped there, however. While Karras's eyes were blood red, even where they should have been white, this battle-brother's eyes were a solid, flawless black, like two spheres of pure polished obsidian. They were the same black as his long shimmering hair – hair that lay like a silk mantle on his shoulders. Karras was as bald as a knarloc egg. It was genetic. All Death Spectres went bald during the gene-seed implant process.

Damned impractical, thought Karras, staring at all that long, shining hair. *What vanity! And look at that face. Not a single scar. Surely this one has never been tested. Surely he is too young and inexperienced to be here.*

It was a remarkable face for more than just its lack of scars, and for more than the rare friendliness apparent in its expression, too.

The unblemished face stared back at Karras with an apparent openness the Death Spectre had seen nowhere else since his arrival.

Something familiar, Karras thought. *Like Ithoric's White Champion. Or Gorlon Xie's Olympiarch.*

Karras was no stranger to the works of the Great Sculptors. For ten thousand years, the worlds of the Imperium had produced a few men each generation in whose hands simple stone became works of such beauty and perfection that they inspired the populations of whole segmenta. Most of these men were eventually commissioned to produce inspirational military works for the Adeptus Munitorum, as much to boost morale as to immortalise the noteworthy. The glorious diorama of Macharius and Sejanus on Ultima Macharia – the famous *End of the Long March* – was one such example, much imitated in the years following its unveiling, but never bettered.

The face of the Space Marine sitting opposite Karras now was more suited to such a sculpture than to a trained killer or living war-machine. Silky black hair framed a forehead of respectable height, a noble brow, a sharp slender nose and a mouth neither too wide nor too small. The planes of the cheekbones were smooth and superbly proportioned. Such symmetry there. Were it not for the all-black eyes, Karras could almost have believed this brother a masterpiece of statuary come to life.

The stranger noted Karras studying him and laughed.

'I know,' he said. 'Too good-looking for the Deathwatch. But don't let that fool you.'

Karras raised an eyebrow.

'Don't mistake this perfection for a badge of inexperience. You were thinking that very thing. Not so?'

'You have the Gift yourself, then,' said Karras with some humour, 'to read others so well.'

'I'm gifted all right, but not in the way you mean. I'll leave sorcery to the likes of you, witchkin.' Karras stiffened at the word, but detected no malice in the tone. 'I'm just used to dealing with false assumptions,' the stranger went on.

'The only Space Marines I've seen without a scar on their faces are neophytes,' countered Karras. 'It doesn't last long.'

'That should tell you something,' said the battle-brother.

'It would tell me that you're a neophyte,' said Karras, 'but the Deathwatch does not recruit neophytes.'

The black-haired battle-brother shovelled a spoonful of thick, sludgy gruel into his mouth.

'You'd think they could add some flavour to the damned stuff,' he groaned. Then, after another swallow, added, 'We share blood, you and I.'

Karras nodded. The colourless skin was the giveaway. Gene-seed mutation. Another reason certain others kept their distance. 'It would seem so. Raptors, perhaps? Revilers?'

The other tutted. 'Now why would you think that? Raven Guard, I'll have you know.'

Karras cursed. Given the stranger's breezy manner, how could he possibly have guessed it? He dropped his spoon in his bowl and stood. Dutifully, and in accordance with ancient tradition, he raised right hand to left pectoral, bowed his head, and intoned gravely, 'We look to Corax and pray for his return. We of the Death Spectres honour the seed that made us.'

The Raven Guard's smile weakened for a moment. He gestured for Karras to sit. A few others in the Refectorum looked over.

'We honour the brothers born of our roots,' he replied. 'May Corax take pride in them and all they do.' It was appropriate in response but not so much in the way it was said. 'Relax, brother. I don't stand much on formality. You've obeyed the forms. Let us put them aside where they belong. How old are you, by the way?'

He spooned another mouthful of gruel into his mouth.

Karras sat stunned. What manner of Raven Guard was this?

'Why did you approach me?' he asked, ignoring the other's question.

'Why not? You were eating alone. Not being shunned, are you?' He looked around almost theatrically, pretending to fear that anyone might see them together. 'Actually, I just wanted to meet the Space Marine who overloaded his implant and bloodied Prophet's nose. He had it coming. If not from you...'

'You keep calling him Prophet,' said Karras. 'I don't understand.'

The Raven Guard snorted. 'He makes more predictions than a back-alley palm-reader. *You're making an error. This strategy will fail. I told you so. Exactly as I foresaw. If you had listened to me...*'

'Ah,' said Karras. 'I'm sure he is delighted with the name.'

'Revels in it,' said the Raven Guard with obvious pleasure.

'And do I have a nickname?' asked Karras.

The Raven Guard indicated the weathered old volume Karras had lain aside while they talked. 'I've taken to calling you Scholar,' he said. 'A little obvious, I admit.'

'Perhaps, but at least I won't take offence.'

'I should have tried harder,' said the Raven Guard, flashing perfect teeth.

He half turned and pointed out a number of others in the Refectorum, quoting their nicknames to Karras. Some were obscure and needed explanation, just as Prophet's had, but others were simple, some bordering on the openly offensive, others given in respect of a particular talent or skill. Of these latter, the last that Karras learned was the nickname of a squat, bulky battle-brother of the Imperial Fists. He was sitting in the far corner with a Black Templar.

'Omni,' said the Raven Guard.

'Why that?'

'You haven't trained with him yet? About the only thing he *can't* do is fit into narrow spaces.' At this, he laughed. 'Heavy weapons, explosives, communications, vehicles, repairs, encryption. I guess he's making up for being so damned short. It looks like his body grew outwards rather than upwards, doesn't it?'

'There's one name you haven't told me,' said Karras, leaning forwards, eyebrow raised.

The Raven Guard made a short bow from his seat.

'My name is Zeed, brother. Siefer Zeed.'

Karras extended his hand and they briefly gripped wrists.

'Well met, Brother Zeed, but don't pretend you haven't earned a nickname yourself. Or are you somehow excluded?'

Zeed had apparently decided he was finished with his gruel. He rose from the stone bench and stepped backwards over it, still facing Karras. He left his bowl on the table.

'They call me Ghost,' he said.

It was Karras's turn to laugh. 'And why do they call you that I wonder? As well to call me the same, given the skin colour we share.'

'It's not that, Scholar,' said Zeed, strangely serious all of a sudden. 'Not at all.'

He turned to leave, but paused a moment and spoke over his shoulder.

'Watch for me in the combat pits if you have the chance. See me fight. You'll see why they call me Ghost... and why this face bears no scars.'

With that, he strode off, leaving Karras to wonder at the strange encounter. Zeed stopped at a few other tables on his way out, greeting battle-brothers from various Chapters, always with a quip or remark. Some shared his good humour. A White Scar by the name of Brother Khaigur particularly enjoyed whatever it was that Zeed said to him, laughing uproariously and pounding the table with big calloused hands. Others merely glared until Zeed moved away. Of those who showed little patience with him, surliest of all was the Ultramarine, Ignacio Solarion. *Prophet.* Karras hadn't noticed him enter the Refectorum. It must have been within the last few minutes. He was seated at a far table beside a small group of Space Marines from progenitor Chapters. Karras saw warriors from the Novamarines and the Sons of Orar among them.

Whatever it was that Zeed said to Solarion, it was clearly far from politic. Solarion snarled aggressively and made to rise, but the Novamarine seated next to him said something back and the Raven Guard shrugged and moved off. Solarion then turned his glare towards Karras, a look that was difficult to read.

If not for this damned implant…

Karras opted not to return the look. Would that he could undo the whole mess.

We should reserve our hate for the xenos, he thought. *Not for each other. Among those who share a sacred duty to mankind, it should never be so.*

He left the Refectorum with half an hour to spare before the beginning of the next cycle. He would sleep for fifteen minutes, he decided. Even so short a rest would allow him to begin the next cycle rejuvenated and ready, his fatigue falling away, minor tissue damage naturally mending. Such was the enhanced constitution of a Space Marine.

But he didn't sleep. Not even for a minute. He settled only into a dissatisfying attempt which was thwarted as his mind turned over all the complications he had encountered thus far. All his notions, all his preconceptions…

Perhaps things would change after the taking of Second Oath. Perhaps after he officially donned the black and was assigned to a kill-team proper… Maybe then everything would change.

Time, of course, would teach him the folly of that belief.

11

Varlan heard the plasteel door click shut behind her as she stepped into the close air and the dim orange glow. All around her, pipes, ducts and snaking wires traced a complex dance on the walls and ceilings, twisting and flowing together like a nest of mating snakes frozen solid mid-coitus. Before her, in the centre of the floor, a metal stair with twin handrails led down into the space port's service tunnels. Like the interior of the concrete hut itself, the tunnel section below was lit by work-lumes – lambent spheres set in the ceiling, recessed, spaced every few metres.

As her boot heels rang on the fourth metal stair, a freight train must have arrived at the space port. She could feel the vibration of the massive vehicle through the handrails as it came to a stop. Good. Her cargo of industrial supplies would be on its way to a city warehouse within the hour. All part of her cover.

At the bottom of the metal steps, she set foot on the stone floor of the underground tunnel. Cautiously, but without actual stealth, she pressed on. She wore no weapons on hip or thigh, not while playing the role of Lady Fara, but then Shianna Varlan was herself a weapon, trained and conditioned on her birth world to superb ability by the finest Darguu[16] master, T'shon Elisur. The Ordo appreciated that, and had built on it with advanced training of their own. If her close-quarters combat abilities were inadequate to neutralise the dangers she faced, the micro-weapons concealed in the rings on either index finger ought to equalise things a little.

She doubted she would need such weapons here. Oroga had

---

16. Darguu – a close-quarters martial discipline emphasising reflexive movement through nerve conditioning.

assured her that Asset 16's codes were still listed as uncompromised. Unless the asset had been broadcasting under duress, the information exchange ought to be a simple matter of protocol.

As if summoned by that very thought, a shadowy shape moved into view at the tunnel junction up ahead. Varlan's heartbeat sped just a fraction. The figure moved into a pool of weak lume-light and stopped. There it stood, awaiting her, back hunched, waist bent, its lopsided shoulders sitting a little too far forwards on its torso. A twisted, impure shape. Varlan felt a wave of revulsion pass through her. From infancy, one was taught to hate the mutant, the heretic, the psyker. The latter, she had come to believe, could be noble and great; His Lordship's astropaths and Navigators, for example, wielded their strange powers only for the good of mankind. The mutant and the heretic, however, were cancers rooted in the very bones of the human race.

And this one is a mutant! A twist!

As she neared him, her revulsion grew.

She stopped two metres from him, noting that he held a compact autopistol levelled at her heart. At this range, depending on the type of rounds he was using, even one shot might lethally pierce the armour mesh woven into her clothes. At least he was cautious, a professional. Both had doubts that needed assuaging before they could proceed.

Without raising her hands from her side, Varlan made a series of gestures with her fingers. The last two represented her callsign for this operation:

White Phoenix.

The little hunchback nodded and, without lowering his weapon, gave a brief finger-sequence of his own with his free hand.

Varlan indicated her satisfaction with a nod and breached the silence between them. 'You'll not need the weapon with me, Sixteen. Let us conclude our business quickly. Ready your opticom for transfer.'

The little man hesitantly tucked his pistol in his waistband, lifted a hand to one eye, and removed the flexible layer of artificial pupil, iris and white that hid the cybernetic augmentation beneath. Lifting her right hand, Shianna Varlan did the same. There they stood for a moment, two very different human beings dedicated to service in the same cause. Varlan towered over Asset 16. She was a living expression of good genetics, of beauty, health and great physical aptitude. He was a bent wretch, barely able to look her in the eye without twisting his ugly head sideways. But His Lordship had use for both, and that was reason enough for Varlan to put aside pride. She took a knee so that their eyes drew level, the better to facilitate a quick, steady transfer without errors.

'Are you ready?' she asked.

In answer, Asset 16 leaned towards her until their opticoms were aligned. A bridge of red laser light appeared between them, lens-to-lens, and the transfer began.

Varlan absorbed it all. She could not consciously process everything as it entered her brain – there was far too much data travelling at speed into the area of her memory assigned to such work – a storage partition, as she thought of it – but, turning a part of her attention to the dataflow, she managed to catch a significant amount.

The transfer lasted eight seconds, the longest she'd ever experienced, and she hadn't been prepared for the nature of the content. The things that Sixteen had seen, had done... As the red bridge blinked out of existence, she fell backwards on her rump, her composure broken. She was breathing in gasps.

'You... I saw... I...'

Asset 16 – Ordimas Arujo, as she now knew him to be – shrugged his misshapen shoulders. He seemed suddenly weary, almost on the verge of collapse, wracked with all he had endured. And rightly so, Varlan judged.

'What would you have done, interrogator?' There was bitterness, even loathing in his voice, but directed at himself, not at her. His actions sickened him. Yet what choice had there been? 'Had I refused, they would have known me for an infiltrator and slain me. And you would come here blind, groping in the frozen dark for the intelligence I have just provided. Would you have acted any different?'

As Varlan pushed herself to her feet, he looked her up and down, taking in her lines, but without any of the animal hunger so obvious in the eyes of men like Captain Dozois. 'As a woman, you would have fared much worse than I under the circumstances.'

She wasn't about to deceive herself. She knew exactly what he meant and shivered in acknowledgment. If the Ordo had sent a female infiltrator...

'I understand what you did,' she told him, 'but it sickens my soul.'

'Do you think it sickens mine any less? Or do you think I enjoyed it? A twisted body reflects a twisted mind – is that not what the Ecclesiarchy tells us?'

'I see your value well enough.'

'You see the value of the mutation, not the man. I risk my life for those that hate me, but a curse on all mutants will come no slower to your lips, I'll wager.'

'Don't presume to know me,' she thundered, angry at his accusation, uncomfortable with the truth in it. 'You will be well rewarded for your success, I'm sure. I came here only for the information you were carrying. Now I have it.'

Though I wish, in the name of all the saints, that I did not.

She found herself struggling with the more dreadful images now stored in her mind. Flashes of his terrible experience kept forcing themselves to the forefront of her awareness, insisting on her attention.

'You were joined with one of them,' she murmured. 'One of the women, the Infected. In front of that foul congregation, you...'

Ordimas's face twisted.

'Don't tell me what I did,' he hissed at Varlan through clenched teeth. 'I know it, and I know *why* I did it too, may the Emperor wash the stain from my soul. I was under His Lordship's direct orders, as you are now. Would you have had me disobey?'

He guesses my thoughts, my inner struggle. He reminds me of my own duty so I will not kill him.

Her mind spun. She was an interrogator. It was one of her sworn duties to kill those who partook in such sinister rites. They were heretics and traitors. Any tribunal in the Imperium would have condemned such a man to torture and death. But this Ordimas was an Ordo asset. He belonged to His Lordship. He lived and died by His Lordship's command. One did not overstep the boundaries of that authority and expect to live.

She could see it all as if the memories were her own: the kidnapping of the other work-crew deep down in the mines; the cart journey into abandoned Arraphel; the strange congregation kneeling in the darkness and the freezing cold.

The sensory data from Ordimas's opticom showed her all this and the rest. She saw the massive cloaked men haul their prisoners off into the dark tunnel. She saw women move to stand on the platform. She saw the tall, strange man – their high-priest or equivalent – moving among his flock, selecting from among them with a touch on the cheek. She saw the chosen leave the throng and moved to stand on the platform, each beside one of the women.

Then the tall man stopped in front of Asset 16.

Ordimas had looked into the face of the cult leader.

The strange priest's irises were a vivid, shimmering gold, the black pupils not round, but shaped like the fluted glass vessel of an hourglass. They were striking: so icy, so composed; so absolutely lacking in doubt or weakness. There were no eyelashes, no eyebrows. The tall man was utterly hairless.

It was no man, thought Varlan. *It was something else. Unnatural. Inhuman.*

She had already begun to suspect what.

'The Master calls upon you, Mykal Durst,' the cult leader had said softly to Ordimas. His gaze flicked briefly to the fake tattoo on Ordimas's neck. She felt the memory of Ordimas's panic. Had the ink smudged? Did the strange priest see through his ruse? 'Stand with one of your sisters. Give, now, in the service of He who raised you up from misery and ignorance. Swell our ranks so that we might know His paradise all the sooner.'

Varlan knew the asset's abject terror as she lived through his memories. Every fibre of him screamed out in fear and horror. His body had wanted to turn and flee, but his mind held on, if only by the thinnest of threads.

Incredible that he retained control!

Knowing that the only other option was discovery and death, Ordimas had taken his place on the stone platform, sick with self-loathing, shivering in the chill air. Varlan saw what followed, saw it through the asset's eyes while he, in turn, saw it through the gene-copied eyes of a dead miner.

What passed on the platform made her gut clench like a vice. All those others, watching in unholy rapture as the ritual proceeded. She knew Ordimas's struggle, knew how close his mind had come to being torn apart.

She thought of the strange children his opticom had recorded in the market square, and knew many such children would follow. From that alone, she knew also the nature of the threat on Chiaro. Asset 16 did not quite see the full picture. He saw the presence of a threat, but not the extent of it. All to the good. Better for this one if he lived the rest of his days in ignorance. As it was, she guessed he would not live long. Whatever substance or activity he turned to seeking distraction from the horror – be it alcohol, drugs or adrenaline – it would eventually kill him.

The truly haunted rarely escape their ghosts.

She forced her mind back to the present and found him staring at her, open concern written on his lumpy face. How long had she been submerged in his past? Long enough by half. It was time to go. The little mutant's weariness had settled over her like a fog.

'Your work in Cholixe is done,' she told him. 'I commend you for your sacrifice. His Lordship chose well, as always.'

The hunchback snorted. 'I wish he'd chosen someone else.'

'If you have personal affairs here, deal with them swiftly and make ready to depart. The ship on which I arrived, the *Macedon*, ought to be leaving within the week. Negotiate passage to the nearest commercial hub. The captain is a greedy man. He will accept your business despite any prejudices, providing the fee is substantial enough. I'm sure His Lordship will call on you before long.'

'Will you be on that ship?' Ordimas asked, voice not quite flat enough to hide the fact that he asked out of concern for her.

Varlan's expression hardened. 'Do not pity me and do not fear for me. There is dangerous work here, but it is work I was trained for.'

How she wished she felt such confidence. In the face of what nested here, what bred here, she could not. 'Do you have adequate funds?'

'A transfer was made yesterday. I have all I need for now.'

'Then our business is concluded. Emperor light your way.'

She was about to turn from him, set to return the way she had come, when a strong, long-fingered hand on her arm stopped her. She recoiled a little by reflex from the mutant's touch, but only briefly.

Ordimas was looking up at her, head tilted awkwardly so he could meet her eyes. She noticed that his opticom was covered once again with its false layer, reminding her to do likewise.

Ordimas licked his lips anxiously. 'You are proud and strong, interrogator. You embody all the finest qualities of the Inquisition. I can see that. But heed my words for your own sake, I beg you. If you must go down into the mines, go down in force. His Lordship has potent military assets at his disposal. You know of whom I speak. Call them here if you can. This corruption, this infection… It goes far beyond what I have seen. I've barely scratched the surface, and yet my part has been played to its end. Yours is just beginning. Guard your life, my lady. It would sadden me to know such beauty had succumbed to such ugliness.'

Both stood silent for a moment, a grim tableau in orange and black, the asset's hand still on Varlan's arm, his words hanging in the cold air between them. Somewhere deeper along the tunnels, generators thrummed, seeming louder now than before. Another freight train rumbled by on the surface. Varlan moved, lowering her arm so that Ordimas's hand slid away. She thought she knew what had moved him to speak. It wasn't just her death. Everyone died sometime, and there was no sorrow to be found in giving one's life in the service of the Emperor. No, not that. The hunchback was referring to a fate far darker, the most vile and unholy of exploitations. Against that, death was a blessing.

She couldn't afford to let that fear take root. She galvanised herself against it. She was an interrogator, class 3, of the Ordo Xenos of the Emperor's own Holy Inquisition.

Stiffening, she said, 'I will not succumb. Be sure of that.'

There was fresh grit in her voice, mixed with ice and fire. The little mutant blinked at her, his warning given, nothing left to say.

Varlan turned and began walking back down the tunnel. She spoke over her shoulder only once.

'Farewell, Sixteen. You do not know me. You have not seen me.'

Ordimas bowed to her retreating back, then vanished.

She listened a moment to the offbeat rhythm of his footfalls. They receded quickly, soon drowned out by the background noise of the space port generators and the buzzing of the overhead lumes.

She strode briskly, eager to rejoin her retinue and find a place to take repast before a much-needed sleep… If she could even manage sleep given the knowledge she had now acquired. She would need the comfort of prayers and mantras at the very least. The security she felt in the company of the twins would help, too. It always did.

In something that barely passed for a whisper, she said, 'Eagle to Shield.'

She listened. Nothing.

'Eagle to Shield,' she repeated.

Again, nothing.

'Eagle to Sword,' she tried. There was no answer.

There were two possibilities: either the tunnels and their machinery were interfering with the vox-net or her aides were incapacitated.

The latter possibility made her break into a run.

Even in heels, she was fast, running on the balls of her feet. The lamps in the ceiling rushed by her. Within moments, she reached the metal stair and flew up it, boots clanging on every second step. She reached the top and was about to throw open the door that led outside when, in her left ear, she heard a burst of static and a tinny voice repeating over and over, 'Shield to Eagle. Shield to Eagle. Do you copy?'

Oroga.

'Eagle copies,' she replied. 'Go ahead Shield.'

'We have a serious problem, Eagle,' voxed Oroga. 'It's an HID[17]. I think we may have been compromised.'

---

17. HID – Human Interference: Deliberate.

12

Karras and nineteen others were ordered to the Central Pankrateon fourteen tortuous cycles after he and Zeed had spoken in the Refectorum. The cycles between had been as brutal and exacting as anything he had so far experienced. One involved being subjected to the cold and pressure of crushing oceanic depths without any breathing apparatus, and having to complete various problems set by the Watch sergeants. There were no oceans on Damaroth, of course, but the tech-priests had managed to create immersion pods that achieved the precise effect. Karras's body drew the oxygen he needed from the icy water that flooded his lungs. It was a new experience for him, being forced to breathe water, and not something he hoped ever to repeat.

Another cycle involved sprinting through kilometres of gas-filled tunnels wearing a hundred kilos of additional weight in the form of old-fashioned, unpowered plate armour. The thick, toxic clouds that billowed from nozzles in the walls attacked his eyes, skin and nasal membrane as he pounded towards the goal, but there was no stopping, no turning back or quitting. His breathing was as shallow as he could make it while still powering his muscles. Without the implanted organs of a Space Marine, he would have fallen down dead within the first twenty metres. As it was, it took him several further cycles to feel properly recovered.

There were other exercises, too, simulating combat in the zero-G void of space, fighting teams of servitor drones in extremes of heat and cold and various types of radiation. It wasn't just a matter of combat in a range of extremes; all of these exercises included tasks to tax the mind as well as the body. The Deathwatch wanted to be sure its operatives could get the job done no matter what challenges they faced.

Compared to such withering tests, close-combat cycles in the Pankrateon sounded like a grand reprieve. Of course, they proved to be anything but. In the coming cycle, the group to which Karras was assigned would train knife, sword, double knife, double sword and empty-hand techniques under the critical eyes of Watch Sergeants Kulle and Coteaz. The latter was a veteran Deathwatch squad leader, originally of the Crimson Fists Chapter, who had famously slain an ork warboss that outweighed him six-to-one at close quarters using only a standard-issue combat blade. The scarred mess of his face, ruined almost beyond recognisable humanity, was ample testimony; Karras could believe the story all too easily looking at that battered visage.

The Pankrateon was a massive close-combat training facility roughly cross-shaped in layout. The main area was a dark central hall, its arched ceiling some thirty metres above a stone floor stained with thousands of years of shed blood. Brothers got cut here, and not infrequently. It was a rule that the flagstones of the Pankrateon did not get washed. Blood spilled was blood honoured, a mark of commitment to the ultimate goal of all this hard work. The Pankrateon exceeded even the kill-blocks in terms of serious injuries reported and formed a part of Deathwatch training every bit as critical.

The high ceiling was supported by cylindrical pillars set eight metres apart and running in two rows down the entire length of the main hall. These were no ordinary pillars. At their base, they boasted a profusion of multi-jointed mechanical arms, each ending in a metal appendage into which could be placed a wide variety of weapons: from swords and hammers to barbed whips and great crushing claws. Set on the surface of each pillar, winking from between the paired sets of arms, were target lights. These glowed red until struck, at which point they would turn momentarily blue. With this change, the arms linked to that light would stop attacking. The servo-skull embedded in stone above the top pair of arms would register the successful strike. Then the light would change back, the arms would reactivate, and the Space Marine would find himself under full assault once again.

Karras, his fatigues growing damp with a light sweat, ducked just as his pillar sent a slashing horizontal blow at his head. Air whooshed above him. He stepped in, careful to check the movement of the other three arms he faced, and stabbed upwards with his training knife.

The tip hit the target light's hard, scratch-proof dome. It went blue and, for a second, the attacking arms froze. Karras stepped out, breathing hard, and rolled his shoulders, readying himself for the pillar-drone's next tireless assault. The pillar's embedded skull sounded a warning tone, the light flickered from blue back to red, and the arms began slicing the air once again, metal claws and sword-blades flashing.

Around Karras, his fellow Deathwatch trainees fought just as hard, grunting with effort as they pushed themselves to keep up with the fighting machines. This was training unlike anything Karras had known. Back at Logopol, the Death Spectres had trained with each other, learning from the mistakes and successes of their kin as much as from their own. But fighting fellow Space Marines was less than ideal given the special remit of the Watch. It was the combat habits and patterns of the main xenos threats which had to be learned and overcome. Karras's pillar fought him according to a pattern taken from sensorium records of a mid-sized tyranid variant, large enough to be a serious threat, but not too large for hand-to-hand combat. Thus, four arms assailed him instead of two, and they were fast, striking like scorpion tails with lethal intent.

The Watch sergeants paced up and down the main hall, watching the unarmoured Space Marines fighting with all they had, barking at them to work harder, fight smarter.

'Keep moving, damn you!' shouted Coteaz through ragged lips. The torn flesh of his cheeks and mouth gave his voice a lisping quality. 'Footwork. Footwork. A stationary Space Marine is a dead Space Marine.'

Karras put a burst of extra energy into his movement, slipped under another assault from the arms bearing knives, and scored another strike on the middle target light. The pillar's skull beeped an alarm and froze. The light turned blue.

'Sergeant,' someone called out.

Karras looked towards the sound. Coteaz limped over to an extremely stocky Space Marine just two pillars away on the left. Then the pillar in front of Karras beeped, and the arms whistled out towards him again, abruptly recalling his attention. His training knife parried a blow that could have given him a very nasty chest wound. As he blocked and slipped another series of blistering swipes, he heard the stocky warrior speak.

'I think I broke it.'

'Don't talk nonsense, Voss. No one has ever...'

'Someone just did. Sorry, sergeant.'

'Dorn's blood! How did–?'

Karras scored another disabling hit on his foe and took the second's respite to glance again in Voss's direction.

The Imperial Fist. The one they're calling Omni.

Voss was by far the shortest Space Marine Karras had ever laid eyes on, but his muscular bulk went a step beyond compensation. His arms, his shoulders, his chest; every muscle group on his squat frame rippled with thick, hard mass. Back on Occludus, it would not have been tolerated. Such muscularity often came at the price of agility and speed.

Then again, perhaps not. In that oh-so-momentary glance, Karras had seen Voss holding up a mechanical arm that he had somehow ripped right out of the training pillar. He lifted it as if offering it to Coteaz in embarrassed tribute. It was a feat that should only have been possible in power armour. Omni had used his bare hands.

Coteaz never got the chance to comment further. At that moment, Sergeant Kulle came storming out of one of the side halls and urged Coteaz to follow him.

'You need to see this,' he insisted.

Coteaz, noting the look in Kulle's eyes, turned from Voss without another word and fell into step behind his fellow Watch sergeant, following him to the Pankrateon's west chamber where one of the facility's two sunken combat pits was located.

Two minutes later, Kulle reappeared and shouted for everyone else to follow him.

Karras withdrew from his combat-drone's active range. The moment he stepped out of the machine's engagement field, the scanners in the servo-skull blinked green, then off.

He fell into step behind the others as they followed Kulle through a short hall of black stone into a room with circular tiers sunk into the floor. There were five of these tiers, in the middle of which was a pit some twelve metres across and four metres deep. From the base of that pit came the sound of harsh impacts, of metal clashing, bursts of staccato sound interspersed with brief pauses. Looking at the other battle-brothers around him as he stepped to the rim, Karras noticed the hard looks on the faces of some, the knowing grins on the faces of others. Reaching the rim, he looked down and saw a whirling, darting blur of a figure being assaulted from three sides by heavy, multi-limbed close-combat servitors.

It was Siefer Zeed. *Ghost*. The alabaster skin and black-silk hair were unmistakable. Like all those present save the Watch sergeants and their Mechanicus support, Zeed wore black training fatigues. They contrasted sharply with his pale form. One of the training servitors sent a blistering diagonal axe-blow towards Zeed's clavicle. The Raven Guard slipped it and struck the servitor's chassis targets with three hard, open-handed blows. The servitor's plasteel torso rang with the impacts.

One of the others servitors, this one armed with a sword and spiked shield, burst forwards while Zeed was withdrawing from the range of the other. For a moment, it looked like the servitor's sword would bite down into Zeed's upper back, but the Raven Guard had noticed the movement behind him. He stepped right as he spun to face his attacker, somehow still managing to keep himself just a hair beyond the range of the others, and threw out a hand to redirect the servitor's downward force at the wrist. The sword bit into the pit's sandy floor at the very moment Zeed moved inside, checking the spiked shield with his right hand and hammering a straight left into the glowing target that represented his enemy's face.

The cybernetic drone staggered backwards, arms out for balance, only to receive a thunderous kick in its plated abdomen. It dropped hard to the sand, striking what passed for its head against the curving granite wall of the pit. There, it twitched a moment, its organic brain rocked, until subroutines kicked in and it began to right itself. In the meantime, Zeed had kicked the legs out from under the third, dropping it to its backside in front of him. It swiped at him from the ground, lashing out with the double short-swords it held, but it could not reach him. He ignored its futile attacks and focused on the axe-wielder, which had begun to close on him again.

Without turning or looking up, Zeed called out, 'Next setting, damn it! They're too slow!'

From a few metres to Karras's right, someone growled and muttered, 'Arrogant fool!'

Someone else grunted in agreement, but no one withdrew from the edge of the pit. Arrogant or not, Zeed was worthy of an audience. Karras saw that he had misjudged the strange battle-brother. That porcelain face was flawless not because he was untested or a gun-shy coward, but because no blade had ever been fast enough to touch it. The same was not true of Zeed's body. One didn't take combat to this level without paying the price. His white skin was laced like a roadmap of hundreds of scars, some broad and deep, a sign of tearing or gouging, some long and fine, where sharp blades had slashed his flesh.

On the other side of the pit's rim, Watch Sergeant Kulle glanced at Coteaz, one eyebrow raised.

'Not I,' said Coteaz to his fellow. 'I won't be responsible for the first Pankrateon death in a century.'

'He can handle it,' said Kulle. 'Look at him. See for yourself.'

Whatever look crossed Coteaz's face then, Karras couldn't read it. The grizzled old Space Marine's visage was too much of a mess to discern any clear expression, but his words were anything but vague. 'All I see is a showboater revelling in attention. The lesson here is of humility and of knowing one's limitations, as you'll see when this all turns ill.'

Karras felt Coteaz was wrong. Down in the pit, Zeed's attention was focused like a las-beam on the deadly ballet in which he had the central role. Zeed never once looked up at the Space Marines ringing the pit, despite the supportive shouts of *Ghost!* from some of those present. The rest watched in either brooding or respectful silence. Zeed was putting his life on the line to test his capabilities and to try to move beyond them. His movements were so fast and precise they almost seemed choreographed. It was mesmerising.

No one would leave while he still fought. If Space Marines respected anything, it was proficiency in battle, and Karras doubted anyone here would honestly argue they were the equal of the Raven Guard in close quarters. Not now. How could they? Karras knew for certain that he himself was not. Had he been permitted to combine his own combat skills with the power of his gift, the story would be quite different, but that lessened Zeed's achievement not one bit.

Ignoring Coteaz's concerns, Watch Sergeant Kulle drew a slate-shaped device from a pocket on his webbing and tapped its face with his index finger. 'Program Orpheus,' he called down into the pit. 'Mind yourself, Raven Guard!'

The Space Marines around the pit could see the change that took place immediately. Activation lights on the servitors' chassis blinked in faster tempo. As aggressive as they had been earlier, they became more so now, leaping to attack in tight coordination with each other, their weapons whistling as they churned the air just inches from Zeed's unprotected flesh.

Unprotected, but fast. Despite the intensity of the new assault, Zeed was somehow always just outside their reach, or just inside the arc of their blows. It was then, once he was inside, that he would strike like bolter-fire, rattling off a rapid series of strikes to his enemies' glowing target lights. He was, in a word, incredible.

Karras didn't dare blink, such was the speed of what played out below. Zeed seemed to have fallen into a kind of trance. Though the warp field suppressor had locked away Karras's powers, he was sure he felt something from the Raven Guard. It was a kind of mindlessness, as if his noisy, cocky, boisterous personality had melted away into the substance of his surroundings. He was one with his opponents, each an inseparable part of this expression of artful violence, and as such, knew every microscopic change in their movement even as it happened. In a way, he was as much a machine now as they were. They could not touch him.

But they do not tire, thought Karras. *And pressed like this, even a Space Marine will exhaust himself eventually.*

Zeed struck the metal knee-joint of one servitor and it staggered, dropping to the ground on its other knee. The Raven Guard leapt forwards, sprang off the downed servitor's exposed shoulder and, with the extra height and momentum, hammered a leaping kick into the head of the drone closing on his right.

Despite being deep in a battle-trance, he summoned his voice.

'Higher, damn it,' he barked up at the Watch sergeants. 'Faster. Make them faster.'

Above the clanging and ringing of the combat below, Karras heard Watch Sergeant Coteaz curse aloud.

Kulle tapped the screen of his slate again. Coteaz grabbed his shoulder. 'No one has gone higher than Orpheus against three drones,' he hissed. 'Don't do this.'

'Someone must raise the bar,' Kulle snapped back, 'or none of us will ever go beyond what we are.'

'Then his blood will stain your honour, not mine. I'll not be party to this.'

For a moment, they stood there, eyes level, communicating so much without need for words. Then Coteaz turned and pushed his way from the edge of the pit, cursing as he went.

'Program Umenides,' Kulle shouted down to Zeed. 'Extremis Ultra. You break new ground today, Raven Guard.'

The shouts of *Ghost!* became louder.

Watching all this, Karras felt a knot twist in his primary stomach. In Kulle's eyes, he now noted something he had seen many times on the battlefield: tunnel-vision. The Watch sergeant's focus had narrowed to encompass only the moment, only that which lay before him. He was not seeing the bigger picture, not staying mindful of the consequences should something go wrong. Together, complicit in this testing beyond limits, Kulle and Zeed risked too much. To have Zeed die here in a training pit, never having taken Second Oath, would stain the honour of the Deathwatch and the Raven Guard both.

Karras felt a weight settle over him. He looked at the battle-brothers on either side. They too, all of them, had eyes and minds only for the deadly game below. It was up to him, then.

Reluctant as he was, Karras began to edge around the pit towards Kulle. Those who found him suddenly blocking their view simply craned their necks to keep watching and settled again once he had passed. The ringing of hard impacts sounded again and again from below. To this was now added grunts of greater and greater physical effort and growls of aggression-fuelled assault.

Then there came a new sound. It was the sound of steel on flesh. A roar of anger followed immediately. Karras's enhanced hearing heard blood spatter on sand.

Extremis Ultra indeed. A fresh rip in the meat of Zeed's left shoulder was pumping blood down his arm. Deep as the wound was, it was only tissue damage. The Raven Guard's enhanced physiology would stop that flow within seconds and a waxy secretion would seal it against further loss. But a wound was a wound. Its significance was greater than the flash of pain it caused. It marked the turning point. While the drones were getting faster and more relentless, Zeed was slowing at last.

Karras reached Kulle, extended a hand, and gripped the Watch sergeant's arm at the elbow.

'How do you see this ending, brother-sergeant?' Karras demanded. 'He has proven himself and more.'

Kulle was surprised at the intrusion, the sudden imposing presence of the red-eyed Death Spectre beside him. Not just any Death Spectre, but a Codicier, senior in his Chapter's Librarius. To a Silver Skull, the will of a Librarian was not something to be ignored.

Kulle looked down at the slate in his hand. The screen showed a graphical representation of the dial he had turned almost all the way to the right. The needle was deep in the red.

Down in the pit, Zeed battered one drone aside with a lateral elbow-strike, kicked another in the chest, and rolled away. When he rose, Karras could see that he was bleeding from a trio of shallow slashes on his chest and back. Nevertheless, his coal-black eyes still blazed with sharp focus. He was enjoying this, revelling in the battle-high.

'Yesss!' he hissed at the drones as they ambled forwards, weapons raised. 'To me, you mindless mannequins! To me!'

His thick blood dripped on the sand between his feet. Karras could smell its ferrous tang mixing with the scent of sweat and hot metal.

Suddenly, the drones froze. Their target lights faded from red to blue. Their arms dropped to their sides, weapons lowered, motors humming to a stop.

Zeed stared at them, momentarily confused, still holding his combat stance.

After a second, he dropped his stance and looked up at the pit's rim. His eyes sought out and found Sergeant Kulle.

'I wasn't done,' said the Raven Guard flatly.

Karras was surprised. He was expecting adrenaline-soaked rage from the long-haired battle-brother, but Zeed seemed to have switched off as easily, and almost as abruptly, as the drones had.

'Look around you, Ghost,' Kulle called down, and Karras noted that even the sergeants had started to use the nickname. 'You have the eye of everyone in the Pankrateon. We all know what you have achieved here today. But you've distracted your brothers from their own training long enough. Extremis Ultra.' He shook his head. 'Truly, you have made a name for yourself today. Let it stand for now. The others must look to their own training if they are ever to rival you in the pit.'

That drew mutterings from some; typical warrior pride. It was pride only, however, without any real conviction behind it. The others couldn't deny Kulle's words. Zeed's proficiency had held them spellbound. He had dominated three armed attackers of inhuman speed and resilience with nothing but his natural weapons: hands, feet, knees and elbows. That he had done so without power armour or even basic combat-plate was the greatest proof of his skill.

Gradually picking up strength, a wave of applause – right fists beating on chests – started on the far side of the pit from Karras and spread right the way around.

Zeed shook his head, but he was smiling. He moved to the edge of the pit directly below Karras and reached up a hand.

'A little help, Scholar?'

Kneeling at the edge, Karras reached down, closed his fingers around Zeed's wrist and stood, hauling him up and over. There they stood, a metre apart, Zeed grinning into Karras's face. He shrugged and indicated his wounds.

'Had to let them get a few shots in.'

The smell of his oxygen-rich blood was strong in such close proximity.

'You fight without peer,' Karras admitted. 'But to die in training is to deny the Emperor his due. Our lives are not ours to spend freely.'

'You sound like a bloody Chaplain.'

'You would not have stopped until they cut you down, brother. I saw it in your eyes.'

'How are we to know our limits,' asked Zeed, 'if we never fully test them?'

'What is the point of knowing your limits if they are the last thing you ever know?' countered the Death Spectre.

The applause bled off, and the others filtered away down the tunnel back into the main hall. There, with ambitions aroused by the spectacle of Zeed's performance, the Space Marines would train harder than ever. Kulle had known that. He had been counting on it. This was not the first time he had exploited a particularly gifted Space Marine to inspire and motivate others. Each of the twenty grizzled warriors in the Pankrateon knew that he alone represented the hopes of his Chapter in meeting the old accords. Zeed might be nigh untouchable in hand-to-hand combat, but they were all Space Marines here. Fresh commitment to their training would, at the very least, lessen the margin between themselves and the display they had just witnessed.

Soon the hall echoed anew with clashing and grunting and blood-chilling battle-cries.

In the pit-chamber, Zeed moved around Karras to address Kulle. 'Thank you for your faith. I know Brother-Sergeant Coteaz had reservations. He left?'

Kulle's voice was carefully neutral. 'The Deathwatch has many brothers to train, Raven Guard. It cannot rest all its hopes on you. Brother Coteaz saw that the training of your brothers was being neglected while they spectated here. In future, I will endeavour to follow his example.'

Zeed shook his head. 'You would have missed quite a show.'

Karras and Kulle both laughed at that.

'By the nine hells, Raven Guard,' said the Silver Skull. 'Arrogance and skill in equal measure. The former will be your downfall one day, I think. As to why I allowed it, well, I'll not call it faith exactly. When one sets a new standard, it opens the way to greater heights for all. You inspired some and bruised the pride of others. All will train harder as a result.'

With that said, Kulle nodded once to each of them, then strode off, returning to his supervisory duties. As he departed, he called back, 'Training isn't over. You've another three hours here. Make it count, both of you.'

Karras watched the sergeant disappear down the corridor.

'Well?' said Zeed.

'Well what?'

The Raven Guard gestured at the pit. 'Train with me. An exchange of techniques. I've never seen a Death Spectre fight.'

'I can't match your speed.'

Zeed swept his glossy hair back over his left ear.

'No one can,' he said and leapt back down to the sandy floor at the bottom. 'But the gain is in the trying. So let's see what you've got.'

13

Varlan followed Aide Primaris Suliman along a bright corridor floored with creamy brown marble. At every ten metres, they passed alcoves housing the shining white busts of various playwrights, artists, actors and writers. There were no political or military figures among them, Varlan noted. No religious icons, either. It attested to what she'd read in the Chiaro dossier. The Lord High Arbitrator was known to spend far more time on the arts than on the practical aspects of planetary rule, no doubt delegating the lion's share of his workload to Suliman and others.

The unimposing little aide led the interrogator towards a set of broad double doors, darkly varnished and detailed with fine carving, watched by two men in the livery of the House Guard. Their uniforms were the purple of the twilight sky over Cholixe, and, though they looked fine and healthy, to Varlan it was clear their role was mostly a mix of decoration and visual deterrent. These were not true fighters like the twins. She got no sense of threat, no subconscious tightening of her gut as she approached them. They had about as much contained violence in them as the alabaster busts lining the hall and if they had ever used those short-barrelled lasguns, it was only on a practice range and not recently, judging by the impeccable condition of the weapons.

Of her own two bodyguards, only the girl Myrda walked behind Varlan. The interrogator had sent Oroga into the city. As she prepared to pass through the double doors at the end of the hall, Varlan thought back to the space port and the moments after her meeting with Asset 16.

She had emerged to find Oroga standing over a body in the darkness.

'Captain Dozois,' he had told her, looking up. 'He was about to follow you inside.'

'He's alive?' Varlan had asked.

'If you want him that way.'

Varlan had considered it. The captain had opted to meddle in her affairs. Not wise. Those that crossed the Inquisition did not live to tell of it. But had Dozois known with whom he was interfering? She doubted that. Had he known her for a servant of the Ordo Xenos, he would never have spent all those weeks trying to bed her. A healthy fear for one's life tended to quell one's carnal appetites. Actually, that would have brought her some much-wanted peace from the start, but the movement of Ordo assets was not the business of civilians and her master had enemies both within and without that would take great interest in her trip to Chiaro.

No. Varlan would wager the captain's life that he had guessed neither her identity nor her affiliation. He did not need to be permanently silenced so long as he had nothing dangerous to say.

'Serious injuries?' she had asked her aide. 'Did he see you?'

'I don't think so, ma'am,' Oroga had answered. 'I struck him from behind. One blow to the base of the skull. He'll have one hell of a headache, but that's all.'

'Good. Get him back on that shuttle. Dump him in the passenger cabin and shoot him up with one cc of psytroprene[18]. Then get out of there. Let him wonder why his head hurts and he can't remember a damned thing. The headache and the missing time should be enough to keep him out of our way. I want you to go into the city. Once you've seen the cargo into storage, set up a safe-house and get the lay of the land. Myrda and I will stay with this Lord Sannra while it suits me. Contact me at his apartments if there's a problem. Questions?'

'None, ma'am. Leave it to me.'

She had. Oroga had hauled the captain's body back towards the *Macedon*'s cargo shuttle under cover of Chiaro's eternal twilight gloom. She and Myrda had ridden with Suliman and his fellows in their armoured cars. Now the double doors were opening and she was about to meet Lord Sannra himself.

Suliman stepped through first, striding into a bright and spacious room with thick burgundy carpeting to announce her.

'Presenting Lady Fara Devanon of House Devanon.'

A tall figure rose from behind a broad desk of dark oak; a broad-shouldered man of about forty. Beneath a waistcoat of House

---

18. Psytroprene – a memory-wiping drug often employed by the Inquisition. A 1cc dose wipes approximately forty minutes of memory in average humans. The lost memories can never be recovered, even by psychic means.

Sannra purple, he wore a white silk shirt with ruffs at collar and neck. He opened his arms and smiled in a gesture of warm welcome. Flanking him on either side were two tall, pale, willowy women – identical twins wearing diamond-studded garments of white gossamer that could barely be called clothes at all. They eyed Varlan critically, then faced each other and sneered, not thinking much of her outfit.

Varlan ignored them beyond the habitual threat assessment.

'Come,' said Nenahem Sannra effusively. 'Enter and be welcome, lady.'

Varlan strode into the room, ignoring Suliman's bow as she passed him.

Sannra came round from the far side of his desk to kiss her hand. He was ten centimetres taller than she and heavily built, but not fat. Whatever his pleasures, he had not fallen into corpulence as so many aristocrats did.

He dismissed his two women with a wave, saying, 'Leave us for now, my swans. I will join you later.'

The women threw Varlan a last contemptuous look as they swept from the room.

'I hear your journey has been a long one, lady,' Sannra continued. 'Sit, please.' He gestured to an ornate, well-padded armchair to Varlan's right, and she accepted with grace. Sannra returned to his own seat on the far side of the desk.

'Sul,' he said, 'have some caff brought in, would you? Are you hungry, lady? Might you appreciate a fruit platter? Something else, perhaps? You need only ask.'

'Very kind, m'lord,' said Varlan, 'but your man Suliman was kind enough to provide a small meal in my room on arrival. It was more than adequate, thank you.'

'Just the caff then, Sul. A great pity you weren't here for dinner, Lady Fara. Barasaur lungs stuffed with chestnuts and glazed with honey. I have a wonderful cook, you know. She's a rare treasure on this Throne-forsaken world.'

'I shall look forward to sampling her work in due course, then.'

'You absolutely must,' said Sannra. 'Now, I've heard so very little about what brings you here, and I'm frankly quite curious. We're very isolated out here. It's a rare honour for me to entertain such a worthy guest, and a cousin of sorts, no less.'

They talked. Varlan said all the things Sannra expected to hear from Lady Fara Devanon. He, in turn, said little that surprised her. He was like many minor nobles given governorships on the edges of the Imperium, desperate for recognition in whatever form it came and equally desperate to prove himself worthy of greater station in life, if only with words. She played to his ego while it served, and guided the conversation into areas that interested her: industrial output, population figures, the religious and political leanings of the people, crime rates and so on. She asked about the Hasmiri and Garrahym both, and remarked on his success in coordinating the operations of two distinct peoples who had little liking for each other. She already knew this was a simple matter of separation, of course – with the two peoples confined to different cities, there hadn't been significant bloodshed between them since before his father's rule – but he took the compliment regardless, and it served her cover.

It was some forty minutes into this first meeting that Varlan sensed Myrda stiffen behind her. She half turned and looked at her bodyguard from the corner of her eye. Myrda had been standing quietly by the door since she and her mistress had entered. She had performed a quick tactical assessment of the room, as she always did, and had indicated *condition yellow* with a quick hand-sign. But now she seemed to be studying it again, slowly and discreetly. She caught Varlan's attention and gave the slightest nod towards one of the grand portraits on the east wall. Varlan glanced over at the painting – a large oil of a surly-looking man in a hunting coat and a long white wig. His left hand, the one in which he held a long wooden pipe, was a steel augmetic.

Lord Sannra noted her gaze. 'My great grandfather,' he said. 'A Navy man for twelve years. Rather stern fellow by all accounts. I never knew him, but the pipe was a gift from the Lord High Commander of Cadia, you know. I still have it.'

'It's a wonderful piece,' said Varlan, making to rise. 'Do you mind?'

'Not at all,' said Sannra, pleased. He pushed his chair back and rose to escort Varlan over to the painting.

For a moment they stood before it in silence, Varlan pretending to appreciate the brushwork. In truth, she was tuning all her senses towards what lay behind the painting.

Yes, Myrda, you clever girl.

'It was painted by Morrico of Piscina. Not my favourite of his works, despite the family connection, but my father adored it.'

'And what happened to his hand?'

Before Sannra could answer, Varlan raised her own hand, index finger extended. There was a sharp crack and a burst of light. From the far side of the canvas came a muffled grunt of pain. A body, doubled in agony, ripped through the canvas and collapsed on the floor at Varlan's feet. A silenced autopistol fell to the floor beside it. The trigger was sensitive. As the pistol hit the floor at an angle, it discharged with a muffled cough. The round shattered a lume in the ceiling. Glass showered Lord Sannra's desk.

Sannra cried out and sprang two metres backwards. When no further shots came, he edged forwards, hands on cheeks, keeping Varlan between himself and the body on the carpet. 'What in the name of Carastina is going on here, lady? What did you just do?'

Varlan ignored him. She crouched over the figure on the floor and checked for a pulse. *Faint.* It was a woman, short and slim with black hair tied in a tight bun. She was neither young nor pretty. *Forty or so. Hard worker.* Her white blouse was stained deep red from the crater Varlan's weapon had left in her chest. She was struggling to breathe.

'A name. Now!' Varlan demanded. 'Who sent you?'

The dying woman's expression changed from one of agony to one of gloating. She bit down hard on something. Blue froth bubbled from between her lips. Varlan shook her. 'No! Warp damn it!' Turning, she barked, 'Myrda, secure this room. No one in or out.'

'Aye, ma'am,' said Myrda, drawing a stun-pistol from beneath her black jacket and turning the lock on the inside of the doors. Outside, the two House Sannra guards started banging and shouting for their employer.

Varlan spoke to Lord Sannra. 'Tell them you are fine. Tell them to be quiet and wait. Order it.'

Sannra gaped. His mouth worked noiselessly for a moment. He looked like a suffocating fish.

'Do it!' snapped Varlan.

Sannra jerked backwards as if slapped, then proceeded to call out to his guards as instructed. They stopped pounding on the doors. When he crouched down beside Varlan again, the lord was pale but his breathing had steadied.

'It's Aga!' he whispered, studying the face of the dead woman. 'One of the senior maids. But she couldn't have known about the crisis tunnel. No one does save Suliman and I.' He stood. 'What was she doing in there? Why the pistol? Did she…? Look here, Lady Fara. What's going on? You just killed one of my maids with that ring of yours. If you're just some noble's daughter here on trade business, then I'm the bloody Lord Marshall of Terra itself! I want answers, now. I'm the governor here!'

'Yes, you are,' hissed Varlan. 'A job you've been doing with your eyes shut, if at all. You don't seem to have noticed the mass disappearances among the Garrahym. You don't seem to have noticed the reports coming in of strange things seen in the mines or on the fringes of your cities.' She gestured at the dead body on the floor. 'You don't seem to notice much at all. One of your own staff was spying on you, perhaps even planning to kill you this day.' *Or me,* she thought, *which is the more likely.* 'How many more might be doing the same, Arbitrator? How safe do you think you are? We both know the guards at your doors are more for show than anything else. Even they might be traitors awaiting an opportune moment.'

Sannra made a scoffing sound, but there was fresh fear in his eyes. It soon gave way to anger. 'You can't come in here and say such things. You can't just shoot the place up like this. I say again, just who the devil are you?'

Time to play her cards, Varlan knew. If she was to get his full cooperation, she had best reveal herself now. Her master would make sure the loose ends were tied up later.

Committed, she reached two fingers down into her bodice and drew a circular pendant from her cleavage. The setting was of intricately worked silver, in the centre of which sat a ruby cut into a perfect disk. The gem was both a button and a lens, and Varlan pressed it, then sat the pendant in the palm of her hand. Above it, a hololithic image of a skull appeared and began to rotate. In the centre of the skull's forehead was a rune: the Inquisitorial 'I' crossed with three short bars, each representing one of the great ordos. After a few seconds the skull vanished to be replaced by the rotating image of a scroll on which were inscribed Varlan's credentials in tiny Gothic runes.

'My name is Shianna Varlan,' she told the astonished aristocrat. 'Interrogator class 3, Ordo Xenos, agent of His Imperial Majesty's Holy Orders of the Inquisition. My word is law, Nenahem Sannra. From the moment I set foot on your world, your authority was superseded. Chiaro faces a crisis it is not equipped to deal with. That is why I have been sent. I have come to aid you. If I can, I will save you.

'But you will do as I command, or you will die.'

14

Tencycles came and went. Times in the kill-block improved. Previous bests were beaten, then beaten again. Accuracy rates with the new weapons and ammunition types went up. Proficiency in race-specific close quarters combat methods rose steadily. And still the Space Marines trained without the power armour to which they had so long been accustomed. At first, eschewing armour throughout the first half of Deathwatch training had seemed a strange, even ill-considered approach to Karras and the others. Ceramite plate and boltgun were badges of honour, the entitlement of those tested to the brink of death – in Karras's case, beyond even that. They were entitlements not easily put aside. But now, some two hundred cycles into the programme, with their performance levels beyond anything the sequestered Space Marines had previously known, the logic behind it could not be faulted.

Dependence could be deadlier than the most lethal of foes.

If a Space Marine of long years' experience could no longer wage war without the iconic armour and weaponry that were his hard-earned right, was he not less than the aspiring Scout he had once been? How could such a one justify his place among the legendary Adeptus Astartes? It was not one's power armour or weapons that made one a Space Marine. It was the man inside – the body, the mind, the spirit, all forged in a training and augmentation regimen that killed far more than it successfully produced. Strip away all the tools of his lethal trade and you changed nothing; a Space Marine was still a Space Marine.

Forged on Occludus, and re-forged here on Damaroth. I am more than I was. And yet, without my powers, how could I not feel so much less?

Only another Librarian could truly understand. A power so great, so multifaceted; a gift of blood, of complicated and ancient lineage – it became part of the soul, woven into the very fabric of the self. When mankind was young, still numbering less than a trillion, people had doubted the evidence before them, doubted that a few could see paths into the future or start a fire with but a thought. The confluence of genetic factors that allowed the birth of the witchblooded was still all too rare. But humans had proliferated, had spread across the stars, the race exploding and expanding. And with the growth of their number came a burgeoning of that evidence. Now, without the eldritch abilities of astropaths and Navigators, without the empyrean fire and fury of sanctioned battlefield psykers, the Imperium would shatter and fragment, and the jaws of the xenos threat would snap shut over the human race forever.

Call us what they will, be it witchkin, witchblood, blackfate or any other name; it is we who hold this Imperium together, even as fools shrink from us and make the warding sign over their hearts when we pass.

He had tried to understand the fear and contempt others bore towards his kind, but they had never known the invigorating sense of freedom and strength his power gave him. To him it seemed that the lives of the ungifted were lived blind. They missed so much that was all around them. They would never see the coruscating aura that flickered and danced like living flame around ancient artefacts that had belonged to heroes or saints. They would never know the joys of watching an enemy's soul dissipate into the ether after being wrenched from its physical body by a killing blow.

It was only natural that one came to rely on so great a gift – as natural as relying on one's eyes to see and one's ears to hear. To Karras, fighting without his gift was like fighting without one of those senses. Suppressing it by choice was like disabling one's own arm before leaping into battle. Senseless.

Yet all Librarians knew the sword was double-edged. He thought back a hundred years and heard his khadit's voice, deep and clear:

'There are enemies in the vastness of space to whom your gift is as nothing. Never forget that. Some can suppress it entirely, even turn it against you. Faced with such foes, your salvation lies in bolt and blade, and in those beside whom you fight. Unleash your power with due caution, for it carries a price and, as with all things, excess is the path to one's undoing.'

It was downtime, the end of another tencycle, as Karras recalled these words. Second Litany had been said, as it always was at the end of a cycle. Ninety minutes remained before the beginning of the next, but Karras had opted not to sleep. Nor had he gone to the Refectorum. Instead, he had come to one of the central keep's many spires seeking silence and solitude. Here he sat, on a deep stone sill before an armourglass window, knees drawn up to his broad chest, looking out at a strange blue snowfall. It was dark and silent up here in the tower heights, and icy cold, but that didn't bother a Space Marine. Karras's breath misted in the air in front of him.

The moon of Damaroth was shrouded from view by thick cloud, but the glow from the fat flakes of eerie blue snow cast a chill light on the ancient stone floor behind him as they drifted against the glass.

So much insecurity still. So much doubt. He should have adjusted fully by now. Others had. He knew he was holding himself back. Still, he couldn't feel entirely angry at himself. So many things seemed to hover just beyond the edge of his awareness, just out of mental reach. Important things. Things he would have perceived if only his power hadn't been locked away. In frustration, he had almost considered tearing out the accursed implant, and not just once since the day of his run-in with the arrogant Ultramarine.

Prophet, indeed!

Karras had reached back over his head, groping blindly for the protruding edge of the metal casing where the warp field suppressor sat like a cold, steel spider on his upper spine, level with his shoulder blades. His fingers had brushed it, but there was no purchase to be gained on its surface. It had been sunk deep into flesh. Besides, he knew he couldn't really pull it out. He believed Lochaine. The implant's artificial ganglia had penetrated his spinal cord and linked themselves to his own. He wasn't about to risk permanent self-paralysis.

I must bear it for now. The time will come.

He thought of the Megir then, of the terrible burden the First Spectre carried, of all he endured for the Chapter and the Imperium itself, suffering in faith and hope, his life-force being burned up far faster than it ought to be, all in the name of the Great Resurrection which Corcaedus had foretold. Shame hit Karras like a wave and he resolved to do better, but a darkness clung to his thoughts. The knowledge that Athio Cordatus would one day take the First Spectre's place twisted Karras's stomach. He didn't think he could stand to see his khadit's life-force bled away by that damnable throne. To know the Shariax was killing the First Spectre even now was almost too much to bear. He sought distraction – something, anything to bring him back to the here and now.

Outside, the snow was getting deeper, the flakes were getting fatter. So strange, that blizzard of gently pulsing blue light. So eerie, the blanket it lay upon the surface of the vast artificial ring. What manner of beings had made this inexplicable place? Were they still out there somewhere – a xenos threat to be purged in blood and fire?

Through the old stone archway on the right, Karras heard the unmistakable beat of a battle-brother's footsteps on the long stone stairwell. The sound echoed up to him from far below. The approaching Space Marine still had long minutes of ascent before he would arrive here, but the sound of those footfalls had already broken Karras's peace.

Perhaps that's just as well, he thought.

He knew by now the identity of the one who approached. The climber's height and weight were written in the sounds of his steps, along with much else besides.

It was Lochaine, Chief Librarian of Damaroth. Dimly, a part of Karras sensed his power, despite the fact that the greater part of his own was sealed from him.

When the footsteps ended, Karras turned to see the huge Storm Warden standing in the arched stone doorway, his face cast in faint blue tones from the snow outside.

'I intrude on you,' said Lochaine.

'Not without welcome,' replied Karras; a polite formality, if not entirely honest.

Lochaine allowed himself a smile and entered the room unhurriedly. He moved to the large recessed sill on which Karras sat and gazed outside.

'Haunting in a way, isn't it?' he said of the glowing snow. 'The Mechanicus remain at a loss to explain it. Samples dissipate too quickly for any proper study.'

'The universe will have its secrets,' said Karras.

Lochaine frowned. 'We trust you as much as any, Death Spectre. If you do not understand by now the need for–'

'I understand well enough. Forgive me. It is I who am the cause of my own dissatisfaction. I feel I should have adapted fully by now. I train to my limits and beyond, and I follow the strictures. I know only too well what I and my Chapter gain by my presence here. But still…'

The implant. The lack of trust. The need to set the core of one's very identity aside.

Lochaine leaned against the opposite side of the stone window frame and glanced out at the pulsing snow. He wore a tunic of rough black cloth belted with a thick silver chain. From the chain hung a small censer, a silver ball with aquila-shaped apertures. Aromatic smoke curled up and around him, clinging to him like the tendrils of some ghostly oceanic creature.

'You have been resisting the hypno-induction process, brother,' said Lochaine. 'More so than most. We've seen it before, of course, but it brings only misery and difficulty. You must let go. We do not ask that you put your Chapter aside. Do we not honour all who stand by the Old Accords? You do no one any favours, least of all yourself. The honour of the Death Spectres will be better served by dropping your barriers. Embrace the Watch as it waits to embrace you. There is great glory to be earned. Do most of the veterans who return not make the rank of captain in time? And how many of those went on to become Chapter Masters? The number might surprise you.'

Karras shivered at that.

Become the master of his Chapter and slowly petrify on the cold seat of the Shariax? Better a death in battle. Better anything but that.

And there it was; the reason he resisted so hard.

I fight out of loyalty to the Megir and to the Order, but it is more than that. I fight out of guilt. I know how he suffers on our behalf.

If Lochaine detected his sudden chill, he chose to let it go unmentioned.

And yet, Karras thought, *it was the Megir and the Menrahir*[19] *who put me forward for Deathwatch service. They would not do so simply to honour me. There is greater purpose to all they do. Emperor, grant me the faith I need to serve that purpose without question. Therein lies my true duty.*

Karras met the eyes of the Deathwatch Librarian.

'Have I been a fool, brother? Is that how you see me?'

Lochaine smiled.

'If only you knew how alike we were, Lyandro. When I was in your place, the Chief Librarian of the Watch at that time almost authorised a mind-wipe, such was my resistance. The Watch Commander, too, thought me beyond all hope of full induction. He judged my recruitment a mistake, but my brothers in the Watch Librarius would not relent. Loyalty is a fine quality, Lyandro, and there is no such thing as *too much*. But how one's loyalties are served and how they are best placed is a thing that needs great consideration.

'Stop fighting it. Let yourself be the warrior this Imperium needs. Service to the Watch does not last forever. It is only temporary.'

'It does not seem so temporary for you,' Karras countered.

Lochaine nodded. 'Many fear permanent secondment at first, eager to return to their brothers, especially before the hypno-induction takes root fully. The Watch makes higher demands of some than of others. But I came to terms with that long ago. The honour of the Storm Wardens is served better by my continued presence here. My name will be writ large in the Halls of Honour when I am gone. Many of my kills already grace the chambers of the Great Ossuary.

---

19. *Menrahir* – the Chapter council of the Death Spectres; from the word menris, meaning 'sage' in Occludian Low Gothic

I am as proud to be Deathwatch as I am to be a Storm Warden. I have made a difference. Brothers survived to return to their Chapters with honour because I stood beside them. I would serve an eternity for that alone. We are the line between life and death to our kill-teams, Lyandro. We live forever in the memories of those we lead. I no longer see things as I once did. Nor shall you.'

Karras gazed out beyond the cold armourglass pane.

'Hypno-induction changes the very way we think. I do not wish to lose my *self*.'

'Nothing is lost, only better shaped to fit needs, as it was when you rose from neophyte to battle-brother. Or would you return to Occludus in disgrace, your mind wiped of all you have seen and learned here? How would that serve the honour of those you love?'

Karras nodded thoughtfully. He realised he would rather die than allow such events to unfold. That was no idle assertion. It was sincere. He had crossed a bridge, and the weight on his soul seemed to rise, to lift away and dissipate like disturbed crows scattering into a winter sky.

Lochaine saw it on his face, that change, like sunlight breaking through clouds.

'I will be all the Deathwatch asks,' said Karras, resolute. 'I will honour the accords. You have my word.'

Lochaine didn't have to read the Death Spectre's aura to believe it.

'I am glad we have reached this point, brother. In truth, we could wait no longer. Things are about to change, for you and for all who have answered the call. Preparatory training is drawing to an end. In seven more cycles, you will be called to take Second Oath. Hypno-induction must be completed before then because, after Second Oath, you will be Deathwatch, and from that moment until the day you are released from service, it is to the Deathwatch that first honour must be served.'

Karras bowed, ready at last, seeing the need.

'There is another important change you should know about,' continued Lochaine. 'Kill-team allocations have been finalised. After Second Oath, they will be announced. You will begin training exclusively with your kill-team, and unit cohesion will be key.'

That, at least, was welcome news. The quirks and moods of just four or five battle-brothers would be far more manageable than dealing with those of almost a hundred.

Lochaine glanced out the window again, his face revealed in profile to Karras as he added, 'You'll return to training in power armour, too, and with a full loadout. Second Oath gives you the right to don the black at last. The Watch sigil will grace your shoulder. Be proud to wear it. So few earn that right. Fewer still wear it for long.' He turned his eyes back to Karras. 'We do our best to recover those that fall and send their remains back to their Chapter worlds. Would that the number were higher.'

'Brother Stephanus,' replied Karras. 'It meant a lot to his company that they were able to inter him in the sacred catacombs.'

'He died well,' said Lochaine. 'As did the Death Spectres who served the Watch before him. May we all meet such a worthy end when the time comes.'

'I fear not death,' said Karras resolutely.

'For you embody it in His Name. It is a fine motto. The name of the Death Spectres is less renowned than some, but know that it is well honoured here, despite your misgivings. I would not have sought you out otherwise. We expect great things from you, Lyandro Karras, despite the special challenges you will most certainly face.'

Lochaine pushed himself from the wall then and strode to the archway leading to the stairs.

'What does that mean, brother?' Karras asked the Storm Warden's broad back. 'Special challenges?'

'Just a few more tencycles, Death Spectre,' said Lochaine as he began his long descent. 'We shall speak again after Second Oath.'

15

The flashlights of the enforcers cast broad beams through the glittering, frost-filled air. Neither Varlan nor her trusty aides needed much light themselves – even the darkest shadows surrendered detail to their top-of-the-line augmetics – but the enforcer squads Lord Sannra had ordered to escort her would have been as blind as earthworms down here without their gear. It was a flustered Sannra, too, who had ordered the railways cleared so that several Viper LAVs[20] could push deep into the mines unhindered, carrying Varlan and her escort. And here they were at last, in the very hall where Ordimas had witnessed the ceremony of the strange and seedy cult.

No bodies, no lit lamps, no sign that anyone had been here recently save recent ash in the wall sconces and braziers, and a profusion of tracks on the icy stone floor. *Yes. Lots of foot traffic.* Oroga was crouched over, studying it while Myrda stood watching Varlan's back, her awareness electrically charged to every sound around them. Both the twins were on *code orange*, ready to respond to any threat.

Oroga looked up and nodded at Varlan.

The tracks are recent, then. They fit Ordimas's experience exactly.

Varlan's gaze moved to the black mouth of the tunnel that led away from the rear of the hall's elevated stage. It was along that tunnel her answers lay.

Looking at the stage, she shuddered, remembering all too sharply the sights she'd seen through Asset 16's opticom.

Here. It all happened right here.

Footsteps sounded behind her, and Varlan turned to find Lieutenant Borges approaching, breath misting from the muzzle filters

20. LAV – Light Armoured Vehicle.

of his rebreather. He stopped a few steps in front of Myrda, who had automatically positioned herself to block his approach. 'You were right, ma'am,' he said, speaking past the deceptively slim bodyguard, voice muffled by his apparatus. 'Recent activity. Too many tracks to make head or tail of.'

Varlan removed her own rebreather to reply. She needn't have, but the strap was pulling painfully at her hair and she wanted to adjust it. The next breath was icy sharp in her lungs, but not intolerable. The powered thermasuit the enforcers had lent her kept her body at a steady temperature, but that too bothered her. It felt close and hot, even in the airy, ice-rimed hall. The control module was belted at her lower back. In a moment, she decided, she would ask Myrda to adjust it.

'I did not expect to find anyone here, lieutenant, but you will take the matter more seriously now, I presume.'

The officer stiffened. 'I assure you, ma'am, I never take my duties any less than that. As I told you, this section of the Underworks has been abandoned for centuries. It was listed as stripped and locked down. Only a mine administrator or a tech-priest could have reopened it.'

'Then a mine administrator or a tech-priest is clearly part of the insurgency.'

'Insurgency? Come now, ma'am. Surely this is just a group of religious nuts who've breathed in a little too much soledite dust.'

'How many people have been reported missing in the last year, lieutenant? How many of those resurfaced soon after. How many children were born in Cholixe? More or less than in preceding years? How much equipment and provision went mysteriously unaccounted for? You see accidents, population increase and theft as all quite separate. I tell you now that they are not. The Civitas here on Chiaro have been caught sleeping. You are damned lucky I arrived when I did. Who can say how close the enemy's knife was to your own throat?'

The lieutenant's brow furrowed, but he bit back whatever reply was forming on his lips. Instead, he asked tersely, 'And what would the inquisitor have us do now?'

'I have told you already that I am an interrogator. In terms of relative authority to your own, it hardly matters, but I'll ask you to stop making the error.'

Borges was flexing his fists now. He was not a man used to being commanded. Nor was he used to being chastised. Who was this bloody woman to show up here and start running the show? And that aristo-fool, Sannra. Since when did he mess in Civitas matters? Better the man lock himself away with his addictions. Lord High Arbitrator in name only, that one. It was the Administratum men and the tech-priests that kept this place running. They left the Civitas to their business, and rightly so. This woman, though…

'My apologies, interrogator,' he offered insincerely. 'What would you have us do now?'

Varlan noted the lack of apology in the man's tone, but it hardly mattered. 'The tunnel at the back,' she told him, pointing. 'If we're to know more, we'll have to go deeper.'

'It means leaving guards with the vehicles,' replied Borges. 'I'll not have those Vipers fall into the hands of this supposed cult.'

'I leave force disposition to you, lieutenant, but let us move quickly. We're not here to sight-see.'

Borges grunted and turned away. When he was out of earshot, Myrda leaned in and spoke to her principal. 'Don't think he likes you much, ma'am.'

'I expect not, Myrda. These people have had it their own way for far too long. That's the problem with fringe worlds. Too much freedom, not enough scrutiny. Come, let's mount the platform.'

She called Oroga over and addressed the twins together. 'We're going deeper. Stay sharp. Asset 16 never went beyond this point. From here, we break new ground. I want any observations you care to make. Anything at all, clear?'

'Clear, ma'am,' said both in unison.

Lieutenant Borges had posted guards on the LAVs by now and had organised his platoon-strength force to move out – forty men minus the guards he'd posted, all in las-proof plate with heavy riot-guns locked and loaded. With a barked command, they all set off, two of Borges's best scouts up front, followed by a six-man fire-team. Behind the fire-team, Varlan and her aides walked with Borges and his second, a big sergeant called Caradine. Behind them came the rest of the force, all in combat helmets and carapace armour. The lieutenant was the only one dressed any differently. Eschewing a helmet, he had opted for a black beret with a golden Civitas crest on the front, a privilege of his rank, but one liable to get him killed if he wasn't careful, Varlan thought. Some of the men muttered from beneath their integrated rebreathers about being sent down into the freezing dark on *a bloody ghost hunt*. Others hushed them, glad of any change to the routine of daily duty on the city streets.

Varlan registered all this with growing irritation. A good officer would have stamped it out. Even better, a good commissar.

Up ahead, the torchlight of the scouts played across curving tunnel walls. The rock had been plastered over, giving everything a smooth surface that glittered with ice crystals. In the ceiling, some two-and-a-half metres above them, there were regular lume-globe fixtures, but there was no power to light them. Some had been broken, but how recently? Fragments of transparent plastek lay on the tunnel floor. They could have been there a day, a year, a century.

'Halt,' hissed one of the scouts from up ahead.

Varlan looked up the tunnel and saw the fire-team in front of her squat down suddenly. The scout who had spoken was pointing something out to his companion. His left hand was raised in a fist to stop everyone behind him.

'Signs of a struggle here,' he said at last over the vox-net. 'Looks recent. Days, maybe a week. Difficult to tell with everything getting frozen so fast. Scuffs on the wall. Boots, fingers. There's a little blood on the left side and on the floor.'

'Anything else?' asked Borges.

The scouts were silent for a few more moments. 'Nothing, sir. Proceeding.'

The platoon continued down the tunnel. They passed several broad chambers – junctions, really – where decisions had to be made. Tracks in the frost led off in every direction. Myrda and Oroga worked with the scouts where there was any doubt. Together, they managed to keep the party on the path most recently used.

'Your people don't need any light,' Borges said to Varlan as they strode through the gloom together. It was an observation, not a question. He had been watching how surely and effortlessly they moved in the gloom. The tunnel currently being traversed was, unlike most so far, wide enough to accommodate two or three people walking abreast. It was five minutes into this particular tunnel that he had decided to break silence with her. Perhaps, she thought, he was coming to terms with her authority now. Perhaps he regretted his earlier manner. *Rightly so.*

'A little,' she told him, 'but not much.' She did not tell him that she, too, boasted low-light vision capability, though hers, unlike the night-vision of the twins, was monocular, provided as it was by her opticom.

'Have they much experience with this sort of thing?'

'This sort of thing?'

'I… I'm not sure what to call it, ma'am. You've spoken of a cult down here. And you're not mistaken about disappearances, but that's always been a hazard of mining on Chiaro. People get lost. There are cave-ins, machinery accidents, all sorts. There are dangerous creatures down here, too. Nightside has its indigenous life. The miners run into them from time to time: tunnel-jellies, volpiad swarms, kinefrachs, all dangerous in their own way. There haven't been any sudden spikes in missing persons. Those reported seem to turn up alive after a few days. I can't speak on the subject of births, mind, but I don't see how that would relate to a cult way down here in the deep tunnels. What the heck would they eat down here? How would they survive? You think they're cannibals?'

Varlan didn't answer that. Speculation was useless right now, and what she did know was not for a mere lieutenant's ears. Instead, she answered his earlier question. 'My people have the highest level of training and the very best military grade augs, lieutenant. Experienced? Let me say this: were I forced to choose between them and an entire company of Imperial Guard, I should still choose the twins. That's not lip-service, I assure you.'

Borges went silent for a while. Varlan could guess what he was thinking:

Who are these bloody people and what are they doing on my planet?

Local law-enforcement were always the same. An inflated sense of importance. They'd know little of the Inquisition or its work. Borges would have checked the Civitas archives and found that no inquisitor had ever set foot on Chiaro before. At least, none that had ever been recorded in the archives to which *he* had access. All he'd know is that Varlan's authority superseded even Lord Sannra's. Exactly how or why would be bothering the breeches off him right now. She saw him studying Myrda and Oroga.

'I should like to see them in action,' the officer said at last.

'Better for all concerned, lieutenant, that you never get the chance.'

Myrda and Oroga overheard. Not difficult. Their hearing was superb. Varlan thought she saw them throw each other a glance. She grinned beneath her rebreather. They had every right to a little shared pride. She had told the Civitas officer no lie when she had said she would choose them over an entire company of Guard. They had proven themselves equal to her expectations in every regard during the three years she had been their principal.

The men in front of her suddenly halted again. Borges's hand flew to the large autopistol at his hip. 'What is it?' he hissed through his throat-vox. 'Gormund, report.'

Varlan fingered the grip of the ornate plasma pistol holstered on her right thigh. On her left, her golden sabre hung, a deadly vibrablade so valuable and steeped in old glory she often felt unworthy of it. His Lordship had made a gift of it, but a gift that came with a warning and a price.

Let it remind you to always give your best, he had told her. *Because any less will not be tolerated. The Ordo has no place for second-raters, Shianna.*

Varlan had made living up to the gift her personal mission.

'End of the tunnel, sir,' one of the scouts voxed back quietly.

Varlan noted how stealthy the enforcers had suddenly become. Good vox discipline, too.

Not as sloppy as I thought, Varlan admitted to herself. *Good.*

'What can you see?' Borges asked his scouts.

'A cavern or a hall, sir. It's massive. Dome-shaped, by the looks of it. Our flashlights aren't quite reaching the far wall.'

'Give me an estimate,' Varlan interrupted.

The two scouts conferred in whispers for a moment.

'Six hundred metres in diameter, we reckon, ma'am. Maybe two hundred metres to the ceiling. Looks like it might be an old shift-station.'

Varlan turned to Borges. 'A shift-station?'

Borges shrugged. 'Back before the train systems were properly installed, work-crews would come into the mines for months, even years, at a time. The tech-priests set up shift-stations for them – a sort of small town for them to live in while they worked down here. They were mostly a mix of habitation, maintenance and ore-processing facilities. After the transport systems were completed, they just started shipping workers in and out for each shift. There's not much call for such places any more.'

'But there *are* others?'

'Aye, a few. Well spread out. I don't see how anyone could live in them, though. No power to them now. The tech-priests used to use geothermal transfer sinks to power them, but when the shift-stations were abandoned, they removed the fusion cells. Honestly, interrogator, if we're looking for people down here, it can't be many, and they're living on a knife-edge. The cold would surely kill them if starvation didn't. None of this makes any sense.'

Varlan didn't contradict him, but she knew better. They weren't looking for *people* as Borges thought of them. Normal men and women couldn't run any kind of rebellion from down here. No, there was nothing normal about the cult that Ordimas Arujo had uncovered.

'What do you think, Caradine?' Borges asked his second-in-command.

Caradine's voice was gruff. It had a hoarse whispering quality to it, the result of having had his throat cut during a skirmish outside a Rockhead bar.

'Sweep-and-clear, sir,' he said. 'Jus' like it were a sector purge topside. Safest way forward, I reckon.'

Borges nodded, then remembered himself and looked to Varlan for confirmation.

'Do it,' said the interrogator.

Borges addressed his force over the vox. 'Right, gentlemen. You know the drill. I want a good, swift sweep-and-clear of the entire chamber. Safeties on unless we have contact. Six-metre spacing. Watch your corners and your angles. A-Squad, take left. B- and C-Squads on centre. D, take right. You report anything to me at once, and I mean anything. We don't know what we're looking at down here, so I want eyes sharp. Squad leaders?'

The four squad leaders, all corporals, voxed back their acknowledgement, and the party moved out of the tunnel mouth and into the gaping space of the dark, silent dome.

Varlan could feel the tension on the biting air. The men didn't talk. Some were afraid. They were used to breaking up wage-riots and drunken brawls. Here in the inky blackness, their imaginations began to work on them, pricking their minds with icy needles of fear.

Bars of torchlight swung to and fro as the men marched steadily forwards. The light picked out scores of squat prefab structures, long abandoned and rimed in ice. Their metal walls shimmered as if encrusted with a billion tiny gems. Here and there, doors hung open like the slack mouths of long dead men. Anxious enforcers peeked into these, sweeping flashlights and gun muzzles from corner to corner, satisfying themselves perhaps a little too quickly that they were unoccupied.

Varlan and the twins walked between and a little behind Squads B and C, accompanied by a tense, tight-lipped Borges and Sergeant Caradine. She watched the men in front as they entered and exited each structure, always in twos. There were several structures to which no easy entry could be gained. The doors and shutters were frozen solidly in place. These, the men swiftly abandoned and moved on, asserting with good reason that they had not been in recent use.

'What's this building?' Varlan asked Borges, gazing up at the tallest structure, a gargantuan monolith of plasteel plate, frosted concrete and broad metal pipes.

'This will be the main power node, ma'am.'

'I want it checked, thoroughly, lieutenant. And these look like storehouses and silos on either side. I want them checked out, too.'

'We can do a cursory sweep, ma'am, but anything else will take bloody hours. You can see for yourself that no one has been in or out of them. Not with those doors frozen solid. We've been down here half a day as it is, and my men are getting tired and hungry, not to mention bloody cold despite the thermasuits. Now, we're with you, have no doubt of that. But we're just thirty-odd men, and I think it's time my lads had a break. We'll finish the first sweep, set up a perimeter, and give them a bit of down-time before we crack open the bigger structures and go room-to-room. What do you say?'

Varlan was about to lash him with an angry reply when someone called out from the darkness, the voice clear and penetrating and chilling beyond even the icy air.

'It sounds like an excellent idea, lieutenant, but I wouldn't worry about that perimeter. It seems you've found what you were looking for. Or rather, it has found you. Welcome, Interrogator Varlan. May I call you Shianna? We've been so looking forward to your arrival. Word travels fast on Chiaro.'

The sudden hard glare of powerful spotlights stabbed at Varlan's organic eye. Her augmetic eye whirred softly, racing to compensate. She threw a hand up, squinting against the brief pain. The speaker gave a cold, clear laugh.

'And now we have you. The Master will be pleased.'

16

Karras sat in the Refectorum, halfway through his gruel, part of his mind occupied by the age-browned pages of the old tome in front of him, the other part turning over the events of the last exercise.

For seven hours, he and nine others had endured the caustic air, strange smells and harsh light inside one of the great pavilions. Eighty kilometres long on a side, the glittering pavilions were no mere botanical gardens, though many of them did contain vast forests of alien vegetation. Instead, each was a kind of reserve with its own special atmosphere and cogitator-controlled gravity, home to a variety of deadly alien organisms that had been brought to Damaroth and, in some cases, bred here.

Incredibly, the tencycle had involved running sniper operations against an entire four hundred-member tribe of imprisoned kroot.

The aliens were armed with the weapons favoured by their kind – powerful, long-barrelled rifles and vicious curving blades. They were well organised, highly skilled, supreme hunters with a long tradition of war. Karras couldn't guess how long they had been at Damaroth, but he suspected most had been born here, raised knowing the reserve as home. They were fiercely territorial. They had established a village in the centre of the pavilion encircled by an abatis made from the trunks of the trees that had stood around it. There was no hope of them ever breaking out, of course. Deadly automated defence systems were in place at every possible exit. The kroot had learned long ago that getting too close to the pavilion's inner walls was a waste of one's life.

They had learned the Gothic tongue of the Imperium, and the vox-speakers fitted throughout the reserve warned them of their intruders and told them they were being hunted. This stirred them into forming furious and excited hunting parties of their own. Karras and the others had to locate, identify and eliminate their pre-assigned targets without becoming prey themselves.

Had he not been burdened with the suppression implant, Karras could have employed his gifts to guide him, cloak him, divert the kroot hunting parties, even to eliminate his target. But all he'd had was a set of camouflaged combat fatigues, a bolter with a single magazine and a standard combat blade.

And knowledge.

Using all he had learned so far at the Watch fortress, he was able to avoid detection, get a good line-of-sight on his mark, and end another alien life.

The kill-shot had snapped that beaked head backwards, spraying the dirt with foul purplish blood.

In truth, his own performance during the exercise was not what occupied Karras as he numbly spooned cold nutriment into his mouth. It was the Ultramarine's performance that held his thoughts. Solarion had been in the same training group once again – the first time since their now infamous confrontation. Today, he had shown himself to be in a different class entirely. Even the Watch sergeant in command of the exercise – one Brother Bastide of the Sable Swords, a combat-proven hard-reconnaissance specialist himself – watched with thin-lipped disbelief as Solarion struck targets that ought to have been well out of range. That he had done so using the fin-stabilised, gas-propelled *Stalker* stealth rounds – something he had never used before, and whose density, balance and aerodynamic qualities he was thus unused to – proved him beyond a mere *natural*. He was, at least in terms of his specialisation, a legitimate prodigy.

Karras wished his respect for the Ultramarine could be pure and untainted, but he was certain it would always be overshadowed by what had passed between them. Perhaps, with the taking of Second Oath, it would no longer matter. They would soon be assigned to kill-teams. Throne willing, the day would soon come after which he'd never see the Ultramarine again. Unless...

He frowned and consciously attempted to centre himself, pushing bitter thoughts from his mind. He focused on the exercise itself and on the lessons it had reinforced, things he had made a habit over countless hard hours spent in the kill-blocks.

Shape, shine, shadow and silhouette. The four 'S's. All must be eliminated lest one give one's position away.

Suddenly, he became aware of a change in the atmosphere around him. He looked up from his bowl. The Refectorum had gone silent.

Some of the battle-brothers had turned where they sat, facing the entrance to Karras's right. There was a tension in the air waiting to break. Karras followed their gaze and saw a tall, broad Space Marine in a tunic of bright red standing in the west archway surveying the room. About his waist was a belt of gold hexagons, each inscribed with hexagrammic glyphs. On forearm and shin, he wore bracers and greaves, also of gold, engraved with richly detailed honour markings. He looked formidable, perhaps a Chapter champion, but of which Chapter?

It was then that Karras noted the horned skull tattoo on the newcomer's neck, a sigil he had seen in books and scrolls only. Never in person. But here it was now, marking its bearer as a Space Marine of the Exorcists.

The warrior finished his survey and marched stiffly into the Refectorum accompanied by Watch Captain Oro, dwarfing everyone present in his armour of Deathwatch black. As they drew level with Karras, who had lowered his spoon and placed it on the table, the Exorcist stopped and turned. He looked down his nose at Karras and stood there, staring silently, assessing for a long moment.

Karras, discomfited by something other than the stare, rose to his feet and addressed Captain Oro.

'Well met, Watch captain.'

'Lyandro Karras,' said the captain, 'This is Darrion Rauth–'

'Of the Exorcists,' Karras finished for him.

The Space Marine in red neither smiled, nor extended his hand. He simply stared. Karras had never seen such hollow, lifeless eyes on a living being – small, pale green eyes without any spark, sunk in dark pits under a low brow. His nose was flat and slightly skewed to the right, as if broken and then either badly reset or ignored completely. The most notable thing about that nose, however, was the deep scar across the bridge. It extended out over the right cheek and down to the jaw line. It was far from the only scar on that weathered, craggy face. Service studs told of long decades spent in battle. The Exorcist's short hair was a dark brownish red streaked with grey, brushed forwards, framing his face.

His eyes fell to the book on the table in front of Karras.

'Ordell's *Advancement of Imperial Man*,' he said. His voice was low and harsh, like grinding rocks. 'Extreme hardship is the root of all strength,' he quoted.

'And self-love is the surest path to one's destruction,' Karras finished, recalling the opening lines of chapter fifty-nine.

Silence hung for a time, broken only when an impatient Captain Oro cleared his throat. The Exorcist paid the captain's hint little attention. He seemed on the verge of saying something important, but he never quite got to it. Instead, he told Karras simply, 'Countless are the paths to destruction, Death Spectre. In the end, we all choose one.'

'Or one chooses us,' Karras returned, but he was thinking, *This one knows my Chapter, though I wear no visible sigil. Someone has spoken to him of me. Did Oro bring him through the Refectorum knowing I was here? Why?*

Something about the encounter made him believe it was no random event.

Rauth spoke once more only. 'I don't believe that. One's doom lies in the choices one makes. There are no excuses.'

To Karras it sounded accusatory, but that made no sense. How could it? As Darrion Rauth and Watch Captain Oro marched from the hall, followed by the eyes of muttering Space Marines on either side, Karras decided the entire encounter had been bewildering.

No. More than bewildering. It had been unsettling in the extreme, for what the others had failed to notice about Darrion Rauth, Karras had noted the moment he had laid eyes on him, despite the suppression of his extra senses. He had thought himself mistaken at first. Fatigued, perhaps. Definitely confused.

But he knew himself better than that.

The absence of any possible explanation changed nothing.

The Exorcist appeared to have no soul.

17

'Contact,' someone bellowed from an avenue on the right.

'Hostiles! All sides!' yelled another desperately.

'The rooftops,' shouted Oroga over the sudden eruption of gunfire all around. He was already moving to put himself in front of Varlan. Myrda, too, had immediately moved to shield the interrogator from fire. From behind, she grabbed her principal by the shoulders and hauled her into the cover of the nearest corner.

'Enemy strength,' Varlan hissed. 'Numbers. How many?'

Oroga shook his head. 'Difficult to say, ma'am, but at least double our own. They knew we were coming.'

On the vox-net, enforcers strung out across the domed space were shouting, desperately trying to coordinate some kind of counter-attack. But between the shouts, screams rang out. The attackers poured fire down on them from the rooftops and from the tunnel mouths on the far side of the shift-station.

Oroga ducked out from behind a metal wall, augs lighting the dark. He saw what the enforcers could not. When he spoke, it was to Varlan.

'Those aren't Guard-issue lasguns. They're using modded mining lasers and las-cutters. Most of them look like miners, too. Some are dressed like enforcers. Those have riot-guns. It's messy, ma'am. Orders?'

'Where the hell is Borges? He has to rally his people now!' She tried to contact him on the vox. 'Lieutenant, this is Varlan. Respond!'

'Damn it, interrogator. What in blazes have you gotten us into?'

'Where are you?'

'I'm in the avenue just north of you.'

Oroga poked his head out again. 'I see him, ma'am. Him and Caradine.'

A bright beam of las-fire flashed towards him, and the bodyguard pulled his head back just in time. The beam struck the ground, vaporising ice and cutting a deep furrow in the stone below. Both of the twins had drawn hellpistols from their shoulder holsters. Varlan had powered up her plasma pistol. The blue-purple glow of its charged energy coils lit the wall against which the three now huddled.

'We need to get you out of here, ma'am,' said Myrda. 'We could break for the tunnel we came through. If we can bottleneck their pursuit, we can do things our way.'

The cold voice from before spoke again. 'Do not throw your lives away. Embrace the Master. You need not die, only evolve. Put down your weapons. You will not be harmed. You will be shown the light.'

It seemed to come from everywhere at once. Varlan shivered, despite sweating inside her thermasuit. Beads rolled down her back, irritating her. She wished she could take the damned thing off. The voice tugged at her, so persuasive, so seductive. Had she not been trained to resist such things, she realised, it would have made her step out into the open. 'Psyker,' she spat. 'Their leader is a psyker. Can you feel it?'

Oroga and Myrda glanced at each other and nodded. They, too, sensed it. Like Varlan, they too had been trained to resist. But the enforcers...

'We have to get you out, ma'am.'

More weapons-fire split the dark, strobing so sharp and bright it lit the cavern like a captive thunderstorm. Varlan winced. 'Borges and Caradine are only about ten metres away, correct?'

Oroga nodded grimly.

'We regroup with them first. Then we pull back with as many of the enforcers as we can. Let's move. Oroga, knock out their lights.'

'Ma'am.'

He broke from cover at a run, firing two shots up towards the nearest rooftops from which the thick beams of spotlights knifed through the chill air. Within a second of each other, both lights exploded, showering hot glass on the shadowy figures operating them.

Varlan and Myrda broke from cover, moving swiftly behind Oroga as he sprinted for the avenue where Borges was pinned down. A figure stepped out from a darkened doorway on Oroga's right, hefting a heavy mining laser, preparing to fire from the hip. Blindingly fast, Oroga swerved towards the figure and launched a blistering right hook. His augmetic arm jolted just before impact, igniting a small propellant charge that made his metal fist jack forwards like a piston. The sound was like a riot-gun discharging. The impact took the shadow's head clean off its shoulders. The body tumbled to the icy floor, dropping the mining laser. Oroga slid back into cover beside Borges and Caradine. Barely a second later, Varlan and Myrda joined him.

Borges was furious, face twisted with impotent rage. 'What the bloody hell is going on here?' he stormed.

'What does it look like, lieutenant? Get your men back to the entry tunnel right now. Tell them to fall back. Staggered retreat. The enemy knows the terrain. They have the numbers. We can't win this here.'

Borges's eyes were almost bugging out of their sockets.

'Now listen here,' he rasped, so close to Varlan's face she could smell the bile on his breath. He was scared, despite the words he spoke next. 'I'm not about to turn and run from a bunch of bloody miners. This is–'

He was drowned out by a staccato burst of gunfire from nearby. Someone howled, high and long, the sound filled with raw agony. An instant later, the scream was cut off. A chilling laugh replaced it, filled with cruelty and malice.

'Throne, man, if you think these are just angry labourers…' hissed Varlan. 'There are men among them with enforcer uniforms and weapons. Somehow I doubt they're just playing dress-up. You've had traitors in your ranks, lieutenant. Emperor alone knows for how long. Is it any wonder they knew we were coming? We can't win this here. They have us on the back foot, and their leader is some kind of psyker. Pull your men out now. Give the command while you still have some left to follow it.'

Scowling, Borges addressed his embattled men over the sound of cracking las-cutter and plasma fire and riot-guns barking in deep reply.

'This is Force Command to all units. Back to the tunnel, all of you. Break contact. We're getting out of here. That's an order.'

'Right,' said Varlan. 'Now we move.'

Just then, shadows burst from the alleys on either side of the squat structure behind which they hid. Myrda's pistol blew a melon-sized hole in the torso of the first before anyone else had even registered it. Varlan herself got the other – the powerful blast of her plasma pistol atomising all but the booted feet of her would-be attacker. Borges and Caradine both winced with pain when the bright flash of Varlan's weapon damned near blinded them with its discharge glow. The air crackled with skin-prickling residual energy.

'Caradine,' barked Varlan, taking charge. 'You're on point. Oroga and Myrda will cover the retreat. Borges, you move with me. We follow Caradine. Get moving, sergeant!'

Caradine was up and running a heartbeat later. Varlan and Borges broke into a run just behind him. Then, the twins moved, their low-light vision picking out threats on the roofs and between the boxy structures.

They ran for what seemed only moments, time compressed by adrenal rush, before Varlan looked past Caradine's shoulders and saw a tunnel mouth ahead. Caradine had guided them incredibly well, not an instant of doubt or hesitation, despite his lack of augmetics or low-light optical gear.

Too well.

The thought slowed her. She put out a hand to stop the others. Something wasn't right about this.

'Caradine,' she called to him. 'How did you–'

Caradine slowed, stopped and turned. He aimed the barrel of his riot-gun right at her chest and grinned. With his left hand, he reached up and took off his combat helmet. Varlan gasped. In the dark, no longer hidden by a visor, his eyes glowed with a strange, unwholesome light.

'Sergeant,' snapped Borges, skidding to a halt beside Varlan. 'What the hell are you doing, man?'

Caradine adjusted his aim and pulled the trigger. There was a bright muzzle flash and a deafening crack. Borges howled in agony and collapsed to the cold cavern floor. Varlan dropped beside him at once. His left leg, she saw, had been blown off at the knee. The sharp smell of his blood mixed with burned cordite.

Caradine strode closer to them, chuckling to himself.

Varlan readied to launch herself at the man as soon as he was within reach of a killing blow. She knew she could disarm and kill him if he would just step into range. Frustratingly, Caradine stopped just beyond it and levelled his gun barrel at her face.

'Now, now,' he said in a gloating, sing-song voice. 'Don't get any ideas, woman.'

Myrda and Oroga fired another volley of shots back down the avenue and turned to find their principal looking down the muzzle of a riot-gun. They would have surged in front of her, giving their lives for her without hesitation, but both judged the distance they would need to cover in a single glance. There was no way they could get in front of Caradine's weapon before he could pull that trigger.

They halted, hissing curses, coiled to spring, but unwilling to take the risk until a better opportunity arose.

'Drop your damned weapons or she dies,' growled Caradine. 'Do it!'

Oroga and Myrda glanced at Varlan. For a second only, the interrogator hesitated. Then she nodded for them to abandon the pistols they held. She knew it would lull Caradine into false confidence. He didn't know how deadly the twins were even without the pistols.

Once the weapons were dropped to the ground, Caradine ordered the twins to kick them away, which they did with equal reluctance.

From the cold cavern floor, Borges spoke through gritted teeth. 'Why, Draz? We've served together for thirteen years. I was there at the birth of your daughter, for Throne's sake!'

Caradine didn't turn his eyes from Varlan as he replied. A tone of almost maniacal zeal had entered his voice. 'You can't possibly imagine the glory that has come to Chiaro, lieutenant. None of you can. Not yet. I was chosen before you. For years, I've served, and you never had a clue. You will know soon enough, though. The Master will grant you wisdom, power, understanding. You'll never get sick. Never get old. You'll be stronger, faster, see in the dark. You'll see the truth once you accept the Master's kiss.'

'You're a bloody madman,' spat Borges. 'Come to your senses!'

'Oh, I assure you he's quite coherent,' said someone from the shadows on the right. Varlan recognised the chilling voice even before she turned. The figure, impressively tall, completely unhurried in its movements, emerged with regal strides from between two stocky hab-blocks. Varlan's opticom showed her his features in stark detail. Her stomach clenched. Here was the priest-like figure who had led the strange ceremony, his tall slender form hidden beneath the folds of his robe, his long staff carried upright in his left hand.

He stopped several metres from Varlan.

'At last we meet face to face,' he said. 'Please, do not try to fight your way out, interrogator. It would be utterly futile, and killing you would be a lamentable waste of good material. Besides, this little skirmish is over. My people are gathering the bodies of your enforcers even as we speak. Listen,' he added, and cocked his head.

The sounds of the fight were dying off. Few shots could be heard. Even as Varlan registered this, the last riot-gun fell silent.

'They will not be wasted, living or dead,' said the cult priest. 'The Master has a role for all of them. They will contribute, one way or another, and the Master's flock shall grow.'

He stepped closer to Varlan now, his movements smooth and fast, then raised a hand and gripped her by her slender jaw. It was what she had been waiting for. This was the time to launch an attack. Her mind sent a lethal impulse to her right arm.

Nothing happened.

She could not move.

The strange priest laughed. 'Something wrong, interrogator?' He turned her head to left and right, appraising her. Varlan, her muscles refusing to respond to her will, could only study him back. His eyes were larger than they should have been, and of a colour unknown in natural human development. The pupils were abnormal, too, each shaped like a rounded hourglass. This was the second time she had noted their strangeness, the first having been through the eyes of Asset 16. The cult priest's teeth were also disturbing, seeming to number more than they should, each the same size and shape, dangerously pointed at the tip with a milky, semi-transparent quality. They made her think of the vicious snagglefish that populated the equatorial rivers of her home world.

This is no man.

'I know what you are,' she spat. 'Xenos hybrid scum.'

The priest laughed and shook his head. 'Do you think you offend me? I may not be a pureblood, but I am blessed, while you are cursed. You know nothing of my race. We do not kill our own. We do not waste our energy in wars among ourselves. Our destiny is too grand for that. You cannot begin to conceive of the coming change. Mankind is pathetic. To us, it is you who are the xenos. But we will not waste you. We will utilise you – fuel for our expansion towards the ultimate destiny of all life. You will understand soon. We will not kill you, Shianna Varlan. Your cells boast too fine a poetry. Instead, you shall make a splendid mother to the next generation of kindred. Yes, and what strong children you will have.'

As the strange priest had spoken, Lieutenant Borges slowly, carefully managed to grip his pistol from beneath his body. He withdrew it and took aim at Sergeant Caradine's head. He couldn't line the shot up properly without giving his intention away, so he used best judgement and hoped for the Emperor's blessing.

Caradine was distracted by the cult leader's words, his face betraying his rapture at standing in such close proximity to the eerie religious figure. Borges said a quick prayer in his mind and pulled the trigger of his autopistol. The shot rang out, deafeningly loud. Caradine's head rocked backwards, a gout of steaming blood leaping into the air to splash on the frozen floor a moment later.

His lifeless body hit the ground with a thud, the riot-gun clattering as it spun away.

The hybrid priest turned, scowling, distracted for just an instant, and Varlan struck at once, a knife-hand strike to the cult leader's throat. It would have killed any normal man. She had used it before to just such effect, stiffened fingers fatally striking a major nerve bundle. But in this instance, her fingers met cold, rigid resistance. They buckled painfully and she hissed at the sharp jolt of agony. One of her fingers broke.

The priest laughed again, showing those innumerable small pointed teeth gleaming in the black hole of his wide mouth. His hand flashed up, cuffing her on the side of the head. Varlan fell, stars reeling in her vision.

Myrda and Oroga were already surging forwards, but it was too late. Powerful figures flooded from the black alleyways on either side, casting off canvas robes to reveal grotesquely misshapen humanoid forms. Each was at least two metres tall, their flesh strangely ribbed and wet-looking. Oroga had a brief glance of body-armour made of some kind of organic resin, but then the giants were on him. He heard Myrda grunt in pain, but there was no chance to look. A bony arm shot out towards him, fingers clenched in a fist. Oroga couldn't believe the speed of it. He had seldom come across anyone or anything that could strike faster than he could. He tried to ride the blow on his metal forearm, but his movement was a fraction of a second too late. The blow connected with his jaw, breaking it, staggering him back towards the wall of the hab behind him. He never hit it. He tripped on something and fell. He registered a hot, sticky wetness that didn't belong in such a cold, stony place as this. He scrambled backwards and looked down at the thing over which he'd fallen. It was the remains of his sister. Her ribcage had been pulled apart and her heart torn straight from her chest. Steam lifted into the air as her blood-slick body quickly cooled.

Fuelled by rage and torment, Oroga loosed a battle-cry and launched himself upwards, determined to have revenge. One of the towering grotesques was already behind him, however. As Oroga came up, the twisted humanoid gripped his jaw in one hand and the back of his head with the other. The strength in those sharp-clawed hands was immense. Oroga heard his own skull crack. Then the giant twisted, sudden and hard. Oroga's connective tissues ripped apart. His head came off in the giant's hands. His body collapsed limp like an empty sack.

All this had taken only seconds, during which Varlan had been slumped on the ground, practically insensate. She was shaken out of it by Borges. He was propped up on one arm, trying to get her to take his gun. His leg was bleeding out like a fountain and his supporting arm kept slipping. He was fading, dying and he knew it.

'Take it,' he hissed at her. 'Kill that bastard while you still–'

Varlan heard a whooshing sound. Wind whipped her hair.

Where Borges's head had been, there was suddenly nothing but wet darkness. His supporting arm gave out. His body flopped to the cavern floor.

Varlan felt sharp fingernails, hard and cold as iron, bite into her upper arms. Without any apparent effort, she was hoisted into the air and slung over the shoulder of one of the grotesques. She found it hard to focus her eyes, still dizzy from the priest's blow. But when the monstrosity that carried her began walking, she saw the priest fall in behind them, eyes locked to hers, such a sickening look of satisfaction on his face. Behind him, other strange figures bent to lift the corpses of Lieutenant Borges, her aides and even that of the traitorous Sergeant Caradine.

A resource. Fuel for the expansion. They waste nothing.

She was the last one left alive, but that was hardly something to be thankful for. Her fate, she knew, would be far worse unless she ended her life right now. A mother, the priest had said. Ordimas Arujo had warned her. She wanted to weep, but that was not something Shianna Varlan ever did. She had a single choice left. Looking down at the rings on her fingers, she knew one of them still held a charge, a single bolt of energy that would be enough to end her life and spare her from the horror to come. *Do it*, she thought. *Kill yourself, Shianna. Don't let them do what they will.*

She almost convinced herself, too, but in the end, she was an interrogator of the Ordo Xenos. Her life was not her own to end. It belonged to the Ordo, and to His Lordship. Her opticom was logging everything in that special partition of her brain. Somehow, His Lordship would find a way to get her out. If not, then at least he would recover the intelligence she was now uniquely positioned to gather. For that, she would endure. It might mean the difference between life and death for countless others.

For just a moment, she wondered if His Lordship had known this might happen. His psykers were powerful. Had he sent her here knowing capture was written in her future? Was it this very circumstance that best served his veiled purpose? No. She couldn't believe that. Mustn't believe it. Her loyalty was the foundation of everything in which she trusted. He would get her out somehow. He would send someone, perhaps even his angels of death.

Until then, I will suffer what I must, observe all I can. Emperor Omniscient, I pray only that salvation come soon, whether rescue or death.

The monstrosity that carried her left the underground dome of the shift-station behind. Narrow, frost-covered walls slid past on either side. The creature was taking her deeper into the old mines. The hybrid priest strode behind, his unblinking eyes always on her. She did not know it then, but they would travel for hours to reach the lair of the so-called Master. All sign of human handiwork would disappear. They would travel through tunnels carved in solid rock by the powerful bio-acids of great prehistoric worms. They would traverse narrow stone walkways and vast echoing caverns cut and shaped by geological time and, at the end of it, they would reach a place Varlan lacked the vocabulary to describe, save that it resembled nothing that could have come from a human mind.

It was here, in this foul place, this alien den of soul-swallowing horror, that Shianna Varlan's slow descent into madness and destruction would begin.

It was here that her children would be born.

18

Ninety-eight Space Marines stood in the great hall, all clad in black robes, their hoods thrown back. Ninety-eight grizzled warriors of the Adeptus Astartes, waiting like statues set in rows of ten, all save the front row of eight in which Lyandro Karras stood.

They gazed up at the vast hovering head of the Watch Commander, Zaharan Jaeger, supreme authority at Damaroth, holo-projected onto the incense-heavy air. As was his right, Jaeger had donned ancient Terminator armour, both to celebrate the day and to lend it an indisputable gravity. The vid-picter that captured his image couldn't quite encompass his massive armoured shoulders and cowl. At the sides, the hovering holo-projection appeared abruptly cropped. Nevertheless, the tech-adepts had done fine work. The raw presence of the giant armoured form in the air above them, almost god-like, was felt by all. It held every eye. Jaeger's voice boomed from vox-grilles set high in the carved stone pillars and buttresses that held up the frescoed ceiling so far overhead.

'Second Oath, my brothers. More significant than you can yet comprehend. It is here today that you truly become Deathwatch. Your training has been intense – a testing time, I know. For some more than others, our doctrines are a thing hard learned. We are no marching army to go knocking on gates, as you are now all too aware. Throne willing, you will return one day to the Chapters that made you, all the more capable of strengthening them with what you've learned, better able to serve their needs, because you were Deathwatch, and you stood as a bastion against that most heinous of tides. The xenos give no quarter. Good. We ask none and never shall. They are beasts, a vermin infestation, a cancer in this universe, and they think mankind mere slaves or prey. Let them. In that very arrogance lies their defeat. They know not our true strength. *Your* strength. For it is you, newest of my Deathwatch brothers, who shall cast them down into dark oblivion.

'Since the Apocryphon Conclave of Orphite IV, the defence of the Imperium from forces inhuman has fallen to us. It is in our strength, our zeal, that mankind unknowingly finds its salvation. We have stood watch for almost ten thousand years. Vigilant, my brothers. Vigilant and bold. And we ask no thanks. Tribute matters little to such as we. Our fight is in the shadows, and in those shadows we must remain. Take pride instead in what you are: first among equals, warriors cast anew in sharper, deadlier form. No filth born of alien blood can rival you. You were Space Marines, but now you transcend even that.

'As you take Second Oath, pour all your commitment into the words you speak. There is no going back. Once you pass through these doors' – here he gestured to an ornately carved portal in the wall on his right – 'you will be bolted into your power armour. On your left shoulder shall be the icon of our sacred order. On your right you shall bear the icon of your Chapter, for your service honours both, and a betrayal is a betrayal to both. Make no mistake about that. The rest of your armour, save the silver left arm, has been painted black, for shadow is your ally in this desperate fight. You don the black and cloak yourself in darkness both. Think on that a moment. Think on how few, even among the greatest you have known, ever get to bear that honour. I hope each of you understand its implications.

'It is a thing of life-changing significance, this oath you take today. Remember the instructions of your Watch sergeants and do as you are bid. Secrecy is law among us. Hold to that. Those who break the oaths made to our order suffer the penalty of death. No exceptions. Those who betray their bond face execution. Those who run are hunted down. Those that came before you understood this. To these laws, each of your Chapters swore when they signed the Old Accord. Renegades and oath-breakers will find no succour among kin, for aiding a renegade is itself a crime. Do not stain the honour of those who sent you. And do not stain the honour of those who have worked so hard to see you succeed.'

Here, Jaeger cast a glance at the Watch sergeants, who stood quietly, heads bowed, by the side of the great dais from which he spoke. His vast hololithic image, however, appeared to look not at the sergeants, but at the glorious banners which hung from brass rods fixed high on the smooth stone walls. Turning back to face the ordered rows of oath-takers, Jaeger continued: 'Now, it is time for you to step forward. The moment has come. We begin with the Librarians. Watch Captain Xavian, call forth the first oath-taker.'

Jaeger stepped away from his golden lectern and his hololith disappeared, like a towering ghost melting back into strange dimensions.

A Watch captain stepped forwards, his black armour chased with gold, embossed with skulls and laurel motifs. His voice was sharp and high, a rapier sound in contrast to the thunder hammer boom of Jaeger's.

'We call upon Ledahn Sandaro Arrexius, Epistolary of the Iron Lords, chosen of his kin, pledged to the service of our order by oath and accord. Come forth. Stand before all and make your pledge.'

Arrexius, a quiet, stern individual with whom Karras had shared only the briefest of words, moved from his place in the front row of Space Marines. Walking solemnly down the central aisle, head bowed, hands pressed to his chest in the sign of the aquila, he looked like a penitent monk. He stopped by the bottom step of the dais. Before him was a block of dark oak, its uppermost surface covered in thick red velvet. Upon this, Arrexius knelt.

Karras watched intently. He breathed deeply, inhaling the rich incense that hung on the air.

I am ready, he told himself. *I am ready.*

The floor trembled a little as Zaharan Jaeger, in his massive Tactical Dreadnought armour, descended the broad marble steps, flanked on his right by Watch Chaplain Qesos. They stopped on the final step and looked down at the bowed and kneeling Arrexius waiting patiently before them.

As they will soon look at me, thought Karras.

Chaplain Qesos gestured towards a group of figures waiting in the left wing of the hall. Two servitors ambled forwards, one carrying a finely crafted tripodal stand of black iron, the other a dish of black ceramite filled with blazing hot coals. They placed these things by Qesos – the dish of coals atop the stand – and shuffled back to their original position.

Qesos gestured again, and a slim male Rothi, face masked in white porcelain as they always were, stepped close to present the Chaplain with a rod of steel topped with the skull-and-bones symbol of the Watch. The Chaplain took it, dismissed the Rothi, and pushed the brand between the glowing coals.

Jaeger spoke.

'Brother Arrexius, look at me now. Look into my eyes as you make your pledge.'

Arrexius looked up into the gold-irised eyes of the titanic figure in front of him.

'Do you, Ledahn Sandaro Arrexius, scion of the Iron Lords, swear your loyal service to the Deathwatch for so long as it may be needed?'

'On the blood of my brothers, so do I swear,' said Arrexius with clenched-jaw conviction.

'Do you, Ledahn Sandaro Arrexius, scion of the Iron Lords, swear to stand tall beside your fellow Space Marines, no matter their Chapter, no matter the scars of the past, to fight side-by-side against the xenos threat at the cost of your very life?'

'On the bones of the primarchs, so do I swear.'

'And do you, Ledahn Sandaro Arrexius, now and forever more scion of the Deathwatch, pledge your very soul to the holding of this order's doctrines, laws and secrets? Swear to this now with all your heart and hold this oath above all else, or forfeit all memory of your time here and be returned to your Chapter in disgrace.'

'On the eternal sacrifice of the Emperor Himself, so do I swear.'

The words rang out, echoing from the walls. It was the most solemn oath any had heard since swearing fealty to their own lords, their Chapter Masters, and to the martial brotherhoods that had forged them.

Jaeger lifted his massive plated arms, servos whirring, pistons hissing, and turned his eyes to the assembly. 'Second Oath is observed. Death be upon all who renege.'

'Second Oath is observed,' intoned the assembled warriors.

The Watch Commander turned his dark eyes back to Arrexius. 'Ready yourself, brother, to accept the mark of your promise.'

Arrexius opened his robe and dropped it back to reveal an upper body thick with that hard, ropey muscle so typical of a Space Marine. His skin was somewhat pale, Karras noted, there being no natural sunlight on Damaroth to turn it brown, and it bore scars and old burns in numbers not easily counted. His back looked like the street map of some bustling hive-city, such was the history of battle written on his flesh. At the base of his skull, Karras could see the shining black metal of the I/O sockets by which a Librarian could interface with a psychic hood. Beneath this, an inch or so down the spine, he saw also the arachnid form of the warp field suppression implant. The sight of it sitting there embedded in a fellow Librarian's flesh caused a brief surge of disgust that Karras had to consciously expunge from his mind.

It won't be long now until they remove the warp-cursed thing, he told himself.

Chaplain Qesos pulled the brand, now white hot, from the coals, gripped Arrexius's left shoulder with his free hand and said, 'Duty and honour never to be forgotten.'

'Duty and honour!' growled Arrexius, bracing himself for the pain to come.

Qesos pushed the glowing brand hard against the Librarian's

bared left pectoral. There was the sound of hissing as skin cells blistered and died, followed by the uppermost layers of tissue beneath. Arrexius tensed, muscles locking hard, and ground his teeth, but he gave no voice to his agony.

Qesos pulled the brand away and returned it to the brazier of coals.

Jaeger spoke again.

'Stand, Brother Ledahn, Space Marine of the Deathwatch!'

Arrexius stood and, after a moment's pause, fixed his robed about himself once more. At the sides of the hall and on the upper levels of the dais itself, the Watch sergeants and Watch captains clashed their armoured fists against their breastplates three times in salute. In the echoing quiet of the great hall, the sound was like thunder. Watch Commander Jaeger gestured once again to the carved doors on the right. Two hunched tech-adepts stood on either side of the doorway, their red shrouds bearing the icons of both the Deathwatch and the Adeptus Mechanicus.

With his oath taken, Arrexius saluted, fist to chest, ignoring the fire in his flesh, and moved off through the doors, followed by the two tech-adepts, both of whom bowed low to him as he strode past.

'Watch Captain Xavian,' boomed Jaeger, 'call forth the next oath-taker.'

'We call upon Morbius Galus,' announced Xavian, 'Codicier of the Doom Eagles, chosen of his kin, pledged to the service of our order by oath and accord. Come forth. Stand before all and make your pledge.'

Galus stepped out into the centre aisle from beside Karras and marched forwards.

And then there was one, thought Karras, for he would be the last of the Librarians to take the oath.

He could feel the weight of the coming moment, the sacrifice this oath demanded. His words would divide his loyalties for the first time in his life. But this was what his Chapter wanted. This was what it had asked of him. This was why he had been sent. He was more at ease with that now. He had given himself up to the hypno-induction, and it had taken effect. His loyalties did not need to be divided merely because he fought under a different banner. He would still wear his order's sigil into war. Serving the Watch meant serving the will of the First Spectre. His mind had been re-conditioned to accept it as truth, and so he did.

Megir, watch over me. Khadit, guide me. Let my actions honour you both.

I shall not fail you.

19

Lord Sannra sat behind his desk, looking down at its richly grained surface, unspeaking, unmoving, numb to the core. He could still hear High Commissioner Taje's boots receding down the corridor outside the room. The man had left in a fury, slamming the heavy doors behind him. Sannra wasn't a man who shrank from a shouting match, and he wasn't intimidated by the Civitas commander, but Taje's words had left him too stunned to take immediate issue.

Sul sat opposite his lord, likewise stunned, gazing into the shadow below the edge of the desk with a thousand-yard stare.

All of them? thought Sannra. *Even that lethal-looking female bodyguard?*

It was in this very room that Lady Devanon – *no, Interrogator Varlan* – had saved him from an assassin's bullet.

His own staff. His own bloody staff!

He glanced over at the wall on his right. In a way, he was glad the painting of the old man was ruined. There had always been an unsettling quality about it, as if the eyes were ever on him, judging him, criticising. Good riddance to it, priceless or not.

The crisis tunnel behind the painting had since been covered with another piece, something far less intrusive, a wonderful oil of the famed fire-trees on Kalhrada.

One day, I shall go there and see them for myself.

He tutted at himself, knowing that such idle thoughts were his attempt to avoid facing the current mess, to shy from the implications of Taje's report.

Forty Civitas enforcers lost. Seven Viper LAVs. And not a sign or word from anyone in the interrogator's group. Taje was right to be angry, of course. Sannra, shaken by the assassination attempt on his own life, hadn't given the High Commissioner ample time to organise a proper response. There hadn't seemed much need. No one really believed the whole of Chiarite society was at risk, did they? Just a miner's revolt, he'd thought it. In fact, it was more the interrogator's fault than his own that Taje's people had vanished. It was she who had demanded the escort, she who had insisted a fully armed expeditionary force must be formed and deployed at once. Maybe they would show up alive. There hadn't been any bodies to speak of. Not yet.

'Vox-comms are notoriously unreliable underground, Sul. Is that not so?'

Sul looked unconvinced, disinclined to pass it off as easily as that, and now Sannra felt his own doubts stealing back over him. He spoke again, keeping his eyes on the bright reds and yellows of the burning trees. 'I suppose if there were any real hope, the High Commissioner wouldn't have been in quite such a state. He ought to know better than either of us. The question is what to do about it. That lovely woman. I doubt we shall be seeing her again. Such a waste!'

Sul seemed on the verge of responding to that, but held his tongue.

Sannra looked at him. 'If you've anything to say, Sul...'

The aide looked up.

'With the greatest respect, m'lord, I feel that this is a matter for law enforcement. Surely our only real priority here is to ensure your personal safety. Whatever the extent of the threat – and it must be significant given that the Inquisition sent an agent at all – I'd say the population of Chiaro and the Imperium in general would be best served by your immediate removal from the area of risk. Forgive me if that sounds small-minded, m'lord, but your wellbeing is always my foremost concern. I can't abide the thought of these rebels or heretics or whatever striking a blow against the nobility.' Now he, too, glanced at the painting which had replaced the old portrait. 'They might not fail a second time.'

Sannra saw his aide shiver at the thought.

Good old Suliman. Such loyalty. I'm lucky to have you.

'A return to the palace at Najra, then? Have the staff prepare for departure. And have my train car readied.'

Sul leaned forwards in his chair and placed his hands flat on his master's desk. 'Forgive me, lord, but Najra is not nearly far enough. Your enemies may already have agents in place there. They may have predicted such a move.'

'Go on.'

'The ship on which the interrogator arrived, m'lord. The *Macedon*. It's still in orbit. The cargo shuttle has already been refuelled and is scheduled to depart in two days' time, according to my contact in the Officio Transportarum. I'm sure the captain – a man by the name of Dozois – could be persuaded to leave earlier. With enough coin in his pocket, of course.'

'Leave Chiaro entirely? Given the crisis, surely I'd face charges of dereliction.'

'Not so, m'lord. The trip could be officially listed as diplomatic under Section 3. It's not unknown for planetary governors to visit subsector neighbours in the interests of securing defence or trade agreements and the like. And I can backdate the official papers. I'm thinking either Melnos or Purdell, both of which have day-night cycles. It would be a welcome change, I'm sure you'll agree.'

Sannra was quiet as he thought about that.

'It couldn't be a long trip,' he told his aide. In his heart, he wanted to leave Chiaro as soon, and for as long, as possible. He enjoyed his position, but he had never loved this planet, just as the planet had no love for humankind. Chiaro seemed to grudge man's presence here. Those who made mistakes, whether on Dayside or Nightside, did not often live to make them again. Were it not for the Nystarean Gorge, men might never have settled here.

'Melnos is the nearest of the two, m'lord,' said Sul. 'Temperate, if a tad under-populated. It's mostly given over to automated agriculture, but the capital should entertain you – the City of Duma. And the Imperial Zoological Gardens are a sight to behold if reports read true. House Agiese hold the governorship. The ruling lord is close to your own age and a gregarious man by all accounts.'

'The gravity, Sul. The gravity.'

'Point eight, m'lord.'

Sul smiled knowingly.

Ah, thought Sannra, *the women will be tall and slender. That settles it.*

'Very well. Make all the necessary preparations. A staff of eight should be enough, yes? And my two best House guards. Blasedale and that other one. The big Hasmiri bruiser, Kaseed. Secure the agreement of this Dozois character. And brief my valet on what to pack for the Melnosi climate.'

Sul rose from his chair with the beginnings of a smile, enthusiastic for his work, glad to have a clear purpose again. He bowed to his master. 'With your leave, m'lord.'

As he was retreating to the door, Sannra called him to a halt.

'One last thing, Sul.'

'M'lord?'

There was a pause. 'I know I don't say it often, but a man in my position ought to recognise the value of his people. Know that I do. Recognise your value, I mean.'

Sul was somewhat taken aback, but only for the briefest instant. 'You need never thank me, m'lord. It's not necessary. The pleasure I derive from serving House Sannra is, and has always been, my greatest reward.'

Sannra grinned at his aide. 'Send in my darling swans. I want to share the news of the trip myself.'

'Very good, sir.'

The little man shuffled away, turning only to close the double doors behind him.

The planetary governor began tapping a runeboard on his desk, calling up hololithic display data. Melnos appeared in miniature, rotating in the space before him.

Yes, thought Sannra. *Taje can deal with this mess on his own. That's his job. I'm sure he and his men don't need the added pressure of worrying about my safety. Besides, I'm due a vacation.*

I may even find another pair of twins.

20

When Ordimas returned, he found the little basement hab in darkness. Part of him had expected Nedra to be awake, awaiting his return from the meeting with White Phoenix. It was very late, however, and the boy had no doubt succumbed to sleep despite his eagerness to see the puppeteer come home safe.

Ordimas let himself in quietly, relying on his augmetic eye to see his way around the hab in the dark.

Sure enough, Nedra lay in his cot, curled up and silent. There was a bowl of salted beans on the table, only half of them eaten. The boy had tried to force himself, but anxiety for Ordimas's safety had robbed him of his appetite.

When he awakes, thought Ordimas, *we will eat well.*

In truth, Ordimas had no appetite of his own. It wasn't just the horrors he had witnessed in the mines – horrors he had been part of, he reminded himself with a sick feeling. He was still enduring some of the after-effects of the nucleocode drug. On leaving the mines, he had sought out a hiding place in the sewers. He would have preferred to weather the effects of the crash in his own cot, of course, but the sight of the miner, Mykal, striding through the hab door would have been too much for poor Nedra. He did not know that Ordimas could take the shape of others. He would have assumed the worst and either attacked what he thought was his one-time abuser, or fled in terror. So Ordimas had endured the crash surrounded by filth and sewer-stink. That was two days ago, and still his head was pounding and his muscles ached incessantly. He didn't think the interrogator had noticed. Feigning weakness was one thing, but genuine weakness had to be covered. Showing it was never a good idea. During their meeting, he had felt his death all too close at hand. He would not have been overly surprised if the woman had tried to execute him.

Ordimas moved to the small kitchen and poured himself a cup of water.

This damned headache is killing me.

He returned to the table in the main room, drew a chair and sat down, weary beyond anything he could remember.

I don't want to do this any more. Maybe I'll just take the boy and leave. No more missions. No more shape-shifting. I'll become a puppeteer for real. It's an honest enough living.

The thought amused him. Surely no puppeteer in Imperial history had ever amassed as much wealth as Ordimas Arujo had. His Lordship paid well, though he asked all too much in return.

Ordimas scowled.

If we run, I'll not be able to access my accounts. Most of that money will be lost to me. Am I really ready to turn my back on it? Throne, I never use it anyway. It just keeps accruing.

Perhaps it was exhaustion. Perhaps it was the long crash of the nucleocode drug. Either way, Ordimas was genuinely caught off-guard when the tall figure dropped heavily from the ceiling and straightened in front of him.

The puppeteer leapt to his feet, his chair crashing to the floor behind him, but, as fast as he was, the intruder was faster. A powerful hand flashed out, catching Ordimas by the throat and lifting him into the air. His feet kicked out uselessly, his legs too short to strike at his attacker.

A strange, sibilant voice hissed from the shadows beneath the figure's hood.

'The Master sends his regards, agent of the Imperium. We enjoyed having you attend our little ceremony.'

Ordimas couldn't speak, couldn't even draw breath. The hand was tight around his neck, cutting off any hope of air. One of his kicking feet connected with the table. His cup smashed on the hab floor. Ordimas looked over to Nedra's cot, certain the sound would wake the boy. Maybe Nedra could get out alive if he moved fast enough.

But Nedra didn't stir, and Ordimas felt his heart sink.

'The boy died quickly,' hissed the intruder, noting the direction of the little mutant's gaze. 'Do not be sad. His flesh and bone will not be wasted. And neither will yours. The Master hopes to integrate your better genetic qualities into a new generation. You should be honoured.'

Now the intruder drew Ordimas closer, and Ordimas kicked again, connecting with full force. It didn't matter. It was like kicking concrete. The figure which held him barely shook at all from the impact. The grip tightened. Ordimas's vision blurred. He felt faint. Dimly, he registered hot breath on his face. He scrabbled for the poisoned blade in his waistband, but his fingers had gone clumsy as he edged towards death. He heard the knife clatter on the floor beneath him – a spirit-crushing sound. With his other hand, he reached up and pulled at the tall intruder's hood. It fell away.

Beneath was a face almost human. Almost, but clearly not.

The skin was bluish purple, the protruding eyes set too wide apart, the teeth too numerous and sharp. There were no lips to speak of; the mouth was a wide, wet slash in glistening flesh.

Hybrid, Ordimas thought. *Hybrid. As my own child will be. And Nedra. Nedra is dead. Throne, I am so tired of all this. Let it end. If death gives me nothing else, at least it will give me peace.*

The hand that gripped him flexed hard. There was a muffled snap.

Ordimas went limp.

Minutes later, a tall dark figure in shapeless robes left the door of the hab, keeping to the shadows, a heavy sack carried over one shoulder, two bodies contained within. The sack-carrier made his way to the nearest manhole and descended into the sewers where he could move with greater speed and less caution.

In time, he would go to the Master's lair, there to cast his kills into the digestion pools. The bodies would be broken down, semi-digested into pungent organic sludge. Their matter would be remade, recast in lethal alien form to serve a higher, purer purpose.

So, too, would all life in the galaxy.

It was inevitable. Nothing could stop that beautiful dark unity.

Eventually, it would devour everything.

21

Sixteen hours after the decision had been made in his office, the Lord High Arbitrator of Chiaro found himself in a well-appointed passenger cabin aboard the *Macedon's* cargo shuttle as it hauled itself up towards orbit. On either side of him sat his tall, pale female companions, their long legs crossed beneath dresses of black silk. Sul stood nearby, ready to serve. In the chair across from the High Arbitrator sat Captain Higgan Dozois.

Lord Sannra would have liked a window. It was many years since he had left terra-firma. He had hoped to watch the curve of the planet fall away underneath him, to watch the stars intensify, but it was not to be. The shuttle's cockpit was built to accommodate a pilot and co-pilot only. Sannra made do with a reasonable amasec from the captain's personal store, which he sipped from a slender, fluted glass.

Higgan Dozois had not been a difficult man to buy. Though neither Sannra nor Sul knew anything about it, Dozois had managed to sell his entire shipment of narcotics with ease. The Rockheads had sent a senior gang lieutenant to negotiate with him. The meeting was tense, neither side quite trusting the other, but the price eventually agreed upon was fair, and the transfer of the drugs went smoothly. The Rockheads ought to make a tidy profit. Dozois got exactly what he'd expected for the yaga. No more. No less. Now, he was just glad to be off that accursed, egg-shaped world. He hadn't felt right since the moment he'd set eyes on it. Since he'd landed on it, he'd had the strangest sensation that he was missing something. At least the headaches had finally stopped.

With the sale of the yaga completed, he had quickly turned his thoughts to his outward journey. The Lord High Arbitrator's sudden and unexpected commission was more than welcome. Melnos wasn't far, and it was in the general direction he had been planning to take. If he had to put on extra airs and graces for a contract this profitable, so be it.

A week's warp transit. A quick shuttle drop. Then off to Syclonis in the Gates of Varl for a resupply.

'I'm confident you'll find the accommodation to your liking,' Dozois told his guests. 'The *Macedon* is a fine ship, if I say so myself. I've certainly never had any complaints. In fact, I believe my last passenger, a lady of House Devanon, was some relation to you. Is that not so? I hope she's well.'

In truth, he hoped she was anything but. Thoughts of her made him confused and disoriented somehow. He remembered his frustration sharply enough. He hoped he'd soon forget it, and he mentioned her now only in a further attempt to curry favour with his well-heeled passenger.

Sannra and his aide shared a dark look. It was the aide who spoke up.

'A very distant relation only. Last we heard, Lady Fara was busily engaged in establishing a business venture in the city. I'm sure she found her passage with you most satisfactory.'

How uncomfortable they are at the very mention of her, thought Dozois. *Hiding something, both of them. I wonder if she made a fool of this Lord Sannra somehow. Perhaps it's best I don't mention her again.*

'I've a very fine dining room aboard,' he said, changing the subject. 'And the gallery on the upper deck provides quite spectacular views on planetary approach.' He gestured around the passenger cabin. 'It will more than make up for the lack of viewports on the shuttle, I assure you.'

Sannra was about to respond when a voice chimed from the speakers in the cabin's corners. 'Captain, forgive the intrusion, but I'm getting orders from both GDC and the Naval defence monitors to turn the shuttle around and head back to port. They… They're telling me the planet has just been placed under quarantine, sir.'

Dozois lost the polite smile he had painted on his face. The voice on the comm belonged to his pilot. He thrust himself forwards in his chair. 'They're telling you what?'

'GDC have us locked, sir, and both of the Navy boats are on intercept headings. If we don't turn back, they say they'll have no choice but to fire on us.'

Lord Sannra gaped. 'Sul?' he said shakily. 'Don't they know I'm on board?'

'All the relevant authorities were informed, my lord. This must be a mistake. It's the only possible explanation. Quarantine, indeed. Who ordered it?'

Dozois spoke to his pilot. 'Barrett, any word on who issued the no-fly order?'

'They say it's by order of the Holy Inquisition, sir. That can't be right, can it?'

Again there was a dark, knowing look that passed between the lord and his aide.

Dozois cursed. 'Whoever issued the damned order, I'm not about to have my ship fired upon. I think we had better do as they say.'

Lord Sannra looked helplessly at Sul, confusion and desperation both written clearly on his face.

'How far are we to the *Macedon*, captain?' asked the aide.

The captain relayed the question to his pilot. The answer came back. Just a little over three minutes, according to the flight cogitator. Sul asked another question and got an answer for that, too. The Naval defence ships were sixteen minutes away. Any missile launched from groundside would take approximately six minutes to reach them. How long it would actually take GDC personnel to prepare a launch was anyone's guess. In all the years men had occupied Chiaro, they had never once been forced to defend the planet. The few missile bases that existed were under-funded, undermanned and poorly maintained.

Sannra wouldn't have gambled much on their not being able to muster a few ground-to-orbit missiles, but Sul seemed ready to play those odds.

'Captain,' said the aide sternly. 'You will proceed to the *Macedon* as planned. Order your pilot to make haste. We will not be turning back.'

'You can't be serious, Sul,' gasped Lord Sannra. 'This is all tied to that damned woman. We have to turn back. We have to! I'm the Lord High Arbitrator. I can't be fired on by my own planet's defenders.'

The aide moved in a blur that defied his age and apparent frailty. Dozois watched in stunned silence as the little man plunged a knife deep into the breast of his lord and master. There was a wet, wheezing sound. Blood boiled up from between the aristocrat's lips. Tears welled in his eyes as they rolled upwards, trying to meet those of his aide, asking why, why this terrible betrayal.

Sul's expression didn't change a bit. Even as he murdered the man he had served for more than thirty years, his expression was calm, almost placid, in stark contrast to the violent act.

The women on either side flew from their seats screaming hysterically. They bolted for the nearest door in a whirl of blonde hair and black fabric. Dozois suddenly wished he was wearing a weapon. With such a prominent passenger on board, he had decided not to, worried that it might send the wrong message. He cursed that decision now.

'What in the Eye of Terror are you doing, man? You've just–'

Suliman ignored him. He turned his eyes to the women and called out, 'Kindred!'

The doors to the passenger cabin slid open. Two towering nightmares of chitin, claw and sinew swung beneath them and into the room. They straightened, and their sickening purple-skinned skulls bumped against the cabin ceiling.

Each was a horror from the darkest nightmares of men, a glistening amalgam of smooth armoured ridges and dark, striated muscle. Their claws were as long as machetes, as black as their soulless eyes and wickedly curved. They looked sharp enough to flense meat from living bone with ease. They stood on two legs, a short useless tail hanging limp behind them, and from their torsos hung four arms, long enough to reach the floor despite their height. But it was their faces that chilled the most – the quasi-human configuration of eyes and nose above a mouth more suited to some grotesque deep-sea monstrosity, the teeth like glass daggers, all set in a head horribly swollen and distorted, veins pulsing at the temples.

Both women fainted at once and hit the floor hard. Dozois, paralysed with fear, felt a hot wetness spread through his breeches from the area of his crotch. He began to shake uncontrollably.

The huge, six-limbed creatures bent over the women and lifted them effortlessly into the air. Blonde hair fell away, revealing two graceful, exposed necks. Alien eyes fixed on them.

'Do it,' hissed Suliman, tugging his knife from the cadaver of his former master. The wound made a sucking sound as the blade came free.

Dozois saw the monsters open their wide, razor-toothed jaws. He saw grotesque purple tongues whip out and back again, leaving raw red craters in pale human flesh. At the centre of those small, fresh wounds, implanted packets of alien DNA began their work, multiplying, diversifying, rewriting.

The beasts lay both women aside then turned their terrible black eyes on Dozois.

Suliman spoke from close by. The captain felt the wet point of a knife at his neck.

'I'm sorry, captain,' said Sul. 'I forgot to mention my family here would be joining us. They managed to clamber aboard while the cargo was being loaded. I hope you don't mind, but, you see, we have something of a mission, they and I. We have to reach Melnos, or any populated planet, really, and your ship is the only chance we have. Now, don't go getting any ideas, will you? You've a full life left ahead of you. A full, rich life still left to live. I'll let you live it, too, so long as you get us to the *Macedon* quickly and get us out of this system. But I assure you, if you don't, you *will* die. And it will be a far more painful experience than poor Lord Sannra's. Mark my words.

'Well, captain? What say you?'

The cargo shuttle docked with the *Macedon* just three minutes later. The body of Lord Nenahem Sannra was left slumped in the shuttle's passenger cabin, his rich clothes soaked in cold, sticky blood.

Despite repeated calls from the Navy monitors and GDC to power down, Captain Higgan Dozois, now ensconced in his command throne with Suliman and his restless, kill-hungry monsters standing over him, ordered the warp engines brought online. He had little choice. He kept telling himself there might be a window later, a chance to turn things around, even to escape, but, as he looked out over the bridge at his terrified crew, all of them desperately trusting him, depending on him to keep them alive, he knew he was stuck. There was no way the crew could overpower Suliman's monsters. When they had first stepped onto the command bridge, two foolhardy ensigns had drawn small-arms and charged the creatures. Dozois had tried to shout them down, but it was too late. The abhorrent, six-limbed aliens had leapt on them, shrugging off their pathetic pistol-rounds without a scratch. In front of everyone, the ensigns had been torn to red tatters by clawed, inhuman hands.

Resistance was a death sentence.

They'll kill us anyway, thought Dozois, *or do what they did to those women. As soon as we're of no further use...*

He wasn't quite sure what he had witnessed back in the shuttle. The Lord High Arbitrator's women were certainly still alive – they had groaned as he and his captors had stepped over them – but the welts on their necks meant something. He just couldn't imagine what.

'Sir,' called out the chief auspex operator, 'those Navy boats are only seven minutes out. They're calling again for us to power down. And I now have three missile contacts approaching. The closest is six minutes off our port side.'

'Engines?' asked Dozois.

His helmsman looked up. 'Engines at sixty-two per cent, captain. We might outrun the missiles, or we could trust to the point-defence turrets to knock them out, but if those Navy ships have forward lance batteries–'

'Warp engines?' asked Dozois, cutting the helmsman off.

'At full now, sir, but the Navigator needs another four minutes of focus before we can breach.'

Sul leaned forwards and spoke low in the captain's ear. 'We'll all die together, captain, if you don't hurry this up. Jump blind if you have to. Just get us away from here. Now.'

'I'll handle it,' snapped Dozois. Before Suliman could add anything, the captain rose from his throne and stormed down from the command dais to the floor of the bridge. 'Mister Sael, step away from your station please. I'll take this one.'

The shocked helmsman stepped back with a nod, his mouth open, but no words coming out. Dozois almost never took the helm himself.

The captain looked at the monitor. It was just as Sael had said. He might outrun the missiles or gun them down. He might even make warp before the Navy ships could open fire. But did he really want to?

The Ecclesiarchy were always banging on about the Emperor of Mankind and of eternal salvation at His side. Dozois had never gone in for it much. He had always lived for the moment. But at that moment, he hoped, truly hoped, that the priests were right, because he wasn't going to ship those monsters to another planet full of innocent people.

Were he to allow the *Macedon*'s destruction at the hands of the Navy or Chiaro GDC, forever after, people would think of he and his crew as traitors or renegades. But, if he could only summon the courage to take responsibility himself, to pre-empt the very destruction he could not now escape, they would know. They would know someone on board had taken a stand.

Holy Emperor, you had better be real.

He hit a quick series of runes, shutting off the ship's overrides and alarm systems. Then, with a sinking heart, he drew a finger across a dial on the monitor, setting the warp engines, which were already at full charge, to overload.

Six seconds. It has been an honour and a pleasure, old girl. If there is a life after this...

'All hands,' he called out, 'brace for warp translation in five, four, three, two, one–'

The warp core implosion and the resulting explosions that ripped through the *Macedon* formed a twisting nexus of strange blue light in the Chiaro sky. It lasted several minutes. The people of Chiaro seldom looked up, but some did and wondered at it.

None would ever know the truth behind the destruction of that ship, not even those aboard the *Ventria* and the *Ultrix*, both of which had been close enough to feel the blast ripple through local space.

But by his last living action, Captain Higgan Dozois – in the eyes of many, a worthless, lecherous, drug-dealing rogue – saved the lives of sixty-four million people, the entire population of the planet Melnos.

At least, for a time.

22

If any had believed Second Oath would mean an easing of the trials faced at Damaroth, they soon discovered just how wrong they were. Kill-team allocations were announced and training resumed almost at once. At first, the Space Marines revelled anew in the upgrades and alterations that had been made to their wargear. The Watch's Techmarines and enginseers were almost unrivalled in what they could achieve. Enhanced tactical data-feeds and real-time automapping, vastly superior low-light vision modes that needed only the slightest luminance to render everything in crystal clarity, sound-suppressive joint and actuator coatings to muffle excess armour noise by almost ninety per cent; the list went on.

The greatest marvel, perhaps, was the layer of tiny photo-reactive cells coating every visible surface of their plate. With an operative's power armour running quiet, stealth systems fully engaged, those cells would absorb and mimic the reflected light, colours and patterns of their surroundings, allowing the wearer to blend into the background like a chameleon. The effect wasn't perfect, especially when in motion, but it was impressive all the same. Karras had never seen anything like it. Between this and the new armaments available to them, the latest Deathwatch members felt all but invincible. But then the true tests began, and they quickly realised that, as hard as things had been *without* their armour, they were harder yet with it.

For Karras in particular, however, things were even harder still.

The Chief Librarian had opted to handle his squad introductions personally. As he and Karras walked a long, candlelit corridor, they talked of what had passed and what was to come. The suppressor on

Karras's spine had been dialled down, allowing him limited access to his powers once more, but it had not been removed entirely as Karras had hoped it would. Patience, Lochaine counselled. As always, there were good reasons behind it. Karras had heard those words all too often by now, but he resigned himself to them. There was nothing he could do in any case. He was granted deeper access to the archives now, yet many were the times his searches hit a brick wall. A flashing pict-screen with the words *Access Denied: Clearance Level Inadequate* remained a common and infuriating sight. Many areas of the facility likewise remained off-limits, though the Great Ossuary, where dead xenos specimens were preserved and displayed, and the Black Cenotaph, the Watch's Hall of Remembrance, were both open to him now during what little downtime he had.

'And you'll be able to select personally from the sensorium archives for your kill-team's sessions in the Librarius,' said Lochaine. 'I'd recommend you keep it varied for obvious reasons.'

Because we don't know what we'll be going up against, thought Karras. *I don't even know who we are.*

Lochaine sensed the Death Spectre's thoughts and the apprehension that attended them. 'There has never been a kill-team without conflicts of personality, Lyandro. That is a reality we have all had to face at some time or another. Our Chapters of origin mark us deeply. They make us who we are. They make us different to those we serve beside when we don the black. It is a difference that should be celebrated, not disdained. It is *that* difference which makes a Deathwatch kill-team unique, able to handle any crisis, to use the element of surprise, and to employ the unexpected. Though you will doubt it at first, you and your kill-team brothers will complement each other well. It is with this in mind that most allocations are made. In your case, however, things were a little… unorthodox.'

Karras stopped and stared at Lochaine.

'Unorthodox?'

Lochaine stopped too and turned, his expression dark. 'It is high time you were told of this. You are not to serve the Deathwatch as others do, Lyandro. The Inquisition has expressly requested that your kill-team – only yours – be placed under the direct aegis of an Ordo Xenos handler. We don't know why.'

Karras gaped. 'What?'

'It happens, though it is the exception rather than the rule. The Ordo Xenos has great need of our services. Their strength lies in intelligence and subterfuge. Ours… Well, you know ours. We share a common cause. The mutual benefits of deep cooperation are significant. When they ask, we do not often say no.' Lochaine paused to let Karras absorb this. Then added, 'Watch Sergeant Kulle was himself assigned to an Inquisition handler. If you have questions, ask him, though there is little he will be able to say openly.'

Karras remained still, letting this new information sink in.

An Inquisition handler? I don't like the sound of that.

Ripples rolled across his psychic awareness, not presaging a truly prescient vision, for he did not have that particular gift, but warning him that this was a matter of great importance, that being assigned to the Ordo Xenos would play a great part in his destiny, for better or worse. It wasn't just a feeling; it had the ring of real knowledge, of undeniable fact.

Lochaine put a hand on Karras's armoured shoulder and urged him to continue walking. Karras fell into step.

'Who is this inquisitor?' Karras asked.

'He has many names.' Lochaine snorted. 'We know him as Lord Arcadius. An alias of course. Some know him as Lord Moldavius. Others as Lord Dromon. None of these are his true name, so far as we can tell. The Inquisition are even more secretive than we are, if you can believe that. The kill-teams already under his command – yes, there are others – know him by his callsign, Sigma.'

Karras was perturbed. He had expected to fight under the auspices of the Watch Commander, or, at the very least, a Watch captain. Space Marines took orders from Space Marines. Anything else was…

'You said this Sigma requested my kill-team specifically?'

'He did.'

'It bothers you, too,' said Karras. 'Something about it bothers you.'

Lochaine kept his eyes on the corridor ahead. Already, a junction could be seen at its end with grand archways leading off in three directions. 'The Ordo Xenos do not think of Space Marines as we do. We see brothers, forged in battle, worthy of respect and honour for the trials we share. We understand each other, even beneath all the diversity and bitter rivalries. At our core, we are the same. They see only assets, an armoured fist to hammer down when things are at their worst, expected to act as commanded and ask no questions. They underestimate us. In this, I see great trouble for you.'

Silence fell, heavy, broken only by the guttering of the flames and the suppressed sound of armoured footfalls.

Shaking off his gloom by force, Lochaine clapped Karras on the shoulder and grinned. 'But not as much trouble as you will cause for them, Death Spectre. I'll take some comfort in that.'

I won't, thought Karras dourly.

They had reached the three arches and Lochaine led Karras through the leftmost one into a small antechamber with worn tapestries on two walls and a set of doors cast in polished bronze, embossed with images of Space Marines in battle. Fine work. In the centre of the chamber was a stone font with simple clay cups set on the rim. 'Drink if you wish,' said Lochaine, gesturing at the water in the font. 'Through that door, your kill-team awaits you.'

The water looked cool and refreshing, and had no doubt been sanctified by Qesos or another of the Watch Chaplains, but Karras declined. 'I'll not keep them waiting any longer.'

Lochaine nodded. He strode forwards and pushed open the bronze doors. Then he gestured for Karras to step through ahead of him.

The room beyond was large and circular, the walls dark red, the stone floor black. A domed ceiling hung high above, supported by columns of cream-coloured marble. In the centre of the room was a round table of polished black crystal, surrounded by massive granite chairs.

Figures in black power armour now rose from four of these chairs, leaving their helmets on the table's surface. Just beyond them, on the far side of the table, the hulking angular form of a Dreadnought took two floor-shuddering steps forwards, exhausts venting promethium fumes, engine rumbling, a low growl in a predator's throat.

On seeing Karras, one of the black figures swore loud and harsh.

Karras locked eyes with him, ground his teeth in abject denial, and spun to face Lochaine. 'You have got to be joking, brother,' he hissed at the Storm Warden. 'By the blood of the primarchs, you have *got* to be joking.'

Lochaine walked towards the table, arms splayed, presenting the others.

'Lyandro Karras,' he said, 'meet Talon Squad.'

ACT III: DEPLOYMENT

ACT III: DEPLOYMENT

'Fear not death, you who embody it in my name.'

– The God-Emperor of Mankind,
Address at Czenoa, 928.M30

1

The sky above Nightside was thick with stars. They glittered like shards of crystal while below them, all was absolute, lifeless black. Chiaro's rimward hemisphere was, on the surface, little more than vast expanses of frozen black rock. If the sun had ever shone here, it was back in the days of the planet's formation, when its axis of rotation wasn't yet pointed straight towards Ienvo, the local star. But that was over a billion years ago. Now, the only photons that ever bounced off this barren land were thrown out by the stars above and, today, by the jets of the three Stormravens that screamed in low over the bed of a large circular crater which the old Mechanicus survey maps called Inorin Majoris.

Above the centre of the crater, the three craft stopped and hung in the freezing air, wing-tip jets blasting downwards, hull nozzles flaring to steady each in position. The second and third hung back while the first adjusted for its drop.

There was a flash from one of the lead craft's under-wing weapons pylons. Something streaked forwards and hit dirt, burying its harpoon-like nose in cold, dead rock. At the tail end of this missile was a pod. It opened like a black flower, spreading steel petals to form a communications relay dish. In the centre of the dish, an antenna emerged, a tiny blue light blinking at its tip. Lower on the pod, a hatch opened, and a small floating object emerged, the size of a human head, trailing a length of thin silvery cable – a communications hard-line.

With its tiny motors throbbing quietly, the head-sized object floated forwards and descended into the black mouth of the shaft in the centre of the crater.

A voice spoke over a vox-link.

'Reaper One in place. Vox-relay deployed. Opening hatches.'

Four doors levered smoothly open on that first craft – one in either side of the short hull, another in the nose, another below the ship's tail. Zip-lines dropped, snaking off into the deep darkness below. Four shadowy shapes emerged, heavy and heavily armed, only the dull light of their visor slits giving them any detail. They dropped fast on the lines, vanishing quickly into the yawning mouth of the old ventilation shaft that gaped at the crater's centre.

Seconds later, a fifth figure slid from the rear hatch and shot downwards on its line. Slung over its neck and shoulder was a sword.

Moments later, a sharp voice reported, 'Infil site secured. Ready for Six's drop.'

'Reaper flight hears you, Alpha. Prepare for delivery.'

The first Stormraven tilted to the left and slid away from the shaft. Reaper Two moved in to take up position.

'Deploying Talon Six,' voxed the pilot.

At the back of the second Stormraven, winches began to whine, spooling out thick, high-tensile, advanced polymer cables. Something big and improbably blocky was lowered into the mouth of the shaft. Impatient growls emanated from within, amplified by the vocaliser grilles on its sloping, thick-armoured front.

Moments later, an irritated bark sounded on the vox-net.

'I'm down.'

'Withdrawing lines,' replied Reaper Two.

Magna-grapples disengaged with a clunk. Cables whipped back up into their reels at speed.

'Reaper Three now moving into position. Dropping mission support package. Stand by.'

A large metal container descended slowly into the darkness beneath. A hundred and twenty metres down, it hit the ground with a clang. One of the dark figures – the shortest and broadest – moved to its door, guided by the glow of its rune panel. Plated fingers tapped in the access code. The door unlocked, jerking forwards a few centimetres as the seals released, then sliding backwards and upwards with an oily, pneumatic hiss. Five gun-servitors rolled out in a line, chest-embedded readouts lighting their grisly faces from below in red. They were ugly things – half machine, half corpse; mind-wiped undead slaves kept alive, so to speak, by nutrifluids and electrical subsystems. Their human arms had been removed at the shoulder, replaced with heavy weaponry fed by the ammo drums riding high on their steel-plated backs. At their waists, their flesh gave way to a chassis with tank-treads in miniature. They chugged and rumbled quietly, and twin trails of greasy exhaust smoke issued from the pipes at their rear. Augmetics sat in place of facial features, their original eyes, nose, lips and tongue having long ago rotted to nothing.

For all their crude appearance, and despite being unable to think beyond basic targeting and threat assessment, they offered solid support in a firefight. They made convenient ammo mules, too.

And they were expendable.

Once the servitors had all emerged, Maximmion Voss went into the container and began hauling out sealed cases. These he lay side-by-side, then tapped a rune to close the cargo crate's door.

'Talon Four confirms support elements unloaded. Take her up.'

'Understood, Four. Deployment complete. Reaper flight wishes you happy hunting, Talon. See you back here for exfiltration. Reaper One, out.'

The Stormravens' jets flared again as they rose high above the crater. Then, in triangular formation, they swung north and roared off into the darkness, turbines throbbing, until they were too far away to hear. The silence and the stillness of the frozen surface returned. Starlight was all that lit the rocks once more. It was as if the three powerful assault craft had never been there at all.

At the bottom of the shaft, proof of the drop remained: six Deathwatch operatives with a mission and the weaponry to achieve it.

Or so they hoped.

2

Karras scanned the broad, circular chamber into which they had descended, his helm optics whirring as they struggled to apply low-light mode to such utter dark. Even a little starlight would have been enough; his upgraded visor technology could have worked with it to make the chamber as bright as a cloudy day, at least to his gene-boosted eyes. But no light reached the bottom of the Inorin vent shaft at all.

'I can't see a damned thing in here,' said Solarion, tapping his helm as if this were a technical problem. 'I thought they finished the vision mode enhancements before we left the Watch fortress.'

'They did,' replied Voss. 'I watched them do it.'

'Talon Squad,' said Karras. 'I want bolter lights on. Lowest setting. We don't want to announce ourselves by throwing shadows all over the place.'

Four dim lights winked on. Four only, for neither Voss nor Chyron, the Dreadnought, carried bolters like the others. Voss carried a flamer, but he would not light the blue flame of the igniter until he was in combat. Chyron was armed with a heavy power fist boasting a small under-arm flamer of its own. His main armament, however, was the formidable assault cannon fixed to his chassis's right shoulder socket.

The rest of the squad gripped bolters that were far from standard, boasting a triple-rail system which allowed for the addition of tactical attachments. On this particular mission, that meant a side-mounted flashlight – now put to use – a small laser range-finder, and an under-barrel grenade launcher, the special rounds for which were stored on the ammunition belts around the Space Marines' plate-armoured waists. Together with the mounted magnoscope on top of the bolter and a shorter barrel length more suited to Deathwatch operations, the gun almost looked like a different weapon to the one most Space Marines were used to, but in every important way, it was essentially the same.

There was a humming noise in the dark, just above Karras, as the servo-skull that accompanied the kill-team moved forwards on its tiny suspensors. When it was five metres in front of the team leader, it stopped. There was an audible click. Its own light – little more than the power of a small candle – formed a hazy sphere around it. The floating skull rotated, lens-eyes surveying the chamber just like the eyes of the Space Marines.

It was an equal mix of geometric and natural forms, this dark, echoing place. Human construction, with its straight lines and sharp angles, speared out from mounds of rough, black, ice-encrusted rock. The floor was flat, or rather, almost flat. Centuries of human passage and the grinding wheels of heavy autocarts had worn tracks into the stone. Karras's eyes followed the tracks to a dozen arched tunnel mouths, only a few of which remained completely clear of rubble. The others had suffered some kind of collapse, blocking them up with thick piles of tumbled rock and great iron beams.

'Machinery,' said Voss from off to Karras's left. He stepped close to the nearest piece, a bulky cargo-lifter toppled on its side, one rigid leg sticking out in the air at an angle. It was a big machine, clumsy-looking and crude, almost as large as Chyron but painted yellow where the temperamental Dreadnought was black. 'Preserved by the ice,' said Voss. 'Not even rusted.' He moved closer and peered into its metal guts. 'No power core and no subsystem control boards.'

There was similar detritus all around them. The kill-team's lights played over hills of twisted metal and boxy shapes. Solarion looked at a dark mass of plasteel and cable in front of him, then began walking in a wide circle, half crouching, the beam of his light pointed to the ground. After a minute, he said, 'This place was abandoned years ago, Karras. No recent tracks. No one has been through here.'

'It's dead,' said Zeed.

'Where is the foe, Alpha?' boomed Chyron. 'I wish to kill something, and I wish to kill it now.'

'This is no purge, Six,' said Karras sharply. 'You know that. You'll kill when I give you leave to kill. Not before.'

Chyron rumbled something to himself, then said, 'The sooner the better. We may not have been sent to purify, Librarian, but there *will* be killing. Mark my words. More than enough for all of us.' The Dreadnought pivoted on his mechanical legs, seeming to address Siefer Zeed directly as he said, 'There always is with tyranids.'

None could mistake the hatred in the Lamenter's voice as he snarled that last word. Did he believe he had found a kindred spirit in the Raven Guard? Certainly, they both hungered for battle, but what Space Marine did not? Even Karras had to acknowledge that part of him which looked forward to the rush, the heightening of senses, the dizzying satisfaction of seeing one's foes cut down.

He glanced up at the servo-skull hovering nearby. Thoughts of glorious battle suddenly dropped away. His brow furrowed beneath his helm. Via the skull's instruments, Sigma could hear all, see all, record all, even take action if need be. To all intents and purposes, that yellowed floating mish-mash of brain, bone and ancient tech *was* Sigma, though the inquisitor's actual physical body remained safely in orbit aboard the *Saint Nevarre*.

Karras thought back to the mission briefing they had attended on that ship, the first and only time they had ever set eyes on the man to whom their solemn Deathwatch oaths had bound them in fate and service.

The briefing room was striking but simple, almost chapel-like with its high arched ceiling some twenty metres above the cold black flagstones of the floor. There were no windows or viewports anywhere, just hydraulic bulkhead doors set in the port and starboard walls. These were so large that the five Space Marines could have walked abreast as they passed under them, if they had wanted to. They were large enough to cause Chyron no trouble. In fact, when the rest of Talon Squad arrived for the briefing, they found the Dreadnought already waiting, his chassis idling with a quiet rumble.

'A tad over-eager, aren't you, Old One?' Zeed jested.

'The inquisitor wished to greet me personally,' boomed the big warrior. 'At least someone on this ship recognises and respects the value of age and experience. Unlike others.'

'I respect you, brother,' replied Zeed. 'I just wish you didn't smoke up the place so much. And you're noisier than a battle tank with a bad axle.'

Chyron growled, but there was no menace behind it. 'One day, little raven, you will be glad to hear that noise. That will be the day Chyron saves your worthless life.'

Zeed laughed aloud. 'I think your own fumes have gone to your head.'

The Lamenter had taken a liking to the Raven Guard. Darrion Rauth and Ignacio Solarion, on the other hand, had not. Solarion threw the long-haired Space Marine a withering glare, wishing he would shut up.

Zeed, as usual, ignored it.

Karras turned on a boot heel and took in the room.

Six weeks. Six weeks aboard the *Saint Nevarre* with no sign of the man who had brought this kill-team together. And now they were in the Ienvo system on their way to the site of their first operation, and the inquisitor had, at last, deigned to call them together. It was the first time any of them had been in the briefing room.

Only one wall bore any real decoration beyond the regularly spaced alcoves in which bowls of scented oil burned, their orange light dancing, causing the room to pulse and move. That wall was dominated at its base by a semi-circular dais on which sat a tall throne of exquisitely carved skulls in black marble. It was a work of fine craftsmanship, but there was something distinctly odd about it; the seat was sized for a normal man, but the height of that seat, roughly three metres above the uppermost level of the dais, meant that no man could easily place himself on it. Clearly, its height was intended to convey status and authority over those assembled below it. As yet, it remained empty.

Behind the throne, the wall bore a towering relief of a somewhat narrow man in hooded robes flanked by huge Space Marines in an armour design dating back to the dark years of the Heresy and its immediate aftermath. The distinctive staff which the hooded man carried marked his identity clearly: none other than Malcador, known as the Sigillite, founder of the Holy Orders of the Inquisition in days when the Emperor still led the Space Marine Legions he had created.

'None were trusted more,' quoted Rauth from behind Karras, 'Unquestioning he was. And unquestionable his faith.'

'His body turned to dust on the wind,' replied Karras, quoting from the same ancient text, Echto's *Dreamer Unsleeping*. 'But his will and his sacrifice took form everlasting in the legacy he left all men.'

'An overrated work,' said a new, unfamiliar voice. 'Ibramin Izavius Echto was born over seven hundred years after the Sigillite's death and held only mid-level clearance in the Great Librarium. His writings are sensationalist speculation and melodrama. Nothing more.'

The voice was clear and sharp, higher than any Space Marine's, but somewhat modulated, given an almost artificial quality by the machinery that transmitted it. The words emanated from small vocaliser grilles in the sculpted eye-sockets of the throne's many skulls. The attention of Talon Squad was drawn to the throne now, for a figure had suddenly appeared there, seated high atop it – a pale, deep-chested, muscular man with a full white beard and piercing blue eyes. He wore black breeches over a bodyglove of black titanium scales, with golden bracers on his forearms and golden greaves on his shins. A red cloak with a high collar hung about his shoulders, fixed there by two silver clasps bearing a heavy skull motif. Between the skulls hung lengths of thick silver brocade. His fingers were spread over the domes of the two black skulls which formed the end of his throne's armrests.

He looked down at them and smiled, but it was a smile as flat and artificial as his voice.

'We meet at last, Talon. I am Sigma and I will be your operational commander until the end of your service with the Deathwatch. You will forgive me for not making a personal introduction sooner, but I prefer to hold my briefings only in the relative security of real space.'

'Then you should have introduced yourself after we boarded at Damaroth,' said Solarion, indignant as ever. 'One does not keep Space Marines waiting, inquisitor or otherwise.'

The bearded man's eyes found him. 'It suited me better to observe you first, son of Guilliman. A handler ought to know his assets' personalities and individual capabilities before he deploys them. For your part, however, you need only know your mission parameters. The burden is lighter on your side, is it not?'

A thrumming sound began, building slowly, coming from a wide circular aperture some five metres across, cut in the centre of the floor. The hole had a railing of black plasteel around it. Maximmion Voss moved to the railing and looked down into the space below.

'That's an impressive hololithic array.'

Three metres below the aperture, a large black hemisphere glittered, its surface pocked with shimmering projection lenses. Even as Voss admired it, a massive three-dimensional object resolved into existence before him, hovering in the air above the hole. It was the icon of the Inquisition rendered at extreme resolution, two metres tall and one across. It looked no less real than anything else in the room.

'Gather before the projection, Talon,' said Sigma. 'It is time you learned some of the details of *Operation Night Harvest*.'

'Some?' challenged Karras, but the inquisitor did not answer.

The skull-and-I vanished and was replaced by the strangest planet Karras had ever seen. It looked like an egg laid on its side, its axis of rotation pointed straight at its sun. The tapering sunward hemisphere was bright and riddled with deep volcanic rifts, while the rounded rimward hemisphere was as black as oblivion. Around the planet's equator, a shadowed gouge extended; a vast canyon spanning the entire circumference of the world.

'This,' said Sigma, 'is the planet Chiaro, a mining world in this very system. A world to which you will soon be deployed.'

He had told them of the intelligence the Ordo had gathered to date, told them of the ranking agent he had sent and of her sudden disappearance. White Phoenix, he called her. He spoke of the augmetic implant in her head and of the critical intelligence it carried. He talked of duty and loyalty, and of getting her out alive. She had always served the Emperor and the Inquisition well, and now she needed help.

Night Harvest, then, was not a kill-mission. It was a tactical rescue and recovery.

Chyron groaned. Zeed shook his head.

Then the inquisitor told them of the nature of the xenos infestation. *Tyranids*.

That changed Chyron's mood. He flexed his vast metal fists restlessly.

The hololith of the planet disappeared to display a range of sickening xenos forms in unpleasantly sharp detail and colour.

The Dreadnought growled and twitched as he looked at them, seeming on the verge of storming forwards to swipe in murderous hatred at their mere image. It was tyranids, after all, which had all but wiped his Chapter from the face of the galaxy.

Sigma rattled off a series of facts and figures supporting the operation and giving the kill-team estimates on enemy strength. The numbers were staggering. No six-man kill-team should rightly have been sent to face such a force, but again he reminded them that this was, for the first half at least, a stealth operation. They were not to reveal their presence until absolutely necessary. To this end, he ordered that Karras suppress his psychic gifts. His ethereal signature had to be muted almost completely.

The reason was simple: the Ordo believed a powerful tyranid genotype was at the root of all the activity. That genotype was a genestealer broodlord.

None present had ever faced such a creature. Karras had read enough on Damaroth and in the Occludian archives to know such a thing was not to be underestimated. Sigma confirmed that, telling them the creature was the perfect killer, one evolved to be every bit as deadly in ethereal battle as it was in physical.

Were the Deathwatch Space Marines to descend into the mines of Chiaro unshielded by pentagrammic wards, and with Karras's gift unsuppressed, they would be located and assessed immediately, and the entire ravening horde would be unleashed upon them.

Chyron and Zeed both voiced enthusiasm for that scenario, envisioning a battle that would fill the mines to bursting with xenos dead, but Sigma was harsh in his reprimand. The recovery of White Phoenix was the objective. Only her successful retrieval would qualify the mission as a success. Anything else would be a disgrace that, he assured them, would stain their names and the honour of their Chapters.

There were questions. Some were answered, and some of those even satisfactorily. But other questions were not. The inquisitor frequently referred to clearance levels and classifications. The kill-team were given only the information they needed. Anything which did not directly contribute to their ability to complete the operation was withheld.

There was tension and anger at this, and in no small amount, but it was tempered by the time they had spent surrounded by secrecy at Damaroth. They were Deathwatch operatives, trained to kill. They longed for combat above all else, a chance to employ the lessons of the Watch sergeants directly against the enemies of mankind. That they would soon be seeing action was foremost in their minds.

With the kill-team finally dismissed, Karras turned to leave with the others. But the pale, bearded man on the high throne called him back.

'Not you, Alpha. I would have words with you alone.'

So Karras stayed and approached the bottom of the dais, looking up at the strange image of the man above him.

'We must work together, you and I,' said Sigma. 'I know that taking orders from a mortal man will be difficult for you – I have other kill-teams under my command, and it has always been difficult at the beginning – but we need each other. The ancient pact between the Ordo and the Deathwatch has held since the Apocryphon Conclave. We provide the intelligence. You do the killing. The sword cuts better when the eye directs its blows, yes? So I ask you now, will we have a problem?'

Karras hadn't answered immediately. A lot about the situation on board the *Saint Nevarre* bothered him. The top six decks were permanently Geller-shielded, meaning any astral projection of his consciousness could not breach their walls. Even the ship's captain, Cashka Redthorne – tall, pretty and keenly intelligent – was denied access despite over a decade in command.

Karras knew the inquisitor resided on those decks, along with the ship's Navigator and astropaths, but only because he sensed them nowhere else on the ship. He had never encountered such internal security on an Imperial vessel before. Was the inquisitor paranoid? Just what was he afraid of?

'This,' said Karras, gesturing up at the body on the throne. 'This is not you.'

'If I told you it was,' said Sigma, 'would you believe me?'

Karras shook his head. 'No more than the names you give for yourself.'

'Good. You are right to doubt. This is mere projection, as you have guessed. My actual appearance, my real name, these are things of no import. Mission data only is what ought to concern you, and on that front you may believe all you see and hear. I want White Phoenix returned to me, Lyandro Karras, no matter her condition. If she cannot be recovered alive, I will settle for her remains, and if not that, then, at the very least, I require the opticom unit implanted in her eye socket. But your highest priority is to bring her back to me. As the leader of this Deathwatch kill-team, and as a Space Marine assigned to my operational command, it is your sworn duty. Members of your team may die in combat to achieve it. I need you to accept that reality now. And I need you to be ready to lay down your own life in order to complete the missions I assign you.'

'But you will not share the full implications of our operations, nor the data you glean if we are successful.'

'I will always give you everything you need to get the job done. No more, no less. You may not always agree with my decisions, but you *will* follow them. I have served the Ordo for a very long time, Codicier, and my authority has the backing of Holy Terra herself.'

He would say no more on the matter of disclosure.

It was far from enough, but it changed nothing. Oaths had been taken. Duty must be served.

But Karras wasn't finished.

'Answer me this, inquisitor. It was you who selected me for command. It was you who put my kill-team together. I heard talk at Damaroth of irregularities. The members of the Watch Council itself seemed less than sanguine about it. There were almost a hundred battle-brothers to choose from, yet you chose us. Darrion Rauth is the first Exorcist ever to serve the Deathwatch, and he serves now only because you yourself brokered an agreement with the Master of his Chapter. I feel there is great significance in this, something I am missing. I suspect you have prescients in your service, gifted seers who may have told you of potentialities you wish to see fulfilled. If they have sensed prime futures in which I or my kill-team factor, you will tell me about it now. We have a right to know.'

The bearded man smiled that plastic smile again. 'I cannot fault the logic behind your supposition, Alpha, but the truth is rather more mundane. Your team was selected by virtue of their talents and by the ways in which each might complement the others. I am aware of the tensions that exist between you now. Time and experience will strengthen your unit cohesion. Like all Space Marines, you will be bonded in battle sooner or later. There is no mystery behind your selection. I simply require the best.'

Karras scowled, certain that this was a lie, but he could not deny the kernel of truth behind it. Lies were always more effective with a little truth mixed in. Throughout the trials on Damaroth, the brothers of Talon Squad had shown themselves to be exemplary specialists. All except Rauth. While the Exorcist was a formidable warrior, his abilities were not as obvious as those of the others. Karras was certain that Rauth had been chosen because he had no discernable soul. Precisely why that was the case still confused him and caused him great concern.

With the silence stretching out between them, it was clear that there was nothing more to be gained from further questions. Sigma had shared all he was willing to share. He dismissed Karras, and the Librarian rejoined the others and the ship's enginseers to offer obeisance to their wargear before deployment.

That had been twenty-two hours ago, before final approach, before loading into the Stormravens. Now, here they were, descending into the bowels of a world carved by contrasts.

As Karras followed Solarion just up ahead, he thought back to the inquisitor's words:

Members of your kill-team may die. Accept that reality now.

The Death Spectre muttered a curse behind the muzzle of his helm. If he had anything to say about it, none of his Space Marines would be dying down here. Not on his watch. Not for that blasted inquisitor and not for anyone else.

'Talon Squad,' voxed the ugly, skull-faced construct, transmitting the words of Sigma via the surface relay, 'I will now key your tracking systems to the relevant locatrix. This will reveal the position of the primary objective, but not the path to it. There are no records of the natural tunnels beyond the mines. Nevertheless, we will continue to grid-reference *six-delta-six-one*, visible on your retinal displays. From there, I will initiate a special mapping procedure. If this servo-skull is damaged before it reaches that waypoint, the likelihood of mission success will drop to less than one per cent. If we are ambushed or discovered, your first priority is to protect this proxy device. Is that understood?'

Karras blink-clicked inside his helm until the retinal display showed him a three-dimensional representation of the known extents of the Nightside Underworks. Blink-clicking a few more times isolated the section of the mine they currently occupied. Their present location was a glowing green dot. The waypoint in question was a blinking white one. The quickest route from here to there was also highlighted – a thin line of pulsating white light. In truth, it looked anything but quick, a convoluted series of twists, turns and drops where the original excavators had burrowed in any and every direction, desperate to strike a rich vein of rare and valuable elements. In a word, the layout of the mines was absolutely chaotic.

'We've got it,' said Karras to the skull. 'Let's hope nothing has happened to collapse any of the key tunnels on our route. Stalker rounds only for now, Talon. Let's try to keep this clean and simple. Solarion, take point. Let me know the moment you see any sign of recent passage.'

'I hear you, Alpha,' replied the Ultramarine brusquely.

There was a tinge of acid on that last word, *Alpha*, said to sound almost like a curse. Karras buried an urge to rise to the bait. Would Solarion still covet command so much when the violence began? Sigma hadn't left them in any doubt at the briefing. They would be staggeringly outnumbered down here once they were compromised, and they *would* be compromised sooner or later. It was inevitable. Once they reached the primary objective, they would kick the nest hard. Everything after that would be a mad run, a fighting retreat back to the exfil point before time ticked out.

'The rest of you know the pattern for this mission. Chyron, you and one of the gun-servitors, GS8, will hold this chamber secure.'

'I need no servitor,' rumbled the Dreadnought.

'You have blind spots just like the rest of us, Lamenter. The gun-servitor will cover those spots. You may be glad of it. This chamber absolutely must not fall. Is that clear? This is the only feasible exfil point for fifty kilometres in any direction. If we lose this ground–'

'Just lead them to me, Death Spectre. Do not keep all the killing for yourselves.'

Karras faced the others. 'I will designate additional rendezvous points as we go. If we have to fall back and you find those RPs compromised, you fight your way here. No matter what happens, brothers, you make sure you are here before the mission chrono runs out. We have less than ten hours. Those Stormravens won't wait.'

With just under ten hours on the chrono, its readout was green. At five hours that would change to yellow. At two hours, orange.

At thirty minutes, the chrono display would turn red.

'Are we clear?' Karras demanded.

Deep, vox-modulated voices answered in the affirmative. The kill-team leader moved them out, and they all bade the Dreadnought what they hoped was a temporary farewell. Solarion, bolter raised to light the way, stalked towards the easternmost tunnel. Sigma's remote presence followed a metre above and behind, throwing out its own weak, candle-glow illumination.

The rest of the team fell in behind them: Karras first, then Rauth,

Voss, and finally Zeed, trailing four of the five gun-servitors in his wake, three of which carried the extra ammunition Voss had secured to their chassis. Strapped to the back of the last gun-servitor was a black case belonging to Sigma. As yet, the inquisitor hadn't opted to share any information about its contents.

Karras wondered if it was some type of bomb. He had dark thoughts of he and his kill-team getting vaporised down here, unable to escape in time while they battled to break free from a glut of alien bodies. Sometimes, he was glad he didn't have the gift of true vision. If he'd had, such thoughts may have augured his doom. Better not to know the manner or moment of one's final, irreversible death until it came to claim you.

Back on Damaroth, Marnus Lochaine had questioned him about his psychic training on Occludus, seemingly surprised that Karras was unable to scry prime futures.

'My gifts are for the battlefield,' Karras had told him. 'I was not blessed with strong prescience like some of my brothers. Since I had little raw talent for it, it was decided early on that my energies would be put to better use on other more combative arts.'

'I see,' Lochaine had said. 'Or perhaps you were not taught to see the future because there are things in it which some do not want you to see.'

The tone, as much as the words themselves, had disturbed Karras at the time. He'd had no response. Lochaine had smiled and waved the comment off, but there had been something in his eyes, and Karras had not liked the look of it.

If it is a bomb, thought Karras, *we'll just have to make sure we get out of here before it blows. Otherwise Talon Squad will be the shortest lived kill-team in history.*

And there won't be anything left of us to send back.

Chyron watched the lights of his fellows dim and vanish as the tunnel curved away. When they were gone, he turned to look at the gun-servitor which remained beside him.

It stood quite still, engine chugging in a soft imitation of Chyron's own. With weapon primed and raised, it scanned the mouths of the chamber exits for sign of enemy movement.

Chyron sighed in his metal sarcophagus. There would be no slaughter here. It was the others that would see bloodshed this day, not he. Of that, he was almost certain. He wished he could go with them, wished he still had a Space Marine body, more than just a brain and organs stuffed into a nutrifluid tank. His chassis was too big for the tunnels. This would be no hunt. The enemy would have to come to him.

With nothing but a mindless servitor for company, and quiet inky darkness all around him, he turned his mind to the glories of the past, and cursed the fate that had left him alive when the rest of his Chapter had died.

Often during times like these, with little to do but await the vengeful slaughter he longed for, his thoughts would turn to death. A part of him, the most self-indulgent part, longed for it. He might have died with honour and glory countless times, but his fate had always been that of the survivor. Even at his worst, lying in red pieces on a blood-sodden moor while the carrion birds tugged at his entrails, death all but certain to claim him, fate had intervened, denying him the peace of oblivion. He was found, lauded as a great hero, and locked into this life-sustaining metal casket to fight on. Pride was one thing, but it had its limits. Let a violent end claim him, take him away to stand with the souls of his lost brothers. He hungered for it, but he would not speed its coming. He had long ago sworn his life, however long, to the service of the Emperor. Even so, centuries had come and gone. Just how much more would the Emperor demand of that oath?

To himself, Chyron rumbled, 'Perhaps today, I will find a worthy doom. Maybe today I shall be granted the release for which I long. Let them come for me, a great tide of them, clamouring for my destruction. Let us die together, the music of their final bestial screams carrying me to the other side, to the brothers that await me. A violent, bloody end. By the red tears of Sanguinius himself, let it be so.'

The servitor beside him twitched a little on hearing the words, and Chyron half imagined it was about to concur. But servitors could not do that. Perhaps part of the wretch's memory-wiped brain felt an impulse to speak in response. Perhaps the Dreadnought's words echoed its own desperate wish.

No. It was just a servitor – no longer a man with words and thoughts of its own.

Nevertheless, we are both denied death for the service we might render, thought Chyron as he looked down at the pallid, socket-covered head of the man-machine.

His sense of pride rose up then, and rebelled against this growing malaise. He felt anger at himself. What was he doing, comparing himself to a servitor? How could he allow such weakness, such self-doubt? They were nothing alike. He, Chyron, was a Lamenter, a mighty battle-brother of the Adeptus Astartes. He had not been made a Dreadnought because he was weak, nor had he committed some crime of heresy or treachery like the man this servitor had once been. Chyron endured because he was strong, resilient, indomitable, relentless. His was a life worth extending, no matter the price, no matter the suffering and the loneliness and the interminable survivor guilt. The Imperium still needed him. The Deathwatch needed him. This upstart Librarian, Karras, and his Talon Squad… They would need him, too, before the day was out.

While filthy xenos still threatened everything his Chapter had ever fought and died to protect, he would go on, his bloodlust insatiable.

One day, when the time was right, death would bring an end to duty.

Let the Emperor decide that day, not he, and not some filthy xenos abomination.

Deep in such thoughts, he walked the chamber's perimeter, chassis lamp lighting his way, his concussive, piston-powered footfalls shaking tiny fragments of ice from the ceiling and the walls.

The old mineworks sensed him, heard him, listened to his restless rumblings as it breathed slow icy breaths, waiting for the maelstrom of violence and slaughter that was to come.

3

Karras was glad of the automapping upgrade the tech-magi had installed in his battle-helm. For the last half-hour, the endless tunnels had blended together until they were all but indistinguishable, an almighty mass of looping, sloping passageways; the frozen, lifeless intestines of Nightside. Talon Squad had come across no signs of recent activity, no animal carcasses, not even so much as a patch of lichen or fungus.

It was too cold and desolate for much life to exist here, but none at all? In times past, Karras knew, it had been different. The Chiaro dossier had listed several large indigenous life forms as potential threats. So far, however, nothing stirred.

He thought of the miners that had once walked these very paths before the local veins dried up. It was not, he guessed, a life any would choose given other options. A malfunctioning thermasuit was a death sentence, as were loss of lighting, cave-ins, gas-pockets and a dozen other common hazards. Then again, the baking heat, deadly radiation and regular seismic activity of Dayside was hardly any better.

Up ahead, Solarion angled right, following the gradual bend and downward slope of the path they trod. Even a Space Marine, his memory flawless, would have struggled with this maze of rough-hewn roads and abandoned machine-cut chambers. Some of the tunnels lacked the telltale signs of human creation. They had not been melted or blasted out, though they bore support stanchions and plasteel safety doors like all the man-made sections. The walls in some of these natural tunnels were almost mirror-smooth, seeming to curve to the contours of a massive tubular body. These,

Karras guessed, were the work of rock-eaters – oversized vermians listed as extinct.

Only their massive blade-like teeth and rings of body segment armour had ever been found, formed of a black material as hard as diamond, yet entirely organic according to Mechanicus Biologis reports. No other physical remains had been discovered in all the planet's centuries of human occupation, and no live specimen had ever been recorded. A part of Karras hoped the giant worms *were* extinct. His team didn't need any extra complications.

Men had exploited the legacy of the rock-eaters. From their earliest days on Chiaro, they had incorporated the creatures' tunnels as part of the mines, branching their own efforts out from them in search of priceless ores.

Karras turned the bend ahead and caught sight of Solarion again.

There was a crackle on the vox. Up ahead, the quality of the light changed. Around Solarion, it no longer shimmered on the ice-rimed tunnel walls.

'I've entered the next chamber,' said the Ultramarine. 'No contacts.'

'Move left, stop at ten metres and wait for orders,' replied Karras. 'We'll do a proper sweep before I decide whether or not this is an appropriate site for an RP.'

'Understood,' Solarion grunted.

Karras emerged into the chamber now, and, with the boosted, green-hued image his optical enhancements provided, saw it to be a vast polygonal hall, its walls cut from pure rock without need of artificial supports. Eight dark archways had been machine-cut into the walls, including the one through which the kill-team had come, leading off down inky tunnels in every compass direction. The ceiling above had been left rough and natural, covered in sharp stalactites that hung like black fangs waiting to bite down on them. Around the perimeter, however, there were several metal stairways reaching to smaller man-made tunnel mouths. Between some of these hung plasteel gantries and platforms. The immediate impression of the entire chamber was that people not only worked here, they had lived here.

A natural cavern the first miners exploited, thought Karras. *I don't like all those exits. Too many angles to cover. On the other hand, there are some good bottlenecks at ground level and enough room to stay mobile during a firefight.*

In ordered rows on the cavern floor, there were several dozen prefab huts and cabins – some quite large, all with flat roofs – along with a number of raised platforms the purpose of which it was no longer possible to guess. Perhaps there had once been a small first-stage refinery operating here. Pipes and ducts criss-crossed large sections of the walls. Huge circular extractors hung silent and motionless in the gloom overhead. An old autocart, its basic cabin-and-flatbed design some eight metres long, lay to the far right in perfect condition, broad wheels frozen stiff to the chamber floor. Whatever purpose this place had once served, from now until the end of this particular mission, it would function as the first of the kill-team's emergency rendezvous points. Karras was satisfied that, despite its shortcomings, it offered a good place to turn and engage pursuing enemy forces without getting locked down.

The others filtered into the chamber now, breaking its long-lived, icy tranquillity. Following Karras's commands, they arranged themselves in a broad line along the chamber's western edge. Four gun-servitors rolled in after them, chugging and shuddering on their compact iron treads.

Karras ordered a sweep. Within minutes, the chamber was proclaimed clear.

Nothing. Not even recent tracks. It was as lifeless as the tunnels that had brought them. The squad gathered in the centre of the chamber and Karras addressed them.

'I'm designating this RP1. It's the closest large chamber with a direct access route to our exfil point. Omni, I want an ammo cache set up on one of the central roofs, one with easy access. A full third of what we have. By the time we return here, we'll have plenty of company.'

'I could rig the chamber for structural collapse, Scholar,' said Voss, 'but it will leave us light on charges.'

Karras thought it over. He looked at the walls, the ceiling. Rigging it all to come down on a pursuing enemy force might make all the difference once things got out of hand, but it didn't look like an ideal place to lay that kind of contingency measure.

No pillars. All the weight is held by the walls. And just how thick are they?

'No. Save them, Omni. There will be more viable options up ahead.'

The inquisitor's servo-skull moved off, drifting towards the thick adamantium plates of an emergency blast door approximately four metres across – a door that was firmly closed. There were many such doors in the more developed sections of the mines, intended to protect men and equipment from gas explosions or other deadly accidents.

'Beyond this door is the way forwards,' said Sigma.

The little skull moved sideways and hovered by a control panel to the left. A tiny mechanical arm extended from its undercarriage and began prodding a runeboard.

Nothing.

Karras walked over to the same control panel and leaned in to study a small aperture in the wall.

'There's no power. Most of the circuits have been stripped out. We'll have to open it manually,' he told the others. 'Two, Three and Five, help me with this.'

There was a glass window behind which Karras could see a handle with yellow and black diagonal stripes. He punched the glass and pulled it. From the middle of each door, a long, thick bar swung out.

'Zeed, Rauth, you take the far one. Solarion and I will take this one.'

With two Space Marines to each door, and with their weapons mag-locked to their thigh plates, they began trying to haul the doors open, but even with superhuman musculature and all the additional strength conferred by their power armour, it was incredibly heavy going. After a minute of straining and swearing, the doors had shifted only half a metre apart.

Voss had finished setting up the ammo cache. He stood watching them for a moment, grinning under his helm. 'You are all pathetic,' he joked. 'My old serf could do better. Prophet, go pull with the others. I'll work this side with Scholar.'

'I've warned you about calling me that,' said Solarion.

'All right, brother, just get over there and start pulling, will you?'

Voss joined Karras on the handle of the left door. He settled into position, gauntleted hands gripping the bar, ready to exert his significant strength. 'Now you'll see something.'

Together with Karras, he heaved, throwing all his power into it, pulling hard with the broad, thick muscles of his unfeasibly wide back. The metal of the door groaned in protest, but it started moving. Within a matter of seconds, the gap had widened from half a metre to two-and-a-half, and most of that was on the left side. There was no need for further effort. They could proceed.

'Don't all thank me at once,' said Voss as the team filtered through into the dark tunnel beyond.

'I can see it now,' said Zeed, 'Maximmion Voss, Imperial Fist, Captain of the Third Company, Master of Doors. Think of the banner iconography. Glorious.'

Even Solarion failed to stifle a snorted laugh.

Rauth and Sigma, however, were silent. Karras noted it and it robbed him of his own grin.

'Stay vigilant, Talon,' he voxed. 'This is enemy ground. Solarion, lead on.'

4

'Alpha. You had better come up here.'

It was the voice of Solarion, tinged with static. Increasing amounts of soledite dust on the icy air were starting to tell on vox-comms the deeper Talon Squad descended. Karras raised a gauntleted first, signalling those behind him to hold position, then he moved forwards down the tunnel to where he could see the Ultramarine's broad silhouette. Drawing up alongside him, Karras didn't need to ask why Talon's point-man had stopped. The tunnel ended abruptly in a mass of fallen rock.

'I saw this coming. This is recent, Karras.'

'Deliberate?'

'No tracks,' said Solarion. 'No explosive residue on the air. From this side, it looks natural, but I can't be sure.'

Karras was silent as he mulled that over. Was it conceivable that someone or something had known they were coming? Between this and the emergency blast door with the missing power core, it was starting to look like a definite possibility. Conventional stealth was one thing – though dropping a multi-tonne monstrosity like Chyron down a hundred-metre vent shaft was far from stealthy – but a psyker of strong ability with his mind turned to the right place at the right time could certainly have detected the arrival of unfamiliar spiritual signatures, even though Karras had suppressed the strength and brightness of his own. But why would another psyker be focused on the Inorin shaft unless… Could it be that the enemy had a true seer among them, one who could glimpse prime futures?

Karras wished he could free his own talents then, if even for a moment only. He might have sent his astral self out at the speed of thought to scour the darkness ahead for such a foe. But, again, Sigma had been emphatic. Without the suppression, this time self-regulated, of Karras's ethereal presence, the enemy leader would sense him in an instant and send his lethal children out en masse to rip them apart. A true seer, however, with genuine prescient ability, could have perceived months, even years ago, that the kill-team would be coming this way. If this cave-in was a response to such a vision then, for all the psychic damping, the pentagrammic wards tattooed on their flesh, the photo-reactive cells on their black armour and the low-light discipline they employed, Talon Squad might well have been compromised already.

Without employing his power, there was no way to be sure.

'Alpha to squad. It's possible that we are being herded into ambuscade. Stay sharp, brothers. I'll not have them get the drop on us.'

'There's a way around,' said Solarion. 'Check the automapper. See that junction three sections back? We can take the south-east tunnel. It's small and cramped, and not as direct, but it will get us to the waypoint.'

'We will lose an additional twenty minutes,' said Karras, 'and we're already running out the chrono. But you're right, brother. That's our only option.'

Karras turned to look at the servo-skull a few metres behind him. Did Sigma have nothing to say? Apparently not. Someone else did, however.

'They underestimate us,' said a hard, almost toneless voice over the link. 'Whatever advantage they think they have, it will not be enough. We are Deathwatch and we encompass their doom. Lead us on, Alpha, ambush or no, and let us prove it to them.'

It was the Exorcist, and he had just addressed Karras directly for the first time since the drop. That in itself was hardly surprising. Karras and the others had soon discovered during training at Damaroth that the Exorcist was a man of very few words, and half of those were obscure literary quotes only Karras ever seemed to recognise.

Rauth's words hung in the air between the five armoured warriors. The kill-team leader could almost feel a tremor of battle-hunger wash over him. He guessed the others felt it, too, but since his talent had to remain suppressed, it could only be a guess.

'Watcher's right,' said Zeed. 'Let them try their ambush. I welcome it.'

On hearing the nickname, Rauth tensed. *Watcher*. It had been given to him because Rauth, for reasons unknown to anyone but himself, rarely took his eyes off the kill-team leader. Even back at Damaroth, this had been true. Since the moment of their meeting in the Refectorum that day, there had been a strange charge in the air between the two Space Marines. Karras had confronted the Exorcist, asking more than once if there was a problem, something he wished to discuss in private. But the Exorcist never answered. It was as if he was waiting for something, and not something positive, judging by his mien. But Karras could not begin to guess what it might be. With no recourse, he had pushed the matter aside, though he was ever aware that Rauth continued to watch him.

Zeed meant no real offence. There was a spirit of camaraderie behind the giving and the usage of the nicknames, but Rauth and Solarion were both a lot less inclined than their fellows to accept theirs.

Karras didn't have time to arbitrate. 'Solarion,' he said, 'lead us back to the junction. But let's keep the pace up. Any more dead-ends will cost us time we can ill afford to spare.'

The Ultramarine moved past Karras without a word.

The rest of the squad fell in behind, with the servitors and Sigma's floating skull in tow. They moved faster than before, conscious that doubling back was costing seconds they could ill afford. Despite their haste, they kept their senses razor-keen for any sign of hostile contact up ahead.

So many 'if's, thought Karras. *And these tunnels are riddled with blind-siding opportunities. If they have a prescient, we're walking right into their game. Why in the name of the Emperor are we really down here, Sigma? I don't believe this is about your loyalty to your people. Critical intel, maybe, but I suspect there's more to it than that.*

What is it about this White Phoenix that you're not telling us?

5

The Space Marines had to hunch over as they traversed the side tunnel that led away from the junction Solarion had mentioned as their only alternative. All but Voss, that is, so much shorter than the others. As they moved along the cramped passageway, pauldrons occasionally scraping on the cold black rock, Zeed half turned to the stocky Imperial Fist.

'At long last, Omni, being so short proves advantageous.'

Voss snorted. 'Do me a favour, paper-face. Take your helmet off. We need more light in here, and you practically glow in the dark.'

The Raven Guard laughed.

'Kill it, you two,' barked Karras from up ahead. 'Talon Three, you should be seeing the next junction.'

'Moving out into it now,' voxed Solarion.

Karras felt something – a tremor, slight at first, but building rapidly. A rain of dust broke the beam of his rail-mounted flashlight.

'Move now,' he snapped at his squad. 'Get to that junction.'

With the exception of Solarion, who was already far up ahead, the rest of the kill-team broke into a crouching run. The tremor got stronger and stronger. A rain of rock and dirt began drumming on helms and pauldrons.

'Seismic?' asked Zeed as he made haste.

'Blood and blazes,' cursed Karras as he ran. 'If I didn't have to suppress my power, I'd know what is happening here.'

'And the enemy leader would perceive you at once,' crackled the inquisitor's voice, relayed through the comms module in the servo-skull's small metal undercarriage. 'The psy-suppression order stands until I say otherwise. The success of this mission depends on it.'

Karras broke from the tunnel and saw Solarion, his back towards him, bolter raised to cover the three tunnel mouths on the other side of a small natural chamber.

'It's still getting stronger,' gasped Voss as he barrelled out behind Karras. 'What in Dorn's name…'

Rauth and Zeed followed, the servo-skull swooping out between them, still trailing its communications lifeline. Last of all came the gun servitors, rolling forwards swiftly on their tracks. Three of them made it out. The last was struck on the skull by a falling rock the size of a power fist. The man-machine's head was smashed, the left hemisphere of its brain pulped to a grisly jelly. Milky nutrifluids pumped out over its neck and shoulders. Then more rocks fell. Just as the servitor's treads were about to take it beyond the lip of the tunnel, it was buried in a rush of heavy black stone.

'By the Spire, that was close,' breathed Zeed, closest of the kill-team to the tunnel mouth that was now, suddenly, just another wall of rock.

Karras checked the servo-skull's communications hard-line and saw that it extended back into the fresh rubble. 'Sigma, are you still with us?'

'Still with you, Alpha,' crackled the inquisitor's voice. 'The hard-line has not been severed. We have comms. Now start clearing this away. The servitor's body must be recovered.'

'That's a negative,' Karras replied. 'We've just had our primary exfil path blocked and the mission-chrono is not on our side. We're not digging out a non-operational servitor. Talon Squad–'

'That servitor was carrying a hexagraphe,' interrupted Sigma. 'Do you know what that is? Because without it, this mission is already over, and the implications for you and your team, Death Spectre, are dire indeed.'

Karras had seen a number of obscure references to hexagraphes in his reading back at Watch Fortress Damaroth. There were several vague mentions of their use, mostly in connection with defensive operations launched against the despised eldar. For a second, he was furious. If the device was so critical to the mission, they should have been issued two – a primary and a back-up – and the Space Marines themselves should have been tasked with carrying them.

But Karras had no idea just how rare or dangerous they were. Did the Ordo Xenos even *have* two?

He glanced over at the three remaining gun-servitors. They would be of no help here. Their upper limbs had been replaced with shoulder-grafted weaponry. It was down to Talon to get their hands dirty.

'Right, brothers,' said Karras. 'Let's dig the damned thing out.'

'I don't think so,' replied Solarion.

Maximmion Voss ignored him, pushed past the others, grabbed the biggest rock as if it weighed nothing, and flung it off to his left where it smashed into a score of smaller pieces.

Resignedly, Zeed and Rauth pitched in seconds later.

Karras stared at Solarion for a moment longer, considering a direct command but certain it would lead to a confrontation he didn't need right now. He left it and began removing debris with the others. A few seconds later, Solarion joined them with only a mumbled curse. Soon, the five Deathwatch Space Marines stood in a half-circle staring down at the mangled form of the permanently offlined gun-servitor.

'Messy,' said Zeed, 'but two of the ammo boxes are still intact.'

He crouched over the ruined man-machine and lifted the grey boxes from the battered metal chassis.

There was a smooth black container strapped to the servitor's broken back. It, like the two ammo boxes, was dented and scraped, but had suffered no more damage than that. The servitor's white body fluids were splashed along one side of it.

'The hexagraphe?' asked Voss.

Sigma's servo-skull drifted over, anti-gravitic motors buzzing, like a fat beetle on the wing.

'Detach it from the body,' he commanded, 'but do not open it. We must not deploy it here, because the moment we do, every psychic eye on this planet will be turned to your location. I say again, keep it sealed.'

'We heard you,' said Voss as he bent and unclasped the container from the pale and twisted torso.

'Strap it to another of the servitors,' Sigma ordered. 'And keep that servitor between you. This operation cannot afford a repeat of what just happened here.'

'If you had told us in the first place,' Zeed countered.

The skull whirled to face him.

'As your Alpha has already pointed out, the mission-chrono is ticking. I suggest you proceed.'

'Solarion,' said Karras. He needed no more words than that.

The Ultramarine had already turned and was walking off towards the tunnel mouth they must enter next. He disappeared into it, his light shimmering on the walls. But the quality of that light had changed again, and Karras noted it. The air wasn't quite as crisp now. He checked his external temperature readout.

It's getting warmer. We're going deeper and it's getting warmer.

According to the automapper projection on his retinal display, they were soon to cross into uncharted territory. It would not be long before they'd have to use the hexagraphe.

And if what Sigma says is correct, the moment we do, it will bring the onslaught right down on top of us.

He hefted his bolter in his hands, comforted by the weapon's reassuring weight, and followed Solarion into the tunnel mouth.

So be it, he thought, gripping the weapon firmly. *It's about time we got to the real business.*

Perhaps the force sword *Arquemann*, sheathed and slung over his left pauldron, felt the same way. Karras couldn't tell. While he kept his inner gates closed to the flow of his power, he was cut off from perceiving the blade's mood.

Be patient, thirsty one, he told the blade regardless. *The killing will come.*

And when it did come, it would hit them all like a perfect storm. One they'd be lucky to survive.

6

Four hours in, and these were no longer the same mines they had entered. Not any more. Signs of human exploitation were non-existent. There were no more support beams or thick plasteel safety doors. No tools had worked these walls. No ore had been pulled from these deep rocks to be taken to the refineries above. These were the planet's natural caves and lava tunnels, at least for the most part. Criss-crossing them at every angle were the passages cut by the diamond-hard teeth of the leviathan rock-eaters.

Karras couldn't shake the feeling that the earlier quake had not been the result of simple tectonics. Was it possible that some of the rock-eaters had survived down here, undiscovered? Or had the quake been caused by something much, much worse?

It was lighter here. Karras studied the nearest wall. Patches of bio-luminescent growth dotted the rock. He reached out and touched one. It was about a centimetre deep at the middle, springy but quite dry. The moment he touched it, patterns of colour rippled across it, and a faint puff of powder rose into the air. His helmet sensors warned him of a mild cytotoxin in that dust, mixed with a trace of hallucinogen – a defence mechanism.

Sigma had urged them beyond the extents of the map projected by their retinal displays. Karras noted the moment on his automapper when the blips indicating his kill-team left the glowing loops of digital tunnels and chambers behind and moved into dark, empty space. They would, Sigma insisted, continue in the general direction of the prime objective until they came to a suitable location from which to deploy the hexagraphe. That meant the next tunnel intersection because, as things stood now, there was no other way to discern the proper path until the strange device was put to use.

'Turn off your lights,' Karras told the others as he thumbed off his own. 'These organisms on the walls provide more than enough illumination for low-light vision mode.'

Voss stopped to study one and noted the same ripple of light and defensive toxin release. 'Interesting reaction. Quite an aggressive response. If this were analysed, I'd wager we'd find tyranid DNA.'

Zeed was unimpressed. 'I didn't come here to fight moss. Five hours in and no hard contact. How sure are we of a xenos infestation? We've seen nothing. How good is your intelligence, Sigma? Because, so far, it looks like no one is home.'

The servo-skull, or rather its operator, ignored him. Still trailing its comms hard-line all the way back to the relay by the Inorin vent, the proxy device continued to move relative to Solarion's position as the Ultramarine stayed on point up ahead.

Whether tyranid organism or not, the moss-like patches cast everything in an eerie bluish glow, not unlike the moon of Damaroth, only nowhere near as bright. In fact, there was something about the quality of light and air here, the tone of the scene, that cast Karras's mind back to his times struggling against the Black River. Perhaps it was the sense of being channelled towards something unknown. Perhaps it was just the sense of confinement with only forward motion possible. Whichever was true, the memories and the sensations they brought with them were unwelcome. Fortunately, they were soon broken by the dry, crackling tones of Sigma speaking through his fleshless floating remote.

'This will suffice, Talon. We will deploy the hexagraphe here.'

Up ahead, Solarion and the floating skull had emerged from the end of the current passage. Karras stopped beside them, finding himself on a broad ledge before a sheer, craggy drop that plunged about thirty metres into a strange glowing pool. Looking over the edge, he noticed masses of crystal below the waters, shimmering in pale hues of blue and green. The water itself was perfectly still.

The rest of the kill-team and their three remaining gun-servitors emerged onto the ledge. Voss whistled as he gazed around the massive cavern. 'Impressive. It reminds me of the caverns on Valaxos. Minus all the dead and dying, of course.'

'Sigma,' said Karras. 'That water looks like it's heavily infused with margonite.'

'It should not be a problem. If there is any effect, it will only be to boost the strength of the device's charge. Think of a psychic hood. It is the margonite folded into the metals which resonates with the gifts of the wearer. We think this is why the broodlord opted to nest so deep in the tunnels. The margonite may be magnifying its powers. The miners had already stripped the upper levels. Regardless, the hexagraphe will work. Take it to the centre of this chamber and extract it from its carrying case.'

The ledge they were on followed the curving cavern wall a short distance to the left, then branched out into the middle of the chamber, forming a natural bridge across the glowing lake below. In the approximate centre, beneath a ceiling dense with stalactites, that bridge split into four sections, each leading off to a different part of the cavern walls. Three of those narrow spans led to dark hollows, like the gaping mouths of dead men. It was down one of these that Talon's primary objective lay. But which?

'G-17,' voxed Karras. 'Come forwards.'

One of the servitors trundled out from behind the others and rolled over to stop in front of the kill-team leader. Karras looked at the servitor's white-fleshed face, lens-eyed and steel-jawed. Its papery skin was the same colour as his own, though for entirely different reasons.

'Turn,' he told the man-machine.

Obediently, the servitor rotated on its treads, presenting its back.

Karras stepped in and removed the case containing the inquisitor's hexagraphe.

'Return to your place in line,' he told the servitor. Wordlessly, it obeyed.

Rauth, Zeed and Solarion kept their weapons raised and their attention on the tunnel entrances. Voss, however, joined Karras to watch him extract the device. His flamer lacked the range to cover the far side of the chamber, and he was curious to see what marvel of technology was so critical to the success of the operation.

Sigma's servo-skull descended to hover a metre over the black case. There was a high-pitched screech from the skull's vox-grille – a pulse-burst code – and the case hissed open, releasing its hydraulic seals. The lid swung up slowly on small pistons. The inner walls of the box were intricately carved with ancient and baroque symbols, only a few of which Karras had ever seen in all his many decades of reading and dedicated study.

Hexagrammic and pentagrammic wards, he thought. *But different from the ones with which we Space Marines are tattooed and branded.*

He wondered at their origin, probably lost long ago in the mists of time, as was so much mankind had once known and had taken for granted. To Karras, the loss of knowledge always seemed particularly tragic.

The device itself sat in a circular depression in the centre of the box and was remarkably unassuming at first glance. A perfect sphere, little bigger than a child's skull, flawlessly smooth and absolutely black. It seemed that such a thing ought to reflect light, but, much like the anti-specular resins used on Deathwatch armour, it did not. In fact, like their armour, it appeared to absorb it. At a casual glance, it might have been mistaken for a hole in space rather than a solid object, but solid it was, for around its middle was a band of ancient lettering, the script extremely fine and gold in colour.

Solarion, standing a metre to Karras's left, glanced over. 'Eldar! I've seen enough runes like that in my time!'

Voss stiffened and spun to regard the inquisitor's floating yellow proxy. 'Is this how the Ordo Xenos conducts its operations? By trusting Space Marine lives to the enemy's tainted artefacts?'

The servo-skull turned its hollow sockets on the Imperial Fist.

'A disappointing and predictable response from a warrior of the Adeptus Astartes, but one I had not expected from you, Talon Four. I had thought your affinity with technology would have taught you the value of looking beyond the source. Put your distaste aside in the name of expedience. This device is our only hope of mapping the tunnels beyond this point and selecting a route to the primary objective. There is no alternative, alien or otherwise.' To Karras, he continued, 'The Ordo has secured a number of hexagraphes over the millennia, and we have spent significant time and resources in their study. Our understanding is, if not complete, at least practical and applicable. We have employed them in the field before with success. We employ this one now, for there is no other way you can complete your mission in the time remaining.'

'The woman is surely dead already,' Zeed protested. 'Forget accursed eldar orbs and all this stealth. Reclassify this as a purge and let me loose. I have genestealers to kill.'

The skull faced him. 'When will you listen, Raven Guard? It is no mere genestealer that rules these depths. The broodlord is a foe beyond even your capabilities and, if you engage it directly, you will not survive. Whether my agent is alive or dead, you are to avoid contact with the broodlord. Do not seek it out. Do not stand your ground when it comes for you. This is no hunt to satisfy your ego and your bloodlust.'

'White Phoenix,' said Zeed. 'Just what is her strategic value? Why are the lives of Space Marines being gambled on her recovery?'

'No more questions,' said Sigma. 'You will proceed as ordered. The scalpel does not ask the surgeon why it cuts.'

That was too much for Zeed. Pride and anger erupted, crashing over his usual good humour and self-control. He moved in a blur, intent on striking down the servo-skull, obliterating it. With little more than a flinch, he covered two metres, but there he stopped, suddenly and abruptly. Karras heard him roar beneath his helm. It was followed by a furious torrent of invective. He realised Zeed was struggling against his own ceramite shell. His greatest asset had been turned against him at the speed of thought.

'Armour lock,' said Sigma coldly. 'Consider it an insurance policy against just such folly as this. Should any of you act to compromise the mission, I can and will disable you.'

The servo-skull rose another metre into the air and turned to face Karras.

'In attempting to damage this proxy, Talon Five has acted against the best interests of the kill-team and this operation. If you cannot elicit proper discipline from your people, Alpha, I will.'

'This is an outrage,' rumbled Voss deep in his throat, stepping forwards to glare at the hovering skull. 'One does not–'

'I agree,' hissed Solarion, cutting him off. 'The Inquisition oversteps the mark. Do not ever utilise this on me, Sigma, I'm warning you now.'

'All of you, listen well,' Sigma snapped at them. 'The Ordo Xenos respects the Adeptus Astartes more, perhaps, than any other body in the Imperium. We know your value. We know what you can do. That respect comes from a long and fruitful cooperation. It is I who selected you, I who respects you most. But the war my Ordo wages is unlike any you have known. Nothing is ever as it seems. Taint and corruption are everywhere. The Imperium is besieged on all sides and in ways you cannot yet imagine. I need your capabilities to help me win that war. What am I to do if you will not listen to orders? Armour lock is a regrettable necessity. It gives me no pleasure to employ it, and I will do so only when pressed. Put your pride aside, work *with* me, and I shall not have to. Siefer Zeed, had I let you strike this servo-skull, you would have ended the mission right here. How many millions would die needlessly then because the Inquisition did not get the critical intelligence it sought? And how much suffering would White Phoenix have endured for nothing? Think on it.'

There was silence, heavy with angst.

'You should have told me,' said Karras at last. 'We should not have found out like this.' He turned to Zeed. 'Your word, Ghost. Recall your oath. Give me your word. I need you back on mission.'

'He pushes us too far, Scholar,' grated the Raven Guard. 'We are scions of the Emperor.'

'And in His name, we took our oath and accepted our secondment. I'll have your word, Ghost,' Karras insisted.

The moment stretched out. At last, gruffly, Zeed answered. 'You have my word, Scholar. I'm back on mission. But it's not the end of this. The Raven Guard are puppets to no one. You speak of cooperation, Sigma. That does *not* mean unilateral control.'

Karras stepped in close and faced Zeed, visor-to-visor. 'While we are Deathwatch, we are assigned to the Ordo, and Sigma has operational command. But I'm the kill-team leader, Ghost. Look at me. I'm Alpha here. I have tactical command. Take orders from me, for your Chapter's honour, if nothing else.'

Zeed tried to nod, but he couldn't. He couldn't even move a finger.

'I gave my word, Scholar.' His voice was low, the heat of his rage bleeding. 'It will stand.'

'Sigma,' said Karras turning. 'Unlock him. We don't have time for this.'

'No,' replied Sigma pointedly, 'we do not'.

There was a sharp burst of high-frequency noise from the servo-skull. Zeed's armour unfroze. He flexed his plated limbs and rolled his shoulders, cursing quietly under his helm.

Be patient, brother, thought Karras. *Let this play out for now. We are bound by oath to do our duty, but this cannot stand. Once we return to the* Saint Nevarre...

With the situation now defused, at least for the moment, Sigma's proxy drifted back down towards the case containing the hexagraphe, ignoring the glares of the giants surrounding it.

Over the link, the inquisitor addressed Karras. 'Alpha, listen closely. It is almost time to unshackle your power. The hexagraphe requires your gifts in order to function. It is a machine designed for a psyker's use. You understand what this means, yes? The broodlord will sense you and send its mind to seek you out. You will feel it watching you, studying, evaluating. The horde will come down on you shortly after. That is unfortunate, but inevitable. We have come as far as we can unnoticed.'

'Just tell me what to do,' Karras demanded.

'Pick it up and hold it out in front of you.'

Fixing his bolter to the mag-lock on his right cuisse, Karras did so. The sphere looked so innocuous in his hand. Did it really warrant so much caution?

'Now release the lock on your power. Let the eldritch energies of the empyrean flow back into you and through you.'

Karras was only too happy to do that. As he felt the swell of ethereal energy within him, he saw the auras around him brighten, and felt *Arquemann*'s soul linking with his once more, the force sword as anxious for battle as the rest of the kill-team.

'With your gift,' said Sigma, 'raise the orb into the air and push it out into the centre of the cavern. There! Hold it there. Good. Now listen carefully. Focus your mind on the hexagraphe as if it were a foe. Attack it with your witchfire. Attempt to destroy it.'

'How will my destroying it help us?'

'You won't. It will absorb the energy and utilise it. You will see. But be ready. Once the energy is sufficient, the device will detonate. The moment it does, you need to throw a psychic shield around yourself and the others, and that includes the servitors. You must protect them from the device's detonation.'

Even Rauth? wondered Karras.

'Do you understand, Alpha? You must shield them immediately.'

'Acknowledged,' said Karras. 'But once the accursed thing has done its job, how are we to know? How do we access the results?'

'From the moment of detonation, a psychic backwash will begin. It will be similar to receiving information via clairvoyance. Of all present, you alone will be able to process the data. Only you will be able to discern it fully, to understand it. To that end, the moment it is safe to do so, you must drop your barrier and open yourself to the psychic resonance. It is only the initial detonation that is dangerous to the others.'

Karras shook his head. 'You have not prepared me adequately for this, Sigma.'

'There are no preparations for this. Trust your Librarius training and your gift and you will see. The resonance will imprint directly on your awareness not only a clear knowledge of the terrain ahead, but the density of life forms and any concentrations of psychic strength. This knowledge will be critical to the survival of the team and the success of this operation. Now attack the hexagraphe, and be ready to shield your squad.'

The others watched, unsettled, uncomfortable with things beyond their understanding and unsure of what they should do. Karras ordered them closer together, the easier to shield them all. Then he began to focus violent energies on the orb.

He spread his feet wider and tensed, allowing his inner gates to widen, channelling a flow that changed from a stream to a crashing torrent. Something in the air changed. The others felt it. Skin prickled beneath thick armour. Karras bared his teeth. He felt so strong, so alive. As balefire manifested around him, licking over the black and silver of his ceramite, he wanted to call out, to roar a battle-cry. It was too long since he had felt this. He bunched his muscles, focused, intense, and the strange white flames surrounding him began to flare taller and brighter.

The others watched as the air darkened the floating orb. It seemed to be swallowing what meagre light existed in these surroundings. Soon its spherical form was lost in a nebulous black shadow that simply hung in the air and continued to grow. As it grew, a screaming sound filled the minds of all present, all of them but one: the Exorcist, Rauth.

Karras began chanting a low mantra, words taught by Cordatus that would concentrate the flow like a laser. Centering his awareness in his lower abdomen, he unleashed a level of energy now that could have ripped a gunship from the sky or could have torn a tank to pieces.

The scream of the strange eldar device reached its peak. Everything went suddenly black. There was a deafening sound, a mighty crack like a great tree splitting. Karras switched focus, throwing up a bubble of psychic defence just in time. Even so shielded, the Space Marines and servitors were buffeted backwards a step. The lambent water below the rocky bridge on which they stood became rough with choppy waves that lapped against the cavern's sheer walls.

Normal light returned, the light of the bioluminescent moss, the crystals and the glowing waters below. There was no sign of the hexagraphe now. None at all.

'Drop the barrier and ready yourself, Librarian!' ordered Sigma.

Karras did so, and the flood of information began, washing over him like a torrent.

In his mind's eye, he saw the tunnels that led from this cavern, thousands of passageways – no, tens of thousands – from lava tubes no wider than a fingertip to massive gaping roads that could accommodate a Thunderhawk in flight. He saw every intersection, every pit, every body of cold, still water, the stalactites, the stalagmites, the flowstones and the deep, undiscovered, untapped veins of margonite, soledite and a thousand other materials from common to priceless.

And then there was the foe.

At first, he sensed only the footsoldiers. Genestealers. Mindless individuals slaved to one far greater. They were deadly enough in their own right. Even alone, a genestealer was capable of killing a Space Marine if only it could engage him at close quarters. They needed no weapons. They *were* weapons, crafted by evolution to the point of absolute lethality. Their speed and stealth allowed them to get close. Their claws and talons could shear through ceramite as if it were little better than tin. Perhaps worse still, they could implant members of a host-species with gene-altering packets of organic material – the genestealer's kiss by which they spread their abhorrent infection, undermining from within all those who would stand in their way.

And there are so many, thought Karras. *Thousands of them. We can hardly hope to make a dent. I see now why this cannot be a purge. By the Throne, if we become trapped down here...*

And yet, the worst was still to come. As the hexagraphe's explosive psychic resonance sped further along the twists and turns, Karras sensed the tyranid nests – vast nurseries filled with new abominations waiting to be born. Not just genestealers. The infestation had already reached a new phase. Other organisms were being born – other variants, larger and smaller both, all lethally specialised expressions of tyranid genetic evolution. And there were people down there – trapped, infected and doomed. One of them had to be White Phoenix.

Suddenly, his awareness was wrenched away from them, yanked forcibly towards something incredibly powerful. He knew it could be only one thing.

He felt another power looking back at him, sensing him, scrutinising him.

He knew it was the broodlord, because he had never sensed anything so cold and so alien. It was a mind utterly inscrutable, and his own withdrew from it on reflex, repelled by the darkness within it.

Here is death, he thought. *Here is the reaper made flesh.*

The motto of his Chapter had never seemed hollow to Karras. Not even for the briefest moment in all his centuries of war.

Fear not death, we who embody it in His name!

He had always been proud to live by those words, to fight under banners bearing them in bold Gothic script. But, by the Throne, those words sounded hollow now. This beast, this tyranid monstrosity from beyond the domain of man… It embodied death with a perfection and authority Karras could not dispute. This was a being perfectly evolved to kill in every conceivable way. Yes, it was the broodlord that embodied death. Not he.

'Insanity,' he groaned, and glared at the servo-skull hovering just in front of him. 'And now it knows us, Sigma. Now it knows who we are and what we are. The horde is mobilising. The hunt has begun. And we are the prey.'

7

Chyron's insides bubbled with anger and impatience. Better they had left him in stasis on the *Saint Nevarre* than drag him down here to stand guard in an empty chamber no one, not even the enemy, cared about.

A black pox on the wretched miners that made the tunnels too small for him. He ought to be with the others. Who knew what they were doing right now? Vox-comms had quickly eroded to nothing but hissing static as the rest of the kill-team had moved further and deeper into the planet's bowels.

He raged at the thought of others seeing combat while he sat here like a glorified watch-dog. By the souls of all those lost, it was an outrage. An outrage!

Looking at the gun-servitor quietly covering the tunnel mouths and passageways at his back, an impulse flickered through him, only momentary, but there nevertheless. It was the urge to obliterate the little man-machine. The servitor had done nothing wrong, but such was the rage within Chyron that no one and nothing was safe when such a mood took him.

He cursed in the old dialect of his swamp-covered home world – a birthplace he had shared with many of his late battle-brothers. Even as he called the old curse to mind, his anger was cooled and was replaced by that deep melancholy to which he was far from a stranger.

Am I the only one left who curses in such a way? Might there not be some remnant of the Chapter out there among the stars, perhaps looking for others who survived the battle with the hive fleet?

The hive fleet in question was the vast tyrannic incursion which had struck the Ultima Segmentum like a sudden, lethal plague. *Hive Fleet Kraken.*

By Terra, there had never been darker days than those. Chyron had been there at the beginning, but his performance against the tyranid vanguard had marked him for Deathwatch service, and he had left his brothers to serve the Watch with honour, believing he would soon return to them with many scars to show – and perhaps even with access to the Watch's advanced weaponry, a factor he had once hoped would help turn the tide.

Scars he had in great abundance, of course. So many, in fact, that his body needed this damned iron box to keep the pieces together. But though he had won honour and more with his deeds, when the time came to end his term of service, there was no Chapter left to which he might return.

As far as Chyron knew, none left alive bore the heart-and-bloody-tear icon of the formerly mighty Lamenters.

He was no fool. Chapters vanished. It happened. The war for dominion over this sprawling galaxy demanded blood by the oceanful. It could not be won without sacrifice. But the knowledge did nothing to salve his spiritual wounds.

There were few places to take solace. One, of course, was in ending the lives of as many foul tyranid spawn as he could hope to encounter. It was why he became so enraged at the thought of others battling while he stood and waited. The other was in that narrow thread of hope, his most fervent wish, that one day, he would see the Chapter icon on another Space Marine's pauldron, and know for sure that Chyron Amadeus Chyropheles was not the last of his kind.

Fight on till then, he told himself. Earn that moment with the blood of your foes.

There was sound from behind him: a metallic clattering and a shuffling that echoed briefly from the high chamber walls.

Chyron turned casually, unconcerned, thinking that perhaps his mindless companion was merely adjusting itself. As he did, there was the sudden roar and flash of ignited rocket fuel.

Something white hot raced from one of the tunnel mouths straight towards Chyron's glacis plate. He saw it spiral towards him almost in slow motion, on a trail of white smoke that stretched out from the tunnel mouth like a ribbon.

He was still turning when it struck him hard and exploded, punching off a thick chunk of armour from the upper left corner of his frontal plate. The impact sent him staggering two steps back.

Had the missile hit him dead centre, he might have joined his fallen brothers there and then.

Bolter-fire erupted from the gun-servitor's weapons, shaking its pale form as it rattled a torrent of rounds into the tunnel mouth so clearly marked by the missile's trail. Screams of agony and the wet sound of internal detonations followed as at least some of the rounds found enemy flesh.

Chyron recovered his balance and was about to add fire of his own when, from at least a dozen passage mouths, armed targets surged forwards, firing and screaming like men possessed.

Bright, thick beams of las-fire licked across Chyron's plate, scoring it, tracing deep lines in the outer layer, but doing little real damage beyond that. Futile, too, was the fusillade of stubber and pistol-fire that rattled off him in bursts of sparks and metal chips.

You cannot harm me. You have made a fatal error in judgement. The price will be your lives!

Chyron fired back, stitching an entire hemisphere of the chamber with a stream of lethal shells from the assault cannon that was his right-side armament. The large-calibre bullets tore through bodies as if they were made of naught but wet tissue. Blood gushed over the cold floor, quickly freezing there in great icy slicks. Corpses, many of them torn in half by the raw power of the weapon, slapped to the ground and lay their steaming, leaking all their heat into the air as their contents slid out to quickly cool.

Between them, Chyron and the gun-servitor met that first wave with such deadly force that the chamber was turned into an absolute slaughterhouse.

The Dreadnought lost all thoughts of regret and self-pity then. All he knew was battle-lust and the joy of slaughter. Who were these foolish people that they attacked a member of the mighty Space Marines? No ordinary member, either. What manner of men would hurl themselves at a Dreadnought?

His arrogance and revelry in bloodshed undid Chyron then.

He heard a clang. A vibration shook through his right side. He tried to turn to see what had happened, but his arc of vision didn't extend to looking down at his own form. It was fixed forwards. He rotated further and saw a strange-looking man with shining yellow eyes backing away from him.

Four arms! He has four arms!

'What have you done?' Chyron roared at him.

Without waiting for an answer, he turned his assault cannon on the retreating figure and opened fire.

The hail of bullets turned the target to bloody mulch. There was nothing left that resembled human form at all. But, no sooner had the strange enemy been obliterated than Chyron discovered what the noise and the shudder had been.

Demo charge!

An explosion rocked him, knocking him from his piston-powered legs, hurling him twenty metres across the icy chamber floor in an uncontrollable skid.

Parts of his right arm and shoulder showered to the ground, a hail of plasteel and adamantium that had only moments before been his primary weapon.

Chyron's HUD went wild with warning lights. Alarms screeched at him.

He ignored them all. With a roar of absolute rage, he struggled to his feet, levering himself upwards with the power fist that was his left hand. He turned his gaze back to the centre of the chamber just in time to see the gun-servitor overwhelmed and torn apart by thick-set men with mining lasers. Others were still pouring from the tunnel mouth, a great surge of armed insanity intent on the Dreadnought's absolute destruction.

Another missile arced out towards him, but he saw it coming and managed to avoid it by a hair's breadth. His sensors blinked a temperature warning as the missile's tail-fire brushed him. It struck the wall a few metres behind him. The concussion wave kicked him forwards and pelted him with a rain of small rocks.

Chyron rose again, set his stance wide and roared at the mob rushing towards him. He lifted his power fist into the air, the weapon crackling with deadly arcs of blue energy.

'To me, you brainless dogs! To me, you twisted fools! Chyron of the Lamenters will teach you how to die!'

8

Still on the rock bridge where they had deployed the eldar psychic mapping device, Karras took a moment to brief the others on the path ahead. The hexagraphe had done its job, and in a remarkable way. To Karras, it was almost like having an automapper inside his brain, only far, far more advanced. He could almost feel the tunnels, feel the currents of hot and cold air that pushed and pulled through them. They were like great calcified arteries leading to yawning caverns that were like vast fossilised hearts.

I know where we must go. I know exactly which route to take. I can even see an exfil path that will cut around the cave-in. What a device, indeed. But if I fall in battle...

'Listen,' he told the others. 'I have to give you this knowledge. I have to share with you the map I have in my head.'

'How do you propose to do that?' asked Zeed. 'Draw it out?'

'I'm going to imprint it directly on your minds. Solarion, come forwards.'

'I don't think so, Karras,' said the Ultramarine. 'You're not messing with *my* mind.'

'Don't waste time, Talon Three. You're on point. You need the information and there's no other way. Or at least none faster.'

Solarion was still reluctant, so Karras stepped straight towards him and thrust his open palm onto the point-man's breastplate. 'Ready yourself. This may cause pain.'

He said it quickly, giving Solarion no real chance to protest further before Karras speared a tendril of psychic force into the Ultramarine's mind and wrote the relevant information directly onto it. When he took his hand away, Solarion crumpled forwards, gasping, breathing hard. As he straightened, he groaned. 'Don't... don't ever do that again.'

'Do you have it?' Karras demanded. 'Can you see?'

Solarion turned his attention inwards for a long quiet moment before he responded.

'Incredible,' he muttered. 'Yes. Yes, I see it. I don't know how you did that, and I don't bloody like it, but I have it all as if I had memorised it from somewhere myself. I know where White Phoenix is. I know where the nurseries are. And, Throne help me, I know where the broodlord is, too.'

'I will go next,' said Zeed, unsettlingly eager, pushing past Solarion to stand before Karras. It was apparent he still wanted a shot at the broodlord, despite the warnings of the inquisitor.

When Solarion, Zeed and Voss had all accepted the psychic transfer, Karras turned in the direction they must follow.

'Wait,' said Voss. 'What about Watcher?'

'He will move with the rest of us,' said Karras. 'He doesn't require the transfer.'

'What?' said Zeed. 'Why not?'

'Drop it, Ghost,' said Karras. 'Check your chrono. Five hours and sixteen minutes until the extraction deadline. Almost half our allotted time gone and we're not even halfway. So we had better pick up the pace. All of us.'

Voss and Zeed threw each other a look. Even with their helms on, they understood each other. It was nothing to do with the chrono. Whatever lay between Karras and Rauth was the real reason the Exorcist was not being imprinted as they had been. They didn't like not knowing. But the tone in Karras's voice said it was the wrong time to push him.

'I'm designating this cavern RP2. Omni, I want these bridges rigged with charges. The next time we pass through here, we'll have a lot of company. The structures in this cavern will work to our advantage. With a minimum of explosives, we can at least slow the genestealers down. They'll have to scale the walls and ceiling to pursue us. Can you manage it?'

'Of course I can, Scholar. A few melta-charges will rip right through these spans.' He leaned over the edge of the rocky bridge under his feet and looked down. 'It's a long drop to the water.'

'Margonite-infused solutions are highly corrosive,' said Karras. 'Anything that falls in there isn't stepping out again. Watch your footing, all of you.'

Voss moved to one of the gun-servitors and began pulling melta-charges from one of the munitions crates. Then he set about placing the charges where they would do the most damage.

'The enemy is on the move,' said Karras. 'Solarion, Zeed, Rauth. I want another ammo cache here. See that crevice by the tunnel mouth behind you? Bolter mags and grenades, well hidden. Two canisters for the flamer. Half of all the spare ammo the servitors are still carrying. The other half we'll need for a cache at RP3.'

'You think we need another rendezvous point?' asked Zeed.

'I do. We're going to burn through a lot of rounds when we hit the nest. We'll need every last cache we can establish once we're falling back.'

Within moments, the tasks had been completed and the Space Marines, plus their three mindless drones, were ready to move deeper into the enemy's lair.

Before they did, Karras opened a secure private channel to the inquisitor.

'Sigma, there's something you need to know. When I read the resonance of the hexagraphe, I sensed the life-force of several human prisoners in the tyranid nurseries. All female. All...' He swore and shook his head. 'All swollen with xenos abominations. Do you copy, Sigma? Do you understand me? They're carrying tyranid young. One of them is White Phoenix. There's no doubt. I recognised the signature of the implant.'

There was no answer. The servo-skull just floated there, trailing its long silver thread like a hovering spider.

'Sigma?' Karras pressed. 'This changes things. Please advise.'

Nothing.

Karras swore again. On the mission channel, he addressed the others. 'Listen up, brothers. We've just lost comms to the *Saint Nevarre*.'

'What?'

'We've lost Sigma. The link is dead. He's offline.'

Voss reached out a hand and tapped the servo-skull. It bobbed gently in mid-air.

'Good bloody riddance,' said Zeed. He snatched the skull out of the air, dropped it to the ground, raised a heavy boot, and crushed it violently.

'What in Dorn's name did you do that for?' demanded Voss.

'It made me feel better.'

'I could have configured it for semi-autonomy and voice command,' complained Voss. 'We could have used it.'

'To what end?'

Voss had no immediate answer.

'Enough,' said Karras. 'It doesn't matter. The drone served its purpose. Now the relay is dead, we have no need of it.'

He felt conflicted about losing Sigma. On one hand, it was

freeing. He was in full command now, as he should have been from the start. The inquisitor had cast a shadow over the mission which had been a source of constant tension from the start. On the other hand, this *was* an Ordo Xenos operation. Sigma still had some important calls to make. White Phoenix carried an alien inside her. That had always been a possibility given the foe they faced, though Karras had truly expected to find the woman dead. Under any other circumstances, a Space Marine would not hesitate to end both those lives. But Sigma had been adamant about recovering his asset alive.

Very well. I'm not about to second guess him. We will follow the last orders as they stand. We will try to keep her alive for extraction, despite her condition. We will drop her at his feet. Let the inquisitor deal with his own mess.

He sensed the horde still heading towards them, getting nearer with every heartbeat. The longer he and his squad spent here, the more time he gave them to fill the tunnels. He pointed to an exit just to the right of a column of milky-coloured flowstone on the far side of the cavern. 'That's where our target lies, brothers. Talon Three, you're on point. Move out.'

Solarion led them out of the shimmering cavern and back into the relative gloom of the old lava-tubes with their patches of glowing blue bioforms.

'One more thing,' said Karras to the others as they moved. 'Safeties off, and I'm rescinding the Stalker round order. They know we're here. We're on assault protocols now. Kill on sight, understand? From now on, we go in hard.'

Karras heard safeties being clicked off up and down the line. Free at last to read the auras around him, he felt, too, the surge of battle-lust in his brothers, and acknowledged his own. But his was tempered by feelings of dread, for unlike the others, his gift – some would say his curse – told him just how many genestealers they faced.

He knew they would not evade the broodlord itself for long.

Down here in the dark, we are five against thousands, to say nothing of the power of their leader. Would that you were with me here, my khadit. Would that I had an entire company of my glorious brothers. I could use such strength and more.

As dauntless and deadly as my squad-brothers are, I fear we are marching into the jaws of certain death.

9

It got steadily warmer as the kill-team pushed on. Warmer and more humid. The curving rock, constantly pressing in on them from four sides, became damp and slick. Veins of metal and crystalline compounds glowed dully, some of them seeming to pulse with a rhythm like a slow, steady heartbeat. Still the tunnels wound further and deeper into the depths.

Karras charted their progress in his head, knowing by virtue of his gift exactly where they were in relation to the maze itself and the beasts that now hunted them. But he was also sharply aware of the data on his retinal display. Vox contact had dropped to a range of only thirty metres. He had heard nothing from Talon Six for hours. He had sensed the Dreadnought's soul in the backwash of the hexagraphe, but it was lost to him now. He didn't know what that meant. Was Chyron still with them? The distance was too great, and the margonite concentration in the walls was too high, to be able to tell with any certainty.

As for the others, since leaving the cavern he'd designated RP2, they had been tense and, for the most part, silent. He could feel their doubts, almost see them with his mind's eye. They rippled across the surface of their souls, like the ripples from a stone dropped in still water. Karras carried those same doubts too, but he couldn't afford to show them. The rest of the kill-team must believe absolutely that he had full confidence in his own command. They had to believe he knew exactly what he was doing, and that meant he had to believe it himself. It was the crux of any authority. The leader had to know best. So he pressed them forwards, guiding them with as little hesitation as possible.

And all the time, he felt the psychic focus of the enemy locked on to him like a laser-targeting beam. The mind of the xenos monstrosity probed at his, looking for weaknesses, chinks in his psychic armour, anything the beast could exploit to get inside his mind and read his intent, or drive him mad with alien thoughts.

But Karras was First Codicier of the Death Spectres. He had fought dark wills before. The wards on his body and the mantras in his mind made him a hard shell to crack. Moreover, he was able to shield the others from similar attempts. He could not hide their presence. Their warrior spirits were strong. With that one glaring exception, their souls shone too brightly to properly mask. Karras might just manage to hide his own, or project it elsewhere, but Solarion, Voss and Zeed were, in ethereal terms, lit up like beacons.

The same was true of the broodlord, of course. Such a nexus of raw power couldn't hide, no matter how much margonite surrounded it. But there was something else. The broodlord wasn't the only powerful presence further down in the tunnels. There seemed to be another locus of energy close to the tyranid leader. The nature of this being was harder to read, for its psychic signature had elements in common with the broodlord, and yet was significantly different, too. Almost human somehow. A corrupted astropath? Impossible to tell as yet.

Up ahead, Solarion was emerging from the end of yet another tunnel and out into a broader space. Karras emerged second. The rest of the kill-team followed him out into a wide cave with a low ceiling lit in shifting patterns of dull orange and red. The heat inside it was intense.

'Not good,' said Voss, stopping on Karras's left. 'The footing will be treacherous here.'

From cracks and craters in the cavern floor, puddles of glowing magma bubbled and churned. Narrow streams of molten rock ebbed from gaps in the walls. The black surface of those walls looked almost like the skin of some vast, burned creature, lambent blood leaking thickly through tears in its fire-crisped flanks. This was not a safe place.

Most of the floor looked solid enough, but looks could kill. Much of what seemed stable might only be the cooled skin of an old bubble, mere millimetres thick. To step on it and break through it might be to plunge one's leg into boiling magma. Even Space Marine power armour would succumb if submerged for a few seconds too long in a substance of such incredible heat.

'Solarion,' said Karras, 'can you find us a route across?'

The cavern had only one exit on the far side – a gaping tunnel mouth, the edges of which had a strange, melted-wax appearance, a result of how the cavern and tunnels had been formed.

Solarion drew his long, serrated combat knife, went into a crouch and, without another word, started edging forwards, probing the ground before him with the point of the sixty-centimetre blade.

Karras ushered Rauth, Zeed and Voss to follow the Ultramarine, slow and steady. Then he turned to the gun-servitors.

'Command code: Bastion,' he told them. 'Cover both exits. Lethal force. All non-identicode-bearing targets viable. Confirm.'

The servitors turned their blank faces towards him. Their vox-speakers crackled.

'GS-18 confirms,' said one. 'Bastion protocol active.'

'GS-11 confirms,' said another. 'Bastion protocol active.'

'GS-5 confirms,' said the last. 'Bastion protocol active.'

Karras glanced down at the ammunition reserves strapped to the back of the servitors' chassis. Each carried grenades of various types and magazines loaded with bolter-rounds. One carried two extra promethium canisters to refuel Voss's flamer. And then there were the remaining melta-charges.

Without turning, Karras ordered the others to a halt.

'Omni,' he said. 'Would you be able to rig these walls?'

'Thinking of using the magma?' Voss asked.

'I'm thinking it would be a damned good deterrent to anything in pursuit.'

Voss paused for a second to consider it.

'It would mean using the last of our charges, Alpha, but I think you're right. It would be easier to breach those walls and cause a magma flood than it would be to collapse the tunnel mouths, for example. And by Dorn, I'd love to see the results.'

'Then I'm designating this chamber RP3,' said Karras. 'It's close enough to the target to be a good first fall-back point and we can give them a proper bloody nose here. The gun-servitors are staying to secure it. Go ahead and rig it, Omni. Solarion, find him a stable path over to the walls. The rest of you stay put for now. We'll do a final weapons check before we move on.'

While Solarion and Voss moved left towards the cave wall, Zeed addressed Karras.

'How long until we see some killing, Scholar?'

'They're almost on us, brother. There's a four-way tunnel intersection about two hundred metres up ahead. I'm guessing we'll have first contact there. Be ready.'

'And yet you choose to leave the gun-servitors here,' said Rauth.

'I do,' said Karras. 'The servitors give off only the merest trace of any kind of psychic residue. In essence, they are almost as soulless as–' He almost said *as you*, but he caught himself. Even so, Rauth must have guessed what was on his mind. 'I'm counting on that to keep them from notice.'

Did the topic of souls disturb Rauth? Was he even aware of his condition? Impossible to tell. Even without his helm, Rauth's face was all but unreadable at the best of times. No emotion ever played out on it, at least none that Karras had seen.

'We'll need their fire-support on the way out,' the kill-team leader continued. 'By then, we'll have the whole nest coming down on us. So I'm keeping them out of the fight until we need them most. Objections?'

No one spoke.

'Good,' said Karras. 'Because I'm Alpha here and the decisions are mine to make. Listen to me and do as I say, and we may yet get out of this alive.'

Karras was presenting as cold and confident a face as possible. In truth, he knew their chances. The odds were almost laughable, but it was not in a Space Marine's constitution to ever give up. They had established three solid fall-back positions, each with ammunition caches. Two were rigged with explosives to buy them extra time in their retreat. If they made it back to the exfil point with the foe on their heels... Well, maybe Chyron would get his fill of killing after all – if he yet lived.

Be patient, Old One, and you may yet extract some revenge for your fallen brothers.

Karras couldn't know then that Talon Six was already waist deep in blood and fire.

Minutes later, with RP3 rigged and ready, Talon Squad followed their point-man out of the blistering chamber and into yet another tunnel that was barely wider than an individual Adeptus Astartes. Unsurprisingly, this caused problems for Maximmion Voss. His broad bulk – from shoulder-to-shoulder a great deal wider than any of the others – forced him to move sideways along the passage.

'Don't get stuck, tree stump,' jibed Siefer Zeed. 'We need this tunnel clear for the journey back.'

Voss snorted. 'Go brush your hair or something.'

Zeed laughed and made another riposte. So it went, back and forwards for a minute or so.

Karras, focused as he was on the dark presence ahead and the kill-team's descent towards it, nevertheless found himself grinning a little at the banter between the two Space Marines. Their rapport was something he envied. It wasn't just a matter of their personalities, either. He recalled some of Damaroth's hardest trials, the ones they had run as a kill-team, heavily poisoned, disoriented and beset by simulated foes. He had seen the way Zeed and Voss had moved together, each complementing the other's strengths, compensating for his weaknesses, all without a word needing to be said between them. *Cohesion*. The Watch captains had stressed its importance. It was something the entire team should have shared. Perhaps in time...

No, thought Karras. *I'm not that naive.*

'Throne and sword, Alpha,' snapped Solarion. 'Will you shut them up?'

Karras's first instinct was to shout the Ultramarine down – these warriors were walking into death's jaws. Let them laugh as they did so. But Solarion wasn't entirely wrong. This was no time to lose focus in favour of levity. He needed all of them razor sharp, fingers on triggers, righteous death-dealing foremost in their minds.

'Omni, Ghost,' he said with some reluctance. 'Ice the vox-chatter, now.'

It was as much of a rebuke as he felt like issuing. For their part, Zeed and Voss conceded, guessing rightly that it was prudent not to press their Alpha too far, and the team moved on. They stepped out into a small, rocky chamber and took up positions covering each of the passage mouths that opened onto it, with the sole exception of the tunnel they had just exited.

'Where are they, Scholar?' demanded Zeed.

'They're closing fast,' said Karras. 'A lot of them. Back-to-back, all of you. Now!'

The kill-team formed a tight fighting circle, bristling with bolter muzzles. Voss lit the igniter at the business end of his flamer.

'How far, Karras?' Solarion asked, voice tinged with tension, rough with the readiness to kill. 'Range?'

Faint scrabbling sounds began to reach their gene-boosted ears, vying for attention with the beating of their hearts and the rushing sound of the increased blood flow in their veins.

Muscles twitched eagerly. Adrenaline levels and body temperatures increased. Their super-human physiologies were primed for combat, ready to fight like no normal man ever could.

The scrabbling sounds got louder.

'Twenty metres,' said Karras. 'Front and sides.'

Louder still; a frantic clatter of claws on rock.

'Fifteen metres, Talon Squad!' said Karras.

Harsh chittering and screeching joined the clatter of the advance now. The sounds came out of the dark, like a vanguard of ghosts sent to cause terror ahead of the physical threat.

'Ten metres,' shouted Karras. 'This is it! Fight well, brothers. For the honour of the Deathwatch and for the glory of your Chapters! Fear not death!'

Shapes burst from the shadows at speed: tall and terrible, a great tangled mass of fang and claw, of chitin armour and long, spidery limbs. The first to emerge came straight for the Space Marines with eyes aglow and jaws dripping, compelled to commit savage and bloody slaughter by the alien mind whose impulses they served.

'Engage!' roared Karras.

Muzzles flashed. Sheets of white flame gushed forth.

Absolute violence swallowed everything.

10

Diamond-hard claws slashed the air just millimetres from Zeed's visor. Had he not been faster, swaying backwards at the last instant, his head would have been taken clean off. The momentum of the savage swing carried the beast too far and it was open for a crucial half-second; a half-second in which, at point-blank range, Zeed unloaded a single bolt-round up through its lower jaw and out the back of its distorted purple head.

Genestealers! Of all the foes to face in tight quarters...

The body dropped hard, revealing others coming straight towards him.

They had to leap the bodies of their dead, giving Zeed a scant few metres' grace before they were on him. Decades of relentless training took over, coordinating his movements, impelling him to lethal action almost without conscious thought. He raised his bolter and put a single round in the forehead of each. Their heads snapped backwards, exploding as the bolts detonated within. But a third creature was coming in low on six limbs, skittering forwards like a scorpion intent on striking down its prey. Suddenly it leapt, long limbs splayed out, ready to attack with any of them.

Zeed knew better than to step backwards, trying to avoid the killing claws. Instead, he lunged forwards with all the power of his legs, slipping inside the monster's guard. As he did, he balled his left hand into a ceramite-plated fist and, with all the momentum available to his gene-boosted, power-armoured body, drove it hard into the monster's face.

The beast's head was jolted backwards, but it didn't stagger. It recovered quickly, lifting its limbs high for a killing blow, screeching with rage. But that screech would be the last sound its throat ever loosed. Zeed whipped his combat knife free from its sheath with his left hand, quick as lightning, and drove it straight through the genestealer's exposed neck. Then he turned away, using all his body-weight to rip the knife free. The serrated blade left almost nothing of the muscle and connective tissue. The genestealer collapsed, crashing to the rocky chamber floor with its neck gaping wide, head lolling at a gruesome angle.

Others were still pouring from the black tunnel mouths. The Raven Guard resumed firing, adding the sound of his bolter to the deafening noise of the others. Ammo counters dropped with frightening speed. Bodies lay everywhere, but the assault didn't seem to be slowing.

'Stand firm!' yelled Karras.

A great sheet of fire roared out from Voss's flamer. Seven distorted alien forms began an agonised dance in the middle of the blaze before they collapsed, their flesh melting off to leave only black and smoking bones.

'Talon Four, cease fire,' ordered Karras. 'Conserve that ammo. This wave is almost at an end!'

Voss slung his flamer in favour of the bolt pistol holstered on his left cuisse. He flicked off the safety just as the last line of genestealers erupted from the tunnels. The Space Marines' guns rattled a deep tattoo. The frenzied aliens were mowed down even as they closed with their prey.

Rauth killed the last of them, putting two bolts in the beast's torso, dead-centre mass. As this last member of the alien assault tumbled dead to the chamber floor in front of him, the Exorcist hit the release catch on his bolter and dumped another empty mag.

Zeed, almost giddy from the combat high, surveyed the charnel house scene before him.

Bodies lay strewn everywhere. Footing was poor; the ground was slick with shining wet viscera. Brass bolt-casings surrounded the feet of the Space Marines, slowly being enclosed in a sea of cooling alien blood.

'That's it?' he asked Karras.

The team leader was reloading his bolter. 'That was a probe, Ghost. The broodlord wanted to see what we can do. Now he knows. If anything, we've just proved that we deserve special attention. They'll be coming for us in real numbers now.'

Voss swapped his pistol out for his flamer again. He looked at the heaps of dead bodies all around them. '*Real* numbers?'

'How many are we talking about, Alpha?' Solarion asked. Tension had robbed his voice of its usual caustic tones.

Karras faced his squad. 'Too many for us to handle, and that's not something I say lightly. Sigma told us this was not to be a purge. There's good reason for that. We can't afford to get locked down and have to fight it out. Look at your chronos, Talon. The readout is yellow, now. So we move fast, or we die here. I'm not planning on the latter.'

Zeed rammed a fresh magazine into his bolter and cocked it. 'Then let's get a move on,' he said, 'because, that taste of combat has left me hungry for more.'

It was here that Karras finally told them all that the kill-team must split up.

Only Rauth did not voice objections, and Karras was hardly surprised. He had the feeling the Exorcist had known all along that this moment would come. Only Rauth was truly invisible to the broodlord's psychic senses. Karras could suppress his gift again, and mute the signature his soul gave off so long as he did not exercise his powers, but he could not mask the others at the same time. To travel as a squad meant being tracked. That left only one course of action.

'We will not be able to retrieve White Phoenix while under assault,' Karras told them. 'Solarion, Voss and Zeed, I need the three of you to head south towards the largest nurseries or hatcheries or whatever the warp they are. Cause as much damage as you can. Wreak havoc on them, a storm of slaughter so great they will have no choice but to send everything they have against you.'

'That's your plan?' raged Solarion. 'Use us as a diversion? Expendable, are we? No, Karras. I don't think so.'

'Listen,' barked Karras. 'There's something you ought to know. Tell them, Rauth. Do it!'

The Exorcist glared at Karras, but he would say nothing. Instead, he stepped away, bolter raised, and covered the exits in silence.

Karras cursed in frustration. 'Then I will tell them. Our Exorcist brother here gives off no spiritual signature. He has no presence in the immaterium. Do you understand me? The enemy cannot track him. They cannot even see him unless they have actual physical line-of-sight.'

He let them process that a moment. 'It means the broodlord does not know he is here.'

'How is that possible?' asked Voss. 'I thought all living things had an ethereal signature. How can a Space Marine lack a soul?'

Karras looked at Rauth, but the Exorcist presented only his back.

Indeed, thought Karras. *A Space Marine with no soul, and yet he lives and fights just as we do. It should not be possible. It goes against everything we know. And yet, here he is.*

There was no time to think on it more. Not here. 'How does not matter,' he told Voss. 'I'm certain that Sigma knew of this... anomaly... and that he planned to have Rauth split off from the rest of the kill-team to recover the woman. I will be going with him as insurance. We cannot risk so much on only one of us.'

'Can the broodlord not see you also?' asked Voss.

'He sees me clearest of all, brother, but only while my power is unshackled. I will suppress it again, now that Rauth and I will be separating from the rest of the squad.'

'You're still using us, Death Spectre,' hissed Solarion.

'Of course I am,' snapped Karras. 'You are members of my kill-team. We have a mission to accomplish, and this is our best chance of success. I am no more using you than Sigma is using all of us, but we are Deathwatch. This is what we do, and we are sworn to it by solemn oath. Let's get the job done and get out of here. We will rendezvous at RP3 and fight our way back to the exfil point together. Is that clear? I expect all three of you to meet us back there. Do not disappoint me.'

'I'm in,' said Zeed. 'I'll take a straight fight over tip-toeing through tunnels with some woman on my back any day.'

'Aye,' said Voss. 'We'll give them a fight, all right.'

They looked at Solarion, who looked back at them blankly for a moment.

With an angry grunt, he finally agreed. 'Very well, Alpha. I'll do as ordered. But know this: if you plan to spend our lives as coin for your own escape, my shade will haunt you for the rest of your days.'

Karras lifted both hands and disengaged the seals of his helm. He lifted it from his head, then he stepped directly in front of Solarion.

'Look into my eyes, brother. Look, damn it! And listen to me now. Whatever you think of me, know that you are respected and valued, a crucial member of my kill-team. More than that, you are my battle-brothers, all of you. And I will not leave you behind. *I will not!*'

His eyes blazed with intensity and emotion, and even Solarion had to admit to himself that he believed him.

'Go south-east for half a kilometre. Move with speed. There is a cavern at the tunnel's end. You already have the knowledge. Visualise it. From there, take the leftmost tunnel. It slopes down towards several of the enemy birthing chambers. There you will unleash your fury on them.'

'How will we know when you have the woman? How will we know when to fall back to the rendezvous point?'

'I cannot mask the woman's soul, nor the signature of the creature in her belly. Once we have her, the broodlord will sense her moving away from the nest. In a fury, it will turn all the forces at its command to her recovery. You will know that we have her when the assault on your own position slackens. Pray for us then, because they will be coming for us. All of them. We will need your strength as soon as you can give it. Hurry to the RP. Without you, Rauth and I will have almost no chance of survival.'

His words sat heavy on the air. It was such a long shot, but all of them had known long odds before – had known them and survived them, if only by the skin of their teeth.

When Karras finished replacing his helm, Voss moved forwards and gripped his wrist tight. 'Emperor watch over you, Scholar.'

'Fight hard, all of you,' replied Karras. 'Do yourselves proud, for the honour of Watch and Chapter both.'

They parted, two moving off into the abyssal black tunnel to the north, three heading south-east as ordered.

Karras felt a weight in his stomach as he and Rauth moved at a heavy trot.

He could not shake the feeling that he had just sent three exemplary Space Marines off to their deaths.

If so, both he and Rauth would not be far behind them.

11

As they ran, Karras glanced sidelong at the recalcitrant Exorcist.

Of all his kill-team operatives, Darrion Rauth was the one about which he knew the least. Save a very few rare exceptions such as the Badab War, the exploits of Rauth's Chapter were shrouded in unusual levels of secrecy. There seemed some link to the Inquisition's Ordo Malleus, but it was vague and tenuous at best, at least as far as records went.

What he did know was that Rauth had earned the nickname Zeed had given him.

Watcher, he calls him, and with ample cause.

Karras would have been a fool not to notice how often Rauth's cold, withering gaze was on him. Worse still, his hand never strayed far from his weapon when in Karras's presence. It was as if he expected violence to erupt at even the unlikeliest of times.

Has he taken it upon himself to act as some kind of bodyguard? Has he been so instructed without my knowing? It can't be that. His manner... It doesn't fit. Then, what?

Together, he and Rauth moved at speed along a slowly-curving downwards tunnel that branched north from the chamber in which they had parted from their fellows, then turned slowly north-east. It was pitch black here. They'd had to activate the rail-mounted lights on their bolters again.

Karras had closed the inner gates on his power almost completely for now. What little he allowed through was spent on forcibly reducing the brightness of his soul and projecting that dimmer ethereal light well away from his true position. It took a certain amount of steady concentration, and while he maintained it, he could not psychically detect enemies that might be nearby, but what he did detect was the change in their surroundings. One only needed eyes for that.

The walls were changing. Instead of bare, natural rock, they had become strangely ribbed, as if the two kill-team operatives were descending down the gullet of some vast creature as yet unnamed.

Karras slowed to study them. Rauth ran on, then noticed Karras was no longer pacing him and stopped. Karras heard the slight shifting of ceramite plates as the Exorcist brought his bolter up.

'What's wrong?'

'The walls,' said Karras. He stepped over to the tunnel surface on his left and angled his bolter's light onto it. 'See for yourself.'

Rauth moved cautiously over to his side and looked down.

Karras reached out a hand and touched the surface. It was as he had suspected. The further they went, the more it became apparent: the walls were organic. They were in the nest for real now. Originally, the tunnel would have been a natural lava tube, or perhaps a path cut by a massive prehistoric rock-eater. But now the rock surface was covered with a shiny, waxy substance marbled with a network of fine lines that looked like veins. Rauth drew his knife from the sheath at his lower back and stabbed the point into the strange wall. The immediate surface was still somewhat soft, being composed of younger, newer growth, but the deeper the point of the blade went, the harder the material became. When Rauth withdrew his knife, the wound he had made began bleeding a thick, sticky substance – sap-like in consistency but with the colour and smell of super-oxygenated blood.

'It bleeds,' said the Exorcist.

Karras nodded. 'It's alive and it's growing on its own, spreading out from the centre of the tyranid nest. We are almost there. The locatrix is not far ahead.'

They moved back to the centre of the tunnel, Rauth sheathing his blade. Side-by-side, they continued at a run down into the darkness. The air was stiflingly hot and humid now, but the filters, seals and regulatory systems of their power armour rendered such changes meaningless in terms of discomfort.

When they had gone a few hundred metres further, and the growth on the walls became noticeably thicker, Karras remarked on the strange shapes their lights now described. The forms on the tunnel walls became more complex in structure. He saw cross-ribbed swellings and serrated spurs. There were thousands of craters clustered in groups, each containing a barnacle-like mouth from which tiny fronds, barely visible, waved. As the Space Marines passed these, they whipped inwards and disappeared completely, the beaks snapping shut with an audible clack.

'We must talk, brother,' said Karras, 'about why the broodlord cannot detect you.'

They kept running, and Rauth made no reply.

'I noticed it the first time we met. You give off no resonance at all. I've never known anything like it.'

It was not a question, and Rauth did not treat it as such.

Karras's tone became sharp.

'As your Alpha,' he said, 'I have a right to know.'

'You know everything you need to,' growled Rauth in reply. 'I have no psychic signature. I do not resonate. Accept it. Use the knowledge to your advantage, as you do now. Do not waste time and energy pressing me for the how and the why. I cannot and will not speak of it. My Chapter has its laws just as yours does.'

Silence fell between them again.

Eventually, Karras said, 'Very well, brother, but the truth will out sooner or later. It always does.'

'Then it will out for you, also. Think on that.'

As they pressed on, Karras dimly sensed the broodlord stirring. He had not expected to, not with his talent closed off to him, but the abomination's aura was throbbing powerfully with psychic thunder, strong enough to feel even with his gift suppressed. It was sending out a terrible impulse, compelling its hordes of chittering killers to move south-east in the direction of the other kill-team members.

Their storm of carnage and destruction had begun.

Karras clenched his teeth, adjusted his grip on his bolter, and increased his pace, acutely conscious that Zeed, Voss and Solarion were fighting to buy him time.

'It has started,' he told Rauth. 'The tyranids move against the others. We must be swift.'

Rauth matched his speed. 'May the Emperor lend them His fury.'

Whatever gulfs of misunderstanding and mistrust lay between Karras and Rauth, against the xenos threat, they were Deathwatch operatives united by oath. It would serve them both to remember that, Karras knew.

He and Darrion Rauth would stand together, fight together, even die together.

And the latter perhaps sooner than either of us might wish.

12

Voss stepped over the body at his feet, jammed his pistol into the genestealer's mouth and blew out the back of its head. It flopped back, twitching, four arms splayed out.

He looked down at it and cursed. These foul creatures were an offence to the eye. Perhaps if they hadn't borne so many features inherited from their host species… But the telltale signs of their parentage were plain for all to see: the thumbed hands, the configuration of facial features, the play of muscles beneath the skin of the neck – all this and more besides.

Corruption, thought Voss. *They twist everything to their own pattern. What guides them? What purpose drives them across so much space just to absorb and multiply?*

Mankind had no answer, but for now, at least, there were still men alive to ask. How much longer would that be so? The tyranids surely represented the greatest threat by far to the Imperium. They were implacable, remorseless, insatiable. There was no bargaining to be had. You killed them, or you were killed.

Zeed stepped past him, sheathing his long knife.

'Not out of breath, I hope, brother.'

Voss grinned beneath his helm. 'Show me to more of them and you'll see.'

Solarion joined them, having surveyed his own kills and reloaded his empty bolter. 'They'll be coming soon enough. Let's move a little deeper and do some more damage.'

Around them lay not only the first wave of genestealers who had been sent to defend this place, but the amniopods and birthing sacs from which the broodlord's vicious progeny were meant to hatch. They wouldn't be hatching now, however. Solarion, Zeed and Voss had torn through the place like a murderous wind before the first genestealer defenders had arrived. Half-formed creatures had spilled out in a wash of nutritional fluids as the Space Marines had wrenched open protective shells and cut through fleshy membranes. They had stamped on these unborn creatures, ending early the lives of beings that would have gone out to claim so many others.

There was no pity in their hearts. The xenos young were simply monsters waiting to grow into full lethality. Their destruction was the Emperor's work.

Solarion took point without being asked, and they moved on, deeper into the heart of the alien nest, looking for the next birthing chamber in which to conduct their righteous slaughter.

They found one soon enough, large and humid, the air thick with noxious gases emitting an unwholesome, acrid stink. But the horde had been fully mobilised against them now, and there was no time to kill the tyranid young before the walls were swarming with full-grown genestealers.

Back at the junction after the assault of the first wave, Zeed had said he wanted more.

Now he got it.

Solarion's breastplate screeched in protest as a talon raked it, tearing a great, jagged rent across its embossed honour-markings and Deathwatch iconography. Warning glyphs flickered to red life, his visor projecting them directly onto his left retina.

ARMOUR INTEGRITY COMPROMISED

The offending creature, hissing and spitting savagely as it readied itself for a killing lunge, suddenly choked out a wet cry and fell to the ground in two pieces separated at the waist. Behind it, the Raven Guard was already moving away, engaging another knot of xenos abominations, bolter blazing, firing one-handed as he gripped his combat knife in his other.

Solarion added his own gunfire, cutting down three large genestealers that were trying to flank Maximmion Voss from the right.

The chitin-covered cavern walls strobed with muzzle flashes. Genestealers were crawling all over them, climbing out from holes between faintly glowing cysts that were swollen close to bursting with embryonic alien forms. Quivering sacks of flesh lay pale pink and glistening wherever there was a corner or crevice. Wall-veins and ribbed umbilici, as white as the eyes of a blindfish, pumped nutrient-thick fluids to clusters of queer eggs that hung from between the stalactites above. Occasionally, a stray bolt would rupture them, and a rain of thick, smelly fluids would fall to the ground. It hardly mattered if it rained on the Space Marines. Their armour was already awash with gore.

The genestealers poured out towards them in numbers seemingly without end. The broodlord's earlier probing attack had convinced it of the threat these armoured intruders represented to its nurseries, to the swelling of its forces and its eventual domination of the planet. It was time to remove that threat.

Even as Solarion revelled in the bloodbath, he recognised that he and his two irreverent Deathwatch brothers could not stand for long against numbers like these. They fought for the sake of Karras and Rauth, but he was less than willing to die for them.

Come on, Death Spectre. Retrieve the woman and get moving so we can pull out of here.

He knew he carried too few rounds to last much longer if the genestealer assault maintained its intensity. Voss was wielding his flamer again, gloriously effective against enemy ranks so dense, and the Imperial Fist was taking an impressive toll on the foe, but sooner or later, his weapon would run dry and there would be no more canisters of promethium to fuel it. Not until they returned to RP3.

If we ever get that chance.

'More contacts,' shouted the Raven Guard. 'Front right, high.'

Solarion looked up. Another wave of hissing, six-limbed forms poured into the nursery chamber from a quivering, fleshy orifice in the ceiling, an obscene sight.

Zeed's bolter barked out a greeting, and four of them fell with shots neatly placed in their brains and breasts. Solarion added three swift kills of his own to his tally. But not all of the genestealers could be killed at a safe distance. There were simply too many for that, and they moved so fast. Even Zeed, supreme at close quarters, would meet his death if the fighting went hand-to-hand. Against one or two at a time, he might just hold his own, but not against more than that.

How much longer, Karras? thought Solarion bitterly. *In Guilliman's name, how much longer?*

If he, Zeed and Voss could only manage to break away from the fight in the next few moments, then maybe, if the Emperor was with them, they might just live to see the end of this damned fools' errand.

He tried not to wonder if the prize was worth his life, nor to wonder how, if they didn't make it back, Sigma would report their increasingly inevitable deaths to their respective Chapters.

13

'In Terra's holy name,' groaned Karras. 'I knew, but to see it with one's own eyes…'

He and Rauth had entered a chamber of grotesque horrors, the sight of which, he knew, would stay with him forever, a reminder of reality's darkest, cruellest face. It was the birthing chamber in which the primary objective awaited them. White Phoenix ought to be here, not just because the locatrix said so, but because this chamber was different from any other they had come across in a single, crucial way:

Women! Dozens of them. They have become a part of the nest, incorporated into it by their captors. Such a gruesome fate.

Karras wanted to turn away, sickened and infuriated.

More than half of the women were fixed to the strange organic walls of the chamber by a mix of dark chitin plates and thick strands of a sticky substance like some kind of tough mucus. The others were half enclosed in equally disgusting organic mounds dotted about the cavern floor. Pools of pungent yellow-brown liquid bubbled and steamed near them. Ropes of semi-translucent flesh fed or withdrew fluids from their bodies, snaking into their noses and mouths. Gratefully, Karras saw that the women's lower bodies were fully encased, though their grossly distended bellies were exposed to the hot, humid air. He had no doubt there were similar organic catheters beneath the chitin, responsible for Throne-knew-what. Those bellies were so stretched by the xenos organisms growing within that the skin had become as translucent as the looping coils of strange umbilici. In some, the Death Spectre could see jostling clusters of embryonic aliens vying with each other for the most comfortable positions. The women playing host to these slithering forms wept and whimpered in an agony that pierced their mindless stupor.

Rauth was murmuring some litany that only those from the Basilica Malefix on Banish could possibly comprehend. His fists were clenched so tight that he had lost feeling in both hands.

'And I saw the true face of darkness behind that veil, and it did blind me with its horror,' quoted Karras numbly.

Rauth looked over at him. 'Uxol Thay's *Necrisod*.'

'Volume three. His visions of the sixth hell.'

Rauth moved forwards, mag-locking his bolter and drawing his combat blade. 'We should not let them suffer like this.'

Karras halted him with a hand on his right pauldron, palm pressed to the horned-skull icon there. 'Agreed, and we *shall* end their misery, but we have a mission to complete, and our brothers are fighting for their lives so we can do just that. We will release them from their suffering after we extricate White Phoenix. Not before. The mission has ultimate priority here. We may be beset at any time.'

Rauth nodded once and brushed off Karras's hand. He kept his blade ready in his own.

Karras checked his retinal display and found what he was looking for.

His battle-helm's subsystems had locked on to the source of a repeating electronic life-signal. A small, red, triangular reticule appeared, marking the precise location of the opticom they had been moving towards all this time. Karras blink-clicked the reticule off and saw a wretched figure lying bound to a pulsing organic structure. It looked part-altar, part-incubator, and on it was White Phoenix, the primary objective.

'That's her,' he said pointing, and strode over to her side.

Looking down at her, he saw deep scratches, crusted thick with blood, on her arms, face, neck and chest.

She fought them.

It hadn't made any difference, but at least she had tried. He turned his eyes to her abdomen and saw that it was horribly distended. She was pregnant like the others, her belly stretched taut with early signs of the chitinous armour which the creature within was already forming. It would emerge ready to protect itself.

That emergence would be no quiet, slithering escape, either. It would rip and tear its way out, bursting forth in a tide of its dying host's blood. Not one of these women would survive the birthing process. The creatures, when ready, would erupt through their flesh, then turn on their mothers and feed on them until nothing was left, not even the teeth, hair and bones.

Eat. Absorb. Incorporate. Spread.

So it went, the tyranid life cycle. It was a thing of absolute simplicity, but the halting of it, the stemming of that tide, was anything but simple. Countless brothers had already fallen in the attempt: Ultramarines at Macragge, Blood Angels and Angels Vermillion at Hollonan, Brother Chyron's own Lamenters at Devlan and Malvolion, and so many more. Many yet would fall, and with no clear hope in sight.

Karras locked his bolter to his cuisse and, leaning forwards, tugged hard at the foul, sticky mass restraining White Phoenix. First, he worked to free her head and neck. With a cracking sound, a handful of chitinous matter came away trailing wet strands and tangles of what looked like human hair. It was the woman's hair. As he pulled more of her bonds away, more hair came with it, falling out so easily. All her nutrients were being leeched away by the alien inside her. Karras paused, wondering if removing her from this abominable apparatus might kill her. She seemed so pale and thin. He had never seen her before, so he could not know that men of great power and influence had once coveted her. She had been an example of superb human genetics once. Now, she was little more than skin and bone. And yet, Sigma would have her returned. He had sent Talon Squad down into the depths of this dark, filth-ridden hellhole to get her back.

Again, he questioned the true motives behind this operation. Just what was her strategic importance to the Ordo Xenos? Well, it hardly mattered for now. Here she was, and it was his job to get her out, whatever Sigma's motives might be.

As he pulled away more of the biomass from her body, he hoped his squad brothers were still alive. Talon was *his* kill-team. They were *his* operatives. *He* was responsible for their survival. But, as tempted as he was to send his astral self out to check on them, he would risk alerting the broodlord to his location. Not yet. It was too early. He just had to trust in their skill and hope they would rendezvous with he and Rauth as planned.

Suddenly, the woman's eyelids fluttered open, surprising Karras and causing him to freeze. She turned her head slowly to regard him.

'She's conscious,' he whispered to Rauth over the link.

The Exorcist, who had been covering the exits while Karras had been busy pulling her out, came closer and leaned in to snatch a brief look.

One of the woman's eyes was completely bloodshot. The other was a gunmetal-grey orb with a glowing red lens for a pupil. 'Space... Marines...,' she murmured.

'Yes,' answered Karras. 'Deathwatch.' Against her barely audible voice, he was all too aware of the grating sharpness of his own, modulated as it was through his helmet's vocaliser. Without knowing quite why he did it, he reached up and removed his helm.

His face was too harsh to be called handsome, criss-crossed as it was with scar tissue and old burns, as pale as snow and with blood-red eyes. But it was a more human face than she had seen in all too long. More than that, it was a Space Marine face, the face of a warrior, the face of her salvation. The woman smiled up at it weakly.

'Kill us all,' she said. 'Don't let us be... be used like this.'

'I was not sent to kill you,' said Karras. 'I was sent to get you out.'

The woman shook her head. 'No,' she told him. 'It was not me he sent you to recover.'

She knows it is Sigma who holds our leash.

He replaced his helmet and addressed Rauth, using the link so she would not hear. 'She wishes death. Would that I could grant it.'

'She is not likely to survive the extraction,' Rauth returned. 'Look at her. Death will come soon enough. Your hand need not hasten it.'

'She believes it is the unborn beast Sigma wants, not her. But he was adamant we try to extract her alive.'

'Then she is mistaken about his interests. Regardless, we should make haste.'

'I will carry her,' said Karras. 'You take point.'

'Very well. But first I shall set the others free.'

They looked again at the walls and grotesque mounds, and at the pitiful creatures trapped there.

'Mankind must wipe out this tyranid cancer,' snarled Karras. 'Surely no other xenos race is as worthy of our hatred and rage.'

Rauth raised his knife.

'No,' said Karras. 'There is not enough time to kill them that way. We will move to the exit and use our grenade launchers. Inferno rounds. We will burn everything to ash.'

So they did, and granted all the Emperor's mercy.

14

Something happened, a sudden change that rippled across the enemy ranks. The genestealers froze in their attack and turned their heads to the north, as if hearing something the three blood-spattered Space Marines could not. Those nearest to passageways and tunnel mouths vanished into them, like great cockroaches scuttling for shadow, but the genestealers closest to the Deathwatch operatives resumed their attack, their targets too close to turn from, still intent on slaying the power-armoured intruders.

Even as he cored the torso of the closest with a triple burst of explosive bolts, Solarion called out over the link to the others. 'That's it. That must be it. They've got her!'

The others made no response, their minds lost in the joys of the killing.

Voss was closest. He had switched to his bolt pistol and knife. The flamer was down to half a canister. With the enemy ranks less dense, he didn't want to waste it. Solarion stormed over to him and gripped the edge of his pauldron. He tried to turn him, but it was no easy task. As well to try and turn Chyron. 'Time to fall back, brother. We must rendezvous with them at RP3. They will need our strength.'

Until the broodlord's silent psychic call, the fighting hadn't eased off for an instant. Checking his chrono, it was hard for the Ultramarine to believe just how briefly he and his fellows had been here. Adrenaline and battle-focus did strange things to one's experience of time. The peak of the genestealer onslaught had lasted only minutes, but it felt a lot longer than that.

No further waves of tyranid organisms were emerging into the chamber now, and those that remained were thinning rapidly in number, cut down by Zeed, who continued to ignore the Ultramarine's calls to pull out.

Lifeless bodies lay where they had fallen, piled together in slick, wet, steaming heaps. Perhaps a dozen live threats remained. A dozen genestealers, still more than enough to kill them all if they got within striking distance.

One dropped from the ceiling, landing with a clatter of chitin behind Voss and Solarion. Long arms flashed out towards the Imperial fist, but the sound of its landing had given the Ultramarine just enough time to turn. He emptied the last three bolts in his mag, blowing big holes in the creature's torso and head, then dumped his empty clip and slid home another.

My second last.

Voss turned to see the creature dead on the cavern floor.

'Thanks, Prophet.'

'Thank me by getting your oversized backside out of here. And stop calling me Prophet.'

They turned to call on Zeed and found the cavern suddenly empty.

'For Throne's sake,' raged Solarion. 'Where in the blasted warp is that idiot?'

He tried the link again and again, voice rising to a shout.

'Get back here Raven Guard. Get back here now, curse you!'

A black figure emerged from one of the far tunnels at a run.

'Let's move,' said Zeed, voice unusually flat. He didn't stop. He ran straight past them and out of the chamber. Voss and Solarion broke into a run behind him.

'What happened, Ghost?' asked Voss. 'What did you see? Is something in pursuit?'

The Raven Guard was being uncharacteristically tight-lipped.

'No,' he told them. 'We need to regroup with the others. I have to speak to Scholar.'

Solarion snorted doubtfully. Voss threw Zeed a curious look. But whatever was bothering Siefer Zeed, he would say no more about it, so they ran in wordless silence, hoping they wouldn't be too late to help the others.

The woman in Karras's arms was bleeding from all the places where they had tugged out tyranid umbilici. Every juddering step Karras took seemed to wrack her with fresh pain, but he couldn't stop. Not now. Not with death breathing down his neck. So he ran, and Darrion Rauth ran with him.

Behind them, genestealers filled the tunnels, screeching and chittering as they raced after their prey.

'Keep going,' shouted Karras. 'RP3 is not far now.'

Intermittently, Rauth would turn and fire a burst of deadly bolts back at their pursuers, but his ammunition supply was getting dangerously low. Since the horde had diverted towards them, he had downed scores of genestealers. But it never seemed to make a difference. There were always more emerging from the walls and ceiling, skittering out from every hole they passed. Karras couldn't turn his own weapons on them, not with the frail woman in his arms. He wrestled with a near overwhelming desire to put her down, unsheathe *Arquemann* from his shoulder, and face the foe. Space Marines did not run.

Suffer not the alien to live.

It was the motto of the Deathwatch, but did the urge behind it belong to him, or to the spirit of the force sword? He could feel the blade's lust for battle. It resonated, like the deep throbbing and pulsing of the air inside an enginarium.

Karras broke from the end of the tunnel and emerged into the junction where he had earlier split the kill-team into two groups. He kept running, Rauth just behind him, boots pounding on the cavern's stone floor. Just as Karras and Rauth were crossing the centre of the tunnel intersection, three shapes careened out of a passage on the left, moving so fast that they almost collided with the kill-team leader. Karras swerved right, trying to shield the woman, and raised the bolt pistol in his right hand. Bolter muzzles whipped upwards to take aim, but recognition came at that very instant. It was Solarion, Voss and Zeed, their armour scored and gouged in a dozen places from the battle in the birthing chamber.

For a split second, the kill-team operatives halted and blinked at each other, stunned by the fact that they were all still alive. Then Karras yelled at them over the link.

'Don't stop now. Keep moving!'

United once more, Talon Squad bolted from the junction, thundering up the tunnel to RP3 just as the genestealers emerged behind them. As they ran, Rauth dropped back behind Voss, taking the rear. Still running, he plucked two grenades from his combat webbing, primed the first, and dropped it.

Seconds later, there was sharp sound, more like an almighty crack than a boom, and a sudden gust of superheated air. Bestial screams followed. In the tight confines of the tunnel, the explosive fragmentation caused impressive casualties. Many died. Many others were badly wounded. But the horde would not stop. They did not feel fear. They served a savage mind without the slightest notion of pity or sorrow.

Fresh, unwounded genestealers thrust aside the bodies of their dead or dying kin and resumed the pursuit. In less than a minute, they were as close as ever.

Rauth dropped his second frag grenade, then pulled his bolter from its mag-lock and put on a burst of extra speed. The designated rendezvous point was just up ahead, less than a hundred metres away. He heard the detonation of the grenade behind him, heard the high screeches that followed. The death toll from the second was as great as the first.

Just ahead of Karras, the light was changing. The rocky walls at the end of the tunnel were rimmed in red from the glow of the slow-flowing magma that ebbed from the pits and cracks in the cavern beyond.

Talon Squad exploded into the chamber.

And stopped.

Before them lay a scene of absolute carnage.

On every side, genestealer bodies lay shredded by the heavy bolter-fire of the three gun-servitors Karras had left behind. Other corpses were burned to black husks on the treacherous pot-holed floor. Pools of bubbling magma had already consumed parts of the dead, leaving an odd scattering of cracked and smoking heads and limbs, so blackened as to be almost beyond recognition.

The sight might have gratified the Deathwatch operatives but for two other elements. Firstly, the gun-servitors left to hold RP3 were strewn liberally around the cavern floor in countless dead pieces, their mechanical and biological components torn to tatters. Secondly, and of far more immediate concern, there were two figures waiting for the kill-team, standing dead-centre in the middle of the baking hot floor.

They were both beings of significant, almost overwhelming psychic power. But beyond that, in appearance at least, the similarities were few.

The smaller of the two was a tall man dressed in finely embroidered robes, with a long jewel-headed staff clutched in his right hand. He looked utterly incongruous in such a place, his face a mask of almost regal calm while all around him bubbles of glowing magma popped and hissed. On closer inspection, it was clear he was not really a man at all. The proportions of his features were off-kilter, somehow simply wrong, and despite his attempts to style himself some kind of high-priest, his eyes glimmered with an unwholesome alien light, to say nothing of their strange pupils. Psychic fire arced and crackled around him.

A magus, thought Karras. *A hybrid psyker.*

He was no weakling, despite his long, narrow frame. But the magus was, by far, the lesser of the two figures, for the other towered over him, at least three metres tall, and that while standing hunched over. It was a thing of nightmare: of heavy, ropey muscle that could pull limbs from torsos with sickening ease; of a super-dense armoured exoskeleton that standard bolts couldn't hope to even chip; of four long arms – two with curving claws like scythes and two with taloned hands – that could rip and shred even the heaviest armour plating as if it were mere tinfoil. Its face was an ugly mass of skin and muscle, ridged with tiny thorns and webbed with thick, pulsing veins. Its teeth – all too many and all too wickedly sharp – sprouted from a lipless slash that was disgustingly wide. This was the broodlord, mighty and murderous, and its appearance hinted only at the least of its power.

Rauth, Zeed and Solarion brought up their bolters, but before they could fire, a wave of raw force struck them from their feet, hurling them backwards against the black chamber walls.

Voss stepped forwards with his flamer and was likewise batted aside as if his heavy body weighed no more than that of a fly. Only Karras stood unassaulted, and he knew it was only because of the groaning, bleeding woman in his arms.

No, not the woman. The damnable parasite in her belly. Whatever genotype it is, it's important to them. That much is clear.

Karras knew better than to think a mere bolter-round would get anywhere near this creature or its hybrid aide. The air around them both shimmered with more than just the heat of the chamber.

They were shielded against attack but, with White Phoenix in his arms, so was Karras. It was a standoff. The broodlord simply stood there, glaring at Karras with eyes devoid of recognisable emotion, irises of pale purple with pupils round and black.

The magus smiled.

Against the walls, the other four members of the kill-team struggled groggily to rise to their feet. Their weapons had been knocked from their hands. They reached for them, but the moment they gripped them again, they were pushed back and pinned against the walls. Again, the force that did this was invisible, but it was incredibly powerful. They all felt the air being crushed from their lungs.

Behind Karras, the scrabbling sounds of the genestealer horde became louder and louder. The creatures reached the edge of the tunnel leading into the chamber and stopped. There they waited in silence, simply watching, awaiting some psychic command-impulse from their master.

The magus spoke.

'So, the venerable Space Marines deign to grace us with a visit.'

His tone was mocking, the words spoken with a strange humming quality, product of vocal cords not quite human. 'And they come as thieves and murderers, as killers of children. How did it feel to kill so many of our unborn back there in the hatcheries? Proud kills to add to your tallies? How mighty you are, indeed.'

Despite the pressure on his chest, Voss managed to growl, 'We'll add you to that tally, abomination!'

The magus barely glanced at him.

'A threat beyond your means to make good, as you are surely well aware by now. You continue to draw breath for one reason, and one reason only. The Master could eviscerate all of you with but a single thought. Even you,' he said to Karras. 'But you may yet live through this if some bargain can be struck. We care not for your lives. Go free and never return. Only, give us the woman. The child she carries belongs to us.'

As the magus spoke, Karras could feel him exerting psychic force, trying to employ unnatural powers of persuasion. It was the very power with which, as cult priest, he had influenced and controlled so many Chiarites, but it was a power wasted on Space Marines. Their minds were too strong, trained to resist, and the pentagrammic wards on their bodies only added to that shield.

'Xenos lies,' grated Zeed, voice straining with the effort of trying to speak without adequate breath. 'I would rather die than bargain with a damned alien.'

'That is not your decision to make, underling,' said the magus. 'I speak to your leader. What say you, blood-gifted one? You have the power. Read my mind, see that I speak the truth. Give us the woman, and leave our tunnels. Simple terms. Non-negotiable. Your position is the weaker here. Surely you see that, yes?'

Karras wasn't so sure. He drew his combat knife from the sheath at his lower back and, with his eyes on the broodlord rather than the magus, he pressed the point of the blade gently to the skin on the swollen belly of the inquisitor's agent.

The broodlord shrieked in rage, the sound so piercing it hurt Karras's ears. The magus stepped forwards, eyes wide, and stretched out a hand in placation. 'No,' he said nervously. 'Don't. I promise you will all die here if you dare harm–'

'If you knew anything about Space Marines,' Karras snarled, 'you would know that we do not fear death. We court it. It is our constant companion. We would be proud to die here, slaughtering as many of your disgusting kin as we can before we fall. And trust me, those numbers would be great. So, no. You are mistaken. Ours is not the weaker position here.'

'Yet you stay your hand,' said the magus. 'You do not strike. Despite your words, you are not so ready to meet your end, I think.'

Karras didn't doubt the magus was lying, trying to play him for a fool. He made a gambit of his own. 'We have other enemies than you,' he told the hybrid. 'Greater enemies against whom some of us have sworn blood-oaths of vengeance. I would see us have that vengeance. And to have it, we must leave here alive, mission accomplished or otherwise. So, very well, you may yet have your beloved parasite, but only if you meet my terms.'

The magus frowned, unsure, but he inclined his swollen, distended head for Karras to proceed. 'Which are?'

'Your master will release my brothers and allow them leave. Once I am satisfied that they are at a safe distance, I shall hand the woman over to you. Do you understand? I will give her to you and then *I* will leave. But so help me, if you attempt to interfere with our departure, we will unleash death on you such as you can scarcely imagine. You have the power, too. Read my mind if you dare and see what will come of betrayal.'

The magus closed his eyes and raised a long-fingered hand to one of the broodlord's massive chitin-covered forearms. He did not read Karras's mind, fearful, perhaps, of some psychic trick. Instead, he was silently conferring with his overlord.

Karras took that opportunity to communicate with the others in Space Marine battle-sign.

All: retreat to exfil point at speed, he ordered.

Do not wait.

He hoped they would trust him and follow his command. He did not intend to martyr himself here. He had already marked the locations of the explosive charges he had ordered Maximmion Voss to place on these very walls. Voss had the detonator, and Karras doubted he could contrive some way for the Imperial Fist to pass it off to him, but it didn't matter. He had other means at his disposal.

Sigma had ordered Talon Squad not to engage the broodlord. But the accursed thing was right here within striking distance, and it was too good a chance to pass up. The footfalls of such a creature heralded the doom of entire worlds.

The monster had to die.

The magus removed his hand from the broodlord's arm and took a step forwards. 'We find your terms acceptable, Space Marine. These others will be allowed to leave. They must go now, before the Master changes his mind.'

Karras, his knife still pressed to the woman's belly, half turned to his kill-team.

'Get out of here, now. All of you. Go.'

They moved around to the other side of the cavern, Karras moving with them as far as he was able. At the mouth of the exit tunnel, Voss hesitated. 'You can't mean to do this, Scholar.'

'Get back to the exfil point,' Karras commanded. 'Fire the signal-round and call in Reaper flight. That's an order.'

'You're abandoning the mission, Karras,' warned Solarion. 'You'll be executed for this.'

'I said go.'

There was much swearing and cursing as they left him there. Voss almost had to be dragged away by the others, but soon they were gone from view. Karras listened to the sound of their boots on the tunnel floor as they ran.

Once the sound had faded, he nodded to the magus.

The hybrid stepped forwards.

'You must see, Space Marine,' he gloated, 'that the destiny of this galaxy – nay, the entire universe – lies with our race, not yours. And yet you humans resist us, struggling futilely against the inevitable day when all you represent will be incorporated. Within our great united race, there is no competition, no treachery or betrayal. There is no selfishness. We are the embodiment of equanimity. All are rendered equal, for we are, in truth, simply cells in a single vast life form. Your species will become part of that, its genes blended with ours to live on forever.'

Not while a single Space Marine still draws breath, swore Karras.

He let the magus rant. He used that moment to send out a psychic tendril seeking his kill-team. They were moving fast, almost hitting the halfway point to RP2. He edged closer to the mouth of the exit tunnel and stopped. His escape route was only two metres behind him now.

He checked his mission chrono and felt his heart speed up. The readout had turned orange.

01:32:01.

01:32:00.

01:31:59.

Time was uncomfortably scarce.

'Enough words,' he told the magus. 'Take her. But move slowly. Any tricks and I'll cut your damned parasite in two.'

The magus carefully laid his ornate staff on the cavern floor, raised both hands in submission, and walked slowly forwards to receive the woman. The broodlord was still, silent, watching Karras with unblinking eyes.

'No deceits, Space Marine,' warned the magus coldly as he neared. 'They would only doom you.'

When he was two metres from Karras, he stopped and turned his hands flat to receive the swollen, sickly body of White Phoenix. 'The birth will occur soon,' he said. 'We must get her back to the nest quickly.' The monster in the woman's belly shifted and thrashed against the walls of its fleshy prison. Karras felt a definite psychic emanation from the parasite. The magus felt it, too. His face lit up as if he were in some kind of rapture.

It was the moment Karras needed. With the magus distracted, he stepped in, whipped up his right leg, and booted the foul hybrid directly in the sternum. There was an almighty crunch of shattering bone and the robed figure flew backwards, hitting the ground hard. His right arm splashed in a pool of molten rock and he screamed, a high and terrible sound. Behind him, the broodlord screamed too and took a lumbering step forwards. The genestealers waiting at the mouth of the opposite tunnel burst into the chamber like floodwaters, flowing around their leader, heading straight for Karras with lethal claws outstretched.

Karras stepped backwards towards his exit, still holding the woman tight in his arms, and mustered power from within. He reached out with astral energies to Voss's explosives, found them on the walls, and ignited their fuses with a single thought. This done, he instantly threw up a powerful bubble of protective energy.

The explosives blasted inwards, rocky debris scything through the air, cutting down several of the genestealers at the sides of the charging mass. Glowing magma erupted from breaches in the black walls and flooded into the room.

The broodlord hissed with rage and threw up a protective screen of its own, against which the magma crashed and surged but could not penetrate.

The magus, on the other hand was too slow to shield himself, still reeling from the pain of his smashed ribs and his blackened, withered arm. He screamed as the molten rock rolled over him, and thrashed wildly in unspeakable pain as it closed over his head and destroyed all trace of him.

Karras saw all this happen in the space of a heartbeat, but he didn't wait around any longer than that. His shield could not be maintained for more than a matter of seconds, not against such constant heat and force. As he was turning to make his escape, he glimpsed the broodlord turn the other way and make its own retreat, the river of magma between them too thick to ford.

So you survive, beast, thought Karras sourly. *But I can still finish my mission if I hurry.*

He raced away from the flooded chamber and pounded up the tunnel towards RP2 with the sagging woman in his arms. He could sense masses of genestealers moving through parallel tunnels to the north and south of his position, racing to try and overtake him. He couldn't allow that. He couldn't let them flank him. He ran with everything he had. They would be wary of harming the woman while the parasite was still inside her, but would it hold them back? Karras doubted his bluff would work a second time, and the magus was gone. He didn't think the broodlord and his purestrain genestealers would be inclined towards verbal negotiations.

He knew he would be seeing the alien overlord again before this mission was over.

Then something bulky suddenly emerged from the tunnel wall in front of him and brought Karras to a sharp, jarring halt.

15

'Did you kill it?' asked a gravel-rough voice.

Karras recognised it at once, relief mixing with anger in equal measure.

'I told you to get to the exfil point!' he snapped.

'Did you *kill* it, Karras?' Darrion Rauth asked again.

Karras shook his head. 'It lives, though the magus is dead.'

He should have guessed the Exorcist might be waiting. Like Karras himself, the magus and the broodlord wouldn't have sensed Rauth hiding there in the tunnel, standing by to offer support.

'Give her to me,' said Rauth. 'Quickly. If the monster shows its face again, you'll need to fight it. You're the only one who can.'

Karras passed the woman gently into the Exorcist's plated arms. 'Be careful. She clings to life by a thread.'

Up ahead, he sensed the others. Then he sensed something else. Waves of genestealers were converging on them from multiple tunnels. Genestealers and something bigger, something different they hadn't yet seen. The broodlord was still to the east, behind them, forced to circle around. But it was hunting them.

Karras and Rauth ran as fast as they could, but even without their precious burden, they wouldn't have been in time. Their three Deathwatch brothers were about to be engaged by significant enemy strength. If Karras and Rauth wanted to regroup with them at all, they would have to find another way around.

The kill-team was once again split in two, with a horde of xenos foes separating them and less than ninety minutes on the mission chrono.

Operation Night Harvest was not going well.

* * *

'Run, you clods!' shouted the Ultramarine.

Zeed and Voss had been laying down a lethal covering fire, burning through ammunition far faster than either would have liked, but now they broke from the fight and turned. In the tunnel up ahead, they could see the Ultramarine facing them. He dropped to a knee with his bolter raised. Zeed heard rounds whipping past his shoulder to embed themselves in the bodies of the genestealers close behind. He didn't turn to look. With the genestealers so numerous and so fast on their feet, a staggered retreat was the only option, but with the chrono ticking, it was far slower then he'd have liked.

Only twenty metres separated the Raven Guard from the Ultramarine when the tunnel wall to the right suddenly exploded. Solarion vanished in a cloud of black dust and stone chips. Behind Zeed, there was a roar and a rush of white light. Voss had turned to punish their pursuers with righteous, cleansing flame. In the tunnel confines, the lethal blast of blazing promethium was inescapable. Scores of the hideous wretches collapsed in withering heat, leaving little but charred husks and ash. Others – those at the farthest extent of the weapon's effective range – screamed and thrashed in agony like wild marionettes, their muscle tissue bubbling and burning as the fire licked at them.

But something was moving in the cloud of dust up ahead. Something big.

Zeed heard a chilling double scream unlike anything he'd heard before. Then he saw it, the frontal section of something large and wormlike, plated in broad rings of glittering black shell. It cast its head about, searching for the Ultramarine, strange multi-part jaws working the air, hoping to bite down on its target.

Zeed still couldn't see Solarion. His view was blocked by the bulk of the monster. But he heard him growl something over the vox-link. In all the noise, it was difficult to make out – a curse of some sort, maybe.

'Omni! Contact front!' Zeed shouted to his friend. 'Something big!'

Voss's flames had bought them a little breathing space. Together, the Raven Guard and the Imperial Fist ran forwards up the tunnel, Zeed firing off rounds at the monstrous armoured worm. That armour, however, was too thick for any bolter-round to penetrate, and if Zeed thought his attack would draw the monster's attention away from Solarion, well, in that regard he was wrong.

'Prophet,' he shouted over the link. 'Respond.'

From the other side of the beast's massive cylindrical bulk, Zeed and Voss could hear three-round bursts of bolter-fire.

'Prophet!' Zeed said again.

'Damn it, Raven Guard,' came the voice at last. 'I'm a little busy here. And don't call me that!'

There was further cursing, then, 'It's no good. I can't even chip the thing. I knew we should have been issued Kraken rounds.'

At least the Ultramarine was to the west of the creature. He could still fall back to RP2, which lay just half a kilometre further up the tunnel. But the vast, wormlike enemy was blocking any hope of Talon Four and Five joining him. Clearly their weapons were inadequate against all that armour plate.

Zeed and Voss were within just a few metres of the creature's bulk now. Zeed slowed, knowing there was nothing in his arsenal to defeat such a beast. Perhaps if they had brought a lascannon, a meltagun, a plasma cannon, or his own beloved master-crafted lightning claws...

But, right now, those peerless claws were somewhere beyond the planet's ionosphere, in orbit aboard the *Saint Nevarre*. Next time, he would insist on choosing his own damned mission loadout, and to hell with Sigma.

Voss, however, had his own ideas. The Imperial Fist surged past Zeed, ran straight up to the side of the worm and thrust his gauntlets deep between two of the monster's exo-skeletal segments. With a booming roar, he threw all his tremendous augmented strength into pushing the sections of black plate apart. Zeed saw glistening purple flesh appear in the gap, soft, wet and sticky.

Vulnerable.

He leapt to Voss's side, thrust his bolter's muzzle against the exposed skin, and emptied half an entire clip deep into the body of the beast.

There was a repeat of the strange double-voiced scream, and the creature whipped its head around, throwing Zeed and Voss back against the wall to their right. But, as it turned to bring its glistening jaws to bear on them, the bolts detonated deep inside its flesh. The rounds, clustered together, caused a massive rupture, blowing out a great section of its body, covering the Space Marines and the tunnel walls in a disgusting shower of gore and chitinous fragments.

The creature slumped dead, rocking slightly from side to side on its rings, pungent smoke rising from the messy crater in its corpse.

Zeed and Voss pushed themselves up and looked at the results of their handiwork.

'Not subtle,' said Zeed, 'but nice.'

'It will do,' Voss agreed. 'I guess the tyranids found rock-eater genes somewhere after all. They must have incorporated them into one of their new bioforms.'

'You think too much, tree stump,' said Zeed, kicking the lifeless mass of the thing with the toe of his boot.

The creature suddenly jolted, and they both levelled their weapons at it with a start, though Zeed's was now already empty. But the thing hadn't returned to life. It was just Solarion, pushing his way past the limply clacking mouthparts to rejoin them.

If Zeed and Voss had expected any thanks, they were mistaken.

'Once you're finished feeling proud of yourselves, perhaps we can get a bloody move on. RP2 is just up ahead.'

He vanished back around the monster's corpse and they could hear him break into a run on the other side, his boots hammering on the rocky tunnel floor.

They looked at each other a moment.

'Sooner or later,' said Zeed, 'I'm going to crack him one in the face.'

'I'll hold him for you,' Voss replied with a grin beneath his helm.

Zeed snorted his disdain for the idea.

'Hardly necessary.'

16

Solarion, Zeed and Voss found RP2 just as they had left it. The water so many metres below the strange natural bridges still cast its eerie white glow up to the cavern's ceiling. The hidden cache of ammunition and grenades was untouched. This was the room in which the inquisitor's hexagraphe had been detonated, but it bore no real trace of that event. The only sign there had ever been a hexagraphe was the orb's case, still lying open where they had left it. Fragments of Sigma's servo-skull were still scattered where Zeed had stamped on it.

Voss covered the point where the rock bridges met in the approximate middle of the cavern while Zeed and Solarion restocked on bolter ammunition. This done, they turned to cover him while he re-supplied himself with flamer fuel.

Then, on the single span of narrow rock that ran west towards the exfil point, they waited, and hoped that Karras and Rauth were somehow still alive.

Seconds felt like minutes. The silence was, in some ways, worse than coming under full assault. After all they had been through, the running and firing, the non-stop pursuit, the storm of slaughter they had rained on the birthing chambers, this relative quiet was unnatural and unsettling.

'What if they don't come?' murmured Zeed. He had just checked his mission-chrono and did not like what he saw. If they left now, just the three of them, they could make it back to RP1 and then to the exfil point with minutes to spare before the extraction deadline. Not many, but enough. Were Scholar or Watcher even still breathing? He almost wished he had powers of clairvoyance himself.

Almost, but not quite. He could never truly wish for a Librarian's gifts. The dark fate often attached to them was too terrible.

There had been nothing from either of them on the link. *That doesn't mean anything,* he told himself. Comms at any kind of range down here were poor at best. Too many rare metals and strange crystals interfering.

How long was one to wait for those that might already be dead? How long did honour and loyalty demand? And what about the woman? Did they have her? Had Karras actually given her back to those monsters to buy their lives?

No. Zeed didn't believe that for one second. No Space Marine would bargain with a filthy xenos. *Suffer not the alien to live.* Karras wouldn't have done it. He'd had a trick up his vambrace, Zeed was sure. Rauth had held back to wait for him. If things had gone awry, Karras had good support. Zeed might not like Rauth all that much, but there was no denying his cold efficiency. The Raven Guard could quite believe the Exorcist had no soul.

No one spoke. All of them, even Solarion, knew that, despite the relentless cycling of the mission chrono, duty and honour bound them together and dictated that they wait until the last possible moment. To return to Sigma without White Phoenix was to return in disgrace, their first Deathwatch operation a disaster. It would suggest that their Chapters had made a mistake in nominating them. It would mean that the Watch Council had made a mistake in approving them for deployment, and it would mean Sigma and the Ordo had made a mistake in trusting them. Alive or dead, they would be judged unworthy of selection.

No, thought Zeed. *I'll not go back to be labelled 'failure' or 'disgrace'. Not by Shrike, not by anyone. Especially not that damnable inquisitor. Not after what I saw back there in the heart of the nest.*

He hoped Karras was on his way. He had to tell him. Let Karras decide whether to inform the others or not.

The sounds of countless claws scraping on rock came to them now, getting louder as the Space Marines listened, accompanied by that distinct screeching and chittering, and the clacking of chitin shell.

'For the Emperor,' said Solarion, cocking his weapon.

'For the primarchs,' said Voss, his flamer held ready.

'For Talon and the Watch,' added Zeed.

The first cluster of horrid alien forms raced into the chamber, the genestealers' powerful legs propelling them at frightening speed, eyes wide, filled with murder.

Bolters answered.

Hunched, ridge-backed bodies began tumbling from the rocky bridge, spinning end over end before splashing into the glowing liquid far below. Dozens fell that way. The bridge was narrow, funnelling the genestealers into a lethal cone of fire. The Space Marines simply couldn't miss. Some of the genestealers, blocked by sheer numbers on the bridge, began to clamber up towards the cavern ceiling, the claws and talons of their double pairs of arms making light work of vertical walls.

'Omni,' shouted Zeed over the raucous rattle of his bolter, 'cover the bridge while we pick the others off the walls and ceiling.'

Voss stepped forwards towards the foe, white flame roaring out in front of him.

Zeed watched his latest kill tumble from overhead, down past the bridge, then targeted another, and another. Focused on the killing, he had all but put Rauth and Karras from his mind.

Then a black shape exploded out from a tunnel mouth on the right. Had the broodlord sent a flanking force?

The Raven Guard almost loosed a bolt at it, but checked himself just in time.

It was Darrion Rauth, sprinting full-tilt with the pale, pathetic figure of White Phoenix in his arms. 'Covering fire!' he was shouting. 'The beast comes!'

Just half a dozen metres behind him, Karras now burst into view, also running as fast as he could, bolt pistol in his left hand, the shimmering force sword *Arquemann* held single-handed in his right.

'Prepare to fall back!' Karras shouted.

A second later, Zeed saw why.

The tyranid broodlord emerged after them at speed. It burst into the cavern with a deafening roar. Its thunderous footfalls shook stone chips loose from the underside of the bridge. It turned to face the Space Marines and screamed.

Voss had just purged a span of the bridge with a blast from his flamer when Rauth reached the junction at its middle. He leapt over the heaps of charred corpses, came level with the rest of the kill-team, dropped to a knee and placed the woman as gently as he could on the ground. Then he ripped his bolter from his right cuisse and shouted, 'Mag!'

Zeed stepped close, still firing, and let the Exorcist strip a fresh magazine from his webbing. Rauth hammered the magazine home into the housing under his bolter's barrel.

'Not that it'll make a damned bit of difference,' he spat and loosed a burst at the broodlord. Zeed saw at once what he meant. The triple-round burst detonated before ever striking the beast, such was the powerful protection of the psychic shell it was projecting around itself.

Karras was almost with them now, vaulting over the smoking bodies that littered the bridge.

'What are you doing?' he yelled. 'Pick her up and run!'

Rauth turned his muzzle towards a knot of genestealers breaking from the far tunnel and pressed the thumb-stud on his under-barrel grenade launcher. There was a dull whomping sound. Half a second later, the high-explosive round struck dead centre, blowing the tyranids apart. Pieces of them rained down on the surface of the lake below. Then Rauth scooped White Phoenix back up into his arms and turned for the exit.

Karras reached the others where they were laying down suppressing fire, and spun. The broodlord had just made the junction at the middle of the bridge. It turned, stance wide, and its eyes tracked Rauth as he sprinted into the west tunnel and disappeared.

'Omni,' said Karras. 'Tell me you still have the detonator for the charges you placed here.' As he said it, he holstered his bolt pistol on his left cuisse and held out his left hand. He had used psychic detonation once already. The broodlord would be wary now. If Karras sent out psychic force to set off the explosives, the monster might react to block it. Conventional means were a safer bet this time around.

Voss passed him a small metal cylinder with a flip-top safety release and a red button on the top. 'You get one shot only with this, Scholar,' he warned.

'I know. Now move out, all of you. Get that woman back to the exfil point. Go!'

There was no argument this time. Zeed and Solarion each loosed a final HE[21] grenade-round from their own launchers, then sprinted from the cavern with Voss. The first detonation, high on the north-east wall, sent a score of badly wounded genestealers tumbling to their deaths. The second detonation struck the broodlord's shield dead-centre. The beast raged and staggered back, but a metre only. When the smoke cleared, it stood unharmed, its furious gaze now locked on Karras. It broke into a lumbering trot, heading straight towards him.

Keep coming, you ugly bastard, cursed the Death Spectre.

With the detonator in one hand and *Arquemann* in the other, he prepared to slay this menace once and for all. Psychic power flowed along his arm and into the ancient crystalline matrix set deep within the rare alloy of the blade. The broodlord felt the concentration of building power. Its cold eyes flicked to the sword then back to Karras's visor.

It didn't slow its advance.

Karras's retinal display told him exactly where all the explosives were. His helm's spectrometer and tracking subsystems had pin-pointed their location by concentrations of scent molecules. The display marked them with small red reticules.

---

21. HE – high-explosive.

The charge of most immediate interest to Karras was the one stuck fast to the side of the bridge just ten metres in front of him – a charge past which the broodlord now ran.

Karras held up the detonator, arm extended straight out.

'Far enough!' he snarled at his enemy. He thumbed the release and hit the switch.

There was a peal of thunder, so sharp and close that it stabbed at his ears.

The broodlord bellowed in outrage as the rock beneath its feet disintegrated into a shower of rubble. Chunks large and small plunged to the glowing waters below. The mighty tyranid plunged, too… Almost. As the bridge fell away beneath it, it leapt powerfully, slamming its upper body into Karras's end of the shattered bridge and scrabbling desperately against gravity. One set of talons found purchase, and it hung for a moment, clawed feet dangling in thin air above a hundred-metre drop. Then it swung another arm up and secured a better grip.

The creature, more physically powerful than any Space Marine, began hauling its heavily armoured body upwards. But, as its head cleared the lip of rock, it found itself looking up into the glowing visor-slits of Karras's battle-helm.

There was a moment when their gazes locked, each combatant looking into the soul of the other. It was a moment Karras had known many times – that moment of shared knowledge between enemies, even across species so vastly different. It was the moment when the victory of one becomes absolute; the moment when the loser knows absolute loss, when the deadly dance is over and they stand apart, separated by inescapable, undeniable fact.

'I win,' said Karras coldly, voice little more than a whisper tremulous with hate.

Arquemann flashed downwards, once, twice, severing those clawed hands at the wrist.

The broodlord gave a long, chilling scream as it fell, a scream that Karras allowed himself to savour, if only for a moment. He didn't stay to watch the monster hit the powerfully corrosive waters so far below. He heard the splash, but he had already turned away and was running; running as fast as his tired, aching legs could manage.

The digits on his mission chrono had turned red. Talon Squad had less than thirty minutes until the extraction deadline.

It might just be enough, Karras told himself as he pounded up the tunnel.

But a self-critical sneer stole over his face.

Who did he think he was he fooling?

17

Zeed, Solarion and Voss raced along the tunnel, plasteel support beams whipping by in the glow of bolter-mounted flashlights. The tunnel curved upwards and to the right, and soon they reached the end of it, to be greeted by a frustrated Rauth.

The Exorcist had placed the woman down. Behind him was the emergency blast door that they had muscled open hours ago.

It was shut tight.

'They got ahead of us,' rasped Rauth. 'This door... It's not designed to be opened from this side. No emergency release, no handles, nothing.'

There was the boom of an explosion from back down the tunnel.

'At least that means the bridge is out,' said Zeed.

'It won't stop them,' said Solarion. 'Even with the broodlord dead, they'll be coming. They still have prey to hunt.' He looked at the slumped woman. 'Maybe they'll come for what's inside her.'

Voss slung his flamer and pushed past the others, walking straight to the door. Rauth was right. The blast door was built to be opened from the other side only, a measure intended to stop doomed and desperate men from inflicting their fate on others, be it deadly gas, a magma flood, or something else entirely.

Voss drew his knife and tried to work the blade into the crack between the heavy adamantium doors.

'No good.'

If he could just get some kind of grip...

They heard Karras approaching fast before he burst into view, *Arquemann* still in hand, the blade still glowing from the psychic charge it had built up. It bathed the end of the tunnel in chill, white light.

'Is it done?' asked Rauth.

Karras nodded as he walked up to Voss's side, eyes on the door.

'It's done. The broodlord has fallen. But it won't count for anything if we can't get back to the exfil point in the next twelve minutes. Check your chronos.'

'I can't open it, Scholar,' said Voss. 'Not without some kind of handhold.'

'Stand back,' Karras told the others. 'Don't let the blade touch you.'

They stepped away as Karras lifted the force sword above his head and made four diagonal slashes in the metal. Two heavy chunks fell away, and Voss had his handholds at last. They weren't much, but they might just be enough.

'Let's see what you've got, Omni,' said Karras, stepping clear.

The Imperial Fist rolled his massive shoulders and stepped in. He pressed his fingers into the space Karras's blade had carved and began to pull the doors sideways.

At first, nothing happened. He threw more power into it, the servos in his armour grinding in complaint. Every muscle in his back strained near to tearing. He roared and raged, and finally a space began to appear, finger-wide at first, then wider, wider, until it was the width of his helm.

Suddenly, something black flashed out from the gap and raked his breastplate, sending out a flash of sparks. Voss fell backwards just as it swiped again. The others looked down at him and saw the two ragged tears on his breastplate.

'Genestealers!' shouted Zeed.

Rauth stepped in and pointed his gun muzzle through the gap. He fired a triple burst. There was an alien scream and the sound of frenzied movement.

Lots of movement.

Voss was on his feet again. 'Stand aside,' he told Rauth. His flamer was already in his hand, the blue igniter hissing in angry anticipation. He pushed the nozzle to the gap and loosed a blinding burst of white fire into the chamber beyond the door. The screams of burning xenos reached their ears.

'There are many,' said Karras. 'Talon, we have to get through here. There's no other way to the Inorin shaft from this side. We have less than ten minutes, brothers. We have to go straight through them.'

'Grenades,' said Voss. 'We roll everything we have through there, make some room, and sprint for the far side.'

'Approved,' said Karras, 'and Solarion, you'll crack a flare as soon as we're in. I want as much light as we can get. Rauth, take the woman and stay between the four of us. We move as a unit. Standard close-protection diamond pattern. Keep the woman safe, but do not fall behind. Cover your fire-sectors. Solarion takes front. Zeed covers the left. Voss, you'll take the rear. I'll take the right side. Keep it tight. Once we reach the tunnel mouth on the far side, move as fast as you can. Zeed, you and Solarion will move to the exfil point with Rauth. Rendezvous with Chyron and fire that damned signal round. We have to let Reaper flight know we're still in this. Voss, you'll hang back with me. Between us, we might be able to buy some time. I don't want to extract under assault.'

'I'm with you, Scholar. What about the cache on the central rooftop?'

'Unless we get hemmed in, ignore it. I don't want a standing battle. Our only goal is the tunnel on the far side. Bless your weapons, brothers. Voss, give those vermin a little gift.'

Voss grinned beneath his helm as he primed the grenades and tossed them through the gap, one after another. There was a series of deafening cracks, accompanied by flashes of bright light and waves of searing fire, and through the gap itself, a spray of dark xenos blood.

Voss threw himself back to the task of wrenching open the adamantium doors. With the gap he had already made, Solarion and Zeed were able to help him, one on either side.

'Are you ready?' Karras demanded of Rauth.

The woman was cradled in the crook of his left arm again, so small against his massive armoured frame. He held his bolt pistol in his right hand, knowing his primary weapon would be too unwieldy to brandish one-handed at a run. It was locked to his right cuisse.

Karras couldn't help thinking how he'd rather the woman wasn't here. He suspected he would very soon need every bit of firepower the kill-team could muster.

At least the broodlord is dead.

'I'm always ready,' grunted Rauth.

'It's open!' Voss called out.

'Talon, move! Remember your fire-sectors. Go!'

They burst into the chamber at a run. Solarion cracked a flare and tossed it.

What they saw almost stopped them dead.

The walls, the floor, the ceiling, every walkway, stair and gantry; everything was literally crawling with tyranid life forms.

The chrono kept counting down. No amount of hoping or praying could slow it.

00:07:34.
00:07:33.
00:07:32.

'Open fire!' shouted Karras. 'Death to the xenos!'

But all he could think was, *More time. We needed more time.*

18

Bolters chugged relentlessly, their barrels growing hot. Purging flames gushed forth in a torrent, twisting side-to-side like a great dancing snake as Voss strafed the murderous ranks of the foe. Under-barrel grenade launchers coughed, their rounds detonating with lethal efficacy, carving great craters of death in the horde. The genestealers were so numerous they were almost packed shoulder to ugly misshapen shoulder. The toll on them was devastating, but they didn't care. They had numbers to spare and then some. There was no end to them. For every ten that were blasted or burned apart, twenty seemed to emerge onto the elevated gantries and walkways around the perimeter of the chamber.

The exit was cut off. It had been from the start. Karras had had no choice. He had ordered them to the rooftop where the cache was. With growing, heart-sickening despair, he watched the chrono tick down as if it was a death clock counting away the seconds until they were overwhelmed.

He couldn't let the others feel this way. It was unworthy. If they had to die, let it be glorious and noble, drowning in the blood of their enemies right up to the end.

'The Emperor is watching you!' he roared at his squad. 'Show him your worth. You are Deathwatch. Best of the best. Show him what that means. Earn honour for your Chapters. Remember your oaths!'

So they fought. They fought like gods of war. The genestealers seethed all around them, moving like an ocean, crashing against the old, frozen prefab structure on which they stood, then scrambling to the roof only to meet the wrath of Voss's flamer. At this range, the weapon was savagely effective, spewing fiery death, cutting a burning swathe through literally hundreds of the foe. But it couldn't last. Even with the additional ammo of the cache – already stripped bare – the moment would come when the last canister ran dry. Voss was ready. He would switch to his bolt pistol and knife. Standard operating protocol. But it meant Karras's plan would never see fruition. He had been meant to help the kill-team leader hold the genestealers off while the others fell back. He couldn't do that effectively with just his sidearm.

Over the link, he shouted to Karras. 'Scholar! Last canister!'

There was no answer. At first, Voss felt his heart speed up. Had the Death Spectre fallen?

But Karras was gunning down genestealers with the others. Gunning them down and making the kind of decision only an Alpha could make.

'All of you, down off the roof. Make for the tunnel. Move as a group, triangle formation, Rauth and the woman in the middle as before.'

'No!' said Zeed. 'I'll not leave this fight to you alone, Scholar. You plan to martyr yourself?'

'You will do as commanded, Talon Squad!'

Balefire had begun to coruscate over his armour, the flickering tongues getting longer with each passing second, with each kill he racked up. *Arquemann* was glowing, pulsing, strapped to his back by its sling. The blade wanted free, free to slaughter enemies of the Chapter to which it belonged. Karras could feel it compelling him to mag-lock his bolter. But that was not why he was ordering the others away.

Two minutes remained on the mission chrono. It was already too late, he knew, but he wasn't ready to believe it was over. If the others would only move clear, maybe, just maybe, he could do something to get them out of here.

'You have to break for the tunnel now. Jump roof-to-roof until you are close. I will buy you the time you need to reach the exfil point, but you must do exactly as I say.'

'Scholar–'

'I'm giving you an order, Talon. Now move!'

There was no arguing with him. The tone of command in his voice was as hard as the rock all around them. But still they hesitated, and he saw that he would have to make a move himself.

'Go!' he shouted at them, then he ran to the edge of the roof and leapt to another, only not in the direction of the exfiltration point. He was trying to draw some of the genestealers in the other direction.

'Don't make me do this for nothing!' he snarled at them.

'Let's move, Talon,' barked Rauth. 'I need cover. Let's go!'

With a last glance at Karras, beset on all sides now by clambering, slavering terrors, the rest of the squad broke from the central roof and headed west to the exit, gunning down and burning all those genestealers unlucky enough to draw near.

Behind them, Karras emptied round after round into chitin-ribbed bodies and hideous, razor-mawed faces. He fired grenades into the densest knots. The kill-count was staggering, and it kept rising, but he was soon down to his last magazine.

Then the trigger clicked that fateful click every warrior dreads in the middle of a conflict – the last round was spent, the mag was empty. He unslung *Arquemann* from his back and gripped it two-handed, as it was meant to be held. Eldritch lightning began arcing between his body and the blade, bright white, bright enough to sear afterimages on the eyes.

The genestealers around him hesitated, sensing the lethal nature of the weapon, its touch utterly deadly. But there were so many pressing at their backs, they could not hold themselves clear. Like a great crashing tide, they surged towards him again.

Karras felt power racing through every fibre of his body. 'You have underestimated me, alien filth!' he bellowed. 'And now you will learn to fear the power of the sons of Occludus!'

The cavern filled with great bolts of lightning. The air shook. Dying creatures screamed as their life force was ripped away from them, their bodies hewn to pieces.

At the far side of the chamber, the rest of Talon Squad had dropped from the roof of the block closest to the exit and had cut a path out through the foe.

Solarion ran in front, point-man as ever. Rauth was just two metres behind him, and behind Rauth came Zeed and Voss. As they bolted up the tunnel with all the speed they could manage, Voss chanced a single, brief glance backwards, looking for the kill-team leader.

He couldn't quite see him. He couldn't quite make sense of what he *did* see. It was so bright back there, his helm's optics struggled to compensate. But he thought he saw hundreds of writhing forms suspended in the air while a figure clad in raging, blinding flame threw great spears of deadly energy out in all directions. Everything those spears of light touched burst into swirls of ash.

There was no time to witness anything more. The others were already pulling ahead.

Voss turned back to them and put on a burst of speed.

The exfiltration point was just up ahead.

But did it even matter any more?

After all, the chrono had stopped counting down minutes ago.

Now, all it read was --:--:--.

19

The exfiltration point looked like a scene from Gaudoleri's famed triptych *Aftermath at Hades*. The circular expanse of the room was awash with blood, littered with the broken bodies of the dead. Four members of Talon Squad – Zeed, Voss, Solarion and Rauth – skidded into the echoing chamber and stopped, their lips forming grim lines behind their visors. They could not see their sixth member at all in this reeking mess. The chamber floor was tacky with cooling crimson. The nearest bodies looked like they had been ripped to pieces. Others nearer the far walls looked like they had been burned in flames or chewed apart by large rounds. Against one wall, more lay in a great mound.

But of Chyron himself, there was no sign.

Before anyone could comment, they heard footfalls from the tunnel behind them, and Karras entered at a tired, staggering run. *Arquemann* was once again slung on his back. When he stopped running, he collapsed to the ground on hands and armoured knees. There were deep gouges, tears and a spidery network of fracture lines all across his armour. His right vambrace had shattered completely. Only the metal frame and black layer of artificial muscle remained.

He was gasping in pain.

Zeed was closest to him. The Raven Guard dropped to his haunches at Karras's side.

'In the name of the primarch, Scholar, I don't know how you did it, but I wish I could've stuck around to watch. Are you wounded?'

Karras, wordless at first, waved him off, then struggled to his feet. His entire body ached. It felt like there was fire in his bones and grinding glass in his brain. It was the second time only in a long life of war that he had been forced to exercise his power like that – not just in the purging of the foe with psychic fire, but also, once he had reached the chamber exit, to collapse the tunnel between here and RP1. It wasn't much, but it would stop the genestealers from harassing them for a while...

... until they circled around and found another way in.

It was dangerous, this excessive use of a power that flowed from the warp of all places. In his head, he had heard the mutterings of inhuman voices, hungry and excited, watching him with gleeful anticipation for the moment he lost control. Those sounds were not something he ever wished to hear again.

'Chyron?' he asked the others.

'No sign,' said Solarion, 'apart from this bloodbath. He must have pulled out at the last minute.'

Karras hoped the old warrior had indeed extracted on time. It made sense.

The rest of us... We all made it back alive. But for what, I wonder?

He had blinked off his chrono display. It was pointless now, just a row of dashes and colons that seemed to say *You Have Failed* more than anything else.

He crossed to the circular space beneath the Inorin vent shaft – the very shaft down which they had infiltrated just over ten hours ago – and looked upwards. At the top, he could make out a tiny circle of starlit space. *Ten hours.* He felt so drained. It was not so much a physical exhaustion – Space Marines could operate at extremes for days on end if need be – but the strain of first suppressing then almost constantly exercising his unique abilities, which had left him close to his mental limits. That last battle had pushed him beyond them. He needed nutriment and a long, unbroken rest.

And a book, he thought. *An ancient, worthy tome in which to lose myself awhile.*

'I knew this would happen, Karras,' Solarion griped, pulling off his helm. 'If we hadn't wasted so much time back–'

The kill-team leader's patience was spent. 'Kill it, Three!' he barked harshly. 'It was always going to be tight. Sigma was unrealistic in his assessment. The broodlord was always going to become a factor.'

Voss, largely ignoring the back-and-forth, had seen something of note among the bodies. He walked over to it and picked it up. 'Now *that* explains a lot.'

He was holding the severed end of Sigma's communications relay cable.

'Burned straight through. It must have taken a las- or plasma-blast during Chyron's little skirmish. I guess he was already engaging the enemy while we were crossing the lake.'

Solarion had been glaring daggers at Karras, but he, like the kill-team leader, didn't have the necessary energy left to keep anger ablaze. 'So what do we do now? For all we know, the *Saint Nevarre* is already heading out of the system.'

'We have Sigma's package,' Karras grated, gesturing at the woman cradled in Rauth's left arm. 'And we're only minutes late. I don't think he'll have given up on us quite yet. Reaper flight may still be in range. The signal round, if you please, brother.'

With some small hope rekindled, the Ultramarine drew a uniquely coloured bolt from his webbing. It was red with white banding. He detached the magazine from under his bolter, pulled the cocking lever back, slid the signal round into the breech and primed it. Then he lifted the bolter vertically, sighted upwards through the mounted scope, squeezed on the trigger and loosed the round.

A second later, the sound of the bolt detonating above the planet's surface returned to them. There was a flash of bluish white light on the chamber floor, perfectly circular, shaped by the vent shaft under which Talon Squad stood.

'So we wait,' said Zeed, 'and hope she's as important to him as we think she is.'

'There's the city, Cholixe, eighty-three kilometres west of here,' Voss replied. 'If it comes down to it, we can make for there. They have a small space port and a subsector comms array.'

Karras looked at the woman again. 'She won't last another hour. Omni, if there's no response to the signal round, do you think you could do something with that relay cable?'

'I don't have the tools to patch in from here, Scholar. I'd need to fix an I/O jack to the end of it before I could do anything else.'

'So, we have to depend on the signal round,' said Zeed.

'If there's no response from Reaper flight within twenty minutes,' said Karras, 'we will grant White Phoenix the Emperor's Mercy, kill the parasite, and make for Cholixe.'

The others nodded silent agreement. All were thinking that the genestealer horde might find a way through to them by then. Zeed, unsatiated even now, actively hoped it.

'Such butchery,' murmured Solarion, looking at the bodies by his feet. 'At least he enjoyed himself in our absence.'

'They were a welcome diversion, Ultramarine,' rumbled a voice, basso profundo, 'from the boredom of awaiting you.'

The hill of corpses against the chamber wall began to shudder and shift. Dead meat slid away. There was the noise of skulls smacking on stone, the slap of lifeless flesh. Chyron rose awkwardly from beneath the pile and turned his slot-visored glacis plate to face them.

'A little hide-and-seek, Old One?' said Zeed with a grin.

Chyron began dragging himself towards the middle of the chamber, and the rest of the kill-team could see just how badly damaged he was. His left leg was a mess, its armour shattered, the pistons and actuators beneath twisted and snagged. His foot made showers of bright yellow sparks as he dragged it along the ground. His right arm was in an even worse state, for almost nothing of the assault cannon remained. All over his chassis his tank-thick armour was gouged, scored, chipped and burned in too many places to count.

He pre-empted their next question.

'Man-portable missile launchers,' he growled. 'The dung-eating cowards fired on me from the shadows, then swarmed on me like ants. And they died like ants – brainwashed men and xenos-bred abominations both.'

At this, the other Deathwatch operatives took a better look at the dead. There were literally hundreds of them, but finding bodies which had not been pulped beyond recognition by the Lamenter's power fist or burned to cinders by his flamer was far from easy. For the most part, Chyron's attackers were, in physical form at least, men like any others. The majority wore miners' overalls and orange thermasuits. Others yet wore the dark uniform and body armour of Civitas enforcers. But there were others, too, and these last were not so much like men. They were taller, boasted larger frames, and those frames were twisted with xenos corruption. Some had extra limbs. Others had sharp triangular teeth peeking out from within their slack mouths. To a Space Marine's eyes, even the relative darkness of the chamber could not hide the unnatural colouring of their skin. These were the tainted by-blows of the genestealer infection, and Chyron had left none here alive.

'Quite a body count,' said Voss.

'Would that the diversion had lasted longer,' returned Chyron. 'Is there anything left to kill down here?'

'Genestealers,' said Voss. 'Leaderless now, thanks to Scholar, but they'll be coming. You may yet have more killing to do.'

'That would be some compensation,' said Chyron. 'I tried to call in the Stormravens via the link when the chrono dropped to five minutes. I wondered why there was no response.'

'Why did you hide under those corpses?' asked Zeed.

Chyron snorted derisively. 'Use your head, little raven. I was left with only my power fist. Would you have me stand here in the middle of the chamber where our enemies could fire missiles on me from a safe distance? I had hoped to ambush more of them as they walked among their dead. But it seemed there were no others to come. Or perhaps they did not want to die.' After a pause he asked, 'Is that the primary objective? That sickly woman? She looks all but dead herself.'

Rauth was still holding her, but it was Zeed who answered. 'I doubt it's the woman herself that Sigma wants.' He looked with distaste at the shifting swollen skin of her belly. It suddenly occurred to him that Chyron, whose Chapter had been all but obliterated by the tyranid race, might recognise she was heavy with forbidden progeny and strike at the woman in a flash of vengeful rage. His power fist would kill both her and her unborn parasite in a single blow. He stepped in front of Rauth, blocking her from view as nonchalantly as possible.

Chyron watched the Raven Guard do this without comment, but he was no fool. He perceived the cause of Zeed's concern, and searched himself for the fury his brother suspected might rise. It wasn't there. In truth, the sight of the woman was so pathetic that it had not occurred to him to strike her and her unborn parasite down. Instead, he rumbled, 'The Inquisition has strange needs. Whatever business they are about this time, they are welcome to it. Give me war, plain and simple, and to the warp with all their intrigues.'

At the mention of Inquisition business, Karras caught Zeed throwing him a meaningful look. He was about to question it when a tinny voice on the link stopped him.

'Reaper One to Alpha. Reaper One to Alpha. Signal round sighted. Better late than never, Talon. We are en route to your location. ETA two minutes. Prep for extraction.'

'Throne and sword!' gasped Solarion. There was no mistaking his relief and joy.

'Praise the Emperor,' added Voss. He and Zeed gripped wrists in mutual congratulation.

'Descended they, from the high heavens, upon wings of fire and steel,' quoted Rauth quietly. 'And lifted were our hearts, and we called them e'er after our salvation.'

Karras didn't recognise that one. Half his mind was occupied by something else. A compulsion of sorts had come over him. He looked at Chyron and made a decision, though he would not understand why until later. Something inside him, a feeling not quite his own, told him that Chyron must not be the last member of the kill-team left in the chamber. Though he could find no logical basis to support that thought, as a psyker, he had learned to trust his instincts in moments like these.

'Alpha to Reaper One. Talon Six will be extracted first. Instruct Reaper Two. Reaper Three will hang back. There are no retrievable support assets. Confirm.'

'Negative, Alpha,' said the flight-group leader. 'We have orders to extract the package first.'

'Reaper flight, Alpha reminds you that you are addressing one of the Emperor's own Space Marines. You will do as I command or face the consequences. Talon Six will be extracted first. Acknowledge.'

There was a moment of tense silence before the pilot replied resignedly, 'Understood, Alpha. Reaper Two moving into position now. Stand by for magna-grapple drop.'

Moments later, the battle-ravaged bulk of Chyron was winched out of sight, vanishing up the long, echoing vent-shaft. Even once he disappeared, Karras could still hear Chyron grumbling and growling about the indignity of being hauled up like a fish on a line.

Reaper Two moved off. Reaper One swung into position and dropped four lines, one of which ended in a body-sized recovery frame of black plasteel. Into this frame, the Space Marines strapped the limp form of White Phoenix. She was still breathing, but the movements of the parasite had increased. She did not have the luxury of time.

The kill-team watched her ascend after Karras gave Reaper One the all-clear to pull her up. Then Solarion, Rauth and Voss each mag-locked their weapons, placed a booted foot into the loop at the bottom of each of the three lines, voxed for the winches to start reeling them up, and began their own rapid climb to the gunship hovering overhead.

Zeed and Karras stood at the bottom, looking up.

'Before we get back to the *Saint Nevarre* and that bastard inquisitor, there's something I think you should know, Scholar,' said the Raven Guard.

Karras looked at him, surprised by the tone. 'I'm listening.'

'Back in the xenos nest, after the horde broke away to hunt you and Watcher, something caught my eye. There was a cave deep at the back. I noticed it when I was clearing out the last of the genestealers. I took a quick look.'

'And?' asked Karras.

'Talon Two, Three and Four are aboard,' reported Reaper One. 'What's that? Alpha, please hold. We're having some kind of trouble with the lines.'

Zeed continued. 'There were several pods there, made of metal. No chitin. These were not tyranid things. They looked more like one-man boarding torpedoes – a diamonite drill for a nose and all the hallmarks of human construction. Big enough for genestealers, Scholar. In fact, when I looked inside, there were marks consistent with genestealers having broken out from within.' The silence that followed his words was thick and heavy with unspoken implications.

A single line dropped down the shaft now. The slack hit the floor in front of them.

'Some kind of trouble with the winches, Alpha,' voxed Reaper One. 'Damned strange. We've had to drop a manual line. You and Five will need to pull yourselves up.'

Karras ordered Zeed to go first. 'I'll be right behind you.'

But Zeed wasn't finished talking. He moved to the rope and grabbed it, but there he stopped and asked, 'You see it, don't you?'

I see it, thought Karras sourly. *The Inquisition. The Ordo Xenos.*

The genestealer infestation on Chiaro had been deliberate, engineered by men against men. But, in the name of Holy Terra, why?

'They'll burn this place out,' continued Zeed, tugging the line to make sure it was secure. 'The mines are almost dry now anyway. It must be why they chose this planet. They won't wait long once we're gone. They can't afford the truth getting out. No one else is getting off this rock. Not after us.'

'Exterminatus,' murmured Karras to himself. The word carried a chill all of its own. A whole world purged of life. Extreme, but what other recourse was there, he supposed, when the civilian population was infected with genestealer taint? It could be rooted out no other way, and it was far too dangerous to risk the chance, even remote, that it might get off-world somehow.

He thought of the woman they had worked so hard to recover, and of the alien creature readying to tear its way out of her womb. Would he ever know why it had been so important to retrieve her? Would he ever know exactly how he and his team had served the Emperor's Will? They had risked their lives, stood on the edge of the abyss and faced their end. Did they not deserve to know? And if Karras ever did discover why, would he feel it justified that a whole planet would pay the price for the games the Inquisition had played here?

That seemed unlikely.

'Say no more on this, Ghost. For now, at least. I've a feeling Sigma monitors all we say and do. Nowhere on the *Saint Nevarre* is secure. For now, just keep your eyes and ears open. Even the best surgeon makes occasional mistakes. Sigma had best be careful lest he get cut by his own scalpel one day.'

'Count on it, Scholar.'

The Raven Guard began his climb, his own muscles working in perfect concert with the tireless artificial fibre-bundles beneath his ceramite plate. Within moments, he was high above Karras, and now the kill-team leader gripped the rope and began his own climb. He was only slightly slower than the Raven Guard, but then nobody moved quite as fast as Siefer Zeed.

Karras had pulled himself some fifteen metres from the ground, and was just about to pass beyond the lower lip of the vent shaft when, suddenly, he stopped. He felt something sharp, bitter, pricking at his psychic awareness; a sense of something deeply wrong. It was only the briefest instant, but in that instant, he knew his sense of victory back at RP2 had been premature.

There was a rushing of air from below. Something powerful grasped his armoured ankle and, with terrifying physical force, hauled him from the rope.

Karras fell two metres and crashed into his attacker. The clip on his webbing cinched tight, arresting a further fall.

He whipped his head around to see the broodlord glaring up at him, spitting and twitching violently as it clung to the rope just below him. The fall into margonite-infused waters had not killed it, but immersion in that dangerous and corrosive solution had melted its flesh horribly and given it an unearthly white glow. Gleaming bone poked out between ragged gaps in the creature's scorched flesh. The stumps where Karras had severed two of its wrists were horribly burned and withered. The other pair of arms, however, still with their sharp-clawed, five-fingered hands, were very much intact and still every bit as lethal.

Releasing its grip on the rope with one of these hands, the beast batted savagely at Karras, once, twice. He spun wildly. His weapons were knocked away and plummeted to clatter hard on the stone of the chamber floor below – all but his combat knife, sheathed on his right greave. *Arquemann*'s strap was severed by the beast's second strike. Karras felt the force sword spin away from him and turned to see where it fell. The blade struck the floor point-first and lodged itself deep and hard in the stone. Karras's hearts sank. He knew his talents would not be able to call the blade back to his hand. Not now.

'Scholar,' shouted Zeed from further up the rope.

The Raven Guard had reversed his climb. He was moving downwards again.

The broodlord lunged, attempting to pass Karras completely and grasp the rope above him, and Karras realised with a start that it did not simply want to kill them all. It was attempting to retrieve the body of the woman. It wanted the unborn thing inside her.

But, as the ruined creature leapt past him, Karras grabbed it and grappled with it, desperate to prevent its ascent. The accursed alien was still physically stronger by far, despite its dreadful wounds. It thrashed and struggled, and beat at Karras with the disfigured limbs that could not clutch the rope.

Karras saw no other option. Right here, right now, he had but a single chance to ensure the mission's success. The cost would be great, but the Black River claimed all in the end – even those who had returned before from its furious astral waters.

With a roar of defiance, he drew his combat knife, stretched up and, gripping the broodlord tight with his other arm, cut the rope with a single hard slash.

Together, they tumbled backwards, plunging to cold, hard rock.

The monster screamed in rage. It was a scream that cut of abruptly when the ground leapt up to strike them both. The impact was brutal. Karras grunted, felt bones shatter. His knife skittered away. Even power armour couldn't protect him completely from a fall like that.

Pain surged through him. Warning glyphs flashed red on his left retina. His right eye was blind. He didn't know why. Several of his armour's subsystems were non-functional. Main systems and motor controls were reporting progressive drops in efficiency. The suit's joints were starting to lock up.

Heavy footfalls – clawed toes on blood-slicked stone – sounded near Karras's head. He looked up with one eye.

The beast stood over him, trembling in rage and pain.

Just one more hideous terror in a galaxy filled with them, thought Karras. *It is not your destiny to rule, monster. Only man can rise above his bestial instincts. Only man can ascend to a higher state of consciousness. For man alone, there is hope of salvation. That is why you and your kind will lose. Always. The future belongs to man.*

The tyranid broodlord crouched over him and raised its clawed hands, ready to rip his armour open like foil and tear the organs from his flesh.

Karras had little life left in him, but he fought back with the only weapon that remained in reach.

He let the power of the immaterium flow through him.

White balefire rose from his body. It flared across his battered armour, and he bent all his will towards the destruction of the beast that was standing over him.

The air crackled with all that ethereal power. Karras heard voices taunting him, voices from the warp, the dark domain from which his power flowed. It was always a risk, always had been, but he was ready for that. He had been trained for it. He cast his inner gates wide and let more of the power flow through him. He turned his mind to the mantras with which the mighty Athio Cordatus had taught him to protect himself.

The broodlord staggered, buffeted by the rising psychic surge. Immediately, the monster turned to its own powerful gifts and battle was joined between the two one last time.

Dimly, Karras could hear voices calling to him on the link, but it was no good. There was nothing they could do for him now. They had the package. They had to get away while the broodlord was held here. Success had a price. Today, the price was his life, as he had always known it would one day be.

The ground beneath the two bitter enemies began to shudder. The stone floor started to crack and chip. Small loose rocks began rising up into the air, lifted on currents of psychic fire. Dust and dirt began to rain down in great drifts from fresh cracks in the chamber's domed ceiling and in the lip of the vent shaft.

Karras sensed a surge in the broodlord's power, fuelled by raw animal rage. The resonance of the unborn xenos parasite was moving away from their location. Reaper One was withdrawing. The broodlord had lost. *Operation Night Harvest*, whatever its true purpose might be, had come to a close. Talon Squad had succeeded.

Now it was time to end this properly, and there was only one way left.

'I die in battle,' Karras spat at the creature. 'And in so doing, earn my rebirth.'

He opened the gates of his mind as wide as he could, far further than he had even risked before. The flow of power was a crashing, raging tide now. The mocking voices from the warp grew louder, closer. The ground beneath him shook as if caught in the middle of a massive seismic cataclysm.

'We die here together, xenos filth,' roared Karras, 'but of the two, only I will live again!'

Great, lethal chunks of rock began to tumble from the ceiling, smashing into the ground to shatter with all the force that weight and gravity could muster.

The beast fought back, its own power rising to meet the flow of Karras's own, strength for strength.

Karras could channel no more. He gave himself over completely to the power that flowed through him, hoping it would be enough. He felt unseen things closing on him from a great distance, but their speed was immeasurably high. He prayed that he and the broodlord would die before his soul was forfeit.

The thick ceiling of the chamber gave a great heave above them and collapsed completely. Absolute finality tumbled towards the locked combatants, thousands of tonnes of sharp black rock spinning end-over-end. Karras loosed a final, raw-throated shout:

'I fear not death, I who–'

He didn't finish it.

20

Silence.

No more chittering voices to drive him mad. No more crashing surge of psychic power testing the limits of his strength and sanity. Nothing.

Just silence.

Silence and pain.

Karras knew death when he felt it. He had embodied it for over a century. He had passed through its dark veil to prove himself worthy of the name Death Spectre. And now he felt it rage through his system, all white fire and black ice, at once burning and freezing his flesh to the deepest core. His plate armour was pierced and torn, the claws of the frenzied tyranid abomination more than equal to the task of ripping a full suit of Space Marine power armour to pieces. One of his hearts – his primary – was all but demolished, and his secondary heart, the organ known as the *Maintainer*, struggled to keep him alive while so much of his blood ran free. Great sticky pools of dark red welled up from the jagged rents in his ceramite shell. The blood itself was far from normal. Even now, the powerful coagulants it contained allowed it to clot, sealing wounds that should have killed him already. But it was too late. Karras had buried himself and the tyranid broodlord in an impossibly deep grave. Here they would lie, tangled in death. But that was all right. To Karras, even this was a victory. He had taken his foe with him. This abomination, at least, would threaten the Imperium no more.

Ah, I hear them. I hear the waters around me now.

His consciousness pulled free of his ruined body and slid beyond the physical world into that familiar passage which led to the next.

It was the Black River. All around him, the great cylinder of dark water surged and splashed. He felt it pulling him.

The broodlord had no presence here.

Of course, it doesn't. As if such a blight on reality could possess a soul!

But there *was* something else here. As Karras was pulled along by the surging currents of the Black River, he became aware of something vast and powerful shifting into his reality from somewhere else. Dread filled him. He had sensed such a presence the last time he had died. Across a century, the memory of that battle on the edge of oblivion returned to him. This thing, this new presence, had the same foul air of that other, and yet this one was far more powerful. Karras knew at once, as the thing began to materialise before him, that here was an enemy he could not overcome.

Its voice, when it finally addressed him, was the voice of a great multitude surrounding him on all sides. The dark waters themselves grew agitated at the sound. Everything seemed to shake and judder, and the pain Karras thought he had left behind with his ruined physical body came suddenly back to him, only now magnified many times with each word the dark being spoke.

'Lyandro Karras,' it hummed and cracked. 'First Codicier of the Death Spectres. Son of Occludus. How exquisite your pain!'

It laughed, and the sound was like a thousand burning needles thrusting into one's flesh.

'Would that I could linger to enjoy it,' the presence continued. 'But I did not breach the boundaries of time and space and interfere in your escape merely to take pleasure in your torment. A greater prize I seek, and nothing else will content me.'

Karras could make little of this. The words themselves were agony to him. He tried to will himself past the being, to be swept swiftly into the eternal Afterworld by the raging waters of the tunnel, but he was fixed firm, and no amount of psychic struggle could free him. He tried to fix his awareness on the dark form now hovering before him, but he could hardly look at it. Something almost physical and utterly irresistible forced his senses away every time.

He did manage to get a sense of the thing, though it made little true sense at all.

Three faces. Five horns. Seven wings. All black as a moonless, starless night.

The black of the void.

The being laughed again, revelling in the inability of the human mind to comprehend both its power and its form.

'You are not dead yet, Lyandro Karras,' the terrible voice said. 'Even now, your physical form fights to remain alive. Will you rise again? Ah, you may just. Only, when you do, you will carry a message for me, for there is one known to you who owes me a debt – a very great debt indeed.'

Karras railed at this lunacy. He was no messenger of daemons. Better that he die once and for all. Let the Black River sweep him away right now. 'I shall carry no message for the likes of you,' he hissed. 'Release me or destroy my soul completely, but you will have nothing from me!'

The being squeezed close around him, and Karras's mind howled with fresh agony.

'You *will* carry this message, Librarian, or I will bring a doom on your beloved Chapter that you can scarcely imagine. Centuries of agony and dishonour, I will rain down on them. They will not escape my wrath for a second. It will not begin today, of course. What is doom without a little anticipation, after all? Let it take a decade to begin. Perhaps even longer. But it will come, a fate so black that their name will be expunged from the records, and it shall be on your head.'

'Empty words, daemon,' spat Karras.

'You know better,' replied the presence. 'There is much the Death Spectres endeavour to keep secret. But it is not so secret as you think. So, you will deliver this message for me, or I will deliver your oh-so-venerable brotherhood into misery, torment and eternal damnation.'

Karras howled in anger and pain. 'I deny you! The words of Chaos sit only on the tongues of liars and traitors. You know nothing. Emperor of Man, deliver me unto silent oblivion. Cut me free from this monstrosity!'

The daemon delighted in this. Its laugh was so deep and potent that it distorted even the shape of the Black River, stretching it here, compressing it there, so that it flexed and strained such as Karras had never seen it do before. There could be no greater testament to the power of this entity. And then it said something that robbed Karras of any confidence he had left.

'The Shariax,' it gloated. 'Such a burden to those who sit upon it.'

Karras fought to stay silent, though a screaming denial echoed in his mind.

'Even now, its power leeches life from your beloved Chapter Master. So it has been with all the First Spectres. Foolish Corcaedus. There is a great price to be paid for sitting on the Glass Throne. Yet the Death Spectres are ever willing to pay it, terrible as it is. And all because of the vision that drove your founder to the very border of madness!'

How can it know this? thought Karras. *Occludus is protected. No daemon could have manifested on such sacred ground. We would have known.*

'What would the Inquisition do, I wonder, on learning of the Shariax? What would your vaunted Lords of Terra think?' Again, it laughed and the sound was a raw, oozing malevolence pressing in on Karras's mind, smothering it, choking it. 'So you *will* carry my message, Lyandro Karras. You will carry it, or we shall discover the terrible power of a secret revealed.'

Karras said nothing. He could find no words. His mind spun. There could be no compact with this abhorrent thing. He could not stain his soul. Far better he were unmade entirely, wiped from existence as if he had never been. But hoping for such was futile. Here he was, and he could do nothing to change it.

Naught but hope for final death. Then, at least, the role of messenger will not fall to me.

The daemon read his thoughts.

'No,' it said simply. 'You shall not die. I have already apportioned some part of my power to sustain you. My strength supplements your own, fuelling your recovery. And I have compelled others, your fellows, to seek you out. They dig even now.' Again, that laugh, so painful, like splashes of acid on open wounds. 'Ever after, you shall owe your survival to me, Librarian. Let the knowledge burn inside you until you do as I have asked.'

Karras could stand no more of this. His sanity was at breaking point. If he lost it, fragile as it currently was, he would be open to full possession. 'Speak your damned message and be gone, warp abomination. I will deliver it or I will not, but speak it now and free me, curse you!'

'Then listen well, insect, for such you are to me. You will tell that treacherous Exorcist cur, Darrion Rauth, that I have forgotten neither him nor his debt. You will tell him this: I will not be denied. What is owed me shall be paid in full. I, Hepaxammon, Prince of Sorrows, will *not* be denied!'

With these last words, the daemon's rage was so great that Karras almost lost himself completely. Countless inner voices invaded his mind, overwhelming it, repeating over and over and over, 'Hepaxammon will not be denied!'

He felt himself diminish, felt his identity, his very consciousness, being drowned out, eroded, burned away. He struggled to grasp hold of it, repeating to himself the mantra that had defined so much of his life – his Chapter's motto:

I fear not death, I who embody it in His name.
I fear not death, I who embody it in His name.
I fear not death…

'…you who embody it in His name!' boomed a fresh voice. It was powerful, all-consuming, almost like that of the daemon Hepaxammon, but this was a single voice, not a multitude, and each word pulsed with soft white light that burned away Karras's agony. Each word muffled the dreadful sound of the daemon's many voices. Muffled them until there were none left at all.

Then something most unlikely intruded over all else.

Karras heard the clapping of pinion feathers.

21

Something small and black shot straight across Karras's field of awareness and struck the daemon's form dead-centre. There was no roar, no howl of rage or indignation, no time for anything like that. In the span of an instant, Karras saw both Hepaxammon and the Black River freeze and shatter as if everything around him were nothing more than a painting on a great sheet of glass. Light blinded him for a moment, but the sound of the beating of wings continued, fading gradually as the source moved off into the distance. When Karras was no longer blinded, he turned his attention in the direction of the sound and saw a black crow disappear over a snow-covered hill.

The cemetery on Occludus!

The sound of the bird's passage diminished to nothing, to be replaced by footsteps crunching in snow. Karras turned.

'Be at ease, khajar. There is little time, and things you must hear.'

Karras was stunned. Stunned and confused.

Athio Cordatus stopped a few metres in front of him and smiled. He was clad in full Terminator armour, but adorned for ceremonial purposes rather than battle. Purity seals fluttered in a wind Karras could not feel. The Chief Librarian's honours, cast in gold, silver and precious gems, glittered in the watery winter sunlight of a late afternoon that could not possibly exist here and now.

Karras knew he was in a mindscape, knew his corporeal form still lay in a grave of thick black rubble back on Chiaro.

Cordatus, it seemed, knew it too.

'Since you are seeing me here, Lyandro,' he said, his smile dropping, 'it is clear that the prime future in which you lie dying beneath the rock of a collapsed mine has come to pass. For you it is the present, and no doubt it seems dark indeed. You have suffered grievous wounds. Would that it were otherwise, my khajar, but take comfort if you can. For all your suffering, we have ample reason to be glad. You will live. And it is on this path alone that the Chapter's greatest hope lies. I could say nothing of this before without affecting the future. Sharing this knowledge now, however, will not close the path you must continue to walk. Had things gone any other way... Well, that hardly matters now. What matters is the going forward. And that is why I have constructed this,' here he gestured to the scene around them, 'so that I might still guide you, though the void of space stretches wide between us.'

Cordatus indicated that Karras should walk with him, and Karras fell into step, dwarfed even at his significant height by the towering bulk of the Terminator armour. It all seemed so real, at least to his visual senses. Here, it seemed, he still had full binocular vision. Each fallen snowflake glittered just as it should. The graves poked from the thick white layer just as he remembered, slabs of black stone inscribed with that ancient script which no one alive could read. But the absence of smells or sensations kept Karras supremely conscious of the ethereal nature of the event.

Could it all be a trick? A vile trap set by Hepaxammon?

No. This is my khadit. I can feel it. I would know.

Almost as if reading him, Cordatus continued, 'The daemon's involvement was something we did not foresee until recently, and the significance of its attention towards you is, as yet, unknown to us. Time is fickle about what it chooses to reveal. You know this. The workings of Chaos have always been hard to read. Nevertheless, the daemon may have its part to play, for good or ill. As of yet, we cannot know. What we do know is this: you will survive. Much work will be needed to restore you, but the inquisitor to whom you are bound, this so-called Sigma, has resources far beyond most. And despite everything, he will want to keep you in his service. He has ambitions of his own, and his psychic coven has pierced the veils and seen hints of your importance to his goals. We cannot perceive those goals. The futures that reveal them are clouded and distorted. We think this is deliberate. Regardless, he will not discharge you from your duties. This is imperative.

'I can give no further detail now without closing futures we must keep open, my khajar, but there will come a moment when Sigma's ambitions and the most desperate hopes of the Chapter will align. Nothing compares in importance to this. Difficult though it may be, do not take too much licence with this man. His tolerance has its limits. Stretch it as you will, but do not break it. As to your new brothers, keep them close. They are your strength. They will see to it that *Arquemann* is recovered. You will need the blade again before long. It, too, has a part to play.'

Karras had questions, all too many of them, but his words, he knew, would be futile. The notion that this was, in any way, a real conversation was false. Cordatus's spirit was not here. This was a construct in every sense, placed along this timeline somewhere in the past in the hope that Karras would live long enough, and make the right choices necessary, to discover it.

Cordatus stopped walking and reached out an armour-plated hand to Karras's shoulder. Karras turned to face him.

'Your brothers and I at Logopol continue to scry with all the power at our disposal, Lyandro. Even the Megir has turned some of his power towards your prime futures. So much is still hidden, but what we have seen thus far gives us great hope – the first real hope the Chapter has had in millennia. The Cadash is real. The Great Resurrection is closer than ever. I never dared to imagine it might come in our lifetime.'

Karras couldn't restrain himself at this.

'The Great Resurrection? Truly, it comes?'

Cordatus, of course, did not hear. He was not really there. Instead, he smiled warmly down at his protégé and said, 'It is no small effort to seed your future with such moments as this, Lyandro. There are risks to both of us. Grave risks. The accidental creation of a single major paradox could undo everything. Thus, these visits together will, by necessity, be few. But where I can, I shall do my best to guide you further wherever the moment demands. For now, though…'

He reached out to Karras, and they both looked down at the powerful armoured hand extended there in the space between them.

'Take it. Take my hand.'

His voice had changed, suddenly and completely. It was not Athio Cordatus.

'Come on, Scholar! Take my hand. Grab on.'

Scholar? When did my khadit ever…?

Bright light exploded in his vision, driving out the snowy mindscape. Karras felt sharp ocular pain. He blinked and tried to turn away. Slowly the pain left him. He blinked again. His right eye was blind after all, but the gene-boosted pupil of the other adjusted quickly.

He saw an armoured hand extended towards him. His eyes moved up the arm to a pauldron embossed with ancient script and a familiar skull motif. He tracked left a little and saw the muzzle of a helmet. Another hand rose and pulled the helmet off to reveal a broad, smiling face, deeply lined and scarred, but friendly and open.

'Omni?' groaned Karras. His throat and lungs felt like they were filled with sharp gravel.

The Imperial Fist beamed down at him.

'Welcome back from the dead, Scholar. You're a hard bastard to kill.'

EPILOGUE

The oil lamps flickered, but no shadows danced. Two figures regarded each other across the table of polished wood, hooded, masked in shadow, almost a perfect reflection of each other. Always the same two figures. Always the same room, the same simple furnishings, none of it real save the two minds that came to meet, to confer in secret, transported to this mindscape by the life-sapping efforts of their respective astropathic choirs.

'The report says he will recover,' said one. 'Fully?'

'My chief medic believes he will require certain augmetics,' answered the other. 'But, if we can get him back to Damaroth quickly, he should be able to return to operational status. The apothecarion there boasts cellular regeneration facilities beyond anything else in the Imperium.'

'Ah. The captured eldar machines.'

'It will take time. The damage was great. All reason says he should have died.'

'Perhaps you underestimated him.'

'You know me better than that. There is something else at play here, but it eludes me.'

'Not for long, I'm sure. And the rest of this Talon Squad, they performed as expected?'

'Predictable to the letter. Underneath it all, Space Marines are cut from one cloth. They do so long to be heroes. Honour and glory constantly cloud their judgement. Their distrust of me remains palpable, but I don't believe they fathom the true extent of Ordo involvement in the Chiaro situation. Their oaths will hold.'

'Good. Keep pushing them. If they really are the ones we need, they will have to endure far more than they did during *Night Harvest*. As to your former interrogator, it is well that she survives. A rare opportunity for us. I had thought to receive only the infant, but the survival of the mother is a tremendous bonus. We must keep her alive after the birth. Once she is stabilised and properly conditioned to our needs, it will be fascinating to see how her offspring responds to her in a Geller-shielded environment. My congratulations. *Blackseed* has borne the very fruit we hoped for. This could not have gone better, old friend. We will have our answers and, perhaps in time, we may have the greatest weapon our Ordo could ever hope to wield.'

'Her stasis pod will be transferred to your frigate as instructed. We expect to reach the transfer coordinates in three weeks.'

'My people will be waiting. And then to Damaroth, yes?'

'Talon Squad will be split up and assigned to one-man operations while their Alpha recovers. I shall deploy Scimitar Squad to Karkarus for *Operation Deadshot*. They ought to be finished with the ork incursion on Ixio by then.'

'Let us hope Talon returns to full strength soon. There can be no rest for us, despite this success. There will be many dead-ends before our long journey is over. Keep searching. Keep exceeding my expectations.'

'And Chiaro?'

'I will authorise the usual action myself later today. The Watch Council at Talasa Prime will back it. The Naval defence monitors will remain to enforce quarantine for now, but a kill-ship will arrive within the week. Nothing will remain.'

'Then, with your permission, I will take my leave. Only, before I go… My sister…'

'She sleeps, my friend, as always. No change. Perhaps the results of *Blackseed* can be turned to her recovery in time. Or perhaps her cure will come via another route entirely. That is why I need you out there, continuing to do what you do best. I can trust no other to the same degree.'

'You have my oath. I will do all that needs doing.'

'I know you will. And together, we will cure her one day. Have faith.'

'Vigilance. And may the Emperor watch over you.'

'Vigilance, old friend. *In nomine Imperator*. We shall speak again soon.'

THE ALIEN HUNTERS

ANDY CHAMBERS

In the empty vastness of the void, a tiny sliver of metal drifted with its crystalline gaze fixed on distant stars. If it were taken from its setting, this artificial satellite would seem large to a man. To a man it would appear as a gnarled tower of steel and brass at the centre of vast spreading sails of silver mesh, like the overgrown stamen at the centre of an unnatural flower. But here in the emptiness between stars it was less than nothing; a tiny and unnoticeable mote on the face of the universe.

Few men would ever see this lonely artefact as it kept its silent vigil down the years. Inside it dwelt only clicking cogitators and thrumming data-stacks. The tireless machine-spirits meticulously marked off the span of centuries as they watched for signs their masters would wish to know of. The tower was called Watch Station Elkin and served the organization known as the Deathwatch.

If the machine-cant of the unliving occupants of Watch Station Elkin could be eavesdropped upon at this juncture, it would have revealed a flurry of activity. Relays opened and closed with a rapid chatter analogous to excitement at the first brush of distant energies.

+Anomalous contact detected: Bearing/98.328. Azimuth/67.201.+

Moments passed as a faint ethereal breeze caressed the far-flung sensor nets of the Watch Station. Weeks or months away in real-space, events had occurred that only now had crossed the intervening distance to reach the artificial eyes and ears of the Station. The spreading ripples betrayed much to the watching machine-spirits. Their brass-bound cogs and gears ground the information into powder, reconstituted it, and sieved it back through data-stacks filled with information on every known contact signature, human or alien. A match was quickly found, one that was disappointingly mundane.

+Contact identified. Analysis confirmed: Warp egress signature of Imperial Pilgrim-class transport vessel verified. Location: Teramus system. 38AU from star, 68 degrees above plane of the ecliptic.+

Lenses locked onto the origin point of the warp signature picked out tell-tale twinkles of light, ones racing far ahead of all tertiary emissions. The clattering cogitators suddenly sped up to fever pitch.

+High energy discharges detected. Spectral output gradient indicates xenos-specific origins.+

+Cogitators II through IV assigned to verify. Processing... Contact confirmed. Cogitators V through XXII activated for cross-correlation.+

+Institute automated blessing protocols.+

+"Blessed be the Omnissiah, blessed be his coming and going, blessed be his servants, blessed be their instruments. Grant us the wisdom of His clarity this day."+

+Automated blessing confirmed. Cogitators V through XXII now active. Begin analysis.+

+Confirmed. Data-stack inquiry confirms weapon signatures most closely match eldar lance parameters. Logged as high probability xenos contact. Activate all remaining idle cogitators. Institute automated celebratory catechism.+

+"Praise be to the Machine-God, through Him our purpose is found."+

The full attention of the Watch Station was now bent on the distant Teramus system. Weeks or months ago, alien-built weapons had been fired in a system that should have no xenos within a hundred light years. Perhaps once in half a century, Watch Station Elkin might detect such an event and such was precisely the purpose for which it was constructed. Slower ripples of energy were arriving now, laggardly waves of electro-magnetism and tardy infrared that betrayed the complexities of the unfolding drama. Each nugget of information was dissected with infinite care and precision; all was logged and recorded by the watching machine-spirits in an ecstasy of purpose.

+Tertiary contacts detected. Engine trace analysis indicates estimated twelve plus unidentified system vessels on intercept course with primary contact.+

+Broadband high power transmission detected. Imperial standard gamma level encryption. Origin point: Pilgrim-class vessel. Recording.+

'...Repeat. This is the *Penitent Wanderer* Imperial transport out of Dhumres. Our warp drive is damaged. Unidentified vessels closing in. We're running but we can't stay ahead of them for long. For the love of Terra, any Imperial vessel in the area please assist. Repeat.'

+Voice print confirmed human origin. Conjecture: Captain of *Penitent Wanderer*. Speech patterns indicate heightened stress levels. Conjecture: Under attack.+

The doomed pleas of the long-dead captain were taken and preserved in crystal and silicon for later examination, assigned with a low priority. Charters and logs were cross-examined to confirm the existence of the *Penitent Wanderer*. Its five-hundred year history of hauling pilgrims and convicts between Dhumres and Vertus Magna were appended to the growing report as a minor footnote.

+Confirmed. Additional low power transmissions detected. Unknown sub-Alpha level encryption. Cogitators II through IV assigned to breaking encryption.+

+Unfocused plasma dispersal detected. Conjecture: Drive loss on Pilgrim-class vessel designated *Penitent Wanderer*.+

+Confirmed. Alpha level encryption defeated. Signal content as follows:+

'There she is, boys! Didn't 'ole Buke tell you there'd be a soft touch for the taking today? Aren't I good to you? Now run her down careful, mind. I don't want her all spread across the belt like last time. Get this right and there's a year's worth of red sacra in it for everyone, got it?'

+Voice print confirmed human origin. Conjecture: Leader of system ships. Speech patterns indicate non-dispersed non-militaristic command structure. Conjecture: Pirate.+

+Subsequent transmission source from *Penitent Wanderer* detected. Confirmed low power broad band signal.+

'Engines are out! Hull integrity at thirty per cent! Their weapons cut straight through the plating like it was nothing! Anyone in range, please help! This is *Penitent Wanderer* under attack in the Teramus system… Emperor's teeth they're coming aboard… Even if you can't get here in time just make sure these bastards pay, get them, I–'

+Subsequent transmissions terminated at source. Naval data cross-reference confirms pirate activity reported around Teramus system. *Penitent Wanderer* logged as overdue, believed total loss. Situation unresolved.+

The dispassionate crystal eyes of Watch Station Elkin observed the dying moments of the *Penitent Wanderer* as the pirates closed in on their prey. The lightning-flicker of xenos weaponry had died away and nothing now remained to excite the interest of their masters, but the machine-spirits faithfully continued recording every detail of the month-old attack. The *Penitent Wanderer* was boarded, gutted and left drifting in the void. The pirate ships vanished back into the slowly tumbling corona of rock around Teramus's star and beyond the reach of the Watch Station's most sensitive detectors.

A report was filed and flagged in the data-stacks alongside hundreds of other incidents. With their work complete, the cogitators subsided into endless slow matriculations once more. In a year, a decade, or a century, their masters would come for the knowledge accumulated by the Watch Station and decide whether to act upon this particular report. Perhaps the nameless captain and his crew would be avenged, perhaps not. To the machine-spirits, and to their Deathwatch masters, simple vengeance was an emotion of no consequence.

Far from Watch Station Elkin and months later, a group of its masters did indeed meet in conclave at the great citadel of Zarabek. A towering edifice orbiting a dying star, Zarabek had once been the last holdfast of the race of Muhlari, a xenos people of tremendous antiquity that had claimed to have walked the stars when mankind was still in its infancy. The Deathwatch had ended the Muhlari centuries ago, slaying their den mothers and burning their sacellum of knowledge in the Purgation of Zarabek. The mighty fortress was purged by promethium fires from top to bottom as the Deathwatch consigned the Muhlari to the Book of Extinctions.

Afterwards, seeing Zarabek as a place both strong and well-hidden, the Deathwatch took it as one of their own. Zarabek became a Watch Fortress, like and unlike a hundred other hidden places scattered across the galaxy and used by the alien-hunting Deathwatch to keep vigil. Generations of serf-artisans began the work of chipping away the obscene carvings of the extinct Muhlari and rendering the fortress fit for service. Centuries later, the ghosts of the unfortunate Muhlari would scarcely recognise their own holdfast. The sinuous, curving Muhlari script covering Zarabek's lofty halls had been completely obliterated with ranks of statuesque Imperial heroes and crowding lines of angular High Gothic creed; elegantly curved pillars and arches had become sharp and angular; vast open spaces once filled with light and life were now dark and sepulchral.

Now the sternly chiselled faces of past heroes overlooked a company of living warriors close to blows. A dozen different Chapter icons were displayed by the assembled Space Marines: fists, claws, daggers, wings, flames, skulls set against green, red, white, yellow, silver and more. Save for this single link back to their parent Chapters, all present wore their power armour repainted in unrelieved black and bearing the silver skull icon of the Deathwatch. Despite this symbolic unity, barely submerged Chapter rivalries were coming to the fore and threatening to break the company apart.

'How can you speak such words? Are we not the Emperor's chosen warriors? Are we not vowed to seize the enemy by the throat at every opening and tear him asunder? Your cowardice sickens me!'

Gottrand's words rang through the grim silence of the Hall of Intentions like a clarion call, arousing snarls and imprecations from his fellow warriors. A score of hulking figures armoured in ceramite and plasteel surrounded him. For Space Marines of the Holy Emperor of Mankind, accusations of cowardice are a matter to be expunged by blood.

Gottrand grinned back at them all without fear. His sharp teeth and long, plaited hair marked him as a member of the Space Wolves Chapter as much as his grey shoulder pad marked with the icon of the wolf rampant. Such wild talk was expected among the brothers of Fenris, where the youngest Space Marine warriors, Blood Claws as they are called, are measured in worth by their gusto and carelessness of danger. His present companions evinced little appreciation for his savage brand of courage.

'Curb your tongue, wolf-cub. Your childish jibes have no place here,' grumbled Battle-Brother Thucyid. His own shoulder bore the black mailed fist against yellow that was the icon of the Imperial Fists Chapter. Stoic and meticulous by nature, the Imperial Fists contrasted the headstrong Space Wolves as night contrasts day.

'While lacking in tact, Brother Gottrand's point is well-made,' offered Brother-Sergeant Courlanth, his shoulder marked by the quartered crimson and gold of the Howling Griffons Chapter. 'What purpose do we serve if not to fight the alien? Why come so far from our respective Chapters, only to sit idle in defiance of the sacred vows we've taken?'

Courlanth addressed these words not to the assembled Space Marines, but to one who sat apart from them on a throne forged of shattered alien bones and broken xenos weaponry. Watch Captain Ska Mordentodt glowered down at his squabbling charges with undisguised contempt. No Chapter badge or icon was borne upon his armour except for the silver skull of the Deathwatch. Which Space Marine Chapter Mordentodt originally hailed from was as unknown and as unknowable as the man himself.

Centuries of devotion to the Deathwatch vigil had rendered the watch captain a distant and forbidding figure. When Mordentodt finally spoke, the company present quieted instantly, not out of fear – for Space Marines know no fear – but out of respect to one that has long sacrificed the fellowship of Chapter brethren for the lonely vigil of the Deathwatch.

'Your vows are ones of obedience and service – a sacred charge to stand vigil among the Deathwatch,' Mordentodt grated. 'The defiance you speak of is defiance only of my authority as captain of this fortress.'

'Such was not my intent, watch captain, as well you must know,' Courlanth said with contrition. 'I wished only to add my voice to Gottrand's that the reports from the Elkinian Reach are disturbing and bear further investigation. Xenos weaponry appearing in the hands of pirates must surely fall within the remit of the Deathwatch.'

'A great many things fall within the remit of the Deathwatch,' Mordentodt replied grimly. 'Hrud migrations, necrontyr tomb-sites, xenarch raids, malgreth sightings, genestealer infestations and more, much more, fall within the remit of this single fortress and the handful of battle-brothers your Chapter Masters permit to stand vigil here.

'In truth, a hundred battle companies would be insufficient for the task. The xenos swarm and multiply beyond the Emperor's Light in such numbers. Where would you have me pluck the brothers needed to chase these pirates into their holes? What should remain unwatched while some of you indulge yourselves in the pursuit of glory?'

Courlanth bowed his head. 'Such decisions are yours and yours alone to make, watch captain. Though this is not my first vigil in the Deathwatch, I am but newly arrived at Zarabek and know nothing of the other commitments you speak of. My apologies if I spoke out of turn.'

Mordentodt made no response to the Howling Griffons sergeant, only gazing stonily out across the faces of the assembled Space Marines for several long moments. At this, a young Techmarine bearing the icon of the Novamarines on his right shoulder quietly stood forward and calmly returned Mordentodt's basilisk glare when it was snapped onto him.

'What is it, Felbaine?' Mordentodt growled. 'Do the machine-spirits seek to usurp my command as well?'

'No, watch captain, I wished only to draw to your attention certain details in the reports I brought back from Watch Station Elkin.'

'I see – more advice. I have a veritable feast of it laid before me this day. Out with it then.'

'I wish to be specific in one regard. The weapons used in the attacks closely match the signature of those used by the degenerate eldar. My xenos-lore is feeble compared to some present, yet even I know that the eldar wield blasphemous technologies of the most potent kind. To find such technology in the hands of pirates is exceptional to say the least.'

Mordentodt's eyes glittered at the mention of the eldar. 'So these pirates found a wreck and looted it,' the watch captain murmured with less conviction. 'It remains a matter of small and distant import compared to many of the others confronting this fortress.'

The Techmarine shook his head regretfully, his single bionic eye and the complex swirl of electoos that marked his cheeks flashing in the gloom. 'With respect, watch captain, even the finest savants of the Adeptus Mechanicus have struggled to maintain eldar artefacts in operative condition. For mere pirates to use and continue to use these weapons, they must be getting help from somewhere or someone – and I believe that is what is truly significant about this matter.'

Mordentodt sat back in his throne, contemplating the Techmarine's words. The implications were clear to all present. Some bargain had been struck between human and alien in the Teramus system. In the eyes of the Deathwatch there was no greater crime. Mordentodt eventually nodded grimly.

'Good. Well done, Felbaine. You apply logic to the problem while others do battle to see only who can bark the loudest. Know also that the Elkinian covenant of Ordo Xenos has also demanded – *demanded* – action be taken in the Reach due to the virtual cessation of shipping between Dhumres and Vertus Magna because of these pirates. The damned inquisitors call upon us because the Imperial Navy is too weak to act and the Imperial Guard too slow... Courlanth, you spoke in favour of this mission – will you now fulfil your oath to accept it?'

'It is my sworn duty to do so, watch captain,' Courlanth replied, 'and my honour to serve the Deathwatch in any way I can.'

'Spoken like a true Howling Griffon,' Mordentodt grunted. 'I meant what I said about other commitments – I can spare no more than five battle-brothers for the Teramus kill-team, including you. Choose now those you would have accompany you from among those here present.'

Courlanth's voice was strong and steady as he named his companions one by one without hesitation. Each came to stand beside him to be eyed jealously by those not chosen.

'I name Brother Maxillus of the Ultramarines for his sharp aim and his honourable role in shared dangers past.'

'I name Brother Thucyid of the Imperial Fists for his strength and stoicism in adversity.'

'I name Brother Felbaine of the Novamarines for his knowledge and wisdom.'

'I name Brother Gottrand for his fervour and to spare those who remain behind at Zarabek from his wailing if he were not permitted to come along.'

This last drew a chuckle from his companions, most of all from Gottrand himself. Mordentodt did not even crack a smile.

'Set aside thoughts of your Chapters,' the watch captain warned. 'All are as one in the Deathwatch. Your only concern should be whether your remains will be returned to your brothers garlanded with honour and success, or failure and ignominy. Get to the arming halls and ready yourselves, the strike cruiser *Xenos Purgatio* departs for the Teramus system within the hour. Do not fail me. Do not fail the Deathwatch.'

The arming halls of Zarabek had been rebuilt from the walled enclosures that had formed the Muhlari sacellum of knowledge. The inquisitors of the Ordo Xenos had pored over the contents of the sacellum for weeks before ordering its complete destruction, to the predictable dismay of some of the attending Adeptus Mechanicus representatives. The Deathwatch had attended to the matter with customary thoroughness, grinding the delicate crystal data repositories into powder, mixing it with the crushed bones of the Muhlari, and shooting into the heart of the dying star nearby.

Now brass cages filled with racks of armaments enclosed the sacellum where libraries of data crystals said to encompass the whole length and breadth of the known universe had been stored. The far end of the cavernous halls was the realm of the Forgemaster. These glowed with ruddy light and rang with a cacophonous hammering where a thousand servitors worked beneath the Forgemaster's direction, churning out munitions for the Deathwatch's endless war against the xenos in all its forms. Everything was made here, from the humblest bolt shell to hundred-metre long cyclonic torpedoes built for the ruin of worlds.

Maxillus emerged from the cages and greeted Sergeant Courlanth with a clenched fist salute. Dark-haired and square-jawed, Maxillus looked every inch the archetypical warrior of Ultramar – so much so that the black of Deathwatch looked incongruous covering his armour. The Ultramarine easily held the hefty weight of a slab-sided Crusade-pattern boltgun upright in his other hand, the weapon's pistol grip fitted so perfectly into his fist that it looked like an extension of him.

'Well met, Maxillus,' Courlanth said warmly, returning the salute before gripping Maxillus by the forearm and slapping him on the shoulder plate. 'Ready your bolter well, brother, we aren't out for a simple afternoon's gaunt-hunting this time.'

Maxillus grinned appreciatively. 'Don't worry, brother, I'll make sure to bring along enough shells for everyone this time.'

Maxillus and Courlanth had fought together before on the moons of Masali, an arid agri-world that formed part of the Realm of Ultramar. They had met as part of a Deathwatch kill-team hunting down the resurgent tyranid broods which could never seem to be fully expunged after the defeat of Hive Fleet Behemoth in the First Tyrannic War.

Courlanth had been on his first vigil with the Deathwatch and feeling acutely aware of the absence of the stalwart Chapter-Brothers of the Howling Griffons that he had fought alongside for decades. Maxillus had inspired his confidence by telling him that a simple afternoon's gaunt-hunting was nothing to get anxious about. In the event, Maxillus's confidence was proven ill-founded and Courlanth's concerns had emerged as being warranted, but both had at least survived to share the tale.

Courlanth found Thucyid in another cage methodically slotting oversized bolt-rounds into the flexible belt feed of his cherished heavy bolter *Iolanth*. The heavy bolter stood over half as tall as a Space Marine, a huge slab of metal any ordinary man could scarcely lift, let alone fire, unaided.

As he took up each shell, the Imperial Fists veteran rubbed it with sanctified oils and whispered a prayer to Dorn and the Emperor to guide it straight and true. Thucyid looked up as Courlanth entered, his practiced hands still blessing and loading the bolt-rounds even as he gazed curiously at the Howling Griffons sergeant. Thucyid was scarred, with blond hair cropped to little more than stubble across his thick-boned skull. Five long-service studs gleamed on Thucyid's brow, plentiful evidence if any were needed of his extensive experience and battle-craft. The Imperial Fist was the first to speak.

'Why choose me, sergeant?' Thucyid said mildly, his hands never stopping as they loaded shell after shell into the link-belt. 'You were right to choose the wolf-pup, I think, his kind are bad at waiting for anything – most of all a fit chance for glory. I think that's why they wind up getting killed chasing the unfit kind so often. But why choose me?'

'Because when you chided Gottrand for his hasty words it was without real anger or challenge, and he subsided at once. The others were ready to fight him on the spot, but you just told him to know his place and he accepted it. I need that kind of stability – and quite possibly heavy firepower too.'

Thucyid still seemed puzzled. 'I suppose you're right – he did quiet down after that, can't understand why myself.'

'I've heard that among the Space Wolves, their veteran warriors wield heavy weapons much as you do, Thucyid, as they have the wisdom to know that winning battles requires fire support as well as the courage to rush into the midst of things. They're called Long Fangs and hold high regard at the Wolves' feasting tables.'

'Ah, so you're saying that you think Gottrand will listen to me because I'm old?' Thucyid said with a twinkle in his eye. 'Old and too slow with *Iolanth* to go rushing off anywhere.'

Courlanth grinned. 'I'm sure *Iolanth* – or more accurately her many offspring – will close the distance for you quickly enough. What shells are you loading for her?'

'Three-to-one mix of mass-reactive to Inferno in this belt, mass-reactive and metal storm in another, all Inferno in a third, Kraken penetrator rounds in a fourth. It's hard to know what we'll need so I've found it's best to prepare for all eventualities.'

'I ask your forgiveness for that lack of knowledge,' the Tech-marine Felbaine said as he entered the cage bearing an ornate casket. 'I did not anticipate that the watch captain would react by sending a kill-team without arranging further reconnaissance of the system first. I fear the confrontation among the brethren drove him into hasty action to seek resolution.'

'Don't underestimate Mordentodt's foresight,' Courlanth said reassuringly. 'Further reconnaissance might have simply scared the pirates away – or more likely their mysterious benefactors – and left us with nothing. A single kill-team is enough to investigate and deal with the threat at the same time.'

'Perhaps, perhaps not,' insisted Felbaine. 'I fear that if we are not strong enough we will only know when it is too late and we have failed.'

'Then we will be avenged,' said Courlanth with finality.

Courlanth found Gottrand emerging from the forges. The Blood Claw had a sour look on his face as he ruefully contemplated his long-bladed chainsword.

'What's wrong now, Gottrand?' Courlanth asked.

'The Forgemaster here hasn't even heard of kraken teeth. On Fenris the Iron Priests must learn to carve them before they can even dream of smelting iron.'

'Significance continues to evade you. What exactly is the problem?'

'This blade is *Hjormir*,' Gottrand declared with pride and a little chagrin, brandishing the weapon with its sharp rows of contra-rotating teeth before Courlanth. 'It has been borne by my Great Company since the days of Russ. The Great Wolf entrusted it to me when I began my vigil so that it might add some new stanzas to its saga.'

'And so?'

'I chipped three of *Hjormir*'s teeth in training, and now I find they cannot be replaced by the Forgemaster. *Hjormir* snarls and whines at me in complaint whenever he is woken, and I fear I will offend his spirit if I bear him into battle in such a state.'

'Gottrand, if your chainsword has truly been fighting since the days of your primarch, its spirit has survived far worse calamities than a few chipped teeth. *Hjormir* will simply have to be remembered for fighting this battle wearing a gap-toothed smile.'

The command bridge of the *Xenos Purgatio* was a cold, cramped, angular space filled with low bulkheads, struts and stanchions that was designed for solidity more than comfort. The ship's Lochos was a gaunt thrall wrapped in a cloak of trailing cables that connected his cranium directly to the ship's primary systems. Ranged around the walls, dozens of niches held more thrall-servitors, each connected to their respective stations. The air was thick with machine-cant as the Lochos guided the kilometres-long vessel out of its docking berth in Zarabek's lower reaches and set it on a course away from the citadel.

Sergeant Courlanth had assembled his kill-team to coordinate his plans with the Lochos of the *Xenos Purgatio* for the coming action. A strike cruiser was capable of carrying a whole company of a hundred Space Marines across the stars and delivering them into the heart of battle via Thunderhawk gunship, drop pod and teleportarium. It had enough firepower to defeat any vessel of its own size, and enough speed to outrun anything greater. The strike cruiser also carried Exterminatus-class weapons that could devastate a world from orbit and expunge all life from it if such were deemed necessary. This vast, world-destroying ship and its thousands of thrall crew members were now theoretically under Courlanth's direct and absolute control, a somewhat dizzying prospect for a mere sergeant like him.

Fortunately, its Lochos – a servant of the Deathwatch permanently bonded to the machine-spirits of his vessel – had centuries of experience to draw upon. He would understand the capabilities and limitations of his ship far better than Courlanth could ever hope to. Unfortunately, the Lochos appeared fully engaged with getting the ship underway for the Teramus system. Courlanth feared to disturb the man-machine from his matriculations in case they ended up making a warp translation into a star, or something worse, thanks to his impatience.

'Felbaine,' the sergeant said at last. 'What can you tell us about the Teramus system? How can we track down our quarry once we arrive?'

The Techmarine gestured to a holo-pit at the centre of the bridge. Skeins and jewels of light sketched an orrery of a star system. 'This is Teramus,' Felbaine explained. 'See here the old, red star at its centre? In some long age past it gradually expanded to its current size and most of the worlds in its orbit were torn apart. The rings of rocky debris you see were formed out of the bones of them.'

'Does anyone live there at all?' asked Thucyid. 'Aside from heretics and pirates I mean – are there no outposts or astropath stations?'

'There used to be mines in the asteroid belts,' said Felbaine, 'but they were abandoned centuries ago. There's really no reason for ships to go to Teramus at all. I confess I was surprised when the watch captain spoke of the Ordo Xenos demanding immediate action over the affair.'

'If I may interject, my lords?' The Lochos's voice was a parchment-thin whisper issuing from speaker-grilles all over the bridge. The lips of his cable-cloaked body standing at the command console did not move. 'Our course is laid in, a task easily done because Teramus is within what you might call a calm channel through warp space. To either side of it lie areas of more tumultuous flux, so a course through Teramus is frequently used. On the passage between Dhumres and Vertus Magna, most Navigators need to translate into the real at Teramus in order to check their bearings or they risk straying into the aforementioned tumult and becoming lost.'

'I understand your meaning, Lochos,' said Courlanth. 'While Teramus itself is of no consequence, it lies on a route of importance.'

'Dhumres and Vertus Magna support a combined population of over ninety billion souls,' Felbaine added. 'Any disruption to their trade and shipping will cause immense privation and eventually disorder.'

'That must be what these eldar are really after,' said Maxillus. 'In Ultramar they are known for being ever-full of trickery and misdirection.'

'We'll make sure we catch some live ones so we can ask them,' joked Gottrand.

'Not if they hear of our arrival. They'll disappear into their rat holes at the first sign of trouble,' said Thucyid.

'It's a fair point,' granted Courlanth. 'Lochos, will you be able to keep the ship undetected when we arrive?'

'Impossible to determine given the unknown capabilities of the enemy,' whispered the Lochos, 'but our translation in-system will be far from the usual arrival points, and I will refrain from using active sensor sweeps to avoid advertising our presence. By using limited manoeuvring thrusts I will keep us undetectable against the background radiation of the star, save by direct observation.'

'Good. And what about locating their base?'

'Again, impossible to determine at this time. Once in the Teramus system it is likely that there will be emissions too weak to register from a Watch Station that will become readily apparent from closer proximity.'

'Very well. We may need to act to draw them out if that doesn't work, but I'm loath to tip our hand if we don't have to. Surprise will be key to victory.'

'I have a question to ask of the Lochos with your permission, sergeant,' said Felbaine. Courlanth nodded curtly in response, wondering what was troubling the Techmarine now.

'Lochos, Watch Captain Mordentodt said that the Imperial Navy was too weak to act, and yet I see recent Navy reports appended to the holo-display of the Teramus system – what can you tell us about those?'

'Three Imperial Navy patrols have been routed through the Teramus system to search for pirates in the past five years,' the Lochos said tonelessly. 'Two found no sign of pirates, the third and most recent failed to report back and is listed as missing presumed lost. Further operations have been suspended until capital ships can be found to reinforce the effort.'

'Then we definitely need the element of surprise,' Courlanth said grimly. 'I will pray that you tread lightly enough to evade detection, Lochos.'

'Have no fear, my lords,' the Lochos replied, 'no effort will be spared to bring you to battle in the manner of your choosing. For now, however, it may be wisest to retire to your Reclusiam while warp translation is achieved. I ask you not to wander the ship; you will find most sections sealed off or hazardous while in flight.'

The *Xenos Purgatio* slid through the churning rock rings of Teramus on minimum power, no more than a sensor-shadow among the hurtling drift of asteroids. No burst of comm-chatter had met its arrival, despite the ship straining every receptor to listen for it. Either the arrival of the Deathwatch strike cruiser had gone unmarked or their enemies were preternaturally well-disciplined. The other possibility, Courlanth silently reflected, was that they had been expected and were blithely drifting into a trap.

The bridge of the strike cruiser was once again alive with quiet machine-cant and drifting clouds of sickly sweet incense from auto-thuribles. Ranks of monotask servitors had already been sifting the available data for hours as they tried to locate a veritable needle in a haystack. Without recourse to active sensor sweeps, they must perforce look for tell-tale emissions that stood out from the natural cacophony of background radiation. Meanwhile, there was little for Courlanth and his kill-team to do but watch and wait while the man-machines ferreted out their target.

In deference to his passengers, the Lochos had configured the holo-pit to project a view of the outside world. Even with this aid the kill-team could see nothing but rolling rocks the size of mountains all around them, jagged-looking and ruddy in the backwash of Teramus's star. After several hours of this unchanging landscape, Gottrand was becoming increasingly restless. Courlanth was beginning to regret his decision to convene the kill-team so early. The hunt could take days rather than hours.

'I still say we issue a challenge,' the Blood Claw declared for the hundredth time, 'and board the first ship they send out. We take a prisoner and make them tell us where their lair can be found.'

'A direct challenge from a Space Marine strike cruiser will only send them running, xenos weaponry or not,' Thucyid said, 'but a faked distress call might produce the desired result.'

'It's simply too risky,' Courlanth declared. 'We have to find their nest before we act or we risk losing our chance to act at all. Our best and probably our only chance to discover the xenos connection will be to infiltrate the interior of their base and strike from within. If we are discovered before that, we have failed before we have even begun.'

'Courlanth is right,' Maxillus said loyally. 'The pirates are alien-tainted scum that need to die too, but the important thing is to find the xenos themselves. If there is a connection here then their corruption may have spread to other worlds too. It's our duty to root out every last vestige of it.'

Gottrand muttered something and turned away, pacing the deck-plates like a caged wolf. Thucyid looked to Courlanth and shrugged, appearing little troubled by the delay. The Imperial Fists were legendary besiegers who knew the value of patience.

'Contact detected,' the Lochos announced. 'A high albedo anomaly, probably the remains of a shipwreck.'

The holo-view swung around to show an apparently entirely identical selection of tumbling rocks. In the shadows of one asteroid, Courlanth could pick out a tell-tale glitter of metal.

'Lochos, take us closer,' the sergeant said. 'As quietly as you can.'

Courlanth felt the gravity fluctuate slightly as the strike cruiser changed course, its giga-tonnage of mass shivering as it manoeuvred on limited power. As his view steadied he saw more gleams coming into sight on the holo-view. There were more wrecks drifting in this sector of Teramus's asteroid belts, a lot more.

'The sheer brazenness of them,' Thucyid muttered in disbelief. 'There must be a hundred wrecks out there. How could the Navy have missed this?'

'The last patrol didn't, and it's probably out there adrift with the rest of them now,' Courlanth replied. 'Lochos, can you gain any notion of the age of these wrecks or how long ago they were taken?'

'Yes, my lord. Plasma core remnants detectable on most of the vessels give an approximation of age through their heat signature degradation. The vast majority of the visible ships were destroyed within the last year, while the oldest wreck is more than a century old.'

'The xenos weaponry has tipped the balance and now the pirates are running wild like a pack of rabid dogs,' Courlanth said grimly. 'With any other predator I would expect to find the freshest carcasses close to the lair. Is it so, Lochos?'

'Allowing for drift there is an apparent nexus of activity,' the Lochos whispered. 'I will indicate it on the holo-view.'

Cross-hairs sprang into place within the holo-view, indicating an island-sized asteroid that at first glance appeared little different from its fellows. Deep cracks were visible in its surface, wide enough and long enough to swallow the *Xenos Purgatio* whole.

'Trace emissions indicate power sources and atmosphere present in some areas of the asteroid. Dispersed ion trails indicate vessels travel to and from it with some frequency. I could find out more through active scans or a closer approach, but either action would substantially increase the chances of our detection.'

'Then ready a Thunderhawk for immediate launch and it can take us quietly in for a closer look.'

'Landing a Thunderhawk gunship on the asteroid will create unavoidable emissions that will almost certainly be detected,' the Lochos warned. Gottrand brightened visibly at the prospect.

'Then we simply won't land the Thunderhawk,' Courlanth countered. 'We'll land without it.'

Courlanth sat in the hold of the Thunderhawk with his kill-team, each of them fully occupied with making final checks of their armour and weaponry in preparation for combat. Theoretically, up to thirty armoured Space Marines could have been carried within that long, narrow space but it seemed crowded holding just the five members of the kill-team. Prayers were murmured and catechisms recited over the thick carapace of ceramite and plasteel that protected their bodies. Their weapons were anointed with sacred oils and given abjurations to the ferocity of their spirits.

'Pay particular attention to your atmospheric seals,' Courlanth bade them, 'and your backpack air scrubbers. We must respect the environment we enter.'

'Ah, when you've fought through plasma storms and acid lakes a little hard vacuum is nothing,' Gottrand joked. 'Are we not Space Marines?' Maxillus and Thucyid groaned at the old joke. Felbaine, looking a little uncomfortable, brought out the ornate casket Courlanth had first seen him carrying in the arming halls.

'I received specific instructions before we left Zarabek,' Felbaine said apologetically, 'that every member of the kill-team was to be outfitted with one of these devices before potentially entering any combat.'

'Eh? What are you talking about, what are they?' Gottrand asked dubiously as Felbaine opened the casket. Inside were five palm-sized, finger-thick discs embossed with a design of skull against a cross.

'Teleport homers,' Felbaine said. 'Devices that allow the *Xenos Purgatio* to lock its teleportarium onto their unique signatures over a considerable distance and through all kinds of interference. With these we can theoretically be recalled to the ship at any time.'

'I don't like that,' Gottrand declared sullenly. 'I don't like that at all. It smacks of going into battle ready to be pulled out of it at the whim of another. I am no puppet to be dangled on a piece of string!'

'Calm yourself, Gottrand,' Courlanth snapped. 'Who gave you these specific instructions, Felbaine?'

'Watch Captain Ska Mordentodt. He said he wanted...' Felbaine paused in momentary discomfort at the implied insult he was about to deliver. 'He said if things went badly he wanted no one left behind under any circumstances – "no Deathwatch corpses for the xenos to despoil" were his exact words.'

'I see,' Courlanth said icily, trying not to show his anger at the implications for his command. 'The watch captain has commanded and we must obey without regard to our foolish notions of pride and honour. Go ahead, Felbaine, fit your damned devices and I will have words with the watch captain after our return with them unused.'

As Felbaine set about spot-welding the disk-shaped devices to the kill-team, Courlanth consulted his inertial map via his armour's autosenses. The Thunderhawk was sliding along unpowered and undetectable, its engines dark since their initial push away from the docking cradles of the *Xenos Purgatio*. Their course described a precise arc which would take them to within a few kilometres of the pirates' asteroid base.

Mountains of rock and tumbling wreckage were all around them, sometimes so close that Courlanth could have opened a hatch and trailed his fingers across them. Micro-gravity effects from the passing asteroids made the Thunderhawk buck and judder, meteorites occasionally rattling off the craft's thick armour plates like hail. The course had been precisely calculated to avoid any direct collision with larger bodies – or at least so the Lochos had assured him.

They would be at their closest approach to the target within just a few minutes. Felbaine was just finishing the last piece of welding. 'Helmets on,' Courlanth ordered before clamping his own into place. There was a momentary sensation of claustrophobia before the autosenses connected and his vision cleared into tactical view with its display of status icons showing reassuringly steady and green. He checked around the rest of the kill-team, receiving the traditional thumbs-up signal from each in turn.

Courlanth stepped to the rear hatch controls and triggered them. Warning lights flashed before the entire rear wall of the hold hinged downward to form a ramp. Beyond the open hatch a rushing blackness was revealed, where the asteroids around them were just barely visible as a turning kaleidoscope of vast interlocking shadows. Courlanth walked onto the ramp, acutely aware of the tenuous grip of his magnetic-soled boots. Below him a vaster shadow was rearing up, its highest peaks painted crimson as they flashed in the light of the distant red giant. The Deathwatch sergeant braced himself at the edge for a moment before quite deliberately hurling himself off.

One after another the kill-team flung themselves after him: Gottrand, Felbaine, Maxillus and Thucyid dropped towards the asteroid, spread-eagled in a perfect echelon behind Courlanth. Above them the Thunderhawk plunged silently onward through the maelstrom of stone until it could reach a safe distance to make a course change and return to the strike cruiser undetected. Thousands of metres below them, the asteroid that was their goal swelled rapidly as it came up to greet them.

Arlon Buke, King Buke the third as he styled himself, chafed uncomfortably in the rich robes he had forced himself to wear. He was hurrying through the twisting, lamp-lit rock tunnels of his kingdom of Bukehall with the robes unceremoniously hitched up around his knees for speed. Some fat Ecclesiarch or adept had died inside the starched folds of silk and satin he wore – dried blood still clotted the rich fur of the collar. But it was the freshest and most impressive looking of the pickings from the space lanes. It would have to do.

His bodyguards clumped along at his back, big men with bigger guns, who Arlon Buke had deemed stupid enough to be intimidating and trustworthy. The bodyguards were being careful not to snigger but he could feel their knowing smirks behind him. Buke didn't like wearing fancy robes. He would much rather be roistering with his men, drinking red sacra and indulging his most base lusts with the most recent acquisitions. There was no time for such happy diversions now. A black bird had flown, the winged messenger had come with fresh demands that he pay up or be replaced. They came so often now it seemed there was no end to them.

In his father's day, Buke could remember the black bird had been seen precisely five times before Arlon had grown big and strong enough to strangle Buke the Second and take his place. Now every month brought word of new gifts and new prices from the winged ones, and Arlon never had the guts to turn any of it down.

The bird had said the Crimsons were coming to collect the latest payment in person, something Buke had always dreaded. The Crimsons were such sticklers for protocol that they looked down on him and mocked what they called his oafish ways at every turn. It didn't stop them dealing with him any more than it had stopped them dealing with his father, or his father's father before him in the first days after the Discovery, but Arlon still hated it. He did feel oafish and stupid around the Crimsons and the hungry, avaricious glitter in their eyes reappeared in his nightmares all too often.

From past experience, Buke knew that dressing in finery shielded him from some tiny part of the Crimsons' disdain. He had a sneaking suspicion that it was because the different clothes made it easier for them to pick him out from among his men and address him directly. The Crimsons really saw them all as just meat, beasts in an enclosure they could cull at will. Buke and his men could only avoid a trip down the hell-mouth by staying useful. Otherwise they might end up being carried off like Buke's father's father had been.

Buke reflexively smoothed the robes down again at the thought, failing to notice the sweaty trails he left on the white satin as he hurried along. The Crimsons weren't due for hours but he had to get things going in case they decided to play games by arriving early. Starting the meeting off with the Crimsons claiming to be insulted by his inattention would not end well for him. Ahead of him the great brass valve that was the main door of the audience chamber was coming into view. Buke slowed down and dropped the hem of his robes, ambling onward with an outward show of stately confidence that he really did not feel. He could hear strains of weird, alien-sounding music coming from within.

They had chosen an impact point a kilometre out from the widest crack in the asteroid, reasoning that would be the most likely location for the base. What had seemed a shadowed crevice through distant telescopes was now revealed as wide valley between twin peaks. As they dropped closer, metal could be seen glittering in the valley and Courlanth knew the pride of vindication. Closer still and details became apparent to his autosenses when boosted to maximum gain: the hunch-backed shapes of system vessels, a spider-web framework of gantries and platforms, sensor dishes and defence turrets pointing at the tumultuous skies. Light and heat plumes betrayed occupation below, but the distance was too great to spot any suited figures.

Courlanth rotated to bring his heels toward the asteroid and folded his arms to his chest. He released a blast of compressed gas from his backpack to give himself a single, hard push downwards and the rocky surface leapt towards him. Seconds later Courlanth crunched into the sloping surface with legs braced, the impact of his armoured boots gouging two craters into the brittle rock. Behind him, Gottrand, Maxillus and Thucyid struck with more or less the same skill. Felbaine unaccountably misjudged his descent and struck with a force his suit's gyro-stabilisers couldn't cope with, sending him tumbling out of control.

The Techmarine half-stumbled, half-skidded away in a cloud of dust and debris, his excess momentum sending him down-slope towards a yawning chasm. Under the asteroid's weak gravity Felbaine was less in danger of falling than flying off the asteroid altogether. It was still a very real danger. The kill-team would lose precious time hunting for him and Felbaine could even become irretrievable in the asteroid belt. A member lost before the operation even began would be a particularly ill omen.

The thoughts raced through Courlanth's head in less time than it takes to tell it. He ached to give direction but he had ordered comm-silence from the outset and was loath to be the one to break it. This was Courlanth's first real test of trust for the kill-team. All of them were members of the Emperor's finest and should be able to resolve the crisis without any orders from him. He was not to be disappointed.

Maxillus was closest and lunged forward without hesitation. The Ultramarine grabbed Felbaine's flailing arm and planted both of his feet and his other hand in a three-point stance for maximum traction. With Maxillus anchoring him, Felbaine managed to bring his own momentum under control and get his own boots properly down on the surface just at the edge of the chasm. Thucyid and Gottrand took up immediate overwatch positions and left Maxillus to his work when they saw what was happening. In less than three seconds, the situation was under control again with nothing but a floating cloud of dust and grit to betray Felbaine's misstep of a moment before.

Courlanth snapped his own attention back towards the pirate lair, looking for any sign that their landing had been seen. No alarm signals rippled the airwaves, no alerted guards appeared above the lip of the chasm; everything seemed quiet. The sergeant released a breath he hadn't realised he had been holding, hearing it whisper away through the tubes of his rebreather. He held up his gauntleted hand with palm outward and fingers spread to order the team to spread out. The kill-team silently moved apart and began to advance with him in low, loping bounds across the rocks.

Within minutes they had reached upper gantries that led down into the valley. Courlanth now had a clear view of a dozen system ships berthed untidily around it. The smallest was no more than a dozen metres in length while the largest was more than a hundred. The ships had the appearance of a selection of haulers and luggers that had been converted for more nefarious activities. They were bedecked with auxiliary engines, covered in crudely painted skulls and had prows barbed with antennae. The landing platforms the ships sat upon dominated all of the other structures in view. Near each platform shutter-like metal doors were sunk into the rock, this last presumably being airlocks leading to underground tunnels.

Courlanth scanned around carefully but he could see no signs of life. Gottrand pointed to his own eye-pieces and then to a set of landing platforms on the far side of the valley. After a few seconds Courlanth detected movement there: an open hatch in the flank of a ship and moving shadows that indicated men at work just out of sight. Felbaine signalled for his attention and moved closer to touch helmets with him. By using direct resonance they were able to talk with no risk of detection.

'The spirit of my auspex-scanner was somewhat disgruntled after my terrible landing,' Felbaine explained, 'but I believe that we're safe to use our communicators. We've passed inside their sensor net and I've found nothing that would pick us up this close.'

'You "believe?"' Courlanth said warily. 'I need certainties, Felbaine, not to risk discovery because you've made another mistake.' He saw the Techmarine tense inside his armour and regretted his harsh words immediately. Courlanth had spoken to Felbaine as he would have done to a Chapter Brother of the Howling Griffons – short and direct, unafraid to offer challenge or criticism. But within the confines of the kill-team, where every battle-brother consciously or unconsciously felt himself to be representing the honour of his own Chapter, it had been too much.

'I am certain our communications won't be detected,' Felbaine replied stiffly, 'but there is always a risk. The decision is yours.'

Felbaine was already castigating himself over his mistake in the landing and criticism had only added fuel to the fires of martyrdom. Courlanth turned back to the squad, struggling to think of how to reassure Felbaine that he still had his sergeant's trust. After a moment the Howling Griffon pointed to the side of his helmet and spoke via communicator.

'Communications cleared for use. Report in.'

'Gottrand, ready.' A small wolf icon sprang into being within Courlanth's autosenses as the Blood Claw spoke.

'Thucyid, ready.' A clenched fist appeared beside the wolf.

'Maxillus, ready.' An Omega sign joined the row of icons.

'Felbaine... ready.' A small sunburst completed the row.

The icons flashed as the suit's communication systems tested their signal strengths and returned a positive green across all of them. When he was satisfied that all was well, Courlanth began rapidly issuing his orders.

'We're here and the enemy has no idea of our presence, so we still have the advantage of surprise. No guards are visible so we'll take ourselves across to the occupied ship on the landing platform and find some prisoners there to question about the rest of the complex. Felbaine, I want you to place melta bombs on the other ships we pass and set them to a forty-minute delay. Take Maxillus with you to guard your back. Gottrand, Thucyid, you're with me. Any questions?'

Silence.

'Move out.'

The five Space Marines split up and disappeared into the shadowy tangle of walkways and gantries. They were rendered almost invisible by their night-black armour and the airless asteroid rendered their progress silent, save for the internal hiss of their retreaters. It seemed as if ghosts of vengeance stalked into the pirates' lair, grim revenants called up to exact retribution for their victims at last.

Buke hauled open the main door into the audience chamber and rushed inside with his robes flapping. Beyond it a wide circular chamber rose in roughly-hewn tiers to a domed ceiling high above. The chamber was the largest open space in Bukehall and many more entrances dotted the upper tiers. Once upon a time it had been the main mining hall, a central hub from which galleries had been cut seeking the rich metal ores of the asteroid. The remains of old mine machines still littered the floor of the chamber, while torn conveyor belts hung uselessly from the upper tiers.

The Discovery had changed everything about Bukehall, changed it completely from the failing mining colony it was then to the pirate den it was now. Directly opposite, Buke could see the open mouth of hell. It looked like just another gallery sunk into the rock from the floor of the chamber. A little wider than the rest perhaps, and maybe a little taller, but unremarkable in itself.

There was no indication that tens, perhaps hundreds of thousands of people had disappeared down that innocuous tunnel and never returned, starting with the first unlucky crew of miners that had been digging it. The weird music was coming out of it, a broken, haunting melody that hovered maddeningly close to the edge of perception.

A dark shape fluttered down from the rocky tiers above to alight on curved claws in front of Buke. The black bird was taller than him and rake-thin, with long limbs that were as narrow as spindles. Magnificent, black-feathered wings extended from above its shoulders to scrape the floor. Dark, malevolent eyes glittered at him from a face dominated by a cruelly hooked beak. The voice that issued from the being was cool, clear and indescribably ancient.

'Buke, Arlon Buke, here to make sure all goes smoothly,' the black bird said, cocking its head to one side. 'You are a wise man, King Arlon Buke.'

'Ha-yes, all the others are coming and the offerings are being brought,' Buke stammered, feeling the sweat running down his face. 'Naturally I came as soon as I heard. We were ready for-for-'

'This one-' the black bird interrupted, pointing a claw to a crumpled, bloody mass on the floor of the chamber. 'This one ran from our presence before the message was delivered. It died horribly. Not all are as wise as Arlon Buke, it seems; not all remember our pacts.'

'I-I remember the pacts we've made with the Crimson Blossom in every detail,' Buke said quickly and succinctly, 'and I regret that my man did not greet you with the proper obeisance, the – ah, the magnificent terror of your appearance must have been too much for him to bear.'

The black bird made a sound but Buke couldn't decide whether it was a snort or a titter as it turned away, flexing its wings noisily.

'May I ask a question to better make preparations to full satisfaction?' Buke ventured tentatively. The predatory, beaked face swung back towards him, half-opened as if in silent laughter.

'Speak your question,' the black bird said.

'What is the music I can hear being played? What is it for?'

'Celebration. A paean to the arrival of one so great that it is necessary to bring beauty as his vanguard into this benighted realm.'

'That's– ah that's wonderful news,' Buke said quietly. 'But what does it mean? Who is coming?'

'Sad, silly king Arlon Buke not to know,' the black bird mocked. 'Rejoice, you are to be in the presence of an archon of High Commorragh within the hour. Pray to your gods and give thanks that you will be permitted to grovel in his presence.'

* * *

As Courlanth crept through the long shadows cast by the pirate ships he got his first good look at them from close quarters. What he had taken for being barbed antennae from a distance were obviously nothing of the kind up close. Felbaine had called them lances and the name was highly appropriate. The xenos weapons were extremely long and slender. They tapered down from a metre-wide bulb-shape at the rear to no more than a hand's-span in width at their tip. The greasy-looking metal they were made of seemed to shimmer oddly between black and olive-green as the light reflected from it. These clearly alien-built weapons were mounted in clusters of twos and threes on the prow plating of the ships, in some cases protruding from holes crudely cut straight through it.

'How are those charges coming along, Felbaine?'

'Almost done, sergeant,' Felbaine's voice replied after a nerve-wracking pause. 'I will not have enough charges to destroy all of the ships, but I have rigged all of the ones along our route satisfactorily.'

'Will the xenos lance-weapons be destroyed?'

'I've placed the melta-charges to cause reactor meltdowns on the ships. I pray that the fires will be intense enough to destroy the alien weapons – they should be by all accounts.'

Courlanth hesitated for a moment. Again Felbaine presented him with uncertainties instead of solid facts, but this time he quelled the urge to demand a more specific answer. The Tech-marine was no doubt simply trying to be as accurate as he could be under the circumstances.

'Good enough,' Courlanth replied. 'Rendezvous with us at the loading dock.'

There were six humans at work inside the ship's hold, although 'work' was a loose definition of their activity. Four stood around watching while two others struggled to free a cargo sled that had spilled part of its load and wedged itself firmly into the rim of the hatch. The four gawkers supplied unhelpful commentary on their comrades' efforts via crude, unencrypted radio.

'Told you – gotta unload the whole thing,' observed one.

'No way you're getting that outta there,' chirped another.

'I already said. Jus' leave it or we're gonna be late,' warned a third.

'...and that'll get us skinned alive for sure,' whined a fourth.

All of the pirates wore light vac-suits that amounted to little more than rubberised coveralls with bubble-like hoods. All were armed with a variety of pistols and vicious-looking knives that were obviously intended to make for a ferocious show. Courlanth surveyed the open hatch critically and decided it would be hard to fit more than one of his fully armoured battle-brothers through it at a time.

'Gottrand, take the lead, I'll cover your back. Remember, I want one alive. Everyone else: overwatch. Gottrand wait – damn it!'

The Space Wolf was already darting out of cover and pounding for the open hatch. Inside it one of the pirates looked up quizzically, some premonition warning him of the danger heading towards him. Gottrand made a powerful leap in the low gravity and slammed both boots full into the wedged cargo sled. His combined mass and momentum popped the sled free like a cork from a bottle and sent it hurtling across the cargo hold. Men scattered with cries of alarm but one was too slow to dodge the caroming sled. He disappeared behind it with a shriek terminated by ugly cracking sounds as it struck the far wall with bone-crushing force.

Gottrand crushed the skull of the first pirate to speak with the butt of his bolt pistol. A split-second later he shot another pirate as they reeled back in horror from the hulking figure that had sprung up in their midst. The mass-reactive bolt went off in the man's chest and burst it open with a spray of gore that blinded the rest. It was an unnecessary nuance. Panic had already gripped the pirates, sending them running and screaming in all directions as they tried to escape.

The Space Wolf's gap-toothed chainsword, *Hjormir*, licked out and slashed through two of the survivors in a single, gory sweep. The last pirate darted around Gottrand and towards the hatch, skidding to a halt as he saw the armoured bulk of Courlanth blocking his path. The pirate opened his mouth to speak – to plead for his life, or curse, or pray – Courlanth never found out. Gottrand's chainsword crashed down through the gore-slicked bubble-hood of the last pirate, its contra-rotating teeth flinging out twin sprays of blood and bone as it chewed through to the spine. Courlanth ground his teeth silently as he bit back anger. The sergeant tried to recall the lesson he had already learned with Felbaine.

'An approach worthy of your Chapter Brothers,' Courlanth grated. 'But what of the prisoner I sought?'

'Fear not, sergeant,' Gottrand replied smugly. 'I had not forgotten.' The Space Wolf dragged the wrecked cargo sled back from the wall to reveal one crushed, mangled, but very much alive pirate behind it. Courlanth slapped aside the autopistol the pirate was trying to raise and seized him by the throat.

'You know that you will die,' Courlanth told the wretch. 'Only the absolution of death will cleanse you of your crimes against the Immortal Emperor of Mankind. You may ease your passing by answering my questions. If you do not, then Gottrand here will crack open your skull and ingest what we need to know from your still-living brain. Do you understand?

'Yes!' the wretch squawked past the grip of Courlanth's steel hard fingers. 'I-I'll tell you anything you want to know!'

'Where did the alien weapons come from? Who maintains them?'

'The Crimsons bring them up from the hell-mouth! When they stop working we take them back and get new ones!'

'Who are these "Crimsons"? Describe them to me.'

'Tall! Thin! Not men! Something older they say, old as daemons! They demand tribute and we give it to them. They give us the guns and lots of red sacra, tell us where to find ships to hit.'

'And what do they demand in return for their help?'

'P-people! All kinds of things, but people most of all! They want slaves to take back to hell with them.'

'You prey upon your fellow men and trade the survivors to xenos as slaves, you deserve a worse death than I have the time to mete out.' Courlanth's fingers tightened inexorably as he struggled to maintain control of himself. 'Now… Tell me where I can find these Crimsons.'

The pirate clan was gathering in the audience chamber in dribs and drabs. They were being slow enough to make Buke nervous and he sent some of his bodyguard off as enforcers to hurry things along. Each crew that arrived dragged along their own tithe for the Crimsons of a dozen or more prisoners chained together. The slave coffles were gradually filling the floor of the chamber in ragged rows. Their suffering generated a low whine of misery throughout the chamber. It had taken Buke some time to notice it, but the sound mingled seamlessly with the weird music emanating from the hell-mouth in a number of disturbing ways.

The black bird had flown up to the tier above the hell-mouth and squatted there, enfolded in its wings like a patient carrion-eater poised over a carcass. It fluttered its wings as the alien music dipped and then swelled suddenly, crying out in a voice modulated so that it cut across the buzzing audience chamber.

'He comes! Grovel before your true master, meat-slaves!' the black bird announced. 'Archon Gharax of the Kabal of the Crimson Blossom approaches!'

Purple light was growing in the hell-mouth, a darkling illumination that seemed to show nothing but shadows. Within it, Buke could see shapes moving, twisted inhuman shapes that were approaching up the tunnel. At the last moment he remembered himself and dropped to his knees, pushing his sweating face down on to the dirt floor. Around the chamber it was as if a silent scythe swept through the other pirates as they all followed Buke's example. The wailing and whimpering of the chained slaves grew more intense as they realised something was happening, the weird music swelling to match it before dropping away to a sudden silence.

'Look up, King Arlon Buke,' the black bird said in hushed tones. 'The archon orders you to meet his gaze.'

Buke looked up from the dirt to see that the hell-mouth was no longer empty. A sinister company of beings now filled it. Each was as inhuman as the black bird but in different ways. There were slender warriors in insect-like armour carrying rail-thin rifles like barbed stingers. There were exotic, half-naked females as alluring as visions from a drug-fuelled dream that bore cruelly hooked knives and a look of awful hunger on their beautiful faces. In the background a trio of hunched, iron-masked creatures clustered around an upright device like a glass-fronted, tube-covered casket at the sight of which Buke was filled with an unspeakable thirst. Beyond them, hulking, furred monsters twice the height of a man filled the hell-mouth with their bulk, their long claws twitching menacingly as they stood quiescent – for now.

At the centre of the horrid company stood two figures who dominated the others as a sun dominates the sky. One was the individual that Buke had dealt with on every occasion previously that the Crimsons had issued from the hell-mouth. This was Maelik Toir. His angular, bone-white face and human-skin robes were not usually a reassuring presence, but on this occasion Buke felt relief to see him. Maelik was the purveyor of many things, most of all the red sacra Buke relied on to maintain his hold over the pirate enclave. Of all the Crimsons Buke had encountered, Maelik was the one who seemed least disgusted at dealing with him, projecting an aura of amused disdain instead of withering contempt.

But Maelik Toir was standing to one side, leaving the centre stage for another that could only be Archon Gharax. The eldar physically stood no taller than the others in his presence, but seemed larger somehow. He was clad in armour like burnished ebony and cloaked with a material so black it seemed to drink light into itself. One hand rested lightly on the gem-encrusted pommel of the long, curving blade sheathed at his side, the other holding a spike-crowned helm evidently just removed. Buke met the gaze of the archon as ordered and found that he could not look away. The alien's pitiless black gaze gripped him like a vice, its crushing presence wringing a gasp from Buke's lungs.

'Impressive, isn't it?' Maelik Toir whispered in his precisely-accented Low Gothic. 'An inheritance from his mother's side – they say that the Lhamaen Yesyr could turn one to stone with the poison of her glance.'

Buke could feel his soul being laid bare beneath the archon's gaze. Every petty malice he had inflicted, every base betrayal he had committed, felt like open pages in the archon's presence. King Arlon

Buke could feel himself being weighed and measured by an intelligence infinitely older and more wicked than his own, his fears, limitations and secrets being picked over and discarded as irrelevances. After what seemed like an eternity, Archon Gharax broke the contact by glancing up toward the higher tiers of the chamber with a faint smile on his face.

'The archon finds you... suitable... to remain in his presence,' Maelik Toir told Buke. 'He will not disgrace himself by giving tongue to slave languages and so will speak through me. Address your replies to me alone, your words will offend his ears.'

Buke grovelled, keeping his face away from the archon's terrible gaze. 'W-we have brought our tithing as promised, illustrious one,' the pirate king stammered. 'We have held up our part in the pact, w-will you uphold yours?'

The words were old, a formula dating back to the Discovery, otherwise Buke would never have dared to use them right now. Maelik Toir nodded approvingly. Men had died horribly for diverging from the words of the pact in the past.

'Yes, Arlon, we will give you what you call the red sacrament in exchange for the slaves you've brought. Let us begin.'

Relieved to have someone else to brutalise, Buke turned on the nearest group of quailing captives and began kicking them to their feet. Stung by a sharp sense of self-preservation other pirates quickly joined him, half-dragging and half-carrying the unfortunates toward the hell-mouth. Maelik Toir examined each captive briefly before sending most onward to be hauled off into the tunnel by the great clawed beasts. One captive was deemed unsuitable and consigned to the casket attended by Maelik's assistants.

Buke and the other pirates salivated to see the machine at work so early in the exchange. The gurgling, reddening tubes surrounding the casket were almost hypnotic as they pumped and purified, distilling drops of the precious red sacra. He had to slap and curse at several of his fellows to remind them to keep the other prisoners moving before they became fractious. Cowed, beaten and emaciated as the prisoners were, even the very dullest of them could see their fate laid out before them now. Many would fight back rather than face being given to the aliens.

The archon stood to one side, surrounded by his warriors and entirely aloof from the proceedings. Buke wondered why the archon had troubled to come as a lord surveying his estates, with no orders to give. He noticed the archon looking expectantly towards the upper tiers of the chamber again and glanced there himself. There was nothing to be seen up there but shadows.

* * *

'We can take them!' Gottrand's guttural sub-vocal whisper came over the comm carrying a thick tocsin accusation with it. Courlanth was failing them as a leader by skulking and hiding when their opponents stood before them. Courlanth was nothing but a contemptible coward.

The kill-team crouched out of sight near the top of the large, circular chamber they had found. Below them were the pirates and their captives. To their left was the contingent of eldar they had just witnessed entering the chamber from a connecting tunnel. The kill-team's view of events was narrow and fish-eyed, a by-product of the fact that Felbaine was using a sensor tendril to spy on them without risk of exposure.

Courlanth stared intently at the view Felbaine was communicating to his own suit's autosenses. By his count at least a dozen eldar were at the tunnel mouth with more behind, with thrice that number of pirates handling the hundreds of prisoners filling the chamber. It was true that the more he delayed the greater the chance they would be discovered became, and yet he hesitated to start a battle that would inevitably kill so many innocents in the cross-fire.

'This is only their meeting point, we have to track them to their lair–' Courlanth began, just as the first wailing prisoners were dragged before the eldar. His heart sank as he saw one of them sent to the torture device the eldar had brought with them. Even now, cold tactical logic would have dictated that the prisoners and even the pirates were of secondary importance to the real goal – that of rooting out the alien. Some in the Deathwatch would sacrifice a million innocents to achieve such a goal without blinking an eye.

But tactical logic could not make it acceptable for Courlanth to sit still and witness aliens torturing and murdering humans at will. He knew the kill-team felt the same way and that only his command had held them back so far. They must act now, even when the logical choice was to wait. Honour demanded it.

Courlanth outlined his plan in a terse series of commands. Wordlessly, Maxillus and Thucyid moved away left and right along the ledge, creeping cautiously to positions where they could maximise their crossfire. Felbaine readied a thick-bodied plasma gun, checking its temperamental coolant rings before setting it to maximal power. Gottrand, for his part, squatted back on his haunches with *Hjormir* in his hands, watching Courlanth expectantly. The Blood Claw had removed his helmet without orders as soon as they had entered the atmosphere-filled tunnels of the asteroid base. Now Gottrand's long braids and coarse beard jutted free in the light gravity, fully lending him the barbaric aspect of his native tribesmen on icy Fenris.

Courlanth hefted his own chainsword and bolt pistol in his hands. He committed his soul to the Emperor with a silent prayer before issuing the final order to begin.

'Execute.'

Thucyid's heavy bolter roared instantly to life, the staccato beat of its fist-sized shells an accompaniment to all that followed. A split second later, Maxillus's bolter added its sharper bark to the thunder of heavy bolts ripping across the chamber.

Courlanth and Gottrand leapt down from the ledge and saw the chamber for the first time with their own eyes. The pale ovals of hundreds of faces stared up at them from the chamber floor, both prisoners and their guards frozen in shock. A few looked up with hope, but most with abject terror at the two black-armoured giants landing in their midst.

'Suffer not the alien to live!' Courlanth shouted, his enhanced voice cutting across the thunder of explosions. His bolt pistol kicked in his hand as it hurled flame-tailed meteors into the nearest pirate guards. Blood sprayed as the explosive bolts punched his chosen targets off their feet with deadly accuracy. Gottrand had already bounded ahead of him, the Blood Claw having leapt down the stepped ledges to the chamber floor with reckless abandon. Courlanth pounded after him, doing his best to avoid crushing the prisoners huddled at his feet.

The chamber was in bedlam, with groups of prisoners turning on their guards while others tried to flee in panic. Panicked pirates were firing indiscriminately in all directions and sometimes cutting each other down in their own crossfire. Even though he felt a few solid slugs rattle off his armour, Courlanth ignored them as he surged after Gottrand. Maxillus was tasked with eliminating the pirates from his vantage point; each bark of his bolter marked another one being pulped by a single bolt round.

The tunnel mouth where the eldar had been gathered was lit by a lurid mass of flames where Thucyid's Inferno rounds had been at work. In the uncertain, flickering light Courlanth briefly glanced lithe eldar bodies twisting and leaping. At that moment Felbaine's plasma gun spoke with a crack like thunder, its actinic blaze flashing down on the eldar torture device like a finger of judgment. The device exploded instantly at the touch of the plasma bolt and sent gobbets of molten matter scything through its attendants. An animalistic howl of pain rang through the chamber, twisting a grim smile onto Courlanth's lips.

Two huge shapes shouldered their way out of the tunnel mouth and rushed at Gottrand. Courlanth recognised the beasts instantly as donorian clawed fiends – alien monstrosities of near legendary size and ferocity. He shouted a warning to the Space Wolf, but giant claws were already sweeping down on him with eye-blurring swiftness.

Arlon Buke had nerved himself up enough to edge a little closer to Maelik's casket in readiness to collect the first harvest of red sacra. It was dangerous stuff to take undiluted – it could kill a man in frothing agony if he took too much – but Buke reasoned he had a good enough tolerance to stand a few drops here and now. He'd earned it, kept up his end of the bargain and dealt with the Crimsons, so he deserved a reward. His mouth, his whole body felt parched in a way that only the red sacra could refresh.

The first explosions surprised Buke so much that he thought some sort of accident had occurred. His instinct for self-preservation threw him to the ground before he had time to think about it. In an instant the scene changed from the more or less orderly handover of slaves to the Crimsons to a roaring, flame-spitting battle. Buke saw a stream of bolter rounds hose across the hell-mouth and splatter it with a wreathe of flames that made it truly worthy of its name. The eldar darted away from the stream of searching bolts with preternatural agility, twisting and leaping incredibly in the low gravity. Some were still caught by the bolts and brutally pounded into bloody, burning ruin but most escaped, scattering among the broken mining machinery in the blink of an eye. The archon swirled his black cloak about himself and vanished with all the alacrity of a stage devil in a morality play.

All around him screams and confusion reigned as the prisoners tried to get away: Curses and shouts among the roar of explosions, the panicky chatter of his clansmen firing their weapons at unseen foes. Buke kept his face in the dirt and crawled towards Maelik's casket, unaware that his rich garb of silk and satin kept him alive as Battle-Brother Maxillus of the Deathwatch methodically picked off the other pirates in the chamber.

Buke raised his face again just in time to see Maelik's casket immolated by a plasma bolt. The delicate structure of metal and crystal shattered outwards as its contents were explosively vaporised. In the same instant, unthinkable pain lashed across one of his eyes and blinded it. He fell back and howled like an animal with the hideous sizzling meat smell of his own burned flesh in his nostrils.

Half-blinded, Buke scrabbled in the dirt with clawing fingers searching for pieces, fragments, anything that might give him hope. Screams and detonations surrounded him but his own world had shrunk to the reach of his arms. His torn hands brushed something smooth and curved that was still hot from the fires. He twisted around trying to focus his one remaining eye on his discovery.

It was a piece of tubing from the casket that was still sealed at one end. His heart leapt to see the tiny puddle of thick red liquid settled in the bottom of it. Weeping and laughing, Buke raised the broken glass to his lips and tilted it back to let the red sacra drop on to his tongue.

Explosions of orgasmic pleasure rolled through his body at the touch of the first drop. The pain from his eye was swept away, lost in a sea of absolute ecstasy. Energy flowed through him, revitalising every part of him from his brain to his glands. Every sense became crystal clear and hyperacute. Buke's pulse pounded in his ears as he struggled to his feet and roared his defiance at the universe. He could feel his muscles rippling, ripening with rich, red blood. He felt strong, stronger than ten men, faster than the wind. Everything he'd experienced from the red sacra before was nothing compared to this.

Buke took a step forwards. Two Space Marines in black armour were in the audience chamber and were cutting their way to the hell-mouth. The Crimson's huge bear-like pets had rushed out of the tunnel to attack them. Bloodlust swept through Buke at the sight. To see Imperial Space Marines, such fearsome giants of legend, dwarfed and overborne by the monsters set his pulse racing even faster. He would join in the victory, tear the hated Space Marines apart with his bare hands and bathe in their blood...

King Arlon Buke sprang forward with his fingers hooked like claws. He rushed into the fray shrieking like a daemon, ducked under the swinging claw of one of his bestial allies and leapt onto one of the Space Marines. The hulking, black-armoured warrior all but ignored Buke, shrugging off his grasp as if the pirate king were nothing but a small and overly rambunctious child. Buke was sent sailing past to land flat on his back beside a ruined mining machine.

Buke roared in frustration and tried to spring to his feet, but at that moment his overwrought heart virtually exploded with the strain it had been placed under. The hyperawareness given to him by the tainted red sacra ensured his dying moments were riven by indescribable agonies that, subjectively at least, lasted a long, long time.

Gottrand attacked the towering fiends like a blood-mad wolverine. A slashing claw of the first fiend was half-severed at the wrist by his long-bladed chainsword, even as his bolt pistol sent round after round ripping into the torso of the second. Courlanth joined the fray, hacking and slashing at the mountainous bulk of the twin monsters. It was as if they hewed at stone, the tough alien flesh resisting blows that would have cleaved a man in two. What injury the Space Marines inflicted seemed only to redouble the monster's fury, putting them in a whirlwind of snapping jaws and reaching claws. They needed help to beat the things quickly.

'Give us supporting fire,' Courlanth ordered. It was a risk to order fire into a melee, but the fiends were big enough to make prominent targets. A split second passed and no supporting fire came in. Gottrand was struck by a blow that sent him reeling, the fiend's claws tearing ragged holes in the Blood Claw's armour.

'Support fire, NOW!' Courlanth snapped as he rushed forward to protect the staggered Space Wolf. Still no bolts came in support. The sergeant realised that Thucyid's heavy bolter no longer sang its song of death.

'Under attack!' Maxillus's voice shouted back urgently. 'Thucyid and Felbaine are down! Poison! They've got–' The comm went dead.

Courlanth's mind reeled as he tried to fend off the gigantic fiends. More than half his team down in moments, what horror had the xenos unleashed? Maxillus had shouted about poison but no toxin should be able to overwhelm a Space Marine's genetic-ally enhanced constitution so quickly. A glancing claw ripped at his shoulder plate and drove him down to one knee.

Courlanth's anger and frustration coiled through him as he surged back to his feet. His chainsword flashed down on the leering, dome-shaped head of the fiend as it leaned in to bite him. Churning monomolecular teeth snarled and spat as they tore their way through the monster's iron-hard cranium before pulping the grey matter inside to slurry. Even brain-panned the monster remained a threat, the reflexive jerk of its claws knocking Courlanth back a dozen metres.

The sergeant skidded to a halt, half-sprawled against a piece of broken machinery and tried to stagger upright. He felt as if he had been hit by a gunship, icons in his autosenses were flashing warning amber as they began to take stock of his armour's condition. He looked up to see Gottrand plunge his sword, *Hjormir*, into the other fiend with an eviscerating uppercut.

Gottrand did not withdraw his blade, instead dropping his bolt pistol so that he could heave the whirling chainsword upward with both hands. The furred giant collapsed, gripping the Space Wolf with its claws in an effort to crush him against its chest, but only succeeding in driving the blade ever deeper. Gottrand staggered free covered virtually head to foot in foul alien ichor.

The sudden silence that enfolded the scene was broken only by the crackle of flames and the moans of the injured. Courlanth looked quickly up to the ledge where Maxillus and the rest of the kill-team should have been, but he could see only shadows.

'Grip like an ice troll,' Gottrand muttered unsteadily. Courlanth saw the Space Wolf's scalp was laid open to the bone, and blood had slicked his braids into a thick mass. There was also the hint of stealthy movements in the shadows, meaning the eldar had not fled. They were still here and they were stalking the two surviving members of the Deathwatch kill-team. An unfamiliar chill ran down Courlanth's spine at the thought.

'Gottrand, we have to get back to the others, I–' Courlanth began before a barrage of shots swept across them. Hypervelocity needles rang off their armour in a scatter of ceramite chips and plasteel fragments. Decades of training took over as both Space Marines moved instantly to attack their assailants. Lithe figures sprang up to bar their path, wild and half-naked eldar that fought with the ferocity of daemons.

Gottrand was rapidly surrounded by darting combatants, his two-handed swings with *Hjormir* too slow and cumbersome to connect with his opponents. As Courlanth turned to assist he barely saw a blade flashing in at his side and had to twist desperately to avoid it. He turned to confront an eldar that seemed to have sprung from nowhere. The alien was clad in polished, insectoid armour with a spike-crowned helm, a black cloak swirling about its shoulders as it wielded a curved blade with fearsome speed and precision.

'My archon wishes you to know that it is Archon Gharax of the Crimson Blossoms that delivers your doom,' a voice called out in precisely accented Low Gothic from another part of the chamber. 'You should feel honoured.'

'Alien scum,' snarled Courlanth in response. 'You will all die!'

'Never, and certainly not by your hand, *sergeant*,' the voice gloated.

Courlanth fought with every ounce of his fury and skill, but the archon quite simply outmatched him. The sergeant felt like a stumbling child as he struggled after the elusive figure, every slash and shot was evaded without seeming effort, while every riposte the archon made left a new gouge in Courlanth's armour. Warning icons were flaring amber and red at the edges of his vision. The alien was toying with him, Courlanth was sure, and the thought of it drove him to new heights of rage.

The sergeant unleashed a furious whirlwind of blows with his chainsword, forcing his opponent to skip backwards a few paces. In the momentary breathing space he snapped open a frequency to the *Xenos Purgatio*.

'Lochos! Immediate kill-team extraction,' Courlanth was sickened by the thought of retreat but his duty was clear. The kill-team had failed and now the Exterminatus weapons on the strike cruiser must be unleashed to obliterate the pirate's nest once and for all. Something dark, terrible and corrupt had taken root in the Teramus system and Courlanth felt shame that it was beyond his strength to overcome it.

Only the hiss of static could be heard through the link. Inhuman laughter rang through the chamber.

'My archon insists that you remain,' the taunting voice called, 'after so much trouble has been taken to bring you here.'

The archon darted forward, deflecting Courlanth's swing with a thrust that slipped inexorably in beneath his guard. The sergeant felt the impact of the point piercing his armoured shell and sheathing itself in his guts. He felt the blade grate against bone as it was withdrawn as quickly as insect's stinger. Courlanth had been injured in worse ways before but this felt completely different. Icy numbness spread out from the wound site and didn't stop spreading. Poison!

The speed of it shocked him. Within a few heartbeats his whole body was unresponsive. The ground lurched beneath Courlanth as his legs buckled and blackness rushed into his sight. His last impressions were of falling forever.

Sight returned, at first without colour, vague splotches of light and shade in a moving pastiche. Courlanth's fogged mind tried to make sense of the scene. He was on his side with his helmet gone and his arms locked somehow behind him. Near him other figures in black armour lay prone on the rocky ground and he could see that their arms and legs were manacled. The sergeant could vaguely feel blood oozing sluggishly from his gut-wound and decided that meant that only a short time had passed. Such a wound would have been fully sealed by his superhuman constitution otherwise.

More detail swam into focus. Nearby was a curious structure, a tall arch of twisted silver and bone that was filled with multicoloured mists. Courlanth recognised it as a warp portal, a gateway into the inter-dimensional pathways the degenerate eldar used to move themselves around the galaxy. Such artefacts were always a curse wherever they turned up. This one had no doubt been lost for millennia until the unwitting asteroid miners unearthed it. Loyal citizens would have reported their discovery but the temptations offered by the eldar had corrupted the miners, turning them into slavers and pirates.

Lithe eldar shapes were moving around the warp gate. One, noting Courlanth's movement, turned and came closer. The sergeant saw a bone-white, angular face as it bent over him with a triumphant grin on its narrow lips.

'Simply amazing, the recuperative properties of your kind,' it said with what seemed genuine affection. It was using the same precisely accented Low Gothic that taunted Courlanth during his battle with the archon. 'After centuries of study you can still surprise me on occasion.'

Courlanth did his best to spit into the face before him but he could only drool. The alien carried on as if it were talking to a pet.

'You're probably thinking this was all for you, aren't you? That we planned to trap some *Deathwatch* here – well, you would be right. Give out some weapons and it's only a matter of time, as I told dear Archon Gharax, before the alien hunters arrive. You see, in Commorragh we have an insatiable hunger for diversion and your kind, your perfect, genetically-enhanced, muscle-bound kind, make for some of the best diversions this tired old galaxy has to offer.

'You will be taken from here to fight and die for our entertainment in the arenas, save perhaps for one or two of you that I will take for my own experiments. My toxin was pleasingly effective on this occasion, but that's no reason to neglect perfect–'

A sudden explosion of white light half-blinded Courlanth and cut off the alien's gloating in mid-sentence. The continuous hammer of bolter-fire split the air in the aftermath, mass-reactive bolts pulping the angular bone-white face in a shower of gore. The sergeant looked up to see figures in black Terminator armour towering above him, the twin flames of their storm bolters stabbing relentlessly as they cut a swath through the shocked eldar. The silver skull of the Deathwatch gleamed on every shoulder. In their midst, the grim face of watch captain Ska Mordentodt cracked in a rare smile as he and his men ruthlessly purged the aliens.

When the bodies were counted Archon Gharax was not found amongst them. Maxillus was dead, killed by a reaction to the toxins brewed by the eldar haemonculus Maelik Toir, while Felbaine was paralysed from the waist down by a spinal injury. The other members of the kill-team responded well to the Brother-Apothecary's ministrations and could stand on their own feet before Ska Mordentodt.

'Remember this day, brothers, teleport homers work better to summon aid than retreat,' the watch captain began.

'You used us as bait,' Courlanth said. He could not keep the bitterness from his words.

'I saved your lives,' Mordentodt reminded him, 'and many others besides by locating the gate. One less hole for the eldar to creep in through and the universe becomes a better place.'

'But why not tell us we had help to call upon at need? Maxillus is dead and Felbaine crippled!'

'The alien has a thousand times a thousand ways to glean such knowledge from you; what chance then of them leading us straight to their most secret places? They had to believe you defeated, just as you had to believe yourselves defeated.' Mordentodt shrugged.

'You volunteered for the mission without any such promises – if I have lied to you it is by giving you help you had no right to expect.'

'So this is the way of the Deathwatch – secrets within our own ranks – never knowing why or when we may be sacrificed to further some other design?'

'This is the way of the Deathwatch,' Mordentodt agreed.

ONYX
CHRIS WRAIGHT

Kaivon had always considered Valmar's Gorge a fortunate posting. He made good money, which he was able to transfer back to his family on Herephalomos Tertius. He planned to work for another two years or so, relying on the crackly vid-bursts of his two daughters and single son that arrived on data-slates with each six-month deep-void transport to keep him sane.

It was hard graft, working the lifters that carried the ore up from the mine-face and into the greedy maws of the processing hoppers. Dangerous, too – the infirmary was usually full of broken limbs, respiratory problems, the occasional cloth-covered corpse – but then everything worth doing, he had always told himself, carried danger with it. The priests reminded them of that often enough, and he paid attention to what the priests told him, and so worked harder.

In any case, there wasn't much else to do on Valmar's Gorge besides work, sleep, and listen to devotional screeds. The rest of the workers, men and women both, were just like him – scraping together enough of a nest-egg to set up somewhere more civilised, keeping sweat-dripped heads low, working the machinery, thinking of better times ahead.

They would come. They all knew that.

The mining installation was small by the ancient standards of the Phalomos ore-belt – a single building cluster occupying a speck on the rocky face of the deep-void asteroid Valmar. There had once been dozens of similar stations – Valmar Primus, Valmar's Edge, Saint Violetta, Karlspar Magna – but they had been mined out over the centuries, and were now abandoned to emptiness. Only

Valmar's Gorge remained in operation, though all knew that even there the workings would one day wind down.

Kaivon occasionally speculated on what would happen when all the worlds of the galaxy had been exploited. The quantity of minerals in the charted Imperium must once have seemed infinite, though he had overheard mutterings from overseers that supplies of all but the most abundant raw materials were becoming harder to locate. Humanity's peerless fecundity, its endless wars and voracious appetites had, over ten thousand years, done the near-impossible and depleted what had once seemed limitless.

Still, that mattered little to him. He was twenty-nine standard years old and, if lucky, could expect to live for twenty more. He'd be reunited with Janna in time, and the children, and they'd petition for a work-slot on an agri-commune, using the product of his labours to procure passage, permits and grease the palms of the officials where necessary.

It was a good plan. It was sober and considered. It was industrious. He was doing his duty and advancing the cause of his family, just as the Imperial cult demanded. Kaivon had every reason to believe that it would cause him to prosper.

The installation itself clung like a limpet to the inner cliff-edge of a vast caldera of gouged rock. The chasm below, broken open by ancient tectonic movements, delved into the very heart of the obsidian-dark asteroid, its edges limned only faintly by a distant sun. Valmar's Gorge was a motley collection of constructions, dominated by the colossal shell of the processing foundries. Mined ores were funnelled into the receiving end via hundreds of trackways, beyond which kilometres-long manufactories beat, sorted, hammered and refined the contents into usable ingots. At the far end of the production lines lay the lifter stations, each capable of berthing massive Grade IX ore-carriers.

The station's accommodation section was tiny in comparison. The main domed assembly hall was capable of holding the roughly five thousand workers who were stationed on the Gorge's edge at any time. Radiating out from that hub were the administratum buildings, the infirmary, the comms station, the chapel complex, the armoury, then the long, grim lines of dormitory blocks. It was all covered and insulated, for Valmar's old terraformed atmosphere was now barely thick enough to breathe. The installation was a precarious thing, established with the sole objective of sucking up the vital resources needed to keep the starships and hive-spires of the Imperium functioning.

One day they all knew it would be gone. All of them believed that day would be a long way off.

Kaivon was returning to his dorm-unit after a five-hour shift at the ore face when it happened.

He was covered in a thick layer of dust, and, as ever, wanted nothing more than a scrape-shower, to dump his fatigues in the corner of his hab-unit and crawl into his bunk. Every muscle throbbed with lactic acid, and his head was beginning to ache. If he could summon the energy, he might take a detour to the infirmary and see if he could grab some anti-inflamm from the dispenser he'd become friendly with.

As he reeled down the corridor with the drunken fatigue-walk that all off-shifters affected, the sodium lamps set in the walls suddenly flickered out. Kaivon stood still, surprised. He could hear the breathing of the other workers around him, all doing the same thing.

Then the lights came on again. Kaivon found that he'd been holding his breath. That surprised him – it was just a power fluctuation.

'End of the world,' said the woman next to him wryly.

'Yeah,' said Kaivon.

He'd got to the end of the corridor and into the dorm-unit's antechamber before the lights failed again. This time, they didn't come back on. Instead, emergency lumens glowed up from the floor, red and flickery.

Now he was unnerved. Everyone else in the antechamber did the same thing – look stupidly up at the low ceiling where the lumens were now unlit. Why were they doing that?

Then he heard it. It was a like the wind moaning across the distant rooftops, except that Valmar's meagre atmosphere had no winds. Something about that noise chilled Kaivon to his stomach – it was like nothing he'd ever heard before, not even on vid-reels.

He went over to a cogitator pillar placed at the centre of the antechamber. It was a communal facility, one capable of patching into the installation grid and showing up processing movements and carrier positions. He brought the pict screen into life and punched in the command for a full system overview.

For a moment, he thought that the system might have gone down with the main lighting grid, as the readings made no sense to him – there were location markers shooting all over the installation schematic, whirring in and out of life like insects. They might have been flyers, but for their speed – nothing moved that fast.

Then he heard a crash from deep in the heart of the installation, followed by more high-pitched whines. An alert klaxon started to sound and was quickly silenced. The emergency lights flickered badly, threatening to plunge them all into darkness.

Kaivon felt his heart thumping hard. Something about what was happening scared the hell out of him. The others, too – they were already hurrying for their dorm-units, shouting contradictory things about core-breaches or processor malfunctions.

Kaivon didn't follow them in. There were procedures for events like this, protocols to be followed. He started to run, jogging back down the corridor he'd walked along, heading towards the installation's heart. If there had been some major systems failure then they had to congregate in the main assembly area and await instruction. He tried to ignore the sweat on his palms as he went. Why was he so scared?

As he closed in on the station centre, he saw that others had had the same idea, and soon dozens of ore-workers and administratum staff were jostling to get into the assembly hall's outer chambers. More crashes made the walls shake, and the high-pitched whine began to mask out all other sounds. Kaivon heard people shouting – or was it shrieking? – from both ahead and behind. He began to doubt whether he was doing the right thing. Perhaps he should have stayed in the dorm-cluster and waited for more data from central command, but by then it was too late, and he was being carried along by the crowds.

They all broke into the domed assembly area, and Kaivon instantly found himself gagging. The air felt painfully thin, as if the hall's outer skin had been pierced and the compensators hadn't kicked in yet. He looked up, towards the high curved roof that covered the main seating area, and his heart missed a beat. A perfectly circular hole had been burned into the apex, and there were intruders streaking down to ground-level on lengths of gossamer-thin wire.

For a moment, all he could do was stare at them. They were outlandish figures, oddly compelling, kitted out in glossy black plate armour with tall, smooth helms. At first Kaivon thought they were human, until he saw the way they moved.

He tried to back up then, to push his way into the doorway again and out of the hall, but the press of bodies kept pushing him inward. More armoured figures emerged, seeming to spin out of the air like black twists of lightning. Crackles of cold energy snaked across the chamber's width, followed by the stink of ammonia.

Kaivon began to panic. Others around him shoved and jostled, and the whole mob surged further in. As they did so, the intruders opened fire.

Their slender-barrelled rifles were near-silent but the projectiles were deadly. Kaivon saw the man in front of him ripped into shreds by a rain of razor-sharp slivers. The dying man's blood splattered hotly across his face, shocking him into immobility.

By then the screaming had started in earnest. Kaivon did what everyone else did – frantically kicked his way through the masses to get out. More bodies exploded around him, throwing blood up against the walls. He heard laughter, but it wasn't human. He was screaming himself by then, tearing at those around him to get to the safety of the doorway. Somehow, propelled by the energy of sheer terror, he made it to the portal before the razor-shards caught up with him, and he stumbled over the threshold.

As he broke clear of the hall, he risked a last look over his shoulder. The intruders were now at floor level and opening fire with their shard-guns. Others were swooping into the crowds on grav-boards, grabbing their prey and hauling them up into the heights. The xenos were killing, but not quickly or cleanly. They were enjoying themselves.

He ran on, feeling vomit rise in his gorge. He staggered down the feeder corridor, knowing they'd be after him soon, knowing he couldn't possibly escape them. As he gave in to primordial urges, running like an animal, only one cogent thought flashed through his terrorised mind.

Why us?

The chamber was lit intriguingly. Inquisitor Aoart Halliafiore of the Ordo Xenos, was a man who enjoyed the theatre of the clandestine, and every station he oversaw was kitted out in an almost parodic image of the secretive. Shadows pooled and clustered. Sigils nestled under the faint glow of lanterns, tracing old lineages back to the distant days of pre-Crusade Terra. Perhaps he even knew what they signified. It was not impossible; the Inquisition had a long memory.

He was a thin, spare man who wore finely tailored robes. The only badge of office he allowed himself was an iron aquila icon on his left breast; otherwise, he could have been any courtier on any civilised world. His skin was smooth, almost youthful despite his several centuries' service, and he had tight features, the result of over-aggressive rejuvenat work. His movements were measured, precise and contained.

He stood in the centre of a circular chamber, illuminated by a single shaft of blue light. Seven giants stood around him, each towering over the slight figure in their midst. They wore black armour, relatively unadorned, in the Mk VII pattern. Only the right pauldrons varied, giving away the Chapter origins of the squad-members: Ultramarines, Dark Angels, Blood Angels, Executioners, Angels Puissant, Iron Shades, Space Wolves. They were helm-less, which was the only other source of variation. Callimachus of the Ultramarines, the squad leader, had a close-cropped, blocky visage. Jocelyn of the Dark Angels wore his dark hair long. The Blood Angel Leonides's pale skin looked almost ghostly in the low light.

Ingvar of the Space Wolves struggled to maintain the icy composure of his brothers. Halliafiore's mannerisms wore at his nerves. The mortal was so quiet, so dry, half-dead, hardly worthy of a warrior's attention. The others were nearly as bad. They were deadly – he had trained with them long enough to know that – but they were... bloodless. None of them, not even the Blood Angel, truly had the rage, the heart.

Perhaps that would come out during the mission. It felt like he had been waiting months for it to come, though it was hard to mark the passage of time in the lightless tunnels of an Inquisitorial fortress.

'This is your target,' said Halliafiore, summoning up a ghostly hololith from his outstretched palm. It showed a schematic star-cluster. Several of the systems were marked with a death's head. 'The Phalamos Belt. Value to the Imperium: production of raw materials, rhodium, magnesium, sundry rare earths. Predated by xenotype eldar, sub-species tertius, for nine standard years. Seven installations lost. Three hive worlds raided, resulting in heavy loss of life and, more to the point, frequent interruption of tithe production.'

The inquisitor's manner, more suited to a scrivener than a lord of the Allfather's everlasting realm, never ceased to grate.

'Study the pattern,' Halliafiore said. 'What do you note?'

Ingvar looked at the star-map, and saw nothing but a trail of destruction. The raid-marks all had a date-stamp on them, which told him nothing.

Xatasch, the spectral member of the Iron Shades Chapter, was the first to respond. 'The mark is incomplete,' he said in his near-whisper.

Halliafiore nodded. 'Elaborate.'

'Xenotype datum 347,' said Xatasch, recalling the element of Deathwatch training pertinent to the species. 'Attack-patterns subordinate to aesthetic considerations. The breed takes pleasure from marking the void in certain symbolic forms. They are tracing a rune.'

The hololith zoomed in, homing down to a point on the edge of the attack distribution. Soon it showed a single point – a remote asteroid bearing the ident 'Valmar'.

'This completes the symbol,' said Halliafiore. 'Xenosavants identify it as the rune yllianua, known to be significant for seven eldar factions operating in the subsector. One of these is of particular interest, given the physical presence, so reports allege, of a flesh-twister.'

Flesh-twister. The colloquial name for the xenos subtype haemonculus, identified in Inquisitorial intelligence as being part of the species' command hierarchy. To catch one on the battlefield was rare, for their attacks were so rapid and so well-coordinated that few records were ever left behind. Ingvar remembered the scarce scraps of vid-footage he'd been shown in orientation training – grainy images of warped, hunched grotesques floating on suspensor cushions, their long clocks hanging with hooks. The purpose of the haemonculi was not fully understood, though it was clear that they were the often the architects of the raids, and therefore the primary target for retribution.

'Then we know where they will strike,' said Callimachus. 'We can protect it.'

The Ultramarine was always keen to propose the squad's course of action, as if itching to gain the inquisitor's approval. Ingvar loathed that and was pleased to see Halliafiore give Callimachus a disdainful look.

'Do you think they would strike, if we were known to be protecting the station?' he asked.

Callimachus glanced at the installation statistics, undeterred. 'Its annual tithe production is significant. Its loss will harm weapon production in the subsector.'

Halliafiore gave him a tight smile that said stop talking now. 'The flesh-twister is the target. It will be disabled, contained and brought here, to be placed under the instruments of information-extraction. All other considerations are negligible.'

The inquisitor turned his pristine visage to the rest of them, looking at them in turn. 'Your first mission, Onyx,' he said, using their squad designation. 'Always a delicate time. Greater tests will come, should you perform adequately.' Hallifiore fixed Ingvar with a particularly lingering gaze. 'Operate as a unit. Do not deviate from the mission parameters.'

He smiled for a final time, just as mirthlessly and perfunctorily as before.

'The Emperor protects,' he said, which told them all that the briefing was at an end.

Tallia ran down the corridor, pushing past the bodies around her. They had lost their heads, all of them, giving into a kind of herd-like panic at the first sign of trouble. Throne, they disgusted her. There were standing orders to follow. In her service in Phalamos's militia she'd had the importance of discipline drilled into her, and the old habits hadn't quite gone away. At forty years of age, and having seen plenty of foulness on the battlefield, she was better equipped to deal with what had just happened on Valmar than most of her counterparts.

The whole place was now slippery with blood. The xenos were beginning to move through the complex. They worked incredibly quick. The Emperor only knew what had happened to the automatic defence grid – it seemed to have shut down as soon as the enemy arrived, perhaps jammed by some forbidden xenotech, or – as was entirely possible – maintained so badly it had failed to detect the incoming threats at all.

Tallia swore aloud in frustration. Valmar's Gorge was such a backwater – she should have arranged a transfer back to Tertius months ago.

She skidded around the last corner before the comms-array chamber, and the volume of bodies lessened. They were all running the other way now, down towards the armoury to kit themselves out and lock themselves in. That was pointless, and would do little but slow the inevitable. The only chance, to the extent that any still existed, was to call for help.

The slide-doors of the comms-chamber were open and gaping. Tallia threw herself inside and punched the lock controls. The doors hissed closed behind her, sealing her into the perfectly dark interior. As the bolts clicked home, she scrabbled around for a lumen activator. Her fingers closed over the controls and she depressed the switch.

Carmine emergency lights flickered briefly, showing up a circular space dominated by a central console. She caught a glimpse of equipment lockers running around the edge of the far wall, each one several metres tall and wide, enough to house the racks of spare machinery needed by the array. Beyond that was the transmission room, stocked with standard message canisters. All she needed to do was get there, slot a distress canister into the proper cogitator housing and activate the transport. It would be relayed through the system network in seconds, hopefully being picked up by a Guard patrol before they were all wiped out.

She stumbled through to the transmission room, tripping on cables snaking across the floor, and the lights blew again. Cursing, she felt her way forward, running her hands over the equipment ahead of her. She traced the outlines of the central console and hurried around it towards the transmission room doorway. Guessing she'd come far enough, she edged out into the dark, her arms outstretched. Her fingers brushed against the door-frame, and she clung on tight.

Too late, she realised that no door-frame was that smooth.

With a lurch of horror, she tried to jerk away from it. A slender fist clasped tightly around her wrist, hauling her back. Two jewelled eyes, slanted like a snake's, glowed in the dark before her.

How long had it been there? Had it been waiting for her the whole time? Or could they even slip through locked doors?

She saw a blade flicker up towards her in the cold blue light of the glowing eye-lenses, and a soft, alien breath from behind a twisted metal vox-grille. It was taking its time.

Tallia hauled with all her might, yanking her arm free with a sudden burst of strength that surprised even her. She managed to scramble away from the creature, falling on to all fours and scrabbling away in panic. Somehow she found the inner doorway in the dark, and scampered through it. Behind her, she could hear a delighted hiss of pleasure and a soft swish as the xenos followed her in.

The emergency lights snapped on again, for just a split-second, showing up the interior of the transmission room. One of the equipment lockers stood open, a black gulf in the otherwise uniform walls.

Then the darkness returned, and she felt the cold grip of an alien hand around her ankle.

She screamed. Terror lodged deep in her psyche ripped the sound from her throat, and though she thrashed again, this time the grip was secure.

For some reason, though, the expected dagger-strike never came. She kept on screaming long after the vice at her ankle relaxed. She would have screamed further, had a metal gauntlet not been clamped over her mouth.

'Be silent,' came a grinding, vox-deepened voice close to her face.

Tallia opened her eyes. A black helm loomed over her, different from the one the xenos had worn. It was far larger, built with the angular bulkiness that marked all Imperial construction. Even in the almost complete darkness, broken only by the faint glow of the lenses above her, she knew what that helm represented.

She could have wept. If it had not been for the crushing sense of awe, she could have grabbed hold of the monster crouching over her and hugged him. As it was, it took all of her scant remaining wits not to move and to do as he had told her.

'We must transmit,' she urged, whispering as she gestured towards the comms mechanism.

The Space Marine rose, activating his armour-lumens so she could see, and shook his head. 'Negative. They believe they are undisturbed.'

He stowed the shortsword he'd used to gut the xenos warrior, and drew his bolter from its holster. As he did so, Tallia noticed the blue-and-white pauldron on his otherwise perfectly black armour. The Space Marine reached into the open equipment locker, located a lasgun, checked the charge and threw it over to her.

'Stay here,' he ordered. 'Do not activate the comms. If they come back, defend yourself with this.'

Tallia nodded mutely. The aura of command possessed by the Space Marine was absolute – if he had ordered her to charge back into the living hell of the assembly area, she would have complied.

'By the Emperor,' she managed to stammer, 'thank you.'

He looked down at her strangely, as if he didn't quite understand. Then he turned and stalked through the outer doors, already searching for the next target.

The empty ore storage hoppers were lined with 50 millimetre-thick adamantium. No light or sound penetrated their interior, and even augur readings were subject to interference. Remaining stationary for six weeks inside those coffin-like spaces had required the partial use of sus-an immersion to shut down peripheral bodily functions, but they had mostly remained conscious, mentally reciting battle-litanies and tactical outlines to remain sharp.

Ingvar had found it harder than the others. He was closeted with Leonides and Prion, neither of whom were troubled by the long inactivity. Prion was complete in himself, perfectly content to slip into the long trance knowing that it would be followed by explosive action. He was a siege specialist, used to boarding actions in the genestealer-infested Aymar Belt, and had spent literally years cooped up in the creaking holds of immense space hulks. Leonides, by contrast, simply enjoyed the subterfuge. Like all Blood Angels, he had a deep-grained appreciation for intrigue, birthed from Baal's complex and radiation-soured culture. Perhaps the hopper reminded him of the coffin-capsule he had once emerged from.

For Ingvar, though, it was torment. He was unable to fully lapse into complete immersion and spent long days waiting fruitlessly for the call to arms. At times he felt close to ripping the locks free and blasting out of the ignominious hiding place, roaring out his defiance before the startled looks of the menials around him.

But that would only have reinforced the verdict his brothers had already formed of him: rash, barbaric and insular.

When the order came, though, flashed across his helm display, he could have screamed with relief.

Operation commences. Enact retrieval action.

Prion stirred instantly, coughing slightly as he swam to full consciousness. Leonides took a moment longer, struggling against the deep trance before snapping back into focus. Ingvar's helm quickly lit up with Xatasch and Vhorr's locator-signals, just a few metres away.

'At last,' he growled, reaching for the locks and slamming them free. The hopper's shell cracked open and cantilevered clear. Ingvar was the first out, grabbing the hopper's edge and swinging himself over. He landed heavily, his muscles sluggish after weeks of inactivity.

Leonides landed next to him more expertly. 'Rusty?' the Blood Angel asked.

Ingvar ignored him and pulled his bolter from his belt. Six of Onyx squad were in a mined-out section of the installation's underbelly, at least three hundred metres above the main workings but a long way below the inhabited sections. Insertion into the unused cavern had been easy enough, given the station's meagre defences and the sloppy guard-rotation, and there had not been a sniff of disturbance since.

From the far side of the cavern, the other two emerged, their black armour glistening from helm-lumens. Ingvar had already learned to identify his battle-brothers solely from the way they carried themselves – Vhorr strutting, Prion heavy, Leonides lithe, Xatasch like a liquid shadow. All of them carried stalker bolters with attached silencers and Deathwatch-issue rounds that would explode with no more noise than a fist crunching into flesh.

They ran their checks and final weapon-rites efficiently, in moments, ensuring the mechanisms were free of defect. Ingvar was still getting used to the sheer perfection of Deathwatch wargear – he had been shocked to discover just how far it outmatched his old Fenrisian battleplate. In it, his senses were sharper, his movements smoother, his reactions even quicker.

'All done?' asked Vhorr, blunt as ever, eager to be going. Ingvar liked Vhorr.

Leonides ran an augur sweep of the levels above. In Callimachus's absence, he was in command. 'Objective located,' he reported calmly. 'Multiple targets, moving out from ingress point. *Shade* incoming. Suffer not the xenos to live.'

They repeated the mantra, then broke out into the dark, heading for the heavy ore-lifts that would take them up into the heart of hell.

Callimachus sped through the dark corridors, the way ahead lit up with his helm's false-colour images. There were no mortals out in the open now. Those who had bolted for the sanctuary of the main assembly hall were already dead or rounded up; the rest were being culled at the xenos' leisure. The squad had precious little time: the entire assault would be over in minutes, after which no ship in the Imperium would be able to catch the fleeing xenos landing craft.

He reached an intersection and crouched against the nearside wall, listening. Standard power armour was audible even to mortal human ears, but his was as quiet as the tech-adepts of the ordo could make it, and if used with care might just fool even a xenos' hearing for the necessary microseconds.

Proximity scans revealed nothing, so his slipped around the corner and ran towards the main dorm-unit antechambers. The volume of screaming was decreasing, which was bad news – the xenos were getting through their prey quickly.

The corridor turned sharply. Beyond the corner, fifty metres ahead of him, he saw the first of them – a slender figure, two metres tall in armour, its helm splattered with gore and skulls of different sizes clattering from chains at its belt. Three humans trailed behind it, blind in the dark, their wrists manacled and spikes driven between their bleeding lips. The eldar warrior had just disabled another and was stooping to shackle its prey for delivery.

Callimachus aimed and fired in one movement, striking the eldar in the chest and hurling it back against the wall. The bolt-round punched through the creature's breastplate, exploding with a wet pop and cracking the shell from within.

A second later and Callimachus was standing over it. He placed the bolter-muzzle against the creature's forehead and fired again. The xenos's head exploded, throwing black brain-matter across the floor.

Two of its human prey stretched their chained hands out to him, moaning weakly as they tried to part bloody lips. Callimachus glanced down at them, just for a fraction of a heartbeat.

That was enough. Another xenos warrior opened fire as it raced down the corridor towards him, moving in a blur of speed, leaping from wall to wall as it came. Callimachus's armour took hits, showered with projectiles that scythed through the upper layer of ceramite.

He fired back one-handed, reaching for his blade, but the xenos closed too quickly, bounding into him and lashing out with a flickering sword. Callimachus missed with his shot and only just managed to parry with his blade. Up close, the eldar's movements were astonishing – like a snake striking, it punched out with its own hooked blade, gouging deep into his pauldron, before loosing a second flurry of shard-projectiles at point-blank range.

One of Callimachus's helm-lenses shattered, and he felt the hiss of cabling rupturing. He swung hard, using his greater bulk in place of speed, and managed to smash the barrels of the xenos' rifle. That didn't slow his enemy, who slashed across Callimachus's breastplate, driving him back with a whirl of ink-dark steel. Callimachus, off-balance, crunched into the corridor's near wall, just managing to block a swipe at his throat. The defence left him exposed, and the xenos whipped a blade-strike into his chest.

The edge never cut. The eldar was blown sideways, limbs bent like a crushed spider. More bolt-rounds slammed into it, pulverising what remained of the brittle armour-shell.

Callimachus looked up to see Ingvar and Vhorr crouched down at the far end of the corridor, both bolters still trained on the eldar's twitching body. He pushed clear of the wall, bent down and cut the xenos's neck.

That had been too close. He would have to learn from it.

'*Shade* incoming?' he asked calmly, noting the interference from his damaged armour-augurs.

Vhorr nodded, as Ingvar, bristling with palpable battle-anger, swept his bolter muzzle back down the other direction. The two of them backed up towards him.

'Two minutes,' said Vhorr.

'They have mustered in the assembly hall,' said Callimachus, setting off. As he did so, the shackled humans on the floor started moaning again.

If there had been time Callimachus would have helped them, but there was none and he kept going. As he did so, Ingvar pushed past him.

'Space Wolf...' warned Callimachus, but it was too late. Ingvar broke the mortals' bonds with his own hands, twisting the metal shackles into pieces. Then he stood up again and looked at Callimachus defiantly.

Callimachus felt the old frustrations flare up instantly. The Space Wolf was impossible to command, chafing against every imposition of authority like a caged beast pacing the bars. He did it to provoke, to challenge and demonstrate his superiority to the orders that bound them.

Savage.

'We move now,' he ordered again, setting off, filing away the slight for another day. 'No more delays.'

Kaivon couldn't stop weeping. As he crawled along the air-duct passages, scraping against the hot metal in the dark, the tears streamed down his face.

The things he'd seen. The things he'd heard. It was burned into his mind now, flash-frames of horror he would never be able to erase. There just shouldn't have been that much cruelty in the universe – and for what? Why did they do it?

He'd seen dead men before, and he'd seen some bad things in the lower hive-levels, but nothing, nothing, compared with what he'd witnessed back in the hab-units. Even when he screwed his eyes closed he still couldn't shift the images of torn skin, the sutures being pulled tight, the extractions, the incisions, the long gouges...

Enough. He had to find a way to get out. He tried to fix his mind on Janna, the family, the old friends back on Tertius, anything to keep his limbs moving and his mind from seizing up.

He'd somehow managed to break free of the central hub, though he was one of only a handful that had done so. There were only a few dozen of the xenos, but they appeared to be everywhere at once, throwing bolas and spiked netting and hauling dozens of human prey at a time.

Right at the end, just before he'd managed to break into the cramped network of air-ducts, he'd seen the worst one of them all, hovering over the entire flesh-carnival like a corrupted saint in a devotional picter. That one had been more twisted than the rest, clad in a cloak of skins and draped with chain-length hooks. Kaivon had seen a withered face, as dry as ash, and eyes that radiated such chilling ennui that his heart had almost stopped beating. The monster had been gazing over the slaughter with a kind of dull-eyed, scientific curiosity, deaf to the horrific tide of screaming.

After that, Kaivon had just run, and run, and run. He knew the ducts wouldn't keep them out for long, but there was nowhere else left to go. He had no idea where he'd crawled to – perhaps over the comms station? Or the chapel units?

He stopped, listening hard. His own heartbeat thudded in his ears, hard and erratic.

For a moment, he thought he'd managed to get away. Then, with a lurch that made him want to gag, he heard the scratching from further down the duct. It was already close, and getting closer. He imagined his pursuer – scrabbling like a spider up the narrow twists, the needles held ready and a collar to drag him back with.

Kaivon pressed on doggedly, fighting against the raw panic that threatened to freeze him up completely. He saw a break ahead, a maintenance panel that he could lift up and drop through. He scurried over to it, fumbling as he tried to lift the security catch.

From behind, the scrabbling got closer, echoing up the shaft, surely no more than a few metres behind him now. His fingers shook, and he slipped on the catch, expecting at any minute to feel the touch of cold fingers on his ankles.

He heard a thin chuckle just as the last catch broke free. There was a thin whine, like a weapon powering up, and the panel broke open.

Kaivon dropped through the duct's floor, carried down by the panel's fall. As he fell, an intense heat passed over him, and he detected the stink of melting metal.

Then he hit the floor, hard. It was a four metre drop, and it nearly stunned him. He reeled, tasting blood in his mouth, knowing his pursuer was right on his heels. He tried to twist onto his back, to at least see what was coming after him, but then agonising pain spiked through his left shoulder. Something thin and metallic had speared him, pinning him to the metal floor. He craned his head, and saw something black, almost insectoid, crouching in the gap in the ceiling. It was going to leap, to follow him down. It was already reaching for something that looked like a cluster of hypodermics.

As he screamed out his terror, he barely noticed the las-beams whipping up from floor-level, one after the other, all aimed with unerring precision. The xenos's armour deflected some of them, but the volume of fire was too much, and it tumbled from the gap, crashing to the floor next to Kaivon.

Kaivon pushed himself away, crying out in pain as his shoulder ripped free from the barbed spear, and shuffled away from the xenos's corpse. In his bewilderment, he had no idea where the las-shots had come from – the chamber was dark, lit only by flickering emergency lumens, and all he saw were more shadows.

'Get away from it,' hissed a woman's voice from floor-level, over by the wall.

Kaivon did as he was told. The woman edged gingerly over to the downed xenos, aimed her weapon carefully at its head, and send another four las-blasts into it. Soon the stench of burning flesh, subtly different to human aromas, filled the chamber.

The woman turned to him. Kaivon was trembling so badly by then it was hard to even focus on her. He was in shock, and couldn't kick himself out of it.

'Any others?' she demanded.

Kaivon could only shake his head. He had no idea.

Tallia hefted her lasgun, unclipping the charge pack and slamming in another. 'Stay down. If any more try to follow, they'll get the same.'

Ingvar broke into the central hub, flanked by Callimachus and Vhorr. For a moment, just a fraction of a second, even his psycho-conditioned senses rebelled.

The domed roof was broken, neatly breached at the apex. Long chains hung down from a circular hole, each one hauling a struggling body up into the gap. More than a hundred humans were being extracted, all impaled on the chains like fish on a line. Many more victims were waiting at floor-level in improvised pens, all of them bearing signs of recent mutilation. The stench of faecal matter and sweat mingled with toxic aromas from the xenos' chem-weapons. Blood and filth swilled freely across the floor, the slick studded with floating eyeballs.

Twenty eldar were corralling the slave-chains, lashing out with barbed whips that sliced chunks of flesh from the shivering victims. Rows of eviscerated corpses hung on hooks from the vaults, their empty rib cages twisting in the thin air, slopping trails of gore to the floor below. The chamber had been turned into a charnel-vision of utter depravity, a slaughterhouse stocked with human meat.

Ingvar's hunt-sense kicked in. The three Deathwatch Space Marines opened fire, each picking his target. At the same time, Prion, Xatasch and Leonides burst in from the far side of the hall and did the same, filling the space with the soft whoosh and thud of stealth-shells impacting.

Taken by surprise, several eldar were downed outright. More were felled as they tried to extract themselves from their torturing, and the numbers rapidly evened.

Ingvar leapt across a railing and ran into the centre of the hall, firing all the while. He saw Leonides charge towards one of the lead slave-takers, peppering its slender body with round after round until the armour blew apart in flecks of ebony. Callimachus, Vhorr and Prion maintained ranged fire, picking out the eldar with merciless accuracy, while Xatasch moved silently to block the far exit.

The xenos had been caught, their attention focused on whatever rites they had come to enact. Even with their peerless reactions, it took time to switch from torture instruments and take up their splinter weaponry.

Ingvar had been told not to use his Fenrisian battle cries on the operation, but as he charged towards them his throat unlocked in a ragged howl of fury. He kept on firing, whirling through the meagre projectile hail that the xenos mustered, smashing his way through the broken seats of the old assembly chamber and towards the nearest enemy. The eldar warrior tried to get a blade up at his throat, but by then Ingvar's momentum was unstoppable – he crashed into it, punching out with his gauntlet and shattering the creature's fragile carapace. His fist plunged up into its viscera, and he hoisted it clear from the floor, bellowing death-curses as its foul blood rained down on him.

'Vlka Fenryka!' he roared, hurling its broken corpse away and sending it slamming into the edge of an overturned torture-slab with satisfaction.

As he tensed to charge on into the remaining xenos, his helm-display flashed with a single command – flesh-twister – and his head snapped up.

The haemonculus emerged into the open, ascending from the piled-high bodies at the centre of the hall. It soared high above the bloody floor, its hide-cloak twisting under the buffeting lift of suspensor columns. All six Space Marines immediately opened fire, and its skeletal body was shrouded in explosions.

That didn't stop it – bolter-detonations splash-patterned across some kind of energy-field. Ingvar could see an impossibly aged face in snatches within, glaring at them with pure contempt. It made some kind of gesture, and the chains hauling bodies up to the dome's aperture fell away, coiling down to the floor in clanging spirals.

The few remaining eldar warriors fought back then, launching splinter-volleys at the Space Marines, but their challenge was no longer significant. Vhorr and Prion filled the chamber with wide-scatter bolter-fire to lock them down while the others pursued the haemonculus.

Leonides was quickest, firing the whole time as he leapt up to grasp at the xenos's chain-tails. His gauntlet grasped on to a flailing length of metal, but his whole body immediately spasmed with fork-lightning, and he slammed to the floor, his armour steaming.

Ingvar ran over to him, scanning for life-signs even as he maintained fire on the haemonculus above. By then, Leonides was already dragging himself back to his feet.

'It's got some tricks,' rasped the Blood Angel, hefting his bolter again.

'As do we,' hissed Xatasch, reaching for a bulbous object at his weapon-belt, one that looked more eldritch and alien than anything else in the chamber. He primed it with a flick, then hurled it at the haemonculus. Before the creature could react, it exploded in a whirl of neon, sending a blast-pattern sheeting out in radial spirals.

The haemonculus's energy-field shattered, exploding like glass, and something like a high-pitched wail broke out amid the carnage. It plummeted, thrashing out with prehensile hook-chains even as Xatasch's arcane weaponry ate through its protective aegis.

Callimachus was already in position, hefting a claw-shaped weapon that looked to have been carved from ivory. He trained its sights on the haemonculus and opened fire just as the creature crashed back to earth. A flare of eye-burning light enveloped the struggling xenos, enclosing it in what looked like rapidly-solidifying crystal. It cried out words that none of them could understand in a voice that sounded like iron nails being dragged across granite. Then the crystalline lattice entirely engulfed it, ending both its screeching and its movements.

When the debris of Xatasch's weapon had subsided, they could see the result – a solid-mass stasis field, with the haemonculus caught in its centre like a wasp in amber. Its outraged scream was frozen on its face, lost amid translucent layers of xenotech.

Ingvar still hated to see that – witch-weapons, forbidden to all but the servants of the ordo. Bolter and blade should have been enough. There was no time to regret their use, though, for with the capture of the haemonculus the remaining eldar warriors were roused into a frenzy. As if their lives depended on it, they came clawing back into the fight. Reinforcements from the rest of the installation came careering back into the hall through unguarded entrances around its edge, cartwheeling and pirouetting as they fired their deadly armour-cutting ammunition.

'Defensive,' ordered Callimachus, hefting his bolter again and laying down a fresh wave of fire.

The Onyx squad members retreated towards the centre of the hall, drawing back to where the haemonculus's stasis-enclosed body lay on the floor surrounded by stray slivers of electric-discharge. As they ceded ground, those humans still capable of speaking cried out for aid, reaching out with bloody hand stumps and eyeless faces. They knew that the bringers of pain were coming among them again, and what sanity remained in them forced them to cleave to the deliverers that had arrived so suddenly.

Ingvar hunkered down next to Vhorr, and the two of them launched bolter-round after bolter-round into the enemy. It felt like they'd already killed all the xenos in the installation, but more emerged all the time, spinning into view as if bursting out of the rockcrete itself. Their already balletic fight-style took on a frenzied edge as they weaved and ducked through the hurricane of shells to get at their prize.

Ingvar watched his ammo-counter tick down to zero, and instinctively reached for his blade. He'd already seen how quickly Callimachus had been outmatched, and relished trying some sword-work out for himself.

Just a little closer... he thought, watching the nearest xenos dance towards him.

Then a massive explosion ripped the roof apart in a cloud of shattering metal and armourglass. A heavy, thudding sound followed, growing louder as the debris bounced around them. The xenos were hurled back, knocked from their feet by the downdraft of enormous engines.

Ingvar didn't need to look up to know what was descending through the annihilated roof-dome. A second later, heavy bolter-fire opened up, carving through the surviving xenos and blasting their fragile outlines into explosive clots of blood and armour-shards. The whole chamber drummed with the rubble of the Thunderhawk's descent, stirred up by the hurricane of the gunship's arrival.

'So, you have something for me?' came Jocelyn's sardonic voice over the squad-comm.

'Open it up,' snapped Callimachus, backing towards the haemonculus's cocoon.

Only then did Ingvar look up. The ink-black outline of the *Shade* hung less than ten metres above them, filling a large chunk of the assembly hall's broken dome and labouring on atmospheric thrusters. Like all Deathwatch-issue craft, it was kitted out with bulky archaeotech artefacts along its flanks, and the only insignia was the deathshead sigil of the Ordo Xenos. Its sponson-mounted heavy bolters juddered on full-power, ripping apart any surviving eldar careless enough to keep moving. As the guns swept the hall, the far walls were lost in blooms of dust and blown masonry.

The gunship dropped down further, and with a screech of metal on metal the fore crew-bay door swung down, revealing an illuminated interior lined with esoteric field-amplifiers. An open casket lay within, twice the height of a man, connected by lengths of cable to the hull.

Once the gunship was hovering two metres up, Callimachus and Leonides leapt into the crew-bay, boosted by their armour-servos. Lengths of adamantium chains clattered down, fastened to the haemonculus's stasis-cocoon by Xatasch and Prion. Ingvar and Vhorr kept up the punishing barrage of shells until their ammo-counters finally clicked empty.

'We leave,' voxed Callimachus from the gunship's interior.

The haemonculus was hoisted into the crew-bay and secured within the casket. Working quickly and expertly, Leonides fastened a series of probes to the exterior of the crystal, and lights began to flicker along the edge of the instruments. By then the others had hoisted themselves up into the gunship's interior.

Ingvar was the last to leave. He looked around the hall for a final time, his attention snagged by the scene of complete destruction. The remnants of the old Imperial architecture slumped amid the pools of blood left by the torturers. Hooks and eviscerators swung from what remained of the ceiling-arch, glistening from the gobbets of flesh still attached.

'Space Wolf,' growled Callimachus.

Ingvar pulled himself over the edge of the crew-bay door and away from the gore-swilled floor. As he did so, the hatch-pistons hissed and pulled tight, closing off his view. *Shade* powered up its thrusters, and lurched towards the broken-tooth edge of what had been the hall's roof.

By the time Ingvar had clambered up into *Shade*'s cockpit, the Thunderhawk was high above the installation. From the nearside real-view portal he could see the sprawling structure clinging to the obsidian surface of the asteroid. There was very little sign of damage, save for the shattered dome of the assembly hall. The far vaster ore-workings were entirely intact, and the gunship's sensors reported the full functioning of all life-support systems.

Five hundred metres away, smouldering gently in Valmar's thin atmosphere, lay the remains of a xenos starship. Its vanes and sails were crumpled, and its swollen hull was open to the elements.

Jocelyn grunted with satisfaction as he powered past the downed eldar vessel. 'It was fast,' he remarked, 'but fragile.'

Ingvar studied the wreckage carefully. The human prey had been herded into it during the assault, hauled through the roof like raw meat. Presumably most were still inside the lightless hold, perhaps alive, or perhaps succumbing to the wounds they had suffered.

Every fibre of his being strained to go back, to at least cut them loose. As *Shade* gained height, the window for opportunity was shrinking quickly.

'I know what you are thinking,' said Callimachus, sitting next to him in the cramped cockpit.

Ingvar looked at him. The Ultramarine's helm had been ravaged by the xenos shard-weapons, and it would take the artificers weeks to restore it. The tone of Callimachus's voice was just as it always was – reasonable, calm, phlegmatic. If Ingvar had defied his commander on Fenris in the way he had done with Callimachus down in the corridors, he would have new scars to adorn the old. That was what infuriated him so much – the reasonableness.

'We could secure the station,' Ingvar said, already knowing all the arguments against but unable not to at least protest. 'Alert the Guard, get them help.'

Callimachus shook his head. 'Mission orders,' he said, though there was no great satisfaction in his voice. 'The system's authorities will respond. They must not know we were here.'

Ingvar's irritation flared up again, and he was about to tell Callimachus what he thought of mission orders when a warning alarm chimed from the command console. Jocelyn immediately banked the Thunderhawk hard to the right and brought it back down close to the asteroid's surface.

'Incoming,' the Dark Angel reported, powering up the gunship's weapons again.

On the far side of the curved horizon, more than one signal had been picked up. They were closing with tell-tale speed – no Imperial vessels moved that fast.

'Xenos, fighter-class,' said Ingvar, taking in the tactical reading and reaching for the gunnery controls. 'We can down them.'

There were four blips on the augurs, nothing that *Shade* couldn't handle. It was just as Jocelyn had said – they were fast, but they were fragile.

'Negative,' ordered Callimachus. 'Resume exit trajectory, full velocity.'

Jocelyn did as he was ordered, and the Thunderhawk screamed along at low-level, leaving the installation far behind.

'We're running?' demanded Ingvar, disbelieving.

Callimachus nodded. 'We are.'

'They'll finish what they started,' protested Ingvar. 'They'll harvest them.'

Callimachus turned on him. Through the broken helm-lens, Ingvar thought he could see an anguished expression on the Ultramarine's face, but it was hard to tell.

'We have what we came for,' Callimachus said. 'Nothing will be allowed to jeopardise that.'

'*Skítja*, we can take them out!'

Callimachus snapped his gauntlet out, catching Ingvar on the chest and slamming him back into the cockpit's inner wall. 'And that is your answer to everything, is it not, Space Wolf?' he snarled. 'Nothing you can't fight, nothing you can't kill.' He shook his head disgustedly. 'They will keep coming, and the longer we stay, the more will come. They bend space in on itself. You know this.'

Callimachus let go. Ingvar's first instinct was a strike out in turn, to avenge the insult, to establish his place in the squad. It was what he would have done on Fenris. If he hadn't, he would not have lasted a week in the packs.

But the Ultramarine had already turned away from him, ready to assist Jocelyn in the task at hand. *Shade* was powering clear at full thrust now, its huge engines augmented with all the forbidden technology the ordo had at its disposal. The pilots had more to worry about than him.

Ingvar, feeling his blood pumping in his temples, glanced down at the tactical display. The xenos craft had pulled out of the pursuit, and had returned to the installation. They were already descending on the ruined dome, no doubt preparing the ground for landing parties.

There was no going back now. *Shade* would make the rendezvous with Halliafiore's command ship as planned, on schedule and with no casualties to report. The flesh-twister would be delivered alive to the tender mercies of the interrogators, and over long decades imprisoned in the void-shielded depths of the Inquisition's darkest oubliette-fortresses would have priceless information extracted.

It was a valuable prize, one worth celebrating. That knowledge would save countless more installations, and ones worth much more to the Imperium than Valmar's Gorge.

Ingvar punched the wall hard, denting the metal and sending a clang resounding around the cockpit's interior. None of the others so much as looked at him – they were already busy with course-plotting, or securing the cargo in place, or just reflecting on a clean first mission.

He imagined how it would be if he could have gone back. He would have drawn his blade and taken on the xenos, bringing them down one by one. They would have come in their dozens, and he would have slaughtered them in their dozens. If they had brought him down, it would have been a fine death, standing between them and the mortals like the warrior-kings of the old ice.

They would be inside the perimeter by now. They would be creeping back through the corridors, their needles already withdrawn and their dark minds turning to vengeance.

Ingvar turned off the scanner. He could already picture Halliafiore's sleek, satisfied face welcoming them back, and more than anything else he had seen on Valmar's Gorge, he knew it would make him sick to his stomach.

The comms room remained dark. Both of them had heard explosions for a long time, like grenades going off. Then there had been the huge booming noise, like a starship coming to land, that had made the whole station shake. They'd felt a massive impact, like a hammer blow against the asteroid's core.

Then, for a while, nothing.

Kaivon was the first to speak. 'Do you think they've done it?' he whispered.

Tallia and he were both crouched in the flickered dark. She still had her lasgun trained on the air-duct opening, her eyes locked on to it with impressive dedication.

Kaivon admired that. She was everything that he wasn't – disciplined, focused. He could hardly stop shaking still, and every time he blinked he saw again the horrible sights that made him want to start weeping again.

Eventually, Tallia relaxed. She lowered the weapon by a fraction, though she kept her finger tight on the trigger.

'They've done it then, have they?' asked Kaivon again, anxious and urgent. He wished he'd seen one of them himself now – an Angel of Death, just as the stories said they were, emerging at the time of darkest need, the protectors of the faithful, the guardians of the immortal soul of humanity.

'He said to stay here,' said Tallia, warily.

Kaivon scrambled to his feet. He found that moving helped him a little. If he started to walk, the trembling ebbed slightly. 'They must have killed them all,' he said, his voice picking up. 'Praise the Emperor!'

Tallia tried to grab him, to haul him back down, but missed the edge of his jacket. 'Remain still!' she hissed.

By then, Kaivon wasn't listening. A kind of euphoria had taken over, an ecstatic release from the vice of fear and nausea that had clamped on him since the first inklings that something was wrong.

He edged into the larger chamber beyond, the one with the central column where Tallia had dragged the two xenos bodies up against the walls. They held little fear for him now, for the true masters of battle were in the station now, and with all his remaining strength Kaivon determined that he would at least lay eyes on them.

They had to be thanked. They had to know, even if it only lasted seconds, that he was grateful, and that their arrival had vindicated every scrap of faith that he had ever possessed, for it was one thing for the priests to tell them that the Emperor's Angels would always be there for them, but it was another thing to have it demonstrated.

He reached the outer door, and paused. The lights had been partially restored on the far side, and he could see a ribbon of red glowing around the joints. Something was moving outside, coming towards the doors. He saw the light broken.

He found himself suddenly unwilling to open the lock. Suddenly, the fear returned, as sharp and debilitating as before.

'Don't open the door!' hissed Tallia, staying where she was and keeping the lasgun trained for firing. 'Get back here!'

He didn't know why he still reached for the lock mechanism. He saw his hand moving long before he realised what he was doing, and the portal slid open.

Tallia opened fire, sending lasbeams fizzing past him and into the dark. A return burst of splinter-shards ended the barrage, somehow missing him entirely and whistling into the chamber beyond. Tallia gurgled and gagged, and the lasbeams ceased.

Kaivon stood perfectly still, his eyes wide, his limbs frozen. Before him, in the dark, hung two glowing lenses, like a snake's eyes. He heard the faint sound of alien breath coming from a glossy mask.

He wanted to scream, but no sound came from his mouth. He wanted to resist as the hooks and the collar came towards him, but his body no longer obeyed his mind's commands.

If he'd had any wits left, he would have wished for death to come quickly, but from somewhere, deep down, despite all the choking fear that consumed him again and made his thoughts sluggish, Kaivon knew that he would be alive yet for a very long time indeed.

As the first of the hooks went in, he couldn't even close his eyes.

MACHINE SPIRIT

NICK KYME

'Tracking…'

The gruff voice issued through a mouth grille, reverberating inside the warrior's battle-helm. Gauntleted fingers rimed with dried blood, the black ceramite chipped from hand-to-hand combat, twisted a dial on the magnoculars.

'Wait…'

A slew of data came through the scopes. The myopic visual of a white, trackless desert was augmented by a scrolling commentary describing wind speed and directionality, mineral composition, temperature and atmospherics in truncated rune-script. The most salient piece of intel was revealed in the hazy image return, however.

Squalls of armour-abrading calcite were whipping across endless dunes farther out, presaging another storm. The more dangerous hazard had yet to reveal itself, but Zaeus knew it was there.

He grunted, annoyed and trying to marshal his temper.

'Any sign, Brother Zaeus?' asked another voice, one partially obscured by the rising wind. What began as a zephyr had developed into a gale.

The more cultured speaker was crouched below Zaeus in a shallow calcite basin where the rest of the kill-team had taken refuge. He looked up expectantly at the Brazen Minotaur through the burning coals of his eyes. An orange drake head upon a black field on his right shoulder guard marked him as a Salamander, and he was supporting a third warrior who carried the sigil of the Imperial Fists. A fourth knelt in silent vigil beside them both, head bowed, while the last of their group was laid in still repose nearby.

'Weather's impeding visual feed,' Zaeus muttered, careful to mask his fatigue. He adjusted the dials again, using small movements that looked too delicate for such a hulking brute.

Despite their power armour, he was more broad-shouldered than the others and his chin jutted as if set in a challenge, even encased by a battle-helm.

Distant shadow figures, like patches of blurred ink on a canvas, resolved through the growing blizzard. The grain and rock whipped about within it *plinked* against Zaeus's shoulder guards. It wore at the gold trim and cracked the black bull icon against its field of flaking white.

Some of the shadow figures were larger than the others, gene-bulked by carapace and outfitted with forearm blades. Zaeus's stomach clenched, as did his jaw, as he remembered the fate of Brother Festaron. The former Star Phantom had killed a swath of the creatures before they'd gutted him. A greater mass of the less developed aliens moved slowly behind the hulks, bowed against the wind. Their avian war-cries, altered slightly by the hybridisation of the thorax, were just audible.

Zaeus counted at least fifty, but he knew there were more. He made a mental note of the ammunition left in his cache. Thirteen hellfire, four kraken rounds, three metal storm and two tangle-web. Including two clips of standard mass-reactive, it wasn't much.

'They have our spoor now,' he told the others.

He reckoned on over three hundred. The kill-team's present condition removed 'combat engagement' as a mission option. It only left 'harass and retreat'. That irritated the Brazen Minotaur like a thorn under a nail and he growled.

'I feel it too, brother,' said Ar'gan, the Salamander. 'The desire to burn them to ash.'

Zaeus lowered the magnoculars and headed back down into the basin where the others were waiting.

'Carfax will be expecting us,' he said, referring to their pilot.

The kneeling warrior, Vortan, looked up from his litany as Zaeus's shadow fell across him.

'How many?' he asked, voice grating, getting to his feet. Vortan was of the Marines Malevolent, and carried a winged bolt of lightning against a yellow background on his guard. He was also a miserable bastard, but hard as adamantium.

Zaeus stopped, racked his bolter's slide, but didn't turn. He wore a bulky armature fitted to his power pack, a servo-arm that flexed in simpatico with his body's movements.

'We will be meeting the Emperor if we stay to find out,' he said.

Vortan sneered, hefting a belt feed around his waist and attaching it to his heavy cannon. 'Fleeing from xenos scum...' He shook his head. 'It's beneath us.'

The Brazen Minotaur sniffed noncommittally, 'Then I shall see you again at the foot of the Golden Throne, brother.' He checked his ammo gauge. 'My count is low,' he muttered, stooping to grab a length of chain looped around Festaron's torso.

Zaeus grunted, and began to heave the body. The trail left by the dead Star Phantom was quickly absorbed by the drifts of calcite. At least his blood wouldn't give them away. Not that it really mattered.

'We should move. Use the storm as cover,' he said, increasing his pace. 'Ar'gan?'

The Salamander was helping up Captain Polino. Both went without battle-helms, and Ar'gan's red eyes flared like hellfires in the blizzard. His face was like a slab of onyx. It stuck out, but then they all did, wearing Deathwatch black.

'So much for the line of Dorn,' Polino rasped, flecking his ashen lips with blood. The Imperial Fist turned moribund, and as he leaned heavily against Ar'gan's shoulder said, 'I'm sorry, brother... I led us to this.'

Hunters had become the hunted, their elite kill-team in danger of extermination by the very filth they were supposed to have already neutralised.

Ar'gan's tone was conciliatory. 'None of us, not even you, Captain Polino, could have anticipated what we found in that nest, their immunity to the nerve toxin.' He nodded to the armoured corpse of Festaron and the fist-sized puncture wound in his breastplate. The Deathwatch had sealed it with a binding solution that kept what was inside dormant. 'But soon the truth here will be exposed and end the Imperium's treaty with the tau by unleashing the wrath of the Inquisition.'

'Only if we escape this Throne-forsaken desert before we share the same demise as our eviscerated comrade,' said Vortan.

Zaeus kept his own counsel. War with the tau had been ongoing for months with no sign of inroads on either side. Negotiation was sought, but certain interested parties within the Inquisition were keen to avoid that. A single kill-team had been dispatched to eliminate the bulk of the alien's forces – a faction of avian mercenaries designated *krootis aviana* by Imperial taxonomers – through the utilisation of an Ordo Xenos nerve toxin that would remove them as a threat. Without their mercenary horde, the tau would be unable to match the Imperium on a war footing. That the nerve toxin had proven less than efficacious grated on the Brazen Minotaur, even if its failure did mean he and his comrades had unearthed a greater threat in their midst.

The Marine Malevolent was still venting. 'We should have broken into that council session and executed every single one of those grey-fleshed dung-eaters.'

'The Imperial officers would have resisted us,' said Zaeus.

'They would have been next before my guns.'

Zaeus believed him. The Marine Malevolent was a singular warrior, driven and harsh to the point of brutality, but he saw only in absolutes and so his view was oft narrow.

Vortan glanced at the Imperial Fist, whispering to Ar'gan, *'He slows us,'* before he looked at the Star Phantom being dragged by Zaeus. *'They both do.'*

As if to make Vortan's point, Captain Polino staggered and would have fallen if not for Ar'gan. Pain reduced his voice to a rasp between clenched teeth.

'Keep moving...'

Ar'gan gave Vortan a dark look that was both a reproach and suggested their captain wasn't going to last much longer. They needed to find Carfax and the gunship before the hunters found them.

Vortan shrugged, engaging the suspensors on his heavy bolter that allowed him to move as fast as the others in his kill-team, even whilst encumbered.

He marched ahead to take point. 'Give me a bearing, Zaeus.'

It was tough to get a reading with so much environmental interference. The retinal lenses of all the helmeted Space Marines were fraught with static, and ghosted with false returns and feedback.

Heat signatures were non-existent and visual confirmation of landmarks, geography or enemies was reduced to almost point-blank. The data stream through scopes or retinal feed was scrambled, useless. But the Brazen Minotaur possessed much better auspex than his brothers, and could cut through the fog of static easily. He sub-vocalised the coordinates of the rendezvous point relative to their position and ex-loaded them to Vortan's lens display.

'I have it,' said the Marine Malevolent. 'Advancing.'

Ar'gan's voice came through Zaeus's comm-feed, low and full of distaste.

'He would sacrifice them both for the mission.'

'As would I, son of Vulkan,' Zaeus replied, 'as should you.' He half-glanced over his shoulder at the Salamander.

'But he is callous to a sharpened edge, brother. We all must be pragmatic, but what Vortan suggests is disrespectful.'

'He is of the Marines Malevolent, and therefore practical to the point of being an utter bastard. I thought your Chapter was familiar with their ways?'

Ar'gan's tone grew darker and there was a scowl in his words, 'That we are, but I cannot condone–'

'Hsst!' Zaeus raised a clenched fist for silence. 'Stop.' It was an order to the entire kill-team, even Captain Polino. The Imperial

Fist was all but incapacitated; as Techmarine, the Brazen Minotaur was next in command.

'Brother?' Vortan asked warily through the feed.

Intensifying storm winds were making it tough to hear, but Zaeus had reacted to something.

The Brazen Minotaur's entire left side, all the way down to his abdomen, was cybernetic, sacrificed to the Machine-God and the glory of the Omnissiah. As well as granting phenomenal strength and endurance, his augmentations also included superlative hearing courtesy of a bionic ear.

Zaeus arched his neck towards the skies. After four seconds, he shouted out, 'Incoming!'

Kraken rounds scudded through the storm-drift, chewing off pieces of carapace that fell in chunks. Vortan heard the creature bleat before it ditched into a nearby dune. Ar'gan was already moving low with his combat-blade drawn. It was acid-edged, fashioned to slice through hardened xenos-chitin like air. The creature was bleeding, one wing broken, the other shredded and incapable of flight when he found it. A jet of caustic bile spewed from its maw, but the Salamander warded it off with his vambrace before ramming the blade into the insect's throat. It shuddered once and was still.

From the shallow ridge, Vortan bellowed, 'More coming!' The *dug-dug* staccato of armour-piercing heavy bolter rounds joined a muzzle flash that spat from the cannon's smoke-blackened mouth. Two of the flyers were cut apart, exploding in a shower of viscous gore that coated Ar'gan's armour.

The Salamander scowled at his battle-brother, but the Marine Malevolent was laughing, loud and raucously. When the cannon *chanked* empty and the belt feed ran slack, his humour evaporated as he went for his sidearm. Before he could slip the pistol from its holster, a stingwing arrowed towards him, flesh-hooks extended. Vortan used the heavy bolter like a club and smacked the creature head-on, crushing its snout and most of its skull. He stamped on its neck, finishing it off.

Zaeus stayed at Polino's side, and also watched over the corpse of Festaron, who would be like carrion to the flyers. The injured captain was doing his best to keep upright, and snapped off loose shots with his bolter.

'Herd them to me if you can, brother-captain,' said Zaeus, eyes keen as he discerned a jagged shape arcing through the drifts. An ululating challenge, foul with alien cadence, resonated from a stingwing's throat as it dived hungrily.

'Here, filth!' Zaeus spat, and swung his servo-arm. The mechanical clamps seized the creature's neck in mid-flight, piling on the pressure until the reinforced chitin buckled and its head came off with a snap. Gore spewed across the Brazen Minotaur's battle-plate, scoring the metal and acid-burning it down to raw grey. Through his bionic, he performed a split-second analysis.

'High concentrations of sulphuric and hydrochloric acid,' he related to the data-corder in his helmet. 'Trace elements of alkali, potential hydrogen levels fourteen or greater. Extremely corrosive, and inconsistent with the bio-strains in-loaded to the kill-team mission brief.'

This he catalogued whilst bringing down another stingwing with a snap shot from his bolter. The designation came from the xenos datacore identified: *tau*. Countless others filled the hard-wired cogitator arrays of the Iron Fortress watch station where Zaeus and his comrades were currently barracked. Interrogating the data from the mission brief and cross-referencing it with previous engagements, he noticed an inter-species correlation with a second organism class.

Tyrannic.

The xeno-form, 'stingwing', was a mutated strain corrupted by genetic hybridisation. It could explain why the nerve toxin had failed, and why the kill-team were running for their lives.

'They're still coming,' breathed Polino.

Zaeus gave him a glance. The Imperial Fist was flagging, his left hand perpetually pressed against his torso. Dark blood flowed freely from the wound through Polino's fingers as his Larraman cells lost the battle against whatever anti-coagulating agents were rife in his dead attacker's bodily juices.

'Hold on,' snarled Zaeus, 'we're almost through them.'

Despite their initial frenzy, the stingwings were peeling off and returning to the larger herd now lost in the sandstorm.

Tracer rounds from Vortan's heavy bolter followed the creatures and a miniature sun erupted from the hellfire shell the Marine Malevolent had loaded, streaking flame across the choked sky. The red dawn was short-lived, however, though Vortan grunted his satisfaction as he watched the burning carcasses of a pair of stingwings spiral earthwards.

'Slightly profligate, brother?' Zaeus suggested upon Vortan's return.

The Marine Malevolent grunted, almost a verbal shrug as he continued on the marked route that would take them back to Carfax and exfiltration.

Ar'gan was farther out and ran to catch up to the rest of the kill-team, who were already moving again.

'How is he?'

Zaeus shook his head, trying to be surreptitious. He need not have bothered. Polino was putting one foot in front of the other, but his eyes were glazed, his expression slackening by the minute.

'We need to get back to Carfax,' the Salamander urged. He spoke through a comm-bead built into his gorget.

'Aye,' Zaeus agreed, taking up the chains wrapped around Festaron. The Brazen Minotaur's eyes were fixed on the hulking ammo hopper attached to Vortan's back. 'But we won't make it.'

'What?' Ar'gan turned swiftly. 'Explain, Techmarine.'

'Those flyers didn't attack us for no reason,' he said. 'They were gauging our strength and our foot speed. Across this terrain,' he gestured to the raging sand storm, 'and in these conditions, we will be fortunate if we get halfway to Carfax before the herd catches us. And then...' He paused to draw his hand across his throat in a cutting motion.

'I didn't mark you for a fatalist, Zaeus.' There was some reproach in the Salamander's tone that the Brazen Minotaur ignored.

'I'm not. I'm a realist, as I thought you Nocturneans were supposed to be.'

Hooting cries, the bleating battle-cant of the hunters, followed them on the breeze.

'Hear that?' said Zaeus, 'They are sending another vanguard to slow us down. It'll be more flyers, but this time with support. This desert is theirs, Ar'gan. In it they are faster, cleverer and more deadly. Make no mistake, we are prey here and our head start has almost been eroded.'

Ar'gan kept up the pace, just less than ten metres behind Vortan and in lockstep with Zaeus. He felt the urge to increase it but Polino was at the edge of his endurance already. He recalled what the Marine Malevolent had said about leaving the Imperial Fist, and dismissed the idea as unworthy.

'How can you know what they're planning, or did they teach you xeno-lexography on the red world too?'

'It's what any hunting pack would do,' Zaeus replied. 'Trammel us with lesser forces to give the horde time to arrive. Once they've encircled us, we will make a last stand and die before we've destroyed even half their number.'

Zaeus had stopped to manipulate a panel affixed to one of his armour's cuffs.

He called out, 'Vortan.'

The Marine Malevolent only half-turned, barely slowing his determined march in the direction of the Thunderhawk and extraction.

'What are you doing? We need to move! I'm not dying on this dust bowl world.'

A minuscule hololith projected from a node attached to the Brazen Minotaur's wrist. There was a small focusing dish appended to it. As he swept his arm around, the landscape was revealed in grainy green, undulating contours.

'I'm mapping the region, searching for weaknesses, a fissure, anything we can use.'

Ar'gan's expression remained concerned as his eyes flicked from the injured Captain Polino to the storm belt now behind them. Somewhere in its depths, the herd were coming.

'Whatever it is you are planning, Zaeus, do it swiftly.'

'Madness. We need to move!' Vortan reasserted, having now come to a dead halt. 'If we march hard we can still reach Carfax and the gunship.'

'And what about our injured and dead?' It sounded more like a suggestion, even coming from Ar'gan's lips. So conflicted was he that the Salamander could not bring himself to face Vortan.

The Marine Malevolent's solution was brutally simple. 'We leave them behind. Both.'

Though he was largely incoherent now, Polino caught enough of the conversation to weigh in himself. He nodded. 'I will make the sacrifice for the rest, and take a heavy toll of the alien filth.'

'Stoic to the end, captain,' said Zaeus, letting a little machine edge grate his voice, 'but you can barely lift your weapon.'

Polino tried, but his entire arm was shaking.

'And, besides,' Zaeus added, 'it wouldn't matter. We still wouldn't reach the gunship. We have a further problem.'

Vortan snarled. 'This Throne-forsaken mission has been fraught with them.'

'Such as?' asked Ar'gan, raising his eyebrow in inquiry.

Zaeus's eyes narrowed behind his retinal lenses as he found what he needed, but his answer had nothing to do with this discovery.

'I have heard nothing from Brother Carfax in over an hour. The Angel Vermillion is likely already dead.'

'Without the ship, so are we,' snapped Vortan. He stomped to where Ar'gan was watching the storm belt. 'So are we to wait here for the end then? Kill as many as we can?'

'You don't sound displeased with that scenario,' suggested the Salamander.

'I want to live, but if doomed then I will at least decide the manner of my destruction.'

Zaeus asked, 'How many charges do you have?'

'A pair of krak grenades and a melta bomb, why?' Ar'gan replied, turning to see Zaeus aiming the focusing dish at a point in front of them. A fractured script beneath the hololith display read: 5.3 km.

'All of you,' Zaeus corrected, looking down at Polino. 'Festaron too, someone check his wargear.'

Vortan did, offering up another krak grenade. 'I have four incendiaries,' he said of his own cache.

'Two melta bombs,' said Polino, still struggling.

'And with mine that makes four, plus the krak grenades.' Zaeus shut down the scanner.

More avian war-cries knifed the air, louder now as the herd slowly emerged from the storm.

'You have a plan, Techmarine?' asked Vortan.

'I do.' Zaeus pointed. 'Ahead, about three kilometres, there is a tectonic imperfection. It's little more than a crack in the desert basin at the moment but with the correct explosive encouragement, I think we can broaden it into a chasm. The fault line is long, easily wide enough to impede the entire herd.'

'And what of the stingwings? A chasm will be no impediment to them,' said Vortan.

'I doubt they'll attack without reinforcement, especially given what we did to them last time.'

The Marine Malevolent grunted in what could have been either derision or approval. 'Which way?' he asked, revealing the truth of his first response.

'North.'

They went north.

Thunder erupted across the desert as a line of explosions obliterated the edge of the basin behind them, plunging it into a deep sinkhole many metres wide and many more across.

It was, as Zaeus had promised, a chasm.

'All our grenades went into making that pretty hole,' remarked Vortan bitterly.

Ar'gan ignored the Marine Malevolent, asking, 'How long will it take them to navigate around it?'

'An hour, maybe two if the Throne is merciful.'

Zaeus was transfixed, his eyes on the vast clouds of expelled earth spewing into the air in dirty white geysers of calcite.

'And what mercy do you think the Throne has shown us so far?' asked Vortan, the sneer half-formed on his face when Zaeus struck him.

The Marine Malevolent crumpled under the blow, like he'd just been charged down by a raging bull.

In many ways, he had.

'A second blow will shatter your collarbone, and you won't be able to lift that cannon of yours any more,' snarled the Brazen

Minotaur. 'Don't think because I am of the Omnissiah now that I forget my heritage. You have been shown mercy. If any of my brothers had been present here instead of me, you would be dead by now for your constant dissent.'

Retaliation crossed Vortan's mind for a split second, Zaeus saw it in the near-perceptible tremor of his fingers, but the Marine Malevolent recognised the error in that and his conduct thus far, so relented.

'We the Watchers, though divided in brotherhood, are as one in our calling,' he said, uttering one of the many catechisms of the order.

Zaeus nodded.

'Accord is preferable to conflict, is it not brother?'

Vortan slowly bowed his head.

'Especially a conflict you would lose. Now,' said Zaeus, 'we make for the ship and hope that Carfax yet lives.'

Brother Carfax was dead. Slumped over the command console, the glacis of the gunship shattered by several dozen bullet holes, the Angel Vermillion had tried to take off when the snipers ventilated him.

Vortan was in the cockpit and placed a gauntleted hand against the dead warrior's brow, closing his eyes, which were still etched with futile anger.

'No way for a warrior like Carfax to pass,' muttered Ar'gan, solemn as the Marine Malevolent murmured a benediction.

'Aye, he was a bloody bastard,' Vortan agreed, lifting his eyes from the corpse. 'Do you remember when he gutted that clade of psykers?'

Ar'gan smirked ferally, giving a glimpse of the fire in his heart, 'The eldar barely had a moment to consult their skeins of fate before Carfax had weighed in with bolter and blade to cut them.'

Vortan laughed warmly at the memory, but Zaeus returning from his inspection curtailed his humour.

'The gunship's inoperable, but I can repair it,' the Techmarine informed them. An icon was flashing on his vambrace.

Abruptly, the mood turned grim.

'How far out is the herd?' asked the Salamander.

'Too close for me to repair the damage and for us to take off.'

'And what is that on your arm?' Vortan gestured to Zaeus's vambrace.

'Carfax engaged the gunship's distress beacon before he died.' When the Techmarine's eyes met the gaze of the others, they were bright and shining behind his retinal lenses. 'It has picked up a signal.'

* * *

...the Emperor's name, here all true servants of the Throne will find sanctuary. In the Emperor's name, here all true servants of the Throne will find sanctuary. In the Emp–

Zaeus killed the feed.

'There are coordinates, and from what I could discern when I interfaced with the ship's long range augurs, they lead to a stronghold.'

Ar'gan had been crouched listening to the looped message, but now he sat up.

'A bastion? Reinforcements?'

'At the very least a way off this rock and back to the Watch.'

The two of them were sitting in the ship's hold. Festaron was laid out in front of them, hands folded across his chest in the sign of the aquila. Polino was resting against a bulkhead, his eyes fluttering. In the dull lambency of the internal lighting, the captain's skin looked sallow and waxy. He gave no indication he had heard either of them.

Ar'gan remained sceptical. 'There was nothing in the mission brief that mentioned an Adeptus Astartes garrison on this world.'

'Perhaps it wasn't relevant. Perhaps it had simply been forgotten. Either way, we must investigate.'

After a moment's thought, Ar'gan nodded.

Vortan was outside, keeping watch through the scopes from a vantage on top of the fuselage.

Three hard raps against the hull was the signal that he had seen something.

Wordlessly, Zaeus and Ar'gan went outside.

The Marine Malevolent handed the magnoculars to Zaeus who augmented the view with his bionic eye.

'It's them, isn't it,' said Vortan.

'Yes,' Zaeus confirmed, checking the internal chrono on his lens display. 'Less than an hour. Mercy wasn't on our side after all.'

'I want to kill them,' the Marine Malevolent declared.

Ar'gan was casting around the ship. Carfax had set it down in a narrow defile, high cliffs on either side that were tough to reach from the ground. It was a good extraction point: hidden, defensible with only two bottlenecks at either end of the valley as realistic points of ingress.

'Zaeus has found a bastion, potential reinforcement,' announced the Salamander. He was still appraising their surroundings when he added, 'We could hold here. Maintain a defensive perimeter until your return.' He looked at the Brazen Minotaur, who looked back impassively through his retinal lenses.

'Three of these turrets are still functional,' Vortan weighed in. 'I can liberate the cannons, set them up behind a makeshift emplacement with the cargo from the hold.' He thumbed towards Ar'gan. 'Salamander takes one, I the other. Both ends of the valley covered. A pity you used all our grenades,' he added wryly. 'We could have mined them too.'

'And Captain Polino?' Zaeus asked.

Now the Marine Malevolent gave a short, snorted laugh. 'He takes the third gun, squeezes the trigger until the moment his fingers give out. He's close to suspended animation coma as it is, but at least this way his contribution might count for something.'

'Agreed,' said Zaeus, giving the scopes to Ar'gan so the Salamander could take a look at the opposition.

'How far's the bastion?' he asked, tweaking the focus. 'Or should I ask how long we need to hold them for?'

'Taking into account the return journey, one hundred and thirty-seven minutes. But the ident-marker on that message was Adeptus Astartes in origin, so reinforcement will be substantial and battle-winning.'

Vortan clapped Zaeus on the shoulder. 'Then bring back angels on wings of screaming death for our salvation, brother.'

'You always were the poet,' said Ar'gan.

The Marine Malevolent corrected him, 'You're mistaking poet for zealot, Salamander.'

Whilst his brothers made ready the defences outside, Zaeus was left alone to explore the hold. Captain Polino was in there too, but inert. Eyes closed, his skin the colour of wax, he might well have been dead. Only the slight murmur of his neck as he breathed fitfully betrayed the ruse.

'Rest easy, brother,' said Zaeus, lifting a hand from the Imperial Fist's shoulder as he went deeper into the hold. It was dark, most of the internal lume-strips shorted out or simply destroyed in the attack that had claimed Carfax's life. If the ambushers were still around they had yet to announce their presence, but Zaeus suspected not. Some of the gunship's contents had been stripped, only that which could easily be carried and reappropriated. It was why the heavy cannon still remained.

Zaeus mouthed a silent prayer of binaric to the Omnissiah that something else had proven too cumbersome for the xenos scavengers and smiled when he saw the cargo crate at the very back of the hold, still unopened.

A luminator attached to his battle-helm snapped on, revealing a dusty access panel. There were no runes upon it in which to punch a code. Instead there was a simple vox-corder. A blurt of binaric from the Brazen Minotaur's mouth grille turned the red lume on the panel to green. Escaping pressure hissed into the cabin and the door to the cargo crate, which was easily as tall again as the Techmarine, opened.

Within, Zaeus found what he sought and quickly set to work.

The low, angry squeal of a rotating belt-track interrupted the defence preparations around the gunship.

Ar'gan looked up from fitting a drum mag into one of the cannons he'd liberated from the Thunderhawk's wing. Vortan was stripping sections of the gunship's ablative armour to form makeshift barricades behind which the Salamander would set up the guns.

'In the name of the Throne…' said Vortan, setting down a chunk of scrap he'd been hammering into shape.

Ar'gan simply stared.

'What did you do?'

'Removed the torso and organics,' Zaeus told them. 'It's crude but will provide much greater land speed across the desert.' He was squatting on the hard metal frame of a track bed, two wide slatted belts of vulcanised rubber grinding either side, providing locomotion. The Techmarine's haptic implants were connected to the simple motor engine that had once been slaved to the cyborganic body of a servitor. Through them, he controlled the vehicle's speed and directionality.

It had taken him approximately four minutes to affect the modification, engage the machine-spirit and drive from the gunship's hold.

'I have a revised estimate for my return,' said Zaeus. 'Eighty-eight minutes. Think you can last that long?' he asked.

'Be on your way, brother,' said Ar'gan.

Vortan finished for the Salamander. 'The chrono's already running.'

Another xenos coming over the ridge line exploded, and Vortan revelled in the destructive fury of the gunship's weapons.

'Yes! Come and taste the wrath!' he bellowed, stitching a line across the narrow aperture into the defile. With a jerk and a grunt, he aimed the cannon upwards to strafe the dwindling swarm of stingwings attempting to attack from above. 'Watch the skies,' he warned his comrades through the comm-feed.

Ar'gan nodded, but had his own problems. His autocannon's drum mag was empty but locked. He couldn't free it to slam home another. Polino's support fire was desultory but no better than that. The captain skirted oblivion now and couldn't be relied upon to hold down a trigger, let alone cover one side of the ravine.

Creatures were spilling into the gorge, a mutant soup of alien limbs, chitinous appendages and snapping mandible claws. They were *krootis aviana* but they were also something else, something altogether more abhorrent.

Aspects that were distinctly avian persisted about the kroot, their long sloping beaks and spine quills protruding from the backs of their heads. Long limbed, they had sharp claws and hooves, capable of impressive foot speed with the ability to wield semi-complex weapons. Natural armour was not one of the kroot's usual traits but these creatures wore a sheath of chitin over their bodies that provided some protection. Others had additional limbs that ended in scything talons. Some were malformed facially, possessing glands not unlike gills through which they could project flesh barbs or trailing hooks.

Despite their evolutionary advantages, an autocannon could render them down into bio-matter easily enough, but only if it could actually fire.

Ar'gan railed at his misfortune, eager to cut them and trying to resist the urge to draw blades and do just that. He was adept at close combat, more so than any of his kill-team brothers. In one sheath he carried a Nocturnean drake-sabre, fashioned from sa'hrk teeth honed to a monomolecular edge, and in the other a Kravian fire-axe. The heavy bladed weapon was a rare specimen of the Kravian machine-cult, a faction of xeno-artificers with obscure ties to the jakaero. A third blade, his back-up or culling knife, was strapped to his thigh.

Against a horde of fifty something kroot-hybrids, its use had limits.

In the end, it was his boot not his blades that prevailed as a swift kick dislodged the drum. Though quick to slam in a replacement, Ar'gan was already overrun.

The creatures had advanced almost to the edge of the gunship's perimeter and the Salamander engaged the cannon's fully automatic fire mode, yanking back the alternator slide and lighting up the muzzle with a roar of star fire.

Swathes of the kroot died, malformed carapaces yielding to the aggressive fury of the high-calibre shells. Organs were pulped, limbs ripped off and bodies transformed into visceral mist. A clutch made it through the barrage, wounded but determined. Ar'gan wedged the trigger down and leapt over the barricade. He took a solid slug to the left shoulder; it scored his guard but left no lasting damage. A second hit mashed against his breastplate, blunted by adamantium. The kroot sniper lined up a third but Ar'gan's combat-knife had left its sheath and was lodged in the creature's throat. It bleated once before crumpling into a wretched heap of quivering mandibles.

The autocannon was still eating through its explosive payload when Ar'gan blocked the claw swipe of a second assailant, seizing its wrist and throwing it into the fusillade. Ululating screaming told the Salamander the threat was neutralised. A third and fourth he killed with two strikes, one an elbow smash to the thorax, the second a pile-driving follow up with his clenched fist that broke the fifth creature's clavicle and went on going into its ribcage. When Ar'gan withdrew his forearm it was steaming with gore and intestinal acids.

Only when the fifth kept coming did the Salamander draw the drake-sabre. It flensed flesh and bone in an eye blink, leaving two halves of a kroot bifurcated along its breastbone. A rapid lunge, like an assassin would use with a punch-dagger but which Ar'gan employed with a full blade, speared another through the heart. The last he decapitated, just as the autocannon was rattling close to empty, having shred the ravine opening to rubble and corpses.

The alien head was still falling as he turned, looking for further prey, his other hand hovering near the hilt of his fire-axe. It remained undrawn – the kroot were slain, but Polino was down.

Ar'gan was already running to the captain when he cried out, 'Vortan!'

The Marine Malevolent was finishing off some dregs with snapshots from his bolter. He was an excellent marksman. Vortan looked up, breathless but exultant from the carnage he had wrought, but rushed over to Polino.

A ragged line of flesh barbs was lodged in the Imperial Fist's upper chest and neck. Fortunately, his armour had borne the brunt of the attack and the cuts weren't deep, but they were envenomed. Polino was fading, descending into full cardiac shock.

'Keep a watch,' Vortan snapped at the Salamander, working at the Imperial Fist's armour clasps so he could remove the front half of his cuirass.

Ar'gan nodded, his gaze returning constantly to the stricken captain, trying to fight off the guilt threatening to impair his ability to follow orders. Mercifully, both sides of the ravine were clear and swamped with settling white dust.

'It was my fault,' he said, surrendering to dismay. 'The drum was jammed. I took too long to–'

'Forget that!' snapped the Marine Malevolent, wrenching off a chunk of Polino's battle-plate and noisily casting it aside. 'Are we still under attack or not?'

'No,' Ar'gan regained his composure, 'the gorge is clear for now.'

'They'll be back.' Vortan stepped back to regard the mess of Polino's bodyglove beneath his armour. It was bloody and it stank like a gretchin had just taken a shit in his breastplate. 'I knew we should have left him.'

Ar'gan scowled, not at the stench but at the wound. 'Putrefaction. It must have been like this for a while. There's a narthecium in the hold,' he said, meeting Vortan's gaze.

'Get it. Quickly.'

Ar'gan returned a few seconds later with a small medical kit. It was rudimentary with gauze, unguents, oils and a small set of tools. It wasn't exactly apothecarion standards but it was still a useable field kit. Vortan had some experience as a field medic and rummaged through the few phials and philtres, ampules and other medicines.

They had resisted its usage until that point, not knowing when it would be most needed. That time had arrived.

'Excise those flesh barbs,' Vortan barked, taking a tube of briny-looking liquid.

Ar'gan had left his shorter combat-blade in the kroot sniper's neck, so took a scalpel from the kit instead and began removing the barbs.

'These things...' he swore, slicing the skin around the wounds carefully so as not to aggravate more of the poison and further envenom it. 'Abominations.'

Vortan's reply was curt, 'All xenos are abominations, fit for extermination and nothing else.' He licked his finger, tasting a droplet of the liquid in the tube before spitting it out with a grimace. 'Should bring him around.' The Marine Malevolent waved the Salamander back, who was done with his improvised surgery anyway.

Vortan had fitted a syringe to the tube and was squeezing out any air bubbles when he said, 'This needs to go into his primary heart. Immediately.'

Polino looked weak, murmuring incoherently, a pained expression gripping his face.

Using a clean scalpel, Ar'gan cut away the section of bodyglove over the Imperial Fist's primary heart to reveal skin. It looked pale and unhealthy.

'How will you pierce the bone?' asked the Salamander, glancing sidelong at either entrance to the ravine. Mercifully, a second wave wasn't coming. Not yet.

'With as much brute force as I can muster.' Vortan rammed the syringe, two-handed, into Polino's chest and depressed the trigger.

Enhanced adrenaline surged into the captain's arteries, flooding his heart with the equivalent of a chemical electro-shock. It was dangerous, especially for someone in the captain's condition. But they were desperate. Polino's eyes snapped open like shutters and he roared, smashing Vortan off his feet with a backhand and kicking Ar'gan in the chest, doubling the Salamander over. Bolt upright, he jerked to standing position and then sagged, breathing heavily.

'Sword of Dorn,' he gasped, spitting blood. 'What did you do to me?' He looked up at Vortan, who was only just now rising, eyes wild.

'I got you back in the fight, sir,' he growled, removing his battered helmet. Polino had dented it and cracked one of the retinal lenses with his punch.

The Imperial Fist looked around.

'Where is Zaeus?'

'Off fetching reinforcements.' Ar'gan grimaced, clutching his bruised chest. Straightening up, he glared at the spent autocannon. Smoke was rising from the ammo feed where it had overheated. Part of the metal was fused and had seized the mechanism.

'It's scrap,' he said, cursing inwardly, 'be more use as a club now.'

'Do we have any other weapons?' asked Polino, trying to get a handle on the tactical situation. Despite his enhanced strategic acumen, he was having trouble focusing.

Vortan spread his arms to encompass the gunship and the makeshift defences.

'This is it. Everything you see.'

Ar'gan looked down at the chrono readout in his vambrace.

'How long?' asked Vortan.

'Eighteen minutes.'

They had lasted only eighteen minutes so far, and already they were down one autocannon and Polino was unlikely to last the duration of the next engagement.

'And the estimated arrival of Zaeus with our reinforcements?' asked Polino.

Shadows were gathering at the edges of the ravine again, heralded by the tell-tale cries of the kroot. A deeper strain joined the shrilling chorus this time, as something larger at the periphery of the kill-team's defences lumbered into view.

Vortan was already on his way back to the autocannon, 'Not soon enough.'

At the edge of the crash site, the kroot had been waiting for him. Zaeus had barely left the ravine when the creatures attacked. He killed them quickly, using up the last of his kraken and hellfire rounds to leave a mess of destroyed carcasses in his wake. The ambush was predictable, Zaeus reasoning that the kroot would have drawn a loose perimeter around the gunship and were using it to bait a trap. It was one the kill-team had gladly fallen into. If nothing else, the Thunderhawk was the only defensible position in the desert and their only means of exfiltration, but only if Zaeus could repair the damage done to the gunship, and then only if they could defeat the horde pursuing them to enable the Techmarine to do it. Kilometres clicked by in the Brazen Minotaur's retinal lens display, as did data describing fault lines, contours, temperature fluctuations and calcite density in the air. Beyond the ravine where he had left his brothers, the storm had not fully abated. It carved shallow grooves into his armour and wore at his Deathwatch black.

He remembered the day he had repurposed it, painted over the colours of his Chapter and taken the sacred oaths of moment of the xenos hunters. Back then, he had barely known the other warriors in his kill-team.

Carfax, so full of choler, his blood always up, had seemed ill-suited as a pilot; the quiet depths of Ar'gan hid a deadly bladesman; Vortan, the bitter and moribund priest, who cradled a heavy bolter like a favoured pet; Polino, the Fist, was as rigid as any son of Dorn but a strong captain; but Festaron, gifted as a field medic, was more open than any Star Phantom Zaeus had known or heard of. Their cultures and ways of war were strange, even anathema to the son of Tauron at first. Giving up the black lion pelt had been hard during that time, but the bond with his new-found brothers made it a worthy sacrifice. Respect and synchronicity had grown between them, and their differences became as boons that strengthened and united rather than weakened the group.

Now they were one, but they were dying and Zaeus raged at the fates that had brought them to this mortal place. He could not fail them.

A chrono counted down in his other retinal lens. It was over twenty-six minutes old already, the harsh terrain adding precious minutes to his arrival at the bastion or whatever was broadcasting the signal. It looped in his helmet vox, repeating the same message over and over. Recently, it had become a taunt rather than a promise of reinforcement.

Zaeus fed more power into the half-track, ignoring the whine of its sand-clogged engine as he pushed the servitor unit to its limit.

'Emperor, make me swift...'

Slowly a bulky structure began to resolve through the storm. Cycling through the optical spectra of his bionic eye, Zaeus discovered it was indeed a fastness, isolated but ironbound with thick buttresses and high, sloping walls.

He resisted the natural urge to charge straight at it, demand audience and bring back warriors to help save his beleaguered brothers.

Common sense tempered his Tauron desires and he eased his speed.

The bastion was dark green, much of its militaristic stencilling eroded by the desert, so he could only guess at its provenance. There was no mistaking the Adeptus Astartes ident-code of the signal. Zaeus switched to a corresponding frequency and spat a blurt of simple binaric that even the most rudimentary codifier could interpret.

I am an ally in need of aid. Cycle down your defences.

The half-track growled the last few kilometres to the installation, slowing as Zaeus approached the shadow of its defence towers.

No answer came from his hails, but the tell-tale muzzles of heavy bolters jutting from lofty firing slits looked threatening. The gun nests sat in a pair of watchtowers, which flanked an open gate. A quick biometric analysis suggested they were unmanned but could be auto-slaved.

Zaeus decided on the direct approach.

'Archeval Zaeus, of the Emperor's Adeptus Astartes,' he declared, letting the engine idle. If there was a data-corder or pict-feeder located in the gate somewhere it would have logged his presence.

Silence.

Time lapsed so loudly Zaeus could almost hear the seconds ticking over on the chrono in his retinal lens. The lion within him stirred, demanding action.

Zaeus looked through the gate but could find no evidence of habitation. The cannons were still, not even auto-tracking.

He snorted, a deep nasal exhalation that speckled the inside of his battle-helm with sputum. Caution was not a trait his Chapter held in much regard. He risked approaching the entryway. Like the walls it was thickly armoured, but gaped wide enough to fit the half-track. Easing down further on the speed to preserve the engine for the return journey, Zaeus passed through but met no resistance.

He met no signs of life or occupation at all.

Stretched in front of him was a large square plaza delineated by what he assumed were barracks or stores. Zaeus examined the signal data again and determined it was emanating from a large blocky structure at the end of the plaza.

Flurries of calcite were drifting across the ground, scuffing the Brazen Minotaur's boots after he had ditched the half-track at the gate to rest its protesting mechanics. He crossed the square of metal plates quickly, trying to banish the itch that the back of his head was in crosshairs, but reached the blocky structure without incident.

Up close, he realised it was some kind of workshop or forge. Perhaps the Chapter here had a Techmarine as part of its garrison. Zaeus prayed to the Omnissiah he was right. It would make repairing the gunship much easier if there were a second pair of mechadendrites devoted to the task.

A heavy door barred access but a simple chain and pulley would open it. Taking the partially corroded links in both hands, Zaeus grunted and heaved. After some initial resistance the chain spilled through his fingers, but the gate was obviously broken and only slid aside halfway to partially reveal the darkness of the workshop within.

He muttered, 'No time for this.' Taking a back step, Zaeus barged the gate using his head and shoulder like a battering ram. It crumpled inwards with a squeal of wrenched metal, and he snarled at his achievement, some of the old Tauron warrior emerging through his Martian conditioning. He could have torn it off its hinges with his servo-arm but old habits were tough to break, and he was feeling pugnacious.

Zaeus ventured into the darkness, his hand on the grip of his bolter.

'Hail, brothers.'

The machine growl of his voice echoed back at him.

In such a large installation, it was possible the warriors who had sent the message were deeper in its confines. It was also possible that a single Space Marine acted as its garrison warden. Such postings were not uncommon. Perhaps their alarums were malfunctioning too, as the Brazen Minotaur's violent entry would certainly have tripped more than one warning klaxon. He penetrated further, but still nothing. From the condition of the ragged machines in the workshop it certainly appeared as if the bastion had suffered from several years of neglect. He found a heavy switch and threw it, igniting a bank of flickering halogen strips above, but the dim light revealed little else but more mechanised decrepitude.

Zaeus's bionic eye added little to that analysis. There were no heat traces, biological or otherwise, but he did detect the hidden Icon Mechanicus inlaid into the back wall. It was only revealed through specific data-interrogation, the likes of which only an adept of the Mechanicus could perform. Whoever had hidden this chamber did not want it found by a casual inspection.

A glance at his bolter confirmed his low ammo count. Zaeus mentally shrugged – hand-to-hand would do just as well if it came to that. Already, he could feel his enhanced physiology priming him for the eventuality of close combat, fuelling his body, heightening his senses and reactions, incrementally increasing his strength and adrenaline levels with every step. For now, Zaeus kept himself in check. Closer inspection of the Icon Mechanicus suggested it might occlude a second gate leading further into the compound.

A quick glance at the chrono showed almost forty-eight minutes had elapsed. Over half his time had passed. He needed to move faster.

A patina of age and a veil of gossamer-thin cobwebs enshrouded ranks and ranks of ancient welders, rivet-punchers, machine lathes and furnaces. As he walked through the graveyard of extinct machines a theory formed. Much of the desert was overrun by the kroot-hybrids. Whilst the high walls of the bastion would keep most casual predators at bay, they might not be proof against a hardier, more adaptive strain of xenos. From his research of the kroot carnivore, Zaeus knew they were a race that had the ability to absorb the traits and characteristics of creatures through ingestion of biological matter. He balked at what species of xenos would evolve through a fusion of kroot and tyranid. So far, the kill-team had seen little of its potential but perhaps in the deeper desert the old garrison of the bastion knew more of such horrors.

Regardless of any possible danger, it was too late now to do anything other than press on. Zaeus had reached the concealed gate and shone a beam of binaric-filled decoding light onto the Icon Mechanicus. It responded instantly, illuminating, the light spreading to a data wire that ran up to the top of the gate describing a hexagonal portal limned in magnesium white.

Gears and motors, extant servos and half-forgotten engines grumbled into life from somewhere below. Zaeus felt the great machine beneath kilometres of rockcrete stirring like a leviathan awakened in an ocean trench. The gate cracked, split into four, each fissure running to a nodal point in the exact centre of the Icon Mechanicus. Monolithic in sheer size, the portal dwarfed Zaeus and he had to crane his neck just to see how far up it would open.

A vast hangar was revealed beyond the gate, immense and echoing. Dust motes thronged the air, which was musty and dryer than the desert. Zaeus's helmet sensorium detected mould spores and the activity of dormant insect life disturbed by his sudden entrance.

But there was no life beyond that, and no death either. He had feared there would be bodies, the empty carcasses of slain battle-brothers and the genetic soup of dead xeno-forms. Neither greeted him, but something else did – something he did not expect.

And as the gloom within was lit up like a firmament of a thousand crimson stars, Zaeus raised his bolter.

He'd been wrong, so wrong about everything. The kroot-hybrids had not come here. Something else had happened to the bastion. Possibly, something even worse...

'Omnissiah,' he breathed, taking up a firing stance.

* * *

The gorge was almost overrun. For over an hour and a half they had held the line with just the weapons salvaged from the gunship and inhuman determination. But after ninety-seven minutes of near relentless assault, ammunition was low and hope with it. Only wrath remained and the fervent desire to sell their lives at the cost of their enemies'.

For Vortan, the price could not be high enough.

He roared, a righteous expression of anger and defiance that merged with the ballistic shout of the cannon punching solid shot into the kroot beast's torso. The Marine Malevolent could hardly miss such a gargantuan creature. Slab-snouted, with two bulky forelimbs that were more simian than avian, it was broad-backed with much shorter rear legs and loped towards Vortan in the manner of an ape. Underneath its ribbed torso were paired rending claws, jutting forward like tusks.

It snorted and snarled, its chitinous body wracked by cannon-fire, then bleated as Vortan found more tender flesh.

'Hate is the surest weapon!' the Marine Malevolent raged, chanting his Chapter's battle-cry as zealous indignation washed over him. 'Suffer not the alien to live!'

The beast was slowing. Blood oozed from its nostrils, foaming with its heavy breath. But it wasn't done, not even close. A half glance at Polino during the barrage revealed the Imperial Fist was in worse shape. He sagged at the gun emplacement, the adrenaline fuelling his system almost spent, his finger locked against the trigger through sheer force of will. He strafed the gorge but his fire was only seventy per cent effective.

'Keep them off me,' Vortan spat down the comm-feed.

A horde of the lesser kroot were scurrying through the narrow aperture of the gorge, abandoning rifles in favour of the deadly gifts granted them through their hybridisation with the tyranid. A swarm of champing tooth and claw was descending on the survivors of the kill-team and only Captain Polino could stop it.

The Imperial Fist barely nodded.

'By Dorn's blood...' It came out as a rasp, strained by fatigue.

'I'll kill them all if I have to,' Vortan snarled through clenched teeth, putting a three-round burst through the kroot beast's skull. It grunted once, spitting up more blood and acid-bile, before slewing to a halt. Momentum carried it forwards, its bulk carving a deep furrow in the calcite.

Polino was down. Hoping to share in his triumph, Vortan only saw the Imperial Fist's gauntleted fingers slipping off the gun before he disappeared behind the barricade. He opened up the feed to Ar'gan.

* * *

They needed to retrench, head back towards the gunship and try to mount some kind of defence. Hold and repel. Victory through attrition – that was the Salamander way.

'Vulkan's fire beats in my breast.' Ar'gan uttered the mantra known and honoured by every fire-born son of Nocturne. With his death so imminent he found comfort in this small act of remembrance.

'Ar'gan.'

The comm-feed crackled in his ear. He didn't risk a glance behind; his side of the gorge was filling up with xenos. Staccato bursts of heavy bolter-fire had turned into an unceasing salvo that would eventually reach its terminus. Ar'gan smiled. When that happened, he would turn to his blades.

For now, he squatted on the gunship's nose cone. He'd stripped off much of the armoured fuselage to gain access to the prow-mounted heavy bolter. The weapon was underslung, half-buried in the dirt, but made for a good makeshift deterrent to ward off the attackers. As he fired, it spat out clods of calcite and mass-reactives. He kept up the punishment.

'Ar'gan.' The comm-feed sounded insistent.

'Speak.'

There was a short pause. Behind him, Ar'gan knew the Marine Malevolent was as hard pressed as he was.

'Polino's not getting back up.'

Something large and hulking bullied its way through a crowd of lesser creatures. Kroot were crushed to paste and broken limbs. It didn't seem to concern the beast.

It was a little way off, tough to discern through the drifts and the swell of alien bodies. But definitely monstrous. It filled the end of the gorge, spined shoulders scraping rock, the suggestion of a tail lashing in irritation behind it... a beak, eye clusters hooded by sheaths of nictitating chitin. Ar'gan absorbed the details, his brain analysing them for potential weaknesses even as he listened to the *chug-chank* of the cannons and heard the tell-tale hollow report of a rapidly diminishing ammo supply.

Vortan was speaking again. It sounded like he was moving.

'We need to retreat.'

'Where?'

'The gunship. We get inside, defend it.'

'We'd be besieged.' Though the Salamander acknowledged he'd considered the same tactic.

A spray of shells cut down a cluster of kroot that had approached the twenty metre mark. *Nothing breaches that line.*

That rule was about to be broken. The fire-axe practically hummed in its scabbard.

Soon... It was like talking to an old friend.

'Have you not noticed, Salamander,' said Vortan, with an edge of irritation, 'we already are.'

Ar'gan could not disagree. He tried to see beyond the horde, for evidence of Zaeus's coming.

Vortan read his thoughts. 'The Techmarine's dead. We're on our own.'

'Meet you inside,' Ar'gan replied as the underslung mount ran dry.

'Where are you going?'

He was already up, leaping off the nose cone, twisting the fire-axe out of its scabbard.

'To kill something.'

The beast was struggling through the neck of the gorge. Everything around it was dead or dying. A landslide would make a poorer bung. A pity they had used up their grenades or he would've already collapsed the rock face to achieve just that.

Instead, he had a beast, some fusion of one monster with another to create a fresh abomination more terrible than both.

Ar'gan was running at it. The fire-axe came alive in his hand, bright as sun-flare.

Eight pairs of milk-white sclera alighted on the Salamander. Nasal pits opened in the monster's neck, drinking in his scent but not finding prey.

+You are the hunted+, Ar'gan told it, his mind cast back to gutting sa'hrk on the Scorian Plain when he was just a boy, when he was mortal.

He had transformed, just as this beast had. The strength of the evolution of both was about to be tested in a bloody survival of the fittest.

Recognising a threat, the monster opened its maw and a barbed proboscis lashed out like a whip. It caught Ar'gan's shoulder, piercing the armour and sending a jolt of pain which his advanced nervous system rerouted so he felt it as a pinch, a slow spread of numbness through his upper arm.

He whirled the fire-axe, severing the monster's proboscis tongue. Left it flopping like a drowning fish in his wake. Ar'gan rolled, ducking under a thick flesh hook that would have impaled him like a sauroch on a Themian's spear. He came up with an arc of fire clenched in his fist. It seared the monster's beak, which snapped like a bird's at the Salamander. Snarling, Ar'gan dug his blade into its snout. It jerked spasmodically, hurt, and wrenched the weapon from his grasp. In a nanosecond, he'd drawn the sa'hrk knife and proceeded to stab it into the creature's neck and face. Acid-bile ruined the blade but Ar'gan kept going, knowing that sometimes frenzy was as valid as any finessed sword tactic.

The monster thrashed against the gorge, squirming and fighting. It managed to angle a shoulder in Ar'gan's direction and released a cluster of dagger-thick spines. Three lodged in the Salamander's vambrace and one struck his chest, went through battle-plate, the epidermis of his bodyglove and scraped into flesh. He was wracked by convulsion, enhanced biology struggling to retard the sudden rush of poison.

Fingertips brushed the hilt of the fire-axe as it came back within reach. Ar'gan lurched forward and took it, ripping the blade free and swinging it two-handed against the monster's neck. The head came off at an awkward angle, spilling gore and bile all over him. Kroot were crawling to get over the corpse. One had crested its back, clinging on despite the monster's last shuddering motions.

Ar'gan disengaged. Poison was turning his limbs to lead, stealing away his vitality and endurance, replacing it with agony. He took it. He was a son of Vulkan, fire-born. It would take more than alien venom to stop him.

The edges of the gunship looked blurred as he turned. He could no longer run. It was a half-limp, half-stagger.

Shrieking, avian noises behind him told Ar'gan he needed to be faster.

'Vortan.' His voice did not sound like his own as opened up the feed. A few minutes and his organs would counteract the poison, dilute it, neutralise it. He didn't have one minute. 'Vortan...' They were almost upon him. Engaging them was suicide. His Lyman's implant picked out eight distinct tonal arrangements. And that was just the first wave.

The feed crackled in his ear.

'Get down!'

Three metres from the gunship, Ar'gan hit the dirt.

Overhead, the air was lit by muzzle fire.

Through a haze of slowly fading poison, Ar'gan saw the Marine Malevolent braced on the roof of the gunship. He carried an autocannon, one hand on the grip at the top of the stock, holding it like a scythe; the other on its trigger. He dampened the recoil by jamming the butt into his stomach. His armour's servos did the rest, steadying his aim.

Eight kroot vanished in the metal storm.

Ar'gan was dragging himself up to his knees, thumbing the release clamp off a grenade from his weapons belt. He rolled it behind him, hard so it would travel, then pitched into the gunship.

A few seconds later, Vortan swung in beside him. The auto-cannon was gone, empty and discarded on the roof. He had Polino's bolter instead.

The captain was lying in the hold along with Festaron. Both were of equal use now.

'Holding out on us, brother?' he asked as the tangle-web grenade exploded behind Ar'gan, filling a five-metre wide area with deadly razor-wire.

'Only for emergency,' the Salamander replied. 'I didn't think it was worth wasting on collapsing that chasm.'

Vortan laughed. It sounded like metal scraping metal.

'Got one of those for me?' Ar'gan pointed to the bolter. Sensation was returning, his body's advanced immune systems finally counteracting the poison.

The Marine Malevolent shook his head. 'Only half a clip, anyway. Not enough to kill all of them.'

'Fortune I kept hold of this then.' Ar'gan brandished the fire-axe.

'You'll have to tell me one day how you came upon that brutal weapon.'

Outside, the horde had recovered from their blooding and was advancing. High pitched war-cries echoed from several directions, colliding in a deafening welter of noise that told the Space Marines they were surrounded.

'One day.'

Ar'gan glanced at the various points of ingress around the gunship.

'The hold has only three access points,' he observed.

'I can probably watch the roof and left side,' said Vortan, racking the bolter's slide.

'Then the right side is mine.' Ar'gan swung the fire-axe in a languid arc to relieve some of the stiffness in his shoulder from the proboscis wound. 'Bet you're wishing we'd have left the others now, eh?'

'No,' said Vortan. 'I like it better that we'll all die together.' He smiled. It was like a dagger slit across his mouth. 'Seems some of your compassion is rubbing off on me.'

Ar'gan met the Marine Malevolent's gaze across the length of the hold. 'I doubt that. Any last words, brother? A benediction perhaps, before we go before the Throne?'

Vortan tapped the bolter's stock, 'This,' he said, then nodding to the Salamander's fire-axe, 'and that are the only words we need now. Kill as many as you can.'

'Would you like to wager on the outcome?' Ar'gan asked.

More grating laughter from the Marine Malevolent cut through the cacophony from the kroot. 'Bolter versus blade? Very well.'

'Good hunting,' said Ar'gan.

Vortan didn't respond, and went to guard the left side of the fuselage.

Embracing the sheer fatality of it all, Ar'gan turned his back on him and took up a ready stance on the right. Through the side hatch a torrent of aliens were swarming towards the stricken gunship.

The chrono on his vambrace was broken, damaged by the spine attack. It stood frozen but flickering, close to two hours.

'Zaeus,' the Salamander said to the air. 'I hope you died well.'

Thunder filled the gorge. It echoed off the walls, rebounded and amplified by the natural close confines. Lightning followed, rippling in flashes along the high, rocky flanks right at the summit.

It wasn't a storm, at least not any natural one. It was fire and it was fury, wrath distilled into an unremitting barrage that tore into the alien horde and savaged it. Missile strikes provided a different tone to the war chorus, dense *fooms* of exhalation ending in a crescendo of earth-trembling impacts and flame.

Kroot bodies were thrown into the air like leaves.

The larger beasts mewled like cattle as their bodies were ripped apart by incendiaries.

'Vortan…' Ar'gan said down the feed.

'I see it! It's on this side of the gorge too.'

A broad smile split the Salamander's lips apart. 'Zaeus isn't dead.'

'If he is, I salute his undead corpse.'

Gunfire rained down from either side of the gorge, angling into a kill box where the kroot were advancing. Ar'gan noticed it wasn't accurate. As the xenos died they began to disperse, gaps appeared in their ranks that the massed fire from above failed to adapt to. Space Marines would not be so profligate.

Straining, Ar'gan tried to ascertain the nature of their saviours, but all he caught were snatches of silhouettes through split-second breaks in the continuous muzzle flare.

The kroot brayed and hooted at their unseen attackers. It took less than three minutes for their resolve to fail. Howling, they fled the gorge, spilling out in a tide in both directions.

They still numbered in the hundreds but the herd was spooked and sought the safety of the desert where the harsh flashes couldn't sting them further.

Slowly, the muzzle flashes faded one by one. Ar'gan detected the harsh *clank* of weapons on empty, the impotent *clack* of vented rocket tubes. Their saviours hadn't stopped firing because the enemy was dead or running; they'd stopped because there was nothing left for them *to* fire.

'What is this?' Ar'gan stepped out from the confines of the gunship.

There was a morass of sundered alien corpses outside.

Vortan joined him from the other side.

'I approve of the massacre, but what just happened?'

The Salamander shook his head. Craning his neck he saw a figure appear at the summit of one of the high walls of the gorge.

Zaeus gave a clipped salute.

'Thought you were dead,' said Vortan through the feed, having followed Ar'gan's gaze.

'You sound disappointed,' the Brazen Minotaur replied.

'Where are the rest of our brothers? Why don't they show themselves?' asked Ar'gan.

Zaeus stepped back from the edge as he manipulated something on his gauntlet the Salamander couldn't see. 'Because they are not exactly our brothers.'

After a few seconds the grind of machine servos resonated throughout the now silent gorge as a host of pallid faces emerged from the shadows.

Most were on tracks, but some stomped forward on piston-like legs or tottered on reverse-jointed stilts. Others still were not like men at all, but merely automated weapon platforms slaved to the Techmarine's will. They were servitors, dozens of them, armed with stubbers and autolaunchers, heavy bolters and shot cannons. Zaeus had found his reinforcements; he had recruited an entire force of dead-eyed cybernetics to his will.

They stared, unthinking, unfeeling at the pair of warriors looking up at them.

'I am sorry I was late,' said Zaeus, 'but as you can see, I was busy.'

The Brazen Minotaur vaulted the edge of the gorge and slid down the sharp incline, grinding a furrow down the rock with his back and shoulders. In a few minutes he was standing with his brothers again.

'Climbing up wouldn't have been so easy,' Vortan griped, but gave a nod of thanks.

Ar'gan clasped the Brazen Minotaur's forearm in a warrior's grip, which Zaeus returned.

'Your arrival was timely, brother.'

Vortan eyed the servitors warily. 'Still need to repair the ship. I assume they aren't coming with us.'

Zaeus gestured to the edges of the gorge where a small cadre of servitors had begun to encroach. Unlike the warrior caste above, these cybernetics were equipped with tools.

'We can be airborne in under an hour.'

'So there was no garrison, no Space Marine bastion,' said Ar'gan. 'The signal was fake?'

'No,' Zaeus replied, 'just a little out of date. Our brothers were long gone but they left an army behind.'

Above, the weapon servitors began to retreat from the edge of the gorge and were lost to the shadows again.

'I thought they were hostile but most were simply dying out. I accessed the doctrina programming of the functional ones, inloaded some new imperatives and led them here.'

'You did all that with ones and zeros, brother?' asked Vortan.

Zaeus snorted, pugnacious. 'It was slightly more complicated than that. But now the protocol I gave them is complete they will revert to their default settings and return to dormancy inside the bastion.'

Vortan laughed again, he had never been so mirthful. 'For the next beleaguered survivors to find.'

Zaeus shook his head. 'This world dies, brother. I have already contacted Inquisitor Vaskiel and provided my report. I am certain her response will be Exterminatus.'

'How soon until we're wings up?' asked Vortan.

'We have ample time. The chrono is no longer running.'

'Do you think they know?' asked Ar'gan, staring at the blank space above them at the edge of the gorge.

'Know what?' Zaeus was directing the remaining servitors in the repairing of the gunship.

'That they saved us but doomed a world.'

'This world was already doomed, but I think perhaps a mote of cognitive recognition remains. A machine-spirit, if not in the literal sense.'

Ar'gan nodded.

'Well, praise the Omnissiah,' said Vortan.

'Praise the Omnissiah,' echoed Ar'gan.

Zaeus stayed silent. Polino would live, so too Vortan and Ar'gan. Carfax and Festaron would be returned to their Chapters with the highest honours, their legacies could live on.

Though he would never forget his Tauron heritage, Zaeus knew he was of the Machine-God now. Flesh or machine, he would serve the Throne and his brothers until duty ended in death. Even in that bleak thought he took comfort as he looked to the horizon.

A train of soldiers were marching. Their hearts still pumped, their limbs still moved, their lungs still drew air, but their minds were empty tombs only filled with what their masters put into them.

Zaeus saluted them as they faded into the storm.

It would rise higher and swallow the entire world in cyclonic death, a million souls consigned to the grave so a trillion more would live on. Then the Deathwatch would come to their worlds too – Zaeus had seen it happen countless times before, and the same thing would repeat.

Without an iota of remorse, he turned his back on the servitors and went to the gunship.

This world had only hours left to it, but there were thousands more in need of purgation. The task of the Deathwatch was endless, their victories unsung.

As he watched his brothers return to the ship, he wondered where they would be bound for next and what they would have to kill.

None of it really mattered. The mission could always be broken down to a single universal truth: suffer not the alien to live.

SWORDWIND

IAN ST. MARTIN

Screaming fire hurls me into eternal night. Silence swallows the flames as the boarding torpedo darts through the void, dark iron and ceramite against the infinite desert that is at once nothing, and everything.

Our shipmaster slips in with audacious grace to knife us into the xenos vessel of our target, trading broadsides with migraine-bright energy weapons. She loses most of her port side getting this close, and by the time she breaks off she trails fire and atmosphere from a thousand points. Servants of the Holy Ordos stream into the void as decks blow apart, tumbling away to suffocate alone in the dark.

It is inconsequential. Billions have died; a few thousand more are beneath notice. They are as expendable as I am, a fact I accept without rancour.

Our quarry has guided its foul kindred through the razing of thirteen Imperial worlds, leaving nothing but corpses in their wake. Our pursuit fleet engages them over the ashes of the thirteenth planet. We have never got this close, and will never get another chance. Four kill-teams are dispatched to take the target's head.

Mine is among a shoal of torpedoes hurtling towards the alien warship. Most, loaded with arcane ordnance of the Inquisition's design, detonate short of the craft, releasing shrouds of null-field particles designed to disrupt psychic ability.

In the pod's ochre light, I regard the ebon giants within. We are indistinguishable in sable ceramite armour but for a shoulder pauldron of each warrior's native brotherhood.

Ero repeats the operations order and his guiding intent. Wasted words. We have all had extensive briefings, hypnotic preparations, repeated drills through mock-ups of what we believe we will find inside. We have pored *over data, learned their disposition, pulled apart their corpses to study their anatomy. We have killed them on world, moon and between the stars. We are as ready as we can be.*

Apothecary Cornac sits beside our commander, his Death Spectres Chapter mark contrasting with the golden iconography of Ero's Imperial Fists. He cycles through the tools of the reductor bolted to his arm. The whining drills set my teeth on edge, a reminder of the almost certainty that we will return with fewer operators than we began with, if any return at all.

The Wolf is singing. The lamentable bastard always sings during insertion, and I have long since resigned his howling to my awareness's periphery.

I glance at Sobor, silent and focused as I am. It was providence that saw us, both Mortifactors, seconded together. To serve within the same kill-team rarer still. A veteran of countless crusades, he has anchored me through our silent wars.

The ident-runes for two of the kill-teams blink out. Dead before contact.

Ero's vox clicks. 'Orders changed,' he says. 'We are realigning as primary assault element, acquisition and destruction of Primary Target One. Emperor guide our hand.'

I open my eyes, the memory clinging behind them as my senses embrace the now. I stand in an umbilical of interlocked iron discs, freezing and thick with the scorched metal scent of the void. Behind me is the *Crystal Saint*, of the Inquisition's Ordo Xenos. Before me the *Endless Night*, system monitor frigate of the Mortifactors Chapter.

My Chapter.

The umbilical is silent. I am alone with what I carry from duties past to future. My hold tightens on two items. I rise and move forward. My service to the Deathwatch is ended.

We barely make egress from the pod before the xenos are upon us. One might mistake them for human from a distance, but their movements put the lie to the thought. Inhumanly tall and slender, the eldar pirouette through our bolter fire, their weapons lashing us with gales of monomolecular shuriken that part ceramite like flesh.

The eldar close into melee. We advance, leveraging our strength against their speed. We must be the swift spear-tip plunged into their throat. Faltering will doom us all.

Five Mortifactors command the *Endless Night*. They incline their heads in deference to their kindred, but remain silent as the frigate follows the Sundered Path, the trail of death and wreckage marking Leviathan's march to Posul, from the system's edge. The hull shivers as we plough through clouds of iron and wreckage.

I have not released what I carry. It is my charge alone; I will bear it the rest of the way as we approach the planet of my birth.

The Wolf is dying. His head thrashes, hanging by sinew as Cornac fights to stabilise him within our defensive circle. Aspirated blood sprays from his lips between Fenrisian curses.

Cornac cannot save him, and instead seeks to save his legacy. He locks the Wolf's head to the deck, punching the reductor into his throat to tear out the progenoid. We do not have time to wait until he dies.

The Wolf calms once Cornac finishes, making peace with his end. I press a grenade into the hand he has left, and move on.

We do not get far before the crump of the detonation. He will never feel the winds of his birth world again.

Posul. For a moment, I see my home world as I remember it, a cloud-curdled sphere of sunless rock, soaked in the blood of savage tribes scattered across its surface. I remember snatches of a childhood drowned in violence. Eating the dead. The last man I killed, his blood and fat still stringing my teeth when the demigods came for me. I was ten, by the Terran standard. I remember defiant beauty, brutal purity in a land of eternal night. Fertile ground to sow the seeds of demigod killers.

I see that, before reality conquers memory, and I see Posul as it is. A shattered, lifeless husk, one amongst the numberless worlds devoured by Leviathan. Generations had lived and died never seeing the break of dawn. Now the sun will never set, shining over the barren wasteland left behind by the swarm.

In orbit is the *Basilica Mortis*, our fortress monastery hanging above Posul like a dark iron crown. It looms like a headstone over our greatest failure. An orphan's monument to the world we could not protect.

Ero sells his life at a chokepoint. My last sight of him is his thunder hammer, felling swathes of eldar with devastating strikes, building walls of bodies around himself like the fortresses his kin are legendary for.

Cornac is incinerated by brightlance fire. Molten shards of him embed my armour.

The gene-seed is lost with him. Their legacies now fall upon me. Oaths of silence consign them to oblivion.

I disable my audio receptors as we cleave through squads of Howling Banshees. Their screams craze spider-web fractures over our armour.

Sobor and I are close. Resistance has swollen with every step towards our target's sanctum. We sprint through the curved halls towards light ahead. Our target lies within.

* * *

The *Endless Night* reaches the end of the Sundered Path. I see shattered bulwarks. Last stands. Acts of valour and sacrifice, laid bare in the open grave of the void.

A dead hive ship hangs in orbit and marks the path's end, wreathed in a nebula of shattered chitin. None are spared the Leviathan's hunger, even their own dead. All that remains after their consumption is a husk, a skeletal frame, bleached and pitted like dead coral. It twists into broken shards along points, like warped armour on a ship's hull. I remember the suicidal boarding action to kill it as it ravaged our fleet. Desperate fighting within a living nightmare swollen with horrors. Acts that had gained the Inquisition's notice, leading to my recruitment into the Deathwatch. I remember triumph rendered mute by the numberless swarms that devoured my world.

We set melta charges to bring down the corridor behind us, and pass into a portal of crackling light. A searing jolt of nausea. Migraine smears of light in colours human eyes were never meant to see. My retinal display flickers, overloads, and resets.

We stand in a sphere at the spine of the eldar warship. It is wraithbone, so thin it is transparent like glass. Our boots sink into perfectly manicured grass. At the centre, a tree flourishes, swaying in a phantom wind. A figure sits before it, back to us in silent repose.

Our target. The eldar witch is here.

Beside him stands a hulking robotic construct, lacquered in the shade of forest at dusk. A stone set into its chest blinks and glows, and it raises its elongated crown to regard us. It takes the halberd it holds at its side into both hands, heat radiating from its chassis in shivering waves.

The sanctum's temperature plummets as the witch's awareness returns to the present. He looks round, regarding us with golden eyes. He turns back, eyes returning to the tree at the sanctum's centre.

'My ancestors bore this here in the days of the collapse,' he whispers in clipped, mellifluous Gothic. 'Generations of Biel-Tan have stood beneath it, a reminder of our past and hope for our future.'

The eldar stands, facing us. His pearl and ivy robes gleam in the sphere's light. Webs of jade energy shiver up the blade of the staff gripped loosely at his side.

'Cunning, attempting to drown my mind,' he gestures to the clouds of null particles glittering around the ship. 'An aggressive failure, ever your hallmark. I do not revel in the necessary destruction of your race, as many of my kin do. Nor shall I revel in your own. But fate sings clearly to me, Mon-Keigh.'

'Have you seen me then, witch,' asks Sobor, 'taking your head?'

A tired smile creases the alien's features as he lowers a crested helm into place.

'You should not have come here.'

The *Endless Night* slows its approach, and I look upon my charge once more. A simple iron case, and a sword of exquisite craftsmanship, a masterwork of ebon adamantium and steel. A blade worthy of a champion.

'Adoni,' Sobor says calmly as he draws his sword. 'I have the target. Engage the construct.'

I blink-send an affirmation as I draw level with the eldar ghost machine. The halberd in its hands crackles with emerald lightning. My axe comes alive at my touch, its power field hissing with killing force.

I empty my bolter into the automaton as it charges, mass-reactive rounds savaging its armour but failing to slow its advance. It slashes out in a blistering arc, the energy field scorching my armour as I roll beneath it. I raise my bolter in a crouch, firing the last charge in my combi-plasma.

The thing howls, a syncopated dirge like a dying man screaming beneath dark waters. Molten wraithbone drools down its glowing torso like wax. It lashes out with the shaft of its halberd. My cuirass is dented as the blow connects, hurling me across the sphere. I spit blood into my helm and feel warmth pool inside my armour. I stand, breath ragged through cracked ribs. The enemy charges again.

I weather its attacks, dodging when I can, blocking when I cannot, fighting to survive its furious assault. It slashes as I raise my bolter. The weapon spins away, my gauntlet crushed into a claw from the force of the blow.

Roaring, I hack my axe into ruin against its head. We grapple before it backhands me away. I let momentum carry me as far as possible from it. The xenos takes a moment to discover the melta charge locked to its side, but a moment is all I need.

I subvocalise the command through broken teeth, and the xenos construct vanishes in a cloud of searing plasma. The sphere behind it superheats. Wraithbone bubbles and liquefies. I brace as its integrity fails, and the sanctum explodes in violent decompression.

I spin into space through a blizzard of shattered wraithbone. Vertigo assails me in greasy tides as razor-sharp slivers spiral around me. My armour seals against the vacuum as best as its brutalised condition allows. I feel the flesh beneath my warped gauntlet freeze. I turn about amidst the maelstrom, searching for Sobor and the eldar while drawing my combat blade.

* * *

I stare at the synthetic skin that covers my left hand. I make a fist. The new flesh creaks like leather as it stretches. Returning to the sword, my eyes trace the scars along its blade.

Posulan runes etch the steel, naming the weapon's bearer before it was Sobor's. I make out a handful of marks, *A-R-T-E*, before the blade ends in jagged termination.

I find Sobor grappling with the eldar witch in the void. His Chapter relic sword is shattered halfway down the blade, his armour broken in countless places. He attacks the xenos psyker with the broken weapon, ferociously displaying the martial skills that made him a Chapter hero. I engage my thruster pack, kicking off from wreckage through the broken shards to reach them.

Sobor bypasses the eldar's guard, slashing into the armour beneath his robes. I am close, yet too far to stop the counter.

The witch gathers hundreds of wraithbone splinters and hurls them forward. Shards tear into Sobor, slicing through armour and sending him spinning away. His ident-rune vanishes from my retinal display. I roar as I close upon the eldar.

I lock the claw of my arm around the xenos and punch my blade into his back. I tear it out, wreathed in gems of his lifeblood, and drive it in again and again.

The present waxes and fades. I am a child again, beneath the sunless skies of Posul. I am hacking a man apart, the length of sharpened bone in my fist sticky with blood. My tribe joins me, prying the flesh apart to feast on the glistening warmth within. We howl to the endless night above. I will eat my fill before he goes cold–

The witch snaps me back to reality, smashing an elbow into my faceplate and sending me reeling. My retinal display crazes, awash with static and warning icons. It resolves and I see him poised to strike, wreathed in emerald lightning reflecting against the blizzard of wraithbone.

The eldar stops short as steel punches through him. Garnet spheres tumble around a broken blade. Sobor appears behind him, armour ruined and straining with effort. He tears the blade up from groin to throat. Vacuum steals the sackcloth-tearing noise of alien flesh splitting. Blood leaps out in arcs.

The eldar spasms.

+Do you fear what the future holds?+ the alien's mind lances into mine with icy spikes.

+You should.+

His mind screams, a thunderous dirge that tears through me with bone-rattling force as he explodes in a blinding flash.

There is a rumbling clunk as the *Endless Night* docks with the *Basilica Mortis*. The bulkhead rolls open. I behold dark stone catacombs, fires burning from black iron braziers at intervals along the halls that do little to dispel the darkness. I smell the mausoleum scent of stone, dust and metal surrendering to the aeons. I smell death. I fight the urge to drop to my knees.

I breathe deeply, inhaling the dead of my Chapter. My lungs fill with the bone dust of fallen Mortifactors that coats the monastery like snow. I feel the strength of those who have found death course through me. The glorious dead and I are one again.

'Brother Adoni.' A robed form steps from the shadows. He draws back the sackcloth hood to reveal a grinning skull. 'You have returned to us.'

I clash my fist to my chest in salute. 'Hail, Astador.'

'What do you bear, son of Posul?'

I raise the sword before him. He knows the blade, as we all do.

'And that?' His helm renders his voice a metallic snarl.

I open the case, enough for him to see within.

He is silent a moment before turning down the corridor. 'Come. The Chapter Master awaits us, brother.'

'Brother.' His voice is faint, the vox turbulent as my armour struggles with catastrophic damage. Activating my recovery beacon, I swim through the void to heed Sobor's call.

'Brother.'

I traverse the madness of the battle's aftermath, through the crystalline tempest. The eldar warship is gone, flown from honest combat. How like all their craven race. My retinal display warns of dozens of breaches, critical power loss, imminent oxygen starvation.

'Brother.'

I find Sobor, nearly indistinguishable from the surrounding wreckage. His armour is scorched and buckled. Torn fibre bundles sputter dirty light, and escaping air gasps through fractures in puffs of freezing mist. His head turns to me as I approach. The relic blade is clenched in his fist.

'I am here.'

Sobor lifts the sword before me. 'This weapon was forged at the Chapter's birth, passed down brother to brother through millennia. It passes to you now, Adoni, as it was passed to me.'

'Sobor, I cannot. I am not worthy.'

'Nor was I,' his voice weakens, wet with blood. 'Fulfil the oath of its return in my stead, brother. This night I join the dead.'

'Enough.' Speaking flecks blood into my helm. 'Your service is not done.'

'See it returned,' Sobor's helmet lenses flicker. His grip on the sword wavers, nearly letting it slip from his grasp. 'Its legacy must not end here, discarded in darkness. Swear this.'

I nod, the grinding of damaged servos muted in the night. 'Upon the sunless world, I swear to you.'

Sobor goes still. I exhale through savaged lungs. Floating beside him, I take the sword as he relinquishes it in death. My vox crackles, detecting exfiltration elements inbound. I slide through the black, forcing blood to my head to remain conscious, watching as the broken eldar tree withers in the darkness, and dies.

'Brother Adoni returns' says Magyar, Chapter Master of the Mortifactors.

I kneel, armoured in the black and bone, left fist pressed to the tombstone floor, right to my chest in salute. He sees me, expecting Sobor to have survived, not the line brother of just three crusades. I could seek venom in the words, but I will not. I agree with him. What I would not give for death to have stolen me into its embrace, for a champion to return to inspire the rebuilding of our Chapter.

Magyar sits in the gloom of the Gallery of Bone, his throne carved from the skeletons of Chapter heroes. Pale slugs of scar tissue pucker his face, old wounds unlike the purple lightning that covers my albino flesh. He wears exquisite Terminator armour carved from bone, its silvered hue matching his dreadlocked hair and forked beard. The very image of death incarnate.

Dark-armoured Terminators flank him, looking upon me from behind death masks carved to resemble howling flensed skulls. Astador stands a step below the throne's dais. Magyar's skeletal winged familiar sits perched upon its master, clicking against his plate with clattering claws as it chitters into his ear.

Sobor was of First Company, eminent even among the heroes of the Mortifactors veteran elite. Magyar holds Sobor's sword in one hand. In the other, taken from the case and presented to him by Astador, is Sobor's skull. The Chapter Master's features are impassive, save the faintest tightening in his jaw.

'And you will say nothing.' It is not a question.

'One word makes me an oath breaker,' my eyes remain on the headstones. 'Oaths kept for more than my honour.'

I hate the words I must speak. Everything within me cries out to proclaim the saga of the brother who cast aside his life to save mine.

'Tell me,' Magyar's eyes leave the sword to regard me. 'Were you there when he fell?'

I remember the night I swore my oath to the Inquisition, never to speak of what I had done, what I had seen. The Inquisitor swore one in return. Swearing what measures he would take against oath breakers, his pet witch touched my mind to show me.

Worlds burning. Fortress monasteries in ruin. Entire Chapters wading their fleets into the roiling nightmare of the Eye.

I look up at Magyar, holding the gaze burning within his coal-dark mask of scar tissue.

'You know what they will do.'

He makes to reply, but his jaw sets, and he says nothing.

The Mortifactors lord rises, the bulk of Terminator plate doing nothing to restrain his predatory grace. He stands over me, torchlight playing flickering shadows over his face.

'Rise,' he says. 'Adoni, you have returned a fallen brother, and this prized weapon of our Chapter. The blade shall be restored with honour amongst our relics. Sobor will join the fallen, interred within our monastery. His spirit is at rest by returning him here.'

I stand.

'You honour me, brother.'

'Indeed. Sobor's death resides in you,' Magyar clasps my shoulder. 'Honour *him*. Your memories are all the tomb his legend shall have.'

'Chaplain,' Magyar regards Astador. 'Assemble the brotherhood. We have fallen to honour once more.'

'We are born into darkness,' Astador stands before the altar at the sepulchre's centre, his incarnadine armour ochre in the torchlight gloom of the massive circular chamber. Bleached skulls of conquered foes cover the walls, staring down without eyes. The square ziggurat of the altar sits beneath a crystal dome ceiling. Posul hangs over us in the void beyond.

I stand with the three Mortifactors companies on the *Basilica Mortis*. There are fewer than two hundred. Leviathan took much of the Chapter, and crusades since have bled us further of warriors we can no longer replace.

'In the endless night of Posul, there was only death. Lives began, and ended, in the bloodletting of our tribes.' Astador's voice is the only sound beyond the thrum of active power armour. Every brother stands armed and armoured. A Mortifactor does not draw breath without a weapon in his hand.

Sobor's skull sits upon the altar. Every campaign, honour and triumph is etched into it in blunt Posulan script. Beside it lies his sword, polished to an ebon sheen.

'Until the *Ultimum Bellator* came. The Emperor's illumination offered us ascension above the savagery of our birth. For millennia we have defended His realms, for without Him none would know meaning in death.

'The most precious gift one can give is that which they deny themselves. For all His might, He who reigns over a million worlds from Terra, has given us something He can never possess.' He anoints Sobor's skull in oil, placing it in an iron bowl.

'Death. For all He has sacrificed, He can never give fully of Himself. We can, and so we must. He has given His life to us, and so we die in His place. Blasphemy is not acknowledging we surpass the Emperor in this way,' Astador shakes his head. 'Blasphemy is recognising a gift and wasting it.

'Sobor was among the greatest of our brotherhood. He has accepted the Emperor's precious gift, shedding his life in His stead. The shadows grow darker for his absence. Those who remain must burn brighter in defence of His realms.' He holds Sobor's sword over the skull.

'Who among you shall do so?'

'I shall,' says Magyar. He runs his palm down the shattered blade, clenching his fist to rain a trickle of blood over the skull.

'I will,' says Althanax, bearer of the Chapter banner. He repeats the act, as does everyone, until Sobor's skull sits submerged in oil and kindred blood.

'With each of the fallen, our flames must burn brighter,' Astador takes up a blazing torch. 'We must give light, and endure burning.' He lowers the torch, and sets the blood alight.

The blood burns away in coils of greasy smoke, filling the cavern with a scent like battle. I watch the flames consume the blood, until only the skull remains. Astador raises it in his hand for all to see.

'We are born in darkness. May we be the Emperor's light until we join the dead.'

'Until we join the dead,' repeats the assembly. Heads bow, and fists touch chests in salute. Quiet descends, each warrior in prayer and contemplation. I look down, frowning as I see my breath feather out from the vents of my helm, and frost crawl over my plate.

A cry rings out, shattering the reverent silence. Brother Librarian Uxbal collapses, blood jetting from his eyes. His armour's crystalline hood flares bright before exploding in a conflagration of warpfire. Aetheric flames leap over Uxbal's prostrate form, their windswept roar marred by his screams. He tears away fistfuls of his face as it weeps away like tallow, collapsing in a charred husk.

There are three other Librarians on the *Basilica Mortis*, and each of them falls to a phantom affliction. Olthis bellows like an animal, charging into the wall of the sepulchre and dashing his head apart against the stone in a cloud of blood and skull fragments.

A soul-curdling scream tears from Ionuth's throat as his body ruptures in flash-mutation. His flesh bursts with spines that dissolve into rolls of glistening fat before hardening into stone. His scream is the one constant in the maelstrom of change, before his flesh shakes itself apart into pale, shivering globs. All of this occurs in the time it takes for us to draw our weapons.

Chief Librarian Zdeno alone endures. Driven to one knee, eyes screwed tight and weeping blood, armour crackling with hoarfrost as he withstands the psychic onslaught. I can hear his teeth breaking in his jaw.

A keening wail shrieks across the vox. The Space Marines recoil at the violent noise. I feel warmth pool in my ears and slide down my face.

The shriek ripples and stutters, becoming a disjointed, lyrical sound. I realise that it is laughter. As suddenly as it began, it vanishes, replaced by the dread-soaked oppression of silence.

'It is undeserved,' a voice pierces the quiet. A female's voice, mellifluous yet edged with barely restrained fury. The one who laughed. *'Undeserved, but I grant you this. I shall have you know the name of the reckoning that has come for you. I am the Bahzakhain. I am exarch, the Swordwind and the Tempest of Blades. Know that in the moments remaining to you.'*

I see Zdeno standing halfway up the steps of the altar.

'Brother?'

He turns, movements sluggish and dreamlike. He raises his hand, pointing to the crystal dome above. I look, seeing only Posul.

'I have come to take from you what you have stolen from us,' she sings as the air trembles.

'A future.'

I blink, and in that instant the void swells with swarming eldar warships. I watch the *Endless Night* break apart as they stream through its wreckage. The *Basilica Mortis* quakes under fire, and again the vox fills with laughter.

It begins as a spark, a single mote of light splitting in two and multiplying until a cloud of sparks spin and twist about like fireflies. They coalesce into a corona of multicoloured light beneath the sepulchre's dome. The corona yawns open, becoming a gateway.

She emerges from the light like the spirit of vengeance made manifest. Her armour is powder white, coiled tight around her lithe musculature. Ivy iconography slides and twists over the plates like living smoke. From her shoulders trail banners of flowing vermilion silk like blood-drenched wings, matching the crested mane of her screaming war helm. She bears a crackling power glaive, its crystalline blade singing as it carves the air. She soars towards Magyar, at the altar's apex.

Togin is a Mortifactor without peer, having served for a century in Magyar's elite guard. In Posul's last nights, Togin slaughtered over a thousand of the Leviathan swarm, allowing the surviving companies to withdraw.

Althanax bears the Chapter banner. He has carried it through every crusade of the Mortifactors' First Company for the last two centuries. The skulls of every race and wicked bastion of Mankind's enemies clatter from his plate on dense black chains.

These are the warriors at Magyar's side as the war maiden descends. These are the warriors she kills before touching the ground. Their bifurcated remains crash to the flagstones like tolling bells. The Chapter banner falls, its fabric drinking the blood of champions that empties onto the stone.

The eldar exarch tilts her head, regarding Magyar, before whipping blood from her glaive. The Chapter Master stoops, gathering the fallen banner and lashing it to his armour like a cloak. He activates his massive war scythe with a hiss of coruscating lightning, and the two clash.

The air shimmers, and hundreds of blinding flares fill the sepulchre. Eldar warriors stream into the chamber, charging and firing weapons. Mortifactors die, eviscerated by shuriken and blasted apart by brightlance fire. The flagstones become slick with blood.

I bury my chainaxe in the head of a charging eldar. I gun the engine, ripping the xenos' head apart in a blur of screaming teeth. Sergeants and captains fight to rally their commands into order amidst the chaos of the ambush. Sporadic fusillades of bolter fire pluck leaping eldar from the air. Dead and dying are ground to mulch underfoot in a churning melee.

I slash through an eldar's torso and watch him collapse, fighting to restrain the steaming coils of his insides as they unspool from the wound. An explosion flings me through the air, smashing me against a mound of rubble. I feel flashes of paralysis, my consciousness flickering in and out. A ringing smothers my hearing. Scarlet warning icons wail in a wash of frenzied static.

I pull my ruined helm off. I turn my head to see Magyar duel the exarch above the melee. He attacks in blurring combinations, martial prowess alloyed with volcanic fury. The exarch flows around his attacks like quicksilver.

Magyar slashes low, a disembowelling strike the exarch evades with a flourishing backflip. Landing in a crouch, she counters with an upward slash, severing Magyar's scythe in two, barely missing the Chapter Master's head with a horizontal reverse strike.

Magyar drops the smoking halves of his scythe, reaching for the gladius at his hip. But his grip falters, and the weapon falls away. My eyes widen as bright blood sheets down from his gorget.

She had not missed. With a sound like a Titan falling, Magyar drops to his knees. His head trembles, and rolls off his shoulders. His body pitches forward, and his blood joins that of his champions in pulsing sprays.

'No!' I scream.

The exarch strides to the altar's edge and raises her arm. Clutched in her fist is Magyar's head, shedding the last of its lifeblood from severed arteries. She holds it aloft for all to see, and releases it. It tumbles down, bouncing against the timeworn steps before disappearing from sight.

An eldar dives onto me, fighting to drive a dagger into my throat. I strain against her, my strength depleted by the crash. Weakness fills my mouth with a taste of bloody ash. I could not save the world that gave me life. I could not save Sobor in the freezing night of the void. Now I have brought about the reckoning that has killed my Chapter Master, while my brothers die around me.

Can I even save myself?

In that moment, I gather the shame, the loss and the failure, and crush them into a supernova of rage. I bite down and leap into wrath's molten embrace. My muscles shiver and twitch as fury lends them new strength.

I clamp hold of the eldar's wrist, snarling as armour splinters and bones crush. My free hand searches for a weapon. It closes around a handle and roaring I swing it up, burying a blade in the eldar's temple. She twitches like a marionette as blood sluices down her armour.

Sobor's sword is in my hand. The weapon my brother had entrusted me to bring home rather than allowing it to vanish into darkness. I wrench it from the corpse and stand, taking a boltgun from the ground.

I throw myself forward, slashing and firing, fighting my way to the altar. I will not watch my Chapter die. I will not vanish into the darkness. I will take my brother's blade, and by the sunless world, I will bury it in the exarch's heart.

As Mortifactors clash against eldar amid the slaughter of the sepulchre, I reach the steps of the altar, and begin to climb.

DEATHWATCH:
KRYPTMAN'S WAR
IAN ST. MARTIN

DRAMATIS PERSONAE

DEATHWATCH CHAPTER

Artemis — Second of the Mortifactors Chapter, watch captain of Kill Team Artemis, Watch Company Tertius, Talasa Prime

Sekor — Second of the Imperial Castellans Chapter, Kill Team Artemis, Watch Company Tertius, Talasa Prime

Haryk Thunderfang — Second of the Space Wolves Chapter, Kill Team Artemis, Watch Company Tertius, Talasa Prime

Lavestus — Second of the White Consuls Chapter, Kill Team Artemis, Watch Company Tertius, Talasa Prime

Imtehan — Second of the Flesh Tearers Chapter, Librarian, Kill Team Artemis, Watch Company Tertius, Talasa Prime

Rogerio — Second of the Crimson Fists Chapter, Kill Team Artemis, Watch Company Tertius, Talasa Prime

Hyphantes — Second of the Scythes of the Emperor Chapter, Kill Team Artemis, Watch Company Tertius, Talasa Prime

Asharbanapal — Second of –REDACTED–, watch master and custodian of watch fortress Furor Shield, The Bladefall

Caltanix	Second of the Black Templars Chapter, watch captain of Kill Team Caltanix, Watch Company Primus, The Bladefall
Pecori	Second of the Blood Angels Chapter, Kill Team Caltanix, Watch Company Primus, The Bladefall
Nulsis	Second of the Novamarines Chapter, Apothecary, Kill Team Caltanix, Watch Company Primus, The Bladefall
Krycses	Second of the Raven Guard Chapter, watch sergeant of Kill Team Krycses, Watch Company Quartus, The Bladefall
Sango Aemna	Indentured shipmaster of the Deathwatch strike frigate *Fatal Redress*

BATTLEFLEET KURBYNOLA

Clovis Nearchus	High Admiral, Master of the *Claw of Damyrov*
Jaroslav Leitz	Commodore, *Claw of Damyrov*

THE INQUISITION

Kryptman	Lord Inquisitor of the Ordo Xenos

'Across the vastness of space, alien races plot the dethroning of the Emperor and the downfall of Humanity. This is the Imperium's call to arms, and nothing shall stand in the way of our righteous crusade.'

– Unattributed

PROLOGUE

'It cannot be done,' whispered the flickering spectre. *'It simply must not be done.'*

Giants of harsh light ringed the darkened chamber, shivering intermittently from hololithic projectors. They encircled the chamber's lone occupant, looming over him as they voiced their sanction.

'The course you set to undertake cannot be allowed,' said the projection of a High Lord. *'Your mandate is to prevent the subjects of the God-Emperor from falling to such a fate.'*

'It is unthinkable,' said another of the projections, an Inquisitorial rosette shining proudly on her uniform.

'It is madness.'

'It is genocide.'

'We are supposed to protect them!'

The man at the centre of the chamber lifted a hand. The projections froze, halted in the heat of their denouncement. The man turned, watching as a lobotomised servitor shuffled forwards on legs of bronze clockwork. The servitor halted a respectful distance from the man, head low, its milky, unfocussed eyes on the floor.

'They have arrived?' asked the man, the pools of light from the projections failing to draw his face from the shadows.

'Affirmation,' choked the servitor through the iron vox grille replacing its teeth.

'Bring them here.'

'Compliance.' The servitor gave a palsied bow, drooling from corpse-blue lips as it turned and limped from the chamber.

The man turned back, looking from face to face at the projections glaring upon him. He sighed. *Each of them wields such formidable power,* he thought. *Yet none of them possesses the foresight to see what is coming. None have the conviction to do what is necessary.*

The corridor leading to the chamber began to resound with the tread of heavy footfalls. The man snapped his fingers, and the glowering projections evaporated, their harsh light replaced by that of hovering glow globes. He turned back to the doorway as it slid open, framing the genhanced warriors standing beyond.

Watch Captain Artemis stepped into the chamber, encased in the sable power armour of the Deathwatch. His three companions entered behind him, wearing the same midnight-lacquered war-plate. All that distinguished the warriors were the right-hand pauldrons of their armour. Artemis wore the bone and black of the Mortifactors Chapter, while his comrades bore the heraldry of the White Consuls, Space Wolves and Imperial Castellans. The Space Marines carried massive weaponry, securely mag-locked to their armour. Stowing their weapons did nothing to diminish the aura of intimidation they exuded. They were war made manifest, the sharpest blade wielded by the Imperium of Man, and in the case of the Deathwatch, there were no deadlier hunters of xenos.

Artemis stopped a pace away from the man, shown in the light to be a slight figure of advanced age wearing simple black robes. Unmistakable, however, was the Inquisitorial rosette hanging from a chain about his neck, and the fire burning in his eyes. The eyes of a man who had condemned planets with a word.

'Lord inquisitor,' said Artemis, the vox grille of his helm rendering his voice into a harsh machine snarl. 'The brotherhood of Talasa Prime has answered the call of the Ordo Xenos.' He reached up, removing his helm with a hiss of balancing air pressure. A face of near-albino flesh and eyes of electric sapphire stared down impassively upon the inquisitor. 'The Deathwatch stands before you in this place. Why?'

'I have summoned you here for a grave purpose,' said the inquisitor.

The Space Marine bearing the markings of the Space Wolves boomed with laughter, crossing his arms as he looked to Artemis. 'Ah, this one summons us? A thin-blooded mortal who speaks as though we were his thralls.'

'Be silent Haryk,' said the Space Marine of the White Consuls. 'We are all servants of the divine Emperor. The Holy Ordo Xenos of the Inquisition stands as Terra's defence against the foul alien, as do we.'

The Space Wolf chuckled in reply.

Artemis raised a hand, and his brothers were silent. 'It is true, you hold no authority over my brothers, inquisitor. But the crusade against the manifold xenos of the galaxy has bonded our purposes.

It is in the continuance of that bond that we answer your call of our own accord.'

'Of course, watch captain,' said the inquisitor.

'Now,' said Artemis, 'tell me of this grave purpose.'

The inquisitor smiled thinly and snapped his fingers. The glow globes extinguished, and a hololithic star chart leapt into the centre of the chamber. The image coalesced around Ultima Segmentum, in the galactic east, focusing further upon a shrouded and indistinct web of stars.

'This is the Octarius sector. An expanse nearly as large as the dominion of Ultramar.'

'That is greenskin territory,' said Artemis. 'Their so-called *empire*.'

'Quite so,' the inquisitor replied. He gestured with his hand, guiding their view away to the outer fringes of the segmentum. 'Deep-void auguries have detected something skirting the galactic rim, pressing into Ultima.' A crimson stripe stitched out from beyond the rim, blinking on the projection.

'Cross-referenced with the data we have, there can be no doubt of what it is.'

The inquisitor turned to the Space Marines, his smouldering gaze locked to Artemis' icy stare. 'It is a tendril of the Great Devourer.'

Haryk and the White Consul exchanged glances. The inquisitor could hear the soft clicks of inter-suit vox communications between them.

'The tyranids?' Artemis held the inquisitor's stare. 'Behemoth has returned?'

'No, this is another strain entirely. We have designated this tendril, and its hive fleet, as Leviathan.'

'Why do you not marshal the battlefleets?' asked Haryk. 'Deploy the full forces at the Inquisition's disposal against such a threat?'

'Because you don't have them, do you?' said Artemis. The inquisitor said nothing as the watch captain stepped closer. 'Cadia burns under another of the Archenemy's black crusades. Every ship, every weapon, every mortal who can carry a weapon is being sent to repel them, bleeding the resources elsewhere white. You don't have anything to stand against this Leviathan.'

'And so,' replied the inquisitor, 'to survive we must adopt new tactics. The Leviathan will enter Ultima Segmentum. We cannot prevent that. But,' he turned, pointing to the hololith of the advancing tyranids, 'what if we could direct its course? Guide it away from Imperial systems, and towards those of a mutual adversary?'

Artemis noted the proximity of the tendril of Leviathan and the ork empire of Octarius. 'You mean to force the tyranids into a war with the greenskins.'

'Impossible,' said the Imperial Castellan, his first words since entering the chamber.

'Sekor.' Artemis raised a fist, silencing the Castellan. The watch captain returned his attention to the inquisitor. 'How?'

The image of Ultima Segmentum collapsed into shards of fractured light. In its place, a disjointed oblong of rock and twisted metal appeared, spinning slowly in the air. Artemis could see the corpses of Imperial vessels riddled throughout the object, backs broken, prows jutting from the rock surrounding them like drowning men desperate for breath. He also saw xenos vessels, some he recognised and some he could not identify, twisted among the amalgamated wreckage.

'This space hulk translated into Ultima Segmentum eighty-six days ago,' said the inquisitor. 'It is travelling along the projected path of the Leviathan. I have seen the ways of the Great Devourer before. This xenos is insidious, infecting targeted systems and worlds with a vanguard in preparation for its arrival.'

'Genestealers,' said Haryk. 'We have dealt with their like in the past.'

'Precisely,' replied the inquisitor. 'You and your team have experience with the genestealer, watch captain. Which makes you eminently suitable for an undertaking such as this.'

The inquisitor's servitor hobbled forth from the shadows, clutching a cylindrical device in its pallid hands.

'This is an experimental weapon,' said the inquisitor, taking the device. 'Still a prototype. It emits a compact stasis field over a small area, rendering anything caught within immobile. When your team makes contact with the genestealer brood infesting the hulk, the device can be used to neutralise a number of them, allowing you to capture them alive.'

'Alive?' asked Haryk. He turned to his comrades. 'Did he just say *alive*?'

'To be seeded into the ork empire,' the inquisitor continued. 'Genestealers are the harbinger of their hive fleet, readying the path for the greater brood to descend. Seeding the captured genestealers will draw the Leviathan to Octarius. The orks have been massing in extraordinary numbers, and the conflict between both xenos could provide the Imperium decades to prepare. The enemy of my enemy–'

'Is still a vile affront to the Emperor!' the White Consul's gladius was half drawn from its sheath in a moment.

Artemis placed a hand upon the White Consul's arm. 'Peace, Lavestus.'

'This is heresy,' Lavestus snarled. 'It is our holy province to visit death upon all xenos. To do any less is betrayal.'

'And yet it is the only chance we have to prevent the Leviathan from a full invasion of our realm.' The inquisitor's voice was steady, his conviction ironclad. 'If we fail to divert them, both the ork and the Leviathan will spill into the Imperium at their full strength, with nothing to stand against them. Rynn's World, Baal, even Ultramar will burn if we do not act.'

Rage emanated from Lavestus, a low growl scratching from his vox grille. Artemis' eyes had never left him, his hand still clamped over the White Consul's arm. With considerable effort, Lavestus sheathed his blade. 'If this gambit fails, inquisitor, I will tear your limbs from you and cast you into the void.'

'The fate of billions rests upon this moment, watch captain.' The inquisitor met Artemis' gaze once more, fire against ice. 'What is your answer? Will you serve?'

The Mortifactor was silent for a few heartbeats. No emotion was betrayed on his pallid features. In a blink the glittering power sword at his hip was free of its sheath, the blade carving the air as it spun in Artemis' grip.

The watch captain drove the blade down into the floor of the chamber, the name 'Exterminatus' etched in fine script down its length. Artemis' eyes had never left the inquisitor. 'The Deathwatch answers your call.'

Haryk snorted. 'Eh, I was too pretty for this life anyway.'

Lavestus seethed, and Sekor remained silent.

Artemis sank to one knee, his comrades doing the same behind him. The watch captain raised his eyes to the frail man standing in the spectral glow of the hololith.

'Lord Inquisitor Kryptman, of His Majesty's Holy Ordo Xenos, hear now this oath of moment, bonding my blade and my blood in thy service.'

PART I

PART 1

ONE

He listened to his world die.

From the throne at the centre of the command dais on the bridge of the Imperial Retribution-class battleship *Claw of Damyrov*, High Admiral Clovis Nearchus shook with tremors of impotent rage. The cries echoed through the vaulted heights of the enormous chamber, issuing from bronze horns, flittering cherub servitors and the carved mouths of gargoyles. The cries of a world being consumed. The cries of apocalypse.

They overlapped each other, each a panicked petition for aid, each rife with confusion that their protectors had abandoned them. Nearchus had ordered that the transmissions continue to play throughout the ship, as it remained at high anchor over the citadel world of Praesidium. The combined forces of the entire system had been gathered there. Its fleets ringed the planet, while its armies were immobilised on its surface, forced to watch as their worlds burned and their populations were massacred. Twenty worlds aflame, while their defenders did nothing.

Their impotence was mandated by the highest authority of the God-Emperor's Inquisition. Questions were heretical. Dissent was met with oblivion. Nearchus' own first officer had railed against their orders, unable to stand idle as the hive city that housed his wife and children was dragged into the maelstrom of two warring xenos races. For his inconstancy, he had been given the Emperor's justice.

The agent of that justice stood just behind Nearchus as he rose from the command throne, gripping the brass railing of the dais. The high admiral felt the itch of active power armour, the heat radiating from a power pack. He smelled the lapping powder and sacred oils anointing the ceramite plate, and the coils of fyceline smoke that lingered in the ceiling buttresses from the mass-reactive boltgun round used to execute his first officer.

Armoured in black, the Space Marine stood as a silent sentinel, red eye-lenses glowing like balefires. A member of the vaunted Deathwatch, he carried the authority of the Inquisition, and upon his right shoulder stood the proud heraldry of the warrior kings of Macragge, noble cobalt against the sable.

There is no nobility in the genhanced warrior, Nearchus thought. *There can be no nobility in this. In watching the slow genocide of billions, without ever knowing why.*

Nearchus steeled himself, watching as a pair of servitors removed what was left of his first officer's body from the bridge. They were clumsy things, leaving smears of crimson across the deck as they gathered up the chunks of flesh. The admiral turned to the silent Space Marine.

'Can you not hear them?' he asked, pointing to a circling cherub screaming in panic. 'Can you not hear the voices of the Emperor's servants, crying out for protection? Is that not your purpose?'

The Space Marine remained silent.

'Our system burns. Billions are dying, our families, our homes. Your masters have forsaken them, and forced us to forsake them as well. Why?' Nearchus demanded, rage lending his voice a growing boldness. 'Are we to sit here and do nothing?'

'No.' The single word boomed from the Space Marine, who slowly turned the eye-lenses of his helm upon Nearchus.

'What then? Tell me, what am I to do? Tell me!'

The Space Marine looked down at Nearchus for a long moment, before turning forwards again, resuming his vigil.

'Duty.'

Artemis rolled into cover, crunching against the remains of the barricade as viridian lightning stitched over his head. Strings of jade energy slashed around him, liquefying walls and scorching the ground into furrows of dirty glass.

The watch captain blinked away a damage rune pulsing on his retinal display, and peered over the barricade.

Phalanxes of silver figures marched out of the smoke in perfect order. Hurricanes of las-fire and solid projectiles blasted into them, smashing much of the front ranks apart. Many of the fallen simply vanished, blinking out of existence, to be reawakened within the labyrinths of their ancient tomb ships. Others slithered back into one piece, their component parts flowing together as they stood.

The gaps formed by those rendered ineffective were filled with silent, cold precision, and the advancing necron warriors levelled their glowing weaponry, firing without breaking stride.

The fortifications around the central bastion of Quaris were aflame after weeks of repelling the endless advance of the necrons. Heavy armour, elite regiments of the Astra Militarum and strategic orbital bombardments had done little to oppose their unstoppable march. Confined to a narrow valley barricade, with ammunition dwindling and casualties mounting, the Astra Militarum had petitioned for aid.

Artemis and his kill team had deployed from the *Fatal Redress* as soon as the rapid strike frigate had entered low orbit. Dropping directly into the enemy ranks, the Space Marines of the Deathwatch had fought a blistering counter, pushing the necrons back and buying the defenders time to consolidate.

Now the xenos had returned, and in far greater numbers.

Artemis slapped a magazine of kraken penetrator rounds into his bolter, looking sidelong at a comrade as he squared up beside him.

'It is a blessing,' said Rogerio, the myriad xenos skulls chained to his armour clattering as he reloaded his weapon, 'to face a foe one can kill again and again.' Hailing from the Crimson Fists, Rogerio had been a veteran of dozens of campaigns as a sternguard before joining the ranks of the Deathwatch. Though his voice was rendered a cold snarl by the bionics that replaced his throat, Artemis could hear the joy and zeal in the old warrior's words.

'I'd settle for them staying dead,' Artemis replied, rising out of cover to snap off a volley of bolter fire. The anti-armour kraken rounds punched through the necron ranks, savaging their skeletal forms too severely for them to reform on the battlefield. He ducked back behind the barricade as the xenos responded with a withering fusillade of gauss cannon fire.

The necron weaponry stripped away the barricade on a molecular level, and Artemis dived back as he was exposed. Rogerio fired bursts from his storm bolter to cover him as the xenos overran the barricade.

'Hyphantes, in the fight!' barked Artemis.

A rumbling shriek of igniting promethium filled the air. The Scythe of the Emperor rocketed down on a pillar of fire, hurling a clutch of frag grenades ahead of him. He hit moments after the detonations, smashing into the tight ranks of the necrons. Capitalising on the moment of confusion, Hyphantes tore into the aliens with twin falxes, whirling the curved blades and slashing through living metal.

Artemis and Rogerio stalked forwards, emptying their bolters into the necrons closing on Hyphantes' rear and flanks, before drawing their melee weapons. Rogerio's spear spun as he lanced through a necron's torso, and Artemis activated the power field of Exterminatus, wreathing the blade in crackling energy as he cleaved into a foe.

In the tight confines of the valley, the superior numbers of the xenos did not give the advantage it could in the open field. The crump of artillery sounded from the fortifications, raining shells down upon the rear phalanxes stymied at the front by the Deathwatch.

'Now, Imtehan!' grunted Artemis, countering a clubbing strike from a gauss cannon to his head by bifurcating the xenos from neck to groin.

Standing alone atop the high ridge framing one side of the valley, Imtehan snarled. Hooking his fingers into claws, the Space Marine tensed. His breath feathered out from between iron teeth as frost crept over his armour. The psychic hood sweeping behind his head crackled as his snarl became a roar. Loose rock and dust lifted around him, spinning, as he reached across towards the opposite ridge.

Tremors shook the ground beneath Artemis' boots. He spared a glance up at the ridge, where Imtehan stood within the eye of a tempest. His roar split the air, lightning dancing over his limbs as he reached out. The dust on the opposite ridge began to tremble and leap upon the air. The tremors spiked in intensity as fissures erupted in the splitting rock.

'Back!' ordered Artemis, as Hyphantes and Rogerio closed to his sides. The xenos had ignored Imtehan, and the battle psyker was primed to show them the cost of such an error.

With the effort of hauling a star from the sky, Imtehan *pulled*.

The ridgeline shattered. Thousands of tons of rock floated for a heartbeat before hurtling down into the valley. The necron phalanxes, with no room to manoeuvre, were obliterated as the valley filled with mounds of rock twenty yards high. Dust fountained into the air, racing through the valley and over the ridgeline. Within moments, the rock settled and the guns went silent.

Imtehan dropped to a knee, snarling as he caught his breath. The sawtooth blade framing the ruby blood drop on his right shoulder became caked with dirt as the frost melted over the dust.

'You are graceless, Flesh Tearer,' said Hyphantes. 'But one can find no fault in your results.'

Imtehan wiped blood from his nose with the back of his gauntlet, smearing it over the brutalised mahogany flesh of his face. 'Remind me how graceful you would be, flayed by necron guns?'

'Consolidate on my position, Imtehan,' said Artemis. He opened a new vox-link with the bastion. 'We have delayed them, colonel. But they are far from defeated.'

'It will give us time to shift our wounded to the rear and consolidate whatever manpower we have left,' the Astra Militarum commander replied over the scratchy vox-link. *'We are in your debt, watch captain.'*

Artemis killed the link as a priority transmission rune blinked on his display. He felt a slight vibration beneath his boots. Peering into the rock for any sign of movement, Artemis opened the channel.

'Go ahead, Sekor.'

'Contact from Fatal Redress,*'* said the Imperial Castellan. Artemis could hear the roar of engines spooling up behind his voice. *'We are being recalled to orbit, emergency condition.'*

'We are still conducting operations here, our mission is incomplete.'

'It appears that it shall remain incomplete, then. The order is coming from a watch master.'

Artemis frowned. He blinked at the vox-link, sharing it across the kill team. 'What is urgent enough to draw us from a combat zone?'

'This is a watch master and the ordo calling us in,' replied Sekor. *'They are not exactly conversationalists.'*

Artemis closed his eyes for a moment, pushing a breath through his teeth. 'Very well, confirmed. We will stand by for immediate extraction.'

'I am en route via Blackstar. Arrival imminent.'

Artemis severed the vox-link. He looked to Rogerio.

'What of this mission, watch captain?' asked the veteran.

'This is no longer our mission.' Artemis turned towards the bastion gateway.

'We will just leave them to their fate, then?' asked Hyphantes, betraying his unease.

Artemis sighed. Hyphantes was young for a Space Marine, freshly inducted into the battle companies of his own vanishing Chapter before being seconded to the Deathwatch. 'We will follow our orders, brother. These soldiers swore oaths to defend the Imperium. They will do their duty, as shall we.'

The kill team gathered at the landing pad of the bastion. Imtehan joined them, his meteor hammer slung over one shoulder as they awaited Sekor.

The Corvus Blackstar was a sleek inverted arrow carving through the sky. Smaller than a Thunderhawk, the drop-ship was an experimental craft, in service only to the Deathwatch. Artemis still marvelled at how quiet the Blackstar was, as the drop-ship settled upon the rockcrete landing apron. Assault ramps lowered on each side of the Blackstar's nose, and the kill team moved to board.

'Watch captain!' Artemis turned to see a wiry man in officer fatigues approach, a flock of aides and lieutenants trailing behind him. 'Something is happening in the valley. Are you going airborne to conduct reconnaissance?'

Artemis stopped, pulling his helm free. He heard the distant sound, metal scraping against stone. He looked down at the colonel.

'We are leaving this world. Our orders have directed us elsewhere.'

The colour drained from the officer's face. 'But, you cannot leave here. Our ammunition is depleted, our soldiers–'

'Will serve the Emperor,' said Artemis. 'Your charge is not to question. You have your walls. Hold them. Do not take a step back. And should you fall, let it be in service. There is glory in that.'

The scraping grew louder as Artemis turned, joining his kill team as they boarded the Blackstar. Hyphantes spared a look back at the group of shocked mortals. Reaching to his shoulder, he tore a scroll of parchment held to his armour with crimson wax, and dropped it to the ground.

'You discard your oath of moment?' asked Imtehan as the Space Marines locked themselves into the crew bay. 'You shame yourself, and us.'

'We all discarded it,' spat Hyphantes. 'We have forsaken them.'

The scraping became a howling din as the Blackstar lifted from the landing pad. Looking out from an observation viewport, Artemis watched the mountains of broken rock shake, the cracks between them glowing with baleful green light.

As the drop-ship turned to blast into the atmosphere, Artemis saw the rock dissolve, washed away by a tide of silver scarabs. Thousands of the necron constructs flowed over the ramparts, consuming everything in their path as phalanxes of necron warriors marched behind their advance. He saw tiny islands in the ocean of silver, desperate last stands by the Imperial defenders, quickly subdued.

'If you became an Adeptus Astartes believing you would forestall the death of innocents,' said Artemis, turning to the Scythe of the Emperor, 'then you have sworn your oaths in vain.'

TWO

The *Fatal Redress* dived through the warp, its crackling Geller field alight with burning daemons. The smaller entities swarmed around the modified Gladius-class frigate, ravenous for the souls of the crew within. Little more than fragments of rage and hunger, they ruined themselves against the bubble of realspace, while immense shapes circled from the depths like oceanic predators. The field held strong, keeping any of the neverborn from breaching.

Artemis had not told his kill team or the crew of the contents of the watch master's message. He had relayed the navigational data to the shipmaster and Navigator, and proceeded to the duelling cages on the lower levels of the ship alone.

The cages were dark, the glow globes ringing the chamber extinguished. The only light to pierce the darkness was the flickering discharge of energy as Exterminatus made contact with the combat servitors. Bladed armatures and whirring chainblades spun through the air in showers of sparks, clattering to the polished rockcrete floor with dull clangs. Each blow illuminated Artemis for an instant as he turned and slashed, countered and riposted, his sword a blur of strobing flashes.

Sekor stepped into the chamber, his eyes adjusting to the lack of light. He made out Artemis' outline, moving with effortless grace as he flowed around the combat servitors. Sekor's augmentations and surgeries allowed him to see in the dark chamber quite easily. But Artemis was a child of the night.

'A taste of home, watch captain?' asked Sekor with a smirk.

The chamber went silent. Sekor watched the outline go still, steam rising from the watch captain's skin.

'Lights.' The glow globes lit with Artemis' command. A native son of the Mortifactors home world of Posul, Artemis had lived his entire mortal life in total darkness before being taken by his Chapter. He stepped out of a ring of severed limbs and bladed armatures, the dismembered combat servitors collapsing in various states of ruination around him.

'Care for a real challenge?' Sekor took a pair of short swords from a rack on the wall, spinning them to loosen his shoulders. 'Or would you prefer continuing to play with your toys in the dark?'

Artemis smiled thinly. 'A curious choice, brother. Twenty years and you have yet to land a blow on me.'

'Yes, well we can't all be like Haryk in the cages.' Sekor chuckled. 'Word is he is leading his pack to Cadia, following that child king of his.'

'Trust Haryk to be at the centre of that storm.' Artemis nodded.

Sekor tossed a short sword to Artemis. 'For now you'll have to content yourself with me.'

Artemis caught the weapon. Both Space Marines wore simple black body gloves, the torso and sleeves hanging from their hips to leave their upper bodies bare. Each was a patchwork of weathered flesh, threaded with ropes of scar tissue. Geometric patterns and lines flowed over Sekor's skin, along with cogwork iconography from his brief apprenticeship on Mars. Artemis' slab-like musculature was undecorated, bearing only the scars of battle.

Artemis turned to slip Exterminatus into its scabbard. Grinning, he spun, catching the overhand slash from Sekor and locking the blades.

'Better,' Artemis leaned forwards, slowly pushing Sekor back. 'I almost couldn't hear you that time.'

Sekor sidestepped, dragging their blades low and coming over the top with a return strike. Artemis weaved aside, and the two circled.

'What of the watch master's message?' asked Sekor, tossing his gladius from hand to hand.

'There was no message,' replied Artemis. 'Only the navigational data for our destination, and the mandate for this team to rendezvous there. Nothing more.'

The watch captain lunged, launching a flurry of lightning cuts and stabs. Sekor closed his guard, forced to his back foot as he waited for an opening to counter. They locked blades again. Artemis pistoned a fist into Sekor's face, stepped behind him and threw him to the ground.

'Was it your lack of attention that saw the Martian priesthood dismiss you from their forges?'

Sekor spat blood onto the rockcrete. He had never confided to

Artemis the infraction that had seen him discharged from his training as a Techmarine, prompting his Chapter to send him to the Deathwatch. He rolled back over his shoulder into a crouch. He looked up, seeing Artemis holding both swords. The watch captain flipped one, offering the grip to Sekor.

'Again.'

Sekor wiped the blood from his mouth, accepting the gladius. 'So where is it we are going then?' he asked as he stood.

'Ultima Segmentum,' replied Artemis. 'To the watch fortress Furor Shield.'

'The Bladefall are stationed there,' Sekor frowned. 'It seems out of character to petition for aid outside of their own chambers.'

'Indeed,' Artemis replied. He sprang forwards, meeting a lunge from Sekor with a sweeping deflection. He shoulder barged inside of the Imperial Castellan's guard, gripping his sword arm and kicking out his legs from under him.

Artemis stood over Sekor, still gripping the warrior's arm by the wrist, his boot pinning his shoulder to the floor.

Sekor winced. 'What are we doing that is so important that we must abandon a mission?' He looked up at Artemis, holding the Mortifactor's frigid gaze. 'Artemis, what do you know that you aren't telling us?'

Artemis remained impassive, releasing his hold on Sekor's wrist as he turned away. 'You know as much as I, brother.' He looked back as he strode from the chamber. 'It will not be long before we arrive. I suggest you spend that time in practice.'

Imtehan knelt in silent repose in the centre of his chamber. Barely more than a cell, the Librarian's austere quarters contained little. An arming rack for his weapons and armour, a simple pallet, and a small table laden with scrolls and tomes was the extent of the room's contents. The flickering candlelight glittered on the frost coating the walls. The Flesh Tearer snarled, struggling to quiet the tremors in his mind.

Wrath radiated from Imtehan's every action. It was the birthright of his Chapter. From the lowliest neophyte to Chapter Master Seth himself, all whose veins carried the blood of the primarch felt a rage that ran marrow-deep. It was their greatest weapon, a fury that had broken sieges and destroyed whole armies where others would have failed.

Yet there was a curse within such ire. Imtehan had watched battle-brothers, veterans of countless campaigns and crusades, succumb to the afflictions of their blood. As unceasing war starved the companies of able warriors, more and more brothers fell to the ranks of the condemned. Taken by the Rage or the Thirst, they donned the crimson saltires and the black armour of the Death Company until death in battle finally claimed them.

For Imtehan and the other psykers of the Flesh Tearers, it was a constant struggle to combat the afflictions within and the ravages of the warp's foul entities from without.

The door to his chamber chimed once. Imtehan pushed a deep breath through his teeth, and stood.

'Enter.'

The door slid open with a rumble. Artemis lowered the hood of his robes, and stepped into the chamber.

'How are you faring, brother?' the watch captain asked.

Imtehan turned to face Artemis. 'I endure. Passage through the Sea of Souls can often be,' the Flesh Tearer searched for the word, unused to Low Gothic, 'demanding, for those with my affliction.'

'Most would call your abilities a boon,' said Artemis. 'I would number among them. Your powers have tilted the balance of battle in our favour a dozen times over.'

'Most,' Imtehan nodded.

But not those born of Cretacia. The Dragon's Cradle bred warriors who distrusted the arcane. Few of the witches born survived within their tribes long enough to gain the notice of the Chapter. Those that did rarely ascended to the ranks of the tearers of flesh.

Librarians were always the first ones chosen to join the ranks of the Deathwatch. Artemis knew that their exile suited Seth, who understood fully that few that were sent returned.

The Flesh Tearer looked at Artemis, smiling thinly. 'I do not begrudge him his sentiment, Mortifactor. We deal in death. You know as well as I that it is not the mandate of the weapon to question its course. I am concerned only with meeting the enemy. Once we do, this weapon will bite, and drink deeply of their blood.'

'You do your kindred credit,' said Artemis. 'I shall leave you to your meditations.'

'Summon me, when you need me,' replied Imtehan, kneeling once more as Artemis walked from the chamber.

Artemis walked through the corridors of the *Fatal Redress*. Servitors passed him at regular intervals, attending to the myriad menial tasks needed to keep the rapid strike vessel operational. The vessel's crew was largely composed of servitors, having very little in the way of human crew members. Due to the secrecy with which the Deathwatch conducted its missions, and the unceasing pace of its operations, having as few mortals manning the decks as possible was an asset. It left less room for mistakes.

With the majority of the ship's human complement stationed on the bridge, the bulk of the *Fatal Redress* remained without heat or light. The near-freezing conditions had no effect upon the servitors, or the Adeptus Astartes who called it home.

Artemis felt at ease within the blackness. He had fought across the galaxy, in all conditions and environments, but the darkness was always home to him. He remembered the endless night of Posul, and the dark passageways of the Mortifactors' fortress-monastery, the Basilica Mortis. It had been more than a century since he had last walked its halls, the scents of ancient stone and bone dust filling the air. He put such reminiscence from his mind as he entered the armoury.

Rogerio stood at the workbenches towards the rear of the large chamber, Hyphantes aiding him in repairs to his bionic eye. The Scythe of the Emperor focussed, fitting the ticking lens assembly into the socket in Rogerio's face.

The Crimson Fist blinked as the bionic locked into place. 'Ah,' he smiled as the lens glowed scarlet. 'Thank you.'

Hyphantes pressed a fist to his chest, and turned to regard Artemis.

'Brothers,' the Mortifactor greeted.

'Hail, Artemis,' replied Rogerio with a nod.

'Watch captain.' Hyphantes bowed. 'I must attend to my armour. By your leave?'

'Proceed.' Artemis turned aside, and Hyphantes strode from the chamber.

'He still resents my decision,' said Artemis. It was not a question.

'He is young,' replied Rogerio. 'Much is expected of him. His kindred have placed a great burden on his shoulders – to return seasoned, with the knowledge and wisdom to rebuild his Chapter.'

'One cannot lead until he learns to follow.'

'He still holds the zeal of a child.' The Crimson Fist pressed a finger to his temple, adjusting the seating of his bionics. 'He still believes that all life can be saved, and has not yet accepted the truth of our galaxy. He never saw Sotha.'

'Few Scythes draw breath that have.'

'One in ten survived the Kraken's fury. A disaster. I understand him. After Rynn's World, my own kindred stood upon the precipice. We could have easily fallen, fading into annihilation as so many Chapters have. He will need his faith, as will his brothers, if they have any hope of survival.'

'Sekor was similar when he first arrived,' said Artemis. 'Obstinate. Hyphantes will adjust. But this is no academy, Rogerio. We are elite, and you have seen the measure of our foes. No amount of faith alone will stop what we will face.'

'Indeed. I relinquished the honour of the First Company to serve here. Combating the alien, setting fire to their worlds and striking at their very hearts – the Deathwatch is the highest honour one can achieve in my Chapter.'

'He must learn in the crucible. He will learn, or his Chapter will have another brother to grieve.'

Rogerio rose, clapping Artemis on the shoulder. 'I will watch over him, brother.' He looked down. 'Sekor should have a look at your arm.'

Artemis lifted his right arm, flexing iron fingers with a rasp of stuttering augmetics. The pistons threading the forearm caught, scraping against impact gouges left by necron blades.

'Do you still feel it?' asked Rogerio, pointing with his own whirring prosthetic.

Artemis frowned, looking over at the Crimson Fist. 'I will have it attended to.'

The translation bell sounded in the armoury, and the chamber was bathed in amber light.

'Gather the team and report to the bridge,' said Artemis. 'We have arrived.'

THREE

Realspace shivered. The light of distant stars blurred as the void before them distorted. Pinpricks of light the colour of bruised flesh winked into being, swelling and melting together to form a tear in reality. The *Fatal Redress* erupted from the tear, translating after sixty-one days in the immaterium. Fledgling daemons clung to the hull, trailing tears of warp light as they burned away with banshee screams.

Artemis stepped through the bulkhead into the controlled bedlam of the bridge. The deck reverberated with each step he took, bearing the weight of his power armour. Naval officers and serfs hurried from point to point, giving orders and confirming screeds of data from cogitators. Servitors twitched at their stations, connected by wires in the ceiling like marionettes.

At the centre of it all was Shipmaster Aemna, relaying orders to runners and her staff as she tapped at the runeboards of her command throne. Her eyes, silver bionics pulsing white, glittered like diamonds in the low light of the bridge.

'Retract viewport shielding,' said Aemna. 'Let's have a look.'

The segmented armour plating covering the forward observation ports, locked in place during warp travel, split, peeling back to provide the bridge with an unobstructed view of the void beyond. Empty space greeted them, with no planets or stars near their translation point.

Artemis came to a halt beside Aemna's throne, inclining his head. 'Shipmaster.'

'Watch captain.' Aemna flashed a smile as she pulled up a hololith of the local sphere of space. 'Doesn't appear to be anything out here.'

'These are the coordinates I provided to you?' asked the Space Marine.

'Affirmative. We lit the engines a touch for a quick burn to reach here from our translation point, but this is it.' Her shining eyes flicked up at Artemis. 'I don't suppose you left anything out?'

'Shipmaster!' a junior officer called, stopping at the command dais and making the sign of the aquila.

Aemna collapsed the hololith, regarding the officer. 'Report.'

'Long-range auspex came back with a flash return. It ghosted our scans but was gone by the next pulse.'

'One of ours?' she asked.

'Inconclusive,' he shook his head. 'But it was there.'

'Shields up,' Aemna stood, smoothing a crease in her uniform. 'I want all crews at their stations, the reactor primed and weapons online within twenty minutes.'

'Aye, ma'am.' The officer saluted again, and set to relaying the shipmaster's orders to the rest of the bridge.

Aemna narrowed her eyes, peering into the void before looking back at Artemis. 'Anything at all?'

Klaxons blared from the trumpets of angels carved into the walls.

'Radiation spike,' shouted a rating from a sensor station. 'Closing in from the port side.'

'Our phantom again?' Aemna shouted back over the klaxons.

'Negative, this is a different signature. It's erratic but constant, and it's big.'

'To my station,' Aemna ordered as she returned to her throne. 'Battle stations. Gunnery, get those breeches loaded, I want broadsides and I want them now. And kill those damned bells!'

The klaxons ceased as the bridge became awash in red light. The crew, finely drilled veterans of the Imperial Navy, hurried to and fro in orchestrated disarray, conducted by the shipmaster.

Aemna read the lines of runes dancing down her viewscreen. 'That…' she blinked, reading the data again, '…that isn't possible.'

'What is it?' asked Artemis.

'The signature bearing in. It's an ork ship,' she shot a sidelong glance at Artemis. 'What is a greenskin ship doing all the way out here?'

'Incoming,' squalled a servitor from the auspex stations, programmed to have its dull voice spike in volume when calling in approaching ordnance. 'Incoming.'

Aemna cursed as the ship shook violently. Crew were hurled to the deck, and sparks vomited from a cluster of stations. Artemis was unmoved, his boots mag-locking to the deck plating.

'Report!' shouted the shipmaster.

'Void shields holding,' called out an officer. 'Hull breaches sustained on decks C-Nine and E-Four, contained.'

'Bring us about,' Aemna snarled. 'Run out our broadsides and get those lances primed!'

The *Fatal Redress* groaned as it manoeuvred at full engine burn, the pearlescent capsule of its void shielding still flickering. Yawning gunports ground open down its flanks, the deck thrumming as the Deathwatch strike frigate's massive weapons batteries came online. Lance turrets tracked from the spinal battlements, turning towards the alien ship rapidly coming into view.

An ugly, ramshackle knob of scrap metal, the ork warship rocketed towards the *Fatal Redress*. Part junkyard, part asteroid, it bristled with oversized weapons arrays, which fired in all directions as it drew closer.

'Where are my guns?' Aemna demanded, tapping furiously at the runeboards of her control throne.

'Broadsides ready in eight minutes,' an officer from the gunnery pits shouted in reply. 'Lances primed in four.'

Aemna cursed again. 'They'll be all over us in four.' Her station chimed, new data appearing in urgent red script.

'Shipmaster, we have another augur return. Contact inbound!' a crewman called, hunched over an augur station.

'Here's our phantom,' Aemna hissed.

'It's fired torpedoes!' shouted the officer.

'Evasive manoeuvres!' ordered Aemna. The ship lurched in a chorus of strained iron as the *Fatal Redress* dived. The torpedoes, launched from an incredible distance, knifed through the void, passing the Deathwatch vessel and smashing into the flank of the ork warship.

Chains of explosions tore down the side of the xenos vessel, breaking the momentum of its assault vector. Armour plating shattered, and a cluster of engines was completely sheared away, leaving it listing and venting atmosphere. Seconds later, an enormous detonation engulfed the ship as another payload struck, reducing the greenskin craft to an expanding cloud of plasma and spinning debris.

'That weapon,' Aemna said, distracted as she flicked through the data on her viewscreen. 'That was a bombardment cannon.'

'Shipmaster! Priority communication inbound. We are being hailed.'

Aemna keyed a sequence into her console. A hololithic projector thrummed as an image sprang into life. A massive figure appeared in the air, armoured in midnight war-plate.

'This is Watch Captain Caltanix of the Deathwatch,' said the figure. *'To our kindred of the* Fatal Redress, *we bid you welcome.'*

FOUR

The Deathwatch battle-barge *Victorious Son* dwarfed the *Fatal Redress*. Spanning over five miles of void-black iron, the titanic warship was nearly five times the size of Artemis' vessel. Spires and crenellations ran down her spine, bristling with weapons batteries, ending at its distinct hammerhead prow. Its bombardment cannons perched on dorsal turret mounts, potent weapons capable of levelling entire cities with a single shot from orbit.

A trio of support craft, each the size of the *Fatal Redress* themselves, peeled off from their escort positions around the *Victorious Son*, making a pass around Artemis' ship. Instruments and tactical hololiths on the bridge crackled with interference as the escorts conducted deep auspex scans before, seemingly satisfied, they returned to their designated support formation.

'Watch Captain Caltanix,' said Artemis to the hololithic projection of the Deathwatch commander. 'We have answered your call to rendezvous here. My crew and I would like to know why you have brought us here, and what an ork vessel is doing this close to Imperial space.'

'*Our astropathic choirs sent that message months ago,*' replied Caltanix, expressionless behind the snarling faceplate of his helm. '*I was not certain if it had reached its destination, or whether you would be able to rally here. I am pleased to be mistaken.*'

'Watch captain–'

The Space Marine raised a hand of flickering light as he leaned to regard someone beyond the projection. '*We are transmitting coordinates to your vessel. Follow us in to Furor Shield, brother, and you shall find the answers to your queries.*'

Caltanix turned away as the hyololithic link cut, ending the transmission. Aemna shot a sidelong glance at Artemis. The Mortifactor kept his gaze locked to the viewports, as the *Victorious Son* began to turn.

'Attend to your duties, shipmaster,' said Artemis, ignoring her stare. 'You have received the coordinates relayed from the *Victorious Son*?'

Aemna nodded, punching commands into her keypad. 'We have them.'

'Good. Match their approach vector and bring us in. I shall be below on the embarkation deck.'

'Aye, watch captain,' said Aemna, rising to issue orders to the crew as Artemis left the bridge.

When the alarm had sounded, Kill Team Artemis had armed themselves swiftly. With the watch captain on the bridge, they had deployed across the remainder of the vessel, in preparation to repel boarders from essential sections of the *Fatal Redress*.

Imtehan had proceeded to the gunnery decks, to ensure boarders could not silence the vessel's guns by slaughtering the pressganged serfs and ratings responsible for hauling enormous shells into the breeches of broadside cannons. Sekor moved to the embarkation deck, ready to vent the hangar bays to the void to displace any xenos assault. Rogerio took up a defensive position in the engineering deck, safeguarding the warp drive and reactor, while Hyphantes posted himself at the sanctum of the vessel's Navigator.

Once the alert lifted, and the ship's bulkheads came out of lockdown, the kill team converged on Sekor's position, meeting Artemis on the embarkation deck.

Artemis entered the main hangar first, seeing Sekor behind a hastily constructed barricade of heavy cargo pods. Setting a bulky multi-melta cannon down beside him, the Imperial Castellan began breaking down a tripod-mounted heavy bolter, stripping a belt of metal storm fragmentation shells from the weapon's breech.

'Greenskins?' Sekor asked without looking up. 'And only one ship?'

'It was a small vessel,' Artemis replied. 'Likely a scout.'

'How often do we see orks with the forethought to conduct reconnaissance?' Sekor hauled the heavy bolter from its tripod, setting it on the deck with a thud.

'Perhaps it was part of a convoy that drifted off course.'

Sekor locked eyes with Artemis. 'You know where we are.'

Artemis did not avoid his gaze.

'You remember when we were here last,' Sekor pressed.

Artemis blinked, closing his bionic hand into a fist. He stepped towards Sekor, clapping a hand on his pauldron. 'We will find answers, brother.'

The bulkhead of a heavy lift ground open, and Rogerio, Imtehan and Hyphantes joined Artemis and Sekor.

'When I heard,' said Rogerio, distractedly scraping an ork skull chained to his armour with his fingertips, 'I was admittedly sceptical, watch captain. A single greenskin ship? Not possible. We cannot afford to tarry here. There are others, and we must bring them to battle.'

'Peace, brother,' said Artemis. 'I suspect we may not have long to wait.'

The *Fatal Redress* fell into formation behind the *Victorious Son*, lighting its engines and following in the battle-barge's wake. The vessels sailed through the void, the midnight iron of their hulls rendering them near invisible to the eye. Skirting the edges of the segmentum, they passed through the empty space between systems, swimming through the black towards their destination.

The watch fortress Furor Shield resembled a sprawling cityscape, as if it had been torn from the surface of a world and cast into the void. Spires and battlemented towers branched in all directions, bristling with launch bays, torpedo silos and weapon emplacements. Dry-dock cradles and scaffolds ringed the star fort, ready to accept returning Deathwatch warships seeking to refit and make repairs. Its surface winked with the light of vast forges, and domed environmental blisters bunched in clusters, providing kill teams with the ability to train in any climate, from lush rain forests to icy tundras.

No two watch fortresses were alike, varying in size, design and capability. Some formed artificial rings orbiting around worlds, others resembled planetoids or small moons. While most were inert, remaining at fixed points of vital strategic importance throughout the Imperium, several watch fortresses were mobile, even capable of travelling through the warp. Furor Shield was one such installation, with a full third of its mass devoted to its powerful plasma engines.

Sekor made preparations for their Corvus Blackstar to launch, readying the drop-ship to transport the kill team onto Furor Shield. Teams of serfs, Mechanicus adepts and servitors swarmed the craft, disconnecting fuel lines, checking vital systems and appeasing its machine-spirit with droning entreaties of binary cant.

Artemis led the kill team up the assault ramps of the Blackstar as Sekor buckled himself into the cockpit. The servitors permanently hard-wired into the stations to either side of him went about their tasks, oblivious to his presence. Sekor's hands danced over the control panels of the drop-ship, and the craft began to thrum as its primary engines spooled up into readiness.

'*Watch captain,*' the voice of Shipmaster Aemna crackled over Artemis' vox.

'Shipmaster?'

'*We are entering close proximity to Furor Shield now, you are free to disengage.*'

'Acknowledged,' Artemis nodded as he locked Exterminatus into an overhead magnetic harness alongside his bolter.

'*Once you clear the hangar, I suggest taking a look.*'

'I have seen watch fortresses many times, shipmaster. This fortress is of similar design to our own of Talasa Prime.'

'*Just take a look,*' said Aemna, before cutting the transmission.

Artemis sighed. He endured the necessary interaction with mortal humans, but found the constant awe with which they regarded nearly everything in the galaxy tedious. He cleared his head, focusing as the Blackstar shuddered. Its assault ramps folded into the fuselage on hissing hydraulics as the drop-ship lifted from the embarkation deck.

'*Stand by,*' announced Sekor over the vox of the crew bay. The drop-ship shook as it accelerated, darting from the hangar of the *Fatal Redress* and into the void. '*And we are clear, inbound for Furor Shield. Watch captain?*'

Artemis rolled his neck. 'What is it, Sekor?'

'*You may want to have a look at this.*'

Artemis quelled his irritation, pushing the restraint harness locking him in place up and away from him. Standing, he passed through the troop compartment towards the opening cockpit hatch. As Artemis entered, he froze.

Slowly, Artemis reached up, unbuckling the seals of his helm and pulling it free with a muted hiss of air pressure. He peered forwards, leaning over Sekor's pilot throne, the shock writ upon his face mirrored by his comrade.

Dozens of warships hung around Furor Shield, the lights of their engines like fireflies in the night. Vessels of every class employed by the Space Marines of the Deathwatch were represented, from the most nimble hunter-destroyers and strike cruisers to the vast silhouette of a battle-barge.

Two, Artemis realised. *There are two battle-barges here.*

This gathering was unprecedented. The sheer number of vessels gathered was beyond anything Artemis had ever seen in a single place. The Deathwatch was continuously deployed on operations across the farthest flung regions of the Imperium. The gathering of all four of the kill teams comprising a watch company was exceptionally rare, a force tasked for only the most urgent of missions. Artemis himself had not been in contact with his kill teams in months, granting them autonomy to conduct operations from Talasa Prime.

The entire fleet of Furor Shield was present. Every kill team. Every company. Nearly two hundred Space Marines in all. It was a staggering force. The Deathwatch had pacified entire systems with less.

'Throne. What could be happening,' asked Sekor, 'to require an entire watch fortress to assemble?'

Artemis took in the massive assembly as the Blackstar made its final approach to Furor Shield.

'What indeed.'

FIVE

The primary embarkation deck of watch fortress Furor Shield thronged with activity. Hundreds of serfs, menials and thralls scurried about the massive hangar, while tech-priests and servitors attended to the multitudes of inbound craft landing each minute.

Drop-ships and rapid attack craft of every kind covered the hangar deck. Most units had adopted the newer Corvus Blackstar, as Artemis had. Some of the more stubborn commanders continued to make use of older craft, arriving in venerable Storm Eagle and Thunderhawk gunships, their hulls littered with litanies and sagas of battles dating back millennia.

Artemis led his kill team down the assault ramps of their Blackstar as crews of serfs attached fuel lines and performed rote maintenance. He had never seen so many Space Marines in one place, let alone from a unit as steeped in autonomous small-unit warfare as the Deathwatch. Hundreds of his brothers stepped down from their gunships, representing Chapters of the Adeptus Astartes from across the Imperium.

A warrior caught Artemis' eye from halfway across the flight deck, bearing the same black and bone heraldry as he. A fellow Mortifactor. Artemis squinted, magnifying the view through his retinal display to make out the name adorning the Space Marine's armour in blunt Posular script. *Sobor*.

The Mortifactor regarded him, brushing his armoured fingertips across his eyes in an ancient salute from the Mortifactors' benighted world. Artemis mirrored the salute in reply, before Sobor turned away to follow his kill team.

'Watch captain,' a low, resonant voice boomed from behind Artemis. He turned, watching as the figure of Watch Captain Caltanix approached, flanked on each side by a Space Marine of the Storm Lords and Salamanders Chapters.

Artemis inclined his head, and the two clasped wrists in the traditional warrior fashion. 'Caltanix.'

'Well met.' Caltanix was tall, even for a Space Marine, standing nearly a head taller than Artemis. The splayed cross of the Black Templars stood proud on his shoulder in pearl and polished jet. He possessed the same blunt, craggy features common among Space Marines, a countenance smashed to ruin by the trials of war time and again. A two-handed power sword, its blade as long as a mortal human is tall, was strapped to his back in an oiled leather scabbard, while a hunched pair of serfs carried his massive shield between them. They muttered from beneath their dark robes, chanting the litanies that covered the shield in hair-fine silver wire.

'What is happening here?' Artemis gestured to the bustling hangar.

'A summons of great import,' Caltanix nodded. 'All of the Bladefall have rallied to the watch master's call. As have you, praise be.'

The Black Templar turned. 'Walk with me.'

Artemis glanced sidelong at Sekor before looking to Caltanix. 'My kill team will accompany me.'

Caltanix gave a fractional bow, the servos of his brutish war-plate snarling. 'As you say, watch captain.'

Artemis walked with Caltanix down the corridor, his kill team following behind.

'What of the ork vessel that attacked us?' asked Artemis. 'There is no record of greenskins this far into the segmentum.'

'Indeed,' replied Caltanix. 'We have been hunting and intercepting small armadas and raiding groups in this space for the better part of a decade. Recently, though, their numbers have dwindled. The one you encountered was among the last we have identified.'

'The orks are massing for an invasion, then? This is why your companies have been recalled here?'

Caltanix halted before a large bronze gateway, intricately detailed with the symbol of the Deathwatch.

'Inscribed upon this portal are the names and Chapters of every Space Marine to have fallen in service to the Bladefall over the centuries,' said Caltanix. 'Every warrior seconded to Furor Shield swears their oaths in the names of these heroes, those who have gone before and whose crusades are now ended.'

The gateway split down its centre, yawning open with a rumble of ancient cogwork.

'Come,' said Caltanix, 'let us explain why you are here.'

* * *

The main strategium of Furor Shield was arranged like a vast amphitheatre. Tiered rows of stone led down to the centre of the chamber in a semicircle, with a single ramp leading down from the opposite wall. The Space Marines of the Bladefall filed into the strategium, assembling by watch company with their watch captains at the fore.

Caltanix led Artemis and his kill team to the bottom of the amphitheatre, gesturing to the first row of benches. Artemis and his team were seated, and Caltanix returned to his place before his company.

Sekor leaned towards Rogerio. 'Brother, have you ever seen anything like this?'

The Crimson Fist shook his head. 'No, never in these numbers. This situation must be dire for them to pull every battle-brother from the line.'

A flight of cherub servitors buzzed over the amphitheatre, settling above the central dais. The diminutive angels brought golden trumpets to their lips, sounding a blaring fanfare. Every Space Marine rose, standing and locking to attention as one.

A doorway in the rear of the amphitheatre opened, flooding the walkway before it with bright light. A procession of robed figures emerged in two columns, swinging bronze censers that trailed twisting clouds of incense. The thralls came to the end of the walkway, proceeding around the edge of the dais.

Next to pass through the doorway was a pair of hulking warriors encased in Terminator armour. They stomped forwards with heavy tread, one brandishing a massive rotary assault cannon, the other armed with lightning claws built into each gauntlet.

Behind the Terminators came the ruler of Furor Shield. Watch Master Asharbanapal strode towards his warriors with the easy grace of one destined for command. He wore exquisitely crafted power armour, adorned with laurels and parchment scrolls pronouncing the victories of the Bladefall. A cloak of crimson silk flowed behind him, its edges held aloft by cherub servitors. He bore no heraldry from the Chapter of his origin, having renounced all ties outside of the Deathwatch when he assumed the mantle of watch master.

In his hands, the watch master held a relic weapon, rare beyond imagining. Its haft was a perfectly balanced rod of adamantium encased in gold, its every surface etched with scrolling names of those who had carried it to war. It ended in an ornate boltgun, accented with pearl and rose gold. Beneath its barrel sat a platinum power blade, honed to a monomolecular edge, itself the length of an Adeptus Astartes power sword.

It was a weapon that had been created and carried by the elite bodyguard of the Emperor himself. A weapon that had held the ramparts upon the holy Throneworld of Terra against the fires of heresy ten thousand years before. Asharbanapal carried the guardian spear as he joined his brethren, a symbol of both his office and his peerless skill as a warrior.

A pace behind the watch master to either side followed the masters of the Reclusiam and Librarius of Furor Shield. Chief Librarian Sugedai, formerly of the White Scars, calmly descended towards the dais, a half smile visible beneath the shadow of his crystalline psychic hood. High Reclusiarch Albanactus, his armour still bearing the heraldry of the Black Templars, was unreadable, his features locked beneath the snarling flayed skull of his helm. Aggression and zealous fury radiated from him like a heat haze.

The watch master's boots touched the dais, and every Space Marine assembled bent the knee. Heads bowed, their fists clashed against their breastplates in salute. Flanked by Sugedai and Albanactus, and the Terminator elite beside them, Asharbanapal raised his guardian spear in one gauntleted fist, bringing the end down against the stone floor with a clang like the tolling of a bell.

'Rise, my brothers,' said the watch master, his voice carrying effortlessly through the vast amphitheatre despite his soft, measured tone. The assembled Space Marines stood as one.

'This is a day of days,' said Asharbanapal. 'The Bladefall have not united in full strength in all of the millennia since their founding. Our stewardship of the Emperor's realms has called you to many places, and measured you against the foulest predations of the xenos.

'Our duties are manifold, our enemies ruthless and insidious. The reclamation of each watch company here will not be without consequence. Threats will arise in our absence, and the blood of the Imperium will be shed. The burden of that choice rests upon my shoulders, my brothers. I did not arrive at it without consideration of its gravity, but the threat that has surfaced eclipses all others.'

The watch master turned, levelling the guardian spear. 'Watch Captain Artemis, of Talasa Prime.'

Artemis went to one knee beneath Asharbanapal's gaze. 'Watch master.'

'Rise, watch captain. You have been summoned here for a purpose.'

Artemis stood. 'I have answered your call, and I obey.'

'You have performed admirably in your service to Talasa Prime and the Deathwatch,' said Asharbanapal. 'You have faced the darkest of the xenos and prevailed against them.'

'You honour me, watch master. I live but in service to the Emperor.'

The watch master flashed a smile for an instant. 'You have even prevailed against the Great Devourer, an enemy that has blighted the Imperium and sown great destruction upon humanity. On one such undertaking, you succeeded in capturing a brood of genestealers alive, in service to Lord Inquisitor Kryptman of the Ordo Xenos. Is that not so?'

Artemis looked up. 'It is as you say, watch master.'

Murmurs of disbelief rippled out across the assembled Space Marines. Muted outrage passed between warriors, suppressed by their sub-commanders. Two hundred faces turned to Artemis, a mixture of anger, shock and fascination colouring their features.

Asharbanapal raised his hands, silencing the clamouring Space Marines before turning back to Artemis.

'A perilous task, watch captain. The purpose of the Deathwatch is the eradication of the xenos, wherever it appears. It is not to be understood, not to be cognised, but to be hated. Nothing but its utter annihilation can be accepted, yes?'

'By the Emperor, it is so,' replied Artemis.

'Why did you capture the tyranid in service to the lord inquisitor?' asked the watch master. 'To what end, what purpose did you undertake this?'

'A vanguard of a new hive fleet was emerging,' said Artemis, 'threatening to spill into Ultima Segmentum. Lord Inquisitor Kryptman sought to direct the tyranids away from Imperial space and into the ork empire of Octarius, to set them upon each other while a defence could be mounted.'

'Indeed,' said Asharbanapal. 'In that, the lord inquisitor succeeded. The hive fleet appointed "Leviathan" descended upon the foul greenskins, turning its ravenous hunger upon their Overfiend and its hordes. All that remained was to wait. Wait for the xenos to rage against one another until only one survived, a broken shadow of its former strength.'

The watch master stepped to the centre of the dais, raising his guardian spear aloft. 'We are here because the Inquisition has *failed*. The conflagration they kindled between our enemies has made them stronger, and their numbers more vast. The more biological matter it devours, the heartier and more numerous the tyranid becomes. And the foul ork, capable only of war, used the fire of battle to multiply far beyond the hordes it wielded before.'

A watch captain bearing the marks of the Iron Hands stood, his voice rendered harsh by extensive bionics. 'Has the Inquisition done nothing to curtail their advance?'

Asharbanapal regarded the Iron Hand, and nodded to Albanactus. The high reclusiarch tapped a command into a data-slate, and a hololithic star chart leapt into view in the air over the central dais. A system blinked and expanded into focus, on the border of the ork empire of Octarius and the tendril of hive fleet Leviathan.

'The Kurbynola System,' began the watch master, gesturing to the hololith. 'A vibrant star encircled by twenty worlds. Agriculture, mineral deposits, and substantial population centres on most of them.

'When the ork conflict with the tyranids began to spill into the Imperium, the Inquisition sought to contain their advance. They deemed the Kurbynola System "non-essential". All defensive resources were withdrawn from the system, confining them to the innermost citadel world of Praesidium. Defenceless, the Kurbynola System was enveloped by the xenos. Within months, both greenskins and tyranids had overrun the outer worlds. After two years, half of the system was razed, their populations butchered, their surfaces rendered uninhabitable.'

Artemis seethed, his bionic arm creaking as his fist tightened. The memories flooded back with his rage, burning in his mind.

–the twisted, claustrophobic passageways of the space hulk. The nightmarish forms of the genestealers, illuminated in the strobing flash of boltgun fire. The floor beneath them buckling and shearing away. Lavestus falling into a swarm of rending claws. Artemis leaping, grabbing hold of his brother as they sank into the howling darkness. His brothers pulling him back, finally hauling him away as he lost his grip. Sprawling as blood sprayed down his armour, his arm gone at the shoulder–

Artemis stood. 'Watch master, where is the lord inquisitor? Kryptman must be brought to account for the billions of the Emperor's servants he has led to the slaughter.'

'The Inquisition shares your sentiment, watch captain. They declared him excommunicated, and their agents scour the Imperium as we speak to find him. Yet nothing he could do would alter our course. Our path is clear. Only we can deter a xenos menace of this magnitude.'

Asharbanapal spread his arms wide, exercising a rhetorical command that made it seem as if he were speaking directly to each Space Marine alone.

'We are the bane of the xenos, my brothers. Now, in its multitudes, it is poised to threaten the entire segmentum. We stand against the invasion of the Leviathan hive fleet, and a greenskin incursion of a scale that has not been seen in nearly ten thousand years. It is for that threat, my kindred, that I have forsaken all other oaths. The Inquisition has failed, and it now falls to the Deathwatch to stand and drive this peril from our shores.'

'My lord,' Caltanix stood, striding down the amphitheatre to stand before the watch master. In a single smooth motion, he drew the longsword from his back and dropped to one knee. Head bowed, he held the sword in both hands. 'Task me with such a crusade. I will burn every world the xenos infest, and marshal our fleet to purge them from the stars. I will lead our brothers and cleanse the Imperium of their taint!'

'No.'

With a single word, the chamber was silent. Caltanix turned, watching as Artemis stepped forwards.

'Watch master, the Deathwatch is a scalpel, not a cudgel,' Artemis said. 'If we are able to draw out the Overfiend of the greenskins and take his head, his hordes will turn upon themselves. Their unity will collapse as it has before.'

'And what of the tyranids?' asked the watch master.

'The greenskins will be in disarray, no longer a united threat to the segmentum but they will still combat the tyranids as much as they will each other. The hive fleet will seek to press their advantage, and we can capitalise on such a diversion to locate the primary hive ships controlling the swarms. If our combined fleets can destroy the hive ships, the tyranids will lose their link to the Hive Mind, becoming feral. Precise, coordinated strikes can cut the heads from our enemies.'

Artemis locked eyes with the watch master. 'My lord, it was the work of my hands, my deeds which brought about the start of this. With your blessing, I would have them bring about its end as well. I will hunt down the greenskin Overfiend and return with its head. With their fleets in conflict they will not notice a single vessel.'

Asharbanapal was silent for a moment, impassive as he looked at Artemis.

'Very well, watch captain. You will take your ship and do as you have said.'

The watch master turned to Caltanix, who was still kneeling before him. 'Caltanix, you and your kill team shall accompany him.'

For a pair of heartbeats Caltanix remained on his knees, his eyes cast to the floor. His facade betrayed nothing, as if carved from cold stone, yet Artemis could see the faintest tremble ripple over the blade the Templar held aloft.

'Brother?' asked Asharbanapal, a soft smile creasing his dusky features.

Caltanix stood, sheathing his longsword and bringing a fist to his chest. 'It will be done, my lord.'

The Iron Hands watch captain stood once more. 'You shall have a kill team of my company as well.'

Artemis bowed. 'I will not fail.'

PART II

SIX

The space between stars caught fire, as hunger warred against wrath.

The Waaagh! of Overfiend Blaktoof, ruler of the ork empire of Octarius, filled the void, hundreds of brutal warships colliding with the enveloping swarm of hive fleet Leviathan. Rockets, mass-driven asteroids and unstable plasma bombs sprayed from each ramshackle vessel as the hive fleet vomited billions of winged horrors from vast bio-ships.

The ork vessels glowed with the fire from thousands of gun turrets bristling their hulls, filling the void around them with ordnance as the tyranids descended. Greenskins in primitive environment suits charged onto the hulls of their ships, slavering for combat. Flocks of ork fighters streamed from terror ships, twisting through space as they engaged the oncoming tyranid fliers.

The bio-ships quivered, organic cannons discharging gouts of acid that burned through ork armour and reduced their ships to boiling slag. Vast grasping tentacles wound about greenskin warships, breaking their backs and dragging them slowly into gaping, razor-toothed maws.

A cluster of ork ships, little more than asteroids with engine arrays bolted onto them, swept through the swarms of tyranid creatures. Firing their engines in starbursts of dirty light, they rammed a bio-ship, smashing into its flank and breaching thick layers of void-hardened chitin. Clouds of flash-freezing ichor burst from the living craft, and thousands of ork warriors clawed their way into the bio-ship with axes and saw-bladed claws. Broods of tyranid warrior organisms, dormant within the bio-ship, roused from their comatose state, tearing from birthing pods and flooding the interior of their vessel to oppose the orks. Tides of chitin smashed against greenskin flesh and scavenged metal, claw against blade.

The orks roared, jubilant at the slaughter even as they fell beneath the waves of gnashing tyranids. War was everything to the greenskins, the sublime goal sought in every act undertaken by an ork. Violence and aggression were their lifeblood, and they hurled themselves into the swarms of Leviathan, ecstatic to shed blood.

The tyranids cut down the orks in droves, the cold instinct of their gestalt intelligence leading the combat forms as other creatures dragged away the dead of both xenos races, their corpses to be consumed and converted to biomass to fuel the hive fleet.

Blood and ichor streamed through the battle, wreathing wreckage and the husks of dead bio-ships in frozen crusts of crimson and purplish black. The light of stars glittered on the frozen corpses of thousands and thousands of xenos, some still locked together as they drifted silently through the dark.

As their fleets mauled one another, the worlds turned below them. The once verdant planets of the Kurbynola System had been reduced to ashen husks, their populations massacred, all organic life devoured. The war between ork and tyranid had raged through the charnel house of Octarius, and now it had erupted into the Imperium of Man.

The *Fatal Redress* slid through the void, its engines dark and reactor cold as it pushed through the fringes of the Kurbynola System. The Deathwatch warship had shot forwards at maximum burn before deactivating its plasma engines, drifting on its momentum. All but the most essential systems onboard the frigate had been shut down to avoid detection, rendering the spear of dark iron indistinguishable from the void around it.

Shipmaster Aemna turned to Artemis. The bridge was dark, with only the most essential stations still receiving power. Servitors drooled, slack and inert at their consoles. Crew members paced from point to point in silence, breathing from bulky rebreather masks now that the life-support systems had been brought to barely survivable levels. The hand-held lamp packs they carried revealed portions of the bridge within cones of weak yellow light.

'How close are we?' asked Artemis, standing beside Aemna's command throne.

'If we managed to maintain our course before cutting our engines,' replied the shipmaster, her voice muffled by her rebreather mask, 'we should reach maximum augur range within the hour. That is, unless they have shifted across the system from our last available scans. It will be difficult to know for sure until we make visual contact. Right now we are running blind.'

The vox-bead in Artemis' helm chimed. The rune for Rogerio blinked insistently on his retinal display.

'Watch captain.' The Crimson Fist's voice crackled over the low-powered vox-link.

'What is it, Rogerio?' replied Artemis, irritated that vox silence had been broken.

'It is the Flesh Tearer,' said Rogerio. Artemis heard the tightness in the veteran's voice. It was rare for him to exude such tension.

'Understood, I am inbound.' Artemis looked down at the shipmaster. 'Notify me of any developments immediately. No alterations to our current course are to be made without my sanction. Do you understand?'

Aemna nodded. 'Aye, watch captain.'

Artemis walked down the darkened corridors of the *Fatal Redress* from the ship's bridge. He was fully armed, his thrumming Mark VIII power armour sealed and ready for combat at a moment's notice. Alongside Rogerio, Hyphantes, Imtehan and Sekor, two full kill teams of the Bladefall prepared themselves within the ship's armouries and barracks, adding another eighteen warriors to join Artemis in the hunt for the greenskin Overfiend.

A roar ripped through the metal bones of the Deathwatch vessel, a deafening howl of wrathful pain. Artemis broke into a run, his heavy boots clanging against the deck plating as he drew closer to the source of the cry.

It had begun as soon as they entered the system. In every place the hideous swarms of the tyranid touched, they radiated a dense synaptic field, projecting the vile presence of their Hive Mind. The field, known as the 'Shadow in the Warp', was anathema to psychic ability, drowning out all connection to the warp. All felt its insidious touch, racking the mortal crew with nightmares, disrupting the abilities of the ship's Navigator and astropathic choir to perform their function, and bringing psykers to the very edge of madness.

Imtehan had sequestered himself within his living quarters as the *Fatal Redress* drew close to the Kurbynola System. As the warship slipped into proximity of the hive fleet, sounds of violence began to issue from the Flesh Tearer's cell, along with furious bellowing from the tormented Librarian.

Artemis possessed an inkling of the affliction that tormented the sons of Sanguinius. He had fought alongside enough of them to appreciate the danger they posed should they succumb. He had witnessed Urbino, a warrior of the Blood Angels, lapse into a frenzy, slaying dozens of hideous genestealers before he himself was killed. Such fury was a powerful weapon, but indiscriminate in whom it harmed. Urbino would have attacked Artemis as easily as he had the xenos.

The line between maintaining control and descending into a mindless berserker was growing thin, and Artemis was wary of the pain driving Imtehan into the same state he had seen consume Urbino.

Another roar rattled the walls of the corridor as Artemis reached the Flesh Tearer's chamber. Rogerio and Caltanix stood vigil at the bulkhead, their weapons at the ready.

'His condition is worse,' said Rogerio, his storm bolter braced across his chest.

'Has he made any effort to leave his cell?' asked Artemis.

Caltanix gestured to the bulkhead, indicating the fist-sized deformations in the thick iron plating. 'No, though it may be a matter of time. His suffering grows the closer we draw to the xenos.'

'Let me speak to him.' The Space Marines turned as they heard the voice.

A warrior strode from the darkness of the corridor. The winged blood drop icon of the Blood Angels Chapter rested on a field of crimson on his pauldron.

'I am Pecori, born of Baal and Angel of the Blood. Our brother stands upon a threshold, his grip tenuous. If you will sanction it, I would seek to hold him from such a fall.'

Artemis considered the Blood Angel. 'Do what you can. We will need every brother we have for this mission. He must overcome this affliction.'

Pecori nodded. Rogerio and Caltanix braced at either side of the bulkhead as Artemis hauled the door open.

The interior of the cell was dark, the lumen strips smashed and torn from their housings. Detritus and fragments of metal and stone covered the floor, clicking beneath Pecori's boots as the Blood Angel entered. As his eyesight adjusted, Artemis saw the cracked rockcrete of the walls, stained crimson from where the Flesh Tearer had beaten his fists bloody against them.

A deep, breathless snarl issued from the dark corner of the chamber. It reminded Artemis of a wounded beast, backed into a corner where it was the most dangerous and unpredictable. He could make out the silhouette of Imtehan, kneeling, with both hands grasping at his skull.

'Shut this door behind me,' Pecori whispered, stepping slowly towards Imtehan. Artemis glimpsed the Flesh Tearer, growling through clenched teeth, fists splitting cracks into the rockcrete floor as he crushed down, before sealing the hatch.

For several minutes, there was silence, punctuated briefly by the snarling roars of Imtehan's anguished rage. Through the thick iron doorway to the cell, Artemis could hear a calm undercurrent weaving through the fury, slow and methodical but with the insistence of the tide. Artemis could not hear the words being spoken, but he could feel the tension as it ebbed away, before the silence asserted itself fully within the darkness of the Flesh Tearer's chambers.

Pecori stepped out into the corridor, closing the hatch behind him.

'What happened?' asked Artemis of the Blood Angel. 'What did you say to him?'

Pecori stared back at Artemis with piercing green eyes. Brushing a lock of platinum blond hair away from his porcelain visage, he raised the hood of the surplice he wore over his armour.

'Only what needed to be said.'

Artemis had departed for the *Fatal Redress'* observation dome after Pecori had calmed Imtehan. He did not know what had transpired between the two sons of Sanguinius, but knew well enough that some secrets were best kept from the light. The psyker was pained, but able to control his suffering. He would be able to fight when the time came.

The observation dome was a blister of armourglass protruding from the spine of the *Fatal Redress*. With its sheath of armoured ceramite retracted, it offered an unobstructed view of the void surrounding the Deathwatch warship, the light of distant stars glittering down upon Artemis as he took in the view.

'In a system of this size,' Artemis turned as he heard the voice behind him, 'jump points along the rim would be teeming with ships. Cargo freighters, Imperial Navy system monitors, all manner of military and commercial craft moving corewards or jumping to adjacent systems.'

Sekor stopped at the edge of the blister, resting his gauntleted hands upon the brass railing encircling the chamber. 'Now, there is nothing. It is silent.'

'Quiet as a tomb,' Artemis agreed.

'Did you know?' Sekor asked, looking up at the emptiness. 'When we boarded that hulk for Kryptman. Did you know that this was what he intended?'

Artemis was silent for a moment. 'No,' he answered. 'I knew the mission, where to go and what we were to do when we arrived, but nothing beyond that.'

'If you had known, would you have done anything to stop it?'

'That is not our province.'

'Then what is?' Sekor rounded on Artemis. 'Our duty is to defend humanity from the predations of the xenos. Lavestus died–'

'Lavestus died in service to the Imperium!' Artemis snapped. His vox-bead chimed, but he blinked it away. 'As must we all if called to do so. Ours is not to question why, Sekor. We do our duty, no matter what the cost may be.'

'You yourself have thrown us into this madness because of what we have done!' Sekor hissed, pointing to the void beyond the dome. 'Is it to avenge the lives of those whose blood is on our hands? Or are you scrambling to salvage your wounded pride?'

'You overstep your bounds, Castellan,' Artemis growled. 'You will still your insubordinate tongue, or I will–'

The watch captain's words were cut off by a thudding impact striking the armourglass dome. Another collision followed, and another, and another. The two Space Marines looked up into the void.

Ork bodies smashed against the observation dome. Frozen and twisted in death, they tumbled over the blister as the *Fatal Redress* ploughed through them. Veils of icy blood droplets cascaded over the frigate like rubies, fields so vast they resembled nebulae. Larger debris and twisted metal drifted around them, and a shadow fell over Artemis and Sekor as the still form of a dead bio-ship reared into view.

Artemis focussed, finally heeding the insistent chime of his vox-bead. He opened the link.

'Watch captain,' cried Aemna, *'ahead of us, we–'*

'I see it, shipmaster,' replied Artemis calmly.

'We are approaching the minimum distance to manoeuvre. We need to change course now!'

'Bring secondary propulsion online, shipmaster.' Artemis turned from Sekor and strode to the bulkhead. 'And avoid notifying both xenos fleets of our arrival, if you please.'

SEVEN

Manoeuvring thrusters set in the prow of the *Fatal Redress* fired in jets of sharp flame, arresting the frigate's momentum and pitching it into a sharp dive. The sleek craft barely scraped free of direct impact with the dead tyranid bio-ship, and several spires and auspex towers along its spinal battlements were sheared away.

Shipmaster Aemna gripped the armrests of her command throne as her vessel shuddered. The vibrations were more unnerving to the crew in the eerie silence that hung over the ship without the gentle rumble of the vessel's reactor. She gritted her teeth, suppressing the anger welling up in her chest.

Aemna had served with the Deathwatch from childhood, climbing the ranks aboard ships of all kinds before taking the helm of the *Fatal Redress*. Conducting dangerous and secretive missions against some of humanity's most terrifying enemies was nothing new to her, but sending her rapid strike frigate alone into a major void engagement between two xenos races was suicidal at best.

The ship ceased its tremors as it cleared the tyranid bio-ship. Aemna barked orders to her crew, firing a short burn from the ventral jets before killing the manoeuvring drives.

A junior officer rushed to her command throne from the vox station pits. 'Ma'am, receiving reports from the upper decks. We have confirmation of multiple contacts cutting into the hull.'

Aemna hissed a quiet curse, opening her vox-link.

'Watch captain, your presence is required on the upper decks. We have tyranids onboard.'

* * *

'Prime all armour void seals,' said Artemis as he chambered a round in his bolt pistol. He had deployed the three kill teams onboard the *Fatal Redress* across the upper decks, braced to repel the xenos they heard clattering and scratching against the ship's hull. 'Activate mag-locks. Close-combat weapons and hellfire rounds only. Pick your targets. Engagement will be at close range and we must minimise damage to the hull.'

Rogerio plodded forwards through the maintenance corridor, his boots clamping to the deck with each step. 'Watch captain!' he called, pointing to the ceiling of the corridor as the metal began to smoulder.

'Be ready.' Artemis waved Hyphantes ahead, stopping to pull Imtehan aside. 'Are you prepared, brother?'

The Flesh Tearer nodded sharply, his shoulders rising and falling with each pained breath. 'I will fight, watch captain. These xenos will die by my hand.'

Artemis clapped his pauldron, indicating a position across the corridor.

Smoke began to curl from the ceiling, the stink of burning metal and ozone thick even through the filters of the Space Marines' helms. The reinforced steel began to liquefy, bubbling as slag drooled down to the floor. Microscopic breaches popped as the hull groaned.

'Brace!' Artemis shouted. The ceiling blew apart as it explosively decompressed. Hard vacuum tore at the Deathwatch warriors, who were held firm to the deck by their mag-locked boots. Heavy bulkheads on either side of the Space Marines slammed down to contain the breach. The silence of the open void muted all noise but the soft chimes of Artemis' retinal display, and the steady sound of his breathing.

For several heartbeats nothing moved. The Space Marines tensed, flexing their grip on their weapons. Darting shadows flashed over the hull breach.

'Contact!' bellowed Hyphantes as a tide of tyranids erupted into the corridor. Hormagaunts, hideous creatures of violet and corpse-white carapace, leapt at the kill team, slashing with scything claws and snapping fanged jaws.

Bolter fire eviscerated the invading xenos. The mutagenic acid encased within the Deathwatch's specialised hellfire rounds boiled the tyranids alive from the inside, reducing them to crumbling husks of scorched meat. More tyranids appeared, hooking their sickle claws into the compromised hull plating and tearing the breach wider.

A hormagaunt leapt onto Rogerio, thrashing as it fought to bury its claws in his chest. He could feel the thump of its powerful hind legs against the deck and hear the screech of its vicious claws through his power armour. The Crimson Fist drew a gladius from his hip, ripping it up and through the vile creature and hurling the bifurcated remains to clash against the walls of the corridor with a dull thud.

Slaved to the united gestalt intelligence of the Hive Mind, the tyranids converged on the hull breach, cutting through the floating corpses of their dead to reach the kill team inside.

Artemis raised his bolt pistol as he drew Exterminatus. A lattice of targeting runes crystalised over his right eye. He fired, the pouncing tyranids rupturing into frozen blooms of ichor and spinning chitin fragments. He whipped Exterminatus across another hormagaunt's thorax, spinning away and on to the next as its innards burst from the gash in slowly tumbling coils.

Sekor and Imtehan fought back to back. As Sekor filled the corridor with withering fire from twin bolt pistols, the Flesh Tearer carved into the xenos assault with his meteor hammer, the saw-toothed spheres of dark iron blurring through chitin and obliterating xenos flesh. The morning star whirled its deadly orbit beside Imtehan as he readied for another wave of tyranids, its twin heads crackling with active power fields as they spun from the chain linking them. Beneath his helm, Imtehan's clenched jaw creaked. Had his organic teeth not been replaced by pegs of dense iron long ago, they would have shattered under the strain of his repressed rage.

Hyphantes locked his bolter to his hip as his magazine depleted, drawing his twin falxes in a blur of energised metal. He howled a jubilant battle cry as he danced into the press of alien claws, relishing the death he dealt to his Chapter's most hated enemy with every swing of his blades. Clouds of frozen ichor surrounded him like gems of tainted amethyst. He punched the tattered remains of a tyranid corpse drifting in front of him away, turning with leaden footfalls in search of new targets.

Silence descended once more, save for the elevated breathing sawing from each of the Space Marines behind their helms. Artemis took advantage of the reprieve to reload his bolt pistol, and opened a vox-link to the rest of the kill team.

'Team, status report.'

'Sekor, no damage.'

'I am unhurt, watch captain,' said Rogerio.

'I endure,' hissed Imtehan, clearly still fighting the battle within his mind.

'Ready for more,' growled Hyphantes, still hunched in a combat stance with his falxes spread wide.

Artemis killed the link and opened another. 'Watch Captain Caltanix, what is your status?'

The vox crackled, flawed with static as the Black Templar replied.

'We had brief contact via a minor hull breach, only a handful of the vile things from when we impacted their hive ship. We put them to the sword. The situation is contained.'

'Understood. Our kill teams will perform overlapping sweeps of the upper decks to confirm the ship is secure before bringing up crews to close the hull breaches.'

'Acknowledged,' Caltanix replied. *'Beginning our sweep now.'*

Artemis closed the vox-link, sending a quick pulse to the bridge confirming their containment of the tyranid incursion to the shipmaster. After a moment, the bulkheads unlocked and slid open, and Artemis waved his kill team forwards to begin their inspection.

Hyphantes sheathed his falxes, picking a severed tyranid head from the air as it spun within a veil of its own ichor. He stared down at the monstrous visage of the creature, frozen in a vicious snarl. For all the black history of the Scythes of the Emperor, this had been his first action against the tyranids. The vile beasts that had devoured honoured Sotha, slaughtered his brothers before him and brought his Chapter to the precipice of extinction.

Slowly, Hyphantes tightened his grasp. The slick plates of carapace began to buckle under the crushing strain. His lips peeled back from bared teeth. The tyranid skull held his furious glare with black unfocussed eyes before fracturing in his grip, collapsing into an expanding cloud of freezing gristle.

'Rest easy, lad.' Rogerio laid a hand on Hyphantes' shoulder. 'This is only just beginning. There will be legions of these xenos filth to be slain soon.'

EIGHT

It had taken four hours for kill teams Artemis and Caltanix to meticulously purge the upper decks. The third Deathwatch unit aboard the *Fatal Redress*, Kill Team Krycses, had waited in reserve, prepared to converge on any surviving tyranids that had penetrated deeper into the ship. By the time crews of servitors arrived to seal the breaches and make repairs, the corridors were caked in blackened carbon where the Space Marines had scoured the passages with searing deluges from heavy flamers.

Artemis entered the strategium of the *Fatal Redress*, his armour still caked in thawing gore that slicked from the ceramite plates in greasy strings. With a dull thud, he set his bolter on the table dominating the chamber and removed his helm. Caltanix and Krycses stepped through the hatch and joined him.

Last to enter was Shipmaster Aemna. She strode into the chamber, and with a flickering stare from her augmetic eyes, a tactical hololith stuttered into being from a purring focusing lens.

'This is the return from our last auspex pulse forty-eight minutes ago. We were able to make two other scans prior to that without detection. Either the xenos remain unaware of our presence, or we are not enough of a threat for them to care.'

Clouds of blinking runes designating ork and tyranid ships crackled in the hololith, entangled in swathes of red and yellow. A single blue icon representing the *Fatal Redress* stood alone, apart from the knot of embattled xenos.

'We need to get closer,' said Caltanix.

'This is the closest we have reached without detection from either fleet,' said Aemna. 'A prospect that grows increasingly unlikely the nearer we draw to them.'

'Shipmaster,' said Artemis. 'Have you been able to determine the relative sizes of the ork vessels in their armada?'

Aemna consulted her data-slate, tapping in a series of commands. The hololith refreshed, with each ork ship's rune bearing a stream of data beside it. 'There is little coordination or formation to be found in their arrangement. While standard Imperial doctrine calls for capital ships to sit at the centre of formations shielded by layers of support craft and escorts, the orks' largest vessels are at the vanguard, pressed the furthest into the hive fleet.'

'Where the fighting is the thickest,' said Watch Sergeant Krycses, the Raven Guard pushing a stray lock of sable hair from his face as he leaned towards the hololith.

Artemis studied the tactical projection. He focussed on the blinking rune of the ork flagship, completely enveloped in tyranid icons.

'Then that is where we must go,' said Artemis with finality. 'That is where we will find the Overfiend.'

Each brother of Kill Team Artemis readied themselves for battle in their own way, conducting rituals and traditions ingrained from service in the Chapters of their origins. While their former allegiances had been cast aside when they ascended to the ranks of the Deathwatch, they still retained the cultures and identities ingrained in them as neophytes.

Rogerio bathed his armour and weapons in twisting coils of incense from a burning censer. The veteran chanted guttural litanies of hate against the greenskin as he prepared to do battle with the most abhorred of all the Crimson Fists' myriad foes. He drew the blade of his gladius across his left palm, pressing his bleeding hand against his armour and leaving a dark handprint on its chest.

Sekor meticulously dismantled each of his weapons down to their simplest components before reassembling them, repeating the ritual twice more for each tool of destruction he would carry on the mission. Imtehan fought in the training pits, centring his turbulent thoughts as he ripped apart a host of combat servitors.

Hyphantes sang. A low, sonorous dirge rang from the walls of his arming chamber as he prayed to crystal vials containing the remains of the warriors who had worn his armour before him. The vials held ash, scraps of fabric and splinters of bone. One contained a measure of blood, dried and crumbled away by time into wine-red dust. Their names adorned his right shoulder pad in flowing script, edged in silver around the golden crossed-scythes icon of his Chapter.

Alone within his own cell, Artemis flicked his gaze over the menagerie of flensed skulls hanging from the walls. Every xenos breed was represented, from the sleek elongated skull of an eldar witch to the brutal, sloped visage of an ork chieftain. He remembered tearing the massive warlord's head from its spine, standing upon mounds of the dead and holding the trophy aloft as he roared in triumph.

Artemis pushed the memory aside and walked to a clay urn set beneath his armour. Opening the urn, he dipped his hands inside, drawing out handfuls of gritty black dust from within. He looked down upon the dark volcanic soil of Posul, ashen from an eternity starved of a star's light. Artemis spread the dust over his flesh in an ancient ritual dating back to the earliest primitive tribes of his night-shrouded home world, who had caked themselves in earth to camouflage their bodies before the hunt.

Once he had finished, robed serfs stepped forwards. They anchored the heavy plates of ceramite armour to Artemis' musculature, drilling the war-plate into place and connecting the interface ports set along his spine with a series of sharp clicks, as other serfs offered reverent prayers to its stirring machine-spirit. His power pack thrummed as it was machined into place, flooding his limbs with strength.

Artemis dismissed the serfs as they finished their appointed tasks. He sprinkled the ashen soil of Posul over the blade of Exterminatus, offering a silent prayer to the spirit of the relic blade. He honoured the bygone warriors of the Deathwatch who had borne it into battle before it had become his inheritance to wield. He clamped a grenade dispenser to his belt, mag-locking his bolter to his left leg and his bolt pistol to the small of his back.

Artemis sheathed Exterminatus, locked the scabbard to his hip and set his helm in the crook of his arm. The time for preparations had ended. The Mortifactor stood upon the brink, the war rushing up to meet him. He had only to leap.

The three kill teams assembled on the embarkation deck of the *Fatal Redress*, a cross-section of the finest warriors of the Imperium of Man.

Caltanix had chosen his own kill team of vanguard veterans to join him. They were consummate close-combat linebreakers, taken from the elite of their Chapters' assault companies. The warriors were heavily drilled in boarding actions and planetary assault, and accounted for the absence of jump packs by doubling their caches of melta bombs. They perched on the deck, some carrying artificer thunder hammers in both hands, others bearing power mauls held loosely behind heavy boarding shields.

Drynn, the Iron Hands watch captain of the fourth watch

company, had sent a kill team comprised primarily of asymmetrical warfare specialists. The eight warriors were encased in irregular power armour, heavily modified by each of the warriors to their own specifications as much as was possible without rousing the ire of the spirits dwelling within the ceramite plate. They excelled in assassination, clandestine operations and sabotage, at their best sowing destruction from deep behind enemy lines. Watch Sergeant Krycses lounged against a supply crate, tossing a combat blade in glittering arcs before catching it on his fingertip.

Artemis stepped onto the embarkation deck, giving a curt nod to his kill team as he placed himself between the three units.

'My brothers,' he began. 'There is little I must say, and so I will exercise brevity. We all know what lies ahead of us. With victory, we end this now, and this system shall remain the only casualty of the Inquisition's folly. We must cut the head from the beast. We must be swift, silent and ruthless. Bring glory to your watch fortresses, and honour to your Chapters. Draw your blades against the predations of the xenos, and purge them from the realms of the Emperor.'

Exterminatus blurred from Artemis' sheath, the power field crackling as it burned Posul's soil from its raised blade. 'Victory!' Artemis boomed, his voice reverberating across the vast chamber.

'*Victory!*' the kill teams roared in reply.

NINE

The *Fatal Redress* was nearly invisible in the void. With short blasts from its manoeuvring jets, it wound through the labyrinth of tumbling debris with glacial slowness.

Within the darkness of the warship's bridge, Shipmaster Aemna waited in her command throne, fingers steepled before her mouth as she watched the ponderous dance of wreckage through the viewscreen. The tension among the crew was thick, a near physical thing. The shipmaster felt relief that the majority of the ship's complement was comprised of mindless servitors, unaffected by the strain afflicting the mortal crew.

The void before them darkened as the shadow of a vast bio-ship passed over the Deathwatch vessel. Undulating tentacles larger than the Imperial frigate swept slowly ahead of the gargantuan creature, grasping in search of prey as it stalked closer to the centre of the space battle. It took several minutes for the shadow to lift as the bio-ship passed.

Aemna released a breath she did not realise she had been holding, running a hand through the stubble of her scalp. Bone-deep exhaustion permeated her and her crew, and the vulnerability of their situation grated on her. She was used to speed, to the rapid traversal of the void as she delivered her deadly cargo of demigod warriors. Without shields, without weapons and barely sipping enough power from the reactors to keep the ship from becoming a tomb, Aemna had never put her vessel in such a fragile, precarious state.

Aemna keyed in a command on her throne's runepad. The *Fatal Redress* gave another short blast from its attitude thrusters, angling the prow towards the heart of the xenos confrontation. The incredible distances separating them rendered the battle as little more than a smudge on the viewscreen, briefly flickering with pinpricks of light as alien warships died.

The crew was silent, their tense, weary eyes fixed to the viewscreen as another blast slid them forwards. The frigate's superstructure groaned softly as it advanced, its momentum carrying them inexorably closer to their target. Aemna ran the calculations through her mind. Barring a collision with the thousands of pieces of debris large enough to smash her vessel into fragments, which represented an uncomfortable amount of the prospective outcome, the *Fatal Redress* was set to ghost by the largest ork capital ship present, close enough to launch the pair of Corvus Blackstars carrying the kill teams to their destination.

If Aemna were able to achieve the insertion without being detected by either fleet, she would maintain her drift, slipping back into and hiding amongst the wreckage until the drop-ships returned. If not, she would light the engines and burn the reactors to slag fleeing to the deepest black. The watch captain would be on his own.

Some outside of the Deathwatch would consider the shipmaster callous, she was sure. Perhaps there was truth to that, but experience had scoured the sympathy that came with ignorance from her. Aemna had served on enough ships and carried enough kill teams to understand better than most the odds of survival for the Space Marines she transported from hot zone to hot zone. Were Artemis and his comrades to meet their destiny, it would not mark the first time she had watched the Emperor's angels of death leap into the jaws of the eternal shadow war against the xenos, never to return.

When the demigod Space Marines were aboard the *Fatal Redress*, they were in command. When not, Aemna's responsibility was the survival of the strike frigate and her crew. The *Fatal Redress* had sailed the stars and brought destruction to the xenos in service to the Deathwatch for over four thousand years. She would not have it brought to ruin on her watch.

The xenos battlefleets began to materialise, solidifying as the *Fatal Redress* drifted closer. The ugly masses of ork ships, an unholy union of scrap iron, asteroids and technology plundered from other races, charged into the hideous organic fleet of the tyranids with their consummate careless fury. Aemna could not recall ever seeing so many ships of either foul species, and seeing them locked against one another in one place chilled her blood. She could not begin to speculate on the mind of the lord inquisitor who had brought this catastrophe about, but knew that whether intended or not, she beheld the greatest threat to emerge against the Imperium after the invasions of the Archenemy assailing the bulwarks of Cadia.

She considered for a moment that the threat before her may be even greater.

The details of her briefing were thin by necessity, and Aemna had learned long ago not to press for information. She blinked, closing her eyelids over the smooth augmetics that had been installed after her masters had taken her eyes. She had been blinded upon ascending to serve in the battlefleets, her eyes removed so that she would never see the secret wars of the Deathwatch with her natural sight. It had been a simple, albeit unmistakably clear gesture. She saw only what the Deathwatch allowed her to see, and existed only as long as the alien hunters deemed her of use.

Still, Aemna's thoughts drifted to the fleets anchored at the core of the system. The combined military of twenty worlds, forced to abandon their duties and bear witness to the destruction of the planets they were oath-sworn to protect. Many ships' captains and crew had met summary execution at the hands of the Deathwatch enforcing the cordon, attempting to peel their ships away to respond to the wash of panicked entreaties for aid.

Aemna struggled to believe that more of the system's defenders had not rebelled. The shipmaster had never known the world of her birth, but the prospect of being forced to watch, powerless, as it burned twisted acid through her veins.

The shipmaster dismissed the thought as an officer hurried to her side, offering a data-slate. Aemna scrolled through the screeds of data, her lips peeling back as she bared her teeth in a snarl.

The lead ork ship was moving. It had changed its vector to bring itself to bear against a trio of enormous hive ships that had just arrived. There was no way Aemna could get close enough to deploy the kill teams without burning her engines.

The shipmaster handed the data-slate back to the officer, and keyed the vox-link on her throne.

'Watch captain, our plans have changed.'

TEN

Artemis stepped through the central aisle of the Corvus Blackstar's crew bay, his booted steps rattling the deck as he passed the seated battle-brothers on both sides. The Deathwatch warriors of his own kill team locked themselves into their restraint thrones beside the eight warriors of Kill Team Krycses, mag-locking weapons beside them or in overhead compartments as they made final preparations for insertion. The watch captain heard whispered prayers and oaths in a dozen languages from the assembled Space Marines, honouring their weapons, beseeching their primarchs or entreating the Emperor Himself to look upon their deeds in the battle to come.

Artemis climbed up to the cockpit, where Sekor was priming the drop-ship's systems to launch. The Imperial Castellan's hands danced over the control panels, running final diagnostics and triple checking that all of the myriad systems of the gunship were operational.

'You look tense, brother-captain,' said Sekor without turning. Artemis did not respond. The Mortifactor glimpsed the other Blackstar through the armourglass canopy, where Caltanix's kill team was mustering for deployment. After the shipmaster had detailed the change to their approach vector, the Deathwatch kill teams had scrambled to prepare their wargear and gunships for launch.

The two drop-ships would need to exit the *Fatal Redress* hangar while the frigate was at full engine burn, timing their departure precisely so that they could intercept the ork capital ship. It was a prospect whose statistical chances of success were objectively laughable.

It was far from ideal, but Artemis had led enough sorties to know that a flexible plan with viable contingencies was essential to prevail over the enemy. He had hoped to avoid adopting this contingency, but fortune, it seemed, had different ideas for him.

'The shipmaster will line us up over the target as she makes her pass,' said Artemis, leaning over Sekor's shoulder. 'You know our window to reach them. Straight across, high burn and get us inside in one piece. Preferably without letting every ork and tyranid onboard know we are there.'

'I have plucked you from the air in freefall within a planet's atmosphere, watch captain.' Artemis could hear the easy smile in Sekor's voice. 'I will get us onto that ship, you have my word on that.'

Artemis clapped Sekor on the shoulder guard, and turned to exit the cockpit. 'Just be ready when those doors open.'

Aemna gripped the railing of her command dais as she barked orders to her crew. The bridge was alive with motion again, as crewmembers rushed through the chamber performing the manifold tasks necessary to reawaken the *Fatal Redress*. Adepts of the Mechanicus encircled the reactor core of the strike frigate down in the engineering decks, conducting the arcane rituals and chants to rouse the vessel's slumbering machine-spirit. Gangs of vat-grown slaves hauled on dense chains, loading gigantic shells into the breeches of the Deathwatch warship's broadside cannons.

The *Fatal Redress* was ready, set for a blistering run into and through the warring xenos fleets. Once she was committed, the frigate would have little opportunity to manoeuvre or change its course, and would only have one chance to catch their foe unawares long enough to deploy the boarding parties.

Aemna took a deep breath as her junior officers sounded off, confirming their readiness. The alien battlefleets were close enough for her to see individual weapons impacts. She watched an ork cruiser ram a tyranid vessel amidships, splitting the squid-like bio-ship in two in an expanding cloud of dark ichor. Aemna watched the same ship become ensnared by the grasping tentacles of another hive ship, its reactor going critical in a sunburst of sickly green radiation as its back was broken.

The shipmaster shook her head, forcing herself to focus.

Just get them onboard, she thought. *Just get them onboard.*

'I want shields raised and weapons ready to fire as soon as we light our engines,' ordered Aemna, standing straight and smoothing a crease from her starched black uniform. 'We will need to punch our way out of here, so get ready for a fight.'

She locked eyes with the deck officer overseeing the propulsion systems. The thin man held her gaze, coming to attention and offering a crisp salute.

'Ready, ma'am.'

Aemna nodded, her shining eyes turning back to the viewscreen. She closed them for a moment. 'Emperor guide our hand.'

Her eyes flashed open. 'Engines to full power, now!'

'Aye, ma'am!' the officer replied, and the bridge erupted into feverish, practised activity. The reactor core of the *Fatal Redress* roared as it breathed once more, flooding the half-frozen decks of the warship with power. Sodium lamps bathed the corridors of the vessel in light, and the thin air was sucked into rescrubbers as they hissed back to life.

The deck of the *Fatal Redress* rumbled. The vessel's engine arrays screamed with the fire of a chained star, launching the Deathwatch strike craft into the frenzy of the battle. The flickering globe of void shields solidified around the craft as it dived into the maelstrom of aliens.

Almost immediately, a shoal of smaller tyranid creatures peeled off from the underside of a nearby bio-ship, curling in towards the *Fatal Redress*.

'Punch through them!' shouted Aemna. 'I want salvoes from all forward torpedo bays, lances ready for what is left.'

A volley of torpedoes burst from launchers in the Deathwatch vessel's plough-like prow, shooting ahead on ribbons of plasma as their internal drives activated. The warheads smashed into the swarm of tyranid interceptors in a chain of detonations. Organic debris rained against the *Fatal Redress* as it knifed through the dissipating blasts, its void shields flaring in ripples of kaleidoscopic colour. Point-defence batteries bracketed the surviving tyranids in hellstorms of laser and artillery fire, taking only moments to hurl them into oblivion to join their hideous kindred.

Aemna cursed. At this pace they would be cut off and obliterated by any of the larger vessels between them and the ork capital ship before they could get anywhere near close enough to launch the drop-ships. They needed to go faster, much faster.

The shipmaster keyed in an emergency sequence on her command throne. Secondary coolant feeds flooded into the propulsion systems, fighting to quench the searing heat of the drives as Aemna pushed the engines beyond acceptable tolerances. The ship rumbled all around her as its point-defence batteries fired without pause at the hordes of converging tyranid and ork interceptors. Migraine-bright beams of lance fire slashed into the larger of the oncoming enemy vessels, leaving hulls cored through as thundering broadsides ruptured greenskin armour and void-hardened tyranid carapace in blasts of fire and twisting shrapnel.

The bridge heaved as the *Fatal Redress* was struck by a barrage of impacts. Sparks fountained from consoles as they caught fire. Crew-members floundered on the deck, screaming, while others fought to put the flames out. Servitors, oblivious to the end, cooked and twitched as their remaining flesh ran from their bodies like wax.

'Get those shields back up!' Aemna staggered to her feet, blinking away the blood that covered her face from a gash on her brow. 'Report!'

'We have a fire on the gunnery decks. Teams are fighting to keep it from spreading to the magazines,' shouted an officer as he sprayed a flaming console with extinguishing foam.

'Hull breaches on decks D-Three, D-Four, E-Eight and G-Twelve,' called out another. Aemna could not locate a face to match to the voice amidst the chaos. 'Bulkheads are sealing but E-Eight and G-Twelve are open to the void.'

'The engines are redlining! Shipmaster, they will go critical if we do not shut them down now!'

'Not an option,' spat Aemna. She pulled up a shaking hololith from a projector in her throne's armrest. She double-checked their approach vector and that of the ships in their path, and then triple-checked it. 'Two hundred and forty seconds and we make it.'

She glared at the gargantuan ork capital ship as it swelled to fill the entire viewscreen.

Just get them onboard.

'Seal all bulkheads. Keep the point-defence batteries screaming but divert power from the broadsides and lances to shields. And open a secure vox-channel to the Navigator's sanctum.'

'Ma'am?' asked a communications officer over the din of the ship shaking itself apart. 'Say again. You need the Navigator?'

'Yes, I do,' Aemna bared her teeth in a defiant grin. 'I intend to do something very foolish.'

ELEVEN

Sekor breathed calmly through the recycled air of his void-sealed power armour. His vision, stained crimson by his retinal display, was awash with technical data – ammunition and fuel readouts, engine temperature gauges and auspex returns, along with dozens of other runes and data screeds jockeying for his attention. He blinked anything not immediately relevant to transparency, shuffling it to his peripheral vision as he focussed on the sealed hangar bay doors before him.

Twenty seconds. That was the projected window Sekor had to deploy from the *Fatal Redress* and be directly over the ork capital ship. The Corvus Blackstar he sat in was a proud, nimble beast. It was faster and more manoeuvrable than the venerable Thunderhawk, yet it was less heavily armoured than the iconic gunship. Its weapons arrays were formidable despite its relatively slim profile, and Sekor had made use of the Blackstar to conduct surgical strafing runs of entrenched xenos strongpoints on more than one occasion.

'*Just get us across, brother,*' said Artemis over the vox. '*Nothing extravagant.*'

The Imperial Castellan looked to either side at the servitors hard-wired into co-pilot and navigator stations.

'Ready to slay the foes of the Emperor, my stalwart companions?'

'Compliance,' they droned in unison.

Sekor smirked and turned his gaze to the hangar bay once more. He spared a glance to the second insertion team beside him. The Techmarine pilot of the Blackstar stood before the craft, offering final ministrations and entreaties to its machine-spirit. Sekor's gaze lingered over the crimson ceramite of the Techmarine's armour, the mantle given upon completing an apprenticeship within the towering forges of Mars, before turning away to focus on his own instruments.

Sekor hoped the Techmarine pilot was skilled. With the madness awaiting them, it would be impossible to maintain any contact or formation in their sprint to the ork ship. Once the doors opened, each of them would be on their own.

Klaxons began to wail. Serfs and tech-adepts scrambled, disconnecting fuel lines and making for the bulkheads. The rune in Sekor's display for Shipmaster Aemna pulsed and issued an insistent chime. Sekor rapped his fist against the cockpit over his head, and slowly fed power to the engines. The drop-ship trembled as the thrusters spooled up, and a series of glyphs counted down in the corner of his eye.

3...

2...

...1

'Here we go,' Sekor whispered.

The hangar bay door flashed open on lightning-fast pneumatics. Sekor shoved the control sticks forwards, and the Corvus Blackstar rocketed out of the hangar and into absolute pandemonium.

The *Fatal Redress* was hit the instant Sekor cleared the hangar bay. A blinding flash surrounded the Corvus Blackstar for an instant before the Deathwatch frigate rolled away, its superstructure aflame and trailing smears of spectral blue plasma from its tortured engines.

'I've lost visual on the *Fatal Redress*,' Sekor barked. He hauled on the control sticks, pushing the engines to their limits as the drop-ship dived down to the revolting monument to xenos ingenuity that was the ork capital ship. The second Blackstar spiralled away to Sekor's port side, immediately lost in the chaos.

'There goes the Templar,' Sekor exhaled sharply, as the ork flagship swelled to consume his view.

The ship was a mountain range of scrap metal, a bulky amalgamation of rusted plates daubed in the vile graffiti of the greenskin. Weapons covered every conceivable surface – macro-cannon batteries, torpedo silos, even ramshackle plasma cannons and lance turrets. Jutting from the ship's blunt prow, shaped into the visage of one of their foul mongrel gods, was the unmistakable silhouette of a nova cannon, looted from the wreck of an Imperial battleship. The cannon jutted from the 'mouth' of the prow, framed by twisted blades of a starship hull in a crude facsimile of curved tusks.

A tyranid bio-ship had latched onto the ork battleship directly ahead of Sekor, adhering itself like an enormous limpet as it worked relentlessly to devour a warship twice its size. Tyranid combat organisms swarmed over the hull of the ork ship in their thousands, leaping into battle against the hordes of orks disgorging from within to oppose them. The hull shivered with thousands upon thousands of warring xenos, entire armies slaughtering each other, the dead spinning away into the void.

Sekor took in the sight in an instant, before a rust-red blur reared up into their path. Collision alarms wailed. Sekor yanked the control sticks to his chest, corkscrewing the Blackstar away from an onrushing ork cruiser just ahead of them as it rammed the tyranid bio-ship. Sickly bioluminescence wormed over the ailing tyranid vessel as it was torn from the ork capital ship, leaving shredded gouges of molten iron where it had adhered itself. It twisted, latching onto the ork cruiser embedded in its flank, and the two tumbled away, grappling for the advantage.

Sekor fought the controls of the Blackstar, arresting its lethal spiral and weaving through the maelstrom of weapons fire and xenos escort ships. Even a glancing hit from anything filling the void around them would leave them as nothing but a cloud of spinning fragments. He rolled the drop-ship over the spine of an ork destroyer as its hull evaporated in a spray of bio-acid. Sekor coaxed more power to the engines, curling the drop-ship back towards the ork capital ship as a rune blinked on his retinal display.

Aemna. The *Fatal Redress*. Sekor caught sight of the Deathwatch strike frigate long enough to realise what the shipmaster intended to do.

'Oh,' Sekor's eyes went wide. 'You stupid, stupid human.'

The space around the *Fatal Redress* began to undulate and shimmer. Instinctively, ork and tyranid ships in proximity to it peeled away in all directions, seeking to put as much distance as possible from the wounded frigate. Sekor watched the vessel's Geller field shimmer into being, as the space in front of it began to tear like a velvet curtain.

Entering into the warp, even in the most calm and calculated conditions possible, was still a feat that was rife with peril. There were reasons Imperial law dictated that jumps occur only at designated points in planetary systems. Even the most flawless translation into the Sea of Souls was a horrifying cataclysm, as reality was torn open to admit the departing vessel into the beyond. Emergency warp translations were nearly always absolutely ruinous to the space around them.

An emergency warp translation conducted in the centre of a void battle was nothing short of apocalyptic.

The *Fatal Redress* dived into the roiling psychic syrup of the immaterium, and those ships too close to the vortex were pulled in as well, ork and tyranid alike. Vessels further away collided into one another under the pull of the translation point, rippling with internal detonations before shattering in clouds of twisted metal and hissing ichor.

'*What was that?*' Artemis demanded, the vox-link in Sekor's helm stuttering and hazed with static.

'The shipmaster just bought us an opening,' Sekor replied, straining against the Blackstar's controls. 'If she didn't just kill us doing it.'

Sekor pushed the engines to maximum, the drop-ship convulsing as it fought at the edge of the translation point's pull. The vortex imploded, dissipating in a flash of tortured energy and flawed light. An ork ship caught halfway when the portal closed spun as the half in realspace broke free, its superstructure crumbling away like fossilised bone.

Sekor banked, pulling the ship onto a direct course towards the ork capital ship. Targeting runes meshed over his retinal display. He snarled as he depressed the firing runes on the control sticks. A withering salvo of energy bolts lanced into the ork ship's hull from the Blackstar's ventral lascannons, and a fusillade of storm-strike missiles leapt from beneath the drop-ship's wings. The hull liquefied under the assault, the armour weakening and shearing away from the exposed decks beneath.

'Brace! Brace!' Sekor roared as he cut the engines and swung the Blackstar ninety degrees. Collision alarms screamed. The interior of the drop-ship was doused in crimson emergency lighting as the drop-ship smashed through the remaining weakened hull plating and ploughed through a scrap heap the size of a small mountain. Sekor fought to stay conscious as the g-force whipped the blood through his body, his vision blurring as a hurricane of scrap filled his view.

The Blackstar spun like a top, carving a gouge through the deck as it finally ground to a halt, partially buried in debris and refuse. The stanchions behind the drop-ship collapsed, burying half the chamber in compressed wreckage.

Sekor exhaled, and punched the buckle at his chest to release himself from the crash webbing of his control throne.

'Adopt defensive protocol Iota-B-Nine,' said Sekor to the servitors, placing them in control of the drop-ship's weapon systems.

'Compliance,' they murmured in affirmation.

'Well, brother-captain,' Sekor said as he jumped down to the crew bay and the dazed kill teams within, 'as you said, nothing extravagant.'

TWELVE

Artemis stormed down the assault ramp of the Corvus Blackstar and into the smoke-wreathed chamber of the ork battleship, bolter raised as Sekor and Rogerio held his flanks. Krycses' team filed down the other assault ramp in practised silence, modified bolters covering all angles of their surroundings. Flickering targeting runes winked in and out across Artemis' retinal display, his armour straining to pinpoint targets amidst the utter disarray of his surroundings.

Mountains of scrap metal reared over the Deathwatch kill teams. The air was a choking miasma of ash, scorched metal and industrial fumes. Rusted debris groaned and tumbled down in clamouring avalanches, reflecting the dirty light of chemical fires that danced against the blackened walls. Every breath was inundated with the dense fungal reek of the ork, and Artemis snarled as he tasted the xenos' foul musk through his helmet filters.

The kill teams fanned across the chamber in silence, directed by curt battle-sign gestures from their commanders. Artemis halted his team quickly, priming his bolter as he heard approaching footsteps.

A mob of diminutive greenskins shuffled through the canyons of junk, attracted by the noise of their arrival. The hunched wretches, used for slave labour or exploited as meat shields in the Overfiend's armies, cackled and shoved at one another, dull light glinting from their beady eyes and the broken tools they clutched.

Kill Team Artemis pressed to either side of the aliens' path, hidden by smoke and mounds of scrap. As the gaggle passed, Rogerio and Sekor drew short blades, stalking behind their prey. It took only moments for the greenskins to die, left in expanding pools of their lifeblood as they choked through slit throats.

A rune flashed on Artemis' visor display. Krycses had located a route out of the chamber. He blinked an affirmation to the Raven Guard, and watched their locator runes slip from the range of his auspex readout as the watch sergeant led his team through the ducts of a vent system at the opposite end of the chamber. Artemis brought up his vox, cycling through the frequencies selected by the kill teams as they planned their assault.

No contact from Caltanix. It was possible that the Black Templar's kill team had boarded beyond range of the vox, or that the scale and material of the xenos craft was interfering with their communications. Perhaps more likely was that their drop-ship had been hit, and was now nothing more than splinters of wreckage in the void.

Artemis cleared his head. Such thinking was devoid of utility, nothing but a distraction in their current situation. No matter what had befallen them, Caltanix and his team were beyond Artemis' aid. Krycses had taken his brothers along one path, and he would guide his own along another, as planned.

Seek and destroy. All had agreed that the best chance to locate and neutralise the Overfiend rested with each kill team moving through the ork vessel autonomously, staying in frequent vox contact to converge upon their target's location when found.

'Could the *Fatal Redress* have survived that warp jump?' asked Hyphantes as the kill team picked their way through the fields of twisted metal.

'Unlikely,' replied Rogerio. 'The superstructure was aflame as they translated. If the Geller field had been damaged they would be vulnerable to any number of predations waiting within the aether.'

'The tyranid hive consciousness drowns out even the Astronomican's light,' hissed Imtehan, his voice strained through gritted teeth. 'Their Navigator made the jump blind.'

'Focus,' Artemis snapped. 'Their fate is irrelevant, and such speculation is done at expense to the moment. If death has taken them then so be it. They have done their duty, and it is now our mandate to do the same.'

'And if they are dead?' asked Sekor, cresting a dune of debris as he scouted ahead. 'Any thought as to how we extract from this madness without them?'

Artemis was silent for a moment before replying. 'There won't be an extraction of any kind if we fail to accomplish our mission. We neutralise our target. Until that happens, no other considerations are relevant.'

Affirmation runes blinked across the watch captain's visor display, the last coming from Sekor.

'Stay alert, all of you. Sekor, have you identified an exit?'

'Affirmative, brother-captain,' Sekor replied. 'Converge on my position.'

The remainder of the kill team closed and hunkered behind cover around the Imperial Castellan. Artemis crouched beside Sekor, following the path he indicated through the canyons of industrial refuse.

'That is how the greenskins we despatched came in,' said Sekor, motioning to a rusted bulkhead fifty yards ahead of their position. 'Though I can guarantee we will be running into more of them going through there.'

'Inevitable,' Artemis replied, checking the ammo counter on his display. He turned to the rest of the kill team. 'We move, fast and hard. Keep it tight and kill anything we hit up against, but don't slow. If we get dragged into a pitched firefight, we are dead. If we get cut off and encircled, we are dead. Stay together, and keep moving.'

The kill team saluted with dull thuds of fists against breastplates. Artemis nodded.

'On me, move out.'

The corridors of the ork ship were wreathed in clouds of toxic smog. The kill team stepped through thick drifts of rust, piled ankle deep like corroded snowfall. Passageways collapsed at random intervals, either from the inherent deterioration of greenskin technology or the constant tremors of the warship burning around them, forcing Artemis and his squad to double back through the labyrinth. The sweltering, humid air was thick with the guttural barks and roars of the greenskins, punctuated by the cold, bloodcurdling shrieks of tyranid combat organisms.

Artemis froze, a mailed fist raised to bring his kill team to a halt behind him as the deck gave a uniquely violent tremor. The Deathwatch warriors felt the iron of the wall come apart before they heard the scream of shearing metal. The wall ruptured like a jagged flower in bloom, sending shrapnel pinwheeling in all directions. Artemis raised a forearm, the fragments of twisted metal sparking from his armour as a blur of purple chitin appeared.

The tyranid warrior sank the scything claws protruding from its upper arms into the deck, arresting its slide in a fountain of sparks. It rose to its full height, head and shoulders taller than Artemis, turning its hideous visage upon the watch captain. The shining black orbs of its eyes glared unblinking from below a wedged crest of armoured chitin, riven by scars and slick with ichor and ork blood. It swung the bio-cannon it cradled in its lower arms towards Artemis, the tubular appendage glowing as it swelled with living plasma.

The tyranid wailed as a mob of charging orks burst from the tear it had made. The roaring greenskins leapt upon the warrior, carving into its armoured hide with axes and firing crude firearms at point-blank range. A scything claw bifurcated one of the orks from collar to hip, but the weight of numbers soon had it hauled to the ground in a storm of hacking blades. The walls were sprayed with dark ichor as they rang with the piggish battle cries of the orks.

Artemis opened fire on the knot of embattled xenos. Sekor fired his bolt pistols, and Rogerio lent his storm bolter's fire to the barrage, a fusillade of mass-reactive death that reduced the grappling aliens to tatters of burst flesh and splintered bone. Gunsmoke twisted from the barrels of the kill team's bolters like sanctified incense as they slammed fresh magazines home.

Hyphantes edged forwards, peering into the newly torn gap in the wall of the passageway. 'Watch captain,' he waved Artemis over.

The kill team gathered beside the Scythe of the Emperor, crouched behind the shorn metal of the breached wall. Artemis leaned out over Hyphantes, silent as he took in the scene before him.

The chamber was immense, a cavern of roughly hewn asteroid threaded with gantries, smoking generators and scrap-iron ducts. It was a factory, a hangar bay and an assembly area all at once, and it was absolutely teeming with warring xenos.

Swarms of tyranids flowed over mobs of braying orks. Larger warrior breeds of the Leviathan hive fleet reaped huge tallies with every slash of their bladed limbs as their hides crawled with whooping greenskin warboys. Ork tanks fired indiscriminately into the churning melee, their gunners oblivious to who or what they killed with the thunderous blasts of their battle cannons. Clattering greenskin walkers, little more than ramshackle cylinders of looted armour plating with shrieking rotary saws bolted to their hulls, threw themselves against the larger tyranids as packs of smaller ripper creatures inundated them with sheer numbers.

The cavern was so vast, its heights carved so high, that the morass of greasy smoke, aerosolised blood and industrial fumes rose and mingled together in the air, condensing to fall back as acid rain upon the heaving armies clashing below. Ochre fog clung to the ground as the rain burned away at the rust floating in reddish-black lakes of alien blood.

Artemis had seen entire battles that were of smaller scale than what was contained within the cavern's jagged walls. Thousands of frenzied xenos of both races fought and died below the watching kill team – and this was just one of the countless battles raging between the two fleets.

'Do we have a visual on our target?' Artemis called out to his comrades. 'Do we see the Overfiend?'

The Space Marines scanned the chaos of the battle below. While it was nearly impossible to distinguish between individual orks, slathered in blood and engine oil, they all had engaged enough greenskin warbands to know that the tyrants who commanded them were always of uniquely prodigious size. From the scattered intelligence they had on the Overfiend, only the Great Enemy, the ork war chieftain Ghazghkull, was larger, itself close to the size of a venerable Dreadnought.

There were dozens of orks that were powerful specimens of their vile breed in the clash below, but none approaching that bulk.

'Negative,' said Rogerio, the mechanical snarl of his augmetic throat still dripping with the acid of his marrow-deep hatred for the ork. 'It is not there.'

'Do we descend?' asked Hyphantes, turning to Artemis. The eagerness in his voice was clear, his grip tight around the hilt of his combi-melta as he charged its under-slung meltagun.

'Going down into that is suicide,' said Sekor, shaking his head. 'We do nothing to find our target by exposing ourselves to that many hostiles.'

'We can skirt around,' growled Imtehan. The Flesh Tearer pointed across the cavern to a series of massive pathways interspersed along the far wall. 'Those passages lead deeper into the ship. That is where our prey lies.'

Artemis nodded in agreement. 'We go in.' He mag-locked his bolter and drew Exterminatus from its scabbard. He pointed the blade at the scaffolding ringing the cavern. 'Circle around. Stick to the gantries above the fray, and stow your bolters. Any contacts we must engage will be neutralised silently.'

A deafening boom ripped through the cavern. An ork tank exploded in a fireball of spinning armour fragments, sending shrapnel knifing through everything within a thirty-yard radius. Hordes of orks and tyranids were eviscerated in the blast. Within moments, the two xenos races had filled the gap once more, trampling their dead as they leapt upon each other.

Artemis turned back to his kill team.

'We do not want to attract their attention. Now move.'

The Deathwatch kill team vaulted over the breach, landing with a crunch of abused metal as they picked their way down into the madness of the cavern.

THIRTEEN

Gunfire stitched up the wall behind Artemis. Streamers of hot phosphorus whizzed by his position as the rounds struck the wall with percussive bangs, showering him with rock dust and bits of metal. He could not tell whether his presence had been discovered by an ork gunner, or if it was just one of the thousands of indiscriminate volleys of gunfire lancing through the cavern. It was impossible to say with any degree of certainty.

Kill Team Artemis had spent two hours negotiating the crumbling catwalks and gantries that encircled the cavern within the ork battleship. They sprinted between points of cover one by one, doing everything possible not to draw the ire of the two xenos races clashing in the bowl of the cavern. The Overfiend's hordes and the swarms of hive fleet Leviathan churned against one another with seemingly inexhaustible numbers, the floor carpeted knee-deep with the dead and dying as their comrades trudged through them without care.

Artemis peered over the ledge of the scaffold he crouched behind. They had navigated over half of the circumference of the cavern towards the tunnel entrance to the network of passageways leading deeper into the greenskin warship, and with any fortune the location of the Overfiend itself. The doorway lay only a few hundred yards from their position.

The watch captain blinked rapidly, cycling through his vox-channels. He had lost contact with the other two kill teams that had boarded the warship with them three hours ago. The ork ship was immense, a dishevelled city of dense asteroid, void-hardened ice and jagged scrap iron. Such materials were likely the primary factor obstructing him from receiving clear auspex returns and vox communications as the Deathwatch navigated through its labyrinthine structure. Artemis had to get deeper into the core of the ship, towards where he knew the other Deathwatch kill teams would be converging in search of the ork warlord.

The steel mesh beneath Artemis trembled as Hyphantes charged towards him in a low sprint, sliding into a crouch beside him in a rasping whir of his armour's servo joints. Hyphantes flexed his grip around his twin falx swords, giving Artemis a sharp nod as he took up a position behind him.

Artemis pulled a melta bomb from his belt, reaching under the gantry and clamping the explosive charge to the underside of the walkway. They had planted explosives at intervals along their path. Once they reached the passageways out of the cavern, the kill team would detonate the charges, detaching the scaffolds from the cavern wall and down onto the heads of the ork and tyranid hordes.

Adhering the melta bomb under the walkway with a hard clunk of magnetism, Artemis slid back from the edge and made ready to move to the next cover point. The clashing xenos made a ferocious din, easily covering the pounding tread of the Space Marine as he sprinted to where Rogerio knelt. The Crimson Fist waited for a moment before Artemis tapped his shoulder, and then shot forwards to the next point.

Cognisant of the tight-quarters combat he was sure to be steeped in during the boarding action, Rogerio had left his spear, a prized Chapter relic dating back to the founding of the Crimson Fists, behind on the *Fatal Redress*. He carried an exquisitely crafted power axe in both hands, its inactive generator snarling as the weapon's leashed machine-spirit hungered for blood to shed.

Rogerio swore a silent oath to himself that, once this mission was concluded, he would scour the stars to find the *Fatal Redress*, wherever the warp's foul currents had carried her. He would reclaim the cherished weapon his Chapter had entrusted him with. It had survived the tumult of his Chapter's near extinction, and Rogerio vowed not to return to Rynn's World without it in hand.

Rogerio came to a halt behind Sekor, the thrum of their active power armour sending thin shivers through the corrugated tin at the edge of the gantry. The cobalt of the Imperial Castellans glittered on Sekor's shoulder pad in the flickering light, the Chapter icon of an armoured arm brandishing a sword in jet at its centre. Wisps of smog clung to Rogerio's war-plate as he rapped his knuckles against the other Space Marine's power pack. Sekor broke from cover and sprinted into the hot mist.

Imtehan skidded behind Artemis, ducking beneath an errant

blast of bio plasma that fizzed and popped as it ate into the rock above them. Artemis began to move from cover when a shockwave nearly threw him from his feet.

A huge detonation rang out from behind him, sending tremors through the gantries with enough force to tear steel mesh, snap rebar and wrench support columns from their housings. Artemis cursed beneath his breath. A stray shell fired by one of the ork tanks had struck one of the melta charges the kill team had laid. The explosion tore an entire section of the scaffolding away, sending it spinning downwards into the battlefield in a cloud of shrapnel and blinding dust.

Imtehan spat a curse from his vox grille, a snarled bark of guttural Cretacian. A horde of orks had detached themselves from the edge of the battlefield, bearing towards the walls to inspect the source of the explosion. At the centre of the throng rumbled an ork tank, the massive greenskin riding atop it stabbing up at their position with a saw-bladed cleaver. The turret began to grind, panning the yawning mouth of its battle cannon towards the kill team.

Now it was Artemis' turn to curse. 'Throne,' he hissed, looking to either side. 'Displace!'

The battle cannon roared, rocking the tank back on its treads and wreathing the orks around it in blue fyceline as it lobbed a high-explosive shell into the scaffolds. The thin metal of the gantries burst into splinters as the shell hit, causing the catwalk beneath Artemis' boots to lurch and groan in a chorus of protesting metal.

'Move!' Artemis pushed Imtehan forwards. The two Space Marines ran along the catwalk, with Hyphantes charging at their heels. Bullets ricocheted and sparked around them, fired by the crude weapons of the orks as they climbed the scaffolds towards them. Hyphantes took aim and fired his combi-melta as he ran, reducing a roaring greenskin's head to a puff of pink mist.

A rocket spiralled, slamming into the catwalk ahead of the Space Marines in a burst of smoke and fire. Artemis cycled through the vision filters of his helm, selecting an enhanced mode that cut through the smoke.

The catwalk ahead of him was gone, sheared away by the ork rocket. A two-yard gap rushed up before him.

'Jump!' Artemis roared as he hurled himself across the gap, crashing down on the other side in a clang of strained metal. He stumbled for a moment before returning to his sprint. Imtehan struck the gantry behind him, a string of Cretacian invective issuing from his helm.

Hyphantes made the leap, clearing the gap and landing on the other side. A support beam beneath the catwalk snapped from the impact, wrenching the length of walkway down. Hyphantes' feet slipped out from under him, landing hard and sliding down the falling walkway. He threw out an arm, seizing hold of the guard railing and arresting his fall at the end of the shorn catwalk.

Hyphantes looked down, his legs dangling above a growing sea of howling green faces. Small-arms fire slashed the air around him, a few lucky shots spanking from his armour and carving deep gouges in the ceramite. He felt a firm grip seize his wrist, and looked up.

'Graceless,' Imtehan hissed, grunting as he hauled Hyphantes back from the edge. The Flesh Tearer looked to Artemis as he rapped his chest with armoured fingers. 'Half a cripple and still I am above the whelp.'

Hyphantes rolled his shoulders, rotating his left arm to clear a hitch from the servo joints. 'My thanks to you, brother.' The Scythe of the Emperor thudded a fist to his chest.

'Another time,' Artemis barked as a burst of gunfire slashed overhead. The Space Marines dashed forwards, meeting Rogerio and Sekor. The Crimson Fist and Imperial Castellan snapped off a blistering salvo of suppressing fire, curbing the tide of orks rising up the walls. They raised their bolters and joined in with the rest of the kill team as they ran the final yards towards the passageways.

The kill team reached a point directly above the tunnel entrance leading into the heart of the ship. Artemis activated the power field of Exterminatus, wreathing the blade in chains of killing light. He slashed down, carving a square into the grating of the walkway. The square fell away, clattering against the sloping rock wall as it pinwheeled to the ground.

Rogerio made the drop first, cratering the wall with his landing. The Crimson Fist veteran punched his right gauntlet out, raking down the slope to slow his fall as he slid. Imtehan went next, followed a moment later by Hyphantes.

'Go!' Artemis fired a burst from his bolter into the mobs of greenskins pounding down the catwalk. Sekor dropped down the gap, producing a thin cylinder from his belt and leaving a trail of dust as he slid down the slope.

The watch captain mag-locked his bolter as he backed to the drop. A howling ork bellowed a challenge, beating his chest with a rusted hatchet. Artemis stepped back, falling from the catwalk.

Sekor looked up, seeing that Artemis had cleared the scaffold. He raised the cylinder in his fist. Sekor triggered the activation rune on the detonator, and an intense flash swallowed the entire gantry. The Space Marine's visor darkened to dull the blinding blast, and a smile touched his lips as he admired the destruction.

The chain of melta bomb detonations sheared the skeletal

network of iron walkways from the wall of the cavern. The storm of jagged metal floated for a moment before tumbling down. The xenos turned, attempting to scatter from the onrushing mass of rebar as its shadow crept over them.

The gantry struck the ork and tyranid hordes in a mushroom cloud of dust and splintered rock. The expanding veil flew out in all directions, swallowing everything in sight. The swarms of rampaging aliens vanished within its suffocating embrace.

Artemis cycled through his vision filters, selecting an infrared overlay to pierce the dust and smoke. He slid to a stop as he reached the ground, joining the rest of his squad as they advanced towards the tunnel entrance. Artemis waved his comrades over to the looming gateway, turning to the noise of rumbling gears approaching from behind them.

A dark shape materialised from the dust, shaking with the clattering roar of hammering engines and grinding treads. The ork battle tank lumbered forwards, its mismatched armour given a ghostly pallor by the rock dust.

The tank's battle cannon ground towards them, the ork commander perched atop its turret roaring as it pounded the roof of the tank. Artemis made ready to leap as a shadow flitted over the tank.

With a high-pitched shriek, a pack of winged tyranid harpies swooped down upon the ork war machine. The hideous flying beasts hooked their talons into the turret, tearing the cannon from its mounting. The ork commander was snatched up between two of the harpies, howling and lashing out with its cleaver before they tore him in half.

More shapes appeared from the dust – the thick, brutish aspects of the orks and the hunched, revolting silhouettes of the tyranids. Artemis spun on his heel, leading the kill team through the gateway and into the mouth of the tunnel.

Sekor threw his last melta bomb as they ran, the charge locking to the ceiling just above the tunnel entrance. Orks streamed in behind them, caked in bloody dust and howling in frustrated rage.

Sekor triggered the detonator. Nothing happened. The Imperial Castellan cursed, pounding the device against his gauntlet.

Artemis halted, spun and brought up his bolter. He took aim and fired. The melta charge exploded, enveloping the tunnel mouth in a blinding flash of superheated plasma. The ceiling collapsed, bringing tons of rock down upon the pursuing xenos and sealing the tunnel behind the Deathwatch kill team. The strangled cries of greenskins and the clicking scrape of dying tyranids sounded weakly from beneath the heap of stone for a moment, before all was silent.

Sekor crushed the detonator in his fist, hurling it to the ground as the kill team advanced into the darkness of the tunnel.

FOURTEEN

The kill team moved in silence through the tunnels of the ork ship. Veils of toxic mist filled the passage to knee height, clinging to the dark armour of the Space Marines. The width of the tunnel varied widely. At points it would constrict to less than an arm's span on either side, before yawning wide enough to allow a Land Raider battle tank to pass through. As with so much of their architecture, the orks displayed no rhyme or reason here. The darkness was almost total, only briefly illuminated by the sparking of the decrepit machinery and faulty cabling threading through the walls. The blackness was no obstacle to the Deathwatch, even without the enhanced infrared vision of their helms.

Artemis smelled the orks before he saw them. The spicy fungal reek of them curled his lip in disgust as he pushed down the bile rising in his throat. He heard their heavy tread, no fewer than a dozen of the brutes lumbering through the poisonous smog towards them.

The tunnel had narrowed, and was barely wide enough to accommodate two of the Space Marines shoulder to shoulder. Rogerio heard the orks a moment after Artemis, his rune pulsing on the watch captain's visor display.

'I see them,' said Artemis, his eyes flicking to his ammo counter. The countless running battles the kill team had fought against the orks and tyranids through the tunnels for the past hours had expended over a third of their ammunition. They would have to reserve their remaining supplies if they were to have any hope of completing their mission, not to mention blasting their way out of the xenos warship afterwards.

'Blades,' Artemis ordered, as he had ordered in the past three skirmishes. Rogerio gave a pleased grunt in reply, hefting his power axe as Artemis drew Exterminatus. 'Hyphantes, Imtehan, kill anything that gets through us. Sekor, make sure nothing moves in behind.'

The kill team stowed bolters and drew their melee weapons as the porcine barks of the orks grew louder. Artemis and Rogerio halted, bracing into fighting stances as the xenos rounded a corner.

The two Space Marines triggered the power fields of their weapons as one. Exterminatus glowed, silver lightning coursing down its blade, while webs of crackling sapphire energy shivered down Rogerio's axe. The orks stopped abruptly, grunting in alarm at the sudden light. They recovered quickly, brandishing cleavers and war mauls, and charged.

Rogerio roared, splitting an ork in half from skull to hips with a brutal overhead strike. He wrenched his axe from the dead alien's guts, smashing aside a clubbing blow from an ork cleaver and taking the beast's head from its shoulders.

'Come to me, kine!' Rogerio snarled as he waded into the ork ranks, his axe flashing with discharging energy with each killing strike. 'Come join those who dared exist in the Emperor's galaxy. Join them in oblivion!'

Exterminatus reaped a gruesome tally as it carved through the howling greenskins. Heads, limbs and weapons spun away into the dark in sprays of stinking blood, the xenos' bodies torn into ribbons of putrid meat by the relic blade.

A massive ork bellowed a savage battle cry and slammed its war maul down at Artemis. The watch captain sidestepped, absorbing the blow on his pauldron. The maul's head struck like a tolling bell, and Artemis felt the layers of ceramite armour fracture as his shoulder dislocated. He growled in anger and rammed his sword forwards, driving the blade up into the beast's ribcage. The ork gave a strangled cry, its foetid breath flecking blood and bits of spoiled meat into Artemis' faceplate as it tottered.

Artemis stumbled as the ork fell onto its back, dragging him to one knee as he finally pulled his sword from its ribcage. His head snapped up as he heard a deep clunk, and he looked up into the barrel of an ork hand cannon.

The greenskin bellowed an incoherent sound that might have been laughter. It aimed its crude weapon, and pulled the trigger.

For all that the tanks and weaponry of the xenos looked as if they had been made from rubbish soldered together by a madman in the dark, and although they appeared to teeter on the verge of self-destruction with every use, ork wargear was brutally effective in the vast majority of cases.

This was not one of those cases.

The ork's firearm exploded in a flash of dirty light and scuds of greasy smoke. Artemis shielded his face with his bracer and came to his feet, his ears ringing as the air cleared. The ork was gone from the waist up. Its squat legs tilted and toppled to the ground at the centre of a circle of blasted rock.

A spinning globe of spiked iron slashed over Artemis' head, crushing the skull of a charging ork. Imtehan stepped forwards and hauled his meteor hammer back on its clattering chain. The morning star wrenched free from the ruin of the greenskin's face in a welter of stinking gore.

Artemis stood, slamming his shoulder against the wall to snap it back into place. He snarled, and gripped Exterminatus in both hands. An ork's head flew from its shoulders as the watch captain charged back into the crushing melee. He passed Rogerio, who crouched over a thrashing ork he was choking the life from as he screamed his hatred down at the beast. The Crimson Fist beat the greenskin's head against the ground until it broke apart, then took up his axe again.

Artemis froze. Instinct stilled his mind for a heartbeat, right before he felt the tremor beneath his boots. He dived back as the bedrock shattered in a cloud of splinters. A gaping maw filled with slavering, diamond-hard fangs emerged from the dust. A pair of huge, mantis-like talons hooked the lip of the breach, levering an undulating serpentine body into the tunnel. Two more sets of smaller talons unfolded, stringed with gelatinous resin, as the massive tyranid reared to the ceiling of the tunnel.

'Contact!' Artemis barked, rolling to his feet and drawing his bolt pistol with his free hand. 'Ravener-breed!'

The ravener struck in a blink. Artemis lapsed into reflex and training, bringing up Exterminatus just in time to deflect a decapitating strike from the monster's talon. Razor-edged chitin burned as it clashed with the power sword's energised blade in a puff of ozone and acrid smoke. Artemis ducked as another talon strike blurred over his head, blasting chunks from the ravener's exoskeleton with his bolt pistol.

The one ork remaining in the tunnel yelped as the ravener snatched it in its two sets of lower limbs. The greenskin bayed as the talons sank into its flesh. The ravener tore the ork into quarters, hurling the spurting chunks aside as it charged the kill team.

'Witness the vengeance of Sotha!' Hyphantes vaulted into the air, vaporising one of the ravener's primary limbs with a blast from his combi-melta. He locked the weapon to his thigh and drew his twin falxes as he descended. He rammed the curved blades of the swords into the tyranid's flank. A shrieking howl tore from the beast as he let his weight drag him to the ground, leaving a pair of haemorrhaging lacerations down the alien's side. Ichor from the wounds sprayed his armour, blinding him for the moment it took the ravener to bring its tail around. The blow smashed Hyphantes against the wall of the tunnel.

Sekor advanced on the ravener, twin bolt pistols blazing. Chunks of the tyranid's spined crest tore away in the mass-reactive firestorm. Sekor's fire halted as his magazines emptied. The ravener surged forwards as he paused to reload. A scything talon slashed across Sekor's chest, hurling him to the ground.

A pained battle cry filled the tunnel. Imtehan charged, his meteor hammer spinning in a deadly orbit above his head. He swung the morning star, crushing chitin and exoskeleton with each impact.

Rogerio stalked to the beast's wounded side, pulling a frag grenade from his belt. He leapt forwards, pouncing on the ravener. He punched into the gaping wound of the tyranid's severed forelimb, sinking his arm shoulder-deep. The ravener screeched, thrashing and sending the Crimson Fist flying.

There was a muted click within the ravener's shoulder, before the inside of the tyranid lit up. The frag grenade detonated, and the creature exploded in a shower of black gore. A jagged section of its snake-like lower torso twitched, trembling for a moment before thudding to the ground in a wash of pulsing ichor.

Artemis hauled Sekor to his feet. The ravener's talon had sheered through his breastplate, and dark blood oozed over the iron aquila emblazoned on his chest.

'It is nothing,' Sekor shook his head, waving Artemis away. 'The wound is already closing.'

Artemis nodded. 'Take a moment, brother.' He turned, walking to where Imtehan and Rogerio were helping Hyphantes up. The Scythe of the Emperor wavered for a moment, steadying himself against the wall before straightening fully.

Artemis looked over his kill team. Each warrior had accumulated wounds during the boarding action, their armour scarred and pitted, the flat black lacquer scorched and abraded away in places down to the steel-grey of the ceramite. The Chapter icons on their pauldrons were marred by xenos blades and claws, and the symbol of the Deathwatch bore similar scars on the silver of their left arms.

His warriors had borne the brunt of the maelstrom, thought Artemis. He was astonished they had not taken casualties.

'Patch your wounds,' Artemis ordered, swapping a fresh magazine into his bolt pistol. 'I want an ammunition inventory in two minutes.'

The Deathwatch kill team knelt in an outwards-facing circle, remaining vigilant for any sign of inbound threats as they performed rites of restoration upon their power armour and counted their remaining ammunition. Artemis did the same, drawing an oiled cloth over Exterminatus to clean the rime of alien blood from its blade. He reloaded his bolter, grimly noting that his remaining magazines had dwindled to half capacity. He breathed deeply. It would have to be enough.

'Watch captain!' Rogerio called out from the edge of their perimeter. Artemis rushed to the side of the Crimson Fist, panning over the darkness ahead with his bolter. He looked to the veteran, who crouched with a hand to the side of his helm.

'I hear something.'

Artemis immediately flicked through the vox frequencies in his helm. 'What do you hear?'

'It…' Rogerio strained to hear over the haze of boiling static. 'It sounds like Watch Sergeant Krycses.'

Artemis found the frequency, listening to the faulty vox-channel as it fizzed and popped with interference. He could barely make out the voice of the Raven Guard. He walked forwards, the signal clearing fractionally the further he went. The rest of the kill team rearmed and followed him down the tunnel.

Artemis began to sprint, tearing loose rock from the ground as he charged forwards. 'To me, brothers!'

The kill team broke into a thundering run behind Artemis. He heard the voice of the Raven Guard flickering between the static. The delivery of the communication was flawed, but the son of Corax's message was clear:

They had located the Overfiend.

FIFTEEN

Watch Sergeant Krycses was a child of shadow.

Born on the airless rock of Deliverance, the boy who would become Krycses had been moulded by darkness from his first moment of life. Abandoned in the monolithic shadow of the Ravenspire, he had been brought within the darkness of its crypts. To this day he did not know the identities of those who had forsaken him, or whether the blood in his veins had been that of spire nobility or gutter transients. Nor could he bring himself to care. He had taken the first step on the path towards ascension. The blood in his veins would soon be that of demigods.

The boy ceased to be human, becoming an apprentice of the night-shrouded masters of the Raven Guard's fortress-monastery. He survived the mutations and surgeries that hardened his bones and swelled his muscles. He endured where other supplicants were broken by the Chapter's perilous trials. He faced the utter blackness of the shadows, and wilfully sank into their cold embrace.

Initiations and proving grounds ended, and service within the Scout Company of the Raven Guard began. He had become one with the shadows, the avenging blade of the primarch, striking down the enemies of the Imperium in silence. It consumed him – the cold calculation and discipline, the stealth. The feeling of watching the light flee from an enemy's eyes, from a hand's span as lifeblood flowed over his combat blade or from the telescopic sight of a sniper rifle miles away. It suited the child of the shadows better than his own flesh.

When the time had come for him to join the battle companies, the warrior who had become Krycses looked upon that mantle, and allowed it to pass from him. He would remain among the Scouts, the coldest talon of the Raven Guard, and his masters acquiesced to his wish.

So his service to the shadow war continued for the next eighty-six years. In that time, there was no enemy of mankind that had not met its end at the kiss of his rifle or the edge of his blades. When the shadow war called him into the ranks of the Deathwatch, those who made war against the most vile fastnesses of the hated alien, he had gone aboard their ebon warships without question. He had put aside the Scout carapace and accepted the strength of power armour then, keeping only the ragged cameleoline cloak he wore as a remnant of his former station.

Krycses almost always remained silent, and his voice scratched as he called out his message into the vox. Quyuk, a peerless tracker of the White Scars who could stalk prey across entire star systems without fail, thrashed at his feet, clutching his throat as bright arterial spray jetted from the wound he was fighting in vain to close. Artek of the Iron Lords hurled a smoke grenade ahead of their position, buying Krycses a handful of seconds as a fusillade of gunfire cut the distant son of the Gorgon down.

Krycses unclamped a thick cylinder of dark metal from the small of his back. His breath hissed calm and even from his helm as ordnance filled the air around him. The Raven Guard iterated his message once more, boosting the vox signal as far as the machine would allow, and set the communication to repeat every ten seconds as he tapped in a series of commands on the cylinder.

The device vibrated softly with the clicking of internal components as a deafening roar blasted through the thinning smoke. Krycses gritted his teeth as a bullet punched through his shoulder, fracturing the stripped-down power armour and shredding the ragged cameleoline cloak that hung about his shoulders.

The Raven Guard looked down upon the beacon as it pulsed insistently for activation. A thick shadow fell over Krycses, accompanied by the pounding of monstrous footsteps. He felt the caress of that familiar darkness, the projected lightlessness he had dwelt within to cut the life from his enemies, close over him to finally take its claim. The irony brought a thin smile to his lips.

Krycses' fist slammed down on the beacon, before the shadows burned away in a storm of fire.

Artemis' eyes locked to the auspex readout on his retinal display as the beacon fired. The signal carried clear, even through the dense walls of rock and scrap iron of the ork warship. The Deathwatch kill team pushed themselves to move faster. All around the

Space Marines, the titanic xenos vessel rumbled and groaned. The blood-maddened cries of greenskins and the endless scratching of thousands upon thousands of tyranids filled the air around them.

Artemis pushed himself harder. He felt the sting of combat stimulants entering his bloodstream from the interface ports that connected him with his armour. The gene-forged warriors of the Adeptus Astartes were capable of staggering acts of sustained physical effort, able to fight on where mortal soldiers would fall to crippling wounds or exhaustion many times over. But they were not invincible. Their armour sustained damage, their bodies accumulated wounds and fatigue, and their weapons hungered for ammunition and grew blunted from protracted battle as surely as any others. They could tire, they could bleed, and they could die.

Artemis followed the beacon's signal like a lifeline. It blinked again as his auspex refreshed, eight hundred yards distant. He began to see the weak glow of a light source ahead. Artemis primed his bolter, slowing his pace.

The light was coming from a string of corroded sodium lamps drilled into the ceiling of the tunnel. They led to a large bulkhead, roughly one and a half times Artemis' height and of distinctly Imperial design. Like the space hulks they so often infested, the greenskins created most of their warships and other weapons of war from amalgamations of pilfered vessels captured during raids.

It sickened Artemis to see the technological perfection of the human race twisted in service to this mongrel scum. He could feel the rage radiating from Rogerio behind him. The veteran had survived the near extinction of his Chapter at the hands of the orks on Rynn's World, and he exemplified the marrow-deep hatred those sons of Dorn felt towards the greenskins.

'They befoul our warships to cobble together their abominations,' Rogerio hissed. 'Brother-captain, when the time comes, let it be me who takes the beast's head.'

'If the sightings of this Overfiend are to be believed,' replied Artemis, 'it will take all of our strength to bring it low.'

The watch captain turned to regard his kill team. He looked at each of his brothers, battered and tested by the crucible of this mission, but unbowed.

Unbroken.

'We stand upon the threshold of the beast,' said Artemis. 'We must be swift, and strike together as one. Hate the xenos, and be ruthless and thorough in its annihilation. We shall cut the head from this horde of barbarian filth and set them upon each other. We will fulfil our oaths of moment, and see this foul tyrant destroyed for daring to exist in the Emperor's galaxy. We strike together!'

Artemis slammed a fist to his chest.

'Together!' his brothers replied, mirroring the salute.

'Suffer not the alien to live,' Artemis snarled, turning and raising a boot to the bulkhead. He slammed down, tearing the rusted hatch from its hinges.

The kill team stormed into a gallery that had been ripped from an Imperial battleship. It was a long corridor, with a buttressed ceiling that soared high above the heads of the Deathwatch warriors. Great armourglass windows filled the walls on either side, giving an uninterrupted view of the chaos of the void conflict between the orks and the Leviathan hive fleet. Crude xenos graffiti covered much of the glass, and heaps of refuse and scrap were strewn across the floor, but the gallery's eerie presence on the greenskin flagship still stopped Artemis in his tracks. It was like staring into the eyes of a dead brother, his body desecrated but unmistakable.

The corridor led to a massive steel gateway, the entrance to an audience chamber where envoys and adjutants would report to the master of the ship. The beacon pulsed, directly ahead. Artemis knew that the Overfiend was waiting behind those doors. All that stood between the Deathwatch kill team and its target was a throng of screaming xenos.

The gallery was the same abattoir the cavern had been. Heaving masses of orks and tyranids clashed, their foul blood fountaining onto the rusted deck. Greenskins bayed their savage war cries as they flung themselves at the scything claws of the tyranids, exhilarated as they revelled in the violence. The swarms of Leviathan came on, an unstoppable tide of monstrosities enslaved by an insatiable hunger.

'Flesh Tearer,' said Artemis, looking back over his shoulder. 'Make us a path.'

'At last.' Imtehan stepped forwards, unlimbering a blackened flamer from his back. He had stowed the flamethrower in the tunnels, where the crushing close quarters and air thick with volatile chemicals made the weapon more of a liability than an asset. The air in the gallery was as clear as it could be on an ork ship.

The blue tongue of the flamer's pilot light flickered beneath the dual barrels of the weapon. Imtehan braced in a wide stance and levelled the barrel at the churning melee. The embattled xenos turned to confront the new threat just as Imtehan depressed the firing stud.

Sheets of chemical fire screamed from the flamer, enveloping ranks of orks and tyranids in a storm of ignited promethium. Ochre green flesh and purple chitin ran like wax, sloughing into heaps of burning fat and ash. Imtehan walked forwards, dragging the flames back and forth over the xenos hordes. Alien howls pierced the flamer's roar as dozens of the creatures burned alive.

The tyranids' vile presence dug deeper into the meat of Imtehan's mind. He gritted his teeth tighter, feeling as though his skull might split from the pressure swelling behind his eyes. He channelled the agony into a snarled litany of hatred as he atomised his foe with holy flame.

Artemis and the rest of the kill team followed in a wedge behind Imtehan, blasting into the xenos with a withering salvo of boltgun fire. Artemis fired flaring blasts from the combi-flamer, setting concentrated knots of greenskins ablaze before its reserve of promethium was depleted. The Flesh Tearer had reaped a fearsome tally with his flamer, and his Deathwatch brothers had pressed deep into the heart of the enemy in his wake – but it would not be enough.

The jet of flame stuttered as the canister of promethium feeding Imtehan's flamer ran dry. Starved of fuel, the weapon ceased its lethal deluge. Imtehan dropped the spent canister with a hollow clang as he reached for another. The enraged xenos broke from their combat with each other and turned to charge at the Deathwatch Space Marines.

'Stand ready!' shouted Artemis, drawing his bolt pistol in one hand and Exterminatus in the other. 'They will swarm to encircle us!'

Kill Team Artemis braced for the imminent onslaught. The watch captain seethed, to be so close to fulfilling his mission only to be cut down at the vile warlord's door. He focussed, set on the grim knowledge that the xenos would pay dearly before he gave his dying breath.

The xenos charged in a thundering stampede of crude boots and scraping claws. They closed, ready to pounce, as a side entrance to the gallery exploded in a flash of superheated air.

A melta blast, Artemis realised.

Dark forms surged out from the shroud of smoke and dust. Lightning chained from within the pall as massive weapons smashed into the alien tide. The charge died as a wedge of armoured figures cut into its flank. Massive boarding shields crushed against the writhing forms of orks and tyranids. Thunder hammers and power mauls crushed chitin and pulped flesh.

At the centre of the storm of whirling death was a champion bearing a sword dark as midnight. The champion tore the aliens apart, cleaving bodies and taking heads with each sweep of his blade.

'Well met, Brother Artemis,' bellowed Caltanix, his words booming from his helmet grille. The Templar raised his longsword in salute before bringing it down to split an ork chieftain in two. 'Let us finish this.'

SIXTEEN

The charging xenos faltered as they were struck on two fronts. The slow, implacable march of the vanguard veterans, with Caltanix at their head, crushed the thrashing aliens against their shield wall as they were shredded by a firestorm of bolter fire from Kill Team Artemis.

After their fusillade, Artemis drew Exterminatus and led his brothers into the melee. The two kill teams of the Deathwatch butchered their way towards each other, leaving the stolen gallery a charnel house of broken alien flesh. As the last of the xenos fell, the Space Marines trudged knee deep through the dead to stand before one another.

'Watch captain.' Caltanix brought the hilt of his longsword to his forehead.

'Hail, Caltanix,' replied Artemis. Xenos blood fizzed and popped from the active blade of Exterminatus, cooking into twisting coils of foul-smelling smoke. He looked upon the vanguard veterans of Kill Team Caltanix. Their wargear bore the same level of damage as Artemis' squad. The broad boarding shields they carried were gouged and cratered from small-arms fire. Patches of their power armour were splintered, the lacquer burned away by the touch of flame and bio-acid. The edges of their swords and hammers were scored and blunted by protracted use. Chainswords offered gap-toothed smiles, their tracked sawblades stripped of half their teeth.

An ivory-helmed Apothecary, bearing the heraldry of the Novamarines, settled to a crouch over a fallen brother. The warrior was surrounded by heaps of dead, half buried himself in the twitching corpses of xenos he had killed.

Caltanix and the Apothecary exchanged a short glance. The

Novamarine shook his head slowly, and readied his reductor. The watch captain stared for a moment, before issuing orders to his brethren to see to their wargear. The veterans split, half of their number keeping watch while the others made quick repairs, replaced tracks of chainsword teeth, and offered prayers to their armour and weapons, before rotating.

Artemis saw the body beneath the Apothecary as the gene-seed was cut loose. It was the Blood Angel, Pecori. Imtehan stared at the body, bearing silent witness as the reductor and bone saws of the Novamarine's narthecium gauntlet did their gruesome work. The Blood Angel's progenoid glands, fleshy masses of pinkish tissue, were sealed within cryo-cylinders and stowed within a case on the Apothecary's belt.

With a careful mix of alacrity and reverence, the Novamarine machined the warrior's pauldron loose and pulled it free. The Apothecary locked the shoulder pad to a harness on his power pack. The crimson war-plate would see the skies of Baal once more, even if the warrior who had worn it would not. Kill Team Caltanix now stood on the strength of seven brothers.

'You have lost kindred,' said Artemis, bringing a fist to his chest.

'Yes, our path carried us through the greenskin birthing chambers.' Artemis could hear the solemn tone in the knight's voice giving over to fury. 'Two of our number fell between there and here. Brother Pecori had been wounded purging a tyranid brood infesting a barricaded causeway. His fall was not... unexpected, by me.'

The Black Templar paused for a moment and rolled his shoulders.

'Nulsis,' said Caltanix. The Novamarine Apothecary rose.

'Kindred.' Nulsis uttered the single word, his voice low and resonant, before stepping away to attend to his chainaxe. Each warrior of Kill Team Caltanix stopped before Pecori's body. They crouched, offering a silent word to their departed, before taking a portion of his armour as Nulsis had done. Deathwatch war-plate was a sacred relic, and priceless beyond measure. Just as the Blood Angel's legacy would live on through his gene-seed, his brothers ensured that his armour would continue on in service to the Deathwatch as well. It was then that Artemis noticed the other sections of armour hanging from the harnesses of the vanguard veterans. None of their fallen's wargear had been left behind, their machine-spirits not forsaken to rot away in ignominy aboard the ork warship.

Nulsis returned to Pecori, now stripped of his armour. He primed a syringe from his narthecium gauntlet, injecting it into the fallen Blood Angel's neck. The modified strain of the mutagenic acid used in the Deathwatch's hellfire boltgun rounds coursed through the Space Marine's body, boiling it away into dust and ash.

The Novamarine gathered Pecori's weapons, an artificer-crafted bolt pistol and power sword of gleaming silver. Nulsis stepped to Caltanix, raising the weapons to him with his head bowed. The knight accepted them, stowing the bolt pistol and sheathing the power sword at his hip.

Caltanix levelled his stare at Artemis. 'These brothers' crusades have ended, but ours has not. Come, we must not tarry now. This foulness must be purged.'

The knight stepped before the massive gateway at the end of the gallery. 'Kindred, help me tear these doors down.'

The thick iron doors of the gateway flashed white-hot as the heat of the melta charges liquefied them to slag. The doors dulled to a deep red as the charges died, and began to bow from the booming pounding of hammer blows. The strikes reverberated through the darkened chamber like the tolling of bells, before the frame of the doorway gave way. The immense doors were sent crashing to the ground with a peal of thunder, revealing twelve giants standing at the threshold.

A thick pall of smoke filled the chamber. Artemis cycled through his vision filters, unable to pierce its toxic veil. Thin static crackled over his retinal display, meaning that a portion of the smoke was from a Deathwatch-issue blind grenade. The beacon pulsed on his auspex, just yards from where he stood. He heard a crashing stomp, and the device's guiding light was extinguished.

Did the Overfiend want us to come here? thought Artemis. It would have constituted a surprising degree of cunning from a greenskin, though this tyrant was anything but typical for its mongrel race.

'Stand!' Caltanix shouted into the chamber. The knight levelled his longsword at the darkness. 'Face the judgement of the Emperor of Mankind, praise be to Him! Show thyself, foul xenos, and die by His avenging hand!'

Silence greeted the Black Templar's challenge. Artemis strained to hear the eager shuffling of metal-shod boots scraping against the bare rockcrete of the floor, the soft clattering of armour plates. He heard the deep, low breathing of multiple entities within the pall. That they did not charge immediately was another stunning feat of discipline for the greenskins.

The silence was broken by a rolling thud. An object bounced from the smoke, rolling slowly towards Caltanix. The knight stopped the object with a mailed boot. It was a Space Marine helm, with etchings of avian motifs and screeds of sharp Lycaen script.

The dead eyes of Watch Sergeant Krycses looked up at Caltanix from behind its tinted visor, as a deafening roar shook the walls. The vocal blast was a physical force, so strong it parted the smoke and cleared it from the room.

A dozen ork warriors of the larger, ruling breed stood before the Space Marines of the Deathwatch, clutching battleaxes and flexing the talons of pneumatic power claws. Scavenged tank plate and dense scrap iron was bent around their limbs to form crude armour, which was slathered in crimson war paint. Their faces were dyed the same arterial red, with their brutish tusks and fangs stained black.

Standing behind the fearsome greenskin berserkers, rising from a vast scrap-iron throne, was the single biggest ork that Artemis had ever seen.

It stood, the throne groaning with relief as it was freed of its oppressive weight. The ork reared to its full height, its hunched posture within its brutish armour still nearly half again the height of a Space Marine.

Chains and lengths of metal cabling dangled in dreadlocks from beneath its jaw, adorned with skulls that clattered like beads against the armour of its chest. More skulls – human, alien and some beyond any recognition – rattled from iron polearm axes that protruded from its shoulders, along with the desecrated helms of more than a dozen Space Marine Chapters. The beast wore a crown of crossed axes, their blades lacquered in scarlet, a match for the crude clan symbol daubed on the banner of rough sackcloth that rose from its back.

One enormous fist ended in scything talons, glowing red with heat from the crackling generators mounted on the crude armour the ork was encased in. The other clutched an immense double-headed axe, itself the size of a mature ork, stained red and covered in greenskin tribal graffiti.

The ork warlord bared its teeth, the cracked fangs and tusks curving from its jaw stained black in the same fashion as its retinue. The beast's maw stretched wide as it issued another tectonic roar. Its praetorians joined in the war cry, shaking their fists and slamming their weapons against their chests.

Artemis' heart sank as he beheld the greenskin warlord.

'This is not the Overfiend,' he said.

'What?' Caltanix hissed.

'This is one of its vile sub-commanders.' Artemis remembered the hypnotic instruction and eidetic recall briefings that had been conducted before their mission. He recognised the beast before him as the warlord of one of the larger clans of greenskins in service to the Overfiend. Roughly translated into Gothic, the ork was known as 'Gorsnik Magash', warboss of the clan designated the 'Blood Axes'. The greenskin was formidable, responsible for spilling the blood of billions and for the pillaging of countless Imperial worlds, but it was not the target the Deathwatch sought to eliminate.

'Overfiend or no,' growled Caltanix, 'this brute dies now.'

SEVENTEEN

The warriors of the Deathwatch stood in silence before Gorsnik Magash and his blood-maddened orks. Caltanix hefted his longsword, placing the ebon blade upon the rim of his boarding shield. The vanguard veterans who formed Kill Team Caltanix stood shoulder to shoulder with their watch captain, grips tight upon the hafts of thunder hammers, power mauls and chainswords as they built their shield wall.

Kill Team Artemis formed a second rank behind Caltanix's line breakers. The barrels of their bolters held steady, aimed over the shoulders of the vanguard veterans. Targeting reticules danced over Artemis' retinal display, settling over each of the orks' heads and locking in brackets of sharp crimson light.

As one, the shield wall saluted in thunder those whom they were about to destroy. Seven weapons clashed against seven shields as they took their first step.

Thrun dun dun DUN!

Another step.

Thrun dun dun DUN!

Another.

Thrun dun dun DUN!

A savage war cry ripped from the throats of the orks as they charged. Kill Team Artemis opened fire, sending streams of mass-reactive death into the oncoming xenos. A bolt-round took one ork through the eye before detonating, the back of its head blowing out in a shower of blood and skull fragments. Another fell as its left knee disappeared in a puff of crimson mist. A burst hit it as it crashed to the ground, tearing its throat away in jets of gore. Bolts ricocheted from the orks' armour, some finding the gaps between plates to score deep wounds that only served to enrage the greenskins further. The vanguard veterans interlocked their shields, weapons ready as the xenos closed to within a few yards.

Ten orks struck the shield wall with the force of a siege hammer. Kill Team Caltanix strained, held their ground, and pushed. Step after grinding step, the vanguard veterans drove forwards. Sword blades and hammers swung over the tops of their shields, while Artemis' kill team fired precision shots at point-blank range into the orks' howling faces.

Caltanix barked an order, and the shield wall froze. He barked again, and the centre of the wall allowed the orks to push them back. The line of Space Marines held, slowly bowing back as the orks pushed deeper into the chevron of shields.

'Now, brother!' Caltanix roared.

Kill Team Artemis swung out from both sides, snapping around the charging orks at their flanks. The xenos found themselves locked within a constricting ring of dark armour.

Artemis triggered the power field of Exterminatus and lanced it through the back of an ork's skull. He tore the blade out sideways, leaving the alien's head hanging by ligaments as it crashed to its knees. The orks thrashed within the tightening circle, crushed closer and closer together. Soon they could not raise their arms, and they howled in frustrated rage as blades found their throats and hammers pulped their skulls.

Rogerio cut the head from the last of the greenskins with his axe. He stooped, gathering the severed head up by its topknot of coarse black hair, and hurled it at the feet of Gorsnik Magash.

The ork warlord looked down at the head of its warrior, before returning the glare of its beady, bloodshot eyes to the Deathwatch Space Marines. A wet, choking rumble issued from the ork's blackened maw. Artemis' face twitched in revulsion at the xenos tyrant's monstrous excuse for laughter.

Magash stomped the head flat in a wet crack of breaking skull, crushing it to a paste and smearing it across the deck. Its talons knifed through the air, their smouldering tips wreathed in heat haze. It took a booming step down from the elevated dais its throne sat upon. The Deathwatch kill teams scrambled to reform as the ork warlord raised its axe overhead and brought it smashing down to the ground.

The impact was seismic. Artemis was hurled from his feet, landing hard on his side with a squeal of grinding ceramite. He rolled to his feet, watching as Magash struck a vanguard veteran of the Dark Angels with the fist of its power claw. The warrior's torso collapsed in a spray of blood, the blow killing him before he smashed against the far wall. A sweep of the ork's axe killed two more, shearing through their shields and sawing through their bodies at the shoulders.

Rogerio roared, rolling beneath the axe's blades and bringing his own to bear. He slashed into the torso of the warlord, drawing fountains of sparks from the looted tank plates as Sekor blasted at its head with his bolt pistols.

Magash twisted, turned and raked its power claw over the Crimson Fist veteran. The superheated talons tore Rogerio's right side open. His power axe spun away, still in the grip of his severed right arm. The ork backhanded Rogerio, swatting him away and sending him hurtling into a wall. The sternguard struck with enough force to crack the rockcrete before falling in a heap.

'Brother!' Hyphantes cried. A howl of rage ripped from the grille of his helm as he leapt upon the back of the greenskin. The Scythe of the Emperor seized hold of the ork's armour with one hand and stabbed down with a falx at Magash's head with the other.

Artemis charged with the other Space Marines, weaving around the devastating attacks of the ork warboss as it rampaged through the chamber. He barely avoided a slash that cut the head from the vanguard veteran behind him.

Hyphantes screamed in anger as the claw crushed his legs. Magash tightened its grip, raising the Space Marine above its head and dashing him against the ground. The ork raised him to do it again as Artemis slashed the claw with Exterminatus, severing a bundle of hydraulic feeds. Oil and fuel sprayed from thrashing hoses, causing the claw to spasm and unlock. Hyphantes slid from between the talons and crashed to the floor.

Artemis ducked below a vicious backhand from the claw, slashing at the talons in a sheet of sparks. The ork moved fast, faster than anything that big should be capable of moving. Artemis readied to slash again on the return swing, and then was spinning through the air as Magash clubbed him aside with the haft of its axe.

Artemis hit the ground hard and rolled. He pushed himself to his knees. Flecks of scarlet dotted the interior of his visor. The spicy scent of his own blood filled his nose and its coppery tang coated his tongue. His vision wavered, blurring and focusing in and out. He saw Hyphantes dragging himself along the ground. Reaching for Artemis. His voice, weak and wet with blood, scratched across the vox-link.

'Brother–'

The axe came down in a blur. Hyphantes writhed, his body locking in convulsions as the ork tyrant wrenched the blade free. The

Space Marine was bisected from collar to hip. Hyphantes remained alive long enough to reach once more for Artemis, before his gauntlet dropped and he went still.

Hyphantes' biometric readout flatlined on Artemis' retinal display. The rune of twin scythes crossed beside it winked dark. Rogerio's biosign flickered below it, the Crimson Fist barely clinging to life. Artemis saw Nulsis hurry to Rogerio's side, fighting to stabilise him.

A needle of ice spiked up Artemis' spine. He threw himself to the side as the greenskin's axe smashed down again, embedding itself halfway into the rockcrete. Battle narcotics and pain suppressants itched through his blood as he brought his bolt pistol up. The percussive bangs of the bolter were numbed by his dazed senses as the weapon bucked in his fist. Mass-reactive rounds spanked off Magash's armour in flashes of sparking metal. The ork tyrant ignored those that found its flesh, the craters erupting on its hide in welters of stinking blood beneath its notice.

Magash heaved, fighting to free its axe from the ground. A dense black chain struck the weapon, following the momentum of a spiked globe as it wrapped tightly around the axe's haft.

Imtehan hauled back on the chain of his meteor hammer and braced his heavy flamer against his hip. He set his feet in a wide stance as he doused the ork in sheets of burning promethium. Magash bayed in savage fury as it thrashed in a cloud of chemical fire. The talons of its power claw lanced through the firestorm, shearing the heavy flamer in half.

The Flesh Tearer hurled the weapon away as it exploded. Heaps of refuse and combustible scrap caught fire, setting the chamber ablaze and filling it with choking black smoke. A weakened wall of the audience chamber collapsed, and the crackle of the flames was joined by the scraping and scratching of inhuman claws.

Tyranids smashed against the gap of the collapsed wall. They sank their long claws into the breach, straining to pull it wider to admit their chittering swarms.

Imtehan fell back as the chain of his meteor hammer snapped. He dodged as Magash charged at him, rolling to the wall where Rogerio lay. Grasping behind him, Imtehan grabbed hold of the Crimson Fist's power axe, bringing the weapon to bear as the ork rounded on him.

It took a thunderous step and was nearly within striking distance when a volley of bolter fire stitched up its side. Artemis and Sekor fired upon the massive ork as the broken wall came down fully. Tyranids boiled into the chamber, leaping upon Magash.

'Artemis,' shouted Sekor. 'We have to turn back!'

'I will not flee from this place!' Artemis snapped, dashing an empty magazine to the ground as he reloaded his weapon.

'If we stay here, we die like the others!' Sekor pressed.

'Then we die!' was Artemis' cold reply.

'This is not our mission! If we die here we will have failed. We fall back now, we live to fight another day. We live to find the Overfiend and end this!'

'He is right.'

Artemis turned to see Caltanix stride from the flames. Fire had scorched the enamel from the knight's armour, exposing the bare metal and ceramite.

'Go, my brothers,' said Caltanix. 'Get clear and find the Overfiend. Nulsis!'

'Brother!' the Novamarine Apothecary shouted back.

'You have the gene-seed of our fallen kindred?'

'I have it.'

'Then go with them.' The knight levelled his sword at Magash. 'Yours is another path, brother-captain,' he said to Artemis, 'and you must walk it as I must walk mine. I will see to it that this monster is banished from the Emperor's light.'

'We cannot–' Artemis began.

'Go now!' Caltanix bellowed.

Artemis roared, emptying the remainder of his bolt pistol's magazine at Magash as it brawled with the leaping tyranids. He lowered the weapon as it clicked empty, and allowed Sekor to turn him. Imtehan and Nulsis lifted Rogerio between them and carried him from the chamber. Standing upon the threshold of the audience chamber, Artemis spared an instant to glance back.

The watch captain saw an image that would not have been out of place stitched in tapestry or depicted in stained glass mosaic in the chapel of any fortress-monastery. The knight stood, sword in hand, alone against a massive inhuman monstrosity. He saw the manifestation of the Imperium of Man, a single light in the darkness, defiant against the encroaching doom that threatened to devour the human race.

Caltanix raised his longsword, its blade glittering with the raging inferno filling the chamber, and charged. A portion of the ceiling collapsed between them, blocking Artemis' view of what occurred next. He offered a silent prayer, and turned with his brothers to run.

EIGHTEEN

Artemis and his kill team sprinted through the frenzy of the ork vessel. Nulsis had given Rogerio a series of chemical injections that triggered the sus-an membrane implanted over the veteran warrior's brain. The Apothecary had induced a state of suspended animation to keep the trauma of the Crimson Fist's wounds from killing him. The enhanced physiology of the Space Marine worked to staunch the worst of the haemorrhaging and knit the body back together, but the severe wounds covering his right side were still oozing dark blood that pattered to the deck.

The Deathwatch Space Marines carried their comrade between them, shifting between bearing his inert form and providing covering fire as they scrambled through the ship's corridors towards the transponder signal of their drop-ship. They skirted around the biggest pockets of clashing xenos, as the tyranids still swarmed through the warship. The deck rumbled beneath the boots of the Space Marines as the greenskin vessel's guns continued to fire at the hideous bio-ships of the Leviathan hive fleet encircling them.

Artemis snapped off a shot from his bolt pistol, watching as a hormagaunt's skull ruptured. He continued to fire disciplined shots over his shoulder as they ran.

As they *fled*.

Acid burned through Artemis' veins. Shame and rage hung from him like cloaks of lead, slowing his steps and flawing his reactions. He had led three kill teams, twenty-five Space Marines of the Deathwatch elite, into this catastrophe. Five remained alive if Rogerio did not succumb to his wounds.

Twenty Space Marines, champions of their respective Chapters.

Dead.

Hyphantes, the hope of a noble brotherhood standing on the precipice of extinction.

Gone.

They had not fallen in glorious battle, selling their lives dearly to complete the Deathwatch's mission to destroy the ork Overfiend. Their deaths had been in vain. They had died for nothing.

Maudlin reflection and self-pity were anathema to a Space Marine. The relentless training, the endurance of the trials, and constant honing in the crucible of war had purged Artemis' soul of such weakness. And in its place, the Chaplains of the Mortifactors, shamans of the endless night of Posul who forged men into demigods, had left one thing in its place.

Hatred.

Hatred that had burned cities and entire worlds to ash. Hatred that had toppled civilizations and rendered whole species extinct. Hatred that had brought the galaxy to heel, and had annihilated the enemies of mankind to keep the Imperium from vanishing into the darkness of oblivion.

Hatred, pure and true and hotter than the heart of a burning star flowed through Artemis. Pity was useless to him. It could not kill, nor could it lead armies against his foes. Pity could not keep him alive. Hatred was a pure, beautiful weapon. And Artemis would wield it.

He would not shrink from surrendering himself before his watch master to answer for his failure. He would stand and account for the lives of the brothers who had fallen under his watch. He would bare his throat to the executioner's blade if it was his master's wish.

But before that, his hatred would see the Overfiend dead.

Kill Team Artemis stormed into the chamber where the Corvus Blackstar drop-ship perched in wait. The wall separating the chamber from the void, breached by the Deathwatch during their landing, had completely sheared away. The splayed landing claws of the drop-ship had held firm. Its ebon hull was scored and pitted from debris that had been torn out into deep space during explosive decompression, but it was intact.

Tiny forms in bulky void suits scrambled over the Blackstar's hull. They pried at the armour plating with crude tools, struggling to strip the drop-ship for salvage. Cruel, hook-nosed green faces squinted through leaded face bowls, waving frantically at each other as they fought over portions of the gunship.

The gretchin burst apart under a hail of bolter fire. Their diminutive bodies spun violently from the drop-ship, smashing against the walls of the chamber or twisting out into the void.

Kill Team Artemis stalked towards the Blackstar, their boots clanging from the deck as their magnetic seals locked and unlocked with their heavy tread. Sekor blink-clicked a series of runes on his visor display, transmitting a signal to the gunship's restless machine-spirit. Clouds of spent bolt casings surrounded the craft, twinkling in the thin light along with the frozen corpses of dozens of orks and the lesser gretchin greenskins. The drop-ship had expended the ammunition reserves of its servitor-manned heavy bolters in defence of the vessel, the few xenos clinging to its hull when the Space Marines returned being the only survivors.

The twin assault ramps at the fore of the Blackstar unlocked, folding down to admit the Space Marines. Nulsis hauled Rogerio up one ramp and through the crew bay, pushing his weightless body towards the drop-ship's austere apothecarion. The rest of the kill team filed up the other ramp, with Sekor climbing into the cockpit.

Sekor pulled the restraint harness down over himself and locked it in place, hands running over the control panels to bring the engines back online. An impact on the armourglass viewport jolted his attention.

The frozen remnants of a greenskin corpse, torn apart in the flayed manner indicative of mass-reactive weapons fire, thumped against the viewport before listing sedately away.

Sekor snorted. 'I suppose I have you to thank for that.'

'Compliance,' murmured one of the servitors.

Sekor looked back over his shoulder at the other servitor. It remained silent.

'Right,' the Space Marine gripped the control sticks as the engines spooled up. The open space before the drop-ship was blocked out by the gargantuan form of a tyranid bio-ship as it rolled past.

'From one fire to the next.'

NINETEEN

The engines of the Corvus Blackstar flared to life, and the drop-ship edged out into the void. A shell exploded a few yards off the right side, sending it corkscrewing to the left.

Sekor hauled on the controls, fighting to bring the Blackstar back under control. He fired the retro thrusters in the craft's nose, breaking the momentum of their spin. Sekor cursed as the force of the correction cracked his head against the control throne. He banked the drop-ship around and down, pushing the engines to put distance from the knot of xenos capital ships mauling one another at the centre of the void conflict.

Artemis clambered up to the cockpit and leant against the control throne.

'Have we cleared their capital ships?'

'We have,' Sekor pulled his helm free, letting it fall to the deck. 'Though it is more dangerous for us out among their more agile escorts and fighter wings than it is in the shadows of the giants.'

Artemis looked down at his comrade. Sekor's face was crusted with black blood from a network of gashes on his brow and nose. One eye was a solid crimson orb, the flesh around it black with trauma bruising.

'What is our plan, brother-captain?'

The gunship rocked as ordnance exploded around it. Sekor looked up at Artemis.

'This system is dead and we cannot rely on the *Fatal Redress*, even if the most likely scenario has not come to pass and it is not being torn to splinters by warp spawn as we speak,' he said.

Artemis looked out through the viewport. A miasma of xenos

ships stretched to fill the void as far as he could see, fighting and manoeuvring and lighting the darkness as they burned.

Artemis unlocked the collar seals of his helm before pulling it off. 'Light our beacon,' he said, running a gauntleted hand through his sweat-plastered hair. 'Take us as far towards the rim as she will go, and we–'

The Blackstar lurched from a violent impact. Artemis mag-locked his boots to the deck, keeping himself from being thrown into the viewport as he gripped the back of Sekor's control throne. Alarm klaxons blared as the cockpit was stained scarlet with emergency lighting.

'Contacts bearing down on us!' Sekor fought against the controls. Streams of tracer fire slashed over the drop-ship as Sekor evaded. 'Fighter-class, must have tracked our engine flare.'

A trio of blocky, rust-coloured fighters swarmed in the Blackstar's wake, streams of fire chattering from their wing-mounted autocannons. The Deathwatch drop-ship weaved through the ork attacks. Sekor swung the Blackstar back towards the larger ships, seeking to lose the fighters in the chaos.

The Deathwatch drop-ship rolled, diving and skimming under the chitinous hull of a bio-ship. One of the ork fighters hesitated and smashed into the tyranid vessel's mottled purple shell. Another drifted too close to the fronds of its grasping tentacles and was snared. The greenskin ship's engines flared in vain as it was slowly hauled into the bio-ship's razor-toothed maw.

Sekor cut the Blackstar's engines, rolling aside as the last ork fighter overshot them. The drop-ship's drives flared back into life as Sekor kept pace with the greenskin. The fighter, a smear of green light on Sekor's auspex readout, rolled and dived as it sought to outmanoeuvre them.

Targeting controls blared in the cockpit as the Blackstar's armaments locked onto the xenos craft. Sekor fired the lascannons. Eye-aching chains of killing light slashed out from beneath the drop-ship's nose. The ork pilot swayed aside, dodging the first volley, but was unable to avoid the next. Sekor's fire struck the fighter in the spine, shearing it in two in a flash of light and expanding gases. Bits of glittering shrapnel clinked from the viewport as Sekor powered through its debris field.

The tyranid bio-ship behind the Blackstar shuddered down its bulbous, pod-like hull. Like a great beast shaking ticks from its hide, it began to shed shoals of lesser tyranid creatures, which peeled away from its skin in pursuit of the kill team. The nimble fliers spread leathery wings as they descended on the Deathwatch drop-ship.

With a silent shriek, the lead xenos unleashed a salvo of tentaclids from beneath their wings. The mindless living missiles darted through the void towards the Blackstar.

'Crones!' barked Sekor. 'We have to shake that ordnance, or their electric pulse will stall our engines.' He banked the drop-ship towards a bulky ork escort bristling with gun batteries.

'What are you doing?' demanded Artemis as the viewport filled with blazing flak.

'Something very stupid.'

Sekor spun the drop-ship into a tight spiral aimed dead centre at the ork warship. He rolled and banked as a firestorm of shells blasted at the Blackstar from the greenskin ship's guns. Streams of fire that missed the Deathwatch craft blasted into the swarm of tyranid hive crones, shredding their bodies and scattering their formation. The volley of tentaclids drew closer.

The Blackstar bucked as an ork round struck home. Shrill klaxons blared within the cockpit, and Artemis heard the whoosh of fire from the crew bay.

'We have a hull breach!' shouted Sekor, fighting the controls with one hand as he clamped his helm back on. 'Go, brother-captain. You see to those fires, I will keep us from becoming a smear on this greenskin bastard's hull.'

Artemis locked his own helm into place and sealed his power armour as he descended from the cockpit to the crew bay.

Sparks fountained from the ceiling, raining down upon Imtehan as he sprayed at the flames spreading through the crew bay with a canister of extinguishing foam. Artemis pulled another canister from a compartment and went to the Flesh Tearer's aid.

'By the blood, what is that imbecile doing up there?' Imtehan snarled as the ship rocked under the force of another impact.

'Keeping us alive,' replied Artemis, as he pushed into the rising flames.

Sparks spat from the control panels as Sekor sent the drop-ship diving towards the ork warship. Flashes of exploding flak filled the viewport, and the armourglass cracked as shrapnel struck the cockpit.

'Proximity alert,' droned the servitors behind Sekor. 'Inbound collision in six seconds.'

Sekor gritted his teeth. He struggled to guide the Blackstar through the firestorm, avoiding the larger rockets and munitions as glancing hits slashed into the hull.

'Inbound collision in four seconds.'

The tentaclids surged closer on the auspex screen as the distance between them and the Space Marines shrank. The ork vessel filled his viewport, so close he could see the individual gun barrels rattling as they hurled explosives at him.

'Inbound collision in two seconds.'

'I know! Throne, terminate proximity warnings,' Sekor snapped.

'Compliance.'

Sekor banked the drop-ship at the last moment. He skimmed along the flank of the ork vessel, lascannons carving a path through the batteries of guns that protruded from the hull like spines.

The tentaclids, guided by synaptic instinct, peeled away from Sekor towards the larger threat. The missiles exploded, showering the ork vessel in crackling chains of jade lightning. The lights studding the greenskin warship winked out in waves, rippling from the site of the impact back across the hull as it lost power and began to list.

Similarly drawn to the greater prey, half of the remaining hive crones dived upon the ork ship's defenceless form, slashing with barbed spurs and dissolving swathes of hull plating with squirts of bio-acid from the fleshy cannons that protruded from their jaws. The other half continued their relentless pursuit of the Blackstar.

Sekor exhaled through gritted teeth. There was no way the drop-ship could keep absorbing such punishment. Even if they weren't vaporised by any of a thousand different equally likely sources, they were burning through their fuel reserves, and any further sustained use of the lascannons would burn their capacitors out.

Sekor looked up as he heard a dull crackling, and watched as a hissing slick of bio-acid began to eat its way towards the cockpit's canopy. Then his attention was snatched away once more as an arrow formation of new contacts strobed on his auspex screen, bearing straight for the Blackstar. The inbound craft would enter maximum weapons range in six seconds.

Sekor breathed, calm and slow, and closed his eyes.

The vox crackled. The voice on the other end, crazed with static, cut through the interference with its urgency.

'Break to port!'

Sekor's eyes snapped open. He wrenched the control sticks, banking the drop-ship to the left as a blur of silver shot past him. He looked back, watching as a squadron of Fury interceptors cut through the swarm of hive crones like a flung javelin. They fired withering volleys of lascannon fire, and launched missiles on twisting contrails to obliterate the tyranid fliers.

A spread of torpedoes stitched across the hulls of the nearby xenos ships at the same moment, sowing destruction and confusion as the sudden attack struck them by surprise.

Another salvo hit, and Sekor began to see tiny silver shapes materialise in the distance. These were not the ebon-hulled warships of the Deathwatch. This was an Imperial battlefleet.

The crenellated blades of Imperial battle cruisers, bristling with gun batteries and banks of lance turrets, powered forwards through the void. Escort craft, frigates, destroyers and corvettes of various designs and tonnages orbited their hulls in support formations, while squadrons of fighters struck ahead to engage the xenos warships.

At their fore, looming like an apex predator of ancient Terra, was a Retribution-class battleship. It dwarfed the other vessels of the battlefleet, its massive plasma drives keeping pace with the more nimble battle cruisers despite its immense tonnage. Vast weapons batteries primed as salvoes of torpedoes continued to fire from its plough-faced prow.

Sekor struggled to fathom where this battlefleet had appeared from. The entire Kurbynola System was a graveyard, and the cordon put in place by the Inquisition ensured that nothing could get in.

Or out.

Sekor realised there was only one place this battlefleet could have come from. He watched as layers of the ork and tyranid fleets came about to engage.

'*Follow us in!*' the voice of the Fury interceptor pilot scratched again over the vox. Sekor brought the drop-ship into their formation, bearing towards the immense blade of the Imperial battleship. If he was right, then things were set to become much more complicated.

A voice, stern, cold and deepened by advanced age boomed across the vox of the Blackstar. Artemis stood, turning to listen as he and Imtehan put the last of the fires out.

'*To the warriors of the Adeptus Astartes Deathwatch Chapter, this is High Admiral Nearchus, servant of the immortal God-Emperor of Man and master of the Battlefleet Kurbynola flagship* Claw of Damyrov. *I have come here for you.*'

PART III

PART III

TWENTY

Battlefleet Kurbynola set in motion the procedures to begin a fighting withdrawal as soon as it had loosed its first torpedo salvo. Thousands and thousands of highly trained crew hurried about their tasks to bring the monumental warships around, from the most senior bridge officers and shipmasters to the lowest indentured ratings who toiled their lives away without ever seeing the light of the stars. Every cog in the vast machine necessary to control an Imperial vessel of war meshed and worked together as the battlefleet conducted its precisely choreographed dance in the heavens.

The escort ships placed themselves in a wedge at the vanguard, running interference against the leading xenos skirmishers and buying the larger vessels the time they needed to turn. The battle cruisers completed their partial rotation first, lending their broadsides and lance batteries to the barrage that scythed down swathes of the charging alien warships.

A tyranid bio-ship died, the bioluminescence that shivered down its hull extinguished as it absorbed the destruction inflicted by a full broadside volley. Ork blockade runners smashed into the armoured chevron of the Imperial vanguard. A destroyer was rammed amidships, breaking its back and overloading its warp core. The vessel erupted into an expanding cloud of wreckage, sending shorn fragments of hull plating spinning into the warships around it. A precision strike from the combined lance batteries of three Imperial ships destroyed the ork craft, slicing it into ragged segments of molten iron.

Sekor followed in the wake of the squadron of Fury interceptors that was escorting him to the *Claw of Damyrov*. The attack craft frequently peeled off in pairs to engage enemy fighters that came too close to the drop-ship, returning to their comrades when the threat had been eliminated or driven off.

Artemis stepped into the Blackstar's apothecarion. The tiny room, little more than a table and a rack of tools and medical supplies, looked as much a war zone as the rest of the ship. While the watch captain and Imtehan had fought to contain the fires spreading through the drop-ship, the Novamarine Apothecary Nulsis had fought his own battle to keep Rogerio alive.

The small medicae chamber's floor was sticky with blood and littered with discarded bindings, tourniquets and empty vials and ampoules. Nulsis stood, knuckles against the table as he studied his charge. He had removed his helm, revealing a noble visage that was endemic in the descendants of Guilliman and the battle-kings of Macragge, despite his many scars.

Rogerio was still. Much of his armour had been cut away and laid in heaps around the table. His torso was brutalised. The attack from Magash that had severed his right arm had torn away much of his right side. Raw flesh and muscle glistened alongside savaged bionics in the apothecarion's sterile light, oozing blood and oil through the swathes of gauze and bio-foam that Nulsis had used to staunch the worst of the haemorrhaging.

'Will he live?' Artemis asked.

'For now,' Nulsis replied, still staring down at Rogerio. 'I have kept him in an induced sus-an hibernation, which will gain him a little time.'

Nulsis turned to face Artemis, his face as cold and expressionless as his steel-grey eyes. 'He needs a full apothecarion if he is going to survive. I've done all that I can with what I have here.'

'Thank you, brother.' Artemis hesitated.

'What is it?'

'I must ask another question of you.'

'Speak it.'

'The Sothan of our number who fell – Hyphantes. Did you recover his gene-seed?'

Nulsis blinked. A slight twitch ticked at his left eye. 'No. It was beyond saving.'

'Very well,' Artemis nodded. 'Thank you, brother.'

'Watch captain,' Nulsis called as Artemis turned to leave.

'Yes?'

'Of the nine who entered that ship with me, the seed of five lies lost within the dead. All of the gene-seed of the Raven Guard's kill team remains there as well. We have all suffered loss on this endeavour.'

Artemis nodded, and turned away.

* * *

No further communications had been sent to the Deathwatch kill team from the battlefleet, nor were any of the Space Marines' hails answered. Artemis climbed up to the cockpit from the crew bay of the Blackstar and stood behind Sekor's pilot throne.

'What brought them here?' asked Sekor, scratching at a patch of newly closed scar tissue at his temple. 'Could it have been the beacon? They would have had to be close for it to reach them, and for them to get here this quickly.'

Artemis watched the Imperial battleship swell to fill the entire cockpit viewport. He suppressed his armour from releasing a dose of combat narcotics into his bloodstream, the interface systems of his war-plate responding to his elevated heart rate and adrenaline.

Tension coiled around the watch captain. Artemis was well aware of the sequestration placed upon the defence forces of the Kurbynola System, ordered by the Inquisition and enforced by the Deathwatch. He speculated on the extent to which the system's destruction had emotionally compromised the high admiral and the other mortals of the Imperial Navy and Astra Militarum relocated to the system's citadel world of Praesidium. He could not relate to their situation, and had neither the desire nor the inclination to try. If the Mortifactor home world of Posul were destroyed, it would do nothing to sway him from fulfilling what duty would demand of him.

If the high admiral had defied his mandate, and sailed the battlefleet here of his own accord, then they were traitors in open rebellion, and Artemis was duty-bound to destroy them. Even if they had departed under orders, Kill Team Artemis was in a precarious position. Artemis did not deign to be at a disadvantage to or to be indebted to mortals.

'Something sent them here,' replied Artemis.

'And Rogerio?' asked Sekor. 'Does he yet live?'

'Aye,' said Artemis. 'He still draws breath. Though he will need the apothecarion of an Adeptus Astartes warship if he is to survive.' The Mortifactor's gaze returned to the *Claw of Damyrov*. 'We will signal the fleet as soon as we are aboard.'

Artemis climbed down from the cockpit. He walked over to Imtehan, sitting in one of the unlocked restraint thrones. With the fires out and the hull breach sealed, the Space Marines had been able to remove their helms and make repairs to their armour. The Flesh Tearer was silent, his dark features impassive as he ran an oiled cloth over the silver blade of Rogerio's power axe.

His eyes flicked up at Artemis as he approached.

'Imperials,' said Imtehan in his humourless growl. 'That they are not where the Inquisition demanded brings ill tidings.'

'We will learn the truth of it,' replied Artemis.

Imtehan grunted, noncommittal. The axe gleamed in his steady grip. 'So, how do you want to play this?'

Artemis wiped the sweat from his brow and rolled his shoulders. 'We do not know what we are walking into.' He laid a hand on Imtehan's shoulder, meeting the Cretacian's gaze with his eyes of electric blue.

'Just be ready.'

The Imperial vanguard broke formation as the xenos response ebbed. Those alien ships remaining were isolated and destroyed or withdrew to return to their fleets. The escorts limped back to their positions supporting their respective capital ships. Many trailed fire and plasma or bore extensive damage to their hulls from the brief but intense fighting.

With the temporary diversion of the Imperial battlefleet gone, the ork and tyranid fleets returned fully to their titanic clash. They did not need to expend ships tracking the withdrawing humans. They were fully aware of the world that was their destination, and it would be only a matter of time before the might of their inhuman empires would darken its skies.

TWENTY-ONE

Commodore Jaroslav Leitz watched as the Space Marine drop-ship lowered onto the primary embarkation deck of the *Claw of Damyrov*. Leitz wiped at the sweat prickling his brow. He had seen one of the Deathwatch craft only once before, the one that had transported Brother Gnaeus to and from the battleship to enforce the mandate issued to Battlefleet Kurbynola by the Inquisition. He took a deep breath as the image of the ebon-clad giant appeared in his mind. It was the closest he had ever come to one of the Emperor's mythical Space Marines. He had felt the ironclad focus of the demigod, and the unique terror of conversing with such a being, however briefly, as the warrior had enacted his mandate.

Like any other citizen of the Imperium, Leitz had grown up hearing legends of the Space Marines, the noble defenders of the Imperium who stood ever vigilant to protect the realms of the God-Emperor. He remembered the joy he had felt when he heard the news that an envoy from a Chapter of the venerable Adeptus Astartes would be arriving on the *Claw of Damyrov*.

Joy that had quickly turned to ashes as Brother Gnaeus of the Deathwatch proclaimed the mandate imposed by the Inquisition. The Space Marines had come not to protect their worlds, but to ensure that no one raised a hand to oppose their very annihilation. To ensure that High Admiral Nearchus, Leitz and every other son and daughter of Kurbynola watched as their home worlds burned. He could still smell the gunsmoke from when the Space Marine had executed Leitz's predecessor. He believed that smell would remain with him for the rest of his days.

That act had brought the newly promoted, now-Commodore

Leitz to the embarkation deck, flanked by an honour guard of senior armsmen, to await this detachment of Space Marines. He could feel the tension radiating from the armsmen, gripping their ceremonial chrome lasrifles with white knuckles. They were angry. Leitz was as well. They were all on edge. And just like Leitz, the powerlessness imposed upon them in the face of the Space Marines only soured that bitterness further.

Leitz cleared his throat, took a deep breath and stood up straighter as the dual assault ramps on either side of the sleek drop-ship's nose lowered on hissing hydraulics.

Three giants clad in dark armour stepped down from the drop-ship assault ramp, the metal ringing with the weight of their heavy tread. The thrum of their war-plate tickled Leitz's eardrums and set gooseflesh rippling over his skin. They looked as though they had clawed their way out from one of the stygian hellscapes of ancient Terran myth. Gouges and impact craters covered the plates of dark ceramite. Blood and other foul liquids slathered the mighty warriors from head to toe, dried to a thick crust that cracked and crumbled from snarling servo joints as they moved.

Baleful red eyes glowed like coals from their snarling masks. Each of the three was fully armed, carrying firearms with barrels the size of a man's fist along with brutal swords and axes. The warrior leading the trio bore a sword as long as Leitz was tall sheathed at his hip.

The Space Marines did not look like the mythical heroes immortalised in statues and stained glass mosaics that had captivated Leitz as a child.

They looked like monsters.

'Hail.' Leitz stepped forwards, giving a short bow and making the sign of the aquila.

The lead Space Marine looked down upon Leitz, saying nothing.

'On behalf of High Admiral Nearchus of Battlefleet Kurbynola, I–'

'Where,' the giant boomed, his voice inhumanly low and given a mechanical edge by his helm, 'is the admiral?'

Leitz swallowed. 'I am his adjutant, I have been tasked with escorting you and your brothers to him.'

The commodore heard muted clicks from the Space Marines, as they communicated with one another on a secure vox-channel, ignoring Leitz.

'My brethren will not accompany me,' replied the lead Space Marine. 'Brother Sekor will stand vigil upon the bridge.'

One of the Space Marines, his pauldron displaying chipped cobalt, stepped away in silence, striding towards the lifts that led to the *Claw of Damyrov*'s bridge.

'Brother Imtehan will attend to your astropathic choir. We have need of it.'

Leitz recognised the saw-toothed blade icon of the Flesh Tearers as another of the demigods departed. He had witnessed a small detachment of their Chapter depopulate an entire cruiser that had committed mutiny during his earliest years as a ship's sub-lieutenant. Six of them had killed every man and woman onboard the seditious vessel, nearly eight thousand people, in two days. Leitz averted his eyes from the Space Marine as he stomped past.

'There is another of our number who remains within our ship.'

Leitz looked back up at the lead Space Marine. The warrior's smouldering gaze had never left him. The demigod gestured to the drop-ship. 'You shall provide him with whatever resources he requires, and do so immediately. I will go with you to your master.'

'Of course, my lord,' Leitz replied.

The Space Marine turned, walking past the commodore and his honour guard. '*I am not your lord.*'

'Then,' said Leitz, fighting to banish the tremor from his voice, 'how may I address you, so that I might announce you properly to High Admiral Nearchus?'

The giant came to a halt, looking back over his shoulder at the officer.

'You will address me as Watch Captain Artemis, of the Deathwatch.'

Leitz bowed again, hurrying to keep pace with the Space Marine as he departed the embarkation deck. The honour guard left them as they came to the lift that would take them to the observation deck, where High Admiral Nearchus waited.

The commodore's stress increased as he squeezed into the small lift. Such proximity to the Space Marine's thrumming armour made him feel as though insects were crawling over his skin. He squeezed his fists tighter in an attempt to make them stop shaking.

It didn't work.

Artemis was silent as the lift ascended through the decks of the *Claw of Damyrov*. He could smell a sour reek emanating from the mortal officer who shared the cramped confines of the pod with him. The same stench he encountered every time he came into contact with mortals. The musk was sharp, primal, and sickeningly biological. The smell of a cornered animal.

Fear.

It radiated from this mortal in great abundance. Artemis sincerely doubted the naval officer had ever drawn the laspistol holstered at his side. He had seen the mortal's kind before. Had this battle-ship been disabled, and its crew ordered to take up arms and repel boarders, crewmembers such as the officer standing beside him would likely not have survived the slaughter.

Mercifully, the ascent to the observation deck was brief. The lift slid open, admitting Artemis and Commodore Leitz onto a broad circular hall at the tip of one of the *Claw of Damyrov*'s spinal crenellations. A ring of void-reinforced crystal ringed the circumference of the chamber, offering a full three hundred and sixty degree view of the void beyond the battleship's hull. The observation deck was of a size that could easily hold hundreds, but there was only one inhabitant waiting. A tall, thin man, his posture hunched by age, stood with his back to the approaching duo, hands clasped behind him as he surveyed the celestial dance.

'High admiral,' began Leitz as they drew close to the figure. 'I present–'

'Thank you, Commodore Leitz,' Admiral Nearchus said without turning. He raised a hand. 'Leave us.'

Leitz swallowed, once again gave a short bow as he made the sign of the aquila, and departed from the observation deck.

The chamber was silent for some time, broken only by the pervasive, gum-aching hum of Artemis' war-plate, before the high admiral spoke.

'We are passing a planet soon.' The man's voice was low, the raw gravel of a man who had spent a lifetime shouting orders. It was stern, paternal, but not without warmth. 'Can you see it?'

Artemis looked past Nearchus, seeing a dark sphere of ochre and grey materialise.

The high admiral gave a short chuckle. 'What am I saying? Of course you can see it.' He turned back, looking at Artemis with deep brown eyes.

'Stand with me.' Nearchus waved Artemis to him. 'I will tell you of it.'

Artemis stepped forwards, stopping beside the high admiral before the crystal panel. Nearchus did not come to the Space Marine's shoulder. Artemis looked back to the void, seeing the twinkling light given off by the *Claw of Damyrov*'s escort ships as the world drew into focus.

'Iljaen.' Nearchus' voice was hushed, almost reverent as he whispered the world's name. Artemis did not need the high admiral to tell him. He had memorised the name of every world in the Kurbynola System, as well as their histories, societies, and the order in which they circled the system's star. Iljaen had been a forested world, a reflection of ancestral Terra in the bygone epochs of its ancient past. It had been verdant, a healthy agricultural contributor and cultural centre in the system, before the xenos had come.

'I am told that it was,' Artemis struggled with the banal conversation that mortals seemed so taken with, 'pleasing in its aesthetic.'

'It was my home,' Nearchus smiled, lost in memory. 'My family owned a farmstead in the hills, when I was young. Orchards, lands for grazing. We would go into the cities during the harvest solstice. The avenues were strewn with flowers. Hanging gardens covered the buildings, so thick and vibrant it was as if nature had taken the land back from us.'

The smile faded from his lips as the *Claw of Damyrov* slowly passed by Iljaen. The idyllic world of the high admiral's birth was now a ruined husk. The planet had been utterly destroyed, and all life had been stripped from its surface, leaving it a cold and barren wasteland. Its two moons, themselves thriving settlements erected to mine their vast mineral deposits, had been shattered by the force of the alien cataclysm. The immense shards of the annihilated satellites, still caught within the gravity of Iljaen's corpse, slowly spread over its orbit like a funeral shroud.

'What are you doing here, admiral?' Artemis finally asked.

'We received a message through our astropathic choirs. With the tyranid hive fleet present, simply receiving it resulted in the loss of half of our astropaths, and even then we recovered only fragments. From what our choirs could decipher, I am told it was a plea from a traveller, on the verge of entering a great storm without eyes to see. A plea to find what they had left behind them in their wake.'

Artemis blinked. The *Fatal Redress*. Shipmaster Aemna must have ordered the telepathic sending before she entered the warp, casting out a call to recover his kill team when she knew she would not be able to herself.

'You have defied the mandate of the Inquisition.'

'For your salvation,' answered Nearchus.

'Irrelevant,' growled Artemis. 'The lives of the Emperor's servants, our lives, mean nothing when weighed against the scale of duty.'

'Watch captain, that is a lesson I have been taught already, is it not? When your brethren departed from our vessels to answer your watch master's summons, they proclaimed to us that any who left the orbit of Praesidium would face summary execution for treason against the Imperium. But each one of us died the day you stripped us from our charge to protect these worlds. We died with our families the day we watched our homelands burn.'

'Then why come for us?'

'To impart a lesson of my own. We both are servants of the Imperium of Mankind. We have both sworn our lives in defence of humanity against the myriad foes that so threaten it. I forfeited my life to rescue you, watch captain, because in spite of whatever parallels we might share, I am *nothing* like you, and I never will be.'

Artemis took a breath, quelling the temper rising in his chest.

'I… understand your desire for vindication against the xenos that have perpetrated this–'

'Xenos?' The high admiral turned to Artemis, eyes wide. His hands trembled into fists, and the skin of his face flushed crimson. '*Xenos?* You dare to lay this desolation at the foot of the alien? The ork and tyranid fleets entered the system only in the past weeks. This system had been murdered, the surfaces of its worlds made graveyards long before they arrived.'

Nearchus rounded on Artemis. 'Our worlds did not die by their vile hands. Our cities were not sacked to sate the unholy bloodlust of the greenskins. Our people, our *children*, were not butchered and rendered down to feed the hunger of the malignant tyranid. No, watch captain, those things were denied to them. By *you*.'

Nearchus stabbed an accusing finger at Artemis' chest. Exterminatus had cleared its sheath, its point against the high admiral's throat before the mortal could blink an eye.

'You forget yourself,' snarled Artemis in a low growl. 'You will account for your insult and your slander, or I *will* take your head.'

Nearchus pressed his throat to the blade hard enough for a thin trickle of blood to run down into the starched indigo of his dress uniform.

'*You* were the Inquisition's agent in this. *You* sought to starve the xenos of the resources this system would provide, to foist them upon each other. *You* came in your ships, and burned each world, one by one. *You* destroyed my home.'

Nearchus' eyes watered and narrowed as he raged at Artemis.

'You did this, Space Marine. To buy respite, to deny the enemy for a moment longer, you took the blood of billions of innocents upon your hands.'

The high admiral leaned as close as he could to Artemis' emotionless helm.

'You have created a wasteland, and called it peace.'

TWENTY-TWO

At the core of the Kurbynola System, a silver orb slowly turned in a careful celestial dance as it patiently circled its star. Thin rings encircled the sphere like glittering haloes. Upon closer inspection, one realised that these were not natural belts of dust and frozen rock. They were defence platforms, shipyards and weapons arrays. The planet below was not silver from natural occurrence, but rather from the vast citadels that covered its surface. If Iljaen had been a simulacrum of Terra's ancestral past, then this world was fashioned to mirror humanity's birthplace in its present state.

There were names given to places such as this. Fortress planet. Citadel world. This one bore the name Praesidium.

Deep-space auguries and auspex arrays on Praesidium's rings tracked the ships of Battlefleet Kurbynola as they approached. Banks of macro cannons and long-range torpedo silos had locked onto and acquired firing solutions for each vessel long before they had entered visual range. The defenders of the citadel world relented as the transponder returns for the Imperial battlefleet were validated. The might of a hundred thousand guns lowered into sentinel vigilance once more.

The *Claw of Damyrov* slowed as it reached the rings of Praesidium, allowing its cruisers and squadrons of escort craft to overtake it as the most heavily damaged ships entered dry dock for repairs. Shoals of tugs and towing craft latched onto their hulls, hauling them into maintenance cradles spread out across the rings.

Artemis watched the fleet break up from the battleship's bridge. The cavernous chamber spread out before the command dais he stood upon in tiers of blinking consoles and crowded control pits.

Servitor stations lined the walls, slotted in as they tirelessly worked to keep the immense warship operational.

Sekor stood beside Artemis. Like the watch captain, he too felt the cocktail of fear and anger emanating from every member of the *Claw of Damyrov*'s crew. He had remained silent for some time when Artemis told him of High Admiral Nearchus' revelation. He had found it as difficult to countenance as Artemis had. That opinion changed, however, as the warships of Battlefleet Kurbynola processed through the wasteland the system had become.

Apocalypse had swallowed the system's worlds, spreading its ruinous touch over everything these mortals had sworn to protect. Calamity was rendered down into reams of scrolling data, whispered reports, and holographic projections gathered by the flagship's sensors. It was not the ravaged devastation of the ork, nor the voracious consumption committed by the tyranid hive fleets. Artemis and Sekor both had served alongside the Inquisition, and they knew the after-effects of cyclonic torpedoes when they saw them. All life on each of the planets had been extinguished. Their surfaces had been set aflame, burned away to glass and barren rock. It could have only been the result of the rarest and most extreme of measures taken by the Imperium.

Exterminatus.

A weapon of last resort used when all other conventional measures had failed, exterminatus was invoked to kill a world in the case of overwhelming infestations by xenos or daemonic cults. To perform such total destruction of a world was a calamity. To invoke exterminatus across an entire system was beyond belief. Yet the proof of it surrounded Artemis as the *Claw of Damyrov* made its way to the system's core.

Sekor had asked Artemis the same question he had been asking himself since Nearchus had told him.

'Why did they not tell us?'

Artemis had no answer for him, but he intended to get one.

As if in concert with his thoughts, Artemis listened as a bell sounded from the auspex stations.

'Translation alert!' called out a crewman. 'Multiple warp ruptures detected.'

Imtehan had voxed Artemis an hour before. He had been successful in sending a message via the *Claw of Damyrov*'s astropathic choir per Artemis' orders, and had returned to the Blackstar drop-ship to aid Nulsis in attending to Rogerio.

Artemis watched as the full might of the Deathwatch fleet of the Bladefall emerged from writhing tears in the warp, corposant and unnatural lightning clinging to their ebon hulls as they returned from their sojourn in the Sea of Souls. The arrivals were dominated by the hammerhead behemoths of two battle-barges translating, one Artemis recognised immediately as the *Victorious Son*.

'High admiral,' called out a junior officer commanding a bank of vox stations. 'We are being hailed.'

A low voice, honeyed yet edged with iron, broke across the bridge.

'*In the name of the Emperor of Mankind, the Deathwatch stands in judgement over this fleet. We carry the authority to grant the Emperor's justice against those who have turned from His service. We demand to know why you have violated your mandate. Failure to surrender your command immediately will be met with your annihilation.*'

Artemis recognised the voice of Watch Master Asharbanapal. High Admiral Nearchus stood from his command throne, drawing breath to respond, when a thundering clang rang out across the bridge, silencing him.

Artemis' fist rose from the brass railing of the command dais, leaving an impression of his dark gauntlet in the metal.

'Watch master, this is Watch Captain Artemis of Talasa Prime. I will give you your reason.'

Artemis stood alone within the strategium of the *Victorious Son*. Space Marine battle-barges were powerful, scarce vessels, highly prized by the Chapters that possessed them. The warships operated as the nerve centre of command and control for any engagements that included them, and the size of their strategiums was testament to that fact. Nearly a hundred generals, admirals and Space Marine commanders could fit within its stone walls, encircling a grand table of hewn onyx as they coordinated the prosecution of the Imperium's wars.

Artemis pulled his helm free and closed his eyes, allowing the silence of the strategium to wash over him in welcome calm. He set his helmet down on the table, breathing in the coolness of the chamber rather than the stale, recycled air of his armour. He took a small comfort in the simple act, though it did nothing to resolve the anger that smouldered within his chest.

When Watch Master Asharbanapal entered the strategium, it was without the fanfare and pageantry that he had indulged in on the watch fortress before his assembled warriors. The watch master was alone and unarmed, though Artemis could hear the rumble of Terminator war-plate just beyond the chamber's doors.

'I would have you know that Brother Rogerio has been stabilised within our apothecarion,' said Asharbanapal.

'Will he live?' asked Artemis.

'As a result of Brother Apothecary Nulsis' attention, he will. While the damage to his body is severe, there are methods that will ensure his service will not end this day. He is a testament to the resilience and fortitude of his Chapter.'

Artemis gritted his teeth, stifling his temper at the watch master's calm banalities.

'Why?'

The watch master arched an eyebrow. 'What?'

'This system, the exterminatus. The lies you told about who did this. Why did you do it?'

Asharbanapal flashed his disarming, charismatic smile, but there was steel in the gesture, like the bright colours of a venomous animal. 'I will excuse the stridency in your tone, watch captain. But I will only do so once.'

'Why, watch master?' asked Artemis, stepping around the edge of the table towards Asharbanapal, calling up a map of the Kurbynola System. 'Why did you not tell me the truth of what happened here?'

'Because it was not necessary that you know,' answered the watch master. 'Doing so would not have altered the fate of this system or its citizens, nor would it have changed the parameters of the mission you failed to achieve.'

Artemis was silent as Asharbanapal continued. 'Mortals do not experience time as we do, watch captain. The shorter lifespans they live compared to ours mean they often fail to grasp the significance of the long-term realities brought about by our actions in the now. They would see the destruction of a system by our hands as a genocide, whereas our duty is to carry out such a task in order to prevent the genocide of a thousand times their number. You know full well that the unenhanced, those not elevated to see the galaxy as we do, debase themselves to emotion, and do so instinctually. The Inquisition is no stranger to wielding deception as a weapon of great power, and nor is the Deathwatch. Laying the deaths of these worlds at the feet of the enemy rallies them to their banners, and coarsens them to endure the true storm that is coming.'

Asharbanapal paused and looked at the glowing hololith.

'Evoking exterminatus upon an entire system was a radical step, that is true enough. But you of all should appreciate the threat we are now facing. The resources of these worlds had to be purged to deny the enemy the use of them against us. Whether their destruction was carried out by our hands or that of the xenos is irrelevant to the slain, but of vital importance to those who remained. The tyranid has already suffered by this deprivation, and were you successful in eliminating the Overfiend, their dual invasion could have been stifled long enough to marshal a comprehensive defence of the segmentum.'

'And what of Praesidium?' asked Artemis. 'The armies and fleets that man its walls, knowing the truth of what happened here?'

Asharbanapal sighed, true solemnity betrayed on his face. 'The Overfiend has always been the key to our efforts here. While we prayed your mission would be successful, we knew that we should have a contingency. I know the ork, watch captain. I have killed it in every condition imaginable. The assembly of legions of Astra Militarum, manning the barricades of a citadel world ringed with warships would be a temptation no greenskin tyrant could resist.'

Asharbanapal stepped in front of Artemis. 'The Overfiend will come to Praesidium, make no mistake of that. And when it arrives at the head of its mongrel hordes, and we have no question of its presence on the surface, we will do to Praesidium what we have done to every other planet in this system.'

'It will be the death of billions,' whispered Artemis.

'Yes,' Asharbanapal held his gaze with unblinking eyes of honey-gold. 'A grim duty done in order to save the lives of trillions. An undertaking I will carry out without hesitation.'

Artemis railed against the watch master's deception, but could not fault his cruel logic. In the cold arithmetic of war, sacrifices are inevitable. Even the loss of an entire system, when weighed against the hundreds and thousands of systems at risk within the segmentum, was a cost that must be paid.

The image of Caltanix, standing alone before the brutish Gorsnik Magash filled Artemis' mind. Rogerio, as the stalwart veteran was brought low by the ork warlord. He saw Nulsis' stone-grey eyes, and heard him speak of the loss he had suffered. He saw Hyphantes as he died.

'Failed,' whispered Artemis.

Asharbanapal frowned, leaning closer. 'What?'

'My mission,' replied Artemis. 'You said that it failed.'

The watch master looked at Artemis, nonplussed.

'When the Overfiend darkens the skies of Praesidium, and goes to its surface with its vile host, I will be there waiting. I will cut its head from its body and shatter the greenskin hordes. I will avenge the deaths of my brothers, and give these soldiers the vengeance they crave as well, whether you stand beside me or not.'

Asharbanapal did not reply. He watched as Artemis turned and gathered his helm from the table.

'I have not failed,' said the watch captain as he donned his helm. 'My mission is not yet complete.'

TWENTY-THREE

'Was this Inquisitor Kryptman's plan all along?' asked Imtehan. The Flesh Tearer had gathered together with Artemis and Sekor in one of the smaller chapels aboard the *Victorious Son*. Standing beneath an onyx statue depicting the Emperor in the warlike aspect of the warrior king and guardian of mankind, the three Space Marines spoke of what was to come next. Artemis had disclosed the details of his conversations with High Admiral Nearchus and the watch master to both of his brothers, as well as the plans set for the inevitable onslaught to come from the Overfiend and hive fleet Leviathan.

'I do not know with certainty,' replied Artemis. The warriors had removed their armour for repair by the battle-barge's serfs and artificers, and now wore robes of heavy black sackcloth. 'Such measures as this would align with a mind such as his.'

'I laud his conviction,' said Imtehan. 'Speaking of such an act is one thing. Possessing the fortitude to see it through, however, is another matter entirely.'

'He has not seen it through,' said Sekor. 'The Inquisition branded him with the Carta Extremis, stripped him of his authority and threw him into exile. Who can say where the old bastard is hiding, living the rest of his wretched life fleeing from the Officio Assassinorum.'

'Where he is now is irrelevant,' said Artemis. Sekor and Imtehan turned to regard the watch captain. 'Whether this was his goal – its success, its failure – it is meaningless to us. All that matters is what is coming.'

'And that is?' asked Imtehan.

'Vindication,' answered Artemis. 'The watch master is correct – the

Overfiend will strike Praesidium, and it will do so soon. The actions of High Admiral Nearchus coming to our aid have likely only hastened its arrival. Legions of the Astra Militarum man the walls of the citadels below us, and Battlefleet Kurbynola stands ready in orbit. Much has been taken from these soldiers. Their homes, their families, the oaths they swore to protect these worlds. The time for them to enact their vengeance is coming. They will face the xenos here at Praesidium, and I will stand beside them when they do.'

Sekor and Imtehan looked at Artemis, their expressions belying their inner conflict. They must have known that this would be his course of action.

'My duty has been left unfulfilled. I swore upon my blood, upon my honour that I would not rest until I had taken the Overfiend's head. I will not forsake that oath now. I will await the greenskin on Praesidium, and when it is dead, Hyphantes and all those who have suffered here will be avenged. I will leave this system with that duty done, or I will die in the attempt.'

Artemis looked to each of his brothers in turn. 'Will you stand with me?'

Imtehan's face screwed up in a feral snarl before going still and impassive once more. 'I will stand with you, Artemis. There must be a reckoning here, and now. Blood must be answered with blood.'

Sekor smirked. 'Seeing as how it is a long fall from here to Praesidium, you two will most likely need a pilot.'

'And an Apothecary.'

The Space Marines turned as a figure stepped into the chapel. Nulsis lowered the hood of his robes as he joined the members of Kill Team Artemis.

'The blood of Caltanix and the vanguard cannot go unavenged. I will stand alongside you in this, watch captain, and do what I must to keep you alive long enough to take the greenskin tyrant's head.'

'What of Rogerio?' asked Sekor.

Nulsis' expression darkened. 'As he is now, he will never wake again.'

Artemis nodded, eyes ablaze as he placed a hand on Nulsis' shoulder. 'Then he shall be avenged as well.'

The watch captain turned to face his brothers. 'We may well be walking the road to our destiny. This is a foe more powerful than any we have faced before. We must not shrink from this duty, and if we are to fall to oblivion, then so be it.'

'And what of the watch master?' asked Imtehan. 'He intends to enact exterminatus as soon as the Overfiend reveals itself.'

'And how will we even get close to it?' asked Sekor. 'If the Overfiend itself makes landfall on Praesidium, the hive fleet will come with it, and it will be at the head of a legion of greenskins.'

'True, brothers,' replied Artemis. 'Which means that, when our opening to strike arrives, we must be swift. And if our enemies are legion, then we must gather a legion of our own.'

The Corvus Blackstar rocketed down through the atmosphere of Praesidium in a blur of flame. The drop-ship had been fully repaired and rearmed once it had been transferred to the *Victorious Son*, its freshly lacquered hull reflecting no light from its sleek, matt surface.

Sekor scrolled through frequencies on the vox-net as they descended. He listened as a dozen different regiments passed orders in a dozen languages through the static and distortion. Armoured battalions, artillery, mechanised infantry and air superiority officers issued orders, rippling their intent out across their respective commands.

No Titan legions, thought Sekor. *They would have helped us now.*

Artemis entered the cockpit, taking his place again behind Sekor's control throne. The last flames of atmospheric entry burned away from the drop-ship, allowing the Space Marines to take in the sight before them on the surface.

Praesidium was a volcanic desert world, its proximity to the Kurbynola System's star rendering its climate inhospitable. Yet, by the technological mastery of the Adeptus Mechanicus, humanity had brought its harsh environment to heel, and erected vast fortifications across its surface. The raging volcanoes studding the planet were dammed and harnessed to power the crackling void shields that protected each of the bastions.

The silver forms of citadels stretched across the planet's surface like star-shaped islands in an ocean of black igneous sand. Artemis leaned closer as the drop-ship approached the largest of the fortresses, watching as shivering tiles of black within its walls resolved into battalions of marching troops.

The drop-ship trembled as the silver inverted wedge of an Imperial Lightning fighter craft closed on either side.

'*Attention*,' the voice of one of the pilots came over the vox. '*Proceed with us to the designated landing zone. Any deviation from your current course will be regarded as an act of hostility.*'

Sekor snorted. 'Acknowledged.' He looked back at Artemis. 'I would not expect the warmest of welcomes, brother-captain.'

'No,' replied Artemis. 'I think not.'

Climbing back down into the crew bay, Artemis approached Imtehan and Nulsis. The Apothecary had busied himself with loading sickle-shaped bolter magazines, and Artemis listened to the *snik snik snik* as the Novamarine slotted the mass-reactive rounds into place. Imtehan had once again elected to attend to Rogerio's power axe, carefully running over the weapon's blade with an oiled cloth.

'What makes you think they will stand with us?' Imtehan asked.

'I don't,' Artemis replied. 'The desire for vengeance burns as hotly within them as it does within us. They will not have to stand with us to stand against the xenos, and that is all we will require of them.'

Artemis had disembarked alone from the Corvus Blackstar upon the main landing pad of Praesidium Primus, the foremost citadel of the fortress-world. He followed an escort of elite shock troopers through the fortification to its command spire, where he joined the assembly he had requested before departing from the *Victorious Son*.

The commanders of the combined forces of the Astra Militarum in the Kurbynola System stood around the central table of the strategium, their muted conversations silenced as the watch captain entered the room.

Artemis was surprised that the majority of the commanders had answered his summons. Representatives of the various armoured divisions, artillery and infantry divisions and fighter squadrons were gathered. The leaders of the Astra Militarum for the system eyed Artemis in silence, their expressions ranging from cold indifference to barely restrained ire. A crackling hololithic projection of High Admiral Nearchus was among their ranks, his pale blue form wavering with occasional interference.

'I have requested this council so that the defence of this world might be coordinated,' said Artemis as he stepped forwards to the table dominating the centre of the strategium.

'Have you, Space Marine?' growled one of the generals bitterly. 'Or have you come to murder us, now that we are all together here in one place?'

A murmur of agreement rippled over the assembly.

'Why not simply kill us as you have killed our worlds?' sneered another commander.

'Why have you come?' demanded another.

Artemis looked around the room. Targeting reticules flickered over each mortal in the strategium. He had known of circumstances where Space Marines had executed mortals for lesser insults. The grim arithmetic coursed through his mind. Even without the use of his bolter, he could kill every man and woman present in the room within two minutes. He allowed himself a moment to savour the temptation, before banishing the thought. That could not be the way through this.

Artemis removed his helm with a hiss of air pressure, setting it down before him as he looked out at the assembled military leaders with eyes of blistering blue.

'The Imperium of Mankind stands alone, a single light in the darkness. Monstrous foes in their legions descend upon it from all sides, desperate to extinguish the flame of humanity and cast the galaxy into darkness for eternity. This is such a foe who has come to your worlds, and who comes this day for your blood. Neither the cruelty of fate, nor the machinations of the Inquisition, nor any other agent can alter that reality. They seek your obliteration.'

'To finish what you have started,' spat a heavyset general bearing the laurels of an artillery battalion, his words greeted by a low murmur of bitter support.

'You will not fight for me,' continued Artemis. 'Nor would I expect you to. Rather, you fight for the homes reduced to ash and ruin. You fight for the blood of the innocents lost. You fight for retribution. You fight for rage. The Emperor looks down upon you and knows your hearts. He has seen the atrocity you have borne, and will watch as you strike back against the enemy to claim the vengeance that is rightfully yours. It is there for each of you.

'Stand upon the walls, look down with defiance upon the enemy in their multitudes, and make war as the avengers of the dead. The avengers of Iljaen, Colxis and Trunidia, of Lunfis and Rygrall and Balinth. Make war this day, as the avengers of Kurbynola.'

Silence filled the strategium. Artemis could sense the adrenaline of the assembled commanders rising. They craved retribution as much as he did, perhaps more. Fury battled within the heart of each man and woman against their mistrust of Artemis and the Deathwatch. Their bitterness and frustration had thinned, but still held their desire for revenge in check.

'I will make war.'

The assembled leaders turned to the one who had spoken. High Admiral Nearchus stood straighter, his eyes hard even through the flickering light of his hololithic projection.

'As I told you before, watch captain, I am already dead. I will not fight for the Inquisition, and I will not fight for you. I will fight for the souls of Kurbynola. I will fight, and walk into annihilation so that their spirits may find peace. The fleet will fight, Space Marine.'

'As will my engines,' rasped the patriarch of a clan of Imperial Knight combat walkers who was more augmetic than flesh. 'House Merovic will walk, and we will make war.'

'For Kurbynola, the Balinthian Rifles will make war.'

'As will the armoured legions of Colxis.'

'We will take to the air,' said a colonel, his uniform bearing the marks of the 981st Air Superiority Corps. 'The xenos will not hold the skies while we draw breath.'

One by one, the assembled commanders committed their warriors, not to Artemis, but to one another, to their honour, and to avenge their fallen. Crisp salutes were offered, and the sign of the aquila was made among the leaders.

A junior officer burst into the strategium.

'Inbound contacts detected in low orbit!'

The wail of sirens filled the air over Praesidium Primus as the sky caught fire. Artemis and a group of senior commanders had stepped out onto the ramparts of the citadel to survey the skies. Teardrops of flame sparked and swelled as they rained down through the atmosphere, leaving fiery contrails in the wake of their entry.

'Disperse orders giving permission to fire to our defensive guns,' barked one of the generals to his adjutant. 'Scramble Lightning squadrons for intercept sorties.'

'No,' said Artemis.

'No?' asked the general incredulously. 'And why, watch captain, is that?'

'Because those are not xenos.'

TWENTY-FOUR

Artemis stood on the running boards atop a Chimera as the troop transport raced to the landing pad. Streams of landers and drop-ships were touching down on Praesidium Primus, filling the sky with the roar of their engines. Every one of the landing craft was black, their hulls bearing the gothic skull iconography of the Deathwatch.

The Chimera rolled to a halt before a growing throng of Space Marines as they disembarked from Corvus Blackstars and heavy landers. Rhino heavy transports and Predator battle tanks rumbled from the open maws of landing craft, clearing the path for the massive Land Raider command tanks that followed in their wake.

Artemis leapt down from the Chimera. The ground beneath his boots quaked with the reverberations of the Deathwatch strike force readying for war.

'Well met, watch captain,' said Asharbanapal at the summit of the heavy lander's loading ramp. He held his guardian spear with easy grace, and was flanked by the hulking forms of his Terminator guard.

Artemis came to a halt before the Deathwatch commander and saluted, his dark gauntlet banging against his chest. 'Hail, watch master. I had not expected you to land a force on the surface.'

'As you said, watch captain. You would be here whether I stood with you or not,' Asharbanapal rested a gauntlet on Artemis' pauldron. 'And we will not stand by while the blood of Caltanix and my company goes unanswered, nor shall we leave our fellow brothers here to stand on their own against its hordes. I have elected that the Bladefall are to stand with you. And we shall not do so alone.'

The watch master gestured to the darkness in the depths of the cavernous lander. 'Your brother has returned to you, watch captain.'

'Rogerio?' asked Artemis. 'He has awoken? Can he speak?'

The deck of the lander boomed with a heavy, ponderous tread. Artemis felt the buzz of energy rippling from heavy power generators, and smelled the smoke and ozone that twisted into the air as the stomping footfalls drew closer.

'*Speak?*'

A massive shape emerged from the lander. A broad, boxy sarcophagus, it stood in a wide stance upon splayed iron claws at the end of a pair of squat, heavily armoured legs. Its blackened hull was adorned with silver plates engraved with golden filigree, extolling a legacy of venerable deeds by legendary heroes. Oath parchments rippled in the wind, fastened to its chassis by discs of red wax. Bolted to its right side was a massive assault cannon, its spinning barrels whirring as they chewed the air in impatience. On its left was a grasping power fist, crackling with energy as its wrist-mounted meltagun hummed with killing power.

Artemis looked upon the hulking assault walker, his eyes transfixed upon the power fist. It was stained crimson.

'I can do far more than speak, brother-captain,' boomed Rogerio from the Dreadnought's vox horn, looking down upon Artemis from a sensor node cluster fashioned to resemble a Space Marine's helm.

Artemis' fist thudded against his breastplate once more in a fervent clash of armour. 'Welcome back, my brother. I am heartened to see you once again.'

'And I you, Artemis,' said Rogerio. 'Now, let us away. Show me these xenos that we shall destroy.'

Artemis had been correct when he had spoken with his brothers. The brief skirmish fought by High Admiral Nearchus and Battlefleet Kurbynola against the clashing forces of the ork Overfiend and hive fleet Leviathan had only hastened the xenos' inevitable advance to the gates of Praesidium.

As the commanders of the Astra Militarum deployed their forces across the many citadels of the fortress-world, the deep-space auguries stationed on the planet's rings detected the coming storm.

Watch Master Asharbanapal had returned to orbit, coordinating the arrangement of the Deathwatch fleet with High Admiral Nearchus from the bridge of the *Victorious Son*. The Imperial warships took up positions, readying themselves for the entangled xenos hordes bearing down upon them.

The ploy to use Praesidium and the legions defending it to lure the aliens had worked. To hive fleet Leviathan, ravenous in its search for bio-mass to replenish its ranks lost in battle against the greenskin, Praesidium was irresistible. The fortress-world was similarly tantalising to the Overfiend's hordes, who came charging towards the Imperial guns with a fanatical thirst for violence.

Against the immense scale of the twin fleets of the xenos, the Imperial ships knew they would not be able to prevent them from making planetfall even if they had wanted to. They would inflict as much damage as possible upon the ork and tyranid fleets before breaking from high anchor, splitting into sub-fleets and squadrons and conducting guerilla lightning attacks against the aliens. Against just one of the opposing fleets, the length of their defence would have been measured in days. Against both combined, the scenario was cut to hours.

High Admiral Nearchus marvelled at the scale of the xenos fleets approaching. He gazed at the grand oculus viewscreen that dominated the front of the *Claw of Damyrov*'s bridge. The fact that the xenos could advance upon them with any sense of coordination while simultaneously mauling one another was a truly chilling sight to behold. On they came, filling the oculus like a plague.

Nearchus had arrayed his ships in the best possible formation alongside the warships of the Deathwatch. Even with the formidable firepower at his command, it would be like holding out an outstretched hand to stop a tidal wave. The water would simply flow over and around it, and in time he would sink beneath its weight, and drown.

The high admiral closed his eyes for a moment, pinching the bridge of his nose. Like all the other defenders of the Kurbynola System, he had been eager to rail against the Inquisition and the Space Marines of the Deathwatch for the ruin they had wreaked to forestall the coming xenos. He had shared their fiery conviction that no threat justified such genocide. Now, finally seeing the scale of their foe, Nearchus understood. He could never forgive what they had done, but now he understood.

'My lord,' Commodore Leitz stepped forwards, coming to a respectful halt one tier below Nearchus on the command dais. 'Auspex confirms that the enemy will reach maximum weapons range in six minutes.'

Nearchus opened his eyes, nodding as he clasped his hands behind his back.

'Run out our guns, commodore,' said the high admiral to his adjutant. 'Our foes have grown slothful quarrelling amongst each other. Let us show them the teeth of a true foe.'

* * *

The void lit with spheres of fire like a chain of infant suns. The combined firepower of the Imperial and Deathwatch fleets filled the space between them and their alien foes with a hurricane of ordnance. Shoals of torpedoes streaked unerringly towards the xenos swarm. The eye-aching brilliance of massed lance fire stitched through the hideous alien attackers, the lightning to the devastating thunder of heavy broadside volleys.

The foremost ranks of the ork and tyranid fleets simply ceased to exist. Bio-ships and ork cruisers vanished in the firestorm, shattered as their wreckage was ploughed through by those coming behind them. Squadrons of Fury interceptors strafed the larger warships before their formations were shattered by swarms of xenos fliers. Any semblance of order and cohesion evaporated as the warring fleets made contact, the precise choreography of traditional void warfare conducted at incredibly long distances erased as the battle devolved into a howling melee in the void.

A bio-ship disappeared in a blinding flash. Seconds later, one of the largest warships in the ork vanguard was similarly obliterated. The prow of the *Victorious Son*, along with the second battle-barge in the Deathwatch fleet, glowed as their titanic nova cannons readied to fire again.

The Imperial forces were reaping a ferocious tally against the xenos, but they were soon overwhelmed. An Imperial grand cruiser broke apart into an expanding cloud of plasma and spinning metal under the thunder of ork guns, while tyranid bio-ships filled their maws with the warships of Battlefleet Kurbynola, still firing their weapons even as they were consumed.

The bridge of the *Claw of Damyrov* was a riotous frenzy. Junior officers sprinted from station to station, shouting over the wail of proximity alarms as they struggled to keep the battlefleet's flagship in the fight.

High Admiral Nearchus leaned heavily against the brass railing of the command dais, bleeding from a gash on his temple. He watched as the oculus viewscreen became completely obscured by the millions of tyranid bio-forms descending on his vessel like locusts. Biting back a curse, he shouted down to Commodore Leitz, who was diligently coordinating the chaos of the bridge like a trained orchestral conductor.

'Send the order, splinter the fleet to their designated rendezvous points,' ordered Nearchus, as the last light on the oculus was swallowed from sight.

'We've done all we can for them on the surface. It's in their hands now.'

TWENTY-FIVE

The sky lit with a false dawn as the last of Praesidium's orbital defence rings was broken. Half visible in the wan light of the volcanic fortress-world, shards the size of cities twisted ponderously from view, or flared as they fell into the atmosphere.

Artemis had received communications from many of the smaller bastions reporting portions of the defence rings crashing into the fortifications. Lightning squadrons had managed to break up some of the fragments, but they could not reach them all. Praesidium Quintus was gone, obliterated in an instant as a fragment of the wreckage that survived re-entry had smashed into it like a mass driver.

The watch captain looked up as the last of the ring's shards broke up in smears of flame. It would not be long now. The last bulwark between the xenos and the surface had been broken, and it was only a matter of time before the invading forces made landfall.

Artemis looked behind him at the blocks of marshalled troops and tanks filing into position behind the walls. They marched up from massive subterranean bunkers that were constructed to shelter refugees from planets across the system in times of emergency. The cavernous holds now stood empty as the Astra Militarum manned the ramparts.

The Deathwatch Space Marine looked back up as the sky began to turn black with vast shapes. They seemed shrouded in storm clouds, a spreading veil that soon blocked out the stifling heat of Praesidium's sun.

Artemis drew Exterminatus smoothly from its scabbard on his hip, raising the blade towards the gathering darkness. Massive guns and flak batteries ground on turrets, angling their gaping barrels at the approaching xenos onslaught.

Artemis tightened his grip, triggering the activation rune of the power sword. The blade flashed with brilliant lightning as the guns of Praesidium Primus hurled their rage at the skies.

The war for Praesidium had begun.

There would be no calm before the storm. No slow procession of landing craft brimming with howling orks, disgorging their war parties away from the range of Praesidium Primus' guns. No gradual massing of the greenskins' confederated tribes until their numbers filled the horizon before they charged the walls. There would not be even the most chaotic and disorganised semblance of orkish strategy employed. The xenos streamed down onto the surface, dragging their war with them like a wildfire spreading to dry woodland.

The void shields of Praesidium Primus rippled with hundreds of impacts as the ork fleet rained down a bombardment from orbit. The shimmering field flared as it withstood the barrage of mass-driven projectiles, radiating in kaleidoscopic colour like an oil spill.

Ork landers filled the skies as they tumbled awkwardly down through the atmosphere. Many were quickly destroyed as the greenskin warships in orbit continued their bombardment of the surface, oblivious to the swathes of their own troops that they slaughtered. Those that survived the fury of their own guns, and those of the Imperial citadels, crashed into the black sand, vast prows slamming down like drawbridges as hosts of whooping orks spilled from their holds. Larger landing craft reached the surface as well, unleashing streams of tanks and the ponderous, hulking forms of scrap-titans.

As the orks filled the skies with their foulness, so too did a deluge of spores sweep down from the firmament. Fleshy spheres of myriad shapes and sizes hurtled down, sheathed in glistening ooze. Some exploded against the void shields of the citadel like artillery, showering the cracking barriers with bone fragments and gouts of bio-acid. A small number of the other pods were small enough that they bypassed the shields completely, passing straight through the energy fields to land behind the fortress walls. Their quivering shapes stretched and tore, eventually rupturing in a fountain of ichor as swarms of writhing tyranids burst out. The ground outside the bastions wriggled like a carpet of chitin as tiny ripper organisms dispersed over the surface.

The ork hordes and tyranid swarms lashed out, devoting as much energy to their continued annihilation of each other as they did to hurling themselves at the walls of the citadels. Streams of las-fire slashed down from the Imperial defenders, slaughtering anything that came near with needle-fine beams of scarlet energy. Artillery boomed, the earth shuddering beneath squadrons of Basilisk tanks which did not have to take aim to hit their targets. The skies were just as frenzied, as Lightning squadrons weaved through walls of flak in dogfights with ork fighters and swooping tyranid fliers.

Artemis took it all in from where he stood on the ramparts. Throughout a century of service to the Deathwatch, having made war in every type of environment against every type of xenos in the galaxy, he had never experienced such a cataclysm. The sky was gone. In its place was a writhing black shroud of inhuman monsters, enveloping the heavens and casting the world below into darkness. There were no single sounds any more, the thunder of exploding shells and roaring aliens meshing with the howls of pain and triumph and a million other sounds that formed the deafening chorus. The noise was incredible, as if Praesidium itself were screaming as its flesh played host to this upheaval.

Fast-reaction forces of elite Tempestus squads and Deathwatch kill teams quickly destroyed any tyranids that breached the void shields of the bastion. Lines of soldiers rotated from the battlements, the barrels of their lasguns glowing from unceasing fire. Each had killed dozens of the xenos that charged through the shimmering canopy of the void shields and threw themselves upon the walls, and some many more than that.

Though their faces were obscured behind rebreathers and darkly visored helms, Artemis could see their conviction plainly. There was fear, its icy claws wrapped about each of their hearts, but it did not slow their pace. Artemis saw reflected in the eyes of the mortal soldiers a grim acceptance that the moment had arrived for destiny to claim them. For months they had watched this storm draw nearer, stripping away everything they had sworn to protect. Now it had come for them, and they sought to meet their end not with a whimper, but with a roar of defiant rage.

Artemis had not expected the discipline he saw represented here by these mortals. He had imagined panic, riots, the air ringing with firing squads executing deserters. There was nowhere for them to desert to, and Artemis sensed they knew that as he looked out over a battlefield that would have made the stygian underworld of the darkest of mythologies pale by comparison. They were afraid, but they faced annihilation and held their ground. They knew theirs was a battle they would not have to fight for long, and accepted that reality with a cold grace that Artemis had not believed mortals could possess. Seeing their worlds burn had deadened them inside, stripping away the animal panic. Only the grim conviction to avenge remained in their eyes.

There was honour in that.

'Admirable,' Artemis said to himself as he watched the last men and women of Kurbynola greet their extinction.

Artemis' visor dimmed as the distant shape of Praesidium Tertius died in fire, its overloaded void shields unable to stop the titanic meteor that smashed down into it like the fist of a pagan god. He waited for the mushroom cloud of smoke and ashen dust to thin, watching as a dark shape emerged.

It was nearly the size of the meteor that had borne it to the surface. It hauled its immense gut packed with devastating weapons forwards on squat, plodding legs. Stubby arms, themselves the size of Land Raiders, protruded from either side, little more than arsenals of battle cannons and missile launchers cobbled together and sheathed in scrap metal. A miasma of smoke and industrial fumes billowed from the haphazard smoke stacks, lingering above the scrap-titan like a diseased halo. At the summit of the hideous machine, carved in crude facsimile of some vile ork deity, static rumbled from vast war horns like building thunder.

The mammoth scrap-titan blared a deafening war cry, throwing anything within distance to the ground and putting the rest of the battlefield's cacophony to shame with its bestial, blood-maddened fury. It was loud enough to send tanks tumbling and knock aircraft from the skies. It was hard enough that it reached Praesidium Primus, drawing skeins of tortured colour across its void shields. It was the roar of an apex predator proclaiming its presence and demanding submission from friend and foe alike. There was only one greenskin with the power to command such a war machine.

'The moment has arrived,' voxed Artemis to the Deathwatch strike force. 'The beast has revealed itself. We go.'

TWENTY-SIX

The Deathwatch staging area was a scene of controlled chaos as they prepared to strike. Darkly armoured warriors donned bulky thruster packs and prayed over their weapons as they filed aboard a wedge of Corvus Blackstar drop-ships. Ahead of them, an entire battalion of battle tanks rumbled as their engines idled before the monolithic gates of Praesidium Primus. At the tip of the spear, mere strides away from the walls that held back the firestorm of clashing xenos, stood the Knights of House Merovic.

Penants and banners rippled from the battle cannons and chainswords that constituted the arms of the venerable combat walkers, displaying a legacy of gallantry over millennia of service to the Imperium. Kill markings and individual honours covered their jade carapaces. An entire warrior lineage shifted in place, eager to be unleashed against the enemy.

Artemis hauled his jump pack onto his back, securing the restraint harness with a chunky click. He whispered a benediction honouring its machine-spirit, and offered prayers to his bolt pistol and to Exterminatus as he locked them to his hips. Looking over towards the hulking form of Rogerio's Dreadnought sarcophagus, Artemis watched as his brother strode with thundering tread towards an arcane platform ringed with hooded tech-magi and esoteric machinery. The Corvus Blackstars were incapable of bearing the weight of the walker, and without access to Thunderhawks or any other heavier conveyances, teleportation would be their sole recourse.

'Are you ready, Brother Rogerio?' asked the watch captain as he clamped a teleportation beacon to his armour. The cylindrical devices were issued throughout the assault force, so that the

Dreadnought could be inserted by any Deathwatch elements that survived to reach the Overfiend.

'They shall sing songs of the ruin I shall wreak amongst their mongrel kind,' came the interred veteran's reply.

'Remember what we must do,' warned Artemis. 'We cannot allow vengeance to cloud our focus.'

'The greenskin you refer to was nothing but a hound,' boomed Rogerio. 'My fury is reserved for the filth that holds its leash.'

Artemis gave the Dreadnought a sharp nod as he turned away.

'Brother-captain,' called Sekor, emerging from Kill Team Artemis' Blackstar.

'Our brothers are in readiness?' asked Artemis.

'Aye, Imtehan and Nulsis are already aboard.'

Artemis noted a brief flicker of hesitation in Sekor's voice, a rarity in the Space Marine's characteristically cocksure manner.

'I wanted to provide you with this, before we departed.'

Sekor handed Artemis a brass cylinder the size of a melta charge. The watch captain accepted the device, his thoughts immediately carrying him back to the darkness of Kryptman's briefing chamber, so many years ago.

'A stasis bomb?' Artemis frowned.

'A design I have been tinkering with, based upon the one given to us by the Inquisition. It will work similarly, though its power supply is smaller, meaning that its detonation will be confined to a much smaller area, and its effect will not last for long.'

Artemis nodded, and clamped the stasis bomb to his thigh. He looked Sekor in the eye, holding the warrior's green stare with his sharp blue gaze.

'Just get us to the target,' said Artemis. 'Nothing extravagant.'

Sekor grinned, looking over the watch captain's shoulder into the skies beyond the citadel. 'Getting to the target alive will be more than extravagant enough, brother-captain.'

A thin smile tugged at Artemis' lips for a moment as the Space Marines gripped wrist-to-wrist.

'Die well, brother,' said Artemis.

'Many, many years from now,' replied Sekor, as the Deathwatch Space Marines donned their helms and boarded the Blackstar.

As the gates of Praesidium Primus rumbled open, the Imperial speartip plunged into hell. The Knights of House Merovic plodded through masses of thrashing xenos, slaying dozens with each blast of their cannons and slash of their chainswords.

Columns of tanks streamed behind them, gumming their tracks with gore as they crushed the bed of corpses beneath them to a paste. They lashed out with the thunder of their guns, shells exploding in geysers of shrapnel and broken alien bodies as they fanned out across the flanks of the Knights.

The ork and tyranid hordes descended upon them immediately. Massed packs of tyranids of all kinds and whooping ork warbands converged upon the Imperial breakout, drawing them into a ferocious firefight. The skies, choked with xenos fliers, cleared for a moment as they swooped down on the Imperials.

Just as the Deathwatch had planned.

With a low whine of engines, a chevron of Corvus Blackstars lifted from their landing pads. The few remaining Lightning fighters formed up around the drop-ships, escorting them through the xenos tempest as they flew like a javelin aimed at the Overfiend.

Corporal Nazia of the 617th Balinthian Rifles stood just beneath the parapet as damnation screamed around her. The sky of Praesidium was gone. In its place was a swarming miasma that defied reason. Nazia had glimpsed it for a moment when it began, but could not look upon it any longer. She had not seen the wedge of Space Marine drop-ships pass overhead, nor where the dark shapes were going.

Her brothers and sisters stood in ranks beside her, awaiting their time to man the ramparts. The din was muted by Nazia's helm and rebreather mask, and the sound of her frenetic breathing was overwhelming. Sweat misted her goggles and she blinked its sting from her eyes. The air shimmered with heat haze above her, as hundreds and hundreds of lasguns fired without pause down into the churning horror that surrounded the citadel. Nazia gripped her own weapon, and shot a quick glance to the soldier standing at her elbow.

'Calm, corporal,' said the man as he caught Nazia looking. His voice betrayed the gravel of age, and the experience that came with it. Sergeant's chevrons adorned the arms of his uniform, and he cradled his own lasgun with the easy comfort earned through a life of soldiery.

Sergeant Maqabee had joined the Astra Militarum as a youth, when the founding tithe came to Colxis. He had warred across the Imperium, through many worlds and against many foes. While in service, patrolling the system and putting down minor insurrections, there had not been a single event or skirmish that he had not linked to a memory of his past service. No matter the situation, it always reminded him of something. He had been the anchor Nazia and her comrades had held fast to amidst the madness they found themselves in, the veteran offering the distraction the troops desperately sought with tales of his campaigns.

'Doesn't this remind you of anything, sergeant?' asked Nazia.

Maqabee did not respond at once, his eyes calm and locked to the parapet. Whistles pierced the air, and the crack of massed las-fire ceased as flag bearers waved signals from watchtowers. The soldiers manning the walls turned, their exhaustion unmistakable as they descended.

Nazia glimpsed the face of a man as he dragged past. His eyes were hooded and glassy, like those of a corpse. Another soldier doubled over as they stumbled past, back arching as he released sick into the confines of his rebreather. Some simply collapsed a few paces behind the lines of waiting troops, their allies and weapons forgotten.

The soldier's eyes blazed into Nazia's mind. There had been terror in them once, but now, in the place of that terror, there was nothing. Numbness, without light or focus, as if the man had died upon those walls, yet his body remained animated. That scared Nazia more than anything.

Another whistle, and Nazia felt the press of soldiers around her push her forwards to the hellscape ahead. Maqabee smoothly charged his lasgun.

'No, lass,' he finally said, turning his dull brown eyes upon her as they prepared to climb to the ramparts.

'I've never seen anything like this before.'

Sekor struggled with the Blackstar's controls as he held the centre of the formation. The craft bucked and jinked as it absorbed dozens of impacts from the streams of xenos weapons fire filling the air. He glimpsed a Lightning sustain a direct hit from a tyranid spore mine, the fighter vanishing in a greasy cloud of jade bio-plasma.

A knot of ramshackle ork vehicles lumbered below the Deathwatch drop-ships, led by a massive ork who danced across the roof of the biggest of them, laughing maniacally and wreathed in electricity from the crown of sparking diodes bolted to its skull. The tanks shook erratically as the spindly cannons mounted to them crackled with growing chains of lightning. The cannons fired, and one of the Blackstars exploded as the ribbons of unstable energy blasted its prow apart. Sekor saw the small shapes of the Space Marines inside tumble out of the spiralling craft, most of them ablaze like the drop-ship as they hurtled lifelessly to the ground.

Sekor gritted his teeth as he passed through another cloud of flak. The Space Marine's eyes went wide as he beheld the sight before him. The immense ork gargant walker was close, and by the Throne, he could *see* the Overfiend. He could see it from miles away.

Standing upon the crown of the gargant's head, the ork king

almost defied description. A godlike knot of ochre green flesh, nearly as wide as it was tall, with the armour of an entire battle tank drilled directly into its slab-like musculature. It staggered Sekor, making the murderous greenskin warlord Gorsnik Magash seem childlike by comparison.

The Overfiend looked up at the approaching drop-ships. Its massive jaw ground low, and the beast roared in feral challenge. Its voice blasted through the gargant's war horns.

The wave of sound hit Sekor's Blackstar like a physical force. The Space Marine fought to stabilise the drop-ship, pushing it into an abrupt dive to avoid a pair of Lightning escorts that were flung together by the force of the Overfiend's tectonic howl.

Sekor hauled back on the controls as a pair of tyranid hive crones tore another of the Blackstars apart.

'Enemy target in maximum weapons range,' murmured the servitors from behind Sekor as his targeting cogitator chimed.

'Fire everything!' shouted Sekor.

'Compliance,' the lobotomised gunners replied with corpse-like calm. The Blackstar's weapons unleashed fire at the gargant. Sekor opened fire with the drop-ship's lascannons, lending the gunship's fire to the barrage that blasted from the remaining Imperial craft as they descended upon the junk-titan.

From across the scrap-iron hide of the gargant, the turrets, cannons and weapons blisters hastily soldered to its hull ground and twisted as they tracked the inbound threat. It appeared as though the gargant had deployed a smokescreen, wreathing the plodding ork machine in fyceline as a fusillade of rockets and flak slashed towards the Blackstars.

'Get that shell up!' Tank commander Joyrll's clipped orders resounded off the claustrophobic interior of the Leman Russ battle tank. He, along with the rest of his regiment, had followed out in the wake of the Space Marine air assault, an armoured spear of one hundred battle tanks of all shapes and sizes plunging into the sea of inhumanity assailing Praesidium. Their crews sang vengeful dirges as they charged, hatred and vindication propelling them into the enemy that had taken everything from them.

It had taken only minutes for their advance to stall. Tracks grew gummed with pulverized flesh in such revolting quantities that vehicles became trapped in the organic quagmire. Ammunition was depleted at staggering rates as commanders fired into an endless ocean of predatory xenos. Tanks were being split off from one another, flooded by howling orks and shrieking tyranids. When the vox had become flooded with the overlapping screams of crews as their hulls, and their bodies, were peeled apart, Joyrll had killed the link.

Smoke filled Joyrll's wounded tank in a suffocating pall, flaring with sparks from where an ork rocket had blown through the left track and killed most of the crew. The only ones remaining alive within the tank were Joyrll and his gunner, the two feverishly working to reload the main cannon of the Leman Russ. Joyrll had not bothered to aim the cannon. He could not have missed if he wanted to, such was the insanity boiling around him. He had to blast a path clear to the nearest allied tank, and see if he could rally to regroup with the others.

He would not die here. He couldn't.

'Throne damn you,' Joyrll hissed, squeezing himself from the firing station down to where the gunner was hauling a shell into the cannon's breech. 'What is wrong with–'

Joyrll stopped cold, mute as he saw his comrade's slumped, twitching form.

A monstrous insectoid face looked up at him from the gunner's ruptured body with milky, lifeless eyes. It grinned with needle-sharp fangs, caked with scarlet as strings of gore slithered down their length.

Joyrll did not even have time to scream as the thing leapt upon him, and sank its fangs deep.

Artemis heard the emergency klaxons blare inside the crew bay of the drop-ship. The chaos of exploding flak increased and Artemis mag-locked his boots to the deck as the craft shuddered violently.

'Hold onto something!' Sekor shouted over the vox. *'We have multiple hostile missile locks!'*

Imtehan calmly rose to stand in the central aisle of the crew bay. He sank to one knee, placing Rogerio's power axe on the deck beside him.

'Take a step from me, brothers,' said the Flesh Tearer as he bowed his head. Nulsis and Artemis backed away from Imtehan, and the psyker began to scream.

He screamed so loudly that Artemis could barely hear the thunder of the guns outside the Blackstar. They sounded somehow baffled, muted. The Flesh Tearer pushed dents into the deck plating as his armoured fingers dug into it. Hoarfrost shimmered and cracked from his power armour as his bloodcurdling cry grew louder.

'What is going on back there?' exclaimed Sekor.

Artemis rushed to look out through a porthole in the Blackstar's fuselage. The drop-ship was surrounded by a sphere of flame. Hundreds of impacts were detonating against the erratic barrier that enveloped the Deathwatch craft.

'A kine shield,' whispered Artemis. 'Sekor, hurry! It is Imtehan. It is killing him! Get us to the target *now*.'

The Blackstar burst through the wall of ork flak, coming close to passing over the gargant.

'*This is as far as I can go*,' shouted Sekor. '*You need to jump now!*'

Nulsis stepped to the drop-ship's rear assault ramp as it lowered. Smoke and wind clawed at his armour in a howling gale as he looked back at Artemis.

The watch captain knelt before Imtehan, drawing level with the Flesh Tearer. 'Stand, brother!'

Imtehan's scream faltered, straining further as he took hold of his power axe with trembling hands. Artemis could not conceive of the agony coursing through the Librarian as he drew power from the warp through the tyranid shadow. Imtehan looked as though he were drowning, his entire being thrown into the act as his body threatened to collapse beneath the monumental strain. He rose, taking one pained, stomping step after another towards the gaping opening, and leapt. Nulsis followed after him, and Artemis stopped for a moment to look down over the churning maelstrom before dropping down into it.

TWENTY-SEVEN

One by one, he felt them die. It was a grievous thing, to watch a comrade fall in battle. To see the men and women you had bonded with through hellish trials go limp within the storm of bullets and blades. But to experience it as a physical sensation, to *feel* the link they shared with you sever without warning – that was something else entirely.

Balas, Patriarch of the Knights of House Merovic, felt every one of his brothers and sisters die. He felt their armour shatter against the howling gale of exploding bombs and boiling acid. He felt the hot wind rake their skin as they were dragged down. He felt the tear and bite of hundreds of claws and crude blades as their sacred forms were carved open. He felt the cold void that took their place, when their hearts beat their last.

Balas was linked to his Knight through the archeotech of its throne mechanicum, as were the others of his lineage. Damage to their hallowed armour manifested through neural interface ports and spinal sockets as physical pain within the bodies of the pilots. They felt every blow, every glancing strike, every deep cut. When another Knight fell in battle, it rippled across the others of its order, wracking them with spasms of agonizing sorrow. Balas felt this over and over, as the xenos stole their light from the world.

A spasm of white-hot pain assailed Balas as he thrashed upon his cockpit throne. He was bleeding so profusely from a dozen points he could taste the metal in the air. His battle cannon was starved of ammunition, little more than a cudgel now as he smashed it into the hordes of gnashing aliens. His chainsword was so caked in inhuman gore that its teeth could no longer turn.

His family was gone. His noble house was reduced to ash and ghosts, their windswept voices joining the choir of those ancestral warriors who had taken Balas' Knight into battle before him. Spitting the chips of a broken tooth from his mouth, Balas waded half-blind into the boiling mass of his foes. Xenos died, obliterated by his weapons and crushed beneath his clawed feet. Balas wheezed, blood spilling down his chin as he raged, determined to drag as many as he could down into the darkness with him. He could not see the Space Marines for whom his house had died, but it was not of consequence any longer.

Balas would be reunited with his kin, and he would not have long to wait.

They fell.

Like teardrops of oil, the Space Marines of Kill Team Artemis plummeted towards the Overfiend who waited atop the gargant.

The battlefield below filled Artemis' vision. Legions of orks, all the more loathsome for their repulsive mimicry of mankind's weapons and technology, continued their slaughter against the tyranids, who were so hideously inhuman that they showed no parallel to humanity at all.

In their midst, standing alone, was the Patriarch of House Merovic. His mount crippled and aflame, the Knight fought surrounded by the dead of his bloodline, an entire lineage lost and never to return. He swung his chainsword, now stripped of its teeth, and wielded his battle cannon like a blunted maul, before collapsing under a swarm of tyranids.

The surviving units of the Imperial armoured assault had ceased their forwards advance as their casualties mounted. Their commander attempted a breakout to stage a fighting withdrawal back to the walls of Praesidium Primus, but his tanks were quickly encircled and slaughtered to the last man by the rampaging xenos.

Artemis twisted in freefall, watching as Sekor took the Blackstar upwards in a steep climb, seeking to clear the range of the xenos guns. The wavering kine shield Imtehan had projected to protect the Blackstar collapsed with a peal of thunder. Artemis watched Sekor weave the drop-ship skilfully through the flak. The agile Blackstar rolled and dipped through the metal storm exploding around it as Sekor guided it with confident grace.

A chime from his visor display drew Artemis' gaze to his altimeter. He did not see the rocket that corkscrewed into the Blackstar's hull, just a flash of flame and smoke in his peripheral vision. His head snapped up, locking to the Blackstar as it lost altitude, trailing fire as it spun.

'Sekor,' voxed Artemis. He heard only crazed static in reply as the drop-ship hurtled groundwards. Sekor's biometric feedback flickered inconsistently on his retinal display, before the Blackstar plunged into the smoke and vanished entirely from his view.

The lumbering armoured cliffside of the gargant rushed up beneath Artemis. A pair of vast doors peeled back across the towering scrap-titan's sloping torso, revealing an immense cannon barrel within.

It made a sound like a god falling as it fired. The blast carved a shallow canyon across the surface of Praesidium as the fortress-world's foremost citadel ceased to exist. Artemis was flung spinning from the force of the weapon firing. He twisted end over end, seeing alternating blurred images of the monstrous gargant and the flaming wreckage of Praesidium Primus.

The altimeter in Artemis' retinal display pulsed urgently. He was falling too fast, and the blast was throwing him too far away from the gargant. Artemis triggered a blast from his jump pack to arrest his spin, bracing to stabilize his freefall as the inertia sought to crush him against his own armour. He fired another sustained burst, slowing his descent and throwing himself back towards the Overfiend's mount.

The other two surviving Blackstars dropped their payloads of Deathwatch Space Marines over the ork junk walker. Artemis watched as one was pulped by flak, and another plucked from the air by a screeching tyranid flier, but the rest managed to land intact upon the gargant's head and shoulders.

Fuel alerts jousted with the altimeter for Artemis' attention as he fired the thruster pack again. He fell over the churning sea of brutality thrashing around the feet of the greenskin scrap god, as the shadow of another behemoth darkened the surface of Praesidium.

It struck with calamity. Swathed in dirty smoke and slick with the gore of the legions it had crushed with its arrival, the charred ovoid capsule that had sheltered it through the cold of the void and the fire of the planet's atmosphere shivered as it sloughed away, exposing a creature seemingly dragged from the depths of humanity's ancestral nightmares.

Spindly, arachnoid legs hauled a hunched insect-like body free of its birthing pod to tower above the battlefield. Enormous bio-cannons and hooked talons tore free of the glistening membranes of the vast creature's womb. Rearing to its full height, it nearly eclipsed the Overfiend's massive walker.

With a chilling screech, the tyranid bio-titan turned to the ork scrap machine. Instinctually, a baying pack of massive carnifex bio-forms swept about in its shadow as it made its way towards the Overfiend's gargant with its knifing gait.

Artemis tumbled in the wake of the bio-titan's crash. He fired the engines of his jump pack, fighting to land atop the gargant as it turned to face the titanic monstrosity bearing down on it. He reached out with grasping fingertips, scraping against its scrap-iron hide. Purchase eluded him. Sparks sprayed from either side as Artemis clawed against the gargant's hull, seeking to arrest his fall down its sloping, distended gut.

Drawing Exterminatus in a reversed grip, Artemis drove the blade down into the scrap-titan's rusted flesh, carving a channel with his momentum until he came to a grinding halt.

A small aperture in the gargant's plough-faced jaw squealed as it was flung open above Artemis. A barking ork emerged, firing wildly at the Space Marine with a smoking junkyard firearm. The Deathwatch warrior dangled one-handed by the grip of Exterminatus as he drew his bolt pistol. The weapon bucked in his fist as it fired. The precisely aimed bolt lanced through one of the greenskin's sunken eyes in a puff of dark blood. The round spun, liquefying the meat within the alien's skull for an instant before detonating. Dirty light kicked out from the entry wound. The ork gave a shallow jump as its head disappeared, all that remained of it reduced to ragged ribbons of stinking meat falling over its shoulders. Artemis leapt upwards, clawing his way to the aperture, and hauled himself inside.

The sweltering interior of the gargant's head bore the same repulsive, erratic madness as all ork technology, with one glaring exception. Everywhere Artemis looked, daubed crudely in ink across the walls or fashioned haphazardly into busts or statues, was the face of the Overfiend. Its dominating armoured underbite, the tusks and fangs stained black with oil and coal dust, its eyes burning with blazing torches or unstable sodium lamps.

Artemis took in all of this in a heartbeat, and fought down the bile rising in his throat. Exterminatus slashed left and right, butchering the greenskins and smaller gretchin wretches within the chamber as Artemis' bolt pistol roared its anger to join the slaughter. This scrap-titan was no effigy to some pagan ork deity. It was the Overfiend itself. The greenskin tyrant had stridden into battle atop a hulking monument to its own ego.

The interior of the gargant rocked as the myriad weapons of the scrap-titan fired at the charging tyranid behemoth. A heavy slapping noise struck the head of the ork walker, and Artemis looked up as pinpricks of light shone down into the chamber amid the sound of hissing metal.

Bio-acid boiled the armour plating of a section of the gargant's head. A whole section of its structure collapsed, throwing packs of orks from its head screaming to the circling carnifexes below. Artemis glimpsed a darkly armoured form among those who fell.

Wan, hellish light from Praesidium flooded in. Artemis sprinted towards the opening. He leapt, burning the rapidly dwindling promethium remaining in his jump pack to lift him to the lip of the gouge in the scrap-titan's crown. He clawed hold of it, the dense armour made pliable like heated wax by the bio-acid. Artemis threw an elbow over the edge, and hauled himself up.

He looked at his target. The xenos chieftain who had brought this system to ruin. The Overfiend brawled in a frenzied melee of Deathwatch Space Marines and his hulking huscarls. Artemis stood, activating Exterminatus in a rush of lightning as he glared at the impossibly large beast, the very image of brutal xenos monstrosity.

And the Overfiend looked back.

TWENTY-EIGHT

The gargant was in flames. Concentrated blasts of bio-acid and living artillery from the tyranid bio-titan had torn sections of the lumbering ork walker into ruin as the two towering combatants fought above the churning chaos of Praesidium's surface. The Overfiend, arch-xenos warlord of the ork empire of Octarius, roared with savage glee as it smashed through the ranks of the Deathwatch Space Marines that encircled it, bathing it in flame and bolter fire. Then a thundering crash of displaced air tore over the melee with a flash of blinding light.

The greenskin's roars soured with rage as a salvo of assault cannon fire stitched up the tank armour bolted to its chest. The boxy shape of Rogerio's Dreadnought walker stomped forwards through the mist of its teleportation, smashing into the Overfiend with a blistering punch from its cracking power fist.

'Die, vile fiend!' bellowed the machine voice of the fallen Crimson Fist. 'Choke on your foul blood and know that you face the vengeance of the Emperor of Man!'

The greenskin colossus grappled with Rogerio, seizing hold of the Dreadnought's hissing power fist in its claw. The Overfiend snarled at the venerable Space Marine as it tightened its adamantium grip. The crimson-lacquered weapon began to buckle under the crushing weight. The Overfiend smashed its other arm into Rogerio's sarcophagus, punching into its armoured hull. It struck again, and again, the power of its clubbing fist building with momentum.

The gargant rocked as a thunderous explosion erupted at its base. One of the scrap-titan's legs collapsed, and the warriors fighting over its hull were flung in every direction as it began to list to one side. The Overfiend broke away from Rogerio, tearing the Dreadnought's power fist from its housing as it fought to balance itself.

With a roaring Cretacian battle cry, Imtehan leapt up behind the Overfiend, Rogerio's power axe gripped in both hands. He drove the energized blade down into the Overfiend's shoulder, in the gap between the creature's massive armour plates. The Flesh Tearer let his weight drag him down to the ground, tearing into the xenos tyrant.

The Overfiend whirled around, lashing out with a clawed fist that Imtehan was barely able to roll beneath. Nulsis opened fire on the ork as it overbalanced, blasting it with searing strikes from his hissing combi-melta between bursts of kraken penetrator bolter rounds. The ork's armour blazed white-hot, and knots of thick blood, dark as pitch, popped through the air as the armour-piercing rounds carved through the plate.

With a bellow of tectonic fury, the Overfiend leapt forwards. Moving faster than anything its size had any right to, it smashed into Nulsis with a clubbing strike. The Apothecary twisted, spinning away to crash in a heap on the gargant's canted scrap plating. It killed another Space Marine, crushing the warrior in its clawed fists and flinging limbs in all directions as it tore the body apart.

The next moments passed as if the scene were trapped in slowly cooling glass. Artemis charged up the slope of the teetering gargant, legs pumping like pistons as he neared the howling Overfiend. A roar breached his bleeding lips as he launched himself in the air. A draconic final blast of promethium, every fume remaining that the feral machine-spirit releasing it could supply, flared from Artemis' jump pack as he rocketed into the beast's chest.

The ceramite of Artemis' pauldron shattered with the impact. The Overfiend grunted in rage, looking down as the Space Marine punched a brass cylinder into a gouge in its armour. The device quivered as Artemis' momentum pushed the two off the ground. The Space Marine bounced from the Overfiend, rolling off to the side and crashing heavily into the rusted gargant's crown. Both began to slide down the tilt of the leaning scrap-titan, towards the precipice and the swarms of howling tyranids waiting below.

The Overfiend punched out a massive claw, digging a gouge into the metal and slowing its fall. With unfathomable rage burning from its beady, scarlet eyes, it began to haul itself up, claw over claw, frothing to butcher the one who had struck it.

Artemis punched down with Exterminatus to anchor himself as he blasted at the oncoming Overfiend with his bolt pistol. The mass-reactive rounds plinked harmlessly from its brutish armour.

Snarling, Artemis fired a shot through the Overfiend's guard, striking one of the beast's eyes in a welter of gore and pus. The Overfiend howled, lifting its claw to clutch at its ragged eye socket, as the stasis bomb detonated.

A blinding flash enveloped the Overfiend. Shivering worms of silver mist wrapped about its limbs and trunk. The beast froze, trapped within the stasis field, unable to do anything to prevent itself from sliding towards the edge of the gargant's head.

The Overfiend of Octarius loosed a stifled, strangled cry, its force titanic enough to breach the stasis field entrapping it, as it hurtled off the edge of the scrap-titan.

The armour plating Artemis had anchored Exterminatus into sheared away. He skittered down the gargant's crown in a shower of sparks, clawing for purchase as the greenskin war machine shuddered from its duel with the bio-titan. Artemis seized a handhold as his legs flew over the edge. He reached out, catching Exterminatus as it tumbled towards the precipice. He slowly released a breath.

Artemis barked in sudden pain as the gargant's hull rippled. He looked down, reason warring with the impossibility of what his eyes were showing him. The Overfiend was alive, hanging from the gargant. It was fighting the suffocating shroud of the stasis bomb, and it was winning. The Overfiend reached up, clawing at Artemis. If it were to fall to its end here, it would take the Space Marine with it. Artemis' armour cracked and shattered like eggshell as the greenskin king tore at it. He felt his leg dislocate as it was wrenched from the hip socket by the ork's brutal strength. Artemis' hold weakened, and he began to lose his grip as the metal bucked and shuddered with impacts.

'*Nay*,' the voice rolled like thunder as a shadow fell over Artemis. He looked up, seeing the gouged, sparking shell of Rogerio's sarcophagus as the wounded Dreadnought levelled his assault cannon over the top of Artemis at the dangling Overfiend.

'There is no escape for you, mongrel beast. Now die, drown in the madness you have wrought!'

The assault cannon was deafening as it fired just over Artemis' head. Spent casings rained down onto him, plinking from his power armour. The Overfiend roared as its arm was ripped apart at the elbow, sending the ork tyrant hurtling into the thrashing masses below. It struggled to free itself, but was still ensnared by the stasis field when it struck the throng of screeching tyranids below. Even its preternatural strength and fury could not aid it, and the Overfiend of Octarius could do little but watch as the mindless swarms of hive fleet Leviathan tore it limb from limb.

The pack of carnifexes in the bio-titan's shadow roared above the slaughter of the greenskin warlord. Artemis watched the frenzy below as the Overfiend was quickly reduced to ribbons of torn meat.

It was dead. The Overfiend was dead.

Artemis felt strong hands grab hold of him and haul him back over the edge. It was Imtehan and Nulsis, their armour split and pitted, but both of them alive. The Novamarine Apothecary supported Artemis with his weight.

'That leg is attached by tendons alone,' he growled, throwing Artemis' arm across his shoulders. The remaining kill teams rallied, forming a condensing ring of black ceramite around the dazed greenskins who still lived atop the gargant.

The scene around Artemis collapsed further into total anarchy. Leaderless, the orks lost any remainder of their barbarian cohesion, and fell in a gory slaughter as the tyranids of hive fleet Leviathan pressed their advantage.

'It is done!' bellowed Rogerio in triumph, as a handful of the Deathwatch Space Marines produced blocky, flickering devices from their armour. Artemis recognised them immediately as teleportation beacons.

'To me, my brothers, as we quit the field in victory!'

The Deathwatch gathered around Rogerio as frost began to coat his ruined shell.

'It is done!'

Artemis felt rippling waves of sickness assail him, the wrenching dislocation and instantaneous sensation of freefall that came with teleportation, before a blinding flash stole the hellish visage of Praesidium from his sight.

TWENTY-NINE

Artemis watched as, true to his word, Watch Master Asharbanapal did to Praesidium what he had done to every other world of the Kurbynola System.

With the ork fleet scattered in the wake of the Overfiend's death, and the majority of the tendril of the Leviathan hive fleet in pursuit of their routed prey, the remaining Deathwatch fleet settled into high orbit above the constellation of ruins that encircled Praesidium.

Artemis had hauled himself out of the packed apothecarion of the *Victorious Son*, limping to an observation screen to watch as the throat of the fortress-world was cut. He could make out the broken silhouette of the *Claw of Damyrov* as the dead battleship sank into the atmosphere of Praesidium, though there was not a soul aboard alive to feel its fire.

The deck beneath Artemis' boots rumbled as the first salvo of cyclonic torpedoes was unleashed. The warheads sailed unerringly for the surface, where they would spark a globe-spanning firestorm, eradicating all life on the planet. In the end, Praesidium would be left a charred, lifeless husk of wind and broken glass, just like the others. It would join its celestial kindred, a silent procession of corpse worlds drifting coldly around the light of an uncaring star.

Upon their rapid return to the *Victorious Son*, Rogerio had been sedated and transported back to the ship's vaults, where he would be attended to by the battle-barge's Mechanicus adepts and Techmarines. Nulsis had carried Artemis to the apothecarion. Once he was convinced the watch captain was stable, he began seeing to the dozens of other grievously wounded Space Marines occupying slabs and lying upon the sterile tiled floor of the chamber.

Artemis did not know of Sekor's fate. There had been scattered retrievals of pockets of Space Marines across the surface before the order for exterminatus had been given. Imtehan had departed from Artemis' side on the watch captain's orders, to scour the ranks of Deathwatch warriors onboard in search of their lost brother.

The first of the warheads exploded, a pinprick of cruel light blooming into an expanding wall of flame that swallowed continents. Its fellows struck soon after, their growing firestorms merging to envelop all of Praesidium in its holocaust.

Victory had never been so momentous, yet its taste so ashen upon Artemis' tongue. The most powerful ork warlord short of the Archfiend Ghazghkull was dead, legions of his vile followers obliterated. The survivors had been thrown into disarray and infighting as a new Overfiend fought to be crowned. Artemis had no way of knowing, but if he had possessed a weakness for games of chance, he would have wagered that the foul brute Gorsnik Magash was likely to inherit that mantle.

The tendril of hive fleet Leviathan was blunted by the continuous war with the orks. The deprivation of bio-mass as a result of the purging of the Kurbynola System had cheated the monstrous xenos of the fuel necessary to continue their invasion of the segmentum. Even now, battle groups and strike forces from the watch fortress Furor Shield were assembling to prevent the weakened tyranids from spilling into the surrounding systems. They were not beaten, but the Imperium had won precious time with the blood of the billions it had lost. When the Leviathan reared its head once again, the Bladefall would be waiting.

Artemis knew in his heart that Asharbanapal had been right. In the face of this threat, any sacrifice made in defence of the Imperium had been necessary. To have done otherwise would have been to betray everything they had sworn to protect. To that extent then, Artemis thought, was Kryptman right as well? Had this been the lord inquisitor's plan all along? And was he even alive to see its fruition?

Artemis did not know. As he watched the world of Praesidium reduced to cinders, he knew only one thing with certainty.

Another war would come. Whether with the inevitable resurgence of Leviathan, another greenskin invasion at the behest of an upstart warboss, the shadowy plots of the eldar, or the unknowable plagues of countless other xenos races that might prey upon the Imperium of Mankind, Artemis knew, in the quiet of that moment, what he had always known.

Another war was coming.

EPILOGUE

He fought alone in the darkness.

Flashes of brilliance blinked out in migraine smears, the only brief light to pierce the gloom given off by a sparking power field as the warrior's blade severed limbs and split bodies. The last of the attackers came on in silence, oblivious to their fallen comrades as they menaced with chainblades and cudgels.

The warrior killed the first in a heartbeat, cleanly severing its head and sending it spinning from its shoulders. The second he killed on his return swing, bifurcating it from collar to groin in a spray of oily fluid.

The final attacker seized the warrior about the waist in a wrestler's grip. The warrior twisted, throwing his opponent down heavily onto its back. The warrior smashed his fist into its face, his sword forgotten by his side as he punched again and again.

His foe's skull protested the first blows. By the fifth, its resilience had gone. By the eighth, it shattered into ruin. One more strike from the warrior reduced the head to a limp bag of crushed gore and protruding skull fragments as his enemy went still.

The warrior panted atop the corpse for a moment, steam curling off his exposed skin in the frigid air. The only sound he could hear was his breathing, and the subtle drips as blood oozed from his knuckles onto the stone floor.

Light flooded the chamber. The warrior instinctively shut his eyes, cursing himself for not detecting the newcomer's arrival.

'Another taste of home?' called out a voice.

Artemis opened his eyes as he stood, looking over as Sekor entered the duelling cages.

'You should let me have a look at that,' said Sekor, pointing to the watch captain's arm.

Artemis looked down upon the whirring bionics of his arm. His eyes ran over the gouges, scars and acid burns covering the iron of the augmetic limb. He saw dark metal fingers, the damaged servos clicking and locking as he drew them together into a numb fist.

'Later.'

Sekor nodded. 'We returned Rogerio to hibernation this morning. He will slumber until we reach Talasa Prime, where the watch master will determine what to do.'

'I spoke with him before, he said as much,' replied Artemis. 'He has borne the scars of this as well as any of us.'

'Perhaps better than most,' said Sekor.

Artemis met Sekor's gaze with eyes of electric sapphire.

'Is this what he wanted?' asked Sekor, inspecting the racks of weapons on the walls but refraining from touching any of them. 'Kryptman? Do you believe this is the end result he sought all those years ago?' The Space Marine spat onto the bare floor of the training circle, watching the saliva eat into the rockcrete.

'Perhaps,' said Artemis, rubbing his closed eyes with his fingertips. 'Though such rumination is pointless for those of our province. The foes have been beaten back from the gates once more, for a time. The Imperium survives for another day. We must return to Talasa Prime, rearm and seek out the *Fatal Redress*, if any of its crew still draw breath.'

Artemis could hear the smile in Sekor's voice. 'We have created a wasteland, and called it peace.'

Artemis' eyes snapped open at the words. Only darkness confronted him. He stared down at the ruin of the combat servitor he crouched over in the inky black as he found himself alone in the duelling cages. The steam of his breath slowly feathered out before him in the cold. He looked over his shoulder, towards the entrance to the cages. The bulkhead was open, spilling cold light across the polished stone floor, but no one stood within its frame.

'No, brother.' The watch captain slowly rose, taking up Exterminatus as he walked from the chamber.

'Never peace.'

RACKINRUIN
BRADEN CAMPBELL

Jerrell had confronted the xenos threat for more than half his life. For the sake and safety of the Imperium, he had staged pre-emptive strikes on eldar pirates, set drahken hatchlings aflame, and ripped the cybernetic limbs from dozens of jorgall. He had faced off against entire platoons of tallerian dog-soldiers. He had been shot with vespid neutron blasters, burned by hrud fusils, and nearly crippled by a chuffian armed with one of their trademark power mauls. The missions had been tough, no doubt, but that was why they were assigned to him. Only he and the specially trained Space Marines who served under him could be trusted to get the job done, and each and every time he had succeeded. His current prey, however, was proving difficult.

Jerrell looked up from the display table upon which he was leaning and took stock of his team. Carbrey, the Sentinel, was double-checking his storm bolter and muttering a litany of hate. Launo, the last remaining Ultramarine, stood with his arms crossed, awaiting his commander's decision. Archelaos, the Dark Angel, stooped his bulk across the opposite side of the display and traced its surface with a beefy, ceramite-plated finger. His face was hidden by a cavernous hood.

The Inquisition unimaginatively called their target 'the jump ship'. Carbrey, on the other hand, had christened it *Rackinruin*, after a mythological void whale said to prowl the segmentum his Chapter called home. Unlike other greenskin spacecraft, *Rackinruin* was able to attain speeds so fantastic as to propel it through the warp. It was covered with ablative amour and shrugged off damage that would have gutted other ships. It had cut a swath across half the galaxy, performing devastating hit-and-run attacks on one forge-world after another. *Rackinruin* had evaded every ambush and defeated every fleet the Imperial Navy had sent up against it.

Jerrell believed all that was about to change. 'Launo,' he barked. 'Prep the boarding torpedo.'

Carbrey looked up from his prayers. 'We'll nay be teleportin' then?' he enquired in his unique dialect.

'Too many variables,' Jerrell replied. *Rackinruin* had evaded the Space Marines thus far because it could accelerate faster than their small cruiser. However, in their last encounter, as the orks had barrelled towards the forge-world of Paskal, they had passed directly through the planet's glittering rings of ice and metallic rock. For precious moments, *Rackinruin*'s speed had dropped dramatically. Following a furious exchange of fire between the two vessels, the orks had sped off again. Behind them they had left a blizzard in space, kilometres long. Whatever kind of engine was powering *Rackinruin* generated a magnetic field so intense that it had caused tons of rock to stick to its sides. It might also scatter their atoms across the void if they tried to materialise near it.

They now hurtled towards the forge-world of Chestirad, famous not only for the weaponry it produced but for its natural satellite. Chestirad's moon was titanic and contained vast deposits of ferrite-236. Jerrell was certain that it would interfere with *Rackinruin*'s power source. Once again it would slow, and as it did, they would attack.

'Coordinates, watch-captain?' Launo asked.

'We'll hit them just below the bridge.'

Archelaos righted himself. 'No. Wait,' he snapped.

Jerrell ground his teeth. Of course, the Dark Angel had some objection. He always did. 'What is it?' he growled.

'I disagree with your choice,' Archelaos said.

Carbrey shook his head, and returned his attention to his weapon. Launo shifted his weight in strained patience.

After a moment, Archelaos added, 'Respectfully.'

Jerrell's eyes narrowed. 'I am tired of having conversations like these,' he said in a low voice. 'I am the watch-captain, and I give the orders.'

Archelaos pulled back his hood. 'I am your Second, and your technical advisor. It's my duty to present you with the best course of action.'

'And what would you have us do?'

Archelaos tapped the display for emphasis. The blue and white schematic they had been studying was suddenly replaced by a pict-capture of *Rackinruin*. 'We board here. Aft quarter. It's the shortest route to their primary engineering core.'

Jerrell shook his head. 'The hull plating is too thick on the rear sections. A torpedo will never be able to punch through.'

'We go in through the engine bell.'

Jerrell was incredulous. 'Are you mad? They are moving at full thrust. Their plasma trail would disintegrate us before we even got near them.'

'I've given this no little amount of thought,' Archelaos said. 'I believe the heat shielding on the torpedo will hold.'

'If you're going to suggest a course of action then make it a plausible one. We'll board them just below the bridge, fight our way in, and slay their leader.'

'We should go in through the engines,' Archelaos repeated. 'We can exit directly into the master control room and eliminate their technical experts.'

'In half an hour that ship will have passed Chestirad's moon and will accelerate beyond our range. We have only this one chance to stop it.'

'Yes,' Archelaos nodded, 'and my plan will do that. Orks can't maintain their ships or weaponry without their engineers.'

'Orks fight less effectively without a commander.'

'Our mission is to is discern why *Rackinruin* can travel the way it does, and then stop it from ransacking more Imperial worlds. We don't need to seek out the ork leaders in order to do that.'

A tense silence suddenly filled the briefing chamber. Jerrell's voice was little more than a growl. 'That almost sounds like cowardice.'

Archelaos's eyes flared. 'What it sounds like,' he said slowly, 'is the recommendation for a surgical strike as opposed to a sledgehammer blow. It is tactically sound, given the time constraints and our low squad strength.'

'Is it what the Dark Angels would do?' he asked.

'Without hesitation.'

'But you are not in your home Chapter any more,' Jerrell said pointedly.

The members of the Deathwatch were drawn from a wide variety of Chapters, and during his term of enrolment, each member was expected to don the sombre battle colours of the Ordo Xenos and work wholeheartedly with those he might not otherwise get along with. It was only natural for everyone to keep some small reminder of home, be it a trinket or pre-battle prayer, a salute or heraldic symbol. Jerrell himself wore a red clenched fist on the left pauldron of his otherwise matt-black Terminator armour that he would never paint over or disgrace.

Archelaos, on the other hand, had dyed his suit as black as space, but it seemed his immersion stopped there. His shoulder plate bore the white winged sword of Caliban. A cluster of pale feathers hung from the hilt of his power sword. He continued to wear the long beige robe and deep hood that were the hallmarks of his Dark Angels brethren.

'The previous order stands.' Jerrell picked up his helmet and stomped heavily out of the room. Launo and Carbrey followed without a word. Behind them, there was a cracking sound as Archelaos slammed his fist down on the display in frustration.

* * *

The boarding torpedo was a windowless, narrow tube. The forefront was occupied by a pilot servitor: the emaciated upper half of a heretic whose punishment was to serve the Ordo Xenos even unto a fiery, crushing death. Behind that five alcoves were recessed into each wall. Jerrell, Launo, and Carbrey each backed into one. Restraints automatically sprung around their feet, waist and shoulders.

Archelaos entered and closed the hatch. He performed a final check on the pilot, and then locked himself into place beside Jerrell.

'Synchronise countdown on your displays,' Jerrell ordered, and in each of their helmets a timer appeared, frozen at ten seconds.

'Ready,' Launo grunted.

'Aye,' Carbrey replied.

'Synched,' Archelaos muttered.

A massive bulkhead slammed down, separating the Space Marines from the pilot. Then, the torpedo rocketed forward with an intensity that would have liquefied the bones of a normal man. The numbers in their displays began to race towards zero, counting off the time until they smashed through *Rackinruin*'s armoured skin.

The actual impact came and went in a heartbeat. From where they were ensconced, Jerrell and the others felt only a single, wrenching lurch. There was a dull thump from behind the blast door, and a staccato clacking as their restraints let go.

'Five seconds!' Jerrell announced. He hoisted his shield in front of him with his left arm, and drew his sword from its scabbard. Both were highly polished and crackled with destructive power.

Launo slid into place behind Jerrell and to his left. The assault cannon mounted to his right arm hummed softly. Carbrey took up position opposite him. Archelaos filled in behind. His storm bolter was decorated in an outlandish pattern of red and green, typical of the Dark Angels.

No one spoke. They simply waited until the bulkhead detonated outwards in a hail of thick shrapnel, and then, as one, they rushed forward.

They emerged into a humid scrapyard that apparently served as a spare parts storage facility. Tall piles of rusted metal and broken machinery, salvaged from countless different planets, lay everywhere. Each pile was being tended to by a multitude of tiny, pale green creatures. They had spindly limbs and grossly oversized noses, and in the dim light looked almost like ork children. Several dozen of them had been turned into gristly chunks by the torpedo's explosive arrival. The rest stood frozen in shock, mouths agape and watery eyes wide. They were alien rabbits caught in the glare of the Emperor's purifying light.

Jerrell pointed towards them wordlessly. The others opened fire, filling the chamber with thunder. Launo's assault cannon, in particular, produced a deafening roar as it swept back and forth. The pathetic little creatures flew apart in droves, or tried to bury themselves under the scrap. A few who were either too brave or too stupid to accept the inevitable tried to fire back with clunky revolvers. The slugs impacted futilely against the Space Marines' Terminator armour. It was over in moments.

Archelaos kicked away a pile of the dead creatures, reached into the folds of his cassock, and produced a bulky scanner. He turned in a slow circle before pointing down a dark corridor to their left.

'This way,' he said.

Jerrell took the lead with Launo and Carbrey by his sides. The walls of the passageway were typically ork: a haphazard collection of metal plates, salvaged over the years from the wreckage of other civilisations, welded together in a slapdash fashion. Everything had the look of refuse about it, broken and corroded.

'Fifty metres,' Archelaos reported, 'then a large open area. There's a shaft or lift of some kind. Should take us straight up to the bridge.'

Behind his faceplate, Jerrell smirked in anticipation. 'That's where it will start,' he said needlessly. They had all received extensive lessons in xeno-behaviour as part of their Deathwatch indoctrination, but Jerrell knew the greenskins well. Nothing was more pleasing to a mob of orks than a close-quarters brawl in which they could dogpile their opponents. It sustained their barbaric natures, but it also required a lot of space.

The 'open area' was two storeys tall and lined with discoloured metal and sparking cables. A large set of double doors was directly opposite them. Three more corridors branched off at odd angles. There was a catwalk above them where several more of the diminutive scrap-tenders cowered. At the Space Marines' approach, they screamed and began to flee. Archelaos aimed his storm bolter at them when a piercing trumpet blast suddenly rang twice, followed by a booming, metallic voice. Its staccato words were harsh and clipped, and in a language familiar to none of them. It cut through their armour's sound filters, and left a ringing in their ears.

Launo spoke in the stillness that followed. 'What was that?'

'*Rackinruin*'s voice,' Carbrey replied.

'You jest?' Launo asked.

The auspex began to chirp before Carbrey could answer. Archelaos glanced down to see clusters of illuminated dots closing in on them from all sides. The wet air was filled with the rushing sound of innumerable, iron-clad boots.

Launo turned down the closest corridor, steadied himself, and let the assault cannon roar. Orks flew apart, dismembered. Archelaos and Carbrey each positioned themselves in a doorway, and emptied the clips of their storm bolters into the rushing throng. The muzzle flashes were blinding in the dank light. Discarded casings piled around their feet. The orks bellowed and cursed and died in droves, but still they came on, pushing closer, closer. They trampled over the bodies of the fallen. Their eyes were as red as blood. Their screaming maws were filled with razor fangs.

In the midst of it all, Jerrell stood smiling. The part of him that would always belong to the Crimson Fists could have stayed there for an eternity. If he could have fought nothing but greenskins from now until death, he would have counted his life well spent. Still, there was a Deathwatch mission to complete. They had to press on.

'Archelaos! Carbrey!' Jerrell thundered. 'Set your charges!'

He ploughed his fist through the lift door and shoved it aside. There was an open platform beyond, large enough to hold the four of them. Immense chains vanished into the black shaft above. Behind him, Launo was firing down one corridor, then another, covering Archelaos and Carbrey as they released the safety locks on the melta bomb each was carrying. They set them for the shortest possible delay, dropped them to the floor, and then backed into the lift. Finally, Launo joined them.

The orks were pressing within melee distance. Carbrey ejected his spent magazine and slapped a fresh one into place. He fired several bursts into the orks at a range so short that blood and brains splashed across his chestpiece and soaked Archelaos's robe. On one side of the platform there was a heavy switch which Jerrell slammed down. The platform made a grinding sound, and began to slowly ascend. Below, they could hear the orks screaming with ferocious bloodlust as their prey escaped.

The bombs the Space Marines had left behind were designed primarily to penetrate thick armoured targets with a concentrated burst of thermal energy. When they detonated seconds later, their power was such that they literally set fire to the air. The orks' flesh was blacked into ash even as their lungs combusted. The walls, floor and ceiling glowed red-hot and liquefied in several places. A roiling, orange fireball raced up the shaft and washed around them. They paid it no heed.

'Report,' Jerrell said.

'No apparent injuries, watch-captain,' Archelaos replied.

'Materiel?'

'Two melta bombs left,' Carbrey answered. 'I'd say fifty per cent ammunition remaining.'

Jerrell turned to Launo. 'Special weapons?'

Wisps of smoke curled from the end of the cannon. 'I used two-thirds of my munitions, but the mechanics are still sound.'

Jerrell nodded, satisfied. 'Then ready yourselves.'

The lift trundled to a stop at *Rackinruin*'s laughably primitive bridge. It was square and cluttered with a mismatched array of cogs, levers, oversized buttons and cranks. There were no view-screens or cogitators, only pipes spouting steam and rusty boxes filled with blinking lights. A massive window dominated one entire wall. A series of piloting chairs were set before it, as was a raised platform featuring a steering wheel of some kind. Scores of the little green creatures milled about, carrying wrenches and hammers and tending to the machinery.

Towering over them were eight hulking orks. Their skin was a deep green hue and their faces meaty. They sported exotic melee weapons and thick sheets of metal plating on their shoulders and chests. Pistons and gears were embedded throughout their bodies at seemingly random points: the greenskin version of bionic augmentation.

Things happened very quickly then. Reacting instinctually, the burly orks moved to close the distance between themselves and the Space Marines. They fired their oversized pistols as they went. Jerrell exited the lift first holding his shield before him. Huge, heavy bullets slammed into it and fragmented. A lucky shot shattered part of his helmet and he noted with cold detachment that he was now blind in his left eye. It mattered little. The other three Space Marines fanned out and opened fire around him. The eight ork lieutenants screamed defiantly and surged forward. The little gretchin, buoyed by the presence of their massive overseers, also gave cackling battle-cries and ran forward. They took no notice as two of them were torn in half by bolter-fire, and crashed into the Space Marines with the force of an avalanche.

The little ones posed no threat, but Jerrell noted that the ork weapons were surrounded by crackling power fields. They would be slow to hit with them, but when they did, they would be enough to test even a Terminator's redundant layers of protection. He had to strike first. He threw his full weight against the orks, shoving two of them back a few paces, and squashing a half dozen of the little runts beneath his foot. He slashed out with his sword, lopping a limb off one and a head from another. Through a red haze, he wondered if Archelaos was doing likewise. He parried two more blows against his shield, and glanced to his left.

The Dark Angel's hood had fallen back off of his helmet. His blade was indiscernible amidst a whirlwind of parries, but even he couldn't stop them all. A rough-hewn claw, mounted to one of the ork's forearms, punched straight through his armour and embedded itself in his chest.

Carbrey and Launo had moved up to reinforce their leaders. They each bore a crushing mechanical glove on their left hands.

The servos in their armour groaned as they wound back and drove them into the foe. Launo punched clear through one of the orks, and sprung back into a riposte. Carbrey, however, swung his entire arm downwards like a lumberjack cleaving logs. He ripped his opponent in half from shoulder to hip, but overextended himself in doing so. A pair of greenskin claws hammered down, catching him between the shoulders. He convulsed, and dropped face first onto the blood-soaked deck plates.

Jerrell roared in anger and came at them like a thing possessed. He chopped and bludgeoned, and before Archelaos or Launo could even react the orks were dead. The remaining gretchin, bereft of their protectors, scrambled and hid, diving for cover behind machinery banks or wriggling up through ventilation shafts. Jerrell stood amidst the carnage, his chest heaving. He stuck his sword into the floor and peeled off his ruined helmet.

Launo dropped to one knee, and rolled Carbrey over. His teeth were clenched as he gave a thick, gurgling sound.

'Easy, brother,' Launo said softly. 'Easy.'

Archelaos looked down. The wound was obviously fatal, and without an Apothecary there was nothing to be done. They had taken the bridge, but at a terrible cost. Now there were only three of them. 'Captain?' he called.

Jerrell didn't respond. He was preoccupied with surveying the dead orks.

'Jerrell!' Archelaos yelled.

Jerrell's head snapped up. His augmented biology was already at work. The gush of blood that had been pouring from his shattered eye socket had reduced to a trickle.

'He isn't here,' Jerrell muttered.

Archelaos stormed over to him. 'What?'

'The ork leader. He's not among them.'

Archelaos looked about quickly. 'You're certain?'

'These bodies are all the same size,' Jerrell sighed. 'Bigger than regular orks, but not one of them larger than the rest.'

Archelaos sheathed his sword. He put his hands on his hips, shook his head, and walked away to scrutinise the crude control panels. Launo appeared beside Jerrell. He had a helmet in his free hand, and held it out.

'Carbrey?' Jerrell asked hopefully.

Launo's posture was supremely rigid. 'Fallen in the service of the Emperor,' he said proudly. 'The watch-captain has need of a new helmet. It would honour our brother if you take his.' Jerrell reached out and took it with a heavy solemnity.

Archelaos cursed and stared out the window. A mottled grey

and brown planet was looming large. 'We're well past Chestirad's moon,' he announced, 'and still under full thrust. This ship is preparing for a low orbital raid.'

'Sir, how can that be?' Launo said to Jerrell. 'We're in control now.'

Archelaos shook his head. The ork machinery made absolutely no sense to him. 'I'm not certain that we are,' he said. 'There might well be controls hidden amongst all this refuse, but it would take weeks to discern them.'

The watch-captain did not reply at first. He was still gazing down at Carbrey's helmet, cradled in his massive hands. 'I should have seen it before. A drive that lets the greenskins leap across space? What could be more valuable? What could be more rare?'

The tilt of Launo's faceplate said that he wasn't following.

'Orks are incapable of building such a thing,' Jerrell elaborated. 'They must have pillaged or stolen it from somewhere. The ork commander would want to stay near it, the better to keep an eye on his treasure.'

Jerrell turned back to Archelaos. His brow was furrowed. 'You were correct. Knocking out *Rackinruin*'s power source would have been far more efficient than trying to usurp command of it. I let my hatred of the orks cloud my tactical sense. Coming to the bridge has not only cost us precious time, but the life of a battle-brother as well.' He swallowed hard. 'I cry your pardon. Both of you.'

'You weren't wrong,' Archelaos corrected. 'We simply come from different Chapters. There were two options, and as watch-captain, you chose the one you thought best.'

Jerrell pointed to their fallen comrade. 'And Carbrey…'

'Will not have died in vain.' Archelaos finished. 'We still have time.'

They left their second-to-last melta bomb behind them, set three minutes later to turn the bridge to slag. The Space Marines would either shut down the engines, or they would ride down to Chestirad's surface atop a cataclysmic fireball. Either way, *Rackinruin*'s pillaging would come to an end this day.

Their journey towards engineering was eerily uneventful. They could hear the little green monstrosities scrabbling about behind the walls and in the shadows, but none of them dared come forth. Jerrell walked in between his remaining two men. 'A ship this size,' he said, 'should be carrying several hundred full-sized orks.'

'Then where are they?' Archelaos asked. He had his sword drawn. The auspex was secured atop his storm bolter using strips torn from his robe.

* * *

Finally, they came to a thick blast door seemingly built by giants. It towered above the Space Marines and was covered with crudely painted glyphs.

Archelaos pulled a heavy wall switch, and it rumbled aside like a rusty curtain. Beyond was a cavernous chamber. The floor was covered ankle-deep with huge bones and fanged, lantern-jawed skulls. Amidst the charnel sat a machine that was of neither greenskin nor Imperial manufacture. It was a perfect sphere, etched in intricate patterns and lit from within by a bright yellow glow. From deep within it came a thrumming sound, like a heart beating in overdrive. Arranged around it stood five enormous orks. Their bodies were covered in layer upon layer of metal armour and cybernetic attachments. Each of them had a large-calibre cannon mounted on one arm. The opposing hand had been replaced by an unwieldy claw. Rusty cables protruded from their heads and torsos. Their faces were gaunt and starved. They stared blankly at the alien sphere as if in a trance.

'Emperor protect us.' Launo's voice was uncharacteristically hoarse. 'It ate them.'

Two sharp notes cut the air, and again came the thundering, alien voice of *Rackinruin*. The orks snapped awake and turned to face the Space Marines. One of them, larger and more heavily plated than the rest, gave a bellow. Then they began trundling forward simultaneously, unleashing a torrent of oversized shells.

Jerrell lifted his shield reflexively. Even so, he felt a massive impact in his right knee. Another tore clean through his right shoulder.

Launo stood his ground, answering back with his assault cannon. When he blew the midsection out of one of the augmented orks, wires and mechanical parts spilled forth where blood and guts should have been. The monstrosity fell over dead. When the greenskins fired at him again, chunks of his Terminator armour spalled inwards, puncturing his organs. He spat blood, went to one knee and fell to the floor.

Archelaos dashed back next to Jerrell, spraying the storm bolter as he went. The rounds sparked and ricocheted off the orks' armour. He glanced at Jerrell, who nodded. They would die in moments if they did not shorten the range of this fight.

Together they rushed forward. Jerrell collided, shield first, into the biggest of the orks and brought his weapon down in a humming arc. There was a fountain of sparks and a screaming of rent metal. The powerful leg servos in Archelaos's suit launched him into the air and he came crashing down, sword first, amongst the rest. A mechanical limb went flying.

Their foes' armour made them slow but their massive claws had enough force to cleave either of the Space Marines in half. Archelaos and Jerrell ducked and parried, moving wholly on instinct. They swept at legs and lopped off heads. The biggest of the orks was the last to go down, and did so only with a combined effort. Jerrell drove his sword into the beast's chest with all his might, as Archelaos slashed it deeply through a hip joint. The deck plating shook as it collapsed.

Archelaos's breathing came in shallow, rapid gasps. His armour was filled with ragged, fist-wide bullet holes. 'We have to... stop the... ship.'

'You've been injured,' Jerrell said.

'Yes, but we've no time for that.'

Together, they turned towards the alien sphere. The orks had obviously tried, in their crude way, to integrate the device into their own mechanical systems. Thick, rusting cables formed a nest at its base, and ran off in all directions. Red paint had been splashed across every surface. Gears and corrugated metal were piled everywhere. There was a cracked display screen recessed into a square box and surrounded by levers and buttons. Archelaos kneeled down and removed his helmet. He leaned in close to examine it. His face was covered with beads of sweat. He saw Chestirad in the foreground, a massive moon in the distance, and two bright dots that obviously represented their cruiser and this abomination of a ship. Alien hieroglyphs scrolled by at a furious rate.

'I've served three enrolments in the Deathwatch,' Jerrell said, slowly reaching out to touch the silver ball. 'I've never seen the like.'

'I have,' Archelaos panted. He began pressing lightened buttons. 'This is khrave technology.'

Jerrell pulled back. 'The mind eaters?' he said, referring to them by their more common name.

'They're really more like... mind copiers,' Archelaos managed. 'They steal memories. Imprint themselves with... personalities that... aren't their own.'

'Are you certain?'

'Quite.' Archelaos smiled grimly to himself. Although he was now certain that he would die in the service of the Deathwatch, he would always be a Dark Angel. Secrets were his forte. 'The orks must have... found this. Tried to use it...'

'And it ended up using them.' Jerrell was suddenly very glad that Archelaos had been assigned to his team. 'Can you disable it?' he asked hopefully.

'Let's pray,' Archelaos muttered, 'that this is... main drive.' He indicated a particular knob and pulled.

The air was cut once again by a piercing alarm that rang on and on. The metallic, alien voice that followed was deafening in its volume.

'Forget it,' Jerrell shouted. He grabbed the final melta bomb in both hands and moved to clamp it on to the metal sphere.

'No, Jerrell!' Archelaos screamed, but it was too late. The moment the bomb made contact, the watch-captain felt a cold presence swirl around inside his skull, rifling through every thought he'd ever had.

The room shook. The alarm became a scream, and the thrumming heartbeat of the khrave machine turned into a single, gut-wrenching tone. A pulse of energy threw the Space Marines across the room to land among the bones. Jerrell felt himself turned inside out for a moment, a tell-tale sign of travel through the warp. Terrible forces pressed around him. Then, as quickly as it had begun, it was over.

Jerrell was still holding the now charred and useless melta bomb. He got up, cast it aside, and walked back to the machine. The image on the screen had changed. Chestirad and its moon were no longer hanging there, replaced instead by a distant star. Ten planets orbited around it. The fourth one was highlighted. Hundreds of bright dots, other starships, were scattered nearby. He knew this beleaguered system. It was home to one of the largest concentrations of orks in the known galaxy; the focal point in three full-scale wars between the Imperium and the greenskins.

'Armageddon, Archelaos,' he laughed. 'Of course it would take us to Armageddon. It brought me to where I'd most like to be.'

Archelaos lay in a motionless, crumpled heap. He was no longer breathing. Jerrell hauled his body into a sitting position against Launo's corpse, and placed the feather crested pommel of his sword into his hand. Then he picked up his own weapons and stood facing the entryway of the chamber.

'We'll take them together,' he said. There was a glint of madness in his eye. 'You and I, brothers at the end.'

Within moments, he knew, this ship would begin filling up with filthy, swearing, murderous orks. They would come in the hundreds, the thousands, and they would find him blocking their way. He couldn't wait to get started.

WEAPONSMITH

BEN COUNTER

Brother-Sergeant Chrysius grabbed a handful of filthy hair and rammed the peon's face into the side of the fuel tank. Bone crunched under the impact. He threw the dead man aside and backed up against the huge cylindrical tank.

His squad hurried into place alongside him. They were his battle-brothers, men he had fought alongside for decades: Vryksus, who had been bested at the Tournament of Blades seven years ago and still wore a black stripe down the centre of his faceplate as a mark of shame; Myrdos, whose study of the Imperial Fists' past heroes made him the tactical brain of the squad; Helian, the monster and Gruz, who treated combat as an art. Assault Squad Chrysius, ready to kill.

The sound of their ceramite soles on the deck was drowned out by the noise of machinery. This level of the station was a fuel depot, where enormous stirring mechanisms churned the vats of starship fuel to keep it from separating and congealing. Between the vats laboured the peons, marked by brands on their faces. They all had the same raised scar blistered up across their lips and crushed noses. Only someone who knew of their allegiance beforehand would recognise the shape of it – a stylised skull with a grille for a mouth, like the face of a steel skeleton. Chrysius had estimated thirty peons held this floor, all of them armed, none of them ready for the wrath of the Imperial Fists.

Twenty-nine, he corrected himself. The body of the man he had just taken down slid to the floor beside him, leaving a glistening slick of blood on the side of the fuel tank.

'Chrysius to command,' he whispered into the vox, for he

habitually fought with his helmet removed and did not want his voice to carry. He went into battle bare-headed because the facial tattoos of his youth, acquired in a half-remembered previous life among the hive gangers of the Devlan Infernus, were his personal heraldry and it was cowardice not to display it. 'In position.'

'The assault has begun,' came the reply from Captain Haestorr. 'Execute, Squad Chrysius.'

Chrysius gave the signal, a clenched fist punched forwards, and his squad charged from their hiding place.

The peons had no idea they were about to be attacked. Even when the Imperial Fists stormed into the open, bolt pistols hammering, the enemy took several seconds to realise it. In those seconds half a dozen men were dead, pinpoint shots blasting heads from shoulders or ripping holes through torsos.

'Helian, Gruz, go high!' ordered Chrysius, pausing amid the carnage to take stock of the situation. A foot ramp led to a series of walkways circling the upper levels of the fuel cylinders. Enemies might be up there, and they would have excellent positions to fire on the Imperial Fists. Brother Helian was first up – half a metre taller than some of the other Imperial Fists, his armour had been altered to fit his frame and even Gruz looked small compared to him.

Chrysius spun around to see three peons taking up firing positions behind a bank of machinery. They had solid projectile guns of simple but effective design, perhaps even capable of putting a hole in power armour at close enough range. Chrysius did not intend to find out.

He ran right at them. It was not the natural reaction for a *human* being faced with a gun, and the peons reacted with shock when they should have blazed every bullet they had at the charging Imperial Fist. But Chrysius was post-human and not afraid of being shot. That was the first thing the hypno-doctrination had weeded out of him.

He vaulted the machinery and crashed down onto the first peon. This one's face was so disfigured by the brand he seemed to have no nose or lips at all, just a torn snarl of blistered flesh that failed to cover his broken teeth. His eyes were yellow, and they rolled back into his head as Chrysius's weight crunched into his ribcage.

Chrysius thrust his chainsword into the belly of the next peon, squeezing the charging stud as he stabbed. The chain teeth chewed through the stomach and spine with a spray of blood and smoke. Chrysius barely even had to look to fire in the opposite direction, into the last peon, leaving three holes in his chest so huge that his upper body flopped away, the centre of the torso completely gone.

'Report. Sound off!' ordered Chrysius. More than ten seconds had passed since battle had been joined. It would be a good way towards its conclusion by now.

'Helian. Nothing up here.' Helian sounded disappointed.

'Myrdos. Four down, am holding.'

'Vryskus. Under fire. Five have fallen to me!'

'Gruz,' voxed Chrysius. 'Gruz, report!'

The reply was the yellow-armoured body of Brother Gruz slamming into the floor ten metres from Chrysius's position. Chrysius ran up to him, grabbed his wrist and hauled him into the cover of the machinery. Gruz's pistol and chainsword lay where he had fallen, the teeth of the chainsword stripped away.

Chrysius glanced at the panel on the forearm of Gruz's armour, where the power armour's sensors read off the user's life signs. His battle-brother was alive.

'Helian!' yelled Chrysius into the vox. 'Helian, what's up there?'

Chrysius saw Helian running along the walkways above. He was firing at something out of sight and return fire, heavier, was hammering back at him.

Chrysius saw a ramp leading up to the tank behind him. It might take him up behind the unseen enemy. He ran for it, bolt pistol held up ready to snap off shots at anything that wasn't Brother Helian. Gunfire stuttered from below him – he would have to leave Myrdos and Vryskus to deal with the peons below.

The great dark shape that barrelled towards him, around the curve of the fuel tank, was too big to be one of the peons. It moved too fast. Chrysius jammed the trigger down by instinct but the shot didn't fell it, and a great weight slammed into him.

It was a Space Marine in battered power armour the colour of smoke-stained steel. The faceplate of the helmet was like the visor of a feudal knight, with dark red eyepieces and a grille over the nose and mouth like a jaw full of steel fangs. That same shape, the stylised, skull-like image, was emblazoned in silver on one black-painted shoulder pad.

An Iron Warrior.

The traitor's weight was on Chrysius and he could barely move. His chainblade was pinned down by his side and his bolt pistol was jammed under the Iron Warrior's torso, the barrel pointing down.

The Imperial Fists had suspected the Iron Warriors had a hand in the taking over of the orbital habitats around Euklid IV, but here was proof. Proof that would kill Chrysius in a matter of seconds if he could not fight like a Space Marine when it counted.

Chrysius let go of his chainsword and forced his arm out, feeling muscles wrenching. He grabbed the back of the Iron Warrior's helmet and yanked it back, forcing the enemy's head back and taking some of the weight off. He drove a foot into the walkway below him and rolled over, throwing the Iron Warrior off.

'Did you think you could hide here like vermin?' gasped Chrysius. 'Hide from the sons of Rogal Dorn?'

'Brave words, whelp of Terra,' replied the Iron Warrior. His voice was a metallic grind, distorted through the helmet filters. He tried to draw a bolter from a scabbard on his waist but Chrysius grabbed his wrist and the two grappled there, face to face, a test of strength with each trying to throw the other down.

The Iron Warrior won.

Chrysius toppled off the walkway, the railing parting underneath him. He slammed hard into the top of the fuel tank amid a tangle of cables and pipes. The Iron Warrior's bolter was out and he snapped off a rattling volley of shots. Chrysius rolled to make himself a moving target as explosive shells hammered home around him. Blooms of flame erupted as fuel lines were ruptured. A ball of fire rushed up, masking Chrysius for the second it took him to get onto his feet.

Chrysius fired blindly through the flames. He counted off the shells in his bolt pistol's magazine, knowing he was outgunned and outmuscled by the enemy.

But this was not just an enemy. This was an Iron Warrior, a Traitor Marine who had engaged the Imperial Fists in battle after bloody battle to test their strength against the scions of Rogal Dorn. Between the two, there was nothing but hate.

Enough hate to propel the Iron Warrior through the fire, closing with Chrysius in a couple of seconds, a combat knife in one hand and the bolter in the other. Chrysius just had time to turn to face his assailant before the knife stabbed home.

Chrysius had earned his laurels through an expertise in hand to hand combat that few Imperial Fists could better. He recognised the strike: a low one to the relatively vulnerable joints between the abdomen of his power armour and the chest plate. Chrysius drove the heel of his hand down, knocked the combat blade off target, and blasted off the remaining shells in his pistol into the Iron Warrior.

One shot rang off the Iron Warrior's shoulder guard, doing nothing more than adding another scar to the pitted paintwork. One hit the chest, blowing a crater in the ceramite but nothing more. A third, the last, punched into the Iron Warrior's thigh, ripping through his thigh joint and blasting muscle and bone apart.

The Iron Warrior bellowed in pain and dropped to one knee. Chrysius was on him. His chainblade was left up on the walkway, but he still had the hands of an Imperial Fist.

He smashed his pistol into the Iron Warrior's face. The weapon shattered but the faceplate buckled, one eye lens popping out.

'There are ten thousand of us,' growled the Iron Warrior as he tried to fend off Chrysius. 'The future is ours. Every–'

Chrysius didn't let the Iron Warrior finish. He drove his fist into his face, feeling nothing but hatred. It was as if there were nothing in the galaxy but Chrysius's fist and the Iron Warrior's steel face, which every blow crumpled and split.

Chrysius's fist pistoned over and over again until the faceplate came apart and he was able to rip the helmet away. He looked into the Iron Warrior's face.

Brother Hestion reached the walkway overlooking the fuel tank. By the time he had vaulted down and reached Chrysius, the Iron Warrior's face had been reduced to a crimson pulp. Chrysius let the body fall, and it clattered limply to his feet.

Hestion handed Chrysius the chainsword he had left on the walkway. 'Good kill, sergeant,' he said.

The edge of night passed across the surface of Euklid IV. The gas giant's upper atmosphere was, in daytime, a mass of firestorms. As night passed the flames became dark, replaced with a grey-black caul of ash speckled with islands of glowing embers.

People had lived here once – humans, citizens of the Imperium, living on the dozens of space stations orbiting the planet. Now whoever lived here could not be described as people at all.

Against the scale of Euklid IV, those orbital stations seemed so tiny and delicate they could barely be thought of as existing at all. And compared to the void that lay beyond it, the planet was an insignificant, infinitesimally tiny fragment of nothing. Even Euklid, the system's star, meant nothing compared to the galaxy. And the galaxy meant nothing compared to the universe.

It was good, thought Chrysius, that a Space Marine rarely had the luxury of time to think about such things.

'Chrysius!' came a familiar voice behind him. Chrysius turned to see another Space Marine entering the observation deck. This one wore the White Scars' livery on one shoulder pad but the rest of his armour was black with silver lettering inscribed. His face was familiar too, half the scalp a metallic shell, one eye a bionic, contrasting with a mouth that smiled easily. His skin, battered and tanned like beaten bronze, was typical of the horse nomads from which his Chapter drew their recruits.

'Kholedei!' said Chrysius. 'My brother. It has been too long!'

The two clasped hands. 'It has,' said Kholedei. 'For all the honour of the Deathwatch, it is good to fight alongside old friends again.'

The last time Chrysius had seen Kholedei, it had been as a joint White Scars and Imperial Fists strike force lifted off from the shattered remains of Hive Mandibus. The city had fallen to a xenos plague which turned the inhabitants into walking incubators for wormlike aliens. The mission had been nothing short of a cull, exterminating every living thing they found. It was a foul, grim business, a merciless grind, when even a Space Marine had been in need of friends. The two had fought alongside each other, their squads merged into one and taking strength from their new comrades.

'I had heard the Deathwatch had sent a kill-team to Euklid IV,' said Chrysius. 'I did not know you would be among them.'

'When I knew we would be in support of the Imperial Fists, I ensured that I would be in the kill-team,' said Kholedei. 'I would not miss the chance to fight alongside the Sons of Dorn again. What news of your squad?'

'Venelus fell at Thorgin,' said Chrysius. 'A shot from an eldar sniper. And Koron at the Fallmarch Expanse, when the *Eternal Sacrifice* was lost.'

'They were fine brothers, Chrysius. We are all diminished by their loss.'

'It is the way of war to take our best,' said Chrysius. 'Vryskus has yet to atone for his defeat at the tournament, though to everyone else but him he has redeemed himself a dozen times over. Myrdos is on his way to taking his own squad. Helian's just the same, of course.'

'Good to know. I hear that you killed an Iron Warrior yourself.'

'That is so,' said Chrysius. 'I was fortunate.'

'A kill that I have not equalled, sergeant,' said Kholedei. 'Aliens aplenty have fallen to me and my team, but an Iron Warrior is something else. I would dearly love to shed the blood of such a traitor. I know of the dishonours they have done to the Imperial Fists.'

'Gruz was wounded,' said Chrysius. 'I am proud to have taken the kill, but not that my battle-brother suffered for it.'

'Then you will avenge him. Just as we avenge our fallen every time we fight. And the next fight will be soon. I have spoken with Captain Haestorr. Given the intelligence the Inquisition gathered on this mission, the enemy will be concentrated in the science facility. We strike there, and strike hard, and the Iron Warriors will be thrown off Euklid IV before they have the chance to mount a defence.'

'What interest does the Ordo Xenos have in Euklid IV?' asked Chrysius.

Kholedei smiled. 'Believe me, the ordo wants the Iron Warriors extinct just as much as we do. They might specialise in hunting the alien, but an enemy is an enemy.'

'Well, that's why we are here. Why are the Iron Warriors here?'

Kholedei looked out through the viewing port. Once this station had been a beautiful place, where the citizens could gather and reflect on the majesty of Euklid IV. Now the place was decaying, the walls spotted with rust and damp, the port smeared with condensation. 'This was an intellectual colony,' said Kholedei. 'Artists, philosophers. Perhaps their meditations uncovered or woke something. A moral threat. Perhaps the Iron Warriors want it. Perhaps they built a science station of enough sophistication to make it valuable to the enemy. It matters little as long as it gives us a time and a place to kill them.'

'I am glad the Inquisition and the Chapter made common cause here,' said Chrysius. 'It is good to have you back, brother.'

'It is good to be back,' said Kholedei. Chrysius recognised that smile, which his old friend only broke out when the chance for competition showed itself. 'I get another chance to show you how a Space Marine really fights.'

Captain Haestorr ascribed to the tactical philosophy that a Space Marine was not a soldier. A soldier could lose his nerve. A soldier would not just walk into the fury of the enemy – he had to be corralled like an animal or cajoled like a child.

A Space Marine was more like a bullet fired from a gun. He went wherever he was pointed, and needed no convincing to inflict fatal damage on anything he hit.

The Imperial Fists' boarding torpedoes slammed into the side of the station. By the lettering stencilled on its side, this station was called the *Enlightenment*. The hull plates came apart under the reinforced prows of the Caestus-pattern boarding rams, as the assault vehicles drove through the multiple levels of protective plating.

Space Marine power armour was proof against the vacuum that ripped everything out of the station's outer hull spaces. After a few seconds to let the gases vent, the prows of the boarding rams opened up and the Imperial Fists emerged, the assault squad first into the breach. They forged into the tangled labyrinth of ventilation ducts and fuel coolant pipes that encased the station's interior.

The enemy knew they were there. Even without any sensors left on the station, the impacts of the rams would have rung throughout the *Enlightenment*. Every Imperial Fist, and the Deathwatch kill-team members who accompanied them, knew this would be a contested boarding. That meant a close quarters fight, a butcher's battle.

It would be against the most hated enemy the Imperial Fists had ever made. They couldn't wait.

* * *

The first sight Chrysius had of the enemy was a blurred, half-glimpsed shape leaping between the laboratory benches. The lab floor was choked with machinery: wires and ducts hanging from the ceiling. An enormous cylindrical structure, an electron microscope, loomed like a monumental sculpture. The enemy had lots of places to hide and the one Chrysius saw, jumping from one piece of cover to the next, was humanoid in a way that was fundamentally wrong. It trailed fronds of skin and its limbs were too long, jointed in the wrong places.

Mutants.

Chrysius's immediate objective was to close with the enemy. It was the first principle of The Doctrines of Assault, sleep-taught to Chrysius during his training. He crashed through the lab equipment, kicking through the bench in front of him, scattering chemical beakers and glassware everywhere. Gunfire was already starting – the staccato thunder of the Imperial Fists' boltguns, and the red flashes of laser fire in return. Chrysius could see more of them now behind barricades of overturned benches and toppled lab gear, dressed in ragtag uniforms of black and yellow, and sporting different mutations. He saw in that glimpse vividly coloured and patterned flesh, claws and stinger tails, tattered wings, scorched and blistered skin.

Hestion was ahead of Chrysius, dropping a shoulder and crashing through a bank of cogitator screens. He slammed into the mutant sheltering behind it and yanked the thing off its feet as the mutant tried to wrench the Imperial Fist's head off with its tentacles. Hestion dashed the mutant against the ground, splitting its head open against the white-tiled floor, and impaled a second mutant through the chest with his chainsword. The whirr of the teeth screeched even above the dying scream and the gunfire, and it was the sound of imminent victory.

Chrysius jumped a barricade of furniture, shooting one of the mutants behind it through the chest before he even landed. It had huge compound eyes and mouthparts like an insect. He swept his chainblade and cut another in two at the waist, his backswing ruining the leg of a third. He barely had time to register what manner of uncleanness had been marked on their flesh before they died, fresh blood spraying across the golden yellow of his armour, the vibrations of cracking bone running up through his feet as he stamped down on them.

More mutants were running into the fray, brought by the screams of their brothers. They were armed with las-weapons and autoguns. Bullets and las-blasts pinged off Hestion's armour as he stood proud, battering down a mutant who charged at him with gun blazing. Hestion was wounded often, and Chrysius had often lectured him on a Space Marine's duty to preserve himself and his wargear as well as destroy the enemy, but Hestion did not have a self-preserving cell in his huge body.

There were hundreds of mutants pouring onto the laboratory deck. Radios were blasting orders and exaltations to kill. Chrysius's squad paused for a moment, the first line of the enemy dead and the next line rushing towards them.

'Hestion! Hold the line and charge on my mark,' ordered Chrysius. 'And get down!'

'Behold the enslavers!' came a braying voice over a vox-caster with speakers mounted on the lab ceiling. 'The heralds of order! The enslavers of your kind! Watch them fall, and revel in their death-cries!'

Chrysius glanced over the cover. The mutants were close. He could see their faces, and the ones with expressions he could read were glassy-eyed, as if they had been hypnotised or mind-wiped.

Dogs, thought Chrysius. Animals, conditioned to attack. The Imperium's malcontents lied to and indoctrinated, and loosed like a pack of dogs.

'Now!' yelled Chrysius, and leapt into the front rank of mutants, into the storm of claws and blades.

Even against this fanatical horde there was glory to be won. The brutal rhythm of violence came easily to Assault-Sergeant Chrysius. They thrust, he parried, reversed and cut, blasted another few bolt shells into them and let them close again, near enough for the pattern to repeat. He saw Brother Myrdos clamber onto the cylinder of the microscope and hack down those who tried to reach him, as if he were a flag planted at the summit of a mountain and the mutants were competing to see who could pull it down first. Somewhere in the thick of it was Hestion, hurling the enemy in every direction, some even clattering against the coolant ducts running across the ceiling.

The enemy relented. They had to – there were only so many of them. As they broke off in twos and threes they were shot down by the bolters of the Imperial Fists behind, directed by Captain Haestorr. The kill-team were there too, firing with lethal precision, each bolter shell shredding a mutant's central mass in a spray of gore.

'Squads, respond!' came the vox on Haestorr's command channel. 'Report all sightings of the Iron Warriors!'

'None here,' replied Chrysius. 'They sent in the fodder. They thought we'd be softened up before we reached them.'

'None yet,' came a voice Chrysius recognised as Kholedei's. 'Squad, free target at will, don't waste your kraken shells. Watch for the Weaponsmith.'

Chrysius dropped to one knee behind a bullet-riddled lab bench. 'Kholedei? Brother Kholedei, can you repeat that?'

There was no answer. The second part of the vox had sounded like it was directed to the Deathwatch kill-team and not the rest of the force. Perhaps it had been a mistake, Kholedei momentarily forgetting to switch channels.

But Chrysius was quite sure of what he had heard. And so had the rest of his squad.

'Sergeant,' said Brother Hestion, who emerged from a bank of machines to join Chrysius. Hestion was covered from head to toe in blood. His bolt pistol was still in its holster, and he had probably killed as many with his bare left hand as with his chainsword. 'Did he say that? About the Weaponsmith?'

'Focus on the enemy, Brother Hestion,' said Chrysius.

'But he did,' said Brother Vryskus, who approached wiping the blood from the blade of the duellist's sabre he used in place of a chainsword. 'We all heard him. I think, sergeant, we all know now why we are here.'

According to the collators of the Imperial Fists' lore – those battle-brothers responsible for recording battle legends and old grudges –Weaponsmith Gurlagorg had been one of the first Iron Warriors ever to break the greatest taboo of the Space Marines. This Iron Warrior, a commander of his Legion, had taken an Imperial Fist prisoner at a long-ago battle, cut open his body and removed the gene-seed organs. The gene-seed, the organ that regulated all the many augmentations of a Space Marine's body, without which he could simply not exist. The gene-seed, created after the genetic pattern of the Primarch Rogal Dorn himself who had in turn been made in the image of the Emperor. A shred of the divine that every Space Marine carried inside him.

Gurlagorg had sought a way to create more Iron Warriors, and had struck upon the idea of harvesting the gene-seed from Imperial Space Marines, corrupting and debasing it, and creating new battle-brothers of his own. It was as blasphemous a concept as ever existed among the Chapter of the Space Marines. Some had even thought that the Traitor Legions, heretics and sworn enemies of mankind though they were, would at least respect the principles of their own creation. But no – Gurlagorg had created a new Iron Warrior from the first gene-seed he took, and set about seeking more to defile with his corrupted sciences.

It was a dangerous story to tell, and the Chapter Masters condemned its spreading. But it was told, hushed and always changing. Gurlagorg was the worst of the worst, as deadly an enemy as the

Imperial Fists had. If ever a roll of the Imperial Fists' deadliest enemies were drawn up, Weaponsmith Gurlagorg would be near the top. Few and powerful would be the names ahead of his.

And now he was orbiting Euklid IV. The Deathwatch knew, and presumably Captain Haestorr and the Chapter's leaders did, too. That was why the Inquisition had sent the kill-team to assist the Imperial Fists in wiping out the Iron Warriors there – because the Inquisition knew that Gurlagorg was a hated enemy of mankind, and that his death would make the galaxy that one degree more sacred.

They had found him. After thousands of years they had found him. And now, after thousands of years, they would kill him.

The deck beyond the laboratory bled from its walls. Where there had once been panels of steel, there was now a blackened bio-mechanical covering of skin, the rotting metal blistered up with pulsing steel veins. Drops of acid pattered from the sagging ceiling and a silver-black ooze bubbled up underfoot. Every warning rune was lit up on the retinas of the Imperial Fists as they warily moved into the science station's core, the filters of their armoured faceplates capturing the worst of the pollutants that turned the air thick and hazy.

Even Assault-Sergeant Chrysius wore his helmet here. The Imperial Fists force spread out through the deck, which stretched most of the rest of the way to the station's centre. The deck was badly warped, forming slopes and hills as it rose and fell, and in places it shuddered underfoot as if ready to give way into the fuel cells and thruster arrays on the station's underside.

'It's a miracle the gravity still works,' voxed Brother Vryskus.

'Speak not too soon, brother,' replied Myrdos. 'Think to the Battle of the *Dark Ascension*. The Night Lords there deactivated their flagship's gravity just as battle was joined, hoping to spread confusion through the Imperial Fists' ranks.'

'Did it work?' asked Vryskus.

'If you were minded to read anything our forefathers wrote, Vryskus, you would know the Imperial Fists were stern and resolute, and were victorious,' said Myrdos testily. 'Our brethren there were ready. So must we be.'

Before Chrysius was a blistered section of the deck where the biomechanical substance was stretched thin. Beneath the surface, suspended in greyish translucent fluid, was an object that looked like a boltgun of an ancient mark. Its lines were undeveloped and its details indistinct, as if it had been moulded from clay. 'They're growing their wargear here,' he said.

'Truly,' said Vryskus, 'no tech-heresy is beyond the Iron Warriors.'

Other blisters held segments of power armour and more weapons, all in various stages of growth. 'We can destroy this on the way out,' voxed Captain Haestorr. 'The Iron Warriors are the objective here.'

'And Weaponsmith Gurlagorg,' replied Chrysius over the command vox. 'If he is here. You cannot deny us that knowledge, captain.'

'Discipline,' replied Haestorr. 'Focus, sergeant. The mission above all else.'

'If the Weaponsmith is on this station then our mission is to kill him,' replied Chrysius. 'As it has been the mission of the Imperial Fists to kill all enemies of mankind.'

'You are ahead of yourself,' voxed Haestorr. 'There is no sign the Weaponsmith is here.'

'The Deathwatch think otherwise,' said Chrysius. He could see Kholedei and the rest of his kill-team moving carefully through the unstable chamber, on one flank of the Imperial Fists' formation. Chrysius could see, along with Kholedei's own White Scars livery, the heraldry of other Space Marine Chapters on the shoulder pads of the kill-team members – a Praetor of Orpheus, a Black Dragon, a Scimitar Guard. Chrysius wondered what it would mean to fight alongside Space Marines whose way of thinking came from the doctrines of a different Chapter, men who might be his brothers as the Emperor's finest but not brothers raised together in war.

'We're closing on the Hazardous Materials Lab,' voxed Sergeant Moxus, whose squad held the opposite flank. 'It's shielded and fortified, if the original blueprints still hold true. If the Iron Warriors make a stand on this station, they will make it there.'

'Captain Kholedei!' ordered Haestorr. 'Bring your demolitions charges forth. We'll blast our way in.'

The kill-team headed to the front where a great bulkhead, the spine of the station, met the corrupted deck. Chrysius saw now the Praetor of Orpheus had the servo-harness and artificer armour of a Techmarine. He attached three large steel canisters to the bulkhead wall and keyed in a command sequence as the kill-team retired beyond the blast zone.

'If the Weaponsmith didn't know we were coming,' said Vryskus bleakly, 'he will soon.'

'Lesser men would call us the forlorn hope,' said Chrysius. 'The first into the breach. A Space Marine calls it the place of the greatest honour, for to us will fall the first blood of the enemy.' Chrysius drew his chainsword. 'To us will fall the Weaponsmith.'

A trio of rapid explosions shuddered the chamber. The cysts burst, spilling half-formed wargear across the floor in a flood of greasy filth. The bulkhead shattered in a blast of red light and flame, and black smoke filled the air.

Through the gloom, Chrysius's auto-senses cut a path through the interior of the Hazardous Materials Lab. Whatever it had once been, it now resembled nothing so much as a temple ripped from whatever dimension had birthed it and transplanted into this space station. Chains hung across the void in the heart of the station, hung with festoons of mangled corpses impaled on the spiked links. Shafts of black steel fell down through the darkness, impaling great altars of carved stone. The laboratory floor had been turned into a maze of altars, the spaces between them choked with bodies and forming a charnel house labyrinth. Statues of monstrous gods and daemons – a dog-headed representation of the Blood God Khorne, a sagging monstrosity of grey stone that was surely Nurgle, the Plague Lord – glowered over the scene, the gemstones in their eyes watching for bloodshed about to begin.

The only remnants of the original lab were the cells. They were of polished steel and now stood on the top of black stone pillars, each one holding a specimen of a different xenos species. Chrysius recognised a genestealer of the Ymargl strain, the harbinger species who moved ahead of the tyranid hive fleets. Another cell held the filth-encrusted mass of a hrud, spacebound scavengers who clothed themselves in exoskeletons of other species' detritus. There was a snake-bodied, four-armed creature among them whose ornate armour suggested ownership by a more sophisticated species who likely used it as a bodyguard or foot soldier. On many of the altars were the corpses of other xenos, some cut open with their innards spread as fodder for soothsayers, other dissected as if for study, their body parts laid out as neatly as a watchmaker's cogs on the sacrificial slabs.

Chrysius took all this in as he led the charge. Half his mind was that of a student of war, sizing up every aspect for cover and fields of fire. The other half saw only the tell-tale shapes of ancient power armour among the heaps of bones and let the recognition of them fill him with hate.

The Iron Warriors. They were here, making their stand in this grand temple to the warp's own gods.

If anyone had asked Chrysius, in that moment, to recite the principles of warfare that had been implanted in his mind in hypno-doctrination, he could not have done so. The glories of Rogal Dorn. The legends of his Chapter. His own name. They were all gone from his mind, replaced by a raw and burning hatred.

Because he had seen the Iron Warrior's face. The one he had killed in the fuel depot. And the image of that face filled his mind, an icon of hatred without equal.

Bolter fire hammered against the shattered bulkhead as Chrysius vaulted the twisted wreckage. Shots burst against his chestplate and greave, but his momentum carried him on. He passed into the dense shadow between two altars, his feet crunching through xenos skeletons.

Black power armour loomed in front of him. The shape was that of a Space Marine but deformed with bulky bionics. One arm was an industrial claw, more suited to carving up slabs of metal in a manufactorum than for using as a hand. Half the head was a metallic skull, crowned with a circle of bronze horns. The single eye in the centre of the faceplate glowed green as it played targeting lasers across Chrysius's body.

Chrysius never gave the Iron Warrior the opportunity to shoot. He closed the gap in two strides and hit the traitor square in the chest.

But it held firm. It was heavier and stronger than Chrysius. It slammed its claw against Chrysius's midriff in a colossal backhand, throwing the Imperial Fist into the black stone of the altar behind him.

Chrysius kicked out, forcing open the gap between himself and the Iron Warrior. It was just enough to bring the point of his chainsword up and drive it forward. The tip sheared through the pistons of the traitor's bionic shoulder, slicing through cables and hoses.

The Iron Warrior laughed. It was a hateful, metallic sound. Chrysius tried to wrench his chainblade back out and the Iron Warrior held up his claw, slamming its blades together as if in mockery, to show Chrysius the weapon that would cut him in half in a handful of seconds.

Another shadow fell against the darkness, black against black. It was Brother Vryskus, his duelling blade arrowing down at the Iron Warrior.

The blade punched into the Iron Warrior's chest. The pressure came off Chrysius for a second and he was free, rolling out from under the Iron Warrior.

The Iron Warrior ignored the injury, pivoting and catching Vryskus between the blades of his claw. Steam spurted from its damaged shoulder as the twin blades slammed closed, slicing Brother Vryskus in half at the waist.

Chrysius felt as if he had been immersed in ice. His blood seemed gone, replaced with freezing gas. He cried out and stabbed his chainblade forward again, this time aiming at the back of the Iron Warrior's head.

The chainsword caught the Iron Warrior in the neck, where the spine joined the skull. The traitor tensed rigid as the chain teeth sawed through the top of his spine and brain stem, pulping the inside of the cranium. The single eyepiece popped and spurted viscous gore down the front of its black armour.

It had taken less than a second. One moment Vryskus had been alive, the next he was dead. Chrysius had seen thousands of deaths, but the death of a brother, of a squad mate, was never the same.

Brother Myrdos, who had bickered with Vryskus minutes before, crunched through the corpses underfoot and stopped dead when he saw Vryskus's helmet, with the black stripe painted down its faceplate, down among the broken bodies. He saw instantly that Vryskus was dead.

'We will mourn him when the Weaponsmith has fallen,' gasped Chrysius.

Myrdos could only nod his agreement before Chrysius stepped over the two dead Space Marines, one traitor and one loyal, and struck further into the altar labyrinth.

The hate had been hot a moment ago. Now Chrysius was filled with ice, and it seemed twice as fierce. He had to be rid of it, this awful freezing pressure building up in his chest, and the only way was to fight on through, kill and maim and avenge with every stroke.

Revenge. He would have revenge. He would carve every unspoken syllable of his hate onto the Weaponsmith's body.

Gunfire streaked from an altar above. Chrysius vaulted up onto the top and saw another Iron Warrior, this one with both hands altered with mutation and bionics into multi-barrelled bolters. It was spraying out the firepower of four or five Imperial Fists, filling the air with burning chains of shrapnel. Chrysius slashed down at one of the Iron Warrior's legs, knocking it onto its back. Myrdos was beside him and leapt on the downed Iron Warrior, stabbing down at its heart. Myrdos's chainsword threw a shower of sparks as it bit into ceramite.

The Iron Warrior threw Myrdos off and, before Chrysius could even swing a return stroke at it, fired a volley at him. One shot caught Chrysius full in the leg and he felt the bones and gristle of his knee blown apart into a bloody-petalled flower of torn skin.

Chrysius fell back. He ordered his body to move in for the kill-stroke, but his body refused to obey him, shocked into disobedience. The Iron Warrior turned to Myrdos and the snarl of its deformed faceplate seemed to sneer as it levelled its bolter barrels at the Imperial Fist.

A massive volley of fire ripped into Myrdos, laying his ribcage open in a bloody mass. One of his arms was blown clean off and another shot punched through his eyepiece, splitting the back of his head open and spilling his brains across the black stone of the altar.

I will mourn later, Chrysius told himself. Time seemed to slow down, leaving him the moments he needed to follow his thoughts. I will weep for him among the shrines and statues of the *Phalanx*. But not yet.

Hanging above the altar was one of the specimen cages – this one containing another genestealer. Chrysius had fought them before, and knew them to be creatures of such viciousness that to take one down, one on one, in close combat was worth a badge of honour that Chrysius had yet to earn. They could be taken down at a distance with no loss, provided they were spotted and targeted in time. Up close, they were a horror.

Chrysius drew his bolt pistol, not moving from his position on his back. He aimed up at the chain holding the cell above the altar.

The Iron Warrior must have assumed Chrysius was trying and failing to aim at it. It blasted off a few bolter shots into the advancing Imperial Fists, then turned back to Chrysius. In the moment that gave him, Chrysius loosed off half his pistol's magazine, and the top of the cage was shredded in a burst of silver shrapnel.

The chain parted and the cell plummeted down. It landed just behind the Iron Warrior, who turned to see what had missed it.

The four clawed limbs of the genestealer inside reached out between the bent bars and grabbed the Iron Warrior by the neck. The alien's head was a mass of tentacles that splayed apart, revealing a beak-like mouthpart. The genestealer dragged the Iron Warrior against its cell, and lashed its tentacles around its helmet.

The beak punched out through the back of the Iron Warrior's face. The Traitor Marine convulsed, bolters firing randomly.

Chrysius forced himself to stand, his ruined leg threatening to buckle under him. There was no pain, even though there should have been too much for his armour's painkiller reserves to mask. He had no room for pain in him now.

The rest of his bolter's magazine was blasted point-blank into the feasting genestealer's head, shattering its alien skull and leaving it slumped in its cell with the dead Iron Warrior still held close.

Part of Chrysius wanted to pick up the remains of Brother Myrdos, carry him far from that battlefield and give him the funeral rites of a brother. He wanted to take Brother Vryskus, too, and bear the two sundered halves of him to the *Phalanx* where they might lie in state as heroes. But that part of Chrysius was a whisper compared to the hate rushing through him – now he was hollow, a desert valley worn smooth by a screaming wind. Everything was scoured away but the will to do violence to the Weaponsmith who had created all this.

Chrysius ran on, leaping down from the blood-slicked altar into the labyrinth. His vision swam with tears as he forced his way through the heaps of skeletons and wreckage. A red glow was ahead of him, and he recognised the heat and colour of molten ceramite. In the forges of the *Phalanx* it was melted down to create new armour plates. He caught the smell of it, breaking through the stench of bodies and boltgun propellant that had made it through the filters of his faceplate.

The forge at the centre of the temple was a structure of barricaded archways. Hundreds of skulls were mounted on spikes on the walls. Gunfire was blasting chunks from the barricades of wreckage the Iron Warriors had set up – the battle had already reached this far into the temple, the Imperial Fists following in the wake of Chrysius's charge and engaging the Iron Warriors from every direction.

The Weaponsmith must be here, in the forge.

In front of one of the barricades was Brother Hestion, the last member of Chrysius's squad. Hestion had charged through the hail of bolter fire to the foot of the barricade. Chrysius watched as he dragged an Iron Warrior over the barricade, flinging it to the floor and pounding a fist into its faceplate.

Another Iron Warrior mounted the barricade and vaulted down. He wielded a power axe with both hands and struck down at Hestion. The blade bit into Hestion's arm and almost cut right through it. Hestion grabbed the Iron Warrior by the throat with his good arm and, with a strength that even a Space Marine could rarely muster, hurled the Iron Warrior into the barricade. Chunks of wreckage and steel beams tumbled down.

Chrysius ran to his battle-brother's side. The Iron Warrior on the floor was trying to get up – Chrysius lanced it through the spine with his chainblade, putting all the momentum of his charge into the sword-thrust. The blade bit deep but did not penetrate far enough to kill the Iron Warrior, who turned and blasted at point-blank range with a bolt pistol.

Chrysius felt the armour over his abdomen dent and shear, but not give way. The bolter round had not penetrated. The next shot would.

Chrysius put a foot against the Iron Warrior's neck, feeling the spikes of pain bursting from his shattered knee. He drove down as best he could, forcing the Iron Warrior's head down, twisted the chainblade and put all of his weight behind it. This time the blade bored through the Iron Warrior's back. Chrysius pulled it almost all the way out and stabbed down again and again, each thrust bubbling up a torrent of gore from the well of blood.

Chrysius looked up to see Hestion and the second Iron Warrior duelling, axe against chainblade. The axe swung in a low arc, aimed at taking out Hestion's legs. Hestion blocked the blow with his weapon but in a flash of light the axe's power field discharged and the chainblade was ripped apart. Loose metal teeth spattered against Chrysius, embedding themselves in his armour like tiny daggers.

Hestion, unarmed now, put both hands around the Iron Warrior's neck. Chrysius fought to get his own chainsword out of the downed Iron Warrior's back but it had jammed tight against the breastplate of fused ribs. Finally it came loose and Chrysius lunged forward but his knee gave way, folding the wrong way underneath him.

The Iron Warrior drove the head of the axe up under Hestion's ribs. The Imperial Fist fell back, the breastplate of his power armour laid open. The Iron Warrior drew up its axe and buried the blade up to the handle in Hestion's exposed chest.

Chrysius cried out wordlessly. The Iron Warrior brought up the axe again and swung it down with such force it split Hestion's torso from shoulder to waist.

Chrysius grabbed the fallen Iron Warrior's bolt pistol from the floor. He dragged himself forward a couple of paces so the shot would be point blank. He unloaded the pistol's remaining ammo into the back of the Iron Warrior, blasting apart the power plant of its armour.

Hestion was still alive. He was the strongest man, Space Marine or otherwise, that Chrysius had ever known and his last act was to grab the Iron Warrior's helmet and wrench it off, before falling to the ground.

The last round of bolter ammo went into the back of the Iron Warrior's head. It blew the back of the traitor's skull apart, throwing brain and skull against the fallen barricade.

Chrysius knew what he would see even before the Iron Warrior tumbled back, its head tilted so that Chrysius looked into dead eyes. He knew what the face would look like. He had seen it earlier, when he had killed the Iron Warrior in the fuel depot. The image had burned into his brain.

And this Iron Warrior was the same.

Chrysius was looking into a human face. Not a monster's face, not the face of a daemon or an inhuman fusion of man and machine. Just a man's face, like a Space Marine. No, not like any – Chrysius himself, with his gang tattoos, looked far more monstrous than this Iron Warrior.

They were men. Space Marines, just like him. Whatever made them the enemy of mankind, it was not the fact they were monsters, debased and savage creatures disfigured by the marks of their heresy. What made them traitors was something inside, something that waited inside every Space Marine.

There was nothing that Chrysius had seen in his life so hateful as a normal, human face on this enemy.

Chrysius struggled across the wreckage to Hestion's body. His battle-brother was dead – his innards were open to the air and Chrysius could see his hearts and lungs motionless amid the gore.

Chrysius pulled himself upright against the ruins of the barricade. Beyond it he could see molten ceramite pouring in sheets, like waterfalls, from above. Here, in the forge, was where the Weaponsmith waited.

Chrysius clambered over the fallen barricade. He reloaded his bolt pistol with hands that shook with pain and physical shock. It did not matter that he was hurt. When he was so full of hate, when it drove him on with such force, he could ignore that. He would suffer later. Now, there was one last kill to be taken.

In the centre of the forge, kneeling beside a black iron anvil, was the Weaponsmith.

The pain all caught up to Chrysius at once. He slumped down, supporting himself with one hand. He wanted to pitch forward onto the floor and let unconsciousness take over, but refused to allow himself such respite.

The Weaponsmith was three-quarters the height of a human, half the height of a Space Marine. It was roughly humanoid, though its limbs were too long for its body and its oversized feet had multi-jointed prehensile toes. Its hands had similarly long fingers, so dextrous they curved back on themselves like snakes. It was covered in red-brown fur. Its face was flat, almost simian, with an underdeveloped nose and wide mouth. It wore no clothing but had a pair of welding goggles clamped to its face and a bandolier of tools strung across its chest.

The anvil beside it was covered in tools and components. As Chrysius watched, it assembled a few into another creation, a spinning armature like a clockwork toy for the amusement of a child. The Weaponsmith let the device fall whereupon it took flight, catching the updraft of hot air from the forge and flitting towards the ceiling like an insect. The Weaponsmith watched it with curiosity, paying no attention to Chrysius at all.

There was no one else in the forge. The Iron Warriors were dead or fighting the main Imperial Fists force outside. Chrysius had been certain he would see the multi-armed servo-harness of Gurlagorg, the steam that belched from the engines and reactors mounted on his archaic armour, the pallid mask of synthetic flesh he wore as a face. But none of those were here, just the strange furred creature beside the anvil.

Another of the barricades fell in, shoved down by the combined weight of two members of Kholedei's Deathwatch kill-team. Kholedei himself followed them in.

'Kholedei!' shouted Chrysius. 'What is this? Where is Gurlagorg?'

Kholedei walked forward slowly. 'Step back, brother, This battle is over.'

'Where is Gurlagorg?' demanded Chrysius again. 'My squad died to get to him. Where is he?'

'Gurlagorg was never here, Brother Chrysius,' said Kholedei.

'But you spoke of the Weaponsmith! We heard you! That was why you were here!'

'And we were,' replied Kholedei, his voice level and calm. 'But I never spoke of Gurlagorg. This creature is of a species possessing a rare technological skill. The Iron Warriors were using it to manufacture wargear for them. It might reasonably be called a weaponsmith. That is what we were here to find.'

'You... you knew we would hear you,' said Chrysius. 'Over the vox. You knew we would believe it was Gurlagorg we were hunting, and you let my squad sacrifice themselves to kill him!' Chrysius aimed his bolt pistol at the alien, which again did nothing to acknowledge any of the Space Marines around it. 'And perhaps I will!'

Kholedei held up a calming hand, but the Space Marine beside him, who wore the golden livery of the Scimitar Guard beside the black of the Deathwatch, had his bolter up and aiming at Chrysius.

'The kraken rounds my kill-team use can punch through even the ceramite of a Space Marine's armour,' said Kholedei. 'Including yours, Brother Chrysius. Though you may not be familiar with the brain stem grafts of the Scimitar Guard, be assured that Brother Shen here can shoot you dead before your finger has finished pulling the trigger. We are here for the alien and we will take him alive. That is our mission, and we will complete it even if we have to go through you. I do not say this lightly, Chrysius. That we bring this alien back to the Inquisition is a matter outweighing either of our lives.'

Chrysius slumped and let his pistol drop. 'We were brothers, Kholedei. At Hive Mandibus you pulled Gruz from the rubble of that blast, and you debated with Vryskus for hours! They were your brothers! You were my brother! You knew we would die for the chance to kill Gurlagorg and you let us believe it anyway.'

'The Iron Warriors were trying to get this alien off the station,' said Kholedei. 'We had to take this position as quickly as we could. That meant spurring the Imperial Fists on to storm this place with all haste, more than combat doctrine would allow. We told you no lies and we fought as sternly as any of you, and for the same end.'

Kholedei knelt beside Chrysius and put a hand on his shoulder, and for a moment Chrysius saw in him the same White Scar who had once fought alongside him. But then that face was gone, replaced with another – the face of a Space Marine sworn to the Inquisition, and not to the battle-brothers at his side. 'And this xenos is a powerful asset to the Inquisition. Even among its own kind, it is a genius. It is responsible for arming whole Black Crusades and now that skill will be used for the good of the Imperium. You may not understand all that we have achieved here, but if you have ever trusted me, trust that it is a greater victory than killing a hundred Gurlagorgs.'

Kholedei waved the Praetors of Orpheus Techmarine forward. He placed cuffs on the alien's wrists and ankles. The xenos did not resist. One of the Techmarine's servo-arms was equipped with a syringe – this injected the alien, which slumped unconscious. The Techmarine picked it up and slung it over his shoulder.

'We must leave,' said Kholedei. 'I will pray for your fallen.'

'They are your fallen, too,' said Chrysius.

With that the kill-team left the forge, moving rapidly back towards the boarding rams. When the main Imperial Fists force breached the barricades, they found nothing but Assault-Sergeant Chrysius, slumped beside the anvil, exhausted and beaten.

Chrysius watched the science station explode and be scattered in the void, shattered by a few demolition charges placed at strategic points. Behind him, on the observation deck, were the bodies of Brothers Hestion, Vryskus and Myrdos, covered in shrouds, for they were in no condition to be viewed. Here they would lie until the Imperial Fists force had loaded their wargear and wounded onto their strike cruiser for the journey back to the *Phalanx*. The dead would be buried there, and their gene-seed would be extracted to be implanted into another generation of battle-brothers. It should have been a consolation.

Chrysius's helmet sat on the workbench in front of him. He had a little time before the force had to leave this place. He had found some paint and a brush among the workmen's tools on the fuel depot. Before he started work he glanced through the viewport again and caught his own face, illuminated by the ruddy light of the dark Euklid IV, covered in the gang tattoos that were far more monstrous than anything he had seen on the faces of the Iron Warriors. There had been nothing monstrous on the face of his friend Kholedei, either, but perhaps it had been there, exploited by the Inquisition to fulfil their mission at any cost – even the cost of fellow Space Marines' lives.

Perhaps Kholedei had been justified. Perhaps the Inquisition's mission had outweighed any Imperial Fist. Chrysius realised now, for the first time, he did not know.

As dawn broke on the far edge of Euklid IV, igniting the planet's atmosphere anew, Sergeant Chrysius began to draw the black stripe down the centre of his helmet. Brother Myrdos had never avenged his shame of losing at the Tournament of Blades. Chrysius doubted he would never avenge his shame, either. But until he did, or more likely until he died, this would be the face he would wear.

THE VORAGO FASTNESS

DAVID ANNANDALE

'To be seconded to the Deathwatch is a great honour,' Captain Vritras had said. 'For the warrior, and for the entire Chapter.'

There had been just enough irony in the captain's tone for Teiras to feel he could respond freely. So he had. 'For an Ultramarine, certainly.'

'And for a Black Dragon?'

'This must be a joke.' He had never heard of any brother from a Chapter of the Twenty-first Founding serving in the Ordo Xenos's force of Adeptus Astartes.

Vritras's smile had been tight-lipped, grim and bitter. 'Of course it is a joke,' he had said. 'The Inquisition is famous for its sense of humour.'

Sense of humour? Perhaps not, Teiras thought now as he approached a massive set of doors aboard the Inquisition battle cruiser *Iudex Ferox*. *But a sense of the perverse? Ah, that's a different story.* And still he looked for the joke.

Beyond the doors was a small theatre. The curving rows of seats descended to a proscenium stage, where a marble lectern was flanked by rows of pict screens and, to the left, a hololith table. There were four other warriors present. They turned to look at him as he worked his way down to take a seat. He ran his eyes over the insignia on their right shoulders, and it seemed to him that here, perhaps, was the punch line. He started to grin.

'Do we amuse you?' growled the Flesh Tearer sitting in the front row.

Teiras shook his head. 'Your pardon, brother. I meant no offence. It is the situation that makes me smile.'

'What do you see that we don't?' the Relictor demanded. He sounded no more friendly than the Flesh Tearer, but had none of the other's defensiveness. There was a haughtiness to his tone.

'He sees a pattern, as now do I.' The speaker sat on the far right and at the rear of the chamber, as far as possible from the dim light of the single lume-strip that ran down the centre of the ceiling. He was the only Space Marine present who wore his helmet, and his right pauldron had no insignia. His livery was of the Deathwatch alone. He was anonymous.

'So do I,' said a soft voice. The Son of Antaeus sat a few rows back from the front, and he was a head taller than any of the others. He was one of the biggest Space Marines that Teiras had ever seen. Only Volos, a fellow Dragon Claw of the Second Company, was larger. Teiras nodded to the Son of Antaeus and took a seat beside him. 'Teiras,' he said. 'Well met.'

'Jern,' said the other, nodding back. He pointed to the others. 'The Flesh Tearer is Utor, and the Relictor is Kyral.' He jerked a thumb over his shoulder. 'And our shadowy friend tells us his name is Gherak.' His gaze focused on Teiras's forehead. 'You'll want to be careful. Our sponsor might decide a head like yours should have a place of honour atop a column.'

'Beauty like mine *is* a rare thing,' Teiras agreed, and showed his fangs. From the centre of his head grew a single horn, the gift of an overproducing ossmodula zygote. Like the other mutated battle-brothers of his Chapter, Teiras had moulded the bone protuberance, teasing out the shape it suggested and sheathing it in adamantium. It was conical, and curved to a lethal point. 'I plan to keep my head where it is,' he said, and as he held up an arm and flexed his fist down, a bone-blade suddenly jutted out from his wrist. The flash of pain as it emerged was so familiar, he didn't even wince.

'I shouldn't worry,' said a new voice. 'Your head is of far more use to me attached to your shoulders.'

Teiras faced forwards as Lord Otto Dagover stalked towards the lectern. The Black Dragon had known the name of the inquisitor whose orders he would be following, but little else. As monstrous as Teiras knew he looked to most mortals, and to more than a few Space Marines with his horn and stone-grey flesh, he was a physical ideal next to the creature that now stood before them. Dagover had so many bionic modifications, he might have passed for a member of the Adeptus Mechanicus were it not for the ostentatious morbidity of his remaining flesh. His ornate power armour was night-black, with silver spines rising along the shoulders and back. He was accompanied by a constant hum of servo-motors, and Teiras wondered how much of Dagover's original being was encased in ceramite, and how much of the ceramite encased anything at all.

Both of his arms, certainly, were artificial. They were longer than a human's, had several joints and ended in iron-clawed fingers that twitched at the air as if searching for prey. Above his shoulders, Dagover's head emerged from his gorget like a malignant tumour. There had been no juvenat treatments for the inquisitor. He wore his centuries and his battle scars like badges of honour and masks of horror. A few strands of grey hair hung like coarse spider's webs from a scalp that flowed like molten wax off his skull. Oversized lenses replaced eyes in something that was not so much a face as it was a hanging curtain of wrinkled, savaged flesh. Hooks pulled back the cheeks to reveal an almost lipless mouth. Teeth poked through, but they weren't genuine fangs like those of Teiras and Utor; they had simply been filed to cruel points.

Draped over the inquisitor's armour, pierced by its spines, was a cloak. It was a meticulously crafted leather patchwork, the different shades of hide suggesting the colours of a noble house. It took a moment for Teiras to realise the cloak was composed of flayed xenos skin.

Dagover's arms reached out and tapped at the screens and table. Picts of a planet appeared on the former, while the table generated a hololith of an immense fortification with a towering spire at its centre. 'Your mission,' he began without preamble, 'concerns the planet Discidia.' His words were amplified by a speaker in his gorget, but his natural voice was still audible, its cancerous rasp overlaid by the electronic scrape. There was just enough delay to create a sepulchral reverberation; the sound was redolent of all the nuances of pain both given and received. 'Your target,' Dagover went on, 'is the Vorago Fastness.' He gestured at the hololith.

Teiras took in just how many structures were contained within the walls displayed before them. There was a sprawling, disorganised quality to the layout, as if the buildings had sprung up over time and been built without regard for anything except the convenience of the moment. There was nothing liveable about the fortification, and it was far too large to be barracks. Judging from the scale of the buildings, the Fastness covered thousands of square kilometres. The meaning of the tower and the height of the walls registered. 'A prison,' he said.

Dagover nodded. 'A most profitable one, thanks in part to its quarries. One in particular also has a certain xeno-archaeological interest. My *colleague*,' he said with weary loathing, 'Inquisitor Salmenau has been overseeing a dig site at this location,' a light began to blink near the north-east wall, 'and his team has found a xenos relic of considerable importance.'

Kyral sat forwards. 'What kind of relic?'

To Teiras's surprise, Dagover answered. 'Early reports point to a cyranax weapon.'

There was a pause. The cyranax watchers were a xenos race that existed somewhere between myth and rumour. Teiras had heard whispers that the creatures possessed world-destroying technology, but he didn't know anything verifiable about them, not even whether or not they still existed. Teiras wasn't sure what was more startling: the nature of the information, or the fact that Dagover had revealed it so readily. The inquisitor smiled, and seemed to chill the air by several degrees. *A sense of humour, by the Throne*, Teiras thought.

Utor broke the silence. 'And the problem is?'

'Other than the fact that Inquisitor Salmenau's judgement makes him an unfit guardian of that weapon? An enemy force has arrived before us to claim the prize.'

'What enemy?' Teiras heard Utor's temper flare at Dagover's tease.

'The ruling council of Discidia has no idea. But their fragmentary intelligence strongly suggests the necrons.'

Teiras fought back a snort of disbelief. A single kill-team against an enemy about which so little was known beyond its utter implacability? Was there more information available than he suspected? 'What connection do the necrons have to the cyranax watchers?' he asked.

'Unknown, if indeed there is one.'

Better and better, Teiras thought. 'Are we really an adequate response to–'

'You are more than adequate,' Dagover interrupted. 'The necron force must be a small one, or all of Discidia would already have fallen, and Inquisitor Salmenau, of all people, has been able to stand up to the siege for a week. Furthermore, it is the will of the Inquisition that Discidia and its resources be preserved intact, not turned to so much glass and cinder by a large-scale war.' He began to shut down the pict screens. 'We will reach Discidia in a week.' He turned to go.

'How long can Inquisitor Salmenau hold out?' Teiras asked.

'His supplies should last for another five days.' The inquisitor's carrion flesh smiled again. 'If we get there too soon, there will be no incentive for him to leave his refuge, now will there?' Then he left the stage, metal and death disappearing back into the shadows.

'Well,' said Jern after a few moments. 'He told us a lot more than I was expecting.'

'But not the important thing,' Teiras observed.

'Which is what?' Kyral asked.

'Why us?'

Black Dragon. Son of Antaeus. Relictor. Flesh Tearer. Two fell results of the Cursed Founding, one member of a Chapter that was dancing on the edge of outright heresy, and one warrior whose genetic makeup was so corrupted that madness was not just a risk but a destiny. And if Gherak felt the need to keep his Chapter allegiance anonymous in *this* company, then his secrets were dark indeed. They were all from Chapters that were, at best, regarded with suspicion by the Inquisition and the more orthodox Adeptus Astartes. At worst, they were the targets of outright ostracism and investigation. The situation was more than bizarre. Not one of them should be in the Deathwatch. Teiras had no idea what game Dagover was playing, but he knew now that he was a long way from seeing the punch line to the inquisitor's joke.

Why us?

The feudal lords of Discidia were a forward-thinking aristocracy. Centuries earlier, the Vorago Fastness had been built with room for a near-infinite prison population. Larger than any one city on the planet, it had been conceived as a means of political control at least as much as a dumping ground for the criminal element. Discidia had the highest incarceration rate of any world in the Maeror subsector. It also had the lowest crime rate. Justice there was rudimentary to the point of being meaningless: any infraction, or even the mere perception of one, resulted in the accused being thrown into Vorago and forgotten. The abysmally short life expectancy in the prison hive kept the population density to merely hellish, rather than impossible.

Faced with such a surplus of space, the wise and benevolent regents of Discidia did the only logical thing: they imported prisoners. They let it be known to all neighbouring systems that here was a location where undesirables of whatever description could be sent and held for a suitable remuneration. And so, for generations had come a flood of inconvenient heirs, rivals and political malcontents, men and women who, for one reason or another, could not simply be assassinated, or whose continued existence was more profitable than their deaths. Those were the prisoners over whom an actual watch was kept, to make sure that they stayed alive for as long as was useful. Over time, the Vorago Fastness had become a profitable enterprise, feeding the wealth of Discidia's growing leisure class, and financing its exploding prison bureaucracy.

But the prison was a source of riches not only for what it held, but also for what it exported. It was built – by design – over many of the planet's richest deposits of benthamite. The stone was hard and smooth as marble, yet had the gloss and shine of obsidian. In its pure state it was as translucent as glass, but when other minerals were introduced it took on colours of extraordinary richness and hue. Its beauty and strength made it highly sought after for the construction of monuments. Very little struck awe into the heart of the masses with quite the same power as the sight of a sunset filtered through the beyond-royal blues and reds of a benthamite triumphal arch. And very little gladdened the hearts of Discidia's nobility quite like the quarrying of one of the subsector's most valuable resources by slave labour.

All of this Teiras learned on the journey to Discidia. A surprising amount he heard from scarified lips of Dagover himself, who seemed to be everywhere in the lead-up to mission launch. Teiras asked him only once why he had put together a kill-team with such a roster. Dagover had only smiled in response. He had tilted his head, and the black lenses of his bionic eyes had flashed with the reflected light of a lume-strip. Teiras was sure the effect was deliberate.

And on the seventh day, the Thunderhawk gunship *Merciless* flew Dagover and the kill-team over the capital city, Carcera Lucrosus, towards the Lord Governor's palace. On Dagover's orders, the pilot came in low, skimming the rooftops. At first, Teiras had thought the approach was strategic, but there was no sign of conflict. The war they were heading for was confined within the walls of Vorago. What he was granted through the viewing block was a thorough perspective of the city. He glanced at Dagover. The inquisitor was watching him closely. *There's something he wants me to see,* Teiras thought. He looked down again, absorbing and evaluating.

Carcera Lucrosus was vast, and its regions varied between forests of glittering spires and shantytown swamps. But the slums were far more sparse, and took up far less real estate than Teiras was used to seeing in a city this size. He also saw none of the ant-like activity he would have expected. The slums were half-empty, some of them wholly deserted, their ramshackle structures collapsed into rubble.

The more affluent areas, on the other hand, were teeming. Sky-reaching needles of ambition and cathedrals of wealth sprouted in enclave after enclave of privilege and entitlement. Architectural follies fought to outdo each other in size and luxury. But the palace, centuries older than any of the buildings that surrounded it, was the grandest monstrosity of them all. Nestled beside the equally monumental outer wall of the Vorago Fastness, it sprawled for blocks, a tasteless concatenation of domes and minarets built beside and on top of each other like a cluster of gold-plated mushrooms. It was an unrestrained explosion of wealth and power. There was no tempering by faith; as evening fell and the *Merciless* lowered itself to the landing pad, Teiras saw a few devotional figures worked into friezes along the bases of some of the domes, but these gestures seemed hollow, mere artistic fillips.

'This is a corrupt city,' Gherak muttered.

Teiras agreed.

Dagover met with Lord Governor Pallens alone. His accompanying servo-skull sent a real-time hololith back to the Space Marines on the Thunderhawk. Teiras studied the updating images closely. The meeting room struck him as simply a throne room with variations. Even though the flicker and the grain of the hololith, the ostentation of the chamber was glaring. Floor-to-ceiling panels alternated between riotous mosaics of gold and benthamite, and enormous mirrors. Wealth and light reflected each other and turned the room into a narcissistic paroxysm. The work tables and pict screens almost disappeared beneath the visual weight of the ornamentation.

Pallens sat on a throne in the centre of the hall. The designs on the floor radiated out from the throne's dais, as if the Lord Governor were the fount of all knowledge in the room. But Pallens was not looking happy. He was a short, heavy-set man draped with too much finery, and he shrank from the sight of Dagover. Now the rays from the dais were so many accusatory fingers, pointing at the callow little man in the big chair. That he was flanked by the other members of the ruling council didn't seem to comfort him much. They were cowering just as badly. But all of them, despite their fear, still had an arrogant glint in their eyes. They resented the necessity of outside intervention, Teiras saw. They wanted a dirty job done so they could get back to the business of accumulating wealth. Over the vox transmission, Teiras heard all sorts of references to piety and worship of the Emperor, and he believed not a one.

Dagover consulted a data-slate. 'These floor plans are entirely accurate?' he asked the functionary who stood before the table. 'There has been no deviation from them at any time during or since the construction of the tower?'

'Those are the amended versions, lord,' the other man said. 'They illustrate the control room as it was built, not as it had been planned.'

Dagover nodded. 'And the power supply?'

'Prepared to your specifications.'

Dagover turned to go.

'When will the Fastness be able to resume normal operations?' Pallens asked. His voice shook, but his greed and arrogance overrode his fear.

'You are asking when Discidia will be free of the vile xenos taint?' Dagover's tone would have stopped the heart of a more intelligent man.

'Yes, yes,' Pallens said. 'Of course. But Vorago has been closed to all traffic in and out since the incident began, and every day that goes by, our economy–'

'Will stagnate and rot until, by the Emperor's good grace and my good will, I say otherwise,' Dagover snarled. He stormed from the hall.

There was nothing useful in that briefing, Teiras thought, as the hololith blinked out. *It was all for show. Why does he want us to see this?*

Teiras examined the bolter shell before inserting it into the magazine. The kraken penetrator round came to a solid adamantium tip. It was a thing of beauty.

The kill-team was loading up before leaving the *Merciless* for the generatorium. Dagover had distributed the equipment they would be deploying against the necrons. Along with the specialised shells, the bolters were Mark IVs with range finders, and the grenades were haywire variants. The weapons were impressive, but they were also, Dagover explained, best guesses. The hope was that the kraken rounds would tear through the enemy's armour, and that the grenades would disrupt the creatures' eldritch energy. The hope, not the certainty.

'We know one thing with absolute certainty about the necrons,' Dagover said as the Deathwatch loaded up. 'And that is that we know *nothing* with certainty. Remember that. Be surprised by nothing. You will be fighting a foe who seems to be composed of nothing but armour. What would incapacitate a man or an ork is a mere inconvenience to a necron. We do not even know if they can be truly killed.'

'Why is that?' Teiras asked.

'They vanish,' said Kyral.

'You've fought them before?'

The Relictor nodded. 'Once. With my Chapter brothers.' He tapped his bolter's magazine. 'Let us hope these are more effective than standard arms.'

'What do you mean "they vanish"?'

'Just that. You'll see. Instead of dying, they simply disappear. They leave no corpses.'

'Nothing to study,' Jern realised. 'Any advice?'

'Hit them as hard and as quickly as possible.'

'Disrupt, paralyse, then exterminate,' Dagover supplied. 'And beware their weapons. As far as we have been able to determine though battlefield observation, their beams flay matter in molecular layers. Organic or inorganic makes no difference. It is simply sliced away to nothing.'

Teiras grimaced. The concept of the xenos weapon was distasteful. It lacked the directness, the brutal truth, of Imperial guns. He loaded the last of the kraken rounds, murmured a prayer of benediction over the magazine, then slammed it home in the bolter. Teiras liked these weapons. He left the *Merciless* eager to put them to the test.

The generatorium was vast. Its massed ranks of immense turbines marched into the distant gloom of the hall beneath a vault whose frescoes depicted the heroic rise and rise of Discidia's ruling caste. The particular blessing of the Emperor that they laid claim to was depicted as nothing less than their due. The walls and floor vibrated with the white-noise hum of the turbines. Here, power for the entire city was produced. Dagover was about to steal all of it for a few crucial seconds.

In an open space before the turbines was the teleporter that had been brought down from the *Iudex Ferox*. It was ancient. There was an artisanal touch to the ornate pylons that surrounded the pad, in the brass keys of the bulky cogitator, and in the inlaid mosaic of runes on the pad itself. This was a relic. A survivor, Teiras suspected, from the Dark Age of Technology. One of the treasures that the Inquisition held for its own particular use.

'It's glorious,' Kyral said. The Relictor ran a gauntlet over the surface of the cogitator. The machine gleamed with the patina of enormous age.

Jern seemed more concerned with the implications of its presence. 'How are we using this?' he asked.

'To teleport into the control room of the Fastness.'

'Control *room*?' Utor protested.

Jern exchanged a look with Teiras. 'Which I am sure,' the Black Dragon said, 'is located at the top of that centrally located tower, just as I am sure that there is no teleport homer to keep us from phasing into the floor or walls.'

'Quite,' Dagover said.

'This is madness,' said Utor.

Teiras looked at Gherak. The other Space Marine said nothing. He stood motionless, waiting, his posture suggesting indifference, as if he had seen this game of the inquisitor's many times before. 'All right,' Teiras said to Dagover. 'What's the trick?'

'Data,' Kyral said, still hovering over the cogitator.

'Very good.' The mask of ravaged flesh beamed, and the effect was obscene. 'Given enough information and power, this teleporter has a flawless precision of beam.' He held up the data-slate. 'Hence my insistence that the floor plans be accurate.'

Teiras felt himself grinning. However magical this equipment, there was a lunatic recklessness to the mission that spoke to him. It held a violent promise, one into which he could sink his fangs. He strode onto the pad. 'Brothers,' he said, 'the xenos foe awaits. Shall we go meet it?'

Reality blinked. The continuity of existence was severed as two spaces conjoined. There was the infinitesimal, but all-encompassing, moment during which the self ceased to be, and then Teiras had being once again.

The teleporter performed as Dagover had promised. The kill-team materialised in a circular chamber about twenty metres in diameter. Armourglas windows, overlooking the full prospect of the Vorago Fastness, ran around the entire periphery. Below them sat banks of cogitators, control panels and pict screens. In the centre of the floor, what looked like an extremely thick pillar was, in fact, an elevator.

Most of these details Teiras did not take in consciously until later. What registered in the moment were the half dozen metal skeletons that stood before him. They did not wear armour because they *were* armour. They were life of a kind, but their shape was death, their faces as unchanging and unforgiving as the bone they resembled. There was little in the eyes of these warriors beyond a driving hatred for anything that did not share their inorganic half-life. And there was no surprise. They raised their weapons and fired.

Teiras threw himself down. A gauss beam struck where his head had been a moment before. It glanced against his helmet, and warning runes lit up in his retinal display. The merest touch of the beam had damaged the ceramite. The light of the beam was the green of corruption and disease. A death ancient, merciless and incomprehensibly alien had found its expression in that light.

The space was too confined for the haywire grenades. Teiras returned fire with his bolter. The kraken rounds punched into the necrons, some going all the way through to the wall behind. A ghoul jerked and stumbled from the hits, its gun bucking up and the beam shearing away the rockcrete of the ceiling.

But the necron didn't fall. It stepped forward. It had been damaged, but it showed no pain. The lack of expression on its face was chilling, because what looked like a helmet was the creature itself, unflinching before the hail of destruction; and still the eyes glowed with that cold, immovable hatred.

Disrupt. Teiras rolled forward and came up like a battering ram against the undead thing's chest. He knocked it to the ground. *Paralyse*. Kneeling on the torso, he snapped out a bone-blade and plunged it into the necron's neck. With a vicious thrust, he severed the thing's head, and yet its hands reached up, seeking to pull off his helmet. *Exterminate*. He brought a fist down, pulverising the skull. There was a spine-grating electronic wail of agony. Then it cut off, and the necron was gone. Its vanishing was another reality blink. Existence cracked and reformed, taking the necron with it. Teiras felt himself twitch, as if he had been violently woken. Around him, there was nothing but a dispersing afterglow of rotted green.

There were other wails, a choir of the damned, as Teiras stood up. His kill-team brothers had destroyed the other machinic ghouls, but even in their passing, the creatures left behind a taint. There was something wrong with the atmosphere of the control room, as if a cemetery had learned rage. Jern's opponent still struggled. The Son of Antaeus, his armour bearing deep scrapes where a flayer beam had touched him, had shot the necron's limbs off, but the thing still tried to squirm forwards to attack him. The five of them watched for a few moments more before Jern dispatched the abomination with a shot to the head.

'A good start,' Utor said.

Kyral snorted. 'We've done little more than alert the main force to our presence.'

'So we strike quickly,' Gherak said. It was the first time he had spoken since they had arrived on Discidia.

'Agreed,' Teiras said. He examined the control room's screens. 'The mining rail network is still running.'

'No doubt being used by the enemy,' Jern said.

Utor grunted. 'Then we can reach them all the faster.' Even through the tone-deadening distortion of the Flesh Tearer's helmet speaker, Teiras heard a false note in Utor's eagerness. It wasn't bravado he was detecting – the Space Marine worried about the prospect of battle did not exist. This was something else. Utor was working hard to hold himself back, Teiras realised. It wasn't battle that worried him: it was his ability to restrain his fall into the Black Rage. His eagerness and surliness were conscious performances, as if by acting the thuggish berserker he could stave off becoming the real thing.

And Dagover probably selected you precisely for that propensity to madness, Teiras thought.

He traced a finger over a hololith map of the prison's rail system. 'This line passes directly in front of the north face of this tower and crosses the dig site.'

Gears engaged and there was a steady mechanical hum as the elevator suddenly began to ascend. The kill-team faced the doors, bolters up. Gherak stepped forward with a heavy flamer. When the doors of the enclosed metal box opened, he flooded the interior with ignited promethium, bathing the group of necrons within with purging fire. The warriors did not feel pain, and they advanced into the control room, but the flame corroded their bodies. Their legs collapsed within a few steps. The Space Marines crushed the flailing skeletons beneath their boots and watched the bodies vanish in a flare of sickly green. Already, Teiras was growing used to their death wail.

The kill-team piled into the smoking elevator. The walls of the cage were scorched black, and a bas-relief frieze at its rear had been melted to ruin. Kyral pulled the lever that operated the lift. There were only two destinations: the base and the control room. The cage dropped with a rattling groan.

Teiras and Jern took up positions at the doors, and burst through them as soon as they opened, into the night and open air of the Vorago Fastness. They unleashed a stream of bolt-fire as they charged, their kraken shells hammering into the ranks of necrons on the rockcrete platform before them. The others followed, and the kill-team hit the enemy with concentrated punch and momentum. Multiple bolters hit one target then the next, and with the sheer volume of fire, the kraken rounds were lethal this time. Kyral threw a haywire grenade at the end of the platform, catching the necrons in its disruption field. It did not paralyse them, but their movements became jerky and their guns would not fire. The ghouls marched forward out of the field. They were even more ghastly as they twitched. They were creatures from the galaxy's nightmares for whom death had become both meaningless and their only calling.

But the few seconds that the grenade bought were enough, and the bolter-fire did the rest. The necrons went down and vanished, leaving behind the echoes of their hate-filled electronic wails and the uncanny flicker of ghost light.

The kill-team moved forward. Teiras knew they hadn't been properly tried yet. The opposition was still organising. Even so, the assault had been a model of its kind. Every member of the team had fought as if amongst his Chapter brethren. There had been no need for verbal communication, barely even a gesture passing between the Space Marines. A good omen, he thought.

The platform ended at the rail line. The trains of the Vorago Fastness were not designed with passengers in mind. With very few exceptions, anyone travelling through the Fastness did so on foot. The trains were for the far more valuable cargo of benthamite. They were crude maglev affairs, long links of shallow freight wagons with the most basic locomotive imaginable. It was a car just large enough to hold a control unit as simple as the cable-lift's. The lever pulled down would set the train in motion. It would travel to the next stop on the line, where sensors would trip the lever back up, releasing the train from the magnetic field and bringing it to a stop.

The kill-team jumped onto the forward freight wagon. Kyral stood on the locomotive car and held the lever down. The wagons were empty, and the train accelerated rapidly.

'We're under way,' Teiras voxed Dagover back on the *Merciless*.

Maglev or not, the train rattled and shook as they plunged through the monstrous landscape of the Vorago Fastness. Over the centuries, a metropolis of improvised structures had risen. It made Teiras think of a collapsed hive. Shacks of sheet metal and primitive hab-blocks constructed from roughly chiselled slabs of stone tumbled over each other. There was no order, no thought to the assemblages, just a desperate grab for whatever space and materials could be had. Many structures had fallen, returning to the rubble from which they had sprung, crushing the souls that had sought refuge inside them.

Between the ruins and tottering agglomerations that would soon be ruins, the ground was hard-packed dirt and stone. The paths were a twisting labyrinth of switchbacks, random forks and dead ends. Some passed through perpetual night as buildings leaned together to form crumbling roofs over the passageways. The ground rose and fell. Some of the higher elevations ran past sunken windows, evidence that the denizens of the Fastness had built over whatever fell. Beneath the surface, geological strata held the record of imprisonment and death. Above the paths, running at the level of the upper floors of the taller buildings, were the maglev tracks. They were a metal web stitching the space of the Fastness together, the trains transporting the native wealth of the earth over the imported squalor of man.

Down those paths, through the windows and doors of the misery expressed in stone, and in the squares of subsiding wreckage, the human population of the Vorago Fastness swarmed and eddied like a blanket of maggots. The movement was desperate. It was a perpetual clawing for survival. Rotting food, weapons of stone and pipe, shelter or the means to build it, blood clans and shifting alliances – these were the currency that paid for another hour of life, another hour of fighting for the means to fight for another hour.

As the mining train raced through the vistas of the prison, Teiras saw moments of collective effort alternate with blood-soaked riots. The resilience of dignity adjoined the plunge into the bestial. He knew that there were good men and women in the cauldron. From Dagover's description, he understood that the political wealth of the prison meant that far more of the inmates were innocent of anything that he would recognise as a crime than were guilty. But wolves and lambs were both represented in the bubbles of hope and vortices of violence. The nature of such a place permitted no alternative.

The train entered the mining zones of the Fastness, where quarries broke up the chaotic squalor of the habitation sectors. Centuries upon centuries of benthamite extraction had created abysses from which rock was hauled by endless cable. Into them, men descended to an existence of slavery in depths so profound that the sky was lost. As the line ran deeper into regions rich in benthamite, the quarries became more numerous, canyons of darkness yawning beneath the train, while overcrowded towers of stone teetered on narrow plateaus between.

The attack came as the train was going to pass under another track. Teiras saw them lined up on the upper rail, waiting, motionless as armed statues. A dozen warriors, three larger and bulkier than the others. They opened up with a constant barrage of gauss energy before the Space Marines were even in range. The beams sliced the maglev track apart.

Teiras glanced down. They were passing over a quarry. The blackness looked eager to receive them. Ahead, on the other side of the gap in the line, was one of the narrow plateaus. 'Too late to stop,' Kyral warned. Teiras leaned over the rear of their cart, bone-blade out. He hacked at the link between carts. Iron parted before adamantium. He cut the rest of the train away just as they hit the gap.

The necrons' flayer beams had not warped the line. They had simply removed any trace of what had been there, reducing ten metres of track to floating atoms. The train rode air and dropped. The front cart, lighter now than the rest of the train, flew a little bit further as it fell. It missed the canyon by metres, slamming into the plateau on a hard diagonal. The kill-team was catapulted from the cart. Teiras curled into a ball and hit the ground like a meteor. He came to a stop when he smashed into the wall of a shack. The unmortared stone collapsed around him. He rose, shrugging off the debris and blinking away the amber warning runes before his eyes. His armour was damaged, but still functional.

The kill-team gathered in the street beside the cart. The landing had killed a dozen prisoners. Their deaths were unavoidable; there was no space in this anthill of humanity for anything to come down without harm. Teiras did not look back at the demolished hab behind him. He turned his attention instead to the street. It was barely four metres across, and moved uphill in a relatively straight line for several hundred metres before taking a sharp bend to the right. Vorago's haphazard architecture leaned over it. The roofs of some of the buildings almost touched each other, sealing the street in permanent night.

'They'll be coming soon,' said Kyral.

'Good,' Utor snarled.

Jern said, 'These structures are a gift.'

'Agreed.' *Ambush paradise*, Teiras thought.

Gherak pointed to a pair of buildings on opposite sides of the street near the top of the hill. 'There,' he said. They looked as stable as anything here was, and they had windows facing each other and looking back down the street.

The Deathwatch charged uphill. Desperate humanity parted before the Space Marines, looking at them with neither hope nor fear, only the feral calculation of survival. Teiras and Jern took the building on the right. There were no stairs between floors. Instead, there were holes cut on alternating sides of each ceiling with a large block of stone placed underneath. An ordinary human could climb to the next floor without too much struggle. The Space Marines leaped. They zigzagged from floor to floor until they reached the top. There were perhaps twenty Fastness denizens here. As Teiras and Jern ran to the windows, a woman approached them. She had short grey hair that looked as if it had been shorn with a knife. Her age was difficult to guess – all the faces here had the worn look of lifetimes of hard experience – but she carried herself with a commanding bearing born of sheer determination.

'My lords, are you here to kill us or save us?' she asked. Her tone was respectful, but unafraid.

'Neither,' said Teiras. 'I'm sorry.' He was.

'And those creatures?'

'They have not come here to kill you specifically, but they will, all the same.'

She nodded. 'Then, my lords, I pray you: do not leave this place unchanged.' Then she stepped back. Other prisoners clustered around her, as if for protection.

What must not go unchanged? Teiras thought. *Us, or the prison?*

With Jern in position, Teiras climbed out the window and up onto the top of the building. He checked the lower end of the street. Nothing yet. There was time to refine the ambush. He loped from rooftop to rooftop, until he was about halfway down the slope. Opposite him, Gherak kept pace. They dropped at the same moment, lying flat on the roofs. The necrons had arrived.

The xenos ghouls had descended from their perch on the maglev line and were now moving up the street in a wedge formation. The spaces between them were so regular, their steps so precisely synchronised, that they could have been a single machine. But the aura of death that radiated from them had nothing to do with the unfeeling and the inorganic. It was as livid as the green of the gauss rifles. As mechanical and emotionless as the actions of the necrons appeared to be, they were motivated by an ineradicable hatred, older than human civilisation.

The necrons sought out the Space Marines through a process of brutal elimination. They simply killed everything in sight. Their gauss beams played over the prisoners, flaying them to the bone in agonising instants. The street erupted with a cascade of fragmented screams and violently shed flesh. The necrons swept the beams back and forth, slicing away the supports of the surrounding structures. The patchwork city collapsed in their wake, stone and blood spilling with a roar to close the street behind the marching abominations.

Teiras looked through his bolter's range finder. He zeroed in on the skull of the leading necron. It was one of the larger ghouls. Invisible beams bounced between the scope and the target, and the precise distance to the xenos appeared as a readout in the sight. Teiras adjusted his aim and fired. He held the gun steady as he pumped a stream of penetrator rounds into the necron's skull. It was like sniping with a bolter. The head disintegrated. The necron phased out in mid-step. Gherak took out another in the next rank. The perfection of the wedge was shattered.

The necrons retaliated. They charged forward and brought their beams to bear on the rooftops. But Teiras and Gherak had already moved on, leaping to the next building down and firing again. Two more ghouls uttered their electronic scream and vanished. The necrons spread their fire wide and low, and all the lopsided, deathtrap piles of stone for a hundred metres on both sides of the street now fell. Teiras saw the destruction coming to his position, and he jumped, dropping ten metres to the ground. He stuck the landing, and felt the jar of impact shoot up his spine. Gherak was also down and at his side in a moment. They were now behind the necron wedge, and they unloaded their clips into the ghouls at the same time as their brothers in the forward positions began shooting. A haywire grenade joined the enfilading fire, and the necrons were stitched with mass-reactive devastation. More were sent back to the hell from which they had crawled.

The ghouls staggered forward, as if against a strong wind, and emerged from the grenade's disruptor field. Beams raging, they toppled the buildings at the head of the street. Kyral, Jern and Utor jumped from the windows and outran the destruction, closing with the necrons and firing still. Teiras and Gherak advanced, and now they were a pincer snapping shut on the enemy.

The remaining necrons split into two groups and charged forward and rear, matching the Deathwatch's aggression, but not the kill-team's speed. The Space Marines came at the ghouls in sudden doglegs and diagonal sprints, keeping their movements unpredictable.

The street was a shrunken space, filled with rubble and smashed bodies. The two forces were in close quarters now. They were seconds from clashing together.

Utor leapt forward, reckless. A beam sideswiped his midsection. The Flesh Tearer fell forward, but then rose to a crouched firing position. His anger roared from the barrel of his gun.

'Brother Utor?' Jern voxed.

'Stupid,' Utor rasped. His breathing was laboured. 'Fine. Fine. Come on, then. Fight.' He spoke with the staccato of strain, but not, Teiras thought, from pain. He was holding back his rage with a slippery grip.

They had all taken glancing hits, but their armour held. Utor had suffered serious tissue loss in his midriff, but his Larraman cells' rapid formation of scar tissue was compensating. His breathing was a constant sub-vocalised growl. He fought with increasing savagery. It was as if every violent gesture was a blow against the madness that promised a deeper violence. But despite the toll it must have been taking on him, Utor's brutal energy was infectious. Teiras felt himself exhilarated by battle. The fury of the Emperor was upon him, and nothing could stem its charge.

The Space Marines moved as one, the genetic insanity of Utor's blood transmuted into an infusion of strategic savagery in his brothers.

Brothers.

Brothers.

Teiras felt the spirit of battle granting them the blessing of unity, turning them into the fingers of a single fist.

They raced over the final metres, taunting fate and lethal weaponry. Crimson runes flashed in Teiras's retinal lenses as a flaying beam glanced against his arm. But the contact was brief and shaken as he unleashed a torrent of bolter shells into the necron's face. Then he was moving forward through the skeleton's shriek and vanishing flash. In his peripheral vision, his brothers were moving with the same grace of perpetual killing.

Ahead of him, the last of the larger, more powerful ghouls levelled its gauss blaster at his chest. Teiras threw himself to one side. The air shrieked with destructive energy and slashed at his armour's flank. The necron adjusted its aim. Teiras tucked himself into a roll underneath the barrel of the gun. Bone-blade unsheathed, Teiras slashed upwards, cutting through the fuel line. The weapon disappeared in a flash of disordered energy, and took the top half of the necron with it.

Teiras stood up. To his left, Jern knocked the barrel of a ghoul's blaster aside with his bolter. The necron countered with inhuman speed, reversing the gun and smashing its stock against the side of Jern's head. The blow would have staggered Teiras, but Jern's only reaction was to slam his bolter down on the necron's crown with such force that the machine head seemed to implode. Then it was gone. The last of the other necrons were also nothing more than the crackle of dissipating energy.

Utor stood over the spot where his foe had been. The growl in his breathing had ratcheted up. He was shifting his weight back and forth from foot to foot, a hunter looking for a reason to spring. Gherak stood in front of him, close enough to get his attention, far enough not to be an immediate threat. His bolter was mag-locked to his thigh, his arms at his side. 'Brother Utor,' Gherak said. 'Are you with us?' His tone was even, measured, neutral. When Utor didn't respond, Gherak repeated the question.

There was a brief pause in the rattling breath.

'We stand with you,' Gherak said. 'We stand in the Emperor's light. Can you feel it? Can you feel His blessing? It is upon our mission, it is upon this action and it is upon you.' He raised his right arm, hand open, palm up. 'Draw strength from His light, brother. Draw focus and clarity. He calls you to our mission, and it is far from over. We still have need of your strength, and of the gift that is yours alone.'

Teiras would have pledged his oath that he *heard* Utor blink. The Flesh Tearer stopped his rocking. 'Brother Gherak,' he said. He clasped forearms with the other Space Marine.

'We are close,' Kyral said. He was consulting the map on his data-slate. 'The target is on the other side of this plateau. A few thousand metres.'

They set off at a quick march. As they passed the wreckage of the building where Jern had been stationed, Teiras saw that the woman who had spoken to them had survived the collapse. She was helping dig for other survivors. She looked up, and Teiras nodded to her. She gazed back, impassive.

The kill-team moved beyond the destruction. Though the road turned at the top of the hill, it was faster to climb over the low houses and move straight towards their destination.

Teiras joined Gherak and opened a private vox-channel. 'You handled Utor well, brother,' he said.

Gherak shrugged. 'The true madness was not upon him.'

'But he was teetering on the edge. You brought him back. I thought your approach demonstrated an unusual understanding.'

'You mean I didn't call for his immediate execution?'

Interesting, Teiras thought. It was the first flash of emotion he had heard from Gherak. 'I meant that to view the call in his blood as in any way a gift takes a rare insight.'

'Do you regard your own mutation as a curse?'

Bless the curse. The refrain of the Black Dragons' holy communion came back to Teiras. 'My Chapter's creed is not that crude,' he answered; *and neither, it seems, is yours,* he thought. He waited for Gherak to speak again, but the other had fallen silent.

The train had taken them north and west from the tower, and by now the kill-team had travelled most of the way to the outer wall. They were, Teiras calculated, approximately level with the Lord Governor's palace. There were no more houses now as they entered mining territory again. There was a rise in the terrain ahead, and from the other side came a pulsing green glow and the *crump* of explosions.

At the crest of the rise, a quarry came into view. This one was not a vertical gulf, more a narrow box canyon. It had been dug into the hill, creating ragged, oppressive cliffs on either side of a steep, uneven slope. From its depths came the unholy flashes and echoing energy crackles of xenos warfare.

The kill-team descended the slope. The broken surface gave the Space Marines plenty of cover. They moved from boulder to boulder. On the other side of a large tumble of stone, they saw the siege. There were ten necron warriors. Before them was a monstrous face fifty metres high, and they were assaulting it with a relentless, untiring, mechanical rhythm. The face bore the disfigurements of a week of unceasing assault. Its features had blurred and crumbled, and what its true character had been was now impossible to determine. It had never been human, that much was sure. Teiras could see the vague suggestion of scales, and its eye sockets were much too far apart, as if the being represented had possessed 180-degree vision. More disturbing yet was that it did not appear to be carved from the rock. At first, Teiras thought that it looked as if it somehow had been *formed* by the rock, as natural an extrusion as a crystal. But that too was wrong. He had the process reversed, he realised. The rock had been formed by the face. Strata exposed by the dig showed the record of metamorphism radiating out from it. Benthamite and all its glory were the mere by-product of the face's creation.

Whatever its composition, the face had withstood days of incessant necron fire. So had the door in its roaring mouth. It was made of the same mysterious stone as the face itself, but its strength, too, was failing at last. It was pitted and crumbling. It had the visual consistency of sponge, even though it was still standing. The necrons eroded it further by the second.

The skeletal warriors were as rooted as turrets, moving only to play their gauss beams over a resisting part of the door. They were directed by a lone figure. It carried a staff that to Teiras resembled a cross between an ecclesiarch's sceptre of office and a spear. He caught a glimpse of the creature's face. It was the expressionless skull of its race, but it had only one eye in the centre of its forehead. The emerald glow of the orb was brighter and more piercing than those of its fellows. Its gaze was one of eternal, unblinking observation, analysis and judgement.

'There is much here to destroy,' Kyral said. He pulled out a melta bomb.

Teiras did the same. The canyon was very narrow, only a few dozen metres wide. The necrons were bunched close together. The invitation was impossible to ignore.

'Let us purge them from the Emperor's sight,' Teiras said.

He and Kyral leaped over the crest of the rubble. They raced down the slope. Halfway down, they were within range, and threw their bombs. The cyclopean necron noticed them and brought its staff to bear at the same moment. It fired. A blistering, shrieking beam slammed into Kyral's chest. The Relictor flew backwards, enveloped by howling light. Then the bombs landed, and there was a different light. This was the light of the Emperor, beyond molten, silver-white as blindness. It swallowed the necrons and their glow of the plague. There was a satisfying unity to the death shrieks. The one-eyed necron was caught at the outer edge of the bombs' radius of effect. Its lower half was liquefied by the heat. Its staff exploded, disintegrating its right arm. It dragged itself forwards a few metres before phasing out, and Teiras was sure he saw hatred in the fading glow of its eye.

Teiras turned to help Kyral, but the Relictor was already on his feet. His chest plate was badly damaged, but whatever the extent of his injuries, he strode on as if they were beneath notice.

'Brother,' Teiras began.

'I require no assistance,' Kyral snapped. He marched the rest of the way to the stone door.

Jern muttered, 'Aristocrat,' as he went past, drawing a snort from Teiras.

They gathered before the ravaged door. The melta bomb attack had damaged it still more, but it had not fallen.

'We are at the door, inquisitor,' Teiras voxed to the *Merciless*.

Dagover opened a general channel. 'Salmenau,' he said, 'let them in. You know you have no choice.'

Several seconds went by, pregnant with resentment. Then the door opened. There was no sound. The unknown stone split into six wedges that withdrew into the sides of the face's mouth. The kill-team moved inside.

The interior was surprisingly small, given the monumental façade. It extended for about thirty metres, was the same in width, and half that in height. The walls, floor and ceiling were smooth and rounded, like the interior of a bubble. Rows of lume-strips had been installed on the ceiling. Along the right-hand wall was a large cogitator and a panoply of excavation and analytical equipment fussed over by a clutch of tech-priests. Power was supplied by a large cable, almost as thick as Teiras's torso. It snaked into the cavern from an opening in the rear wall, near the ceiling. It must have been fed in through the top of the hill, and linked to a power source via the maglev tracks.

The weapon crouched in the middle of the floor. It was fifteen metres long, and two thirds of that comprised a monstrous barrel wide enough to take metre-thick shells – if indeed those were what it fired. Teiras couldn't begin to guess whether it was a projectile or energy weapon. Its body was articulated, and it rested on four insect-like legs. Teiras's lip curled. The cannon was an utterly and disgustingly alien object. There was also something about its design, its machinic mimicry of life, that reminded him of the necrons' guns. There was a connection, he realised. The nature of the link between the necrons and the cyranax watchers was as obscure as the watchers themselves, but the fact of the link was clear. There was a dark logic behind the necrons' presence here, and their pursuit of this gigantic weapon.

Facing the Deathwatch were Inquisitor Salmenau and the survivors of his team. Salmenau had clearly not been expecting serious combat. He was flanked by an Imperial Guard veteran, a man whose facial scars were so extensive that his face had become two eyes glaring out from a mass of thick, leathery tissue, an angry pink in colour. He had also been injured. His combat fatigues hung oddly on his left side, as if chunks of his body were missing. He was soaked in his blood. It seemed to Teiras that standing beside his master was all that the man could still do. The others were scholars, not fighters. They held lasrifles, but would be lucky not to shoot off their own heads.

Salmenau stood in marked contrast to Dagover. They were, Teiras knew, close to the same age, but Salmenau had undergone aggressive juvenat treatments. He seemed much younger, though there was a brittle tautness to his youth. His clothes were torn from combat, but after two weeks of being besieged, he didn't have a hair out of place. The cut of his breeches and coat was severe but stylish. His hand rested on the pommel of a power sword. He was no less grotesque than the massively armoured vulture that waited back on the Thunderhawk.

Dagover's voice crackled from multiple speakers. 'You aren't going to be difficult about this, Armand, are you? There really wouldn't be any point.'

'You cannot have it, Otto.'

'Why not? You don't appear to be doing anything useful with it. If you were going to use it, you would have done so days ago.'

Salmenau paled. 'Such xenos obscenities are to be studied, then destroyed. I would die before risking such a taint to my soul.'

'Which you were about to do. You Amalathians are so hidebound, I'm surprised your pious caution hasn't led you to extinction.'

'You must not take the weapon.'

'Are you going to stop us?'

The scholars were trembling. One of them moaned, but they did not drop their guns. Teiras respected them for that.

Salmenau turned to the kill-team. 'You are being led down the path to heresy and treason,' he said. 'Step off it, for all our sakes.'

Teiras remained still. Dagover's enthusiasm for xenos technology disturbed him, but he had no wish to cast judgement, not when the Black Dragons were often denounced as abominations. And the oath he had sworn on his and the Chapter's honour was to serve the Inquisition in the person of Otto Dagover. The other Space Marines made no move, either.

Salmenau stepped directly in front of the weapon's barrel. 'You will have to kill me,' he said.

'Spare us the melodrama,' Dagover began.

He didn't finish. The room erupted with green light as a barrage of gauss beams blasted through the open door. Teiras hurled himself down and to the side, out of the direct line of fire. Jern hit the ground hard, smoke pouring from his damaged power unit. Salmenau ducked under the weapon, which the necrons' shots avoided, but his retinue was taken apart in seconds, bodies stripped and anatomised.

Teiras crawled forward with his brothers. He was able to stand once he reached the raging 'O' of the stone mouth, staying in cover on the right-hand side. He took a quick look outside. The necrons were coming in force. He saw dozens of warriors, many of them the hulking variants they had fought on the street. At the head of the army came a figure whose tattered robes could not disguise a terrible majesty. It wielded a massive war scythe and towered over its troops, a monarch of death and machinic night. Its skeletal jaw parted, hurling a stream of alien curses as it closed in.

Salmenau scrabbled to the cogitator and turned some dials. There was a hum of power. The chamber glowed faintly and the door began to close. It was sluggish, and the necron fire ate at the wedges. The door stopped dead, leaving an oval about the size of a man. Gherak and Jern took up positions at the gap. Gherak crouched, Jern stood, and they loosed a steady stream of bolter-fire at the advancing ghouls, staggering reloads so the mass-reactive hell never stopped.

Teiras gave them further support. Warriors vanished in crackling glows, but the advance barely slowed. The door continued to erode. The arithmetic was unavoidable. The kill-team only had so many bolter clips. Not nearly enough.

'Ambush,' Gherak growled. 'They gave up part of their force so we would give them access.'

Teiras could almost admire the strategic precision of the necrons' sacrifice. They had abandoned just enough of their number to make that force convincing. It had never occurred to him that he had been gunning down bait.

'This barrier will not last,' Jern said.

Ducking just under the barrel of Jern's bolter, Teiras directed his fire at the approaching noble. The necron didn't even acknowledge the attack. The shells bounced off its form. Teiras thumbed a krak grenade from his belt and hurled it through the gap. The explosion immolated the two foot soldiers on either side of the lord, but the leader marched on without pause. It was less than thirty metres from the door.

Teiras looked back. Kyral was huddled over the back of the weapon. 'Brother Teiras,' he called.

Teiras dropped another warrior, then joined the Relictor. Utor took his place at the door.

Kyral pointed at the power cable. 'That links to the main generatorium for the Fastness. That should be enough power. I think I can connect the weapon. I see enough parallels to other relics of my experience.'

Use the xenos weapon? Teiras thought. The concept was disgusting. And yet...

'This is not done lightly,' Kyral said. He pointed to the disintegrating door. 'Or shall we die in purity and leave this to the necrons?'

Salmenau glared, but drew a laspistol and went to engage in symbolic defence of the entrance.

'I should be able to keep the power connected and flowing,' Kyral began.

'And I must pull the trigger,' Teiras finished. It was midway down the enormous barrel, shaped as if for a handheld weapon, but on a cannon the size of a major artillery piece. Teiras wrapped both arms around the firing mechanism. He watched the door.

The malevolent green intensified. The barrier did not glow so much as become translucent. The gap widened. Teiras's proximity to the weapon was the only thing that saved his life. Salmenau reeled back from the opening, clutching at the perfectly sheared stump where his right hand had been. Utor, Jern and Gherak kept up the fire, even as their armour lost layers to the stray hits they did not move fast enough to avoid. Teiras listened to Utor's breathing. As if sensing he was monitored, Utor announced, 'Do not fear, brothers. If we are to meet the Emperor this day, I shall do so with a clear spirit.'

There was a flash of energy and green corruption. The door vanished. The necrons surged forward, led by their lord. It swung its scythe at Jern with blinding speed and shattered his pauldron. He fell, but was not cut in half. Teiras's eyes widened at Jern's strength. It was as if he wore a second suit of armour.

Utor had pulled his chainsword and was decapitating the warriors almost as quickly as they crossed the threshold to the chamber. Almost. The tide was pushing him back. A group of three converged on Gherak. He roared and threw himself into their midst. Others joined the attack. Individually, they were weaker than a Space Marine, but they fought with a terrible collective precision. Gherak sank under the attack.

Then he threw the attackers off and swung a chainaxe. And as he did so, he burst into flame.

At first, Teiras thought that Gherak had been hit by a flamer. Then he saw that the Space Marine himself was the source of the fire.

Teiras felt a moment of astonishment at the depths of Dagover's game. A Flame Falcon. The most cursed Chapter of the Cursed Founding, the most ill-fated of the Black Dragons' cousins. Declared Excommunicate by the Inquisition, they had, Teiras had always believed, been exterminated, and yet here was one, no doubt existing at the pleasure of Dagover.

What agenda am I aiding by fighting for this man? Teiras thought. But then Kyral shouted '*Now!*' and Teiras thought, *I fight for my brothers.*

The Deathwatch warriors threw themselves back and down.

The necron lord had reached the cannon and it swung its scythe at Teiras.

Teiras heaved back, and fired the gun.

It was as if he had personally triggered a nova cannon. The world vanished in a flash of quasar silver streaked with infernal red. Energies he could not begin to fathom sprang into being. Microseconds merged with eternity. Creation was the negation of all that stood in its path. There was a silent roar so huge it buried all sound except, deep within the core, something that sounded like a hissing whisper.

The light and the sound of otherness faded. In their wake came the almost reassuring rhythm of massive but conventional explosions. And in a straight line from the weapon: nothing. The necrons had vanished. So had a large section of the slope. A wake of pure destruction stretched as far as Teiras could see.

Behind him, Kyral, dazed, was picking himself up. The power cable was a twisting, burning wreck. Teiras imagined the immense recoil of the weapon transformed into annihilating feedback.

He had to know. He tore out of the chamber and scrambled up the cliff wall, punching handholds into the rock face where none presented themselves. It took him less than a minute to reach the top of the rise, and he was in time to see the last of what had been wrought. He had been right. The energy of the recoil had travelled back over the entire power network of the Fastness. The maglev web flashed orange and white, molten tracks dropping down like burning logs. Power nodes were exploding all over the Fastness, bright spheres of light and death in the night. In the distance, the tower swayed. It was the centre of the grid. The generatoria at its base were massive in power, and now massive in death. There was a huge flash. God-flames engulfed its entire height, and moments later the sound arrived, hammering the air and ground with a hollow blast of doom. The tower collapsed straight down, folding again and again in on itself.

Then there were only glows and echoes, and the anticipation of aftermath.

'You are a Recongregator,' Teiras said. Helmet under his arm, he was standing in Dagover's study aboard the *Iudex Ferox*. Gargoyles and the statues of martyred saints lined the walls.

The inquisitor was seated behind a massive desk. Its surface was covered in books whose titles Teiras was content not to examine. Crouched in his armour, his long bionic arms flicking through papers, Dagover reminded him of a scarab. 'And?' Dagover asked. He did not sound displeased that Teiras knew of his radical faction within the Inquisition.

'I want to know what we just did.'

Dagover snorted. 'It is not your place to ask.'

'I realise that. Nonetheless.'

Dagover nodded, that ghastly smile forming once again. 'Why don't you tell me what you think we accomplished.'

'We destroyed a necron raiding force. We also managed to shut down all power, and thus all security measures, of the Vorago Fastness, punch a large hole through its outer wall, and do considerable damage to the city beyond, including bisecting the Lord Governor's palace.'

'Quite,' Dagover said, the grin becoming even wider and more hideous. 'And...?'

'And the prison population has flooded into Carcera Lucrosus. We have effectively unleashed a civil war on Discidia.'

Dagover nodded. 'Would you say that the existing political order on Discidia was worth preserving?'

'No.' Teiras was surprised at how easily the answer came.

'So the wealth of the planet has been preserved, and a regime that was unworthy of the Emperor's light has fallen,' Dagover summed up.

'And this is how it is replaced?' Teiras asked, incredulous.

'You and I agree that the Lord Governor and his cronies were corrupt, but they kept well within the letter of Imperial law. They paid their tithes. They violated no edicts. And their political friends were many. I could not act directly.'

Teiras noticed Dagover's use of the first-person. 'You planned this from the beginning?'

'You flatter me. I took advantage of the opportunity that the necron attack provided.' The inquisitor leaned forward. 'But now, matters have changed as an unintended consequence of a necessary action.' He became deadly serious. 'Creative destruction is necessary for the salvation of the Imperium, Black Dragon,' he said. 'Do not doubt it.'

Teiras thought of the grotesque spectacle that the capital city had presented to him, and found that, indeed, he could not doubt what Dagover said. 'You plan to control the outcome?'

The smile again. 'Whatever faction wins will know that deviation from the good of the Imperium will be met with a most terrible judgement. In the end, a new, more pure order will arise. And so we have another small step towards galactic renewal.'

'That weapon is unlikely to fire again.' It lay in the hold of the *Iudex Ferox*. The back half had been turned to slag.

'No one on the planet will know that.'

The rest of the kill-team was waiting for him outside the study. Gherak had removed his helmet. Teiras looked from one Adeptus Astartes to the next. *We are the damned*, he thought, *fighting for the redemption of the Imperium*.

'Well?' Jern asked.

'Our missions will not lack for interest.'

'Was his visitor present?' Gherak asked.

'Visitor?'

'The ship that docked beside ours while we were on the surface. It sent a shuttle over about an hour ago.'

Teiras shook his head. 'There was no one else there but Dagover.'

'Well, old friend?' Dagover asked.

One of the statues moved. Shadows pulled away from grey armour. Canoness Setheno did not remove her helmet, but Dagover felt her gaze behind it. It was a sensation of discomfort that never faded. 'Your evaluation of the Black Dragon was correct,' Setheno said.

'I understand Inquisitor Lettinger is about to descend upon his company.'

'Then so shall I.'

The pitiless cold of her voice lingered long after she was gone.

STORM OF DAMOCLES

JUSTIN D HILL

DRAMATIS PERSONAE

DEATHWATCH STATION PICKET'S WATCH

Jotunn — Space Wolf, Watch-Commander

Domitian — Imperial Fists Librarian

WATCH COMPANY VIGIL

Nergui — White Scar, captain

KILL TEAM PRIMUS

Priam — Marine Errant

Gualtino — Angels of Redemption

Tula — Star Phantom

Nidal — Warmonger

Ellial — Mortifactor

KILL TEAM ORION

'Last' Leonas — Black Consul

Aslon — Brazen Claw

Brand — Destroyer

Branstonio — Ultramarine

Solovax — Black Guard

KILL TEAM FAITH

Konrad Raimer — Black Templar

Cadvan — Storm Giant, veteran Techmarine pilot

Sardegna — Scion of Sanguinius

Harath — Salamander

Nestia — Crimson Fist

Atilio — Ultramarine

Olbath — Aurora Chapter

Elianus	Howling Griffon
Ragris	Celebrant, Vanguard Veteran
Imano	Lamenter, Vanguard Veteran

KILL TEAM ZEAL: ON LOAN FROM WATCH FORTRESS TALASSA PRIME

Corith	Brazen Minotaur
Eadmund	Brotherhood of a Thousand
Iason	Carcharodon
Hadrian	Black Shield
Moaz Khileni	Raven Guard
Cadmus	Dark Angel
Cerys	Imperial Fist
Mateo Nuoros	Crimson Fist
Kallos	Ultramarines Tyranid War veteran

DEATHWATCH PERSONAE

Loni Ferral	Shipmaster, strike cruiser *Nemesis*

WHITE SCARS FOURTH COMPANY, 'THE TULWAR BROTHERHOOD'

Batbayar Khan	Captain, commander of White Scars Fourth Company, Master of Blades
Khulan	Apothecary
Ganzorig	Honour Guard Fourth Company, standard bearer
Törömbaater	Scout sergeant, Fourth Company

SEPT KE'LSHAN

Aun'ui Hoo'nan	Ethereal

Fireblade M'au	Base commander
Shas'vre Gru'eb	Commander, Security Orbital VX-223
Fio'ui K'or	Earth caste technician
Shas'vre N'loo	Instructor
Shas'vre O'man	Commander, Terrestial Defence Rig
Bro'bul	Air caste commander, Kir'qath defender
Kor'el Um'ng	Commander, Kir'qath defender
Shas'vre Rs'tu	Defence force, Kir'qath defender
Fio'ui Ph'al	Earth caste, chief technician, M'Yan'Ral Base

MU'GULATH BAY VETERANS

Shas'vre Ch'an	Sept Au'taal, Stormsurge pilot
Shas'el Sham'bal	Sept Elsy'eir
Shas'vre Po'lco	Sept N'dras
Shas'vre Mysto	Stormsurge pilot
Shas'el Reet'u	Stormsurge gunner

CADET

Shas'ui H'an	Sept Sa'cea, Stormsurge gunner

PART ONE
THE SEARCH

CHAPTER ONE

LOCATION: MOON QX-937, SEXTON SYSTEM, DAMOCLES GULF, 999.M41

Captain Nergui of the Deathwatch stopped his bike at the top of one of the foothills and looked out into the void. To his left were the uncountable stars that made up the galaxy, the home of humanity, the hope for survival.

To the right were the empty shadows of the Eastern Fringe, where the wide-flung spiral arms threw a last few fingers of light out into the vast night. The light of these lonely stars was bright against the black. But it was to the shadows between them that he turned his gaze, and stared into the darkness. It was always the darkness from which his enemies – the foes of all mankind – came.

He unclasped his helmet and set it into the crook of his elbow. He had sent two kill teams out on this mission but neither of them had returned, and now he was desperate for answers, for a hint of what had happened to them.

This was the third rock they'd visited in as many days, just one of thousands that drifted through the less hospitable parts of the gas clouds in the Damocles Gulf. But what was strange about this one was that it had an atmosphere: thin, sulphurous, but an atmosphere nonetheless.

Nergui turned around. A light appeared over the southern horizon, coming low and winding towards him in great sweeping parabolas. It was Cadvan, formerly of the Storm Giants, searching in the Corvus Blackstar.

'Captain. There's nothing here,' Cadvan voxed as he approached to

within half a mile. The moon was empty apart from an archaic tau communication hub on the southern pole, which did not look like it had been touched for decades.

'No,' Nergui said. 'But this was the last known position of Kill Team Primus.'

He could hear Cadvan grunt. Brother Cadvan was a big, flame-haired, thunder hammer of a warrior. He was the newest recruit to Nergui's chamber and had proved himself the master of saying the obvious. He didn't do subtleties. 'Well. They're not here now.'

Nergui knew arguing with a Storm Giant would be a waste of breath, however sulphurous. 'No,' he said, 'they're not. But they *were* here, and I want to find out what happened to them.'

He closed the vox-link before Cadvan could respond.

Cadvan was right though. There was nothing here, so why did the air reek of xenos taint?

Ahead of Nergui rose the lip of a great crater where some ancient asteroid had smashed into the moon, leaving behind a scar miles wide. Nergui skidded his bike – *Ganbold* – up the loose scree of the rise, using his knees to turn the handlebars. All Chogoreans learnt to ride horses as soon as they were big enough to balance upon a saddle, and they treated their bikes in the same casual way. Riding without hands was a trick White Scars learnt as Scouts, allowing them to fire and reload as they rode down their foes. He did it unconsciously now, knowing when to touch the handlebars just long enough to steady the bike over a rock or round a landmine, and turned towards the next low peak.

Dust and pebbles sprayed out behind as Nergui accelerated up a bare slab of copper-veined black rock. A fissure opened up suddenly before him, and he swerved past, the engine note rising as the incline steepened. He only took hold of the handlebars when the scree got so thick that he had to zigzag his way up. He brought his bike to where the rim of the crater fell precipitously before him, and paused.

Far below, the land was flat and plain, except for where sulphur pools slowly bubbled and spluttered, and the dark circles of smaller craters dotted the land in irregular patterns. Nergui was unusual among the veterans of the Deathwatch in that battle damage had not rendered it necessary to restore his vision. He looked out with narrowed yellow eyes over the boulder fields, craters and sulphur pools, silent except for the gentle hiss of atmosphere and the low revving of his bike. The Corvus made a low pass three miles to the west, banking off towards the polar region.

'I've seen something,' Nergui voxed and revved his bike forwards, over the edge of the crater. His wheels bounced once, twice on the rocks, and then there was nothing but thin air, and the exquisite sense of falling.

Nergui's bike crunched as the reinforced suspension took the impact of hitting the bottom slopes of the crater. Once, twice he bounced. He had to hold on with one hand as *Ganbold* hit rocks and loose scree, the wheels screaming and the tyres beginning to smoke as he reached dangerous speeds, but still he clung on, grinning with the challenge.

In a few seconds the drop began to flatten out, the slopes less sheer as the crater wall approached the bottom. He gunned the engine, bouncing and roaring over fissures and boulders, until the crater levelled out as he approached the centre.

The armour was half buried, about ten miles from the cliff top, in the empty boulder field. Nergui caught it with one hand as he brought *Ganbold* to a skidding halt. The ceramite was blistered and melted, the charred edges dented and scratched, but despite the damage it was unmistakably the shoulder pad from a suit of Mark VI Corvus armour.

He looked around further. Just a shoulder pad. Nothing else. Nergui cursed. No body, no gun, no sign of what had stripped away the layers of ceramite plating. He dusted the dirt from the patches of unmelted armour. Enough of the insignia remained for him to recognise it as the badge of the Marines Errant: a flaming star on a background of midnight blue.

This was Brother Priam's.

He engaged his vox, spoke tersely. 'Cadvan. Bring Domitian here.'

The Storm Giant's voice crackled back. *'What is it?'*

Nergui did not bother answering, but kicked *Ganbold* forwards.

The last telepathic relay had come from this moon. Kill Team Primus were amongst the best the Chapter had – eight of the finest veterans, honed through decades of battle against the alien. Priam had more augmetic parts than an Iron Hand – 'Easy to wound,' he'd laughed, 'but hard to kill.' It was the same for Ellial. Tula. Octavian. Nidal, even. Each of these warriors could have been a captain, like himself. He had led them many times. They could not just have disappeared. There *had* to be more evidence. A clue.

Searching further, Nergui found a few more scraps of Priam's Mark VI power armour – a knee plate and an ankle fitting – and a spare underslung magazine for his combi-bolter. If he knew Priam, the Marine Errant had either made it away from the main battle, to draw the enemy off, or – more likely – he had been the last survivor.

The Corvus Blackstar grew from a dark spot to a blur as it skimmed in over the eastern horizon, just yards from the ground, a line of dust rising in its wake. Even at this speed it would take fifty seconds to reach him. He was about to investigate a deep crater fifty yards to the right when he shivered – an involuntary response, as though ice were dripping down the back of his neck.

'Don't do that,' he almost said, as Librarian Domitian's psychic presence slid into his consciousness, but by then the mind of the Imperial Fists psyker was within him.

There were no words, as such, just compulsions.

+I'm here,+ it seemed to say. +Show me what you have found.+

Nergui held up the shoulder pad and inspected it as though he were looking at it for the first time.

+Ah.+ Domitian was seeing through his eyes. +Priam.+

'Yes.' Nergui shook himself and forced his gaze away from the shoulder pad, but the Librarian's presence had gone.

Nergui had served with all kinds of Librarians in his time. His Chapter's own Stormseers, of course, who revelled in shamanistic rituals and totems, creating a mystery of it all, and then many Librarians from other Chapters. Blood Angels. Space Wolves. The strangest had been the Black Dragon Epistolary named Ulgon. He had bony protrusions on his skull and arms that he used in combat, and he had kept himself very much to himself, and the rest of them had been happy about that.

Ulgon's Chapter had called him back. Nergui doubted he'd have lasted much longer. You could tell the brothers who were destined for death. There was a Lamenters Librarian who had dreamt that he was destined to die on Terra. He had joked about it for a while, but when they were given the mission to clear the drifting hulk named *Heart of Terra*, he had gone silent, and they knew he'd understood. He had held the genestealers back as the rest of his kill team withdrew to a defensible position. It was a good death. It helped, Nergui thought, when you knew it was coming.

But Domitian, the former Imperial Fist, was almost *normal*, at times, Nergui thought. You could almost forget that he wielded such power. But he had the odd habit of entering your mind too much, too invasively, as if he forgot that others did not have his abilities.

Domitian's mind touched Nergui's for a moment.

+We are nearly there.+

'I can see.' Nergui liked to speak the words aloud, even when his interlocutor was just a voice inside his head.

Nergui watched the Corvus approach and lift for a moment, as retro engines fired blue flames. The down-draught threw up a great cloud of grit as it settled on its landing gear, and Cadvan waved as he powered the craft down and checked his screen readings.

The dust was still settling when one of the fore-facing landing ramps lowered and a single figure marched down – small, for a Space Marine, slight, almost. Delicate. Poised. Intense.

Domitian knew all that Nergui had seen, but sometimes he acted as if he did not have the access to others' minds that he did.

'So,' he said, 'you have found Priam's armour.'

Nergui nodded. 'Yes.'

He held out the shoulder pad. Domitian took it and sighed. 'Was it over there?'

Nergui nodded.

'I found these as well,' Nergui said. He held out the other pieces. Domitian smiled pleasantly and nodded.

'Yes, I saw. Now, stay back. Your presence will only obscure the traces. I shall go and see if there is anything left.'

Cadvan jumped down from the Corvus Blackstar's cockpit, his reinforced power-armoured boots crunching into the dust. He took off his helmet and held it in one hand as he strode towards Nergui. The scar across Cadvan's cheek gave the Storm Giant's mouth a lopsided grin. He saw the damage to Priam's shoulder pad and said, 'So they're dead?'

Nergui nodded. 'Priam most likely is.'

Cadvan gave a low and humourless chuckle. 'Has he found anything?' He nodded towards where Domitian was pacing slowly across the ground.

Nergui shook his head. 'Not yet.'

Cadvan waited for a moment. 'Do you think they all died here?'

Nergui was silent for a long time, then he nodded and said, 'Perhaps.'

Cadvan liked to talk. He stood there for a while, as if thinking of something else to say, then seemed to change his mind and wandered back towards the Corvus.

Nergui let him go. He preferred to be alone. He watched Domitian move in a deliberate zigzag pattern, his psychic searchlight straining into the past, away from Nergui, looking for warp echoes of what had happened. Nergui's thoughts began to drift for a moment, before the sudden presence of the Librarian's mind made him shudder and his body stiffened.

+They died here.+

'All of them?'

+All, I cannot tell. But more than one or two. The sense of death is thick. Some xenos, also.+

'Where are their bodies?'

+Not here. But their presence remains. I feel anger. Frustration. Betrayal.+

'Betrayal?'

+It is not hard to grasp what messages the dead leave behind them. The images that are easiest to read are related to the strongest emotions.+

Nergui turned and regarded the scene. It was as if the battlefield had been scoured clean. He strode to the Corvus and swung himself up to stand on the wing. He had seen the crater from the heights and he brought that image back to mind, seeing it differently now.

The smaller crater patterns were not asteroid strikes. Understanding went through him like a blade. He saw it all clearly. The clusters were where massive ordnance had been brought to bear.

Jumping down from the Corvus, he jogged to the nearest crater. There were lumps of molten copper, ripped from the ore by the intensity of the blasts. He knelt, rubbed his fingers in the dirt, and lifted them to his nose.

The scent had the unmistakable tang of plasma.

'They made their stand here,' he said. He could see it all. Where they had fallen back, desperate for shelter. Where they had split into pairs, dividing their pursuers, where each crater trail came to an end.

He took *Ganbold* and roared over to the farthest cluster, nearly half a mile away from where the Corvus' engines were turning over. Three overlapping craters marked the place. He shuddered. Brothers had died here.

Nergui stopped suddenly, skidded round, bent from the saddle and plucked a spent brass bolt shell as easily as a Chogorean boy would swing from the saddle to pluck a ball from the ground.

Hellstrike round. Fired within the last month. He was about to move on when he saw a skull lying in the dirt. A tiny thing, no larger than a simian's head, plated with gold and with facetted eyes of shaped red crystal.

He felt a cold shiver, as he did when Domitian entered his mind, but Domitian's presence was nowhere near him.

Nergui clicked his vox-link open. 'Domitian. I've found Ellial's totem.'

Domitian's mind was with him instantly. +Bring it to me.+

Brother Ellial had come to the Deathwatch from the Mortifactors Chapter.

The home world of the Mortifactors, Posul, was doomed to perpetual darkness, and that darkness had entered their souls, into their ways of being and ways of relating to the galaxy. Nergui had once been sent as an emissary to the Chapter.

He remembered landing on their fortress-monastery – a vast star fort in high orbit. The landing bay walls were decorated with the oversized bones of thousands of Space Marines. No body was complete. Femurs were arranged in spiral patterns. Shoulder blades into another. It had seemed disrespectful to display the bones of the dead warriors in this way.

A guide had appeared, hooded and pale.

'This way,' the guide had said, before leading him across the hallowed silence of the entrance hall to an arch of skulls. Adeptus Astartes' skulls, Nergui saw, with distaste, some of the bones yellow with age and still bearing the violent marks of their death blows.

He had met the Chapter under a chandelier of ribs and scapulae, with skulls as the setting for the tallow candles. He had politely refused food and the Chapter Master had seen through his manners.

'You will find recruits from our Chapter the most stalwart of all, for we do not fear death,' the Chapter Master had explained, his face hidden in shadow. 'We embrace it, for when we die, our souls are united with the Emperor on the Golden Throne.'

He'd brought Ellial back with him that time.

They'd served together for years, and before battle the Mortifactor always closed his eyes in meditation, his hearts almost stopping and his breathing slowing to a slight flare of the nostrils, once or twice a minute. It was the manner of the Mortifactors to withdraw like this before combat, just as it was the manner of the Space Wolves to brag and laugh at danger. Seconds before battle, Ellial would be sitting, eyes closed, body relaxed, and moments before the first shot his eyes would snap open.

'We commune with the primarch, and all the brothers that have gone before us. They are our ancestors, in a manner of speaking,' Ellial had told him. He'd been sitting in his cell – a shrine, really, to death – surrounded by the skulls of enemies he had taken. They were stacked up the walls and angled over into an arched ceiling of jaws and eye sockets, and the skulls of things that had no eyes – like the nicassar head that he had taken and which held pride of place in his room, the bulges in the thin, bird-like skull showing where the psychic glands had formed.

'What do your Chapter believe?' Ellial had asked, and Nergui laughed.

'We do not think about death,' he'd said.

Ellial had blinked in surprise. 'No?'

Nergui had shaken his head. 'No. We do not care for such things. We care for the wind in our hair, the blood of our foes, the ferocity of our assault. And after death, we sleep, because the battle is done.'

And that was enough.

Ellial was one of those who had been changed by his time within the Deathwatch. He had stopped drinking the blood of his foes, although he'd never given up collecting their skulls, or entering a near-death state of meditation as he approached battle.

The tiny gold-plated skull was Ellial's totem, the thing he meditated upon when he wished to go into a deep trance. As Nergui's fingers touched it he flinched, as if stung. There was a psychic presence there. He had the strangest feeling that Ellial was standing next to him.

As he rode *Ganbold* back, he held the tiny skull in his hand, as a Chogorean boy would carry a wounded bird, and he gave it to Domitian with due reverence.

Domitian closed his eyes and focused.

'He's here,' Domitian gasped before he was quite ready to speak. 'He has stayed, knowing we would find him. But he is weak. No one else could have held his presence so long after death. Only a Mortifactor. I must concentrate.'

The temperature began to drop.

Nergui's nose began to drip. He wiped it and saw a smear of blood on his armour. The cold was precipitating acid from the air. It was starting to corrode his nasal lining.

'*What is happening?*' Cadvan voxed. '*Your readings are showing that you are bleeding.*'

'It's Domitian. He's got Ellial's totem skull. He's communing with it.'

The Storm Giant was one of those brothers whose attitude was unchanged by the proximity of other Chapters and traditions.

'Throne!' he said. '*Tell me when they're done.*'

Nergui stayed on, even as the noxious gases thickened about Domitian, creating a yellow mist of sulphuric acid. Nergui could feel the bite in his throat now. There was blood in his lungs. The blood in his nose had clotted but the scab hung like a red icicle, before he brushed it away.

Domitian staggered from the acidic mist, his drawn face white. Fresh red blood dripped from his nostrils and ears, and even from the corner of his human eye. He coughed, and there was blood there too. Even the black of his armour had been eaten away to reveal the yellow of his Chapter, and in patches raw metal. He made a gesture which said, *I cannot speak*.

Nergui felt the cold, wet, icy touch of Domitian's presence slipping into his skull again. The world went dark. He resisted briefly, as he felt the Librarian taking over his mind. For a moment he was sitting in a Corvus, holding a storm shield, eyes closed as the craft bucked, weaved and lurched over hills and craters, gullies – and then he understood.

This was Ellial's memory, as the Mortifactor had passed it on to Domitian.

Nergui braced himself as he prepared to watch the last moments of Ellial's life.

CHAPTER TWO

A golden light stabs through the darkness. It does not blind. It is warm upon his face. There is singing, distant voices, calling to him.

'Faith in the Emperor,' a machine-spirit's servitor voice intones. 'Hatred steels our resolve. The alien cannot embrace the Emperor. To attempt understanding with the xenos is folly. You must destroy, and put understanding to the side. You shall rest in the comfort of the Emperor when the battle is done...'

The voice is the automated chant of the Corvus' machine-spirit. It speaks to him in the same moment that he basks in the light of the Astronomican. His mind exists in both places. The here and now, the present and the other. He feels the tilt as the Corvus Blackstar banks and accelerates to the right. He breathes through his nose, circles in and out, impossibly long and slow. A voice comes as if from far away.

'I'm taking her in. Landing in six, five, four...'

At 'one' the inside of the Corvus snaps into light. In one hand he holds a storm shield, in the other a combi-plasma. He is already moving.

Nidal, the Warmonger, is first out and then Tula, the Star Phantom, engaging his multi-melta as he follows. Priam, the Marine Errant, rests his combi-plasma on his lap. He turns and looks at Ellial.

'Welcome back,' he says.

'I always come back,' Ellial says. His hand slams the disengagment studs. He jumps down as the Corvus hovers a few yards above the ground, smells sulphur and dust through his helmet's sensor array, and the distinctive peppery scent of tau.

Next moment, Ellial is crouched at the crater lip. This is a mission to destroy a tau communication relay, but what he sees is all wrong. The wrong buildings, the wrong doorways. What they have discovered is a small city of domes and gun turrets.

Nidal, the Warmonger, lets out a low whistle. 'Throne!' he says. 'Look what we have found!'

The pain of possession made Nergui retch. He saw the kill team moving out to observe the tau base. He saw Ellial moving through the landscape. The Mortifactor's last seconds came at him in vivid and fragmented flashes. For a moment, Nergui dropped back into his own mind. He found himself on all fours, but then Domitian's mind gripped the back of his neck like a vice, and he arched his back in agony.

+You must see this.+

'We have contacts,' Ellial says.

The pilot, Gualtino of the Angels of Redemption, gives a short whistle. 'Holy Throne,' he voxes. 'What are they doing?'

'Nidal is taking picts. We'll scout them out, and then get out of here. Jotunn has to see this or he won't believe it.'

There is a sound like tearing cloth. Ellial rolls to the side as his retinal lens display flares an incandescent green. Rock showers on him. He is half buried. He kicks to get his legs back, and Nidal's marker turns red. There is a smoking crater where he had been standing. Ellial has only minor wounds. He engages his bolter, rolls to the side, and sees a streak of blue as a pair of Razorsharks rips across the sky, contrails flaring white in the thin atmosphere. There are plumes of explosions that stitch closer, throwing up dark clouds of fractured rock. Another tau fighter screeches overhead, banking as drones drop from its belly in a long stream.

Ellial puts two rounds into each, knocking them out as they turn towards him. One explodes, two more spin, winged to the floor, and the third comes on, tilting closer. He fires a third shot which blows it into pieces that pirouette down to the ground.

'More contacts!' Priam voxes. There is a hiss and puff of melta fire. A skimming Piranha nose plugs the earth and spins over and over, slowing with each spin, before exploding in a hail of black fragments. He curses as the sky is suddenly full of contrails and drones, banking fighters and scouts.

'They have our position,' Tula is shouting.

Gualtino is swinging back around to try to extract them.

'I'll hold them off,' he hisses, banking as a gun rig lands to fire its railguns. The Corvus Blackstar brackets a team of fire warriors. In the background comes the blast of railguns. Then he says, 'Holy Throne! Look at those battlesuits.'

Ellial has mistaken them for Riptides. But now he sees. There are a hundred of them, in the colours of at least ten septs that he knows, surging over the sentry lines with giant bounds, their shoulder-mounted railguns primed and ready.

Then there is a Riptide! The battlesuits are dwarfed by this new construction. One of the giant battlesuits, in the pale colours of Vior'la, pauses for a moment, thrusters dampening recoil, and then it fires.

The ground explodes in a great gout of rock and spinning debris. Ellial rolls to the side. Suddenly it seems they are all firing. The world goes dark as shots hammer about him. All is rock and fire and debris and pain. It goes on for what feels like an age: blast, explosion, pain.

Gualtino is racing back in. 'Are you still there, brothers?' he voxes.

There is a long pause. 'Still here,' Ellial manages to say. His legs are stumps. He grits his teeth against the pain. 'But I might be alone now.'

Something vast rears up before him. It blots out the thin light of the sun.

For a moment the world goes dark. Then impossibly bright.

And hot.

And then it is done.

Nergui found himself coughing and choking. He threw back his head, and saw Domitian kneeling beside him.

The blood had started dripping from his eye again. It rimmed his socket with red.

+You saw.+

'Yes,' Nergui said, and coughed and shook his head. He pushed himself to his feet, and held Domitian's wrist to drag him up as well. The Librarian leant on him for a moment, and Nergui swayed. 'Throne, yes. I understand now. What were those things? They had no chance against such an enemy. We must take word back. We must counter this thing.'

Domitian caught the White Scar with one hand and held him up as they limped back towards the Corvus. Cadvan was aboard, starting up the engines.

The ramps lowered and Nergui helped Domitian up.

'Listen,' the White Scar said. 'Don't ever do that again. Take me over. Without warning me.' He hit the button to bring the ramps back up. They did not bother to strap themselves in as the Corvus' engines whined and the craft lifted into the air.

'I was losing him,' Domitian said. 'His soul, I mean. I wanted you to see what he saw.'

'I know.' Nergui wiped the scabs of blood from the corners of his eyes. 'I saw it all. But just warn me next time.'

'Find anything?' Cadvan voxed, as the ramps closed behind them.

'Oh yes,' Nergui voxed back. We have found something, he thought.

CHAPTER THREE

It was not usual for a Deathwatch shipmaster to stand on the landing deck to await the return of a kill team, but Shipmaster Loni Ferral far from ordinary.

She was small, even for a human, but her diminutive size only made her tougher, like foil crushed by a mighty fist into a tight ball. Her face had been handsome once, despite the severe fringe, but years of rejuvenat had given her a slightly waxy look, while years of service with the Deathwatch had given her unaugmented eye a mean and wary light. At her side she carried a bolt pistol, and she'd used it a number of times, when the fighting had become desperate.

Ferral saw the Corvus Blackstar settle on the landing decks of the Deathwatch strike cruiser *Nemesis*, and watched the black-power-armoured Space Marines stride towards her. She had positioned herself by the doors to the private chambers of the warriors and addressed Nergui as he approached.

'Did you find them?'

Nergui paused, took off his helmet and looked down. There was dried blood on his cheeks, and his eyes were rimmed with red. It was a point of pride for Ferrel that she alone of the bridge crew did not tremble when speaking with one of the Adeptus Astartes, but she caught her breath for a moment. 'Was there a fight?'

'No,' Nergui said.

'Then why the blood?'

'Sulphur,' he told her. 'The atmosphere became acidic.'

She seemed unimpressed – if a member of the Adeptus Astartes was going to bleed, her face seemed to say, there better be a damn good reason for it. Something better than environmental hazards.

'You should have put your helmet on.'

He did not laugh. 'It is superficial. I wanted to smell the place where my brothers died.'

Among the human crew members, only she was privy to the purpose of the mission. 'So you found them?'

Nergui absentmindedly brushed away the dried blood from one cheek. 'We found traces of them.'

She looked back to where tracked servitors were fussing about the Corvus Blackstar: reloading, checking, promethium pipes already refilling her tanks. 'But there are no bodies.'

'No. But they died there nonetheless. Domitian felt it.'

'What killed them?' she said. 'Don't tell me it was the atmosphere.'

'No. It was not the sulphur. It was the tau.'

Shipmaster Ferral did not have a sense of humour, though her habit of speaking bluntly was sometimes mistaken for jest – to the distinct disadvantage of her crew. 'Looks like your prey fought back.'

Nergui nodded. 'Yes, it does that.'

'In the wild it is the hunter who kills the prey. Not the other way round.'

'This is not the wilds of some planet, shipmaster. This is the way of the galaxy. Kill or be killed. The hunted adapts, or it dies. And this enemy has adapted.'

She stiffened. 'I have commanded auspex sweeps of the whole system, but found nothing.'

Nergui turned for a moment as *Ganbold* was loaded onto one of the armoury carriages and carried with due reverence into the armoury lift. He waited until the lift doors had closed, and then he turned back to her. 'I do not think they are still here. The xenos have made great efforts to hide their presence. Whatever was there a month ago is now gone.'

'Where to?'

Nergui remembered the size of those battlesuits, and his jaw hardened. 'That is what we need to find out.'

She sighed. 'So we have accounted for Kill Team Primus. But what of Kill Team Orion? Do we keep searching for them?'

Nergui paused for a moment. 'No,' he said. 'We do not. What I saw there – I must take news back. Our commander must hear. Now, please excuse me.'

Nergui's cell was a plain chamber with a bed, an armoury and a vast round viewport that looked out across the upper portside weapon batteries. He kept reliving the moment when Ellial had seen the Riptide and the new battlesuit side by side. Their enemy had evolved in a way that repelled him. The urge to kill was strong. They were not just xenos, they were a deadly bacteria that multiplied and learned and changed.

Humanity would not be safe if even one of their foul race was left alive.

He closed his eyes, meditated upon the images that he had seen from Ellial's mind, going over each one moment by moment, gleaning every scrap of information.

He did not sleep for three days, and it was not until he felt the warp drive being engaged that his eyes snapped open. He had given his orders for the return to Picket's Watch, but now – after long and deep thought – something nagged at him.

Nergui jumped up suddenly and strode out into the central corridor. To the left the walls were warm and throbbed with the heat of the ship's core reactor. To the right the Adeptus Astartes' cells opened out to the port side of the *Nemesis*, at the base of the bridge spires. It would have taken Nergui an hour to climb the long stairs up to the bridge, and sometimes he did this, timing himself and trying to beat his best. It helped to keep the mind active on long voyages.

This time he took the lift, and just in time. Shipmaster Ferral was preparing for the jump into warp space as he entered. He felt the human crew stiffen at his presence. They stared into their instruments and avoided looking in his direction. It was an effect he was almost entirely oblivious to.

Shipmaster Ferral was sitting in her throne, issuing a series of commands, when an alarm sounded.

'What is that?' she said.

'Long-range anomalous readings,' the Master of Auspex reported.

'Let me see.' It was Nergui who spoke. The Master of Auspex was an augmented human, and he visibly wilted as Nergui turned his full attention upon him. He held out a sheath of reports in a shaking hand.

Nergui inspected the readings. 'Anomalous readings from so far beyond the Mandeville point?'

The Master of Auspex nodded.

Nergui nodded. 'We must investigate.'

Shipmaster Loni Ferral had been hovering on the edge of the conversation and she stepped in now, her voice tense. 'Captain Nergui. Your orders were to move to the Mandeville point with all speed. It will take us two days, at least, to investigate those readings. May I suggest...'

Nergui did not bother listening to the suggestion. He turned his back on the shipmaster and waited for the suggestion to end, before saying, with due honorifics, 'Shipmaster Ferral. My orders have changed. I want to find out if that is their ship, and if any of my brothers are still alive.'

The readings were correct. They found a burned hulk, two and a half days past the Mandeville point, within the dark, cold heart of a nebula made up of her own frozen clouds of oxygen and water and hydrogen – still venting thin trails of gas from the gaping holes in her flanks.

Kill Team Primus had set out on their mission aboard the six hundred-year-old strike cruiser *Troilus* – a hardy vessel, retrofitted with extra slabs of ablative armour along her sides, a suite of generators, and three vast dorsal lance batteries, unusual for a ship of this class, which gave her a formidable punch against any foe.

Domitian appeared on the bridge just as Nergui was about to call him. His eyes had lost their glassy tiredness, and he approached the round viewport with steady steps.

'I have done as you asked,' the Librarian said.

Nergui did not hold out much hope. 'And did you feel any… presence, brother?'

Domitian shook his head. 'I have felt out for life. But there is none.'

Nergui nodded. Sometimes there were pockets of life aboard a destroyed ship, airlocks that had remained secure, human crews sheltering in the depths of the engines or about the warmth of the reactor cores. Or one of the Adeptus Astartes, whose enhanced physiques and armour allowed them to survive in places no ordinary human could. 'And did you sense anything else?'

Domitian shook his head. 'Nothing.'

Nergui looked at the wreck. He had flown on the *Troilus* many times. She had a fine crew. It hurt him to see the gaping holes along the hull, thick slabs of armour melted and peeled away. Her fuselage was bent and broken. She had been blasted down to the structural spine, long after she would have stopped posing any threat. But most chilling of all were the three great dorsal turrets, with their massive lance arrays. All three of them remained in the cruising position, pointing straight forwards. 'They did not even have a chance to fire back. They were ambushed.'

'They knew what they were doing,' Domitian said. He put a hand to Nergui's arm, and spoke earnestly. 'And you were right to send them here. Remember what you saw. They found *something*.'

Nergui remembered the images he had seen. An armed camp, hidden in the depths of empty space, a hundred newly developed battlesuits raining fire down upon a single kill team. 'Yes, they found something. But what?'

'Captain,' the shipmaster's voice came again.

Nergui turned.

Ferral cleared her throat. 'I have logged the location of the *Troilus*. When we return to Picket's Watch I suggest we send a reclamation craft to bring her home, but for now we have information of importance that must be brought back with all speed. Do I have your permission to make the translation now?'

'Yes,' he said. 'We can leave.'

CHAPTER FOUR

Nowhere in the Imperial archives did it tell who Picket of the Picket's Watch was, but archeo-scribes recorded that the foundation of the fortress dated to the days of the Great Crusade, when it was a sentinel on the vast emptiness of the Damocles Gulf.

The earliest extant archival record was by Archeo-scribe Nay-lor, attached to Explorator Fleet Beaconfire, whose footnotes recorded that Picket's Watch had been an outpost of the Imperial Fists Legion – although there was evidence of an earlier watch fortress, of human design, probably dating back to the Age of Strife.

What the Imperial Fists legionaries had been guarding against no record survived to tell, but they built Westkeep: a massive bastion of stone and ceramite, with void shield generators, hidden gun batteries and murderous enfilading fields of fire.

It was possible, the author of the history mused, that Picket's Watch had been built to mark the edge of habitable space. Or it could be that whatever threat those ancient Legiones Astartes had perceived had faded, or been wiped out. Now the Damocles Gulf was a quiet region of space, Nay-lor stated: safe, predictable, thoroughly colonised. One of the more stable regions of the Imperium of Mankind.

Nay-lor's treatise had been written in 789.M35, when the Explorator Fleet Beaconfire passed through on its way across the gulf. That statement about this being a safe region of space had been true then. The expedition had successfully crossed the Damocles Gulf and found worlds that had never been visited before by emissaries of the Adeptus Mechanicus. On their journey they had found one world, named T'au. *Predominantly arid – possible uses: grox cultivation on semi-arid savannah regions,* the official reports had read. *Currently inhabited by indigenous xenos race. Have just mastered fire. Suggest extermination landing. Clearance expected one to six months.*

That report had been logged, recorded and filed safely away when it reached Terra, and T'au scheduled for clearance before it was made suitable for human colonisation. A sudden warp storm had cut the region off for over six thousand years, and when the first rogue traders pushed back into this area of space, they found that the tau race had evolved from a virtual stone age to a culture of high sophistication and technological heresy, spanning three hundred light years.

For thousands of years Picket's Watch had been sustained by a skeleton crew of servitors, but with the threat now expanding across the Damocles Gulf, it found itself on a new front line. It was taken over by the Deathwatch. They reinforced the outer wards, with massive batteries and emplacements, buttressed towers and bastions set around the impregnable fortress of Westkeep. And so it became a frontier outpost, home to the Second Chamber of the Warriors of Talassa Prime – Guardians of the Eastern Fringe.

But despite the vast bombardment cannons and automated lance batteries, its chief defence was secrecy. And it was to this hidden outpost that Nergui's ship, *Nemesis*, returned, bearing the news of the loss of Kill Team Primus and the strike cruiser *Troilus*.

Their Navigator steered them through the swirling warp to this lone rock, lost in the black void of true space, and while the *Nemesis* manoeuvred slowly into her assigned dock, a black Thunderhawk bearing the insignia of the Deathwatch brought Cadvan, Domitian and Nergui down to the starport.

Automated gun platforms tracked their descent. They disembarked and made their way towards the dark, solid bulk of Westkeep.

'Shall I come with you?' Domitian voxed.

Nergui shook his head. 'It is not necessary. I must tell the commander first.'

'So be it,' Domitian said.

Nergui watched as the slight figure of the Librarian and giant Cadvan crossed the flagstones of the inner courtyard and disappeared into the shadows of Carnot's Bastion, then he turned to the vast, heavy block of Westkeep.

Slaved heavy bolters tracked Nergui's progress as he started up the broad rockcrete steps. As he strode up, a bell rang out from the top of Westkeep, a single note marking the loss of his brothers. It seemed the tidings of the fate of Kill Team Primus had arrived before him. Ferral must have sent a message ahead. She should not have done that. It was not right for a human, even a shipmaster, to get involved in the affairs of the Deathwatch.

The augmented door wards had their black hoods pulled low over their faces. They stood back, shotguns braced to chests, and bowed as Nergui's shadow passed across the threshold. The servitors' slack-jawed faces had sad and melancholic looks, as if even they understood the loss that the Second Chamber had suffered.

A dark-cowled adept bowed. 'The commander is in the Old Feast Hall. We heard of your losses, captain,' he ventured. 'We are sorry…'

'Yes. We're all sorry,' Nergui snapped.

Nergui descended four levels down into the hidden fastness of Picket's Watch, past Carnot's Library, where two automated savants wheeled up towards their respective lecterns, low lights illuminating ancient leather-bound tomes as their metal fingers carefully turned each page.

The sparring chamber was strangely quiet, although he could hear the distant thud from the firing range. It sounded like Olbath. He had a distinctive one-two style of firing. Head and heart, he called it.

Nergui took the third corridor on the right, descending the broad and gently worn steps that led to the Old Feast Hall. Only authorised personnel were permitted to enter the lower levels, where the past centuries lay like fine dust on the floor, and the lower he went the more conscious he was that he was stepping into history – where the Imperial Fists once held vigil over the borders of the galaxy.

At the antechamber entrance, the lintels were carved with twin axes and above the lintel a clenched fist icon held three lightning bolts in its grip.

The Old Feast Hall was the only place in Westkeep where the Imperial Fists iconography had not been replaced with that of the Deathwatch. Why this was so, Nergui did not know. But there was a boldness and confidence in those Legion emblems that seemed to say, *We are humanity's guardians. We do not fear the emptiness of space.*

Theirs had not been a secretive mission, he was sure. Here on the edges of known space those ancient warriors had gloried in humanity's achievement. But their watch had ended, their Legion had been broken up, and the Chapter born in its stead was unable to maintain the resources necessary to man hundreds of watchposts.

Nergui passed under the arch of dressed stone into the Old Feast Hall. After so long in corridors and low chambers, he stepped into the vaulted room and felt the ceilings lift above his head to a cathedral space. He had seen it once lit as it must have been when the Imperial Fists filled the benches.

The arched ceiling was gilded with icons of Rogal Dorn, the Great Crusade and the Emperor Ascendant that must have taken decades to finish. The sight of these ancient images had taken his breath away for a moment. They had been so hopeful, coming as they did from before the days of the Great Heresy.

There had once been benches for the entire company of Imperial Fists. Now the Deathwatch could barely maintain more than three kill teams here. And despite the years of fighting, the dangers had only increased. The feast benches had been long since cleared away, and now the room was empty except for the tombs of ancient warriors that lined the walls, and a lone figure, standing in the corner, at the black marble shrine of St Hallows.

And it was here, in the ancient shadows, that Commander Jotunn liked to keep his watch.

'White Scar…' Jotunn the Space Wolf's voice was so deep and resonant it made the stones of the ancient fortress tremble. Nergui paused mid-step. Watch-Commander Jotunn – the Lone Wolf – only addressed brothers by their Chapter names when he was angry, and now, as his great hunched form turned, Nergui could see that the Space Wolf's long fangs were bared in a snarl. 'Where are my warriors, White Scar?'

Nergui stopped two sword lengths away. 'Kill Team Primus was destroyed. Domitian found Ellial's presence on a moon in the Sexton Sector.'

Jotunn faced the White Scar. His finely artificed black power armour was almost as old as the fortress itself. His face was drawn with age and the puckered red marks of old scars, while his white beard hung in long plaits that reached down to his knees.

'I gave you my best kill team, White Scar,' the Lone Wolf growled.

Nergui was defiant. 'Yes, commander. You did. And I sent them out to do their duty, which is to fight the xenos.'

There was a low rumble of anger. The Lone Wolf came almost to the edge of the shadows.

'Do you see this empty hall? I cannot spare warriors!'

Nergui did not need to look. He knew what the darkness obscured. The walls were covered with an assortment of shoulder pads, xenos skulls, bolt pistols, lovingly polished hellfire bolter rounds, eldar swords, grotesque and screaming masks, chequerboard faces with wickedly curved features, a loaxtl's withered front claw, the flensed jaw bone of a carnifex prime. Each totem was carefully inscribed in High Gothic script with the name of a fallen member of the Deathwatch.

Jotunn picked out a green spirit stone with the name Mortifax chiselled into the surface, but where the names usually ended with a Chapter symbol, there was an empty shield, without emblem or marking.

'Do you know who Mortifax was, White Scar?'

Nergui shook his head.

'His real name was Kaspar Dabanville. He was of the Sons of Medusa Chapter. He rose to great fame among his brothers. For a hundred and six years he was a great warrior within the Deathwatch. He hated the eldar, and pursued them mercilessly from world to world, burning and razing their ancient shrines and scattered communities. He led an entire chamber – seven kill teams – on a raid into the webway on the world of Brand's Gate. It was a trap that the xenos had laid for him. They killed each of his warriors, one by one, until only he was left, surrounded, wounded and alone.

'And do you know what they did to him?'

Nergui shook his head.

'They let him return to Brand's Gate. Alive. Shamed. It was there that he took the black. He held himself to higher standards than anyone else. He became a Black Shield and painted over all trace of his former Chapter, and went back to being a simple warrior. He even changed his name to Mortifax to symbolise his contrition.'

'Why do you tell me this, commander?'

'I tell you this because there is no mercy in this galaxy,' Jotunn said. 'There is no room for the weak or the stupid. The hunters became the hunted. It is the way of the galaxy. Only the strongest and fiercest and most cunning will survive. You have to think like the xenos we hunt. You have to understand them, to know what they are thinking, even though their thoughts are abhorrent. You have to understand their logic, even though their thoughts are illogical. You have to hate them! But you must never underestimate their evil and their cunning. You have failed to outthink, out-reason, outguess your foes. Not doing so, Captain Nergui, is the worst kind of failure.'

Jotunn touched the spirit stone, and a glow appeared within it – as if there were a firefly trapped inside – that slowly faded again.

Nergui found the xenos object disgusting. He stroked his moustaches and said, 'It was no failure.'

'What do you mean, no failure?'

'You have not heard?'

Jotunn's fangs showed for a moment. 'No. I have not heard.'

'Kill Team Primus found something.'

There was a pause, and the ancient Space Wolf moved towards him. Nergui could see his eyes gleaming with reflected candlelight, like a cat's, and bared fangs as the Space Wolf growled.

'What?' he rumbled.

'They found something that the tau do not want us to know even exists. The xenos cleaned the site of the battle. They destroyed the *Troilus* and towed it out past the Mandeville point, into dead space. They scoured the system and thought they had left nothing that could leave a trace. And they were almost successful.'

'*Almost?*'

'Yes. But they overlooked this.' He held up the gold-plated simian skull that Ellial had used as a totem. The red crystal eyes glittered. 'Ellial's presence remained. Domitian communed with him. I saw what he saw.'

The Lone Wolf was like a ghost in the darkness. 'What did he see, White Scar?'

Nergui described the large complex, the number of buildings, the gun emplacements and the hab zones, and the Lone Wolf listened patiently. At the end Nergui said, 'And there was a type of battlesuit we have not seen before.'

'Describe it to me.'

'Larger than their usual battlesuits. They carry the same calibre railgun as their ships, but shoulder-mounted, on a suit that can deploy onto the battlefield via jump pack or aerial insertion. I saw one being deployed. It looks like a Titan killer.' He drew himself up. 'I would class them as an extreme threat. And what is more, there were nearly a hundred of them, with at least twelve separate sept markings, including Vior'la, Ke'lshan and Sa'cea.'

The Space Wolf sank back into the shadows. 'The finest warrior worlds of the tau, working together?' His fangs showed once more. 'What could this be, this secret base that disappears when we find it? That is protected so well, my finest warriors are wiped out? That has so many of these new weapons of war? And where the septs cooperate? Nergui. You have done well. We know the base is no longer on this moon. But where could it be?'

'It did not appear to be a production facility.'

Jotunn nodded. 'No. Not with so many septs working together. Then what do you think it was?'

'I do not know,' he said. 'Unless, perhaps, it is a training facility.'

'Where pilots are brought to be inducted...' Jotunn growled. 'Whatever it is, Nergui, if the enemy value it, you must find it and destroy it.'

Nergui bowed. 'I shall, commander.'

As he marched back across the dark and empty chamber, Jotunn called out after him.

'What about Kill Team Orion? Where are they?'

Nergui turned and faced the Space Marine. 'I do not know.'

'You stopped looking?'

'I thought the appearance of these battlesuits meant I had to return here. To consult with you.'

Jotunn's fangs were bared. 'I might be able to help. We had an astropathic signal while you were gone, from the strike cruiser *Robidoux*. Two weeks ago.'

Nergui started forwards. 'Tell me.'

'Yes. Leonas led them in a boarding action of a tau emissary craft that was heading towards the Sexton Sector. Leonas and his team were trapped. The captain of the *Robidoux* was heading for the Mandeville point. If she ever got there, I do not know.'

'The Sexton Sector? So they would use the route through the Distaf Nebula? I will go and see what I can find,' Nergui said.

Jotunn nodded.

Nergui turned back to the darkness of the hall. His enhanced vision could make out the xenos trophies that stretched up to the vaulted ceiling, weapons and names as ancient as the Imperium of Mankind itself. His was a fight that seemed endless, unwinnable at times. But all that mattered was the fight itself.

Without war, there was no hope.

CHAPTER FIVE

'Last' Leonas refused to die.

He spat fresh blood from his mouth. Bile burned his throat. No, it was not bile, it was the shots that had wounded him. He kicked and moaned as he relived that moment. The knowledge that he was alone and surrounded by tau.

It was supposed to be an ambassador's ship. Lightly defended, a respectfully sized bodyguard – easy, in short, to overwhelm. It *should* have been easy.

Half the squad were in Terminator armour, the other half in power armour, so that they could keep moving, rocking the enemy back with lightning body punches.

Their Thunderhawk had come in unseen and blasted its way into the docking bay. It landed long enough to drop the kill team, as its own automated weapon systems knocked out bulkheads, ripped through tau drones and shredded the first team of fire warriors who came sprinting into the hall, their commander shouting orders as his warriors knelt and fired.

The mission itself had gone well. They'd cut a path through the ship, leaving dead tau slumped against bulkheads and lying in heaps where they had fallen. The bridge been taken after a brief assault, and they'd killed all within and torn the databanks from their cases.

It was the fight out that had gone badly. How were they to know that this craft was carrying a tau ethereal? They had carried the xenos tech, battling their way back out against twice as much opposition as they had faced on the way in, and each moment they were slowed meant the enemy could bring more warriors to bear. The fire warriors fought with a tenacity and resolve that was exemplary.

Leonas and Brothers Aslon and Brand had dragged themselves wounded to the Thunderhawk. Leonas' magazines had clicked empty as he stood on the ramp and covered the retreat of the Terminators. The three of them had strode slowly backwards, shoulder to shoulder, assault cannons tearing up the mobile tau bulkheads, as plasma rounds made the air crackle with ozone.

It had all gone wrong when the Thunderhawk lifted and a lucky shot ignited a fuel cable in the gunship's second engine. A small fire spread in seconds, until the whole wing was ablaze, and he remembered the face of Branstonio as the Thunderhawk crashed.

'Throne,' he had said. 'Let's get out there and die with honour.'

They had fought a three-hour battle across the landing zone, trapped, encircled, running low on ammunition, without hope of rescue. They'd used the wreckage of their own Thunderhawk as cover until one by one his brothers had been picked off. Aslon and Branstonio were incinerated when the Thunderhawk's port-side fuel tank exploded. He had no idea what killed Brand, but Solovax of the Black Guard died cursing the xenos.

Leonas had taken a plasma bolt to the side, and something big enough had hit him on the side of the head, making an egg-shell dent in his skull. His clips were empty, but still he had fought on, battering the foe with the butt of his weapon – bucking, snarling, clawing at faces, tearing off helmets, breaking bones in his grip. He had killed ten, a score, he had lost count, and then the world had become fire.

It did not matter. All that mattered was that he stayed alive. He could not die.

Leonas was the last. He would not die, he *could* not die.

Leonas twitched as the dreams tore like old curtains and reality pushed her ugly snout into his consciousness.

He moaned and tried to turn back over into his delirium, but he could not. There was light in his eyes, his nose was full of scabbed blood, one of his hearts had failed and the other one was skipping beats, sending dizzy palpitations through his wounded body.

The plasma had seared a hole straight through his chest. He could feel fluids dripping into his core as his body tried to repair the seared innards of his flesh, despite the fact that the edges scabbed and the pain was…

…bearable. He was of the Adeptus Astartes. He was the weapon that had conquered the whole galaxy on behalf of the Emperor of Mankind. He could conquer pain. All it took was concentration. He slowed his breathing. He concentrated.

He knew the xenos observed him from behind the armoured glass screen. He could feel their wonder as scabs formed on his wounds and he came back to life, when they were sure that he had died. But he did not care. He had to survive. He was the last. He could not die.

A door opened. One of Leonas' eyes was bruised shut. The other opened just enough for him to see the room. It was plain, cream, smooth, unmistakably alien.

He took in the bulkhead's location, the way it opened, sliding to the left, in case he had to prise it open. A figure walked towards him. It was a human, female: a short, plump woman with a stud in her nostril and long blonde hair. She wore what looked like the grey flak armour of an Imperial Guard major, but underneath she wore a suit of xenos design. Where she would have worn the aquila was the round black-and-white symbol of a tau sept.

'Can you speak?' she asked. She was trembling. He wanted to kill her for her treachery to her species, and it took a moment's concentration to hold back the desire to reach out.

'Lord, can you speak?' she asked again.

He lay still for a long time.

'If you speak, I can help you,' she said. He saw that she kept well back out of arm's reach. She had that much sense at least.

'I am Major Jerym,' she said. 'Of Sept Bork'an.' She came forwards a little.

Leonas had picked up enough to know that Bork'an was the centre of learning for the tau, and the chiefmost of their military academies.

She came a little closer still. 'We thought you were dead.'

He laughed at the idea. It was simple. He *could* not die.

'When you started moving we brought you here. It is for your good. It is for all our good. You'll understand that at some point. It is better that way.'

Leonas opened his good eye fully. He could tell from the look on her face that it was a baleful sight, looking into the red eyes of a Black Consuls Space Marine.

'Better for whom?' he spat.

She took a step back. He could smell her fear. It sparked something within him. Confidence. Violence. The pride of his kind. He slowed his heart. It had enough to deal with. He tried to smile, but the left side of his face was swollen. There were bits of teeth still in the bloody recesses of his mouth. His right hand twitched for a bolter or a blade.

'You are disarmed,' she said.

He laughed. 'If you were just a little closer I would break your neck.'

'You're sick,' she told him.

'I'm not sick. I'm wounded. There's a distinct difference.'

'Rest. I will speak to you later. We're taking you back.'

'Back where?'

'You will see.'

Leonas laughed, even though it hurt, and it brought a gout of fresh blood from his mouth. 'Look what you made me do,' he said, as he struggled to lift a hand to wipe the blood away.

'You will understand,' she said, 'or we will have to hand you over.'

'Who to?'

'To the others,' she said. 'We have claimed the first right. But there are others. Younger, brasher. They want to have their chance with you. They will not be as kind as us. It would be easier if you conform.'

Leonas spat at the word 'conform'. The acid hit her full in the face, and she screamed and stumbled back.

He pulled at his restraints, but he was held fast. The door opened. He had a brief glimpse of a thin, grey-skinned tau dressed in long white robes with thick cuffs that were turned back.

'I cannot do anything with him,' his interviewer hissed.

After that a team of tau came in with pain-prods and stun-shields. They surrounded Leonas and beat him down, and the electrocharges in the spiked ends brought grunts of startled pain through his clenched teeth.

When he woke there was fresh blood oozing down his face and from his ears. His hands had been bound. There were tubes in his arms, a tube up his nose. His heart was more erratic. Another of his teeth was broken, his arms leaden. Even opening his good eye was an effort.

And then he saw why. They were pumping something into his veins. Sedatives. Pacifiers.

He closed his eyes.

He wanted to retch. He wanted to sleep. He wanted it to be over.

No, a voice within him said.

You are the last, Leonas.

You *cannot* die.

The next interrogator came after hours of flashing lights and blaring sirens. He came in the darkness, as if that would hide him from the Space Marine's sight, padding stealthily into the room, as if Leonas could not hear him. Then he spoke. A human, but one with a slight accent that Leonas could not locate.

'You will die, here, Space Marine,' he whispered. 'Look at you! You are weak, and broken! All your brute strength could not save you against the united power of our forces. You think you are strong, but you are weak. We shall break you all. One by one, as we destroy your corrupt empire. We bring the Greater Good! We shall triumph. All that you hold dear shall be washed away. There will be nothing left. Not your Chapter, not your Emperor, not even the Golden Throne upon which He rots. We shall replace the darkness with light. Terror with peace. War with Trade. We are the servants of the Greater Good.'

The lights returned with a sudden hum of lumens. Leonas tried to lift a hand, but it had been strapped down. He felt the lights' heat upon his face as his pupils shrank to pinheads within his green eyes. He blinked for a moment as his enhanced physique responded.

Human male, buck-toothed, mid-forties according to standard Terran years, no visible weapon, no armour, grey uniform, Sept Ke'lshan – and just beyond the reach of his boot.

The man glared down at Leonas.

'Look at you! Tethered like a beast. You are worthless. You are stupid. You are crude and brutal. What do you know of the Greater Good? You like your life in darkness. You think the light of a candle flame is illumination. You could not understand what it is to live in the bright light of day. The light of knowledge and understanding. Your Imperium is dead. It is worthless. It is rotten to the core. We are the future…'

Leonas closed his eyes as buck-tooth kept up his tirade. Just a little closer, he thought, and I shall have you. One kick and I will stave this buck-toothed fool's skull in.

'Are you done yet, traitor?' Leonas said in the end. 'Take your tricks away. I do not fear you! You try to hide in darkness and light, but I see your face, and I shall remember, and I will take vengeance.'

Buck-tooth laughed at him. And the sirens and flashing lights started up again.

They lasted a week this time.

On the eighth day a third man came in. He was dressed in a double-breasted yellow jacket, fastened with buttons that carried the sept badge of the Elsy'eir. He held up a hand and cleared his throat, and the noise and flashing stopped. A single gentle light lit the room. Leonas forced himself to sit up, woozily shaking his head.

They had increased the dosage, and his body was struggling to counter its effects.

His hands were clamped down with leather straps about his wrists and forearms. He shook his head slowly, like a stunned bull that has one last charge in it.

The man waited. He was a neat little figure, sitting there before him. He drew up a three-legged stool and sat down, hands folded precisely on a data-slate in his lap. He had a thin neck, large head and grey hair swept across his wide forehead. 'Hello,' he said. 'Please don't glare at me. I am here to help you.'

The man waited as Leonas sat up and opened his good eye before speaking. 'Hello,' he said. 'My name is Roboute.'

'You're called Roboute?'

The man seemed nonplussed. 'Yes,' he said.

Leonas could not hold back his laughter. He could imagine telling Branstonio that he had met a traitor named Roboute. He could picture the Ultramarine's fury.

The man continued a little peevishly. 'Now can we get along? We don't have much time.'

Leonas was still laughing. 'No?'

'No. I'm the last.'

'The last what?'

The man gave a thin smile. 'The last chance. *Your* last chance, in fact.'

'Chance of what?'

'Life.'

Leonas laughed once more. 'My life is mine. You cannot take it from me.'

'Oh, but I can.' The man seemed incredibly pleased with himself. 'You see, I am the last. If you do not agree to talk to me, then we shall vent you out of the nearest airlock.'

'And you think that will kill me?'

'Yes,' the man said, simply. 'If you keep your mouth shut then, yes, I am reliably informed so by our scientist brothers – a poor translation of the exact word, but never mind. If you are voided and keep your mouth shut I am told that the air in your lungs will expand at such a rate that it will tear you apart from the inside. That would be almost instantaneous death. Even with the ribcage you possess, the air will find a way out. The softest way, generally. Through your stomach, or your neck. It will tear through the soft organs and turn you inside out within moments. Seconds. A second, really, to be precise.

'If you don't hold your breath you may survive a few seconds. I suppose, before cold and the void kill you. A normal human would survive seconds. You might survive minutes. But yes. It will kill you.' The man forced a smile. 'So. Perhaps you will cooperate.'

'What do you want to talk about?' Leonas said. He swept his hands over the wounds on his body. 'I am in some pain.'

'Yes, but you are healing so quickly.'

'Am I?'

'Yes. *They* thought that you would not survive,' Roboute said.

'I have to survive,' Leonas said.

Roboute frowned, put his stylus to his mouth and sucked it for a moment. 'You keep saying that. Please explain.'

There was a dull thud and the ship trembled for a moment.

Leonas waited. There was another thud. Far off but distinctive.

A siren sounded. Leonas sat up abruptly and the interrogator's eyes widened in surprise.

'My,' he said. 'You have healed quickly!'

Leonas flexed his forearms and the bindings creaked as his muscles swelled and stretched them wide. He tugged at the holding straps. One hand burst free and then the other. Roboute's face expressed a moment of boggle-eyed surprise as Leonas reached across and caught him by the throat. The neck was so thin it was easy to snap.

'I told you,' Leonas said, dropping the dead body to the floor. 'I cannot die.'

CHAPTER SIX

LOCATION: CANNIS GAS CLOUD, DAMOCLES GULF, 999.M41

Without psykers, the tau could not make translations into the warp, but they had learnt to make short hops through the edge of the immaterial and real space, sticking to pre-ordained 'stepping stones'. This particular transit point, deep in the Cannis gas cloud, was known to connect to the Sexton Sector. It was what the tau thought was a safe transit route, but its location had been known to the Deathwatch for some time.

And now the *Nemesis* waited, systems low, barely ticking over, watching the empty space.

Nergui stood before the *Nemesis'* bridge viewport and watched the tau ships as an eagle watches the deer on the Chogorean plains, waiting his moment.

The strike cruiser had been in a state of preparedness for over two weeks. Rumours of the loss of a kill team had filtered down among the human crew. All of them were keen to strike a blow against the enemy. All of them were hungry for violence.

It was the waiting that strained nerves. Kill Team Faith were ready for immediate deployment. The bridge crew were tense. Nergui gave no sign or movement.

An alarm sounded from the auspex scanners as a tau convoy slowed almost to a stop, their white hulls pale against the darkness of the void.

The xenos ships readied their gravitic drives. If the Deathwatch were to attack, it had to be now, but the captain made no move.

Only Shipmaster Ferral dared disturb the Space Marine. Her boots clipped out a regular beat as she strode towards the viewport. She had a sheath of reports in her hands.

'Our guns are ready. Give the word, Captain Nergui, and we shall attack.' There was a long pause. Her voice was tense. 'If we do not, then we will lose the chance.'

Still no answer.

'Captain Nergui. Permission to engage the foe? My gun crews are ready. We could just take out a few of their transports and slip into warp space before their escorts have time to react. After the loss of Kill Team Primus...'

'No,' he said, and when she started to argue he spoke over her. 'I do not doubt the bravery or skill of you or your crew, shipmaster. But we are hunting something far more important than this. We will not let vengeance get in our way.' He gave the huddled transports before them a contemptuous nod.

'May I know what?'

'An emissary-class craft, bound for the Sexton Sector. Damaged in some way. Wounded.' Domitian had seen it in the Emperor's Tarot. 'Wounded' was the word he'd used.

'Wounded' seemed an odd word to use for a craft, but there were some mysteries about which it was better not to know.

Ferral looked down and seemed to remember the thing she was carrying in her hand.

'This arrived,' she said. She held out a sealed message from the astropathic chambers. It was a standard bulletin from Agrellan. Clearance code vermillion.

The language was terse and impersonal.

Imperial Task Force Retribution had closed on Agrellan, under Lord Admiral Hawke's command, and engaged the tau defences. The *Will of Iron* had been lost. The *Herald of Terra* had been forced to retire. The first Imperial Guard landings had taken place. The results were mixed. House Terryn had lost twelve Knights within the first day. The tau had a new battlesuit.

Nergui's hearts beat a little faster as he read on with a growing sense of hatred and anger.

A new battlesuit, the thing that Kill Team Primus had found on Moon QX-937. Designated *Stormsurges* by the enemy. His eyes scanned through the pages, seeing the name, over and over.

The Space Marine rolled the vellum scroll back up and held it tight in his fist. He gave no visible reaction, but he felt personally responsible. Worse than that, he felt sick at the thought of the damage the enemy had done with these new weapons. It had been his mission to find them and destroy them, and he was no closer to that than he had been six months earlier. When he had three entire kill teams.

Ferral cleared her throat. The tau ships were still there, and it was hard for her to pass up the opportunity to strike a blow against the foe. She ran a hand through her short-cropped hair, shaking it back from her neck. 'Do you think this emissary craft will come?'

'Yes,' Nergui said. 'It has been seen in the Tarot.'

As he spoke, the first of the tau ships seemed to pulse as it skimmed into the immaterium. In ten minutes they were all gone, and the space before them was empty once more, except for the light of distant stars.

It was three days later that a lone tau ship tore into real space at the Cannis gas cloud, heading back towards the Eastern Fringe. It slowed rapidly, slewing off vapour contrails from its wide-spread wings.

'Emissary craft,' the Master of Auspex reported, and Ferral sent word to Nergui.

The Space Marine was on the bridge in moments. Ferral handed him data reports but he did not look at them, striding straight to the viewport. The ship's port drive was running on half power. *Wounded.* He knew in an instant. 'That is it. Prepare for the attack.'

His order was so sudden that Ferral thought she had misheard.

Nergui turned on her. 'Prepare your ship for the assault,' he told her. 'I am taking Kill Team Faith in.'

The emissary craft went through standard protocol defensive manoeuvres as it prepared its gravitic drives for the next hop across space. The air caste captain was a veteran of many years, and had made a point of hailing each of the other captains they had met along this route. The last convoy had passed through this point only days before, reporting no signs of an enemy. Shields were raised. Scanners made perfunctory interrogations of the area, and drones were deployed before the ship made the next jump.

The gravitic drive was powering up when the alarms sounded. A single ship, the scanners reported. Alarm signals flared as the attackers moved to assault positions. Scanners showed a spread of torpedoes burning towards them. The captain remained calm but tense. He deployed counter-drones, set all automated gun turrets to attack mode.

One by one the torpedoes were hit with precise fire. The captain of the emissary craft slewed his ship around, scrambling to find an escape route. But the real attack had been launched half an hour before. A spread of three Caestus assault rams – too small to pick up amongst the space debris – powered towards the emissary craft. The first warning the bridge crew had was when one of them made visual contact. He stared and pointed through the bridge windows. It was hard to pick out anything so small until a drone exploded. Then they saw it: a blunt, brutal shape.

The captain shouted for defences to be reconfigured against short-range targets. The air caste crew dashed to their controls, the fire warriors at the bridge door engaging their pulse weapons. Evasive manoeuvres were ordered, and through the skill of the crew, the technologically advanced ship began to bank to the right as close-range drones moved to intercept the attackers.

The Caestus batted the drones out of the way. Shots whizzed about the assault ram. They seared scorch marks into the thick slabs of reinforced ceramite plating, and had almost no effect. The Caestus kept coming, and as it filled the viewport the wing-mounted meltas flared. Then the bridge of the emissary craft was filled with molten steel and globes of reinforced glass. There was a moment of noise as the Caestus smashed through the wide viewport. At the same time, the atmosphere suddenly vented in a roar of air. The air caste crew were sucked out of the hissing gaps around the hull of the Caestus. Within seconds the entire bridge crew was dead or had been vomited out into the void, pain and horror forever frozen upon their faces as the twinned assault ramps slammed down, and a single black-armoured Terminator strode out, assault cannon spitting out trails of murderous steel.

Nergui's preferred style of battle combined speed and power in a devastating strike. He liked to drop from orbit like an eagle, jump pack lifting him from foe to foe, or ride his bike across the empty spaces. The slow and ponderous Terminator armour was not natural to him. He had not even left the assault ramp before he cursed its slowness. While it made him almost invulnerable to attack, it made him too slow. He crunched through the ruin of the emissary craft's bridge, punched his chainfist through the sealed blast doors, kicked the bent panels to the side and forced his way through.

As the vacuum of space sucked the air from the next corridor, it blasted towards him in a hail of debris. A startled fire warrior slammed full into his body. For a moment the warrior was held there by the force of the exiting air, mouth working soundlessly in the vacuum before it sucked him out and he spiralled into space.

Nergui was already at the second door, carving through it and standing back to let the next section of the ship expel its contents. He must have found a mess hall of some kind, for large pots and plates and eating utensils went past in a sloppy blizzard of what he guessed was food. There were chunks in the mix: chunks that were tau and human. A hundred of them, he thought, as they started to catch and clog up the hole he had carved.

His chainfist widened the hole and then the whole clot of food and bodies and furniture tore the rest of the door away, and it was all he could do to hold his footing.

Nergui kicked through the next door, and a squad of fire warriors greeted him. These had had time to engage their void suits, and magnetic boots held them to the floor as they lowered their pulse carbines and doused him in a hail of searing fire. His Terminator suit was older than the tau race. He fired. The hail of shots cut through the tau bodies as a shredder went through straw on an agri world. As their bodies were ripped apart, he was already stepping through the gore and engaging the next foes.

As Nergui advanced, the second Caestus assault ram hit the beleaguered emissary craft. Nergui felt the tau ship shudder at the impact.

We have them now, he thought.

Konrad Raimer's Caestus assault ram hit the tau ship on the fifth deck, just below the secondary engines. The Black Templar was a grey and grizzled veteran with nearly a hundred years within the Deathwatch to his name. He loved the darkness inside a suit of Terminator armour, relished the power, the fury, the weaponry it gave him.

He fired his heavy flamer as soon as the ramp doors slammed down. The corridor filled with fumes as the jet of promethium spilled out into the mess room. Off-duty tau warriors fell backwards before the incinerating flames. Behind Konrad three more Terminators strode out.

Sardegna, a Scion of Sanguinius, lowered the muzzle of his storm bolter and fired. Cadvan blocked a burst of plasma with his storm shield and brought his thunder hammer over his head in a crushing blow that crumpled a close-action battlesuit into the floor. Olbath of the Aurora Chapter fired his storm bolter in the familiar staccato pattern of paired shots: head and heart, head and heart.

The trailing shots punched fire warriors from their feet, exploded within them, showering their comrades with gore. Cadvan led the way, storm shield swatting away the few desultory shots, thunder hammer crackling with blue threads of power.

Nergui kept moving into the tau ship, carving his way through bulkheads and into its heart. His role was to cause maximum destruction. He drew the defenders towards him, mowed them down with torrents of murderous fire.

He had been inside the ship for just over sixty-four seconds when the third impact came. Nergui felt the ship tremble.

Even within his Terminator armour Nergui flinched at the cold touch on his neck as Domitian's mind found his own.

+In.+

Librarian Domitian was the Angel of Death in his suit of black artificer armour: a thing of sombre craftsmanship, visor sockets glowing, his psychic hood crackling with static overflow as he reached out through the ship, his gamma-plus level psychic presence a many-tendrilled thing, touching each mind.

His psychic power stunned everyone who felt it. It left the tau and their human allies slumped and drooling in mental shock. Frost rimed the corridor walls as Domitian searched for his brother.

It took him seven seconds to find his target, and when he did he reached out to Nergui and Konrad.

+He is alive.+

Leonas ripped the tubes from his veins, and staggered up. His head still hurt, and the wound in his side leaked blood and internal fluids, but he was alive, he told himself, and he could still fight.

The tau guards had no idea what was coming for them. They ducked back behind the bulkheads and stared in horror at the naked torso of the Space Marine, hammering the plexiglass screen, leaving bloody smears against the pane. The roar of battle came closer, and ice began to craze the monitor screens before them. One of the fire warriors tried to open the door to shoot. As he fumbled with the lock the door burst from its hinges and the Space Marine ripped the carbine from him.

Leonas fumbled with the mechanism for a moment, before giving up and smashing the guard in the face with the butt of the gun. By the time the others fought their way to him, Leonas stood in a room of the dead. He finally got the carbine to work as one by one the three Terminators pushed their way inside. He knew them by their Chapter markings. Konrad with heavy flamer, Sardegna with the heavy bolter, Cadvan with thunder hammer and storm shield, Olbath with his gilt-worked storm bolter.

'What kept you?' he said.

Konrad wasn't one for jokes. He spoke through his vox-grille.

'Are there any others?'

'Not that I know of,' Leonas said. Then more seriously. 'No. They're all dead.'

'Are you sure?'

'I'm sure. They don't have the same pressure. I can't die, you see.'

+Time to go.+ Domitian's mind spoke to them all simultaneously. Konrad made no reaction. +Let's get out of here.+

+We have him.+

The Librarian's message came as Nergui slammed another magazine into his bolter.

'How is he?'

+Angry we took so long.+

What was left of the fire warriors made way for a pair of close-assault battlesuits. The corridor was suddenly full of photon grenades and a blizzard of red burst cannon rounds. Nergui swore through gritted teeth as his underslung storm bolter jammed.

'Hazard battlesuit,' he hissed, as a third battlesuit engaged its jump pack and powered up the corridor. 'I'm retreating to my transport.'

The assault cannon was low on ammo. He moved too slowly, and cursed as a hail of burst cannon rounds smacked into his gut. His system internals flared red as circuits failed. He slammed the jammed assault cannon against the wall. His left leg was dragging. He slammed it again, and this time it clicked into firing mode, and he opened up, wildly spraying the corridor. The battlesuits ducked back. Nergui had a moment's warning as something landed behind him. He twisted too late.

There was a flash of light, and his helmet's readings flared red. His armour's leg had seized up completely and his assault cannon clicked empty. He punched his chainfist into the chest of the suit that had ambushed him. The ceramite teeth spun for a moment on the armour casing, before breaking through to the soft interior.

Nergui kept pushing until the razor sharp teeth found flesh and his left visor lens was splattered with gore. His suit's left leg was still shut down, so he half-dragged himself back along the corridor. He could see his Caestus only a hundred feet away, but at this rate it might just as well have been a league.

Mission objectives had him dragging out the databanks, but that would be impossible now. 'Can you help?' he hissed.

Domitian's presence was immediate.

+I was just waiting for you to ask.+

The Librarian's mind was operating at distance. It swept through the corridor in a stunning blast. Nergui felt it.

'Careful,' he voxed.

+I wanted to make sure.+

As Nergui's vision cleared he saw hazard suits hanging motionless in the air, their pilots unconscious. Nergui limped through the ruins of the ship's bridge, cutting the wall of databanks open and dragging them up the Caestus ramps. Tau were nothing if not efficient. The databanks came in large blocks that could easily be fitted and removed from their casing.

It took a minute before he had salvaged all he could. He punched the ramp controls closed.

'Disengage,' he commanded the machine-spirit and the Caestus snarled and trembled as the engines roared to full power. There was a hiss and screech of glass and steel, and then they were out in the void.

Nergui cursed as he dragged his malfunctioning leg up the boom and slumped down at the far end, exhausted. Next time just go in power armour, he thought, and then took in a deep breath and voxed the *Nemesis*.

'On our way back. We've got Leonas.'

CHAPTER SEVEN

News had spread through the crew that they had recovered one of the members of Kill Team Orion. Nergui could feel the change in mood. Even the servitors who had gathered on the landing deck seemed to move with a sharpness and a speed that was unlike them. He hailed the tech officer.

'Recover the data,' he said as they carefully unloaded the recovered xenos equipment, 'and report to me as soon as possible.'

The tech officer bowed. 'We will do all that we can.'

It was a week's journey back through the warp to Picket's Watch. A team of servitors re-established power for the databanks, repairing broken cables and then coaxing out the reams of tau information.

The Space Marines had little need for sleep. They worked constantly, comparing Imperial star charts to those of the tau, finding known points of reference, and slowly piecing together a picture of tau movements to and from the Agrellan Warzone.

When they had inputted it all, the holo-charts glowed with criss-crossing web-lines of xenos activity. Its scale and sophistication repelled them all. Supply hubs, refuelling stations, convoy protection teams, automated drone sentries, human worlds secretly compliant, all enabling the massive movement of the invasion fleet that had smashed through to Agrellan. Konrad located two new routes that had appeared only a Terran week before the appearance of the Stormsurges.

'This is how they are transporting their new battlesuits,' he said with grim conviction.

Domitian's slight face followed the lines on the chart that the

Black Templar was pointing to. 'You're right,' he said. 'We will feed the information through to Navy command. But those routes are too well defended for us to attack.'

They stared at the glowing charts.

Konrad scowled. 'We have to do something,' he snapped.

'You're right,' Nergui said. 'We have to find the heart of the enemy.'

Konrad snarled in frustration. 'So where do we attack?'

Nergui paused. 'The question is not where, but what. I will speak to Leonas.'

There was an honour guard of adepts assembled to watch Leonas' return to Picket's Watch. They stood by the front gate. Nergui let them celebrate, but he was tense. The Stormsurge had to be stopped somehow. The enemy had to be weakened. The coming meeting with Jotunn troubled him as he led his warriors up the steps and into the Westkeep. After so many setbacks, the return of Leonas should have put a fresh energy into their steps, but now they knew much more about the new suits the tau had deployed, and unless they could do something to hinder their foe, the future of the battle at Agrellan and the fate of the Eastern Fringe hung in the balance.

The entrance hall was hung with Deathwatch banners, each proudly telling of victories over the xenos. It was a cold and draughty chamber, the red and black tiles usually unoccupied except for the door wards and the occasional servo-skull that hummed across the empty space.

This time, as they crested the top step and nodded to the door wards, they saw a new kill team standing in the entrance way. It seemed that Jotunn's request for aid from Talassa Prime had borne fruit, though one kill team was hardly enough in this battle. They should have been sent a hundred brothers, or more.

Nergui stepped forwards. Their leader – a Brazen Minotaur – had a tyranid skin thrown over one pauldron. He was a square hulk of a warrior, with curly black hair and a face that must once have been handsome before half of it had been torn away. The steel plates beneath did little to soften his arrogant air.

'I am Brother Corith,' he said. 'We come from Talassa Prime. Word is that you have lost two kill teams, against the tau.'

'We have,' Nergui said. 'You are aware of the state of the battle for Agrellan?'

'We are,' Corith said. 'And we are ready.' He turned to the others. 'We are Kill Team Zeal.'

He introduced his brothers. A Carcharodon was the first to step forwards. He was almost softly spoken. 'I am Iason. We are glad to join your fight.'

Next was a Space Marine with a formal, almost bookish look about him, with a grey shoulder pad marked with the letter 'M' in black. Nergui frowned. 'Greetings, brother. I do not know that sigil.'

'Brotherhood of a Thousand,' the warrior said, taking Nergui's hand in a firm grip. 'I am Eadmund.'

'Ah,' Nergui said. 'I have never served with a brother of your Chapter. But I have heard of your exploits. You liberated the Mostar System from the Darellian.'

Eadmund smiled. 'The dog-soldiers. Yes. I was honoured to be part of that victory when I was a just a Scout.'

Nergui gave a brief nod.

The next was a Dark Angel, his black hood drawn over a lean and grizzled face.

'I am Cadmus,' the warrior whispered. Behind him was an Imperial Fist named Cerys, Mateo Nuoros, a Crimson Fist, and Kallos, an Ultramarine – but it was the last who caught Nergui's attention.

'Greetings, Black Shield,' he said. The warrior bore no Chapter markings, nothing that might identify him, just plain black power armour, a silver left arm, and a helmet etched with threads of silver, which traced the faint outline of a skull.

'I am Hadrian,' the dark-haired warrior said. His eyes were violet, and his skin almost white. 'Of the Deathwatch.'

'Welcome,' Nergui said. Black Shields were bad luck and they did not need any bad luck at the moment. As the kill teams shook hands, the Black Shield, Hadrian, turned and looked to Leonas. 'I have heard of you, brother. You are the one they called the "Last"?'

'Yes,' Leonas said. 'I am.'

Corith's skin pulled against the steel plates in his face as he snorted at the exchange. 'The last what?'

'I am Leonas of the Black Consuls Chapter.'

The Brazen Minotaur clearly spent less time than his fellows in the librariums. 'And what of it?'

Leonas fixed him with a hard stare. 'Do you not know? The Black Consuls were destroyed in battle at Goddeth Hive. Probably when you were still a Scout, learning how to clean a bolter.'

The Brazen Minotaur sneered at the insult, but Leonas spoke over him. 'At the time there were seven of us who were not with the Chapter. Three of us were on a pilgrimage to the Shrine of our Primogenitor on Ultramar. The other four were serving with the Deathwatch. For a while there was talk of refounding our Chapter. There still is, sometimes, but no decision came, so we resolved to join the Deathwatch. That was three and a half centuries ago. Brother Agrys died that same year, fighting the Demiurge Incursion. Brother Soktritas was lost to the Great Devourer. Brothers Cylus and

Nikanos were sent to Vraks. Their gene-seed was never recovered. Brother Kyriakos was interred into a Dreadnought, on Watch Fortress Callax. He was last seen holding the breach, locked in combat with the dark eldar. Until six months ago there was only me, and Razlon. He served the Throne in Segmentum Pacificus. But now, I hear that he too is dead. I am the only one left. Deathwatch is my Chapter now. When I die the Black Consuls shall be no more than a note in the histories of the Imperium of Mankind.'

The sneer had softened somewhat, and the Brazen Minotaur held his tongue. But the Black Shield, Hadrian, frowned. 'The Segmentum Pacificus is far from here. How do you know he is dead?'

'I saw it in my dream,' Leonas said. 'Just as I saw Brother Konrad would come to release me.'

Iason, the Carcharodon, made the sign of the aquila, but Hadrian laughed. The Deathwatch was tolerant of all the Chapters who served with them.

'Good,' Nergui said. 'I shall leave the pleasantries to you. Now, please excuse me, I must report to our watch-commander.'

'Ah,' Corith said. 'The Lone Wolf? He said he would see you in the morning. He is busy.'

'At what?'

Corith smiled. 'He did not tell me.'

CHAPTER EIGHT

Nergui spent the night in meditation, but no answers came. An hour before daybreak there was a scrape on his door. An adept bowed.

'Here, lord,' he said. 'This has just arrived.'

The parchment had come from the Tower of the Astropath. Nergui broke the wax seal and unrolled the parchment. It bore greetings from his Chapter, the White Scars.

Nergui read the message and smiled. The Emperor had delivered.

As Nergui made his way down to the feast hall the only light came from distant stars that glimmered in the high gothic windows. There was a pensive feel to the air, which Nergui did not think was entirely of his own imagination. The Lone Wolf only secluded himself when there was a matter of great import. The air smelt of burned meat and knucklebones were spread out across the floor. The Lone Wolf had been communing with the fates, escrying the paths in his own, particular way. Jotunn turned as soon as Nergui entered.

'Ah!' he said. 'At last. The eagle returns. What have you found, Nergui? Have you brought me news?'

The two of them met in the middle of the great hall. Nergui drew in a deep breath.

'Yes,' he said. 'I think we have good news.'

Jotunn put his head back and laughed. His fangs glinted in the dim light and he rubbed his pale hands together. 'Nergui – it is not often that you give me good news! Come tell, what have you found?'

Nergui slowly laid out the data-slates for the Lone Wolf to inspect: vox transcripts, reams of picts, supply lists. The Space Wolf leafed through them all, taking it in, building up each fragment into a picture that made sense. At last he let out a low grunt. 'We cannot attack the transport lines. They are too heavily guarded. But we could pass on their location to others.'

Nergui nodded. 'We have. The Imperial Navy could strike them here, at Major's Point. Or here, even. But it would require a bold captain to go so far into enemy space and once there, how long could they remain exposed, so close to the Fi'irious Sept?'

'These are not for us.'

'No. But here. Look at this.'

Nergui presented the information he had gleaned from the data banks and that Leonas had reported to them. 'The battlesuits are coming from the tau empire. This was where Kill Team Primus discovered the tau base in the Sexton Sector. See these transport routes? After that they move here, to the Distaf Nebula. See, as I move time forwards, the routes of these ships changes. See the movements into this system. The tau call this place Sh'anshi. I have checked the records. It is the same as the Imperial planet Proth.'

Jotunn frowned at the data-slate before him. 'Proth. What is this place?'

'Ice world, mainly. Limited mining. It was abandoned during warp storm Hades.'

Jotunn's pink eyes narrowed. 'What use would the enemy have for a place like Proth?'

'No one has any interest in Proth, which makes it invaluable to our foes. I think they are taking crew from Agrellan and training them how to use the new battlesuits. See. We have a plan of a base, here. It does not say so, but I would guess this is what was found by Kill Team Primus. And it is what has been built on Proth.'

The Space Wolf looked. There was an orbital defence platform at the north pole. Three hunter cadres. Xenos auxiliaries. He snorted. 'This does not look like a training facility, it looks like a fortress!'

'Exactly. A training facility that is well defended.'

'But why is this place so important that the enemy defend it with such strength? Why do they take such care to hide it from us?'

'As they expand they are coming up against new problems that their old systems and structures cannot cope with. Here, in the outer regions, they are having to pool the strength of their septs. Evolution is something they have excelled at. What I saw from Ellial's visions has to have been some kind of pilot training facility for the new Stormsurge. If we strike this place and destroy it, we will rob them of months of battle-trained warriors.'

Jotunn smiled briefly. 'I see, Nergui. But to attack this place would mean destroying it in one strike. Killing all the crews. And I have less than twenty warriors left. How can we attack such a place with hope for success?'

Nergui returned his gaze. 'We cannot.'

The White Scar's face was inscrutable, but Jotunn had a nose for such things.

'You have a plan?'

'I have more than a plan. I have this.' Nergui held up the roll of parchment.

Jotunn read it and scowled. 'A White Scars strike cruiser has slipped out of the warp. A week's flight away. How does this help? Kor'sarro is already engaged on Agrellan. He has sworn to find Shadowsun and kill her. If this ship has strayed off course, he will be eager for them to catch up. He will not let you take his warriors. You are chasing lightning. They will not help.'

The Space Wolf screwed the parchment up and dropped it onto the scattered knucklebones at his feet.

'The ship that has arrived is the *Northwind*,' Nergui said. It is the flagship of the Tulwar Brotherhood, the Fourth Company of White Scars. Kor'sarro Khan leads the *Third* Company.' Nergui let that fact sink in for a moment. 'The Fourth Company are bound for Chogoris, to defend her from invasion. The warp has blown her off course. I have seen a little of the ways of the galaxy, and when a company of the White Scars loses sight of the Astronomican and becomes stranded, just as we need their help, then I am not one to pass over that opportunity.'

'What good will they be to us?' Jotunn demanded. 'The White Scars do not serve the Deathwatch. If they are bound for Chogoris, then to Chogoris they will go.'

'Not necessarily.'

The Lone Wolf snarled. 'Speak no more in riddles, White Scar. Tell me plain. If you have a plan, then announce it!'

'I shall. The Fourth Company of White Scars is led by the Master of Blades. We were Scouts together, once, riding our bikes over the bones of our foes. I taught him how to strip a boltgun. His name is Batbayar Khan. I know how to persuade him to help our cause. In fact I have already sent word to his strike cruiser, telling him how he can gain his company great glory…'

'And?'

'The eagle flies to the glove for the easy meal.'

Jotunn let out a snort of laughter. 'You are crafty as you are devious, White Scar. When does their cruiser arrive?'

'Four days.'

Jotunn slapped the White Scar on the arm. Nergui had to brace himself against the blow.

'Go!' Jotunn roared. 'Meet this brother of yours. See if he will eat your scraps.'

CHAPTER NINE

Westkeep was crowned with a wonder of Dark Age technology: the double-barrelled defence laser that bore the name Dorn's Fury. It had always been the last line of defence for the citadel, when secrecy failed. Back-up generators, batteries and overload circuits spiralled down into the keep's core, deep in the rock upon which the citadel stood.

As the White Scars strike cruiser *Northwind* approached to within five hundred miles, Dorn's Fury turned towards it, the weapon's machine-spirit locking on to the approaching craft, the double barrels tracking it as it sped closer.

The captain of the *Northwind* sent a curt message. Nergui stood at Jotunn's side.

'Batbayar Khan is tetchy,' the Lone Wolf rumbled in his chest. 'He says he will not continue unless our defence laser is disengaged. He wants me to disarm our only protection? It is preposterous. Who is this khan and how dare he tell me what I should do?'

'Do as he says,' Nergui said. 'He is not bluffing. If he leaves we lose a company of the Adeptus Astartes and the chance to throw back our foes. If we step Dorn's Fury down you lose nothing but your pride.'

Jotunn growled. 'What is a warrior without pride? I do not like this. Are there things you are not telling me, Nergui of the White Scars?'

'Yes,' Nergui laughed. 'Many things.' The sound of laughter was a rarely heard sound within Picket's Watch. But as the last echoes of it died away, Nergui's face was serious. 'But we need Batbayar. I do not think Jotunn of the Space Wolves, Watch-Commander of Picket's Watch, will die from the loss of his pride.'

Jotunn turned his back. 'I am Jotunn of the Deathwatch,' he hissed. 'I was old when this Batbayar was a mewling babe at his mother's breast. I do not take orders from a pompous young pup!'

'Do as he says,' Nergui said.

The Lone Wolf turned his albino pink eyes on the White Scar. Jotunn loved Dorn's Fury. It spoke to his soul. He saw the ancient gun as a kindred spirit. It was how he saw the Deathwatch: ancient, tough, defiant, isolated, deadly against its foes. Disarming the ancient gun was emasculation. Surrender.

There was a long pause.

'It will please Batbayar Khan. He is... proud. Overly so, at times, but if I meet him, I can turn him to our cause.'

Jotunn growled deep in his chest. It was a low rumble that set the air vibrating. He nodded.

'Have it done then. Order Dorn's Fury to disengage. But I hold you responsible, White Scar.'

Nergui put a hand to the Space Wolf's pauldron. 'Thank you. Trust me, I will bring him to our cause.'

Nergui was in the librarium when the servo-skull found him, its lenses whirring as it focused on the White Scar's face. Satisfied it had found the right recipient, its memory logs played back the broadcast message in a staccato voice. 'The White Scars strike cruiser *Northwind* has docked with the orbital platform, captain.'

Nergui took a deep breath. He was ready. 'Is my Thunderhawk prepared?'

'Yes.' The skull hovered, lenses whirring once more.

As he sat in the Deathwatch Thunderhawk that carried him up to the *Northwind*, Nergui prepared himself for his meeting with his gene-brothers. He felt apprehensive, in a way that disturbed him.

There were ghosts in his past that he had long thought banished, but they haunted him now.

The last time Nergui had fought with his gene-brothers was on Gastrond IV. He'd led the Second Company – the Firefist Brotherhood. His hand had shaken with the magnitude of this honour. The objective of that long campaign was to kill a greenskin war-chief named Blackfist. He'd cornered the xenos forces on the plains of Brenax Secundus, and Blackfist had led the whole ork horde against them. Nergui remembered how the flat plains were dark with the foe, a black cloud of exhaust fumes above their heads, the sky raining lead as the beasts fired their weapons wildly into the air.

Nergui had led the charge, a whole company as one, firing their side-mounted bolters into the masses of orks. Smaller greenskins sped forwards on crude bikes to meet them, and Nergui had cut through the creatures like a warm blade through wax, prompting a great roar of anger and terror and exultation. The xenos seemed to love nothing more than a battle, even one in which they were destined to be destroyed.

Blackfist was a vast hulk of fangs and neck and gap-tusked jaws, riding a bike of enormous proportions and unique manufacture. He had come for Nergui through the desperate melee. The tusked giant had bellowed his fury, the great metal jaws of his power armour working crudely in time with his own. Nergui had emptied a full magazine of bolter shells into Blackfist's machine, but the ramshackle bike had only given up fifty feet from him, slewing to a halt in a billowing cloud of burning fumes.

Blackfist had jumped free and bounded towards Nergui, still bellowing with the same long breath, chainaxes whirling. The ork's keenest bodyguards had charged with him. Nergui rode one down, put bolter shells through the next and saved his power lance for their leader. The explosive charge caught Blackfist under the chin. A jolt went through the ork's body, but he did not seem to notice, even when Nergui's tulwar sliced one muscled limb down to the thick bone.

Nergui had made three passes before Blackfist understood that he was dead. He had fallen backwards, still snarling as his heels drummed the earth.

The death of their leader only drove the greenskins to a higher pitch of fury as each one tried to outdo the other, to claim the title of warchief. The fighting was furious. Nergui's left pauldron was ripped from his armour. He had a dozen rents in his war-plate. His blood clotted in the dust of battle. In the end, Nergui had stood alone, eagle banner in one hand, tulwar in the other.

He flinched just reliving the moment. Nergui had thought himself done. His confidence had drawn him too deep into the enemy. And what point in killing the leader, if the beast had a hundred heads?

He was a blur of steel, a typhoon of fury. He was as slippery as a river dragon, made of mist and clouds.

'Jaghatai!' he had raged, and he had felt the power of his primarch fill him with the fury of a steppes gale. He was destruction. He was death. He was a sublime killer, and his warriors saw his stand, as the piles of greenskin dead rose up about him, and their will and drive and relentless skill with blade and bolter drove the greenskins back.

He had a moment to draw breath. Dark liquids oozed from his suit, and foul greenskin blood covered his arm from his hand to his shoulder. And then he saw how many of his warriors he had lost to the xenos, and a furious fire burned within him that would lead him eventually to this place: serving with the Deathwatch.

His charge had been foolish. It had risked too much. He had lost too many of his brothers, and Nergui felt his pride tarnished. Was his time with the Deathwatch an attempt to make up for this, he wondered? That battle had been decades ago. He had not ridden with his gene-brothers since.

The realisation hit him with a feeling akin to loss. He missed his gene-brothers.

CHAPTER TEN

Cadvan was flying Nergui's Thunderhawk up to the *Northwind*. The Storm Giant had tried a number of times to start up a conversation, but each time Nergui had answered with a single word, and by the time the gunship arrived – a black dot alongside the vast white gun batteries of the *Northwind* – the pilot had fallen silent.

And silence suited Nergui.

He felt the vibration as they passed through the airlock into the upper port-side landing deck, felt the landing gear touch down. He heard the hiss as the atmosphere of the Deathwatch Thunderhawk equalised with that aboard the *Northwind*, heard his own heavy footsteps as he strode out of the dark into the brightly lit landing bay.

'No one's here to greet you,' Cadvan voxed.

'No,' Nergui said. 'Maybe they do not think one of their own needs to be greeted.'

'Maybe they do not think you are one of them any more.'

Nergui did not answer. He had spent so long in the shadows of Picket's Watch that the glare of the lumen globes on the plain white walls, with their lightning strike imagery, seemed too bright, too stark. But as he stepped onto the side landing ramp Nergui had the odd sense that he was *home*.

Across the long wall were four Thunderhawks, all emblazoned with the lightning strike of the White Scars and the crossed tulwars of the Fourth Company. Two servitors were loading missiles into the underwing hard points, while across the flight deck a trio of tracked servitors were attending to an ancient Fire Raptor, *Obos*. Steam vented from its engine exhausts as the turbofans wound down, and a wheel-track servitor moved across the chevroned landing deck with a fuel hose connector where its right shoulder should be.

Nergui had flown *Obos* once, long, long ago. He crossed the deck and reached out his hand to the Fire Raptor's fuselage. He could feel the hum of the machine-spirit, fierce and eager, and he felt it recognised him as one of its own. He patted its ablative armour in a way that reminded him of his father stroking the muzzle of his black stallion. It shocked him, for a moment, to see the black of his glove against the white of the White Scars craft.

He had barely noticed the colour of his armour for years. But here, he saw himself in a new light. Black, not white. Secretive, not exultant.

A White Scars Apothecary entered the deck. His long black hair was pulled back in a knot so tight it pulled the skin of his forehead up.

He had a steel jaw and three ritual scars down what remained of each cheek. A voice sounded but hismouth did not move, and for a moment Nergui thought that there was a third interlocutor somewhere, but it was this warrior who spoke.

'I am Khulan,' he said. 'Announce yourself, stranger in black.'

Nergui turned full towards him. 'I am Nergui Khan, of the White Scars.'

'Khan no longer,' the words came, and as Nergui strode towards the Apothecary, he saw the speaker inside the steel mouth.

'No,' Nergui said, 'but still a White Scar. And as a brother I seek your khan.'

'Batbayar Khan?'

Nergui nodded.

'Your hand, brother.' As Nergui let him take it there was a sharp prick. Nergui pulled his hand back and saw blood. 'Forgive me,' Khulan said, lifting his arm to see the readings on his narthecium. 'I was sent here to see if you were really who you claim to be.'

Nergui gave a humourless laugh. 'The Tulwar Brotherhood have sunk low if this is the way you greet brothers now.'

'Forgive me. Dealings with the Deathwatch are never straightforward. I do not like to expose my khan to unnecessary dangers. He does that well enough for himself. You bear the gene-seed of the White Scars so I shall trust that you are indeed Nergui.' The Apothecary bowed. 'Batbayar is my khan and he asked me to greet you.'

'And this is his greeting?'

'This way,' Khulan said. 'Welcome to the *Northwind*, home of the Fourth Company, the Tulwar Brotherhood, scourge of the enemies of Mankind.'

'What was that about?' Cadvan voxed.

'It's how we do things,' Nergui voxed back. After a moment's thought he added, 'Leave me to it now,' and closed the link.

Nergui followed Khulan through corridors that could have belonged to any of the ships within the White Scars Chapter. The walls were plain and white, adorned with occasional tapestries of felted yak hair, woven totems in niches, scroll paintings, bells of cast bronze: all the symbols of Chogorean power.

Nergui remembered the days when he rode on the front of his mother's horse, and felt a strange pang at the thought of riding with his people again.

Nergui followed Khulan along the corridors, to the Hall of the Warriors. His palms were clammy and he could not tell what exactly it was that made his hearts beat so fast.

The great brass doors were shut, their ring-handles – each a ton in weight – tied with red and white silk scarves. Two bronze dragons were emblazoned into the wall on either side of the gateway. One devoured a greenskin, the other held a necron pyramid in its claws. Beneath them was a stylised image of the Empty Lands of Chogoris, where the wild tribes lived and warred and supplied the new recruits, and where Nergui and Batbayar had grown up as children, Nergui from the Chaoge, Batbayar from the Tufan.

By the time the doors swung open his eyes had become used to the bright glare of white, but through the doors he saw that the Hall of the Warriors was dark, except for the low light of yak-butter wall lamps, the single flames reflected in the wide bowls in which they burned. The ceiling hung with coils of unlit incense. Embroidered banners covered each wall, the images lost, only the glint of silver and golden thread revealing depictions of massed armies of white-clad warriors.

The vast hall echoed as Nergui strode inside, Khulan at his shoulder. The unpolished marble flagstones rang as he paced into the centre of the room and stopped as the main doors shut behind him.

Suddenly the hall was filled with the growl of fifty bikes sweeping in from side doors. Within moments he and Khulan stood in the centre of concentric circles of bikers, each going about in opposite directions. Nergui felt the sudden proximity of so many of his gene-brothers exhilarating, almost overwhelming. The roar of engines, the stink of promethium fuel, the acrid scent of the yak-oil they used to tie back their hair – all this woke the White Scar within Nergui and he longed to leap on a bike and ride.

'They have not forgotten Nergui,' he thought. 'And Nergui has not forgotten them.'

One of the warriors veered suddenly out of the circle and accelerated towards him, his rear tyre skidding as he braked to a sudden halt, and the front of the bike, where the bolter muzzles jutted out, tapped gently against Nergui's black knee pad. The rider tore off his helmet. This was not Batbayar but a young warrior with a face that was proud, arrogant and ugly beneath thick black brows that met in the middle.

His mouth was harsh.

'Who summoned us?' he demanded.

'I am Nergui.'

The other warrior gave him a contemptuous nod. 'What is your tribe?'

'Chaoge.'

The other warrior snorted and slammed his fist into his power-armoured chest. 'I am of the Red Tangut.'

This was Batbayar's doing, Nergui knew. Chaoge and Red Tangut tribes were blood enemies. Nergui knew he would have to fight.

'What is your name, Red Tangut?'

The other warrior punched his chest-plate with his left fist. 'I am Ganzorig.'

Nergui grinned. 'First blood,' he said.

Ganzorig put out his hand and another of the warriors with the Red Tangut scars on his cheeks pulled a Chogorean power axe from his back and put it into Ganzorig's hand.

'That is a big weapon for a duel,' Nergui said and conspicuously left his tulwar sheathed.

Ganzorig pressed the activation stud, and the blade of the power axe crackled blue. 'It is typical of a Chaoge to try and wriggle from a fight.'

Nergui felt more alive than he had done for years. He was a child again, on the steppes, with the smell of wood smoke in his nose, flocks to guard, and a constant threat of wolves and enemies. He dropped into a fighting stance. 'Come, Ganzorig of the Red Tangut.'

Ganzorig leapt at him, power axe already swinging down in a terrifying blow. Nergui twisted and the blade slammed into the slabs he had been standing on. He made no effort to strike back, but let Ganzorig of the Red Tangut swing backhanded, overhead, body swipes, face-butts.

'Draw your weapon, Chaoge!' Ganzorig snarled, but Nergui did not need a weapon to beat a Red Tangut. He was a black blur, always just out of reach of the swinging blade. Ganzorig grunted and cursed, sweat starting to spray from his bald pate. His face grew uglier with anger as his frustration grew.

'Fight!' he hissed. 'Are you a coward?'

Nergui skipped back out of his range. Ganzorig swung wildly at his head and Nergui ducked in low, caught the axe haft in one hand, and drove the other fist into Ganzorig's face.

The other warrior was thrown backwards. He cursed, spat a piece of tooth onto the ground as he lifted the axe, and readied for another swing.

Nergui pointed to the flagstones at their feet.

The spittle was red.

Sometimes it was the precision blow that killed the foe. The shot of a lone sniper, not the rage of a hundred warriors.

'Don't bring an axe next time,' Nergui said as he held out his hand. Ganzorig cursed and bowed stiffly.

'Well fought, Chaoge,' he said, in a manner that implied there was no honour in Nergui's win.

There was laughter like a clap of thunder. A Land Speeder descended from the dark heights of the hall, where the incense coils hung.

A white-clad warrior stood on one of the Land Speeder's vanes. It flew down along one side of the hall and banked sharply to come around the other side. As the Land Speeder made its third pass the warrior leapt from its vane and landed with a heavy thud that cracked the marble flags at Nergui's feet. It was Batbayar Khan.

He had aged, of course. His moustaches now hung to his chest, and they were shot with steel grey, but his face still looked youthful, and the light in his dark eyes glittered.

'Greetings, brother!' he roared, his bone charms rattling as he held Nergui at arm's length. 'I told Ganzorig to lose,' he said. 'I did not know if you had forgotten how to fight. You have been away from the hunt for too long. When will you ride with us again? The wind misses your call, brother. The skies miss the wind of your passing. The hunt misses your speed. *I* miss you, brother!'

Nergui found himself laughing with his old comrade. It came to him again, how much he missed his Chapter – a sudden, sharp pain, the same sense of loss. He bowed his head. 'As soon as my service here is done.'

'When will that be?' Batbayar roared. Nergui could not answer. Batbayar still held him by the shoulders but as he took in Nergui's armour the khan's face looked pained. 'I thought you had summoned me to ask me to take you away from here. To colour your armour white. It should not be black. Black is not your colour, brother.'

'I need your help,' Nergui said.

The hint of a shadow passed across Batbayar's face, but he said, 'Speak! What Batbayar can do, he shall. But I must warn you. I have been summoned back to Chogoris. There are dark tidings, brother.'

'I know them,' Nergui said. 'I have heard. But still, I have need of your help.'

Batbayar held out his hand. 'Speak then. What is it?'

Nergui told him.

There was a moment's pause and Batbayar turned his head to give Nergui a sideways look. 'You want me to destroy a xenos factory?' Batbayar's reaction seemed to waver between insulted and disappointed. His eyes narrowed and there was a hint of anger in his voice. 'Do you mock me?'

Nergui shook his head. 'I do not mock.'

Batbayar's temper flared for a moment. 'I am Batbayar Khan! I lead the Fourth Company, the Tulwar Brotherhood. I shall not carry the eagle banner into battle against such a petty target. It is like taking a boltgun to hunt a rat.' He spat out the last words with distaste, then called to the horde. 'Nergui, it cannot be you. It is an imposter. Warriors! Come!' he shouted. 'Let us go!'

Each squad peeled away to either side. Immediately the hall was filled with the sound of bikes. 'Wait!' Nergui shouted, and the roar of bikes subsided for a moment as the khan turned back to face the black-armoured figure.

'You think there is no glory here, Batbayar of the Tufan, Khan of the Fourth Company. Is that all the Tulwar Brotherhood want? Glory? These xenos are tough as steel. They are as fast as an eagle. They are as slippery as a snake, and they bite!'

Batbayar looked back and laughed with contempt. 'Chogoris calls me. She is under attack. I am needed where there are foes I can kill. Foes worthy of my fury! I will leave two squads. Twenty brothers. No more.'

Batbayar whistled and the Land Speeder swept in like a summoned eagle, swooping down to the centre of the room. As Batbayar set one foot on the wing, Nergui shouted once more, 'Kor'sarro Khan has not found the tau an easy foe.'

The words hung in the air for a moment, and Batbayar turned, his foot still resting on the Land Speeder's wing. 'Kor'sarro Khan fights the tau… I had almost forgotten. Has he not defeated them yet?'

'He has not.'

'And has he not killed their commander yet?'

'He has not.'

Batbayar paused. There was a note of expectancy in the revving engines of the bikes. Nergui took his chance.

'Kor'sarro Khan has suffered great troubles on Agrellan. He has lost many brothers. If you win victory where he has not, then what glory would that bring for the Tulwar Brotherhood and their khan?'

Batbayar took his foot off the Land Speeder, and the roar of bike engines stilled for a moment. The khan looked at Nergui for a long time. 'I do not smell deceit,' he said. 'Nor do I see it. But I feel it.'

'I do not lie,' Nergui said. He nodded towards Khulan. 'I came here in good faith. I am Nergui of the Chaoge. It was your Apothecary who tested my blood, as if I were a lie clad in power armour.'

Batbayar seemed taken aback. 'If Khulan did this thing, I did not command it.'

'Maybe not, khan. But you did not forbid it either, and there is guilt in the absence of command.'

'You speak to me of guilt?' Batbayar's anger flared again.

'Yes,' Nergui said. 'There is guilt in omission, just as there is guilt in inaction. I come here to ask for your help, and you deny me. That makes you guilty.'

Batbayar thumped a clenched fist against the intricately worked breast of his suit of Mark VIII power armour. 'I am not guilty. Chogoris burns. The tribes have fallen back to the Empty Lands. They hide from the enemy that comes from the sky.'

'If you destroy this place, it will not take you more than a month. Can Chogoris last that long? I say yes. We know our people. They do not succumb. They do not bow. They fight and they die, and in killing their enemies they are glad to die.'

Batbayar paused for a long time, considering. 'I would like to help you, but Kor'sarro has the Eagle Brotherhood on Agrellan. To have two companies fighting the tau... Are these xenos worthy of so many of our Chapter? We would just get in each other's way.'

'What if I told you Shadowsun was on this planet that I wish you to attack?'

Batbayar Khan put up a hand and the roar of bikes came to a sudden halt. For a moment it seemed that the only thing moving in the room was the dust and fumes of their exhausts. A sly smile played about Batbayar's lips. 'I knew you were hiding something, Nergui of the Chaoge. I could smell it on you. It hangs about you like a cloud of flies over yak's dung. Tell me true. Is this Shadowsun on the planet?'

It was like pushing at an open door. Nergui could not hold himself back. The lie came easily, even to his own gene-brother. 'Yes. We think she is there. You do the killing. The glory will be all yours.'

Batbayar licked his lips. 'I could bring her head to Kor'sarro Khan. As a gift from the Tulwar Brotherhood. Both our companies could return to Chogoris.' Batbayar smiled as he savoured the thought. 'Kor'sarro would not be pleased.'

Nergui frowned and nodded. 'Oh, no. He would not.' It was as if the decades of separation had never been. The two of them slipped back into their old friendship. 'Kor'sarro has worked so hard to find her. He has lost so many of his warriors. He has sworn to kill her.'

'He would be foresworn,' Batbayar laughed, and then remembered himself. 'Poor Kor'sarro. We should not shame him so.'

'No,' Nergui said. 'We should not.'

'We should not,' Batbayar sighed. 'But let us do it anyway!'

CHAPTER ELEVEN

As soon as he returned from the *Northwind*, Nergui started putting his plan into action.

Kill Team Zeal were to lead the way, preparing the ground before the rest arrived.

Nergui gave them their orders, and came to see them off.

He stood with Corith at the side of the landing port as the others climbed aboard the shuttle. Their strike cruiser, the *Valete*, was ready above them.

'Remember. Secrecy is paramount.'

Corith nodded curtly. 'I understand.'

They clasped forearms.

'Good winds,' Nergui said. It was a traditional White Scars farewell, and Corith nodded.

'I shall see you there,' the Brazen Minotaur said.

Nergui stood alone as he watched their Thunderhawk lift off and disappear into the black of the galaxy. In his mind's eye he could trace them up to the docks, aboard the strike cruiser *Valete*, and then out towards the Mandeville point. He never liked to be left behind, but as he turned to walk back towards the inner courtyard, he consoled himself that soon the rest of them would be following.

Leonas was in the inner courtyard when he returned. 'How was it meeting your gene-brothers again?' he asked.

'It has brought back many… memories.'

'Do you want to return to them?'

Nergui smiled. 'No. Not yet.' He thought about saying more, but the Black Consul did not have the option of returning to his Chapter, and so he held his tongue.

'When are we leaving?' Leonas asked.

'As soon as the White Scars are ready.'

'Aren't you coming to the Remembering?'

Nergui cursed. 'No. I must speak with Jotunn. Be there for me.'

Leonas nodded. 'I shall.'

Sometimes Westkeep reminded him of Quan Zhou, the fortress-monastery of the White Scars.

It bore the nickname of the Fort of Ten Thousand Doors. But deep, deep in the old palace's heart were the remains of an older temple, and occasionally Nergui had found himself walking there, on steps worn almost flat with age.

The depths of Picket's Watch had the same ancient air about them. The same smell, the same damp touch, the same musty air that had lingered there for centuries, undisturbed, and barely even breathed. It was to those deepest chambers that Jotunn summoned him. The Lone Wolf had insisted. 'See Kill Team Zeal off, then come to me. I shall be waiting on the first level.'

'The first?'

'Yes,' Jotunn had said. 'You have never been so deep before?'

'No.'

'Don't worry. You will find the way.'

The conversation echoed through Nergui's mind as he took the long stair down. The blast doors opened at his touch, and he went through doorways he had not known even existed.

The stairs plunged past ground level, deep into the heart of the rock, the steps no longer slabs of masonry, but carved from the mountain itself. The White Scar passed ancient chambers where narrow shafts of light from lumen-globes stabbed down to the dark hollows, where the dust of xenos bones lay thick on the floor, past crude shrines of uncarved rock, where paintings of extinct xenos races lined the wall, down to where the hum of the vast generatorium was just an echo.

Nergui's enhanced vision could only make out rough shapes of light and dark. This was the purest darkness, which had lain undisturbed for millennia. He put out a hand to feel his way. The walls fell away to either side as he stepped into the dark mouth of the cave, and he felt his skin prickle.

He spoke to the darkness. 'Are you there?'

He felt he was being watched, and marched with one hand out into the centre of the cave. Then there was light from across the cavern.

Faint, distant, wan – but it was enough to illuminate the white head of Jotunn.

'You have come,' the Lone Wolf growled. 'Now follow.'

Nergui followed the Space Wolf down another staircase of worn steps. The air grew colder. The steps became irregular and there was a faint hum.

'I did not think there was anything down here,' Nergui said after they had passed ancient doors, each marked with the clenched fist.

'There is much down here, brother. There is much that you do not know that dates back to times beyond our ken. These are the ancient catacombs. I will show them to you, perhaps. It is where the Imperial Fists laid their most honoured warriors.'

The Space Wolf stopped at a brass door set into the rock. It bore no sigil, just a pair of holes in the interlocking ceramite plates. Jotunn fitted the two prongs of his clavis key into the lock. There was a faint hiss as the door unsealed, and then it swung open before them.

'What is this place?'

'It is named the Ubliet, though that is a poor name, for this part of the fortress is used for many things,' Jotunn said. 'It is a place of keys and doors and hidden chambers. It is where all doors are locked. It is both a prison and a safe. It is the deepest vaults of our fortress.'

Nergui stopped and put a hand to his ear. He turned and looked behind him, but the corridor was empty. 'I heard my mother's voice,' he said. 'I heard a shout. She called me by the name she used when I was a child.'

Jotunn sniffed the air. 'All I smell is us,' he said.

'There!' Nergui said. 'I heard her again.'

'You heard our enemies. Some of the things locked away here have refused to die. They are too dangerous to be let out. One of those touched your mind.'

Nergui listened again. There was a strange call, like a muffled voice. It came clearer this time. 'Shao-shao!' his mother called to him. It meant 'little one.'

Jotunn watched Nergui's face intently. 'What do you know of the Nicassar?'

'Little.'

'They are creatures that the tau have used, in a way we are not yet sure about. Domitian is studying this. They are psychic. They sleep for years, sometimes. They are strange to us. But when they dream their minds lash out emotions. When we took this one, its dreams were all of war and violence. Now, it dreams of home. So when its psychic tendrils touch your mind, it brings forth memories so vivid and real, you are convinced that they are true.'

'Is it safe to keep this thing here?'

'Nothing is safe in this world,' Jotunn said. 'Least of all the xenos. But if it was not safe, I would not have brought you. Come, follow me.'

Nergui did as he was told. Shao-shao, he heard over and over, and had to will himself not to turn and look.

'Do you know what I hear when I pass the Nicassar's chamber?' Jotunn said as they approached another doorway.

'Wolves howling?'

'No.' Jotunn grinned long, yellow fangs. 'I hear the bell chime for our lost brothers.'

The interlocking blast doors rolled back, and the corridor that was revealed was lit with low lume-globes. There were ten niches to either side, which appeared to have once held statues or busts, perhaps, but which were now empty, and at the end another door.

Again Jotunn inserted the twin prongs of the clavis key. There was another low hiss as cold air escaped, and the lume-globes flickered to life, revealing a wide gallery.

The door closed behind them and Nergui looked about him in wonder. To either side suits of ancient armour stood in gothic alcoves. The air was warm. It had a clean, fresh feel. Nergui stopped before the first suit, finely crafted Mark VI armour with ornate black scrollwork about the chest-plate and greaves. The next was an ancient suit of armour, with gold-trimmed greaves and gloves. It had once belonged to Watch-Captain Titus, who had founded this fortress, his three-flanged maul still gripped in the suit's fist.

In the next niche was a suit of Terminator armour, and beside it was a twin-headed power axe with a handle of solid steel, cast with the shapes of coiling serpents.

'That belonged to my predecessor,' Jotunn said. 'With it he slew the Tyrant of Rangarr. A single blow to the neck.'

At the end was a suit of silver armour.

'Do not touch,' Jotunn said quickly.

Nergui pulled his hand back. 'Mark II,' he said in wonder. There was a pause. 'What is that sigil?'

'That is the symbol of Malcador.'

The suit had been cared for and cleaned, but there were nicks in the armour, scratches and dents where it had seen combat.

'Can it still be used?'

'It could,' Jotunn said. 'But the spirit of the armour would have to be placated before it could be painted black. There are only so many times that a suit of armour can be changed.'

'What colour was it before?'

'I cannot tell you. It is beyond the reach of the sagas of my Chapter, and the sagas we tell ourselves here. But I did not bring you here to wonder about such things, Nergui. Come, follow me.'

Jotunn led him along niches holding weapons: beautifully crafted boltguns, swords, axes, a pair of curved tulwars such as the White Scars used, but it was at the end of the row that they stopped before an exquisitely damasked halberd. Jotunn stepped forwards and lifted the blade from its mountings. The blade was wide, the shaft solid brass, a pair of gold-worked bolters incorporated into the weapon, the magazines fashioned in the shape of coiled serpents.

'This is a guardian spear,' Jotunn said. 'Forged in the Holy Palace on Terra.' The Space Wolf spoke with awe. He turned it in the light so that they could see the fine damasking of light and dark in the blade. 'There are over a thousand rods of steel folded in this blade,' Jotunn said at last, his voice lowered. 'I counted them once. No smith could fashion this now. Not even among the Salamanders. Harath said that there was a blade with eight hundred folds that he had seen. But nothing like this. And,' he said, giving Nergui a long look, 'there were hundreds of these weapons made. Thousands, even. Once.'

Nergui's mouth was dry as he ran his hands along a weapon that was as old as the Imperium itself.

'Why bring me here?'

'What use are weapons if they are not used?' Jotunn said.

'You are going to risk it in battle?'

'We shall not fail,' Jotunn said. 'We are few and our enemy are many. This will inspire each of us to fight harder.' As he spoke the bell in the high tower rang out. A single note that brought a deep silence after, which stretched on, before another mournful knell.

Nergui knew he should have been there, and he lowered his head in silence.

The Remembering had begun.

As the bell rang Leonas led the members of Kill Team Faith into the armoury furnace chamber.

In the centre of the room a vast crucible was half embedded into the rockcrete floor. Red flames and black smoke licked up about its heavy stand as the bellows drove a storm of sparks up from the furnace floor, and the colour of the molten steel inside went from black to red to glowing yellow – the surface washed by flames.

One by one the Adeptus Astartes entered. When all the warriors were gathered, the arco-smiths bowed and filed out. 'All who are living, and who remember, are gathered here.' As Leonas spoke, the bellows whined and sparks flew up from the crucible fires, until the metal within was white.

Leonas stepped to the edge of the wide crucible. One by one the other Space Marines stepped forwards to join him. They stood in a circle, their faces uplit with the glowing light. High above them, in the chapel, a lone bell rang out a steady knell. One toll for each year of service that the lost Space Marines had given to the Deathwatch. When the count reached thirty-seven, 'Last' Leonas put his hand over the crucible. He did not flinch at the heat as he held out his bare arm and opened his fist. A metal ingot dropped onto the crust of molten slag. It broke under the weight and showed cracks of dull red fire that widened to yellow. The lead ingot sank slowly, dissolving as it did so, until it was a thin lozenge and the name inscribed upon it was lit from beneath by fire.

The inscription read: *Nidal Franz, Warmonger*.

The words glowed brighter as the bar dissolved, before finally slipping into the molten liquid and fading from sight.

Konrad Raimer, the grizzled Black Templar, carried the tablet with Priam's name. Sardegna, the Scion of Sanguinius, held the tablet of Gualtino. Harath carried Tula's. Elianus carried Branstonio's. Each of them stepped forwards, bearing their ingot. Each one spoke the name of their lost brothers, and the darkness heard and remembered as each lead tablet fell into the crucible and was devoured.

The last to fall was carried by Cadvan, the Storm Giant. The name read *Ellial, Mortifactor*. As the glowing ingot began to dissolve at the edges, they chanted.

'They died holding back the darkness of the alien. Let their memory bring light. Let their legacy be death to the xenos.'

The forge bell rang, a different note to the death knell that had rung above, and the arco-smiths filed back into the room, their goggle eyes reflecting the light of the furnace as their vox-grille mouths began chanting the litany of perfect casting. As the crucible tilted, the Deathwatch warriors stood back. Molten metal lit up the grooves in the floor. There were hundreds of moulds, in neat lines of glowing lead, cooling from white to yellow to red, and then a dull, shiny black.

The Ritual of Casting was complete. The mould cases opened and hundreds of bolter shells rattled into the basin before them.

'Last' Leonas lifted his up. *Nidal*, it read, with the Warmonger's sword-and-skull icon emblazoned on the side. It was a lucky sign to pick out the same name you had put in. One by one they took their pick.

Harath, the Salamander, was always last. He chanted an old Nocturne smith's charm as he reached in with his ungloved hand and took a handful of the fresh, hot shells. 'I shall honour you all,' he said.

As the Space Marines returned to their chambers the names of the fallen were inscribed in the wall of the feast hall, and the high bell tolled a melancholy note.

The Remembering was done.

The note of the bell changed from grief to one that sounded vengeance, and the fortress of Picket's Watch began to charge with anticipation.

Thunderhawks were fuelled, ammo-carriages brought up missiles from the armoury, tech-savants checked over Land Speeders, Rhinos were cleaned and loaded onto the lifters – even the Land Raider, *Moab's Revenge*, was brought out of seclusion, her promethium tanks checked and refitted and tested once more.

Now it was time for war.

CHAPTER TWELVE

In their own quarters, and in their own ways, the warriors of Kill Team Faith spent their last hours in Picket's Watch, preparing for their mission.

In his painted chambers, Sardegna of the Scions of Sanguinius examined the fine tracery of the stone block before him. The statue is there, so the old masters liked to say – the trick is in uncovering it. But it was odd thinking of his primarch locked inside this white marble slab. Sardegna bent once more and tapped away the line of Sanguinius' wing. He would free him from it, as he had freed him so many times before. It was the perfect way to prepare for battle, to feel your hearts slow almost to nothing, your breathing become measured, the only sound in the world the clang of the mission bell, and the gentle tap of hammer and chisel upon stone.

Next to Sardegna's chambers were those of Imano, the Lamenter.

Imano and Ragris the Celebrant were wrestling as the bell tolled. Imano tipped Ragris over, and the Celebrant fell on his back with a grunt that drove the wind from his lungs for a moment before the other let go.

'Two,' Imano said, grinning as he wiped the sand from his shoulders.

They were both stripped to the waist, their massive torsos crisscrossed with scars, their chests heaving with exertion.

Ragris cursed as he pushed himself up, dusted the sand off his hands, and went immediately back to the opening stance.

'Again!' he said.

Imano laughed. He was the master of this kind of battle. 'You do not need to prove anything,' he said.

'Again!' Ragris spat.

Imano strode into the ring, feigning indifference. Ragris came at him like a python. It was over in a matter of seconds, Ragris lying flat on his back again.

He cursed and punched the floor.

'How did you do that?' he said.

Imano laughed. He did not give away his secrets.

'I will not stop until I have beaten you,' Ragris said, as he dusted his shoulders off once more.

'It could be a long time,' Imano said.

'I can do it.'

Below them, in rooms just above the gateway, Olbath of the Aurora Chapter stood in his fighting pit and wiped the sweat from his eyes. He was not satisfied. Again, he told himself, as he went through his Chapter's attack drill, pacing to the end of the long chamber and taking up his stance.

He slowed his breathing down and concentrated on the energy within himself. Control the power within you, his Chapter taught. Learn the strength of the quiet. The resolve of the silent. The patience of the leopard. There were a hundred and eight steps to the drill. The upper cut, the pommel drive, the explosive break, the feigned sting, the mantis strike.

Olbath ran through the drill three more times before he was satisfied, then turned to see Cadvan leaning against the wall.

The Storm Giant's presence irritated Olbath. The irritation gave him an edge as he worked through the last moves, harder and faster now, and at the end he slammed his pistol back into its holster and rested the chainsword on his shoulder pad.

'I wish you would not do that,' Olbath said.

Cadvan did not care. 'Nervous?'

Olbath made a non-committal sound.

Cadvan smiled. 'This is your first battle with the Deathwatch?'

Olbath was used to Cadvan's taunts.

'It is,' Olbath said, and stuck out his chin defiantly. 'So?'

Cadvan was the largest Space Marine Olbath had ever seen. The red-haired warrior looked down on him and smiled. 'There was another warrior from the Aurora Chapter once. His name was Kalgah. He fell against the Great Devourer.'

Olbath was not sure what kind of response was called for here. 'I did not know him.'

'No,' Cadvan said. 'You would not. But he saved me, and Storm Giants do not forget such things. Understand?'

'No,' Olbath said.

Cadvan laughed and turned to go. At the doorway he turned

and spoke seriously, for once. 'Let me know if you ever… need a brother at your side.'

Then he was gone, and Olbath was not quite sure what had happened.

Atilio the Ultramarine strode the empty corridors with an almost obsessive manner. He had been stationed here for nine years and this was the third watch fortress he had been attached to, and the loneliest. But he found peace in movement.

He could not wait to return to his Chapter, to Ultramar, to see once more the shrine of Roboute Guilliman. To thank him for deliverance. But he quelled this yearning. It did not help a warrior fight.

On the seventh toll of the bell, he passed Harath the Salamander on his way back from the forge.

'Greetings, brother,' the Salamander said. 'I was looking for you.' He held something out in his dark hand.

Atilio took it and saw immediately what it was: a bolt round with the name 'Branstonio' upon it.

'He was of your Chapter. You should take revenge for him.'

Atilio's fingers closed about it. 'Thank you,' he said.

It was an exercise in persistence, 'Last' Leonas thought, tattooing a Space Marine. No sooner was the skin cut than it healed into thick scar tissue. You had to cut deep, he'd found, and rub caustic black powder into the wound.

Leonas sat cross-legged on the floor of his chambers and tested the point of the knife against his thumb. His enhanced musculature made his skin taut as a drum skin. He began to chant the Song of Tollon, the Master of Sanctity, who bore Lorgar's Bane in battle, and pressed the knife into his flesh.

It was both painful and slow, but it helped focus the mind as he worked his flesh.

All the other rooms on this side of Westkeep were locked and empty, so when he heard footsteps from the far end of his corridor, he knew they were coming to his chambers. He also knew they belonged to Konrad, the Black Templar. His footsteps had a distinctive heel-clip note as he walked.

Konrad cast a slight shadow as he stood in the doorway.

'What are you doing?' he demanded.

Leonas blew on his skin as the scab formed. He did not bother to look up, but said, 'Tattooing my arm.'

'I heard the Black Consuls kept strictly to the Codex?'

'They do,' Leonas said.

'There is room for such tribal markings?'

'There is now,' Leonas said, lifting a round flap of skin away, so he could mark it before it healed. The caustic salts stung, but not all pain was evil, he'd found. He pressed it down for a few seconds to let the Larraman cells seal the wound, then he inspected his handiwork.

Konrad came into the room. 'What name?'

'The name of an impetuous fool named Razlon.'

'If you did not like this warrior, then why tattoo yourself with his name?'

'Because I swore I would do so,' Leonas said. He had almost finished the outer rim of the disc upon his arm. He pressed the flap down for a few seconds, and looked up. 'Why are you here, Black Templar?'

'You are part of Kill Team Faith now. I like to know the warriors that serve with me.'

Leonas nodded. That made sense. He carefully ground the point of his knife back to a razor's edge.

'The edge is lost so quickly,' he said. 'You have to keep honing it, don't you find?'

'Are we talking blades or warriors?'

Leonas laughed. 'Both.'

'So tell me. I know nothing about the Black Consuls.'

'You say it as if it is our fault. You are from the Black Templars?'

Konrad nodded. 'I am.' He turned to show his shoulder pad with its distinctive cross and sword icons.

'Second Founding, from the gene-seed of the Imperial Fists?'

'Yes,' Konrad snapped.

Leonas looked up from his tattoo. 'See, I know all about *your* Chapter. But you know nothing of mine. We too were Second Founding. Our warriors were brought from the seventy-second Chapter of the Ultramarines. As a home we were given the star fort *Noctis Obscurum*, which once guarded the skies above Macragge. Our commander was Arrias Cordos, who was known as the Bane of Lorgar. He earnt his name in the Cleansing of the Orbstar. He pursued our foes through the Orbstar System, leading his Chapter from the *Noctis Obscurum*.

'We were a crusading Chapter like your own. One of twenty Chapters named the Astartes Praeses. I can see that at least you have heard of them. We each made a solemn vow to guard the Eye of Terror, to take the fight to the greatest enemy of mankind. Our foe was not the xenos, but our former brothers, who had turned to evil.

'Our home, the *Noctis Obscurum*, was almost impregnable. Or so we thought. But one year our Chapter was lured out to fight, and our star fort was infiltrated by the dark eldar. They found a way aboard as we made a jump through the warp. None of us knew they were there. While the Chapter was fighting, they overpowered the skeleton crew and overloaded the warp drives.'

He blew on the cut.

'Our Chapter came home, victorious, to find their home, their armoury, their history was gone.' He blew once more. 'All this happened before my birth. When I was young there were still a few members of the Chapter who remembered the *Noctis Obscurum*. It was our experience with the dark eldar that brought us closer to the Deathwatch. We sent some of our greatest warriors to the Deathwatch, and they brought all their expertise against the xenos.'

'But it was not the dark eldar who wiped you out?'

'Oh no. They did not. That happened later. We had many enemies, some older than the dark eldar. We found our foe, the *Infidus Imperator*, once the flagship of the Word Bearers, in orbit around the planet of Yearsli. We brought them to bay at last at Goddeth Hive. As we broke down the final defences, the traitors ignited the reactors within the hive. In the explosion, half the planet was broken away and our entire Chapter was lost, including the axe of our founder, Lorgar's Bane.'

Leonas looked up. He had almost finished the image above Razlon's name. It was a tau sept mark. 'You are wondering how I survived. I was not there. I was on pilgrimage to Macragge. To the shrine of Roboute Guilliman,' he said. 'I remember standing by his tomb, looking at the face, and I thought of all the stories I had heard. All the dreams that our gene-father had for our race. The light, the beauty, and the vision he had. And I console myself with that. When I die and my Chapter's story is finally done, then we will have left the galaxy a less dark place than it might have been. And that light still shines. That hope. It is all we have left. The battle for the good of mankind.'

'The Greater Good?' Konrad said. He chuckled at his own joke. 'You sound like the foe.'

Leonas remembered his time with the xenos. How they had tried to break him.

'Yes,' Leonas said. 'The Greater Good.'

For a long time Konrad did not speak.

'I have seen that there is a black mark against your name,' the Black Templar said.

Leonas smiled as he rubbed black into his wound. 'Ah. So *that* is why you are here.'

'If you join my kill team I have to know what transgression you committed.'

Leonas blew on the scab as it sealed the wound. 'I wanted vengeance.'

'Do not speak in riddles.'

'Three years ago I was on a mission in the Cellebos Warzone when I heard that a high-ranking demagogue of the Word Bearers was fighting there. I took my kill team without orders to hunt him down.'

'And did you find him?'

Leonas looked up and caught the Black Templar's eye. 'Yes. He had horns where his mouth had been. He was a dreadful, twisted thing, more terrible to behold than any xenos I have seen, because once he was like us. We could barely make out what he was saying. He no longer knew what was true and what was false. Whatever he had been, he was now debased. He was a mad, mewling thing by the time I put a bolt round through his skull.'

Leonas ground the edge of his knife once more. 'So, as a punishment I was sent here, to the Eastern Fringes, on the far edge of the universe, far from all that I knew. And now, I fight xenos.'

He inspected his new tattoo, and then held it out for the Black Templar to admire.

'Very detailed,' the Black Templar said, in a tone that was forbearing of such deviant behaviour. 'But it is a xenos marking.'

'It is,' Leonas said. 'It is the mark of the Sept Ke'lshan. I put it there so I will remember.' Leonas tapped the side of his head. 'I have so much to remember. So many debts I have to repay. I am the last, remember.' Leonas turned to show his back. It was covered in script. Names, Konrad realised as he curled his lip in disgust. Leonas' back was covered with names.

'The names of the nine hundred and eighty-four of our Chapter who died at Goddeth Hive,' Leonas told him. He turned back to Konrad. 'On Cyclopeia the gangers had a tradition of writing the names of their dead gangers on their bodies. We brought this tradition back when our brothers were lost.' He turned his shoulder towards the Black Templar.

Konrad gave a snort. 'Who will bear your name on their skin?'

Leonas laughed. 'Me,' he said, and tore open his top to show his own name in curling Gothic script emblazoned across his chest.

The Black Templar frowned. 'But does that mean…?'

'Yes,' Leonas said. 'I've already died.'

Konrad laughed at that. He put a hand out. 'You are welcome among us, Brother Leonas. I hope the dead fight well.'

PART TWO
THE HUNT

CHAPTER THIRTEEN

It took nearly a week for the *Valete* to drift towards the target, power systems barely functioning. Now, at last Kill Team Zeal's Corvus Blackstars were within range of Proth.

Moaz Khileni was going in first. A bandolier of jammers slung about his chest, he crouched in shadows as the Corvus lifted off from the landing bay, the fuselage rattling as it passed through the airlock and out into the vacuum of space.

Only when he felt the craft rattle as it slipped into the high atmosphere did he stand. His mission was to disable the listening stations that covered the planet. He had to move carefully to avoid banging his jump pack on the roof of the craft.

'*Approaching the southern pole,*' the Dark Angel, Cadmus, said.

There was a hiss of wind as the rear landing ramp lowered. Moaz stepped forwards to the edge of the opening and looked down. They were flying above the equatorial range, where the landscape was brown and dusty. It soon gave way to tundra and the brilliant ice fields of the polar regions. From this high the sky was distinctly curved, a blue nimbus ringing the horizon.

Moaz had seen many battlefields and planets in his eighty-four years. Most of them had started off like this: the view of an unknown world seen from the open doorway of a Stormraven or Thunderhawk. Entering from high orbit with nothing but a jump pack was what the Raven Guard excelled at. It was what they were made for. To strike from the sky, when most enemies looked towards the land for their foes.

Moaz stepped to the edge and felt the ramp shudder beneath his power-armoured footsteps. The emptiness seemed to suck at him, to beg him to step forwards and embrace it. They were passing into night now, the land below turning dark until all that was left was the blue nimbus and the shadowed mass of the planet.

'We're approaching drop zone,' Cadmus voxed.

There was no answer. Moaz had already embraced the void and was falling head first into the night.

Moaz accelerated to thousands of yards per second. At a height of two miles he began to reach atmosphere and the temperature readings in his suit climbed. Friction began to heat his power armour. The black paint started to burn. Black on black, it did not matter. *That is why we wear the black*, one of his Scout masters had told him when he was learning the ways of the Raven Guard.

As he fell he stabilised his fall until his arms and legs were flung back, like the barbs of a black arrow. In the earth, he could make out the dry beds of ancient river systems. The meandering channels ended in the vast white salt pans. His enhanced vision searched for a suitable canyon and found one within moments. Three hundred feet deep, funnelling out into a dry river bed.

From a height of one mile, the gap towards which he was falling was nothing but a black line. It grew slowly at first. He was falling at a hundred yards a second. Seventeen seconds until impact.

He altered his body shape as effortlessly as a raven would adjust a tail feather and he started to veer towards the gap. He changed direction again, lining up with the narrow mouth of the canyon, always adjusting, altering, aligning.

He counted down the seconds to impact. Five, four, three. The canyon was only four yards wide. Moaz wobbled as it rushed towards him, filling his vision.

Moaz overloaded his retros, blasting back against his momentum. He hit a projecting rock and pulverised it, then bounced twice more before landing so hard his chin hit his knees. His vision went dark for a moment as the blood drained from his cranium, his muscles tensing in response, both hearts slowing momentarily as amber readings flashed inside his helmet and he forced blood up and around his body.

An unaugmented human would have died from organ failure at the shock of that deceleration. Moaz Khileni shook himself and rose slowly. He checked his readings, got his bearings within seconds and started towards his first target.

It was only twenty miles distant. He slipped out of the canyon mouth. He was a shadow.

Moaz found the first listening station three Terran hours after landing. The tower rose twenty feet into the air, with four splayed feet and a cupola sensor scanning the skies above the planet. He twisted the first of the jammers from his bandolier, engaged the power, set the timer and then slipped it into the housing.

By the second morning he had attached a jammer to another fifteen sensor towers. By the fourth day he had travelled nearly a thousand miles. By the time he reached the north pole he would have covered a corridor a mile wide across the whole planet. The tau thought that they had shrouded their world with sensors, but when the timer clicked in, the jammers would create an area over which the tau would be entirely blind.

And along that strip would come their doom.

CHAPTER FOURTEEN

LOCATION: TAU WORLD SH'ANSHI

At the same time as Moaz landed at the southern pole, a tau craft touched down at the base named M'Yan'Ral.

The silhouette of a fire warrior wearing a well-worn black leather greatcoat like a cloak from his shoulders appeared in the doorway, and all across the flats of the hastily erected starport facility there was a hush from the assembled fighters and earth caste engineers.

Shas'vre Ch'an drew in a short breath through his thin, leathery lips as he leant on his staff. Sh'anshi was a bleak place, he thought, as he took in the four low mountains that surrounded Base M'Yan'Ral, then the ice-flats, the kroot camp, the planetary defence turrets and the low domes of the tau training station, with its triple rings of mobile defence.

So this was it, Ch'an thought, as he leant on his cane and took the first steps down.

He had come straight from Mu'gulath Bay, a vampire of a planet that had sucked blood deep into its earth. After the noise and violence of that world this place was silent and white and frozen. But what he noticed most was the stillness of the air. Given ten tau'cyr or so, the earth caste could make this place habitable. A hundred tau'cyr and it could even be a pleasant place, worthy of colonisation. Maybe even as sublime as his own home world of Au'taal: a gentle place of lakes and rivers, and mountain retreats where the ascetic could retire to contemplate the Greater Good. Other tau considered them lazy, but there had been nothing lacking in the warriors he had fought with.

It saddened Ch'an when he thought of how many of his sept – who were cultured and learned in all the arts of the tau race – had lost their lives on Mu'gulath Bay. It was for the Greater Good, of course, but he had started to have the feeling that the Greater Good would not include him, or the armies that he had sailed with nine tau'cyr ago.

He, at least, was still alive. But there were only so many times he could survive battle, and each time he fought he seemed to leave parts of himself behind. The last time had been the worst. It had been on Mu'gulath Bay, in the ruins of a hive, with thousands of gue'la refugees streaming from the burning city. The Imperials had fired indiscriminately, killing many of their own kind. He had been trying to protect them with his Stormsurge when he'd been hit. It was the enemy you never saw that were the most dangerous, he'd always said, and he'd ignored his own wisdom. Ch'an had spent so long in the rehabilitation ward, he had thought he would be refused permission to return to the battlefront. He had begged for active service, and in the end his commander had come to his bed.

'You will be sent away,' the commander said.

'Back to Au'taal?'

'No,' his commander had said. 'I cannot tell you where you are going. I can say nothing more.'

Ch'an had gleaned the rest from the earth caste technicians who'd brought him here. This was a forward training base, and he was to be both instructor and pupil. It was an honour, he reminded himself, as he caught a glimpse of a distant Stormsurge striding back to the domes of the base. But it wouldn't be the same. He'd miss the thrill of being part of something vast and mobile, like the kauyon assault on Mu'gulath Bay when they had taken three hive cities in one day. He would miss the down-to-earth humour of the fire warrior teams he brought into battle; he would miss the thrill of swooping in and setting his stabilisers into the ground, and letting his gunner open fire.

By the time Ch'an had limped to the bottom of the ramp, the crowd were staring intently at him in that odd way the earth caste had.

'I am Fio'ui K'or,' one of them said. 'We are Sept Ke'lshan. We are honoured to have you here, Shas'vre Ch'an.'

Ch'an thanked him and then the silence returned.

'This way,' Fio'ui K'or said, and bowed, and Ch'an limped after him.

Fio'ui K'or led him to where a skimmer floated, waiting, and helped Ch'an mount the steps and then closed the dome over his head.

'I will bring you to the camp,' Fio'ui K'or said. He climbed in beside Ch'an and fitted his three-fingered hand into the steering mechanism, and they accelerated away.

The tau flew across the crater field. Ch'an found it hard to go at their pace. He wondered, not for the first time, how the earth caste managed to get anything done. They moved so slowly, he thought. They thought slowly too. Ch'an tried to make conversation as they crossed the ice flats to the camp, but his heart wasn't in it and Fio'ui K'or was a little staccato in his replies, and eventually they were passing a tethered krootox when the conversation faltered.

'How many kroot are here?' Ch'an said when he spotted the low shaggy yurts of the kroot camp, half buried into the ice.

'A hundred,' Fio'ui K'or said. His flat, dark face was impassive, hands fixed on the steering disc. 'There are thirty-seven hounds, fifty-four kroot and nine krootox.'

'They can survive the cold?'

'They are from Yuun'chen. Ice world. Genome mixed with local fauna named Yuun'chen ice bear.'

Shas'vre Ch'an nodded and leant his head against the domed windowpane. There were four of the new NG-4 terrestrial defence rigs – their low domes and twin-linked railguns an unmistakable silhouette. The farthermost one was at the top of a rocky crag that stood up straight through the ice, as if it were a spear that had been driven through the ice cap. At the top he could see what appeared from this distance to be the kind of flies found on gue'la worlds. Black, dirty, noisy.

The earth caste saw what he was looking at. 'Vespid,' he said.

'Vespid?'

'They come from the planet Vespid,' Fio'ui K'or said without irony.

Ch'an nodded. Not very imaginative, he thought. They must have been discovered by one of the more dour sept worlds. 'What are they like?'

There was a pause. 'They are a little slow,' Fio'ui said.

Ch'an nodded. And that was coming from an earth caste. He had fought with kroot on Mu'gulath Bay. He'd rather liked them until he'd found them squatting in the trenches, eating their way along the bodies of dead Imperial Guardsmen. He had never come across vespids before.

'What do they eat?' he asked.

The earth caste frowned. 'I do not know.'

'Not flesh, I hope.' The technician kept his mouth shut. Ch'an left him alone for a while, then said, 'This place is secret?'

'Oh yes,' Fio'ui said. 'Very secret.'

'So why all these defences?'

'Just in case.'

'Just in case of what?'

'In case the enemy find us again.'

'They found it before?'

'Once. Yes,' Fio'ui said. 'We had to move. We cannot be found.'

Ch'an nodded. Experience had taught him that the more heavily defended a place was, the more someone wanted to find and destroy it. And now he knew they were being hunted he turned and looked about him. It was an instinctive movement, born from so long spent in deadly warzones. It was a dead warrior who did not check behind him.

Ch'an's eyes scanned the starport, the kroot camp, the distant crags that rose up to the defence turrets, but he saw nothing.

They were nearly at the base. He closed his eyes for a moment, and wished he could hold this moment of peace and silence a little longer. From what he knew of a warrior's life, silence and stillness never lasted long.

Tidings travelled faster than earth caste fio'ui, it seemed. As the transporter came to a slow halt alongside the main dome, Ch'an saw a crowd of fio'la workers staring up expectantly, their flat faces and wide nostrils flaring in the cold air. They had a slightly nervous air to them, their three-fingered hands clasped together in a gesture of honour and supplication.

'This is Shas'vre Au'taal Ch'an,' Fio'ui K'or announced. The fio'la looked on without blinking.

Shas'vre Ch'an felt foolish as he swung his leg over the side of the passenger compartment. He leant heavily on his cane as he limped down to the crowd and they stood back silently, watching him pass, the hero of Mu'gulath Bay. It was as if they could not quite believe he was still alive.

Sometimes he could not either. Ch'an set his cane and bowed.

'Greetings, brothers,' he said. 'And what is your honoured sept?'

It was a formal greeting, perhaps too formal for a fire caste to use with fio'la, but the tau of Au'taal were famed for their manners, and he liked to keep these traditions up, despite everything.

'Ke'lshan,' their leader said. 'We are all Ke'lshan. It is the honour of our sept to defend you all.'

'Indeed?' he said, as if he were learning this for the first time.

It depressed him, to be honest, to learn that he was to be seconded to Sept Ke'lshan. They were a hard, dour bunch, with little room in their minds for arts or pleasure or harmony.

'Honoured one. We were glad when we heard that you had survived.'

'Yes,' he said. 'I survived when many others did not.'

'We all wish you much luck.'

'Please,' Fio'ui K'or said and led him towards the dome. 'This way. The commander is keen to meet you.'

The command dome stood a little way off from the larger hab-dome. There were sandbags about its entrance, which kept off the wind.

Ch'an was led into an office, and through a door guarded by two fire warriors in the grey-and-black armour of Ke'lshan, yellow sept markings on the sides of their helmets and pulse carbines that were held close to their chests. As he moved towards the doorway, one of them stepped in front of him.

'You cannot enter with that,' the fire warrior said.

Ch'an shook them off. A voice from the office called out in question.

'Sire. He has brought this gue'la object. We cannot allow anyone to bring gue'la artefacts into this camp. It is procedure.'

'What do you mean, you cannot allow?'

'There might be gue'la objects within it. Tracing devices.'

Ch'an pushed the fire warriors from him. 'There are no tracing devices within this jacket.'

'Stand back,' a voice called, and the two Ke'lshan fire warriors obeyed. Ch'an cast them a furious look as he pulled the black jacket over his shoulders. Their commander strode out. He took Ch'an in, and guessed correctly who he was.

'Welcome to M'Yan'Ral,' he said. 'I am Fireblade M'au. We are honoured by your presence, Shas'vre Ch'an. But I am the commander here, on behalf of my sept. We are entrusted with your safety and all those on this camp. So, I am afraid you will have to give up this... trophy.'

Fireblade M'au had the nasal twang of a Ke'lshan warrior that grated on Ch'an's nerves. 'I have fought for our empire for longer than some of you have been alive, and this jacket has been with me every step of the way. If you want me here to train your crews, then you leave this with me. It is my totem.' The urgency of Ch'an's words surprised them all.

Fireblade M'au smiled and nodded. 'We can make an exception for our honoured guest. Just this time.' He nodded to the two fire warriors. 'Show the esteemed warrior to his quarters.'

'Sorry, shas'vre,' Fio'ui K'or said as they crossed the well-trodden ice to the hab-dome.

'It's nothing,' Ch'an said, but he was still shaking as they reached the hab-dome's doors.

They passed through the doors, and there was a blast of warm air as they closed behind them. The dome wound down into the ice, with rows of dorms overlooking a central sunken Ke'lshan rock garden. It was a fairly standard design, with sublevels no doubt, where stores and ammunition could be kept. Ke'lshan was not known for foresight or originality.

'We have nearly seven hundred students here. They are drawn from all the septs.'

'So I heard.'

'As you know, this runs counter to previous practice. Before now, septs tended to work alone. This was not harmonious. Most High One Aun'ui Hoo'nan wished the septs to work together in this. The need is great.'

'That it is,' Ch'an said.

Fio'ui K'or stopped for a moment. 'Apologies, honoured one. You have been on Mu'gulath Bay. Is it a beautiful world?'

'No. Not really.' Ch'an paused. 'It is polluted and foul. You know the gue'la.'

The earth caste nodded slowly and solemnly. 'Yes. I hoped it would be beautiful. We have given so many lives. So much towards it.'

Emotion was rare in an earth caste.

'It might be one day,' Ch'an said. 'Given time and work.'

Fio'ui K'or nodded. 'You are from Au'taal. I always wished to see Au'taal.'

'Maybe you will.'

'I dream of it sometimes. It is the most radiant world, is it not?'

Ch'an had never imagined an earth caste dreaming. 'Yes,' he said after a moment's consideration. 'It is.'

Fio'ui K'or pressed his hands together, interlocking the four digits on each hand. 'I hope to see it one day. But I do not think it will happen.'

They moved on, the brief flash of emotion passing, and Fio'ui K'or went back to facts and figures. They were probably safer ground. 'The hab block is three quarters underground,' he said. 'It is better for insulation and protection. There is no way through the ice, and the camp is protected by six planetary defence turrets.'

'Six? I only saw four.'

'There are two more in the outer hills. They are the older NG-23 variety. Much bigger than the ones you saw.'

Ch'an knew the NG-23s. They were weapons of an impressive scale, with generators to match. But they were largely stationary once deployed, which made them increasingly unsuitable for the kind of warfare that the tau had developed. The newer versions were fitted with more efficient gravitational drives. On the flat they could move at half the speed of a Devilfish.

He realised that he had drifted off for a moment. Fio'ui K'or was still talking. 'Have you seen the new XV9 battlesuits?'

'No,' Ch'an said. 'I have not.'

'Fireblade M'au has one. I will see if we can get one for you to try. They are impressive. You will think so too. Everyone thinks so.'

Fio'ui K'or touched a corrugated pipe that wound around the inner wall of the stairwell. 'We have installed back-up generators here,' he said. 'We also have extra generators for the dome shield. You see, we have thought of everything.'

Ch'an said nothing. If experience had taught him anything, it was that expressions like that were always misplaced.

'Here,' Fio'ui K'or said when they got to the bottom, and they looked into a wide circular underground chamber, ringed with hab blocks, their neat, regular armourglass windows tinted against the glare. 'I will let you go in and find your bunk. It is bunk number Y-445-A.'

'Y-445-A,' Ch'an repeated, and nodded, forcing a smile. 'Thank you.'

All tau establishments were built and ordered to the same harmonious plan, so he knew what his room would be like before he got there, and he was not surprised: it was a tall and narrow room with four double bunk beds, two on either side of the cell. A thin lume-strip lit the chamber when the window tint was turned up to night levels. The only thing that did surprise him was the holo-vista of the Western Lakes on his home sept of Au'taal. The isles were wreathed with mist, and the ultraviolet tones had been enriched. Underneath was written in simple letters of an archaic style a line of poetry from a famous fire warrior named D'fu: *The burning of this fire, the years run out too soon.*

There was the low hissing from a sleeping warrior across the room. Shas'vre Ch'an threw his pack onto one of the empty beds and from the bunk above him there was a creak as a mottled head appeared, eyes widening in surprise.

'It's you!' he said. Then he blushed a deep shade of purple, and fumbled with his greetings. 'Apologies, master!' he said. 'We were not expecting you so soon.'

'We arrived early,' Shas'vre Ch'an said. 'It is a good habit for a warrior to have.'

The other fire warrior sat up, swung his hooves over the side of the bunk, dropped onto the floor and bowed low.

'Shas'vre,' he said. 'We are deeply honoured!'

Ch'an gave him a long look and the cadet blushed. 'Apologies. My honoured name is Shas'ui Sa'cea H'an.' H'an bowed low, his pigmentation on the ultraviolet scale cooling as he mastered his sudden burst of excitement. 'I am a cadet. We are to be bonded.'

'Are we?' Shas'vre Ch'an said.

He tried to hide his discomfort. For an old timer like him, it felt wrong for warriors of different septs to be brought together like this, but Mu'gulath Bay had taken such a toll on the Tau Empire that this was what the ethereals had demanded. The other one blushed purple again and hung his head in an almost child-like gesture. 'I was one of the top students to graduate from my intake of Ves'oni'Vash.'

Shas'vre Ch'an pursed his lips in a thoughtful manner. 'So we're sending infants and the ancient into battle together. There must be a poem in there somewhere.'

Whispers were running along the corridor. 'Shas'vre Ch'an is here! Shas'vre Ch'an!' There was a clatter of hooves as other cadets filled the doorway in a silent crowd. One of them reached out to touch the black leather overcoat that he wore. 'We did not believe it, master, that you were really coming back to fight. A-a-after your wounds...'

'I serve the Greater Good,' Shas'vre Ch'an said. He made a low clacking sound, that was almost like a laugh. 'The reports of my death were a little premature.' He took off his overcoat, threw it onto the bed and sat down, grateful to take the weight from his damaged leg. 'Now, when does training start?'

'Class begins again after noontide.'

The look in Ch'an's eyes gave away the fact he was not quite clear on whether noontide was close or not.

'In three dec,' H'an added helpfully. 'But as you have just landed, perhaps we could ask the Commander M'au to let you rest until tomorrow.'

Ch'an grunted in appreciation. 'There is no time to rest. I will start with you. But now, if you will excuse me, brothers, I have come straight from Mu'gulath Bay. I am a little tired. I shall lie down and sleep.'

Ch'an used both hands to swing his stiff leg up. He laid his cane by his side, pulled the black leather overcoat up over his body and closed his eyes.

CHAPTER FIFTEEN

Ch'an had given himself a week to lose his patience. He did not make it through the first afternoon's session, in one of the sub-level lecture theatres.

A pale Ke'lshan warrior named N'loo relayed footage from Mu'gulath Bay.

'This is another successful kauyon engagement,' he droned, and showed footage of a fleet of drones swooping over the hilltop fortified Imperial position. It had been prepared in depth, with rockcrete bunkers, twinned trench support systems and gun emplacements at each of the six forts that offered enfilading fire to each other and to the long wall sections.

'See how they keep the heads of the enemy warriors down. Then look. This is a new use of the Stormsurge, a tactical variation developed on Ke'lshan known as the Petalled Sword.'

He played the footage of a lone Stormsurge landing in the middle of the compound. One foot crushed the command Chimera while the other kicked a power lift sentinel that tried to engage it. The air was suddenly full of airburst fragments, and then it opened up with its pulse battle cannon from point-blank range. The forts all faced outwards, and their guns swivelled helplessly as the Stormsurge singled each one out from behind with a blast of its pulse battle cannon. One shot was enough to destroy a fort, the ammunitions inside raining the troops with debris. Six shots and all the forts were neutralised; fire warriors were already deploying from their Devilfish and mopping up the last defenders.

'This is called the Stunned Krootox,' N'loo started. He almost smiled. 'It was a name I came up with myself, for reasons that I believe will be obvious.'

N'loo loved to hear the sound of his own voice. After an hour, Ch'an could not hold himself back. He stood up. 'Excuse me, honoured one. May I speak?'

N'loo faltered to a stop. There was an embarrassed silence as Ch'an pushed himself up on his cane. 'My name is Shas'vre Ch'an. You will forgive me interrupting like this. My body has been broken beyond my years. I am delighted to see so many victories over our enemies, but I have fought the gue'la many times, even though it was with the forces of my sept of Au'taal, which I know many of you do not consider to be within the top rank, or even second rank of fighting septs.

'But even we have found that the gue'la are not entirely stupid. They have a base and evil cunning, and they will be learning our methods of war as much as we learn them here. And they will find ways to counter them. It is our strategy that we should be three steps ahead of them at all times. It is by speed, power and innovation that we destroy our enemies. You give us footage of all these victories, but you know as well as I that we are losing Stormsurge crews faster than we can replace them.

'We should not be studying our victories but our failures. I would like to see our failures on Mu'gulath Bay. Then we can learn from that. *Then* we can break our enemy on their own anvil.'

Ch'an let himself sink back onto his stool.

N'loo had coloured a deep ultraviolet. His nostrils flared and he bowed briefly. 'I will bring us to the failures of our esteemed commander. We will consider this in the second half of the kai'rotaa.'

'Do we have that time?'

The instructor's mouth opened in shock and there was a stir as some of the warriors there made a low and disapproving hissing sound, and turned their heads. Ch'an pushed himself to his feet again. 'Forgive me, teacher. I was on Mu'gulath Bay and it is terrible. We have all heard about the Imperium of Mankind, how their kingdom stretches for tau'cyr of travel. Many tau'cyr. The numbers of their worlds are legion. The power of their empire is vast.'

He made a gesture to the black coat he wore. 'This jacket was taken from the body of a warrior they name the *Kom'sr*. His duty is to make sure his warriors fight. He uses this stick.' He gestured towards the cane that he leant on. 'He drives his men forwards like cattle, and if they fail, he speaks to them and then he shoots them in the head.'

There was a stunned silence among the cadets. How could a warrior kill one of his own?

'I have seen this happen. Many times. That is the way of our enemy. I wear this coat to remind me of the nature of the foe we face. They are cruel, they are merciless, they are uncivilised and they are evil. I use that word with much thought. I, like many of you, have fought alongside our gue'vesa allies, and they use a word that I should quote here – *in-human*. But they are many and we are few. We are like a...' he paused for the right comparison, 'a fl'aat bee when the fanged honey bear comes to break into his hive. The bear is stronger, more powerful. Why, he is the master of his world. But each bee has a sting, even though it may kill him when he delivers it. We are those bees. The gue'la empire can crush us with just a single claw of its mighty fist. We have to deliver such a blow to it at Mu'gulath Bay that it pulls back its paw in pain and shock. Then we must pursue it from one planet to the next and we must drive it away, as the hive of bees drive off the bear.'

Ch'an's anger had got the better of him. His words died away and were greeted with silence, then a scattering of applause that grew in strength and feeling.

Ch'an took in a deep breath and bowed stiffly before sitting down. Half the listeners seemed scandalised, the other half delighted. H'an touched his arm.

'Well said!' he whispered. 'About time someone told them!'

That evening Ch'an and H'an were to suit up for their first test flight.

The suiting bay lay towards the top of the firing range, a long, low building with a row of gates for the Stormsurge battlesuits to pass through. It was a short distance from the hab-dome. Ch'an's leg had stiffened as he sat, and the cold of the crossing had done it no good either. He used both hands to lower himself, wincing as the limb jammed against the knee brace.

'I'm fine,' he said. He felt strange emotions of fear and trepidation. 'Take my jacket off.' He watched as it was hung on a peg by the door.

'I shall make sure that no one touches it,' the earth caste technician, Fio'o Bork'an Koba'ashi, reported. His assistant was earnest as he helped Ch'an into the pilot's bay. 'I have adjusted the stirrups,' the young assistant said. He spoke quickly and breathlessly around the veteran.

'Thank you,' Ch'an said, adjusting the controls, and then pulled the pilot's vision helm onto his head. Ch'an slid his hands into the controls and welcomed the feeling of becoming the machine, without old wounds, a stiff leg, or the unpleasant memories. Machines had no memories, he thought as he flexed the arms and bent the legs as if for a giant spring.

They'd updated it. This was a newer version than he had been using on Mu'gulath Bay. The holo-graphs did not lag as much.

He started the power generator as H'an slipped into the seat beside him. His last gunner had been from Au'taal, of course. His name was... P'ort'a, and he'd hum his favourite lines of poetry as he fired. When battle was at its worst, he would chant *The Ballad of O'pon'sa*. He was the one who really deserved the title of ace, Ch'an thought, as H'an flicked the gun systems on.

'Live fire exercise two hundred and seventy-six,' H'an dictated into the system log. 'Cluster rockets, one through four – check. Destroyer missile – check. Flamers engaged – check. Pulse driver cannon – check. Shields engaged – check. Secondary generator, full power – check. All weapon systems active and engaged.'

The Stormsurge lurched forwards on its massive legs.

'Right,' Ch'an said, 'let's see how this thing moves.'

For the first hour, Ch'an was fine, but when they started the war-game simulator programme, he felt his hands begin to shake. He closed his eyes and tried to focus, but for a moment he was back on Mu'gulath, dropping from a Manta into the maelstrom of battle. Even the descent was terrifying as searing tracers and missiles arced towards him, their contrails of white falling gracefully behind them.

'Is all well, master?' H'an asked.

Ch'an closed his eyes to find the inner peace. For him it was the view of the Western Lakes on Au'taal, with the sacred mountain, Fi'jen, in the background, reflected on its mirrored surface. He held that image in his mind for a moment, just as he had when he hung from the bottom of a Manta, praying that they would not be shot out of the sky. But as soon as he opened his eyes he felt the panic return, and in irritation he lurched forwards as the thrusters flared, making the opening of the target range in two great bounds.

'What is wrong with this machine?'

H'an looked at him in concern. 'Master,' he said. 'Are you sure you are well?'

There were beads of sweat on Ch'an's brow. He wiped them away and closed his eyes once more. I am fine, he told himself. But the Stormsurge did not move. It stood motionless for what seemed an age. Ch'an sat in the pilot's carriage and breathed deeply.

'The suit is faulty.'

'Is it?'

'Yes,' Ch'an said. He closed his eyes again.

'Shall we go back?' H'an said. 'Fio'ui K'or can check it.'

Ch'an paused and then nodded. 'Yes,' he said. 'I think that would be good.'

Ch'an managed to get them back into the suiting dome, and Fio'o Bork'an was there to open the hatch.

Ch'an could not get out fast enough. As he dragged himself from the machine, he caught his bad leg on the rim and gritted his teeth against the pain.

'Apologies,' Fio'ui K'or said. 'I will check the suit straight away.'

'My thanks,' Ch'an said as he took Fio'o Bork'an's hand. He grabbed his leather jacket and sucked in long breaths.

By this time H'an had climbed out. 'Are you sure you are well?' he asked.

'Yes,' Ch'an said. 'You are very kind. I think I will lie down.'

Ch'an had not long closed his eyes and started to breathe slowly when someone shook his shoulder.

'Shas'vre Ch'an.' It was a Ke'lshan voice. He sat up and saw the pale face of N'loo staring down at him. 'Commander M'au has summoned you. You are to come at once.'

N'loo marched with Ch'an to the lift and out into the snow. M'au did not make him wait long, having Ch'an brought in as the commander sat cross-legged on the floor.

'Sit,' M'au gestured, but Ch'an tapped his leg. 'It is easier if I stand.'

'As you wish.' M'au drew himself up. 'Shas'vre Ch'an,' he said, his voice straining with fury. 'I hear that yesterday you interrupted a training session with talk of jackets and gue'la and shooting your own troops.'

'Yes, sire. I did.'

'What do you mean by this?'

Ch'an started to speak but M'au cut him off. 'You were criticising our training. You do not think we are teaching the cadets properly. You are typical of the warriors of Au'taal. You think yourself above all others. You hide your laziness behind contempt. You are separate, when strength comes from being whole. This is the way of the Tau Empire. We work together as one. We do not pursue individual aims and goals. What is it you want, Shas'vre Ch'an? Personal glory?'

'No, Shas'el.'

'Then do not criticise us again. Is that clear? I keep a strict grip on this camp. We are all working towards the Greater Good.' Ch'an turned towards the door but Fireblade M'au called him back. 'One more thing. I made an exception before, but I think I made a mistake. Please take off that filthy jacket. I know what it stands for. You disrespect us all by wearing such a thing.'

Fireblade M'au called one of his guards forwards. The fire warrior took the jacket from Ch'an's shoulders, first one side, then the other. 'Burn that filthy thing.'

Ch'an was stiff as he stood before the commander.

'I expect you to support our efforts here, Ch'an. Do you understand?'

'Yes, Fireblade.'

'Dismissed.'

CHAPTER SIXTEEN

Ch'an lay in his bunk all that afternoon. Whenever he closed his eyes he felt his heart pounding, he heard the thunder of battle and he felt himself falling as his Stormsurge burned about him.

He lay there throughout the afternoon and into eventide. His dorm mates stayed away out of respect and H'an stood at the door to ward off the chain of concerned warriors who came to visit.

'He is unwell,' he said. 'It was a long flight. He is going to meditate. Yes, he was most impressed with the improvements in the stabilisation controls. He liked the rotary controls. Yes.'

The sound of the evening bell brought him back. He sat up and touched his brow. He was cold, he thought. Damp. It was an unhealthy sight for a tau. H'an was sitting at the end of the bed. He looked concerned. 'The cooks have prepared a feast.' Ch'an made no response. 'It is in your honour, shas'vre.'

Ch'an sat up slowly. He nodded. 'I'll come,' he said.

'I could bring you something.'

'No,' Ch'an said. 'I am fine.'

The food sharing hall was a wide, low-sided chamber, dug under the ice, with rows of long benches and tables. When Ch'an limped in that eventide, the whole cadre of Stormsurge pilots and gunners stood and started the low hooting noise that marked deep respect. He hooted with them in return and they all sat and went on with their meals.

Ch'an moved slowly along, bowing to the chief warriors who came forward to greet him personally. The cadre was a mix of veterans and new graduates. It was so strange to see a room full of a mix of septs. He could see the markings of Elsy'eir, T'olku, Ksi'm'yen, Uan'Voss and Dal'yth, amongst others.

Some of the warriors had the smooth flat faces of young fire warriors, each one with the honour Ch'ay symbol, for elite graduates.

It was easy to spot the veterans. They had a slightly haunted look about them, as if they knew how thin their shadows were. Ch'an knew many of them by face or reputation. Shas'vre N'dras Po'lco, with the almost-black leather hide of his sept, had almost a hundred kills. Shas'vre Mysto, who greeted him with stiff formality, had a Warhound Titan to his name. Shas'el Reet'u, who had lost a finger and part of his skull on Mu'gulath Bay, was credited with driving back an Imperial tank brigade single-handedly. And at the end he saw an old fellow, Shas'el Elsy'eir Sham'bal, who had fought with him in the first battle of Mu'gulath Bay.

'So they sent you here too!' Sham'bal said. 'Must be bad if they're bringing an old thin-lip like you back.'

'I thought the same when I saw you here.'

'I revolunteered.'

'You did? Then you're a fool.'

Sham'bal made a respectful gesture which meant, will you honour me by sitting and eating with me? After a few refusals, Ch'an accepted.

'I wanted to keep fighting,' Sham'bal said at last. 'I lay in my bed and thought about what would happen if the gue'la ever landed on Au'taal. They would dig her mountains for coal. They would burn her forests. Rip down the arches. They would turn it into a rank and polluted place. I had to go back and fight. I knew that I would never see her again. But I would give my life making sure that my home lived on. We would give other worlds the chance to flourish and bloom, as Au'taal does.'

They took it in turns serving each other the choicest pieces from the platter before them. For a while they talked of Au'taal, and the times they had met there by the Western Lakes, and recalled their battles.

'So how did you end up here?' Ch'an said.

Sham'bal shook his head. 'I was at an awards ceremony when an earth caste by the name of Fio'o Bork'an Koba'ashi…'

'Oh, I met him this morning.'

'Well. He was very excited. This was a tau'cyr ago, or more. He said he had helped develop a new weapon that would counter the titans of the enemy. It was the Stormsurge KV122 at the time. A little heavier. More armour on the front, but too slow. He wanted me to pilot it as they perfected the torso controls. So I helped out. I recommended a lighter chassis. I went through four development stages. There was a problem with the recoil. Then Fio'o Bork'an

Koba'ashi came up with the idea of stabilisers. I helped him with those. And when it was done, and perfect, and deadly, how could I leave it and say goodbye? I had to try it out myself. In combat. Against the foe. I just had to!'

Ch'an made the distinctive chuckle deep in his throat. He understood.

They ate for a while, before Sham'bal said, 'I felt needed. That this battle for Mu'gulath Bay is bigger than anything before.'

Ch'an nodded. 'If it were not for Shadowsun…'

'She is very fine,' Sham'bal nodded.

'Even she is rumoured to have made…' he paused, and the last word came out with a look of distaste, '…mistakes.'

The word 'mistakes' lingered in the air.

There was a long silence.

'I heard what happened this morning,' Sham'bal said at last.

'What do you mean?'

'Your machine malfunctioned.'

'No. It was me.' Ch'an forced a smile. 'I was a little unwell.'

Sham'bal put out a hand and rested it on the back of Ch'an's. 'You could retire, you know.'

Ch'an felt the clamminess returning to his forehead. He slowed his breathing, swallowed and nodded.

'We cannot let the gue'la change us. We cannot let go of what it means to be tau. Not just the success, but also the art, the songs, the poetry, the tolerance, peace, productivity, innovation.

'Just imagine a galaxy which was full of gue'la and only gue'la. Just imagine the horror and the devastation.'

Sham'bal shuddered. 'And the ignorance,' he said.

Ch'an's eyes were wide with passion. 'Yes!' he hissed. 'The ignorance!'

As the food sharing hall emptied, Sham'bal called for a jug of wine and laid out two small ceremonial cups.

'We should drink to remember our old fellows,' he said, and poured two cups.

They drank them back and poured two more.

When they reached the bottom of the pot, Ch'an started a song. The words were his own, set to an ancient Elsy'eir tune. They spoke of hope and light, when the darkness and stupidity pressed close. Sham'bal picked up as Ch'an sang the chorus, and the hall fell silent as all the warriors listened to the song. One by one, like a flame being passed from one candle to another, each of the warriors sang the melody. Even the earth caste servants came out of the kitchens and hung their heads with strange and rare emotions.

Tomorrow, Ch'an swore, he would get back into the Stormsurge, and he would not fail.

CHAPTER SEVENTEEN

Shipmaster Ferral brought the news of their successful translation directly to Nergui's chamber. Kill Team Faith kept to their own decks for the two weeks it took the strike cruiser *Nemesis* to make the warp jump. The corridors of the Space Marine quarters were silent, except for the thud of a distant boltgun.

Nergui's chambers were at the base of the bridge, looking out over the dorsal lance batteries. She felt her pulse rising as she turned left from the lift and tapped gently on his door. It opened in moments, Nergui's black-armoured shape filling the doorway.

It always surprised her, when she had been away for more than a few weeks – the size and proportions of the Adeptus Astartes. She flinched.

His voice was a deep rumble. 'Shipmaster.'

For a moment she forgot why she had come, and then it came out in a rush. 'We have made contact with the *Valete*. They report the insertion successful.'

'Thank you, shipmaster,' Nergui said. 'Has Batbayar's *Northwind* arrived yet?'

'Not yet, sire.'

'Let me know as soon as that happens. Until then, we remain in blackout.'

'Yes, sire,' she said, and the door closed.

Two days later, the *Northwind* exited the warp with a sudden flash of blue energy, her gun batteries and launch bays wreathed in tendrils of warp energy as she hit real space. Shipmaster Ferral brought the *Nemesis* alongside the *Northwind*, and when the two strike cruisers – one black, one white – came to within a hundred miles of each other, a black Thunderhawk launched from the *Nemesis*, bound for the White Scars.

On board, Nergui was tense at the thought of returning to his brothers' craft.

He had enjoyed it too much, he thought, and the voice of his mother in the catacombs of Picket's Watch had woken memories he had thought long forgotten.

The Thunderhawk landed in the same bay as before, but now the White Scars Thunderhawks had gone, and there was only the venerable Fire Raptor, *Obos*, with attentive servitors milling along her fuselage. As Nergui came down the assault ramp, Ganzorig strode out to greet him. If there were any hard feelings between Nergui and the Red Tangut they appeared to have been buried.

'Welcome, captain,' the White Scar said. 'The khan is eager to see you. He asked me to tell you to come to the Eyrie. I can summon a servo-skull to show you the way.'

Nergui marched into the White Scars ship. 'No. I know the way.'

The Eyrie was a nickname Nergui and Batbayar had for the observation tower that rose up behind the bridge. It was the highest point you could reach on a strike cruiser. You could look back over the engines, into the darkness of space, or forwards along the spine of the craft, or out to either side, over the gun batteries. It was Nergui's favourite place on a cruiser – a place where he could stand and watch and think.

Batbayar had clearly remembered this.

The White Scars he passed did not even give him a second glance. It was as if they could see through the black on his armour to the white beneath. As if they had accepted him as one of their own.

Nergui thought the guards on the bridge lift would say something, but they stood aside and let him pass. He entered the lift and punched in the access code, and felt himself being carried up through the decks, past the bridge access point, up to the observation tower.

The lift opened out into the centre of a small domed chamber. Thirty feet across, the armourglass gave clear visibility overhead as well as below, the floor plates affording a viewer the odd sensation of walking in space.

Batbayar stood with his back to the lift. He was alone, except for a pair of servo-skulls that hovered in the air behind him.

'Ah!' the khan said as Nergui entered. 'You were right. There's nothing better after the claustrophobia of a warp jump than standing here and feeling the openness of the galaxy all about you.'

Nergui joined him and they stood staring out into the darkness. Somewhere, ahead of them, lay their target.

'So,' Batbayar said, 'what news?'

'Our advance teams are already on the planet. They will prepare the ground and when all is ready we attack. Not until then, understand?'

'Of course,' Batbayar said. He tapped his thigh with a gauntleted hand. 'Have they found Shadowsun?'

'Not yet,' Nergui said.

'I can just see Kor'sarro's face!' He chuckled to himself. 'It will be a great aid for our Chapter, if I bring our leader home as well. If I bring you home too... Nergui Khan's return would be a boon in our hour of need.'

Nergui laid out a map of the planet before them. 'The production facility is here,' he said. He pointed to a plateau near the northern pole of the planet. 'The camp lies in the middle of this valley. On each of these crags there are NG-4 planetary defence platforms. We will deal with these. There are six hunter cadres with strong air support. I will lead the attack on the landing port. There are vespid warriors here, and a kroot camp here. Their threat is not negligible.'

'How many battlesuits?' asked Batbayer

'Thirty suits of various classes, as well as the larger, newer ones in production'

'A hundred?'

'Yes. They are your target. The production facility here.'

If Batbayar was intimidated by this he did not show it. 'Good,' he said. 'We will sear it from the galaxy. Is it protected?'

'We will destroy the generators. There are a number of possible routes of attack. Our team have disabled a route along here.' Nergui traced a line along the planet.

Batbayar looked at the other with barely suppressed amusement. 'You have spent too long with the Deathwatch, my friend. Remember how you used to lead your company to battle, with drop pods and assault squads raining from the sky? Tell me, does the eagle still fly?'

'I fly,' Nergui said.

'Join us then! Fly with our warriors as we plummet from the sky! We shall draw chainswords together once more.'

There was a long pause. Nergui laughed. 'That would be fine, wouldn't it? Black and white together!'

'You see it too!' The khan paced up and down, extoling the virtues of battle and combat, and the ways of the White Scars. Then he grabbed Nergui's hand. 'Paint your armour white!' The khan was serious. 'My Techmarines are ready. They can do what must be done.

Come out of the shadows. Black is not a colour for a White Scar. It is the colour of hiding. Of shadows. It is the colour of burned timbers. Of the exhaust smoke that we leave in our wake. Wear white once more. I will give you command of the Fourth Company.'

Nergui took a deep breath to answer but Batbayar held up a hand. 'Do not answer. But think on it. Swing your sword with us. Kill the foes with us. Hunt them. Add the roar of your bike to our charge. Where is *Ganbold*? How your bike must miss the company of our bikes. Is it not alone?'

Nergui smiled as he imagined his own return. Part of him wished for nothing more... 'I heard my mother's voice a month ago,' he said.

Batbayar looked at him. 'Your mother?'

Nergui nodded. 'She was calling me. I was in the Empty Lands, standing with the goats as my father mounted up. I was trying to lift a kid that was too weak to suckle, and she called out to me, "shao-shao!"'

Batbayar frowned as his amusement turned to concern. He snorted, 'I don't even remember which of my father's wives was my mother!'

'Of course it was not really her. The memory was prompted by a psychic presence,' Nergui said. 'But it was a true memory.'

'So?'

'I have not thought of Chogoris for a long time. I hope I see it before I die. Of course my mother will be dead. My whole family will have died out a hundred years ago. But that is not why I hope to return. I would like to see my tribe once more, the Chaoge. When I think of fighting the aliens, it is the Chaoge I think of. Not hive slummers or agri worlds, or even the marble arcades of Ultramar. I think of my people, picking their way from summer pasture to winter hole, herding their grox. And it is them I fight for.'

'Then come back with me! After this is over. Come back to Chogoris!'

Nergui had to force the words out. 'I cannot join you.'

'Cannot, or will not?'

'I have sworn a vow, and until that is complete I cannot leave the Deathwatch.'

'What is the vow?'

'I cannot say.'

Batbayar let out a shout of anger and frustration. 'I come to the aid of your brothers. Will you not do me the small honour of returning to us?'

'I will do all that I can,' Nergui said, but Batbayar cursed in frustration – and the black and the white moved apart.

CHAPTER EIGHTEEN

Ch'an was furious as he limped towards Commander M'au's office.

The guard stepped before him. 'Shas'vre Ch'an. Should you not be teaching our cadets?'

Ch'an tried to go round him but the guards reacted quickly, blocking the door, so he shouted over their heads.

A shadow appeared, as Commander M'au made his way from his office to the door. He acted surprised to see Ch'an here, and made a point of checking his chronometer. 'This morning you are scheduled to be instructing Cohort Ar on the gue'la strategies.'

Ch'an nodded. 'Yes, honourable one. I have asked Sham'bal to perform this duty for me.'

'If I wanted Sham'bal to teach Cohort Ar, then I would have scheduled that myself,' M'au said.

'I heard something that I thought was urgent. That there are gue'la on this planet.'

M'au feigned surprise. 'Who told you this?'

'You don't deny it?'

Fireblade M'au drew himself up. 'There is nothing to deny. A kroot claimed to have seen one fall from the sky. I have three hunter cadres out searching for it. They have found nothing. No body. No trace. Nothing. Every time the kroot tell me they have seen something it is the same. They are a little unreliable.'

Ch'an cut him off. 'This has happened before?'

'What?'

'The camp has been discovered?'

'How do you know?'

'That does not matter.'

Fireblade M'au's eyes narrowed. He put his fingers together and nodded slowly. 'Yes, once. The intruders were eliminated. Last time we sent the cadets straight into battle, but the losses were too high. It is vital that the training and bonding of crews is performed in the correct manner. Most High One Aun'ui Hoo'nan has thought on this most deeply. We have tightened security. Sweeps are being made. All we need is a week, then the training will be finished and the cohort deployed to Mu'gulath Bay. Once your cohort is ready, this base shall be moved again. It is all under control.'

Ch'an struggled to counter this. He stammered for moment. 'If there is an intruder then he cannot have flown through space to reach us. It means there is a ship up there. Our enemies are upon us.'

'If there was an intruder then don't you think we would have found it? We have a Defender patrolling the system, a security orbital above our heads, and the planet is covered with listening devices. You are not afraid, are you? I have heard what happened during the simulation. Maybe you cannot face fighting any more...'

Ch'an could barely contain his fury. 'It is not fear that makes me speak, but the vision of victory to which I hold dear. If we have been found we must relocate to a safe location. They will come for us. I have seen them – they are terrible.'

'If,' Commander M'au repeated Ch'an's own word. He drew himself up. 'Ke'lshan Sept has been granted the honour of guarding this facility and we take our duty seriously. I have sent my best hunter cadres out. The kroot too are hunting for signs. If anything landed here, we will find it.

'The Most High One is aware of the risks. A move at this point, when the crews are being bonded, will result in an unacceptable delay. This cadre of pilots and gunners need to be deployed to Mu'gulath Bay. Training will be completed within six days. Until then, the risk is not negligible, but it is acceptable.' Ch'an started to argue once more and Fireblade M'au bowed suddenly. Aun'ui Hoo'nan was standing in the doorway.

'We have nothing to fear,' the ethereal said.

Ch'an opened his mouth. He struggled for a moment, then bowed deeply. 'Apologies. I did not know that you were aware of this, and that the matter had been considered.'

'Do not feel guilt. We need your wisdom. We need you to lead. By example. Am I right in hearing that you have not yet completed the Mu'gulath Bay simulation?'

Ch'an shook. 'Yes,' he said.

'Please go to Cohort Ar. You have much experience that they will need in the coming battle. I would like you to share that with them. Show them. Lead them. Do the simulation. I have confidence in your abilities.'

Ch'an's voice was a croak. 'Thank you, Most Honoured One. I will be glad to help.'

Ch'an limped back towards the instructional dome.

He felt giddy and deflated as he entered the food sharing hall. From the noise, Cohort S'a'an were on the firing range. Cohort Y'ap and Ar had both entered the hall at the same time. Ch'an took his tray and turned, but there was no place for him to sit, and no one made way for him.

'Shas'vre!' a voice said, and he turned and saw H'an holding an empty tray. 'I missed you this morning.'

'I was giving a talk to Cohort Ar.'

H'an nodded and leant in closer to speak. 'We heard you had gone to see Fireblade M'au.'

Ch'an felt his hand trembling, and he put his tray down and poured himself a cup of water. 'I did.'

'Was it about the simulation?'

'No,' Ch'an said.

'Everyone is talking.'

'About what?'

H'an didn't like to say.

'I am no coward,' Ch'an said.

'I do not think you are, but the Greater Good has been decided.'

'Maybe the Most High One is wrong,' Ch'an said quietly. H'an's face blanched for a moment. No one spoke against the ethereals. They were the supreme minds of their society. It was like a well frog trying to speak of the ocean. Mere fire warriors were unable to contemplate such lofty things. He leant forwards and took Ch'an's three fingers in his own, pressing hard in both warning and concern.

'Please don't say that again,' he said.

Ch'an started to argue, but H'an put up his hand. 'Promise me you will not say such a thing again...' He struggled for the words. 'If you do I will lose all respect for you.'

As evening fell Ch'an stood in the top chamber of the hab-dome, and looked out from the armourglass windows. All day, security had been visibly tightening. That afternoon the krootox were released. Mobile gun rigs made an ostentatious display as they moved to the high crags on Vespid Rock. Devilfish moved in outer rim defensive patterns, and a Riptide appeared suddenly, its jump pack flaring as it crested the distant ridge, knees bending before it jumped once more, skimming low across the ground.

Behind him H'an was playing another cadet at sho'gi. The other cadets were crowded round. H'an appeared to be winning. Ch'an listened to their banter with a detached air. He saw his reflection in the oval armourglass window and the sight of his own body shocked him. The galaxy had not been kind to him. It had taken him in its palm and crushed and broken him. And now this was what was left.

'I am tired,' he said to the others, and took the lift down to his dorm. In the sunken garden, a fire warrior was meditating, and in the lit windows he saw others talking, sleeping, revising for the next day's exercises. The chime rang for lights out.

Ch'an turned back to his bunk, but for once sleep did not come. He tossed and turned, let out an irritated sigh, sat up, and walked back to the window.

H'an heard the door latch click and sat up. Ch'an was gone.

H'an thought for a moment, and decided that he should follow. He slipped from his bunk and lifted the latch.

CHAPTER NINETEEN

The corridor was empty and quiet, apart from the gentle hum of the hab-dome's generator. There was no sign of Ch'an or any guards. The sunken garden was empty. The lift door stood open, the lights dimmed, unused.

H'an felt his panic growing as he began to run up the winding stairs, but the doors were closed and secure. There were fire warriors outside. A mobile gun rig moved slowly past with crew walking behind.

The sight of them calmed his panic.

He spun about and saw a figure sitting in the low red light of the dome. It was Ch'an.

'What are you doing?' H'an demanded as he hurried across the open space.

Ch'an turned and looked up. 'I could not sleep,' he said. There was a bundle in his lap. 'I feel it. They are coming for us. The Most Honoured One is... mistaken.'

'I asked you not to say that,' H'an said.

Ch'an looked down into his lap and the cadet put a hand out to the older warrior's shoulder. 'Forgive me. It is a veteran's sense. They found this place before. They will find it again. The silence always shatters.'

There was a pause. 'It's late,' H'an said. He stood, but Ch'an did not move.

After a long pause the veteran said, 'H'an. Will you do something for me?'

'What?'

'Will you bond with me?'

H'an hesitated.

'They are coming,' Ch'an said. 'We must be ready. If we are to fight, then we must be bonded.'

'But we were forbidden from bonding until our pairings have been selected.'

'You have to stop thinking like a cadet,' Ch'an said. 'You are about to go to war. Do you know how many of the last cohort are still alive? Less than half. Mu'gulath Bay is a thirsty planet. We have trained each day together. If we are to serve together in a Stormsurge, then we should bond.'

It went against all the theory that H'an had learnt in the Auspicious Warrior Graduate School on Bork'an, where the ceremony was held at the time of graduation, as a rite of passage, but he saw the look in the old warrior's eyes and the beads of sweat about his head, and inclined his head in a respectful gesture. 'If you wish, Shas'vre. I do not have a knife. May we use yours?'

Ch'an nodded. 'Yes,' he said. He lifted the bundle in his lap, and H'an saw a bonding knife there. 'Good. I have all that we need.'

'Where should we go?'

Young warriors had such ideas. Ch'an laughed. 'Here will do as well as any,' he said.

Ch'an dimmed the red lume-strip. He lit a candle, took out his bonding kit and unrolled the ceremonial cloth which held the knife. He lifted it in both hands.

Most of the knives that H'an had seen were new, freshly issued to newly appointed Shas'vre, but this one had a worn scabbard, with knotwork of red cord about the top and a handle that had been held many times. It looked ancient. It looked like a knife from the tales of old.

Darkness added a certain solemnity to the occasion. 'It is ready,' Ch'an said, and laid the wrapping cloth over his wrist. He handed one scarf to H'an and took one for himself. They were old as well, and had the scent of cordite about them.

'They have been used,' Ch'an said, by way of explanation.

They tied the scarves of bonding about their heads, and then Ch'an started the ceremony of ta'lissera. There was none of the formal standing and bowing and ritual chanting that H'an had learnt in graduate school, but it felt much more real despite this. It felt like the ceremony his ancient forebears had carried out as they prepared for battle. Earnest, full of meaning, solemn unto death. At the end, Ch'an held out his palm and touched the knife to it. He clenched his fingers about it, and then drew the knife so that it cut the grey skin of the open palm. His face was drawn and tight. His life blood dripped out, purple droplets falling to the floor at their hooves.

'Though the suns shall be sundered, though the mists of destruction shall blind us, I shall stay true to you, to ourselves, and to the Greater Good. So I swear by this line on my palm,' he said. 'I shall fulfil my bond to you, unto death and beyond, brother in arms.'

Ch'an handed the knife to H'an. He held the blade, drew in a deep breath, then put the edge to his palm, clenching his own fist around it. At that moment H'an understood why this ceremony had been held on to by his people when so much else had been let go. He understood what it meant to look another warrior in the eye, and pledge to him your brotherhood. He understood that they would fight and die together, if need be.

He spoke the words and began to pull the ancient knife through his clenched fist. The pain made him feel sick. He felt clamminess on his brow. He kept pulling the knife until the whole thing was smeared with his blood.

Ch'an held out his bloody hand, and H'an grasped it. 'Blood to blood, my brother, we shall fight as one for the Greater Good.'

'Now,' Ch'an said. 'When the time comes, we shall be ready.'

H'an slept fitfully that night. His palm throbbed, and he only seemed to fall asleep moments before suit drills began at the fourth dec.

It was dark outside as they crossed to the suiting dome. Flecks of snow were falling hard against H'an's cheeks.

'How is your palm?' Ch'an asked.

'It is fine,' H'an said.

Ch'an nodded and they did not speak again until they were inside the suiting dome, their Stormsurge standing silently waiting for them.

Ch'an was brusque and business-like as they went through the suiting rituals. H'an dropped into place and the earth caste technicians closed the suit hatches up, and he found himself scrambling to keep up with the opening checks.

'Generator. Check. Guns armed. Check. Shield engaged. Check. Ready for combat, shas'vre.'

Ch'an grunted in reply, and they paused for a moment at the opening of the firing range. 'Commencing Mu'gulath Bay simulator seven-eight-four,' he announced.

'Simulation seven-eight-four beginning,' an earth caste technician answered, with just a hint of excitement in his voice. Earth caste could be so, well, earth caste.

'Let's go,' Ch'an said. He sidestepped and lumbered forwards.

The veteran seemed calm and focused in a way that H'an had not seen before. 'You are different this morning,' he said at last.

'Focus,' Ch'an said as their suit stomped across the open tundra.

A decoy Titan's head appeared over the top of the rocks, miles to their right. On Mu'gulath Bay they reckoned you had six seconds to kill a Titan before it brought its own weapons to bear.

'Enemy sighted,' Ch'an's voice rattled through the routine announcements with all the slick, practised air of the ace that he was. 'Engage,' he said, bending the legs and bracing the feet.

At four seconds H'an fired. There was a glorious burst of energy from the secondary generator, a flash of incandescent light that spanned the ultraviolet and infrared spectrums. A first time hit. A hole ripped through the decoy, a steaming crater burned into the ice-cliff behind.

At the end, as they climbed out of their suits, the earth caste's voice sounded excited. 'The suit did not malfunction?'

'No,' Ch'an said. 'Nor the pilot.'

Fio'ui K'or bowed to them both. 'Full marks on firing.'

'We achieved full marks?' Ch'an said.

The earth caste nodded.

Ch'an frowned. 'We shouldn't have. Don't look so pleased with yourself.' H'an's pigmentation darkened. 'This course should be made harder. Attrition rates among new crews are too high. I have been on Mu'gulath Bay. We should train for that. Real war.'

H'an watched Ch'an limp away with a sense of deflation. He shared a look with K'or.

'He is very brave,' the earth caste said.

'He is,' H'an said.

After the noontide meal, H'an made his way down to the sunken garden.

'Shas'ui H'an,' a voice called out.

Shas'el Sham'bal was sitting cross-legged against a rock. 'I see that you have bonded,' he said.

H'an held up his bandaged hand, and nodded.

'It is a great honour to be joined with Shas'vre Ch'an.'

'It is,' H'an said. 'Believe me. I understand that.'

'But it is dangerous too,' the older warrior said.

'What do you mean?'

He took H'an's bandaged hand in his own. 'Look at your hand. It has one scar. Ch'an's hand has many lines. Ch'an's life-thread is strong. It is like a thread of steel that rubs against those that are bonded with it. It wears the other threads out, and breaks them, though it does not mean to.'

H'an lowered his head. 'I understand that, Shas'el. But if that is my fate, then so be it. I shall accept it. It will be for the Greater Good.'

Sham'bal nodded. 'The Greater Good.'

CHAPTER TWENTY

For two days Moaz had been making good time. It was too easy, almost. But a sense had grown on him. He paused, low in the broken ice field, and tried to remember what it meant. It came back to him slowly… It was like having a shadow. Something behind him, just out of sight: a presence. It came to him that this was what it felt like to be *hunted*.

The Raven Guard looked back, his helm-enhanced vision scanning the tundra for heat traces or movement. Nothing, just miles of icy waste, broken here and there by black boulders and places where the grox herds had scraped the ice away. Just flat snow and ice-fields, and the distant passing of a grox herd moving slowly south to better grazing.

They were a hardy winter variant, with shaggy long red hair, wide horns and thick, tough necks. The bull was a thick-necked beast. Ten cows around him. The bull snorted, and swung its horned head about, but it was looking away from him, back along the way that Moaz had come.

The bull had sensed the same thing. Whatever was tracking him had swung wide to come in under the glare of the sunset. He found a ledge under an ice-crag to sit and wait, combat knife loose in its scabbard and a silencer round in his stalker-pattern bolter. An hour later Moaz spotted it, five miles behind him, a low shape, nose pressed to the ground, following the route that he had taken – a kroot hound. It was some kind of tracking beast with beak and claws. He held his fire, needing to know if there was more than one.

It took half an hour for them to show themselves. The kroot hound led, sniffing the air for a moment, then lowered its head to the ice once more. Then another kroot hound appeared, and a third, and then a craggy kroot hunter, bent almost as low as his hounds, taking long loping strides. The pack master had a shaggy white pelt, a hunting rifle and a bandolier of skinning knives across his back, and a black beak and narrow, yellow eyes. He lowered his head to sniff in a manner just like the hounds.

Moaz watched the creatures for a long while. He could shoot, of course, but he was not sure that he could kill them all. Bodies would betray his presence.

He scanned ahead. There was a valley opening ten miles to the north west. It would be a short detour but it would hem his pursuers in, and then he could destroy them.

It took Moaz three hours to reach the valley mouth. It was narrow, with steep, snow-covered slopes: the perfect killing zone. He headed straight along the bottom, then doubled back, scaling the left-hand slopes, looking for a place where he could count his pursuers.

He found a ledge and dug his feet in for good purchase. He loaded hellfire rounds into his stalker-pattern boltgun as the pack of kroot hounds entered the mouth of the valley, the hunter loping after them. Seven hounds, he counted, with one pack master. As the hounds bounded up the defile, Moaz lifted the muzzle, found the head of the pack master, and traced as he bent to sniff the ground. Just a little further.

The shaggy beaked head turned towards where he was sitting. It was as if he could hear the Space Marine. Moaz saw the beaked head in the crosshairs of the bolter, the blinking yellow eyes – which turned and stared straight up to where he was sitting.

Moaz understood his mistake.

The pack master's narrow yellow eyes were not looking at him, they were looking behind him. A low grunt gave Moaz a bare moment's warning.

The blade missed him by inches. It hit bedrock as Moaz twisted and turned. A second blade slammed down. Moaz's boot connected with a thin, hard shin, then the kroot was on him, beak scraping against his armour. He got both legs under it and kicked out, but it was stronger than he had imagined. His boltgun was knocked out of his hand. Thin, hard fingers scrabbled for his throat. He caught one leathery neck in a fist. He felt it snapping at his arm, the razor sharp teeth cutting through to the flesh beneath as he ground his fingers together.

They slid down the slope. The kroot flailed at him in a mad flurry of blows. Moaz kneed it in the head to make it let go, dragged his arm out of its beak, grabbed his gun from the snow, and fired.

The stalker-pattern boltgun was much too long for hand-to-hand combat. It gave a low thud and hiss as the round fired at the first assailant. If he hit, it had no effect. He fired again and the other kroot jumped on his back, knife scoring lines in his armour as it searched for his jugular.

Moaz threw it over his head and fired into it. The mass-reactive hellfire round hit the thing in the neck, the explosive bolt ripping through the tight tendons as toxins sent the kroot's muscles into spasms.

Moaz ducked the other kroot and fired a round into its belly. The hellfire round exploded in a mess of gore.

Moaz saw a blur of movement and skidded down the ice cliff, using a hand to steady himself. Snow tumbled down about him as he descended in an avalanche of his own making. He saw his foe scrambling along the bottom of the ice cliff. A shot rang out. He felt it hurtling past his ear and slowed himself for a moment. Four more shots rang out. He was getting a sense of their numbers now. He was the one who had been driven into an ambush.

He had to kill them all, or the whole mission would be thrown into jeopardy. He took one out from the other side of the crag. It fell back against the snow, and then slid down the slope, hitting the ground in a dark, crumpled heap. Something whizzed past his ear again. All around him kroot were standing and firing.

He counted three more kroot warriors on the slopes nearby, six more on the slopes opposite. One of them was kneeling to fire. Moaz took it down with a shot to the head. He scrambled higher, fired again. Another kill. The kroot hounds were bounding up the slopes towards him. Moaz needed more time. He scrambled higher up the steep slopes. Just as he reached the top he ran into something huge. He found himself staring into a great yellow eye. A vast black beak opened in a hiss.

Krootox, he cursed. It did not look friendly.

CHAPTER TWENTY-ONE

Moaz put a second hellfire round into the krootox as it snapped at him. It slowed for a moment and he fired twice more. The acid began to work at once, seeping into wounds that the shrapnel had already blasted through the creature's internal tissues. A shot to the eyeball finished it off, but a second creature bounded towards him. The rider's spear slammed into his face, crazing his visor. He ducked as the creature crashed into him with the force of a hammer. His visor was a blur of ice and snow and feathers, and the krootox stood over him, pecking and squawking even as he pumped hellfire rounds up into its body.

The rider was on him. Moaz twisted out of its grasp, slammed a foot onto the kroot's spear shaft, and then drove the muzzle of his bolter into its gut. He fired. There was red all over the snow as he pulled his boltgun free of the remains, and turned.

Seven kroot hounds, and five more warriors. He took the warriors down as they tried to flee up the valley wall opposite. The hellfire rounds were deadly. Even a miss could cover a target in a spray of bubbling acid. Nothing could survive a direct hit.

He was moving for a better vantage point when he spotted a blur in the corner of his eye. He ducked as a savage blade glanced off his helm. His head rang with the blow. He came at it from the side. It was taller than him, with a serrated beak, round yellow eyes and a heavy rusted blade that looked like it had been looted from a greenskin. It swung at him again and he stepped inside the blow and caught the kroot hunter with an uppercut. It let out a grunt as he slammed it back against the ice wall.

It rolled to the side, and came back with a backhand blow,

followed up by an overhead swipe and a third savage blow. The blade hissed through the air in front of him, scoring a deep graze across the aquila on his chest-plate. He dropped low and drew his combat knife, and drove into the thing, hitting it low in the gut and knocking it backwards.

Its torso was skinny and slippery in his hands, the arms and legs long and incredibly powerful. He drove it back against the ice wall and they rolled on the ground, tearing and clawing at each other.

Moaz felt them slide towards the lip of the ledge and threw his weight over the edge, dragging the kroot with him. Its beak was clamped on his shoulder. He turned so that the kroot hunter cushioned his fall as they bounced off the first crag, took the second bounce on his back, and then they were tumbling down the lower slopes.

Moaz tore through the rest, until there was only one kroot left.

Half an hour later Moaz found its trail. It had escaped through the mouth of the valley and headed west with two hounds. The hounds gave the hunter's location away. Moaz shot one in the shoulder as it leapt over a rock.

The other was sniffing the pool of blood when the next shot hit it in the head. The hunter laid low for over an hour, and Moaz slowly circled in for the kill.

It knew he was there, unblinking yellow eyes turning to face him as he looked through the scope. The strangeness of having the prey look you in the eye had thrown him last time. This time he was ready.

It was a xenos. It had to die.

When at last he found the body, Moaz stood over the hunter to check that it was dead. The hellfire round had caught it in the back, and his quarry had kept going for nearly half a mile.

He bent down to touch its arm. He flinched back as the head turned towards him and the yellow eyes opened.

It seemed to be speaking to him.

He bent down, trying to hear what it was saying, but could not. He took off his helmet and felt the icy touch of the planet on his cheek, and the kroot blinked and spoke again.

Moaz did not know the tongue. He did not care about what language it spoke, but bent and put the stalker-pattern boltgun to its head. 'The Emperor hates you,' he said and put a bolt into its skull.

CHAPTER TWENTY-TWO

Moaz covered the last hundred miles in less than four hours, found the designated spot and cursed. This was the place Kill Team Zeal were supposed to rendezvous, but he was two days late, and there was no one else here.

He had not slept for four days and the exertion was beginning to show. He crouched in a low hollow half a mile south of the tau space port and took out his magnoculars. The tau facility was well guarded. There was no sign of the rest of his kill team.

He ducked back as a flight of drones went overhead, one leap-frogging the other as they scouted the land. He could not vox so close to the enemy, but he risked a quick crackle of static on his personal channel: two crackles in quick succession.

Nothing. He had started moving round the space port when he heard his vox-unit come to life – just a hint of static, before the signal dropped. He moved forwards, keeping to the shadows, and the signal came again, closer this time. He crouched down, unable to see anything, and risked sending a brief signal back. Just a crackle of static in return.

Moaz moved forwards at a run now, dropping into an icy hollow as a Devilfish passed within twenty feet of him, blue screens lighting up the gunner's face as he looked straight through the Raven Guard.

A hand clasped his arm. Moaz twisted, knife out, but already there was a knife at his own throat.

'I have been waiting for you,' Hadrian said.

Moaz laughed. 'Well done, brother! I have taught you well,' he said and put his own knife away. 'Now, if I had slept in the last four days…!'

'I wondered why you were making so much noise. What happened though? You should have been here two days ago.'

There wasn't time to go over it all. 'I was delayed,' Moaz said.

'Were you seen?'

The Raven Guard had to admit it. 'Yes. Kroot hunters. I killed them all. It took longer than I thought.'

'The jammers are fitted?'

'All of them. They will start jamming in about...' he checked the chronometer inside his helmet, 'ten minutes.'

The Black Shield had dropped in three days after Moaz, manoeuvred slowly to within half a mile of the star base and, for the last three weeks, had watched and recorded all the little routines of the camp. The times of meals. The patterns of movement. The deployment of forces. He knew it all. They were almost ready to attack.

'Get your bolter ready,' Hadrian said. 'You're just in time.'

He opened the vox-link to the ships in orbit. 'He is here,' Hadrian said. 'Yes. Yes. Understood.' He closed the vox-link. 'Nergui says we are ready to go.'

As he spoke he took a homing beacon from his belt, placed it down and set the signal pulsing. There was a slight hum as it started up, and then the note changed as the *Nemesis* locked on to it. A light flashed to show a drop-unit was inbound.

Hadrian loaded his bolter. 'Come on,' he said. 'Let's give them room.'

CHAPTER TWENTY-THREE

The Northwind was running on almost no power, her systems barely ticking over as she slid through the thick gas clouds of the Distaf Nebula. In the Eyrie, Batbayar Khan had his honour guard in attendance. They stood with legs braced wide and arms folded as they stared down at the planet they were about to attack.

'I have a question, great khan.'

Batbayar scowled, his brows coming together as Ganzorig stepped forwards.

'Speak,' Batbayar said.

'Tell me, great khan, why does the Tulwar Brotherhood fight this war, when there is battle on our home world?'

There was a sudden stillness. Batbayar turned on the banner bearer. 'Ganzorig, are you afraid?'

The other warrior smarted. 'You know the answer to that,' he said. 'I fear nothing, except failure.'

'I tell you why we fight today. We were born on a world of wide plains, good for riding and hunting. But we are Adeptus Astartes! We have been raised above others. We are stronger, fiercer, braver. The galaxy is our steppe land. We ride where we choose. We hunt our enemies and we kill them! That is the reason we fight. But more than that. We fight today because our brothers need us. Kor'sarro Khan is set on killing this Shadowsun. If we kill her then we bring two companies home to Chogoris... What a victory that would be!'

As he spoke something began to appear over the planet. It slid slowly into view, a pale cupola with an underslung array of pulse cannons and railguns that could even smash through a craft as powerful as the *Northwind*.

'That is the orbital defence platform,' Apothecary Khulan said as he stood at his khan's shoulder. 'Are you sure the Deathwatch will be able to destroy that?'

'My brother has promised me,' Batbayar said. 'Let us see if he is true to his word.'

Ganzorig marched forwards. 'Why do we not just blow it out of the sky?'

Batbayar smiled indulgently. 'I know. That would be a fine thing, wouldn't it? To sweep in now, before they even know we are here. But no. The Deathwatch want to help. Let them do their work for you.'

'Maybe that is where Shadowsun is,' Khulan said.

No one spoke. Batbayar scowled, but he said nothing. 'If Shadowsun is here, she is mine. Make sure all the sergeants know that. The minute she is spotted, I want to know.'

There was a brief hiss as the lift opened behind them, and Nergui strode out.

'I have just been in contact with my kill teams on the planet. They are in position. We can start the attack.'

Batbayar pointed towards the defence platform. 'And your teams are able to take that out as well?'

'Yes,' Nergui said. 'Three of our brothers are on the planet already. The rest of their team will destroy the defence platform. The others will ensure that there is no resistance to your strike. And then you can do the rest.'

Ganzorig spoke. 'The Deathwatch are confident.'

Nergui looked at him. 'It is a xenos construction. Killing xenos is what we do.'

It was little more than five minutes before Batbayar Khan was sweeping onto the flight deck, riding on his Land Speeder Tempest, legs braced wide. His bear-skin cloak flapped behind him, and his long moustaches trailed over his shoulder pads with the wind of his passing. The air filled with the roar of his warriors as they saluted him and Batbayar made a long, circuitous sweep about the chamber before he jumped down to the dais, where the lightning strike of the White Scars was emblazoned in red upon the wall. 'We have hunted and killed, but there are always more foes for us upon the steppes. Some of you fight today for the first time. Some of you are scarred with years of battle.

'We fight because Kor'sarro Khan needs our help as he leads the Eagle Brotherhood against the xenos. But first another brother needs us.

'The xenos have crafted a new weapon that has driven our forces back over and over. They are weak in the face of it, and Nergui, my brother, has located their production facility. We go to destroy it. Will you ride with me, brothers? Will you follow in my wake and bring destruction to our foes? Will you bring glory to the eagle banner – for it shall be watching you, and the ghosts of our forefathers will see you fight and they shall remember!'

Each time he asked a question there was a roar of 'Yes!' Even Ganzorig roared as the bikers lifted their hunting lances in salute. Batbayar held out his arms. 'The planet we strike today is hidden. The enemy think they can take worlds from our Great Father. Show them no mercy. Show them that there is no place they can hide from us! We shall hunt them, we shall find them, and we shall destroy them!'

Squad by squad the White Scars roared up the ramps, and one by one the Thunderhawks lifted, and then the gunships poured out into the silence of the void.

PART THREE
THE KILL

CHAPTER TWENTY-FOUR

Kill Team Zeal had been the first into the Proth System, so it was fitting that they made the first strike. While Moaz and Hadrian moved into their final positions, the others loaded into a boarding torpedo that burned a lone course towards the pale mass of Security Orbital VX-223. The single torpedo barely registered on the tau system monitors. Its size was, in space terms, barely a mote of dust, and compared to most celestial objects, it was moving at a crawl. It was not until a last defence drone picked it up on an automated sweep of the upper quadrant that the torpedo was even flagged as a potential threat.

By the time an alarm rang on the bridge and a remote gun turret lined it up in its sights, the torpedo was less than ten seconds from impact. Twin railguns fired a dazzling set of bracketing rounds at the object, but these coincided with the boarding torpedo's impact thrusters firing on full. Its acceleration was so sudden that the carefully computed shots fell short, blasting out into the void.

'Countdown commencing.' The machine-spirit of the boarding torpedo had a stern female voice, full of bile and hatred for the xenos.

In the cramped space three warriors from Kill Team Zeal waited. Corith, Eadmund and Iason each stood ready in their black Terminator armour. The low red light of the torpedo's core flickered as the auxiliary thrusters flared in the final moments before collision. Their harnesses braced them for the impact. There was a roar of melta charges, screaming metal, and then the staccato pop of stun grenades being fired into the cavity beyond.

The first tube held an automated assault cannon. As the ramps crashed down, the machine-spirit filled the empty chamber with a storm of shells. 'Tube two,' it announced, barely a second after the first, and the bracing straps dropped away as the tube entrance slammed down, filling the interior with light and smoke.

Corith, the Brazen Minotaur, led this mission. 'Hatred is a gift from the Emperor,' he voxed, tearing through an armoured bulkhead. 'Use it well.'

As he ripped through the last of the structural bars blocking their way, Eadmund hosed flames from one side of the chamber to the other. They appeared to have hit a service conduit. There were the burning remains of an earth caste team in the far corner of the chamber.

'We are too high,' Corith voxed, but he had already planned the fastest route to the bridge and shared it via their helm displays. 'Remember our mission. Disable, disorientate, destroy!'

The boots of the three suits of Terminator armour were like thunder. Eadmund went first, filling each room with burning promethium. At the third intersection a team of grey-armoured fire warriors made a brief and spirited stand, filling the corridor with micro-bursts of incandescent blue plasma, before they were driven back by Eadmund with heavy losses.

There were two more brief stands from the fire warriors as they put up a brave and commendable resistance. But in the close confines of the security orbital's corridors and bulkheads, they were outgunned by the terrible ferocity of Kill Team Zeal.

Eadmund fought off ambushers with brief but deadly rounds of assault cannon fire. The tau commander responded with admirable speed, but even as the fire warriors were being marshalled, Kill Team Zeal were within a hundred feet of their target.

'Hostiles,' Corith voxed as he cut through the blast door and was met by a hailstorm of blue plasma. His armour flashed an amber warning. Corith slashed at the remains of the bulkhead, and then kicked his way through.

There had to be twenty fire warriors at least. Corith stomped forwards, lightning claws tearing through them. Kallos led the way as the other Terminators drove through and fired.

It was over in seconds. Promethium flames, assault cannon rounds and lightning claws turned the generator room into a smoking charnel house.

In the command hub of Security Orbital VX-223 sirens began to wail. The impact made the metal flooring tremble. There were shouts and orders.

Warning symbols flashed. An earth caste technician took a moment to locate the point of entry. 'They have hit us just above the gunnery decks,' he confirmed.

The air caste commander shouted desperately for the scanners to find something to shoot at: 'We have been boarded. They have to have come from somewhere!'

The sound of fighting and explosions drifted up through the decks. Defence measures were being taken. Shas'vre Gru'eb was in command of the third shift. He was buckling on his body armour as he ran into the command hub with his elite warriors around him.

'All combat teams scrambled. I have counter-assault drones. Fire warriors. Combat suits. I can confidently assure you that this assault will be contained.'

'Gunnery decks compromised,' another technician reported.

Shas'vre Gru'eb stared at the readings. 'Seal off the Lower Third Quadrant.'

No one questioned his order. This was life and death now. There was no time to consider the fate of the tau who were locked into compromised sectors.

Shas'vre Gru'eb's presence restored a moment of calm and control over the situation. He put in motion a series of countermeasures and the volume within the room rose as each took over a part of the defence. Raising shields. Redirecting power supplies. Shutting blast doors. Unlocking the close-quarter battlesuits.

'Find where they are coming from,' he ordered when there was a second thud.

'Impact in the lower decks,' a croaky-voiced earth caste technician reported.

'Visuals!' Gru'eb demanded.

The earth caste technician's voice came back thirty seconds later with a visual from the gun drone sent to investigate. The boarding torpedo appeared empty.

'Decoy,' Shas'vre Gru'eb said with characteristic confidence. 'Leave it.'

His voice betrayed the strain as he redeployed the station's defence forces, but as he tried to get an answer from a commander in the Lower Third Quadrant, there was a third impact, much closer than the last two. The command deck shook violently. The lights flickered. Within seconds there was the scent of burning and the distinctive patter of bolters. Shas'vre Gru'eb's response was immediate. 'All cadres within two quadrants report to command hub. Gun drones redeploy. Kill on sight.'

There was an explosion and the blast doors rattled.

Shas'vre Gru'eb's pulse carbine had remained slung across his back. He swung the strap back across his body, and loaded a fresh powercell. There was no time to get into his battlesuit. 'I will try to hold them,' he told the earth and air caste crew.

He took thirty fire warriors with him at a jog. The blast doors were sealed behind him and moments later the sound of fighting filled the corridor outside.

Cadmus, the Dark Angel, led the remaining members of Kill Team Zeal out of the third boarding torpedo. The Dark Angel knew all the known configurations of tau orbital stations. It took him less than a second to guess the mark of this particular platform.

'Urchin four-three-zero,' he announced. 'The control centre is this way.'

The Imperial Fist, Cerys, cursed. His targeting matrix was ghosting. He reloaded his multi-melta and fired. The second time he compensated for the faulty system, and as the smoke cleared he saw that the blast doors had been reduced to dripping slag. The shower of molten metal had caused devastation in the corridor beyond. Searing beads of blue plasma lanced through the smoke. He snarled as a light dazzled him. A fraction of a second later there was a blast and a stink of burned flesh inside his helm.

He tried to find a target, but he felt tears on his cheeks and he could not open his eyes. 'I'm hit,' he cursed as he slammed into a bulkhead. He shook his head. 'Visor.'

A hand caught his arm. 'Got you,' Cadmus voxed. 'Nuoros. We'll need you up front.'

It was not easy manoeuvring Terminator armour in the tight, low corridors of the tau orbital.

'Covering you all,' Nuoros, the Crimson Fist, voxed. There was a hollow patter as his storm shield took the brunt of the incoming fire.

'Leave me,' Cerys hissed, but the hand did not let go.

'Can you see?' Cadmus hissed.

The Imperial Fist shook his head from side to side. 'Go on.'

'We are not leaving you,' Cadmus voxed.

The fire warriors had thrown up a hasty barricade of monitors and consoles and whatever else they could throw in the way of the attackers. Nuoros' power axe smashed a way through in seconds. He drove the xenos off as Cerys tried to open his eyes. His left eye was gone, he was sure, but his right eye burned as he blinked away the tears, and there were flares of light and dark as the helm cleared of noxious fumes.

'Helm systems are coming back,' he said after a moment's pause. 'It's getting better.'

The first thing he saw through his streaming eye was Cadmus' black helm staring intently at him.

'Can you see?' the Dark Angel voxed.

'Yes,' Cerys hissed. 'Just about.'

'Good. Stay close,' Cadmus told him.

The last stretch of corridor was crammed with fire warriors. Their leader was screaming as he sprinted down the corridor towards them. Behind him his warriors knelt and fired. Sparks flew. The air rang as grenades bounced and exploded. Two rounds hit Cadmus in the midriff, scorching insignificant marks in his Terminator armour. He clicked his assault cannon into action. The barrel whirled as he strode forwards. By the time he had reached the blast doors, his gun barrels were starting to smoke and the floor was slick with the blood of the dead.

Nuoros cut through another pair of blast doors with his axe. 'We have reached the command entrance,' he voxed as he kicked his way inside and punched the activation stud of his axe.

In the command hub the crew of earth and air castes looked at each other as they listened and tried to guess what was happening outside. 'Surely our warriors will hold them off,' the air caste commander said. His attendants nodded. Shas'vre Gru'eb had seemed so competent. There was no doubting his bravery. And he had thirty fire warriors, all armed and ready.

Despite all this, the noise grew louder, and closer. Something hammered on the blast doors. It sounded eerily like a tau hand, desperate to get in.

'They're coming!' a technician shouted, his dry voice tight with terror. There were screams of tau, the roar of shooting, the stink of gue'la.

Another tau threw himself on the locking mechanism. 'Closed. Locked and secured!' he declared. He checked his readings and almost smiled with relief as the hammering started again. 'The bulkheads are closed and locked,' he repeated.

There was a shout as a crackling blue axe suddenly appeared through the metal. Then a great hand, flaring with blue light, crumpled the reinforced doorway and tore a chunk away. In three rips there was enough room for a foot, which kicked away the rest of the door, and then the gue'la were inside, and the command deck filled with the sound of dying.

The command hub was full of smoke and fires and fumes from the shattered consoles.

'Command hub destroyed,' Cadmus voxed.

Corith's voice came back, heavy with exertion. 'Charges laid along the power ducts. Six minutes until detonation.'

Nuoros led Cadmus and Cerys back through the scattered and wounded defenders. As they strode along the ruined corridors, the Dark Angel raised a vox-link to the *Nemesis*.

'Charges laid,' he announced. 'We are making our way back. Cerys is hit. He is with us. We are going to get him out.'

They found a team of fire warriors battling with the boarding torpedo's machine-spirit. They scattered as the thud of the Terminators echoed down the corridor, and Nuoros helped the Imperial Fist back into his harness.

Cadmus' magazines were almost empty as he backed up the assault ramp. As soon as he reached the top, it slammed closed.

'Disengaging,' the machine-spirit announced.

The retro rockets blasted them free.

Thirty seconds after their torpedo had blasted out into the void, the charges blew. It took a few seconds for the overload to become critical, and then the super-heated cables ignited and a series of explosions in the lower decks spread rapidly as fireballs raced through the interior.

Without the command hub to section the blazes off they reached the magazines and a cascade of detonations rose up through the spine of the platform as the plasma bays ignited.

Security Orbital VX-223 exploded in a ball of blue flame and debris.

The crew of the tau escort-class Defender had spent the last month in diligent sweeps of the system. With its multi-arc railgun battery and recently modified and upgraded suite of torpedoes, the crew of this sturdy vessel were confident that they could fight off anything that strayed into their vicinity. So, they listened in astonishment as Security Orbital VX-223 was boarded by an unseen enemy.

'Is this an exercise?' their commander hissed, but the wild chatter that came over the intercoms was too chilling and convincing. You could not fake that terror as the bridge crew defended themselves. There was the sudden noise of gunfire and then the link was lost.

'Visual,' Kor'el Um'ng, air caste commander, ordered, and as the long craft swung about to come to the aid of the Security Orbital, its multi-arc railgun panned for targets. 'Power to shields and close-range fire turrets.'

'Shields raised,' a keen technician reported. 'All power subbed to anti-boarding defence arrays. Railgun charging.'

Automated quad ion turrets scanned close space, searching for boarding vessels.

Kor'el Um'ng bent over the consoles. 'Bring us close. I cannot see what has attacked them.'

The Defender accelerated towards the Security Orbital as fires ignited on its underside. They watched in astonishment as Security Orbital VX-223 exploded in a shower of burning debris.

Kor'el Um'ng hailed his Shas'vre. His voice was calm. 'Security Orbital lost. Prepare for possible boarding attack.'

'Maximising all defences,' Shas'vre Rs'tu responded. 'Battlesuits deployed on all levels. We shall contain and then expel intruders.'

A siren blared, and one of the earth caste technicians pointed through the wide clear dome of the defence platform. A vast white shape was powering towards them.

'Enemy identified. Gue'la.'

The Defender's shields flared as the White Scars strike cruiser opened fire. The barriers flickered and held. As soon as the chief gunner reported 'Railgun charged,' Kor'el Um'ng gave the order to return fire.

The vast railgun fired a solid munition the size of a land ship at a velocity unhindered by atmosphere. The energy of its passage lit a searing trail though the near-vacuum of space.

The first shot caused the shields of the White Scars strike cruiser to flare and already the second railgun was being brought to bear. But as it focused its energies on the enemy before it, a black shape came at it from the opposite direction, and opened up.

Nemesis' dorsal lance batteries fixed the smaller craft in their sights, and fired as one.

The Defender's gravitic shielding was overwhelmed by pinpoint lance strikes at the same time as the bombardment cannons spat fury across the void. The ordnance ripped great holes through the defence platform. Some of them tore right through, others exploded within, wreaking terrible carnage and setting off the generators in a ring of explosions that broke the Defender into three pieces, which peeled away from one another and tumbled burning to the planet's surface.

The world had been stripped of its last defences, the way for the planetary assault was now clear.

CHAPTER TWENTY-FIVE

On the hill overlooking the starport, the southern terrestrial defence rig remained on automated watch as Shas'vre O'man lost his third game of p'ao. He shook his head in disgust at himself and went outside while Shas'ui K'len collected his winnings.

O'man threw on his coat and ducked through the exit hatch, rubbing his three-fingered hands against the cold. As he stood he saw a flare in the night sky. It grew in brightness until it was a star, gleaming – a star that started to fall to earth. By the time he ducked back in, Shas'ui K'len had turned the intercom on full. They listened in astonishment to the panicked exchanges from Orbital Security Platform VX-223. They heard the wild chatter as the crew defended themselves, and then there was the sudden noise of gunfire and the link was lost.

Shas'vre O'man vaulted into the gunner's seat as a siren began to wail. The scanners had been blank five minutes ago. Now three blips showed up as clear marks on his targeter. Three mid-sized cruisers. He swung around to face the nearest of the enemy spacecraft.

'Deploy stabilisers!' he commanded, and the giant gun rig braced itself as its twin railguns traversed upwards, their generators beginning to whine as they powered up for the first shot.

Reports were coming through fast now as all the terrestrial defence rigs began to react. As information began to appear about the probable angle of attack, some of the great rigs lifted on their jet packs, looking for improved lines of fire, while others deployed stabilisers and charged their railguns for firing.

Shas'vre O'man had one of the best teams in the outfit. He was desperate to get the first kill, and had already calculated the attack vectors of an approaching gue'la spacecraft.

'Targeting alien craft,' he reported. 'Estimated time to firing, four seconds.' The electromagnetic generator whine reached a pitch of readiness. He made final adjustments for the distortion in the atmosphere and fired a solid projectile at speeds many times that of sound.

It still took eight seconds before his targeter confirmed a hit.

'Reloading,' Shas'ui K'len called as the railgun's whine rose in pitch again. The six piston stabilisers that ringed the gun rig adjusted for recoil. The gue'la craft was not even bothering to take evasive manoeuvres. A drone alarm sounded.

'Intruders,' O'man called.

'Gue'la approaching from the north!' K'len shouted. O'man pulled up the visual on his screen. There was a bike, bouncing through the snow.

'Lone gue'la?' he checked, as the targeting matrix locked on to the spaceship.

'Affirmative,' K'len reported. 'Drones deploying.'

In his helmet he could hear the targeting locks as the rig's deployment of four drones aimed and fired. In the chamber the intruder alarm was still sounding. The main railgun powered up with a whine of electromagnetic force. As it fired, a cloud of snow rose about it, vibrant with the concussive aftershock. As he waited for the confirmation of a hit, O'man turned to his targeter. 'Have the drones contained the threat?'

'Hit!' the targeter shouted. K'len checked outside. The gue'la rode a crude bike one-handed. It seemed impossible that one warrior would attack a weapon of war so vast and powerful it could knock out targets in space. But this warrior was.

'Where are the drones?' O'man demanded.

'They are silent!' K'len shouted.

'Take him down.' Shas'vre O'man's voice betrayed a sudden sense of panic. 'Get out there and deal with it.'

There was a rack of pulse rifles on the wall. K'len grabbed a pair and tossed them to the warriors next to him. 'Let's go!'

Kallos, Tyrannic War veteran of the Ultramarines Chapter, had been deployed from a Corvus Blackstar an hour earlier, his bike leaping from the hovering craft and landing with an explosion of snow and a crunch of suspension. This was how he loved to fight – alone, able to strike and move and strike once more. He had already disabled a pair of automated sentry drones and had come at this vast NG-4 terrestrial defence rig from the north, unseen, lying low as a Devilfish patrol hummed by, and now moving in for the kill.

The vast rig was a low dome, with a squat railgun pointing

towards the sky. Its stabilisers had been driven deep into the ground. It fired with a crack of concussive energy that made the snow jump for hundreds of feet.

It disappeared for a moment as a fog of ice was thrown up about it. The turret swivelled and lined up for another shot. A drone appeared, targeter lights searching for him. Kallos fired one-handed as he wove from side to side. He knocked the first one down, and it fell smoking to the ground. Three more came for him. Kallos picked them off, the last one showering the ice with fragments of armour and wire and smouldering alloys.

His bike jumped over a hollow. Shapes emerged from the rig's rear exit hatch.

He skidded as pulse rifle shots lanced towards him, then started returning fire. The twin-linked bolters hit a fire warrior in the chest and punched him back into the snow. He killed another before the third ran back inside, as hellfire rounds exploded about him.

The rig's gravitic drive engaged, but its stabilisers had been driven too deep into the snow for it to come free. It shuddered as they held for a moment too long, then broke free with a low hiss, and the whole rig lifted and began to rise with a shower of snow and ice.

Kallos tore a melta bomb from his belt. By the time he had approached, the rig was already twenty feet above him. He engaged the magnetic clamp and hurled the melta bomb towards the rig's underbelly. It hit with a satisfying clunk.

He swung his bike around and accelerated clear. The melta charge tore a hole in the rig's belly, ripping through the power relays. The gravitational drive failed immediately. The vast gun rig lurched dangerously as the crew struggled to regain control, and then it slipped sideways and slammed into the ground with a shower of ice.

Kallos dismounted, slammed a fresh magazine of hellfire rounds into his bolter and strode towards the smoking gun rig. There was something almost tragic in such a vast weapon of war being unable to defend itself against a lone warrior, like him. It reminded him of a fearsome creature of the sea, left stranded and immobile as the waves retreated. He dragged the rear access hatch open. His helm's sensors cut through the smoke and debris. Five crew still living. His helm retina display was already lining them up in neat order.

Five hellfire shots rang out.

Kallos' black-booted feet crunched back towards his bike, as smoke continued to rise from the ruins of the gun rig.

Tau Objective One accomplished, Kallos swung a leg over the back of his bike and settled into his seat. This bike had kept him alive through the Tyrannic Wars. He trusted it as if it were a brother. He swung the front round as the tau camp lit up with floating gun rigs, Devilfish and the low red pilot lights of squadrons of drones, streaming out searching for foes.

The trick with any pugilist starting to rock backwards was to just keep hitting them until they fell over.

The back wheel spun for a moment as Kallos accelerated down the hillside. A drop pod left a long white contrail as it burned through the high atmosphere. He watched for a moment as it slammed into the ground with a great cloud of dust, and allowed himself a moment of brief satisfaction.

The direct assault phase had begun.

CHAPTER TWENTY-SIX

In his command centre on M'Yan'Ral, Fireblade M'au stared at the contradictory information from sensor towers and drones, and could not understand what the readings were telling him. He could not contact either the Security Orbital or the kir'qarth, and now he was trying to raise a link to the next tau waystation to call for assistance.

At least, he thought, the enemy were still in space. With shields raised and their formidable terrestrial defence rigs, they should be able to hold off any enemy until assistance could be brought. Until then he needed to understand what was happening.

'Find those missing patrols!' he called to his aide, as Fio'ui Ph'al, chief earth caste technician of the base, came back after a thorough scan of read-outs.

'Nothing, Shas'o,' the technician reported with Ke'lshan certainty. 'There is no trace. I have checked all the sensor drones and towers. There has been no infiltration. I can assure you that there are no enemies upon this planet.'

Fireblade M'au was not one for excessive displays of emotion, but he slammed his hand down, the three fingers splayed out wide. 'Then what is that noise?'

The earth caste could hear the explosions as well as any of them, but he hesitated for a moment in confusion. 'This doesn't make sense,' he said. 'I see no way that the enemy could have infiltrated our defences.'

Fireblade M'au slammed his fist down again. 'We are being attacked, and you have no trace of enemies landing. Nothing?'

The earth caste began to tremble. 'Nothing!'

Fireblade M'au cursed as drone-captured pict-feeds of a piranha nose-diving into the lower slopes of Vespid Rock played on his visuals.

'Something shot that down,' he said.

Fio'ui Ph'al turned to his attendants and the earth caste bent over their instruments in a manner that showed that the readings made no sense to them.

'No sign of infiltration,' one of them said after a long pause.

Fireblade M'au cursed them again. 'Then what is attacking us? I want answers. There are five hundred sensor turrets on this planet. One of them must be able to tell you something!' He paced up and down the row of earth caste technicians. There was an air of tension as they flicked through screens, their flat, grey faces uplit by the glowing monitors, their long slender fingers punching buttons. An alarm went off, and one of the technicians jumped and hurried to shut it down as another explosion erupted to the south.

The ice beneath them trembled.

'What was that?' Commander M'au shouted.

This time the readings were clear. 'Southern terrestrial planetary defence rig has… exploded.'

Two more explosions made the building rattle.

'Get the shields up!' he shouted.

There was a moment of frantic slamming of buttons and checking of display readings. 'The shields are already up,' one of the earth caste attendants said. His voice was hesitant.

'How can they be up… unless the enemy are among us?' M'au said, as realisation dawned on them all. 'They *are* among us. All hunter cadres here to defend the base. Urgent call. Our defences have been compromised. Get me the other terrestrial defence rig commanders. Ask them to commence fire…'

'Links are down.'

M'au slammed his hand against the central column. He calmed himself for a moment. They had conquered whole swathes of Taros with less forces than he had here now. 'I want all forces armed and ready. Mantas, Stormsurges. Everything. We have to assume this is a critical situation.'

The orders were relayed along all the lines that were still working. Something roared overhead. A trail of missiles slammed into a Riptide. An explosion tore it apart and scattered smoking fragments for hundreds of yards in all directions.

'Where is our air support?' M'au shouted.

A drone pict-feed showed the space port. 'Mantas are destroyed.'

'They have been shot down?' M'au was incredulous.

'No, Fireblade. They did not make it off the ground.'

Fireblade M'au shouted for his bodyguard. 'You will take your two best warriors and defend the Most Honoured One. The rest of you, with me. Get my battlesuit ready. It is time to fight.'

CHAPTER TWENTY-SEVEN

The ice flats of the space port facility erupted in chaos as six death-storm drop pods slammed onto the flats. One hit a Manta's broad wing, smashing through to the ground beneath, before its payload of missiles exploded, flipping the huge craft onto its side where it began to burn.

The rest landed safely, their five assault ramps slamming down as assault cannons and missiles were unleashed into crews and craft alike. Within seconds the whole starport began to burn, as acrid smoke drifted across the facility.

Through the tumult rode Ultramarine Kallos, of Kill Team Zeal, his cape of tyranid hide flapping out behind him as he raced his bike along the lines of craft, picking out any that had escaped destruction. In his ear he could hear all the vox chatter of the Deathwatch kill teams as they fulfilled their missions.

Cadmus and Corith and the teams that had attacked the orbital station were racing planetwards in their Corvus Blackstar. Moaz had found a good place to hunker down and pick key targets off with his stalker-pattern bolter. Hadrian was somewhere on the other side of the space port directing the drop pods of Kill Team Faith. They were inbound already. Nergui had taken two of their brothers and they were falling from low orbit with their jump packs, ready to block any enemy counterattacks.

Kallos skidded to a halt by a Tigershark, slammed on a melta charge and kicked the bike around. You could not take something as large as a Manta or Tigershark with a single melta bomb, unless you knew *exactly* where to place them. Kallos had learnt much from fighting the Great Devourer, where only precision shots at eyes or into the mouths of carnifexes could hope to bring the creatures down. The Deathwatch specialised in such information. Kallos had found the Deathwatch libraries full of precise observations. He had spent years learning the anatomy of harpies and tervigons, where a Tigershark's gravitic drive was situated, and how the xenos had tried to mask this fault in the AX10 model. It took him bare moments to pick his spot.

With the first he blew out the power cables that linked the cockpit to the steering thrusters. With the next he lit the port-side fuel tank, knowing it would soon bleed through to the main generator casing. The main generator whined as it failed and overheated, and the secondary explosion ripped through the vast craft as he accelerated along the lines of parked fliers, setting more charges. He passed a Deathstorm drop pod and heard the assault cannons reload as the machine-spirit identified him as a friendly target. He did not pause. He targeted a fuel tank behind him and it detonated as the first rounds hit it. Black smoke roiled skywards. Kallos was already swinging round the base of a burning Tigershark. Two Mantas were burning. He locked a melta bomb to the next. A shadow fell over him. A Manta was rising to the left. Smoke billowed about it as it displaced the air. He cursed and kicked his bike round a cylindrical fuel-hub, the engine screaming as he accelerated towards it.

He flicked a melta charge from the bandolier hung over the front of his bike and lobbed it up, but it failed to attach. A drone disengaged from the Manta's right wing and swung its twin-linked guns towards him as he reared up on the bike's back wheel and fired his front-mounted combi-plasmas into the Manta's belly.

At this range he couldn't miss. Both shots exploded on its underside, but it seemed almost unaffected as it rotated in the air above him. He cursed again and fired his bolter one-handed. A hellfire round hit the drone square on and its systems failed in rapid succession as the acids did their work.

'One Manta has got away,' he voxed.

For a moment there was silence. Then from the inbound Corvus, Cadmus spoke. The enmity was clear. *'You let one go, Kallos?'*

'I hit it,' the Ultramarine said as he swerved to avoid a second drone's fire. 'But it was too large.'

As a drone laced the ground with incendiaries, Kallos drove one-handed, ducking under the Tigershark, round the observation tower and behind a fuel float, where an earth caste technician's grey face peered out from under the wheels.

Kallos shot him in the chest, clamped a melta charge to the square fuel carriage and paused. 'The Manta is flying south. The White Scars must be warned.'

Nergui's voice suddenly crackled in their helmets. His voice faded in and out, but Kallos got the gist of what he was saying.

'Yes, a Manta,' Kallos hissed as he kicked his bike round a corner and met a pair of tau air caste pilots running in a strangely weightless bounce towards their crafts. They shouted something as they saw him. He slammed the first with his bike, tripped the second with a foot, skidded his bike round and put two bolts into its head.

Nergui's voice was suddenly loud in Kallos' earpiece. He looked up and could see the flames of the White Scar's jump pack as he began to slow his descent.

'*I see it.*' Nergui's voice was indistinct for a moment. '*Throne,*' he cursed. '*It's almost in range.*'

Nergui had never lost the White Scars' love of the pinpoint strike. He had carried this method of war through to the Deathwatch, where he had specialised in the use of the jump pack to deal the foe a crushing blow. He named it the Eagle Strike: it was unseen, unstoppable, deadly. He had perfected it through ceaseless practice, falling like a stone and then firing his thrusters at the very last moment. He had spent years stationed at Talassa Prime, training others in this art. Moaz had been one of his first pupils, and was perhaps the only one who had bettered Nergui at it.

Today the White Scar stood with Elianus of the Howling Griffons and Imano, the Lamenter, in the black Thunderhawk. The rear ramp shuddered as he led them out. They were more than a mile above the ground. For a moment they stood facing into clouds.

'Ready?' Nergui voxed.

The two answered in affirmative. Nergui stepped off the end, and was gone.

Elianus jumped straight after. Imano, the Howling Griffon, always went last. 'So I can clear up your mess,' he liked to say.

They fell head first, locking on to the homing beacons set by Hadrian, senses honed and alert, weapons ready. Halfway through the fall the columns of black smoke cut off visual contact. It was then they heard the reports from the ground that a Manta was aloft.

'This should not have happened,' Nergui cursed, but there was no time for arguments. He switched to the personal channel with Imano and Elianus as he changed his angle of flight. 'Follow me.'

As they came through the smoke, they could see the target below them and the Manta swinging round towards the south. It was wider than a Baneblade was long, and yet it moved with a strange speed and grace typical of these xenos. It started to accelerate. The distance made it look slow at first, but as they fell towards it they could see it moved at speed.

'It's going too fast,' Elianus hissed as he struggled to change his angle of attack.

Nergui did not respond. He was an eagle in the sky above Chogoris, falling towards its prey. All the world was the Manta, the roar of the air passing his helmet, and the fury of the righteous.

The Manta's wing lifted as it banked. He fired his jump pack too late and the vast wing slammed his knees against his chin. Something cracked in his jaw. His retinal display froze for a moment as he caught a wing strut and dragged himself out along the central fuselage.

The wing-mounted drones spun in their sockets and fired. '*With you!*' Elianus voxed, but the Manta was rolling side to side in an effort to dislodge them, and he mistimed his jump pack's thrust, slammed down the length of the Manta's flat top, and scraped along the wing as he scrabbled for purchase. He managed to catch a hold of the engine intake, but as the Manta accelerated with punishing force, his fingers were wrenched free, and he tumbled back and out in its wake.

Imano came in higher. He hit the Manta just behind the port drone. His mag-locks slammed onto the Manta's wing and held, and he grunted in pain as he was body slammed backwards along the craft's surface. It took a moment for him to turn to the side to engage a melta bomb, only to find that his charge had been thrown clear by the force of his landing.

The port-side drone swung about and fired. Imano felt the impacts across his chest-plate as he grabbed a krak grenade from his belt. The explosive blew a hole deep enough to reach the Manta's core.

Rounds struck his pauldron. A drone had swung about and was firing at him at almost point-blank range. Warning runes began to flash red.

He put three hellfire rounds into the front of the drone. The bio-acids fizzed as they burned through metal plating.

Imano dropped a melta bomb into the blackened hole, disengaged his mag-lock and kicked free. The charge blew a hole a hand span wide in the upper wing, but failed to take out any critical systems. It was like a gnat bite on a behemoth.

Only Nergui was left, hanging precariously from an engine inlet on the central fuselage. He snarled as he forced himself along it. The acceleration of the Manta made it an effort just to drag himself forwards. Fire was coming from all directions. There was a stab of pain in his left side, but it only made him more determined. He pulled himself to the front of the craft. 'Suffer not the alien to fly,' he hissed as he slammed three melta charges onto the top of the pilot's cabin, disengaged his mag-locks at the same time, and tumbled off into the Manta's slipstream.

The Manta roared into the distance. Three seconds after Nergui had disengaged, the melta charges blew. The force of the blast struck straight down into the main chamber of the Manta, killing the shas'vre and half his hunter cadre instantly. It crippled the craft's gravitational drive and filled the pilots' cabin with beads of molten steel.

Both air caste pilots were killed in moments, and as the gravitational field upon which the great craft floated began to fail, its nose tilted down and it slammed straight into the ground, skidding for three hundred yards before tipping over and exploding in a great fireball.

Nergui switched back to broadcast mode on his vox. 'Manta down. The skies are clear.'

CHAPTER TWENTY-EIGHT

Shas'vre Ch'an woke with a start.

For a moment he was back on Mu'gulath Bay, the dust of the cinderplains clogging up his ventilation ducts, surrounded by burning Imperial tanks, thick billowing smoke, shots and screams of the dying. Through the smoke he saw a new Imperial division charging towards them, alarms sounding in his battlesuit as the enemy began to fire.

And then he was in his dorm. In bunk Y-445.

The dream was over, but the alarms were still sounding.

His heart was racing as he pushed himself up. There was sweat on his leathery brow.

H'an slid down, eyes puffy with sleep. 'What is it?'

Ch'an was already moving towards the door. 'Quick! We're being attacked.'

The dome's corridors were already filling up as the secure doors slammed down. Ch'an and H'an pushed past the rushing fire warriors to the lift. They were herding everyone down to the sublevels. It had been locked down.

'The stairs,' Ch'an said.

He should have brought his stick. Ch'an cursed himself and put a hand to the wall to help himself along.

Something exploded outside. The hab-dome's shields were still up, but the complex shook, and the lights flickered out for a moment. H'an steadied the older warrior. 'We're supposed to stay inside,' he said.

'Don't be stupid!' The retort was stinging. 'Do you want to die here, like this?'

'But Fireblade M'au… The Most Honoured One…'

Ch'an nodded. 'Yes. They were wrong! The gue'la have found us. If we can get to the suiting chambers, we can get into a Stormsurge.'

The building rocked again. The shields were still holding, though the room shook violently. Ch'an dragged himself up the wide stairs. The air smelt of cordite and plasma. The lights flickered as the ground trembled with the low thuds of explosions.

Tracers wound up into the darkness. A Riptide briefly strobed the night as its railgun fired. A drop pod landed beyond the void shield. As it hit the ground the petals slammed down, and then the yard was full of shooting as a flight of piranhas swept overhead, destroying it in moments.

At the exit there was a crowd of warriors trying to push past the guards at the door. The shas'vre was a serious young Ke'lshan. His voice did not carry. He kept repeating, 'You must stay inside. Here we can protect you. Here you will be safe. Please do not try to push past us. The attack will be repelled. All our forces have been mobilised. Sept Ke'lshan is honoured to have this great duty. Down to the sublevels!'

He had twenty guards with him, half of them facing outwards, their fingers pressed to their ear-beads, engaged in a tense conversation. Ch'an cursed. There was no way out here. They had to trust to Sept Ke'lshan, but survival had taught Ch'an one thing: it was sometimes better to work alone.

His fingers were tight on H'an's sleeve. 'We have to get out there. We have to fight. Is there another way?'

H'an thought for a moment. 'There's an exit through the kitchens. It opens out behind the generators.'

'Let's go!'

They turned and pushed through the warriors who were coming up the stairs. One of them was Sham'bal. He grabbed Ch'an's arm. 'Any idea what's happening?'

'The gue'la have found us!' Ch'an shouted back. 'The Ke'lshan won't let us leave. We're going through the kitchen. We have to get out. We have to fight them.'

They took the back spiral to the kitchens, Sham'bal bent low as he hurried down the corridor. A rocket went off just overhead and the explosion rocked the building. Two more followed, each one impacting in the air above them.

'Shields are still up,' Sham'bal shouted.

Ch'an looked up for a moment. The shields could not hold indefinitely. He pushed the cadets and pilots before him. The food sharing hall was scattered with the remains of half-eaten meals that had been abandoned. The kitchen doors were open. Ch'an led them into the darkened room. The hum of refrigeration units was drowned out by the noise of approaching battle. They pushed past and one of the running warriors knocked a fridge door open. Its contents spilt out in a shower of tins. Ch'an tripped and H'an fell with the weight of him.

Ch'an let out a moan. The pain in his leg was excruciating. He felt sick. It was as if his bones had broken once more.

'Are you well, master?' H'an said.

Ch'an pushed himself up. He could not speak for a moment. He swallowed, drew in a deep breath and nodded. 'You landed on my leg,' he managed to say. H'an was appalled. 'It's fine. Just help me up.' Ch'an was unsteady on his feet and threw an arm over H'an's shoulders.

'Gently,' Ch'an managed to say. He felt nauseous. He blinked to try to clear his head. He had to find a battlesuit. He had to fight for his people. His sept. His civilisation.

Sham'bal's mind was already ahead of him, in his Stormsurge suit, starting up the systems. His mind ran through all the checks, slammed the generator on and stomped out, weapons primed.

'Come!' he hissed to the others. 'Come!'

The kitchen service doors were shut, only the thin crack of light showing where the two portals met in the middle. A Vas'talos pilot was already at the door, punching in an access code as the others bunched up in anticipation. Sham'bal turned. Ch'an had fallen behind. He had an arm draped over his cadet's shoulder, and the two were moving slowly about the sharp edges of the cutting counters.

Ch'an saw his friend waiting and forced a smile. 'You lead them!' he said. 'But don't let them take all the suits. Leave one for us!'

Sham'bal nodded. The sept code was recognised. As the doors slid upwards the cold air rushed in. It stank of battle. Flames guttered bright against the night sky and the first warriors were ducking through the opening when someone shouted a warning.

'Shut the doors!' Sham'bal shouted, but it was too late.

Silhouetted against the light were the giant shapes of gue'la warriors.

'Back!' Sham'bal shouted. 'Back!' The doors slid wide open, and the room was full of sparks and fury as rounds ricocheted about them.

Sham'bal found himself lying under a table, his neck at a sharp angle, his head pressed down onto the soft black tiles. He did not feel any pain, but he knew he had been hit. He could see the hole in his chest, could see the long black smear that he had left down the white wall.

His mind flickered back to being in a Stormsurge suit. He loved the height the suit gave him, looking down on the world as he bent the suit's legs and prepared to fire. As his eyes opened, he saw a shadow. It was three times his height, eye sockets lit with a dull red light as they turned towards him.

He saw the gun muzzle point, saw the flash of a round being fired, and the flare that followed it.

Shas'el Sham'bal closed his eyes and felt himself inside the Stormsurge… and then his fantasy ended as the snub-nosed hellfire and its payload of bio-acids ripped through him.

The shooting went on for what seemed like an age, slowing from a storm to an irregular patter. H'an lay on the floor of the kitchens with Ch'an under him.

'Master,' he hissed.

Ch'an squeezed his arm in response to show that he was here and alive. They scrabbled behind the fridge door, drew their legs up tight to their bodies and tried not to breathe.

The gunshots came closer. H'an realised with a chill that the gue'la were moving inside, executing each warrior. Someone cursed the gue'la. Another shouted the name of her sept. Ch'an put a finger on H'an's arm.

The cadet turned. He was bonded to this veteran warrior, and the look in Ch'an's face – flat, solemn, impassive – calmed him for a moment.

There were harsh alien voices, the unmistakable sound of a fresh magazine being slammed into a gun and another shot rang out as the footsteps came closer. The look in the older warrior's eyes was of warning. H'an understood. There could be no sound or they would both die.

CHAPTER TWENTY-NINE

'Last' Leonas had been tense as the kill teams assembled for the briefing on the *Nemesis*, but there was no need. All of them had known that there was only one Space Marine who could lead the attack on the hab-dome – and it had to be him.

He was the only surviving member of Kill Team Primus. He had been captured and tortured. He had many grievances, but most of all, he had a lot to prove.

Cadvan brought the Corvus Blackstar in so low that they could hear the scrape of snow as they skimmed over the surface, and Leonas had been the first out – leaping from the front hatch and landing with a crunch.

Cadvan banked up and away, as Leonas led the kill team forwards at a run.

He ran straight into the path of fifty fire warriors and a trio of their smaller battlesuits, skimming towards them.

'Contacts,' Leonas voxed and fired his plasma gun. He hit a drone with the first shot, one of the battlesuits with the next. The plasma punched it back into the path of the fire warriors.

The fight was ferocious and brutal. Ragris cut one of battlesuits apart with his power axe as he was hit in the back by a bolt of plasma. He burned alive inside his suit. None of them could help him.

'Atilio!' Leonas voxed. The Ultramarine had the storm shield. He should be here to cover them, but what was left of Atilio was slumped against a lump of wreckage. Even his storm shield had been deformed by the power of the blast that had killed him. They were out in the open, outnumbered and out-gunned, and he had already lost two brothers.

It was fifty yards to the hab-dome's doors. There was only one thing for it, Leonas thought, as his lightning claw crackled with furious blue light – and he charged.

The Corvus Blackstar had brought Konrad Raimer and his men to within five hundred yards of the hab-dome without the enemy even knowing that they were there. They deployed without resistance, marching across the open snow, guns ready to fire. Sardegna's heavy bolter had knocked a heavy gun drone out, and then they were at the back door.

Domitian had insisted they attack the service entrance, and as they approached the sealed doorway, Konrad pulled a melta charge from his belt.

Before he could set the charge in place the door began to rise.

'I told you,' Domitian voxed.

'It seems you were right,' Konrad said.

The tau were astonished to see Space Marines at their back door. The front ones fell back in terror as those behind pushed forwards. All of them died. And then Konrad's squad were inside, moving through what appeared to be a kitchen, executing the survivors.

Domitian led his warriors in over the mangled bodies of the tau. While the guards wore Ke'lshan grey, these bodies wore badges of a multitude of different septs.

'Thirty-two tau confirmed dead,' he voxed. 'Entering hab-dome now.'

It was fifteen feet to the third battlesuit, Leonas reckoned, as he led the charge on the front gate. The suit was already skimming about to face him, underslung plasmas heating rapidly.

Leonas' combi-plasma was already spent. He held the gun out before him and pumped the enemy with bolt-rounds. At such short range, the mass-reactive shots slammed into the battlesuit's armour, knocking the foe off balance.

But not, Leonas realised, for long enough.

The twin barrels of the battlesuit swung towards him.

He found the sept markings. Ke'lshan, he saw with fury.

I am going to die at the hands of the Ke'lshan and with me shall end the ten-thousand-year history of the Black Consuls Chapter, he thought. This was not how he imagined his brotherhood ending, on an unknown planet in the Damocles Gulf, charging into a host of foes.

Leonas had saved the round imprinted with *Nidal* until now. He slammed it into his bolter and roared his fury as his power-armoured legs forced his massive bulk towards the enemy, firing wildly.

There was a muffled crack in his vox as the battlesuit fired. The globe of plasma shed white flames as it spat from the twinned barrels. Leonas' visor compensated, dimming the world to soften the glare of the shot. Warning runes flared as the plasma impacted on his armour, and he knew that in a second, as the plasma tore through the layers of ablative ceramite, he would be dead.

But then the heat was gone. The shots had scored a groove through his shoulder guard, and he was still driving forwards, with only two strides between them.

Leonas laughed as he realised that his enemy had just fired both his guns and missed, and as Moaz's voice came in his ear, he understood.

'I spoiled his aim. Now you kill him!' the Raven Guard sniper voxed.

Leonas plunged the points of his lightning claw through the belly of the battlesuit and ripped out part of the crew inside. He felt more cracks of the stalker-pattern boltgun, and realised that he was hearing the shots through Moaz's vox-link.

Leonas did not pause. He singled out the fire warrior leader, cut him into shreds with his lightning claw, and kept moving.

'Keep it up,' Moaz voxed, and Leonas heard the muffled crack in his earbud and felt the bolt-rounds whizz past his helmet.

Harath, the Salamander, was the only warrior still beside him, killing tau fire warriors with a master-crafted thunder hammer. The two of them waded through the fire warriors, mowing the enemy down.

'I'm with you!' a voice shouted, and the Black Shield, Hadrian, appeared, bolt pistol in one hand, power sword in the other, cutting his way through the foe. 'Come!' the Black Shield voxed. 'The cadets are inside the hab-dome!'

Leonas wiped the splattered blood from his helm lenses and saw both that the enemy were dead and that there were more – hundreds of them – coming at a run from the south west with two Devilfish and a Hammerhead approaching from the direction of the starport.

Wherever Moaz was, it was obvious that he had to get clear.

'I've got trouble,' he voxed suddenly, and Leonas started sprinting towards the hab-dome's gates.

'Follow me!' he shouted to Harath and Hadrian as he slammed vengeance rounds into his storm bolter and fired wildly as he charged. 'Let's get inside!'

Leonas reached the gates of the hab-dome. The entire team were wounded.

He kicked a way through the doorway as the Hammerhead fired

and the shot landed short, showering them with dirt and ice. Hadrian and Harath were right behind him. They had to keep moving inside. They had to disable the shield and find the cadets.

It was furious hand-to-hand killing with the three Space Marines working as one. Harath was a stalwart. Hadrian fought with murderous speed. The defence stubbornly clogged the corridors. They were fire warriors, as far as he could tell, though there were others mixed in. Earth caste, he thought, their bodies packed in with the rest. Two battlesuits.

It took nearly two minutes to clear the defenders at the head of the stairwell and more fire warriors were coming into the hab-dome behind them. Hadrian was keeping them at bay.

This mission was going badly wrong.

'No sign of tau,' Leonas voxed, then, as fire warriors appeared behind them, he added, 'I thought the White Scars were drawing off the enemy!'

He ducked back as what looked like a stealth battlesuit appeared across the dome. A searing stab of blue plasma lit the corridor from within. Leonas felt the shot pass inches in front of him, then lifted his storm bolter and fired. He had no idea if he had hit or not, but jumped out. He was furious.

'What are the White Scars doing?' he said, as he ran into a squad of fire warriors and emptied a magazine into them.

They were going too slowly. 'We're being bogged down!' he voxed. 'Nergui? Konrad?'

There was no response.

'Domitian!'

Nothing. Leonas' storm bolter magazine clicked empty. He slammed it into the face of a fire warrior and felt bones break. Tightly synchronised plans tended to unravel. Leonas cursed. It was taking too long for the White Scars to strike, and they still had not managed to get the hab-dome's shields down.

CHAPTER THIRTY

The footsteps had long since passed through the kitchen, but H'an did not dare move.

He was shivering with cold and terror. Ch'an reached out and took his hand.

'Come,' he said. 'We must go. We must fight!'

From inside the stairwell there was the echo of gunfire. H'an closed his eyes as if he could will it all away. 'Come!' Ch'an dragged at H'an's arm, but his gunner would not move. Ch'an pulled him. 'Come!' the veteran said again. 'We must fight!'

Ch'an dragged H'an from the ground, and pulled him through the ruins of the kitchen.

The smell of burned skin and blood was thick on the air. The door had been jammed open, the control hatch shot away. H'an gazed out at the scene before him in a flat-faced look of horror.

The space port burned as fuel dumps lit the sky, and tracers and pulse rounds stabbed into the night. The planetary defence turrets were burning like beacons on the four hills. There were heaps of dead fire warriors, lying where they had fallen.

A Ke'lshan fire warrior ran from the direction of Fireblade M'au's command dome. A sniper shot rang out, and the warrior fell as if punched in the side of the head, and did not move again.

H'an was terrified. But he drew strength from his bonded pilot. 'Will we make it?' he hissed.

'I cannot say,' Ch'an said. 'But we have to make the effort.'

Ch'an set off. H'an watched him, limping across the ice and then crouching as he ran. He caught the older warrior up, put his arm under his armpit and took his weight.

The two – pilot and gunner – struggled across the ice. A stray round hissed past their heads and Ch'an fell behind a defensive barrier.

H'an touched something warm. At his feet a disembowelled Ke'lshan fire warrior was already beginning to stiffen with cold. He recoiled and wiped the gore from his palm.

The defensive line led to within thirty feet of the suiting domes.

'Let's crawl,' Ch'an said.

It was a painfully slow process. There were dead warriors lying where they had fought, but the battle had passed on, and the suiting dome seemed quiet and silent.

It took ten minutes for H'an to pull Ch'an across the compacted snow. At last they came to the entrance.

H'an reached up and slammed the access stud but it did not move. 'Locked,' he hissed, and pounded on the door with his fist.

'Try the code.'

A missile exploded fifty feet away and the flash blinded H'an for a moment. He managed to punch the code in. The door hummed and slid open.

As it closed behind them, Ch'an rose to his feet. Above them, each standing in its chamber, ten Stormsurge battlesuits stood waiting, batteries charged, guns loaded, ready for battle.

Ch'an turned to his bonded gunner and the two of them clasped hands.

'They are waiting for us,' Ch'an said, and slowly and solemnly the two warriors approached the battlesuit, and bowed.

CHAPTER THIRTY-ONE

Aun'ui Hoo'nan's personal quarters were in a separate complex. As soon as he had left his command bunker, Fireblade M'au knew that his first duty was to ensure the ethereal's safety. He gave orders for his battlesuit to be made ready and then went to personally inform Aun'ui Hoo'nan of the danger.

The ethereal was sitting in his meditation chamber, his robes arranged about him and his hands folded neatly in his lap. He spoke with slow and deliberate tones, seemingly unaware of the explosions outside. At one point he looked up and said, 'Fireblade. Do you think the facility is in danger?'

Another boom sounded from the direction of the space port. The explosion made the ground tremble. Fireblade M'au thought about this and said, 'No. We have assessed the risk. Our fire warriors are being recalled from their forward bases. Hunter Cadres Three and Nine are both within minutes of the base. Hunter Cadre Five will be here within half a dec. Seven and Four are also on their way.'

The ethereal took in the information and nodded slowly. 'You are concerned, though, for my safety.'

Fireblade M'au bowed. 'Always.'

The ethereal nodded. 'And you would like me to go somewhere… more steadfast.'

Fireblade M'au bowed once more. 'Yes, Most Honoured One. I have asked for a chamber to be made ready for you in the sub-levels. I have sent the great strength of Hunter Cadre One there. They will protect both you and the cadets. The safety of you and the cadets is my prime concern. My warriors and I will make sure that you are secure.'

Aun'ui Hoo'nan thought for a moment, then nodded. 'As you wish.'

It was too dangerous for Aun'ui Hoo'nan to cross the open ground between his personal quarters and the hab-dome, so a Devilfish was brought up, and an honour guard of Ke'lshan fire warriors stood around him as the ethereal was escorted into the back.

'Apologies,' Fireblade M'au said. 'We have not had sufficient time to make this more comfortable.'

Aun'ui Hoo'nan smiled. 'Do not trouble yourself,' he said. 'This is a moment of trial for us all.'

The fire warriors stood guard as the ethereal was made comfortable, and Fireblade M'au stepped inside and personally oversaw the whole process. Aun'ui Hoo'nan seemed almost apologetic for the inconvenience he was causing, and his humility only made their feelings for him more intense. He was both wise and humble. He was greater than them in all things. Fireblade M'au felt this as keenly as the others. At the end he bowed once more and apologised.

'I have no doubt,' Aun'ui Hoo'nan said, 'that you will deal with this threat. You have been chosen, Fireblade M'au. You are one of our sept's finest warriors. You will honour our sept. Of that, I am sure.'

Fireblade M'au bowed a third time and then dismounted. As the rear hatch closed he slammed his hand onto the fuselage as a signal for the driver to set off. A pair of Devilfish escorted it across the yard to the hab-dome. He watched them enter the dome's transport hatch in single file, and did not leave until he had the report that they were safe inside.

He led his bodyguards to his personal armoury, issuing orders all the time to his hunter cadre's shas'vre. 'Secure the hab-dome. All cadets are to wait in the sublevel. Aun'ui Hoo'nan must be protected within the substructure. If any of the enemy break in then they must be resisted with all strength. Reinforcements are on the way.'

A tau philosopher once said that there was no greater unity than between bonded warriors, or a warrior and his battlesuit.

It was so with Fireblade M'au. When he was harnessed inside his Crisis suit he felt greater than he had been before. He scrolled through the internal data logs and flexed the arms of his XV8. His right arm had a double-barrelled plasma rifle, the left a long shield generator – the most up-to-date Ke'lshan could equip him with.

He sat back in his suit's cabin. The hatches closed about him; lights, monitors, gun readings all came to life at his touch. He sent out a message to all shas'vres. 'Fireblade M'au is now personally leading the defence of M'Yan'Ral.'

With those words his battlesuit lifted from the ground and his shas'vre bodyguards trailed after with a cohort of drones in close support.

Fireblade M'au rallied the remains of the M'Yan'Ral guards as the attack on the hab dome started. The speed and power of the attack had rocked his forces back.

Earth caste technicians fed him constant streams of information, gleaned from drone observations, turrets and teams of fire warriors. Pict-feeds fed into his battlesuit from drones and observation turrets. The gue'la were few in number. No more than twenty, he was sure. His confidence rose with each minute as the attack on the hab-dome stalled and drone pict-feeds showed dead gue'la. Their drop pods had exhausted their ammunition by now, or had been knocked out by precision strikes from the Hammerheads. Three Razorsharks had managed to get aloft and were hunting a biker across the crater fields. A team of stealthsuits had tracked down a sniper and were playing a deadly game of cat and mouse through the wreckage of the starports. The vespid claimed to have killed a gue'la near their rock. They had joined up with Hunter Cadres Three and Nine, and both of them were skimming over the snow to join him. Kroot patrols were being brought in as the hunter cadres came across them.

Pathfinders were to join the Devilfish and Hammerheads to clear the space port of remaining infiltrators. His Crisis suits and fire warrior strike teams were to storm the hab-dome after the infiltrators and kill them before they managed to fight their way through to the sublevels.

The stresses of managing a camp of cadets began to lift from his shoulders. Fireblade M'au smiled for the first time in months, as he began marshalling his hunter cadres into their attack formations. This was war. It was what he was born for. It was what he *excelled* at.

The upset would be unfortunate, but it would be contained, he decided. The honour of Sept Ke'lshan would be enhanced. As he considered this, a new pict-feed streamed into his battlesuit displays.

It was an infrared image from a pathfinder team attached to Hunter Cadre Five. He paused for a moment, not believing what he saw. A new gue'la, largely mechanised, with strong air support.

His optimism ebbed. But there was no time for shock. The gue'la had caught them out a second time. But war was all about outmanoeuvring the enemy. It was about surprise and overwhelming force delivered with a pinpoint precision.

He started redeploying his forces to counter this new threat.

Leading an impromptu force of vespid, pathfinders, Devilfish and a Hammerhead, Fireblade M'au nagged away at the flanks of the White Scars time and again. His railgun's shots left great steaming craters in the ice, and every time the White Scars tried to move forwards he engaged them in a deadly game of cat and mouse.

Each time the gue'la bikes and speeders tried to turn his flank or encircle him, the tau commander pulled his forces back, regrouping for another strike. As the White Scars columns drove inexorably forwards he became more reckless.

'They cannot be allowed near to the hab-dome. Stall them. As soon as the hunter cadres arrive we will destroy them.'

Fireblade M'au would not let Sept Ke'lshan's honour be besmirched. They would meet this threat and destroy it.

CHAPTER THIRTY-TWO

The Fire Raptor *Obos* led the Thunderhawks and escorts of the Fourth Company of White Scars in over the route that Moaz had created through the dead zone in the remote sensor fields. Inside the tight confines of their transports the White Scars warriors were exultant – even the machine-spirits seemed to sense the joyful mood among the warriors, as a Chogorean steed will sense the mood of its rider and stretch out her neck so that the mane flies free.

Battle was in the souls of the White Scars. Few Chapters approached danger with such joy. It was a wild, dangerous and exultant thrill. They were weapons made flesh, and they were going to do what they lived for: kill the enemies of mankind. It made them laugh out loud as they waited inside the Thunderhawks.

The Fire Raptor's machine-spirit searched for targets. Behind the gunship the four White Scars Thunderhawks followed in formation, two carrying a load of Razorbacks and Predators, as a pair of Stormravens flew on the flanks and Stormtalons brought up the rear.

The flight came in low over the snow, their engines kicking up a great tail of ice dust behind them. For the first twenty-five minutes they encountered no opposition beyond a heavy drone flight, whose targeting matrix immediately identified the craft as hostiles and tried to make a stand. *Obos* lined the three drones up and its twin-linked avenger bolt cannons fired. The ancient craft slowed for a moment with the backward force of her guns and the drones disintegrated before their internal logic systems could broadcast an alarm.

Without their remote sensors to show them where the targets might be, the automated gun turrets sat idle and inactive as the

White Scars roared overhead. The White Scars cut straight through the outer defences and were seven minutes from contact when they encountered the first fire team patrols. There were two Devilfish – their crews were dismounted and exchanging news when one of them saw *Obos* and shouted.

The two crews were dashing back to their transports when a hunter-killer missile hit one of the craft halfway up the nose cone. It exploded in a shower of flaming debris at the same time as the second was hit in the rear port engine. The explosion knocked out the grav drives, and it slammed to the ice, rear first, hissing smoke from its fuel lines. The pilot bailed out just as a pair of well-aimed lascannon shots hit the main body and the inside exploded, sending a sheet of flame venting from the open hatches. Flaming bodies tumbled out. One of the fire warriors knelt to fire his pulse rifle.

His shots seared the Fire Raptor's ceramite plating. The shas'vre was desperately trying to raise the nearest pathfinder team when the avenger bolt cannon whirred. Brass casings rained down as it hosed the wreckage with fist-sized mass-reactive shells.

A freezing mist of ice and blood rose where the tau had been. It billowed as the flight passed overhead, and slowly settled as they moved on, revealing a scene of utter destruction.

They were five minutes from contact when a third Devilfish, racing to investigate the lost cadres, hastily turned tail having seen the assault flight coming in low. A Land Speeder cut it off as it tried to circle away, a multi-melta shot winging it and causing it to spin out of control and crash nose first into a fist of a black rock.

Scout Sergeant Törömbaater jumped from the Land Speeder as it swung around for another shot. He approached to within ten feet of the burning wreck as the Thunderhawks roared overhead.

'No survivors,' he laughed and slammed his bolt pistol back into its holster.

The Land Speeder came back round for him and he jumped and caught the foot plate, swinging himself up as the pilot raced after the other fliers.

Two miles from the target, the Thunderhawk transporters lowered their landing gear and settled in the snow as their engines powered down for a moment. The Predators and Razorbacks disengaged from under the Thunderhawks' fuselage, gun turrets already tracking for targets as they took up flanking positions. One by one the Thunderhawks' front ramps slammed forwards and the white bikes roared out like steppe wolves eager for the kill.

Payloads empty, the Thunderhawks roared back into the air, swinging back to retreat to a safe distance, while the Stormravens and Stormtalons positioned themselves in close support. Fifty bikers charged forwards, with Batbayar leading them, pennants flying from the banner-poles on the back of his bike, *Qorchi*. The vehicle was a steed as old as the Chapter itself, a thing of simple and elegant lines, the horse-shaped head at the front lowered as if in a charge, a melta gun jutting out from the prow. In his hand Batbayar carried a great single-edged cutlass, named Greenfire. It crackled with eldritch light as he powered his bike forwards, moustaches streaming behind him.

He remained always ahead of his warriors, but right behind him came Ganzorig, the eagle banner held in his out-flung fist, riding one-handed. Around them both was the honour guard of the Tulwar Brotherhood, each one wielding an ancient power sword, and then came the squads of White Scars arranged in a great V formation, with Land Speeders, attack bikes and fliers roaring in behind.

Batbayar raised Greenfire to the skies and roared a war-cry ten thousand years old.

'For the Khan and the Emperor!'

Batbayar Khan drove his columns onwards with relentless energy, always countering ambushers with squadrons of bikes and Land Speeders, and aerial attack runs.

He was the khan of the Tulwar Brotherhood, and he would not be held back. At last he broke through a swarm of drones and the way to the production facility was open.

Batbayar Khan was exultant as he led the charge straight towards the production facility. There was nothing better than the wind in your hair, the smell of promethium and the roar of chainswords, eager as hunting hounds.

Ganzorig pointed to a stealth team trying to return to their transport. They were right in the path of the White Scars onslaught, and there was no escape.

Their drones came straight towards the Space Marines in a futile effort to slow Batbayar down. They were barely a bump under the wheels of the bikers.

The stealth team turned and realised they were never going to escape. Five of them formed up bravely. Batbayar drove one down as he shot another. Ganzorig speared a third, and the heads of the others were claimed by warriors in the first and sixth squads.

The bikers crested a low rise, and there before them was the camp – already burning. Gun rigs were deploying in a line before the starport. The Tulwar Brotherhood were upon them before they could even deploy their stabilisers.

They rode the first line down. The crews were beheaded, their gun rigs destroyed by melta fire. The second at least managed to get off a salvo of shots before *Obos* roared in. Her avenger bolt cannon made a sound like ripping steel as its mass-reactive fire strafed along the line of rigs, tearing crew and weapon chassis apart, while the accompanying Stormravens' twin-linked lascannons blew holes through the armoured compartments as if they were wax.

The third line of mobile gun rigs managed to get away. All three of them headed left, seeking to outflank the White Scars. They paused at a distance of half a mile to fire quick shots at the enemy. But the flankers had been outflanked. The White Scars spread the wings of their attack wide, and Scout bikers and Land Speeders caught the tau unawares, and destroyed them.

It was only the charge of the kroot that saved the base from being overrun in the first minutes. While half of their three hundred warrior strength was out on patrol, the rest had reacted with alarm and were waiting in their camp for the attack, armed and ready.

None had come, and kroot messengers that had been sent out to the base had not reported back, so until they saw an enemy their shapers had come together in council and decided to wait, and watch.

The White Scars assault was the first enemy they had seen and their shapers had no doubt that the tau masters would want them to fight. They came out of their camp in a wild mob of white-pelted warriors, feathers streaming, rifles clenched in knotty fists, their heads thrown back in their wild and high-pitched war cries. About them loped the shaggy kroot hounds, while the krootox riders shook their spears as they held on to their beasts' backs.

Batbayar saw the kroot break out of their camp and knew that he could not leave them untouched on his flanks, so the khan led the charge straight into the heart of the kroot warband.

He slew a great shaggy kroot that swung at him with its rifle butt, drove his sword through another and slammed at least three to the ground with the momentum of his bike. He must have killed fifteen of the kroot before his charge began to slow. The khan was suddenly surrounded by snapping beaks.

Batbayar was exultant as the enemy's jaws tore at him. His tulwar blade cut through three kroot braves in a single backswing. He punched a krootox so hard he could hear the crunch of bone inside its avian skull, and killed the second with a thrust straight to its cold-blooded heart.

Batbayar gloried in his conquest. He roared out the battle cry of the Tulwar Brotherhood and Ganzorig lifted the eagle banner, and the sight of it filled the hearts of the Fourth Company with the righteous joy of killing.

The charge of the Tulwar Brotherhood had slowed for a moment, like a chainsword catching on a bone, but as the banner was displayed Batbayar drove forwards once more, his bike splattered with blood, the wheels bucking as he rode over the bodies of their foes.

Within moments they were through. Seven White Scars lay dead, as promethium fumes mixed with the red mist that hung in the air around their bodies.

The charge of the kroot gave Fireblade M'au precious moments to redeploy his forces.

Surviving strike teams used their Devilfish to take the high ground to the right of the space port. Their burst cannons threw enfilading fire into the squads of White Scars. Land Speeder Storms drove them off for a moment, before the first vespid flight repulsed them in turn.

While Space Marine Scouts battled on the wings, Batbayar did not slow, but pressed the attack despite the withering fire from gun rigs and Hammerheads. Many of his guards about him were cut down as pathfinders brought in precision missile strikes with deadly accuracy.

The leading companies of White Scars faltered under the combined firepower, before vanguard veterans led Assault Marines into the attack.

There was a brief but stiff fight. Chainswords slashed through wing and bone. Lumps of xenos flesh rained down, while broken vespids hit the ground with dull thuds. Within less than a minute the vespids had broken.

The route to the Stormsurge production facility was open.

'Follow me, my sons!' Batbayar roared, swinging his bike around and racing forwards. 'Find Shadowsun and win the Tulwar Brotherhood eternal glory!'

CHAPTER THIRTY-THREE

Ch'an slid into the pilot's seat and buckled himself in as H'an scrambled to get the gun generators up to full power.

'All charged,' H'an reported as Ch'an plugged into the pict and voice feeds from the units around him.

'Ch'an?' Commander M'au spoke the name with his distinctive Ke'lshan nasal twang.

M'au's position flashed up on the holo-display before Ch'an. He was leading his battlesuits and vespids in a sweeping counter-punch from the east. Ch'an almost flipped the intercom to mute, but he drew in a deep breath and answered, 'Yes, Fireblade.'

'The hab-dome has been struck. I am leading my guard there. We shall hold them off until support arrives. Let them see you. Draw them off. I shall do the rest.'

'Affirmative,' Ch'an answered. 'For the Greater Good.'

'For the Greater Good,' Fireblade M'au answered. Ch'an powered the Stormsurge out of the suiting bay.

The battle looked so different from this high up. He could see so much more and his infrared night vision showed a massive gue'la attack from the south. Fires burned all across the space port.

It was clear where the chief danger lay. Ch'an took three great strides forwards, bracing one foot on the wreck of a Manta as H'an scrambled to align the shoulder-mounted railgun.

'Ready to fire,' H'an told him.

Alarms chimed within the cockpit as a gue'la flier dived towards them.

'Take that out first,' Ch'an told his gunner, and H'an switched to missile launcher and bracketed the flier in his targeting matrix.

A missile arced out and hit the enemy aircraft straight on the nose. It exploded and veered wildly over the shoulder of the Stormsurge, crashing into the ice.

'Moving left,' Ch'an warned.

H'an was already preparing cluster rockets. The Stormsurge rattled as the rockets fired off in a gathering storm, obscuring the gue'la for a moment behind an expanding wall of smoke. The gue'la leader was on his bike, emerging unscathed from the smoke cloud, swatting away a desperate pair of drones that pulled back and turned once more to fire.

'Charging the main gun,' he reported.

Ch'an was always moving. A second and a third gue'la flier roared overhead. Something hit the Stormsurge in the thigh.

'Full charge,' he reported, as he assessed the damage.

'We're limping,' H'an noted.

Ch'an was intent on killing. 'It takes more than that to bring this suit down.' He redeployed the stabilisers. 'Bracing for fire. Take them down!'

H'an lined up the leader as the gue'las skidded round a burning gun rig. The Stormsurge's shoulder mounted blastcannon swung about as the targeters locked on.

'Full charge,' he reported as he centred the gue'la leader within his targeting brackets. 'Fire.'

The Stormsurge shook as the blastcannon's negatively charged induction fields accelerated a ball of superheated plasma out at blinding speeds. H'an's targeting screen flared green as the superheated plasma struck, and when the flare had gone, all he saw was a smoking hole where the rock had been turned to glass.

CHAPTER THIRTY-FOUR

Nergui's plan had been to drive the tau down into the sublevels. Once the enemy were confined within a tight space, Jotunn's drop pod would smash into the hab-dome and he would lead the others in wiping out the entire Stormsurge cohort. The plan, as so often happened, was starting to fray at the edges.

Konrad just hoped that it was not going to come apart entirely.

'This is all taking too long,' the Black Templar cursed as he shook his chainsword to dislodge a piece of armour stuck between its teeth. He had led his team into the sublevels, but they were having to cut their way through the defenders, which wasn't the plan.

+I can feel fear. I can feel excitement. It glows with their thoughts. It must be the cadets. It is not far now. We are closing on him.+

Domitian's presence was brief. His mind was involved elsewhere.

Konrad ducked back as his armour took another salvo of enemy fire. Warning runes were flashing all over. Even his suit of the finest Mark VIII power armour was starting to fail.

'Leonas?' Konrad voxed.

In his helmet he could hear the roar of bolters.

'We're getting there,' Leonas voxed back. Though it wasn't really true – they were stuck as well, halfway down the hab-dome's stairs, trapped in a three-way junction with tau reinforcements pouring in behind them.

'We can't stay here!' Hadrian, the Black Shield, voxed as he used his power sword to widen a hole in the staircase bulkhead. Harath had taken a plasma shot to the side. He could move, but not much, and their enemies were coming up behind them.

'Battlesuits,' Harath spat.

Leonas risked a glance.

One of the tau's Crisis battlesuits was skimming down the corridor and pressed close behind it were squads of fire warriors. Leonas only had two krak grenades left. He lobbed both of them at the battlesuit and sprayed the corridor with his bolter before he caught a glimpse of another battlesuit, this time firing burst cannons.

'Domitian,' he called. There was no reply.

'Nergui?' He voxed on the White Scar's personal channel and when there was no response, he switched to open. 'Where is Nergui?'

The Librarian's mind-voice was distant. +He is helping his gene-brothers.+

'I didn't know Batbayar needed help.'

There was a touch of humour. +Batbayar does not know it either. I have had to help him.+

'Nergui should be here,' Konrad snarled.

+He will be. He is coming now. I feel his presence.+

On the strike cruiser *Nemesis*, the Lone Wolf waited in the darkness of his personal drop pod. The doors were sealed. His braces were clamped shut. His fist was clenched on the shaft of his guardian spear. His eyes were closed as if sleeping, as the vox chatter from below filled his helm.

There was a moment of stillness before a battle. The Lone Wolf exulted in it. It seemed endless and eternal. It was the quiet of the hunter before he strikes. It was the moment when a bow was drawn. It was the instant before the trigger was pulled. It was the pause before he struck.

Jotunn could hear alarm in the voices of his warriors. He let it wash over him, as the sea washes over the hidden rocks. It could not be long now.

Nergui's voice was breathless when he picked up the vox chatter. He'd lost Imano to a sniper shot, and Elianus' jump pack was malfunctioning so he was foot-slogging his way towards the hab-dome. He heard the voices of Konrad and Leonas' teams. 'You're in the hab-dome?' he asked.

'*Affirmative,*' Leonas voxed back. '*There are hundreds of them. Battlesuits. Harath is wounded. Konrad is in the sublevels with Domitian. The attack is slowing…*'

'Understood.' Nergui's voxed message was clipped and short. 'I'm on my way.'

Fireblade M'au led the counterattack on the hab-dome. The attackers were now trapped as his bodyguard of Crisis battlesuits worked with him – a deadly combination of formidable armour and destructive weaponry.

M'au was impressed with the responsiveness of the XV8. The gue'la were armed with a kind of bolt-round he had not come across before. It had killed one of his guard in moments, so now he went first.

His long shield saved him a number of times as he fought his way into the ruin of the hab-domes. His double-barrelled plasma rifle caught one gue'la full in the chest and left him a slumped ruin.

'Vespid attack,' he ordered, and the stingwing support swept in along the corridor, their leathery pinions flapping furiously, their neutron blasters making a mockery of the gue'la's power armour.

As the gue'la fired at the vespids, Fireblade M'au used his jump pack to leap closer.

He could see the foe now – black-armoured gue'la.

'For Ke'lshan!' he ordered and, long shield held high, he fired.

Leonas fired a salvo of hellfire rounds into the next battlesuit, and prayed that the bio-acids would slow it down at least. There was a moment's pause in Nergui's voice, and a low grunt as if the White Scar had just cut an enemy down, then Leonas could hear the metallic thud of a melta bomb being clamped in place. Nergui's voice came back a few moments later.

'Generator has been destroyed,' he voxed on all channels. 'The shield is down.'

There was a pause, before a new voice joined the vox chatter.

It brought hope and faith to the hearts of all the Deathwatch who heard it. The low growl was unmistakable. It was defiance in the face of darkness. Resolution in the shadow of the xenos. It was belief in their right to wrest the galaxy for mankind.

'Thank you, brothers,' Watch-Commander Jotunn whispered. 'I am coming in.'

Leonas counted the seconds.

He felt the impact as Jotunn's drop pod smashed through the armourglass dome, crashed down along the curved dorm windows, and finally landed in the hab's sunken garden, half tilted against the walls.

Two of the drop pod's five ramps refused to open. But Jotunn only needed one. He was a blur of black Terminator armour as he stomped out, guardian spear lowered and already firing.

The Lone Wolf was free among the enemy. With two great sweeps of his blade, Jotunn cut through a crowd of fire warriors who blocked his way. A smaller battlesuit leapt out into the air above him but he shrugged off its burst cannon shots. Despite the bulk of his Terminator armour the Space Wolf moved with a terrible speed. As the battlesuit landed in front of the sublevel doors, Jotunn lowered his shoulder and drove it into the tau's waist. There was a crunch of struts as he crumpled it in two, then, with a casual swing of the guardian spear, he cut the battlesuit – and its pilot – in half.

Jotunn knew the ways of the xenos. He was a whirlwind of death as he drove the tau back before him. He would not, he could not, be slowed. He feared nothing but failure, and as he battled into the sublevels the desperate fire warriors ran onto his blade in an effort to slow him down.

'There's an ethereal here,' Jotunn voxed. It was simple. He could tell from the way that the enemy were dying. This was why they had been slowed down so much. Nergui's intelligence had failed to locate this variable. It made the success of the mission even more precarious. When defending an ethereal, fire warriors fought with a stubbornness that was impressive to any.

'Throne!' Leonas said. *'Are you sure?'*

'Do you doubt my word, Leonas of the Black Consuls?' Jotunn was barely out of breath as he fought his way through. There was humour in his voice. 'Domitian! Find where the ethereal is hiding.'

There was a long pause before the Librarian's mind touched his.

+I have found him.+

'Do not kill him. Just show me where,' Jotunn said. 'I will do the rest.'

Domitian's mind was like a wall of fire as it threw the tau back, and behind the psychic bow-wave strode Jotunn – a giant of black fury. Domitian led him on the most direct route. Jotunn fought his way through the packed fire warriors. Their shots scoured the black paint from his armour, so that it was worn down to the bare ceramite in places. But nothing stopped the Space Wolf.

He cut his way down the steps to the sublevel bunkers, and the further he went, the weaker Domitian's mind became.

+This is as far as I can project.+ The Librarian's mind was barely a whisper in his own. +The ethereal is within this chamber.+

Jotunn glared at the bulkhead before him. He slapped a pair of melta bombs onto its seal.

The blasts ripped a hole large enough for him to get his hands through, and he tore the edges of the doors open and pushed himself inside.

Five Crisis battlesuits stood in defiant guard of their ethereal leader.

The Space Wolf charged.

This was the first time he'd seen one of this type of battlesuit in the flesh. The Lone Wolf sensed that he was facing the commander of the foe and looked forward with grim relish to the moment he could kill the enemy leader in battle.

The guardian spear fired individually inscribed bolter shells that Jotunn himself had crafted. They punched through the armour plating of the Crisis suits and exploded inside, ripping their interiors apart with a hail of steel fragments.

Two of the battlesuits fell before he even reached them. Two more were cut down by his ancient blade, and the last one tried to fire a fusion blast at him from point-blank range, but Jotunn twisted out of the path of the shot and rammed the guardian spear through its chest, killing the pilot within.

The XV9 stepped forwards. It was armed with long shield and double-barrelled plasma rifle. Jotunn sidestepped the plasma shot as he charged.

He drove the XV9 into the wall with such force he felt the armoured battlesuit crack. He drove again and again, then let the ruined suit slide to the floor. A hellfire bolt-shell killed the pilot inside.

Jotunn strode to the sealed blast doors. They were marked with a vast Ke'lshan symbol. He hammered on it with his armoured fist.

'Open in the name of the Emperor of Mankind,' he roared and clamped a melta charge onto it. The door did not open. It exploded. Jotunn kicked the remains away and stooped to enter.

Inside was a small meditation chamber, hung with scrolls of tau script. Jotunn growled as he smelt his foe. The ethereal had been knocked back into the corner of the room by the force of the blast. He paced towards it, fangs exposed. The ethereal shrank back. It was always thus. The xenos quivered before the judgement of mankind.

The xenos had the temerity to speak. The Space Wolf did not know the words. He did not care. Learning the speech of the foe only opened you up to their lies – all within the Deathwatch knew that in understanding lay madness.

As Jotunn stood over it, the ethereal held some symbol of office up towards Jotunn, as if warding the Space Marine off.

Jotunn ripped it from him and flung it against the wall.

The ethereal was still speaking.

Jotunn answered with a roar. He let the twin barrels of his guardian spear speak for him.

CHAPTER THIRTY-FIVE

The earth exploded beneath Batbayar Khan's bike. He let out a low Chogorean curse as he found himself lying on the edge of a crater, *Qorchi*, his beloved mount twisted and scorched, both tyres burning. His armour runes were flashing in warning as he shoved himself up.

The warriors of his honour guard lay dead around him. Only Ganzorig still moved; the eagle banner had almost slipped from his hand. Batbayar seized it from his equerry's fist, but the dying Space Marine would not let go.

'Be still, Ganzorig. It is I, Batbayar Khan, who takes this. You have done well. You did not allow the banner to fall.'

Ganzorig held on for a moment, but Batbayar pushed his hand away. 'Your khan has it,' he said. 'Sleep well, my brother.'

Ganzorig's last words were lost as his broken body gave in to a score of fatal wounds and his twin hearts stopped.

'Khulan!' Batbayar shouted.

As the smoke cleared, the Apothecary's bike came into view. 'Khan! We feared you were dead.'

Batbayar laughed as he held the eagle banner high. 'It takes more than these xenos to kill the khan of the Tulwar Brotherhood! Now give me your bike. Take their gene-seed. Our brothers fought well.'

Batbayar leapt onto the Apothecary's bike. A furious battle was raging overhead as the White Scars air support hunted the enemy craft down. He watched as *Obos* banked round in a wide curve and lined the Stormsurge up in its sights. It was standing on a low rise, its back to the burning hab-dome. 'Leave the Stormsurge to me,' he ordered the crew of the Fire Raptor. 'For the Khan and the Emperor!'

* * *

The Stormsurge fired twice more, but this time the White Scars had seen what it could do and they had learnt their lesson well. The bikers spread wide so that the blasts only killed a few of their number, and while the Stormsurge tried to get a bead on the khan, he was too fast and too wily for it, and the Stormsurge was alone.

Batbayar led his warriors around wrecks and along defiles, playing a dangerous game of cat and mouse with the Stormsurge, which was being gradually hemmed in by the White Scars.

'I am the khan,' Batbayar ordered as he raced across the snow flats, 'and I want that kill.'

Ch'an knew they were running out of time. He could sense it as more and more systems started to flash with warning signals.

H'an was oblivious. All the gunner focused on was the shot and the kill, but even as they fought, the gue'la fliers were taking their toll as they fired into the Stormsurge's exposed flanks and rear.

'Bring me around,' H'an said.

'Bringing you round,' Ch'an told him.

'Steady.'

Ch'an gritted his teeth. He could feel the suit's pain as it stumbled on a half-ruined leg. They were being hemmed in and there was nothing he could do about it. No way out.

They did not train for this in the academy. This was not how battles were supposed to happen, but they had been hit in so many places, were shorn of all their advantages, at the same time and with such violence, speed, surprise and precision, that there was no way the hunter cadres could react in time.

'They're gaining,' H'an said.

They needed time to power up the railgun. Ch'an backed towards the hab-dome, but the Stormsurge had taken significant damage and as he took another step back the battlesuit stumbled.

'Repelling assaulters,' H'an reported. 'Rocket clusters!'

The Stormsurge rattled violently as the salvo fired.

Ch'an saw gue'la through the smoke. If he didn't get them out of there now, they were dead tau. He tried to step away but the systems failed and one of his generators shut down. He had to override the heat warning indicators.

H'an's voice became tense. 'Assault imminent.'

'I am trying,' Ch'an voxed. He felt the suit groaning as the railgun's electromagnetic drives began to whine. They were spent. 'If you have anything left, fire it now,' he hissed.

H'an seemed to suddenly understand that they were doomed. The blastcannon was out. All he had left was the fragmentation projector. It fired off, filling the air with shrapnel. Some of it hit the

Stormsurge. It rocked for a moment, and managed to stay upright, swaying drunkenly, like a prize fighter who has been beaten to the edge of the fighting pit, but will not fall.

Batbayar trapped the Stormsurge on a low rise.

The towering battlesuit rocked as Batbayar stopped his bike, swung his leg over the handlebars and stared up at it, fists on his hips.

Across the battlefield his warriors were victorious as they drove surviving tau into the wilds and cleared the skies of any opposition. His honour guard were dead. His banner bearer had given up his gene-seed so that another might tread the path of the White Scars, but he had led and he had conquered, and victory was sweetest when it was bitterly won, like this. There was no dishonour in death. Death was the end for all of them. All that mattered was to win a glorious end that the White Scars might remember in poems, and that those poems might find their way back to Chogoris, and the yurts of his tribe, where his people might remember him and his deeds, and be glad.

The bikes formed a crescent behind their khan as he handed the eagle banner to Sergeant Tenzig of the Second Squad. The Stormsurge's systems were failing. Sparks flew from its groin pistons and as one of its legs gave way it sank to one knee, as if kowtowing before him.

Batbayar stopped in front of the machine. He would do it the honour of killing it himself. He judged the places where the crew were encased, and he struck with impeccable pose – his sword a sudden blur leaving two neat holes in the Stormsurge's torso.

Blood trickled out from each, as the Stormsurge fell forwards.

CHAPTER THIRTY-SIX

Batbayar led the survivors of his company towards the Stormsurge production facility.

Land Speeders and Stormtalons had already destroyed the last drones that refused to leave their assigned stations and the ice was littered with their burning remains, as well as those of a last flight of vespids who had fallen back to the tower. 'This is the place,' Scout Sergeant Törömbaater announced. 'But there is no production facility.'

Batbayar strode in through the open doors, hands on hips as he surveyed the insides. 'Shadowsun?'

'Nothing,' the Scout sergeant reported.

Batbayar paced forwards. There were long rows of suiting bays and in each one stood a Stormsurge battlesuit. They had a menacing air about them, even in their sedentary state, but there was nothing here that spoke of production. 'There must be another level,' Batbayar said. 'Find it!'

Törömbaater licked his lips before he spoke. 'Khan. We have searched the place. There is nothing else here. No production facility. Nothing.'

Batbayar spun about in fury. 'I do not believe you. Why would the tau defend this place with such ferocity if there was nothing here worth defending?'

As he spoke the khan had an unpleasant feeling. 'Where is Nergui?'

He looked at his warriors, but none of them knew.

'Where is Nergui!' Batbayar roared.

A voice answered. 'I am here.'

The khan turned to stare as the Deathwatch captain paced through the empty hangars. His helmet was under his arm. His black armour was criss-crossed with the blood-splatter that came from close-up sword work. Batbayar smelt deceit. His eyes were wide with fury. 'Have you killed her?'

'Shadowsun?'

'Yes!'

'No. She is not here.'

Batbayar strode towards him. 'Not here? Will men say that she has made a fool of me, as she has Kor'sarro?'

'No. She was never here.'

Batbayar could barely believe what he was hearing. 'Why then did we attack this place, when we could be winning glory for the Tulwar Brotherhood on Chogoris itself?'

Nergui looked pained. 'I cannot tell you,' he said at last.

'You cannot? Yet you led me to believe that she was here…! Are you fooling with me?'

'No, brother.'

'Don't call me brother. If you are a White Scar then you call me khan!'

Nergui was impassive. 'No, Khan Batbayar of the Tangut Tribe.'

Batbayar struck his brother with an open hand. Nergui stumbled back, but did not lift a hand except to wipe the blood away from his cheek. Batbayar turned on his heel and strode from the building.

'You are no brother of mine,' Batbayar spat, then turned to his warriors. 'Melta bomb this place. And everything in it.'

CHAPTER THIRTY-SEVEN

The Corvus Blackstar waited for the extraction as the hab-dome smoked. Konrad was the last to climb up from the sublevel. His joints were sticky with the congealing blood of the tau. They had found the cadets and they had massacred them all. They were so low on ammunition by then they'd had to finish the job by hand.

Konrad had personally killed a hundred and thirty of them. Leonas was just behind him with over a hundred and ten. Hadrian had a kill count of only seventy-nine.

'I was covering you both,' he said. 'Someone has to keep watch.'

Moaz, the Raven Guard, was standing with one foot up on the ramp. He'd taken a couple of hits in his chest, and he was clearly exhausted. The surviving members of Faith were already inside.

Konrad felt nothing. 'You're coming with us?' he said to the Raven Guard.

Moaz nodded.

'What's happened to the rest of your team?' he asked.

'They've gone back already.'

'Domitian?'

'With Zeal.'

Konrad nodded and climbed aboard the Corvus. Sardegna and Elianus were leaning on their guns. Hadrian was resting. On the floor were laid out five Space Marines. He knew them from their Chapter markings.

Ragris, Celebrant.
Atilio, Ultramarines.
Olbath, Aurora Chapter.
Imano, Lamenters.

Only the last one surprised him. 'What happened to Sardegna?'

The hole in his chest showed where the fusion blaster had cut straight through him.

'His luck ran out,' Leonas said. 'When they made their last stand.'

Konrad shook his head. It seemed a waste to have lost the Scion of Sanguinius right at the end of the battle.

'All aboard,' Leonas voxed Cadvan, the pilot, and slapped the side of the Blackstar.

'*I'm taking her up,*' Cadvan voxed back. '*Hold on.*'

They mag-locked their boots to the floor and tensed as the Blackstar made a vertical take-off, banking round for one last look at the tau camp. The White Scars had raised two great piles of heads. One was of flesh, the other a hundred and one Stormsurge heads, in a great mound of mixed sept colours. The field where they had fought was broken with craters and smoking ruins, many of them of Imperial design. At the edge of the battlefield, while a Stormtalon patrolled, a last White Scars Thunderhawk was loading the dead as servitors reclaimed an immobilised Predator. 'How many did they lose?'

'Twenty-seven,' Leonas said.

'I wonder what will happen with yours,' Konrad said. 'You know. When your last battle has been fought.'

Leonas nodded. He had often wondered the same thing.

'The Administratum will have a place for it. The last Black Consul. It could go in a museum,' said Konrad.

'I'll look after it until then,' Leonas said.

Jotunn usually took his own Blackstar, but this time he waited while Nergui made one last effort to speak to Batbayar.

'The khan is busy,' Khulan told him, after he had pushed to the very door of Batbayar's Thunderhawk. His bike lay by the side of the gunship, carefully loaded onto a stretcher crate.

'I would like to see him,' Nergui said.

'I know,' Khulan said. 'But he does not want to see you, Nergui of the Chaoge. And he is khan, and you are not.'

Nergui nodded. This was the way of the White Scars. He held out an offering. 'I brought him this.'

He held out a head.

Khulan looked at it. 'Is that Shadowsun?'

Nergui shook his head.

'Why would we want this ethereal's head, Nergui?'

'It is an offering.'

'Of what?'

'Regret,' Nergui said.

'There is no way back to the past. It is vain to regret and to wish. All there is, is now.'

Nergui nodded. He dropped the ethereal's head at Khulan's feet, and then turned and walked away. The Lone Wolf was waiting for him in the dark corner of the Blackstar.

It had been a long time since Nergui had seen the albino warrior in the light of day. The Space Wolf's pink eyes were tired and bloodshot. 'Did they take it?' he growled.

'No.'

'I said they would not.'

'And you were right. I knew it myself, but I still had to try. They were my brothers once. And may be again.'

Jotunn wiped the blood from his gauntlets and glanced at the pile of Stormsurge heads. 'So we killed them all.'

'All of them,' he said.

'You know there must be more of these sites scattered through the Damocles Gulf. Places where our enemies are planning treachery and violence against us.'

'Well,' Nergui nodded, 'there is one less now.'

WHITEOUT

ANDY CLARK

Crimson light bathed Lothar Redfang as the drop pod plummeted through Atrophon's atmosphere.

He grinned fiercely around at the rest of the Deathwatch kill team as their craft juddered and shook.

'The fires out there would roast us in a heartbeat, eh? We're in the hands of the Allfather now!'

The Ultramarine, Sergeant Cantos, didn't respond. Sor'khal, the White Scar, scowled.

'We trust our lives to a damned machine, Fenris. That's all.'

Lothar's reply was overridden by the grinding voice of the Iron Hand, Brother Gorrvan.

'I have advised on seven previous occasions, Brother Sor'khal. Statistical chance of drop pod mechanical failure is less than zero seven two. You have virtually no cause for concern.'

Sor'khal snorted.

'*Virtually*, he says.'

Oblivious to the irony, Gorrvan continued.

'Brother Redfang, this vehicle is a device of the Omnissiah. If you fear for your safety, pray not to your Allfather but to Him.'

'A Space Wolf fears nothing!' barked Lothar. 'Hot Fenrisian blood in these veins! Not like that sump-oil you got in you!' The Space Wolf's brash laugh faltered as he realised none of his brothers were joining in. Gorrvan stared blankly, and Sor'khal's scowl deepened. Brother Kordus, of the Raven Guard, merely tilted his head slightly and regarded Lothar askance.

'What?' muttered Lothar. 'None of you got a sense of humour?'

'Battle is no laughing matter, Brother Redfang,' declared Sergeant

Cantos, 'and before us lies a fierce one. Brothers, three minutes to impact. Make ready.'

Immediately, the kill team began checking equipment while muttering benedictions to the machine-spirits. Helms were locked in place. Sor'khal's narthecium clicked and whirred as he tested its functionality. Kordus reached across to where his jump pack was mag-locked to the drop pod's central column, fingers dancing over the pack's activation runes. As they worked, Cantos ran through a final brief, reiterating the key points of his squad's strategos briefing with the typical thoroughness of a veteran Ultramarine.

'As you know, the orks of Waaagh! Dregsmasha invaded Atrophon eighteen months ago. Atrophon militia were reinforced by the Catachan Jungle Fighters. However, extreme wintry conditions on the planet have worked against them.'

'Worse,' he continued, 'the orks have deployed a string of super-weapons, to their great advantage. They carried Frostclaw Ridge with volleys of gravity bombs, deployed super-heavy war effigies in the fight for Honorium, and undermined the Ironfields with tunnelling machines.'

'Strategos link these inventions to an ork mechanic named Badklaw,' put in Gorrvan. 'Their augur-skull probes have ascertained his location amid the factorums of the Strakendorf Peninsula.'

'However,' continued Cantos, 'that information is useless to the Astra Militarum. Eighteen hours ago, the greenskins staged a push on the Strakendorf front. The Catachans and Atrophons fell back over the River Strakk, demolishing its primary bridges behind them. This has bought the defenders time to marshal their forces. However, it has cut them off from the orks.'

'Cowards,' grunted Sor'khal.

'Just men,' offered Brother Kordus quietly, 'but not us.'

Sergeant Cantos nodded. 'Correct. The Emperor has blessed us with the ability to take the fight to our foe. Judging by pattern matching of rising energy signatures within the ork's factorum stronghold, it has been estimated we have approximately six hours until Badklaw's latest device reaches completion. Then our target likely moves up to join the attack on the Strakendorf front.'

'Then we kill him first, eh?'

Sor'khal shot Lothar a humourless grin.

'First sensible thing I've heard you say, Fenris.'

Lothar grinned back, baring his canines.

The next moment, the drop pod's electrosconces pulsed and an urgent chime rang from its vox-casters.

'Collision warning!' barked Cantos.

'Not buildings,' gritted Sor'khal as he gripped his restraint harness, 'we're still in clear sky!'

'Then what…?'

Lothar never finished his question as, with a sudden, shocking bang of metal on metal, the pod was slammed sideways. The lights went out, and Lothar felt gravity crush him back into his harness as the drop pod spun wildly. Alarm tones pinged and whooped, and Lothar let out a groan of effort as he braced against the forces clamping him like a vice.

There was a thunderous impact and everything went black.

Lothar's vision swam as it returned, light and shadow churning in a sluggish, nauseating ballet. Pain pulsed in his skull. For several heartbeats, disorientation tried to drag him back down into unconsciousness. With a defiant growl, Lothar forced his eyes to focus. The Space Wolf's helmet chron told him he had only been unconscious for a handful of minutes. The fact that he was still breathing told him that, whatever else had happened, he was still alive.

Lothar sat up, grimacing, and realised he'd been staring up into a thick snowstorm. Sor'khal was crouched next to him, checking readings on his narthecium.

'Ah! Fenris lives.' The White Scar stood, extending a gauntlet to help Lothar up. As Sor'khal hauled him to his feet, the Space Wolf took in his surroundings. The two of them stood shin deep in a snowdrift, engulfed by the shadow of a ruined hab-block. Snow fell thickly, dragged this way and that by gusting winds that Lothar's auto-senses warned were well below freezing. Through the murk, the Space Wolf could see more skeletal ruins all around. Blasted habs loomed over the snowy streets like ghosts.

'The crash landing knocked you senseless,' said Sor'khal. 'Our pod came down in this ruin and we dragged you clear. Damn machine managed to fire its retros just in time to stop us being smashed to bits. By the Emperor's grace we all came away in one piece, more or less.'

'Was it the Iron Hand's impossible failure?'

Brother Sor'khal shook his head and turned away, jogging off through the snow with his bolter ready. Lothar followed, drawing his own weapons as he went.

'No failure,' said the White Scar over his shoulder, 'Gorrvan was right about that. Something hit us, ork aircraft most likely. Emperor knows no Imperial pilot would be aloft in this mess.' They crunched across a road junction, picking their way around the half-buried wreckage of a Chimera and its slain occupants.

'Mess?' scoffed Lothar. 'On Fenris we'd spar in this without armour!'

Sor'khal glanced back at him. 'In that case, on Fenris you must all be deficient.'

Lothar's booming laugh was swallowed by the muffling shroud of snow.

'Hah, remind me to bash your teeth in for that sometime, eh?'

'You're welcome to try, Fenris. If Laedas couldn't take me, you don't stand a chance.'

'Laedas?'

'Our former squad mate. The Imperial Fist who got torn apart by genestealers just so we could enjoy your sorry company. I liked that big bastard – we all did. And he was twice the warrior you are.'

Lothar's rejoinder was drowned out by the howl of a jump pack as Brother Kordus dropped from the sky in front of them.

'The sergeant is in the cathedrum up ahead. Problem.'

Sor'khal gestured around.

'You mean, besides being stuck in a snowstorm on the wrong side of an uncrossable river?'

Kordus paused for a moment.

'Yes.'

With that, he turned, fired his pack, and soared away into the falling snow.

'All talk, that one,' grumbled Sor'khal as they pressed on. Lothar chuckled, then pulled up short.

'Wait. Wrong side of the river?'

'Did I not mention that? Vox is shot to hell with all this stuff in the air – we can barely reach each other, let alone anyone useful. Come on, Fenris, the sergeant will have a plan.'

They found their battle-brothers in the blasted ruin of the cathedrum of the Emperor Resplendent. Shattered figures in stained glass stared down at them with cracked and sorrowful eyes. Snow fell through rents in the domed roof and had piled in drifts across the nave. The Kill Team's briefing had indicated that, while the orks had not yet made it across the River Strakk on foot, their aircraft had been pounding the city for days. It seemed they had been thorough. Lothar frowned as he took in the tangles of fire-blackened bodies strewn around the cathedrum's ruined interior. Many of the Atrophon citizenry would have gathered here to pray for salvation, now finding only death as the bombs fell. Lothar felt anger surge hot in his chest at the pitiful sight. These people would be avenged.

Cantos, Gorrvan and Kordus were at the far end of the building, staring out through a hole in the cathedrum's east wall. Sor'khal and Lothar moved up to stand alongside them.

'It is good that you are unharmed, Brother Redfang,' grated Gorrvan, his voice echoing through the ruin.

'We Space Wolves are made of sterner stuff, Iron Hand,' said Redfang. 'Needn't worry about me, eh?'

'My concern was not for you,' responded Gorrvan. 'If your inability to endure the crash had left you compromised, that weakness would have negatively impacted our chances of mission success.'

Sor'khal snorted, but his amusement died as he followed Sergeant Cantos's gaze.

'Oh…'

Before them, the fire-blackened city dropped away steeply, marching down to the banks of the River Strakk. Through the tattered snowfall, they could see the river churning with breathtaking fury, great white crests of foam boiling upon its surface. The far bank was obscured, but from their briefing they knew the Strakk to be more than a kilometre wide and extremely fast-flowing. Even a Space Marine wouldn't survive an attempt at crossing it. Yet the river was not the problem.

'Is that…?' Sor'khal began.

'Indeed,' Cantos cut in.

'Didn't they…?'

'Evidently not.'

'So we should…?'

'Absolutely.'

Sor'khal blew out a breath.

'Well. Let's get going then, eh?'

Cantos nodded.

'Brothers, we move. Twenty-foot spread to maintain visibility, assume hostile contact as possible. Kordus, stay high. Gorrvan, see if you can get a vox-link to Atrophon High Command. They need to know about this.'

As the Space Marines clambered through the rent in the cathedrum's wall and set off at a jog, the snow swirled about them. Ahead, the river thundered along beneath the un-demolished span of Strakkendorf's third primary bridge.

The bridge was enormous, a plasteel and ferrocrete monument to the might of the Imperium of Man. It consisted of three roadways, each wide enough to accommodate a trio of Baneblades driving abreast, and separated by jutting, armoured barriers. At intervals, towering support columns rose from the churning waters of the Strakk to bear the bridge's weight. From what the kill team saw as they advanced from the west bank towards the bridge's mid-point, each support was a substantial building in its own right, studded with access hatches, snow-choked gantries, stairways and ladders. Thick steel cables stretched between the supports, the wind singing a cold dirge between them.

As they reached the centre of the bridge, the kill team were confronted by the most imposing structure yet. Here stood a mighty fortress, a bastion wall of armoured ferrocrete that incorporated the central support columns and stretched the entire width of the bridge. A vast marble aquila spread its wings across the fortress's imposing facade. Heavy gun emplacements and banks of darkened floodlights studded it. At its feet, the three roadways plunged into darkened tunnels, and it was here, within the blackened maw of the central tunnel, that the Deathwatch found a code-locked door leading into the fortress proper.

Cantos ordered Gorrvan to gain access, reasoning that such a structure would boast hardened vox-relays and military-grade augurs. The survival of a bridge across the Strakk changed the wider strategic picture enormously, and the sergeant was determined to gain access to up-to-date intelligence before his Kill Team made their next move. Leaving the Iron Hand to work on the code-lock, the rest of the squad spread out to scout their surroundings.

Lothar stepped from darkness into murky, snow-curdled daylight. He stared east, along the span of the bridge, scouring the swirling snow for signs of movement. The immensity of the fortress loomed above him, lights dark and guns mute and inactive.

'This is Lothar. I'm at the eastern mouth of the central tunnel. Not seeing anything.' He waited for a few moments, the hiss of the vox underpinning the moan of the wind through the tunnel.

'Kordus,' came the Raven Guard's quiet tones over the vox. 'Eastern mouth of left-hand tunnel. The auspex is showing some unusual energy spikes nearby.'

'I've got the same on the right,' came Sor'khal's gruff voice.

'Elaborate.' Cantos's clipped tones cut through the background static. 'What are you seeing, brothers?'

'One signature, approximately two hundred metres to the east,' reported Kordus. 'Large, constant and concurrent with a shield generator or sizeable weapon system.'

'Again, same,' added Sor'khal. 'Doesn't look orkish, sergeant. Too steady.' For a few moments, the vox was quiet, then Cantos's voice came again.

'Understood. Hold your positions, brothers. We'll know more once Gorrvan gets this door open.'

Lothar gritted his teeth in frustration, snapping a quick glance at his helmet chron. Four hours and forty minutes remaining. He checked his own auspex, banging it against his armoured thigh when its readout remained annoyingly neutral. The device flickered, then a stuttering signature appeared on its screen.

'This is Lothar,' he voxed. 'I think my auspex got damaged in the crash. It's just picked up another signature. The fix can't be right, though.'

'Explain,' replied Cantos.

'Looks like I'm stood right on it, more or less,' replied Lothar, scowling at the flickering readout. Exasperated, the Space Wolf gave up on the damaged device and peered out along the bridge once more. He narrowed his eyes and increased his helm's magnification as he caught the suggestion of a large, humped shadow a little way east. Something he had missed amidst the swirling snow. Lothar raised his bolt pistol and chainsword, readying for a fight, but the shape wasn't moving.

Curious now, the Space Wolf decided to investigate. He crunched forward with a hunter's caution, wolf-tail totems whipping in the wind, until the shape resolved itself into a wrecked, snow-buried vehicle.

Still wary of potential foes lurking in the snowfall, Lothar moved up to the blackened wreck. It was a Taurox, lying stricken on its side in a snowbank like the corpse of some slain beast. The vehicle had clearly been gutted by fire, its hull torn open by what looked to have been forceful explosions against its rear armour. Lothar took in Catachan regimental markings on the wreck's scorched hull and, as he dug out the snow around it, he found several of its ill-fated passengers. Fire-blackened mummies in the tattered remains of Catachan uniforms, the dead men had been twisted by the agony of their deaths and then frozen solid by the sub-zero conditions. Once more, Lothar found his anger stirring at the sight of proud soldiers of the Emperor so diminished and defiled. He looked away from their clawing hands and screaming, black-fleshed skulls, and rose to his feet.

'Cantos,' he voxed, 'I've found something. About a hundred feet east of the tunnel. It's a wrecked Catachan Taurox and what's left of those riding in it. Coming this way at speed, I'd say, then took a few rockets to its arse and went up in flames.'

'Brother Redfang,' came the reply, 'you were ordered to hold position.'

'Aye, but then I saw this mess.'

'Evidently,' came the dry response. 'Well, as you're there, what's your assessment?' Lothar thought for a moment, eyes roving across the bleak and empty roadways of the bridge.

'Not part of the evacuation,' he responded eventually. 'If the orks had disrupted then there'd be wrecks everywhere, not just this one. Stragglers, maybe?'

'Or sappers?' voxed Sor'khal. 'Trying to blow the bridge? The greenskins might have caught them before they could finish the job. They tried to run and... boom.'

Lothar nodded slowly as he stared at the wreck. Perhaps. Just then, Gorrvan's monotone cut across the vox.

'Brothers, the machine-spirits have been rendered compliant. We have access.'

'Good work, brother,' responded Cantos. 'Kordus, keep watch. If the orks know this bridge is open, they may be on their way. The rest of you, regroup with Brother Gorrvan. We shall find our answers inside.'

Minutes later, the kill team, minus Kordus, stood around Gorrvan in the stronghold's cavernous command chamber. Cantos and Sor'khal had removed their helmets. The Iron Hand, meanwhile, knelt in data-communion with the fortification's cogitator bank. The kill team had found the fortress's systems powered down and its hatches locked tight, rendered inert by the garrison during their retreat. Now, Gorrvan was restoring power one system at a time, lumin globes and data-banks flickering back to life all around. Mechadendrites stretched from the Iron Hand's gauntlets into the cogitator's ports, and every few moments he twitched, or emitted a blurt of binary.

Sor'khal grimaced with distaste. Sergeant Cantos clapped a gauntlet against his comrade's shoulder guard.

'I know you mistrust machines, brother. But this is necessary. We need to know why the bridge wasn't demolished. We need to know if it's a viable route of advance.'

Lothar stopped pacing and turned.

'Advance?'

'Yes, brother. You disagree?'

The Space Wolf frowned, opened his mouth to speak and paused. Cantos's ice-blue eyes bored into him. The sergeant's paired service studs glinted in the half-light as a reminder that he was many decades Lothar's senior.

'Cantos...' Lothar began.

'Brother-sergeant to you.' Cantos' voice was not raised, but it cut like a combat knife.

'*Brother-sergeant*. The Atrophons and Catachans think this bridge is down. Reckon they think they're safe, eh? But they're not – there's a great big hole in their shield wall.'

'"Shield wall", Brother Redfang?'

Lothar banged his gauntlet against a datastack in exasperation.

'You know what I mean! If we leave, what's stopping the orks rolling straight over this bridge and catching the Astra Militarum taking a squat in the snow?'

Brother Sor'khal frowned. 'They've not crossed the bridge yet, or we'd have been neck deep in greenskins already. Maybe this was just the chance? A bunch of orks catch up to the Catachans and kill them, then carry their rampage off somewhere else? These are orks, Fenris. You know they're not much for strategy.'

'I know they do whatever you least expect, and when you least expect it,' replied Lothar. 'For all we know, they left themselves a way in on purpose, and the whole Waaagh! is approaching right now!'

Sergeant Cantos nodded.

'A fair assessment, Brother Lothar. But we have a mission. Already we're out of position, and time is against us.'

'But we can't…'

'We can,' interrupted the sergeant, 'and we must. I've no more desire than you to leave a hole in the Imperial defences. But our target takes precedence.'

'Besides,' put in Sor'khal, 'how are we going to demolish a bridge? Tell me that, Fenris. Shoot it with bolters till it falls down? We'll be here a while.'

'By the Allfather! I'm not saying we demolish anything! I'm saying we hold the damn bridge like real warriors.'

'Hold it?' replied Cantos sceptically. 'With what? Five battle-brothers? Rash foolishness.'

'More like heroism,' retorted Lothar angrily. 'Think of the glory!'

Sergeant Cantos's eyes flashed with anger.

'We are not here for glory, Brother Redfang. We are here to complete our mission. If you can't grasp the difference, I'll send you back to Fenris where you can engage in all the wasteful glory hunting you please.'

Lothar growled, the sound raw and angry. Sergeant Cantos stood, a cold stare locked with the Space Wolf's. The grate of Gorrvan's voice punctured the moment.

'Sergeant. Brother Redfang may be correct.' Cantos turned his glare from Lothar to Gorrvan.

'Explain.'

'I have interrogated the machine-spirits and data-logs. When the stronghold garrison pulled back, they did indeed leave a team of Catachan sappers to take care of the bridge itself. I believe we can safely assume that they did not succeed. However, they seem only to have been interrupted at the last moment.'

'The energy signatures!' exclaimed Lothar. 'They got their charges set, but didn't have time to blow the bridge?'

'I believe so,' nodded Gorrvan, 'I have inloaded our squad's auspex data. Cross-referencing with the Catachans' logged demolitions schematic, I believe there are two extremely large plasma bombs located a short distance east of here, and another in the support girders beneath this fortress. In addition, though meteorological conditions are becoming increasingly adverse, long-range auspex suggests dramatically increased movement on the river's east bank.'

'This may have been deliberate, then,' nodded Cantos grimly. 'The orks have left themselves an attack route, and now they gather to exploit it.'

'And in this throne-damned weather, no-one's realised,' said Sor'khal. 'But then, surely they'll be on their way?'

As though summoned by Sor'khal's words, Kordus's voice crackled over the vox.

'Enemy movement in the east. Scattered infantry and light vehicles crossing the bridge towards your position. Numbers unclear.'

Sor'khal exchanged a look with Cantos.

'Sergeant?' For a moment, Cantos stared intently into the middle distance. Lothar drew breath to speak, but Sor'khal motioned him to stay quiet.

'Very well,' said Cantos. 'Brother Gorrvan, I assume we are still cut off from Atrophon high command?' The Iron Hands legionary nodded.

'Correct. Long-range vox contact is impossible at this time.'

'Then we must deal with this matter ourselves. A random greenskin incursion into the Imperial lines was troubling, but an acceptable risk. This is not random. There will be little gain to the Imperium if we eliminate our target at the expense of the entire Atrophon war effort.'

'So we fight?' asked Lothar eagerly.

'Yes, Brother Redfang. We fight. But not for glory, and not in some forlorn last stand. We still have a mission to complete. Gorrvan?'

'Yes, sergeant?'

'The plasma charges. How difficult would it be for us to rouse their machine-spirits?' For a moment, Gorrvan retched binary. From Kordus came three insistent vox-pips. Situation urgent, orders required.

'Viable,' grated Gorrvan. 'The data-logs indicate that the charges require only the final rituals of arming to synchronise them in a data-choir with this cogitator bank.'

'Good. Exfiltration? We need to be on the eastern bank when this bridge comes down.'

'There are maintenance and drainage ducts running through the bridge superstructure just below surface level,' replied Gorrvan after a pause. 'Large enough for us to move along at a run, all the way to the eastern bank. Some systems are still inactive, sergeant. I cannot promise that the duct-ways are fully accessible, or that the foe will not have found a way into them. However, I calculate a seventy-six per cent chance that they will provide a suitable, uncontested exfiltration route once the charges are primed.'

'It will have to do,' barked Cantos, donning his helm. 'Gorrvan, remain here, provide us with strategic oversight and guide us in the arming rituals. And get the east-facing servitor guns up and running as your first priority. Sor'khal, Redfang, with me. We'll press on and prime those charges.'

'Sergeant, I'll take the bomb below the stronghold,' voxed Kordus, 'I can reach it quicker than any of you.'

'Agreed,' replied Cantos. 'Once all charges are set, we fall back here. That should lure the orks onto the stronghold's guns and, while they are fully distracted, we slip away through the ducts before the charges blow.'

Sor'khal nodded.

'No more bridge. No more orks. Brilliant. By the Khan, then, brothers, let us be about our duty!'

The Space Marines emerged into gloom of the central tunnel once more, the door's code-lock rune flashing from green to red behind them. Now only Gorrvan would be able to unlock that portal from the central command chamber. Cantos led his brothers at a run to the eastern mouth of the tunnel, where they ducked down for a moment with weapons held ready.

Lothar stared hard along the bridge, noting that the weather was worsening fast. Already the crashed Taurox and its slain cargo were lost to sight amid the wind-whipped snow. He could hear engines snorting and snarling out there, but couldn't yet see the foe.

'With me,' voxed Cantos, 'Lothar left flank, Sor'khal right.'

The three Space Marines loped out along the bridge, steadying themselves against shrieking gusts of icy wind. As they jogged along the bridge, their boots crunched in the snow and the sound of motors and crude bellowing voices got steadily louder.

'You are now less than one hundred metres from the charges,' voxed Gorrvan. 'There appear to be two, one to either side of the bridge.'

Just at that moment, the first of the foe loomed from the swirling snow. The orks were huge beasts, as tall as the Space Marines themselves and easily as broad. Despite the icy cold they were clad in ragged cloth and scrappy armour that left much of their green flesh exposed. As the hulking silhouettes emerged from the storm, Lothar grinned in recognition.

'Contact left,' he snarled and, raising his bolt pistol, shot the first beast through the face. The ork's head exploded in a wet spray. Behind it, its comrades roared in anger, but Lothar was already charging. A few crude slugs whined off his armour in showers of sparks, then he was in amongst the greenskins, his chainsword howling. His first stroke lopped a greenskin's head from its shoulders. His second hacked through the haft of a scrap-iron axe and severed the arm holding it. An ork hatchet clanged against Lothar's shoulder guard, hacking a chunk from the ceramite and driving the Space Wolf to one knee. In return, he drove his chainsword into the ork's guts and snarled his satisfaction as the alien's innards sprayed red across the snow.

More orks closed in, a metal club crunching into Lothar's chest with enough force to crack the black carapace beneath. The Space Wolf growled as he tasted blood in his mouth.

Bolters thundered as Lothar's brothers joined him. Cantos and Sor'khal gunned down the greenskins with practised skill, the muzzle flare from their weapons lighting the snowbanks with its strobing glare. Within moments only butchered meat remained, pools of xenos blood steaming as it swiftly cooled and froze.

'...sily recognisable. Vox me whe... cated the charges.' Cantos paused, one hand pressed to the side of his helm.

'Brother Gorrvan, repeat. You're breaking up.' Static whistled through the vox.

'We need to move,' muttered Sor'khal, scanning the whirling snow. 'That was just the first handful. The sound of fighting brings the bastards running.'

Lothar revved his chainsword.

'Let them come. *Stormtooth* hungers for their blood!'

'Atmospheri... terference is increasi... sergeant,' voxed Gorrvan. 'Reiterati... each charge is located at the ba... a support column, and will be easily recogni... Vox me when... located the charges.'

'Acknowledged,' replied Cantos. 'Sor'khal, take the left-hand side of the bridge. Brother Redfang, right. I will remain central and retain their attention while you complete the rituals. Go.'

The two Deathwatch brothers nodded, turned, and forged off into the snow. Cantos remained where he was, stood alone amid the orks' contorted corpses. Engines roared, louder now and getting swiftly closer. Cantos raised his combi-melta and waited.

Brother Kordus triggered his jump pack, launching himself from the gantry. Snow whipped around him as he flew through the air, auto-senses overlaying his vision with trajectories and the wireframe mapping of the bridge's structure. For a long moment he sailed through white nothingness, the thuggish wind trying to bludgeon him off course, before his boots clanged down on another strut. He stood on a censer-spar that jutted precipitously from the bridge's underside. Far below, the river churned and roared. The Raven Guard calmly calculated his next leap, ignoring the wind screaming around him, then fired his jump pack's thrusters again. As he flew, he listened to his brothers' vox chatter. Sor'khal and Redfang had almost reached their charges now, and Cantos was engaging another wave of greenskins. Kordus had no doubt they would complete their duties, even the newcomer. Meanwhile, he would see to his task.

Kordus's leap carried him down, under the ferrocrete mass of the bridge and into its shadow. Down here, a vast cradle of gantries, girders and cables helped support the stronghold, lest its weight pull it down into the fury of the Strakk. He landed on a long, wide girder and paused, getting a fix on the energy signature of the plasma charge. With whipping snow and shadow all around, the Raven Guard's visibility was now down to a few metres at best; his helm's auto-senses would have to be his eyes.

Kordus's contemplation was broken as a bullet whined off the girder to his left. Another clanged from his helm, then more were raining around him. Obeying ingrained training, Kordus triggered his jump pack and executed a twisting, evasive leap to carry him out of danger. He crossed the vaulted space between two spars then cut his engines suddenly to drop like a stone. Kordus fell several metres and grabbed the edge of a lower platform as it flashed up at him out of the murk. Swinging into shadow, he waited, twin hearts thudding steadily, aware of the constant, hungry roar of the river far below. More gunfire rattled, then petered out. His assailants had lost him. Hopefully.

Scouring the gloom, Kordus saw the foe as flickering heat-signatures. The creatures swarming along the cables and girders weren't orks. They were smaller, gangling things that clung on for dear life as they climbed. Gretchin, a whole mob of them heading right for the plasma charge. He could see its power readings from here, and gauged that the device was nestled close to a support column directly below the stronghold's main mass. It wasn't far away. Kordus pulled himself up with one fluid motion. The Raven Guard crouched, palmed a frag grenade, and drew his bolt pistol. He would need to be quick.

Lothar was almost at the plasma charge, and could see it pulsing green through the snow when the orks struck. Only the sudden howl of his instincts saved him. Lothar threw himself sideways, a smoke-belching rocket whipping over his head. The projectile corkscrewed into the bridge and exploded. He hit the ground, rolled, and came up with his pistol raised. The snow around him erupted as a mob of orks burst from hiding. They were clad in a jarring grey and red pattern that Lothar realised was meant to be camouflage, and many had a crossed-axe glyph smeared crudely on their skin or wargear.

'Die, filth,' snarled the Space Wolf, blasting the ork with the smoking rocket launcher off its feet. The next greenskin roared and shot Lothar point-blank, cracking his armour and sending him staggering back. The Space Wolf howled with rage and charged, sawing his chainsword into the ork's face. Blood and broken teeth sprayed, even as Lothar's next two shots blew chunks of flesh from another assailant. The ork came on, despite the craters blasted in its torso, and Lothar took a resounding blow to his helm, amber warning runes flickering in the corners of his vision. Spinning, the Space Wolf brought his blade whirring around in an arc and hacked the head from his tenacious foe. As this latest ork fell, neck-stump jetting gore, the last of Lothar's attackers lost their nerve and fled. His instincts bayed at him to give chase, but he had a mission to complete. Instead, he dropped to one knee next to the humming bulk of the plasma charge and stared in incomprehension at the wires and cables that spilled from its innards.

'Gorrvan, I'm at the bomb. What in the Allfather's name do I do now?'

For a few moments there was silence, followed by the sound of Cantos engaging the orks somewhere behind him. Muffled bolter fire thudded through the air, interwoven with bestial greenskin warcries. Lothar grinned fiercely at the sound of something exploding with a hoarse boom. For an Ultramarine, he thought, it sounded like Cantos could really fight. Suddenly, Gorrvan's voice broke through the choppy static.

'...rother Redfang... see a panel with a ...echanicus cog. It... about ha... way up the dev...'

For a moment, Lothar was at a loss. Then his eyes found the panel. 'Got it.'

'Ver... ood. Intoning the thir... cantica... of the Omniss... pre... the red rune ne... the pane...'

Lothar scowled. The wind howled around him, gathering pace by the second. A particularly fierce gust snatched a clutch of icicles from a gantry high above, flinging them down to shatter upon his armoured shoulders.

'...n the circumstance... think we can dispense with the chanting. Just hit the red rune Brother Redfa...'

Lothar grunted and thumped his fist against the blinking red rune. With a puff of incense, the panel slid aside, revealing a nest of wires and switches. Squatting amongst them was a device that Lothar recognised. A melta bomb. A secondary charge, presumably placed to violently dissuade tampering. As the panel opened, a runic display on the small charge's front began to count downward.

'Fenrir's arse,' cursed Lothar. 'There's a bomb here, Gorrvan. Another one, and its machine-spirit doesn't like me! Now what?'

'Ah,' came Gorrvan's response.

'*Ah?* What do I do?' snarled Lothar. For long, agonising seconds, the only response was static, hissing and whistling through the vox. Lothar's twin hearts thudded, and every nerve screamed at him to get clear, but he had a duty to discharge.

'Gorrvan? Gorrvan! By the Allfather, you metal bastard, if you don't tell me what to do right now this thing's going to blow my head off!'

Finally, Gorrvan's voice returned, still infuriatingly unruffled.

'Remain cal… Brother, I will hel… you. Thr… wires shoul… from the top of the melta charge, yes?'

Lothar searched frantically, sweat rolling down the back of his neck as the runes counted down towards zero.

'No… yes! I see them. Now what?'

'…ood. Rip out the … ed and blue. Lea… the green.'

Sliding his thick, armoured fingers into the bomb's workings, Lothar gingerly grasped the wires and, with a muttered prayer, yanked them out. For a second more the rune counter spiralled downwards, and then it blinked and went dark.

A breath that Lothar hadn't realised he was holding escaped his lips in a rush.

'Brother Lo… ar, do you sti… live?'

Lothar barked a humourless laugh. 'I do, Gorrvan. I do. I owe you a debt, brother.'

'You are ver… elcome, Brother Redfa… but no debt has… en incurred. Your immolation, along with… plasma charge, would ha… been sub-optimal for our chances of missio… uccess. Now… the panel, do you se… switches?'

'Aye.'

'…ount along fro… the left… ick the third switch…'

Lothar swore as the signal finally deteriorated into a roar of static. With a wary glance at the huge, pulsing bomb, Lothar counted the switches from the left and placed his finger on the third one.

'Hope this is right, brother,' he muttered. 'Don't want another mechanical failure eh?' Wincing, Lothar flicked the switch.

* * *

At the same moment, Kordus, having monitored Gorrvan's instructions to Lothar, flicked his own switch and gunned down another two gretchin. Already, heaps of the vile creatures lay scattered around the platform, blown apart by bolts and frag grenades. The rest had hunkered down behind struts and spars, preferring to pelt Kordus with fire from a safe distance. He was bleeding from several superficial wounds, his armour a mess of bullet-scars, but as the charge's rune flashed from red to green he knew he'd completed his task.

'Charge primed, Gorrvan,' he voxed. 'Returning.' The wind screamed, its ferocity increasing with each moment. As he watched, several gretchin were plucked from the nearest gantry and sent spinning away into the storm with reedy shrieks of terror.

Steeling himself, Kordus took a running leap into the maelstrom, jump pack roaring as it propelled him past a knot of greenskins and into the darkness. He landed with a clang, steadied himself, leapt again, and again. His auto-senses warned him the wind speed and temperature were becoming untenable for flight. A storm of ice chipped and scratched at his armour. Yet just a couple more jumps would carry him up onto the bridge's surface.

At that moment, his vox coughed static in his ear, along with Cantos's ragged, distorted voice.

'...rothers, if any of you... hear this... plete the mission... can't... hold...'

Kordus was little given to displays of emotion, but he had fought with Cantos on a dozen battlefields, and he swore as he heard the pain and defiance in his sergeant's voice. Desperate urgency gripped the Raven Guard, and he took a running leap before firing his jump pack once more. Heavy with accumulating ice, the engines burned hard for a moment, sputtered, then cut out. Kordus stretched desperately for the nearest strut, just grasping the frozen metal. Behind his faceplate, Kordus's black eyes widened with horror as his fingers slithered off the rime of ice, then he fell wordlessly towards the roaring river below.

Sor'khal pounded through the snow. Behind him, hidden amid the snowstorm, his plasma charge was primed. Ahead, even over the wind, he could hear roars and gunfire. The snow parted, and the White Scar cursed. Cantos was on his knees in the snow, blood running freely from his rent armour. The wreck of a ramshackle ork transport burned nearby, as did several blasted bikes. Orks were piled high around the heroic Ultramarine, yet more still surrounded him. Sor'khal ran faster, drawing his power sword from its sheathe. A massive, armoured ork with a roaring chain-cleaver loomed over the sergeant, its face split in a hideous leer. Then it raised its weapon to deliver the killing blow.

'Cantos!'

The cleaver swept down, only to slam against a chainsword inches above Cantos's head. Sparks flew, and the huge ork roared its outrage. Lothar Redfang surged forward, driving the greenskin back with a series of lightning-fast cuts. The ork punched the Space Wolf in the face, denting his face-plate and shattering one eyepiece. Rallying, Lothar feinted high then swung low and hacked off his foe's leg. The ork leader crashed down, only to sink its tusks into Redfang's thigh. Blood jetted as ceramite parted under the immense pressure of the ork's jaws. With a roar of pain the Space Wolf rammed his whirring blade through the ork's eye socket, causing its head to come apart with gratifying violence. By this time, Sor'khal had reached his brothers, impaling another ork, then pounding bolt shells into several more.

'Get the sergeant up,' voxed Lothar, parrying a whirltoothed axe. Sor'khal nodded, only to be sent staggering as another huge, armoured ork shoulder-charged him. The White Scar and the greenskin exchanged a vicious flurry of blows, and Sor'khal roared in pain as his opponent managed to ram its rusted blade through the armoured cables protecting his midriff. Blood welled through the wound and the ork roared its victory, pushing the blade deeper. Its eyes widened as Sor'khal bellowed a curse of his own. The Apothecary slammed his armoured fist repeatedly into his attacker's face until bone broke and blood spurted. As his foe leaned desperately away from the punches, Sor'khal jammed his narthecium up, under its jaw. Drills whined, armour separators cracked out through bone and sinew, and the White Scar messily tore off the ork's jaw.

Showered in greenskin blood, Sor'khal kicked his gagging, dying attacker into the snow. He wrenched the beast's blade from his stomach and hurled it contemptuously away.

'Are you alive, brother?' Sor'khal answered Lothar's question with a pained nod, before sliding one shoulder under Cantos's arm and hauling the sergeant to his feet. Already, Sor'khal's gene-enhanced metabolism was at work, clotting the flow of blood from his wound and beginning to heal the catastrophic damage that would have killed a lesser man thrice over. Cantos, however, was more sorely wounded. Blood dribbled in ropes through the cracked vox-grille of his helm, and welled slowly from a dozen savage rents in his armour. He grunted in pain, but managed to get his feet under him all the same.

'Lothar,' growled Sor'khal. 'We need to fall back, now!'

The Space Wolf rammed his chainsword through an ork's throat, before backing towards his brothers.

'Agreed. They're thick as hook-tics on a kraken, eh?'

The Deathwatch retreated along the bridge, firing as they went. The enemy were all around, but the howling, snowy gale hampered the orks worse than the Space Marines. Though their ferocious resilience made them all but immune to the cold, the xenos still had to labour for every step. Meanwhile, the Deathwatch had servo-motors to help power their limbs, and gyroscopic stabilisers to keep them upright. Still, all three were hard-pressed and cursing the orks' incredible tenacity by the time the silhouette of the stronghold rose through the snow.

'Gorrvan,' voxed Sor'khal. 'Cover would be good!'

'…oing what I can, Brother Sor'khal. The storm has compromised the servit… guns' targeting augurs. I cannot risk triggering them at this time. They may hit you.'

'Perfect,' spat Sor'khal, blasting another ork as it loomed from the snowstorm. It took the round to its shoulder, staggering as blood and meat exploded from the wound before roaring its defiance and charging again. Sor'khal cursed and shot it square in the face, sending its headless body flopping back into the snow. Sergeant Cantos activated his vox.

'Brother Kordus?' he gasped, 'Where are you? We need to go…'

Silence answered him, and Sor'khal swore again as his bolter clicked uselessly. An ork slammed into him and Cantos, spilling them all into the snow. Sor'khal's helm hit ferrocrete as the greenskin landed atop him. The alien cracked one big green fist into his face-plate, breaking the ceramite and drawing blood.

Meanwhile, Lothar fought ever-increasing odds. He tried to reach his fallen brothers, but several huge orks hurled themselves at him all at once. He crushed in his first assailant's skull and shot the next, but the third managed to hack its blade into his shoulder. Howling with pain, Lothar headbutted the greenskin, only to be knocked off his feet as an ork shell exploded nearby.

'Sor'khal,' he groaned, trying to crawl towards the Apothecary. He saw the White Scar's assailant deliver another clubbing blow. Then a black shape hit the ork like a thunderbolt. Engines roaring, Kordus tackled the greenskin off his brother, snapping its neck as they tumbled to a stop. Standing, the Raven Guard rattled off a volley of shells, gunning down a pair of masked greenskins before they could fire their bulky flame-throwers.

'My thanks, brother,' voxed Sor'khal. 'Thought I was dead.'

'What happened?' asked Lothar, as he staggered to join them. Kordus calmly shot another ork through the throat as it burst into view.

'This storm,' replied the Raven Guard. 'Fell. Climbed. Not really the time for long explanations.'

'I concur,' cut in Gorrvan, 'you need to exfiltrate. Augur shows ork tanks moving up the bridge in great force.'

'Well let us in then, brother!'

'Negative, Brother Redfang. There is a duct hatch beneath the snow about five metres to your left. Enter there, it will be quicker. I will finish setting the timer then catch you up.'

'Understood,' grated Cantos. 'Get those guns firing the moment we're clear.'

A rune flashed on their auto-senses, as Gorrvan showed his brothers their exit route. While Kordus laid down covering fire and Sor'khal busied himself with Cantos's wounds, Lothar swiftly dug down and hauled open the heavy hatch. A dark tunnel lay below, and the Fenrisian winced.

'Like crawling down a troll's gullet,' he muttered. Then he loudly announced, 'Who's first?'

'Go,' ordered Cantos, 'Sor'khal and I will follow. Kordus, rearguard.' Lothar nodded, then dropped into the hole. As he did so he saw Kordus blazing away while Sor'khal helped Cantos to his feet. This was his pack, he thought with a surprised surge of pride, these and Gorrvan. He heard his brothers drop down behind, heard the hatch clang down, then the sudden roar of the servitor guns opening fire at last. The tunnel shook and dust trickled with each heavy concussion.

'Twenty minutes,' voxed Gorrvan. 'Move, brothers.'

Some minutes later, Lothar emerged from the tunnel's exit amid a ruin that flanked the bridge on the eastern bank. The place had been gutted by fire, but it was cover, and there were no orks inside. He could hear them without, voices raised in warcries. The storm was lessening, and the servitor guns of the stronghold thundered in the distance as the orks poured across the bridge and into their fire.

Sor'khal emerged behind him, still aiding Cantos, and Kordus jogged from the shadowed tunnel a moment later.

'Gorrvan?' asked Cantos. Lothar shook his head.

'Brother Gorrvan,' voxed Cantos. 'Location?'

'Stronghold command chamber, sergeant,' came the reply. Sor'khal swore. Cantos closed his eyes. Lothar, meanwhile, lunged back towards the tunnel exit, only to be physically restrained by Kordus.

'By the Allfather, Gorrvan, what're you thinking?' yelled Lothar.

'It was the storm, brothers. Remote detonation was impossible while it persisted.'

'So you stayed to do it manually.' Sergeant Cantos's tone was weary.

'Confirmed. Meteorological augury indicated when the storm would abate. I simply fed that data to your helm chrons.'

'So get out now!' urged Sor'khal.

'Negative, brother. Five servitor guns are dry.' Gorrvan's words were punctuated for a moment by the choppy roar of his bolter. 'The greenskins have breached the east wing, and several have already reached this chamber. If I leave, detonation is uncertain. Logic dictates that I stay.' For a moment, silence fell, then Cantos opened his vox again.

'Your sacrifice will be remembered, Brother Gorrvan. Your Chapter will be notified.'

'Thank you, sergeant. I calculate that you still possess an eighty-two per cent chance of mission success. Please prove me correct.'

'We'll kill him for you, brother,' growled Lothar. 'I swear it on the Fang.'

'Again, Brother Lothar, my tha–'

And then, like a new sun dawning among the Atrophon snows, the plasma charges went up. A monstrous flash of light came first, followed by a thunderous roar that grew louder and louder. The blast wave rolled out, causing the ruin to shake violently and rubble to crash down around them. As one, the Space Marines were thrown from their feet, the earth shaking furiously beneath them. A vast fireball rose skyward, wreckage raining down around it. The brothers of the Kill Team clung to the juddering ground as their shelter came apart and toppled down upon them like an avalanche. For a while detonations continued, accompanied by the monolithic roar of the bridge collapsing into the Strakk.

Then it was finally over.

A short while later, rubble shifted on the east bank of the Strakk. With groans of exertion, the surviving brothers of the Deathwatch heaved fallen masonry off of themselves, clambering bloody and bruised into the smoky daylight. Blackened ork corpses lay everywhere, many crushed under chunks of ferrocrete or scrap metal. Here and there, flaming wreckage still blazed, and ash swirled thick in the midst of the snow. Lothar stared at the destruction they'd wrought.

'Impressive…' he breathed.

The span of the bridge still rose from the east bank, but it terminated a little way out across the river. Most of it had been vaporised, or devoured by the hungry Strakk. Now, two stubs of bridge jutted from opposite banks, severed cables swinging and creaking in the wind.

'Not an ork left alive,' noted Sor'khal. Cantos, his wounds patched for now, stepped painfully up next to him.

Lothar lowered his gaze for a moment. 'Our brother shall have a seat in the Allfather's feasting hall, eh?'

Cantos nodded grimly.

'Indeed. There'll be scattered survivors, but the Imperial lines are safe. Gorrvan would be pleased, may the Omnissiah keep him.'

Kordus tested his jump pack's engines, nodding with satisfaction as they burned steady again.

'More likely, Gorrvan would lecture us on the inefficiency of standing around talking.'

Lothar chuckled.

'You're right. Come on, brothers, we've an ork to kill, and only four hours left to do it in.'

'And some glory to win?' offered Cantos with a wry smile.

'No, sergeant,' replied Lothar, showing his fangs, 'not glory. Revenge.'

Cantos nodded. 'Revenge then. Brothers, for Gorrvan.'

Filled with new resolve, the brothers of the Deathwatch struck out into the snow, making for the outskirts of the factorum district. Somewhere ahead lay their quarry. At their backs, the falling flakes erased their footprints as they vanished into the white.

MISSION: ANNIHILATE

GAV THORPE

'And you didn't think it was worth checking the signal before starting the countdown, brother-captain?' Haryk Thunderfang's bass rumble was tinged with disappointment rather than anger. The Space Wolf looked around the chamber, the glow from his eye lenses reflecting off cobalt-like stone, glittering along silvery circuitry inlays that covered every surface.

'The mission is more important than our survival, Haryk,' replied Artemis, brother-captain of the Deathwatch, leader of the kill-team. 'The necron tomb complex's destruction is our only concern.'

'I find it more problematic that we were capable of teleporting in with the cyclotronic detonator, but are now incapable of getting out. How could we be blocked from teleporting one way?' The question came from Lavestus, seconded to the Deathwatch from the White Consuls.

'I don't think we were a threat until we teleported in,' said Sekor. The youngest, he was often left behind to pilot the Thunderhawk gunship, but on this occasion they had teleported directly from their ship, *Fatal Redress*.

'Another explanation is that this part of the tomb complex is shielded from teleporting, which is why we landed half a kilometre from our target coordinates. We head back to the landing point.' Artemis strode back towards the trapezoid doorway through which they had entered, the door turned to steaming slag by a melta bomb a few minutes earlier.

'Let's get going then,' said Haryk, hefting his plasma reaper.

Ahead of the Space Wolf, Artemis took a step into the passageway and then stopped. A scratching sound echoed down the triangular corridor. Something glittered in the distance just as a noise like a rusty blade being pulled down a metal plate assaulted the ears of the Space Marines.

'Scarabs!' Artemis had only time to bark the warning before a tide of small, multi-limbed metal beetles, each the size of his hand, poured towards him, scuttling along floor and walls with equal ease.

Opening fire with metal storm rounds, the kill-team blew away the first swathe of necron constructs, but more followed, their metallic mandibles clicking open and closed, compound-lensed eyes glowing green with alien energy. They advanced into the swarm, weapons spitting destruction.

'We're going to run out of time,' said Sekor. The chrono-display had counted down below three minutes.

'Attack! Cut through them!' Artemis combined command with action, drawing his power sword to slash through a handful of constructs. He stepped into the gap he had cleaved, firing his bolt pistol to destroy more scarabs.

Haryk joined the brother-captain and opened fire with the plasma reaper. A storm of blasts streamed along the passageway, each tiny star miniscule compared to the bolt of a normal plasma gun, but still enough to punch through the armoured carapace of a scarab with ease. The whine of energy cells recharging replaced the skittering of metal claws.

'Quickly, they will return soon enough,' said Artemis, breaking into a run along the empty corridor.

The walls started to shine, a sickly yellow glow streaming along what Artemis had thought to be veins in the rock. By this dim light he could see mechanoid skeletons entombed within the material itself, rictus-faced skulls grinning at him from the depths.

'We were wrong,' said Sekor. 'This pyramid complex isn't guarding a subterranean tomb. It is the tomb!'

'Even better that it will soon be nothing more than a cloud of ash and particles, Emperor be praised,' replied Lavestus.

They burst into the octagonal hall where they had first teleported into the tomb. It was nearly a hundred metres across and fifty high. One wall was dissolving. The blue stone slewed away to reveal shaft after shaft filled with scarabs. Awakening artificial eyes bathed the black armour of the Deathwatch warriors with a jade glow.

Artemis tried to lock on to the teleport signal again, but his attempt was met by a dull growl from the teleport homer and a smear of nonsense across the display affixed to his right wrist. He took a moment to gauge what was happening as the others opened fire on the swarm of constructs pouring out of the wall towards them. Past the flicker of plasma charges and metal storm bolts,

Artemis noticed something was amiss. The scarabs were not trying to attach themselves to the Deathwatch members. From past records, he knew that scarabs often clung to their victims and detonated themselves, destroying both. Why were they not doing the same?

'Does this seem at all familiar?' said Haryk, blasting apart half a dozen scarabs with a burst of plasma. 'I mean, a countdown that is going to destroy us all, fighting against an alien terror waking up around us?'

'Shut up, Haryk,' said Artemis, trying to concentrate.

He noticed that many of the constructs were not attacking, but were slipping past the Space Marines to disappear down one of the other corridors. A few were heading towards the cyclotronic device.

'Keep them away from the detonator, I have a theory,' Artemis told his companions, setting off after the errant scarabs. The small constructs ignored him as he pounded past, crushing them underfoot.

Less than a hundred metres long, the passage opened up into another tomb chamber. The scarabs hurled themselves at a wall, blowing themselves up to shatter the azure blocks. Amongst them was something a lot larger, several times the mass of Artemis. It floated just above the ground, six bulky legs curled up beneath it, two more limbs extended towards the far wall where green energy beams sliced through the stone-like substance.

Looking past, Artemis saw something within the structure of the tomb, taller and wider than the necron warriors they had passed earlier. Through the diminishing layers of protective cobalt, his gaze met a trio of glowing eyes. He felt a strange moment of connection to the ancient buried thing; they despised each other in equal measure.

Checking his teleport homer, Artemis realised that the jamming signal was emanating from the spider-like construct, which was continuing to ignore him in its efforts to cut free the necron commander. He ejected his bolt pistol's magazine and slammed in kraken penetrator rounds. Lining up his shots, he fired six times, every bolt punching into the mechanical arachnid between head and body. Sparks flew as it fell to the ground, smaller eruptions jerking its body from within.

'The signal!' crowed Sekor. 'It's back.'

'Fatal Redress, evac teleport, now!' barked Artemis.

With shards of stone crashing to the floor around it, the necron lord erupted from its sarcophagus. Artemis fired his pistol. The bolt clanged from the forehead of the necron commander, leaving a bright scar in the living metal.

'Stay dead this time,' he growled. A moment later, a soul-wrenching sickness churned in his stomach and the world disappeared.

As Artemis was deposited on the strike vessel above Norantis XIX, the tomb complex was engulfed by a sphere of plasma and nuclear fire.

THE INFINITE TABLEAU

ANTHONY REYNOLDS

One of them was about to die.

They stood at the epicentre of the battle, beneath a sky that was burning, and it seemed as though time stood still. The black-armoured paragon of humanity brought a golden-winged power sword around in a crackling two-handed killing strike. His pale face was twisted in hatred, and his eyes were tinged red with blood-rage. Despite the thickness of his enemy's bull-like neck, the blow was perfectly timed, delivered with all his gen-hanced and armour-augmented strength.

His opponent was a hulking, green-skinned monster that stood over two and half metres tall. It lived only for battle and knew – nay, cared for – nothing else. It roared as it swung its chugging chain-glaive around in a brutal arc, a blow that could carve the Space Marine clean in two.

Either blow would be mortal if it landed. Both would land within a single heartbeat.

One of them was about to die.

His rage was a vile, black thing dwelling deep within him. His force of will kept it coiled and bound for now, but it was growing stronger day by day, year by year. He knew that there would come a day when it *would* overcome him. All that would be left was the beast within.

Today would not be that day.

He repeated it to himself silently, like a mantra. *Today is not that day.* He forced himself to unclench his fists, and took a deep breath. The anger always came when he felt trapped, or when he felt that his fate was not his own to direct.

The gunship shuddered, but not from incoming fire. The native-born called the scouring winds that whipped across the ice floes the *skree-tha* – the witch-howling. He could understand why. Even enclosed within the ceramite-reinforced shell of the gunship, the roar of the straining engines was drowned out by the screaming, banshee wail outside.

The winds buffeted them hard, slamming the craft from side to side as they hurtled over the vast, empty expanse of ice. It lifted them sharply, threatening to rip the gunship's wings off, before pulling them down, dragging the nose towards the ice floe below.

'Cassiel,' said a voice behind him. It was Tanaka. 'Will you not sit?'

Cassiel did not reply. Nor did he make to return to his restraint harness. He could feel the White Scar's reproachful gaze upon his back, but he ignored it. Had he remained seated, his anger would have blossomed.

He filled the doorway of the gunship's cockpit, his already oversized frame made more massive still by his black power armour. One shoulder pad was dull silver and bore the Inquisition's iconography. The other was blood red, and had the heraldry of his Chapter – the Blood Angels – sculpted in bas-relief upon its curved surface.

Cassiel peered over the shoulder of the ship's pilot, his expression dark. He had taken up the position as soon as they had entered the moon's atmosphere. He'd been unable to bear being restrained any longer.

'We are nearing the distress beacon, sir,' said the gunship pilot, his voice crackling through into Cassiel's earpiece. Despite their close proximity, the howling gale made the vox necessary.

'How long?' said Cassiel.

'Two minutes.'

Cassiel looked over his shoulder, back into the red-lit gloom of the gunship's hold. Twelve black-clad storm troopers were seated back there, strapped in tightly. They were elite soldiers, trained from childhood to serve the Ordo Xenos. Their bodies had been enhanced, making them bigger, stronger and faster than regular humans. Nevertheless, they were dwarfed by Cassiel and the other two members of his kill-team.

'Two minutes to touchdown,' Cassiel said, his words being relayed into the ear of every soldier onboard. 'Be ready.'

'We should be able to see the ship any moment now,' said the pilot. 'There.'

Cassiel leaned forward, brushing a strand of dark blond hair back from his eyes. The storm made it almost impossible to see anything at all beyond the ice-fogged cockpit. Everything was a swirling wall of white.

Then he saw what the human pilot's augmented vision had

picked out a moment earlier: a dark, bug-like shuttle crouched low on the ice. It was just a shadow at first, but solidified as the gunship drew in close. It was half-buried in ice and snow. Another few hours, and it would be completely hidden.

Beside the ship, he could see a dark fissure in the ice: a massive crack that extended out into the storm.

'We're here,' Cassiel said.

Cassiel was the first to step onto the ice, his black armour a stark contrast to his surroundings. How many worlds had he set foot upon now? How many foes had fallen beneath the long golden-winged blade, *Aruthel*, that he wore slung across his back? He had stopped counting long ago.

His face was as pale and cold as his surroundings. He might have resembled a classical statue, carved from pale marble, but for the trio of parallel scars that crossed his face, twisting his lips and puckering his skin; a memento of his encounter with a chameleonic xenos beast two years past.

The gale whipped at Cassiel's shoulder-length hair and the tabard draped across his armour. Ice slashed at his cheeks, and he was forced to narrow his eyes against the biting gale. He breathed in deeply. The cold was as sharp as a knife in his lungs. Without a sealed enviro-suit, an unaugmented human would have been dead within a minute in these conditions. Cassiel was far from unaugmented, however, and he made a point of breathing the air of every planet he visited, even if only for a moment.

A pair of large, black-clad figures clomped out onto the ice behind him.

Tanaka, hefting his heavy bolter, and Var'myr of the Mortifactors, his boltgun held across his chest. These were his adopted battle brothers, his kill-team.

He had fought alongside Tanaka for over a decade – they had both started their tenure with the Deathwatch at the same time. Var'myr was a newcomer, having joined the ranks of the Ordo Xenos fewer than six months ago. There had been others before him, but they were gone now: Svorgar of the Space Wolves had been decapitated by a clawed fiend on the nightworld of Jar'Mun'Gar; Ryzmor of the Carcharodons had been ripped limb from limb by the magicks of eldar witches in the ruins of Delthasur; Titus Constantine of the White Consuls had been released back to his Chapter with honour after the successful purging of Alanthus.

As much as Cassiel yearned to return to his Chapter, it was a privilege to fight alongside such esteemed warriors.

'Var'myr, scan the area.'

A servo-skull hovered at the Mortifactor's shoulder, its mechanical left eye blinking red. Once, that skull had belonged to one of his battle-brothers. They were a morbid Chapter, a fact reinforced by the bones strung across Var'myr's armour.

'Go. Seek,' the Mortifactor said, his voice deep and sombre. The servo-skull swung out into the storm, as ordered. The winds buffeted it – Cassiel heard Tanaka chuckle at the sight – but the device compensated swiftly, gyros buzzing. It commenced a wide sweep of the area, scanning and recording.

He glanced at the White Scar. Tanaka met his gaze, his dark obsidian eyes glinting with humour. His face was gnarled and weathered, the colour of tanned leather.

'I like this place,' Tanaka said, shouting to be heard above the gale and the dying whine of the gunship's engines.

'I see nothing redeemable about it,' said Var'myr.

'Bah!' said Tanaka. 'You know nothing! This cold is good. It lets you know you are still alive.'

'I know I'm alive because I *am* alive,' said Var'myr. 'I don't need the cold to tell me that.'

Var'myr assessed the skull's findings, reading from the auspex built into his left forearm. The entire arm was bionic from the shoulder down.

'The scan is clear,' he said. He snapped the data-screen back into his vambrace, and the armoured plate clicked into place around it like a shell. 'There is nothing living within a hundred kilometres, nor any heat signature or radiation. This is a dead world.'

'Lieutenant, secure a perimeter,' Cassiel ordered over the vox, and the storm troopers who had been standing by moved out onto the ice, flowing around the three Space Marines with their hellguns at the ready.

As they took up support positions, Cassiel and his brothers marched towards the silent shuttle squatting upon the ice. It was a bulbous, ugly ship resembling a fat-bodied insect. Its six articulated legs clung to the ice, and a pair of large eye-like portal-windows were positioned at the front of its 'head'. Through them, Cassiel could see three vacant seats, where the pilot, co-pilot and navigator would normally be seated. There were no lights inside.

With crisp orders, Cassiel directed Var'myr and a pair of storm troopers to search the ship while Tanaka checked the ravine.

Cassiel pulled on his helm; the slicing storm was stinging his eyes. Once he had worn a helmet of shining gold, but since his indoctrination into the Deathwatch he had worn nothing but their traditional black. Among the Blood Angels, the only warriors who wore black were the holy Chaplain-wardens of the Chapter, and the damned warriors of the Death Company.

He walked around the exterior of the shuttle, scrutinising it for signs of battle damage. The nose and wingtips were blackened, but this looked like charring from orbital entry; it had not been brought down by weapons-fire. Var'myr stepped down from the explorator vessel just as he finished his circuit.

'Nothing,' said the Mortifactor, shaking his head. His servo-skull had returned to him, and was once more hovering at his shoulder.

Var'myr fell in beside Cassiel, and the pair trudged into the wind to join the vague figure of Tanaka, standing some way off and staring into the storm. The White Scar was almost completely hidden by swirling ice that seemed to confuse even the advanced sensory arrays of Cassiel's battle plate.

'Speak your mind,' said Cassiel. Var'myr was taciturn at best, silent and sullen at worst, but in the brief time they had known each other, Cassiel felt he was beginning to learn how to read those silences.

'We should never have been sent here,' said Var'myr. 'We ought to have joined the other strike teams in the final assault. We earned that, at least.'

'Watch-Commander Haldaron felt that our presence was needed here,' said Cassiel, keeping his voice neutral. 'It is no smear on our honour.'

'It is,' said Var'myr. 'The greenskin warlord's head should have been ours to claim. By now, someone else will probably have it.'

In truth, Cassiel tended to agree, but that was not helpful.

'I would hope so,' he said, 'else the brute still lives. Put it from your mind, brother. We are here now, and we have been given our duty.'

They joined the heavy bolter wielding White Scar, standing on the edge of the immense ice fissure. Steam was rising from the gaping rift, making it impossible to gauge its depth. It was narrow, little more than two metres across at any point, and extended further than the eye could see.

'You think they went down there?' asked Cassiel.

'Where else?' replied Tanaka.

'Then that is where we shall go too.'

Var'myr sent his servo-skull down into the crack, red beams of light from its sensors scanning and documenting.

'Seismic activity opened this crack twelve days ago,' said Var'myr, tapping his data-slate. 'The whole area is unstable. There are… seventeen active volcanic rifts within an eighty-kilometre radius of this location.'

'How deep is it?' said Cassiel.

'Nine metres, here,' said Var'myr, reading the output upon his forearm screen. 'Deeper… *much* deeper further along.'

'Is the ground solid at the bottom of the fissure, just here?'

'It is.'

'Good,' said Cassiel.

'It is unstable, however,' said Var'myr. 'Another tremor could seal this crack at any moment. You are not thinking of–'

Before the Mortifactor could finish, Cassiel stepped off the ice floe, dropping silently down into the gaping fissure.

The sound of wind down in the narrow defile was even more unearthly than it was up on the ice floe, though it was out of the worst of the gale. The sheer walls of ice were a brilliant, luminous blue – the first real colour that he had seen on this moon – and almost completely transparent in places where the ice was near flawless. Steam vented up from narrower cracks underfoot.

A flurry of ice and snow fell down around him, and Tanaka landed in a crouch a half-second later. He grinned at Cassiel as he rose to his feet. Var'myr landed a moment later, amid a small avalanche of ice.

'You took your time, brother,' said Cassiel.

The Mortifactor did not deign to answer. Up above, the storm troopers were readying their rappelling lines.

'They went this way,' said Tanaka, pointing. 'But they did not come back.'

'Did your ancestors tell you that?' said Var'myr.

'The tracks on the ground tell me that.'

Cassiel led the way. In places the ice canyon was so narrow that their shoulder plates scratched deep furrows in the ice. Their progress was not swift, but after a time they came to a low opening in one of the canyon walls. Hot steam spewed from the gap.

Var'myr's servo-skull disappeared into the steam. It reappeared a moment later, its red eye blinking impatiently. Tanaka scowled at it, and it darted back into the steam like a rebuked hound. It reappeared a moment later, hanging just behind Tanaka's shoulder, and Cassiel smirked. The White Scar caught sight of it, and swore in his own, guttural dialect.

'Irritating thing,' he said, swatting at it. 'Away!'

It darted back, just out of reach. Cassiel wondered how much sentience remained within the skull – it seemed to delight in taunting the White Scar whenever possible. 'Var'myr, control your creature,' he said.

'It's just a machine,' replied the Mortifactor mildly.

'Here,' Tanaka muttered, pointing out the tell-tale marks in the ice. 'They widened the entrance with chainblades.'

'Not enough, though,' said Var'myr. Though the aperture was large enough for a regular human to get through, there was no chance that any of the three Deathwatch brothers could pass.

'Move aside,' Cassiel ordered. He would not sully *Aruthel*'s blade with such a mundane duty, nor did he need to. With a grunt he struck the ice with his gauntleted fist, dislodging a massive chunk. Within the space of a minute he had cleared an opening that he and his team could negotiate, followed a few moments later by the storm troopers.

Cassiel once again took up the lead, ice grinding against his armour. The steam made rivulets of condensation run down the lenses of his helm. Some way on, the passage opened up into an irregular cave formation, its floor at a steep angle. Ice-crystals formed by the volcanic updrafts filled the space. It was easy to see which path the explorers had taken – they merely had to follow the path of crushed crystals.

There was a surprising amount of light within the caves, even as they clambered, slid and crawled deeper beneath the ice floe. It was a diffuse, cold glow, which seemed to radiate from the very ice itself. A rumble of seismic activity shook the ground underfoot, ice fell from the slanted roof, and spider-web cracks appeared in the walls around them.

'We do not want to be here any longer than necessary,' said Cassiel, brushing melt-water from his shoulders.

Eighty metres below the ice floe, having traversed more than a kilometre from their starting point, the Space Marines came upon what the explorator team had been sent to find.

Cassiel dropped down into a large cavern, ice crunching underfoot. He was decidedly conscious of the millions of tonnes of glacier hanging above him, even more so as another ice-quake rumbled. It was groaning like a ship in the void. The walls seemed to close in, shifting and altering their position as the ice floe shuddered, and fresh cracks inched their way across the walls, clouding their previously transparent surfaces. Cassiel forced himself to breathe calmly, controlling his inner rage.

Tanaka and Var'myr joined him, dropping down into the cavern after him. It was as large as the embarkation deck of a battle-barge. The floors were uneven, rising and falling at acute angles, almost meeting the jagged ceiling in places and falling away into sheer deadfalls that sank hundreds of metres further down in others. Traversing the chamber was slow, and a clear line of sight from one side to the other was difficult, for pillars of crystal linked floor to roof and clusters of needle-like ice fanned out from wall and floor.

The storm troopers descended into the cavern in the kill-team's wake. At a silent signal from their lieutenant, they broke off into pairs, each advancing via a different route. Their training was obvious; they moved swiftly but silently, covering each other and scanning constantly for threats.

It was Var'myr who first saw it.

'Cassiel,' he said, drawing his sergeant's attention.

It was located towards the back of the cavern, jutting some four metres from the ice. The exposed section was curved and gleaming black, as if made from obsidian: a four-sided arc, like part of a large, incomplete ring. Judging by the curve of it, Cassiel guessed that the whole thing could have a diameter of over twenty metres, most of which appeared to be embedded in the ice, a dark shadow that curved away beneath their feet.

The cavern darkened considerably around it, as if the black stone were absorbing the light. Strange symbols marked its surface.

Tanaka swore in his guttural tongue.

'What is it?' asked Var'myr.

'I don't know,' said Cassiel. 'A weapon of some kind, but not one made by any human hand. Who knows how long it's been down here. Can you get a reading on it?'

'No,' said Var'myr, fingers sliding through the data relaying across his forearm-mounted auspex. 'This glacier is more than one hundred and fifty thousand years old, however.'

Cassiel shook his head. Such a timeframe was unfathomable.

'We know the Adeptus Mechanicus got this far,' he said. 'What happened to them?'

No answer was forthcoming.

The kill-team circled around the curved structure, keeping their weapons ready. There was something about it that made Cassiel's skin itch. Its geometry was somehow abhorrent; its glossy surfaces made him uneasy.

'There are some mysteries that humanity was not meant to know,' said Tanaka. 'This thing should have remained buried.'

'The entire region is becoming increasingly unstable,' said Var'myr. 'It will probably soon be buried beneath another fifty million tonnes of ice, regardless of what we do.'

'It is not enough,' said Cassiel. 'Even if it were buried at the centre of this moon, the Adeptus Mechanicus would come looking for it again, now they know it is here. They wouldn't be able to help themselves. We have to destroy it.'

'Destroy it?' said Var'myr. 'It's been down here for Guilliman knows how many tens of thousands of years. What danger can it pose?'

'Where is the explorator team, Mortifactor?' Tanaka asked, by way of an answer.

'We have to destroy it,' Cassiel said. 'We cannot trust the Mechanicus to leave this undisturbed.'

'Then let us do so, and be on our way,' said Var'myr. 'Those rumblings are becoming more frequent.'

'I thought your Chapter did not fear death, Mortifactor,' said Tanaka.

'Death, we do not fear,' said Var'myr, his voice cold. 'That does not mean that we invite it. Dying pointlessly, before one's duty is done, is a blasphemy.'

Cassiel opened up a vox-channel to the storm trooper lieutenant. 'I need the melta-charges brought forward,' he said. Even with his helm on, it was clear that Var'myr was glaring at Tanaka. And Cassiel knew the White Scar well enough to guess that he was smiling behind his own faceplate at having riled the Mortifactor.

'Tanaka,' Cassiel said. 'Help me with the charges. Var'myr, determine where to place them. I want nothing to remain of this thing.'

Cassiel turned away, paused, and turned back. 'And don't touch it.'

The White Scar fell in beside Cassiel, and the two of them clambered down towards the storm troopers picking their way through the chamber.

'Why antagonise him, brother?' Cassiel said via a closed channel. 'Is it really necessary?'

'Mortifactors,' Tanaka replied. 'They take themselves so seriously. And this one's ignorance offends me.'

'We were young once ourselves, my brother,' said Cassiel.

Tanaka laughed. 'You sound like an old man,' he said. 'Me? I'm in my prime!'

Cassiel smiled. Tanaka was one hundred and twenty-two years older than him, and looked it, with his weathered face and grey-streaked hair. His smile slipped however, and he paused, narrowing his eyes.

The ice dropped steeply away to the side of the ridge they were traversing, disappearing into a hollow. Steam billowed up from below, obscuring his sight.

'What is it?' said Tanaka, suddenly serious.

'Probably nothing,' said Cassiel. 'Go ahead. Collect the melta-charges. I'll be with you in a moment.'

Tanaka shrugged, and continued on down to meet the storm troopers. Cassiel eased himself off the side of the ridge, and climbed down into the steam, finding adequate handholds in the ice wall.

The descent was short, and soon his feet met the ground once more. Steam billowed around him, and moisture that would turn to ice as soon as he was away from the volcanic updraft beaded upon his armour.

He advanced, stepping gingerly, ensuring that the ground would take his weight before moving forward. He squinted, peering through the fog and steam.

'*Blood of Sanguinius*,' he breathed as the vapours parted.

A dozen bodies were scattered before him, half buried in the ice. Each corpse had been skinned, exposing frozen, dripping musculature. It appeared as though something had fed upon them: chunks of flesh had been torn from the bone, and entrails lay scattered. It was clear to Cassiel from the tortured poses, silent screams and anguished expressions on skinless faces that these horrors had been enacted while these people were still alive.

He saw an iron cog-wheel embedded in the forehead of one of the tortured bodies – the holy symbol of the Adeptus Mechanicus. He'd found the missing explorators.

That was when the screaming began.

Cassiel was up the sheer cliff in an instant, barely touching it. His long blade *Aruthel* was unsheathed, humming with power. He didn't even remember drawing it.

Two detonations echoed through the cavern. Bolter fire.

'Lieutenant, pull your soldiers back and regroup,' he ordered. 'Kill-team, to me.'

Another scream. Cassiel broke into a run, drawing his ornate bolt pistol as he rushed towards the piteous cry. He saw blood spray across an angled wall of ice. More than one of the storm troopers was down. Cassiel strained to locate a target as he ran.

There. Target lock.

A hunched thing of tortured flesh and blood, hands ending in half-metre talons slick with gore. It ripped open the throat of a storm trooper, unleashing a fresh torrent of red. It pressed its face into the gushing fountain – drinking, or perhaps just revelling in the sensation.

It was an easy mark, even at a run.

Cassiel's bolt pistol barked. Two shots struck the target, one in the back, one at the base of the neck. Those detonations should have ripped the creature – man? – to pieces, but they did not. Its flesh was torn, exposing dark metal bones.

Sprawling, the creature righted itself and swung towards him with a snarl. Its face was a dull metal skull draped in dead flesh. Its eye sockets were hollow pits, dark and fathomless, but tiny pinpricks of light lay deep within them, like cold green stars glinting in the void. Gore caked its jaw. Viscera dripped from its hollow ribcage.

A necron warrior, then, but like none that Cassiel had ever encountered before.

More of the creatures were among the storm troopers spread throughout the cavern, ripping and tearing. Shouts and screams echoed in the gloom. Hellguns whined as they powered up, then barked as their power was unleashed, sending angry red beams cutting across the open space. He heard Var'myr open fire again, and Tanaka incanting a tribal war-chant before his heavy bolter ripped across the cavern in a ceaseless stream of fire.

Cassiel quickly closed the distance with his foe. It was edging towards him, moving on all fours like a beast. He fired on it again as he ran. The bolt slammed it onto its back – its chest was a blackened ruin, but its metallic ribcage still held. Cassiel sprang off an uneven ice-boulder, leaping high, *Aruthel* humming in his hands. He came down on top of the deathly creature, landing with one knee upon its chest, buckling it inwards. He drove his blade into the beast's cranium, forcing it deep. It gargled a death rattle, and the pinpricks of light in its empty sockets faded.

A scream came from nearby and he spun, whipping *Aruthel* free. A storm trooper had fallen to one knee, and blood was pooling beneath him. Another of the skeletal creatures draped in dead, frozen flesh was hauling itself up from the ice beneath the Ordo Xenos soldier, its talons hooked into the man's leg.

Sheathing his blade, Cassiel took two bounding steps and grabbed the bloodied necron around its neck, hauling it off the stricken trooper. It thrashed like a feral beast, lashing at Cassiel with its talons.

Using his forward momentum, Cassiel slammed it against an ice wall, sending out a spread of cracks across its surface. He forced the creature's head back and sent a bolt from his pistol up into its metallic brainpan. He released his hold on it, and it flopped to the ground, broken, its skull a ruin of twisted metal.

He turned away, scanning for fresh targets.

He made to re-enter the fray when one of the creatures leapt onto his back, spitting and snarling, its talons slashing at his collar. While it could not breach his armoured plates, the flexible fibre-bundles at his joints – and his neck – were not so well protected. Razored claws sliced through to his flesh, carving deep into his shoulder.

Cassiel threw it off with a curse, warning icons flashing before his eyes. He didn't feel any pain. All he felt was the urge to kill – the urge to taste blood, though the creature had none to shed.

It was the one that he had just put down: its ruptured skull was reknitting itself, flowing like liquid silver back into its original form. Cassiel gripped *Aruthel* in both hands and carved the blade in at its neck. It raised its bladed claws to ward off the blow, but all it achieved was to lose both hands, along with its head. Cassiel kicked the metal cranium away.

'Beware,' he said across an open channel. 'They are self-repairing. Their fallen rise again.'

The foul creatures were setting upon the corpses of the storm troopers – and those who were not yet dead – ripping and tearing. Their talons eagerly sliced away the soldiers' carapace armour, exposing the flesh within, and they tore into it with relish, expertly flensing skin from muscle and bone. Others buried their faces in stomach cavities and throats, snapping and jerking. They snarled and spat at each other, like wild animals fighting over the spoils.

Cassiel snapped off a pair of angry shots, smashing two of the feeding beasts back. The others seemed oblivious or uncaring of the danger, intent on gorging themselves... though they were creatures of little more than metal and malice, with no flesh to feed. Every chunk of meat they swallowed simply flopped, wet and glistening, from their hollow ribcages to the ice, yet they seemed driven by an insatiable, ravenous hunger. It was obscene.

The ice cracked beneath his feet, and a taloned hand shot up and locked around his leg. Swivelling *Aruthel* in one hand into a downward grip, Cassiel thrust the blade down into the ice, skewering the creature's head even before it had emerged.

More of the creatures were appearing, and those that fell simply rejoined the savage attack moments later, their mortal injuries repaired. The storm troopers were being butchered. The survivors had formed a tight knot of defiance in the centre of the cavern, dragging the wounded with them. The storm trooper lieutenant was at their centre, barking orders and snapping off shots with her hellpistol. Cassiel saw her die a moment later, yanked to the ground with her throat torn out, and he cursed.

Cassiel felt torn. Part of him desperately wanted to pull his team out, to save those soldiers who still drew breath. Duty was his life, however. It had been built into his genes. The mission was paramount.

'We must finish this,' he barked.

The Blood Angels sergeant moved through the slaughter with a grace that belied his size. Spinning, wielding his blade in a two-handed grip, he cut the legs from beneath one of the deathly creatures rushing at him frenziedly. Still turning, he sliced the blade through the torso of another, carving it neatly in two. *Aruthel* sang a keening wail as it sliced through the air.

Briefly free of assailants, Cassiel joined the knot of storm troopers and took up a position at their fore. Tanaka joined him, walking steadily backwards, his heavy bolter coughing death. Each controlled burst of fire smashed the enemy backwards, and Cassiel saw metal limbs shorn from bodies, yet even that damage was being repaired.

'Something is happening,' said Tanaka, in between bursts.

'I see it,' growled Cassiel.

Beneath their feet, green light was glowing up through the ice. It was coming from the black xenos structure that curved underneath them.

One of the creatures leapt at Cassiel from a ledge above, talons extended to impale him. Before he could raise his weapon, a kraken bolt struck it from the side and its skull disintegrated into shards of metal. Cassiel looked up to see Var'myr staring down his smoking bolter from his position up at the curved black obelisk. He nodded his thanks, and the Mortifactor inclined his head in acknowledgement. Cassiel saw several fallen creatures around Var'myr's position, and another pinned beneath his boot, thrashing wildly. The Mortifactor had not been idle.

Cassiel's gaze was drawn to the black obelisk behind Var'myr. Green light was spilling from the glyphs and symbols upon its surface.

'Var'myr,' said Cassiel. 'Fall back.'

The Mortifactor bent down towards the screeching, flailing creature trapped beneath his boot. He grasped its skull in one huge hand and, with a violent wrench, tore it loose.

'A keepsake,' he declared as he stood upright.

Then he shuddered, and the metal skull slipped from his fingers.

A glowing blade of green light emerged from Var'myr's chest, transfixing him. Then the blade was sharply retracted, and Var'myr slid to his knees.

A towering being stood behind the fallen Mortifactor. It was as different from the hunched, flesh-wearing creatures as night was from day. Tall and broad-shouldered, it would have loomed over even Cassiel and the tallest of his Chapter brothers. Its skeletal limbs were a gleaming silver and it was decked in heavy plates of black obsidian. It carried a three-metre halberd ending in a humming blade of pure energy. With a swift motion, it brought the weapon around in a lethal arc, and took off Var'myr's head.

'No!' bellowed Cassiel.

The air behind the deathly metal being shimmered and distorted, and more armoured figures materialised. The nature of the curved obelisk was now clear. It was not a weapon, as Cassiel had suspected at first, but something far worse.

It was a *gateway*.

Five of the elite, armour-clad beings stood up there now. They bore a mix of energy-bladed halberds and one-handed axes, though their blades were similar, made of nothing more than crackling energy.

Var'myr's servo-skull hovered just above the Mortifactor's corpse, its red eye flickering. Then it too was cut down, carved in two by an energy blade.

The air shimmered, like silver-dust catching the light, and a final figure appeared, materialising within their protective cordon. It was a creature of alien, yet undeniably regal, bearing.

This newcomer was stooped, and its protectors towered over it, yet it exuded a palpable aura of dominance. It wore a cloak of golden scales and a gleaming cowl, and its ribcage was armoured in polished ebony. Its skeletal limbs were bound in circlets of gold and obsidian and covered in xenos hieroglyphs, and it leaned upon a golden staff topped with a flaring winged icon pulsing with viridian radiance.

It stared around its surroundings, craning its neck one way then the other, like a vulture. Its gaze swept across the ice cavern before settling upon Cassiel. It held his gaze, eyes burning with deathless, pitiless fire. It croaked something indecipherable, speaking in a language that had already been dead a million years before the birth of humanity. It was the voice of the crypt, conjuring images of dust and dry sands. This was no unthinking automaton, Cassiel realised. This was an impossibly ancient being, filled with bitterness and anger, bound within a shell of metal.

The creature jabbed a skeletal finger in the Blood Angel's direction, and spoke again in its dead language. Tall shields of glowing green light sprang to life upon the off-weapon arms of the axe-wielding guardians, and they stepped to the fore, forming a protective shield wall.

Then, as one, the necrons began to advance.

Cassiel's rage was threatening to overwhelm him, and he struggled to control it. It would be so easy to give in…

His vision began to cloud, a reddish tinge over everything he saw, and the pounding of his hearts – his secondary beating now, too – drowned out all else. His lips curled back, and had he not been wearing his black-painted helm, his elongated canines would have been exposed.

Var'myr's blood, spreading from his headless corpse, was almost painfully bright. Everything else was as nothing… except for his foes. He glared at the advancing xenos warriors, and a shameful, animal growl rumbled from his vox-grille. His grip tightened on the haft of his blade as he prepared to attack.

No.

He must remain in control. His duty demanded it.

He forced himself to breathe deeply, and forcibly loosened his grip on the blade. The red haze began to clear, though it hung around the fringes of his vision, ready to descend again at any moment. The black tendrils of his hatred recoiled, temporarily, and once more it retreated to its lair. Its time would come.

'Storm troopers,' he growled. 'Be ready. My brother and I will hold them. Split, and get around behind them. Use the charges. Destroy that gateway.'

'How do we hold them?' asked Tanaka.

'We kill them.'

'Yes. That would do it.'

At Cassiel's direction, the storm troopers divided into two groups, each carrying a case of demolition charges, and they peeled off to each flank.

Cassiel glanced over at his White Scar brother, the last of his kill-team.

'Ready?' he said.

In answer, the White Scar planted his feet wide and brought his heavy bolter around to bear, the built-in suspensors steadying his aim. Squeezing and holding the trigger, he unleashed a blazing torrent of fire. It was virtually a solid stream of large-calibre bolts he sent roaring across the ice cavern, and the sound was deafening.

Tanaka's onslaught tore across the enemy, but their advance did not slow. The shield bearers at their fore tightened their formation, shields interlocking as the heavy bolter fire hammered into them. The shimmering barrier flashed brightly as each heavy bolter round struck, absorbing their energy, creating a flickering strobe as shot after shot rained upon them. Each shot rebounded off this seemingly impenetrable wall, hurled away with the same velocity as it was delivered. Heavy bolter rounds ricocheted across the ice cavern, filling the air.

One round skimmed just over the rim of one of the shields and took one of the foes in the head. The resultant detonation demolished its skull, and it fell heavily. Its brethren gave it no mind, simply stepping over the body to continue their relentless march. A moment later, it rose again.

The necrons altered the angle of their shields, and the warriors of the Ordo Xenos suddenly found Tanaka's stream of bolter fire being redirected back at them.

Cassiel was struck in the shoulder, half spinning him, and other rounds screamed by him, missing by scant centimetres.

He turned his head instinctively, registering an incoming bolt a fraction of a second before it took him between the eyes. It still struck a glancing blow, and the resulting detonation ruined his vision in a haze of grainy static, and kicked his neck to one side.

He tore his helmet off. The whole left hemisphere was a mess of torn metal and fractured ceramite, and his left eye lens was shattered. He could feel blood trickling down his temple. He cast the ruined helm aside.

The head of one of the storm troopers disappeared in a red mist, and another was torn bodily in two as a stream of fire cut through his midsection.

Tanaka cut off his volley with an anguished cry, aghast at the carnage he had wrought. No storm trooper had been left standing. Their blood was sprayed across the ice.

One of the flesh-wearers took its opportunity, leaping upon the White Scar as he stared in horror at the dead. He tried to raise his weapon, but he was too slow and the creature too close. It thrust its talons into his faceplate. Two of the blades smashed straight through his visor lenses, driving deep into his brain. He died instantly, slumping to the ground.

Cassiel roared, his fury surging to the surface, and this time he made no attempt to quash it. He hurled his bolt pistol aside and hacked into Tanaka's killer with his blade. His lips drew back in a snarl, exposing his dagger-like canines and he tasted blood on his lips. His blade rose and fell, hacking and slicing. Only when the creature was rendered into a dozen separate sections did he stop. Even then, those parts quivered on the ice, pulling themselves back together, but Cassiel gave it no more thought. He lifted his reddened gaze, breathing heavily, and focused on the xenos lord and his phalanx of guardians.

He closed the distance quickly, his fury lending him speed. Twenty metres. Fifteen. Ten. He gripped his long blade in a double-handed grip, drawing it back for a powerful strike.

He sprang lightly off one foot, angling his leap to take him slightly to the side and past the closest guardian's shield. He turned in the air as he leapt, and rather than bringing his blade around in arc, he drove it down in a powerful two-handed thrust. It sank deep, driven down behind his enemy's armoured ribcage. Cassiel swiftly withdrew the blade, pulling it free even before his feet had touched the ground.

He instantly threw himself into a roll as a glowing-bladed halberd swung out, humming through the air. It passed harmlessly above him, and he rammed *Aruthel* up into his would-be killer as he rose. The blade punched up under the ribcage, thrusting up through its body. The tip burst from the top of its metal cranium, green sparks dancing wildly along its length. He yanked the blade free and the creature collapsed.

He lifted the sword in a horizontal parry, sensing rather than seeing a blow coming at him from behind. His blade crackled and gave off the smell of ozone as it met the downward strike of an energy halberd. The force of the blow drove him to his knees, but he was up in a second, snarling and spitting, stepping in close.

Still holding his blade two-handed, he slammed its pommel up into his opponent's skull twice in quick succession, jerking its head back but doing little real damage. It backhanded him across the side of his face, sending him sprawling.

With an animalistic snarl, Cassiel rose, swinging his blade around in a lethal arc. One of the warriors that he had already dropped was rising once more, its damage self-repairing. He chopped its legs out from under it and rammed *Aruthel* down into its skull as it toppled to the ground. An energy shield slammed into him, shocking him and sending him stumbling. An overhead blow came crashing down upon him. Cassiel took it upon his blade before ripping around in a screaming arc, neatly cutting the creature in two.

He stood before the xenos lord now, having fought his way in behind its guardians. It glared at him with its baleful green orbs. A burst of mechanised sound emerged from its throat. It took a moment for Cassiel to realise that it was laughing at him.

It stepped forward, thrusting its staff at his chest. Cassiel batted the blow aside and lunged, the move perfectly timed. His blade slid between the lord's slit of a mouth, silencing its ugly laughter. With a roar, he pressed forward, using all his strength and weight to ram *Aruthel* home until the hilt struck its face, a full metre and a half of blade protruding out from the back of its neck.

Even as the light died in the xenos being's eyes, its appearance changed. Its body grew larger in stature, heavy armoured plates appearing on its shoulders and chest, and the shape of its cranium altering. Before Cassiel's eyes, its metal physiology had morphed into that of one of its bodyguards.

'What–' he began, startled by this unexpected transformation.

He felt the hairs on the back of his neck stiffen, and there was a crackling sound behind him.

A blow struck him squarely in the back, accompanied by a sound akin to a thunderclap.

He was slammed flat, twitching involuntarily. Green-tinged lightning danced across his armour. He struggled to push himself to his feet, but his muscles were convulsing uncontrollably, and he could not rise.

The xenos lord stood behind him. It had taken over the body of another of its bodyguards and stood now in its place, looking down upon him, croaking its ugly laughter.

One of the guardians, newly reformed from the damage Cassiel had wrought upon it, stepped forward with its blade ready. The xenos lord barked something in its indecipherable dead language, and the guardian halted, warily. Hunched and cowled, the lord shuffled in, leaning over Cassiel, regarding him closely.

It was so close that he could see the intricate circuitry behind its armoured ribcage, and smell its repugnant stink, a strange mix of battery acid, oil and dust. *Aruthel* lay on the ice, just half a metre away. He could kill this abomination in an instant, he was sure, and he strained to regain control of his body. The convulsions were passing. His fingers twitched, and the veins in his neck bulged.

With a roar, he shot his hand out and grabbed the blade.

He was too slow, however. The ancient xenos placed its hand upon his chest, skeletal metal fingers spread wide. A pulse of energy passed into Cassiel's body. He gasped, his eyes wide – in that instant, Cassiel's twin hearts ceased to beat, and his breathing halted.

'You... are... *mine*,' the necron lord said, his hand still upon the fallen Space Marine's chest.

One of them was about to die.

They stood at the epicentre of the battle, beneath a sky that was burning, and it seemed as though time stood still. The black-armoured paragon of humanity brought a golden-winged power sword around in a crackling two-handed killing strike. His pale face was twisted in hatred, and his eyes were tinged red with blood-rage. Despite the thickness of his enemy's bull-like neck, the blow was perfectly timed, delivered with all his genhanced and armour-augmented strength.

His opponent was a hulking green skinned monster that stood over two and half metres tall. It lived only for battle and knew – nay, cared for – nothing else. It roared as it swung its chugging chain-glaive around in a brutal arc, a blow that could carve the Space Marine clean in two.

Either blow would be mortal if it landed. Both would land within a single heartbeat.

But that heartbeat would never come.

Trazyn the Infinite stepped between the two frozen combatants, inspecting his latest acquisition. He peered into the Space Marine's eyes. Life blazed there, along with a frenzied, insane fury. He knew that the enhanced human creature could see him. He knew that its conscious mind still remained, trapped forever within the prison of its own body. If it were not so, then his display would be lacking.

Satisfied, he shuffled across the battlefield, past hundreds more frozen statues, each carefully positioned as per his grand design. Some were firing weapons or swinging blades. Others were dying, trapped forever in the moment of their deaths. It was glorious.

The holographic burning sky and the red-sanded earth flickered as he reached the edge of the display. Once again he stood upon the gleaming obsidian deck of his infinite gallery.

Trazyn strode away, his staff clicking sharply with each step. He walked his halls, past countless other displays with primitive creatures of every description, breed and race; all arrayed and carefully posed; all living, trapped until the end of time. He passed beings that had died out half a million years earlier – some whose loss was mourned by the galaxy at large, and others that had simply disappeared without note.

There were hundreds of displays on this deck alone, many of them far grander than his latest, humble effort. Thousands more decks lay above and below.

Trazyn gave them no more thought. His mind was already moving on to his next project.

He rubbed his metal hands in glee. It would be a masterpiece.

ABOUT THE AUTHORS

Steve Parker is the author of the Warhammer 40,000 novels *Deathwatch*, *Rynn's World*, *Gunheads* and *Rebel Winter*, along with the novella *Survivor* and a plethora of short stories featuring the Deathwatch kill-team Talon Squad, the Crimson Fists and various Astra Militarum regiments. He lives and works in Scotland.

Andy Chambers is the author of the Path of the Dark Eldar series and the related novella *The Masque of Vyle*, along with the Necromunda novel *Survival Instinct* and a host of short stories. He has more than twenty years' experience creating worlds dominated by war machines, spaceships and dangerous aliens. He lives and works in Nottingham.

Chris Wraight is the author of the Horus Heresy novels *Scars* and *The Path of Heaven*, the Primarchs novel *Leman Russ: The Great Wolf*, the novella *Brotherhood of the Storm* and the audio drama *The Sigillite*. For Warhammer 40,000 he has written *Vaults of Terra: The Carrion Throne*, *Watchers of the Throne: The Emperor's Legion*, the Space Wolves novels *Blood of Asaheim* and *Stormcaller*, and the short story collection *Wolves of Fenris*, as well as the Space Marine Battles novels *Wrath of Iron* and *Battle of the Fang*. Additionally, he has many Warhammer novels to his name, including the Time of Legends novel *Master of Dragons*. Chris lives and works near Bristol, in south-west England.

Nick Kyme is the author of the Horus Heresy novels *Deathfire*, *Vulkan Lives*, and *Sons of the Forge*, the novellas *Promethean Sun* and *Scorched Earth*, and the audio dramas *Censure* and *Red-Marked*. His novella *Feat of Iron* was a *New York Times* bestseller in the Horus Heresy collection, *The Primarchs*. Nick is well known for his popular Salamanders novels, including *Rebirth* and the Tome of Fire trilogy, the Space Marine Battles novel *Damnos*, and numerous short stories. He has also written fiction set in the world of Warhammer, most notably the Time of Legends novel *The Great Betrayal* and the Age of Sigmar story 'Borne by the Storm', included in the novel *Warstorm*. He lives and works in Nottingham, and has a rabbit.

Ian St. Martin has written the Warhammer 40,000 novels *Lucius: The Faultless Blade* and *Deathwatch: Kryptman's War*, along with the short stories 'Adeptus Titanicus: Hunting Ground', 'City of Ruin' and 'In Wolves' Clothing' for Black Library. He lives and works in Washington DC, caring for his cat and reading anything within reach.

Braden Campbell is the author of *Shadowsun: The Last of Kiru's Line* for Black Library, as well as the novella *Tempestus*, and several short stories. He is a classical actor and playwright, and a freelance writer, particularly in the field of role playing games. Braden has enjoyed Warhammer 40,000 for nearly a decade, and remains fiercely dedicated to his dark eldar.

Ben Counter has two Horus Heresy novels to his name – *Galaxy in Flames* and *Battle for the Abyss*. He is the author of the Soul Drinkers series and *The Grey Knights Omnibus*. For Space Marine Battles, he has written *The World Engine* and *Malodrax*, and has turned his attention to the Space Wolves with the novella *Arjac Rockfist: Anvil of Fenris* as well as a number of short stories. He is a fanatical painter of miniatures, a pursuit that has won him his most prized possession: a prestigious Golden Demon award. He lives in Portsmouth, England.

David Annandale is the author of the Horus Heresy novels *Ruinstorm* and *The Damnation of Pythos*, and the Primarchs novel *Roboute Guilliman: Lord of Ultramar*. He has also written *Warlord: Fury of the God-Machine*, the Yarrick series, several stories involving the Grey Knights, including *Warden of the Blade*, and *The Last Wall*, *The Hunt for Vulkan* and *Watchers in Death* for The Beast Arises. For Space Marine Battles he has written *The Death of Antagonis* and *Overfiend*. He is a prolific writer of short fiction set in The Horus Heresy, Warhammer 40,000 and Age of Sigmar universes. David lectures at a Canadian university, on subjects ranging from English literature to horror films and video games.

Justin D Hill is the author of the Warhammer 40,000 novel *Cadia Stands*, the Space Marine Battles novel *Storm of Damocles* and the short stories 'Last Step Backwards', 'Lost Hope' and 'The Battle of Tyrok Fields', following the adventures of Lord Castellan Ursarkar E. Creed. He has also written 'Truth Is My Weapon', and the Warhammer tales 'Golgfag's Revenge' and 'The Battle of Whitestone'. He lives ten miles uphill from York, where he is indoctrinating his four children in the 40K lore.

Andy Clark has written the Warhammer 40,000 novels *Kingsblade* and *Shroud of Night*, as well as the short story 'Whiteout', the Age of Sigmar short story 'Gorechosen', and the Warhammer Quest Silver Tower novella *Labyrinth of the Lost*. Andy works as a background writer for Games Workshop, crafting the worlds of Warhammer Age of Sigmar and Warhammer 40,000. He lives in Nottingham, UK.

Gav Thorpe is the author of the Horus Heresy novels *Deliverance Lost*, *Angels of Caliban* and *Corax*, as well as the novella *The Lion*, which formed part of the *New York Times* bestselling collection *The Primarchs*, as well as several audio dramas including the bestselling *Raven's Flight* and *The Thirteenth Wolf*. He has written many novels for Warhammer 40,000, including *Rise of the Ynnari: Ghost Warrior*, *Jain Zar: The Storm of Silence* and *Asurmen: Hand of Asuryan*. He also wrote the Path of the Eldar and Legacy of Caliban trilogies, and two volumes in The Beast Arises series. For Warhammer, Gav has penned the End Times novel *The Curse of Khaine*, the Time of Legends trilogy, *The Sundering*, and much more besides. He lives and works in Nottingham.

Anthony Reynolds is the author of the Horus Heresy novella *The Purge*, audio drama *Khârn: The Eightfold Path* and short stories 'Scions of the Storm' and 'Dark Heart'. In the Warhammer 40,000 universe, he has written the novel *Khârn: Eater of Worlds*, alongside the audio drama *Chosen of Khorne*, also featuring Khârn. He has also penned the Word Bearers trilogy and many short stories. Hailing from Australia, he is currently settled on the west coast of the United States.